JOHN GALSWORTHY

Janice
Christmas
1981
love Pat

JOHN
GALSWORTHY

JOHN GALSWORTHY

The Forsyte Saga

The Man of Property
In Chancery
To Let

A Modern Comedy

The White Monkey
The Silver Spoon
Swan Song

Heinemann/Octopus

The Man of Property first published in Great Britain in 1906
In Chancery first published in Great Britain in 1920
To Let first published in Great Britain in 1921
The White Monkey first published in Great Britain in 1924
The Silver Spoon first published in Great Britain in 1926
Swan Song first published in Great Britain in 1928

This edition first published in 1976 by
William Heinemann Limited
15–16 Queen Street, London W1
in association with
Octopus Books Limited
59 Grosvenor Street, London W1

ISBN 0 7064 0572 2

Printed in Great Britain by
Jarrold & Sons Ltd, Norwich

Contents

Introduction

JOHN GALSWORTHY is the most thoroughly English novelist since Dickens. The background, characters and situations which he creates in his work comprise a literary edifice as solid, imposing and specifically English as Lloyd's, the Stock Exchange and the Bank of England. But his novels are by no means inanimate masses of verbal masonry which sit immovable on their foundations as mere triumphs of a writer's architectural and engineering ability. To take the simile further one might say that the noble and imposing façades are illuminated by the artist's creative *son et lumière*, the tragedy, comedy and irony of life observed and transmuted into the highlights and shadows of fiction.

John Galsworthy was born in 1867 and came from Devonshire landed gentry stock. He was educated at Harrow and New College, Oxford where he took an honours degree in law in 1889. He was called to the bar by Lincoln's Inn but preferred to travel and sailed in merchant ships to the Far East, meeting at one point that other literary voyager, Joseph Conrad. His first book was a collection of stories entitled *From the Four Winds* (1897) which he wrote under the name 'John Sinjohn', a pseudonym retained for three further books, two novels and a second collection of stories. A novel, *The Island Pharisees* (1904), was the first to appear under his own name and in 1906 came *The Man of Property*, the first of that great series 'The Forsyte Saga' and 'A Modern Comedy'.

The two greatest literary influences on Galsworthy were not, as it happens, English writers, but Russian and French. In his youth he read and re-read the works of Turgenev and Maupassant and although his own books are as firmly part of the society and ways of his own country as the carved mahogany furniture, the dark-green velvet upholstery, and the saddle of mutton traditionally set on Forsyte dinner tables, his view of the dying society which he describes is as affectionate and sensible of its charm as it is ironic.

The Forsyte Saga, continued in *A Modern Comedy* (1929), charts the course of successive generations and the tenacity of the possessive instinct–so evident in Soames Forsyte–through the half-century that included the great War, the birth and rise of socialism and the appearance of those cracks in the social structure that became so inevitably and visibly irreparable fissures. Galsworthy himself said of *The Forsyte Saga* that 'it cannot be absolved from the charge of embalming the upper middle-class life'. But it is that triumph of preservation that allows readers today to enter a vanished way of life and to experience and be captivated by it again and again on both the printed page and so outstandingly on the television screen.

Galsworthy was a skilled and successful dramatist and it was in recognition of both novels and plays that in 1929 he was awarded the order of merit and in 1932, the year of his death, the Nobel Prize for Literature. But his most enduring memorial is his work of which he said: 'If the upper middle class, with other classes, is destined to "move on" into amorphism, here, pickled in these pages, it lies under glass for strollers in the wide and ill-arranged museum of Letters to gaze at. Here it rests, preserved in its own juice: The Sense of Property.'

FORSYTE FAMILY TREE

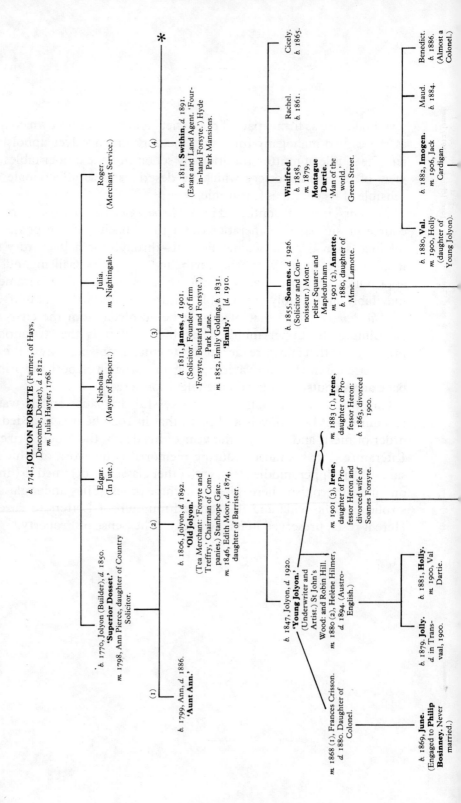

b. 1741, **JOLYON FORSYTE** (Farmer, of Hays, Dencombe, Dorset), d. 1812.
m. Julia Hayter, 1768.

(1)

b. 1799, Ann, d. 1886. **'Aunt Ann.'**

(2)

b. 1770, Jolyon (Builder), d. 1850. **'Superior Dosset.'** m. 1798, Ann Pierce, daughter of Country Solicitor.

b. 1806, Jolyon, d. 1892. **'Old Jolyon,'** (Tea Merchant: 'Forsyte and Treffry,' Chairman of Companies.) Stanhope Gate. m. 1846, Edith Moor, d. 1874, daughter of Barrister.

b. 1847, Jolyon, d. 1920. **'Young Jolyon.'** (Underwriter and Artist.) St John's Wood: and Robin Hill. m. 1880, Helène Hilmer, d 1894. (Austro-English.)

m. 1868 (1), Frances Crisson. d 1880. Daughter of Colonel.

m. 1901 (3), **Irene**, daughter of Professor Heron and divorced wife of Soames Forsyte.

m. 1883 (1), **Irene**, daughter of Professor Heron. b. 1863, divorced 1900.

b. 1869, **June.** (Engaged to **Philip Bosinney**. Never married.)

b. 1879, **Jolly.** d in Transvaal, 1900.

b. 1881, **Holly.** m. 1900, Val Dartie.

Edgar. (In Jute.)

Nicholas. (Mayor of Bosport.)

(3)

b. 1811, **James**, d. 1901. (Solicitor. Founder of firm 'Forsyte, Bustard and Forsyte.') Park Lane. m. 1852, Emily Golding, b. 1831. **'Emily,'** [d. 1910.

b. 1855, **Soames.** d. 1926. (Solicitor and Connoisseur.) Montpelier Square: and Mapledurham. m. 1901 (2), **Annette**, b. 1880, daughter of Mme. Lamotte.

Winifred. b. 1858, m. 1879. **Montague Dartie.** 'Man of the world.' Green Street.

b. 1880, **Val.** m. 1900, Holly (daughter of Young Jolyon).

b. 1882, **Imogen.** m. 1906, Jack Cardigan.

Maud. b. 1884.

Benedict. b. 1886. (Almost a Colonel.)

Julia. m. Nightingale.

Roger. (Merchant Service.)

(4)

*

b. 1811, **Swithin**, d. 1891. (Estate and Land Agent. 'Four-in-hand Forsyte.') Hyde Park Mansions.

Rachel. b. 1861.

Cicely. b. 1865.

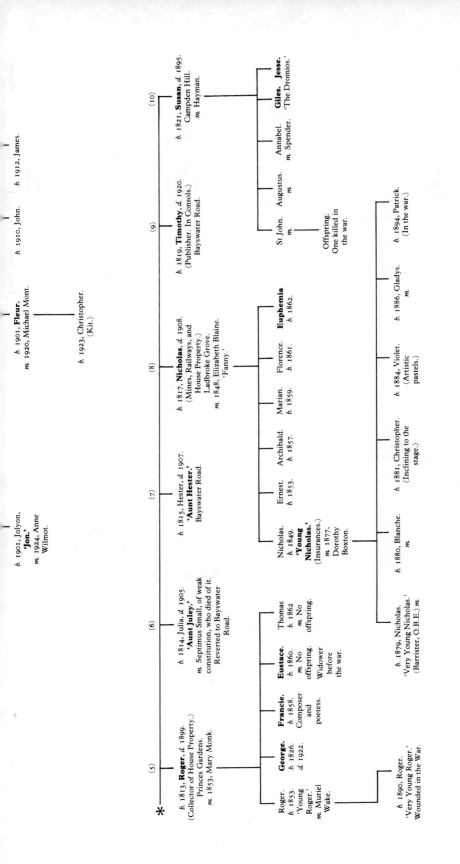

(5)

b. 1813, **Roger**, *d.* 1899. (Collector of House Property.) Princes Gardens. *m.* 1853, Mary Monk.

Roger. *b.* 1853. 'Young Roger.' *m.* Muriel Wake.

b. 1890, Roger. 'Very Young Roger.' Wounded in the War.

(6)

b. 1814, Julia, *d.* 1905. 'Aunt Juley.' *m.* Septimus Small, of weak constitution, who died of it. Reverted to Bayswater Road.

George. *b.* 1826. *d.* 1922.

Francie. *b.* 1858. Composer and poetess.

Eustace. *b.* 1860. *m.* No offspring. Widower before the war.

Thomas *b.* 1862 *m.* No offspring.

(7)

b. 1815, Hester, *d.* 1907. 'Aunt Hester.' Bayswater Road.

Nicholas. *b.* 1849. 'Young Nicholas.' (Insurances.) *m.* 1877, Dorothy Boxton.

Ernest. *b.* 1853.

Archibald. *b.* 1857.

b. 1879, Nicholas. 'Very Young Nicholas.' (Barrister, O.B.E.) *m.*

b. 1880, Blanche. *m.*

b. 1881, Christopher. (Inclining to the stage.)

(8)

b. 1817, **Nicholas**, *d.* 1908. (Mines, Railways, and House Property.) Ladbroke Grove. *m.* 1848, Elizabeth Blaine. 'Fanny.'

Marian. *b.* 1859.

Florence. *b.* 1861.

Euphemia *b.* 1862.

b. 1884, Violet. (Artistic pastels.)

b. 1886, Gladys. *m.*

(9)

b. 1819, **Timothy**, *d.* 1920. (Publisher. In Consols.) Bayswater Road.

St John. *m.*

Augustus. *m.*

Offspring. One killed in the war.

b. 1894, Patrick. (In the war.)

(10)

b. 1821, **Susan**, *d.* 1895. Campden Hill. *m.* Hayman.

Annabel. *m.* Spender.

Giles. Jesse. 'The Dromios.'

b. 1901, Jolyon, **'Jon,'** *m.* 1924, Anne Wilmot.

b. 1901, **Fleur.** *m.* 1920, Michael Mont.

b. 1910, John.

b. 1912, James.

b. 1923, Christopher. (Kit.)

The Forsyte Saga

BOOK I

The Man of Property

THE FORSYTE SAGA
To my wife

I dedicate the Forsyte Saga
in its entirety,
believing it to be of all my work
the least unworthy of one
without whose encouragement, sympathy,
and criticism
I could never have become even
such a writer as I am

THE MAN OF PROPERTY

'. . . You will answer
The slaves are ours . . .'

Merchant of Venice

TO EDWARD GARNETT

PART I

I

'AT HOME' AT OLD JOLYON'S

Those privileged to be present at a family festival of the Forsytes have seen that charming and instructive sight—an upper middle-class family in full plumage. But whosoever of these favoured persons has possessed the gift of psychological analysis (a talent without monetary value and properly ignored by the Forsytes), has witnessed a spectacle, not only delightful in itself, but illustrative of an obscure human problem. In plainer words, he has gleaned from a gathering of this family—no branch of which had a liking for the other, between no three members of whom existed anything worthy of the name of sympathy—evidence of that mysterious concrete tenacity which renders a family so formidable a unit of society, so clear a reproduction of society in miniature. He has been admitted to a vision of the dim roads of social progress, has understood something of patriarchal life, of the swarmings of savage hordes, of the rise and fall of nations. He is like one who, having watched a tree grow from its planting—a paragon of tenacity, insulation, and success, amidst the deaths of a hundred other plants less fibrous, sappy, and persistent—one day will see it flourishing with bland, full foliage, in an almost repugnant prosperity, at the summit of its efflorescence.

On June 15, 1886, about four of the afternoon, the observer who chanced to be present at the house of old Jolyon Forsyte in Stanhope Gate, might have seen the highest efflorescence of the Forsytes.

This was the occasion of an 'At Home' to celebrate the engagement of Miss June Forsyte, old Jolyon's grand-daughter, to Mr Philip Bosinney. In the bravery of light gloves, buff waistcoats, feathers and frocks, the family were present—even Aunt Ann, who now but seldom left the corner of her brother Timothy's green drawing-room, where, under the ægis of a plume of dyed pampas grass in a light blue vase, she sat all day reading and knitting, surrounded by the effigies of three generations of Forsytes. Even Aunt Ann was there; her inflexible back and the dignity of her calm old face personifying the rigid possessiveness of the family idea.

When a Forsyte was engaged, married, or born, the Forsytes were present; when a Forsyte died—but no Forsyte had as yet died; they did not die; death being contrary to their principles, they took precautions against it, the instinctive precautions of highly vitalised persons who resent encroachments on their property.

About the Forsytes mingling that day with the crowd of other guests, there was a more than ordinary groomed look, an alert, inquisitive assurance, a brilliant respectability, as though they were attired in defiance of something. The habitual sniff on the face of Soames Forsyte had spread through their ranks; they were on their guard.

The subconscious offensiveness of their attitude has constituted old Jolyon's 'at home' the psychological moment of the family history, made it the prelude of their drama.

The Forsytes were resentful of something, not individually, but as a family; this resentment expressed itself in an added perfection of raiment, an exuberance of family cordiality, an exaggeration of family importance, and–the sniff. Danger–so indispensable in bringing out the fundamental quality of any society, group, or individual–was what the Forsytes scented; the premonition of danger put a burnish on their armour. For the first time, as a family, they appeared to have an instinct of being in contact with some strange and unsafe thing.

Over against the piano a man of bulk and stature was wearing two waistcoats on his wide chest, two waistcoats and a ruby pin instead of the single satin waistcoat and diamond pin of more usual occasions, and his shaven, square, old face, the colour of pale leather, with pale eyes, had its most dignified look, above his satin stock. This was Swithin Forsyte. Close to the window, where he could get more than his fair share of fresh air, the other twin, James–the fat and the lean of it, old Jolyon called these brothers–like the bulky Swithin, over six feet in height, but very lean, as though destined from his birth to strike a balance and maintain an average, brooded over the scene with his permanent stoop; his grey eyes had an air of fixed absorption in some secret worry, broken at intervals by a rapid, shifting scrutiny of surrounding facts; his cheeks, thinned by two parallel folds, and a long, clean-shaven upper lip, were framed within Dundreary whiskers. In his hands he turned and turned a piece of china. Not far off, listening to a lady in brown, his only son Soames, pale and well-shaved, dark-haired, rather bald, had poked his chin up sideways, carrying his nose with that aforesaid appearance of 'sniff', as though despising an egg which he knew he could not digest. Behind him his cousin, the tall George, son of the fifth Forsyte, Roger, had a Quilpish look on his fleshy face, pondering one of his sardonic jests.

Something inherent to the occasion had affected them all.

Seated in a row close to one another were three ladies–Aunts Ann, Hester (the two Forsyte maids), and Juley (short for Julia), who not in first youth had so far forgotten herself as to marry Septimus Small, a man of poor constitution. She had survived him for many years. With her elder and younger sister she lived now in the house of Timothy, her sixth and youngest brother, on the Bayswater Road. Each of these ladies held fans in their hands, and each with some touch of colour, some emphatic feather or brooch, testified to the solemnity of the opportunity.

In the centre of the room, under the chandelier, as became a host, stood the head of the family, old Jolyon himself. Eighty years of age, with his fine, white hair, his dome-like forehead, his little, dark grey eyes, and an immense white moustache, which drooped and spread below the level of his strong jaw, he had a patriarchal look, and in spite of lean cheeks and hollows at his temples, seemed master of perennial youth. He held himself extremely upright, and his shrewd, steady eyes had lost none of their clear shining. Thus he gave an impression of superiority to the doubts and dislikes of smaller men. Having had his own way for innumerable years, he had earned a prescriptive right to it. It would never have occurred to old Jolyon that it was necessary to wear a look of doubt or of defiance.

Between him and the four other brothers who were present, James, Swithin, Nicholas, and Roger, there was much difference, much similarity. In turn, each of these four brothers was very different from the other, yet they, too, were alike.

Through the varying features and expression of those five faces could be marked a certain steadfastness of chin, underlying surface distinctions, marking a racial stamp, too prehistoric to trace, too remote and permanent to discuss—the very hall-mark and guarantee of the family fortunes.

Among the younger generation, in the tall, bull-like George, in pallid strenuous Archibald, in young Nicholas with his sweet and tentative obstinacy, in the grave and foppishly determined Eustace, there was this same stamp—less meaningful perhaps, but unmistakable—a sign of something ineradicable in the family soul.

At one time or another during the afternoon, all these faces, so dissimilar and so alike, had worn an expression of distrust, the object of which was undoubtedly the man whose acquaintance they were thus assembled to make.

Philip Bosinney was known to be a young man without fortune, but Forsyte girls had become engaged to such before, and had actually married them. It was not altogether for this reason, therefore, that the minds of the Forsytes misgave them. They could not have explained the origin of a misgiving obscured by the mist of family gossip. A story was undoubtedly told that he had paid his duty call to Aunts Ann, Juley, and Hester, in a soft grey hat—a soft grey hat, not even a new one—a dusty thing with a shapeless crown. 'So extraordinary, my dear—so odd!' Aunt Hester, passing through the little, dark hall (she was rather short-sighted), had tried to 'shoo' it off a chair, taking it for a strange, disreputable cat—Tommy had such disgraceful friends! She was disturbed when it did not move.

Like an artist for ever seeking to discover the significant trifle which embodies the whole character of a scene, or place, or person, so those unconscious artists—the Forsytes—had fastened by intuition on this hat; it was their significant trifle, the detail in which was embedded the meaning of the whole matter; for each had asked himself: 'Come, now, should *I* have paid that visit in that hat?' and each had answered 'No!' and some, with more imagination than others, had added: 'It would never have come into my head!'

George, on hearing the story, grinned. The hat had obviously been worn as a practical joke! He himself was a connoisseur of such.

'Very haughty!' he said, 'the wild Buccaneer!'

And this *mot*, 'the Buccaneer', was bandied from mouth to mouth, till it became the favourite mode of alluding to Bosinney.

Her aunts reproached June afterwards about the hat.

'We don't think you ought to let him, dear!' they had said.

June had answered in her imperious brisk way, like the little embodiment of will she was:

'Oh! what does it matter? Phil never knows what he's got on!'

No one had credited an answer so outrageous. A man not know what he had on? No, no!

What indeed was this young man, who, in becoming engaged to June, old Jolyon's acknowledged heiress, had done so well for himself? He was an architect, not in itself a sufficient reason for wearing such a hat. None of the Forsytes happened to be architects, but one of them knew two architects who would never have worn such a hat upon a call of ceremony in the London season. Dangerous—oh, dangerous!

June, of course, had not seen this, but, though not yet nineteen, she was notorious. Had she not said to Mrs Soames—who was always so beautifully dressed—that feathers were vulgar? Mrs Soames had actually given up wearing feathers, so dreadfully downright was dear June!

These misgivings, this disapproval and perfectly genuine distrust, did not prevent the Forsytes from gathering to old Jolyon's invitation. An 'At Home' at Stanhope Gate was a great rarity; none had been held for twelve years, not indeed, since old Mrs Jolyon died.

Never had there been so full an assembly, for, mysteriously united in spite of all their differences, they had taken arms against a common peril. Like cattle when a dog comes into the field, they stood head to head and shoulder to shoulder, prepared to run upon and trample the invader to death. They had come, too, no doubt, to get some notion of what sort of presents they would ultimately be expected to give; for though the question of wedding gifts was usually graduated in this way—'What are *you* givin'? Nicholas is givin' spoons!'—so very much depended on the bridegroom. If he were sleek, well-brushed, prosperous-looking, it was more necessary to give him nice things; he would expect them. In the end each gave exactly what was right and proper, by a species of family adjustment arrived at as prices are arrived at on the Stock Exchange—the exact niceties being regulated at Timothy's commodious, red-brick residence in Bayswater, overlooking the Park, where dwelt Aunts Ann, Juley, and Hester.

The uneasiness of the Forsyte family has been justified by the simple mention of the hat. How impossible and wrong would it have been for any family, with the regard for appearances which should ever characterise the great upper middle-class, to feel otherwise than uneasy!

The author of the uneasiness stood talking to June by the further door; his curly hair had a rumpled appearance as though he found what was going on around him unusual. He had an air, too, of having a joke all to himself.

George, speaking aside to his brother Eustace, said:

'Looks as if he might make a bolt of it—the dashing buccaneer!'

This 'very singular-looking man', as Mrs Small afterwards called him, was of medium height and strong build, with a pale, brown face, a dust-coloured moustache, very prominent cheekbones, and hollow cheeks. His forehead sloped back towards the crown of his head, and bulged out in bumps over the eyes, like foreheads seen in the lion-house at the Zoo. He had sherry-coloured eyes, disconcertingly inattentive at times. Old Jolyon's coachman, after driving June and Bosinney to the theatre, had remarked to the butler:

'I dunno what to make of 'im. Looks to me for all the world like an 'alf-tame leopard.'

And every now and then a Forsyte would come up, sidle round, and take a look at him.

June stood in front, fending off this idle curiosity—a little bit of a thing, as somebody once said, 'all hair and spirit', with fearless blue eyes, a firm jaw, and a bright colour, whose face and body seemed too slender for her crown of red-gold hair.

A tall woman, with a beautiful figure, which some member of the family had once compared to a heathen goddess, stood looking at these two with a shadowy smile.

Her hands, gloved in French grey, were crossed one over the other, her grave, charming face held to one side, and the eyes of all men near were fastened on it. Her figure swayed, so balanced that the very air seemed to set it moving. There was warmth, but little colour, in her cheeks, her large, dark eyes were soft. But it was at her lips—asking a question, giving an answer, with that shadowy smile—that men looked; they were sensitive lips, sensuous and sweet, and through them seemed to come warmth and perfume like the warmth and perfume of a flower.

The engaged couple thus scrutinised were unconscious of this passive goddess. It was Bosinney who first noticed her, and asked her name.

June took her lover up to the woman with the beautiful figure.

'Irene is my greatest chum,' she said. 'Please be good friends, you two!'

At the little lady's command they all three smiled; and while they were smiling, Soames Forsyte, silently appearing from behind the woman with the beautiful figure, who was his wife, said:

'Ah! introduce me too!'

He was seldom, indeed, far from Irene's side at public functions, and even when separated by the exigencies of social intercourse, could be seen following her about with his eyes, in which were strange expressions of watchfulness and longing.

At the window his father, James, was still scrutinising the marks on the piece of china.

'I wonder at Jolyon's allowing this engagement,' he said to Aunt Ann. 'They tell me there's no chance of their getting married for years. This young Bōsinney' (he made the word a dactyl in opposition to general usage of a short o) 'has got nothing. When Winifred married Dartie, I made him bring every penny into settlement—lucky thing, too—they'd ha' had nothing by this time!'

Aunt Ann looked up from her velvet chair. Grey curls banded her forehead, curls that, unchanged for decades, had extinguished in the family all sense of time. She made no reply, for she rarely spoke, husbanding her aged voice; but to James, uneasy of conscience, her look was as good as an answer.

'Well,' he said, 'I couldn't help Irene's having no money. Soames was in such a hurry; he got quite thin dancing attendance on her.'

Putting the bowl pettishly down on the piano, he let his eyes wander to the group by the door.

'It's my opinion,' he said unexpectedly, 'that it's just as well as it is.'

Aunt Ann did not ask him to explain this strange utterance. She knew what he was thinking. If Irene had no money she would not be so foolish as to do anything wrong; for they said—they said—she had been asking for a separate room; but, of course, Soames had not—

James interrupted her reverie:

'But where,' he asked, 'was Timothy? Hadn't he come with them?'

Through Aunt Ann's compressed lips a tender smile forced its way:

'No, he had not thought it wise, with so much of this diphtheria about; and he so liable to take things.'

James answered:

'Well, *he* takes good care of himself. I can't afford to take the care of myself that he does.'

Nor was it easy to say which, of admiration, envy, or contempt, was dominant in that remark.

Timothy, indeed, was seldom seen. The baby of the family, a publisher by profession, he had some years before, when business was at full tide, scented out the stagnation which, indeed, had not yet come, but which ultimately, as all agreed, was bound to set in, and, selling his share in a firm engaged mainly in the production of religious books, had invested the quite conspicuous proceeds in three per cent. Consols. By this act he had at once assumed an isolated position, no other Forsyte being content with less than four per cent. for his money; and this isolation had slowly and surely undermined a spirit perhaps better than commonly endowed with caution. He had become almost a myth—a kind of incarnation of security haunting the background of the Forsyte universe. He had never committed the imprudence of marrying, or encumbering himself in any way with children.

James resumed, tapping the piece of china:

'This isn't real old Worcester. I s'pose Jolyon's told you something about the young man. From all *I* can learn, he's got no business, no income, and no connection worth speaking of; but then, I know nothing—nobody tells me anything.'

Aunt Ann shook her head. Over her square-chinned, aquiline old face a trembling passed; the spidery fingers of her hands pressed against each other and interlaced, as though she were subtly recharging her will.

The eldest by some years of all the Forsytes, she held a peculiar position amongst them. Opportunists and egotists one and all—though not, indeed, more so than their neighbours—they quailed before her incorruptible figure, and, when opportunities were too strong, what could they do but avoid her!

Twisting his long, thin legs, James went on:

'Jolyon, he will have his own way. He's got no children—' and stopped, recollecting the continued existence of old Jolyon's son, young Jolyon, June's father, who had made such a mess of it, and done for himself by deserting his wife and child and running away with that foreign governess. 'Well,' he resumed hastily, 'if he likes to do these things, I s'pose he can afford to. Now, what's he going to give her. I s'pose he'll give her a thousand a year; he's got nobody else to leave his money to.'

He stretched out his hand to meet that of a dapper, clean-shaven man, with hardly a hair on his head, a long, broken nose, full lips, and cold grey eyes under rectangular brows.

'Well, Nick,' he muttered, 'how are you?'

Nicholas Forsyte with his bird-like rapidity and the look of a preternaturally sage schoolboy (he had made a large fortune, quite legitimately, out of the companies of which he was a director), placed within that cold palm the tips of his still colder fingers and hastily withdrew them.

'I'm bad,' he said, pouting—'been bad all the week; don't sleep at night. The doctor can't tell why. He's a clever fellow, or I shouldn't have him, but I get nothing out of him but bills.'

'Doctors!' said James, coming down sharp on his words, '*I've* had all the doctors in London for one or another of us. There's no satisfaction to be got out of *them*; they'll tell you anything. There's Swithin now. What good have they done him? There he is; he's bigger than ever; he's enormous; they can't get his weight down. Look at him!'

Swithin Forsyte, tall, square, and broad, with a chest like a pouter pigeon's in its plumage of bright waistcoats, came strutting towards them.

'Er—how are you?' he said in his dandified way, aspirating the 'h' strongly (this difficult letter was almost absolutely safe in his keeping)—'how are you?'

Each brother wore an air of aggravation as he looked at the other two, knowing by experience that they would try to eclipse his ailments.

'We were just saying,' said James, 'that *you* don't get any thinner.'

Swithin protruded his pale round eyes with the effort of hearing.

'Thinner? I'm in good case,' he said, leaning a little forward, 'not one of your thread-papers like you!'

But, afraid of losing the expansion of his chest, he leaned back again into a state of immobility, for he prized nothing so highly as a distinguished appearance.

Aunt Ann turned her old eyes from one to the other. Indulgent and severe was her look. In turn the three brothers looked at Ann. She was getting shaky. Wonderful woman! Eighty-six if a day; might live another ten years, and had never been strong. Swithin and James, the twins, were only seventy-five, Nicholas a mere baby of seventy or so. All were strong, and the inference was comforting. Of all forms of property their respective healths naturally concerned them most.

'I'm very well in myself,' proceeded James, 'but my nerves are out of order. The least thing worries me to death. I shall have to go to Bath.'

'Bath!' said Nicholas. 'I've tried Harrogate. *That's* no good. What I want is sea air. There's nothing like Yarmouth. Now, when I go there I sleep—'

'My liver's very bad,' interrupted Swithin slowly. 'Dreadful pain here,' and he placed his hand on his right side.

'Want of exercise,' muttered James, his eyes on the china. He quickly added: 'I get a pain there, too.'

Swithin reddened, a resemblance to a turkey-cock coming upon his old face.

'Exercise!' he said. 'I take plenty: I never use the lift at the Club.'

'I didn't know,' James hurried out. 'I know nothing about anybody; nobody tells me anything.'

Swithin fixed him with a stare, and asked:

'What do you do for a pain there?'

James brightened.

'I,' he began, 'take a compound—'

'How are you, uncle?'

And June stood before him, her resolute small face raised from her little height to his great height, and her hand outheld.

The brightness faded from James's visage.

'How are *you*?' he said, brooding over her. 'So you're going to Wales to-morrow to visit your young man's aunts? You'll have a lot of rain there. This isn't real old Worcester.' He tapped the bowl. 'Now, that set I gave your mother when she married was the genuine thing.'

June shook hands one by one with her three great-uncles, and turned to Aunt Ann. A very sweet look had come into the old lady's face; she kissed the girl's cheek with trembling fervour.

'Well, my dear,' she said, 'and so you're going for a whole month?'

The girl passed on, and Aunt Ann looked after her slim little figure. The old lady's round, steel-grey eyes, over which a film like a bird's was beginning to come, followed her wistfully amongst the bustling crowd, for people were beginning to say good-bye; and her finger-tips, pressing and pressing against each other, were busy again with the recharging of her will against that inevitable ultimate departure of her own.

'Yes,' she thought, 'everybody's been most kind, quite a lot of people come to congratulate her. She ought to be very happy.'

Amongst the throng of people by the door—the well-dressed throng drawn from the families of lawyers and doctors, from the Stock Exchange, and all the innumerable avocations of the upper-middle class—there were only some twenty per cent. of Forsytes, but to Aunt Ann they seemed all Forsytes—and certainly there was not much difference—she saw only her own flesh and blood. It was her world, this family, and she knew no other, had never perhaps known any other. All their little secrets, illnesses, engagements, and marriages, how they were getting on, and whether they were making money—all this was her property, her delight, her life; beyond this only a vague, shadowy mist of facts and persons of no real significance. This it was that she would have to lay down when it came to her turn to die; this which gave to her that importance, that secret self-importance, without which none of us can bear to live; and to this she clung wistfully, with a greed that grew each day. If life were slipping away from her, *this* she would retain to the end.

She thought of June's father, young Jolyon, who had run away with that foreign girl. Ah! what a sad blow to his father and to them all. Such a promising young fellow! A sad blow, though there had been no public scandal, most fortunately, Jo's wife seeking for no divorce! A long time ago! And when June's mother died, six years ago, Jo had married that woman, and they had two children now, so she had heard. Still, he had forfeited his right to be there, had cheated her of the complete fulfilment of her family pride, deprived her of the rightful pleasure of seeing and kissing him of whom she had been so proud, such a promising young fellow! The thought rankled with the bitterness of long-inflicted injury in her tenacious old heart. A little water stood in her eyes. With a handkerchief of the finest lawn she wiped them stealthily.

'Well, Aunt Ann?' said a voice behind.

Soames Forsyte, flat-shouldered, clean-shaven, flat-cheeked, flat-waisted, yet with something round and secret about his whole appearance, looked downwards and aslant at Aunt Ann, as though trying to see through the side of his own nose.

'And what do *you* think of the engagement?' he asked.

Aunt Ann's eyes rested on him proudly; the eldest of the nephews since young Jolyon's departure from the family nest, he was now her favourite, for she recognised in him a sure trustee of the family soul that must so soon slip beyond her keeping.

'Very nice for the young man,' she said; 'and he's a good-looking young fellow; but I doubt if he's quite the right lover for dear June.'

Soames touched the edge of a gold-lacquered lustre.

'She'll tame him,' he said, stealthily wetting his finger and rubbing it on the knobbly bulbs. 'That's genuine old lacquer; you can't get it nowadays. It'd do well in a sale at Jobson's.' He spoke with relish, as though he felt that he was cheering up his old aunt. It was seldom he was so confidential. 'I wouldn't mind having it myself,' he added; 'you can always get your price for old lacquer.'

'You're so clever with all those things,' said Aunt Ann. 'And how is dear Irene?'

Soames's smile died.

'Pretty well,' he said. 'Complains she can't sleep; she sleeps a great deal better than I do,' and he looked at his wife, who was talking to Bosinney by the door.

Aunt Ann sighed.

'Perhaps,' she said, 'it will be just as well for her not to see so much of June. She's such a decided character, dear June!'

Soames flushed; his flushes passed rapidly over his flat cheeks and centred between his eyes, where they remained, the stamp of disturbing thoughts.

'I don't know what she sees in that little flibbertigibbet,' he burst out, but noticing that they were no longer alone, he turned and again began examining the lustre.

'They tell me Jolyon's bought another house,' said his father's voice close by; 'he must have a lot of money—he must have more money than he knows what to do with! Montpelier Square, they say; close to Soames! They never told me—Irene never tells me anything!'

'Capital position, not two minutes from me,' said the voice of Swithin, 'and from my rooms I can drive to the Club in eight.'

The position of their houses was of vital importance to the Forsytes, nor was this remarkable, since the whole spirit of their success was embodied therein.

Their father, of farming stock, had come from Dorsetshire near the beginning of the century.

'Superior Dosset Forsyte', as he was called by his intimates, had been a stonemason by trade, and risen to the position of a master-builder. Towards the end of his life he moved to London, where, building on until he died, he was buried at Highgate. He left over thirty thousand pounds between his ten children. Old Jolyon alluded to him, if at all, as 'A hard, thick sort of man; not much refinement about him.' The second generation of Forsytes felt indeed that he was not greatly to their credit. The only aristocratic trait they could find in his character was a habit of drinking Madeira.

Aunt Hester, an authority on family history, described him thus:

'I don't recollect that he ever did anything; at least, not in *my* time. He was er—an owner of houses, my dear. His hair about your Uncle Swithin's colour; rather a square build. Tall? No—not very tall' (he had been five feet five, with a mottled face); 'a fresh-coloured man. I remember he used to drink Madeira; but ask your Aunt Ann. What was *his* father? He—er—had to do with the land down in Dorsetshire, by the sea.'

James once went down to see for himself what sort of place this was that they had come from. He found two old farms, with a cart track rutted into the pink earth, leading down to a mill by the beach; a little grey church with a buttressed outer wall, and a smaller and greyer chapel. The stream which worked the mill came bubbling down in a dozen rivulets, and pigs were hunting round that estuary. A haze hovered over the prospect. Down this hollow, with their feet deep in the mud and their faces towards the sea, it appeared that the primeval Forsytes had been content to walk Sunday after Sunday for hundreds of years.

Whether or no James had cherished hopes of an inheritance, or of something rather distinguished to be found down there, he came back to town in a poor way, and went about with a pathetic attempt at making the best of a bad job.

'There's very little to be had out of that,' he said; 'regular country little place, old as the hills.'

Its age was felt to be a comfort. Old Jolyon, in whom a desperate honesty welled up at times, would allude to his ancestors as: 'Yeoman—I suppose very small beer.' Yet he would repeat the word 'yeoman' as if it afforded him consolation.

They had all done so well for themselves, these Forsytes, that they were all what is called 'of a certain position'. They had shares in all sorts of things, not as yet—with the exception of Timothy—in Consols, for they had no dread in life like that of 3 per cent. for their money. They collected pictures, too, and were supporters of such charitable institutions as might be beneficial to their sick domestics. From their father, the builder, they inherited a talent for bricks and mortar. Originally, perhaps, members of some primitive sect, they were now in the natural course of things members of the Church of England, and caused their wives and children to attend with some regularity the more fashionable churches of the Metropolis. To have doubted their Christianity would have caused them both pain and surprise. Some of them paid for pews, thus expressing in the most practical form their sympathy with the teachings of Christ.

Their residences, placed at stated intervals round the park, watched like sentinels, lest the fair heart of this London, where their desires were fixed, should slip from their clutches, and leave them lower in their own estimations.

There was old Jolyon in Stanhope Place; the Jameses in Park Lane; Swithin in the lonely glory of orange and blue chambers in Hyde Park Mansions—he had never married, not he!—the Soameses in their nest off Knightsbridge; the Rogers in Prince's Gardens (Roger was that remarkable Forsyte who had conceived and carried out the notion of bringing up his four sons to a new profession. 'Collect house property—nothing like it!' he would say; '*I* never did anything else!')

The Haymans again—Mrs Hayman was the one married Forsyte sister—in a house high up on Campden Hill, shaped like a giraffe, and so tall that it gave the observer a crick in the neck; the Nicholases in Ladbroke Grove, a spacious abode and a great bargain; and last, but not least, Timothy's on the Bayswater Road, where Ann, and Juley, and Hester, lived under his protection.

But all this time James was musing, and now he inquired of his host and brother what he had given for that house in Montpelier Square. He himself had had his eye on a house there for the last two years, but they wanted such a price.

Old Jolyon recounted the details of his purchase.

'Twenty-two years to run?' repeated James; 'the very house I was after—you've given too much for it!'

Old Jolyon frowned.

'It's not that I want it,' said James hastily; 'wouldn't suit my purpose at that price. Soames knows the house, well—he'll tell you it's too dear—his opinion's worth having.'

'I don't,' said old Jolyon, 'care a fig for his opinion.'

'Well,' murmured James, 'you *will* have your own way—it's a good opinion. Good-bye! We're going to drive down to Hurlingham. They tell me June's going to Wales. You'll be lonely to-morrow. What'll you do with yourself? You'd better come and dine with us!'

Old Jolyon refused. He went down to the front door and saw them into their barouche, and twinkled at them, having already forgotten his spleen—Mrs James facing the horses, tall and majestic with auburn hair; on her left, Irene—the two husbands, father and son, sitting forward, as though they expected something, opposite their wives. Bobbing and bounding upon the spring cushions, silent, swaying to each motion of their chariot, old Jolyon watched them drive away under the sunlight.

During the drive the silence was broken by Mrs James.

'Did you ever see such a collection of rumty-too people?'

Soames, glancing at her beneath his eyelids, nodded, and he saw Irene steal at him one of her unfathomable looks. It is likely enough that each branch of the Forsyte family made that remark as they drove away from old Jolyon's 'At Home'.

Amongst the last of the departing guests the fourth and fifth brothers, Nicholas and Roger, walked away together, directing their steps alongside Hyde Park towards the Praed Street Station of the Underground. Like all other Forsytes of a certain age they kept carriages of their own, and never took cabs if by any means they could avoid it.

The day was bright, the trees of the Park in the full beauty of mid-June foliage; the brothers did not seem to notice phenomena, which contributed, nevertheless, to the jauntiness of promenade and conversation.

'Yes,' said Roger, 'she's a good-lookin' woman, that wife of Soames's. I'm told they don't get on.'

This brother had a high forehead, and the freshest colour of any of the Forsytes; his light grey eyes measured the street frontage of the houses by the way, and now and then he would level his umbrella and take a 'lunar', as he expressed it, of the varying heights.

'She'd no money,' replied Nicholas.

He himself had married a good deal of money, of which, it being then the golden age before the Married Women's Property Act, he had mercifully been enabled to make a successful use.

'What was her father?'

'Heron was his name, a Professor, so they tell me.'

Roger shook his head.

'There's no money in that,' he said.

'They say her mother's father was cement.'

Roger's face brightened.

'But he went bankrupt,' went on Nicholas.

'Ah!' exclaimed Roger, 'Soames will have trouble with her; you mark my words, he'll have trouble–she's got a foreign look.'

Nicholas licked his lips.

'She's a pretty woman,' and he waved aside a crossing-sweeper.

'How did he get hold of her?' asked Roger presently. 'She must cost him a pretty penny in dress!'

'Ann tells me,' replied Nicholas, 'he was half-cracked about her. She refused him five times. James, he's nervous about it, I can see.'

'Ah!' said Roger again; 'I'm sorry for James; he had trouble with Dartie.' His pleasant colour was heightened by exercise, he swung his umbrella to the level of his eye more frequently than ever. Nicholas's face also wore a pleasant look.

'Too pale for me,' he said, 'but her figure's capital!'

Roger made no reply.

'I call her distinguished-looking,' he said at last–it was the highest praise in the Forsyte vocabulary. 'That young Bosinney will never do any good for himself. They say at Burkitt's he's one of these artistic chaps–got an idea of improving English architecture; there's no money in that! I should like to hear what Timothy would say to it.'

They entered the station.

'What class are you going? I go second.'

'No second for me,' said Nicholas; 'you never know what you may catch.'

He took a first-class ticket to Notting Hill Gate; Roger a second to South Kensington. The train coming in a minute later, the brothers parted and entered their respective compartments. Each felt aggrieved that the other had not modified his habits to secure his society a little longer; but as Roger voiced it in his thoughts:

'Always a stubborn beggar, Nick!'

And as Nicholas expressed it to himself:

'Cantankerous chap Roger always was!'

There was little sentimentality about the Forsytes. In that great London, which they had conquered and become merged in, what time had they to be sentimental?

2

OLD JOLYON GOES TO THE OPERA

At five o'clock the following day old Jolyon sat alone, a cigar between his lips, and on a table by his side a cup of tea. He was tired, and before he had finished his cigar he fell asleep. A fly settled on his hair, his breathing sounded heavy in the drowsy silence, his upper lip under the white moustache puffed in and out. From between the fingers of his veined and wrinkled hand the cigar, dropping on the empty hearth, burned itself out.

The gloomy little study, with windows of stained glass to exclude the view, was full of dark green velvet and heavily-carved mahogany—a suite of which old Jolyon was wont to say: 'Shouldn't wonder if it made a big price some day!'

It was pleasant to think that in the after life he could get more for things than he had given.

In the rich brown atmosphere peculiar to back rooms in the mansion of a Forsyte, the Rembrandtesque effect of his great head, with its white hair, against the cushion of his high-backed seat, was spoiled by the moustache, which imparted a somewhat military look to his face. An old clock that had been with him since before his marriage fifty years ago kept with its ticking a jealous record of the seconds slipping away for ever from its old master.

He had never cared for this room, hardly going into it from one year's end to another, except to take cigars from the Japanese cabinet in the corner, and the room now had its revenge.

His temples, curving like thatches over the hollows beneath, his cheek-bones and chin, all were sharpened in his sleep, and there had come upon his face the confession that he was an old man.

He woke. June had gone! James had said he would be lonely. James had always been a poor thing. He recollected with satisfaction that he had bought that house over James's head. Serve him right for sticking at the price; the only thing the fellow thought of was money. Had he given too much, though? It wanted a lot of doing to—. He dared say he would want all his money before he had done with this affair of June's. He ought never to have allowed the engagement. She had met this Bosinney at the house of Baynes—Baynes and

Bildeboy, the architects. He believed that Baynes, whom he knew—a bit of an old woman—was the young man's uncle by marriage. After that she'd been always running after him; and when she took a thing into her head there was no stopping her. She was continually taking up with 'lame ducks' of one sort or another. This fellow had no money, but she must needs become engaged to him—a harum-scarum, unpractical chap, who would get himself into no end of difficulties.

She had come to him one day in her slap-dash way and told him; and, if it were any consolation, she had added:

'He's so splendid; he's often lived on cocoa for a week!'

'And he wants you to live on cocoa too?'

'Oh no; he is getting into the swim now.'

Old Jolyon had taken his cigar from under his white moustaches, stained by coffee at the edge, and looked at her, that little slip of a thing who had got such a grip of his heart. He knew more about 'swims' than his grand-daughter. But she, having clasped her hands on his knees, rubbed her chin against him, making a sound like a purring cat. And, knocking the ash off his cigar, he had exploded in nervous desparation:

'You're all alike: you won't be satisfied till you've got what you want. If you must come to grief, you must; *I* wash my hands of it.'

So, he had washed his hands of it, making the condition that they should not marry until Bosinney had at least four hundred a year.

'*I* shan't be able to give you very much,' he had said, a formula to which June was not unaccustomed. 'Perhaps this What's-his-name will provide the cocoa.'

He had hardly seen anything of her since it began. A bad business! He had no notion of giving her a lot of money to enable a fellow he knew nothing about to live on in idleness. He had seen that sort of thing before; no good ever came of it. Worst of all, he had no hope of shaking her resolution; she was as obstinate as a mule, always had been from a child. He didn't see where it was to end. They must cut their coat according to their cloth. He would not give way till he saw young Bosinney with an income of his own. That June would have trouble with the fellow was as plain as a pike-staff; he had no more idea of money than a cow. As to this rushing down to Wales to visit the young man's aunts, he fully expected they were old cats.

And, motionless, old Jolyon stared at the wall; but for his open eyes, he might have been asleep. . . . The idea of supposing that young cub Soames could give him advice! He had always been a cub, with his nose in the air! He would be setting up as a man of property next, with a place in the country! A man of property! H'mph! Like his father, he was always nosing out bargains, a cold-blooded young beggar!

He rose, and, going to the cabinet, began methodically stocking his cigar-case from a bundle fresh in. They were not bad at the price, but you couldn't get a good cigar nowadays, nothing to hold a candle to those old Superfinos of Hanson and Bridger's. *That* was a cigar!

The thought, like some stealing perfume, carried him back to those wonderful nights at Richmond when after dinner he sat smoking on the terrace of the Crown and Sceptre with Nicholas Treffry and Traquair and Jack Herring and Anthony Thornworthy. How good his cigars were then. Poor old Nick!—dead, and Jack Herring—dead, and Traquair—dead of that wife of his, and Thornworthy—awfully shaky (no wonder, with his appetite).

Of all the company of those days he himself alone seemed left, except

Swithin, of course, and *he* so outrageously big there was no doing anything with him.

Difficult to believe it was so long ago; he felt young still! Of all his thoughts, as he stood there counting his cigars, this was the most poignant, the most bitter. With his white head and his loneliness he had remained young and green at heart. And those Sunday afternoons on Hampstead Heath, when young Jolyon and he went for a stretch along the Spaniard's Road to Highgate, to Child's Hill, and back over the Heath again to dine at Jack Straw's Castle—how delicious his cigars were then! And such weather! There was no weather now.

When June was a toddler of five, and every other Sunday he took her to the Zoo, away from the society of those two good women, her mother and her grandmother, and at the top of the bear-den baited his umbrella with buns for her favourite bears, how sweet his cigars were then!

Cigars! He had not even succeeded in outliving his palate—the famous palate that in the fifties men swore by, and speaking of him, said: 'Forsyte—the best palate in London!' The palate that in a sense had made his fortune—the fortunes of the celebrated tea men, Forsyte and Treffry, whose tea, like no other man's tea, had a romantic aroma, the charm of a quite singular genuineness. About the house of Forsyte and Treffry in the City had clung an air of enterprise and mystery, of special dealings in special ships, at special ports, with special Orientals.

He had worked at that business! Men did work in those days! these young pups hardly knew the meaning of the word. He had gone into every detail, known everything that went on, sometimes sat up all night over it. And he had always chosen his agents himself, prided himself on it. His eye for men, he used to say, had been the secret of his success, and the exercise of this masterful power of selection had been the only part of it all that he had really liked. Not a career for a man of his ability. Even now, when the business had been turned into a Limited Liability Company, and was declining (he had got out of his shares long ago), he felt a sharp chagrin in thinking of that time. How much better he might have done! He would have succeeded splendidly at the Bar! He had even thought of standing for Parliament. How often had not Nicholas Treffry said to him: 'You could do anything, Jo, if you weren't so d-damned careful of yourself?' Dear old Nick! Such a good fellow, but a rackety chap! The notorious Treffry! *He* had never taken any care of himself. Se he was dead. Old Jolyon counted his cigars with a steady hand, and it came into his mind to wonder if perhaps he had been *too* careful of himself.

He put the cigar-case in the breast of his coat, buttoned it in, and walked up the long flights to his bedroom, leaning on one foot and the other, and helping himself by the banister. The house was too big. After June was married, if she ever did marry this fellow, as he supposed she would, he would let it and go into rooms. What was the use of keeping half a dozen servants eating their heads off?

The butler came to the ring of his bell—a large man with a beard, a soft tread, and a peculiar capacity for silence. Old Jolyon told him to put his dress clothes out; he was going to dine at the Club.

'How long had the carriage been back from taking Miss June to the station? Since two? Then let him come round at half-past six.'

The Club which old Jolyon entered on the stroke of seven was one of those political institutions of the upper middle class which have seen better days. In spite of being talked about, perhaps in consequence of being talked about, it betrayed a disappointing vitality. People had grown tired of saying that the

'Disunion' was on its last legs. Old Jolyon would say it, too, yet disregarded the fact in a manner truly irritating to well-constitutioned Clubmen.

'Why do you keep your name on?' Swithin often asked him with profound vexation. 'Why don't you join the 'Polyglot'? You can't get a wine like our Heidsieck under twenty shillin' a bottle anywhere in London;' and, dropping his voice, he added: 'There's only five thousand dozen left. I drink it every night of my life.'

'I'll think of it,' old Jolyon would answer; but when he did think of it there was always the question of fifty guineas entrance fee, and it would take him four or five years to get in. He continued to think of it.

He was too old to be a Liberal, had long ceased to believe in the political doctrines of his Club, had even been known to allude to them as 'wretched stuff', and it afforded him pleasure to continue a member in the teeth of principles so opposed to his own. He had always had a contempt for the place, having joined it many years ago when they refused to have him at the 'Hotch Potch' owing to his being 'in trade'. As if he were not as good as any of them! He naturally despised the Club that *did* take him. The members were a poor lot, many of them in the City—stockbrokers, solicitors, auctioneers, what not! Like most men of strong character but not too much originality, old Jolyon set small store by the class to which he belonged. Faithfully he followed their customs, social and otherwise, and secretly he thought them 'a common lot'.

Years and philosophy, of which he had his share, had dimmed the recollection of his defeat at the 'Hotch Potch'; and now in his thoughts it was enshrined as the Queen of Clubs. He would have been a member all these years himself, but, owing to the slipshod way his proposer, Jack Herring, had gone to work, they had not known what they were doing in keeping him out. Why! they had taken his son Jo at once, and he believed the boy was still a member; he had received a letter dated from there eight years ago.

He had not been near the 'Disunion' for months, and the house had undergone the piebald decoration which people bestow on old houses and old ships when anxious to sell them.

'Beastly colour, the smoking-room!' he thought. 'The dining-room is good.'

Its gloomy chocolate, picked out with light green, took his fancy.

He ordered dinner, and sat down in the very corner, at the very table perhaps (things did not progress much at the 'Disunion', a Club of almost Radical principles) at which he and young Jolyon used to sit twenty-five years ago, when he was taking the latter to Drury Lane, during his holidays.

The boy had loved the theatre, and old Jolyon recalled how he used to sit opposite, concealing his excitement under a careful but transparent nonchalance.

He ordered himself, too, the very dinner the boy had always chosen—soup, whitebait, cutlets, and a tart. Ah! if he were only opposite now!

The two had not met for fourteen years. And not for the first time during those fourteen years old Jolyon wondered whether he had been a little to blame in the matter of his son. An unfortunate love-affair with that precious flirt Danaë Thornworthy, now Danaë Pellew, Anthony Thornworthy's daughter, had thrown him on the rebound into the arms of June's mother. He ought perhaps to have put a spoke in the wheel of their marriage; they were too young; but after that experience of Jo's susceptibility he had been only too anxious to see him married. And in four years the crash had come! To have approved his son's conduct in that crash was, of course, impossible; reason and training—that combination of potent factors which stood for his principles—told him of this impossibility, but his heart cried out. The grim remorselessness of that business had no pity for hearts. There was June, the atom with flaming hair, who had climbed all over him, twined and twisted herself about him—about his heart that was made to be the play-thing and beloved resort of tiny helpless things. With characteristic insight he saw he must part with one or with the other; no half measures could serve in such a situation. In that lay its tragedy. And the tiny, helpless thing prevailed. He would not run with the hare and hunt with the hounds, and so to his son he said good-bye.

That good-bye had lasted until now.

He had proposed to continue a reduced allowance to young Jolyon, but this had been refused, and perhaps that refusal had hurt him more than anything, for with it had gone the last outlet of his penned-in affection; and there had come such tangible and solid proof of rupture as only a transaction in property, a bestowal or refusal of such, could supply.

His dinner tasted flat. His pint of champagne was dry and bitter stuff, not like the Veuve Clicquots of old days.

Over his cup of coffee, he bethought him that he would go to the opera. In *The Times*, therefore—he had a distrust of other papers—he read the announcement for the evening. It was 'Fidelio'.

Mercifully not one of those new-fangled German pantomimes by that fellow Wagner.

Putting on his ancient opera hat, which with brim flattened by use, and huge capacity, looked like an emblem of greater days, and pulling out an old pair of very thin lavender kid gloves smelling strongly of Russia leather, from habitual proximity to the cigar-case in the pocket of his overcoat, he stepped into a hansom.

The cabs rattled gaily along the streets, and old Jolyon was struck by their unwonted animation.

'The hotels must be doing a tremendous business,' he thought. A few years ago there had been none of these big hotels. He made a satisfactory reflection on some property he had in the neighbourhood. It must be going up in value by leaps and bounds! What traffic!

But from that he began indulging in one of those strange impersonal speculations, so uncharacteristic of a Forsyte, wherein lay, in part, the secret of his supremacy amongst them. What atoms men were, and what a lot of them! And what would become of them all?

He stumbled as he got out of the cab, gave the man his exact fare, walked up to the ticket office to take his stall, and stood there with his purse in his hand—he always carried his money in a purse, never having approved of that habit of carrying it loosely in the pockets, as so many young men did nowadays. The official leaned out, like an old dog from a kennel.

'Why,' he said in a surprised voice, 'it's Mr Jolyon Forsyte! So it is! Haven't seen you, sir, for years. Dear me! Times aren't what they were. Why! you and your brother, and that auctioneer—Mr Traquair, and Mr Nicholas Treffry—you used to have six or seven stalls here regular every season. And how are *you*, sir? We don't get younger!'

The colour in old Jolyon's eyes deepened; he paid his guinea. They had not forgotten him. He marched in, to the sounds of the overture, like an old war-horse to battle.

Folding his opera hat, he sat down, drew out his lavender gloves in the old way, and took up his glasses for a long look round the house. Dropping them at last on his folded hat, he fixed his eyes on the curtain. More poignantly than ever he felt that it was all over and done with him. Where were all the women, the pretty women, the house used to be so full of? Where was that old feeling in the heart as he waited for one of those great singers? Where that sensation of the intoxication of life and of his own power to enjoy it all?

The greatest opera-goer of his day! There was no opera now! That fellow Wagner had ruined everything; no melody left, nor any voices to sing it. Ah! the wonderful singers! Gone! He sat watching the old scenes acted, a numb feeling at his heart.

From the curl of silver over his ear to the pose of his foot in its elastic-sided patent boot, there was nothing clumsy or weak about old Jolyon. He was as upright—very nearly—as in those old times when he came every night; his sight was as good—almost as good. But what a feeling of weariness and disillusion!

He had been in the habit all his life of enjoying things, even imperfect things—and there had been many imperfect things—he enjoyed them all with moderation, so as to keep himself young. But now he was deserted by his power of enjoyment, by his philosophy, and left with this dreadful feeling that it was all done with. Not even the Prisoners' Chorus, nor Florestan's Song, had the power to dispel the gloom of his loneliness.

If Jo were only with him! The boy must be forty by now. He had wasted fourteen years out of the life of his only son. And Jo was no longer a social pariah. He was married. Old Jolyon had been unable to refrain from marking his appreciation of the action by enclosing his son a cheque for £500. The cheque had been returned in a letter from the 'Hotch Potch', couched in these words:

MY DEAREST FATHER,
  Your generous gift was welcome as a sign that you might think worse of me. I return it, but should you think fit to invest it for the benefit of the little chap (we call him Jolly) who bears our Christian and, by courtesy, our surname, I shall be very glad.
  I hope with all my heart that your health is as good as ever.

Your loving son,
Jo.

The letter was like the boy. He had always been an amiable chap. Old Jolyon had sent this reply:

MY DEAR JO,
  The sum (£500) stands in my books for the benefit of your boy, under the name of Jolyon Forsyte, and will be duly credited with interest at 5 per cent. I hope that you are doing well. My health remains good at present.

With love, I am,
Your affectionate Father,
Jolyon Forsyte.

And every year on the 1st January he had added a hundred and the interest. The sum was mounting up—next New Year's Day it would be fifteen hundred and odd pounds! And it is difficult to say how much satisfaction he had got out of that yearly transaction. But the correspondence had ended.

In spite of his love for his son, in spite of an instinct, partly constitutional, partly the result, as in thousands of his class, of the continual handling and watching of affairs, prompting him to judge conduct by results rather than by principle, there was at the bottom of his heart a sort of uneasiness. His son ought, under the circumstances, to have gone to the dogs; that law was laid down in all the novels, sermons, and plays he had ever read, heard, or witnessed.

After receiving the cheque back there seemed to him to be something wrong somewhere. Why had his son not gone to the dogs? But, then, who could tell?

He had heard, of course—in fact, he had made it his business to find out—that Jo lived in St. John's Wood, that he had a little house in Wistaria Avenue with a garden, and took his wife about with him into society—a queer sort of society, no doubt—and that they had two children—the little chap they called Jolly (considering the circumstances the name struck him as cynical, and old Jolyon both feared and disliked cynicism), and a girl called Holly, born since the marriage. Who could tell what his son's circumstances really were? He had capitalised the income he had inherited from his mother's father, and joined Lloyd's as an underwriter; he painted pictures, too—water-colours. Old Jolyon knew this, for he had surreptitiously bought them from time to time, after chancing to see his son's name signed at the bottom of a representation of the River Thames in a dealer's window. He thought them bad, and did not hang them because of the signature; he kept them locked up in a drawer.

In the great opera-house a terrible yearning came on him to see his son. He remembered the days when he had been wont to slide him, in a brown holland suit, to and fro under the arch of his legs; the times when he ran beside the boy's pony, teaching him to ride; the day he first took him to school. He had been a loving, lovable little chap! After he went to Eton he had acquired, perhaps, a little too much of that desirable manner which old Jolyon knew was only to be obtained at such places and at great expense; but he had always been companionable. Always a companion, even after Cambridge—a little far off, perhaps, owing to the advantages he had received. Old Jolyon's feeling towards our public schools and 'Varsities never wavered, and he retained touchingly his attitude of admiration and mistrust towards a system appropriate to the highest in the land, of which he had not himself been privileged to partake. . . . Now that June had gone and left, or as good as left him, it would have been a comfort to see his son again. Guilty of this treason to his family, his principles, his class, old Jolyon fixed his eyes on the singer. A poor thing—a wretched poor thing! And the Florestan a perfect stick!

It was over. They were easily pleased nowadays!

In the crowded street he snapped up a cab under the very nose of a stout and much younger gentleman, who had already assumed it to be his own. His route lay through Pall Mall, and at the corner, instead of going through the Green Park, the cabman turned to drive up St. James's Street. Old Jolyon put his hand through the trap (he could not bear being taken out of his way); in turning, however, he found himself opposite the 'Hotch Potch', and the yearning that had been secretly with him the whole evening prevailed. He called to the driver to stop. He would go in and ask if Jo still belonged there.

He went in. The hall looked exactly as it did when he used to dine there with Jack Herring, and they had the best cook in London; and he looked round with the shrewd, straight glance that had caused him all his life to be better served than most men.

'Mr Jolyon Forsyte still a member here?'

'Yes, sir; in the Club now, sir. What name?'

Old Jolyon was taken aback.

'His father,' he said.

And having spoken, he took his stand, back to the fire-place.

Young Jolyon, on the point of leaving the Club, had put on his hat, and was in the act of crossing the hall, as the porter met him. He was no longer young, with hair going grey, and face—a narrower replica of his father's, with the same large drooping moustache—decidedly worn. He turned pale. This meeting was terrible after all those years, for nothing in the world was so terrible as a scene. They met and crossed hands without a word. Then, with a quaver in his voice, the father said:

'How are you, my boy?'

The son answered:

'How are you, Dad?'

Old Jolyon's hand trembled in its thin lavender glove.

'If you're going my way,' he said, 'I can give you a lift.'

And as though in the habit of taking each other home every night they went out and stepped into the cab.

To old Jolyon it seemed that his son had grown. 'More of a man altogether,' was his comment. Over the natural amiability of that son's face had come a rather sardonic mask, as though he had found in the circumstances of his life the necessity for armour. The features were certainly those of a Forsyte, but the expression was more the introspective look of a student or philosopher. He had no doubt been obliged to look into himself a good deal in the course of those fifteen years.

To young Jolyon the first sight of his father was undoubtedly a shock—he looked so worn and old. But in the cab he seemed hardly to have changed, still having the calm look so well remembered, still being upright and keen-eyed.

'You look well, Dad.'

'Middling,' old Jolyon answered.

He was the prey of an anxiety that he found he must put into words. Having got his son back like this, he felt he must know what was his financial position.

'Jo,' he said, 'I should like to hear what sort of water you're in. I suppose you're in debt?'

He put it this way that his son might find it easier to confess.

Young Jolyon answered in his ironical voice:

'No! I'm not in debt!'

Old Jolyon saw that he was angry, and touched his hand. He had run a risk. It was worth it, however, and Jo had never been sulky with him. They drove on, without speaking again, to Stanhope Gate. Old Jolyon invited him in, but young Jolyon shook his head.

'June's not here,' said his father hastily: 'went off to-day on a visit. I suppose you know that she's engaged to be married?'

'Already?' murmured young Jolyon.

Old Jolyon stepped out, and, in paying the cab fare, for the first time in his life gave the driver a sovereign in mistake for a shilling.

Placing the coin in his mouth, the cabman whipped his horse secretly on the underneath and hurried away.

Old Jolyon turned the key softly in the lock, pushed open the door, and beckoned. His son saw him gravely hanging up his coat, with an expression on his face like that of a boy who intends to steal cherries.

The door of the dining-room was open, the gas turned low; a spirit-urn hissed on a tea-tray, and close to it a cynical-looking cat had fallen asleep on the dining-table. Old Jolyon 'shoo'd' her off at once. The incident was a relief to his feelings; he rattled his opera hat behind the animal.

'She's got fleas,' he said, following her out of the room. Through the door in the hall leading to the basement he called 'Hssst!' several times, as though assisting the cat's departure, till by some strange coincidence the butler appeared below.

'You can go to bed, Parfitt,' said old Jolyon. 'I will lock up and put out.'

When he again entered the dining-room the cat unfortunately preceded him, with her tail in the air, proclaiming that she had been through this manoeuvre for suppressing the butler from the first.

A fatality had dogged old Jolyon's domestic stratagems all his life.

Young Jolyon could not help smiling. He was very well versed in irony, and everything that evening seemed to him ironical. The episode of the cat; the announcement of his own daughter's engagement. So he had no more part or parcel in her than he had in the Puss! And the poetical justice of this appealed to him.

'What is June like now?' he asked.

'She's a little thing,' returned old Jolyon; 'they say she's like me, but that's their folly. She's more like your mother–the same eyes and hair.'

'Ah! and she is pretty?'

Old Jolyon was too much of a Forsyte to praise anything freely; especially anything for which he had a genuine admiration.

'Not bad looking–a regular Forsyte chin. It'll be lonely here when she's gone, Jo.'

The look on his face again gave young Jolyon the shock he had felt on first seeing his father.

'What will you do with yourself, Dad? I suppose she's wrapped up in him?'

'Do with myself?' repeated old Jolyon with an angry break in his voice. 'It'll be miserable work living here alone. I don't know how it's to end. I wish to goodness–' He checked himself, and added: 'The question is, what had I better do with this house?'

Young Jolyon looked round the room. It was peculiarly vast and dreary, decorated with the enormous pictures of still life that he remembered as a boy–sleeping dogs with their noses resting on bunches of carrots, together with onions and grapes lying side by side in mild surprise. The house was a white elephant, but he could not conceive of his father living in a smaller place; and all the more did it all seem ironical.

In his great chair with the book-rest sat old Jolyon, the figurehead of his family and class and creed, with his white head and dome-like forehead, the representative of moderation, and order, and love of property. As lonely an old man as there was in London.

There he sat in the gloomy comfort of the room, a puppet in the power of great forces that cared nothing for family or class or creed, but moved, machine-like, with dread processes to inscrutable ends. This was how it struck young Jolyon, who had the impersonal eye.

The poor old Dad! So this was the end, the purpose to which he had lived with such magnificent moderation! To be lonely, and grow older and older, yearning for a soul to speak to!

In his turn old Jolyon looked back at his son. He wanted to talk about many things that he had been unable to talk about all these years. It had been impossible to seriously confide to June his conviction that property in the Soho quarter would go up in value; his uneasiness about that tremendous silence of Pippin, the superintendent of the New Colliery Company, of which he had so long been chairman; his disgust at the steady fall in American Golgothas, or even to discuss how, by some sort of settlement, he could best avoid the payment of those death duties, which would follow his decease. Under the influence, however, of a cup of tea, which he seemed to stir indefinitely, he began to speak at last. A new vista of life was thus opened up, a promised land of talk, where he could find a harbour against the waves of anticipation and regret; where he could soothe his soul with the opium of devising how to round off his property and make eternal the only part of him that was to remain alive.

Young Jolyon was a good listener; it was his great quality. He kept his eyes fixed on his father's face, putting a question now and then.

The clock struck one before old Jolyon had finished, and at the sound of its striking his principles came back. He took out his watch with a look of surprise:

'I must go to bed, Jo,' he said.

Young Jolyon rose and held out his hand to help his father up. The old face looked worn and hollow again; the eyes were steadily averted.

'Good-bye, my boy; take care of yourself.'

A moment passed, and young Jolyon, turning on his heel, marched out at the door. He could hardly see; his smile quavered. Never in all the fifteen years since he had first found out that life was no simple business, had he found it so singularly complicated.

3

DINNER AT SWITHIN'S

In Swithin's orange and light-blue dining-room, facing the Park, the round table was laid for twelve.

A cut-glass chandelier filled with lighted candles hung like a giant stalactite above its centre, radiating over large gilt-framed mirrors, slabs of marble on the tops of side-tables, and heavy gold chairs with crewel worked seats. Everything betokened that love of beauty so deeply implanted in each family which has had its own way to make into Society, out of the more vulgar heart of Nature. Swithin had indeed an impatience of simplicity, a love of ormolu, which had always stamped him amongst his associates as a man of great, if somewhat luxurious taste; and out of the knowledge that no one could possibly enter his rooms without perceiving him to be a man of wealth, he had derived a solid and prolonged happiness such as perhaps no other circumstance in life had afforded him.

Since his retirement from house agency, a profession deplorable in his estimation, especially as to its auctioneering department, he had abandoned himself to naturally aristocratic tastes.

The perfect luxury of his latter days had embedded him like a fly in sugar; and his mind, where very little took place from morning till night, was the junction of two curiously opposite emotions, a lingering and sturdy satisfaction that he had made his own way and his own fortune, and a sense that a man of his distinction should never have been allowed to soil his mind with work.

He stood at the sideboard in a white waistcoat with large gold and onyx buttons, watching his valet screw the necks of three champagne bottles deeper into ice-pails. Between the points of his stand-up collar, which—though it hurt him to move—he would on no account have had altered, the pale flesh of his under-chin remained immovable. His eyes roved from bottle to bottle. He was debating, and he argued like this: 'Jolyon drinks a glass, perhaps two, he's so careful of himself. James, he can't take his wine nowadays. Nicholas'—Fanny and he would swill water, he shouldn't wonder! Soames didn't count; these young nephews—Soames was thirty-eight—couldn't drink! But Bosinney? Encountering in the name of this stranger something outside the range of his philosophy, Swithin paused. A misgiving arose within him! It was impossible to tell! June was only a girl, in love too! Emily (Mrs James) liked a good glass of champagne. It was too dry for Juley, poor old soul, she had no palate. As to Hatty Chessman! The thought of this old friend caused a cloud of thought to obscure the perfect glassiness of his eyes: He shouldn't wonder if she drank half a bottle!

But in thinking of his remaining guest, an expression like that of a cat who is just going to purr stole over his old face: Mrs Soames! She mightn't take much, but she would appreciate what she drank; it was a pleasure to give her good wine! A pretty woman—and sympathetic to him!

The thought of her was like champagne itself! A pleasure to give a good wine to a young woman who looked so well, who knew how to dress, with charming manners, quite distinguished—a pleasure to entertain her. Between the points of his collar he gave his head the first small, painful oscillation of the evening.

'Adolf!' he said. 'Put in another bottle.'

He himself might drink a good deal, for, thanks to that p— prescription of Blight's, he found himself extremely well, and he had been careful to take no lunch. He had not felt so well for weeks. Puffing out his lower lip, he gave his last instructions:

'Adolf, the least touch of the West India when you come to the ham.'

Passing into the anteroom, he sat down on the edge of a chair, with his knees apart; and his tall, bulky form was wrapped at once in an expectant, strange, primeval immobility. He was ready to rise at a moment's notice. He had not given a dinner-party for months. This dinner in honour of June's engagement had seemed a bore at first (among Forsytes the custom of solemnising engagements by feasts was religiously observed), but the labours of sending invitations and ordering the repast over, he felt pleasantly stimulated.

And thus sitting, a watch in his hand, fat, and smooth, and golden, like a flattened globe of butter, he thought of nothing.

A long man, with side-whiskers, who had once been in Swithin's service, but was now a greengrocer, entered and proclaimed:

'Mrs Chessman, Mrs Septimus Small!'

Two ladies advanced. The one in front, habited entirely in red, had large, settled patches of the same colour in her cheeks, and a hard, dashing eye. She walked at Swithin, holding out a hand cased in a long, primrose-coloured glove:

'Well, Swithin,' she said, 'I haven't seen you for ages. How are you? Why, my dear boy, how stout you're getting!'

The fixity of Swithin's eye alone betrayed emotion. A dumb and grumbling anger swelled his bosom. It was vulgar to be stout, to talk of being stout; he had a chest, nothing more. Turning to his sister, he grasped her hand and said in a tone of command:

'Well, Juley.'

Mrs Septimus Small was the tallest of the four sisters; her good, round old face had gone a little sour; an innumerable pout clung all over it, as if it had been encased in an iron wire mask up to that evening, which, being suddenly removed, left little rolls of mutinous flesh all over her countenance. Even her eyes were pouting. It was thus that she recorded her permanent resentment at the loss of Septimus Small.

She had quite a reputation for saying the wrong thing, and, tenacious like all her breed, she would hold to it when she had said it, and add to it another wrong thing, and so on. With the decease of her husband the family tenacity, the family matter-of-factness, had gone sterile within her. A great talker, when allowed, she would converse without the faintest animation for hours together, relating, with epic monotony, the innumerable occasions on which Fortune had misused her; nor did she ever perceive that her hearers sympathised with Fortune, for her heart was kind.

Having sat, poor soul, long by the bedside of Small (a man of poor constitution), she had acquired the habit, and there were countless subsequent occasions when she had sat immense periods of time to amuse sick people, children, and other helpless persons, and she could never divest herself of the feeling that the world was the most ungrateful place anybody could live in. Sunday after Sunday she sat at the feet of that extremely witty preacher, the Rev. Thomas Scoles, who exercised a great influence over her; but she succeeded in convincing everybody that even this was a misfortune. She had passed into a proverb in the family, and when anybody was observed to be peculiarly distressing, he was known as 'a regular Juley'. The habit of her mind would have killed anybody but a Forsyte at forty; but she was seventy-two, and had never looked better. And one felt that there were capacities for enjoyment about her which might yet come out. She owned three canaries, the cat Tommy, and half a parrot—in common with her sister Hester; and these poor creatures (kept carefully out of Timothy's way—he was nervous about animals), unlike human beings, recognising that she could not help being blighted, attached themselves to her passionately.

She was sombrely magnificent this evening in black bombazine, with a mauve front cut in a shy triangle, and crowned with a black velvet ribbon round the base of her thin throat; black and mauve for evening wear was esteemed very chaste by nearly every Forsyte.

Pouting at Swithin, she said:

'Ann has been asking for you. You haven't been near us for an age!'

Swithin put his thumbs within the armholes of his waistcoat, and replied:

'Ann's getting very shaky; she ought to have a doctor!'

'Mr and Mrs Nicholas Forsyte!'

Nicholas Forsyte, cocking his rectangular eyebrows, wore a smile. He had succeeded during the day in bringing to fruition a scheme for the employment of a tribe from Upper India in the gold-mines of Ceylon. A pet plan, carried at last in the teeth of great difficulties—he was justly pleased. It would double the output of his mines, and, as he had often forcibly argued, all experience tended to show that a man must die; and whether he died of a miserable old age in his own country, or prematurely of damp in the bottom of a foreign mine, was surely of little consequence, provided that by a change in his mode of life he benefited the British Empire.

His ability was undoubted. Raising his broken nose towards his listener, he would add:

'For want of a few hundred of these fellows we haven't paid a dividend for years, and look at the price of the shares. I can't get ten shillin's for them.'

He had been at Yarmouth, too, and had come back feeling that he had added at least ten years to his own life. He grasped Swithin's hand, exclaiming in a jocular voice:

'Well, so here we are again!'

Mrs Nicholas, an effete woman, smiled a smile of frightened jollity behind his back.

'Mr and Mrs James Forsyte! Mr and Mrs Soames Forsyte!'

Swithin drew his heels together, his deportment ever admirable.

'Well, James, well, Emily! How are you, Soames? How do you *do*?'

His hand enclosed Irene's, and his eyes swelled. She was a pretty woman—a little too pale, but her figure, her eyes, her teeth! Too good for that chap Soames!

The gods had given Irene dark brown eyes and golden hair, that strange combination, provocative of men's glances, which is said to be the mark of a weak character. And the full, soft pallor of her neck and shoulders, above a gold-coloured frock, gave to her personality an alluring strangeness.

Soames stood behind, his eyes fastened on his wife's neck. The hands of Swithin's watch, which he still held open in his hand, had left eight behind; it was half an hour beyond his dinner-time—he had had no lunch—and a strange primeval impatience surged up within him.

'It's not like Jolyon to be late!' he said to Irene, with uncontrollable vexation. 'I suppose it'll be June keeping him!'

'People in love are always late,' she answered.

Swithin stared at her; a dusky orange dyed his cheeks.

'They've no business to be. Some fashionable nonsense!'

And behind this outburst the inarticulate violence of primitive generations seemed to mutter and grumble.

'Tell me what you think of my new star, Uncle Swithin,' said Irene softly.

Among the lace in the bosom of her dress was shining a five-pointed star, made of eleven diamonds.

Swithin looked at the star. He had a pretty taste in stones; no question could have been more sympathetically devised to distract his attention.

'Who gave you that?' he asked.

'Soames.'

There was no change in her face, but Swithin's pale eyes bulged as though he might suddenly have been afflicted with insight.

'I dare say you're dull at home,' he said. 'Any day you like to come and dine with me I'll give you as good a bottle of wine as you'll get in London.'

'Miss June Forsyte—Mr Jolyon Forsyte! . . . Mr Boswainey! . . .'

Swithin moved his arm, and said in a rumbling voice:

'Dinner now—dinner!'

He took in Irene, on the ground that he had not entertained her since she was a bride. June was the portion of Bosinney, who was placed between Irene and his fiancée. On the other side of June was James with Mrs Nicholas, then old Jolyon with Mrs James, Nicholas with Hatty Chessman, Soames with Mrs Small, completing the circle to Swithin again.

Family dinners of the Forsytes observe certain traditions. There are, for instance, no *hors d'œuvres*. The reason for this is unknown. Theory among the younger members traces it to the disgraceful price of oysters; it is more probably due to a desire to come to the point, to a good practical sense deciding at once that *hors d'œuvres* are but poor things. The Jameses alone, unable to withstand a custom almost universal in Park Lane, are now and then unfaithful.

A silent, almost morose, inattention to each other succeeds to the subsidence into their seats, lasting till well into the first entrée, but interspersed with remarks such as, 'Tom's bad again; I can't tell what's the matter with him!'–'I suppose Ann doesn't come down in the mornings!'–'What's the name of your doctor, Fanny? Stubbs? He's a quack!'–'Winifred? She's got too many children. Four isn't it? She's as thin as a lath!'–'What d'you give for this sherry, Swithin?' Too dry for me!'

With the second glass of champagne, a kind of hum makes itself heard, which, when divested of casual accessories and resolved into its primal element, is found to be James telling a story, and this goes on for a long time, encroaching sometimes even upon what must universally be recognised as the crowning point of a Forsyte feast–'the saddle of mutton'.

No Forsyte has given a dinner without providing a saddle of mutton. There is something in its succulent solidity which makes it suitable to people 'of a certain position'. It is nourishing and–tasty; the sort of thing a man remembers eating. It has a past and a future, like a deposit paid into a bank; and it is something that can be argued about.

Each branch of the family tenaciously held to a particular locality–old Jolyon swearing by Dartmoor, James by Welsh, Swithin by Southdown, Nicholas maintaining that people might sneer, but there was nothing like New Zealand. As for Roger, the 'original' of the brothers, he had been obliged to invent a locality of his own, and with an ingenuity worthy of a man who had devised a new profession for his sons, he had discovered a shop where they sold German; on being remonstrated with, he had proved his point by producing a butcher's bill, which showed that he paid more than any of the others. It was on this occasion that old Jolyon, turning to June, had said in one of his bursts of philosophy:

'You may depend upon it, they're a cranky lot, the Forsytes–and you'll find it out, as you grow older!'

Timothy alone held apart, for though he ate saddle of mutton heartily, he was, he said, afraid of it.

To anyone interested psychologically in Forsytes, this great saddle-of-mutton trait is of prime importance; not only does it illustrate their tenacity, both collectively and as individuals, but it marks them as belonging in fibre and instincts to that great class which believes in nourishment and flavour, and yields to no sentimental craving for beauty.

Younger members of the family indeed would have done without a joint altogether, preferring guinea-fowl, or lobster salad–something which appealed to the imagination, and had less nourishment–but these were females; or, if not, had been corrupted by their wives, or by mothers, who having been forced to eat saddle of mutton throughout their married lives, had passed a secret hostility towards it into the fibre of their sons.

The great saddle-of-mutton controversy at an end, a Tewkesbury ham commenced, together with the least touch of West India–Swithin was so long over this course that he caused a block in the progress of the dinner. To devote himself to it with better heart, he paused in his conversation.

From his seat by Mrs Septimus Small, Soames watched. He had a reason of his own connected with a pet building scheme, for observing Bosinney. The architect might do for his purpose; he looked clever, as he sat leaning back in his chair, moodily making little ramparts with bread-crumbs. Soames noted his dress clothes to be well cut, but too small, as though made many years ago.

He saw him turn to Irene and say something, and her face sparkle as he often saw it sparkle at other people—never at himself. He tried to catch what they were saying, but Aunt Juley was speaking.

Hadn't that always seemed very extraordinary to Soames? Only last Sunday dear Mr Scoles had been so witty in his sermon, so sarcastic: '"For what," he had said, "shall it profit a man if he gain his own soul, but lose all his property?"' That, he had said, was the motto of the middle class; now, what *had* he meant by that? Of course, it might be what middle-class people believed—she didn't know; what did Soames think?

He answered abstractly: 'How should I know? Scoles is a humbug, though, isn't he?' For Bosinney was looking round the table, as if pointing out the peculiarities of the guests, and Soames wondered what he was saying. By her smile Irene was evidently agreeing with his remarks. She seemed always to agree with other people.

Her eyes were turned on himself; Soames dropped his glance at once. The smile had died off her lips.

A humbug? But what did Soames mean? If Mr Scoles was a humbug, a clergyman—then anybody might be—it was frightful!

'Well, and so they are!' said Soames.

During Aunt Juley's momentary and horrified silence he caught some words of Irene's that sounded like: 'Abandon hope, all ye who enter here!'

But Swithin had finished his ham.

'Where do you go for your mushrooms?' he was saying to Irene in a voice like a courtier's; 'you ought to go to Snileybob's—he'll give 'em you fresh. These *little* men, they won't take the trouble!'

Irene turned to answer him, and Soames saw Bosinney watching her and smiling to himself. A curious smile the fellow had. A half-simple arrangement, like a child who smiles when he is pleased. As for George's nickname—'The Buccaneer'—he did nt think much of that. And, seeing Bosinney turn to June, Soames smiled too, but sardonically—he did not like June, who was not looking too pleased.

This was not surprising for she had just held the following conversation with James:

'I stayed on the river on my way home, Uncle James, and saw a beautiful site for a house.'

James, a slow and thorough eater, stopped the process of mastication.

'Eh?' he said. 'Now, where was that?'

'Close to Pangbourne.'

James placed a piece of ham in his mouth, and June waited.

'I suppose *you* wouldn't know whether the land about there was freehold?' he asked at last. '*You* wouldn't know anything about the price of land about there?'

'Yes,' said June; 'I made inquiries.' Her little resolute face under its copper crown was suspiciously eager and aglow.

James regarded her with the air of an inquisitor.

'What? You're not thinking of buying land?' he ejaculated, dropping his fork.

June was greatly encouraged by his interest. It had long been her pet plan that her uncles should benefit themselves and Bosinney by building country houses.

'Of course not,' she said. 'I thought it would be such a splendid place for—you or—someone to build a country house!'

James looked at her sideways, and placed a second piece of ham in his mouth.

'Land ought to be very dear about there,' he said.

What June had taken for personal interest was only the impersonal excitement of every Forsyte who hears of something eligible in danger of passing into other hands. But she refused to see the disappearance of her chance, and continued to press her point.

'You ought to go into the country, Uncle James. I wish I had a lot of money; I wouldn't live another day in London.'

James was stirred to the depths of his long thin figure; he had no idea his niece held such downright views.

'Why don't you go into the country?' repeated June; 'it would do you a lot of good!'

'Why?' began James in a fluster. Buying land—what good d'you suppose I can do buying land, building houses?—I couldn't get four per cent. for my money!'

'What does that matter! You'd get fresh air.'

'Fresh air!' exclaimed James; 'what should I do with fresh air—'

'I should have thought anybody liked to have fresh air,' said June scornfully.

James wiped his napkin all over his mouth.

'You don't know the value of money,' he said, avoiding her eye.

'No! and I hope I never shall!' and, biting her lip with inexpressible mortification, poor June was silent.

Why were her own relations so rich, and Phil never knew where the money was coming from for to-morrow's tobacco. Why couldn't they do something for him? But they were so selfish. Why couldn't they build country houses? She had all that naïve dogmatism which is so pathetic, and sometimes achieves such great results. Bosinney, to whom she turned in her discomfiture, was talking to Irene, and a chill fell on June's spirit. Her eyes grew steady with anger, like old Jolyon's when his will was crossed.

James, too, was much disturbed. He felt as though someone had threatened his right to invest his money at five per cent. Jolyon had spoiled her. None of *his* girls would have said such a thing. James had always been exceedingly liberal to his children, and the consciousness of this made him feel it all the more deeply. He trifled moodily with his strawberries, then, deluging them with cream, he ate them quickly; they, at all events, should not escape him.

No wonder he was upset. Engaged for fifty-four years (he had been admitted a solicitor on the earliest day sanctioned by the law) in arranging mortgages, preserving investments at a dead level of high and safe interest, conducting negotiations on the principle of securing the utmost possible out of other people compatible with safety to his clients and himself, in calculations as to the exact pecuniary possibilities of all the relations of life, he had come at last to think purely in terms of money. Money was now his light, his medium for seeing, that without which he was really unable to see, really not cognisant of phenomena; and to have this thing, 'I hope I shall never know the value of money!' said to his face, saddened and exasperated him. He knew it to be nonsense, or it would have frightened him. What was the world coming to?

Suddenly recollecting the story of young Jolyon, however, he felt a little comforted, for what could you expect with a father like that! This turned his thoughts into a channel still less pleasant. What was all this talk about Soames and Irene?

As in all self-respecting families, an emporium had been established where family secrets were bartered, and family stock priced. It was known on Forsyte 'Change that Irene regretted her marriage. Her regret was disapproved of. She ought to have known her own mind; no dependable woman made these mistakes.

James reflected sourly that they had a nice house (rather small) in an excellent position, no children, and no money troubles. Soames was reserved about his affairs, but he must be getting a very warm man. He had a capital income from the business—for Soames, like his father, was a member of that well-known firm of solicitors, Forsyte, Bustard and Forsyte—and had always been very careful. He had done quite unusually well with some mortgages he had taken up, too—a little timely foreclosure—most lucky hits!

There was no reason why Irene should not be happy, yet they said she'd been asking for a separate room. He knew where that ended. It wasn't as if Soames drank.

James looked at his daughter-in-law. That unseen glance of his was cold and dubious. Appeal and fear were in it, and a sense of personal grievance. Why should he be worried like this? It was very likely all nonsense; women were funny things! They exaggerated so, you didn't know what to believe; and then, nobody told him anything, he had to find out everything for himself. Again he looked furtively at Irene, and across from her to Soames. The latter, listening to Aunt Juley, was looking up under his brows in the direction of Bosinney.

'He's fond of her, I know,' thought James. 'Look at the way he's always giving her things.'

And the extraordinary unreasonableness of her disaffection struck him with increased force. It was a pity, too, she was a taking little thing, and he, James, would be really quite fond of her if she'd only let him. She had taken up lately with June; *that* was doing her no good, that was certainly doing her no good. She was getting to have opinions of her own. He didn't know what she wanted with anything of the sort. She'd a good home, and everything she could wish for. He felt that her friends ought to be chosen for her. To go on like this was dangerous.

June, indeed, with her habit of championing the unfortunate, had dragged from Irene a confession, and, in return, had preached the necessity of facing the evil, by separation, if need be. But in the face of these exhortations, Irene had kept a brooding silence, as though she found terrible the thought of this struggle carried through in cold blood. He would never give her up, she had said to June.

'Who cares?' June cried; 'let him do what he likes—you've only to stick to it!' And she had not scrupled to say something of this sort at Timothy's; James, when he heard of it, had felt a natural indignation and horror.

What if Irene were to take it into her head to—he could hardly frame the thought—to leave Soames? But he felt this thought so unbearable that he at once put it away; the shady visions it conjured up, the sound of family tongues buzzing in his ears, the horror of the conspicuous happening so close to him, to one of his own children! Luckily, she had no money—a beggarly fifty pounds a year! And he thought of the deceased Heron, who had had nothing to leave her, with contempt. Brooding over his glass, his long legs twisted under the table, he quite omitted to rise when the ladies left the room. He would have to speak to Soames—would have to put him on his guard; they could not go on like this, now that such a contingency had occurred to him. And he noticed with sour disfavour that June had left her wine-glass full of wine.

'That little thing's at the bottom of it all,' he mused; 'Irene'd never have thought of it herself.' James was a man of imagination.

The voice of Swithin roused him from his reverie.

'I gave four hundred pounds for it,' he was saying. 'Of course it's a regular work of art.'

'Four hundred! H'm! that's a lot of money!' chimed in Nicholas.

The object alluded to was an elaborate group of statuary in Italian marble, which, placed upon a lofty stand (also of marble), diffused an atmosphere of culture throughout the room. The subsidiary figures, of which there were six, female, nude, and of highly ornate workmanship, were all pointing towards the central figure, also nude, and female, who was pointing at herself; and all this gave the observer a very pleasant sense of her extreme value. Aunt Juley, nearly opposite, had had the greatest difficulty in not looking at it all the evening.

Old Jolyon spoke; it was he who had started the discussion.

'Four hundred fiddlesticks! Don't tell me you gave four hundred for *that*?'

Between the points of his collar Swithin's chin made the second painful oscillatory movement of the evening. 'Four—hundred—pounds, of English money; not a farthing less. I don't regret it. It's not common English—it's genuine modern Italian!'

Soames raised the corner of his lip in a smile, and looked across at Bosinney. The architect was grinning behind the fumes of his cigarette. Now, indeed, he looked more like a buccaneer.

'There's a lot of work about it,' remarked James hastily, who was really moved by the size of the group. 'It'd sell well at Jobson's.'

'The poor foreign dey-vil that made it,' went on Swithin, 'asked me five hundred—I gave him four. It's worth eight. Looked half-starved, poor dey-vil!'

'Ah!' chimed in Nicholas suddenly, 'poor. seedy-lookin' chaps, these artists; it's a wonder to me how they live. Now, there's young Flageoletti, that Fanny and the girls are always havin' in, to play the fiddle; if he makes a hundred a year it's as much as ever he does!'

James shook his head. 'Ah!' he said, '*I* don't know how they live!'

Old Jolyon had risen, and, cigar in mouth, went to inspect the group at close quarters.

'Wouldn't have given two for it!' he pronounced at last.

Soames saw his father and Nicholas glance at each other anxiously; and, on the other side of Swithin, Bosinney, still shrouded in smoke.

'I wonder what *he* thinks of it?' thought Soames, who knew well enough that this group was hopelessly *vieux jeu*; hopelessly of the last generation. There was no longer any sale at Jobson's for such works of art.

Swithin's answer came at last. 'You never knew anything about a statue. You've got your pictures, and that's all!'

Old Jolyon walked back to his seat, puffing his cigar. It was not likely that he was going to be drawn into an argument with an obstinate beggar like Swithin, pig-headed as a mule, who had never known a statue from—a straw hat.

'Stucco!' was all he said.

It had long been physically impossible for Swithin to start; his fist came down on the table.

'Stucco! I should like to see anything you've got in your house half as good!'

And behind his speech seemed to sound again that rumbling violence of primitive generations.

It was James who saved the situation.

'Now, what do *you* say, Mr Bosinney? You're an architect; you ought to know all about statues and things!'

Every eye was turned upon Bosinney; all waited with a strange, suspicious look for his answer.

And Soames, speaking for the first time, asked:

'Yes, Bosinney, what do you say?'

Bosinney replied coolly:

'The work is a remarkable one.'

His words were addressed to Swithin, his eyes smiled slyly at old Jolyon; only Soames remained unsatisfied.

'Remarkable for what?'

'For its naïveté.'

The answer was followed by an impressive silence; Swithin alone was not sure whether a compliment was intended.

4

PROJECTION OF THE HOUSE

Soames Forsyte walked out of his green-painted front door three days after the dinner at Swithin's, and looking back from across the Square, confirmed his impression that the house wanted painting.

He had left his wife sitting on the sofa in the drawing-room, her hands crossed in her lap, manifestly waiting for him to go out. This was not unusual. It happened, in fact, every day.

He could not understand what she found wrong with him. It was not as if he drank! Did he run into debt, or gamble, or swear; was he violent; were his friends rackety; did he stay out at night? On the contrary.

The profound, subdued aversion which he felt in his wife was a mystery to him, and a source of the most terrible irritation. That she had made a mistake, and did not love him, had tried to love him and could not love him, was obviously no reason.

He that could imagine so outlandish a cause for his wife's not getting on with him was certainly no Forsyte.

Soames was forced, therefore, to set the blame entirely down to his wife. He had never met a woman so capable of inspiring affection. They could not go anywhere without his seeing how all the men were attracted by her; their looks, manners, voices, betrayed it; her behaviour under this attention had been beyond reproach. That she was one of those women–not too common in the Anglo-Saxon race–born to be loved and to love, who when not loving are not living, had certainly never even occurred to him. Her power of attraction he regarded as part of her value as his property; but it made him, indeed, suspect that she could give as well as receive; and she gave him nothing! 'Then why did she marry him?' was his continual thought. He had forgotten his courtship; that year and a half when he had besieged and lain in wait for her, devising schemes for her entertainment, giving her gifts, proposing to her periodically, and keeping her other admirers away with his perpetual presence. He had forgotten the day when, adroitly taking advantage of an acute phase of her dislike to her home surroundings, he crowned his labours with success. If he remembered anything, it was the dainty capriciousness with which the gold-haired, dark-eyed girl had treated him. He certainly did not remember the look on her face–strange, passive, appealing–when suddenly one day she had yielded, and said that she would marry him.

It had been one of those real devoted wooings which books and people praise, when the lover is at length rewarded for hammering the iron till it is malleable, and all must be happy ever after as the wedding bells.

Soames walked eastwards, mousing doggedly along the shady side.

The house wanted doing up, unless he decided to move into the country and build.

For the hundredth time that month he turned over this problem. There was no use in rushing into things! He was very comfortably off, with an increasing income getting on for three thousand a year; but his invested capital was not perhaps so large as his father believed–James had a tendency to expect that his children should be better off than they were. 'I can manage eight thousand easily enough,' he thought, 'without calling in either Robertson's or Nicholl's.'

He had stopped to look in at a picture shop, for Soames was an 'amateur' of pictures, and had a little room in No. 62, Montpelier Square, full of canvases, stacked against the wall, which he had no room to hang. He brought them home with him on his way back from the City, generally after dark, and would enter this room on Sunday afternoons, to spend hours turning the pictures to the light, examining the marks on their backs, and occasionally making notes.

They were nearly all landscapes with figures in the foreground, a sign of some mysterious revolt against London, its tall houses, its interminable streets, where his life and the lives of his breed and class were passed. Every now and then he would take one or two pictures away with him in a cab, and stop at Jobson's on his way into the City.

He rarely showed them to anyone; Irene, whose opinion he secretly respected and perhaps for that reason never solicited, had only been into the room on rare occasions, in discharge of some wifely duty. She was not asked to look at the pictures, and she never did. To Soames this was another grievance. He hated that pride of hers, and secretly dreaded it.

In the plate-glass window of the picture shop his image stood and looked at him.

His sleek hair under the brim of the tall hat had a sheen like the hat itself; his cheeks, pale and flat, the line of his clean-shaven lips, his firm chin with its greyish shaven tinge, and the buttoned strictness of his black cut-away coat, conveyed an appearance of reserve and secrecy, of imperturbable, enforced composure; but his eyes, cold, grey, strained-looking with a line in the brow between them, examined him wistfully, as if they knew of a secret weakness.

He noted the subjects of the pictures, the names of the painters, made a calculation of their values, but without the satisfaction he usually derived from this inward appraisement, and walked on.

No. 62 would do well enough for another year, if he decided to build! The

times were good for building, money had not been so dear for years; and the site
he had seen at Robin Hill, when he had gone down there in the spring to inspect
the Nicholl mortgage–what could be better! Within twelve miles of Hyde Park
Corner, the value of the land certain to go up, would always fetch more than he
gave for it; so that a house, if in really good style, was a first-class investment.

The notion of being the one member of his family with a country house
weighed but little with him; for to a true Forsyte, sentiment, even the sentiment
of social position, was a luxury only to be indulged in after his appetite for more
material pleasure had been satisfied.

To get Irene out of London, away from opportunities of going about and
seeing people, away from her friends and those who put ideas into her head!
That was the thing! She was too thick with June! June disliked him. He
returned the sentiment. They were of the same blood.

It would be everything to get Irene out of town. The house would please her,
she would enjoy messing about with the decoration, she was very artistic!

The house must be in good style, something that would always be certain to
command a price, something unique, like that last house of Parkes, which had a
tower; but Parkes had himself said that his architect was ruinous. You never
knew where you were with these fellows; if they had a name they ran you into no
end of expense and were conceited into the bargain.

And a common architect was no good–the memory of Parkes's tower
precluded the employment of a common architect.

This was why he had thought of Bosinney. Since the dinner at Swithin's he
had made enquiries, the result of which had been meagre, but encouraging:
'One of the new school.'

'Clever?'

'As clever as you like–a bit–a bit up in the air!'

He had not been able to discover what houses Bosinney had built, nor what
his charges were. The impression he gathered was that he would be able to
make his own terms. The more he reflected on the idea, the more he liked it. It
would be keeping the thing in the family, with Forsytes almost an instinct; and
he would be able to get 'favoured-nation', if not nominal terms–only fair,
considering the chance to Bosinney of displaying his talents, for this house
must be no common edifice.

Soames reflected complacently on the work it would be sure to bring the
young man; for, like every Forsyte, he could be a thorough optimist when there
was anything to be had out of it.

Bosinney's office was in Sloane Street, close at hand, so that he would be able
to keep his eye continually on the plans.

Again, Irene would not be so likely to object to leave London if her greatest
friend's lover were given the job. June's marriage might depend on it. Irene
could not decently stand in the way of June's marriage; she would never do
that, he knew her too well. And June would be pleased; of this he saw the
advantage.

Bosinney looked clever, but he had also–and it was one of his great
attractions–an air as if he did not quite know on which side his bread were
buttered; he should be easy to deal with in money matters. Soames made this
reflection in no defrauding spirit; it was the natural attitude of his mind–of the
mind of any good business man–of all those thousands of good business men
through whom he was threading his way up Ludgate Hill.

Thus he fulfilled the inscrutable laws of his great class–of human nature itself—when he reflected, with a sense of comfort, that Bosinney would be easy to deal with in money matters.

While he elbowed his way on, his eyes which he usually kept fixed on the ground before his feet, were attracted upwards by the dome of St Paul's. It had a peculiar fascination for him, that old dome, and not once, but twice or three times a week, would he halt in his daily pilgrimage to enter beneath and stop in the side aisles for five or ten minutes, scrutinising the names and epitaphs on the monuments. The attraction for him of this great church was inexplicable, unless it enabled him to concentrate his thoughts on the business of the day. If any affair of peculiar moment, or demanding peculiar astuteness, was weighing on his mind, he invariably went in, to wander with mouse-like attention from epitaph to epitaph. Then retiring in the same noiseless way, he would hold steadily on up Cheapside, a thought more of dogged purpose in his gait, as though he had seen something which he had made up his mind to buy.

He went in this morning, but, instead of stealing from monument to monument, turned his eyes upwards to the columns and spacings of the walls, and remained motionless.

His uplifted face, with the awed and wistful look which faces take on themselves in church, was whitened to a chalky hue in the vast building. His gloved hands were clasped in front over the handle of his umbrella. He lifted them. Some sacred inspiration perhaps had come to him.

'Yes,' he thought, 'I must have room to hang my pictures.'

That evening, on his return from the City, he called at Bosinney's office. He found the architect in his shirt-sleeves, smoking a pipe, and ruling off lines on a plan. Soames refused a drink, and came at once to the point.

'If you've nothing better to do on Sunday, come down with me to Robin Hill, and give me your opinion on a building site.'

'Are you going to build?'

'Perhaps,' said Soames; 'but don't speak of it. I just want your opinion.'

'Quite so,' said the architect.

Soames peered about the room.

'You're rather high up here,' he remarked.

Any information he could gather about the nature and scope of Bosinney's business would be all to the good.

'It does well enough for me so far,' answered the architect. 'You're accustomed to the swells.'

He knocked out his pipe, but replaced it empty between his teeth; it assisted him perhaps to carry on the conversation. Soames noted a hollow in each cheek, made, as it were, by suction.

'What do you pay for an office like this?' said he.

'Fifty too much,' replied Bosinney.

This answer impressed Soames favourably.

'I suppose it *is* dear,' he said. 'I'll call for you on Sunday about eleven.'

The following Sunday therefore he called for Bosinney in a hansom, and drove him to the station. On arriving at Robin Hill, they found no cab, and started to walk the mile and a half to the site.

It was the 1st of August—a perfect day, with a burning sun and cloudless sky—and in the straight, narrow road leading up the hill their feet kicked up a yellow dust.

'Gravel soil,' remarked Soames, and sideways he glanced at the coat Bosinney wore. Into the side-pockets of this coat were thrust bundles of papers, and under one arm was carried a queer-looking stick. Soames noted these and other peculiarities.

No one but a clever man, or, indeed, a buccaneer, would have taken such liberties with his appearance; and though the eccentricities were revolting to Soames, he derived a certain satisfaction from them, as evidence of qualities by which he must inevitably profit. If the fellow could build houses, what did his clothes matter?

'I told you,' he said, 'that I want this house to be a surprise, so don't say anything about it. I never talk of my affairs until they're carried through.'

Bosinney nodded.

'Let women into your plans,' pursued Soames, 'and you never know where it'll end.'

'Ah!' said Bosinney, 'women are the devil!'

This feeling had long been at the bottom of Soames's heart; he had never, however, put it into words.

'Oh!' he muttered, 'so you're beginning to–' He stopped, but added, with an uncontrollable burst of spite: 'June's got a temper of her own–always had.'

'A temper's not a bad thing in an angel.'

Soames had never called Irene an angel. He could not so have violated his best instincts, letting other people into the secret of her value, and giving himself away. He made no reply.

They had struck into a half-made road across a warren. A cart-track led at right angles to a gravel-pit, beyond which the chimneys of a cottage rose amongst a clump of trees at the border of a thick wood. Tussocks of feathery grass covered the rough surface of the ground, and out of these the larks soared into the haze of sunshine. On the far horizon, over a countless succession of fields and hedges, rose a line of downs.

Soames led till they had crossed to the far side, and there he stopped. It was the chosen site; but now that he was about to divulge the spot to another he had become uneasy.

'The agent lives in that cottage,' he said; 'he'll give us some lunch–we'd better have lunch before we go into this matter.'

He again took the lead to the cottage, where the agent, a tall man named Oliver, with a heavy face and grizzled beard, welcomed them. During lunch, which Soames hardly touched, he kept looking at Bosinney, and once or twice passed his silk handkerchief stealthily over his forehead. The meal came to an end at last, and Bosinney rose.

'I dare say you've got business to talk over,' he said; 'I'll just go and nose about a bit.' Without waiting for a reply he strolled out.

Soames was solicitor to this estate, and he spent nearly an hour in the agent's company, looking at ground-plans and discussing the Nicholl and other mortgages; it was as it were by an afterthought that he brought up the question of the building site.

'Your people,' he said, 'ought to come down in their price to *me*, considering that I shall be the first to build.'

Oliver shook his head.

'The site you've fixed on, sir,' he said, 'is the cheapest we've got. Sites at the top of the slope are dearer by a good bit.'

'Mind,' said Soames, 'I've not decided; it's quite possible I shan't build at all. The ground-rent's very high.'

'Well, Mr Forsyte, I shall be sorry if you go off, and I think you'll make a mistake, sir. There's not a bit of land near London with such a view as this, nor one that's cheaper all things considered; we've only to advertise to get a mob of people after it.'

They looked at each other. Their faces said very plainly: 'I respect you as a man of business; and you can't expect me to believe a word you say.'

'Well,' repeated Soames, 'I haven't made up my mind; the thing will very likely go off!' With these words, taking up his umbrella, he put his chilly hand into the agent's, withdrew it without the faintest pressure, and went out into the sun.

He walked slowly back towards the site in deep thought. His instinct told him that what the agent had said was true. A cheap site. And the beauty of it was, that he knew the agent did not really think it cheap; so that his own intuitive knowledge was a victory over the agent's.

'Cheap or not, I mean to have it,' he thought.

The larks sprang up in front of his feet, the air was full of butterflies, a sweet fragrance rose from the wild grasses. The sappy scent of the bracken stole forth from the wood, where, hidden in the depths, pigeons were cooing, and from afar on the warm breeze came the rhythmic chiming of church bells.

Soames walked with his eyes on the ground, his lips opening and closing as though in anticipation of a delicious morsel. But when he arrived at the site, Bosinney was nowhere to be seen. After waiting some little time, he crossed the warren in the direction of the slope. He would have shouted, but dreaded the sound of his voice.

The warren was as lonely as a prairie, its silence only broken by the rustle of rabbits bolting to their holes, and the song of the larks.

Soames, the pioneer leader of the great Forsyte army advancing to the civilisation of this wilderness, felt his spirit daunted by the loneliness, by the invisible singing, and the hot sweet air. He had begun to retrace his steps when he at last caught site of Bosinney.

The architect was sprawling under a large oak tree, whose trunk, with a huge spread of bough and foliage, ragged with age, stood on the verge of the rise.

Soames had to touch him on the shoulder before he looked up.

'Hallo! Forsyte,' he said, 'I've found the very place for your house! Look here!'

Soames stood and looked, then he said coldly:

'You may be very clever, but this site will cost me half as much again.'

'Hang the cost, man. Look at the view!'

Almost from their feet stretched ripe corn, dipping to a small dark copse beyond. A plain of fields and hedges spread to the distant grey-blue downs. In a silver streak to the right could be seen the line of the river.

The sky was so blue, and the sun so bright, that an eternal summer seemed to reign over this prospect. Thistledown floated round them, enraptured by the serenity of the ether. The heat danced over the corn, and, pervading all, was a soft, insensible hum, like the murmur of bright minutes holding revel between earth and heaven.

Soames looked. In spite of himself, something swelled in his breast. To live here in sight of all this, to be able to point it out to his friends, to talk of it, to possess it! His cheeks flushed. The warmth, the radiance, the glow, were sinking into his senses as, four years before, Irene's beauty had sunk into his senses and made him long for her. He stole a glance at Bosinney, whose eyes, the eyes of the coachman's 'half-tame leopard', seemed running wild over the landscape. The sunlight had caught the promontories of the fellow's face, the bumpy cheek-bones, the point of his chin, the vertical ridges above his brow; and Soames watched this rugged, enthusiastic, careless face with an unpleasant feeling.

A long, soft ripple of wind flowed over the corn, and brought a puff of warm air into their faces.

'I could build you a teaser here,' said Bosinney, breaking the silence at last.

'I dare say,' replied Soames dryly. 'You haven't got to pay for it.'

'For about eight thousand I could build you a palace.'

Soames had become very pale–a struggle was going on within him. He dropped his eyes and said stubbornly:

'I can't afford it.'

And slowly, with his mousing walk, he led the way back to the first site.

They spent some time there going into particulars of the projected house, and then Soames returned to the agent's cottage.

He came out in about half an hour, and, joining Bosinney, started for the station.

'Well,' he said, hardly opening his lips, 'I've taken that site of yours, after all.'

And again he was silent, confusedly debating how it was that this fellow, whom by habit he despised, should have overborne his own decision.

5

A FORSYTE MÉNAGE

Like the enlightened thousands of his class and generation in this great City of London, who no longer believe in red velvet chairs, and know that groups of modern Italian marble are '*vieux jeu*', Soames Forsyte inhabited a house which did what it could. It owned a copper door-knocker of individual design, windows which had been altered to open outwards, hanging flower-boxes filled with fuchsias, and at the back (a great feature) a little court tiled with jade-green tiles, and surrounded by pink hydrangeas in peacock-blue tubs. Here, under a parchment-coloured Japanese sunshade covering the whole end, inhabitants or visitors could be screened from the eyes of the curious while they drank tea and examined at their leisure the latest of Soames's little silver boxes.

The inner decoration favoured the First Empire and William Morris. For its size, the house was commodious; there were countless nooks resembling birds' nests, and little things made of silver were deposited like eggs.

In this general perfection two kinds of fastidiousness were at war. There lived here a mistress who would have dwelt daintily on a desert island; a master whose daintiness was, as it were, an investment, cultivated by the owner for his advancement, in accordance with the laws of competition. This competitive daintiness had caused Soames in his Marlborough days to be the first boy into white waistcoats in summer, and corduroy waistcoats in winter, had prevented him from ever appearing in public with his tie climbing up his collar, and induced him to dust his patent-leather boots before a great multitude assembled on Speech Day to hear him recite Molière.

Skin-like immaculateness had grown over Soames, as over many Londoners; impossible to conceive of him with a hair out of place, a tie deviating one-eighth of an inch from the perpendicular, a collar unglossed! He would not have gone without a bath for worlds–it was the fashion to take baths; and how bitter was his scorn of people who omitted them!

But Irene could be imagined, like some nymph, bathing in wayside streams, for the joy of the freshness and of seeing her own fair body.

In this conflict throughout the house the woman had gone to the wall. As in the struggle between Saxon and Celt still going on within the nation, the more impressionable and receptive temperament had had forced on it a conventional superstructure.

Thus the house had acquired a close resemblance to hundreds of other houses with the same high aspirations, having become: 'That very charming little house of the Soames Forsytes, quite individual, my dear–really elegant!'

For Soames Forsyte–read James Peabody, Thomas Atkins, or Emmanuel Spagnoletti, the name in fact of any upper middle-class Englishman in London with any pretensions to taste; and though the decoration be different, the phrase is just.

On the evening of August 8, a week after the expedition to Robin Hill, in the dining-room of this house–"quite individual, my dear–really elegant!"–Soames and Irene were seated at dinner. A hot dinner on Sundays was a little distinguishing elegance common to this and many others. Early in married life Soames had laid down the rule: 'The servants must give us hot dinner on Sundays–they've nothing to do but play the concertina.'

The custom had produced no revolution. For–to Soames a rather deplorable sign–servants were devoted to Irene, who, in defiance of all safe tradition, appeared to recognise their right to a share in the weaknesses of human nature.

The happy pair were seated, not opposite each other, but rectangularly, at a handsome rosewood table; they dined without a cloth–a distinguishing elegance–and so far had not spoken a word.

Soames liked to talk during dinner about business, or what he had been buying, and so long as he talked Irene's silence did not distress him. This evening he had found it impossible to talk. The decision to build had been weighing on his mind all the week, and he had made up his mind to tell her.

His nervousness about this disclosure irritated him profoundly; she had no business to make him feel like that–a wife and a husband being one person. She had not looked at him since they sat down; and he wondered what on earth she had been thinking about all the time. It was hard, when a man worked as he did, making money for her–yes, and with an ache in his heart–that she should sit there, looking–looking as if she saw the walls of the room closing in. It was enough to make a man get up and leave the table.

The light from the rose-shaded lamp fell on her neck and arms–Soames liked her to dine in a low dress, it gave him an inexpressible feeling of superiority to the majority of his acquaintance, whose wives were contented with their best high frocks or with tea-gowns, when they dined at home. Under that rosy light her amber-coloured hair and fair skin made strange contrast with her dark brown eyes.

Could a man own anything prettier than this dining-table with its deep tints, the starry, soft-petalled roses, the ruby-coloured glass, and quaint silver furnishing; could a man own anything prettier than the woman who sat at it? Gratitude was no virtue among Forsytes, who, competitive, and full of common sense, had no occasion for it, and Soames only experienced a sense of exasperation amounting to pain, that he did not own her as it was his right to own her, that he could not, as by stretching out his hand to that rose, pluck her and sniff the very secrets of her heart.

Out of his other property, out of all the things he had collected, his silver, his pictures, his houses, his investments, he got a secret and intimate feeling; out of her he got none.

In this house of his there was writing on every wall. His business-like temperament protested against a mysterious warning that she was not made for him. He had married this woman, conquered her, made her his own, and it seemed to him contrary to the most fundamental of all laws, the law of possession, that he could do no more than own her body—if indeed he could do that, which he was beginning to doubt. If anyone had asked him if he wanted to own her soul, the question would have seemed to him both ridiculous and sentimental. But he did so want, and the writing said he never would.

She was ever silent, passive, gracefully averse; as though terrified lest by word, motion, or sign she might lead him to believe that she was fond of him; and he asked himself: 'Must I always go on like this?'

Like most novel readers of his generation (and Soames was a great novel reader), literature coloured his view of life; and he had imbibed the belief that it was a question of time. In the end the husband always gained the affection of his wife. Even in those cases—a class of book he was not very fond of—which ended in tragedy, the wife always died with poignant regrets on her lips, or if it were the husband who died—unpleasant thought—threw herself on his body in an agony of remorse.

He often took Irene to the theatre, instinctively choosing the modern Society plays with the modern Society conjugal problem, so fortunately different from any conjugal problem in real life. He found that they too always ended in the same way, even when there was a lover in the case. While he was watching the play Soames often sympathised with the lover; but before he reached home again, driving with Irene in a hansom, he saw that this would not do, and he was glad the play had ended as it had. There was one class of husband and wife that had just then come into fashion, the strong, rather rough, but extremely sound man, who was peculiarly successful at the end of the play; with this person Soames was really not in sympathy, and had it not been for his own position, would have expressed his disgust with the fellow. But he was so conscious of how vital to himself was the necessity for being a successful, even a 'strong, husband', that he never spoke of a distaste born perhaps by the preserve processes of Nature out of a secret fund of brutality in himself.

But Irene's silence this evening was exceptional. He had never before seen such an expression on her face. And since it is always the unusual which alarms, Soames was alarmed. He ate his savoury, and hurried the maid as she swept off the crumbs with the silver sweeper. When she had left the room, he filled his glass with wine and said:

'Anybody been here this afternoon?'

'June.'

'What did *she* want?' It was an axiom with the Forsytes that people did not go anywhere unless they wanted something. 'Came to talk about her lover, I suppose?'

Irene made no reply.

'It looks to me,' continued Soames, 'as if she were sweeter on him than he is on her. She's always following him about.'

Irene's eyes made him feel uncomfortable.

'You've no business to say such a thing!' she exclaimed.

'Why not? Anybody can see it.'

'They cannot. And if they could, it's disgraceful to say so.'

Soames's composure gave way.

'You're a pretty wife!' he said. But secretly he wondered at the heat of her reply; it was unlike her. 'You're cracked about June! I can tell you one thing: now that she has the Buccaneer in tow, she doesn't care twopence about you and you'll find it out. But you won't see so much of her in future; we're going to live in the country.'

He had been glad to get his news out under cover of this burst of irritation. He had expected a cry of dismay; the silence with which his pronouncement was received alarmed him.

'You don't seem interested,' he was obliged to add.

'I knew it already.'

He looked at her sharply.

'Who told you?'

'June.'

'How did she know?'

Irene did not answer. Baffled and uncomfortable, he said:

'It's a fine thing for Bosinney; it'll be the making of him. I suppose she's told you all about it?'

'Yes.'

There was another pause and then Soames said:

'I suppose you don't *want* to go?'

Irene made no reply.

'Well, I can't tell what you want. You never seem contented here.'

'Have my wishes anything to do with it?'

She took the vase of roses and left the room. Soames remained seated. Was it for this that he had signed that contract? Was it for this that he was going to spend some ten thousand pounds? Bosinney's phrase came back to him: 'Women are the devil!'

But presently he grew calmer. It might have been worse. She might have flared up. He had expected something more than this. It was lucky, after all, that June had broken the ice for him. She must have wormed it out of Bosinney; he might have known she would.

He lighted his cigarette. After all, Irene had not made a scene! She would come round—that was the best of her; she was cold, but not sulky. And, puffing the cigarette smoke at a lady-bird on the shining table, he plunged into a reverie about the house. It was no good worrying; he would go and make it up presently. She would be sitting out there in the dark, under the Japanese sunshade, knitting. A beautiful, warm night. . . .

In truth, June had come in that afternoon with shining eyes, and the words: 'Soames is a brick! It's splendid for Phil—the very thing for him!'

Irene's face remaining dark and puzzled, she went on:

'Your new house at Robin Hill, of course. What? Don't you know?'

Irene did not know.

'Oh! then, I suppose I oughtn't to have told you!' Looking impatiently at her friend, she cried: 'You look as if you didn't care. Don't you see, it's what I've been praying for—the very chance he's been wanting all this time. Now you'll see what he can do,' and thereupon she poured out the whole story.

Since her own engagement she had not seemed much interested in her friend's position; the hours she spent with Irene were given to confidences of her own; and at times, for all her affectionate pity, it was impossible to keep out of her smile a trace of compassionate contempt for the woman who had made such a mistake in her life—such a vast, ridiculous mistake.

'He's to have all the decorations as well—a free hand. It's perfect—' June broke into laughter, her little figure quivered gleefully; she raised her hand, and struck a blow at a muslin curtain. 'Do you know I even asked Uncle James—' but, with a sudden dislike to mentioning that incident, she stopped; and presently, finding her friend so unresponsive, went away. She looked back from the pavement, and Irene was still standing in the doorway. In response to her farewell wave, Irene put her hand to her brow, and, turning slowly, shut the door. . . .

Soames went to the drawing-room presently, and peered at her through the window.

Out in the shadow of the Japanese sunshade she was sitting very still, the lace on her white shoulders stirring with the soft rise and fall of her bosom.

But about this silent creature sitting there so motionless, in the dark, there seemed a warmth, a hidden fervour of feeling, as if the whole of her being had been stirred, and some change were taking place in its very depths.

He stole back to the dining-room unnoticed.

6

JAMES AT LARGE

It was not long before Soames's determination to build went the round of the family, and created the flutter that any decision connected with property should make among Forsytes.

It was not his fault, for he had been determined that no one should know. June, in the fullness of her heart, had told Mrs Small, giving her leave only to tell Aunt Ann—she thought it would cheer her, the poor old sweet! for Aunt Ann had kept her room now for many days.

Mrs Small told Aunt Ann at once, who, smiling as she lay back on her pillows, said in her distinct, trembling old voice:

'It's very nice for dear June; but I hope they will be careful—it's rather dangerous!'

When she was left alone again, a frown, like a cloud presaging a rainy morrow, crossed her face.

While she was lying there so many days the process of recharging her will went on all the time; it spread to her face, too, and tightening movements were always in action at the corners of her lips.

The maid Smither, who had been in her service since girlhood, and was spoken of as 'Smither—a good girl—but so slow!'—the maid Smither performed every morning with extreme punctiliousness the crowning ceremony of that ancient toilet. Taking from the recesses of their pure white band-box those flat, grey curls, the insignia of personal dignity, she placed them securely in her mistress's hands, and turned her back.

And every day Aunts Juley and Hester were required to come and report on Timothy; what news there was of Nicholas; whether dear June had succeeded in getting Jolyon to shorten the engagement, now that Mr Bosinney was building Soames a house; whether young Roger's wife was really–expecting; how the operation on Archie had succeeded; and what Swithin had done about that empty house in Wigmore Street, where the tenant had lost all his money and treated him so badly; above all, about Soames; was Irene still–still asking for a separate room? And every morning Smither was told: 'I shall be coming down this afternoon, Smither, about two o'clock. I shall want your arm, after all these days in bed!'

After telling Aunt Ann, Mrs Small had spoken of the house in the strictest confidence to Mrs Nicholas, who in her turn had asked Winifred Dartie for confirmation, supposing, of course, that, being Soames's sister, she would know all about it. Through her it had in due course come round to the ears of James. He had been a good deal agitated.

'Nobody,' he said, 'told him anything.' And, rather than go direct to Soames himself, of whose taciturnity he was afraid, he took his umbrella and went round to Timothy's.

He found Mrs Septimus and Hester (who had been told–she was so safe, she found it tiring to talk) ready, and indeed eager, to discuss the news. It was very good of dear Soames, they thought, to employ Mr Bosinney, but rather risky. What had George named him? 'The Buccaneer!' How droll! But George was always droll! However, it would be all in the family–they supposed they must really look upon Mr Bosinney as belonging to the family, though it seemed strange.

James here broke in:

'Nobody knows anything about him. I don't see what Soames wants with a young man like that. I shouldn't be surprised if Irene had put her oar in. I shall speak to–'

'Soames.' interposed Aunt Juley, 'told Mr Bosinney that he didn't wish it mentioned. He wouldn't like it to be talked about, I'm sure, and if Timothy knew he would be very vexed, I–'

James put his hand behind his ear:

'What?' he said. 'I'm getting very deaf. I suppose I don't hear people. Emily's got a bad toe. We shan't be able to start for Wales till the end of the month. There's always something!' And, having got what he wanted, he took his hat and went away.

It was a fine afternoon, and he walked across the Park towards Soames's, where he intended to dine, for Emily's toe kept her in bed, and Rachel and Cicely were on a visit in the country. He took the slanting path from the Bayswater side of the Row to the Knightsbridge Gate, across a pasture of short, burnt grass, dotted with blackened sheep, strewn with seated couples and strange waifs lying prone on their faces, like corpses on a field over which the wave of battle has rolled.

He walked rapidly, his head bent, looking neither to the right nor left. The appearance of this park, the centre of his own battlefield, where he had all his life been fighting, excited no thought or speculation in his mind. These corpses flung down there from out the press and turmoil of the struggle, these pairs of lovers sitting cheek by jowl for an hour of idle Elysium snatched from the monotony of their treadmill, awakened no fancies in his mind; he had outlived that kind of imagination; his nose, like the nose of a sheep, was fastened to the pastures on which he browsed.

One of his tenants had lately shown a disposition to be behindhand in his rent, and it had become a grave question whether he had not better turn him out at once, and so run the risk of not re-letting before Christmas. Swithin had just been let in very badly, but it had served him right—he had held on too long.

He pondered this as he walked steadily, holding his umbrella carefully by the wood, just below the crook of the handle, so as to keep the ferrule off the ground, and not fray the silk in the middle. And, with his thin, high shoulders stooped, his long legs moving with swift mechanical precision, this passage through the Park, where the sun shone with a clear flame on so much idleness—on so many human evidences of the remorseless battle of Property raging beyond its ring—was like the flight of some landbird across the sea.

He felt a touch on his arm as he came out at Albert Gate.

It was Soames, who, crossing from the shady side of Piccadilly, where he had been walking home from the office, had suddenly appeared alongside.

'Your mother's in bed,' said James; 'I was just coming to you, but I suppose I shall be in the way.'

The outward relations between James and his son were marked by a lack of sentiment peculiarly Forsytean, but for all that the two were by no means unattached. Perhaps they regarded one another as an investment; certainly they were solicitous of each other's welfare, glad of each other's company. They had never exchanged two words upon the more intimate problems of life, or revealed in each other's presence the existence of any deep feeling.

Something beyond the power of word-analysis bound them together, something hidden deep in the fibre of nations and families—for blood, they say, is thicker than water—and neither of them was a cold-blooded man. Indeed, in James love of his children was now the prime motive of his existence. To have creatures who were parts of himself, to whom he might transmit the money he saved, was at the root of his saving; and, at seventy-five, what was left that could give him pleasure, but—saving? The kernel of life was in this saving for his children.

Than James Forsyte, notwithstanding all his 'Jonah-isms', there was no saner man (if the leading symptom of sanity, as we are told, is self-preservation, though without doubt Timothy went too far) in all this London, of which he owned so much, and loved with such a dumb love, as the centre of his opportunities. He had the marvellous instinctive sanity of the middle class. In him—more than in Jolyon, with his masterful will and his moments of tenderness and philosophy—more than in Swithin, the martyr to crankiness—Nicholas, the sufferer from ability—and Roger, the victim of enterprise—beat the true pulse of compromise; of all the brothers he was least remarkable in mind and person, and for that reason more likely to live for ever.

To James, more than to any of the others, was 'the family' significant and dear. There had always been something primitive and cosy in his attitude towards life; he loved the family hearth, he loved gossip, and he loved grumbling. All his decisions were formed of a cream which he skimmed off the family mind; and, through that family, off the minds of thousands of other families of similar fibre. Year after year, week after week, he went to Timothy's, and in his brother's front drawing-room—his legs twisted, his long white whiskers framing his clean-shaven mouth—would sit watching the family pot simmer, the cream rising to the top; and he would go away sheltered, refreshed, comforted, with an indefinable sense of comfort.

Beneath the adamant of his self-preserving instinct there was much real softness in James; a visit to Timothy's was like an hour spent in the lap of a mother; and the deep craving he himself had for the protection of the family wing reacted in turn on his feelings towards his own children; it was a nightmare to him to think of them exposed to the treatment of the world, in money, health, or reputation. When his old friend John Street's son volunteered for special service, he shook his head querulously, and wondered what John Street was about to allow it; and when young Street was assegaied, he took it so much to heart that he made a point of calling everywhere with the special object of saying, 'He knew how it would be–he'd no patience with them!'

When his son-in-law Dartie had that financial crisis, due to speculation in Oil Shares, James made himself ill worrying over it; the knell of all prosperity seemed to have sounded. It took him three months and a visit to Baden-Baden to get better; there was something terrible in the idea that but for his, James's, money, Dartie's name might have appeared in the Bankruptcy List.

Composed of a physiological mixture so sound that if he had an earache he thought he was dying, he regarded the occasional ailments of his wife and children as in the nature of personal grievances, special interventions of Providence for the purpose of destroying his peace of mind; but he did not believe at all in the ailments of people outside his own immediate family, affirming them in every case to be due to neglected liver.

His universal comment was: 'What can they expect? I'll have it myself, if I'm not careful!'

When he went to Soames's that evening he felt that life was hard on him. There was Emily with a bad toe, and Rachel gadding about in the country; he got no sympathy from anybody; and Ann, she was ill–he did not believe she would last through the summer; he had called there three times now without her being able to see him! And this idea of Soames's, building a house, *that* would have to be looked into. As to the trouble with Irene, he didnt know what was to come of that–anything might come of it!

He entered 62, Montpelier Square with the fullest intentions of being miserable.

It was already half-past seven, and Irene, dressed for dinner, was seated in the drawing-room. She was wearing her gold-coloured frock–for, having been displayed at a dinner-party, a soirée, and a dance, it was now to be worn at home–and she had adorned the bosom with a cascade of lace, on which James's eyes riveted themselves at once.

'Where do you get your things?' he said in an aggravated voice. 'I never see Rachel and Cicely looking half so well. That rose-point, now–that's not real!'

Irene came close, to prove to him that he was in error.

And, in spite of himself, James felt the influence of her deference, of the faint seductive perfume exhaling from her. No self-respecting Forsyte surrendered at a blow; so he merely said: He didn't know–he expected she was spending a pretty penny on dress.

The gong sounded, and, putting her white arm within his, Irene took him into the dining-room. She seated him in Soames's usual place, round the corner on her left. The light fell softly there, so that he would not be worried by the gradual dying of the day; and she began to talk to him about himself.

Presently, over James came a change, like the mellowing that steals upon a fruit in the sun; a sense of being caressed, and praised, and petted, and all without the bestowal of a single caress or word of praise. He felt that what he was eating was agreeing with him; he could not get that feeling at home; he did not know when he had enjoyed a glass of champagne so much, and, on inquiring the brand and price, was surprised to find that it was one of which he had a large stock himself, but could never drink; he instantly formed the resolution to let his wine merchant know that he had been swindled.

Looking up from his food, he remarked:

'You've a nice lot of things about the place. Now, what did you give for that sugar-sifter? Shouldn't wonder if it was worth money!'

He was particularly pleased with the appearance of a picture on the wall opposite, which he himself had given them:

'I'd no idea it was so good!' he said.

They rose to go into the drawing-room, and James followed Irene closely.

'That's what I call a capital little dinner,' he murmured, breathing pleasantly down on her shoulder, 'nothing heavy—and not too Frenchified. But *I* can't get it at home. I pay my cook sixty pounds a year, but *she* can't give me a dinner like that!'

He had as yet made no allusion to the building of the house, nor did he when Soames, pleading the excuse of business, betook himself to the room at the top, where he kept his pictures.

James was left alone with his daughter-in-law. The glow of the wine, and of an excellent liqueur, was still within him. He felt quite warm towards her. She was really a taking little thing; she listened to you, and seemed to understand what you were saying; and, while talking, he kept examining her figure, from her bronze-coloured shoes to the waved gold of her hair. She was leaning back in an Empire chair, her shoulders poised against the top—her body, flexibly straight and unsupported from the hips, swaying when she moved, as though giving to the arms of a lover. Her lips were smiling, her eyes half-closed.

It may have been a recognition of danger in the very charm of her attitude, or a twang of digestion, that caused a sudden dumbness to fall on James. He did not remember ever having been quite alone with Irene before. And, as he looked at her, an odd feeling crept over him, as though he had come across something strange and foreign.

Now what was she thinking about—sitting back like that?

Thus when he spoke it was in a sharper voice, as if he had been awakened from a pleasant dream.

'What d'you do with yourself all day?' he said. 'You never come round to Park Lane!'

She seemed to be making very lame excuses, and James did not look at her. He did not want to believe that she was really avoiding them—it would mean too much.

'I expect the fact is, you haven't time,' he said; 'you're always about with June. I expect you're useful to her with her young man, chaperoning, and one thing and another. They tell me she's never at home now; your Uncle Jolyon he doesn't like it, I fancy, being left so much alone as he is. They tell me she's always hanging about for this young Bosinney; I suppose he comes here every day. Now, what do *you* think of him? D'you think he knows his own mind? He seems to me a poor thing. I should say the grey mare was the better horse!'

The colour deepened in Irene's face, and James watched her suspiciously.

'Perhaps you don't quite understand Mr Bosinney,' she said.

'Don't understand him! James hurried out. 'Why not?—you can see he's one of these artistic chaps. They say he's clever—they all think they're clever. You know more about him than I do,' he added; and again his suspicious glance rested on her.

'He is designing a house for Soames,' she said softly, evidently trying to smooth things over.

'That brings me to what I was going to say,' continued James; 'I don't know what Soames wants with a young man like that; why doesn't he go to a first-rate man?'

'Perhaps Mr Bosinney is first-rate!'

James rose, and took a turn with bent head.

'That's it,' he said, 'you young people, you all stick together; you all think you know best!'

Halting his tall, lank figure before her, he raised a finger, and levelled it at her bosom, as though bringing an indictment against her beauty:

'All I can say is, these artistic people, or whatever they call themselves, they're as unreliable as they can be; and my advice to *you* is, don't you have too much to do with him!'

Irene smiled; and in the curve of her lips was a strange provocation. She seemed to have lost her deference. Her breast rose and fell as though with secret anger; she drew her hands inwards from their rest on the arms of her chair until the tips of her fingers met, and her dark eyes looked unfathomably at James.

The latter gloomily scrutinised the floor.

'I tell you my opinion,' he said, 'it's a pity you haven't got a child to think about, and occupy you!'

A brooding look came instantly on Irene's face, and even James became conscious of the rigidity that took possession of her whole figure beneath the softness of its silk and lace clothing.

He was frightened by the effect he had produced, and, like most men with but little courage, he sought at once to justify himself by bullying.

'You don't seem to care about going about. Why don't you drive down to Hurlingham with us? And go to the theatre now and then. At your time of life you ought to take an interest in things. You're a young woman!'

The brooding look darkened on her face; he grew nervous.

'Well, I know nothing about it,' he said, 'nobody tells me anything. Soames ought to be able to take care of himself. If he can't take care of himself he mustn't look to me—that's all—'

Biting the corner of his forefinger he stole a cold, sharp look at his daughter-in-law.

He encountered her eyes fixed on his own, so dark and deep, that he stopped and broke into a gentle perspiration.

'Well, I must be going,' he said after a short pause, and a minute later rose, with a slight appearance of surprise, as though he had expected to be asked to stop. Giving his hand to Irene, he allowed himself to be conducted to the door, and let out into the street. He would not have a cab, he would walk, Irene was to say good-night to Soames for him, and if she wanted a little gaiety, well, he would drive her down to Richmond any day.

He walked home, and going upstairs, woke Emily out of the first sleep she had had for four-and-twenty hours, to tell her that it was his impression things were in a bad way at Soames's; on this theme he descanted for half an hour, until at last, saying he would not sleep a wink, he turned on his side and instantly began to snore.

In Montpelier Square Soames, who had come from the picture room, stood invisible at the top of the stairs, watching Irene sort the letters brought by the last post. She turned back into the drawing-room; but in a minute came out, and stood as if listening. Then she came stealing up the stairs, with a kitten in her arms. He could see her face bent over the little beast, which was purring against her neck. Why couldn't she look at him like that?

Suddenly she saw him, and her face changed.

'Any letters for me?' he said.

'Three.'

He stood aside, and without another word she passed on into the bedroom.

7

OLD JOLYON'S PECCADILLO

Old Jolyon came out of Lord's cricket ground that same afternoon with the intention of going home. He had not reached Hamilton Terrace before he changed his mind, and hailing a cab, gave the driver an address in Wistaria Avenue. He had taken a resolution.

June had hardly been at home at all that week; she had given him nothing of her company for a long time past, not, in fact, since she had become engaged to Bosinney. He never asked her for her company. It was not his habit to ask people for things! She had just that one idea now—Bosinney and his affairs—and she left him stranded in his great house, with a parcel of servants, and not a soul to speak to from morning to night. His club was closed for cleaning; his Boards in recess; there was nothing, therefore, to take him to the City. June had wanted him to go away; she would not go herself, because Bosinney was in London.

But where was he to go by himself? He could not go abroad alone; the sea upset his liver; he hated hotels. Roger went to a hydropathic—he was not going to begin that at his time of life, those new-fangled places were all humbug!

With such formulas he clothed to himself the desolation of his spirit; the lines down his face deepening, his eyes day by day looking forth with the melancholy that sat so strangely on a face that was wont to be strong and serene.

And so that afternoon he took his journey through St. John's Wood, in the golden light that sprinkled the rounded green bushes of the acacias before the little houses, in the summer sunshine that seemed holding a revel over the little gardens; and he looked about him with interest; for this was a district which no Forsyte entered without open disapproval and secret curiosity.

His cab stopped in front of a small house of that peculiar buff colour which implies a long immunity from paint. It had an outer gate, and a rustic approach.

He stepped out, his bearing extremely composed; his massive head, with its drooping moustache and wings of white hair, very upright, under an excessively large top hat; his glance firm, a little angry. He had been driven into this!

'Mrs Jolyon Forsyte at home?'

'Oh, yes sir!—what name shall I say, if you please, sir?'

Old Jolyon could not help twinkling at the little maid as he gave his name. She seemed to him such a funny little toad!

And he followed her through the dark hall, into a small double drawing-room, where the furniture was covered in chintz, and the little maid placed him in a chair.

'They're all in the garden, sir; if you'll kindly take a seat, I'll tell them.'

Old Jolyon sat down in the chintz-covered chair, and looked around him. The whole place seemed to him, as he would have expressed it, pokey; there was a certain—he could not tell exactly what—air of shabbiness, or rather of making two ends meet, about everything. As far as he could see, not a single piece of furniture was worth a five-pound note. The walls, distempered rather a long time ago, were decorated with water-colour sketches; across the ceiling meandered a long crack.

These little houses were all old, second-rate concerns; he should hope the rent was under a hundred a year; it hurt him more than he could have said, to think of a Forsyte—his own son—living in such a place.

The little maid came back. Would he please to go down into the garden?

Old Jolyon marched out through the french windows. In descending the steps he noticed that they wanted painting.

Young Jolyon, his wife, his two children, and his dog Balthasar, were all out there under a pear tree.

This walk towards them was the most courageous act of old Jolyon's life; but no muscle of his face moved, no nervous gesture betrayed him. He kept his deep-set eyes steadily on the enemy.

In those two minutes he demonstrated to perfection all that unconscious soundness, balance, and vitality of fibre that made of him and so many others of his class the core of the nation. In the unostentatious conduct of their own affairs, to the neglect of everything else, they typified the essential individualism, born in the Briton from the natural isolation of his country's life.

The dog Balthasar sniffed round the edges of his trousers; this friendly and cynical mongrel—offspring of a liaison between a Russian poodle and a fox-terrier—had a nose for the unusual.

The strange meetings over, old Jolyon seated himself in a wicker chair, and his two grandchildren, one on each side of his knees, looked at him silently, never having seen so old a man.

They were unlike, as though recognising the difference set between them by the circumstances of their births. Jolly, the child of sin, pudgy-faced, with his tow-coloured hair brushed off his forehead, and a dimple in his chin, had an air of stubborn amiability, and the eyes of a Forsyte; little Holly, the child of wedlock, was a dark-skinned, solemn soul, with her mother's grey and wistful eyes.

The dog Balthasar, having walked round the three small flowerbeds, to show his extreme contempt for things at large, had also taken a seat in front of old Jolyon, and, oscillating a tail curled by Nature tightly over his back, was staring up with eyes that did not blink.

Even in the garden, that sense of things being pokey haunted old Jolyon; the wicker chair creaked under his weight; the garden-beds looked 'daverdy'; on the far side, under the smut-stained wall, cats had made a path.

While he and his grandchildren thus regarded each other with the peculiar scrutiny, curious yet trustful, that passes between the very young and the very old, young Jolyon watched his wife.

The colour had deepened in her thin, oval face, with its straight brows, and large grey eyes. Her hair, brushed in fine, high curves back from her forehead, was going grey, like his own, and this greyness made the sudden vivid colour in her cheeks painfully pathetic.

The look on her face, such as he had never seen there before, such as she had always hidden from him, was full of secret resentments, and longings, and fears. Her eyes, under their twitching brows, stared painfully. And she was silent.

Jolly alone sustained the conversation; he had many possessions, and was anxious that his unknown friend with extremely large moustaches, and hands all covered with blue veins, who sat with legs crossed like his own father (a habit he was himself trying to acquire), should know it; but being a Forsyte, though not yet quite eight years old, he made no mention of the thing at the moment dearest to his heart—a camp of soldiers in a shop window, which his father had promised to buy. No doubt it seemed to him too precious; a tempting of Providence to mention it yet.

And the sunlight played through the leaves on that little party of the three generations grouped tranquilly under the pear tree, which had long borne no fruit.

Old Jolyon's furrowed face was reddening patchily, as old men's faces redden in the sun. He took one of Jolly's hands in his own; the boy climbed on to his knee, and little Holly, mesmerised by this sight, crept up to them; the sound of the dog Balthasar's scratching arose rhythmically.

Suddenly young Mrs Jolyon got up and hurried indoors. A minute later her husband muttered an excuse, and followed. Old Jolyon was left alone with his grandchildren.

And Nature with her quaint irony began working in him one of her strange revolutions, following her cyclic laws into the depths of his heart. And that tenderness for little children, that passion for the beginnings of life which had once made him forsake his son and follow June, now worked in him to forsake June and follow these littler things. Youth, like a flame, burned ever in his breast, and to youth he turned, to the round little limbs, so reckless, that wanted care, to the small round faces so unreasonably solemn or bright, to the treble tongues, and the shrill, chuckling laughter, to the insistent tugging hands, and the feel of small bodies against his legs, to all that was young and young, and once more young. And his eyes grew soft, his voice, and thin, veined hands soft, and soft his heart within him. And to those small creatures he became at once a place of pleasure, a place where they were secure, and could talk and laugh and play; till, like sunshine, there radiated from old Jolyon's wicker chair the perfect gaiety of three hearts.

But with young Jolyon following to his wife's room it was different.

He found her seated on a chair before her dressing-glass with her hands before her face.

Her shoulders were shaking with sobs. This passion of hers for suffering was mysterious to him. He had been through a hundred of these moods; how he had survived them he never knew, for he could never believe they *were* moods, and that the last hour of his partnership had not struck.

In the night she would be sure to throw her arms round his neck, and say: 'Oh! Jo, how I make you suffer!' as she had done a hundred times before.

He reached out his hand, and, unseen, slipped his razor-case into his pocket.

'I can't stay here,' he thought, 'I must go down!' Without a word he left the room, and went back to the lawn.

Old Jolyon had little Holly on his knee; she had taken possession of his watch; Jolly, very red in the face, was trying to show that he could stand on his head. The dog Balthasar, as close as might be to the tea-table, had fixed his eyes on the cake.

Young Jolyon felt a malicious desire to cut their enjoyment short.

What business had his father to come and upset his wife like this? It was a shock, after all these years! He ought to have known; he ought to have given them warning; but when did a Forsyte ever imagine that his conduct could upset anybody! And in his thoughts he did old Jolyon wrong.

He spoke sharply to the children, and told them to go to their tea. Greatly surprised, for they had never heard their father speak sharply before, they went off, hand in hand, little Holly looking back over her shoulder.

Young Jolyon poured the tea.

'My wife's not the thing to-day,' he said, but he knew well enough that his father had penetrated the cause of that sudden withdrawal, and almost hated the old man for sitting there so calmly.

'You've got a nice little house here,' said old Jolyon with a shrewd look; 'I suppose you've taken a lease of it!'

Young Jolyon nodded.

'I don't like the neighbourhood,' said old Jolyon; 'a ramshackle lot.'

Young Jolyon replied: 'Yes, we're a ramshackle lot.'

The silence was now only broken by the sound of the dog Balthasar's scratching.

Old Jolyon said simply: 'I suppose I oughtn't to have come here, Jo; but I get so lonely!'

At these words young Jolyon got up and put his hand on his father's shoulder.

In the next house someone was playing over and over again 'La Donna é mobile' on an untuned piano; and the little garden had fallen into shade, the sun now only reached the wall at the end, whereon basked a crouching cat, her yellow eyes turned sleepily down on the dog Balthasar. There was a drowsy hum of very distant traffic; the creepered trellis round the garden shut out everything but sky, and house, and pear tree, with its top branches still gilded by the sun.

For some time they sat there, talking but little. Then old Jolyon rose to go, and not a word was said about his coming again.

He walked away very sadly. What a poor miserable place. And he thought of the great, empty house in Stanhope Gate, fit residence for a Forsyte, with its huge billiard-room and drawing-room that no one entered from one week's end to another.

That woman, whose face he had rather liked, was too thin-skinned by half; she gave Jo a bad time he knew! And those sweet children! Ah, what a piece of awful folly!

He walked towards the Edgware Road, between rows of little houses, all suggesting to him (erroneously no doubt, but the prejudices of a Forsyte are sacred) shady histories of some sort or kind.

Society, forsooth, the chattering hags and jackanapes–had set themselves up to pass judgment on *his* flesh and blood! A parcel of old women! He stumped his umbrella on the ground, as though to drive it into the heart of that unfortunate body, which had dared to ostracise his son and his son's son, in whom he could have lived again!

He stumped his umbrella fiercely; yet he himself had followed Society's behaviour for fifteen years–had only to-day been false to it!

He thought of June, and her dead mother, and the whole story, with all his old bitterness. A wretched business!

He was a long time reaching Stanhope Gate, for, with native perversity, being extremely tired, he walked the whole way.

After washing his hands in the lavatory downstairs, he went to the dining-room to wait for dinner, the only room he used when June was out–it was less lonely so. The evening paper had not yet come; he had finished *The Times*, there was therefore nothing to do.

The room faced the backwater of traffic, and was very silent. He disliked dogs, but a dog even would have been company. His gaze, travelling round the walls, rested on a picture entitled: 'Group of Dutch fishing boats at sunset'; the *chef d'œuvre* of his collection. It gave him no pleasure. He closed his eyes. He was lonely! He oughtn't to complain, he knew, but he couldn't help it: He was a poor thing–had always been a poor thing–no pluck! Such was his thought.

The butler came to lay the table for dinner, and seeing his master apparently asleep, exercised extreme caution in his movements. This bearded man also wore a moustache, which had given rise to grave doubts in the minds of many members of the family–especially those who, like Soames, had been to public schools, and were accustomed to niceness in such matters. Could he really be considered a butler? Playful spirits alluded to him as: 'Uncle Jolyon's Nonconformist'; George, the acknowledged wag, had named him: 'Sankey'.

He moved to and fro between the great polished sideboard and the great polished table inimitably sleek and soft.

Old Jolyon watched him, feigning sleep. The fellow was a sneak–he had always thought so–who cared about nothing but rattling through his work, and getting out to his betting or his woman or goodness knows what! A slug! Fat too! And didn't care a pin about his master!

But then against his will, came one of those moments of philosophy which made old Jolyon different from other Forsytes:

After all, why should the man care? He wasn't paid to care, and why expect it? In this world people couldn't look for affection unless they paid for it. It might be different in the next–he didn't know, he couldn't tell! And again he shut his eyes.

Relentless and stealthy, the butler pursued his labours, taking things from the various compartments of the sideboard. His back seemed always turned to old Jolyon; thus, he robbed his operations of the unseemliness of being carried on in his master's presence; now and then he furtively breathed on the silver, and wiped it with a piece of chamois leather. He appeared to pore over the quantities of wine in the decanters, which he carried carefully and rather high, letting his beard droop over them protectingly. When he had finished, he stood for over a minute watching his master, and in his greenish eyes there was a look of contempt:

After all, this master of his was an old buffer, who hadn't much left in him!

Soft as a tom-cat, he crossed the room to press the bell. His orders were 'dinner at seven'. What if his master were asleep; he would soon have him out of that; there was the night to sleep in! He had himself to think of, for he was due at his club at half-past eight!

In answer to the ring, appeared a page-boy with a silver soup-tureen. The butler took it from his hands and placed it on the table, then, standing by the open door, as though about to usher company into the room, he said in a solemn voice:

'Dinner is on the table, sir!'

Slowly old Jolyon got up out of his chair and sat down at the table to eat his dinner.

8

PLANS OF THE HOUSE

All Forsytes, as is generally admitted, have shells, like that extremely useful little animal which is made into Turkish delight; in other words, they are never seen, or if seen would not be recognised, without habitats, composed of circumstance, property, acquaintances, and wives, which seem to move along with them in their passage through a world composed of thousands of other Forsytes with their habitats. Without a habitat a Forsyte is inconceivable–he would be like a novel without a plot, which is well known to be an anomaly.

To Forsyte eyes Bosinney appeared to have no habitat, he seemed one of those rare and unfortunate men who go through life surrounded by circumstance, property, acquaintances, and wives that do not belong to them.

His rooms in Sloane Street, on the top floor, outside which, on a plate, was his name, 'Philip Baynes Bosinney, Architect', were not those of a Forsyte. He had no sitting-room apart from his office, but a large recess had been screened off to conceal the necessaries of life–a couch, an easy chair, his pipes, spirit-case, novels, and slippers. The business part of the room had the usual furniture; an open cupboard with pigeon-holes, a round oak table, a folding wash-stand, some hard chairs, a standing desk of large dimensions covered with drawings and designs. June had twice been to tea there under the chaperonage of his aunt.

He was believed to have a bedroom at the back.

As far as the family had been able to ascertain his income, it consisted of two consulting appointments at twenty pounds a year, together with an odd fee once in a way, and–more worthy item–a private annuity under his father's will of one hundred and fifty pounds a year.

What had transpired concerning that father was not so reassuring. It appeared that he had been a Lincolnshire country doctor of Cornish extraction, striking appearance, and Byronic tendencies–a well-known figure, in fact, in his county. Bosinney's uncle by marriage, Baynes, of Baynes and Bildeboy, a Forsyte in instincts if not in name, had but little that was worthy to relate of his brother-in-law.

'An odd fellow!' he would say: 'always spoke of his three eldest boys as "good creatures, but so dull"; they're all doing capitally in the Indian Civil! Philip was the only one *he* liked. I've heard him talk in the queerest way; he once said to me: "My dear fellow, never let your poor wife know what you're thinking of!" But I didn't follow his advice; not I! An eccentric man! He would say to Phil: "Whether you live like a gentleman or not, my boy, be sure you die like one!" and he had himself embalmed in a frock-coat suit, with a satin cravat and a diamond pin. Oh, quite an original, I can assure you!'

Of Bosinney himself Baynes would speak warmly, with a certain compassion: 'He's got a streak of his father's Byronism. Why, look at the way he threw up his chances when he left my office; going off like that for six months with a knapsack, and all for what?–to study foreign architecture–foreign! What could he expect? And there he is–a clever young fellow–doesn't make his hundred a year! Now this engagement is the best thing that could have happened–keep him steady; he's one of those that go to bed all day and stay up all night, simply because they've no method; but no vice about him–not an ounce of vice. Old Forsyte's a rich man!'

Mr Baynes made himself extremely pleasant to June, who frequently visited his house in Lowndes Square at this period.

'This house of Mr Soames's–what a capital man of business–is the very thing for Philip,' he would say to her; 'you mustn't expect to see too much of him just now, my dear young lady. The good cause–the good cause! The young man must make his way. When I was his age I was at work day and night. My dear wife used to say to me: "Bobby, don't work too hard, think of your health"; but I never spared myself!'

June had complained that her lover found no time to come to Stanhope Gate.

The first time he came again they had not been together a quarter of an hour before, by one of those coincidences of which she was a mistress, Mrs Septimus Small arrived. Thereon Bosinney rose and hid himself, according to previous arrangement, in the little study, to wait for her departure.

'My dear,' said Aunt Juley, 'how thin he is! I've often noticed it with engaged people; but you mustn't let it get worse. There's Barlow's extract of veal; it did your Uncle Swithin a lot of good.'

June, her little figure erect before the hearth, her small face quivering grimly, for she regarded her aunt's untimely visit in the light of a personal injury, replied with scorn:

'It's because he's busy; people who can do anything worth doing are never fat!'

Aunt Juley pouted; she herself had always been thin, but the only pleasure she derived from the fact was the opportunity of longing to be stouter.

'I don't think,' she said mournfully, 'that you ought to let them call him "The Buccaneer"; people might think it odd, now that he's going to build a house for Soames. I do hope he will be careful; it's so important for him; Soames has such good taste!'

'Taste!' cried June, flaring up at once; 'I wouldn't give that for his taste, or any of the family's!'

Mrs Small was taken aback.

'Your Uncle Swithin,' she said, 'always had beautiful taste! And Soames's little house is lovely; you don't mean to say you don't think so!'

'H'mph!' said June, 'that's only because Irene's there!'

Aunt Juley tried to say something pleasant:

'And how will dear Irene like living in the country?'

June gazed at her intently, with a look in her eyes as if her conscience had suddenly leaped up into them; it passed; and an even more intent look took its place, as if she had stared that conscience out of countenance. She replied imperiously:

'Of course she'll like it; why shouldn't she?'

Mrs Small grew nervous.

'I didn't know,' she said, 'I thought she mightn't like to leave her friends.

Your Uncle James says she doesn't take enough interest in life. *We* think—I mean Timothy thinks—she ought to go out more. I expect you'll miss her very much!'

June clasped her hands behind her neck.

'I do wish,' she cried, 'Uncle Timothy wouldn't talk about what doesn't concern him!'

Aunt Juley rose to the full height of her tall figure.

'He never talks about what doesn't concern him,' she said.

June was instantly compunctious; she ran to her aunt and kissed her.

'I'm very sorry, Auntie; but I wish they'd let Irene alone.'

Aunt Juley, unable to think of anything further on the subject that would be suitable, was silent; she prepared for departure, hooking her black silk cape across her chest, and, taking up her green reticule:

'And how is your dear grandfather?' she asked in the hall. 'I expect he's very lonely now that all your time is taken up with Mr Bosinney.' She bent and kissed her niece hungarily, and with little mincing steps passed away.

The tears sprang up in June's eyes; running into the little study, where Bosinney was sitting at the table drawing birds on the back of an envelope, she sank down by his side and cried:

'Oh, Phil! it's all so horrid!' Her heart was as warm as the colour of her hair.

On the following Sunday morning, while Soames was shaving, a message was brought him to the effect that Mr Bosinney was below, and would be glad to see him. Opening the door into his wife's room, he said:

'Bosinney's downstairs. Just go and entertain him while I finish shaving. I'll be down in a minute. It's about the plans, I expect.'

Irene looked at him, without reply, put the finishing touch to her dress and went downstairs.

He could not make her out about this house. She had said nothing against it, and, as far as Bosinney was concerned, seemed friendly enough.

From the window of his dressing-room he could see them talking together in the little court below.

He hurried on with his shaving, cutting his chin twice. He heard them laugh, and thought to himself: 'Well, they get on all right, anyway!'

As he expected, Bosinney had come round to fetch him to look at the plans. He took his hat and went over.

The plans were spread on the oak table in the architect's room; and pale, imperturbable, inquiring Soames bent over them for a long time without speaking.

He said at last in a puzzled voice:

'It's an odd sort of house!'

A rectangular house of two storeys was designed in a quadrangle round a covered-in court. This court, encircled by a gallery on the upper floor, was roofed with a glass roof, supported by eight columns running up from the ground.

It was indeed, to Forsyte eyes, an odd house.

'There's a lot of room cut to waste,' pursued Soames.

Bosinney began to walk about, and Soames did not like the expression on his face.

'The principle of the house,' said the architect, 'was that you should have room to breathe—like a gentleman!'

Soames extended his finger and thumb, as if measuring the extent of the distinction he should acquire, and replied:

'Oh! yes; I see.'

The peculiar look came into Bosinney's face which marked all his enthusiasms.

'I've tried to plan a house here with some self-respect of its own. If you don't like it, you'd better say so. It's certainly the last thing to be considered—who wants self-respect in a house, when you can squeeze in an extra lavatory?' He put his finger suddenly down on the left division of the centre oblong: 'You can swing a cat here. This is for your pictures, divided from this court by curtains; draw them back and you'll have a space of fifty-one by twenty-three six. This double-faced stove in the centre, here, looks one way towards the court, one way towards the picture-room; this end wall is all window; you've a south-east light from that, a north light from the court. The rest of your pictures you can hang around the gallery upstairs, or in the other rooms. In architecture,' he went on—and though looking at Soames he did not seem to see him, which gave Soames an unpleasant feeling—'as in life, you'll get no self-respect without regularity. Fellows tell you that's old-fashioned. It appears to be peculiar, anyway: it never occurs to us to embody the main principle of life in our buildings; we load our houses with decoration, gimcracks, corners, anything to distract the eye. On the contrary, the eye should rest; get your effects with a few strong lines. The whole thing is regularity—there's no self-respect without it.'

Soames, the unconscious ironist, fixed his gaze on Bosinney's tie, which was far from being in the perpendicular; he was unshaven too, and his dress not remarkable for order. Architecture appeared to have exhausted his regularity.

'Won't it look like a barrack?' he inquired.

He did not at once receive a reply.

'I can see what it is,' said Bosinney, 'you want one of Littlemaster's houses—one of the pretty and commodious sort, where the servants will live in garrets, and the front door be sunk so that you may come up again. By all means try Littlemaster, you'll find him a capital fellow, I've known him all my life!'

Soames was alarmed. He had really been struck by the plans, and the concealment of his satisfaction had been merely instinctive. It was difficult for him to pay a compliment. He despised people who were lavish with their praises.

He found himself now in the embarrassing position of one who must pay a compliment or run the risk of losing a good thing. Bosinney was just the fellow who might tear up the plans and refuse to act for him; a kind of grown-up child!

This grown-up childishness, to which he felt so superior, exercised a peculiar and almost mesmeric effect on Soames, for he had never felt anything like it in himself.

'Well,' he stammered at last, 'it's—it's certainly original.'

He had such a private distrust and even dislike of the word 'original' that he felt he had not really given himself away by this remark.

Bosinney seemed pleased. It was the sort of thing that *would* please a fellow like that! And his success encouraged Soames.

'It's—a big place,' he said.

'Space, air, light,' he heard Bosinney murmur, 'you can't live like a gentleman in one of Littlemaster's—he builds for manufacturers.''

Soames made a deprecating movement; he had been identified with a gentleman; not for a good deal of money now would he be classed with manufacturers. But his innate distrust of general principles revived. What the deuce was the good of talking about regularity and self-respect? It looked to him as if the house would be cold.

'Irene can't stand the cold!' he said.

'Ah!' said Bosinney sarcastically. 'Your wife! She doesn't like the cold? I'll see to that; she shan't be cold. Look here!' he pointed to four marks at regular intervals on the walls of the court. 'I've given you hot-water pipes in aluminium casings; you can get them with very good designs.'

Soames looked suspiciously at these marks.

'It's all very well, all this,' he said, 'but what's it going to cost?'

The architect took a sheet of paper from his pocket.

'The house, of course, should be built entirely of stone, but, as I thought you wouldn't stand that, I've compromised for a facing. It ought to have a copper roof, but I've made it green slate. As it is, including metal-work, it'll cost you eight thousand five hundred.'

'Eight thousand five hundred?' said Soames. 'Why, I gave you an outside limit of eight!'

'Can't be done for a penny less,' replied Bosinney coolly. 'You must take it or leave it!'

It was the only way, probably, that such a proposition could have been made to Soames. He was nonplussed. Conscience told him to throw the whole thing up. But the design was good, and he knew it—there was completeness about it, and dignity; the servants' apartments were excellent too. He would gain credit by living in a house like that—with such individual features, yet perfectly well-arranged.

He continued poring over the plans, while Bosinney went into his bedroom to shave and dress.

The two walked back to Montpelier Square in silence, Soames watching him out of the corner of his eye.

The Buccaneer was rather a good-looking fellow—so he thought—when he was properly got up.

Irene was bending over her flowers when the two men came in.

She spoke of sending across the Park to fetch June.

'No, no,' said Soames, 'we've still got business to talk over!'

At lunch he was almost cordial, and kept pressing Bosinney to eat. He was pleased to see the architect in such high spirits and left him to spend the afternoon with Irene, while he stole off to his pictures, after his Sunday habit. At tea-time he came down to the drawing-room, and found them talking, as he expressed it, nineteen to the dozen.

Unobserved in the doorway, he congratulated himself that things were taking the right turn. It was lucky she and Bosinney got on; she seemed to be falling into line with the idea of the new house.

Quiet meditation among his pictures had decided him to spring the five hundred if necessary; but he hoped that the afternoon might have softened Bosinney's estimates. It was so purely a matter which Bosinney could remedy if he liked; there must be a dozen ways in which he could cheapen the production of a house without spoiling the effect.

He awaited, therefore, his opportunity till Irene was handing the architect his first cup of tea. A chink of sunshine through the lace of the blinds warmed her cheek, shone in the gold of her hair, and in her soft eyes. Possibly the same gleam deepened Bosinney's colour, gave the rather startled look to his face.

Soames hated sunshine, and he at once got up to draw the blind. Then he took his own cup of tea from his wife, and said, more coldly than he had intended:

'Can't you see your way to do it for eight thousand after all? There must be a lot of little things you could altar.'

Bosinney drank off his tea at a gulp, put down his cup, and answered:

'Not one!'

Soames saw that his suggestion had touched some unintelligible point of personal vanity.

'Well,' he agreed, with sulky resignation; 'you must have it your own way, I suppose.'

A few minutes later Bosinney rose to go, and Soames rose too, to see him off the premises. The architect seemed in absurdly high spirits. And watching him walk away at a swinging pace, Soames returned moodily to the drawing-room, where Irene was putting away the music, and, moved by an uncontrollable spasm of curiosity, he asked:

'Well, what do you think of "The Buccaneer"?'

He looked at the carpet while waiting for her answer, and he had to wait some time.

'I don't know,' she said at last.

'Do you think he's good-looking?'

Irene smiled. And it seemed to Soames that she was mocking him.

'Yes,' she answered: 'very.'

9

DEATH OF AUNT ANN

There came a morning at the end of September when Aunt Ann was unable to take from Smither's hands the insignia of personal dignity. After one look at the old face, the doctor, hurriedly sent for, announced that Miss Forsyte had passed away in her sleep.

Aunts Juley and Hester were overwhelmed by the shock. They had never imagined such an ending. Indeed, it is doubtful whether they had ever realised that an ending was bound to come. Secretly they felt it unreasonable of Ann to have left them like this without a word, without even a struggle. It was unlike her.

Perhaps what really affected them so profoundly was the thought that a Forsyte should have let go her grasp on life. If one, then why not all!

It was a full hour before they could make up their minds to tell Timothy. If only it could be kept from him! If only it could be broken to him by degrees!

And long they stood outside his door whispering together. And when it was over they whispered together again.

He would feel it more, they were afraid, as time went on. Still, he had taken it better than could have been expected. He would keep his bed, of course!

They separated, crying quietly.

Aunt Juley stayed in her room, prostrated by the blow. Her face, discoloured by tears, was divided into compartments by the little ridges of pouting flesh which had swollen with emotion. It was impossible to conceive of life without

Ann, who had lived with her for seventy-three years, broken only by the short interregnum of her married life, which seemed now so unreal. At fixed intervals she went to her drawer, and took from beneath the lavender bags a fresh pocket-handkerchief. Her warm heart could not bear the thought that Ann was lying there so cold.

Aunt Hester, the silent, the patient, that backwater of the family energy, sat in the drawing-room, where the blinds were drawn; and she, too, had wept at first, but quietly, without visible effect. Her guiding principle, the conservation of energy, did not abandon her in sorrow. She sat, slim, motionless, studying the grate, her hands idle in the lap of her black silk dress. They would want to rouse her into doing something, no doubt. As if there were any good in that! Doing something would not bring back Ann! Why worry her?

Five o'clock brought three of the brothers, Jolyon and James and Swithin: Nicholas was at Yarmouth, and Roger had a bad attack of gout. Mrs Hayman had been by herself earlier in the day, and, after seeing Ann, had gone away, leaving a message for Timothy—which was kept from him—that she ought to have been told sooner. In fact, there was a feeling amongst them all that they ought to have been told sooner, as though they had missed something; and James said:

'I knew how it'd be; I told you she wouldn't last through the summer.'

Aunt Hester made no reply; it was nearly October, but what was the good of arguing; some people were never satisfied.

She went up to tell her sister that the brothers were there. Mrs Small came down at once. She had bathed her face, which was still swollen, and though she looked severely at Swithin's trousers, for they were of light blue—he had come straight from the club, where the news had reached him—she wore a more cheerful expression than usual, the instinct for doing the wrong thing being even now too strong for her.

Presently all five went up to look at the body. Under the pure white sheet a quilted counterpane had been placed, for now, more than ever, Aunt Ann had need of warmth; and, the pillows removed, her spine and head rested flat, with the semblance of their life-long inflexibility; the coif banding the top of her brow was drawn on either side to the level of the ears, and between it and the sheet her face, almost as white, was turned with closed eyes to the faces of her brothers and sisters. In its extraordinary peace the face was stronger than ever, nearly all bone now under the scarce-wrinkled parchment of skin—square jaw and chin, cheekbones, forehead with hollow temples, chiselled nose—the fortress of an unconquerable spirit that had yielded to death, and in its upward sightlessness seemed trying to regain that spirit, to regain the guardianship it had just laid down.

Swithin took but one look at the face, and left the room; the sight, he said afterwards, made him very queer. He went downstairs shaking the whole house, and, seizing his hat, clambered into his brougham, without giving any directions to the coachman. He was driven home, and all the evening sat in his chair without moving.

He could take nothing for dinner but a partridge, with an imperial pint of champagne. . . .

Old Jolyon stood at the bottom of the bed, his hands folded in front of him. He alone of those in the room remembered the death of his mother, and though he looked at Ann, it was of that he was thinking. Ann was an old woman, but death had come to her at last—death came to all! His face did not move, his gaze seemed travelling from very far.

Aunt Hester stood beside him. She did not cry now, tears were exhausted—her nature refused to permit a further escape of force; she twisted her hands, looking, not at Ann, but from side to side, seeking some way of escaping the effort of realisation.

Of all the brothers and sisters James manifested the most emotion. Tears rolled down the parallel furrows of his thin face; where he should go now to tell his troubles he did not know; Juley was no good, Hester worse than useless! He felt Ann's death more than he had ever thought he should; this would upset him for weeks!

Presently Aunt Hester stole out, and Aunt Juley began moving about, doing 'what was necessary', so that twice she knocked against something. Old Jolyon, roused from his reverie, that reverie of the long, long past, looked sternly at her, and went away. James alone was left by the bedside; glancing stealthily round, to see that he was unobserved, he twisted his long body down, placed a kiss on the dead forehead, then he, too, hastily left the room. Encountering Smither in the hall, he began to ask her about the funeral, and, finding that she knew nothing, complained bitterly that, if they didn't take care, everything would go wrong. She had better send for Mr Soames—he knew all about that sort of thing; her master was very much upset, he supposed—he would want looking after; as for her mistresses, they were no good—they had no gumption! They would be ill too, he shouldn't wonder. She had better send for the doctor; it was best to take things in time. He didn't think his sister Ann had had the best opinion; if she'd had Blank she would have been alive now. Smither might send to Park Lane any time she wanted advice. Of course, his carriage was at their service for the funeral. He supposed she hadn't such a thing as a glass of claret and a biscuit—he had had no lunch!

The days before the funeral passed quietly. It had long been known, of course, that Aunt Ann had left her little property to Timothy. There was, therefore, no reason for the slightest agitation. Soames, who was sole executor, took charge of all arrangements, and in due course sent out the following invitation to every male member of the family:

To—
  Your presence is requested at the funeral of Miss Ann Forsyte, in Highgate Cemetery, at noon of
  Oct. 1st. Carriages will meet at 'The Bower', Bayswater Road, at 10.45. No flowers by request.
  R.S.V.P.

The morning came, cold, with a high, grey, London sky, and at half-past ten the first carriage, that of James, drove up. It contained James and his son-in-law Dartie, a fine man, with a square chest, buttoned very tightly into a frock coat, and a sallow, fattish face adorned with dark, well-curled moustaches, and that incorrigible commencement of whisker which, eluding the strictest attempts at shaving, seems the mark of something deeply ingrained in the personality of the shaver, being especially noticeable in men who speculate.

Soames, in his capacity of executor, received the guests, for Timothy still kept his bed; he would get up after the funeral; and Aunts Juley and Hester would not be coming down till all was over, when it was understood there would be lunch for anyone who cared to come back. The next to arrive was Roger, still limping from the gout, and encircled by three of his sons—young Roger, Eustace, and Thomas. George, the remaining son, arrived almost immediately afterwards in a hansom, and paused in the hall to ask Soames how he had found undertaking pay.

They disliked each other.

Then came two Haymans—Giles and Jesse—perfectly silent, and very well dressed, with special creases down their evening trousers. Then old Jolyon alone. Next, Nicholas, with a healthy colour in his face, and a carefully veiled sprightliness in every movement of his head and body. One of his sons followed him, meek and subdued. Swithin Forsyte and Bosinney arrived at the same moment, and stood bowing precedence to each other, but on the door opening they tried to enter together; they renewed their apologies in the hall, and Swithin, settling his stock, which had become disarranged in the struggle, very slowly mounted the stairs. The other Hayman; two married sons of Nicholas, together with Tweetyman, Spender, and Warry, the husbands of married Forsyte and Hayman daughters. The company was then complete, twenty-one in all, not a male member of the family being absent but Timothy and young Jolyon.

Entering the scarlet and green drawing-room, whose apparel made so vivid a setting for their unaccustomed costumes, each tried nervously to find a seat, desirous of hiding the emphatic blackness of his trousers. There seemed a sort of indecency in that blackness and in the colour of their gloves—a sort of exaggeration of the feelings; and many cast shocked looks of secret envy at 'The Buccaneer', who had no gloves, and was wearing grey trousers. A subdued hum of conversation rose, no one speaking of the departed, but each asking after the other, as though thereby casting an indirect libation to this event, which they had come to honour.

And presently James said:

'Well, I think we ought to be starting.'

They went downstairs, and, two by two, as they had been told off in strict precedence, mounted the carriages.

The hearse started at a foot's pace; the carriages moved slowly after. In the first went old Jolyon with Nicholas; in the second, the twins, Swithin and James; in the third, Roger and young Roger; Soames, young Nicholas, George, and Bosinney followed in the fourth. Each of the other carriages, eight in all, held three or four of the family; behind them came the doctor's brougham; then, at a decent interval, cabs containing family clerks and servants; and at the very end, one containing nobody at all, but bringing the total cortège up to the number of thirteen.

So long as the procession kept to the highway of the Bayswater Road, it retained the foot's pace, but, turning into less important thoroughfares, it soon broke into a trot, and so proceeded, with intervals of walking in the more fashionable streets, until it arrived. In the first carriage old Jolyon and Nicholas were talking of their wills. In the second the twins, after a single attempt, had lapsed into complete silence; both were rather deaf, and the exertion of making themselves heard was too great. Only once James broke this silence:

'I shall have to be looking about for some ground somewhere. What arrangements have you made, Swithin?'

And Swithin, fixing him with a dreadful stare, answered:

'Don't talk to me about such things!'

In the third carriage a disjointed conversation was carried on in the intervals of looking out to see how far they had got, George remarking, 'Well, it was time that the poor old lady "went".' He didn't believe in people living beyond seventy. Young Nicholas replied mildly that the rule didn't seem to apply to the Forsytes. George said he himself intended to commit suicide at sixty. Young

Nicholas, smiling and stroking a long chin, didn't think *his* father would like the theory; he had made a lot of money since he was sixty. Well, seventy was the outside limit; it was then time, George said, for them to go and leave their money to their children. Soames, hitherto silent, here joined in; he had not forgotten the remark about the 'undertaking', and, lifting his eyelids almost imperceptibly, said it was all very well for people who never made money to talk. He himself intended to live as long as he could. This was a hit at George, who was notoriously hard up. Bosinney muttered abstractly 'Hear, hear!' and, George yawning, the conversation dropped.

Upon arriving, the coffin was borne into the chapel, and, two by two, the mourners filed in behind it. This guard of men, all attached to the dead body by kinship, was an impressive and singular sight in the great city of London, with its overwhelming diversity of life, its innumerable vocations, pleasures, duties, its terrible hardness, its terrible call to individualism.

The family had gathered to triumph over all this, to give a show of tenacious unity, to illustrate gloriously that law of property underlying the growth of their tree, by which it had thriven and spread, trunk and branches, the sap flowing through all, the full growth reached at the appointed time. The spirit of the old woman lying in her last sleep had called them to this demonstration. It was her final appeal to that unity which had been their strength–it was her final triumph that she had died while the tree was yet whole.

She was spared the watching of the branches just out beyond the point of balance. She could not look into the hearts of her followers. The same law that had worked in her, bringing her up from a tall, straight-backed slip of a girl to a woman strong and grown, from a woman grown to a woman old, angular, feeble, almost witch-like, with individuality all sharpened and sharpened, as all rounding from the world's contact fell off from her–that same law would work, was working, in the family she had watched like a mother.

She had seen it young, and growing, she had seen it strong and grown, and before her old eyes had time or strength to see any more, she died. She would have tried, and who knows but she might have kept it young and strong, with her old fingers, her trembling kisses–a little longer; alas! not even Aunt Ann could fight with Nature.

'Pride comes before a fall!' In accordance with this, the greatest of Nature's ironies, the Forsyte family had gathered for a last proud pageant before they fell. Their faces to right and left, in single lines, were turned for the most part impassively toward the ground, guardians of their thoughts; but here and there, one looking upward, with a line between his brows, seemed to see some sight on the chapel walls too much for him, to be listening to something that appalled. And the responses, low-muttered, in voices through which rose the same tone, the same unseizable family ring, sounded weird, as though murmured in hurried duplication by a single person.

The service in the chapel over, the mourners filed up again to guard the body to the tomb. The vault stood open, and, round it, men in black were waiting.

From that high and sacred field, where thousands of the upper middle class lay in their last sleep, the eyes of the Forsytes travelled down across the flocks of graves. There–spreading to the distance, lay London, with no sun over it, mourning the loss of its daughter, mourning with this family, so dear, the loss of her who was mother and guardian. A hundred thousand spires and houses, blurred in the great grey web of property, lay there like prostrate worshippers before the grave of this, the oldest Forsyte of them all.

A few words, a sprinkle of earth, the thrusting of the coffin home, and Aunt Ann had passed to her last rest.

Round the vault, trustees of that passing, the five brothers stood, with white heads bowed; they would see that Ann was comfortable where she was going. Her little property must stay behind, but otherwise, all that could be should be done.

Then severally, each stood aside, and putting on his hat, turned back to inspect the new inscription on the marble of the family vault:

SACRED TO THE MEMORY OF

ANN FORSYTE

THE DAUGHTER OF THE ABOVE

JOLYON AND ANN FORSYTE,

WHO DEPARTED THIS LIFE THE 27TH DAY OF

SEPTEMBER, 1886,

AGED EIGHTY-SEVEN YEARS AND FOUR DAYS

Soon perhaps, someone else would be wanting an inscription. It was strange and intolerable, for they had not thought somehow, that Forsytes could die. And one and all they had a longing to get away from this painfulness, this ceremony which had reminded them of things they could not bear to think about—to get away quickly and go about their business and forget.

It was cold, too; the wind, like some slow, disintegrating force, blowing up the hill over the graves, struck them with its chilly breath; they began to split into groups, and as quickly as possible to fill the waiting carriages.

Swithin said he should go back to lunch at Timothy's, and he offered to take anybody with him in his brougham. It was considered a doubtful privilege to drive with Swithin in his brougham, which was not a large one; nobody accepted, and he went off alone. James and Roger followed immediately after; they also would drop into lunch. The others gradually melted away, old Jolyon taking three nephews to fill up his carriage; he had a want of those young faces.

Soames, who had to arrange some details in the cemetery office, walked away with Bosinney. He had much to talk over with him, and, having finished his business, they strolled to Hampstead, lunched together at the Spaniard's Inn, and spent a long time in going into practical details connected with the building of the house; they then proceeded to the tram-line, and came as far as the Marble Arch, where Bosinney went off to Stanhope Gate to see June.

Soames felt in excellent spirits when he arrived home, and confided to Irene at dinner that he had had a good talk with Bosinney, who really seemed a sensible fellow; they had had a capital walk too, which had done his liver good—he had been short of exercise for a long time—and altogether a very satisfactory day. If only it hadn't been for poor Aunt Ann, he would have taken her to the theatre; as it was, they must make the best of an evening at home.

'The Buccaneer asked after you more than once,' he said suddenly. And moved by some inexplicable desire to assert his proprietorship, he rose from his chair and planted a kiss on his wife's shoulder.

PART II

I

PROGRESS OF THE HOUSE

The winter had been an open one. Things in the trade were slack; and as Soames had reflected before making up his mind, it had been a good time for building. The shell of the house at Robin Hill was thus completed by the end of April.

Now that there was something to be seen for his money, he had been coming down once, twice, even three times a week, and would mouse about among the débris for hours, careful never to soil his clothes, moving silently through the unfinished brickwork of doorways, or circling round the columns in the central court.

And he would stand before them for minutes together, as though peering into the real quality of their substance.

On April 30 he had an appointment with Bosinney to go over the accounts, and five minutes before the proper time he entered the tent which the architect had pitched for himself close to the old oak tree.

The accounts were already prepared on a folding table, and with a nod Soames sat down to study them. It was some time before he raised his head.

'I can't make them out,' he said at last; 'they come to nearly seven hundred more than they ought!'

After a glance at Bosinney's face, he went on quickly:

'If you only make a firm stand against these builder chaps you'll get them down. They stick you with everything if you don't look sharp. Take ten per cent. off all round. I shan't mind its coming out a hundred or so over the mark!'

Bosinney shook his head:

'I've taken off every farthing I can!'

Soames pushed back the table with a movement of anger, which sent the account sheets fluttering to the ground.

'Then all I can say is,' he flustered out, 'you've made a pretty mess of it!'

'I've told you a dozen times,' Bosinney answered sharply, 'that there'd be extras. I've pointed them out to you over and over again!'

'I know that,' growled Soames; 'I shouldn't have objected to a ten-pound note here and there. How was I to know that by "extras" you meant seven hundred pounds?'

The qualities of both men had contributed to this not inconsiderable discrepancy. On the one hand, the architect's devotion to his idea, to the image of a house which he had created and believed in—had made him nervous of being stopped, or forced to the use of make-shifts; on the other, Soames's not less true and whole-hearted devotion to the very best article that could be obtained for the money, had rendered him averse to believing that things worth thirteen shillings could not be bought for twelve.

'I wish I'd never undertaken your house,' said Bosinney suddenly. 'You come down here worrying me out of my life. You want double the value for your money anybody else would, and now that you've got a house that for its size is not to beaten in the county, you don't want to pay for it. If you're anxious to be off your bargain, I daresay I can find the balance above the estimates myself, but I'm d—d if I do another stroke of work for you!'

Soames regained his composure. Knowing that Bosinney had no capital, he regarded this as a wild suggestion. He saw, too, that he would be kept indefinitely out of this house on which he had set his heart, and just at the crucial point when the architect's personal care made all the difference. In the meantime there was Irene to be thought of! She had been very queer lately. He really believed it was only because she had taken to Bosinney that she tolerated the idea of the house at all. It would not do to make an open breach with her.

'You needn't get into a rage,' he said. 'If I'm willing to put up with it, I suppose *you* needn't cry out. All I meant was that when you tell me a thing is going to cost so much, I like to—well, in fact, I—like to know where I am.'

'Look here!' said Bosinney, and Soames was both annoyed and surprised by the shrewdness of his glance. 'You've got my services dirt cheap. For the kind of work I've put into this house, and the amount of time I've given to it, you'd have had to pay Littlemaster or some other fool four times as much. What you want, in fact, is a first-rate man for a fourth-rate fee, and that's exactly what you've got!'

Soames saw that he really meant what he said, and, angry though he was, the consequences of a row rose before him too vividly. He saw his house unfinished, his wife rebellious, himself a laughing-stock.

'Let's go over it,' he said sulkily, 'and see how the money's gone.'

'Very well,' assented Bosinney. 'But we'll hurry up, if you don't mind. I have to get back to take June to the theatre.'

Soames cast a stealthy look at him, and said: 'Coming to our place, I suppose, to meet her?' He was always coming to their place!

There had been rain the night before—a spring rain, and the earth smelt of sap and wild grasses. The warm, soft breeze swung the leaves and the golden buds of the old oak tree, and in the sunshine the blackbirds were whistling their hearts out.

It was such a spring day as breathes into a man an ineffable yearning, a painful sweetness, a longing that makes him stand motionless, looking at the leaves of grass, and fling out his arms to embrace he knows not what. The earth gave forth a fainting warmth, stealing up through the chilly garment in which winter had wrapped her. It was her long caress of invitation, to draw men down to lie within her arms, to roll their bodies on her, and put their lips to her breast.

On just such a day as this Soames had got from Irene the promise he had asked her for so often. Seated on the fallen trunk of a tree, he had promised for the twentieth time that if their marriage were not a success, she should be as free as if she had never married him!

'Do you swear it?' she had said. A few days back she had reminded him of that oath. He had answered: 'Nonsense! I couldn't have sworn any such thing!' By some awkward fatality he remembered it now. What queer things men would swear for the sake of women! He would have sworn it at any time to gain her! He would swear it now, if thereby he could touch her—but nobody could touch her, she was cold-hearted!

And memories crowded on him with the fresh, sweet savour of the spring wind—memories of his courtship.

In the spring of the year 1881 he was visiting his old school-fellow and client, George Liversedge, of Branksome, who, with the view of developing his pine woods in the neighbourhood of Bournemouth, had placed the formation of the company necessary to the scheme in Soames's hands. Mrs Liversedge, with a sense of the fitness of things, had given a musical tea in his honour. Late in the course of this function, which Soames, no musician, had regarded as an unmitigated bore, his eye had been caught by the face of a girl dressed in mourning, standing by herself. The lines of her tall, as yet rather thin, figure, showed through the wispy, clinging stuff of her black dress, her black-gloved hands were crossed in front of her, her lips slightly parted, and her large, dark eyes wandered from face to face. Her hair, done low on her neck, seemed to gleam above her black collar like coils of shining metal. And as Soames stood looking at her, the sensation that most men have felt at one time or another went stealing through him—a peculiar satisfaction of the senses, a peculiar certainty, which novelists and old ladies call love at first sight. Still stealthily watching her, he at once made his way to his hostess, and stood doggedly waiting for the music to cease.

'Who is that girl with yellow hair and dark eyes?' he asked.

'That—oh! Irene Heron. Her father, Professor Heron, died this year. She lives with her stepmother. She's a nice girl, a pretty girl, but no money!'

'Introduce me, please,' said Soames.

It was very little that he found to say, nor did he find her responsive to that little. But he went away with the resolution to see her again. He effected his object by chance, meeting her on the pier with her stepmother, who had the habit of walking there from twelve to one of a forenoon. Soames made this lady's acquaintance with alacrity, nor was it long before he perceived in her the ally he was looking for. His keen scent for the commercial side of family life soon told him that Irene cost her stepmother more than the fifty pounds a year she brought her; it also told him that Mrs Heron, a woman yet in the prime of life, desired to be married again. The strange ripening beauty of her stepdaughter stood in the way of this desirable consummation. And Soames, in his stealthy tenacity, laid his plans.

He left Bournemouth without having given himself away, but in a month's time came back, and this time he spoke, not to the girl, but to her stepmother. He had made up his mind, he said; he would wait any time. And he had long to wait, watching Irene bloom, the lines of her young figure softening, the stronger blood deepening the gleam of her eyes, and warming her face to a creamy glow; and at each visit he proposed to her, and when that visit was at an end, took her refusal away with him, back to London, sore at heart, but steadfast and silent as the grave. He tried to come at the secret springs of her resistance; only once had he a gleam of light. It was at one of those assembly dances, which afford the only outlet to the passions of the population of seaside watering-places. He was sitting with her in an embrasure, his senses tingling with the contact of the waltz. She had looked at him over her slowly waving fan; and he had lost his head. Seizing that moving wrist, he pressed his lips to the flesh of her arm. And she had shuddered—to this day he had not forgotten that shudder—nor the look so passionately averse she had given him.

A year after that she had yielded. What had made her yield he could never make out; and from Mrs Heron, a woman of some diplomatic talent, he learnt nothing. Once after they were married he asked her: 'What made you refuse me so often?' She had answered by a strange silence. An enigma to him from the day that he first saw her, she was an enigma to him still. . . .

Bosinney was waiting for him at the door; and on his rugged, good-looking face was a queer, yearning, yet happy look, as though he too saw a promise of bliss in the spring sky, sniffed a coming happiness in the spring air. Soames looked at him waiting there. What was the matter with the fellow that he looked so happy? What was he waiting for with that smile on his lips and in his eyes? Soames could not see that for which Bosinney was waiting as he stood there drinking in the flower-scented wind. And once more he felt baffled in the presence of this man whom by habit he despised. He hastened on to the house.

'The only colour for those tiles,' he heard Bosinney say, 'is ruby with a grey tint in the stuff, to give a transparent effect. I should like Irene's opinion. I'm ordering the purple leather curtains for the doorway of this court; and if you distemper the drawing-room ivory cream over paper, you'll get an elusive look. You want to aim all through the decorations at what I call—charm.'

Soames said: 'You mean that my wife has charm?'

Bosinney evaded the question.

'You should have a clump of iris plants in the centre of that court.'

Soames smiled superciliously.

'I'll look into Beech's some time,' he said, 'and see what's appropriate!'

They found little else to say to each other, but on the way to the station Soames asked:

'I suppose you find Irene very artistic?'

'Yes.' The abrupt answer was as distinct a snub as saying: 'If you want to discuss her you can do it with someone else!'

And the slow sulky anger Soames had felt all the afternoon burned the brighter within him.

Neither spoke again till they were close to the station, then Soames asked:

'When do you expect to have finished?'

'By the end of June if you really wish me to decorate as well.'

Soames nodded. 'But you quite understand,' he said, 'that the house is costing me a lot beyond what I contemplated. I may as well tell you that I should have thrown it up, only I'm not in the habit of giving up what I've set my mind on!'

Bosinney made no reply. And Soames gave him askance a look of dogged dislike—for in spite of his fastidious air and that supercilious taciturnity, Soames, with his set lips and his squared chin, was not unlike a bulldog. . . .

When, at seven o'clock that evening, June arrived at 62, Montpelier Square, the maid Bilson told her that Mr Bosinney was in the drawing-room; the mistress—she said—was dressing, and would be down in a minute. She would tell her that Miss June was here.

June stopped her at once.

'All right, Bilson,' she said, 'I'll just go in. You needn't hurry Mrs Soames.'

She took off her cloak, and Bilson, with an understanding look, did not even open the drawing-room door for her, but ran downstairs.

June paused for a moment to look at herself in the little old-fashioned silver mirror above the oaken rug chest—a slim, imperious young figure, with a small resolute face, in a white frock, cut moon-shaped at the base of the neck too slender for her crown of twisted red-gold hair.

She opened the drawing-room door softly, meaning to take him by surprise. The room was filled with a sweet hot scent of flowering azaleas.

She took a long breath of the perfume, and heard Bosinney's voice, not in the room, but quite close, saying:

'Ah! there were such heaps of things I wanted to talk about and now we shan't have time!'

Irene's voice answered: 'Why not at dinner?'

'How can one talk—'

June's first thought was to go away, but instead she crossed to the long window opening on the little court. It was from there that the scent of the azaleas came, and, standing with their backs to her, their faces buried in the golden-pink blossoms, stood her lover and Irene.

Silent but unashamed, with flaming cheeks and angry eyes, the girl watched.

'Come on Sunday by yourself—we can go over the house together—'

June saw Irene look up at him through her screen of blossoms. It was not the look of a coquette, but—far worse to the watching girl—of a woman fearful lest that look should say too much.

'I've promised to go for a drive with Uncle—'

'The big one! Make him bring you; it's only ten miles—the very thing for his horses.'

'Poor old Uncle Swithin!'

A wave of the azalea scent drifted into June's face; she felt sick and dizzy.

'Do! ah! do!'

'But why?'

'I must see you there—I thought you'd like to help me—'

The answer seemed to the girl to come softly, with a tremble from amongst the blossoms: 'So I do!'

And she stepped into the open space of the window.

'How stuffy it is here!' she said; 'I can't bear this scent!'

Her eyes, so angry and direct, swept both their faces.

'Were you talking about the house? *I* haven't seen it yet, you know—shall we all go on Sunday?'

From Irene's face the colour had flown.

'I am going for a drive that day with Uncle Swithin,' she answered.

'Uncle Swithin! What does he matter? You can throw him over!'

'I am not in the habit of throwing people over!'

There was a sound of footsteps, and June saw Soames standing just behind her.

'Well! if you are all ready,' said Irene, looking from one to the other with a strange smile, 'dinner is too!'

2

JUNE'S TREAT

Dinner began in silence; the women facing one another, and the men.

In silence the soup was finished—excellent, if a little thick, and fish was brought. In silence it was handed.

Bosinney ventured: 'It's the first spring day.'

Irene echoed softly: 'Yes—the first spring day.'

'Spring!' said June: 'there isn't a breath of air!' No one replied.

The fish was taken away, a fine fresh sole from Dover. And Bilson brought champagne, a bottle swathed around the neck with white.

Soames said: 'You'll find it dry.'

Cutlets were handed, each pink-frilled about the legs. They were refused by June, and silence fell.

Soames said: 'You'd better take a cutlet, June; there's nothing coming.'

But June again refused, so they were borne away. And then Irene asked: 'Phil, have you heard my blackbird?'

Bosinney answered: 'Rather—he's got a hunting-song. As I came round I heard him in the Square.'

'He's such a darling!'

'Salad, sir?' Spring chicken was removed.

But Soames was speaking: 'The asparagus is very poor. Bosinney, glass of sherry with your sweet? June, you're drinking nothing!'

June said: 'You know I never do. Wine's such horrid stuff!'

An apple charlotte came upon a silver dish. And smilingly Irene said: 'The azaleas are so wonderful this year!'

To this Bosinney murmured: 'Wonderful! The scent's extraordinary!'

June said: 'How *can* you like the scent? Sugar, please, Bilson.'

Sugar was handed her, and Soames remarked: 'This charlotte's good!'

The charlotte was removed. Long silence followed. Irene, beckoning said: 'Take out the azaleas, Bilson. Miss June can't bear the scent.'

'No, let it stay,' said June.

Olives from France, with Russian caviare, were placed on little plates. And Soames remarked: 'Why can't we have the Spanish?' But no one answered.

The olives were removed. Lifting her tumbler, June demanded: 'Give me some water, please.' Water was given her. A silver tray was brought, with German plums. There was a lengthy pause. In perfect harmony all were eating them.

Bosinney counted up the stones: 'This year—next year—some time—'

Irene finished softly: 'Never. There was such a glorious sunset. The sky's all ruby still—so beautiful!'

He answered: 'Underneath the dark.'

Their eyes had met, and June cried scornfully: 'A London sunset!'

Egyptian cigarettes were handed in a silver box. Soames, taking one, remarked: 'What time's your play begin?'

No one replied, and Turkish coffee followed in enamelled cups.

Irene, smiling quietly, said: 'If only—'

'Only what?' said June.

'If only it could always be the spring!'

Brandy was handed; it was pale and old.

Soames said: 'Bosinney, better take some brandy.'

Bosinney took a glass; they all arose.

'You want a cab?' asked Soames.

June answered: 'No. My cloak, please, Bilson.' Her cloak was brought.

Irene, from the window, murmured: 'Such a lovely night! The stars are coming out!'

Soames added: 'Well, I hope you'll both enjoy yourselves.'

From the door June answered: 'Thanks. Come, Phil.'

Bosinney cried: 'I'm coming.'

Soames smiled a sneering smile, and said: 'I wish you luck!'

And at the door Irene watched them go.

Bosinney called: 'Good night!'

'Good night!' she answered softly. . . .

June made her lover take her on the top of a bus, saying she wanted air, and there sat silent, with her face to the breeze.

The driver turned once or twice, with the intention of venturing a remark, but thought better of it. They were a lively couple! The spring had got into his blood, too; he felt the need for letting steam escape, and clucked his tongue, flourishing his whip, wheeling his horses, and even they, poor things, had smelled the spring, and for a brief half-hour spurned the pavement with happy hoofs.

The whole town was alive; the boughs, curled upward with their decking of young leaves, awaited some gift the breeze could bring. New-lighted lamps were gaining mastery, and the faces of the crowd showed pale under that glare, while on high the great white clouds slid swiftly, softly, over the purple sky.

Men in evening dress had thrown back overcoats, stepping jauntily up the steps of clubs; working folk loitered; and women—those women who at that time of night are solitary—solitary and moving eastward in a stream—swung slowly along with expectation in their gait; dreaming of good wine and a good supper, or, for an unwonted minute, of kisses given for love.

Those countless figures, going their ways under the lamps and the moving sky, had one and all received some restless blessing from the stir of spring. And one and all, like those clubmen with their opened coats, had shed something of caste, and creed, and custom, and by the cock of their hats, the pace of their walk, their laughter, or their silence, revealed their common kinship under the passionate heavens.

Bosinney and June entered the theatre in silence, and mounted to their seats in the upper boxes. The piece had just begun, and the half-darkened house, with its rows of creatures peering all one way, resembled a great garden of flowers turning their faces to the sun.

June had never before been in the upper boxes. From the age of fifteen she had habitually accompanied her grandfather to the stalls, and not common stalls, but the best seats in the house towards the centre of the third row, booked by old Jolyon, at Grogan and Boyne's, on his way home from the City, long before the day; carried in his overcoat pocket, together with his cigar-case and his old kid gloves, and handed to June to keep till the appointed night. And in those stalls—an erect old figure with a serene white head, a little figure, strenuous and eager, with a red gold head—they would sit through every kind of play, and on the way home old Jolyon would say of the principal actor: 'Oh, he's a poor stick! You should have seen little Bobson!'

She had looked forward to this evening with keen delight; it was stolen, chaperone-less, undreamed of at Stanhope Gate, where she was supposed to be at Soames's. She had expected reward for her subterfuge, planned for her lover's sake; she had expected it to break up the thick, chilly cloud, and make the relations between them—which of late had been so puzzling, so tormenting—sunny and simple again as they had been before the winter. She had come with the intention of saying something definite; and she looked at the stage with a furrow between her brows, seeing nothing, her hands squeezed together in her lap. A swarm of jealous suspicions stung and stung her.

If Bosinney was conscious of her trouble, he made no sign.

The curtain dropped. The first act had come to an end.

'It's awfully hot here!' said the girl; 'I should like to go out.'

She was very white, and she knew—for with her nerves thus sharpened she saw everything—that he was both uneasy and compunctious.

At the back of the theatre an open balcony hung over the street; she took possession of this, and stood leaning there without a word, waiting for him to begin.

At last she could bear it no longer.

'I want to say something to you, Phil,' she said.

'Yes?'

The defensive tone of his voice brought the colour flying to her cheeks, the words flying to her lips: 'You don't give me a chance to be nice to you; you haven't for ages now!'

Bosinney stared down at the street. He made no answer.

June cried passionately: 'You know I want to do everything for you—that I want to be everything to you—'

A hum rose from the street, and, piercing it with a sharp 'ping', the bell sounded for the raising of the curtain. June did not stir. A desperate struggle was going on within her. Should she put everything to the proof? Should she challenge directly that influence, that attraction which was drawing him away from her? It was her nature to challenge, and she said: 'Phil, take me to see the house on Sunday!'

With a smile quivering and breaking on her lips, and trying, how hard! not to show that she was watching she searched his face, saw it waver and hesitate, saw a troubled line come between his brows, the blood rush into his face. He answered: 'Not Sunday, dear; some other day!'

'Why not Sunday? I shouldn't be in the way on Sunday.'

He made an evident effort and said: 'I have an engagement.'

'You are going to take—'

His eyes grew angry; he shrugged his shoulders, and answered: 'An engagement that will prevent my taking you to see the house!'

June bit her lip till the blood came, and walked back to her seat without another word, but she could not help the tears of rage rolling down her face. The house had been mercifully darkened for a crisis, and no one could see her trouble.

Yet in this world of Forsytes let no man think himself immune from observation.

In the third row behind, Euphemia, Nicholas's youngest daughter, with her married sister, Mrs Tweetyman, were watching.

They reported at Timothy's, how they had seen June and her fiancé at the theatre.

'In the stalls?' 'No, not in the–' 'Oh, in the dress circle of course. That seemed to be quite fashionable nowadays with the young people!'

Well–not exactly. In the–Anyway, *that* engagement wouldn't last long. They had never seen anyone look so thunder and lightningy as that little June! With tears of enjoyment in their eyes, they related how she had kicked a man's hat as she returned to her seat in the middle of an act, and how the man had looked. Euphemia had a noted, silent laugh, terminating most disappointingly in squeaks; and when Mrs Small, holding up her hands, said: 'My dear! Kicked a ha-at?' she let out such a number of these that she had to be recovered with smelling-salts. As she went away, she said to Mrs Tweetyman: 'Kicked a ha-at!' Oh! I shall die.'

For "that little June" this evening, that was to have been "her treat", was the most miserable she had ever spent. God knows she tried to stifle her pride, her suspicion, her jealousy!

She parted from Bosinney at old Jolyon's door without breaking down; the feeling that her lover must be conquered was strong enough to sustain her till his retiring footsteps brought home the true extent of her wretchedness.

The noiseless 'Sankey' let her in. She would have slipped up to her own room, but old Jolyon, who had heard her entrance, was in the dining-room doorway.

'Come in and have your milk,' he said. 'It's been kept hot for you. You're very late. Where have you been?'

June stood at the fireplace, with a foot on the fender and an arm on the mantelpiece, as her grandfather had done when he came in that night of the opera. She was too near a breakdown to care what she told him.

'We dined at Soames's.'

'H'm! the man of property! His wife there–and Bosinney?'

'Yes.'

Old Jolyon's glance was fixed on her with the penetrating gaze from which it was so difficult to hide; but she was not looking at him, and when she turned her face, he dropped his scrutiny at once. He had seen enough, and too much. He bent down to lift the cup of milk for her from the hearth, and, turning away, grumbled: 'You oughtn't to stay out so late: it makes you fit for nothing.'

He was invisible now behind his paper, which he turned with a vicious crackle; but when June came up to kiss him, he said: 'Good night, my darling,' in a tone so tremulous and unexpected, that it was all the girl could do to get out of the room without breaking into the fit of sobbing that lasted her well on into the night.

When the door was closed, old Jolyon dropped his paper, and stared long and anxiously in front of him.

'The beggar!' he thought. 'I always knew she'd have trouble with him!'

Uneasy doubts and suspicions, the more poignant that he felt himself powerless to check or control the march of events, came crowding upon him.

Was the fellow going to jilt her? He longed to go and say to him: 'Look here, you sir! Are you going to jilt my granddaughter?' But how could he? Knowing little or nothing, he was yet certain, with his unerring astuteness, that there was something going on. He suspected Bosinney of being too much at Montpelier Square.

'This fellow,' he thought, 'may not be a scamp; his face is not a bad one, but he's a queer fish. I don't know what to make of him. I shall never know what to make of him! They tell me he works like a nigger, but I see no good coming of it. He's unpractical, he has no method. When he comes here, he sits as glum as a monkey. If I ask him what wine he'll have, he says: 'Thanks, any wine.' If I offer him a cigar, he smokes it as if it were a twopenny German thing. I never see him looking at June as he ought to look at her; and yet he's not after her money. If she were to make a sign, he'd be off his bargain to-morrow. But she won't—not she! She'll stick to him! She's an obstinate as fate—she'll never let go!'

Sighing deeply, he turned the paper; in its columns perchance he might find consolation.

And upstairs in her room June sat at her open window, where the spring wind came, after its revel across the Park, to cool her hot cheeks and burn her heart.

3

DRIVE WITH SWITHIN

Two lines of a certain song in a certain famous old school's song-book run as follows:

> 'How the buttons on his blue frock shone tra-la-la!
> How he carolled and he sang, like a bird! . . .'

Swithin did not exactly carol and sing like a bird, but he felt almost like endeavouring to hum a tune, as he stepped out of Hyde Park Mansions, and contemplated his horses drawn up before the door.

The afternoon was as balmy as a day in June, and to complete the simile of the old song, he had put on a blue frock-coat, dispensing with an overcoat, after sending Adolf down three times to make sure that there was not the least suspicion of east in the wind; and the frock-coat was buttoned so tightly around his personable form that, if the buttons did not shine, they might pardonably have done so. Majestic on the pavement he fitted on a pair of dog-skin gloves; with his large bell-shaped top hat, and his great stature and bulk he looked too primeval for a Forsyte. His thick white hair, on which Adolf had bestowed a touch of pomatum, exhaled the fragrance of opoponax and cigars—the celebrated Swithin brand, for which he paid one hundred and forty shillings the hundred, and of which old Jolyon had unkindly said, he wouldn't smoke them as a gift; they wanted the stomach of a horse! . . .

'Adolf!'

'Sare!'

'The new plaid rug!'

He would never teach that fellow to look smart; and Mrs Soames, he felt sure, had an eye!

'The phæton hood down; I am going–to–drive–a–lady!'

A pretty woman would want to show off her frock; and well–he was going to drive a lady! It was like a new beginning to the good old days.

Ages since he had driven a woman! The last time, if he remembered, it had been Juley; the poor old soul had been as nervous as a cat the whole time, and so put him out of patience that, as he dropped her in the Bayswater Road, he had said: 'Well i'm d—d if I ever drive you again!' And he never had, not he!

Going up to his horses' heads, he examined their bits; not that he knew anything about bits–he didn't pay his coachman sixty pounds a year to do his work for him, that had never been his principle. Indeed, his reputation as a horsey man rested mainly on the fact that once, on Derby Day, he had been welshed by some thimble-riggers. But someone at the club, after seeing him drive his greys to the door–he always drove grey horses, you got more style for the money, some thought–had called him 'Four-in-hand Forsyte'. The name having reached his ears through that fellow Nicholas Treffry, old Jolyon's dead partner, the great driving man–notorious for more carriage accidents than any man in the kingdom–Swithin had ever after conceived it right to act up to it. The name had taken his fancy, not because he had ever driven four-in-hand, or was ever likely to, but because of something distinguished in the sound. Four-in-hand Forsyte! Not bad! Born too soon, Swithin had missed his vocation. Coming upon London twenty years later, he could not have failed to have become a stockbroker, but at the time when he was obliged to select, this great profession had not as yet become the chief glory of the upper middle class. He had literally been forced into auctioneering.

Once in the driving-seat, with the reins handed to him, and blinking over his pale old cheeks in the full sunlight, he took a slow look round. Adolf was already up behind; the cockaded groom at the horses' heads stood ready to let go; everything was prepared for the signal, and Swithin gave it. The equipage dashed forward, and before you could say Jack Robinson, with a rattle and flourish drew up at Soames's door.

Irene came out at once and stepped in–he afterwards described it at Timothy's–'as light as–er–Taglioni, no fuss about it, no wanting this or wanting that'; and above all, Swithin dwelt on this, staring at Mrs Septimus in a way that disconcerted her a good deal, 'no silly nervousness'! To Aunt Hester he portrayed Irene's hat. 'Not one of your great flopping things, sprawling about, and catching the dust, that women are so fond of nowadays, but a neat little'–he made a circular motion of his hand–'white veil–capital taste.'

'What was it made of?' inquired Aunt Hester, who manifested a languid but permanent excitement at any mention of dress.

'Made of?' returned Swithin; 'now how should *I* know?'

He sank into silence so profound that Aunt Hester began to be afraid he had fallen into a trance. She did not try to rouse him herself, it not being her custom.

'I wish somebody would come,' she thought; 'I don't like the look of him!'

But suddenly Swithin returned to life. 'Made of?' he wheezed out slowly, 'what should it be made of?'

They had not gone four miles before Swithin received the impression that Irene liked driving with him. Her face was so soft behind that white veil, and her dark eyes shone so in the spring light, that whenever he spoke she raised them to him and smiled.

On Saturday morning Soames had found her at her writing-table with a note written to Swithin, putting him off. Why did she want to put him off? he asked. She might put her own people off when she liked, he would not have her putting off *his* people!

She had looked at him intently, had torn up the note, and said: 'Very well!'

And then she began writing another. He took a casual glance presently, and saw that it was addressed to Bosinney.

'What are you writing to *him* about?' he asked.

Irene, looking at him again with that intent look, said quietly: 'Something he wanted me to do for him!'

'Humph!' said Soames. 'Commissions! You'll have your work cut out if you begin that sort of thing!' He said no more.

Swithin opened his eyes at the mention of Robin Hill; it was a long way for his horses, and he always dined at half-past seven, before the rush at the Club began; the new chef took more trouble with an early dinner—a lazy rascal!

He would like to have a look at the house, however. A house appealed to any Forsyte, and especially to one who had been an auctioneer. After all, he said the distance was nothing. When he was a younger man he had had rooms at Richmond for many years, kept his carriage and pair there, and drove them up and down to business every day of his life. Four-in-hand Forsyte they called him! His T-cart, his horses had been known from Hyde Park Corner to the Star and Garter. The Duke of Z— wanted to get hold of them, would have given him double the money, but he had kept them; know a good thing when you have it, eh? A look of solemn pride came portenously on his shaven square old face, he rolled his head in his stand-up collar, like a turkey-cock preening himself.

She was really a charming woman! He enlarged upon her frock afterwards to Aunt Juley, who held up her hands at his way of putting it.

Fitted her like a skin—tight as a drum; that was how he liked 'em, all of a piece, none of your daverdy, scarecrow women! He gazed at Mrs Septimus Small, who took after James—long and thin.

'There's style about her,' he went on, 'fit for a king! And she's so quiet with it too!'

'She seems to have made quite a conquest of you, anyway,' drawled Aunt Hester from her corner.

Swithin heard extremely well when anybody attacked him.

'What's that?' he said. 'I know a—pretty—woman when I see one, and all I can say is, I don't see the young man about that's fit for her; but perhaps—you—do, come, perhaps—you—do!'

'Oh?' murmured Aunt Hester, 'ask Juley!'

Long before they reached Robin Hill, however, the unaccustomed airing had made him terribly sleepy; he drove with his eyes closed, a life-time of deportment alone keeping his tall and bulky form from falling askew.

Bosinney, who was watching, came out to meet them, and all three entered the house together; Swithin in front making play with a stout gold-mounted Malacca cane, put into his hand by Adolf, for his knees were feeling the effects of their long stay in the same position. He had assumed his fur coat to guard against the draughts of the unfinished house.

The staircase—he said—was handsome! the baronial style! They would want some statuary about! He came to a standstill between the columns of the doorway into the inner court and held out his cane inquiringly.

What was this to be—this vestibule, or whatever they called it? But gazing at the skylight, inspiration came to him.

'Ah! the billiard-room!'

When told it was to be a tiled court with plants in the centre, he turned to Irene:

'Waste this on plants? You take my advice and have a billiard-table here!'

Irene smiled. She had lifted her veil, banding it like a nun's coif across her forehead, and the smile of her dark eyes below this seemed to Swithin more charming than ever. He nodded. She would take his advice, he saw.

He had little to say of the drawing- or dining-room, which he described as 'spacious'; but fell into such raptures as he permitted to a man of his dignity, in the wine-cellar, to which he descended by some steps, Bosinney going first with a light.

'You'll have room here,' he said, 'for six or seven hundred dozen—a very pooty little cellar!'

Bosinney having expressed the wish to show them the house from the copse below, Swithin came to a stop.

'There's a fine view from here,' he remarked; 'you haven't such a thing as a chair?'

A chair was brought him from Bosinney's tent.

'You go down,' he said blandly; 'you two! I'll sit here and look at the view.'

He sat down by the oak tree in the sun; square and upright, with one hand stretched out, resting on the knob of his cane, the other planted on his knee; his fur coat thrown open, his hat, roofing with its flat top the pale square of his face; his stare, very blank, fixed on the landscape.

He nodded to them as they went off down through the fields. He was, indeed, not sorry to be left thus for a quiet moment of reflection. The air was balmy, not too much heat in the sun; the prospect a fine one, a remarka–. His head fell a little to one side; he jerked it up and thought: Odd! He–ah! They were waving to him from the bottom! He put up his hand and moved it more than once. They were active–the prospect was remarka–. His head fell to the left, he jerked it up at once; it fell to the right. It remained there; he was asleep.

And asleep, a sentinel on the top of the rise, he appeared to rule over this prospect–remarkable–like some image blocked out by the special artist of primeval Forsytes in Pagan days, to record the domination of mind over matter!

And all the unnumbered generations of his yeoman ancestors, wont of a Sunday to stand akimbo surveying their little plots of land, their grey unmoving eyes hiding their instinct with its hidden roots of violence, their instinct for possession to the exclusion of all the world–all these unnumbered generations seemed to sit there with him on the top of the rise.

But from him, thus slumbering, his jealous Forsyte spirit travelled far, into God-knows-what jungle of fancies; with those two young people, to see what they were doing down there in the copse–in the copse where the Spring was running riot with the scent of sap and bursting buds, the song of birds innumerable, a carpet of bluebells and sweet growing things, and the sun caught like gold in the tops of the trees; to see what they were doing, walking along there so close together on the path that was too narrow; walking along there so close that they were always touching; to watch Irene's eyes, like dark thieves, stealing the heart out of the Spring. And a great unseen chaperon, his spirit was there, stopping with them to look at the little furry corpse of a mole, not dead an hour, with his mushroom and silver coat untouched by the rain or dew; watching over Irene's bent head, and the soft look of her pitying eyes; and over that young man's head, gazing at her so hard, so strangely. Walking on with them, too, across the open space where a wood-cutter had been at work, where the bluebells were trampled down, and a trunk had swayed and staggered down from its gashed stump. Climbing it with them, over, and on to the very edge of the copse, whence there stretched an undiscovered country, from far away in which came the sounds, 'Cuckoo–cuckoo!'

Silent, standing with them there, and uneasy at their silence! Very queer, very strange!

Then back again, as though guilty, through the wood–back to the cutting, still silent, amongst the songs of birds that never ceased, and the wild scent–hum! what was it–like that herb they put in–back to the log across the path.

And then unseen, uneasy, flapping above them, trying to make noises, his Forsyte spirit watched her balanced on the log, her pretty figure swaying, smiling down at that young man gazing up with such strange, shining eyes; slipping now–a-ah! falling, o-oh! sliding–down his breast; her soft, warm body clutched, her head bent back from his lips; his kiss; her recoil; his cry: 'You must know–I love you!' Must know–indeed, a pretty–? Love! Hah!

Swithin awoke; virtue had gone out of him. He had a taste in his mouth. Where was he?

Damme! He had been asleep!

He had dreamed something about a new soup, with a taste of mint in it.

Those young people–where had they got to? His left leg had pins and needles.

'Adolf!' The rascal was not there; the rascal was asleep somewhere.

He stood up, tall, square, bulky in his fur, looking anxiously down over the fields, and presently he saw them coming.

Irene was in front; that young fellow–what had they nicknamed him–'The Buccaneer!'–looked precious hang-dog there behind her; had got a flea in his ear, he shouldn't wonder. Serve him right, taking her down all that way to look at the house! The proper place to look at a house from was the lawn.

They saw him. He extended his arm and moved it spasmodically to encourage them. But they had stopped. What were they standing there for, talking–talking? They came on again. She had been giving him a rub, he had not the least doubt of it, and no wonder, over a house like that–a great ugly thing, not the sort of house *he* was accustomed to.

He looked intently at their faces with his pale, immovable stare. That young man looked very queer!

'You'll never make anything of this!' he said tartly, pointing at the mansion; 'too new-fangled!'

Bosinney gazed at him as though he had not heard; and Swithin afterwards described him to Aunt Hester as 'an extravagant sort of fellow–very odd way of looking at you–a bumpy begger!'

What gave rise to this sudden piece of psychology he did not state; possibly Bosinney's prominent forehead and cheek-bones and chin, or something hungry in his face, which quarrelled with Swithin's conception of the calm satiety that should characterise the perfect gentleman.

He brightened up at the mention of tea. He had a contempt for tea–his brother Jolyon had been in tea; made a lot of money by it–but he was so thirsty, and had such a taste in his mouth, that he was prepared to drink anything. He longed to inform Irene of the taste in his mouth–she was so sympathetic–but it would not be a distinguished thing to do; he rolled his tongue round and faintly smacked it against his palate.

In a far corner of the tent Adolf was bending his cat-like moustaches over a kettle. He left it at once to draw the cork of a pint-bottle of champagne. Swithin smiled and, nodding at Bosinney, said: 'Why, you're quite a Monte Cristo!' This celebrated novel—one of the half-dozen he had read—had produced an extraordinary impression on his mind.

Taking his glass from the table, he held it away from him to scrutinise the colour; thirsty as he was, it was not likely that he was going to drink trash! Then, placing it to his lips, he took a sip.

'A very nice wine,' he said at last, passing it before his nose; 'not the equal of my Heidsieck!'

It was at this moment that the idea came to him which he afterwards imparted at Timothy's in this nut-shell: 'I shouldn't wonder a bit if that architect chap were sweet upon Mrs Soames!'

And from this moment his pale, round eyes never ceased to bulge with interest of his discovery.

'The fellow,' he said to Mrs Septimus, 'follows her about with his eyes like a dog—the bumpy begger! I don't wonder at it—she's a very charming woman, and, I should say, the pink of discretion!' A vague consciousness of perfume clinging about Irene, like that from a flower with half-closed petals and a passionate heart, moved him to the creation of this image. 'But I wasn't sure of it,' he said, 'till I saw him pick up her handkerchief.'

Mrs Small's eyes boiled with excitement.

'And did he give it her back?' she asked.

'Give it back?' said Swithin: 'I saw him slobber on it when he thought I wasn't looking!'

Mrs Small gasped—too interested to speak.

'But *she* gave him no encouragement,' went on Swithin; he stopped and stared for a minute or two in the way that alarmed Aunt Hester so—he had suddenly recollected that, as they were starting back in the phæton, she had given Bosinney her hand a second time, and let it stay there too. . . . He had touched his horses smartly with the whip, anxious to get her all to himself. But she had looked back, and she had not answered his first question; neither had he been able to see her face—she had kept it hanging down.

There is somewhere a picture, which Swithin has not seen, of a man sitting on a rock, and by him, immersed in the still, green water, a sea-nymph lying on her back, with her hand on her naked breast. She has a half-smile on her face—a smile of hopeless surrender and of secret joy. Seated by Swithin's side, Irene may have been smiling like that.

When, warmed by champagne, he had her all to himself, he unbosomed himself of his wrongs; of his smothered resentment against the new chef at the club; his worry over the house in Wigmore Street, where the rascally tenant had gone bankrupt through helping his brother-in-law—as if charity did not begin at home; of his deafness, too, and that pain he sometimes got in his right side. She listened, her eyes swimming under their lids. He thought she was thinking deeply of his troubles, and pitied himself terribly. Yet in his fur coat, with frogs across the breast, his top hat aslant, driving this beautiful woman, he had never felt more distinguished.

A coster, however, taking his girl for a Sunday airing, seemed to have the same impression about himself. This person had flogged his donkey into a gallop alongside and sat, upright as a waxwork, in his shallopy chariot, his chin settled pompously on a red handkerchief, like Swithin's on his full cravat; while his girl, with the ends of a fly-blown boa floating out behind, aped a woman of fashion. Her swain moved a stick with a ragged bit of string dangling from the end, reproducing with strange fidelity the circular flourish of Swithin's whip, and rolled his head at his lady with a leer that had a weird likeness to Swithin's primeval stare.

Though for a time unconscious of the lowly ruffian's presence, Swithin presently took it into his head that he was being guyed. He laid his whip-lash across the mare's flank. The two chariots, however, by some unfortunate fatality continued abreast. Swithin's yellow, puffy face grew red; he raised his whip to lash the coster-monger, but was saved from so far forgetting his dignity by a special intervention of Providence. A carriage driving out through a gate forced phæton and donkey-cart into proximity; the wheels grated, the lighter vehicle skidded, and was overturned.

Swithin did not look round. On no account would he have pulled up to help the ruffian. Serve him right if he had broken his neck!

But he could not if he would. The greys had taken alarm. The phæton swung from side to side, and people raised frightened faces as they went dashing past. Swithin's great arms, stretched at full length, tugged at the reins. His cheeks were puffed, his lips compressed, his swollen face was of a dull, angry red.

Irene had her hand on the rail, and at every lurch she gripped it tightly. Swithin heard her ask:

'Are we going to have an accident, Uncle Swithin?'

He gasped out between his pants: 'It's nothing; a—little fresh!'

'I've never been in an accident.'

'Don't you move!' He took a look at her. She was smiling, perfectly calm. 'Sit still,' he repeated. 'Never fear, I'll get you home!'

And in the midst of all his terrible efforts, he was surprised to hear her answer in a voice not like her own:

'*I don't care if I never get home!*'

The carriage giving a terrific lurch, Swithin's exclamation was jerked back into his throat. The horses, winded by the rise of a hill, now steadied to a trot, and finally stopped of their own accord.

'When'—Swithin described it at Timothy's—'I pulled 'em up, there she was as cool as myself. God bless my soul! she behaved as if she didn't care whether she broke her neck or not! What was it she said: "I don't care if I never get home!"' Leaning over the handle of his cane, he wheezed out to Mrs Small's terror: 'And I'm not altogether surprised, with a finickin' feller like young Soames for a husband!'

It did not occur to him to wonder what Bosinney had done after they had left him there alone; whether he had gone wandering about like the dog to which Swithin had compared him; wandering down to that copse where the spring was still in riot, the cuckoo still calling from afar; gone down there with her handkerchief pressed to his lips, its fragrance mingling with the scent of mint and thyme. Gone down there with such a wild, exquisite pain in his heart that he could have cried out among the trees. Or what, indeed, the fellow had done. In fact, till he came to Timothy's, Swithin had forgotten all about him.

4

JAMES GOES TO SEE FOR HIMSELF

Those ignorant of Forsyte 'Change would not, perhaps, foresee all the stir made by Irene's visit to the house.

After Swithin had related at Timothy's the full story of his memorable drive, the same, with the least suspicion of curiosity, the merest touch of malice, and a real desire to do good, was passed on to June.

'And what a *dreadful* thing to say, my dear!' ended Aunt Juley; 'that about not going home. What did she mean?'

It was a strange recital for the girl. She heard it flushing painfully, and, suddenly, with a curt handshake, took her departure.

'Almost rude!' Mrs Srnall said to Aunt Hester when June was gone.

The proper construction was put on her reception of the news. She was upset. Something was therefore very wrong. Odd! She and Irene had been such friends!

It all tallied too well with whispers and hints that had been going about for some time past. Recollections of Euphemia's account of the visit to the theatre–Mr Bosinney always at Soames's? Oh, indeed! Yes, of course, he *would* be–about the house! Nothing open. Only upon the greatest, the most important provocation was it necessary to say anything open on Forsyte 'Change. This machine was too nicely adjusted; a hint, the merest trifling expression of regret or doubt, sufficed to set the family soul–so sympathetic–vibrating. No one desired that harm should come of these vibrations–far from it; they were set in motion with the best intentions, with the feeling that each member of the family had a stake in the family soul.

And much kindness lay at the bottom of the gossip; it would frequently result in visits of condolence being made, in accordance with the customs of Society, thereby conferring a real benefit upon the sufferers, and affording consolation to the sound, who felt pleasantly that someone at all events was suffering from that from which they themselves were not suffering. In fact, it was simply a desire to keep things well-aired, the desire which animates the Public Press, that brought James, for instance, into communication with Mrs Septimus, Mrs Septimus with the little Nicholases, the little Nicholases with who-knows-whom, and so on. That great class to which they had risen, and now belonged, demanded a certain candour, a still more certain reticence. This combination guaranteed their membership.

Many of the younger Forsytes felt, very naturally, and would openly declare, that they did not want their affairs pried into; but so powerful was the invisible, magnetic current of family gossip that for the life of them they could not help knowing all about everything. It was felt to be hopeless.

One of them (young Roger) had made an heroic attempt to free the rising generation by speaking of Timothy as an 'old cat'. The effort had justly recoiled upon himself; the words, coming round in the most delicate way to Aunt

Juley's ears, were repeated by her in a shocked voice to Mrs Roger, whence they returned again to young Roger.

And, after all, it was only the wrong-doers who suffered; as, for instance, George, when he lost all that money playing billiards; or young Roger himself, when he was so dreadfully near to marrying the girl to whom, it was whispered, he was already married by the laws of Nature; or again Irene, who was thought, rather than said, to be in danger.

All this was not only pleasant but salutary. And it made so many hours go lightly at Timothy's in the Bayswater Road; so many hours that must otherwise have been sterile and heavy to those three who lived there; and Timothy's was but one of hundreds of such homes in this City of London—the homes of neutral persons of the secure classes, who are out of the battle themselves, and must find their reason for existing in the battles of others.

But for the sweetness of family gossip, it must indeed have been lonely there. Rumours and tales, reports, surmises—were they not the children of the house, as dear and precious as the prattling babes the brother and sisters had missed in their own journey? To talk about them was as near as they could get to the possession of all those children and grandchildren after whom their soft hearts yearned. For though it is doubtful whether Timothy's heart yearned, it is indubitable that at the arrival of each fresh Forsyte child he was quite upset.

Useless for young Roger to say: 'Old cat!'—for Euphemia to hold up her hands and cry: 'Oh! those three!' and break into her silent laugh with the squeak at the end. Useless, and not too kind.

The situation which at this stage might seem, and especially to Forsyte eyes, strange—not to say 'impossible'—was, in view of certain facts, not so strange after all.

Some things had been lost sight of.

And first, in the security bred of many harmless marriages, it had been forgotten that Love is no hot-house flower, but a wild plant, born of a wet night, born of an hour of sunshine; sprung from wild seed, blown along the road by a wild wind. A wild plant that, when it blooms by chance within the hedge of our gardens, we call a flower; and when it blooms outside we call a weed; but, flower or weed, whose scent and colour are always wild.

And further—the facts and figures of their own lives being against the perception of this truth—it was not generally recognised by Forsytes that, where this wild plant springs, men and women are but moths around the pale, flame-like blossom.

It was long since young Jolyon's escapade—there was danger of a tradition again arising that people in their position never cross the hedge to pluck that flower; that one could reckon on having love, like measles, once in due season, and getting over it comfortably for all time—as with measles, on a soothing mixture of butter and honey—in the arms of wedlock.

Of all those whom this strange rumour about Bosinney and Mrs Soames reached, James was the most affected. He had long forgotten how he had hovered, lanky and pale, in side-whiskers of chestnut hue, round Emily, in the days of his own courtship. He had long forgotten the small house in the purlieus of Mayfair, where he had spent the early days of his married life, or rather, he had long forgotten the early days, not the small house, a Foryste never forgot a house—he had afterwards sold it at a clear profit of four hundred pounds.

He had long forgotten those days, with their hopes and fears and doubts about the prudence of the match (for Emily, though pretty, had nothing, and he himself at that time was making a bare thousand a year), and that strange, irresistible attraction that he had drawn him on, till he felt he must die if he could not marry the girl with the fair hair, looped so neatly back, the fair arms emerging from a skin-tight bodice, the fair form decorously shielded by a cage of really stupendous circumference.

James had passed through the fire, but he had passed also through the river of years that washes out the fire; he had experienced the saddest experience of all–forgetfulness of what it was like to be in love.

Forgotten! Forgotten so long that he had forgotten even that he had forgotten.

And now this rumour had come upon him, this rumour about his son's wife; very vague, a shadow dodging among the palpable, straightforward appearances of things, unreal, unintelligible as a ghost, but carrying with it, like a ghost, inexplicable terror.

He tried to bring it home to his mind, but it was no more use than trying to apply to himself one of those tragedies he read of daily in his evening paper. He simply could not. There could be nothing in it. It was all their nonsense. She didn't get on with Soames as well as she might, but she was a good little thing–a good little thing!

Like the not inconsiderable majority of men, James relished a nice little bit of scandal, and would say, in a matter-of-fact tone, licking his lips: 'Yes, yes–she and young Dyson; they tell me they're living at Monte Carlo!'

But the significance of an affair of this sort–of its past, its present, or its future–had never struck him. What it meant, what torture and raptures had gone to its construction, what slow, over-mastering fate had lurked within the facts, very naked, sometimes sordid, but generally spicy, presented to his gaze. He was not in the habit of blaming, praising, drawing deductions, or generalising at all about such things; he simply listened rather greedily, and repeated what he was told, finding considerable benefit from the practice, as from the consumption of a sherry and bitters before a meal.

Now, however, that such a thing–or rather the rumour, the breath of it–had come near him personally, he felt as in a fog, which filled his mouth full of a bad, thick flavour, and made it difficult to draw breath.

A scandal! A possible scandal!

To repeat this word to himself thus was the only way in which he could focus or make it thinkable. He had forgotten the sensations necessary for understanding the progress, fate, or meaning of any such business; he simply could no longer grasp the possibilities of people running any risk for the sake of passion.

Amongst all those persons of his acquaintance, who went into the City day after day and did their business there, whatever it was, and in their leisure moments bought shares, and houses, and ate dinners, and played games, as he was told, it would have seemed to him ridiculous to suppose that there were any who would run risks for the sake of anything so recondite, so figurative, as passion.

Passion! He seemed, indeed, to have heard of it, and rules such as 'A young man and a young woman ought never to be trusted together' were fixed in his mind as the parallels of latitude are fixed on a map (for all Forsytes, when it comes to 'bed-rock' matters of fact, have quite a fine taste in realism); but as to anything else–well, he could only appreciate it at all through the catch-word 'scandal'.

Ah! but there was no truth in it—could not be. He was not afraid; she was really a good little thing. But there it was when you got a thing like that into your mind. And James was of a nervous temperament—one of those men whom things will not leave alone, who suffers tortures from anticipation and indecision. For fear of letting something slip that he might otherwise secure, he was physically unable to make up his mind until absolutely certain that, by not making it up, he would suffer loss.

In life, however, there were many occasions when the business of making up his mind did not even rest with himself, and this was one of them.

What could he do? Talk it over with Soames? That would only make matters worse. And, after all, there was nothing in it, he felt sure.

It was all that house. He had mistrusted the idea from the first. What did Soames want to go into the country for? And, if he must go spending a lot of money building himself a house, why not have a first-rate man, instead of this young Bosinney, whom nobody knew anything about? He had told them how it would be. And he had heard that the house was costing Soames a pretty penny beyond what he had reckoned on spending.

This fact, more than any other, brought home to James the real danger of the situation. It was always like this with these 'artistic' chaps; a sensible man should have nothing to say to them. He had warned Irene, too. And see what had come of it!

And it suddenly sprang into James's mind that he ought to go and see for himself. In the midst of that fog of uneasiness in which his mind was enveloped the notion that he could go and look at the house afforded him inexplicable satisfaction. It may have been simply the decision to do something—more possibly the fact that he was going to look at a house—that gave him relief.

He felt that in staring at an edifice of bricks and mortar, of wood and stone, built by the suspected man himself, he would be looking into the heart of that rumour about Irene.

Without saying a word, therefore, to anyone, he took a hansom to the station and proceeded by train to Robin Hill; thence—there being no 'flies', in accordance with the custom of the neighbourhood—he found himself obliged to walk.

He started slowly up the hill, his angular knees and high shoulders bent complainingly, his eyes fixed on his feet, yet neat for all that, in his high hat and his frock-coat, on which was the speckless gloss imparted by perfect superintendence. Emily saw to that; that is, she did not, of course, see to it—people of good position not seeing to each other's buttons, and Emily was of good position—but she saw that the butler saw to it.

He had to ask his way three times; on each occasion he repeated the directions given him, got the man to repeat them, then repeated them a second time, for he was naturally of a talkative disposition, and one could not be too careful in a new neighbourhood.

He kept assuring them that it was a *new* house he was looking for; it was only, however, when he was shown the roof through the trees that he could feel really satisfied that he had not been directed entirely wrong.

A heavy sky seemed to cover the world with the grey whiteness of a whitewashed ceiling. There was no freshness or fragrance in the air. On such a day even British workmen scarcely cared to do more than they were obliged, and moved about their business without the drone of talk that whiles away the pangs of labour.

Through spaces of the unfinished house, shirt-sleeved figures worked slowly, and sounds arose—spasmodic knockings, the scraping of metal, the sawing of wood, with the rumble of wheel-barrows along boards; now and again the foreman's dog, tethered by a string to an oaken beam, whimpered feebly, with a sound like the singing of a kettle.

The fresh-fitted window-panes, daubed each with a white patch in the centre, stared out as James like the eyes of a blind dog.

And the building chorus went on, strident and mirthless under the grey-white sky. But the thrushes, hunting amongst the fresh-turned earth for worms, were silent quite.

James picked his way among the heaps of gravel—the drive was being laid—till he came opposite the porch. Here he stopped and raised his eyes. There was but little to see from this point of view, and that little he took in at once; but he stayed in his position many minutes, and who shall know of what he thought.

His china-blue eyes under white eyebrows that jutted out in little horns, never stirred; the long upper lip of his wide mouth, between the fine white whiskers, twitched once or twice; it was easy to see from that anxious, rapt expression, whence Soames derived the handicapped look which sometimes came upon his face. James might have been saying to himself: 'I don't know—life's a tough job.'

In this position Bosinney surprised him.

James brought his eyes down from whatever bird's nest they had been looking for in the sky to Bosinney's face, on which was a kind of humorous scorn.

'How do you do, Mr Forsyte! Come down to see for yourself?'

It was exactly what James, as we know, *had* come for, and he was made correspondingly uneasy. He held out his hand, however, saying:

'How are you?' without looking at Bosinney.

The latter made way for him with an ironical smile.

James scented something suspicious in this courtesy. 'I should like to walk round the outside first,' he said, 'and see what you've been doing!'

A flagged terrace of rounded stones with a list of two or three inches to port had been laid round the south-east and south-west sides of the house, and ran with a bevelled edge into mould, which was in preparation for being turfed; along this terrace James led the way.

'Now what did *this* cost?' he asked, when he saw the terrace extending round the corner.

'What should you think?' inquired Bosinney.

'How should I know?' replied James, somewhat nonplussed; 'two or three hundred, I dare say!'

'The exact sum!'

James gave him a sharp look, but the architect appeared unconscious, and he put the answer down to mishearing.

On arriving at the garden entrance, he stopped to look at the view.

'That ought to come down,' he said, pointing to the oak tree.

'You think so?' You think that with the tree there you don't get enough view for your money?'

Again James eyed him suspiciously—this young man had a peculiar way of putting things: 'Well,' he said, with a perplexed, nervous emphasis, 'I don't see what you want with a tree.'

'It shall come down to-morrow,' said Bosinney.

James was alarmed. 'Oh,' he said, 'don't go saying I said it was to come down! *I* know nothing about it!'

'No?'

James went on in a fluster: 'Why, what should I know about it? It's nothing to do with me! You do it on your own responsibility.'

'You'll allow me to mention your name?'

James grew more and more alarmed: 'I don't know what you want mentioning my name for,' he muttered; 'you'd better leave the tree alone. It's not your tree!'

He took out a silk handkerchief and wiped his brow. They entered the house. Like Swithin, James was impressed by the inner court-yard.

'You must have spent a dooce of a lot of money here,' he said, after staring at the columns and gallery for some time. 'Now, what did it cost to put up those columns?'

'I can't tell you off-hand,' thoughtfully answered Bosinney, 'but I know it was a deuce of a lot!'

'I should think so,' said James. 'I should—' He caught the architect's eye and broke off. And now, whenever he came to anything of which he desired to know the cost, he stifled that curiosity.

Bosinney appeared determined that he should see everything, and had not James been of too 'noticing' a nature, he would certainly have found himself going round the house a second time. He seemed so anxious to be asked questions, too, that James felt he must be on his guard. He began to suffer from his exertions, for, though wiry enough for a man of his long build, he was seventy-five years old.

He grew discouraged; he seemed no nearer to anything, had not obtained from his inspection any of the knowledge he had vaguely hoped for. He had merely increased his dislike and mistrust of this young man, who had tired him out with his politeness, and in whose manner he now certainly detected mockery.

The fellow was sharper than he had thought, and better-looking than he had hoped. He had a 'don't care' appearance that James, to whom risk was the most intolerable thing in life, did not appreciate; a peculiar smile, too, coming when least expected; and very queer eyes. He reminded James, as he said afterwards, of a hungry cat. This was as near as he could get, in conversation with Emily, to a description of the peculiar exasperation, velvetiness, and mockery, of which Bosinney's manner had been composed.

At last, having seen all that was to be seen, he came out again at the door where he had gone in; and now, feeling that he was wasting time and strength and money, all for nothing, he took the courage of a Forsyte in both hands, and, looking sharply at Bosinney, said:

'I dare say you see a good deal of my daughter-in-law; now, what does *she* think of the house? But she hasn't seen it, I suppose?'

This he said, knowing all about Irene's visit—not, of course, that there was anything in the visit, except that extraordinary remark she had made about 'not caring to get home'—and the story of how June had taken the news!

He had determined, by this way of putting the question, to give Bosinney a chance, as he said to himself.

The latter was long in answering, but kept his eyes with uncomfortable steadiness on James.

'She *has* seen the house, but I can't tell you what she thinks of it.'

Nervous and baffled, James was constitutionally prevented from letting the matter drop.

'Oh!' he said, 'she has seen it? Soames brought her down, I suppose?'

Bosinney smilingly replied, 'Oh, no!'

'What, did she come down alone?'

'Oh, no!'

'Then—who brought her?'

'I really don't know whether I ought to tell you who brought her.'

To James, who knew that it was Swithin, this answer appeared incomprehensible.

'Why!' he stammered, 'you know that—' but he stopped, suddenly perceiving his danger.

'Well,' he said, 'if you don't want to tell me, I suppose you won't! Nobody tells me anything.'

Somewhat to his surprise Bosinney asked him a question.

'By the by,' he said, 'could you tell me if there are likely to be any more of you coming down? I should like to be on the spot!'

'Any more?' said James bewildered, 'why should there be more? I don't know of any more. Good-bye.'

Looking at the ground he held out his hand, crossed the palm of it with Bosinney's, and taking his umbrella just above the silk, walked away along the terrace.

Before he turned the corner he glanced back, and saw Bosinney following him slowly—'slinking along the wall', as he put it to himself, 'like a great cat.' He paid no attention when the young fellow raised his hat.

Outside the drive, and out of sight, he slackened his pace still more. Very slowly, more bent than when he came, lean, hungry, and disheartened, he made his way back to the station.

The Buccaneer, watching him go so sadly, felt sorry perhaps for his behaviour to the old man.

5

SOAMES AND BOSINNEY CORRESPOND

James said nothing to his son of this visit to the house; but, having occasion to go to Timothy's one morning on a matter connected with a drainage scheme which was being forced by the sanitary authorities on his brother, he mentioned it there.

It was not, he said, a bad house. He could see that a good deal could be made of it. The fellow was clever in his way, though what it was going to cost Soames before it was done with he didn't know.

Euphemia Forsyte, who happened to be in the room—she had come round to borrow the Rev. Mr Scole's last novel, *Passion and Paregoric*, which was having such a vogue—chimed in.

'I saw Irene yesterday at the Stores; she and Mr Bosinney were having a nice little chat in the Groceries.'

It was thus, simply, that she recorded a scene which had really made a deep and complicated impression on her. She had been hurrying to the silk department of the Church and Commercial Stores–that Institution than which, with its admirable system, admitting only guaranteed persons on a basis of payment before delivery, no emporium can be more highly recommended to Forsytes–to match a piece of prunella silk for her mother, who was waiting in the carriage outside.

Passing through the Groceries her eye was unpleasantly attracted by the back view of a very beautiful figure. It was so charmingly proportioned, so balanced, and so well clothed, that Euphemia's instinctive propriety was at once alarmed; such figures, she knew, by intuition rather than experience, were rarely connected with virtue–certainly never in her mind, for her own back was somewhat difficult to fit.

Her suspicions were fortunately confirmed. A young man coming from the Drugs had snatched off his hat, and was accosting the lady with the unknown back.

It was then that she saw with whom she had to deal; the lady was undoubtedly Mrs Soames, the young man Mr Bosinney. Conceiling herself rapidly over the purchase of a box of Tunisian dates, for she was impatient of awkwardly meeting people with parcels in her hands, and at the busy time of the morning, she was thus quite unintentionally an interested observer of their little interview.

Mrs Soames, usually somewhat pale, had a delightful colour in her cheeks; and Mr Bosinney's manner was strange, though attractive (she thought him rather a distinguished-looking man, and George's name for him, 'The Buccaneer'–about which there was something romantic–quite charming). He seemed to be pleading. Indeed, they talked so earnestly–or, rather, he talked so earnestly, for Mrs Soames did not say much–that they caused, inconsiderately, an eddy in the traffic. One nice old General, going towards Cigars, was obliged to step quite out of the way, and chancing to look up and see Mrs Soames's face, he actually took off his hat, the old fool! So like a man!

But it was Mrs Soames's eyes that worried Euphemia. She never once looked at Mr Bosinney until he moved on, and then she looked after him. And, oh, that look!

On that look Euphemia had spent much anxious thought. It is not too much to say that it had hurt her with its dark, lingering softness, for all the world as though the woman wanted to drag him back, and unsay something she had been saying.

Ah, well, she had had no time to go deeply into the matter just then, with that prunella silk on her hands; but she was 'very *intriguée*–very!' She had just nodded to Mrs Soames, to show her that she had seen; and, as she confided, in talking it over afterwards, to her chum Francie (Roger's daughter), 'Didn't she look caught out just? . . .'

James, most averse at the first blush to accepting any new confirmatory of his own poignant suspicions, took her up at once.

'Oh,' he said, 'they'd be after wallpapers no doubt.'

Euphemia smiled. 'In the Groceries!' she said softly; and, taking *Passion and Paregoric* from the table, added: 'And so you'll lend me this, dear Auntie? Good-bye!' and went away.

James left almost immediately after; he was late as it was.

When he reached the office of Forsyte, Bustard and Forsyte, he found

Soames sitting in his revolving chair, drawing up a defence. The latter greeted his father with a curt good-morning, and, taking an envelope from his pocket, said:

'It may interest you to look through this.'

James read as follows:

309D, SLOANE STREET,
May 15.

DEAR FORSYTE,

The construction of your house being now completed, my duties as architect have come to an end. If I am to go on with the business of decoration, which at your request I undertook, I should like you to clearly understand that I must have a free hand.

You never come down without suggesting something that goes counter to my scheme. I have here three letters from you, each of which recommends an article I should never dream of putting in. I had your father here yesterday afternoon, who made further valuable suggestions.

Please make up your mind, therefore, whether you want me to decorate for you, or to retire, which on the whole I should prefer to do.

But understand that, if I decorate, I decorate alone, without interference of any sort.

If I do the thing, I will do it thoroughly, but I must have a free hand.

Yours truly,
PHILIP BOSINNEY.

The exact and immediate cause of this letter cannot, of course, be told, though it is not improbable that Bosinney may have been moved by some sudden revolt against his position towards Soames—that eternal position of Art towards Property—which is so admirably summed up, on the back of the most indispensable of modern appliances, in a sentence comparable to the very finest in Tacitus:

THOS. T. SORROW,
Inventor.
BERT. M. PADLAND,
Proprietor.

'What are you going to say to him?' James asked.

Soames did not even turn his head. 'I haven't made up my mind,' he said, and went on with his defence.

A client of his, having put up some buildings on a piece of ground that did not belong to him, had been suddenly and most irritatingly warned to take them off again. After carefully going into the facts, however, Soames had seen his way to advise that his client had what was known as a title by possession, and that, though undoubtedly the ground did not belong to him, he was entitled to keep it, and had better do so; and he was now following up this advice by taking steps to—as the sailors say—'make it so.'

He had a distinct reputation for sound advice; people saying of him: "Go to young Forsyte—a long-headed fellow!' and he prized this reputation highly.

His natural taciturnity was in his favour; nothing could be more calculated to give people, especially people with property (Soames had no other clients), the impression that he was a safe man. And he *was* safe. Tradition, habit, education, inherited aptitude, native caution, all joined to form a solid professional honesty, superior to temptation from the very fact that it was built on an innate avoidance of risk. How could he fall, when his soul abhorred circumstances which render a fall possible—a man cannot fall off the floor!

And those countless Forsytes, who, in the course of innumerable transactions concerned with property of all sorts (from wives to water rights), had occasion for the services of a safe man, found it both reposeful and profitable to confide in Soames. That slight superciliousness of his, combined with an air of mousing amongst precedents, was in his favour too—a man would not be supercilious unless he knew!

He was really at the head of the business, for though James still came nearly every day to see for himself, he did little now but sit in his chair, twist his legs, slightly confuse things already decided, and presently go away again, and the other partner, Bustard, was a poor thing, who did a great deal of work, but whose opinion was never taken.

So Soames went steadily on with his defence. Yet it would be idle to say that his mind was at ease. He was suffering from a sense of impending trouble, that had haunted him for some time past. He tried to think it physical—a condition of his liver—but knew that it was not.

He looked at his watch. In a quarter of an hour he was due at the General Meeting of the New Colliery Company—one of Uncle Jolyon's concerns; he should see Uncle Jolyon there, and say something to him about Bosinney—he had not made up his mind what, but something—in any case he should not answer this letter until he had seen Uncle Jolyon. He got up and methodically put away the draft of his defence. Going into a dark little cupboard, he turned up the light, washed his hands with a piece of brown Windsor soap, and dried them on a roller towel. Then he brushed his hair, paying strict attention to the parting, turned down the light, took his hat, and saying he would be back at half-past two, stepped into the Poultry.

It was not far to the offices of the New Colliery Company in Ironmonger Lane, where, and not at the Cannon Street Hotel, in accordance with the more ambitious practice of other companies, the General Meeting was always held. Old Jolyon had from the first set his face against the Press. What business—he said—had the Public with his concerns!

Soames arrived on the stroke of time, and took his seat alongside the Board, who, in a row, each Director behind his own inkpot, faced their Shareholders.

In the centre of this row old Jolyon, conspicuous in his black, tightly-buttoned frock-coat and his white moustaches, was leaning back with finger-tips crossed on a copy of the Directors' report and accounts.

On his right hand, always a little larger than life, sat the Secretary, 'Down-by-the-starn' Hemmings; an all-too-sad sadness beaming in his fine eyes; his iron-grey beard, in mourning like the rest of him, giving the feeling of an all-too-black tie behind it.

The occasion indeed was a melancholy one, only six weeks having elapsed since that telegram had come from Scorrier, the mining expert, on a private mission to the Mines, informing them that Pippin, their Superintendent, had committed suicide in endeavouring, after his extraordinary two years' silence, to write a letter to his Board. That letter was on the table now; it would be read to the Shareholders, who would of course be put into possession of all the facts.

Hemmings had often said to Soames, standing with his coat-tails divided before the fireplace:

'What our Shareholders don't know about our affairs isn't worth knowing. You may take it from me, Mr Soames.'

On one occasion, old Jolyon being present, Soames recollected a little unpleasantness. His uncle had looked up sharply and said: 'Don't talk nonsense, Hemmings! You mean that what they *do* know isn't worth knowing!' Old Jolyon detested humbug.

Hemmings, angry-eyed, and wearing a smile like that of a trained poodle, had replied in an outburst of artificial applause: 'Come, now, that's good, sir–that's very good. Your uncle *will* have his joke!'

The next time he had seen Soames he had taken the opportunity of saying to him: 'The chairman's getting very old–I can't get him to understand things; and he's so wilful–but what can you expect, with a chin like his?'

Soames had nodded.

Everyone knew that Uncle Jolyon's chin was a caution. He was looking worried to-day, in spite of his General Meeting look; he (Soames) should certainly speak to him about Bosinney.

Beyond old Jolyon on the left was little Mr Booker, and he, too, wore his General Meeting look, as though searching for some particularly tender shareholder. And next him was the deaf director, with a frown; and beyond the deaf director, again, was old Mr Bleedham, very bland, and having an air of conscious virtue–as well he might, knowing that the brown-paper parcel he always brought to the Board-room was concealed behind his hat (one of that old-fashioned class of flat-brimmed top-hats which go with very large bow ties, clean-shaven lips, fresh cheeks, and neat little white whiskers).

Soames always attended the General Meeting; it was considered better that he should do so, in case 'anything should arise!' He glanced round with his close, supercilious air at the walls of the room, where hung plans of the mine and harbour, together with a large photograph of a shaft leading to a working that had proved quite remarkably unprofitable. This photograph–a witness to the eternal irony underlying commercial enterprise–still retained its position on the wall, an effigy of the directors' pet, but dead, lamb.

And now old Jolyon rose, to present the report and accounts.

Veiling under a Jove-like serenity that perpetual antagonism deep-seated in the bosom of a director towards his shareholders, he faced them calmly. Soames faced them too. He knew most of them by sight. There was old Scrubsole, a tar man, who always came, as Hemmings would say, 'to make himself nasty,' a cantankerous-looking old fellow with a red face, a jowl, and an enormous low-crowned hat reposing on his knee. And the Rev. Mr Boms, who always proposed a vote of thanks to the chairman, in which he invariably expressed the hope that the Board would not forget to elevate their employees, using the word with a double e, as being more vigorous and Anglo-Saxon (he had the strong Imperialistic tendencies of his cloth). It was his salutary custom to buttonhole a director afterwards, and ask him whether he thought the coming year would be good or bad; and, according to the trend of the answer, to buy or sell three shares within the ensuing fortnight.

And there was that military man, Major O'Bally, who could not help speaking, if only to second the re-election of the auditor, and who sometimes caused serious consternation by taking toasts–proposals rather–out of the hands of persons who had been flattered with little slips of paper, entrusting the said proposals to their care.

These made up the lot, together with four or five strong, silent shareholders, with whom Soames could sympathise–men of business, who liked to keep an eye on their affairs for themselves, without being fussy–good, solid men, who came to the City every day and went back in the evening to good, solid wives.

Good, solid wives! There was something in that thought which roused the nameless uneasiness in Soames again.

What should he say to his uncle? What answer should he make to this letter?
. . . 'If any shareholder has any question to put, I shall be glad to answer it.' A soft thump. Old Jolyon had let the report and accounts fall, and stood twisting tortoiseshell glasses between thumb and forefinger.

The ghost of a smile appeared on Soames's face. They had better hurry up with their questions! He well knew his uncle's method (the ideal one) of at once saying: 'I propose, then, that the report and accounts be adopted.' Never let them get their wind–shareholders were notoriously wasteful of time!

A tall, white-bearded man, with a gaunt, dissatisfied face, arose:

'I believe I am in order, Mr Chairman, in raising a question on this figure of £5,000 in the accounts. "To the widow and family"' (he looked sourly round), '"of our late superintendent", who so–er–ill-advisedly (I say ill-advisedly) committed suicide, at a time when his services were of the utmost value to this Company. You have stated that the agreement which he has so unfortunately cut short with his own hand was for a period of five years, of which one only had expired–I–'

Old Jolyon made a gesture of impatience.

'I believe I am in order, Mr Chairman–I ask whether this amount paid, or proposed to be paid, by the Board to the–er–deceased–is for services which might have been rendered to the Company had he not committed suicide?'

'It is in recognition of past services, which we all know–you as well as any of us–to have been of vital value.'

'Then, sir, all I have to say is, that the services being past, the amount is too much.'

The shareholder sat down.

Old Jolyon waited a second and said: 'I now propose that the report and–'

The shareholder rose again: 'May I ask if the Board realises that it is not their money which–I don't hesitate to say that if it were their money–'

A second shareholder, with a round, dogged face, whom Soames recognised as the late Superintendent's brother-in-law, got up and said warmly, 'In my opinion, sir, the sum is not enough!'

The Rev. Mr Boms now rose to his feet. 'If I may venture to express myself,' he said, 'I should say that the fact of the–er–deceased having committed suicide should weigh very heavily–*very* heavily with our worthy chairman. I have no doubt it has weighed with him, for–I say this for myself and I think for everyone present (hear, hear)–he enjoys our confidence in a high degree. We all desire, I should hope, to be charitable. But I feel sure' (he looked severely at the Superintendent's brother-in-law) 'that he will in some way, by some written expression, or better perhaps by reducing the amount, record our grave disapproval that so promising and valuable a life should have been thus impiously removed from a sphere where both its own interests and–if I may say so–*our* interests so imperatively demanded its continuance. We should not–nay, we may not–countenance so grave a dereliction of all duty, both human and divine.'

The reverend gentleman resumed his seat. The late Superintendent's brother-in-law again rose: 'What I have said I stick to,' he said, 'the amount is not enough!'

The first shareholder struck in: 'I challenge the legality of the payment. In my opinion this payment is not legal. The Company's solicitor is present; I believe I am in order in asking him the question.'

All eyes were now turned upon Soames. Something had arisen!

He stood up, close-lipped and cold; his nerves inwardly fluttered, his attention tweaked away at last from contemplation of that cloud looming on the horizon of his mind.

'The point,' he said in a low, thin voice, 'is by no means clear. As there is no possibility of future consideration being received, it is doubtful whether the payment is strictly legal. If it is desired, the opinion of the court could be taken.'

The Superintendent's brother-in-law frowned, and said in a meaning tone: 'We have no doubt the opinion of the court could be taken. May I ask the name of the gentleman who has given us that striking piece of information? Mr Soames Forsyte? Indeed!' He looked from Soames to old Jolyon in a pointed manner.

A flush coloured Soames's pale cheeks, but his superciliousness did not waver. Old Jolyon fixed his eyes on the speaker.

'If,' he said, 'the late Superintendent's *brother-in-law* has nothing more to say, I propose that the report and accounts–'

At this moment, however, there rose one of those five silent, stolid shareholders, who had excited Soames's sympathy. He said:

'I deprecate the proposal altogether. We are expected to give charity to this man's wife and children, who, you tell us, were dependent on him. They may have been; I do not care whether they were or not. I object to the whole thing on principle. It is high time a stand was made against this sentimental humanitarianism. The country is eaten up with it. I object to my money being paid to these people of whom I know nothing, who have done nothing to earn it. I object *in toto*; it is not business. I now move that the report and accounts be put back, and amended by striking out the grant altogether.'

Old Jolyon had remained standing while the strong, silent man was speaking. The speech awoke an echo in all hearts, voicing, as it did, the worship of strong men, the movement against generosity, which had at that time already commenced among the saner members of the community.

The words 'it is not business' had moved even the Board; privately everyone felt that indeed it was not. But they knew also the chairman's domineering temper and tenacity. He, too, at heart, must feel that it was not business; but he was committed to his own proposition. Would he go back upon it? It was thought to be unlikely.

All waited with interest. Old Jolyon held up his hand; dark-rimmed glasses depending between his finger and thumb quivered slightly with a suggestion of menace.

He addressed the strong, silent shareholder.

'Knowing, as you do, the efforts of our late Superintendent upon the occasion of the explosion at the mines, do you seriously wish me to put that amendment, sir?'

'I do.'

Old Jolyon put the amendment.

'Does anyone second this?' he asked, looking calmly round.

And it was then that Soames, looking at his uncle, felt the power of will that was in that old man. No one stirred. Looking straight into the eyes of the strong, silent shareholder, Old Jolyon said:

'I now move, "That the report and accounts for the year 1886 be received and adopted." You second that? Those in favour signify the same in the usual way. Contrary–no. Carried. The next business, gentlemen–'

Soames smiled. Certainly Uncle Jolyon had a way with him!

But now his attention relapsed upon Bosinney. Odd how that fellow haunted his thoughts, even in business hours.

Irene's visit to the house—but there was nothing in that except that she might have told him; but then, again, she never did tell him anything. She was more silent, more touchy every day. He wished to God the house were finished, and they were in it, away from London. Town did not suit her; her nerves were not strong enough. That nonsense of the separate room had cropped up again!

The meeting was breaking up now. Underneath the photograph of the lost shaft Hemmings was button-holed by the Rev. Mr Boms. Little Mr Booker, his bristling eyebrows wreathed in angry smiles, was having a parting turn-up with old Scrubsole. The two hated each other like poison. There was some matter of a tar-contract between them, little Mr Booker having secured it from the Board for a nephew of his, over old Scrubsole's head. Soames had heard that from Hemmings, who liked to gossip, more especially about his Directors, except, indeed, old Jolyon, of whom he was afraid.

Soames awaited his opportunity. The last shareholder was vanishing through the door, when he approached his uncle, who was putting on his hat.

'Can I speak to you for a minute, Uncle Jolyon?'

It is uncertain what Soames expected to get out of this interview.

Apart from that somewhat mysterious awe in which Forsytes in general held old Jolyon, due to his philosophic twist, or perhaps—as Hemmings would doubtless have said—to his chin, there was, and always had been, a subtle antagonism between the younger man and the old. It had lurked under their dry manner of greeting, under their noncommittal allusions to each other, and arose perhaps from old Jolyon's perception of the quiet tenacity ('obstinacy', he rather naturally called it) of the young man, of a secret doubt whether he could get his own way with him.

Both these Forsytes, wide asunder as the poles in many respects, possessed in their different ways—to a greater degree than the rest of the family—that essential quality of tenacious and prudent insight into 'affairs', which is the high-water mark of their great class. Either of them, with a little luck and opportunity, was equal to a lofty career; either of them would have made a good financier, a great contractor, a statesman, though old Jolyon, in certain of his moods—when under the influence of a cigar or of Nature—would have been capable of, not perhaps despising, but certainly of questioning, his own high position, while Soames, who never smoked cigars, would not.

Then, too, in old Jolyon's mind there was always the secret ache that the son of James—of James, whom he had always thought such a poor thing, should be pursuing the paths of success, while his own son—!

And last, not least—for he was no more outside the radiation of family gossip than any other Forsyte—he had now heard the sinister, indefinite, but none the less disturbing rumour about Bosinney, and his pride was wounded to the quick.

Characteristically, his irritation turned not against Irene but against Soames. The idea that his nephew's wife (why couldn't the fellow take better care of her—oh! quaint injustice! as though Soames could possibly take more care!) should be drawing to herself June's lover, was intolerably humiliating. And seeing the danger, he did not, like James, hide it away in sheer nervousness, but owned with the dispassion of his broader outlook, that it was not unlikely; there was something very attractive about Irene!

He had a presentiment on the subject of Soames's communication as they left the Board-room together, and went out into the noise and hurry of Cheapside. They walked together a good minute without speaking, Soames with his mousing mincing step, and old Jolyon upright and using his umbrella languidly as a walking-stick.

They turned presently into comparative quiet, for old Jolyon's way to a second Board led him in the direction of Moorgate Street.

Then Soames, without lifting his eyes, began: 'I've had this letter from Bosinney. You see what he says; I thought I'd let you know. I've spent a lot more than I intended on this house, and I want the position to be clear.'

Old Jolyon ran his eyes unwillingly over the letter.

'What he says is clear enough,' he said.

'He talks about "a free hand",' replied Soames.

Old Jolyon looked at him. The long suppressed irritation and antagonism towards this young fellow, whose affairs were beginning to intrude upon his own, burst from him.

'Well, if you don't trust him, why do you employ him?'

Soames stole a sideway look. 'It's much too late to go into that,' he said. 'I only want it to be quite understood that if I give him a free hand, he doesn't let me in. I thought if you were to speak to him, it would carry more weight!'

'No,' said old Jolyon abruptly; 'I'll have nothing to do with it!'

The words of both uncle and nephew gave the impression of unspoken meanings, far more important, behind. And the look they interchanged was like a revelation of this consciousness.

'Well,' said Soames, 'I thought, for June's sake, I'd tell you, that's all; I thought you'd better know I shan't stand any nonsense!'

'What is that to me?' old Jolyon took him up.

'Oh! I don't know,' said Soames, and flurried by that sharp look he was unable to say more. 'Don't say I didn't tell you,' he added sulkily, recovering his composure.

'Tell me,' said old Jolyon; 'I don't know what you mean. You come worrying me about a thing like this. *I* don't want to hear about your affairs, you must manage them yourself!'

'Very well,' said Soames immovably, 'I will!'

'Good morning, then,' said old Jolyon, and they parted.

Soames retraced his steps, and going into a celebrated eating house, asked for a plate of smoked salmon and a glass of Chablis; he seldom ate much in the middle of the day, and generally ate standing, finding the position beneficial to his liver, which was very sound, but to which he desired to put down all his troubles.

When he had finished he went slowly back to his office, with bent head, taking no notice of the swarming thousands on the pavements, who in their turn took no notice of him.

The evening post carried the following reply to Bosinney:

> FORSYTE, BUSTARD AND FORSYTE,
> Commissioners for Oaths,
> 2001, BRANCH LANE, POULTRY, *E. C.*,
> *May 17, 1887.*

DEAR BOSINNEY,

I have received your letter, the terms of which not a little surprise me. I was under the impression that you had, and have had all along, a 'free hand'; for I do not recollect that any suggestions I have been so unfortunate as to make, have met with your approval. In giving you, in accordance with your request, this 'free hand', I wish you to clearly understand that the total cost of the house as handed over to me completely decorated, inclusive of your fee (as arranged between us), must not exceed twelve thousand pounds—£12,000. This gives you an ample margin, and, as you know, is far more than I originally contemplated.

I am,

Yours truly,

SOAMES FORSYTE.

On the following day he received a note from Bosinney:

PHILIP BAYNES BOSINNEY,

Architect,

309D, SLOANE STREET, S.W.

May 18.

DEAR FORSYTE,

If you think that in such a delicate matter as decoration I can bind myself to the exact pound, I am afraid you are mistaken. I can see that you are tired of the arrangement, and of me, and I had better, therefore, resign.

Yours faithfully,

PHILIP BAYNES BOSINNEY.

Soames pondered long and painfully over his answer, and late at night in the dining-room, when Irene had gone to bed, he composed the following:

62 MONTPELIER SQUARE, S.W.,

May 19, 1887.

DEAR BOSINNEY,

I think that in both out interests it would be extremely undesirable that matters should be so left at this stage. I did not mean to say that if you should exceed the sum named in my letter to you by ten or twenty or even fifty pounds there would be any difficulty between us. This being so, I should like you to reconsider your answer. You have a 'free hand' in the terms of this correspondence, and I hope you will see your way to completing the decorations, in the matter of which I know it is difficult to be absolutely exact.

Yours truly,

SOAMES FORSYTE.

Bosinney's answer, which came in the course of the next day, was:

May 20.

DEAR FORSYTE,

Very well.

PH. BOSINNEY.

6

OLD JOLYON AT THE ZOO

Old Jolyon disposed of his second meeting—an ordinary Board—summarily. He was so dictatorial that his fellow directors were left in cabal over the increasing domineeringness of old Forsyte, which they were far from intending to stand much longer, they said.

He went out by Underground to Portland Road station, whence he took a cab and drove to the Zoo.

He had an assignation there, one of those assignations that had been lately growing more frequent, to which his increasing uneasiness about June and the 'change in her', as he expressed it, was driving him.

She buried herself away, and was growing thin; If he spoke to her he got no answer, or had his head snapped off, or she looked as if she would burst into tears. She was as changed as she could be, all through this Bosinney. As for telling him about anything, not a bit of it!

And he would sit for long spells brooding, his paper unread before him, a cigar extinct between his lips. She had been such a companion to him ever since she was three years old! And he loved her so!

Forces regardless of family or class or custom were beating down his guard; impending events over which he had no control threw their shadows on his head. The irritation of one accustomed to have his way was roused against he knew not what.

Chafing at the slowness of his cab, he reached the Zoo door; but, with his sunny instinct for seizing the good of each moment, he forgot his vexation as he walked towards the tryst.

From the stone terrace above the bear-pit his son and his two grandchildren came hastening down when they saw old Jolyon coming, and led him away towards the lion-house. They supported him on either side, holding one to each of his hands, whilst Jolly, perverse like his father, carried his grandfather's umbrella in such a way as to catch people's legs with the crutch of the handle.

Young Jolyon followed.

It was as good as a play to see his father with the children, but such a play as brings smiles with tears behind. An old man and two small children walking together can be seen at any hour of the day; but the sight of old Jolyon, with Jolly and Holly, seemed to young Jolyon a special peep-show of the things that lie at the bottom of our hearts. The complete surrender of that erect old figure to those little figures on either hand was too poignantly tender, and being a man of an habitual reflex action, young Jolyon swore softly under his breath. The show affected him in a way unbecoming to a Forsyte, who is nothing if not undemonstrative.

Thus they reached the lion-house.

There had been a morning fête at the Botanical Gardens, and a large number of Forsy—that is, of well-dressed people who kept carriages—had brought them on to the Zoo, so as to have more, if possible, for their money before going back to Rutland Gate or Bryanston Square.

'Let's go to the Zoo,' they had said to each other; 'it'll be great fun!' It was a shilling day; and there would not be all those horrid common people.

In front of the long line of cages they were collected in rows, watching the tawny, ravenous beasts behind the bars await their only pleasure of the four-and-twenty hours. The hungrier the beast, the greater the fascination. But whether because the spectators envied his appetite, or, more humanely, because it was so soon to be satisfied, young Jolyon could not tell. Remarks kept falling on his ears: 'That's a nasty-looking brute, that tiger!' 'Oh, what a love! Look at his little mouth!' 'Yes, he's rather nice! Don't go too near, mother.'

And frequently, with little pats, one or another would clap their hands to their pockets behind and look round, as though expecting young Jolyon or some disinterested-looking person to relieve them of the contents.

A well-fed man in a white waistcoat said slowly through his teeth: 'It's all greed; they can't be hungry. Why, they take no exercise.' At these words a tiger snatched a piece of bleeding liver, and the fat man laughed. His wife, in a Paris-model frock and gold nose-nippers, reproved him: 'How can you laugh, Harry? Such a horrid sight!'

Young Jolyon frowned.

The circumstances of his life, though he had ceased to take a too personal view of them, had left him subject to an intermittent contempt; and the class to which he had belonged—the carriage class—especially excited his sarcasm.

To shut up a lion or tiger in confinement was surely a horrible barbarity. But no cultivated person would admit this.

The idea of its being barbarous to confine wild animals had probably never even occurred to his father, for instance; he belonged to the old school, who considered it at once humanising and educational to confine baboons and panthers, holding the view, no doubt, that in course of time they might induce these creatures not so unreasonably to die of misery and heart-sickness against the bars of their cages, and put the society to the expense of getting others! In his eyes, as in the eyes of all Forsytes, the pleasure of seeing these beautiful creatures in a state of captivity far outweighed the inconvenience of imprisonment to beasts whom God had so improvidently placed in a state of freedom! It was for the animals' good, removing them at once from the countless dangers of open air and exercise, and enabling them to exercise their functions in the guaranteed seclusion of a private compartment! Indeed, it was doubtful what wild animals were made for but to be shut up in cages!

But as young Jolyon had in his constitution the elements of impartiality, he reflected that to stigmatise as barbarity that which was merely lack of imagination must be wrong; for none who held these views had been placed in a similar position to the animals they caged, and could not, therefore, be expected to enter into their sensations.

It was not until they were leaving the gardens—Jolly and Holly in a state of blissful delirium—that old Jolyon found an opportunity of speaking to his son on the matter next his heart. 'I don't know what to make of it,' he said, 'if she's to go on as she's going now, I can't tell what's to come. I wanted her to see the doctor, but she won't. She's not a bit like me. She's your mother all over. Obstinate as a mule! If she doesn't want to do a thing, she won't, and there's an end of it!'

Young Jolyon smiled; his eyes had wandered to his father's chin. 'A pair of you,' he thought, but he said nothing.

'And then,' went on old Jolyon, 'there's this Bosinney. I should like to punch the fellow's head, but I can't, I suppose, though—I don't see why you shouldn't,' he added doubtfully.

'What has he done? Far better that it should come to an end, if they don't hit it off!'

Old Jolyon looked at his son. Now they had actually come to discuss a subject connected with the relations between the sexes he felt distrustful. Jo would be sure to hold some loose view or other.

'Well, I don't know what *you* think,' he said; 'I dare say your sympathy's with him—shouldn't be surprised; but *I* think he's behaving precious badly, and if he comes my way I shall tell him so.' He dropped the subject.

It was impossible to discuss with his son the true nature and meaning of Bosinney's defection. Had not his son done the very same thing (worse, if possible) fifteen years ago? There seemed no end to the consequences of that piece of folly!

Young Jolyon was also silent; he had quickly penetrated his father's thought, for, dethroned from the high seat of an obvious and uncomplicated view of things, he had become both perceptive and subtle.

The attitude he had adopted towards sexual matters fifteen years before, however, was too different from his father's. There was no bridging the gulf.

He said coolly: 'I suppose he's fallen in love with some other woman?'

Old Jolyon gave him a dubious look. 'I can't tell,' he said; 'they say so!'

'Then it's probably true,' remarked young Jolyon unexpectedly; 'and I suppose *they*'ve told you who she is?'

'Yes,' said old Jolyon—'Soames's wife.'

Young Jolyon did not whistle. The circumstances of his own life had rendered him incapable of whistling on such a subject, but he looked at his father, while the ghost of a smile hovered over his face.

If old Jolyon saw, he took no notice.

'She and June were bosom friends!' he muttered.

'Poor little June!' said young Jolyon softly. He thought of his daughter still as a babe of three.

Old Jolyon came to a sudden halt.

'I don't believe a word of it,' he said, 'it's some old woman's tale. Get me a cab, Jo, I'm tired to death!'

They stood at a corner to see if an empty cab would come along, while carriage after carriage drove past, bearing Forsytes of all descriptions from the Zoo. The harness, the liveries, the gloss on the horses' coats, shone and glittered in the May sunlight, and each equipage, landau, sociable, barouche, Victoria, or brougham seemed to roll out proudly from its wheels:

> 'I and my horses and my men you know,
> Indeed the whole turn-out have cost a pot.
> But we were worth it every penny. Look
> At Master and at Missis now, the dawgs!
> Ease with security—ah! that's the ticket!'

And such, as everyone knows, is fit accompaniment for a perambulating Forsyte.

Amongst these carriages was a barouche coming at a greater pace than the others, drawn by a pair of bright bay horses. It swung on its high springs, and the four people who filled it seemed rocked as in a cradle.

This chariot attracted young Jolyon's attention; and suddenly, on the back seat, he recognised his Uncle James, unmistakable in spite of the increased whiteness of his whiskers; opposite, their backs defended by sun-shades, Rachel Forsyte and her elder but married sister, Winifred Dartie, in irreproachable toilettes, had posed their heads haughtily, like two of the birds they had been seeing at the Zoo; while by James's side reclined Dartie, in a brand-new frock-coat buttoned tight and square, with a large expanse of carefully shot linen protruding below each wristband.

An extra, if subdued, sparkle, an added touch of the best gloss or varnish characterised this vehicle, and seemed to distinguish it from all others, as though by some happy extravagance—like that which marks out the real 'work of art' from the ordinary 'picture'—it were designated as the typical car, the very throne of Forsytedom.

Old Jolyon did not see them pass; he was petting poor Holly, who was tired, but those in the carriage had taken in the little group; the ladies' heads tilted suddenly, there was a spasmodic screening movement of parasols; James's face protruded naïvely, like the head of a long bird, his mouth slowly opening. The shield-like rounds of the parasols grew smaller and smaller and vanished.

Young Jolyon saw that he had been recognised, even by Winifred, who could not have been more than fifteen when he had forfeited the right to be considered a Forsyte.

There was not much change in *them*! He remembered the exact look of their turn-out all that time ago: Horses, men, carriage–all different now, no doubt–but of the precise stamp of fifteen years before; the same neat display, the same nicely calculated arrogance–ease with security! The swing exact, the pose of the sun-shades exact, exact the spirit of the whole thing.

And in the sunlight, defended by the haughty shields of parasols, carriage after carriage went by.

'Uncle James has just passed with his female folk,' said young Jolyon.

His father looked black. 'Did your uncle see us? Yes? Hmph! What's *he* want, coming down into these parts?'

An empty cab drove up at this moment, and old Jolyon stopped it.

'I shall see you again before long, my boy!' he said. 'Don't you go paying any attention to what I've been saying about young Bosinney–I don't believe a word of it!'

Kissing the children who tried to detain him, he stepped in and was borne away.

Young Jolyon, who had taken Holly up in his arms, stood motionless at the corner, looking after the cab.

7

AFTERNOON AT TIMOTHY'S

If old Jolyon, as he got into his cab, had said: 'I *won't* believe a word of it!' he would more truthfully have expressed his sentiments.

The notion that James and his womankind had seen him in the company of his son had awakened in him not only the impatience he always felt when crossed, but that secret hostility natural between brothers, the roots of which– little nursery rivalries–sometimes toughen and deepen as life goes on, and, all hidden, support a plant capable of producing in season the bitterest fruits.

Hitherto there had been between these six brothers no more unfriendly feeling than that caused by the secret and natural doubt that the others might be richer than themselves; a feeling increased to the pitch of curiosity by the approach of death–that end of all handicaps–and the great 'closeness' of their man of business, who, with some sagacity, would profess to Nicholas ignorance of James's income, to James ignorance of old Jolyon's, to Jolyon ignorance of Roger's, to Roger ignorance of Swithin's, while to Swithin he would say most irritatingly that Nicholas must be a rich man. Timothy alone was exempt, being in gilt-edged securities.

But now, between two of them at least, had arisen a very different sense of injury. From the moment when James had the impertinence to pry into his affairs–as he put it–old Jolyon no longer chose to credit this story about Bosinney. His granddaughter slighted through a member of 'that fellow's' family! He made up his mind that Bosinney was maligned. There must be some other reason for his defection.

June had flown out at him, or something; she was as touchy as she could be!

He would, however, let Timothy have a bit of his mind, and see if he would go on dropping hints! And he would not let the grass grow under his feet either, he would go there at once, and take very good care that he didn't have to go again on the same errand.

He saw James's carriage blocking the pavement in front of 'The Bower'. So they had got there before him—cackling about having seen him, he dared say! And farther on, Swithin's greys were turning their noses towards the noses of James's bays, as though in conclave over the family, while their coachmen were in conclave above.

Old Jolyon, depositing his hat on the chair in the narrow hall, where that hat of Bosinney's had so long ago been mistaken for a cat, passed his thin hand grimly over his face with its great drooping white moustaches, as though to remove all traces of expression, and made his way upstairs.

He found the front drawing-room full. It was full enough at the best of times—without visitors—without anyone in it—for Timothy and his sisters, following the tradition of their generation, considered that a room was not quite 'nice' unless it was 'properly' furnished. It held, therefore, eleven chairs, a sofa, three tables, two cabinets, innumerable knicknacks, and part of a large grand piano. And now, occupied by Mrs Small, Aunt Hester, by Swithin, James, Rachel, Winifred, Euphemia, who had come in again to return *Passion and Paregoric* which she had read at lunch, and her chum Frances, Roger's daughter (the musical Forsyte, the one who composed songs), there was only one chair left unoccupied, except, of course, the two that nobody ever sat on—and the only standing room was occupied by the cat, on whom old Jolyon promptly stepped.

In these days it was by no means unusual for Timothy to have so many visitors. The family had always, one and all, had a real respect for Aunt Ann, and now that she was gone, they were coming far more frequently to 'The Bower', and staying longer.

Swithin had been the first to arrive, and seated torpid in a red satin chair with a gilt back, he gave every appearance of lasting the others out. And symbolising Bosinney's name 'the big one', with his great stature and bulk, his thick white hair, his puffy immovable shaven face, he looked more primeval than ever in the highly upholstered room.

His conversation, as usual of late, had turned at once upon Irene, and he had lost no time in giving Aunts Juley and Hester his opinion with regard to this rumour he heard was going about. No—as he said—she might want a bit of flirtation—a pretty woman must have her fling; but more than that he did not believe. Nothing open; she had too much good sense, too much proper appreciation of what was due to her position, and to the family! No sc—, he was going to say 'scandal', but the very idea was so preposterous that he waved his hand as though to say—'but let that pass!'

Granted that Swithin took a bachelor's view of the situation—still what indeed was not due to that family in which so many had done so well for themselves, had attained a certain position? If he *had* heard in dark, pessimistic moments the words 'yeomen' and 'very small beer' used in connection with his origin, did he believe them?

No! he cherished, hugging it pathetically to his bosom, the secret theory that there was something distinguished somewhere in his ancestry.

'Must be,' he once said to young Jolyon, before the latter went to the bad. 'Look at us, *we've* got on! There must be good blood in us somewhere.'

He had been fond of young Jolyon: the boy had been in a good set at college, had known that old ruffian Sir Charles Fiste's sons—a pretty rascal one of them had turned out, too; and there was style about him—it was a thousand pities he had run off with that foreign girl—a governess too! If he must go off like that, why couldn't he have chosen someone who would have done them credit! And what was he now?—an underwriter at Lloyd's; they said he even painted pictures—pictures! Damme! he might have ended as Sir Jolyon Forsyte, Bart., with a seat in Parliament and a place in the country!

It was Swithin who, following the impulse which sooner or later urges thereto some member of every great family, went to the Herald's Office, where they assured him that he was undoubtedly of the same family as the well-known Forsites with an 'i', whose arms were 'three dexter buckles on a sable ground gules', hoping no doubt to get him to take them up.

Swithin, however, did not do this, but having ascertained that the crest was a 'pheasant proper', and the motto 'For Forsite', he had a pheasant proper placed upon his carriage and the buttons of his coachman, and both crest and motto on his writing-paper. The arms he hugged to himself, partly because, not having paid for them, he thought it would look ostentatious to put them on his carriage, and he hated ostentation, and partly because he, like any practical man all over the country, had a secret dislike and contempt for things he could not understand—he found it hard, as anyone might, to swallow 'three dexter buckles on a sable ground gules'.

He never forgot, however, their having told him that if he paid for them he would be entitled to use them, and it strengthened his conviction that he was a gentleman. Imperceptibly the rest of the family absorbed the 'pheasant proper', and some, more serious than others, adopted the motto; old Jolyon, however, refused to use the latter, saying that it was humbug—meaning nothing, so far as he could see.

Among the older generation it was perhaps known at bottom from what great historical event they derived their crest; and if pressed on the subject, sooner than tell a lie—they did not like telling lies, having an impression that only Frenchmen and Russians told them—they would confess hurriedly that Swithin had got hold of it somehow.

Among the younger generation the matter was wrapped in a discretion proper. They did not want to hurt the feelings of their elders, nor to feel ridiculous themselves; they simply used the crest. . . .

'No,' said Swithin, 'he had had an opportunity of seeing for himself, and what he should say was that there was nothing in her manner to that young Buccaneer or Bosinney, or whatever his name was, different from her manner to himself; in fact, he should rather say . . .' But here the entrance of Frances and Euphemia put an unfortunate stop to the conversation, for this was not a subject which could be discussed before young people.

And though Swithin was somewhat upset at being stopped like this on the point of saying something important, he soon recovered his affability. He was rather fond of Frances—Francie, as she was called in the family. She was so smart, and they told him she made a pretty little pot of pin-money by her songs; he called it very clever of her.

He rather prided himself indeed on a liberal attitude towards women, not seeing any reason why they shouldn't paint pictures, or write tunes, or books even, for the matter of that, especially if they could turn a useful penny by it; not at all–kept them out of mischief. It was not as if they were men!

'Little Francie', as she was usually called with good-natured contempt, was an important personage, if only as a standing illustration of the attitude of Forsytes towards the Arts. She was not really 'little', but rather tall, with dark hair for a Forsyte, which, together with a grey eye, gave her what was called a 'Celtic appearance'. She wrote songs with titles like 'Breathing Sighs', or 'Kiss me, Mother, ere I die', with a refrain like an anthem:

> 'Kiss me, Mother, ere I die:
> Kiss me–kiss me, Mother, ah!
> Kiss, ah! kiss me e–ere I–
> Kiss me, Mother, ere I d–d–die!'

She wrote the words to them herself, and other poems. In lighter moments she wrote waltzes, one of which, the 'Kensington Coil', was almost national to Kensington, having a sweet dip in it. Thus:

It was very original. Then there were her 'Songs for Little People', at once educational and witty, especially 'Gran'ma's Porgie', and that ditty, almost prophetically imbued with the coming Imperial spirit, entitled 'Black him in his little eye'.

Any publisher would take these, and reviews like 'High Living', and the 'Ladies Genteel Guide' went into raptures over: 'Another of Miss Francie Forsyte's spirited ditties, sparkling and pathetic. We ourselves were moved to tears and laughter. Miss Forsyte should go far.'

With the true instinct of her breed, Francie had made a point of knowing the right people–people who would write about her, and talk about her, and people in Society, too–keeping a mental register of just where to exert her fascinations, and an eye on that steady scale of rising prices, which in her mind's eyes represented the future. In this way she caused herself to be universally respected.

Once, at a time when her emotions were whipped by an attachment–for the tenor of Roger's life, with its whole-hearted collection of house property, had induced in his only daughter a tendency towards passion–she turned to great and sincere work, choosing the sonata form, for the violin. This was the only one of her productions that troubled the Forsytes. They felt at once that it would not sell.

Roger, who liked having a clever daughter well enough, and often alluded to the amount of pocket-money she made for herself, was upset by this violin sonata.

'Rubbish like that!' he called it. Francie had borrowed young Flageoletti from Euphemia, to play it in the drawing-room at Prince's Gardens.

As a matter of fact Roger was right. It *was* rubbish, but–annoying! the sort of rubbish that wouldn't sell. As every Forsyte knows, rubbish that sells is not rubbish at all–far from it.

And yet, in spite of the sound common sense that fixed the worth of art at what it would fetch, some of the Forsytes—Aunt Hester, for instance, who had always been musical—could not help regretting that Francie's music was not 'classical'; the same with her poems. But then, as Aunt Hester said, they didn't see any poetry nowadays, all the poems were 'little light things'. There was nobody who could write a poem like 'Paradise Lost', or 'Childe Harold'; either of which made you feel that you really had read something. Still, it was nice for Francie to have something to occupy her; while other girls were spending money shopping she was making it! And both Aunt Hester and Aunt Juley were always ready to listen to the latest story of how Francie had got her price increased.

They listened now, together with Swithin, who sat pretending not to, for these young people talked so fast and mumbled so, he never could catch what they said!

'And I can't think,' said Mrs Septimus, 'how you do it. I should never have the audacity!'

Francie smiled lightly. 'I'd much rather deal with a man than a woman. Women are so sharp!'

'My dear,' cried Mrs Small, 'I'm sure we're not.'

Euphemia went off into her silent laugh, and, ending with the squeak, said, as though being strangled: 'Oh, you'll kill me some day, auntie.'

Swithin saw no necessity to laugh; he detested people laughing when he himself perceived no joke. Indeed, he detested Euphemia altogether, to whom he always alluded as 'Nick's daughter, what's she called—the pale one?' He had just missed being her godfather—indeed, would have been, had he not taken a firm stand against her outlandish name. He hated becoming a godfather. Swithin then said to Francie with dignity: 'It's a fine day—er—for the time of year.' But Euphemia, who knew perfectly well that he had refused to be her godfather, turned to Aunt Hester, and began telling her how she had seen Irene—Mrs Soames—at the Church and Commercial Stores.

'And Soames was with her?' said Aunt Hester, to whom Mrs Small had as yet had no opportunity of relating the incident.

'*Soames* with her? Of *course* not!'

'But was she all alone in London?'

'Oh, no; there was Mr Bosinney with her. She was *perfectly* dressed.'

But Swithin, hearing the name Irene, looked severely at Euphemia, who, it is true, never did look well in a dress, whatever she may have done on other occasions, and said:

'Dressed like a lady, I've no doubt. It's a pleasure to see her.'

At this moment James and his daughters were announced. Dartie, feeling badly in want of a drink, had pleaded an appointment with his dentist, and, being put down at the Marble Arch, had got into a hansom, and was already seated in the window of his club in Piccadilly.

His wife, he told his cronies, had wanted to take him to pay some calls. It was not in his line—not exactly. Haw!

Hailing the waiter, he sent him out to the hall to see what had won the 4.30 race. He was dog-tired, he said, and that was a fact; had been drivin' about with his wife to 'shows' all the afternoon. Had put his foot down at last. A fellow must live his own life.

At this moment, glancing out of the bay window—for he loved this seat whence he could see everybody pass—his eye unfortunately, or perhaps fortunately, chanced to light on the figure of Soames, who was mousing across the road from the Green Park side, with the evident intention of coming in, for he, too, belonged to 'The Iseeum'.

Dartie sprang to his feet; grasping his glass, he muttered something about 'that 4.30 race', and swiftly withdrew to the cardroom, where Soames never came. Here, in complete isolation and a dim light, he lived his own life till half-past seven, by which hour he knew Soames must certainly have left the club.

It would not do, as he kept repeating to himself whenever he felt the impulse to join the gossips in the bay-window getting too strong for him—it absolutely would not do, with finances as low as his, and the 'old man' (James) rusty ever since that business over the oil shares, which was no fault of his, to risk a row with Winifred.

If Soames were to see him in the club it would be sure to come round to her that he wasn't at the dentist's at all. He never knew a family where things 'came round' so. Uneasily, amongst the green baize card-tables, a frown on his olive-coloured face, his check trousers crossed, and patent-leather boots shining through the gloom, he sat biting his forefinger, and wondering where the deuce he was to get the money if Erotic failed to win the Lancashire Cup.

His thoughts turned gloomily to the Forsytes. What a set they were! There was no getting anything out of them—at least, it was a matter of extreme difficulty. They were so d—d particular about money matters; not a sportsman amongst the lot, unless it were George. That fellow Soames, for instance, would have a fit if you tried to borrow a tenner from him, or, if he didn't have a fit, he looked at you with his cursed supercilious smile, as if you were a lost soul because you were in want of money.

And that wife of his (Dartie's mouth watered involuntarily), he had tried to be on good terms with her, as one naturally would with any pretty sister-in-law, but he would be cursed if the–(he mentally used a coarse word)–would have anything to say to him–she looked at him, indeed, as if he were dirt–and yet she could go far enough, he wouldn't mind betting. He knew women; they weren't made with soft eyes and figures like that for nothing, as that fellow Soames would jolly soon find out, if there were anything in what he had heard about this Buccaneer Johnny.

Rising from his chair, Dartie took a turn across the room, ending in front of the looking-glass over the marble chimney-piece; and there he stood for a long time contemplating in the glass the reflection of his face. It had that look, peculiar to some men, of having been steeped in linseed oil, with its waxed dark moustaches and the little distinguished commencements of side whiskers, and concernedly he felt the promise of a pimple on the side of his slightly curved and fattish nose.

In the meantime old Jolyon had found the remaining chair in Timothy's commodious drawing-room. His advent had obviously put a stop to the conversation, decided awkwardness having set in. Aunt Juley, with her well-known kind-heartedness, hastened to set people at their ease again.

'Yes, Jolyon,' she said, 'we were just saying that you haven't been here for a long time; but we mustn't be surprised. You're busy, of course? James was just saying what a busy time of year–'

'Was he?' said old Jolyon, looking hard at James. 'It wouldn't be half so busy if everybody minded their own business.'

James, brooding in a small chair from which his knees ran uphill, shifted his feet uneasily, and put one of them down on the cat, which had unwisely taken refuge from old Jolyon beside him.

'Here, you've got a cat here,' he said in an injured voice, withdrawing his foot nervously as he felt it squeezing into the soft, furry body.

'Several,' said old Jolyon, looking at one face and another; 'I trod on one just now.'

A silence followed.

Then Mrs Small, twisting her fingers and gazing round with pathetic calm, asked: 'And how is dear June?'

A twinkle of humour shot through the sternness of old Jolyon's eyes. Extraordinary old woman, Juley! No one quite like her for saying the wrong thing!

'Bad!' he said; 'London don't agree with her—too many people about, too much clatter and chatter by half.' He laid emphasis on the words, and again looked James in the face.

Nobody spoke.

A feeling of its being too dangerous to take a step in any direction, or hazard any remark, had fallen on them all. Something of the sense of the impending, that comes over the spectator of a Greek tragedy, had entered that upholstered room, filled with those white-haired, frock-coated old men, and fashionably attired women, who were all of the same blood, between all of whom existed an unseizable resemblance.

Not that they were conscious of it—the visits of such fateful, bitter spirits are only felt.

Then Swithin rose. He would not sit there, feeling like that—*he* was not to be put down by anyone! And, manœuvring round the room with added pomp, he shook hands with each separately.

'You tell Timothy from me,' he said, 'that he coddles himself too much!' Then, turning to Francie, whom he considered 'smart', he added: 'You come with me for a drive one of these days.' But this conjured up the vision of that other eventful drive which had been so much talked about, and he stood quite still for a second, with glassy eyes as though waiting to catch up with the significance of what he himself had said; then, suddenly recollecting that he didn't care a damn, he turned to old Jolyon: 'Well, good-bye, Jolyon! You shouldn't go about without an overcoat; you'll be getting sciatica or something!' And, kicking the cat slightly with the pointed tip of his patent-leather boot, he took his huge form away.

When he had gone everyone looked secretly at the others, to see how they had taken the mention of the word 'drive'—the word which had become famous, and acquired an overwhelming importance, as the only official—so to speak—news in connection with the vague and sinister rumour clinging to the family tongue.

Euphemia, yielding to an impulse, said with a short laugh: 'I'm glad Uncle Swithin doesn't ask me to go for drives.'

Mrs Small, to reassure her and smooth over any little awkwardness the subject might have, replied: 'My dear, he likes to take somebody well dressed, who will do him a little credit. I shall never forget the drive he took me. It was an experience!' And her chubby round old face was spread for a moment with a strange contentment; then broke into pouts, and tears came into her eyes. She was thinking of that long ago driving tour she had once taken with Septimus Small.

James, who had relapsed into his nervous brooding in the little chair, suddenly roused himself. 'He's a funny fellow, Swithin,' he said, but in a half-hearted way.

Old Jolyon's silence, his stern eyes, held them all in a kind of paralysis. He was disconcerted himself by the effect of his own words—an effect which seemed to deepen the importance of the very rumour he had come to scotch; but he was still angry.

He had not done with them yet—No, no—he would give them another rub or two!

He did not wish to rub his nieces, he had no quarrel with them—a young and presentable female always appealed to old Jolyon's clemency—but that fellow James, and, in a less degree perhaps, those others, deserved all they would get. And he, too asked for Timothy.

As though feeling that some danger threatened her younger brother, Aunt Juley suddenly offered him tea: 'There it is,' she said, 'all cold and nasty, waiting for you in the back drawing-room, but Smither shall make you some fresh.'

Old Jolyon rose: 'Thank you,' he said, looking straight at James, 'but I've no time for tea, and—scandal, and the rest of it! It's time I was home. Good-bye, Julia; good-bye, Hester; good-bye, Winifred.'

Without more ceremonious adieux, he marched out.

Once again in his cab, his anger evaporated, for so it ever was with his wrath—when he had rapped out, it was gone. Sadness came over his spirit. He had stopped their mouths, maybe, but at what a cost! At the cost of certain knowledge that the rumour he had been resolved not to believe was true. June was abandoned, and for the wife of that fellow's son! He felt it was true, and hardened himself to treat it as if it were not; but the pain he hid beneath this resolution began slowly, surely, to vent itself in a blind resentment against James and his son.

The six women and one man left behind in the little drawing-room began talking as easily as might be after such an occurrence, for though each one of them knew for a fact that he or she never talked scandal, each one of them also knew that the other six did; all were therefore angry and at a loss. James only was silent, disturbed to the bottom of his soul.

Presently Francie said: 'Do you know, I think Uncle Jolyon is terribly changed this last year. What do *you* think, Aunt Hester?'

Aunt Hester made a little movement of recoil: 'Oh, ask your Aunt Julia!' she said; 'I know nothing about it.'

No one else was afraid of assenting, and James muttered gloomily at the floor: 'He's not half the man he was.'

'I've noticed it a long time,' went on Francie; 'he's aged tremendously.'

Aunt Juley shook her head; her face seemed suddenly to have become one immense pout.

'Poor dear Jolyon,' she said, 'somebody ought to see to it for him!'

There was again silence; then, as though in terror of being left solitarily behind, all five visitors rose simultaneously, and took their departure.

Mrs Small, Aunt Hester and their cat were left once more alone, the sound of a door closing in the distance announced the approach of Timothy.

That evening, when Aunt Hester had just got off to sleep in the back bedroom that used to be Aunt Juley's before Aunt Juley took Aunt Ann's, her door was opened, and Mrs Small, in a pink night-cap, a candle in her hand, entered: 'Hester!' she said. 'Hester!'

Aunt Hester faintly rustled the sheet.

'Hester,' repeated Aunt Juley, to make quite sure that she had awakened her,

'I am quite troubled about poor dear Jolyon. *What.*' Aunt Juley dwelt on the word, 'do you think ought to be done?'

Aunt Hester again rustled the sheet, her voice was heard faintly pleading: 'Done? How should I know?'

Aunt Juley turned away satisfied, and closing the door with extra gentleness so as not to disturb dear Hester, let it slip through her fingers and fall to with a 'crack'.

Back in her own room, she stood at the window gazing at the moon over the trees in the Park, through a chink in the muslin curtains, close drawn lest anyone should see. And there, with her face all round and pouting in its pink cap, and her eyes wet, she thought of 'dear Jolyon', so old and so lonely, and how she could be of some use to him; and how he would come to love her, as she had never been loved since—since poor Septimus went away.

8

DANCE AT ROGER'S

Roger's house in Prince's Gardens was brilliantly alight. Large numbers of wax candles had been collected and placed in cut-glass chandeliers, and the parquet floor of the long, double drawing-room reflected these constellations. An appearance of real spaciousness had been secured by moving out all the furniture on to the upper landings, and enclosing the room with those strange appendages of civilisation known as 'rout' seats.

In a remote corner, embowered in palms, was a cottage piano, with a copy of the 'Kensington Coil' open on the music-stand.

Roger had objected to a band. He didn't see in the least what they wanted with a band; he wouldn't go to the expense, and there was an end of it. Francie (her mother, whom Roger had long since reduced to chronic dyspepsia, went to bed on such occasions) had been obliged to content herself with supplementing the piano by a young man who played the cornet, and she so arranged with palms that anyone who did not look into the heart of things might imagine there were several musicians secreted there. She made up her mind to tell them to play loud—there was a lot of music in a cornet, if the man would only put his soul into it.

In the more cultivated American tongue, she was 'through' at last—through that tortuous labyrinth of makeshifts, which must be traversed before fashionable display can be combined with the sound economy of a Forsyte. Thin but brilliant, in her maize-coloured frock with much tulle about the shoulders, she went from place to place, fitting on her gloves, and casting her eye over it all.

To the hired butler (for Roger kept only maids) she spoke about the wine. Did he quite understand that Mr Forsyte wished a dozen bottles of the champagne from Whiteley's to be put out? But if that were finished (she did not suppose it would be, most of the ladies would drink water, no doubt), but if it were, there was the champagne cup, and he must do the best he could with that.

She hated having to say this sort of thing to a butler, it was so *infra dig*; but what could you do with father? Roger, indeed, after making himself consistently disagreeable about the dance, would come down presently, with his fresh colour and bumpy forehead, as though he had been its promoter; and he would smile, and probably take the prettiest woman in to supper; and at two o'clock, just as they were getting into the swing, he would go up secretly to the musicians and tell them to play 'God save the Queen', and go away.

Francie devoutly hoped he might soon get tired, and slip off to bed.

The three or four devoted girl friends who were staying in the house for this dance, had partaken with her, in a small, abandoned room upstairs, of tea and cold chicken-legs, hurriedly served; the men had been sent out to dine at Eustace's club, it being felt that they must be fed up.

Punctually on the stroke of nine arrived Mrs Small alone. She made elaborate apologies for the absence of Timothy, omitting all mention of Aunt Hester, who, at the last minute, had said she could not be bothered. Francie received her effusively, and placed her on a rout seat, where she left her, pouting and solitary in lavender-coloured satin—the first time she had worn colour since Aunt Ann's death.

The devoted maiden friends came now from their rooms, each by magic arrangement in a differently coloured frock, but all with the same liberal allowance of tulle on the shoulders and at the bosom—for they were, by some fatality, lean to a girl. They were all taken up to Mrs Small. None stayed with her more than a few seconds, but clustering together, talked and twisted their programmes, looking secretly at the door for the first appearance of a man.

Then arrived in a group a number of Nicholases, always punctual—the fashion up Ladbroke Grove way; and close behind them Eustace and his men, gloomy and smelling rather of smoke.

Three or four of Francie's lovers now appeared, one after the other; she had made each promise to come early. They were all clean-shaven and sprightly, with that peculiar kind of young-man sprightliness which had recently invaded Kensington; they did not seem to mind each other's presence in the least, and wore their ties bunching out at the ends, white waistcoats, and socks with clocks. All had handkerchiefs concealed in their cuffs. They moved buoyantly, each armoured in professional gaiety, as though he had come to do great deeds. Their faces when they danced, far from wearing the solemn look of the dancing Englishman, were irresponsible, charming, suave; they bounded, twirling their partners at great pace, without pedantic attention to the rhythm of the music.

At other dancers they looked with a kind of airy scorn—they, the light brigade, the heroes of a hundred Kensington 'hops'—from whom alone could the right manner and smile and step be hoped.

After this the stream came fast; chaperones silting up along the wall facing the entrance, the volatile element swelling the eddy in the larger room.

Men were scarce, and wallflowers wore their peculiar, pathetic expression, a patient, sourish smile which seemed to say: 'Oh, no! don't mistake me, *I* know you are not coming up to me. I can hardly expect that!' And Francie would plead with one of her lovers, or with some callow youth: 'Now, to please me, do let me introduce you to Miss Pink; such a nice girl, really!' and she would bring him up, and say: 'Miss Pink—Mr Gathercole. *Can* you spare him a dance?' Then Miss Pink, smiling her forced smile, colouring a little, answered: 'Oh! I think so!' and screening her empty card, wrote on it the name of Gathercole, spelling it passionately in the district that he proposed, about the second extra.

But when the youth had murmured that it was hot, and passed, she relapsed into her attitude of hopeless expectation, into her patient, sourish smile.

Mothers, slowly fanning their faces, watched their daughters, and in their eyes could be read all the story of those daughters' fortunes. As for themselves, to sit hour after hour, dead tired, silent, or talking spasmodically—what did it matter, so long as the girls were having a good time! But to see them neglected and passed by! Ah, they smiled, their eyes stabbed like the eyes of an offended swan; they longed to pluck young Gathercole by the slack of his dandified breeches and drag him to their daughters—the jackanapes!

And all the cruelties and hardness of life, its pathos and unequal chances, its conceit, self-forgetfulness and patience, were presented on the battlefield of this Kensington ballroom.

Here and there, too, lovers—not lovers like Francie's, a peculiar breed, but simply lovers—trembling, blushing, silent, sought each other by flying glances, sought to meet and touch in the mazes of the dance, and now and again dancing together, struck some beholder by the light in their eyes.

Not a second before ten o'clock came the James's—Emily, Rachel, Winifred (Dartie had been left behind, having on a former occasion drunk too much champagne at Roger's), and Cicely the youngest, making her début; behind them, following in a hansom from the paternal mansion where they had dined, Soames and Irene.

All these ladies had shoulder-straps and no tulle—thus showing at once, by a bolder exposure of flesh, that they came from the more fashionable side of the Park.

Soames, sidling back from the contact of the dancers, took up a position against the wall. Guarding himself with his pale smile, he stood watching. Waltz after waltz began and ended, couple after couple brushed by with smiling lips, laughter, and snatches of talk; or with set lips, and eyes searching the throng; or again, with silent parted lips, and eyes on each other. And the scent of festivity, the odour of flowers, and hair, of essences that women love, rose suffocatingly in the heat of the summer night.

Silent, with something of scorn in his smile, Soames seemed to notice nothing; but now and again his eyes, finding that which they sought, would fix themselves on a point in the shifting throng, and the smile die off his lips.

He danced with no one. Some fellows danced with their wives; his sense of 'form' had never permitted him to dance with Irene since their marriage, and the God of the Forsytes alone can tell whether this was a relief to him or not.

She passed, dancing with other men, her dress, iris-coloured, floating away from her feet. She danced well; he was tired of hearing women say with an acid smile: 'How beautifully your wife dances, Mr Forsyte—it's quite a pleasure to watch her!' Tired of answering them with his sidelong glance: 'You think so?'

A young couple close by flirted a fan by turns, making an unpleasant draught. Francie and one of her lovers stood near. They were talking of love.

He heard Roger's voice behind, giving an order about supper to a servant. Everything was very second-class! He wished that he had not come! He had asked Irene whether she wanted him; she had answered with that maddening smile of hers: 'Oh no!'

Why *had* he come? For the last quarter of an hour he had not even seen her. Here was George advancing with his Quilpish face; it was too late to get out of his way.

'Have you seen "The Buccaneer"?' said this licensed wag; 'he's on the warpath–hair cut and everything!'

Soames said he had not, and crossing the room, half-empty in an interval of the dance, he went out on the balcony and looked down into the street.

A carriage had driven up with late arrivals, and round the door hung some of those patient watchers of the London streets who spring up to the call of light or music; their faces, pale and upturned above their black and rusty figures, had an air of stolid watching that annoyed Soames: Why were they allowed to hang about; why didn't the bobby move them on?

But the policeman took no notice of them; his feet were planted apart on the strip of crimson carpet stretched across the pavement; his face, under the helmet, wore the same stolid, watching look as theirs.

Across the road, through the railings, Soames could see the branches of trees shining, faintly stirring in the breeze, by the gleam of the street lamps; beyond, again, the upper lights of the houses on the other side, so many eyes looking down on the quiet blackness of the garden; and over all, the sky, that wonderful London sky, dusted with the innumerable reflection of countless lamps; a dome woven over between its stars with the refraction of human needs and human fancies–immense mirror of pomp and misery that night after night stretches its kindly mocking over miles of houses and gardens, mansions and squalor, over Forsytes, policemen, and patient watchers in the streets.

Soames turned away and, hidden in the recess, gazed into the lighted room. It was cooler out there. He saw the new arrivals, June and her grandfather, enter. What had made them so late? They stood by the doorway. They looked fagged. Fancy Uncle Jolyon turning out at this time of night! Why hadn't June come to Irene, as she usually did, and it occurred to him suddenly that he had seen nothing of June for a long time now.

Watching her face with idle malice, he saw it change, grow so pale that he thought she would drop, then flame out crimson. Turning to see at what she was looking, he saw his wife on Bosinney's arm coming from the conservatory at the end of the room. Her eyes were raised to his, as though answering some question he had asked, and he was gazing at her intently.

Soames looked again at June. Her hand rested on old Jolyon's arm; she seemed to be making a request. He saw a surprised look on his uncle's face; they turned and passed through the door out of his sight.

The music began again–a waltz–and, still as a statue in the recess of the window, his face unmoved, but no smile on his lips, Soames waited. Presently, within a yard of the dark balcony, his wife and Bosinney passed. He caught the perfume of the gardenias that she wore, saw the rise and fall of her bosom, the languor in her eyes, her parted lips, and a look on her face that he did not know. To the slow, swinging measure they danced by, and it seemed to him that they clung to each other; he saw her raise her eyes, soft and dark, to Bosinney's and drop them again.

Very white, he turned back to the balcony, and leaning on it, gazed down on the Square; the figures were still there looking up at the light with dull persistency, the policeman's face, too, upturned and staring, but he saw nothing of them. Below, a carriage drew up, two figures got in and drove away. . . .

That evening June and old Jolyon sat down to dinner at the usual hour. The girl was in her customary high-necked frock, old Jolyon had not dressed.

At breakfast she had spoken of the dance at Uncle Roger's, she wanted to go;

she had been stupid enough, she said, not to think of asking anyone to take her. It was too late now.

Old Jolyon lifted his keen eyes. June was used to go to dances with Irene as a matter of course! And deliberately fixing his gaze on her, he asked: 'Why didn't she get Irene?'

No! June did not want to ask Irene; she would only go if–if her grandfather wouldn't mind just for once–for a little time!

At her look, so eager and so worn, old Jolyon had grumblingly consented. He did not know what she wanted, he said, with going to a dance like this, a poor affair, he would wager; and she no more fit for it than a cat! What she wanted was sea air, and after his general meeting of the Globular Gold Concessions he was ready to take her. She didn't want to go away? Ah! she would knock herself up! Stealing a mournful look at her, he went on with his breakfast.

June went out early and wandered restlessly about in the heat. Her little light figure that lately had moved so languidly about its business was all on fire. She bought herself some flowers. She wanted–she meant to look her best. *He* would be there! She knew well enough that he had a card. She would show him that she did not care. But deep down in her heart she resolved that evening to win him back. She came in flushed, and talked brightly all lunch; old Jolyon was there, and he was deceived.

In the afternoon she was overtaken by a desperate fit of sobbing. She strangled the noise against the pillows of her bed, but when at last it ceased she saw in the glass a swollen face with reddened eyes, and violet circles round them. She stayed in the darkened room till dinner-time.

All through that silent meal the struggle went on within her. She looked so shadowy and exhausted that old Jolyon told 'Sankey' to countermand the carriage, he would not have her going out. She was to go to bed! She made no resistance. She went up to her room and sat in the dark. At ten o'clock she rang for her maid.

'Bring some hot water, and go down and tell Mr Forsyte that I feel perfectly rested. Say that if he's too tired I can go to the dance by myself.'

The maid looked askance, and June turned on her imperiously. 'Go,' she said, 'bring the hot water at once!'

Her ball dress still lay on the sofa, and with a sort of fierce care she arrayed herself, took the flowers in her hand, and went down, her small face carried high under its burden of hair. She could hear old Jolyon in his room as she passed.

Bewildered and vexed, he was dressing. It was past ten, they would not get there till eleven; the girl was mad. But he dared not cross her–the expression of her face at dinner haunted him.

With great ebony brushes he smoothed his hair till it shone like silver under the light; then he, too, came out on the gloomy staircase.

June met him below, and, without a word, they went to the carriage.

When, after that drive which seemed to last for ever, she entered Roger's drawing-room, she disguised under a mask of resolution a very torment of nervousness and emotion. The feeling of shame at what might be called 'running after him' was smothered by the dread that he might not be there, that she might not see him after all, and by that dogged resolve–somehow, she did not know–to win him back.

The sight of the ballroom, with its gleaming floor, gave her a feeling of joy, of triumph, for she loved dancing, and when dancing she floated, so light was she, like a strenuous, eager little spirit. He would surely ask her to dance, and if he danced with her it would all be as it was before. She looked about her eagerly.

The sight of Bosinney coming with Irene from the conservatory, with that strange look of utter absorption on his face, struck her too suddenly. They had not seen–no one should see–her distress, not even her grandfather.

She put her hand on Jolyon's arm and said very low:

'I must go home, Gran; I feel ill.'

He hurried her away, grumbling to himself that he had known how it would be.

To her he said nothing; only when they were once more in the carriage, which by some fortunate chance had lingered near the door, he asked her: 'What is it, my darling?'

Feeling her whole slender body shaken by sobs, he was terribly alarmed. She must have Blank to-morrow. He would insist upon it. He could not have her like this. . . . There, there!

June mastered her sobs and, squeezing his hand feverishly, she lay back in her corner, her face muffled in a shawl.

He could only see her eyes, fixed and staring in the dark, but he did not cease to stroke her hand with his thin fingers.

9

EVENING AT RICHMOND

Other eyes besides the eyes of June and of Soames had seen 'those two' (as Euphemia had already begun to call them) coming from the conservatory; other eyes had noticed the look on Bosinney's face.

There are moments when Nature reveals the passion hidden beneath the careless calm of her ordinary moods–violent spring flashing white on almond-blossom through the purple clouds; a snowy, moonlit peak, with its single star, soaring up to the passionate blue; or against the flames of sunset, an old yew tree standing dark guardian of some fiery secret.

There are moments, too, when, in a picture-gallery, a work, noted by the casual spectator as '★ ★ ★ Titian–remarkably fine', breaks through the defences of some Forsyte better lunched perhaps than his fellows, and holds him spellbound in a kind of ecstasy. There are things, he feels–there are things here which–well, which are things. Something unreasoning, unreasonable, is upon him; when he tries to define it with the precision of a practical man, it eludes him, slips away, as the glow of the wine he has drunk is slipping away, leaving him cross and conscious of his liver. He feels that he has been extravagant, prodigal of something; virtue has gone out of him. He did not desire this glimpse of what lay under the three stars of his catalogue. God forbid that he should know anything about the forces of Nature! God forbid that he should admit for a moment that there are such things! Once admit that, and where was he? One paid a shilling for entrance and another for the programme.

The look which June had seen, which other Forsytes had seen, was like the sudden flashing of a candle through a hole in some imaginary canvas, behind which it was being moved—the sudden flaming-out of a vague, erratic glow, shadowy and enticing. It brought home to onlookers the consciousness that dangerous forces were at work. For a moment they noticed it with pleasure, with interest, then felt they must not notice it at all.

It supplied, however, the reason of June's coming so late and disappearing again without dancing, without even shaking hands with her lover. She was ill, it was said, and no wonder.

But here they looked at each other guiltily. They had no desire to spread scandal, no desire to be ill-natured. Who would have? And to outsiders no word was breathed, unwritten law keeping them silent.

Then came the news that June had gone to the seaside with old Jolyon.

He had carried her off to Broadstairs, for which place there was just then a feeling, Yarmouth having lost caste, in spite of Nicholas, and no Forsyte going to the sea without intending to have an air for his money such as would render him bilious in a week. That fatally aristocratic tendency of the first Forsyte to drink Madeira had left his descendants undoubtedly accessible.

So June went to the sea. The family awaited developments; there was nothing else to do.

But how far—how far had 'those two' gone? How far were they going to go? Could they really be going at all? Nothing could surely come of it, for neither of them had any money. At the most a flirtation, ending, as all such attachments should, at the proper time.

Soames's sister, Winifred Dartie, who had imbibed with the breezes of Mayfair—she lived in Green Street—more fashionable principles in regard to matrimonial behaviour than were current, for instance, in Ladbroke Grove, laughed at the idea of there being anything in it. The 'little thing'—Irene was taller than herself, and it was real testimony to the solid worth of a Forsyte that she should always thus be a 'little thing'—the little thing was bored. Why shouldn't she amuse herself? Soames was rather tiring; and as to Mr Bosinney—only that buffoon George would have called him the Buccaneer—she maintained that he was very *chic*.

This dictum—that Bosinney was *chic*—caused quite a sensation. It failed to convince. That he was 'good-looking in a way' they were prepared to admit, but that anyone could call a man with his pronounced cheek-bones, curious eyes, and soft felt hats *chic* was only another instance of Winifred's extravagant way of running after something new.

It was that famous summer when extravagance was fashionable, when the very earth was extravagant, chestnut trees spread with blossom, and flowers drenched in perfume, as they had never been before; when roses blew in every garden, and for the swarming stars the nights had hardly space; when every day and all day long the sun, in full armour, swung his brazen shield above the Park, and people did strange things, lunching and dining in the open air. Unprecedented was the tale of cabs and carriages that streamed across the bridges of the shining river, bearing the upper middle class in thousands to the green glories of Bushey, Richmond, Kew, and Hampton Court. Almost every family with any pretensions to be of the carriage class paid one visit that year to the horse-chestnuts at Bushey, or took one drive amongst the Spanish chestnuts of Richmond Park. Bowling smoothly, if dustily, along, in a cloud of their own creation, they would stare fashionably at the antlered heads which the great slow deer raised out of a forest of bracken that promised to autumn lovers such cover as was never seen before. And now and again, as the amorous perfume of chestnut flowers and fern was drifted too near, one would say to the other: 'My dear! What a peculiar scent!'

And the lime flowers that year were of rare prime, near honey-coloured. At the corners of London squares they gave out, as the sun went down, a perfume sweeter than the honey bees had taken—a perfume that stirred a yearning unnameable in the hearts of Forsytes and their peers, taking the cool after dinner in the precincts of those gardens to which they alone had keys.

And that yearning made them linger amidst the dim shapes of flower-beds in the failing daylight, made them turn, and turn, and turn again, as though lovers were waiting for them—waiting for the last light to die away under the shadow of the branches.

Some vague sympathy evoked by the scent of the limes, some sisterly desire to see for herself, some idea of demonstrating the soundness of her dictum that there was 'nothing in it'; or merely the craving to drive down to Richmond, irresistible that summer, moved the mother of the little Darties (of little Publius, of Imogen, Maud, and Benedict) to write the following note to her sister-in-law:

June 30.

DEAR IRENE,

I hear that Soames is going to Henley to-morrow for the night. I thought it would be great fun if we made up a little party and drove down to Richmond. Will you ask Mr Bosinney, and I will get young Flippard.

Emily (they called their mother Emily—it was so *chic*) will lend us the carriage. I will call for you and your young man at seven o'clock.

Your affectionate sister,

WINIFRED DARTIE.

'Montague believes the dinner at the Crown and Sceptre to be quite eatable.'

Montague was Dartie's second and better-known name—his first being Moses; for he was nothing if not a man of the world.

Her plan met with more opposition from Providence than so benevolent a scheme deserved. In the first place young Flippard wrote:

DEAR MRS. DARTIE,

Awfully sorry. Engaged two deep.

Yours,

AUGUSTUS FLIPPARD.

It was late to send into the byways and hedges to remedy this misfortune. With the promptitude and conduct of a mother, Winifred fell back on her husband. She had, indeed, the decided but tolerant temperament that goes with a good deal of profile, fair hair and greenish eyes. She was seldom or never at a loss; or if at a loss, was always able to convert it into a gain.

Dartie, too, was in good feather. Erotic had failed to win the Lancashire Cup. Indeed, that celebrated animal, owned as he was by a pillar of the turf, who had secretly laid many thousands against him, had not even started. The forty-eight hours that followed his scratching were among the darkest in Dartie's life.

Visions of James haunted him day and night. Black thoughts about Soames mingled with the faintest hopes. On the Friday night he got drunk, so greatly was he affected. But on Saturday morning the true Stock Exchange instinct triumphed within him. Owing some hundreds, which by no possibility could he pay, he went into town and put them all on Concertina for the Saltown Borough Handicap.

As he said to Major Scrotton, with whom he lunched at the Iseeum: 'That little Jew boy, Nathans, had given him the tip. He didn't care a cursh. He wash in–a mucker. If it didn't come up–well then, damme, the old man would have to pay!'

A bottle of Pol Roger to his own cheek had given him a new contempt for James.

It came up. Concertina was squeezed home by her neck–a terrible squeak! But, as Dartie said: 'There was nothing like pluck!'

He was by no means averse to the expedition to Richmond. He would 'stand' it himself! He cherished an admiration for Irene, and wished to be on more playful terms with her.

At half-past five the Park Lane footman came round to say: Mrs Forsyte was very sorry, but one of the horses was coughing!

Undaunted by this further blow, Winifred at once despatched little Publius (now aged seven) with the nursery governess to Montpelier Square.

They would go down in hansoms and meet at the Crown and Sceptre at 7.45.

Dartie, on being told, was pleased enough. It was better than going down with your back to the horses! He had no objection to driving down with Irene. He supposed they would pick up the others at Montpelier Square and swop hansoms there?

Informed that the meet was at the Crown and Sceptre, and that he would have to drive with his wife, he turned sulky and said it was d—d slow!

At seven o'clock they started, Dartie offering to bet the driver half a crown he didn't do it in the three-quarters of an hour.

Twice only did husband and wife exchange remarks on the way.

Dartie said: 'It'll put Master Soames's nose out of joint to hear his wife's been drivin' in a hansom with Master Bosinney!'

Winifred replied: 'Don't talk such nonsense, Monty!'

'Nonsense!' repeated Dartie. 'You don't know women, my fine lady!'

On the other occasion he merely asked: 'How am I looking? A bit puffy about the gills? That fizz old George is so fond of is a windy wine!'

He had been lunching with George Forsyte at the Haversnake.

Bosinney and Irene had arrived before them. They were standing in one of the long french windows overlooking the river.

Windows that summer were open all day long, and all night too, and day and night the scents of flowers and trees came in, the hot scent of parching grass and the cool scent of the heavy dews.

To the eye of the observant Dartie his two guests did not appear to be making much running, standing there close together, without a word. Bosinney was a hungry-looking creature–not much go about *him*!

He left them to Winifred, however, and busied himself to order the dinner.

A Forsyte will require good, if not delicate feeding, but a Dartie will tax the resources of a Crown and Sceptre. Living, as he does, from hand to mouth, nothing is too good for him to eat; and he will eat it. His drink, too, will need to be carefully provided; there is much drink in this country 'not good enough' for a Dartie; he will have the best. Paying for things vicariously, there is no reason why he should stint himself. To stint himself is the mark of a fool, not of a Dartie.

The best of everything! No sounder principle on which a man can base his life, whose father-in-law has a very considerable income, and a partiality for his grandchildren.

With his not unable eye Dartie had spotted this weakness in James the very first year after little Publius's arrival (an error); he had profited by his perspicacity. Four little Darties were now a sort of perpetual insurance.

The feature of the feast was unquestionably the red mullet. This delectable fish, brought from a considerable distance in a state of almost perfect preservation, was first fried, then boned, then served in ice, with Madeira punch in place of sauce, according to a recipe known to a few men of the world.

Nothing else calls for remark except the payment of the bill by Dartie.

He had made himself extremely agreeable throughout the meal; his bold, admiring stare seldom abandoning Irene's face and figure. As he was obliged to confess to himself, he got no change out of her—she was cool enough, as cool as her shoulders looked under their veil of creamy lace. He expected to have caught her out in some little game with Bosinney; but not a bit of it, she kept up her end remarkably well. As for that architect chap, he was as glum as a bear with a sore head—Winifred could barely get a word out of him; he ate nothing, but he certainly took his liquor, and his face kept getting whiter, and his eyes looked queer.

It was all very amusing.

For Dartie himself was in capital form, and talked freely, with a certain poignancy, being no fool. He told two or three stories verging on the improper, a concession to the company, for his stories were not used to verging. He proposed Irene's health in a mock speech. Nobody drank it, and Winifred said: 'Don't be such a clown, Monty!'

At her suggestion they went after dinner to the public terrace overlooking the river.

'I should like to see the common people making love,' she said, 'it's such fun!'

There were numbers of them walking in the cool, after the day's heat, and the air was alive with the sound of voices, coarse and loud, or soft as though murmuring secrets.

It was not long before Winifred's better sense—she was the only Forsyte present—secured them an empty bench. They sat down in a row. A heavy tree spread a thick canopy above their heads, and the haze darkened slowly over the river.

Dartie sat at the end, next to him Irene, then Bosinney, then Winifred. There was hardly room for four, and the man of the world could feel Irene's arm crushed against his own; he knew that she could not withdraw it without seeming rude, and this amused him; he devised every now and again a movement that would bring her closer still. He thought: 'That Buccaneer Johnny shan't have it all to himself! It's a pretty tight fit, certainly!'

From far down below on the dark river came drifting the tinkle of a mandoline, and voices singing the old round:

> 'A boat, a boat, unto the ferry,
> For we'll go over and be merry,
> And laugh, and quaff, and drink brown sherry!'

And suddenly the moon appeared, young and tender, floating up on her back from behind a tree; and as though she had breathed, the air was cooler, but down that cooler air came always the warm odour of the limes.

Over his cigar Dartie peered round at Bosinney, who was sitting with his arms crossed, staring straight in front of him, and on his face the look of a man being tortured.

And Dartie shot a glance at the face between, so veiled by the overhanging shadow that it was but like a darker piece of the darkness shaped and breathed on; soft, mysterious, enticing.

A hush had fallen on the noisy terrace, as if all the strollers were thinking secrets too precious to be spoken.

And Dartie thought: 'Women!'

The glow died above the river, the singing ceased; the young moon hid behind a tree, and all was dark. He pressed himself against Irene.

He was not alarmed at the shuddering that ran through the limbs he touched, or at the troubled, scornful look of her eyes. He felt her trying to draw herself away, and smiled.

It must be confessed that the man of the world had drunk quite as much as was good for him.

With thick lips parted under his well-curled moustaches, and his bold eyes aslant upon her, he had the malicious look of a satyr.

Along the pathway of sky between the hedges of the tree-tops the stars clustered forth; like mortals beneath, they seemed to shift and swarm and whisper. Then on the terrace the buzz broke out once more, and Dartie thought: 'Ah! he's a poor, hungry looking devil, that Bosinney!' and again he pressed himself against Irene.

The movement deserved a better success. She rose, and they all followed her.

The man of the world was more than ever determined to see what she was made of. Along the terrace he kept close at her elbow. He had within him much good wine. There was the long drive home, the long drive and the warm dark and the pleasant closeness of the hansom cab—with its insulation from the world devised by some great and good man. That hungry architect chap might drive with his wife—he wished him joy of her! And conscious that his voice was not too steady, he was careful not to speak; but a smile had become fixed on his thick lips.

They strolled along towards the cabs awaiting them at the farther end. His plan had the merit of all great plans, an almost brutal simplicity—he would merely keep at her elbow till she got in, and get in quickly after her.

But when Irene reached the cab she did not get in; she slipped, instead, to the horse's head. Dartie was not at the moment sufficiently master of his legs to follow. She stood stroking the horse's nose, and, to his annoyance, Bosinney was at her side first. She turned and spoke to him rapidly in a low voice; the words 'That man' reached Dartie. He stood stubbornly by the cab step, waiting for her to come back. He knew a trick worth two of that!

Here, in the lamp-light, his figure (no more than medium height), well squared in its white evening waistcoat, his light overcoat flung over his arm, a pink flower in his button-hole, and on his dark face that look of confident, good-humoured insolence, he was at his best—a thorough man of the world.

Winifred was already in her cab. Dartie reflected that Bosinney would have a poorish time in that cab if he didn't look sharp! Suddenly he received a push which nearly overturned him in the road. Bosinney's voice hissed in his ear: 'I am taking Irene back; do you understand?' He saw a face white with passion, and eyes that glared at him like a wild cat's.

'Eh?' he stammered. 'What? Not a bit! You take my wife!'

'Get away!' hissed Bosinney—'or I'll throw you into the road!'

Dartie recoiled; he saw as plainly as possible that the fellow meant it. In the space he made Irene had slipped by, her dress brushed his legs. Bosinney stepped in after her.

'Go on!' he heard the Buccaneer cry. The cabman flicked his horse. It sprang forward.

Dartie stood for a moment dumbfounded; then, dashing at the cab where his wife sat, he scrambled in.

'Drive on!' he shouted to the driver, 'and don't you lose sight of that fellow in front!'

Seated by his wife's side, he burst into imprecations. Calming himself at last with a supreme effort, he added: 'A pretty mess you've made of it, to let the Buccaneer drive home with her; why on earth couldn't you keep hold of him? He's mad with love; any fool can see that!'

He drowned Winifred's rejoinder with fresh calls to the Almighty; nor was it until they reached Barnes that he ceased a Jeremiad, in the course of which he had abused her, her father, her brother, Irene, Bosinney, the name of Forsyte, his own children, and cursed the day when he had ever married.

Winifred, a woman of strong character, let him have his say, at the end of which he lapsed into sulky silence. His angry eyes never deserted the back of that cab, which, like a lost chance, haunted the darkness in front of him.

Fortunately he could not hear Bosinney's passionate pleading—that pleading which the man of the world's conduct had let loose like a flood; he could not see Irene shivering, as though some garment had been torn from her, nor her eyes, black and mournful, like the eyes of a beaten child. He could not hear Bosinney entreating, entreating, always entreating; could not hear her sudden, soft weeping, nor see that poor, hungry-loooking devil, awed and trembling, humbly touching her hand.

In Montpelier Square their cabman, following his instructions to the letter, faithfully drew up behind the cab in front. The Darties saw Bosinney spring out, and Irene follow, and hasten up the steps with bent head. She evidently had her key in her hand, for she disappeared at once. It was impossible to tell whether she had turned to speak to Bosinney.

The latter came walking past their cab; both husband and wife had an admirable view of his face in the light of a street lamp. It was working with violent emotion.

'Good-night, Mr Bosinney!' called Winifred.

Bosinney started, clawed off his hat, and hurried on. He had obviously forgotten their existence.

'There!' said Dartie, 'did you see the beast's face? What did I say? Fine games!' He improved the occasion.

There had so clearly been a crisis in the cab that Winifred was unable to defend her theory.

She said: 'I shall say nothing about it. I don't see any use in making a fuss!'

With that view Dartie at once concurred; looking upon James as a private preserve, he disapproved of his being disturbed by the troubles of others.

'Quite right,' he said; 'let Soames look after himself. He's jolly well able to!'

Thus speaking, the Darties entered their habitat in Green Street, the rent of which was paid by James, and sought a well-earned rest. The hour was midnight, and no Forsytes remained abroad in the streets to spy out Bosinney's wanderings; to see him return and stand against the rails of the Square garden, back from the glow of the street lamp; to see him stand there in the shadow of trees, watching the house where in the dark was hidden she whom he would have given the world to see for a single minute—she who was now to him the breath of the lime trees, the meaning of the light and the darkness, the very beating of his own heart.

10

DIAGNOSIS OF A FORSYTE

It is in the nature of a Forsyte to be ignorant that he is a Forsyte; but young Jolyon was well aware of being one. He had not known it till after the decisive step which had made him an outcast; since then the knowledge had been with him continually. He felt it throughout his alliance, throughout all his dealings with his second wife, who was emphatically not a Forsyte.

He knew that if he had not possessed in great measure the eye for what he wanted, the tenacity to hold on to it, the sense of the folly of wasting that for which he had given so big a price—in other words, the 'sense of property'—he could never have retained her (perhaps never would have desired to retain her) with him through all the financial troubles, slights, and misconstructions of those fifteen years; never have induced her to marry him on the death of his first wife; never have lived it all through, and come up, as it were, thin, but smiling.

He was one of those men who, seated cross-legged like miniature Chinese idols in the cages of their own hearts, are ever smiling at themselves a doubting smile. Not that this smile, so intimate and eternal, interfered with his actions, which, like his chin and his temperament, were quite a peculiar blend of softness and determination.

He was conscious, too, of being a Forsyte in his work, that painting of water-colours to which he devoted so much energy, always with an eye on himself, as though he could not take so unpractical a pursuit quite seriously, and always with a certain queer uneasiness that he did not make more money at it.

It was, then, this consciousness of what it meant to be a Forsyte, that made him receive the following letter from old Jolyon, with a mixture of sympathy and disgust:

SHELDRAKE HOUSE,
BROADSTAIRS,
July 1.

MY DEAR JO,

(The Dad's handwriting had altered very little in the thirty odd years that he remembered it.)

We have been here now a fortnight, and have had good weather on the whole. The air is bracing, but my liver is out of order, and I shall be glad enough to get back to town. I cannot say much for June, her health and spirits are very indifferent, and I don't see what is to come of it. She says nothing, but it is clear that she is harping on this engagement, which is an engagement and no engagement, and—goodness knows what. I have grave doubts whether she ought to be allowed to return to London in the present state of affairs, but she is so self-willed that she might take it into her head to come up at any moment. The fact is someone ought to speak to Bosinney and ascertain what he means. I'm afraid of this myself, for I should certainly rap him over the knuckles, but I thought that you, knowing him at the club, might put in a word, and get to ascertain what the fellow is about. You will of course in no way commit June. I shall be glad to hear from you in the course of a few days whether you have succeeded in gaining any information. The situation is very distressing to me, I worry about it at night. With my love to Jolly and Holly.

I am,
Your affect. father,
JOLYON FORSYTE.

Young Jolyon pondered this letter so long and seriously that his wife noticed his preoccupation, and asked him what was the matter. He replied: 'Nothing.'

It was a fixed principle with him never to allude to June. She might take alarm, he did not know what she might think; he hastened, therefore, to banish from his manner all traces of absorption, but in this he was about as successful as his father would have been, for he had inherited all old Jolyon's transparency in matters of domestic finesse; and young Mrs Jolyon, busying herself over the affairs of the house, went about with tightened lips, stealing at him unfathomable looks.

He started for the club in the afternoon with the letter in his pocket, and without having made up his mind.

To sound a man as to 'his intentions' was peculiarly unpleasant to him; nor did his own anomalous position diminish this unpleasantness. It was so like his family, so like all the people they knew and mixed with, to enforce what they called their rights over a man, to bring him up to the mark; so like them to carry their business principles into their private relations!

And how that phrase in the letter–'You will, of course, in no way commit June'–gave the whole thing away.

Yet the letter, with the personal grievance, the concern for June, the 'rap over the knuckles', was all so natural. No wonder his father wanted to know what Bosinney meant, no wonder he was angry.

It was difficult to refuse. But why give the thing to him to do? That was surely quite unbecoming; but so long as a Forsyte got what he was after, he was not too particular about the means, provided appearance were saved.

How should he set about it, or how refuse? Both seemed impossible. So, young Jolyon!

He arrived at the club at three o'clock, and the first person he saw was Bosinney himself, seated in a corner, staring out of the window.

Young Jolyon sat down not far off, and began nervously to reconsider his position. He looked covertly at Bosinney sitting there unconscious. He did not know him very well, and studied him attentively for perhaps the first time; an unusual-looking man, unlike in dress, face, and manner to most of the other members of the club–young Jolyon himself, however different he had become in mood and temper, had always retained the neat reticence of Forsyte appearance. He alone among Forsytes was ignorant of Bosinney's nickname. The man was unusual, not eccentric, but unusual; he looked worn, too, haggard, hollow in the cheeks beneath those broad, high cheek-bones, though without any appearance of ill-health, for he was strongly built, with curly hair that seemed to show all the vitality of a fine constitution.

Something in his face and attitude touched young Jolyon. He knew what suffering was like, and this man looked as if he were suffering.

He got up and touched his arm.

Bosinney started, but exhibited no sign of embarrassment on seeing who it was.

Young Jolyon sat down.

'I haven't seen you for a long time,' he said. 'How are you getting on with my cousin's house?'

'It'll be finished in about a week.'

'I congratulate you!'

'Thanks–I don't know that it's much of a subject for congratulation.'

'No?' queried young Jolyon; 'I should have thought you'd be glad to get a long job like that off your hands; but I suppose you feel it much as I do when I part with a picture–a sort of child?'

He looked kindly at Bosinney.

'Yes,' said the latter more cordially, 'it goes out from you and there's an end of it. I didn't know you painted.'

'Only water-colours; I can't say I believe in my work.'

'Don't believe in it? Then how can you do it? Work's no use unless you believe in it!'

'Good,' said young Jolyon; 'it's exactly what I've always said. By-the-by, have you noticed that whenever one says "Good", one always adds "it's exactly what I've always said!" But if you ask me how I do it, I answer, because I'm a Forsyte.'

'A Forsyte! I never thought of you as one!'

'A Forsyte,' replied young Jolyon, 'is not an uncommon animal. There are hundreds among the members of this club. Hundreds out there in the streets; you meet them wherever you go!'

'And how do you tell them, may I ask?' said Bosinney.

'By their sense of property. A Forsyte takes a practical–one might say a common-sense–view of things, and a practical view of things is based fundamentally on a sense of property. A Forsyte, you will notice, never gives himself away.'

'Joking?'

Young Jolyon's eye twinkled.

'Not much. As a Forsyte myself, I have no business to talk. But I'm a kind of thoroughbred mongrel; now, there's no mistaking you. You're as different from me as I am from my Uncle James, who is the perfect specimen of a Forsyte. His sense of property is extreme, while you have practically none. Without me in between, you would seem like a different species. I'm the missing link. We are, of course, all of us the slaves of property, and I admit that it's a question of degree, but what I call a "Forsyte" is a man who is decidedly more than less a slave of property. He knows a good thing, he knows a safe thing, and his grip on property–it doesn't matter whether it be wives, houses, money, or reputation–is his hall-mark.'

'Ah!' murmured Bosinney. 'You should patent the word.'

'I should like,' said young Jolyon, 'to lecture on it: "Properties and quality of a Forsyte. This little animal, disturbed by the ridicule of his own sort, is unaffected in his motions by the laughter of strange creatures (you or I). Hereditarily disposed to myopia, he recognises only the persons and habitats of his own species, amongst which he passes an existence of competitive tranquillity."'

'You talk of them,' said Bosinney, 'as if they were half England.'

'They are,' repeated young Jolyon, 'half England, and the better half, too, the safe half, the three per cent half, the half that counts. It's their wealth and security that makes everything possible; makes your art possible, makes literature, science, even religion, possible. Without Forsytes, who believe in none of these things, but turn them all to use, where should we be? My dear sir, the Forsytes are the middlemen, the commercials, the pillars of society, the corner-stones of convention; everything that is admirable!'

'I don't know whether I catch your drift,' said Bosinney, 'but I fancy there are plenty of Forsytes, as you call them, in my profession.'

'Certainly,' replied young Jolyon. 'The great majority of architects, painters, or writers have no principles, like any other Forsytes. Art, literature, religion, survive by virtue of the few cranks who really believe in such things, and the many Forsytes who make a commercial use of them. At a low estimate, three-fourths of our Royal Academicians are Forsytes, seven-eighths of our novelists, a large proportion of the Press. Of science I can't speak; they are magnificently represented in religion; in the House of Commons perhaps more numerous than anywhere; the aristocracy speaks for itself. But I'm not laughing. It is dangerous to go against the majority—and what a majority!' He fixed his eyes on Bosinney: 'It's dangerous to let anything carry you away—a house, a picture, a—woman!'

They looked at each other. And, as though he had done that which no Forsyte did—given himself away, young Jolyon drew into his shell. Bosinney broke the silence.

'Why do you take your own people as the type?' said he.

'My people,' replied young Jolyon, 'are not very extreme, and they have their own private peculiarities, like every other family, but they possess in a remarkable degree those two qualities which are the real tests of a Forsyte—the power of never being able to give yourself up to anything soul and body, and the ''sense of property''.'

Bosinney smiled: 'How about the big one, for instance?'

'Do you mean Swithin?' asked young Jolyon. 'Ah! in Swithin there's something primeval still. The town and middle-class life haven't digested him yet. All the old centuries of farmwork and brute force have settled in him, and there they've stuck, for all he's so distinguished.'

Bosinney seemed to ponder. 'Well, you've hit your cousin Soames off to the life,' he said suddenly. '*He'll* never blow his brains out.'

Young Jolyon shot at him a penetrating glance.

'No,' he said; 'he won't. That's why he's to be reckoned with. Look out for their grip! It's easy to laugh, but don't mistake me. It doesn't do to despise a Forsyte; it doesn't do to disregard them!'

'Yet you've done it yourself!'

Young Jolyon acknowledged the hit by losing his smile.

'You forget,' he said with a queer pride, 'I can hold on, too—I'm a Forsyte myself. We're all in the path of great forces. The man who leaves the shelter of the wall—well—you know what I mean. I don't,' he ended very low, as though uttering a threat, 'recommend every man to—go—my—way. It depends.'

The colour rushed into Bosinney's face, but soon receded, leaving it sallow-brown as before. He gave a short laugh, that left his lips fixed in a queer, fierce smile; his eyes mocked young Jolyon.

'Thanks,' he said. 'It's deuced kind of you. But you're not the only chaps that can hold on.' He rose.

Young Jolyon looked after him as he walked away, and, resting his head on his hand, sighed.

In a drowsy, almost empty room the only sounds were the rustle of news-papers, the scraping of matches being struck. He stayed a long time without moving, living over again those days when he, too, had sat long hours watching the clock, waiting for the minutes to pass—long hours full of the torments of uncertainty, and of a fierce, sweet aching; and the slow, delicious agony of that season came back to him with its old poignancy. The sight of Bosinney, with his haggard face, and his restless eyes always wandering to the clock, had roused in him a pity, with which was mingled strange, irresistible envy.

He knew the signs so well. Whither was he going—to what sort of fate? What kind of woman was it who was drawing him to her by that magnetic force which no consideration of honour, no principle, no interest could withstand; from which the only escape was flight.

Flight! But why should Bosinney fly? A man fled when he was in danger of destroying hearth and home, when there were children, when he felt himself trampling down ideals, breaking something. But here, so he had heard, it was all broken to his hand.

He himself had not fled, nor would he fly if it were all to come over again. Yet he had gone farther than Bosinney, had broken up his own unhappy home, not someone else's. And the old saying came back to him: 'A man's fate lies in his own heart.'

In his own heart! The proof of the pudding was in the eating—Bosinney had still to eat his pudding.

His thoughts passed to the woman whom he did not know, but the outline of whose story he had heard.

An unhappy marriage! No ill-treatment—only that indefinable malaise, that terrible blight which killed all sweetness under Heaven; and so from day to day, from night to night, from week to week, from year to year, till death should end it!

But young Jolyon, the bitterness of whose own feelings time has assuaged, saw Soames's side of the question too. Whence should a man like his cousin, saturated with all the prejudices and beliefs of his class, draw the insight or inspiration necessary to break up this life? It was a question of imagination, of projecting himself into the future beyond the unpleasant gossip, sneers, and tattle that followed on such separations, beyond the passing pangs that the lack of the sight of her would cause, beyond the grave disapproval of the worthy. But few men, and especially few men of Soames's class, had imagination enough for that. A deal of mortals in this world, and not enough imagination to go round! And sweet heaven, what a difference between theory and practice; many a man, perhaps even Soames, held chivalrous views on such matters, who, when the shoe pinched, found a distinguishing factor that made of himself an exception.

Then, too, he distrusted his judgment. He had been through the experience himself, had tasted to the dregs the bitterness of an unhappy marriage, and how could he take the wide and dispassionate view of those who had never been within sound of the battle? His evidence was too first-hand—like the evidence on military matters of a soldier who has been through much active service, against that of civilians who have not suffered the disadvantage of seeing things too close. Most people would consider such a marriage as that of Soames and Irene quite fairly successful; he had money, she had beauty; it was a case for compromise. There was no reason why they should not jog along, even if they hated each other. It would not matter if they went their own ways a little so long as the decencies were observed—the sanctity of the marriage tie, of the common home, respected. Half the marriages of the upper classes were conducted on these lines: Do not offend the susceptibilities of Society; do not offend the susceptibilities of the Church. To avoid offending these is worth the sacrifice of any private feelings. The advantages of the stable home are visible, tangible, so many pieces of property; there is no risk in the *status quo*. To break up a home is at the best a dangerous experiment, and selfish into the bargain.

This was the case for the defence, and young Jolyon sighed.

'The core of it all,' he thought, 'is property, but there are many people who would not like it put that way. To them it is "the sanctity of the marriage tie"; but the sanctity of the marriage tie is dependent on the sanctity of the family, and the sanctity of the family is dependent on the sanctity of property. And yet I imagine all these people are followers of One who never owned anything. It is curious!'

And again young Jolyon sighed.

'Am I going on my way home to ask any poor devils I meet to share my dinner, which will then be too little for myself or, at all events, for my wife, who is necessary to my health and happiness? It may be that after all Soames does well to exercise his rights and support by his practice the sacred principle of property which benefits us all, with the exception of those who—suffer by the process.'

And so he left his chair, threaded his way through the maze of seats, took his hat, and languidly up the hot streets crowded with carriages, reeking with dusty odours, wended his way home.

Before reaching Wistaria Avenue he removed old Jolyon's letter from his pocket, and tearing it carefully into tiny pieces, scattered them in the dust of the road.

He let himself in with his key, and called his wife's name. But she had gone out, taking Jolly and Holly, and the house was empty; alone in the garden the dog Balthasar lay in the shade snapping at flies.

Young Jolyon took his seat there, too, under the pear tree that bore no fruit.

I I

BOSINNEY ON PAROLE

The day after the evening at Richmond Soames returned from Henley by a morning train. Not constitutionally interested in amphibious sports, his visit had been one of business rather than pleasure, a client of some importance having asked him down.

He went straight to the City, but finding things slack, he left at three o'clock, glad of this chance to get home quietly. Irene did not expect him. Not that he had any desire to spy on her actions, but there was no harm in thus unexpectedly surveying the scene.

After changing to Park clothes he went into the drawing-room. She was sitting idly in the corner of the sofa, her favourite seat; and there were circles under her eyes, as though she had not slept.

He asked: 'How is it you're in? Are you expecting somebody?'

'Yes—that is, not particularly.'

'Who?'

'Mr Bosinney said he might come.'

'Bosinney. He ought to be at work.'

To this she made no answer.

'Well,' said Soames, 'I want you to come out to the Stores with me, and after that we'll go to the Park.'

'I don't want to go out; I have a headache.'

Soames replied: 'If ever I want you to do anything, you've always got a headache. It'll do you good to come and sit under the trees.'

She did not answer.

Soames was silent for some minutes; at last he said: 'I don't know what your idea of a wife's duty is. I never have known!'

He had not expected her to reply, but she did.

'I have tried to do what you want; it's not my fault that I haven't been able to put my heart into it.'

'Whose fault is it, then?' He watched her askance.

'Before we were married you promised to let me go if our marriage was not a success. Is it a success?'

Soames frowned.

'Success,' he stammered–'it would be a success if you behaved yourself properly!'

'I have tried,' said Irene. 'Will you let me go?'

Soames turned away. Secretly alarmed, he took refuge in bluster.

'Let you go? You don't know what you're talking about. Let you go? How can I let you go? We're married, aren't we? Then, what are you talking about? For God's sake don't let's have any of this sort of nonsense! Get your hat on and come and sit in the Park.'

'Then, you won't let me go?'

He felt her eyes resting on him with a strange, touching look.

'Let you go!' he said; 'and what on earth would you do with yourself if I did? You've got no money!'

'I could manage somehow.'

He took a swift turn up and down the room; then came and stood before her.

'Understand,' he said, 'once and for all, I won't have you say this sort of thing. Go and get your hat on!'

She did not move.

'I suppose,' said Soames, 'you don't want to miss Bosinney if he comes!'

Irene got up slowly and left the room. She came down with her hat on.

They went out.

In the Park, the motley hour of mid-afternoon, when foreigners and other pathetic folk drive, thinking themselves to be in fashion, had passed; the right, the proper, hour had come, was nearly gone, before Soames and Irene seated themselves under the Achilles statue.

It was some time since he had enjoyed her company in the Park. That was one of the past delights of the first two seasons of his married life, when to feel himself the possessor of this gracious creature before all London had been his greatest, though secret, pride. How many afternoons had he not sat beside her, extremely neat, with light grey gloves and faint, supercilious smile, nodding to acquaintances, and now and again removing his hat!

His light grey gloves were still on his hands, and on his lips his smile sardonic, but where the feeling in his heart?

The seats were emptying fast, but still he kept her there, silent and pale, as though to work out a secret punishment. Once or twice he made some comment, and she bent her head, or answered 'Yes' with a tired smile.

Along the rails a man was walking so fast the people stared after him when he passed.

'Look at that ass!' said Soames; 'he must be mad to walk like that in this heat!'

He turned; Irene had made a rapid movement.

'Hallo!' he said, 'it's our friend the Buccaneer!'

And he sat still, with his sneering smile, conscious that Irene was sitting still, and smiling too.

'Will she bow to him?' he thought.

But she made no sign.

Bosinney reached the end of the rails and came walking back amongst the chairs, quartering his ground like a pointer. When he saw them he stopped dead and raised his hat.

The smile never left Soames's face; he also took off his hat.

Bosinney came up, looking exhausted, like a man after hard physical exercise; the sweat stood in drops on his brow, and Soame's smile seemed to say: 'You've had a trying time, my friend!' . . . 'What are *you* doing in the Park?' he asked. 'We thought you despised such frivolity!'

Bosinney did not seem to hear; he made his answer to Irene: 'I've been round to your place; I hoped I should find you in.'

Somebody tapped Soames on the back, and spoke to him; and in the exchange of those platitudes over his shoulder, he missed her answer and took a resolution.

'We're just going in,' he said to Bosinney; 'you'd better come back to dinner with us.' Into that invitation he put a strange bravado, a stranger pathos: 'You can't deceive me,' his look and voice seemed to be saying, 'but see–I trust you–I'm not afraid of you!'

They started back to Montpelier Street together, Irene between them. In the crowded streets Soames went on in front. He did not listen to their conversation; the strange resolution of trustfulness he had taken seemed to animate even his secret conduct. Like a gambler, he said to himself: 'It's a card I dare not throw away–I must play it for what it's worth. I have not too many chances.'

He dressed slowly, heard her leave her room and go downstairs, and, for full five minutes after, dawdled about in his dressing-room. Then he went down, purposely shutting the door loudly to show that he was coming. He found them standing by the hearth, perhaps talking, perhaps not; he could not say.

He played his part out in the farce, the long evening through–his manner to his guest more friendly than it had ever been before; and when at last Bosinney went, he said: 'You must come again soon; Irene likes to have you to talk about the house!' Again his voice had the strange bravado and the stranger pathos; but his hand was as cold as ice.

Loyal to his resolution, he turned away from their parting, turned away from his wife as she stood under the hanging lamp to say good-night–away from the sight of her golden head shining so under the light, of her smiling mournful lips; away from the sight of Bosinney's eyes looking at her, so like a dog's looking at its master.

And he went to bed with the certainty that Bosinney was in love with his wife.

The summer night was hot, so hot and still that through every opened window came in but hotter air. For long hours he lay listening to her breathing.

She could sleep, but he must lie awake. And, lying awake, he hardened himself to play the part of the serene and trusting husband.

In the small hours he slipped out of bed, and passing into his dressing-room, leaned by the open window.

He could hardly breathe.

A night four years ago came back to him–the night but one before his marriage; as hot and stifling as this.

He remembered how he had lain in a long cane chair in the window of his sitting-room off Victoria Street. Down below in a side street a man had banged at a door, a woman had cried out; he remembered, as thought it were now, the sound of the scuffle, the slam of the door, the dead silence that followed. And then the early water-cart, cleansing the reek of the streets, had approached through the strange-seeming, useless lamp-light; he seemed to hear again its rumble, nearer and nearer, till it passed and slowly died away.

He leaned far out of the dressing-room window, over the little court below, and saw the first light spread. The outlines of dark walls and roofs were blurred for a moment, then came out sharper than before.

He remembered how that other night he had watched the lamps paling all the length of Victoria Street; how he had hurried on his clothes and gone down into the street, down past houses and squares, to the street where she was staying, and there had stood and looked at the front of the little house, as still and grey as the face of a dead man.

And suddenly it shot through his mind, like a sick man's fancy: What's *he* doing?–that fellow who haunts me, who was here this evening, who's in love with my wife–prowling out there, perhaps, looking for her as I know he was looking for her this afternoon; watching my house now, for all I can tell!

He stole across the landing to the front of the house, stealthily drew aside a blind, and raised a window.

The grey light clung about the trees of the square, as though Night, like a great downy moth, had brushed them with her wings. The lamps were still alight, all pale, but not a soul stirred–no living thing in sight!

Yet suddenly, very faint, far off in the deathly stillness, he heard a cry writhing, like the voice of some wandering soul barred out of heaven, and crying for its happiness. There it was again–again! Soames shut the window shuddering.

Then he thought: 'Ah, it's only the peacocks across the water.'

12

JUNE PAYS SOME CALLS

Old Jolyon stood in the narrow hall at Broadstairs inhaling that odour of oilcloth and herrings which permeates all respectable seaside lodging-houses. On a chair–a shiny leather chair, displaying its horse-hair through a hole in the top left-hand corner–stood a black despatch-case. This he was filling with papers, with *The Times*, and a bottle of eau-de-Cologne. He had meetings that day of the 'Globular Gold Concessions' and the 'New Colliery Company, Limited', to which he was going up, for he never missed a Board; to 'miss a Board' would be one more piece of evidence that he was growing old, and this his jealous Forsyte spirit could not bear.

His eyes, as he filled that black despatch-case, looked as if at any moment they might blaze up with anger. So gleams the eye of a schoolboy, baited by a ring of his companions; but he controls himself, deterred by the fearful odds against him. And old Jolyon controlled himself, keeping down, with his masterful restraint now slowly wearing out, the irritation fostered in him by the conditions of his life.

He had received from his son an unpractical letter, in which by rambling generalities the boy seemed trying to get out of answering a plain question. 'I've seen Bosinney,' he said; 'he is not a criminal. The more I see of people the more I am convinced that they are never good or bad—merely comic or pathetic. You probably don't agree with me!'

Old Jolyon did not; he considered it cynical to so express oneself; he had not yet reached that point of old age when even Forsytes, bereft of those illusions and principles which they have cherished carefully for practical purposes but never believed in, bereft of all corporeal enjoyment, stricken to the very heart by having nothing left to hope for—break through the barriers of reserve and say things they would never have believed themselves capable of saying.

Perhaps he did not believe in 'Goodness' and 'Badness' any more than his son; but as he would have said: He didn't know—couldn't tell; there might be something in it; and why, by an unnecessary expression of disbelief, deprive yourself of possible advantage?

Accustomed to spend his holidays among the mountains, though (like a true Forsyte) he had never attempted anything too adventurous or too foolhardy, he had been passionately fond of them. And when the wonderful view (mentioned in Baedeker—'fatiguing but repaying') was disclosed to him after the effort of the climb, he had doubtless felt the existence of some great, dignified principle crowning the chaotic strivings, the petty precipices, and ironic little dark chasms of life. This was as near to religion, perhaps, as his practical spirit had ever gone.

But it was many years since he had been to the mountains. He had taken June there two seasons running, after his wife died, and had realised bitterly that his walking days were over.

To that old mountain-given confidence in a supreme order of things he had long been a stranger.

He knew himself to be old, yet he felt young; and this troubled him. It troubled and puzzled him, too, to think that he, who had always been so careful, should be father and grandfather to such as seemed born to disaster. He had nothing to say against Jo—who could say anything against the boy, an amiable chap?—but his position was deplorable, and this business of June's nearly as bad. It seemed like a fatality, and a fatality was one of those things no man of his character could either understand or put up with.

In writing to his son he did not really hope that anything would come of it. Since the ball at Roger's he had seen too clearly how the land lay—he could put two and two together quicker than most men—and, with the example of his own son before his eyes, knew better than any Forsyte of them all that the pale flame singes men's wings whether they will or no.

In the days before June's engagement, when she and Mrs Soames were always together, he had seen enough of Irene to feel the spell she cast over men. She was not a flirt, not even a coquette—words dear to the heart of his generation, which loved to define things by a good, broad, inadequate word—but she was dangerous. He could not say why. Tell him of a quality innate in some women—a seductive power beyond their own control! He would but answer: 'Humbug!' She was dangerous, and there was an end of it. He wanted to close his eyes to that affair. If it was, it was; *he* did not want to hear any more about it—he only wanted to save June's position and her peace of mind. He still hoped she might once more become a comfort to himself.

And so he had written. He got little enough out of the answer. As to what young Jolyon had made of the interview, there was practically only the queer sentence: 'I gather that he's in the stream.' The stream! What stream? What was this new-fangled way of talking?

He sighed and folded the last of the papers under the flap of the bag; he knew well enough what was meant.

June came out of the dining-room and helped him on with his summer coat. From her costume, and the expression of her little resolute face, he saw at once what was coming.

'I'm going with you,' she said.

'Nonsense, my dear; I go straight into the City. I can't have you racketing about!'

'I must see old Mrs Smeech.'

'Oh, your precious "lame ducks"!' grumbled out old Jolyon. He did not believe her excuse, but ceased his opposition. There was no doing anything with that pertinacity of hers.

At Victoria he put her into the carriage which had been ordered for himself—a characteristic action, for he had no petty selfishness.

'Now, don't you go tiring yourself, my darling,' he said, and took a cab on into the City.

June went first to a back street in Paddington, where Mrs Smeech, her 'lame duck', lived—an aged person, connected with the charring interest; but after half an hour spent in hearing her habitually lamentable recital, and dragooning her into temporary comfort, she went on to Stanhope Gate. The great house was closed and dark.

She had decided to learn something at all costs. It was better to face the worst, and have it over. And this was her plan: To go first to Phil's aunt, Mrs Baynes, and, failing information there, to Irene herself. She had no clear notion of what she would gain by these visits.

At three o'clock she was in Lowndes Square. With a woman's instinct when trouble is to be faced, she had put on her best frock, and went to the battle with a glance as courageous as old Jolyon's itself. Her tremors had passed into eagerness.

Mrs Baynes, Bosinney's aunt (Louisa was her name), was in her kitchen when June was announced, organising the cook, for she was an excellent housewife, and, as Baynes always said, there was 'a lot in a good dinner'. He did his best work after dinner. It was Baynes who built that remarkably fine row of tall crimson houses in Kensington which compete with so many others for the title of 'the ugliest in London'.

On hearing June's name, she went hurriedly to her bedroom, and, taking two large bracelets from a red morocco case in a locked drawer, put them on her white wrists—for she possessed in a remarkable degree that 'sense of property', which, as we know, is the touchstone of Forsyteism, and the foundation of good morality.

Her figure, of medium height and broad build, with a tendency to embonpoint, was reflected by the mirror of her white-wood wardrobe, in a gown made under her own organisation, of one of those half-tints, reminiscent of the distempered walls of corridors in large hotels. She raised her hands to her hair, which she wore *à la* Princesse de Galles, and touched it here and there, settling it more firmly on her head, and her eyes were full of an unconscious realism, as though she were looking in the face one of life's sordid facts, and making the best of it. In youth her cheeks had been of cream and roses, but they were mottled now by middle age, and again that hard, ugly directness came into her eyes as she dabbed a powder-puff across her forehead. Putting the puff down, she stood quite still before the glass, arranging a smile over her high, important nose, her chin (never large, and now growing smaller with the increase of her neck), her thin-lipped, down-drooping mouth. Quickly, not to lose the effect, she grasped her skirts strongly in both hands and went downstairs.

She had been hoping for this visit for some time past. Whispers had reached her that things were not all right between her nephew and his fiancée. Neither of them had been near her for weeks. She had asked Phil to dinner many times; his invariable answer had been 'Too busy'.

Her instinct was alarmed, and the instinct in such matters of this excellent woman was keen. She ought to have been a Forsyte; in young Jolyon's sense of the word, she certainly had that privilege, and merits description as such.

She had married off her three daughters in a way that people said was beyond their deserts, for they had the professional plainness only to be found, as a rule, among the female kind of the more legal callings. Her name was upon the committees of numberless charities connected with the Church—dances, theatricals, or bazaars—and she never lent her name unless sure beforehand that everything had been thoroughly organised.

She believed, as she often said, in putting things on a commercial basis; the proper function of the Church, of charity, indeed, of everything, was to strengthen the fabric of 'Society'. Individual action, therefore, she considered immoral. Organisation was the only thing, for by organisation alone could you feel sure that you were getting a return for your money. Organisation—and again, organisation! And there is no doubt that she was what old Jolyon called her—'a "dab" at that'—he went further, he called her 'a humbug'.

The enterprises to which she lent her name were organised so admirably that by the time the takings were handed over, they were indeed skim milk divested of all cream of human kindness. But as she often justly remarked, sentiment was to be deprecated. She was, in fact, a little academic.

This great and good woman, so highly thought of in ecclesiastical circles, was one of the principal priestesses in the temple of Forsyteism, keeping alive day and night a sacred flame to the God of Property, whose altar is inscribed with those inspiring words: 'Nothing for nothing, and really remarkably little for sixpence.'

When she entered a room it was felt that something substantial had come in, which was probably the reason of her popularity as a patroness. People liked something substantial when they had paid money for it; and they would look at her—surrounded by her staff in charity ballrooms, with her high nose and her broad, square figure, attired in a uniform covered with sequins—as though she were a general.

The only thing against her was that she had not a double name. She was a power in upper middle-class society, with its hundred sets and circles, all intersecting on the common battlefield of charity functions, and on that battlefield brushing skirts so pleasantly with the skirts of Society with the capital 'S'. She was a power in society with the smaller 's', that larger, more significant, and more powerful body, where the commercially Christian institutions, maxims, and 'principle' which Mrs Baynes embodied, were real life blood, circulating freely, real business currency, not merely the sterilised imitation that flowed in the veins of smaller Society with the larger 'S'. People who knew her felt her to be sound—a sound woman, who never gave herself away, nor anything else, if she could possibly help it.

She had been on the worst sort of terms with Bosinney's father, who had not infrequently made her the object of an unpardonable ridicule. She alluded to him now that he was gone as her 'poor, dear, irreverend brother'.

She greeted June with the careful effusion of which she was a mistress, a little afraid of her as far as a woman of her eminence in the commercial and Christian world could be afraid—for so slight a girl June had a great dignity, the fearlessness of her eyes gave her that. And Mrs Baynes, too, shrewdly recognised that behind the uncompromising frankness of June's manner there was much of the Forsytes. If the girl had been merely frank and courageous, Mrs Baynes would have thought her 'cranky', and despised her; if she had been merely a Forsyte, like Francie—let us say—she would have patronised her from sheer weight of metal; but June, small though she was—Mrs Baynes habitually admired quantity—gave her an uneasy feeling; and she placed her in a chair opposite the light.

There was another reason for her respect—which Mrs Baynes, too good a churchwoman to be worldly, would have been the last to admit—she often heard her husband describe old Jolyon as extremely well off, and was biased towards his grand-daughter for the soundest of all reasons. To-day she felt the emotion with which we read a novel describing a hero and an inheritance, nervously anxious lest, by some frightful lapse of the novelist, the young man should be left without it at the end.

Her manner was warm; she had never seen so clearly before how distinguished and desirable a girl this was. She asked after old Jolyon's health. A wonderful man for his age; so upright and young looking, and how old was he? Eighty-one! She would never have thought it! They were at the sea! Very nice for them; she supposed June heard from Phil every day? Her light grey eyes became more prominent as she asked this question; but the girl met the glance without flinching.

'No,' she said, 'he never writes!'

Mrs Baynes's eyes dropped; they had no intention of doing so, but they did. They recovered immediately.

'Of course not. That's Phil all over—he was always like that!'

'Was he?' said June.

The brevity of the answer caused Mrs Baynes's bright smile a moment's hesitation; she disguised it by a quick movement, and spreading her skirts afresh, said: 'Why, my dear—he's quite the most harum-scarum person; one never pays the slightest attention to what *he* does!'

The conviction came suddenly to June that she was wasting her time; even were she to put a question point-blank, she would never get anything out of this woman.

'Do you see him?' she asked, her face crimsoning.

The perspiration broke out on Mrs Baynes's forehead beneath the powder.

'Oh yes! I don't remember when he was here last—indeed, we haven't seen much of him lately. He's so busy with your cousin's house; I'm told it'll be finished directly. We must organise a little dinner to celebrate the event; do come and stay the night with us!'

'Thank you,' said June. Again she thought: 'I'm only wasting my time. This woman will tell me nothing.'

She got up to go. A change came over Mrs Baynes. She rose too; her lips twitched, she fidgeted her hands. Something was evidently very wrong, and she did not dare ask this girl, who stood there, a slim, straight little figure, with her decided face, her set jaw, and resentful eyes. She was not accustomed to be afraid of asking questions—all organisation was based on the asking of questions!

But the issue was so grave that her nerve, normally strong, was fairly shaken; only that morning her husband had said: 'Old Mr Forsyte must be worth well over a hundred thousand pounds!'

And this girl stood there, holding out her hand—holding out her hand!

The chance might be slipping away—she couldn't tell—the chance of keeping her in the family, and yet she dared not speak.

Her eyes followed June to the door.

It closed.

Then with an exclamation Mrs Baynes ran forward, wobbling her bulky frame from side to side, and opened it again.

Too late! She heard the front door click and stood still, an expression of real anger and mortification on her face.

June went along the Square with her bird-like quickness. She detested that woman now—whom in happier days she had been accustomed to think so kind. Was she always to be put off thus, and forced to undergo this torturing suspense?

She would go to Phil himself, and ask him what he meant. She had the right to know. She hurried on down Sloane Street till she came to Bosinney's number. Passing the swing-door at the bottom, she ran up the stairs, her heart thumping painfully.

At the top of the third flight she paused for breath, and holding on to the banisters, stood listening. No sound came from above.

With a very white face she mounted the last flight. She saw the door, with his name on the plate. And the resolution that had brought her so far evaporated.

The full meaning of her conduct came to her. She felt hot all over; the palms of her hands were moist beneath the thin silk covering of her gloves.

She drew back to the stairs, but did not descend. Leaning against the rail she tried to get rid of a feeling of being choked; and she gazed at the door with a sort of dreadful courage. No! she refused to go down. Did it matter what people thought of her? They would never know! No one would help her if she did not help herself! She would go through with it.

Forcing herself, therefore, to leave the support of the wall, she rang the bell. The door did not open, and all her shame and fear suddenly abandoned her; she rang again and again, as though in spite of its emptiness she could drag some response out of that closed room, some recompense for the shame and fear that visit had cost her. It did not open; she left off ringing and, sitting down at the top of the stairs, buried her face in her hands.

Presently she stole down, out into the air. She felt as though she had passed through a bad illness, and had no desire now but to get home as quick as she could. The people she met seemed to know where she had been, what she had been doing; and suddenly—over on the opposite side, going towards his rooms from the direction of Montpelier Square—she saw Bosinney himself.

She made a movement to cross into the traffic. Their eyes met, and he raised his hat. An omnibus passed, obscuring her view; then, from the edge of the pavement, through a gap in the traffic, she saw him walking on.

And June stood motionless, looking after him.

13

PERFECTION OF THE HOUSE

'One mockturtle, clear; one oxtail; two glasses of port.'

In the upper room at French's, where a Forsyte could still get heavy English food, James and his son were sitting down to lunch.

Of all eating-places James liked best to come here; there was something unpretentious, well-flavoured, and filling about it, and though he had been to a certain extent corrupted by the necessity for being fashionable, and the trend of habits keeping pace with an income that *would* increase, he still hankered in quiet City moments after the tasty flesh-pots of his earlier days. Here you were served by hairy English waiters in aprons; there was sawdust on the floor, and three round gilt looking-glasses hung just above the line of sight. They had only recently done away with the cubicles, too, in which you could have your chop, prime chump, with a floury potato, without seeing your neighbours, like a gentleman.

He tucked the top corner of his napkin behind the third button of his waistcoat, a practice he had been obliged to abandon years ago in the West End. He felt that he should relish his soup—the entire morning had been given to winding up the estate of an old friend.

After filling his mouth with household bread, stale, he at once began: 'How are you going down to Robin Hill? You going to take Irene? You'd better take her. I should think there'll be a lot that'll want seeing to.'

Without looking up, Soames answered: 'She won't go.'

'Won't go? What's the meaning of that? She's going to live in the house, isn't she?'

Soames made no reply.

'I don't know what's coming to women nowadays,' mumbled James; 'I never used to have any trouble with them. She's had too much liberty. She's spoiled—'

Soames lifted his eyes. 'I won't have anything said against her,' he said unexpectedly.

The silence was only broken now by the supping of James's soup.

The waiter brought the two glasses of port, but Soames stopped him.

'That's not the way to serve port,' he said; 'take them away and bring the bottle.'

Rousing himself from his reverie over the soup, James took one of his rapid shifting surveys of surrounding facts.

'Your mother's in bed,' he said; 'you can have the carriage to take you down. I should think Irene'd like the drive. This young Bosinney'll be there, I suppose, to show you over?'

Soames nodded.

'I should like to go and see for myself what sort of a job he's made finishing off,' pursued James. 'I'll just drive round and pick you both up.'

'I am going down by train,' replied Soames. 'If you like to drive round and see, Irene might go with you, I can't tell.'

He signed to the waiter to bring the bill, which James paid.

They parted at St Paul's, Soames branching off to the station, James taking his omnibus westwards.

He had secured the corner seat next the conductor, where his long legs made it difficult for anyone to get in, and at all who passed him he looked resentfully, as if they had no business to be using up his air.

He intended to take an opportunity this afternoon of speaking to Irene. A word in time saved nine; and now that she was going to live in the country there was a chance for her to turn over a new leaf! He could see that Soames wouldn't stand very much more of her goings on!

It did not occur to him to define what he meant by her 'goings on'; the expression was wide, vague, and suited to a Forsyte. And James had more than his common share of courage after lunch.

On reaching home, he ordered out the barouche, with special instructions that the groom was to go too. He wished to be kind to her, and to give her every chance.

When the door of No. 62 was opened he could distinctly hear her singing, and said so at once, to prevent any chance of being denied entrance.

Yes, Mrs Soames was in, but the maid did not know if she was seeing people.

James, moving with the rapidity that ever astonished the observers of his long figure and absorbed expression, went forthwith into the drawing-room without permitting this to be ascertained. He found Irene seated at the piano with her hands arrested on the keys, evidently listening to the voices in the hall. She greeted him without smiling.

'Your mother-in-law's in bed,' he began, hoping at once to enlist her sympathy. 'I've got the carriage here. Now, be a good girl and put on your hat and come with me for a drive. It'll do you good!'

Irene looked at him as though about to refuse, but, seeming to change her mind, went upstairs, and came down again with her hat on.

'Where are you going to take me?' she asked.

'We'll just go down to Robin Hill,' said James, spluttering out his words very quick; 'the horses want exercise, and I should like to see what they've been doing down there.'

Irene hung back, but again changed her mind and went out to the carriage, James brooding over her closely, to make quite sure.

It was not before he had got her more than half-way that he began: 'Soames is very fond of you—he won't have anything said against you; why don't you show him more affection?'

Irene flushed, and said in a low voice: 'I can't show what I haven't got.'

James looked at her sharply; he felt that now he had her in his own carriage, with his own horses and servants, he was really in command of the situation. She could not put him off; nor would she make a scene in public.

'I can't think what you're about,' he said. 'He's a very good husband!'

Irene's answer was so low as to be almost inaudible among the sounds of traffic. He caught the words: 'You are not married to him!'

'What's that got to do with it? He's given you everything you want. He's always ready to take you anywhere, and now he's built you this house in the country. It's not as if you had anything of your own.'

'No.'

Again James looked at her; he could not make out the expression on her face. She looked almost as if she were going to cry, and yet—

'I'm sure,' he muttered hastily, 'we've all tried to be kind to you.'

Irene's lips quivered; to his dismay James saw a tear steal down her cheek. He felt a choke rise in his own throat.

'We're all fond of you,' he said, 'if you'd only'—he was going to say, 'behave yourself', but changed it to—'if you'd only be more of a wife to him.'

Irene did not answer, and James, too, ceased speaking. There was something in her silence which disconcerted him; it was not the silence of obstinacy, rather that of acquiescence in all that he could find to say. And yet he felt as if he had not had the last word. He could not understand this.

He was unable, however, to long keep silence.

'I suppose that young Bosinney,' he said, 'will be getting married to June now?'

Irene's face changed. 'I don't know,' she said; 'you should ask *her*.'

'Does she write to you?'

'No.'

'How's that?' said James. 'I thought you and she were such great friends.'

Irene turned on him. 'Again,' she said, 'you should ask *her*!'

'Well,' flustered James, frightened by her look, 'it's very odd that I can't get a plain answer to a plain question, but there it is.'

He sat ruminating over his rebuff, and burst out at last:

'Well, I've warned you. You won't look ahead. Soames, he doesn't say much, but I can see he won't stand a great deal more of this sort of thing. You'll have nobody but yourself to blame, and, what's more, you'll get no sympathy from anybody.'

Irene bent her head with a little smiling bow. 'I am very much obliged to you.'

James did not know what on earth to answer.

The bright hot morning had changed slowly to a grey, oppressive afternoon; a heavy bank of clouds, with the yellow tinge of coming thunder, had risen in the south, and was creeping up. The branches of the trees drooped motionless across the road without the smallest stir of foliage. A faint odour of glue from the heated horses clung in the thick air; the coachman and groom, rigid and unbending, exchanged stealthy murmurs on the box, without ever turning their heads.

To James's great relief they reached the house at last; the silence and impenetrability of this woman by his side, whom he had always thought so soft and mild, alarmed him.

The carriage put them down at the door, and they entered.

The hall was cool, and so still that it was like passing into a tomb; a shudder ran down James's spine. He quickly lifted the heavy leather curtains between the columns into the inner court.

He could not restrain an exclamation of approval.

The decoration was really in excellent taste. The dull ruby tiles that extended from the foot of the walls to the verge of a circular clump of tall iris plants, surrounding in turn a sunken basin of white marble filled with water, were obviously of the best quality. He admired extremely the purple leather curtains drawn along one entire side, framing a huge white-tiled stove. The central partitions of the skylight had been slid back, and the warm air from outside penetrated into the very heart of the house.

He stood, his hands behind him, his head bent back on his high, narrow shoulders, spying the tracery on the columns and the pattern of the frieze which ran round the ivory-coloured walls under the gallery. Evidently, no pains had been spared. It was quite the house of a gentleman. He went up to the curtains and, having discovered how they were worked, drew them asunder and disclosed the picture-gallery, ending in a great window taking up the whole end of the room. It had a black oak floor, and its walls, again, were of ivory white. He went on throwing open doors and peeping in. Everything was in apple-pie order, ready for immediate occupation.

He turned round at last to speak to Irene, and saw her standing over in the garden entrance, with her husband and Bosinney.

Though not remarkable for sensibility, James felt at once that something was wrong. He went up to them, and, vaguely alarmed, ignorant of the nature of the trouble, made an attempt to smooth things over.

'How are you, Mr Bosinney?' he said, holding out his hand. 'You've been spending money pretty freely down here, I should say!'

Soames turned his back and walked away. James looked from Bosinney's frowning face to Irene's, and, in his agitation, spoke his thoughts aloud: 'Well, I can't tell what's the matter. Nobody tells me anything! And, making off after his son, he heard Bosinney's short laugh, and his: 'Well, thank God! You look so–' Most unfortunately he lost the rest.

What had happened? He glanced back. Irene was very close to the architect, and her face not like the face he knew of her. He hastened up to his son.

Soames was pacing the picture-gallery.

'What's the matter?' said James. 'What's all this?' Soames looked at him with his supercilious calm unbroken, but James knew well enough that he was violently angry.

'Our friend,' he said, 'has exceeded his instructions again, that's all. So much the worse for him this time.'

He turned round and walked back towards the door. James followed hurriedly, edging himself in front. He saw Irene take her finger from before her lips, heard her say something in her ordinary voice, and began to speak before he reached them:

'There's a storm coming on. We'd better get home. We can't take you, I suppose, Mr Bosinney? No, I suppose not. Then, good-bye!' He held out his hand. Bosinney did not take it, but, turning with a laugh, said:

'Good-bye, Mr Forsyte. Don't get caught in the storm!' and walked away.

'Well,' began James, 'I don't know–'

But the sight of Irene's face stopped him. Taking hold of his daughter-in-law by the elbow, he escorted her towards the carriage. He felt certain, quite certain, they had been making some appointment or other. . . .

Nothing in this world is more sure to upset a Forsyte than the discovery that something on which he has stipulated to spend a certain sum has cost more. And this is reasonable, for upon the accuracy of his estimates the whole policy of his life is ordered. If he cannot rely on definite values of property, his compass is amiss; he is adrift upon bitter waters without a helm.

After writing to Bosinney in the terms that have already been chronicled, Soames had dismissed the cost of the house from his mind. He believed that he had made the matter of the final cost so very plain that the possibility of its being again exceeded had really never entered his head. On hearing from Bosinney that his limit of twelve thousand pounds would be exceeded by something like four hundred, he had grown white with anger. His original estimate of the cost of the house completed had been ten thousand pounds, and he had often blamed himself severely for allowing himself to be led into repeated excesses. Over this last expenditure, however, Bosinney had put himself completely in the wrong. How on earth a fellow could make such an ass of himself Soames could not conceive; but he had done so, and all the rancour and hidden jealousy that had been burning against him for so long was now focused in rage at this crowning piece of extravagance. The attitude of the confident and friendly husband was gone. To preserve property–his wife–he had assumed it, to preserve property of another kind he lost it now.

'Ah!' he had said to Bosinney when he could speak, 'and I suppose you're perfectly contented with yourself. But I may as well tell you that you've altogether mistaken your man!'

What he meant by those words he did not quite know at the time, but after dinner he looked up the correspondence between himself and Bosinney to make quite sure. There could be no two opinions about it–the fellow had made himself liable for that extra four hundred, or, at all events, for three hundred and fifty of it, and he would have to make it good.

He was looking at his wife's face when he came to this conclusion. Seated in her usual seat on the sofa, she was altering the lace on a collar. She had not once spoken to him all the evening.

He went up to the mantelpiece, and contemplating his face in the mirror, said: 'Your friend the Buccaneer has made a fool of himself; he will have to pay for it!'

She looked at him scornfully, and answered: 'I don't know what you are talking about!'

'You soon will. A mere trifle, quite beneath your contempt–four hundred pounds.'

'Do you mean that you are going to make him pay that towards this hateful house?'

'I do.'

'And you know he's got nothing?'

'Yes.'

'Then you are meaner than I thought you.'

Soames turned from the mirror, and unconsciously taking a china cup from the mantelpiece, clasped his hands around it, as though praying. He saw her bosom rise and fall, her eyes darkening with anger, and taking no notice of the taunt, he asked quietly:

'Are you carrying on a flirtation with Bosinney?'

'No, I am not!'

Her eyes met his, and he looked away. He neither believed nor disbelieved her, but he knew that he had made a mistake in asking; he never had known, never would know, what she was thinking. The sight of her inscrutable face, the thought of all the hundreds of evenings he had seen her sitting there like that soft and passive, but so unreadable, unknown, enraged him beyond measure.

'I believe you are made of stone,' he said, clenching his fingers so hard that he broke the fragile cup. The pieces fell into the grate. And Irene smiled.

'You seem to forget,' she said, 'that cup is not!'

Soames gripped her arm. 'A good beating,' he said, 'is the only thing that would bring you to your senses,' but turning on his heel, he left the room.

14

SOAMES SITS ON THE STAIRS

Soames went upstairs that night with the feeling that he had gone too far. He was prepared to offer excuses for his words.

He turned out the gas still burning in the passage outside their room. Pausing, with his hand on the knob of the door, he tried to shape his apology, for he had no intention of letting her see that he was nervous.

But the door did not open, nor when he pulled it and turned the handle firmly. She must have locked it for some reason, and forgotten.

Entering his dressing-room, where the gas was also alight and burning slowly, he went quickly to the other door. That too was locked. Then he noticed that the camp-bed which he occasionally used was prepared, and his sleeping-suit laid out upon it. He put his hand up to his forehead and brought it away wet. It dawned on him that he was barred out.

He went back to the door, and rattling the handle stealthily, called: 'Unlock the door, do you hear. Unlock the door!'

There was a faint rustling, but no answer.

'Do you hear? Let me in at once—I insist on being let in!'

He could catch the sound of her breathing close to the door, like the breathing of a creature threatened by danger.

There was something terrifying in his inexorable silence, in the impossibility of getting at her. He went back to the other door, and putting his whole weight against it, tried to burst it open. The door was a new one—he had had them renewed himself, in readiness for their coming in after the honeymoon. In a rage he lifted his foot to kick in the panel; the thought of the servants restrained him, and he felt suddenly that he was beaten.

Flinging himself down in the dressing-room, he took up a book.

But instead of the print he seemed to see his wife—with her yellow hair flowing over her bare shoulders, and her great dark eyes—standing like an animal at bay. And the whole meaning of her act of revolt came to him. She meant it to be for good.

He could not sit still, and went to the door again. He could still hear her, and he called: 'Irene! Irene!'

He did not mean to make his voice pathetic. In ominous answer, the faint sounds ceased. He stood with clenched hands, thinking.

Presently he stole round on tiptoe, and running suddenly at the other door, made a supreme effort to break it open. It creaked, but did not yield. He sat down on the stairs and buried his face in his hands.

For a long time he sat there in the dark, the moon through the skylight above laying a pale smear that lengthened slowly towards him down the stairway. He tried to be philosophical.

Since she had locked her doors she had no further claim as wife and he would console himself with other women!

It was but a spectral journey he made among such delights—he had no appetite for these exploits. He had never had much, and he had lost the habit. He felt that he could never recover it. His hunger could only be appeased by his wife, inexorable and frightened, behind these shut doors. No other woman could help him.

This conviction came to him with terrible force out there in the dark.

His philosophy left him; and surly anger took its place. Her conduct was immoral, inexcusable, worthy of any punishment within his power. He desired no one but her, and she refused him!

She must really hate him, then! He had never believed it yet. He did not believe it now. It seemed to him incredible. He felt as though he had lost for ever his power of judgment. If she, so soft and yielding as he had always judged her, could take this decided step—what could not happen?

Then he asked himself again if she were carrying on an intrigue with Bosinney. He did not believe that she was; he could not afford to believe such a reason for her conduct—the thought was not to be faced.

It would be unbearable to contemplate the necessity of making his marital relations public property. Short of the most convincing proofs he must still refuse to believe, for he did not wish to punish himself. And all the time at heart—he *did* believe.

The moonlight cast a greyish tinge over his figure, hunched against the staircase wall.

Bosinney was in love with her! He hated the fellow, and would not spare him now. He could and would refuse to pay a penny piece over twelve thousand and fifty pounds—the extreme limit fixed in the correspondence; or rather he would pay, he would pay and sue him for damages. He would go to Jobling and Boulter and put the matter in their hands. He would ruin the impecunious beggar! And suddenly—though what connection between the thoughts?—he reflected that Irene had no money either. They were both beggars. This gave him a strange satisfaction.

The silence was broken by a faint creaking through the wall. She was going to bed at last. Ah! Joy and pleasant dreams! If she threw the door open wide he would not go in now!

But his lips, that were twisted in a bitter smile, twitched; he covered his eyes with his hands. . . .

It was late the following afternoon when Soames stood in the dining-room window gazing gloomily into the Square.

The sunlight still showered on the plane trees, and in the breeze their gay broad leaves shone and swung in rhyme to a barrel-organ at the corner. It was playing a waltz, an old waltz that was out of fashion, with a fateful rhythm in the notes; and it went on and on, though nothing indeed but leaves danced to the tune.

The woman did not look too gay, for she was tired; and from the tall houses no one threw her down coppers. She moved the organ on, and three doors off began again.

It was the waltz they had played at Roger's when Irene had danced with Bosinney; and the perfume of the gardenias she had worn came back to Soames, drifted by the malicious music, as it had been drifted to him then, when she passed, her hair glistening, her eyes so soft, drawing Bosinney on and on down an endless ballroom.

The organ woman plied her handle slowly; she had been grinding her tune all day—grinding it in Sloane Street hard by, grinding it perhaps to Bosinney himself.

Soames turned, took a cigarette from the carven box, and walked back to the window. The tune had mesmerised him, and there came into his view Irene, her sunshade furled, hastening homewards down the Square, in a soft, rose-coloured blouse with drooping sleeves that he did not know. She stopped before the organ, took out her purse, and gave the woman money.

Soames shrank back and stood where he could see into the hall.

She came in with her latch-key, put down her sunshade, and stood looking at herself in the glass. Her cheeks were flushed as if the sun had burned them; her lips were parted in a smile. She stretched her arms out as though to embrace herself, with a laugh that for all the world was like a sob.

Soames stepped forward.

'Very—pretty!' he said.

But as though shot she spun round, and would have passed him up the stairs. He barred the way.

'Why such a hurry?' he said, and his eyes fastened on a curl of hair fallen loose across her ear.

He hardly recognised her. She seemed on fire, so deep and rich the colour of her cheeks, her eyes, her lips, and of the unusual blouse she wore.

She put up her hand and smoothed back the curl. She was breathing fast and deep, as though she had been running, and with every breath perfume seemed to come from her hair, and from her body, like perfume from an opening flower.

'I don't like that blouse,' he said slowly, 'it's a soft, shapeless thing!'

He lifted his finger towards her breast, but she dashed his hand aside.

'Don't touch me!' she cried.

He caught her wrist; she wrenched it away.

'And where may you have been?' he asked.

'In heaven—out of this house!' With those words she fled upstairs.

Outside—in thanksgiving—at the very door, the organ-grinder was playing the waltz.

And Soames stood motionless. What prevented him from following her?

Was it that, with the eyes of faith, he saw Bosinney looking down from that high window in Sloane Street, straining his eyes for yet another glimpse of Irene's vanished figure, cooling his flushed face, dreaming of the moment when she flung herself on his breast—the scent of her still in the air around, and the sound of her laugh that was like a sob.

PART III

I

MRS MACANDER'S EVIDENCE

Many people, no doubt, including the editor of the *Ultra Vivisectionist*, then in the bloom of its first youth, would say that Soames was less than a man not to have removed the locks from his wife's doors, and after beating her soundly resumed wedded happiness.

Brutality is not so deplorably diluted by humaneness as it used to be, yet a sentimental segment of the population may still be relieved to learn that he did none of these things. For active brutality is not popular with Forsytes; they are too circumspect, and, on the whole, too soft-hearted. And in Soames there was some common pride, not sufficient to make him do a really generous action, but enough to prevent his indulging in an extremely mean one, except, perhaps, in very hot blood. Above all this true Forsyte refused to feel himself ridiculous. Short of actually beating his wife, he perceived nothing to be done; he therefore accepted the situation without another word.

Throughout the summer and autumn he continued to go to the office, to sort his pictures and ask his friends to dinner.

He did not leave town; Irene refused to go away. The house at Robin Hill, finished though it was, remained empty and ownerless. Soames had brought a suit against the Buccaneer, in which he claimed from him the sum of three hundred and fifty pounds.

A firm of solicitors, Messrs Freak and Able, had put in a defence on Bosinney's behalf. Admitting the facts, they raised a point on the correspondence which, divested of legal phraseology, amounted to this: To speak of 'a *free* hand in the terms of this correspondence' is an Irish bull.

By a chance, fortuitous but not improbable in the close borough of legal circles, a good deal of information came to Soames's ear anent this line of policy, the working partner in his firm, Bustard, happening to sit next at dinner at Walmisley's, the Taxing Master, to young Chankery, of the Common Law Bar.

The necessity for talking what is known as 'shop', which comes on all lawyers with the removal of the ladies, caused Chankery, a young and promising advocate, to propound an impersonal conundrum to his neighbour, whose name he did not know, for, seated as he permanently was in the background, Bustard had practically no name.

He had, said Chankery, a case coming on with a 'very nice point'. He then explained, preserving every professional discretion, the riddle in Soames's case. Everyone, he said, to whom he had spoken, thought it a nice point. The issue was small unfortunately, 'though d—d serious for his client, he believed'–Walmisley's champagne was bad but plentiful–a judge would make short work of it, he was afraid. He intended to make a big effort–the point was a nice one. What did his neighbour say?

Bustard, a model of secrecy, said nothing. He related the incident to Soames, however, with some malice, for this quiet man was capable of human feeling, ending with his own opinion that the point *was* 'a very nice one'.

In accordance with his resolve, our Forsyte had put his interests into the hands of Jobling and Boulter. From the moment of doing so he regretted that he had not acted for himself. On receiving a copy of Bosinney's defence, he went over to their offices.

Boulter, who had the matter in hand, Jobling having died some years before, told him that in his opinion it was rather a nice point; he would like counsel's opinion on it.

Soames told him to go to a good man, and they went to Waterbuck, Q.C., marking him ten and one, who kept the papers six weeks and then wrote as follows:

'In my opinion, the true interpretation of this correspondence depends very much on the intention of the parties, and will turn upon the evidence given at the trial. I am of opinion than an attempt should be made to secure from the architect an admission that he understood he was not to spend at the outside more than twelve thousand and fifty pounds. With regard to the expression, "a free hand in the terms of this correspondence", to which my attention is directed, the point is a nice one; but I am of opinion that upon the whole the ruling in "Boileau *v.* The Blasted Cement Co., Ltd." will apply.'

Upon this opinion they acted, administering interrogatories, but to their annoyance Messrs Freak and Able answered these in so masterly a fashion that nothing whatever was admitted, and that without prejudice.

It was on October 1 that Soames read Waterbuck's opinion, in the dining-room before dinner. It made him nervous; not so much because of the case of 'Boileau *v.* The Blasted Cement Co., Ltd.', as that the point had lately begun to seem to him, too, a nice one; there was about it just that pleasant flavour of subtlety so attractive to the best legal appetites. To have his own impression confirmed by Waterbuck, Q.C., would have disturbed any man.

He sat thinking it over, and staring at the empty grate, for though autumn had come, the weather kept as gloriously fine that year as though it were still high August. It was not pleasant to be disturbed; he desired too passionately to set his foot on Bosinney's neck.

Though he had not seen the architect since the last afternoon at Robin Hill, he was never free from the sense of his presence–never free from the memory of his worn face with its high cheekbones and enthusiastic eyes. It would not be too much to say that he had never got rid of the feeling of that night when he heard the peacock's cry at dawn–the feeling that Bosinney haunted the house. And every man's shape that he saw in the dark evenings walking past, seemed that of him whom George had so appropriately named the Buccaneer.

Irene still met him, he was certain; where, or how, he neither knew, nor asked, deterred by a vague and secret dread of too much knowledge. It all seemed subterranean nowadays.

Sometimes when he questioned his wife as to where she had been, which he still made a point of doing, as every Forsyte should, she looked very strange. Her self-possession was wonderful, but there were moments when, behind the mask of her face, inscrutable as it had always been to him, lurked an expression he had never been used to see there.

She had taken to lunching out too; when he asked Bilson if her mistress had been in to lunch, as often as not she would answer: 'No, sir.'

He strongly disapproved of her gadding about by herself, and told her so. But she took no notice. There was something that angered, amazed, yet almost amused, him about the calm way in which she disregarded his wishes. It was really as if she were hugging to herself the thought of a triumph over him.

He rose from the perusal of Waterbuck, Q.C.'s opinion, and, going upstairs, entered her room, for she did not lock her doors till bed-time—she had the decency, he found, to save the feelings of the servants. She was brushing her hair, and turned to him with strange fierceness.

'What do you want?' she said. 'Please leave my room!'

He answered: 'I want to know how long this state of things between us is to last? I have put up with it long enough.'

'Will you please leave my room?'

'Will you treat me as your husband?'

'No.'

'Then I shall take steps to make you.'

'Do!'

He stared, amazed at the calmness of her answer. Her lips were compressed in a thin line; her hair lay in fluffy masses on her bare shoulders, in all its strange golden contrast to her dark eyes—those eyes alive with the emotions of fear, hate, contempt, and odd, haunting triumph.

'Now, please, will you leave my room?'

He turned round and went sulkily out.

He knew very well that he had no intention of taking steps, and he saw that she knew too—knew that he was afraid to.

It was a habit with him to tell her the doings of his day: how such and such clients had called; how he had arranged a mortgage for Parkes; how that long-standing suit of Fryer *v.* Forsyte was getting on, which, arising in the preternaturally careful disposition of his property by his great-uncle Nicholas, who had tied it up so that no one could get at it at all, seemed likely to remain a source of income for several solicitors till the Day of Judgment.

And how he had called in at Jobson's, and seen a Boucher sold, which he had just missed buying of Talleyrand and Sons in Pall Mall.

He had an admiration for Boucher, Watteau, and all that school. It was a habit with him to tell her all these matters, and he continued to do it even now, talking for long spells at dinner, as though by the volubility of words he could conceal from himself the ache in his heart.

Often, if they were alone, he made an attempt to kiss her when she said good-night. He may have had some vague notion that some night she would let him; or perhaps only the feeling that a husband ought to kiss his wife. Even if she hated him, he at all events ought not to put himself in the wrong by neglecting this ancient rite.

And why did she hate him? Even now he could not altogether believe it. It was strange to be hated!—the emotion was too extreme; yet he hated Bosinney, that Buccaneer, that prowling vagabond, that night-wanderer. For in his thoughts Soames always saw him lying in wait—wandering. Ah, but he must be in very low water! Young Burkitt, the architect, had seen him coming out of a third-rate restaurant, looking terribly down in the mouth!

During all the hours he lay awake, thinking over the situation, which seemed to have no end—unless she should suddenly come to her senses—never once did the thought of separating from his wife seriously enter his head. . . .

And the Forsytes! What part did they play in this stage of Soames's subterranean tragedy?

Truth to say, little or none, for they were at the sea.

From hotels, hydropathics, or lodging-houses, they were bathing daily; laying in a stock of ozone to last them through the winter.

Each section, in the vineyard of its own choosing, grew and culled and pressed and bottled the grapes of a pet sea air.

The end of September began to witness their several returns.

In rude health and small omnibuses, with considerable colour in their cheeks, they arrived daily from the various termini. The following morning saw them back at their vocations.

On the next Sunday Timothy's was thronged from lunch till dinner.

Amongst other gossip, too numerous and interesting to relate, Mrs Septimus Small mentioned that Soames and Irene had not been away.

It remained for a comparative outsider to supply the next evidence of interest.

It chanced that one afternoon late in September, Mrs MacAnder, Winifred Dartie's greatest friend, taking a constitutional, with young Augustus Flippard, on her bicycle in Richmond Park, passed Irene and Bosinney walking from the bracken towards the Sheen Gate.

Perhaps the poor little woman was thirsty, for she had ridden long on a hard, dry road, and, as all London knows, to ride a bicycle and talk to young Flippard will try the toughest constitution; or perhaps the sight of the cool bracken grove, whence 'those two' were coming down, excited her envy. The cool bracken grove on the top of the hill, with the oak boughs for roof, where the pigeons were raising an endless wedding hymn, and the autumn, humming, whispered to the ears of lovers in the fern, while the deer stole by. The bracken grove of irretrievable delights, of golden minutes in the long marriage of heaven and earth! The bracken grove, sacred to stags, to strange tree-stump fawns leaping around the silver whiteness of a birch-tree nymph at summer dusk!

This lady knew all the Forsytes, and having been at June's 'at home', was not at a loss to see with whom she had to deal. Her own marriage, poor thing, had not been successful, but having had the good sense and ability to force her husband into pronounced error, she herself has passed through the necessary divorce proceedings without incurring censure.

She was therefore a judge of all that sort of thing, and lived in one of those large buildings, where in small sets of apartments, are gathered incredible quantities of Forsytes, whose chief recreation out of business hours is the discussion of each other's affairs.

Poor little woman, perhaps she was thirsty, certainly she was bored, for Flippard was a wit. To see 'those two' in so unlikely a spot was quite a merciful 'pick-me-up'.

At the MacAnder, like all London, Time pauses.

This small but remarkable woman merits attention; her all-seeing eye and shrewd tongue were inscrutably the means of furthering the ends of Providence.

With an air of being in at the death, she had an almost distressing power of taking care of herself. She had done more, perhaps, in her way than any woman about town to destroy the sense of chivalry which still clogs the wheel of civilisation. So smart she was, and spoken of endearingly as 'the little MacAnder'!

Dressing tightly and well, she belonged to a Women's Club, but was by no means the neurotic and dismal type of member who was always thinking of her rights. She took her rights unconsciously, they came natural to her, and she knew exactly how to make the most of them without exciting anything but admiration amongst that great class to whom she was affiliated, not precisely perhaps by manner, but by birth, breeding, and the true, the secret gauge, a sense of property.

The daughter of a Bedfordshire solicitor, by the daughter of a clergyman, she had never, through all the painful experience of being married to a very mild painter with a cranky love of Nature, who had deserted her for an actress, lost touch with her requirements, beliefs, and inner feeling of Society; and, on attaining her liberty, she placed herself without effort in the very thick of Forsyteism.

Always in good spirits, and 'full of information', she was universally welcomed. She excited neither surprise nor disapprobation when encountered on the Rhine or at Zermatt, either alone or travelling with a lady and two gentlemen; it was felt that she was perfectly capable of taking care of herself; and the hearts of all Forsytes warmed to that wonderful instinct, which enabled her to enjoy everything without giving anything away. It was generally felt that to such women as Mrs MacAnder should we look for the perpetuation and increase of our best type of woman. She had never had any children.

If there was one thing more than another that she could not stand it was one of those soft woman with what men called 'charm' about them, and for Mrs Soames she always had an especial dislike.

Obscurely, no doubt, she felt that if charm were once admitted as the criterion, smartness and capability must go to the wall; and she hated—with a hatred the deeper that at times this so-called charm seemed to disturb all calculations—the subtle seductiveness which she could not altogether overlook in Irene.

She said, however, that she could see nothing in the woman—there was no 'go' about her—she would never be able to stand up for herself—anyone could take advantage of her, that was plain—she could not see, in fact, what men found to admire!

She was not really ill-natured, but, in maintaining her position after the trying circumstances of her married life, she had found it so necessary to be 'full of information', that the idea of holding her tongue about 'those two' in the Park never occurred to her.

And it so happened that she was dining that very evening at Timothy's, where she went sometimes to 'cheer the old things up', as she was wont to put it. The same people were always asked to meet her: Winifred Dartie and her husband; Francie, because she belonged to the artistic circles, for Mrs MacAnder was known to contribute articles on dress to 'The Ladies Kingdom Come'; and for her to flirt with, provided they could be obtained, two of the Hayman boys, who, though they never said anything, were believed to be fast and thoroughly intimate with all that was latest in smart Society.

At twenty-five minutes past seven she turned out the electric light in her little hall, and wrapped in her opera cloak with the chinchilla collar, came out into the corridor, pausing a moment to make sure she had her latch-key. These little self-contained flats were convenient; to be sure, she had no light and no air, but she could shut it up whenever she liked and go away. There was no bother with servants, and she never felt tied as she used to when poor, dear Fred was always about, in his mooney way. She retained no rancour against poor dear Fred, he was such a fool; but the thought of that actress drew from her, even now, a little bitter, derisive smile.

Firmly snapping the door to, she crossed the corridor, with its gloomy, yellow-ochre walls, and its infinite vista of brown, numbered doors. The lift was going down; and wrapped to the ears in the high cloak, with every one of her auburn hairs in its place, she waited motionless for it to stop at her floor. The iron gates clanked open; she entered. There were already three occupants, a man in a great white waistcoat, with a large, smooth face like a baby's, and two old ladies in black, with mittened hands.

Mrs MacAnder smiled at them; she knew everybody; and all these three, who had been admirably silent before, began to talk at once. This was Mrs MacAnder's successful secret. She provoked conversation.

Throughout a descent of five storeys the conversation continued, the lift-boy standing with his back turned, his cynical face protruding through the bars.

At the bottom they separated, the man in the white waistcoat sentimentally to the billiard-room, the old ladies to dine and say to each other: 'A dear little woman!' 'Such a rattle!' and Mrs MacAnder to her cab.

When Mrs MacAnder dined at Timothy's, the conversation (although Timothy himself could never be induced to be present) took that wider, man-of-the-world tone current among Forsytes at large, and this, no doubt, was what put her at a premium there.

Mrs Small and Aunt Hester found it an exhilarating change. 'If only,' they said, 'Timothy would meet her!' It was felt that she would do him good. She could tell you, for instance, the latest story of Sir Charles Fiste's son at Monte Carlo; who was the real heroine of Tynemouth Eddy's fashionable novel that everyone was holding up their hands over, and what they were doing in Paris about wearing bloomers. She was so sensible, too, knowing all about that vexed question, whether to send young Nicholas's eldest into the navy as his mother wished, or make him an accountant, as his father thought would be safer. She strongly deprecated the navy. If you were not exceptionally brilliant or exceptionally well connected, they passed you over so disgracefully, and what was it after all to look forward to, even if you became an admiral–a pittance! An accountant had more chances, but let him be put with a good firm, where there was no risk at starting!

Sometimes she would give them a tip on the Stock Exchange; not that Mrs Small or Aunt Hester ever took it. They had indeed no money to invest; but it seemed to bring them into such exciting touch with the realities of life. It was an event. They would ask Timothy, they said. But they never did, knowing in advance that it would upset him. Surreptitiously, however, for weeks after they would look in that paper, which they took with respect on account of its really fashionable proclivities, to see whether 'Bright's Rubies' or 'The Woollen Mackintosh Company' were up or down. Sometimes they could not find the name of the company at all; and they would wait until James or Roger or even Swithin came in, and ask them in voices trembling with curiosity how that 'Bolivia Lime and Speltrate' was doing–they could not find it in the paper.

And Roger would answer: 'What do you want to know for? Some trash! You'll go burning your fingers–investing your money in lime, and things you know nothing about! Who told you?' and ascertaining what they had been told, he would go away and, making inquiries in the City, would perhaps invest some of his own money in the concern.

It was about the middle of dinner, just, in fact, as the saddle of mutton had been brought in by Smither, that Mrs MacAnder, looking airily round, said: 'Oh! and whom do you think I passed today in Richmond Park? You'll never guess—Mrs Soames and—Mr Bosinney. They must have been down to look at the house!'

Winifred Dartie coughed, and no one said a word. It was the piece of evidence they had all unconsciously been waiting for.

To do Mrs MacAnder justice, she had been to Switzerland and the Italian lakes with a party of three, and had not heard of Soames's rupture with his architect. She could not tell, therefore, the profound impression her words would make.

Upright and a little flushed, she moved her small, shrewd eyes from face to face, trying to gauge the effect of her words. On either side of her a Hayman boy, his lean, taciturn, hungry face turned towards his plate, ate his mutton steadily.

These two, Giles and Jesse, were so alike and so inseparable that they were known as the Dromios. They never talked, and seemed always completely occupied in doing nothing. It was popularly supposed that they were cramming for an important examination. They walked without hats for long hours in the gardens attached to their house, books in their hands, a fox-terrier at their heels, never saying a word, and smoking all the time. Every morning, about fifty yards apart, they trotted down Campden Hill on two lean hacks, with legs as long as their own, and every morning about an hour later, still fifty yards apart, they cantered up again. Every evening, wherever they had dined, they might be observed about half-past ten, leaning over the balustrade of the Alhambra promenade.

They were never seen otherwise than together; in this way passing their lives, apparently perfectly content.

Inspired by some dumb stirring within them of the feelings of gentlemen, they turned at this painful moment to Mrs MacAnder, and said in precisely the same voice: 'Have you seen the—?'

Such was her surprise at being thus addressed that she put down her fork; and Smither, who was passing, promptly removed her plate. Mrs MacAnder, however, with presence of mind, said instantly: 'I must have a little more of that nice mutton.'

But afterwards in the drawing-room she sat down by Mrs Small, determined to get to the bottom of the matter. And she began:

'What a charming woman, Mrs Soames; such a sympathetic temperament! Soames is a really lucky man!'

Her anxiety for information had not made sufficient allowance for that inner Forsyte skin which refuses to share its troubles with outsiders; Mrs Septimus Small, drawing herself up with a creak and rustle of her whole person, said, shivering in her dignity:

'My dear, it is a subject we do not talk about!'

2

NIGHT IN THE PARK

Although with her infallible instinct Mrs Small had said the very thing to make her guest 'more intriguée than ever', it is difficult to see how else she could truthfully have spoken.

It was not a subject which the Forsytes could talk about even among themselves—to use the word Soames had invented to characterise to himself the situation, it was 'subterranean'.

Yet, within a week of Mrs MacAnder's encounter in Richmond Park, to all of them—save Timothy, from whom it was carefully kept—to James on his domestic beat from the Poultry to Park Lane, to George the wild one, on his daily adventure from the bow window at the Haversnake to the billiard-room at the 'Red Pottle', was it known that 'those two' had gone to extremes.

George (it was he who invented many of those striking expressions still current in fashionable circles) voiced the sentiment more accurately than anyone when he said to his brother Eustace that 'the Buccaneer' was 'going it'; he expected Soames was about 'fed up'.

It was felt that he must be, and yet, what could be done? He ought perhaps to take steps; but to take steps would be deplorable.

Without an open scandal which they could not see their way to recommending, it was difficult to see what steps could be taken. In this impasse, the only thing was to say nothing to Soames, and nothing to each other; in fact, to pass it over.

By displaying towards Irene a dignified coldness, some impression might be made upon her; but she was seldom now to be seen, and there seemed a slight difficulty in seeking her out on purpose to show her coldness. Sometimes in the privacy of his bedroom James would reveal to Emily the real suffering that his son's misfortune caused him.

'*I* can't tell,' he would say; 'it worries me out of my life. There'll be a scandal, and that'll do him no good. I shan't say anything to him. There might be nothing in it. What do you think? She's very artistic, they tell me. What? Oh, you're a 'regular Juley'! Well, I don't know; I expect the worst. This is what comes of having no children. I knew how it would be from the first. They never told me they didn't mean to have any children—nobody tells me anything!'

On his knees by the side of the bed, his eyes open and fixed with worry, he would breathe into the counterpane. Clad in his nightshirt, his neck poked forward, his back rounded, he resembled some long white bird.

'Our Father—' he repeated, turning over and over again the thought of this possible scandal.

Like old Jolyon, he, too, at the bottom of his heart set the blame of the tragedy down to family interference. What business had that lot—he began to think of the Stanhope Gate branch, including young Jolyon and his daughter, as 'that lot'—to introduce a person like this Bosinney into the family? (He had heard George's soubriquet, 'The Buccaneer', but he could make nothing of that—the young man was an architect.)

He began to feel that his brother Jolyon, to whom he had always looked up and on whose opinion he had relied, was not quite what he had expected.

Not having his eldest brother's force of character, he was more sad than angry. His great comfort was to go to Winifred's, and take the little Darties in his carriage over to Kensington Gardens, and there, by the Round Pond, he could often be seen walking with his eyes fixed anxiously on little Publius Dartie's sailing-boat, which he had himself freighted with a penny, as though convinced that it would never again come to shore; while little Publius—who James delighted to say was not a bit like his father—skipping along under his lee, would try to get him to bet another that it never would, having found that it always did. And James would make the bet; he always paid—sometimes as many as three or four pennies in the afternoon, for the game seemed never to pall on little Publius—and always in paying he said: 'Now, that's for your money-box. Why, you're getting quite a rich man!' The thought of his little grandson's growing wealth was a real pleasure to him. But little Publius knew a sweet-shop, and a trick worth two of that.

And they would walk home across the Park, James's figure, with high shoulders and absorbed and worried face, exercising its tall, lean protectorship, pathetically unregarded, over the robust child-figures of Imogen and little Publius.

But those Gardens and that Park were not sacred to James. Forsytes and tramps, children and lovers, rested and wandered day after day, night after night, seeking one and all some freedom from labour, from the reek and turmoil of the streets.

The leaves browned slowly, lingering with the sun and summer-like warmth of the nights.

On Saturday, October 5, the sky that had been blue all day deepened after sunset to the bloom of purple grapes. There was no moon, and a clear dark, like some velvety garment, was wrapped around the trees, whose thinned branches, resembling plumes, stirred not in the still, warm air. All London had poured into the Park, draining the cup of summer to its dregs.

Couple after couple, from every gate, they streamed along the paths and over the burnt grass, and one after another, silently out of the lighted spaces, stole into the shelter of the feathery trees, where, blotted against some trunk or under the shadow of shrubs, they were lost to all but themselves in the heart of the soft darkness.

To fresh-comers along the paths, these forerunners formed but part of that passionate dusk, whence only a strange murmur, like the confused beating of hearts, came forth. But when that murmur reached each couple in the lamp-light, their voices wavered, and ceased; their arms enlaced, their eyes began seeking, searching, probing the blackness. Suddenly, as though drawn by invisible hands, they, too, stepped over the railing, and, silent as shadows, were gone from the light.

The stillness, enclosed in the far, inexorable roar of the town, was alive with the myriad passions, hopes, and loves of multitudes of struggling human atoms; for in spite of the disapproval of that great body of Forsytes, the Municipal Council—to whom Love had long been considered, next to the Sewage Question, the gravest danger to the community—a process was going on that night in the Park, and in a hundred other parks, without which the thousand factories, churches, shops, taxes, and drains, of which they were custodians, were as arteries without blood, a man without a heart.

The instincts of self-forgetfulness, of passion, and of love, hiding under the trees, away from the trustees of their remorseless enemy, the 'sense of property', were holding a stealthy revel, and Soames, returning from Bayswater–for he had been alone to dine at Timothy's–walking home along the water, with his mind upon that coming lawsuit had the blood driven from his heart by a low laugh and the sound of kisses. He thought of writing to *The Times* the next morning, to draw the attention of the editor to the condition of our parks. He did not, however, for he had a horror of seeing his name in print.

But starved as he was, the whispered sounds in the stillness, the half-seen forms in the dark, acted on him like some morbid stimulant. He left the path along the water and stole under the trees, along the deep shadow of little plantations, where the boughs of chestnut trees hung their great leaves low, and there was blacker refuge, shaping his course in circles that had for their object a stealthy inspection of chairs side by side against tree-trunks, of enlaced lovers, who stirred at his approach.

Now he stood still on the rise overlooking the Serpentine, where, in full lamp-light, black against the silver water, sat a couple who never moved, the woman's face buried on the man's neck–a single form, like a carved emblem of passion, silent and unashamed.

And, stung by the sight, Soames hurried on deeper into the shadow of the trees.

In this search, who knows what he thought and what he sought? Bread for hunger–light in darkness? Who knows what he expected to find–impersonal knowledge of the human heart–the end of his private subterranean tragedy–for, again, who knew, but that each dark couple, unnamed, unnameable, might not be he and she?

But it could not be such knowledge as this that he was seeking–the wife of Soames Forsyte sitting in the Park like a common wench! Such thoughts were unconceivable; and from tree to tree, with his noiseless step, he passed.

Once he was sworn at; once the whisper, 'If only it could always be like this!' sent the blood flying again from his heart, and he waited there, patient and dogged, for the two to move. But it was only a poor thin slip of a shop-girl in her draggled blouse that passed him, clinging to her lover's arm.

A hundred other lovers, too, whispered that hope in the stillness of the trees, a hundred other lovers clung to each other.

But shaking himself with sudden disgust, Soames returned to the path, and left that seeking for he knew not what.

3

MEETING AT THE BOTANICAL

Young Jolyon, whose circumstances were not those of a Forsyte, found at times a difficulty in sparing the money needful for those country jaunts and researches into Nature, without having prosecuted which no water-colour artist ever puts brush to paper.

He was frequently, in fact, obliged to take his colour-box into the Botanical Gardens, and there, on his stool, in the shade of a monkey-puzzler or in the lee of some india-rubber plant, he would spend long hours sketching.

An art critic who had recently been looking at his work had delivered himself as follows:

'In a way your drawings are very good; tone and colour, in some of them certainly quite a feeling for Nature. But, you see, they're so scattered; you'll never get the public to look at them. Now, if you'd taken a definite subject, such as "London by Night", or "The Crystal Palace in the Spring", and made a regular series, the public would have known at once what they were looking at. I can't lay too much stress upon that. All the men who are making great names in Art, like Crum Stone or Bleeder, are making them by avoiding the unexpected; by specialising and putting their works all in the same pigeon-hole, so that the public know at once where to go. And this stands to reason, for if a man's a collector, he doesn't want people to smell at the canvas to find out whom his pictures are by; he wants them to be able to say at once: "A capital Forsyte!" It is all the more important for you to be careful to choose a subject that they can lay hold of on the spot, since there's no very marked originality in your style!'

Young Jolyon, standing by the little piano, where a bowl of dried rose leaves, the only produce of the garden, was deposited on a bit of faded damask, listened with his dim smile.

Turning to his wife, who was looking at the speaker with an angry expression on her thin face, he said:

'You see, dear?'

'I do *not*,' she answered in her staccato voice, that still had a little foreign accent; 'your style *has* originality.'

The critic looked at her, smiled deferentially, and said no more. Like everyone else, he knew their history.

The words bore good fruit with young Jolyon; they were contrary to all that he believed in, to all that he theoretically held good in his Art, but some strange, deep instinct moved him against his will to turn them to profit.

He discovered therefore one morning that an idea had come to him for making a series of water-colour drawings of London. How the idea had arisen he could not tell; and it was not till the following year, when he had completed and sold them at a very fair price, that in one of his impersonal moods, he found himself able to recollect the Art critic, and to discover in his own achievement another proof that he was a Forsyte.

He decided to commence with the Botanical Gardens, where he had already made so many studies, and chose the little artificial pond, sprinkled now with an autumn shower of red and yellow leaves, for though the gardeners longed to sweep them off, they could not reach them with their brooms. The rest of the gardens they swept bare enough, removing every morning Nature's rain of leaves; piling them in heaps, whence from slow fires rose the sweet, acrid smoke that, like the cuckoo's note for spring, the scent of lime trees for the summer, is the true emblem of the fall. The gardeners' tidy souls could not abide the gold and green and russet pattern on the grass. The gravel paths must lie unstained, ordered, methodical, without knowledge of the realities of life, nor of that slow and beautiful decay that flings crowns underfoot to star the earth with fallen glories, whence, as the cycle rolls, will leap again wild spring.

Thus each leaf that fell was marked from the moment when it fluttered a good-bye and dropped, slow turning, from its twig.

But on that little pond the leaves floated in peace, and praised heaven with their hues, the sunlight haunting over them.

And so young Jolyon found them.

Coming there one morning in the middle of October, he was disconcerted to find a bench about twenty paces from his stand occupied, for he had a proper horror of anyone seeing him at work.

A lady in a velvet jacket was sitting there, with her eyes fixed on the ground. A flowering laurel, however, stood between, and, taking shelter behind this, young Jolyon prepared his easel.

His preparations were leisurely; he caught, as every true artist should, at anything that might delay for a moment the effort of his work, and he found himself looking furtively at this unknown dame.

Like his father before him, he had an eye for a face. This face was charming!

He saw a rounded chin nestling in a cream ruffle, a delicate face with large dark eyes and soft lips. A black 'picture' hat concealed the hair; her figure was lightly poised against the back of the bench, her knees were crossed; the tip of a patent leather shoe emerged beneath her skirt. There was something, indeed, inexpressibly dainty about the person of this lady, but young Jolyon's attention was chiefly riveted by the look on her face, which reminded him of his wife. It was as though its owner had come into contact with forces too strong for her. It troubled him, arousing vague feelings of attraction and chivalry. Who was she? And what doing there, alone?

Two young gentlemen of that peculiar breed, at once forward and shy, found in the Regent's Park, came by on their way to lawn tennis, and he noted with disapproval their furtive stares of admiration. A loitering gardener halted to do something unnecessary to a clump of pampas grass; he, too, wanted an excuse for peeping. A gentleman, old and, by his hat, a professor of horticulture, passed three times to scrutinise her long and stealthily, a queer expression about his lips.

With all these men young Jolyon felt the same vague irritation. She looked at none of them, yet was he certain that every man who passed would look at her like that.

Her face was not the face of a sorceress, who in every look holds out to men the offer of pleasure; it had none of the 'devil's beauty' so highly prized among the first Forsytes of the land; neither was it of that type, no less adorable, associated with the box of chocolate; it was not of the spiritually passionate, or passionately spiritual order, peculiar to house-decoration and modern poetry; nor did it seem to promise to the playwright material for the production of the interesting and neurasthenic figure, who commits suicide in the last act.

In shape and colouring, in its soft persuasive passivity, its sensuous purity, this woman's face reminded him of Titian's 'Heavenly Love', a reproduction of which hung over the sideboard in his dining-room. And her attraction seemed to be in this soft passivity, in the feeling she gave that to pressure she must yield.

For what or whom was she waiting, in the silence, with the trees dropping here and there a leaf, and the thrushes strutting close on grass touched with the sparkle of the autumn rime?

Then her charming face grew eager, and, glancing round, with almost a lover's jealousy, young Jolyon saw Bosinney striding across the grass.

Curiously he watched the meeting, the look in their eyes, the long clasp of their hands. They sat down close together, linked for all their outward discretion. He heard the rapid murmur of their talk; but what they said he could not catch.

He had rowed in the galley himself! He knew the long hours of waiting and the lean minutes of a half-public meeting; the tortures of suspense that haunt the unhallowed lover.

It required, however, but a glance at their two faces to see that this was none of those affairs of a season that distract men and women about town; none of those sudden appetites that wake up ravening, and are surfeited and asleep again in six weeks. This was the real thing! This was what had happened to himself! Out of this anything might come!

Bosinney was pleading, and she so quiet, so soft, yet immovable in her passivity, sat looking over the grass.

Was he the man to carry her off, that tender, passive being, who would never stir a step for herself? Who had given him all herself, and would die for him, but perhaps would never run away with him!

It seemed to young Jolyon that he could hear her saying: 'But, darling, it would ruin you!' For he himself had experienced to the full the gnawing fear at the bottom of each woman's heart that she is a drag on the man she loves.

And he peeped at them no more; but their soft, rapid talk came to his ears, with the stuttering song of some bird that seemed trying to remember the notes of spring: Joy–tragedy? Which–which?

And gradually their talk ceased; long silence followed.

'And where does Soames come in?' young Jolyon thought. 'People think she is concerned about the sin of deceiving her husband! Little they know of women! She's eating, after starvation–taking her revenge! And Heaven help her–for he'll take his.'

He heard the swish of silk, and, spying round the laurel, saw them walking away, their hands stealthily joined. . . .

At the end of July old Jolyon had taken his grand-daughter to the mountains; and on that visit (the last they ever paid) June recovered to a great extent her health and spirits. In the hotels, filled with British Forsytes–for old Jolyon could not bear a 'set of Germans', as he called all foreigners–she was looked upon with respect–the only grand-daughter of that fine-looking, and evidently wealthy, old Mr Forsyte. She did not mix freely with people–to mix freely with people was not June's habit–but she formed some friendships, and notably one in the Rhône Valley, with a French girl who was dying of consumption.

Determining at once that her friend should not die, she forgot, in the institution of a campaign against Death, much of her own trouble.

Old Jolyon watched the new intimacy with relief and disapproval; for this additional proof that her life was to be passed amongst 'lame ducks' worried him. Would she never make a friendship or take an interest in something that would be of real benefit to her?

'Taking up with a parcel of foreigners,' he called it. He often, however, brought home grapes or roses, and presented them to this 'Mam'zelle' with an ingratiating twinkle.

Towards the end of September, in spite of June's disapproval, Mademoiselle Vigor breathed her last in the little hotel at St Luc, to which they have moved her; and June took her defeat so deeply to heart that old Jolyon carried her away to Paris. Here, in contemplation of the 'Venus de Milo' and the 'Madeleine', she shook off her depression, and when, towards the middle of October, they returned to town, her grandfather believed that he had affected a cure.

No sooner, however, had they established themselves in Stanhope Gate than he perceived to his dismay a return of her old absorbed and brooding manner. She would sit, staring in front of her, her chin on her hand, like a little Norse spirit, grim and intent, while all around in the electric light, then just installed, shone the great drawing-room brocaded up to the frieze, full of furniture from Baple and Pullbred's. And in the huge gilt mirror were reflected those Dresden china groups of young men in tight knee breeches, at the feet of full-bosomed ladies nursing on their laps pet lambs, which old Jolyon had bought when he was a bachelor and thought so highly of in these days of degenerate taste. He was a man of most open mind, who, more than any Forsyte of them all, had moved with the times, but he could never forget that he had bought these groups at Jobson's, and given a lot of money for them. He often said to June, with a sort of disillusioned contempt:

'*You* don't care about them! They're not the gimcrack things you and your friends like, but they cost me seventy pounds!' He was not a man who allowed his taste to be warped when he knew for solid reasons that it was sound.

One of the first things that June did on getting home was to go round to Timothy's. She persuaded herself that it was her duty to call there, and cheer him with an account of all her travels; but in reality she went because she knew of no other place where, by some random speech, or roundabout question, she could glean news of Bosinney.

They received her most cordially: and how was her dear grandfather? He had not been to see them since May. Her Uncle Timothy was very poorly, he had had a lot of trouble with the chimney-sweep in his bedroom; the stupid man had let the soot down the chimney! It had quite upset her uncle.

June sat there a long time, dreading, yet passionately hoping, that they would speak of Bosinney.

But paralysed by unaccountable discretion, Mrs Septimus Small let fall no word, neither did she question June about him. In desperation the girl asked at last whether Soames and Irene were in town—she had not yet been to see anyone.

It was Aunt Hester who replied: Oh yes, they were in town, they had not been away at all. There was some little difficulty about the house, she believed. June had heard, no doubt! She had better ask her Aunt Juley!

June turned to Mrs Small, who sat upright in her chair, her hands clasped, her face covered with innumerable pouts. In answer to the girl's look she maintained a strange silence, and when she spoke it was to ask June whether she had worn night-socks up in those high hotels where it must be so cold of a night.

June answered that she had not, she hated the stuffy things; and rose to leave. Mrs Small's infallibly chosen silence was far more ominous to her than anything that could have been said.

Before half an hour was over she had dragged the truth from Mrs Baynes in Lowndes Square, that Soames was bringing an action against Bosinney over the decoration of the house.

Instead of disturbing her, the news had a strangely calming effect; as though she saw in the prospect of this struggle new hope for herself. She learnt that the case was expected to come on in about a month, and there seemed little or no prospect of Bosinney's success.

'And whatever he'll do I can't think,' said Mrs Baynes; 'it's very dreadful for him, you know—he's got no money—he's very hard up. And we can't help him,

I'm sure. I'm told the money-lenders won't lend if you have no security, and he has none—none at all.'

Her embonpoint had increased of late; she was in the full swing of autumn organisation, her writing-table literally strewn with the menus of charity functions. She looked meaningly at June, with her round eyes of parrot-grey.

The sudden flush that rose on the girl's intent young face—she must have seen spring up before her a great hope—the sudden sweetness of her smile, often came back to Lady Baynes in after years (Baynes was knighted when he built that public Museum of Art which has given so much employment to officials, and so little pleasure to those working-classes for whom it was designed).

The memory of that change, vivid and touching, like the breaking open of a flower, or the first sun after long winter, the memory, too, of all that came after, often intruded itself, unaccountably, inopportunely on Lady Baynes, when her mind was set upon the most important things.

This was the very afternoon of the day that young Jolyon witnessed the meeting in the Botanical Gardens, and on this day, too, old Jolyon paid a visit to his solicitors, Forsyte, Bustard, and Forsyte, in the Poultry. Soames was not in, he had gone down to Somerset House; Bustard was buried up to the hilt in papers in that inaccessible apartment, where he was judiciously placed, in order that he might do as much work as possible; but James was in the front office, biting a finger, and lugubriously turning over the pleadings in Forsyte *v.* Bosinney.

This sound lawyer had only a sort of luxurious dread of the 'nice point', enough to set up a pleasurable feeling of fuss; for his good practical sense told him that if he himself were on the Bench he would not pay much attention to it. But he was afraid that this Bosinney would go bankrupt and Soames would have to find the money after all, and costs into the bargain. And behind this tangible dread there was always that intangible trouble, lurking in the background, intricate, dim, scandalous, like a bad dream, and of which this action was but an outward and visible sign.

He raised his head as old Jolyon came in, and muttered: 'How are you, Jolyon? Haven't seen you for an age. You've been to Switzerland, they tell me. This young Bosinney, he's got himself into a mess. I knew how it would be!' He held out the papers, regarding his elder brother with nervous gloom.

Old Jolyon read them in silence, and while he read them James looked at the floor, biting his fingers the while.

Old Jolyon pitched them down at last, and they fell with a thump amongst a mass of affidavits in '*re* Buncombe, deceased', one of the many branches of that parent and profitable tree, 'Fryer *v.* Forsyte'.

'I don't know what Soames is about,' he said, 'to make a fuss over a few hundred pounds. I thought he was a man of property.'

James's long upper lip twitched angrily; he could not bear his son to be attacked in such a spot.

'It's not the money—' he began, but meeting his brother's glance, direct, shrewd, judicial, he stopped.

There was a silence.

'I've come in for my will,' said old Jolyon at last, tugging at his moustache.

James's curiosity was roused at once. Perhaps nothing in this life was more stimulating to him than a will; it was the supreme deal with property, the final inventory of a man's belongings, the last word on what he was worth. He sounded the bell.

'Bring in Mr Jolyon's will,' he said to an anxious, dark-haired clerk.

'You going to make some alterations?' And through his mind there flashed the thought: 'Now, am I worth as much as he?'

Old Jolyon put the will in his breast pocket, and James twisted his long legs regretfully.

'You've made some nice purchases lately, they tell me,' he said.

'I don't know where you get this information from,' answered old Jolyon sharply. 'When's this action coming on? Next month? I can't tell what you've got in your minds. You must manage your own affairs; but if you take my advice, you'll settle it out of court. Good-bye!' With a cold handshake he was gone.

James, his fixed grey-blue eyes corkscrewing round some secret anxious image, began again to bite his finger.

Old Jolyon took his will to the offices of the New Colliery Company and sat down in the empty Board Room to read it through. He answered 'Down-by-the-starn' Hemmings so tartly when the latter, seeing his chairman seated there, entered with the new Superintendent's first report, that the Secretary withdrew with regretful dignity; and sending for the transfer clerk, blew him up till the poor youth knew not where to look.

It was not—by George—as he (Down-by-the-Starn) would have him know, for a whipper-snapper of a young fellow like him, to come down to that office, and think that he was God Almighty. He (Down-by-the-starn) had been head of that office for more years than a boy like him could count, and if he thought that when he had finished all his work, he could sit there doing nothing, he did not know him, Hemmings (Down-by-the-starn), and so forth.

On the other side of the green baize door old Jolyon sat at the long, mahogany-and-leather board table, his thick, loose-jointed, tortoise-shell eye-glasses perched on the bridge of his nose, his gold pencil moving down the clauses of his will.

It was a simple affair, for there were none of those vexatious little legacies and donations to charities, which fritter away a man's possessions and damage the majestic effect of that little paragraph in the morning papers accorded to Forsytes who die with a hundred thousand pounds.

A simple affair. Just a bequest to his son of twenty thousand, and 'as to the residue of my property of whatsoever kind whether realty or personalty or partaking of the nature of either—upon trust to pay the proceeds rents annual produce dividends or interest thereof and thereon to my said grand-daughter June Forsyte of her assigns during her life to be for her sole use and benefit and without, etc. . . . and from and after her death or decease upon trust to convey assign transfer or make over the said last-mentioned lands hereditaments premises trust moneys stocks funds investments and securities or such as shall then stand for and represent the same unto such person or persons whether one or more for such intents purposes and uses and generally in such manner way and form in all respects as the said June Forsyte notwithstanding coverture shall by her last Will and Testament or any writing or writings in the nature of a will testament or testamentary disposition to be by her duly made signed and published direct appoint or make over give and dispose of the same. And in default, etc. . . . Provided always . . .' and so on, in seven folios of brief and simple phraseology.

The will had been drawn by James in his palmy days. He had foreseen almost every contingency.

Old Jolyon sat a long time reading this will; at last he took half a sheet of paper from the rack and made a prolonged pencil note; then buttoning up the will, he caused a cab to be called and drove to the offices of Paramor and Herring, in Lincoln's Inn Fields. Jack Herring was dead, but his nephew was still in the firm, and old Jolyon was closeted with him for half an hour.

He had kept the hansom, and on coming out, gave the driver the address–3, Wistaria Avenue.

He felt a strange, slow satisfaction, as though he had scored a victory over James and the man of property. They should not poke their noses into his affairs any more; he had just cancelled their trusteeships of his will; he would take the whole of his business out of their hands and put it into the hands of young Herring, and he would move the business of his companies too. If that young Soames were such a man of property, he would never miss a thousand a year or so; and under his great white moustache old Jolyon grimly smiled. He felt that what he was doing was in the nature of retributive justice, richly deserved.

Slowly, surely, with the secret inner process that works the destruction of an old tree, the poison of the wounds to his happiness, his will, his pride, had corroded the comely edifice of his philosophy. Life had worn him down on one side, till, like that family of which he was the head, he had lost balance.

To him, borne northwards towards his son's house, the thought of the new disposition of property, which he had just set in motion, appeared vaguely in the light of a stroke of punishment, levelled at that family and that society of which James and his son seemed to him the representatives. He had made a restitution to young Jolyon, and restitution to young Jolyon satisfied his secret craving for revenge–revenge against Time, sorrow, and interference, against all that incalculable sum of disapproval that had been bestowed by the world for fifteen years on his only son. It presented itself as the one possible way of asserting once more the domination of his will; of forcing James, and Soames, and the family, and all those hidden masses of Forsytes–a great stream rolling against the single dam of his obstinacy–to recognise once and for all that *he would be master*. It was sweet to think that at last he was going to make the boy a richer man by far than that son of James, that 'man of property'. And it was sweet to give to Jo, for he loved his son.

Neither young Jolyon nor his wife were in (young Jolyon indeed was not back from the Botanical), but the little maid told that she expected the master at any moment.

'He's always at 'ome to tea, sir, to play with the children.'

Old Jolyon said he would wait; and sat down patiently enough in the faded, shabby drawing-room, where, now that the summer chintzes were removed, the old chairs and sofas revealed all their threadbare deficiencies. He longed to send for the children; to have them there beside him, their supple bodies against his knees; to hear Jolly's: 'Hallo, Gran!' and see his rush; and feel Holly's soft little hand stealing up against his cheek. But he would not. There was solemnity in what he had come to do, and until it was over he would not play. He amused himself by thinking how with two strokes of his pen he was going to restore the look of caste so conspicuously absent from everything in that little house; how he could fill these rooms, or others in some larger mansion, with triumphs of art from Baple and Pullbred's; how he could send little Jolly to Harrow and Oxford (he no longer had faith in Eton and

Cambridge, for his son had been there); how he could procure little Holly the best musical instruction, the child had a remarkable aptitude.

As these visions crowded before him, causing emotion to swell his heart, he rose and stood at the window, looking down into the little walled strip of garden, where the pear tree, bare of leaves before its time, stood with gaunt branches in the slow gathering mist of the autumn afternoon. The dog Balthasar, his tail curled tightly over a piebald, furry back, was walking at the farther end, sniffing at the plants, and at intervals placing his leg for support against the wall.

And old Jolyon mused.

What pleasure was there left but to give? It was pleasant to give, when you could find one who would be thankful for what you gave—one of your own flesh and blood! There was no such satisfaction to be had out of giving to those who did not belong to you, to those who had no claim on you! Such giving as that was a betrayal of the individualistic convictions and actions of his life, of all his enterprise, his labour, and his moderation, of the great and proud fact that, like tens of thousands of Forsytes before him, tens of thousands in the present, tens of thousands in the future, he had always made his own, and held his own, in the world.

And, while he stood there looking down on the smut-covered foliage of the laurels, the black-stained grass-plot, the progress of the dog Balthasar, all the suffering of the fifteen years that he had been baulked of legitimate enjoyment mingled its gall with the sweetness of the approaching moment.

Young Jolyon came at last, pleased with his work, and fresh from long hours in the open air. On hearing that his father was in the drawing-room, he inquired hurriedly whether Mrs Forsyte was at home, and being informed that she was not, heaved a sigh of relief. Then putting his painting materials carefully in the little coat-closet out of sight, he went in.

With characteristic decision old Jolyon came at once to the point. 'I've been altering my arrangements, Jo,' he said. 'You can cut your coat a bit longer in the future—I'm settling a thousand a year on you at once. June will have fifty thousand at my death, and you the rest. That dog of yours is spoiling the garden. I shouldn't keep a dog, if I were you!'

The dog Balthasar, seated in the centre of the lawn, was examining his tail.

Young Jolyon looked at the animal, but saw him dimly, for his eyes were misty.

'Yours won't come short of a hundred thousand, my boy,' said old Jolyon; 'I thought you'd better know. I haven't much longer to live at my age. I shan't allude to it again. How's your wife? and—give her my love.'

Young Jolyon put his hand on his father's shoulder, and, as neither spoke, the episode closed.

Having seen his father into a hansom, young Jolyon came back to the drawing-room and stood, where old Jolyon had stood, looking down on the little garden. He tried to realise all that this meant to him, and, Forsyte that he was, vistas of property were opened out in his brain; the years of half rations through which he had passed had not sapped his natural instincts. In extremely practical form, he thought of travel, of his wife's costume, the children's education, a pony for Jolly, a thousand things; but in the midst of all he thought, too, of Bosinney and his mistress, and the broken song of the thrush. Joy—tragedy! Which? Which?

The old past—the poignant, suffering, passionate, wonderful past, that no money could buy, that nothing could restore in all its burning sweetness—had come back before him.

When his wife came in he went straight up to her and took her in his arms; and for a long time he stood without speaking, his eyes closed, pressing her to him, while she looked at him with a wondering, adoring, doubting look in her eyes.

4

VOYAGE INTO THE INFERNO

The morning after a certain night on which Soames at last asserted his rights and acted like a man, he breakfasted alone.

He breakfasted by gaslight, the fog of late November wrapping the town as in some monstrous blanket till the trees of the Square even were barely visible from the dining-room window.

He ate steadily, but at times a sensation as though he could not swallow attacked him. Had he been right to yield to his overmastering hunger of the night before, and break down the resistance which he had suffered now too long from this woman who was his lawful and solemnly constituted helpmate?

He was strangely haunted by the recollection of her face, from before which, to soothe her, he had tried to pull her hands—of her terrible smothered sobbing, the like of which he had never heard, and still seemed to hear; and he was still haunted by the odd, intolerable feeling of remorse and shame he had felt, as he stood looking at her by the flame of the single candle, before silently slinking away.

And somehow, now that he had acted like this, he was surprised at himself.

Two nights before, at Winifred Dartie's, he had taken Mrs MacAnder into dinner. She had said to him, looking in his face with her sharp, greenish eyes: 'And so your wife is a great friend of that Mr Bosinney's?'

Not deigning to ask what she meant, he had brooded over her words.

They had roused in him a fierce jealousy, which, with the peculiar perversion of this instinct, had turned to fiercer desire.

Without the incentive of Mrs MacAnder's words he might never have done what he had done. Without their incentive and the accident of finding his wife's door for once unlocked, which had enabled him to steal upon her asleep.

Slumber had removed his doubts, but the morning brought them again. One thought comforted him: No one would know—it was not the sort of thing that she would speak about.

And, indeed, when the vehicle of his daily business life, that needed so imperatively the grease of clear and practical thought, started rolling once more with the reading of his letters, those nightmare-like doubts began to assume less extravagant importance at the back of his mind. The incident was really not of great moment; women made a fuss about it in books; but in the cool judgment of right-thinking men, of men of the world, of such as he recollected often received praise in the divorce court, he had but done his best to sustain the sanctity of marriage, to prevent her from abandoning her duty, possibly, if she were still seeing Bosinney, from— No, he did not regret it.

Now that the first step towards reconciliation had been taken, the rest would be comparatively–comparatively–

He rose and walked to the window. His nerve had been shaken. The sound of smothered sobbing was in his ears again. He could not get rid of it.

He put on his fur coat and went out into the fog; having to go into the City, he took the underground railway from Sloane Square station.

In his corner of the first-class compartment filled with City men the smothered sobbing still haunted him, so he opened *The Times* with the rich crackle that drowns all lesser sounds, and, barricaded behind it, set himself steadily to con the news.

He read that a Recorder had charged a grand jury on the previous day with a more than usually long list of offences. He read of three murders, five manslaughters, seven arsons, and as many as eleven–a surprisingly high number–rapes, in addition to many less conspicuous crimes, to be tried during a coming Sessions; and from one piece of news he went on to another, keeping the paper well before his face.

And still, inseparable from his reading, was the memory of Irene's tear-stained face, and the sounds from her broken heart.

The day was a busy one, including, in addition to the ordinary affairs of his practice, a visit to his brokers, Messrs Grin and Grinning, to give them instructions to sell his shares in the New Colliery Co., Ltd., whose business he suspected, rather than knew, was stagnating (this enterprise afterwards slowly declined, and was ultimately sold for a song to an American syndicate); and a long conference at Waterbuck, Q.C.'s chambers, attended by Boulter, by Fiske, the junior counsel, and Waterbuck, Q.C., himself.

The case of Forsyte v. Bosinney was expected to be reached on the morrow, before Mr Justice Bentham.

Mr Justice Bentham, a man of common sense rather than too great legal knowledge, was considered to be about the best man they could have to try the action. He was a 'strong' judge.

Waterbuck, Q.C., in pleasing conjunction with an almost rude neglect of Boulter and Fiske, paid to Soames a good deal of attention, by instinct or the sounder evidence of rumour, feeling him to be a man of property.

He held with remarkable consistency to the opinion he had already expressed in writing, that the issue would depend to a great extent on the evidence given at the trial, and in a few well-directed remarks he advised Soames not to be too careful in giving that evidence. 'A little bluffness, Mr Forsyte,' he said, 'a little bluffness,' and after he had spoken he laughed firmly, closed his lips tight, and scratched his head just below where he had pushed his wig back, for all the world like the gentleman-farmer for whom he loved to be taken. He was considered perhaps the leading man in breach of promise cases.

Soames used the Underground again in going home.

The fog was worse than ever at Sloane Square station. Through the still, thick blur, men groped in and out; women, very few, grasped their reticules to their bosoms and handkerchiefs to their mouths; crowned with the weird excrescence of the driver, haloed by a vague glow of lamp-light that seemed to drown in vapour before it reached the pavement, cabs loomed dim-shaped ever and again, and discharged citizens bolting like rabbits to their burrows.

And these shadowy figures, wrapped each in his own little shroud of fog, took no notice of each other. In the great warren, each rabbit for himself, especially those clothed in the more expensive fur, who afraid of carriages on foggy days, are driven underground.

One figure, however, not far from Soames, waited at the station door.

Some buccaneer or lover, of whom each Forsyte thought: 'Poor devil! looks as if he were having a bad time!' Their kind hearts beat a stroke faster for that poor, waiting, anxious lover in the fog; but they hurried by, well knowing that they had neither time nor money to spare for any suffering but their own.

Only a policeman, patrolling slowly and at intervals, took an interest in that waiting figure, the brim of whose slouch hat half hid a face reddened by the cold, all thin, and haggard, over which a hand stole now and again to smooth away anxiety or renew the resolution that kept him waiting there. But the waiting lover (if lover he were) was used to policemen's scrutiny, or too absorbed in his anxiety, for he never flinched. A hardened case, accustomed to long trysts, to anxiety, and fog, and cold, if only his mistress came at last. Foolish lover! Fogs last until the spring; there is also snow and rain, no comfort anywhere; gnawing fear if you bring her out, gnawing fear if you bid her stay at home!

'Serve him right; he should arrange his affairs better!'

So any respectable Forsyte. Yet, if that sounder citizen could have listened at the waiting lover's heart, out there in the fog and the cold, he would have said again: 'Yes, poor devil! he's having a bad time!'

Soames got into his cab and, with the glass down, crept along Sloane Street, and so along the Brompton Road, and home. He reached his house at five.

His wife was not in. She had gone out a quarter of an hour before. Out at such a time of night, into this terrible fog! What was the meaning of that?

He sat by the dining-room fire, with the door open, disturbed to the soul, trying to read the evening paper. A book was no good—in daily papers alone was any narcotic to such worry as his. From the customary events recorded in the journal he drew some comfort. 'Suicide of an actress'–'Grave indisposition of a Statesman' (that chronic sufferer)–'Divorce of an army officer'–'Fire in a colliery'–he read them all. They helped him a little—prescribed by the greatest of all doctors, our natural taste.

It was nearly seven when he heard her come in.

The incident of the night before had long lost its importance under stress of anxiety at her strange sortie into the fog. But now that Irene was home, the memory of her broken-hearted sobbing came back to him, and he felt nervous at the thought of facing her.

She was already on the stairs; her grey fur coat hung to her knees, its high collar almost hid her face, she wore a thick veil.

She neither turned to look at him nor spoke. No ghost or stranger could have passed more silently.

Bilson came to lay dinner, and told him that Mrs Forsyte was not coming down; she was having the soup in her room.

For once Soames did not 'change'; it was, perhaps, the first time in his life that he had sat down to dinner with soiled cuffs, and, not even noticing them, he brooded long over his wine. He sent Bilson to light a fire in his picture-room, and presently went up there himself.

Turning on the gas, he heaved a deep sigh, as though amongst these treasures, the backs of which confronted him in stacks around the little room, he had found at length his peace of mind. He went straight up to the greatest treasure of them all, an undoubted Turner, and, carrying it to the easel, turned its face to the light. There had been a movement in Turners, but he had not been able to make up his mind to part with it. He stood for a long time, his pale, clean-shaven face poked forward above his stand-up collar, looking at the picture as though he were adding it up; a wistful expression came into his eyes; he found, perhaps, that it came to too little. He took it down from the easel to put it back against the wall; but, in crossing the room, stopped, for he seemed to hear sobbing.

It was nothing—only the sort of thing that had been bothering him in the morning. And soon after, putting the high guard before the blazing fire, he stole downstairs.

Fresh for the morrow! was his thought. It was long before he went to sleep. . . .

It is now to George Forsyte that the mind must turn for light on the events of the fog-engulfed afternoon.

The wittiest and most sportsmanlike of the Forsytes had passed the day reading a novel in the paternal mansion at Prince's Gardens. Since a recent crisis in his financial affairs he had been kept on parole by Roger, and compelled to reside 'at home'.

Towards five o'clock he went out, and took a train at South Kensington Station (for everyone to-day went Underground). His intention was to dine, and pass the evening playing billiards at the Red Pottle—that unique hostel, neither club, hotel, nor good gilt restaurant.

He got out at Charing Cross, choosing it in preference to his more usual St. James's Park, that he might reach Jermyn Street by better lighted ways.

On the platform his eyes—for in combination with a composed and fashionable appearance, George had sharp eyes, and was always on the look-out for fillips to his sardonic humour—his eyes were attracted by a man who, leaping from a first-class compartment, staggered rather than walked towards the exit.

'So ho, my bird!' said George to himself; 'why, it's "the Buccaneer!"' and he put his big figure on the trail. Nothing afforded him greater amusement than a drunken man.

Bosinney, who wore a slouch hat, stopped in front of him, spun round, and rushed back towards the carriage he had just left. He was too late. A porter caught him by the coat; the train was already moving on.

George's practised glance caught sight of the face of a lady clad in a grey fur coat at the carriage window. It was Mrs Soames—and George felt that this was interesting!

And now he followed Bosinney more closely than ever—up the stairs, past the ticket-collector into the street. In that progress, however, his feelings underwent a change; no longer merely curious and amused, he felt sorry for the poor fellow he was shadowing. 'The Buccaneer' was not drunk, but seemed to be acting under the stress of violent emotion; he was talking to himself, and all that George could catch were the words 'Oh, God!' Nor did he appear to know what he was doing, or where going; but stared, hesitated, moved like a man out of his mind; and from being merely a joker in search of amusement, George felt that he must see the poor chap through.

He had 'taken the knock'—'taken the knock!' And he wondered what on earth Mrs Soames had been saying, what on earth she had been telling him in the railway carriage. She had looked bad enough herself! It made George sorry to think of her travelling on with her trouble all alone.

He followed close behind Bosinney's elbow–a tall, burly figure, saying nothing, dodging warily–and shadowed him out into the fog. There was something here beyond a jest! He kept his head admirably, in spite of some excitement, for in addition to compassion, the instincts of the chase were roused within him.

Bosinney walked right out into the thoroughfare–a vast muffled blackness, where a man could not see six paces before him; where, all around, voices or whistles mocked the sense of direction; and sudden shapes came rolling slow upon them; and now and then a light showed like a dim island in an infinite dark sea.

And fast into this perilous gulf of night walked Bosinney, and fast after him walked George. If the fellow meant to put his 'two-penny' under a bus, he would stop it if he could! Across the street and back the hunted creature strode, not groping as other men were groping in that gloom, but driven forward as though the faithful George behind wielded a knout; and this chase after a haunted man began to have for George the strangest fascination.

But it was now that the affair developed in a way which ever afterwards caused it to remain green in his mind. Brought to a standstill in the fog, he heard words which threw a sudden light on these proceedings. What Mrs Soames had said to Bosinney in the train was now no longer dark. George understood from those mutterings that Soames had exercised his rights over an estranged and unwilling wife in the greatest–the supreme act of property.

His fancy wandered in the fields of this situation; it impressed him; he guessed something of the anguish, the sexual confusion and horror in Bosinney's heart. And he thought: 'Yes, it's a bit thick! I don't wonder the poor fellow is half cracked!'

He had run his quarry to earth on a bench under one of the lions in Trafalgar Square, a monster sphynx astray like themselves in that gulf of darkness. Here, rigid and silent, sat Bosinney, and George, in whose patience was a touch of strange brotherliness, took his stand behind. He was not lacking in a certain delicacy–a sense of form–that did not permit him to intrude upon this tragedy, and he waited, quiet as the lion above, his fur collar hitched above his ears, concealing the fleshy redness of his cheeks, concealing all but his eyes with their sardonic, compassionate stare. And men kept passing back from business on the way to their clubs–men whose figures shrouded in cocoons of fog came into view like spectres, and like spectres vanished. Then even in his compassion George's Quilpish humour broke forth in a sudden longing to pluck these spectres by the sleeve and say:

'Hi, you Johnnies! You don't often see a show like this! Here's a poor devil whose mistress has just been telling him a pretty little story of her husband; walk up, walk up! He's taken the knock, you see.'

In fancy he saw them gaping round the tortured lover; and grinned as he thought of some respectable, newly-married spectre enabled by the state of his own affections to catch an inkling of what was going on within Bosinney; he fancied he could see his mouth getting wider and wider, and the fog going down and down. For in George was all that contempt of the middle-class–especially of the married middle-class–peculiar to the wild and sportsmanlike spirits in its ranks.

But he began to be bored. Waiting was not what he had bargained for.

'After all,' he thought, 'the poor chap will get over it; not the first time such a thing has happened in this little city!' But now his quarry again began muttering words of violent hate and anger. And following a sudden impulse George touched him on the shoulder.

Bosinney spun round.

'Who are you? What do you want?'

George could have stood it well enough in the light of the gas-lamps, in the light of that everyday world of which he was so hardy a connoisseur; but in this fog, where all was gloomy and unreal, where nothing had that matter-of-fact value associated by Forsytes with earth, he was a victim to strange qualms, and as he tried to stare back into the eyes of this maniac, he thought:

'If I see a bobby, I'll hand him over; he's not fit to be at large.'

But waiting for no answer, Bosinney strode off into the fog, and George followed, keeping perhaps a little farther off, yet more than ever set on tracking him down.

'He can't go on long like this,' he thought. 'It's God's own miracle he's not been run over already.' He brooded no more on policemen, a sportsman's sacred fire alive again within him.

Into a denser gloom than ever Bosinney held on at a furious pace; but his pursuer perceived more method in his madness—he was clearly making his way westwards.

'He's really going for Soames!' thought George. The idea was attractive. It would be a sporting end to such a chase. He had always disliked his cousin.

The shaft of a passing cab brushed against his shoulder and made him leap aside. He did not intend to be killed for the Buccaneer, or anyone. Yet, with hereditary tenacity, he stuck to the trail through vapour that blotted out everything but the shadow of the hunted man and the dim moon of the nearest lamp.

Then suddenly, with the instinct of a town-stroller, George knew himself to be in Piccadilly. Here he could find his way blindfold; and freed from the strain of geographical uncertainty, his mind returned to Bosinney's trouble.

Down the long avenue of his man-about-town experience, bursting, as it were, through a smirch of doubtful amours, there stalked to him a memory of his youth. A memory, poignant still, that brought the scent of hay, the gleam of moonlight, a summer magic, into the reek and blackness of this London fog—the memory of a night when in the darkest shadow of a lawn he had overheard from a woman's lips that he was not her sole possessor. And for a moment George walked no longer in black Piccadilly, but lay again, with hell in his heart, and his face to the sweet-smelling dewy grass, in the long shadow of poplars that hid the moon.

A longing seized him to throw his arm round the Buccaneer and say: 'Come, old boy. Time cures all. Let's go and drink it off!'

But a voice yelled at him, and he started back. A cab rolled out of blackness, and into blackness disappeared. And suddenly George perceived that he had lost Bosinney, He ran forward and back, felt his heart clutched by a sickening fear, the dark fear that lives in the wings of the fog. Perspiration started out on his brow. He stood quite still, listening with all his might.

'And then,' as he confided to Dartie the same evening in the course of a game of billiards at the Red Pottle, 'I lost him.'

Dartie twirled complacently at his dark moustache. He had just put together a neat break of twenty-three, failing at a 'jenny'. 'And who was *she*?' he asked.

George looked slowly at the 'man of the world's' fattish, sallow face, and a little grim smile lurked about the curves of his cheeks and his heavy-lidded eyes.

'No, no, my fine fellow,' he thought. 'I'm not going to tell *you*.' For though he mixed with Dartie a good deal, he thought him a bit of a cad.

'Oh, some little love-lady or other,' he said, and chalked his cue.

'A love-lady!' exclaimed Dartie—he used a more figurative expression. 'I made sure it was our friend Soa—'

'Did you?' said George curtly. 'Then, damme, you've made an error!'

He missed his shot. He was careful not to allude to the subject again till, towards eleven o'clock, having, in his poetic phraseology, 'looked upon the drink when it was yellow', he drew aside the blind and gazed out into the street. The murky blackness of the fog was but faintly broken by the lamps of the Red Pottle, and no shape of mortal man or thing was in sight.

'I can't help thinking of that poor Buccaneer,' he said. 'He may be wandering out there now in that fog. If he's not a corpse,' he added with strange dejection.

'Corpse!' said Dartie, in whom the recollection of his defeat at Richmond flared up. '*He's* all right. Ten to one if he wasn't tight!'

George turned on him, looking really formidable, with a sort of savage gloom on his big face.

'Dry up!' he said. 'Don't I tell you he's "taken the knock"!'

5

THE TRIAL

On the morning of his case, which was second in the list, Soames was again obliged to start without seeing Irene, and it was just as well, for he had not as yet made up his mind what attitude to adopt towards her.

He had been requested to be in court by half-past ten to provide against the event of the first action (a breach of promise) collapsing, which, however, it did not, both sides showing a courage that afforded Waterbuck, Q.C., an opportunity for improving his already great reputation in this class of case. He was opposed by Ram, the other celebrated breach of promise man. It was a battle of giants.

The Court delivered judgment just before the luncheon interval. The jury left the box for good, and Soames went out to get something to eat. He met James standing at the little luncheon-bar, like a pelican in the wilderness of the galleries, bent over a sandwich with a glass of sherry before him. The spacious emptiness of the great central hall, over which father and son brooded as they stood together, was marred now and then for a fleeting moment by barristers in wig and gown hurriedly bolting across, by an occasional old lady or rusty-coated man, looking up in a frightened way, and by two persons, bolder than their generation, seated in an embrasure arguing. The sound of their voices arose, together with a scent as of neglected wells, which, mingling with the odour of the galleries, combined to form the savour, like nothing but the emanation of a refined cheese, so indissolubly connected with the administration of British justice.

It was not long before James addressed his son.

'When's your case coming on? I suppose it'll be on directly. I shouldn't wonder if this Bosinney'd say anything; I should think he'd have to. He'll go bankrupt if it goes against him.' He took a large bite at his sandwich and a mouthful of sherry. 'Your mother,' he said, 'wants you and Irene to come and dine to-night.'

A chill smile played round Soames's lips; he looked back at his father. Anyone who had seen the look, cold and furtive, thus interchanged, might have been pardoned for not appreciating the real understanding between them. James finished his sherry at a draught.

'How much?' he asked.

On returning to the court Soames took at once his rightful seat on the front bench beside his solicitor. He ascertained where his father was seated with a glance so sidelong as to commit nobody.

James, sitting back with his hands clasped over the handle of his umbrella, was brooding on the end of the bench immediately behind counsel, whence he could get away at once when the case was over. He considered Bosinney's conduct in every way outrageous, but he did not wish to run up against him, feeling that the meeting would be awkward.

Next to the Divorce Court, this court was, perhaps, the favourite emporium of justice, libel, breach of promise, and other commercial actions being frequently decided there. Quite a sprinkling of persons unconnected with the law occupied the back benches, and the hat of a woman or two could be seen in the gallery.

The two rows of seats immediately in front of James were gradually filled by barristers in wigs, who sat down to make pencil notes, chat, and attend to their teeth; but his interest was soon diverted from these lesser lights of justice by the entrance of Waterbuck, Q.C., with the wings of his silk gown rustling, and his red, capable face supported by two short, brown whiskers. The famous Q.C. looked, as James freely admitted, the very picture of a man who could heckle a witness.

For all his experience, it so happened that he had never seen Waterbuck, Q.C., before, and, like many Forsytes in the lower branch of the profession, he had an extreme admiration for a good cross-examiner. The long, lugubrious folds in his cheeks relaxed somewhat after seeing him, especially as he now perceived that Soames alone was represented by silk.

Waterbuck, Q.C., had barely screwed round on his elbow to chat with his Junior before Mr Justice Bentham himself appeared—a thin, rather hen-like man, with a little stoop, clean-shaven under his snowy wig. Like all the rest of the court, Waterbuck rose, and remained on his feet until the Judge was seated. James rose but slightly; he was already comfortable, and had no opinion of Bentham, having sat next but one to him at dinner twice at the Bumley Tomms'. Bumley Tomms was rather a poor thing, though he had been so successful. James himself had given him his first brief. He was excited, too, for he had just found out that Bosinney was not in court.

'Now, what's he mean by that?' he kept on thinking.

The case having been called on, Waterbuck, Q.C., pushing back his papers, hitched his gown on his shoulder, and, with a semicircular look around him, like a man who is going to bat, arose and addressed the court.

The facts, he said, were not in dispute, and all that his lordship would be asked was to interpret the correspondence which had taken place between his client and the defendant, an architect, with reference to the decoration of a house. He would, however, submit that this correspondence could only mean one very plain thing. After briefly reciting the history of the house at Robin Hill, which he described as a mansion, and the actual facts of expenditure, he went on as follows:

'My client, Mr Soames Forsyte, is a gentleman, a man of property, who would be the last to dispute any legitimate claim that might be made against him, but he has met with such treatment from his architect in the matter of this house, over which he has, as your lordship has heard, already spent some twelve–some twelve thousand pounds, a sum considerably in advance of the amount he had originally contemplated, that as a matter of principle–and this I cannot too strongly emphasise–as a matter of principle, and in the interests of others, he has felt himself compelled to bring this action. The point put forward in defence by the architect I will suggest to your lordship is not worthy of a moment's serious consideration.' He then read the correspondence.

His client, 'a man of recognised position', was prepared to go into the box, and to swear that he never did authorise, that it was never in his mind to authorise, the expenditure of any money beyond the extreme limit of twelve thousand and fifty pounds, which he had clearly fixed; and not further to waste the time of the court, he would at once call Mr Forsyte.

Soames then went into the box. His whole appearance was striking in its composure. His face, just supercilious enough, pale and clean-shaven, with a little line between the eyes, and compressed lips; his dress in unostentatious order, one hand neatly gloved, the other bare. He answered the questions put to him in a somewhat low but distinct voice. His evidence under cross-examination savoured of taciturnity.

'Had he not used the expression, "a free hand"?'

'No.'

'Come, come!'

The expression he had used was 'a free hand in the terms of this correspondence'.

'Would he tell the court that that was English?'

'Yes!'

'What did he say it meant?'

'What it said!'

'Was he prepared to deny that it was a contradiction in terms?'

'Yes.'

'He was not an Irishman?'

'No.'

'Was he a well-educated man?'

'Yes!'

'And yet he persisted in that statement?'

'Yes.'

Throughout this and much more cross-examination, which turned again and again around the 'nice point', James sat with his hand behind his ear, his eyes fixed upon his son.

He was proud of him! He could not but feel that in similar circumstances he himself would have been tempted to enlarge his replies, but his instinct told him that this taciturnity was the very thing. He sighed with relief, however, when Soames, slowly turning, and without any change of expression, descended from the box.

When it came to the turn of Bosinney's Counsel to address the Judge, James redoubled his attention, and he searched the court again and again to see if Bosinney were not somewhere concealed.

Young Chankery began nervously; he was placed by Bosinney's absence in an awkward position. He therefore did his best to turn that absence to account.

He could not but fear—he said—that his client had met with an accident. He had fully expected him there to give evidence; they had sent round that morning both to Mr Bosinney's office and to his rooms (though he knew they were one and the same, he thought it was as well not to say so), but it was not known where he was, and this he considered to be ominous, knowing how anxious Mr Bosinney had been to give his evidence. He had not, however, been instructed to apply for an adjournment, and in default of such instruction he conceived it his duty to go on. The plea on which he somewhat confidently relied, and which his client, had he not unfortunately been prevented in some way from attending, would have supported by his evidence, was that such an expression as a 'free hand' could not be limited, fettered, and rendered unmeaning, by any verbiage which might follow it. He would go further and say that the correspondence showed that whatever he might have said in his evidence, Mr Forsyte had in fact never contemplated repudiating liability on any of the work ordered or executed by his architect. The defendant had certainly never contemplated such a contingency, or, as was demonstrated by his letters, he would never have proceeded with the work—a work of extreme delicacy, carried out with great care and efficiency, to meet and satisfy the fastidious taste of a connoisseur, a rich man, a man of property. He felt strongly on this point, and feeling strongly he used, perhaps, rather strong words when he said that this action was of a most unjustifiable, unexpected, indeed unprecedented character. If his lordship had had the opportunity that he himself had made it his duty to take, to go over this very fine house and see the great delicacy and beauty of the decorations executed by his client—an artist in his most honourable profession—he felt convinced that not for one moment would his lordship tolerate this, he would use no stronger word than, daring attempt to evade legitimate responsibility.

Taking the text of Soames's letters, he lightly touched on 'Boileau v. The Blasted Cement Company, Limited'. 'It is doubtful,' he said, 'what that authority has decided; in any case, I would submit that it is just as much in my favour as in my friend's.' He then argued the 'nice point' closely. With all due deference he submitted that Mr Forsyte's expression nullified itself. His client not being a rich man, the matter was a serious one for him; he was a very talented architect, whose professional reputation was undoubtedly somewhat at stake. He concluded with a perhaps too personal appeal to the Judge, as a lover of the arts, to show himself the protector of artists, from what was occasionally—he said occasionally—the too iron hand of capital. 'What,' he said, 'will be the position of the artistic professions, if men of property like this Mr Forsyte refuse, and are allowed to refuse, to carry out the obligations of the commissions which they have given.' . . . He would now call his client, in case he should at the last moment have found himself able to be present.

The name Philip Baynes Bosinney was called three times by the ushers, and the sound of the calling echoed with strange melancholy throughout the court and galleries.

The crying of this name, to which no answer was returned, had upon James a curious effect: it was like calling for your lost dog about the streets. And the creepy feeling that it gave him, of a man missing, grated on his sense of comfort and security—on his cosiness. Though he could not have said why, it made him feel uneasy.

He looked now at the clock—a quarter to three! It would be all over in a quarter of an hour. Where could the young fellow be?

It was only when Mr Justice Bentham delivered judgment that he got over the turn he had received.

Behind the wooden plateau by which he was fenced from more ordinary mortals, the learned Judge leaned forward. The electric light, just turned on above his head, fell on his face, and mellowed it to an orange hue beneath the snowy crown of his wig; the amplitude of his robes grew before the eye; his whole figure, facing the comparative dusk of the court, radiated like some majestic and sacred body. He cleared his throat, took a sip of water, broke the nib of a quill against the desk, and, folding his bony hands before him, began.

To James he suddenly loomed much larger than he had ever thought Bentham would loom. It was the majesty of the law; and a person endowed with a nature far less matter-of-fact than that of James might have been excused for failing to pierce this halo, and disinter therefrom the somewhat ordinary Forsyte, who walked and talked in everyday life under the name of Sir Walter Bentham.

He delivered judgment in the following words:

'The facts in this case are not in dispute. On May 15 last the defendant wrote to the plaintiff, requesting to be allowed to withdraw from his professional position in regard to the decoration of the plaintiff's house, unless he were given "a free hand". The plaintiff, on May 17, wrote back as follows: "In giving you, in accordance with your request, this free hand, I wish you to clearly understand that the total cost of the house as handed over to me completely decorated, inclusive of your fee (as arranged between us) must not exceed twelve thousand pounds." To this letter the defendant replied on May 18: "If you think that in such a delicate matter as decoration I can bind myself to the exact pound, I am afraid you are mistaken." On May 18 the plaintiff wrote as follows: "I did not mean to say that if you should exceed the sum named in my letter to you by ten or twenty or even fifty pounds there would be any difficulty between us. You have a free hand in the terms of this correspondence, and I hope you will see your way to completing the decorations." On May 20 the defendant replied thus shortly: "Very well."

'In completing these decorations, the defendant incurred liabilities and expenses which brought the total cost of this house up to the sum of twelve thousand four hundred pounds, all of which expenditure has been defrayed by the plaintiff. This action has been brought by the plantiff to recover from the defendant the sum of three hundred and fifty pounds expended by him in excess of a sum of twelve thousand and fifty pounds, alleged by the plaintiff to have been fixed by this correspondence as the maximum sum that the defendant had authority to expend.

'The question for me to decide is whether or no the defendant is liable to refund to the plaintiff this sum. In my judgment he is so liable.

'What in effect the plaintiff has said is this: "I give you a free hand to complete these decorations, provided that you keep within a total cost to me of twelve thousand pounds. If you exceed that sum by as much as fifty pounds, I will not hold you responsible; beyond that point you are no agent of mine, and I shall repudiate liability." It is not quite clear to me whether, had the plaintiff in fact repudiated liability under his agent's contracts, he would, under all the circumstances, have been successful in so doing; but he has not adopted this course. He has accepted liability, and fallen back upon his rights against the defendant under the terms of the latter's engagement.

'In my judgment the plaintiff is entitled to recover this sum from the defendant.

'It has been sought, on behalf of the defendant, to show that no limit of expenditure was fixed or intended to be fixed by this correspondence. If this were so, I can find no reason for the plaintiff's importation into the correspondence of the figures of twelve thousand pounds and subsequently of fifty pounds. The defendant's contention would render these figures meaningless. It is manifest to me that by his letter of May 20 he assented to a very clear proposition, by the terms of which he must be held to be bound.

'For these reasons there will be judgment for the plaintiff for the amount claimed with costs.'

James sighed, and stooping, picked up his umbrella, which had fallen with a rattle at the words 'importation into this correspondence'.

Untangling his legs, he rapidly left the court; without waiting for his son, he snapped up a hansom cab (it was a clear, grey afternoon) and drove straight to Timothy's, where he found Swithin; and to him, Mrs Septimus Small, and Aunt Hester, he recounted the whole proceedings, eating two muffins not altogether in the intervals of speech.

'Soames did very well,' he ended; 'he's got his head screwed on the right way. This won't please Jolyon. It's a bad business for that young Bosinney; he'll go bankrupt, I shouldn't wonder,' and then after a long pause, during which he had stared disquietly into the fire, he added:

'He wasn't there—now why?'

There was a sound of footsteps. The figure of a thick-set man, with the ruddy brown face of robust health, was seen in the back drawing-room. The forefinger of his upraised hand was outlined against the black of his frock-coat. He spoke in a grudging voice.

'Well, James,' he said; 'I can't—I can't stop.' And turning round, he walked out.

It was Timothy.

James rose from his chair. 'There!' he said; 'there! I knew there was something wro—' He checked himself, and was silent, staring before him, as though he had seen a portent.

6

SOAMES BREAKS THE NEWS

On leaving the courts Soames did not go straight home. He felt disinclined for the City, and drawn by need for sympathy in his triumph, he, too, made his way, but slowly and on foot, to Timothy's in the Bayswater Road.

His father had just left; Mrs Small and Aunt Hester, in possession of the whole story, greeted him warmly. They were sure he was hungry after all that evidence. Smither should toast him some more muffins, his dear father had eaten them all. He must put his legs up on the sofa; and he must have a glass of prune brandy too. It was so strengthening.

Swithin was still present, having lingered later than his wont, for he felt in want of exercise. On hearing this suggestion, he 'pished'. A pretty pass young men were coming to! His own liver was out of order, and he could not bear the thought of anyone else drinking prune brandy.

He went away almost immediately, saying to Soames: 'And how's your wife? You tell her from me that if she's dull, and likes to come and dine with me quietly, I'll give her such a bottle of champagne as she doesn't get every day.' Staring down from his height on Soames he contracted his thick, puffy, yellow hand as though squeezing within it all this small fry, and throwing out his chest he waddled slowly away.

Mrs Small and Aunt Hester were left horrified. Swithin was so droll!

They themselves were longing to ask Soames how Irene would take the result, yet knew that they must not; he would perhaps say something of his own accord, to throw some light on this, the present burning question in their lives, the question that from necessity of silence tortured them almost beyond bearing; for even Timothy had now been told, and the effect on his health was little short of alarming. And what, too, would June do? This, also, was a most exciting, if dangerous, speculation!

They had never forgotten old Jolyon's visit, since when he had not once been to see them; they had never forgotten the feeling it gave all who were present, that the family was no longer what it had been—that the family was breaking up.

But Soames gave them no help, sitting with his knees crossed, talking of the Barbizon school of painters, whom he had just discovered. These were the coming men, he said: he should not wonder if a lot of money were made over them; he had his eye on two pictures by a man called Corot, charming things; if he could get them at a reasonable price he was going to buy them—they would, he thought, fetch a big price some day.

Interested as they could not but be, neither Mrs Septimus Small nor Aunt Hester could entirely acquiesce in being thus put off.

It was interesting—most interesting—and then Soames was so clever that they were sure he would do something with those pictures if anybody could; but what was his plan now that he had won his case; was he going to leave London at once and live in the country, or what was he going to do?

Soames answered that he did not know, he thought they should be moving soon. He rose and kissed his aunts.

No sooner had Aunt Juley received this emblem of departure than a change came over her, as though she were being visited by dreadful courage; every little roll of flesh on her face seemed trying to escape from an invisible, confining mask.

She rose to the full extent of her more than medium height and said: 'It has been on my mind a long time, dear, and if nobody else will tell you, I have made up my mind that—'

Aunt Hester interrupted her: 'Mind, Julia, you do it'—she gasped—'on your own responsibility!'

Mrs Small went on as though she had not heard: 'I think you *ought* to know, dear, that Mrs MacAnder saw Irene walking in Richmond Park with Mr Bosinney.'

Aunt Hester, who had also risen, sank back in her chair and turned her face away. Really Juley was too—she should not do such things when she—Aunt

Hester was in the room; and, breathless with anticipation, she waited for what Soames would answer.

He had flushed the peculiar flush which always centred between his eyes; lifting his hand, and, as it were, selecting a finger, he bit a nail delicately; then, drawing it out between set lips, he said: 'Mrs MacAnder is a cat!'

Without waiting for any reply, he left the room.

When he went into Timothy's he had made up his mind what course to pursue on getting home. He would go up to Irene and say:

'Well, I've won my case, and there's an end of it! I don't want to be hard on Bosinney; I'll see if we can't come to some arrangement; he shan't be pressed. And now let's turn over a new leaf! We'll let the house and get out of these fogs. We'll go down to Robin Hill at once. I–I never meant to be rough with you! Let's shake hands–and–' Perhaps she would let him kiss her and forget!

When he came out of Timothy's his intentions were no longer so simple. The smouldering jealousy and suspicion of months blazed up within him. He would put an end to that sort of thing once and for all; he would not have her drag his name in the dirt! If she could not or would not love him, as was her duty and his right–she should not play him tricks with anyone else! He would tax her with it; threaten to divorce her! That would make her behave; she would never face that. But–but–what if she did? He was staggered; this had not occurred to him.

What if she did? What if she made him a confession? How would he stand then? He would have to bring a divorce!

A divorce! Thus close, the word was paralysing, so utterly at variance with all the principles that had hitherto guided his life. Its lack of compromise appalled him; he felt like the captain of a ship, going to the side of his vessel, and with his own hands throwing over the most precious of his bales. This jettisoning of his property with his own hand seemed uncanny to Soames. It would injure him in his profession. He would have to get rid of the house at Robin Hill, on which he had spent so much money, so much anticipation–and at a sacrifice. And she! She would no longer belong to him, not even in name! She would pass out of his life, and he–he should never see her again!

He traversed in the cab the length of a street without getting beyond the thought that he should never see her again!

But perhaps there was nothing to confess, even now very likely there was nothing to confess. Was it wise to push things so far? Was it wise to put himself into a position where he might have to eat his words? The result of this case would ruin Bosinney; a ruined man was desperate, but–what could he do? He might go abroad, ruined men always went abroad. What could *they* do–if indeed it *was* '*they*'–without money? It would be better to wait and see how things turned out. If necessary, he could have her watched. The agony of his jealousy (for all the world like the crisis of an aching tooth) came on again; and he almost cried out. But he must decide, fix on some course of action before he got home. When the cab drew up at the door, he had decided nothing.

He entered, pale, his hands moist with perspiration, dreading to meet her, burning to meet her, ignorant of what he was to say or do.

The maid Bilson was in the hall, and in answer to his question: 'Where is your mistress?' told him that Mrs Forsyte had left the house about noon, taking with her a trunk and bag.

Snatching the sleeve of his fur coat away from her grasp, he confronted her.

'What?' he exclaimed; 'what's that you said?' Suddenly recollecting that he must not betray emotion, he added: 'What message did she leave?' and noticed with secret terror the startled look of the maid's eyes.

'Mrs Forsyte left no message, sir.'

'No message; very well, thank you, that will do. I shall be dining out.'

The maid went downstairs, leaving him still in his fur coat, idly turning over the visiting-cards in the porcelain bowl that stood on the carved oak rug chest in the hall.

Mr and Mrs Bareham Culcher.	Lady Bellis.
Mrs Septimus Small.	Miss Hermione Bellis.
Mrs Baynes.	Miss Winifred Bellis.
Mr Solomon Thornworthy.	Miss Ella Bellis.

Who the devil were all these people? He seemed to have forgotten all familiar things. The words 'no message—a trunk, and a bag', played hide-and-seek in his brain. It was incredible that she had left no message, and, still in his fur coat, he ran upstairs two steps at a time, as a young married man when he comes home will run up to his wife's room.

Everything was dainty, fresh, sweet-smelling; everything in perfect order. On the great bed with its lilac silk quilt was the bag she had made and embroidered with her own hands to hold her sleeping things; her slippers ready at the foot; the sheets even turned over at the head as though expecting her.

On the table stood the silver-mounted brushes and bottles from her dressing-bag, his own present. There must, then, be some mistake. What bag had she taken? He went to the bell to summon Bilson, but remembered in time that he must assume knowledge of where Irene had gone, take it all as a matter of course, and grope out the meaning for himself.

He locked the doors and tried to think, but felt his brain going round; and suddenly tears forced themselves into his eyes.

Hurriedly pulling off his coat, he looked at himself in the mirror.

He was too pale, a greyish tinge all over his face; he poured out water and began feverishly washing.

Her silver-mounted brushes smelt faintly of the perfumed lotion she used for her hair; and at this scent the burning sickness of his jealousy seized him again.

Struggling into his fur, he ran downstairs and out into the street.

He had not lost all command of himself, however, and as he went down Sloane Street he framed a story for use, in case he should not find her at Bosinney's. But if he should? His power of decision again failed; he reached the house without knowing what he should do if he did find her there.

It was after office hours, and the street door was closed; the woman who opened it could not say whether Mr Bosinney were in or no; she had not seen him that day, not for two or three days; she did not attend to him now, nobody attended to him, he—

Soames interrupted her, he would go up and see for himself. He went up with a dogged, white face.

The top floor was unlighted, the door closed, no one answered his ringing, he could hear no sound. He was obliged to descend, shivering under his fur, a chill at his heart. Hailing a cab, he told the man to drive to Park Lane.

On the way he tried to recollect when he had last given her a cheque; she could not have more than three or four pounds, but there were her jewels; and with exquisite torture he remembered how much money she could raise on these; enough to take them abroad; enough for them to live on for months! He tried to calculate; the cab stopped, and he got out with the calculation unmade.

The butler asked whether Mrs Soames was in the cab, the master had told him they were both expected to dinner.

Soames answered: 'No, Mrs Forsyte has a cold.'

The butler was sorry.

Soames thought he was looking at him inquisitively, and remembering that he was not in dress clothes, asked: 'Anybody here to dinner, Warmson?'

'Nobody but Mr and Mrs Dartie, sir.'

Again it seemed to Soames that the butler was looking curiously at him. His composure gave way.

'What are you looking at?' he said. 'What's the matter with me, eh?'

The butler blushed, hung up the fur coat, murmured something that sounded like: 'Nothing, sir, I'm sure, sir,' and stealthily withdrew.

Soames walked upstairs. Passing the drawing-room without a look, he went straight up to his mother's and father's bedroom.

James, standing sideways, the concave lines of his tall, lean figure displayed to advantage in shirt-sleeves and evening waistcoat, his head bent, the end of his white tie peeping askew from underneath one white Dundreary whisker, his eyes peering with intense concentration, his lips pouting, was hooking the top hooks of his wife's bodice. Soames stopped; he felt half choked, whether because he had come upstairs too fast, or for some other reason. He–he himself had never–never been asked to–

He heard his father's voice, as though there were a pin in his mouth, saying: 'Who's that? Who's that? What d'you want?' His mother's: 'Here, Félice, come and hook this; your master'll never get done.'

He put his hand up to his throat and said hoarsely:

'It's I–Soames!'

He noticed gratefully the affectionate surprise in Emily's: 'Well, my dear boy?' and James's, as he dropped the hook: 'What, Soames! What's brought you up? Aren't you well?'

He answered mechanically: 'I'm all right,' and looked at them, and it seemed impossible to bring out his news.

James, quick to take alarm, began: 'You don't look well. I expect you've taken a chill–it's liver, I shouldn't wonder. Your mother'll give you–'

But Emily broke in quietly: 'Have you brought Irene?'

Soames shook his head.

'No,' he stammered, 'she–she's left me!'

Emily deserted the mirror before which she was standing. Her tall, full figure lost its majesty and became very human as she came running over to Soames.

'My dear boy!' My *dear* boy!'

She put her lips to his forehead and stroked his hand.

James, too, had turned full towards his son; his face looked older.

'Left you!' he said. 'What d'you mean–left you? You never told me she was going to leave you.'

Soames answered surlily: 'How could I tell? What's to be done?'

James began walking up and down; he looked strange and stork-like without a coat. 'What's to be done?' he muttered. 'How should I know what's to be done? What's the good of asking me? Nobody tells me anything, and then they come and ask me what's to be done; and I should like to know how I'm to tell them! Here's your mother, there she stands; *she* doesn't say anything. What *I* should say you've got to do is to follow her.'

Soames smiled; his peculiar, supercilious smile had never before looked pitiable.

'I don't know where she's gone,' he said.

'Don't know where she's gone!' said James. 'How d'you mean, don't know where she's gone? Where d'you suppose she's gone? She's gone after that young Bosinney, that's where she's gone. I knew how it would be.'

Soames, in the long silence that followed, felt his mother pressing his hand. And all that passed seemed to pass as though his own power of thinking or doing had gone to sleep.

His father's face, dusky red, twitching as if he were going to cry, and words breaking out that seemed rent from him by some spasm in his soul.

'There'll be a scandal; I always said so.' Then, no one saying anything: 'And there you stand, you and your mother!'

And Emily's voice, calm, rather contemptuous: 'Come, now, James! Soames will do all that he can.'

And James, staring at the floor, a little brokenly: 'Well, I can't help you; I'm getting old. Don't you be in too great a hurry, my boy.'

And his mother's voice again: 'Soames will do all he can to get her back. We won't talk of it. It'll all come right, I dare say.'

And James: 'Well, I can't see how it can come right. And if she hasn't gone off with that young Bosinney, my advice to you is not to listen to her, but to follow her and get her back.'

Once more Soames felt his mother stroking his hand, in token of her approval, and as though repeating some form of sacred oath, he muttered between his teeth: 'I will!'

All three went down to the drawing-room together. There, were gathered the three girls and Dartie; had Irene been present, the family circle would have been complete.

James sank into his arm-chair, and except for a word of cold greeting to Dartie, whom he both despised and dreaded, as a man likely to be always in want of money, he said nothing till dinner was announced. Soames, too, was silent; Emily alone, a woman of cool courage, maintained a conversation with Winifred on trivial subjects. She was never more composed in her manner and conversation than that evening.

A decision having been come to not to speak of Irene's flight, no view was expressed by any other member of the family as to the right course to be pursued; there can be little doubt, from the general tone adopted in relation to events as they afterwards turned out, that James's advice: 'Don't you listen to her, follow her and get her back!' would, with here and there an exception, have been regarded as sound, not only in Park Lane, but amongst the Nicholases, the Rogers, and at Timothy's. Just as it would surely have been endorsed by that wider body of Forsytes all over London, who were merely excluded from judgment by ignorance of the story.

In spite then of Emily's efforts, the dinner was served by Warmson and the footman almost in silence. Dartie was sulky, and drank all he could get; the girls seldom talked to each other at any time. James asked once where June was, and what she was doing with herself in these days. No one could tell him. He sank back into gloom. Only when Winifred recounted how little Publius had given his bad penny to a beggar did he brighten up.

'Ah!' he said, 'that's a clever little chap. I don't know what'll become of him if he goes on like this. An intelligent little chap, I call him!' But it was only a flash.

The courses succeeded one another solemnly under the electric light, which glared down on the table, but barely reached the principal ornament on the walls, a so-called 'Sea Piece by Turner', almost entirely composed of cordage and drowning men. Champagne was handed, and then a bottle of James's prehistoric port, but as by the chill hand of some skeleton.

At ten o'clock Soames left; twice in reply to questions he had said that Irene was not well; he felt he could no longer trust himself. His mother kissed him with her large soft kiss, and he pressed her hand, a flush of warmth in his cheeks. He walked away in the cold wind, which whistled desolately round the corners of the streets, under a sky of clear steel-blue, alive with stars; he noticed neither their frosty greeting, nor the crackle of the curled-up plane leaves, nor the night women hurrying in their shabby furs, nor the pinched faces of vagabonds at street corners. Winter was come! But Soames hastened home, oblivious; his hands trembled as he took the late letters from the gilt wire cage into which they had been thrust through the slit in the door.

None from Irene.

He went into the dining-room; the fire was bright there, his chair drawn up to it, slippers ready, spirit case, and carven cigarette-box on the table; but after staring at it all for a minute or two he turned out the light and went upstairs. There was a fire, too, in his dressing-room, but her room was dark and cold. It was into this room that Soames went.

He made a great illumination with candles, and for a long time continued pacing up and down between the bed and the door. He could not get used to the thought that she had really left him, and as though still searching for some message, some reason, some reading of all the mystery of his married life, he began opening every recess and drawer.

There were her dresses; he had always liked, indeed insisted, that she should be well-dressed—she had taken very few; two or three at most, and drawer after drawer, full of linen and silk things, was untouched.

Perhaps after all it was only a freak, and she had gone to the seaside for a few days' change. If only that were so, and she were really coming back, he would never again do as he had done that fatal night before last, never again run that risk—though it was her duty, her duty as a wife; though she did belong to him—he would never again run that risk; she was evidently not quite right in her head!

He stooped over the drawer where she kept her jewels; it was not locked, and came open as he pulled; the jewel-box had the key in it. This surprised him until he remembered that it was sure to be empty. He opened it.

It was far from empty. Divided, in little green velvet compartments, were all the things he had given her, even her watch, and stuck into the recess that contained the watch was a three-cornered note addressed 'Soames Forsyte' in Irene's handwriting.

'I think I have taken nothing that you or your people have given me.' And that was all.

He looked at the clasps and bracelets of diamonds and pearls, at the little flat gold watch with a great diamond set in sapphires, at the chains and rings, each in its nest, and the tears rushed up in his eyes and dropped upon them.

Nothing that she could have done, nothing that she *had* done, brought home to him like this the inner significance of her act. For the moment, perhaps, he understood nearly all there was to understand—understood that she loathed him, that she had loathed him for years, that for all intents and purposes they were like people living in different worlds, that there was no hope for him, never had been; even that she had suffered—that she was to be pitied.

In that moment of emotion he betrayed the Forsyte in him—forgot himself, his interests, his property—was capable of almost anything; was lifted into the pure ether of the selfless and unpractical.

Such moments pass quickly.

And as though with the tears he had purged himself of weakness, he got up, locked the box, and slowly, almost trembling, carried it with him into the other room.

7

JUNE'S VICTORY

June had waited for her chance, scanning the duller columns of the journals morning and evening, with an assiduity which at first puzzled old Jolyon; and when her chance came, she took it with all the promptitude and resolute tenacity of her character.

She will always remember best in her life that morning when at last she saw amongst the reliable Cause List of *The Times* newspaper, under the heading of Court XIII, Mr Justice Bentham, the case of Forsyte v. Bosinney.

Like a gambler who stakes his last piece of money, she had prepared to hazard her all upon this throw; it was not her nature to contemplate defeat. How, unless with the instinct of a woman in love, she knew that Bosinney's discomfiture in this action was assured, cannot be told—on this assumption, however, she laid her plans, as upon a certainty.

Half-past eleven found her at watch in the gallery of Court XIII, and there she remained till the case of Forsyte v. Bosinney was over. Bosinney's absence did not disquiet her; she had felt instinctively that he would not defend himself. At the end of the judgment she hastened down and took a cab to his rooms.

She passed the open street door and the offices on the three lower floors without attracting notice; not till she reached the top did her difficulties begin.

Her ring was not answered; she had now to make up her mind whether she would go down and ask the caretaker in the basement to let her in to await Mr Bosinney's return, or remain patiently outside the door, trusting that no one would come up. She decided on the latter course.

A quarter of an hour had passed in freezing vigil on the landing before it occurred to her that Bosinney had been used to leave the key of his rooms under the door-mat. She looked and found it there. For some minutes she could not decide to make use of it; at last she let herself in and left the door open that anyone who came might see she was there on business.

This was not the same June who had paid the trembling visit five months ago; those months of suffering and restraint had made her less sensitive; she had dwelt on this visit so long, with such minuteness, that its terrors were discounted beforehand. She was not there to fail this time, for if she failed no one could help her.

Like some mother beast on the watch over her young, her little quick figure never stood still in that room, but wandered from wall to wall, from window to door, fingering now one thing, now another. There was dust everywhere, the room could not have been cleaned for weeks, and June, quick to catch at anything that should buoy up her hope, saw in it a sign that he had been obliged, for economy's sake, to give up his servant.

She looked into the bedroom; the bed was roughly made, as though by the hand of man. Listening intently, she darted in and peered into his cupboards. A few shirts and collars, a pair of muddy boots—the room was bare even of garments.

She stole back to the sitting-room, and now she noticed the absence of all the little things he had set store by. The clock that had been his mother's, the field-glasses that had hung over the sofa; two really valuable old prints of Harrow, where his father had been at school, and last, not least, the piece of Japanese pottery she herself had given him. All were gone; and in spite of the rage roused within her championing soul at the thought that the world should treat him thus, their disappearance augured happily for the success of her plan.

It was while looking at the spot where the piece of Japanese pottery had stood that she felt a strange certainty of being watched, and, turning, saw Irene in the open doorway.

The two stood gazing at each other for a minute in silence; then June walked forward and held out her hand. Irene did not take it.

When her hand was refused, June put it behind her. Her eyes grew steady with anger; she waited for Irene to speak; and thus waiting, took in, with who-knows-what rage of jealousy, suspicion, and curiosity, every detail of her friend's face and dress and figure.

Irene was clothed in her long grey fur; the travelling cap on her head left a wave of gold hair visible above her forehead. The soft fullness of the coat made her face as small as a child's.

Unlike June's cheeks, her cheeks had no colour in them, but were ivory white and pinched as if with cold. Dark circles lay round her eyes. In one hand she held a bunch of violets.

She looked back at June, no smile on her lips; and with those great dark eyes fastened on her, the girl, for all her startled anger, felt something of the old spell.

She spoke first, after all.

'What have you come for?' But the feeling that she herself was being asked the same question made her add: 'This horrible case. I came to tell him—he has lost it.'

Irene did not speak, her eyes never moved from June's face, and the girl cried:

'Don't stand there as if you were made of stone!'

Irene laughed: 'I wish to God I were!'

But June turned away. 'Stop!' she cried, 'don't tell me! I don't want to hear! I don't want to hear what you've come for. I don't want to hear!' And like some uneasy spirit, she began swiftly walking to and fro. Suddenly she broke out:

'I was here first. We can't both stay here together!'

On Irene's face a smile wandered up, and died out like a flicker of firelight. She did not move. And then it was that June perceived under the softness and immobility of this figure something desperate and resolved; something not to be turned away, something dangerous. She tore off her hat and, putting both hands to her brow, pressed back the bronze mass of her hair.

'You have no right here!' she cried defiantly.

Irene answered: 'I have no right anywhere–'

'What do you mean?'

'I have left Soames. You always wanted me to!'

June put her hands over her ears.

'Don't! I don't want to hear anything–I don't want to know anything. It's impossible to fight with you! What makes you stand like that? Why don't you go?'

Irene's lips moved; she seemed to be saying: 'Where should I go?'

June turned to the window. She could see the face of a clock down in the street. It was nearly four. At any moment he might come! She looked back across her shoulder, and her face was distorted with anger.

But Irene had not moved; in her gloved hands she ceaselessly turned and twisted the little bunch of violets.

The tears of rage and disappointment rolled down June's cheeks.

'How *could* you come?' she said. 'You have been a false friend to me!'

Again Irene laughed. June saw that she had played a wrong card and broke down.

'Why have you come?' she sobbed. 'You've ruined my life, and now you want to ruin his!'

Irene's mouth quivered, her eyes met June's with a look so mournful that the girl cried out in the midst of her sobbing: 'No, no!'

But Irene's head bent till it touched her breast. She turned and went quickly out, hiding her lips with the little bunch of violets.

June ran to the door. She heard the footsteps going down and down. She called out: 'Come back, Irene! Come back!'

The footsteps died away. . . .

Bewildered and torn, the girl stood at the top of the stairs. Why had Irene gone, leaving her mistress of the field? What did it mean? Had she really given him up to her? Or had she–? And she was the prey of a gnawing uncertainty. . . . Bosinney did not come. . . .

About six o'clock that afternoon old Jolyon returned from Wistaria Avenue, where now almost every day he spent some hours, and asked if his grand-daughter were upstairs. On being told that she had just come in, he sent up to her room to request her to come down and speak to him.

He had made up his mind to tell her that he was reconciled with her father. In future bygones must be bygones. He would no longer live alone, or practically alone, in this great house; he was going to give it up, and take one in the country for his son, where they could all go and live together. If June did not like this, she could have an allowance and live by herself. It wouldn't make much difference to her, for it was a long time since she had shown him any affection.

But when June came down, her face was pinched and piteous; there was a strained, pathetic look in her eyes. She snuggled up in her old attitude on the arm of his chair, and what he said compared but poorly with the clear, authoritative, injured statement he had thought out with much care. His heart felt sore, as the great heart of a mother-bird feels sore when its youngling flies and bruises its wing. His word halted, as though he were apologising for having at last deviated from the path of virtue and succumbed, in defiance of sounder principles, to his more natural instincts.

He seemed nervous lest, in thus announcing his intentions, he should be setting his grand-daughter a bad example; and now that he came to the point, his way of putting the suggestion that, if she didn't like it, she could live by herself and lump it, was delicate in the extreme.

'And if, by any chance, my darling,' he said, 'you found you didn't get on with them, why, I could make that all right. You could have what you liked. We could find a little flat in London where you could set up, and I could be running to continually. But the children,' he added, 'are dear little things!'

Then, in the midst of this grave, rather transparent, explanation of changed policy, his eyes twinkled. 'This'll astonish Timothy's weak nerves. That precious young thing will have something to say about this, or I'm a Dutchman!'

June had not yet spoken. Perched thus on the arm of his chair, with her head above him, her face was invisible. But presently he felt her warm cheek against his own, and knew that, at all events, there was nothing very alarming in her attitude towards his news. He began to take courage.

'You'll like your father,' he said–'an amiable chap. Never was much push about him, but easy to get on with. You'll find him artistic and all that.'

And old Jolyon bethought him of the dozen or so water-colour drawings all carefully locked up in his bedroom; for now that his son was going to become a man of property, he did not think them quite such poor things as heretofore.

'As to your–your stepmother,' he said, using the word with some little difficulty, 'I call her a refined woman–a bit of a Mrs Gummidge, I shouldn't wonder–but very fond of Jo. And the children,' he repeated–indeed, this sentence ran like music through all his solemn self-justification–'are sweet little things!'

If June had known, those words but reincarnated that tender love for little children, for the young and weak, which in the past had made him desert his son for her tiny self, and now, as the cycle rolled, was taking him from her.

But he began to get alarmed at her silence, and asked impatiently: 'Well, what do you say?'

June slid down to his knee, and she in her turn began her tale. She thought it would all go splendidly; she did not see any difficulty, and she did not care a bit what people thought.

Old Jolyon wriggled. H'm! then people *would* think! He had thought that after all these years perhaps they wouldn't! Well, he couldn't help it! Nevertheless, he could not approve of his grand-daughter's way of putting it–she ought to mind what people thought!

Yet he said nothing. His feelings were too mixed, too inconsistent for expression.

No–went on June–she did not care; what business was it of theirs? There was only one thing–and with her cheek pressing against his knee, old Jolyon knew at once that this something was no trifle: As he was going to buy a house in the country, would he not–to please her–buy that splendid house of Soames's at Robin Hill? It was finished, it was perfectly beautiful, and no one would live in it now. They would all be so happy there!

Old Jolyon was on the alert at once. Wasn't the 'man of property' going to live in his new house, then? He never alluded to Soames now but under this title.

'No'–June said–'he was not; she knew that he was not!'

How did she know?

She could not tell him, but she knew. She knew nearly for certain! It was most unlikely; circumstances had changed! Irene's words still rang in her head:

'I have left Soames! Where should I go?'

But she kept silence about that.

If her grandfather would only buy it and settle that wretched claim that ought never to have been made on Phil! It would be the very best thing for everybody, and everything–everything might come straight!

And June put her lips to his forehead and pressed them close.

But old Jolyon freed himself from her caress, his face wore the judicial look which came upon it when he dealt with affairs. He asked: What did she mean? There was something behind all this–had she been seeing Bosinney?

June answered: 'No; but I have been to his rooms.'

'Been to his rooms? Who took you there?'

June faced him steadily. 'I went alone. He has lost that case. I don't care whether it was right or wrong. I want to help him; and *I will!*'

Old Jolyon asked again: 'Have you seen him?' His glance seemed to pierce right through the girl's eyes into her soul.

Again June answered: 'No; he was not there. I waited, but he did not come.'

Old Jolyon made a movement of relief. She had risen and looked down at him; so slight, and light, and young, but so fixed, and so determined; and disturbed, vexed, as he was, he could not frown away that fixed look. The feeling of being beaten, of the reins having slipped, of being old and tired, mastered him.

'Ah!' he said at last, 'you'll get yourself into a mess one of these days, I can see. You want your own way in everything.'

Visited by one of his strange bursts of philosophy, he added: 'Like that you were born; and like that you'll stay until you die!'

And he, who in his dealings with men of business, with Boards, with Forsytes of all descriptions, with such as were not Forsytes, had always had his own way, looked at his indomitable grandchild sadly–for he felt in her that quality which above all others he unconsciously admired.

'Do you know what they say is going on?' he said slowly.

June crimsoned.

'Yes–no. I know–and I don't know–I don't care!' and she stamped her foot.

'I believe,' said old Jolyon, dropping his eyes, 'that you'd have him if he were dead!'

There was a long silence before he spoke again.

'But as to buying this house–you don't know what you're talking about!'

June said that she did. She knew that he could get it if he wanted. He would only have to give what it cost.

'What it cost! You know nothing about it. I won't go to Soames–I'll have nothing more to do with that young man.'

'But you needn't; you can go to Uncle James. If you can't buy the house, will you pay this lawsuit claim? I know he is terribly hard up–I've seen it. You can stop it out of my money!'

A twinkle came into old Jolyon's eyes.

'Stop it out of your money! A pretty way! And what will you do, pray, without your money?'

But secretly the idea of wresting the house from James and his son had begun to take hold of him. He had heard on Forsyte 'Change much comment, much rather doubtful praise of this house. It was 'too artistic', but a fine place. To take from the 'man of property' that on which he had set his heart would be a crowning triumph over James, practical proof that he was going to make a man of property of Jo, to put him back in his proper position, and there to keep him secure. Justice once for all on those who had chosen to regard his son as a poor, penniless outcast.

He would see, he would see! It might be out of the question; he was not going to pay a fancy price, but if it could be done, why, perhaps he would do it!

And still more secretly he knew that he could not refuse her.

But he did not commit himself. He would think it over—he said to June.

8

BOSINNEY'S DEPARTURE

Old Jolyon was not given to hasty decisions; it is probable that he would have continued to think over the purchase of the house at Robin Hill, had not June's face told him that he would have no peace until he acted.

At breakfast next morning she asked him what time she should order the carriage.

'Carriage!' he said, with some appearance of innocence; 'what for? *I'm* not going out!'

She answered: 'If you don't go early, you won't catch Uncle James before he goes into the City.'

'James! What about your Uncle James?'

'The house,' she replied, in such a voice that he no longer pretended ignorance.

'I've not made up my mind,' he said.

'You must! You must! Oh! Gran—think of me!'

Old Jolyon grumbled out: 'Think of you—I'm always thinking of you, but you don't think of yourself; you don't think what you're letting yourself in for. Well, order the carriage at ten!'

At a quarter-past he was placing his umbrella in the stand at Park Lane—he did not choose to relinquish his hat and coat; telling Warmson that he wanted to see his master, he went, without being announced, into the study and sat down.

James was still in the dining-room talking to Soames, who had come round again before breakfast. On hearing who his visitor was, he muttered nervously: 'Now, what's *he* want, I wonder?'

He then got up.

'Well,' he said to Soames, 'don't you go doing anything in a hurry. The first thing is to find out where she is—I should go to Stainer's about it; they're the best men, if they can't find her, nobody can.' And suddenly moved to strange softness, he muttered to himself: 'Poor little thing! *I* can't tell what she was thinking about!' and went out blowing his nose.

Old Jolyon did not rise on seeing his brother, but held out his hand, and exchanged with him the clasp of a Forsyte.

James took another chair by the table and leaned his head on his hand.

'Well,' he said, 'how are you? We don't see much of *you* nowadays!'

Old Jolyon paid no attention to the remark.

'How's Emily?' he asked; and waiting for no reply, went on: 'I've come to see you about this affair of young Bosinney's. I'm told that new house of his is a white elephant.'

'I don't know anything about a white elephant,' said James, 'I know he's lost his case, and I should say he'll go bankrupt.'

Old Jolyon was not slow to seize the opportunity this gave him.

'I shouldn't wonder a bit!' he agreed; 'and if he goes bankrupt, the "man of property"–that is, Soames'll be out of pocket. Now, what I was thinking was this: If he's not going to live there–'

Seeing both surprise and suspicion in James's eye, he quickly went on: 'I don't want to know anything; I suppose Irene's put her foot down–it's not material to me. But I'm thinking of a house in the country myself, not too far from London, and if it suited me I don't say that I mightn't look at it, at a price.'

James listened to this statement with a strange mixture of doubt, suspicion, and relief, merging into a dread of something behind, and tinged with the remains of his old undoubted reliance upon his elder brother's good faith and judgment. There was anxiety, too, as to what old Jolyon could have heard and how he had heard it; and a sort of hopefulness arising from the thought that if June's connection with Bosinney were completely at an end, her grandfather would hardly seem anxious to help the young fellow. Altogether he was puzzled; as he did not like either to show this, or to commit himself in any way, he said.

'They tell me you're altering your will in favour of your son.'

He had not been told this; he had merely added the fact of having seen old Jolyon with his son and grandchildren to the fact that he had taken his will away from Forsyte, Bustard and Forsyte. The shot went home.

'Who told you that?' asked old Jolyon.

'I'm sure I don't know,' said James; 'I can't remember names–I know somebody told me. Soames spent a lot of money on this house; he's not likely to part with it except at a good price.'

'Well,' said old Jolyon, ' if he thinks I'm going to pay a fancy price, he's mistaken. I've not got the money to throw away that he seems to have. Let him try and sell it at a forced sale, and see what he'll get. It's not every man's house, I hear!'

James, who was secretly also of this opinion, answered: 'It's a gentleman's house. Soames is here now if you'd like to see him.'

'No,' said old Jolyon, 'I haven't got as far as that; and I'm not likely to, I can see that very well, if I'm met in this manner!'

James was a little cowed; when it came to the actual figures of a commercial transaction he was sure of himself, for then he was dealing with facts, not with men; but preliminary negotiations such as these made him nervous–he never knew quite how far he could go.

'Well,' he said, 'I know nothing about it. Soames, he tells me nothing; I should think he'd entertain it–it's a question of price.'

'Oh!' said old Jolyon, 'don't let him make a favour of it!' He placed his hat on his head in dudgeon.

The door was opened and Soames came in.

'There's a policeman out here,' he said with his half smile, 'for Uncle Jolyon.'

Old Jolyon looked at him angrily, and James said: 'A policeman? I don't know anything about a policeman. But I suppose *you* know something about

him,' he added to old Jolyon with a look of suspicion: 'I suppose you'd better
see him!'

In the hall an inspector of police stood stolidly regarding with heavy-lidded
pale-blue eyes the fine old English furniture picked up by James at the famous
Mavrojano sale in Portman Square. 'You'll find my brother in there,' said
James.

The inspector raised his fingers respectfully to his peaked cap and entered
the study.

James saw him go in with a strange sensation.

'Well,' he said to Soames, 'I suppose we must wait and see what he wants.
Your uncle's been here about the house!'

He returned with Soames into the dining-room, but could not rest.

'Now what *does* he want?' he murmured again.

'Who?' replied Soames: 'the inspector? They sent him round from Stanhope
Gate, that's all I know. That "nonconformist" of Uncle Jolyon's has been
pilfering, I shouldn't wonder!'

But in spite of his calmness, he too was ill at ease.

At the end of ten minutes old Jolyon came in.

He walked up to the table, and stood there perfectly silent pulling at his long
white moustaches. James gazed up at him with opening mouth: he had never
seen his brother look like this.

Old Jolyon raised his hand and said slowly:

'Young Bosinney has been run over in the fog and killed.'

Then standing above his brother and his nephew, and looking down at them
with his deep eyes: 'There's—some—talk—of—suicide,' he said.

James's jaw dropped. '*Suicide!* What should he do that for?'

Old Jolyon answered sternly: 'God knows, if you and your son don't!'

But James did not reply.

For all men of great age, even for all Forsytes, life has had bitter experiences.
The passer-by, who sees them wrapped in cloaks of custom, wealth, and
comfort, would never suspect that such black shadows had fallen on their
roads. To every man of great age—to Sir Walter Bentham himself—the idea of
suicide has once at least been present in the ante-room of his soul; on the
threshold, waiting to enter, held out from the inmost chamber by some chance
reality, some vague fear, some painful hope. To Forsytes that final renunciation of property is hard. Oh! it is hard! Seldom—perhaps ever—can they
achieve it; and yet, how near have they not sometimes been!

So even with James! Then in the medley of his thoughts, he broke out: 'Why, I
saw it in the paper yesterday: 'Run over in the fog!' They didn't know his
name!' He turned from one face to the other in his confusion of soul; but
instinctively all the time he was rejecting that rumour of suicide. He dared not
entertain this thought, so against his interest, against the interest of his son, of
every Forsyte. He strove against it; and as his nature ever unconsciously
rejected that which it could not with safety accept, so gradually he overcame
this fear. It was an accident! It must have been!

Old Jolyon broke in on his reverie.

'Death was instantaneous. He lay all yesterday at the hospital. There was
nothing to tell them who he was. I am going there now; you and your son had
better come too.'

No one opposing this command he led the way from the room.

The day was still and clear and bright, and driving over to Park Lane from

Stanhope Gate, old Jolyon had had the carriage open. Sitting back on the padded cushions, finishing his cigar, he had noticed with pleasure the keen crispness of the air, the bustle of the cabs and people; the strange, almost Parisian, alacrity that the first fine day will bring into London streets after a spell of fog or rain. And he had felt so happy; he had not felt like it for months. His confession to June was off his mind; he had the prospect of his son's, above all, of his grandchildren's company in the future (he had appointed to meet young Jolyon at the Hotch Potch that very morning to discuss it again); and there was the pleasurable excitement of a coming encounter, a coming victory, over James and the 'man of property' in the matter of the house.

He had the carriage closed now; he had no heart to look on gaiety; nor was it right that Forsytes should be seen driving with an inspector of police.

In that carriage the inspector spoke again of the death:

'It was not so very thick just there. The driver says the gentleman must have had time to see what he was about, he seemed to walk right into it. It appears that he was very hard up, we found several pawn tickets at his rooms, his account at the bank is overdrawn, and there's this case in to-day's papers;' his cold blue eyes travelled from one to another of the three Forsytes in the carriage.

Old Jolyon watching from his corner saw his brother's face change, and the brooding, worried look deepen on it. At the inspector's words, indeed, all James's doubts and fears revived. Hard–up–pawn–tickets–an overdrawn account! These words that had all his life been a far-off nightmare to him, seemed to make uncannily real that suspicion of suicide which must on no account be entertained. He sought his son's eye; but lynx-eyed, taciturn, immovable, Soames gave no answering look. And to old Jolyon watching, divining the league of mutual defence between them, there came an over-mastering desire to have his own son at his side, as though this visit to the dead man's body was a battle in which otherwise he must single-handed meet those two. And the thought of how to keep June's name out of the business kept whirring in his brain. James had his son to support him! Why should he not send for Jo?

Taking out his card-case, he pencilled the following message:

'Come round at once. I've sent the carriage for you.'

On getting out he gave this card to his coachman, telling him to drive as fast as possible to the Hotch Potch Club, and if Mr Jolyon Forsyte were there to give him the card and bring him at once. If not there yet, he was to wait till he came.

He followed the others slowly up the steps, leaning on his umbrella, and stood a moment to get his breath. The inspector said: 'This is the mortuary, sir. But take your time.'

In the bare, white-walled room, empty of all but a streak of sunshine smeared along the dustless floor, lay a form covered by a sheet. With a huge steady hand the inspector took the hem and turned it back. A sightless face gazed up at them, and on either side of that sightless defiant face the three Forsytes gazed down; in each one of them the secret emotions, fears, and pity of his own nature rose and fell like the rising, falling waves of life, whose wash those white walls barred out now for ever from Bosinney. And in each one of them the trend of his nature, the odd essential spring, that moved him in fashions minutely, unalterably different from those of every other human being, forced him to a different attitude of thought. Far from the others, yet inscrutably close, each stood thus, alone with death, silent, his eyes lowered.

The inspector asked softly:

'You identify the gentleman, sir?'

Old Jolyon raised his head and nodded. He looked at his brother opposite, at that long lean figure brooding over the dead man, with face dusky red and strained grey eyes; and at the figure of Soames white and still by his father's side. And all that he had felt against those two was gone like smoke in the long white presence of Death. Whence comes it, how comes it—Death? Sudden reverse of all that goes before; blind setting forth on a path that leads to—where? Dark quenching of the fire! The heavy, brutal crushing-out that all men must go through, keeping their eyes clear and brave unto the end! Small and of no import, insects though they are! And across old Jolyon's face there flitted a gleam, for Soames, murmuring to the inspector, crept noiselessly away.

Then suddenly James raised his eyes. There was a queer appeal in that suspicious troubled look: 'I know I'm no match for you', it seemed to say. And, hunting for a handkerchief, he wiped his brow; then, bending sorrowful and lank over the dead man, he too turned and hurried out.

Old Jolyon stood, still as death, his eyes fixed on the body. Who shall tell of what he was thinking? Of himself, when his hair was brown like the hair of that young fellow dead before him? Of himself, with his battle just beginning, the long, long battle he had loved; the battle that was over for this young man almost before it had begun? Of his grand-daughter, with her broken hopes? Of that other woman? Of the strangeness, and the pity of it? And the irony, inscrutable, and bitter, of that end? Justice! There was no justice for men, for they were ever in the dark!

Or perhaps in his philosophy he thought: 'Better to be out of it all! Better to have done with it, like this poor youth. . . .'

Someone touched him on the arm.

A tear started up and wetted his eyelash. 'Well,' he said, 'I'm no good here. I'd better be going. You'll come to me as soon as you can, Jo,' and with his head bowed he went away.

It was young Jolyon's turn to take his stand beside the dead man, round whose fallen body he seemed to see all the Forsytes breathless and prostrated. The stroke had fallen too swiftly.

The forces underlying every tragedy—forces that take no denial, working through cross-currents to their ironical end, had met and fused with a thunder-clap, flung out the victim and flattened to the ground all those that stood around.

Or so at all events young Jolyon seemed to see them, lying around Bosinney's body.

He asked the inspector to tell him what had happened, and the latter, like a man who does not every day get such a chance, again detailed such facts as were known.

'There's more here, sir, however,' he said, 'than meets the eye. I don't believe in suicide, nor in pure accident, myself. It's more likely I think he was suffering under great stress of mind, and took no notice of things about him. Perhaps you can throw some light on these.'

He took from his pocket a little packet and laid it on the table. Carefully undoing it, he revealed a lady's handkerchief, pinned through the folds with a pin of discoloured Venetian gold, the stone of which had fallen from the socket. A scent of dried violets rose to young Jolyon's nostrils.

'Found in his breast pocket,' said the inspector; 'the name has been cut away!'

Young Jolyon with difficulty answered: 'I'm afraid I cannot help you!' But vividly there rose before him the face he had seen light up, so tremulous and glad, at Bosinney's coming! Of her he thought more than of his own daughter, more than of them all—of her with the dark, soft glance, the delicate passive face, waiting for the dead man, waiting even at that moment, perhaps, still and patient in the sunlight.

He walked sorrowfully away from the hospital towards his father's house, reflecting that this death would break up the Forsyte family. The stroke had indeed slipped past their defences into the very wood of their tree. They might flourish to all appearance as before, preserving a brave show before the eyes of London, but the trunk was dead, withered by the same flash that had stricken down Bosinney. And now the saplings would take its place, each one a new custodian of the sense of property.

'Good forest of Forsytes!' thought young Jolyon—'soundest timber of our land!'

Concerning the cause of this death—his family would doubtless reject with vigour the suspicion of suicide, which was so compromising! They would take it as an accident, a stroke of fate. In their hearts they would even feel it an intervention of Providence, a retribution—had not Bosinney endangered their two most priceless possessions, the pocket and the hearth? And they would talk of 'that unfortunate accident of young Bosinney's', but perhaps they would not talk—silence might be better!

As for himself, he regarded the bus-driver's account of the accident as of very little value. For no one so madly in love committed suicide for want of money; nor was Bosinney the sort of fellow to set much store by a financial crisis. And so he too rejected this theory of suicide, the dead man's face rose too clearly before him. Gone in the hey-day of his summer—and to believe thus that an accident had cut Bosinney off in the full sweep of his passion was more than ever pitiful to young Jolyon.

Then came a vision of Soames's home as it now was, and must be hereafter. The streak of lightning had flashed its clear uncanny gleam on bare bones with grinning spaces between, the disguising flesh was gone. . . .

In the dining-room at Stanhope Gate old Jolyon was sitting alone when his son came in. He looked very wan in his great arm-chair. And his eyes travelling round the walls with their pictures of still life, and the masterpiece 'Dutch fishing-boats at Sunset' seemed as though passing their gaze over his life with its hopes, its gains, its achievements.

'Ah! Jo!' he said, 'is that you? I've told poor little June. But that's not all of it. Are you going to Soames's? *She's* brought it on herself, I suppose; but somehow I can't bear to think of her, shut up there—and all alone.' And holding up his thin, veined hand, he clenched it.

9

IRENE'S RETURN

After leaving James and old Jolyon in the mortuary of the hospital, Soames hurried aimlessly along the streets.

The tragic event of Bosinney's death altered the complexion of everything.

There was no longer the same feeling that to lose a minute would be fatal, nor would he now risk communicating the fact of his wife's flight to anyone till the inquest was over.

That morning he had risen early, before the postman came, had taken the first-post letters from the box himself, and, though there had been none from Irene, he had made an opportunity of telling Bilson that her mistress was at the sea; he would probably, he said, be going down himself from Saturday to Monday. This had given him time to breathe, time to leave no stone unturned to find her.

But now, cut off from taking steps by Bosinney's death—that strange death, to think of which was like putting a hot iron to his heart, like lifting a great weight from it—he did not know how to pass his day; and he wandered here and there through the streets, looking at every face he met, devoured by a hundred anxieties.

And as he wandered, he thought of him who had finished his wandering, his prowling, and would never haunt his house again.

Already in the afternoon he passed posters announcing the identity of the dead man, and bought the papers to see what they said. He would stop their mouths if he could, and he went into the City, and was closeted with Boulter for a long time.

On his way home, passing the steps of Jobson's about half-past four, he met George Forsyte, who held out an evening paper to Soames, saying:

'Here! Have you seen this about the poor Buccaneer?'

Soames answered stonily: 'Yes.'

George stared at him. He had never liked Soames; he now held him responsible for Bosinney's death. Soames had done for him—done for him by that act of property that had sent the Buccaneer to run amok that fatal afternoon.

'The poor fellow,' he was thinking, 'was so cracked with jealousy, so cracked for his vengeance, that he heard nothing of the omnibus in that infernal fog.'

Soames had done for him! And his judgment was in George's eyes.

'They talk of suicide here,' he said at last. '*That* cat won't jump.'

Soames shook his head. 'An accident,' he muttered.

Clenching his fist on the paper, George crammed it into his pocket. He could not resist a parting shot.

'H'mm! All flourishing at home? Any little Soameses yet?'

With a face as white as the steps of Jobson's, and a lip raised as if snarling, Soames brushed past him and was gone.

On reaching home and entering the little lighted hall with his latch-key, the first thing that caught his eye was his wife's gold-mounted umbrella lying on the rug chest. Flinging off his fur coat, he hurried to the drawing-room.

The curtains were drawn for the night, a bright fire of cedar-logs burned in the grate, and by its light he saw Irene sitting in her usual corner on the sofa. He shut the door softly and went towards her. She did not move, and did not seem to see him.

'So you've come back?' he said. 'Why are you sitting here in the dark?'

Then he caught sight of her face, so white and motionless that it seemed as though the blood must have stopped flowing in her veins; and her eyes, that looked enormous, like the great, wide, startled brown eyes of an owl.

Huddled in her grey fur against the sofa cushions, she had a strange resemblance to a captive owl, bunched in its soft feathers against the wires of a cage. The supple erectness of her figure was gone, as though she had been broken by cruel exercise; as though there were no longer any reason for being beautiful, and supple, and erect.

'So you've come back,' he repeated.

She never looked up, and never spoke, the firelight playing over her motionless figure.

Suddenly she tried to rise, but he prevented her; it was then that he understood.

She had come back like an animal wounded to death, not knowing where to turn, not knowing what she was doing. The sight of her figure, huddled in the fur, was enough.

He knew then for certain that Bosinney had been her lover; knew that she had seen the report of his death—perhaps, like himself, had bought a paper at the draughty corner of a street and read it.

She had come back then of her own accord, to the cage she had pined to be free of—and taking in all the tremendous significance of this, he longed to cry: 'Take your hated body, that I love, out of my house! Take away that pitiful white face, so cruel and soft—before I crush it. Get out of my sight; never let me see you again!'

And, at those unspoken words, he seemed to see her rise and move away, like a woman in a terrible dream, from which she was fighting to awake—rise and go out into the dark and cold, without a thought of him, without so much as the knowledge of his presence.

Then he cried, contradicting what he had not yet spoken: 'No; stay there!' And turning away from her, he sat down in his accustomed chair on the other side of the hearth.

They sat in silence.

And Soames thought: 'Why is all this? Why should I suffer so? What have I done? It is not my fault!'

Again he looked at her, huddled like a bird that is shot and dying, whose poor breast you see panting as the air is taken from it, whose poor eyes look at you who have shot it, with a slow, soft, unseeing look, taking farewell of all that is good—of the sun, and the air, and its mate.

So they sat, by the firelight, in the silence, one on each side of the hearth.

And the fume of the burning cedar logs, that he loved so well, seemed to grip Soames by the throat till he could bear it no longer. And going out into the hall he flung the door wide, to gulp down the cold air that came in; then without hat or overcoat went out into the Square.

Along the garden rails a half-starved cat came rubbing her way towards him, and Soames thought: 'Suffering! when will it cease, my suffering?'

At a front door across the way was a man of his acquaintance named Rutter, scraping his boots, with an air of 'I am master here'. And Soames walked on.

From far in the clear air the bells of the church where he and Irene had been married were pealing in 'practice' for the advent of Christ, the chimes ringing out above the sound of traffic. He felt a craving for strong drink, to lull him to indifference, or rouse him to fury. If only he could burst out of himself, out of this web that for the first time in his life he felt around him. If only he could surrender to the thought: 'Divorce her—turn her out! She has forgotten you. Forget her!'

If only he could surrender to the thought: 'Let her go—she has suffered enough!'

If only he could surrender to the desire: 'Make a slave of her—she is in your power!'

If only even he could surrender to the sudden vision: 'What does it all matter?' Forget himself for a minute, forget that it mattered what he did, forget that whatever he did he must sacrifice something.

If only he could act on an impulse!

He could forget nothing; surrender to no thought, vision, or desire; it was all too serious; too close around him, an unbreakable cage.

On the far side of the Square newspaper-boys were calling their evening wares, and the ghoulish cries mingled and jangled with the sound of those church bells.

Soames covered his ears. The thought flashed across him that but for a chance, he himself, and not Bosinney, might be lying dead, and she, instead of crouching there like a shot bird with those dying eyes—

Something soft touched his legs, the cat was rubbing herself against him. And a sob that shook him from head to foot burst from Soames's chest. Then all was still again in the dark, where the houses seemed to stare at him, each with a master and mistress of its own, and a secret story of happiness or sorrow.

And suddenly he saw that his own door was open, and black against the light from the hall a man standing with his back turned. Something slid, too, in his breast, and he stole up close behind.

He could see his own fur coat flung across the carved oak chair; the Persian rugs, the silver bowls, the rows of porcelain plates arranged along the walls, and this unknown man who was standing there.

And sharply he asked: 'What is it you want, sir?'

The visitor turned. It was young Jolyon.

'The door was open,' he said. 'Might I see your wife for a minute, I have a message for her?'

Soames gave him a strange, sidelong stare.

'My wife can see no one,' he muttered doggedly.

Young Jolyon answered gently: 'I shouldn't keep her a minute.'

Soames brushed by him and barred the way.

'She can see no one,' he said again.

Young Jolyon's glance shot past him into the hall, and Soames turned. There in the drawing-room doorway stood Irene, her eyes were wild and eager, her lips were parted, her hands outstretched. In the sight of both men that light vanished from her face; her hands dropped to her sides; she stood like stone.

Soames spun round and met his visitor's eyes, and at the look he saw in them, a sound like a snarl escaped him. He drew his lips back in the ghost of a smile.

'This is my house,' he said: 'I manage my own affairs. I've told you once—I tell you again; we are not at home.'

And in young Jolyon's face he slammed the door.

BOOK II
In Chancery

IN CHANCERY

'Two households both alike in dignity,
From ancient grudge break to new mutiny.'

Romeo and Juliet

TO JESSIE AND JOSEPH CONRAD

PART I

I

AT TIMOTHY'S

The possessive instinct never stands still. Through florescence and feud, frosts and fires, it followed the laws of progression even in the Forsyte family which had believed it fixed for ever. Nor can it be dissociated from environment any more than the quality of potato from the soil.

The historian of the English 'eighties and 'nineties will, in his good time, depict the somewhat rapid progression from self-contented and contained provincialism to still more self-contented if less contained imperialism—in other words, the 'possessive' instinct of the nation on the move. And so, as if in conformity, was it with the Forsyte family. They were spreading not merely on the surface, but within.

When, in 1895, Susan Hayman, the married Forsyte sister, followed her husband at the ludicrously low age of seventy-four, and was cremated, it made strangely little stir among the six old Forsytes left. For this apathy there were three causes. First: the almost surreptitious burial of old Jolyon in 1892 down at Robin Hill—first of the Forsytes to desert the family grave at Highgate. That burial, coming a year after Swithin's entirely proper funeral, had occasioned a great deal of talk on Forsyte 'Change, the abode of Timothy Forsyte on the Bayswater Road, London, which still collected and radiated family gossip. Opinions ranged from the lamentation of Aunt Juley to the outspoken assertion of Francie that it was 'a jolly good thing to stop all that stuffy Highgate business'. Uncle Jolyon in his later years—indeed, ever since the strange and lamentable affair between his grand-daughter June's lover, young Bosinney, and Irene, his nephew Soames Forsyte's wife—had noticeably rapped the family's knuckles; and that way of his own which he had always taken had begun to seem to them a little wayward. The philosophic vein in him, of course, had always been too liable to crop out of the strata of pure Forsyteism, so they were in a way prepared for his interment in a strange spot. But the whole thing was an odd business, and when the contents of his will became current coin on Forsyte 'Change, a shiver had gone round the clan. Out of his estate (£145,304 gross, with liabilities £35 7s. 4d.) he had actually left £15,000 to 'whomever do you think, my dear? To *Irene*!' that runaway wife of his nephew Soames; Irene, a woman who had almost disgraced the family, and—still more amazing—was to him no blood relation. Not out and out, of course; only a life interest—only the income from it! Still there it was; and old Jolyon's claim to be the perfect Forsyte was ended once for all. That, then, was the first reason why the burial of Susan Hayman—at Woking—made little stir.

The second reason was altogether more expansive and imperial. Besides the house on Campden Hill, Susan had a place (left her by Hayman when he died) just over the border in Hants, where the Hayman boys had learned to be such good shots and riders, as it was believed, which was of course nice for them and creditable to everybody; and the fact of owning something really countrified seemed somehow to excuse the dispersion of her remains—though what could have put cremation into her head they could not think! The usual invitations, however, had been issued, and Soames had gone down and young Nicholas, and the will had been quite satisfactory so far as it went, for she had only had a life interest; and everything had gone quite smoothly to the children in equal shares.

The third reason why Susan's burial made little stir was the most expansive of all. It was summed up daringly by Euphemia, the pale, the thin: 'Well, *I* think people have a right to their own bodies, even when they're dead.' Coming from a daughter of Nicholas, a Liberal of the old school and most tyrannical, it was a startling remark—showing in a flash what a lot of water had run under bridges since the death of Aunt Ann in '88, just when the proprietorship of Soames over his wife's body was acquiring the uncertainty which had led to such disaster. Euphemia, of course, spoke like a child, and had no experience; for though well over thirty by now, her name was still Forsyte. But, making all allowances, her remark did undoubtedly show expansion of the principle of liberty, decentralisation and shift in the central point of possession from others to oneself. When Nicholas heard his daughter's remark from Aunt Hester he had rapped out: 'Wives and daughters! There's no end to their liberty in these days. I knew that "Jackson" case would lead to things—lugging in habeas corpus like that!' He had, of course, never really forgiven the Married Woman's Property Act, which would so have interfered with him if he had not mercifully married before it was passed. But, in truth, there was no denying the revolt among the younger Forsytes against being owned by others; that, as it were, Colonial disposition to own oneself, which is the paradoxical forerunner of Imperialism, was making progress all the time. They were all now married, except George, confirmed to the Turf and the Iseeum Club; Francie, pursuing her musical career in a studio off the King's Road, Chelsea, and still taking 'lovers' to dances; Euphemia, living at home and complaining of Nicholas; and those two Dromios, Giles and Jesse Hayman. Of the third generation there were not very many—young Jolyon had three, Winifred Dartie four, young Nicholas six already, young Roger had one, Marian Tweetyman one; St John Hayman two. But the rest of the sixteen married—Soames, Rachel and Cicely of James's family; Eustace and Thomas of Roger's; Ernest, Archibald and Florence of Nicholas's; Augustus and Annabel Spender of the Haymans'—were going down the years unreproduced.

Thus, of the ten old Forsytes twenty-one young Forsytes had been born; but of the twenty-one young Forsytes there were as yet only seventeen descendants; and it already seemed unlikely that there would be more than a further unconsidered trifle or so. A student of statistics must have noticed that the birth rate had varied in accordance with the rate of interest for your money. Grandfather 'Superior Dosset' Forsyte in the early nineteenth century had been getting ten per cent for his, hence ten children. Those ten, leaving out the four who had not married, and Juley, whose husband Septimus Small had, of course, died almost at once, had averaged from four to five per cent for theirs, and produced accordingly. The twenty-one whom they produced were now getting barely three per cent in the Consols to which their fathers had mostly tied the Settlements they made to avoid death duties, and the six of them who had been reproduced had seventeen children, or just the proper two and five-sixths per stem.

There were other reasons, too, for this mild reproduction. A distrust of their earning powers, natural where a sufficiency is guaranteed together with the knowledge that their fathers did not die, kept them cautious. If one had children and not much income, the standard of taste and comfort must of necessity go down; what was enough for two was not enough for four, and so on–it would be better to wait and see what Father did. Besides, it was nice to be able to take holidays unhampered. Sooner in fact than own children, they preferred to concentrate on the ownership of themselves, conforming to the growing tendency–*fin de siècle*, as it was called. In this way, little risk was run, and one would be able to have a motor-car. Indeed, Eustace already had one, but it had shaken him horribly, and broken one of his eye teeth; so that it would be better to wait till they were a little safer. In the meantime, no more children! Even young Nicholas was drawing in his horns, and had made no addition to his six for quite three years.

The corporate decay, however, of the Forsytes, their dispersion rather, of which all this was symptomatic, had not advanced so far as to prevent a rally when Roger Forsyte died in 1899. It had been a glorious summer, and after holidays abroad and at the sea they were practically all back in London, when Roger with a touch of his old originality had suddenly breathed his last at his own house in Princes Gardens. At Timothy's it was whispered sadly that poor Roger had always been eccentric about his digestion–had he not, for instance, preferred German mutton to all the other brands?

Be that as it may, his funeral at Highgate had been perfect, and coming away from it Soames Forsyte made almost mechanically for his Uncle Timothy's in the Bayswater Road. The 'Old Things'–Aunt Juley and Aunt Hester–would like to hear about it. His father–James–at eighty-eight had not felt up to the fatigue of the funeral; and Timothy himself, of course, had not gone; so that Nicholas had been the only brother present. Still, there had been a fair gathering; and it would cheer Aunts Juley and Hester up to know. The kindly thought was not unmixed with the inevitable longing to get something out of everything you do, which is the chief characteristic of Forsytes, and indeed of the saner elements in every nation. In this practice of taking family matters to Timothy's in the Bayswater Road, Soames was but following in the footsteps of his father, who had been in the habit of going at least once a week to see his sisters at Timothy's, and had only given it up when he lost his nerve at eighty-six, and could not go out without Emily. To go with Emily was of no use, for who could really talk to anyone in the presence of his own wife? Like James in the old days, Soames found time to go there nearly every Sunday, and sit in the little drawing-room into which, with his undoubted taste, he had introduced a good deal of change and china not quite up to his own fastidious mark, and at least two rather doubtful Barbizon pictures, at Christmastides. He himself, who had done extremely well with the Barbizons, had for some years past moved towards the Marises, Israels, and Mauve, and was hoping to do better. In the riverside house which he now inhabited near Mapledurham he had a gallery, beautifully hung and lighted, to which few London dealers were strangers. It served, too, as a Sunday afternoon attraction in those week-end parties which his sisters, Winifred or Rachel, occasionally organised for him.

For though he was but a taciturn showman, his quiet collected determinism seldom failed to influence his guests, who knew that his reputation was grounded not on mere æsthetic fancy, but on his power of gauging the future of market values. When he went to Timothy's he almost always had some little tale of triumph over a deal to unfold, and dearly he loved that coo of pride with which his aunts would greet it. This afternoon, however, he was differently animated, coming from Roger's funeral in his neat dark clothes–not quite black, for after all an uncle was but an uncle, and his soul abhorred excessive display of feeling. Leaning back in a marqueterie chair and gazing down his uplifted nose at the sky-blue walls plastered with gold frames, he was noticeably silent. Whether because he had been to a funeral or not, the peculiar Forsyte build of his face was seen to the best advantage this afternoon–a face concave and long, with a jaw which divested of flesh would have seemed extravagant: altogether a chinny face, though not at all ill-looking. He was feeling more strongly than ever that Timothy's was hopelessly 'rum-ti-too', and the souls of his aunts dismally mid-Victorian. The subject on which alone he wanted to talk–his own undivorced position–was unspeakable. And yet it occupied his mind to the exclusion of all else. It was only since the spring that this had been so, and a new feeling grown up which was egging him on towards what he knew might well be folly in a Forsyte of forty-five. More and more of late he had been conscious that he was 'getting on'. The fortune, already considerable when he conceived the house at Robin Hill which had finally wrecked his marriage with Irene, had mounted with surprising vigour in the twelve lonely years during which he had devoted himself to little else. He was worth to-day well over a hundred thousand pounds, and had no one to leave it to–no real object for going on with what was his religion. Even if he were to relax his efforts, money made money, and he felt that he would have a hundred and fifty thousand before he knew where he was. There had always been a strongly domestic, philoprogenitive side to Soames; baulked and frustrated, it had hidden itself away, but now had crept out again in this his 'prime of life'. Concreted and focused of late by the attraction of a girl's undoubted beauty, it had become a veritable prepossession.

And this girl was French, not likely to lose her head, or accept any unlegalised position. Moreover, Soames himself disliked the thought of that. He had tasted of the sordid side of sex during those long years of forced celibacy, secretively, and always with disgust, for he was fastidious, and his sense of law and order innate. He wanted no hole and corner liaison. A marriage at the Embassy in Paris, a few months' travel, and he could bring Annette back quite separated from a past which in truth was not too distinguished, for she only kept the accounts in her mother's Soho restaurant; he could bring her back as something very new and chic with her French taste and self-possession, to reign at 'The Shelter' near Mapledurham. On Forsyte 'Change and among his riverside friends it would be current that he had met a charming French girl on his travels and married her. There would be the flavour of romance, and a certain *catchet* about a French wife. No! He was not at all afraid of that; it was only this cursed undivorced condition of his, and–and the question whether Annette would take him, which he dared not put to the touch until he had a clear and even dazzling future to offer her.

In his aunts' drawing-room he heard with but muffled ears those usual questions: How was his dear father? Not going out, of course, now that the weather was turning chilly? Would Soames be sure to tell him that Hester had found boiled holly leaves most comforting for that pain in her side; a poultice every three hours, with red flannel afterwards. And could he relish just a little pot of their very best prune preserve–it was so delicious this year, and had such a wonderful effect. Oh! and about the Darties–*had* Soames heard that dear Winifred was having a most distressing time with Montague? Timothy thought she really ought to have protection. It was said–but Soames mustn't take this for certain–that he had given some of Winifred's jewellery to a dreadful dancer. It was such a bad example for dear Val just as he was going to college. Soames had not heard? Oh, but he must go and see his sister and look into it at once! And did he think these Boers were really going to resist? Timothy was in quite a stew about it. The price of Consols was so high, and he had such a lot of money in them. Did Soames think they must go down if there was a war? Soames nodded. But it would be over very quickly. It would be so bad for Timothy if it wasn't. And of course Soames's dear father would feel it very much at his age. Luckily poor dear Roger had been spared this dreadful anxiety. And Aunt Juley with a little handkerchief wiped away the large tear trying to climb the permanent pout on her now quite withered left cheek; she was remembering dear Roger, and all his originality, and how he used to stick pins into her when they were little together. Aunt Hester, with her instinct for avoiding the unpleasant, here chimed in: Did Soames think they would make Mr Chamberlain Prime Minister at once? He would settle it all so quickly. She would like to see that old Kruger sent to St Helena. She could remember so well the news of Napoleon's death, and what a relief it had been to his grandfather. Of course she and Juley–'We were in pantalettes then, my dear'–had not felt it much at the time.

Soames took a cup of tea from her, drank it quickly, and ate three of those macaroons for which Timothy's was famous. His faint, pale, supercilious smile had deepened just a little. Really, his family remained hopelessly provincial, however much of London they might possess between them. In these go-ahead days their provincialism stared out even more than it used to. Why, old Nicholas was still a Free Trader and a member of that antediluvian home of Liberalism, the Remove Club–though, to be sure, the members were pretty well all Conservative now, or he himself could not have joined; and Timothy, they said, still wore a nightcap. Aunt Juley spoke again. Dear Soames was looking so well, hardly a day older than he did when dear Ann died, and they were all together, dear Jolyon, and dear Swithin, and dear Roger. She paused and caught the tear which had climbed the pout on her right cheek. Did he–did he ever hear anything of Irene nowadays? Aunt Hester visibly interposed her shoulder. Really, Juley was always saying something! The smile left Soames's face, and he put his cup down. Here was his subject broached for him, and for all his desire to expand, he could not take advantage.

Aunt Juley went on rather hastily:

'They say dear Jolyon first left her that fifteen thousand out and out; then of course he saw it would not be right, and made it for her life only.'

Had Soames heard that?

Soames nodded.

'Your cousin Jolyon is a widower now. He is her trustee; you know that, of course?'

Soames shook his head. He did know, but wished to show no interest. Young Jolyon and he had not met since the day of Bosinney's death.

'He must be quite middle-aged by now,' went on Aunt Juley dreamily. 'Let me see, he was born when your dear uncle lived in Mount Street; long before they went to Stanhope Gate—in December, '47, just before the commune. He's over fifty! Fancy that! Such a pretty baby, and we were all so proud of him; the very first of you all.' Aunt Juley sighed, and a lock of not quite her own hair came loose and straggled, so that Aunt Hester gave a little shiver. Soames rose, he was experiencing a curious piece of self-discovery. That old wound to his pride and self-esteem was not yet closed. He had come thinking he could talk of it, even wanting to talk of his fettered condition, and—behold! he was shrinking away from this reminder by Aunt Juley, renowned for her Malapropisms.

Oh, Soames was not going already!

Soames smiled a little vindictively, and said:

'Yes, good-bye. Remember me to Uncle Timothy!' And, leaving a cold kiss on each forehead, whose wrinkles seemed to try and cling to his lips as if longing to be kissed away, he left them looking brightly after him—dear Soames, it had been so good of him to come to-day, when they were not feeling very—!

With compunction tweaking at his chest Soames descended the stairs, where was always that rather pleasant smell of camphor and port wine, and house where draughts are not permitted. The poor old things—he had not meant to be unkind! And in the street he instantly forgot them, repossessed by the image of Annette and the thought of the cursed coil around him. Why had he not pushed the thing through and obtained divorce when that wretched Bosinney was run over, and there was evidence galore for the asking! And he turned towards his sister Winifred Dartie's residence in Green Street, Mayfair.

2

EXIT A MAN OF THE WORLD

That a man of the world so subject to the vicissitudes of fortune as Montague Dartie should still be living in a house he had inhabited twenty years at least would have been more noticeable if the rent, rates, taxes, and repairs of that house had not been defrayed by his father-in-law. By that simple if wholesale device James Forsyte had secured a certain stability in the lives of his daughter and his grandchildren. After all, there is something invaluable about a safe roof over the head of a sportsman so dashing as Dartie. Until the events of the last few days he had been almost supernaturally steady all this year. The fact was he had acquired a half share in a filly of George Forsyte's, who had gone irreparably on the Turf, to the horror of Roger, now stilled by the grave. Sleeve-links, by Martyr, out of Shirt-on-fire, by Suspender, was a bay filly, three years old, who for a variety of reasons had never shown her true form. With half ownership of this hopeful animal, all the idealism latent somewhere in Dartie, as in every other man, had put up its head and kept him quietly ardent for months past. When a man has something good to live for, it is astonishing how sober he becomes; and what Dartie had was really good—a three to one chance for an autumn handicap, publicly assessed at twenty-five to one. The old-fashioned heaven was a poor thing beside it, and his shirt was on the daughter of Shirt-on-fire. But how much more than his shirt depended on this grand-daughter of Suspender! At that roving age of forty-five, trying to Forsytes—and, though perhaps less distinguishable from any other age, trying even to Darties—Montague had fixed his current fancy on a dancer. It was no mean passion, but without money, and a good deal of it, likely to remain a love as airy as her skirts; and Dartie never had any money, subsisting miserably on what he could beg or borrow from Winifred—a woman of character, who kept him because he was the father of her children, and from a lingering admiration for those now-dying Wardour Street good looks which in their youth had fascinated her. She, together with anyone else who would lend him anything, and his losses at cards and on the Turf (extraordinary how some men make a good thing out of losses), were his whole means of subsistence; for James was now too old and nervous to approach, and Soames too formidably adamant. It is not too much to say that Dartie had been living on hope for months. He had never been fond of money for itself, had always despised the Forsytes with their investing habits, though careful to make such use of them as he could. What he liked about money was what it bought—personal sensation.

'No real sportsman cares for money,' he would say, borrowing a 'pony' if it was no use trying for a 'monkey'. There was something delicious about Montague Dartie. He was, as George Forsyte said, a 'daisy'.

The morning of the Handicap dawned clear and bright, the last day of September, and Dartie, who had travelled to Newmarket the night before, arrayed himself in spotless checks and walked to an eminence to see his half of the filly take her final canter. If she won he would be a cool three thou. in pocket—a poor enough recompense for the sobriety and patience of these weeks of hope, while they had been nursing her for this race. But he had not been able to afford more. Should he 'lay it off' at the eight to one to which she had advanced? This was his single thought while the larks sang above him, and the grassy downs smelled sweet, and the pretty filly passed, tossing her head and glowing like satin. After all, if he lost it would not be he who paid, and to 'lay off' would reduce his winnings to some fifteen hundred—hardly enough to purchase a dancer out and out. Even more potent was the itch in the blood of all the Darties for a real flutter. And turning to George, he said: 'She's a clipper. She'll win hands down; I shall go the whole hog.' George, who had laid off every penny, and a few besides, and stood to win, however it came out, grinned down on him from his bulky height, with the words: 'So ho, my wild one!' for after a chequered apprenticeship weathered with the money of a deeply complaining Roger, his Forsyte blood was beginning to stand him in good stead in the profession of owner.

There are moments of disillusionment in the lives of men from which the sensitive recorder shrinks. Suffice it to say that the good thing fell down. Sleeve-links finished in the ruck. Dartie's shirt was lost.

Between the passing of these things, and the day when Soames turned his face towards Green Street, what had not happened!

When a man with the constitution of Montague Dartie has exercised self-control for months from religious motives, and remains unrewarded, he does not curse God and die, he curses God and lives, to the distress of his family.

Winifred—a plucky woman, if a little too fashionable—who had borne the brunt of him for exactly twenty-one years, had never really believed that he would do what he now did. Like so many wives, she thought she knew the worst, but she had not yet known him in his forty-fifth year, when he, like other men, felt that it was now or never. Paying on the 2nd of October a visit of inspection to her jewel-case, she was horrified to observe that her woman's crown and glory was gone—the pearls which Montague had given her in '85, when Benedict was born, and which James had been compelled to pay for in the spring of '87 to save scandal. She consulted her husband at once. He 'pooh-poohed' the matter. They would turn up! Nor till she said sharply: 'Very well, then, Monty, I shall go down to Scotland Yard *myself*,' did he consent to take the matter in hand. Alas! that the steady and resolved continuity of design necessary to the accomplishment of sweeping operations should be liable to interruption by drink. That night Dartie returned home without a care in the world or a particle of reticence. Under normal conditions, Winifred would merely have locked her door and let him sleep it off, but torturing suspense about her pearls had caused her to wait up for him. Taking a small revolver from his pocket and holding on to the dining-table, he told her at once that he did not care a cursh whether she lived s'long as she was quiet; but he himself wash tired o'life. Winifred, holding on to the other side of the dining-table, answered:

'Don't be a clown, Monty. Have you been to Scotland Yard?'

Placing the revolver against his chest, Dartie had pulled the trigger several times. It was not loaded. Dropping it with an imprecation, he had muttered: 'For shake o' the children,' and sank into a chair. Winifred, having picked up the revolver, gave him some soda-water. The liquor had a magical effect. Life had ill-used him; Winifred had never 'unshtood'm'. If he hadn't the right to take the pearls he had given her himself, who had? That Spanish filly had got'm. If Winifred had any 'jection he w'd cut—her—throat. What was the matter with that? (Probably the first use of that celebrated phrase—so obscure are the origins of even the most classical language!)

Winifred, who had learned self-containment in a hard school, looked up at him and said: 'Spanish filly! Do you mean that girl we saw dancing in the Pandemonium Ballet? Well, you are a thief and a blackguard.' It had been the last straw on a sorely loaded consciousness; reaching up from his chair Dartie seized his wife's arm, and recalling the achievements of his boyhood, twisted it. Winifred endured the agony with tears in her eyes, but no murmur. Watching for a moment of weakness, she wrenched it free; then placing the dining-table between them, said between her teeth: 'You are the limit, Monty.' (Undoubtedly the inception of that phrase—so is English formed under the stress of circumstance.) Leaving Dartie with foam on his dark moustache, she went upstairs and, after locking her door and bathing her arm in hot water, lay awake all night, thinking of her pearls adorning the neck of another, and of the consideration her husband had presumably received therefor.

The man of the world awoke with a sense of being lost to that world, and a dim recollection of having been called a 'limit'. He sat for half an hour in the dawn and the arm-chair where he had slept—perhaps the unhappiest half-hour he had ever spent, for even to Dartie there is something tragic about an end. And he knew that he had reached it. Never again would he sleep in his dining-room and wake with the light filtering through those curtains bought by Winifred at Nickens and Jarveys with the money of James. Never again eat a devilled kidney at that rosewood table, after a roll in the sheets and a hot bath. He took his note-case from his dress coat pocket. Four hundred pounds, in fives and tens—the remainder of the proceeds of his half of Sleeve-links, sold last night, cash down, to George Forsyte, who, having won over the race, had not conceived the sudden dislike to the animal which he himself now felt. The ballet was going to Buenos Aires the day after to-morrow, and he was going too. Full value for the pearls had not yet been received; he was only at the soup.

He stole upstairs. Not daring to have a bath or shave (besides, the water would be cold), he changed his clothes and packed stealthily all he could. It was hard to leave so many shining boots, but one must sacrifice something. Then, carrying a valise in either hand, he stepped out on to the landing. The house was very quiet—that house where he had begotten his four children. It was a curious moment, this, outside the room of his wife, once admired, if not perhaps loved, who had called him 'the limit'. He steeled himself with that phrase, and tiptoed on; but the next door was harder to pass. It was the room his daughters slept in. Maud was at school, but Imogen would be lying there; and moisture came into Dartie's early morning eyes. She was the most like him of the four, with her dark hair and her luscious brown glance. Just coming out, a pretty thing! He set down the two valises. This almost formal abdication of fatherhood hurt him. The morning light fell on a face which worked with real emotion. Nothing so false as penitence moved him; but genuine paternal feeling, and that melancholy of 'never again'. He moistened his lips; and complete irresolution for a moment paralysed his legs in their check trousers. It was hard—hard to be thus compelled to leave his home! 'D—n it!' he muttered, 'I never thought it would come to this.' Noises above warned him that the maids were beginning to get up. And grasping the two valises, he tiptoed on downstairs. His cheeks were wet, and the knowledge of that was comforting, as though it guaranteed the genuineness of his sacrifice. He lingered a little in the rooms below to pack all the cigars he had, some papers, a crush hat, a silver cigarette-box, a Ruff's Guide. Then, mixing himself a stiff whisky and soda, and lighting a cigarette, he stood hesitating before a photograph of his two girls in a silver frame. It belonged to Winifred. 'Never mind,' he thought; 'she can get another taken, and I can't!' He slipped it into the valise. Then, putting on his hat and overcoat, he took two others, his best malacca cane, an umbrella, and opened the front door. Closing it softly behind him, he walked out, burdened as he had never been in all his life, and made his way round the corner to wait there for an early cab to come by. . . .

Thus had passed Montague Dartie in the forty-fifth year of his age from the house which he had called his own. . . .

When Winifred came down and realised that he was not in the house, her first feeling was one of dull anger that he should thus elude the reproaches she had carefully prepared in those long wakeful hours. He had gone off to Newmarket or Brighton, with that woman as likely as not. Disgusting! Forced to a complete reticence before Imogen and the servants, and aware that her father's nerves would never stand the disclosure, she had been unable to refrain from going to Timothy's that afternoon, and pouring out the story of the pearls to Aunts Juley and Hester in utter confidence. It was only on the following morning that she noticed the disappearance of that photograph. What did it mean? Careful examination of her husband's relics prompted the thought that he had gone for good. As that conclusion hardened she stood quite still in the middle of his dressing-room, with all the drawers pulled out, to try and realise what she was feeling. By no means easy! Though he was 'the limit' he was yet her property, and for the life of her she could not but feel the poorer. To be widowed yet not widowed at forty-two; with four children, made conspicuous, an object of commiseration! Gone to the arms of a Spanish jade! Memories, feelings, which she had thought quite dead, revived within her, painful, sullen, tenacious. Mechanically she closed drawer after drawer, went to her bed, lay on it, and buried her face in the pillows. She did not cry. What was the use of that? When she got off her bed to go down to lunch, she felt as if only one thing could do her good, and that was to have Val home. He—her eldest boy—who was to go to Oxford next month at James's expense, was at Littlehampton taking his final gallops with his trainer for Smalls, as he would have phrased it, following his father's diction. She caused a telegram to be sent to him.

'I must see about his clothes,' she said to Imogen; 'I can't have him going up to Oxford all anyhow. Those boys are so particular.'

'Val's got heaps of things,' Imogen answered.

'I know; but they want overhauling. I hope he'll come.'

'He'll come like a shot, Mother. But he'll probably skew his exam.'

'I can't help that,' said Winifred. 'I want him.'

With an innocent shrewd look at her mother's face, Imogen kept silence. It was father, of course! Val did come 'like a shot' at six o'clock.

Imagine a cross between a pickle and a Forsyte and you have young Publius Valerius Dartie. A youth so named could hardly turn out otherwise. When he was born, Winifred, in the hey-day of spirits, and the craving for distinction, had determined that her children should have names such as no others had ever had. (It was a mercy—she felt now—that she had just not named Imogen Thisbe.) But it was to George Forsyte, always a wag, that Val's christening was due. It so happened that Dartie dining with him, a week after the birth of his son and heir, had mentioned this aspiration of Winifred's.

'Call him Cato,' said George, 'it'll be damned piquant!' He had just won a tenner on a horse of that name.

'Cato!' Dartie had replied—they were a little 'on' as the phrase was even in those days—'it's not a Christian name.'

'Hallo, you!' George called to a waiter in knee breeches. 'Bring me the *Encyc'pedia Brit.* from the library, letter C.'

The waiter brought it.

'Here you are!' said George, pointing with his cigar. 'Cato—Publius Valerius by Virgil out of Lydia. That's what you want. Publius Valerius is Christian enough.'

Dartie, on arriving home, had informed Winifred. She had been charmed. It was so 'chic'. And Publius Valerius became the baby's name, though it afterwards transpired that they had got hold of the inferior Cato. In 1890, however, when little Publius was nearly ten, the word 'chic' went out of fashion, and sobriety came in; Winifred began to have doubts. They were confirmed by little Publius himself, who returned from his first term at school complaining that life was a burden to him—they called him Pubby. Winifred—a woman of real decision—promptly changed his school and his name to Val, the Publius being dropped even as an initial.

At nineteen he was a limber, freckled youth with a wide mouth, light eyes, long dark lashes, a rather charming smile, considerable knowledge of what he should not know, and no experience of what he ought to do. Few boys had more narrowly escaped being expelled—the engaging rascal. After kissing his mother and pinching Imogen, he ran upstairs three at a time, and came down four, dressed for dinner. He was awfully sorry, but his 'trainer', who had come up too, had asked him to dine at the Oxford and Cambridge; it wouldn't do to miss—the old chap would be hurt. Winifred let him go with an unhappy pride.

She had wanted him at home, but it was very nice to know that his tutor was so fond of him. He went out with a wink at Imogen, saying:

'I say, Mother, could I have two plover's eggs when I come in?—cook's got some. They top up so jolly well. Oh! and look here—have you any money?—I had to borrow a fiver from old Snobby.'

Winifred, looking at him with fond shrewdness, answered:

'My dear, you *are* naughty about money. But you shouldn't pay him to-night, anyway; you're his guest.' How nice and slim he looked in his white waistcoat and his dark thick lashes!

'Oh, but we may go to the theatre, you see, Mother; and I think I ought to stand the tickets; he's always hard up, you know.'

Winifred produced a five-pound note, saying:

'Well, perhaps you'd better pay him, but you mustn't stand the tickets too.'

Val pocketed the fiver.

'If I do, I can't,' he said. 'Good-night, Mum.'

He went out with his head up and his hat cocked joyously, sniffing the air of Piccadilly like a young hound loosed in covert. Jolly good biz! After that mouldy old slow hole down there!

He found his 'tutor', not indeed at the Oxford and Cambridge, but at the Goat's Club. This 'tutor' was a year older than himself, a good-looking youth, with fine brown eyes and smooth dark hair, a small mouth, an oval face, languid, immaculate, cool to a degree, one of those young men who without effort establish moral ascendancy over their companions. He had missed being expelled from school a year before Val, had spent that year at Oxford, and Val could almost see a halo round his head. His name was Crum, and no one could get through money quicker. It seemed to be his only aim in life dazzling to young Val, in whom, however, the Forsyte would stand apart, now and then, wondering where the value for that money was.

They dined quietly, in style and taste; left the club smoking cigars, with just two bottles inside them, and dropped into stalls at the Liberty. For Val the sound of comic songs, the sight of lovely legs, were fogged and interrupted by haunting fears that he would never equal Crum's quiet dandyism. His idealism was roused; and when that is so, one is never quite at ease. Surely he had too wide a mouth, not the best cut of waistcoat, no braid on his trousers, and his lavender gloves had no thin black stitchings down the back. Besides, he laughed too much—Crum never laughed, he only smiled, with his regular dark brows raised a little so that they formed a gable over his just drooped lids. No! he would never be Crum's equal. All the same, it was a jolly good show, and Cynthia Dark simply ripping. Between the acts Crum regaled him with particulars of Cynthia's private life, and the awful knowledge became Val's that, if he liked, Crum could go behind. He simply longed to say: 'I say, take me!' but dared not, because of his deficiencies; and this made the last act or two almost miserable. On coming out, Crum said: 'It's half an hour before they close; let's go on to the Pandemonium.' They took a hansom to travel the hundred yards, and seats costing seven-and-six apiece because they were going to stand, and walked into the Promenade. It was in these little things, this utter negligence of money, that Crum had such engaging polish. The ballet was on its last legs and night, and the traffic of the Promenade was suffering for the moment. Men and women were crowded in three rows against the barrier. The whirl and dazzle on the stage, the half dark, the mingled tobacco fumes and women's scent, all that curious lure to promiscuity which belongs to

Promenades, began to free young Val from his idealism. He looked admiringly in a young woman's face, saw she was not young, and quickly looked away. Shades of Cynthia Dark! The young woman's arm touched his unconsciously; there was a scent of musk and mignonette. Val looked round the corner of his lashes. Perhaps she *was* young, after all. Her foot trod on his; she begged his pardon. He said:

'Not at all; jolly good ballet, isn't it?'

'Oh, I'm tired of it; aren't you?'

Young Val smiled—his wide, rather charming smile. Beyond that he did not go—not yet convinced. The Forsyte in him stood out for greater certainty. And on the stage the ballet whirled its kaleidoscope of snow-white, salmon-pink, and emerald-green, and violet, and seemed suddenly to freeze into a stilly spangled pyramid. Applause broke out, and it was over! Maroon curtains had cut it off. The semi-circle of men and women round the barrier broke up, the young woman's arm pressed his. A little way off disturbance seemed centring round a man with a pink carnation, Val stole another glance at the young woman, who was looking towards it. Three men, unsteady, emerged, walking arm in arm. The one in the centre wore the pink carnation, a white waistcoat, a dark moustache; he reeled a little as he walked. Crum's voice said slow and level: 'Look at that bounder, he's screwed!' Val turned to look. The 'bounder' had disengaged his arm and was pointing straight at them. Crum's voice, level as ever, said:

'He seems to know you!' The 'bounder' spoke:

'H'llo!' he said. 'You f'llows, look! There's my young rascal of a son!'

Val saw. It was his father! He could have sunk into the crimson carpet. It was not the meeting in this place, not even that his father was 'screwed'; it was Crum's word 'bounder', which, as by heavenly revelation, he perceived at that moment to be true. Yes, his father looked a bounder with his dark good looks, and his pink carnation, and his square, self-assertive walk. And without a word he ducked behind the young woman and slipped out of the promenade. He heard the word 'Val' behind him, and ran down deep-carpeted steps past the chuckers-out, into the square.

To be ashamed of his own father is perhaps the bitterest experience a young man can go through. It seemed to Val, hurrying away, that his career had ended before it had begun. How could he go up to Oxford now amongst all those chaps, those splendid friends of Crum's, who would know that his father was a 'bounder'! And suddenly he hated Crum. Who the devil was Crum, to say that? If Crum had been beside him at that moment, he would certainly have been jostled off the pavement. His own father—his own! A choke came up in his throat, and he dashed his hands down deep into his overcoat pockets. Damn Crum! He conceived the wild idea of running back and finding his father, taking him by the arm and walking about with him in front of Crum; but gave it up at once and pursued his way down Piccadilly. A young woman planted herself before him. 'Not so angry, darling!' He sighed, dodged her, and suddenly became quite cool. If Crum ever said a word, he would jolly well punch his head, and there would be an end of it. He walked a hundred yards or more, contented with that thought, then lost its comfort utterly. It wasn't simple like that! He remembered how, at school, when some parent came down who did not pass the standard, it just clung to the fellow afterwards. It was one of those things nothing could remove. Why had his mother married his father, if he was a 'bounder'? It was bitterly unfair—jolly low-down on a fellow to give him a 'bounder' for father. The worst of it was that now Crum had spoken the word, he realised that he had long known subconsciously that his father was not 'the clean potato'. It was the beastliest thing that had ever happened to him—beastliest thing that had ever happened to any fellow! And, down-hearted as he had never yet been, he came to Green Street and let himself in with a smuggled latch-key. In the dining-room his plover's eggs were set invitingly, with some cut bread and butter, and a little whisky at the bottom of a decanter—just enough, as Winifred had thought, for him to feel himself a man. It made him sick to look at them, and he went upstairs.

Winifred heard him pass, and thought: 'The dear boy's in. Thank goodness! If he takes after his father I don't know what I shall do! But he won't—he's like me. Dear Val!'

3

SOAMES PREPARES TO TAKE STEPS

When Soames entered his sister's little Louis Quinze drawing-room, with its small balcony, always flowered with hanging geraniums in the summer, and now with pots of Lilium Auratum, he was struck by the immutability of human affairs. It looked just the same as on his first visit to the newly-married Darties twenty-one years ago. He had chosen the furniture himself, and so completely that no subsequent purchase had ever been able to change the room's atmosphere. Yes, he had founded his sister well, and she had wanted it. Indeed, it said a great deal for Winifred that after all this time with Dartie she remained well-founded. From the first Soames had nosed out Dartie's nature from underneath the plausibility, *savoir faire*, and good looks which had dazzled Winifred, her mother, and even James, to the extent of permitting the fellow to marry his daughter without bringing anything into settlement—a fatal thing to do.

Winifred, whom he noticed next to the furniture, was sitting at her Buhl bureau with a letter in her hand. She rose and came towards him. Tall as himself, strong in the cheek-bones, well tailored, something in her face disturbed Soames. She crumpled the letter in her hand, but seemed to change her mind and held it out to him. He was her lawyer as well as her brother.

Soames read, on Iseeum Club paper, these words:

> You will not get chance to insult in my own again. I am leaving country to-morrow. It's played out. I'm tired of being insulted by you. You've brought on yourself. No self-respecting man can stand it. I shall not ask you for anything again. Good-bye. I took the photograph of the two girls. Give them my love. I don't care what your family say. It's all their doing. I'm going to live new life.
> M.D.

This after-dinner note had a splotch on it not yet quite dry. He looked at Winifred—the splotch had clearly come from her; and he checked the words: 'Good riddance!' Then it occurred to him that with this letter she was entering that very state which he himself so earnestly desired to quit—the state of a Forsyte who was not divorced.

Winifred had turned away, and was taking a long sniff from a little gold-topped bottle. A dull commiseration, together with a vague sense of injury, crept about Soames's heart. He had come to her to talk of his own position, and get sympathy, and here was she in the same position, wanting of course to talk of it, and get sympathy from him. It was always like that! Nobody ever seemed to think that he had troubles and interests of his own. He folded up the letter with the splotch inside, and said:

'What's it all about, now?'

Winifred recited the story of the pearls calmly.

'Do you think he's really gone, Soames? You see the state he was in when he wrote that.'

Soames, who, when he desired a thing, placated Providence by pretending that he did not think it likely to happen, answered:

'I shouldn't think so. I might find out at his club.'

'If George is there,' said Winifred, 'he would know.'

'George?' said Soames; 'I saw him at his father's funeral.'

'Then he's sure to be there.'

Soames, whose good sense applauded his sister's acumen, said grudgingly: 'Well, I'll go round. Have you said anything in Park Lane?'

'I've told Emily,' returned Winifred, who retained that 'chic' way of describing her mother. 'Father would have a fit.'

Indeed, anything untoward was now sedulously kept from James. With another look round at the furniture, as if to gauge his sister's exact position, Soames went out towards Piccadilly. The evening was drawing in—a touch of chill in the October haze. He walked quickly, with his close and concentrated air. He must get through, for he wished to dine in Soho. On hearing from the hall porter at the Iseeum that Mr Dartie had not been in to-day, he looked at the trusty fellow and decided only to ask if Mr George Forsyte was in the club. He was. Soames, who always looked askance at his cousin George, as one inclined to jest at his expense, followed the page-boy slightly reassured by the thought that George had just lost his father. He must have come in for about thirty thousand, besides what he had under that settlement of Roger's, which had avoided death duty. He found George in a bow-window, staring out across a half-eaten plate of muffins. His tall, bulky, black-clothed figure loomed almost threatening, though preserving still the supernatural neatness of the racing man. With a faint grin on his fleshy face, he said:

'Hallo, Soames! Have a muffin?'

'No, thanks,' murmured Soames; and, nursing his hat, with the desire to say something suitable and sympathetic, added:

'How's your mother?'

'Thanks,' said George; 'so-so. Haven't seen you for ages. You never go racing. How's the City?'

Soames, scenting the approach of a jest, closed up and answered:

'I wanted to ask you about Dartie. I hear he's—'

'Flitted, made a bolt to Buenos Aires with the fair Lola. Good for Winifred and the little Darties. He's a treat.'

Soames nodded. Naturally inimical as these cousins were, Dartie made them kin.

'Uncle James'll sleep in his bed now,' resumed George; 'I suppose he's had a lot off you, too.'

Soames smiled.

'Ah! You saw him further,' said George amicably. 'He's a real rouser. Young

Val will want a bit of looking after. I was always sorry for Winifred. She's a plucky woman.'

Again Soames nodded. 'I must be getting back to her,' he said; 'she just wanted to know for certain. We may have to take steps. I suppose there's no mistake?'

'It's quite O.K.,' said George–it was he who invented so many of those quaint sayings which have been assigned to other sources. 'He was drunk as a lord last night; but he went off all right this morning. His ship's the *Tuscarora*;' and, fishing out a card, he read mockingly:

'"Mr Montague Dartie, Poste Restante, Buenos Aires." I should hurry up with the steps, if I were you. He fairly fed me up last night.'

'Yes,' said Soames; 'but it's not always easy.' Then, conscious from George's eyes that he had roused reminiscence of his own affair, he got up and held out his hand. George rose too.

'Remember me to Winifred. You'll enter her for the Divorce Stakes straight off, if you ask me.'

Soames took a sidelong look back at him from the doorway. George had seated himself again and was staring before him; he looked big and lonely in those black clothes. Soames had never known him so subdued. 'I suppose he feels it in a way,' he thought. 'They must have about fifty thousand each, all told. They ought to keep the estate together. If there's a war, house property will go down. Uncle Roger was a good judge, though.' And the face of Annette rose before him in the darkening street; her brown hair and her blue eyes with their dark lashes, her fresh lips and cheeks, dewy and blooming in spite of London, her perfect French figure. 'Take steps!' he thought. Re-entering Winifred's house he encountered Val, and they went in together. An idea had occurred to Soames. His cousin Jolyon was Irene's trustee, the first step would be to go down and see him at Robin Hill. Robin Hill! The odd–the very odd feeling those words brought back! Robin Hill–the house Bosinney had built for him and Irene–the house they had never lived in–the fatal house! And Jolyon lived there now! H'm! And suddenly he thought: 'They say he's got a boy at Oxford! Why not take young Val down and introduce them! It's an excuse! Less bald–very much less bald!' So, as they went upstairs, he said to Val:

'You've got a cousin at Oxford; you've never met him. I should like to take you down with me to-morrow to where he lives and introduce you. You'll find it useful.'

Val receiving the idea with but moderate transports, Soames clinched it.

'I'll call for you after lunch. It's in the country–not far; you'll enjoy it.'

On the threshold of the drawing-room he recalled with an effort that the steps he contemplated concerned Winifred at the moment, not himself.

Winifred was still sitting at her Buhl bureau.

'It's quite true,' he said; 'he's gone to Buenos Aires, started this morning–we'd better have him shadowed when he lands. I'll cable at once. Otherwise we may have a lot of expense. The sooner these things are done the better. I'm always regretting that I didn't–' he stopped and looked sidelong at the silent Winifred. 'By the way,' he went on, 'can you prove cruelty?'

Winifred said in a dull voice:

'I don't know. What is cruelty?'

'Well, has he struck you, or anything?'

Winifred shook herself and her jaw grew square.

'He twisted my arm. Or would pointing a pistol count? Or being too drunk to undress himself, or– No–I can't bring in the children.'

'No,' said Soames; 'no. I wonder! Of course, there's legal separation–we can get that. But separation! Um!'

'What does it mean?' asked Winifred desolately.

'That he can't touch you, or you him; you're both of you married and unmarried.' And again he grunted. What was it, in fact, but his own accursed position, legalised! No, he would not put her into that!

'It must be divorce,' he said decisively; 'failing cruelty, there's desertion. There's a way of shortening the two years, now. We get the Court to give us restitution of conjugal rights. Then if he doesn't obey, we can bring a suit for divorce in six months' time. Of course, you don't want him back. But they won't know that. Still, there's the risk that he might come. I'd rather try cruelty.'

Winifred shook her head. 'It's so beastly.'

'Well,' Soames murmured, 'perhaps there isn't much risk so long as he's infatuated and got money. Don't say anything to anybody, and don't pay any of his debts.'

Winifred sighed. In spite of all she had been through, the sense of loss was heavy on her. And this idea of not paying his debts any more brought it home to her as nothing else yet had. Some richness seemed to have gone out of life. Without her husband, without her pearls, without that intimate sense that she made a brave show above the domestic whirlpool, she would now have to face the world. She felt bereaved indeed.

And into the chilly kiss he placed on her forehead, Soames put more than his usual warmth.

'I have to go down to Robin Hill to-morrow,' he said, 'to see young Jolyon on business. He's got a boy at Oxford. I'd like to take Val with me and introduce him. Come down to "The Shelter" for the week-end and bring the children. Oh! by the way, no, that won't do; I've got some other people coming.' So saying, he left her and turned towards Soho.

4

SOHO

Of all quarters in the queer adventurous amalgam called London, Soho is perhaps least suited to the Forsyte spirit. 'So-ho, my wild one!' George would have said if he had seen his cousin going there. Untidy, full of Greeks, Ishmaelites, cats, Italians, tomatoes, restaurants, organs, coloured stuffs, queer names, people looking out of upper windows, it dwells remote from the British Body Politic. Yet has it haphazard proprietory instincts of its own, and a certain possessive prosperity which keep its rents up when those of other quarters go down. For long years Soames's acquaintanceship with Soho had been confined to its Western bastion, Wardour Street. Many bargains had he picked up there. Even during those seven years at Brighton after Bosinney's death and Irene's flight, he had bought treasures there sometimes, though he had no place to put them; for when the conviction that his wife had gone for good at last became firm within him, he had caused a board to be put up in Montpelier Square:

FOR SALE
The Lease of this Desirable Residence
Enquire of Messrs Lesson and Tukes, Court Street, Belgravia.

It had sold within a week—that desirable residence in the shadow of whose perfection a man and a woman had eaten their hearts out.

Of a misty January evening, just before the board was taken down, Soames had gone there once more, and stood against the Square railings, looking at its unlighted windows, chewing the cud of possessive memories which had turned so bitter in the mouth. Why had she never loved him? Why? She had been given all she had wanted, and in return had given him, for three long years, all he had wanted—except, indeed, her heart. He had uttered a little involuntary groan, and a passing policeman had glanced suspiciously at him who no longer possessed the right to enter that green door with the carved brass knocker beneath the board 'For sale'! A choking sensation had attacked his throat, and he had hurried away into the mist. That evening he had gone to Brighton to live. . . .

Approaching Malta Street, Soho, and the Restaurant Bretagne, where Annette would be drooping her pretty shoulders over her accounts, Soames thought with wonder of those seven years at Brighton. How had he managed to go on so long in that town devoid of the scent of sweet-peas, where he had not even space to put his treasures? True, those had been years with no time at all for looking at them—years of almost passionate money-making, during which Forsyte, Bustard and Forsyte had become solicitors to more limited companies than they could properly attend to. Up to the City of a morning in a Pullman car, down from the City of an evening in a Pullman car. Law papers again after dinner, then the sleep of the tired, and up again next morning. Saturday to Monday was spent at his club in town—curious reversal of customary procedure, based on the deep and careful instinct that while working so hard he needed sea air to and from the station twice a day, and while resting must indulge his domestic affections. The Sunday visit to his family in Park Lane, to Timothy's, and to Green Street; the occasional visits elsewhere had seemed to him as necessary to health as sea air on weekdays. Even since his migration to Mapledurham he had maintained those habits until—he had known Annette. Whether Annette had produced the revolution in his outlook, or that outlook had produced Annette, he knew no more than we know where a circle begins. It was intricate and deeply involved with the growing consciousness that property without anyone to leave it to is the negation of true Forsyteism. To have an heir, some continuance of self, who would begin where he left off—ensure, in fact, that he would not leave off—had quite obsessed him for the last year and more. After buying a bit of Wedgwood one evening in April, he had dropped into Malta Street to look at a house of his father's which had been turned into a restaurant—a risky proceeding, and one not quite in accordance with the terms of the lease. He had stared for a little at the outside—painted a good cream colour, with two peacock-blue tubs containing little bay trees in a recessed doorway—and at the words 'Restaurant Bretagne' above them in gold letters, rather favourably impressed. Entering, he had noticed that several people were already seated at little round green tables with little pots of fresh flowers on them and Brittany-ware plates, and had asked of a trim waitress to see the proprietor. They had shown him into a back room, where a girl was sitting at a simple bureau covered with papers, and a small round table was laid for two. The impression of cleanliness, order, and good taste was confirmed when the girl got up, saying: 'You wish to see *Maman, Monsieur?*' in a broken accent.

'Yes,' Soames had answered, 'I represent your landlord; in fact, I'm his son.'

'Won't you sit down, sir, please? Tell *Maman* to come to this gentleman.'

He was pleased that the girl seemed impressed, because it showed business instinct; and suddenly he noticed that she was remarkably pretty—so remarkably pretty that his eyes found a difficulty in leaving her face. When she moved to put a chair for him, she swayed in a curious subtle way, as if she had been put together by someone with a special secret skill; and her face and neck, which was a little bared, looked as fresh as if they had been sprayed with dew. Probably at this moment Soames decided that the lease had not been violated; though to himself and his father he based the decision on the efficiency of those illicit adaptations in the building, on the signs of prosperity, and the obvious business capacity of Madame Lamotte. He did not, however, neglect to leave certain matters to future consideration, which had necessitated further visits, so that the little back room had become quite accustomed to his spare, not unsolid, but unobtrusive figure, and his pale chinny face with clipped moustache and dark hair not yet grizzling at the sides.

'*Un Monsieur très distingué,*' Madame Lamotte found him; and presently, '*Très amical, très gentil,*' watching his eyes upon her daughter.

She was one of those generously built, fine-faced, dark-haired French-women, whose every action and tone of voice inspire perfect confidence in the thoroughness of their domestic tastes, their knowledge of cooking, and the careful increase of their bank balances.

After those visits to the Restaurant Bretagne began, other visits ceased—without, indeed, any definite decision, for Soames, like all Forsytes and the great majority of their countrymen, was a born empiricist. But it was this change in his mode of life which had gradually made him so definitely conscious that he desired to alter his condition from that of the unmarried man to that of the married man remarried.

Turning into Malta Street on this evening of early October, 1899, he bought a paper to see if there was any after-development of the Dreyfus case—a question which he had always found useful in making closer acquaintanceship with Madame Lamotte and her daughter, who were Catholic and anti-Dreyfusard.

Scanning those columns, Soames found nothing French, but noticed a general fall on the Stock Exchange, and an ominous leader about the Trans-vaal. He entered, thinking: 'War's a certainty. I shall sell my Consols.' Not that he had many, personally, the rate of interest was too wretched; but he should advise his companies—Consols would assuredly go down. A look, as he passed the doorways of the restaurant, assured him that business was good as ever, and this, which in April would have pleased him, now gave him a certain uneasiness. If the steps which he had to take ended in his marrying Annette, he would rather see her mother safely back in France, a move to which the prosperity of the Restaurant Bretagne might become an obstacle. He would have to buy them out, of course, for French people only came to England to make money; and it would mean a higher price. And then that peculiar sweet sensation at the back of his throat, and a slight thumping about the heart, which he always experienced at the door of the little room, prevented his thinking how much it would cost.

Going in, he was conscious of an abundant black skirt vanishing through the door into the restaurant, and of Annette with her hands up to her hair. It was the attitude in which of all others he admired her—so beautifully straight and rounded and supple. And he said:

'I just came in to talk to your mother about pulling down that partition. No, don't call her.'

'*Monsieur* will have supper with us? It will be ready in ten minutes.' Soames, who still held her hand, was overcome by an impulse which surprised him.

'You look so pretty to-night,' he said, 'so very pretty. Do you know how pretty you look, Annette?'

Annette withdrew her hand and blushed. 'Monsieur is very good.'

'Not a bit good,' said Soames, and sat down gloomily.

Annette made a little expressive gesture with her hands, a smile was crinkling her red lips untouched by salve.

And, looking at those lips, Soames said:

'Are you happy over here, or do you want to go back to France?'

'Oh, I like London. Paris, of course. But London is better than Orleans, and the English country is so beautiful. I have been to Richmond last Sunday.'

Soames went through a moment of calculating struggle. Mapledurham! Dared he? After all, dared he go so far as that, and show her what there was to look forward to! Still! Down there one could say things. In this room it was impossible.

'I want you and your mother,' he said suddenly, 'to come for the afternoon next Sunday. My house is on the river, it's not too late in this weather; and I can show you some good pictures. What do you say?'

Annette clasped her hands.

'It will be lovelee. The river is so beautiful.'

'That's understood, then. I'll ask Madame.'

He need say no more to her this evening, and risk giving himself away. But had he not already said *too* much? Did one ask restaurant proprietors with pretty daughters down to one's country house without design? Madame Lamotte would see, if Annette didn't. Well! there was not much that Madame did not see. Besides, this was the second time he had stayed to supper with them; he owed them hospitality. . . .

Walking home towards Park Lane—for he was staying at his father's—with the impression of Annette's soft clever hand within his own, his thoughts were pleasant, slightly sensual, rather puzzled. Take steps! What steps? How? Dirty linen washed in public? Pah! With his reputation for sagacity, for far-sightedness and the clever extrication of others, he, who stood for proprietory interests, to become the plaything of that law of which he was a pillar? There was something revolting in the thought! Winifred's affair was bad enough! To have a double dose of publicity in the family! Would not a liaison be better than that—a liaison, and a son he could adopt? But dark, solid, watchful Madame Lamotte blocked the avenue of this vision. No! that would not work. It was not as if Annette could have a real passion for him; one could not expect that at his age. If her mother wished, if the wordly advantage were manifestly great—perhaps! If not, refusal would be certain. Besides, he thought: 'I'm not a villain. I don't want to hurt her; and I don't want anything underhand. But I do want her, and I want a son! There's nothing for it but divorce—somehow —anyhow—divorce!' Under the shadow of the plane trees, in the lamp-light, he passed slowly along the railings of the Green Park. Mist clung there among the bluish tree shapes, beyond range of the lamps. How many hundred times he had walked past those trees from his father's house in Park Lane, when he was quite a young man; or from his own house in Montpelier Square in those four years of married life! And to-night, making up his mind to free himself if he could of that long useless marriage tie, he took a fancy to walk on, in at Hyde Park Corner, out at Knightsbridge Gate, just as he used to when going home to Irene in the old days. What could she be like now?—How had she passed the years since he last saw her, twelve years in all, seven already since Uncle Jolyon left her that money! Was she still beautiful? Would he know her if he saw her? 'I've not changed much,' he thought; 'I expect she has. She made me suffer.' He remembered suddenly one night, the first on which he went out to dinner alone—an Old Marlburian dinner—the first year of their marriage. With what eagerness he had hurried back; and, entering softly as a cat, had heard her playing. Opening the drawing-room door noiselessly, he had stood watching the expression on her face, different from any he knew, so much more open, so confiding, as though to her music she was giving a heart he had never seen. And he remembered how she stopped and looked round, how her face changed back to that which he did know, and what an icy shiver had gone through him, for all that the next moment he was fondling her shoulders. Yes, she had made him suffer! Divorce! It seemed ridiculous, after all these years of utter separation! But it would have to be. No other way! 'The question,' he thought with sudden realism, 'is—which of us? She or me? She deserted me. She ought to pay for it. There'll be someone, I suppose.' Involuntarily he uttered a little snarling sound, and, turning, made his way back to Park Lane.

5

JAMES SEES VISIONS

The butler himself opened the door, and closing it softly, detained Soames on the inner mat.

'The master's poorly, sir,' he murmured. 'He wouldn't go to bed till you came in. He's still in the dining-room.'

Soames responded in the hushed tone to which the house was now accustomed.

'What's the matter with him, Warmson?'

'Nervous, sir, I think. Might be the funeral; might be Mrs Dartie's comin' round this afternoon. I think he overheard something. I've took him in a negus. The mistress has just gone up.'

Soames hung his hat on a mahogany stag's horn.

'All right, Warmson, you can go to bed; I'll take him up myself.' And he passed into the dining-room. . . .

James was sitting before the fire, in a big armchair, with a camel-hair shawl, very light and warm, over his frock-coated shoulders, on to which his long white whiskers drooped. His white hair, still fairly thick, glistened in the lamplight; a little moisture from his fixed, light grey eyes stained the cheeks, still quite well coloured, and the long deep furrows running to the corners of the clean-shaven lips, which moved as if mumbling thoughts. His long legs,

thin as a crow's, in shepherd's plaid trousers, were bent at less than a right
angle, and on one knee a spindly hand moved continually, with fingers wide
apart and glistening tapered nails. Beside him, on a low stool, stood a half-
finished glass of negus, bedewed with beads of heat. There he had been sitting,
with intervals for meals, all day. At eighty-eight he was still organically sound,
but suffering terribly from the thought that no one ever told him anything. It is,
indeed, doubtful how he had become aware that Roger was being buried that
day, for Emily had kept it from him. She was always keeping things from him.
Emily was only seventy! James had a grudge against his wife's youth. He felt
sometimes that he would never have married her if he had known that she
would have so many years before her, when he had so few. It was not natural.
She would live fifteen or twenty years after he was gone, and might spend a lot
of money; she had always had extravagant tastes. For all he knew, she might
want to buy one of these motor-cars. Cicely and Rachel and Imogen and all the
young people–they all rode those bicycles now, and went off goodness knows
where. And now Roger was gone. He didn't know–couldn't tell! The family
was breaking up. Soames would know how much his uncle had left. Curiously,
he thought of Roger as Soames's uncle, not as his own brother. Soames! It was
more and more the one solid spot in a vanishing world. Soames was careful; he
was a warm man; but he had no one to leave his money to. There it was! He
didn't know! And there was that fellow Chamberlain! For James's political
principles had been fixed between '70 and '85, when 'that rascally Radical' had
been the chief thorn in the side of property, and he distrusted him to this day, in
spite of his conversion; he would get the country into a mess, and make money
go down before he had done with it. A stormy petrel of a chap! Where was
Soames? He had gone to the funeral, of course, which they had tried to keep
from him. He knew that perfectly well; he had seen his son's trousers. Roger!
Roger in his coffin! He remembered how, when they came up from school
together from the West, on the box seat of the old Slowflyer in 1824, Roger had
got into the 'boot' and gone to sleep. James uttered a thin cackle. A funny
fellow–Roger–an original! He didn't know! Younger than himself, and in his
coffin! The family was breaking up. There was Val going to the university; he
never came to see him now. He would cost a pretty penny up there. It was an
extravagant age. And all the pretty pennies that his four grandchildren would
cost him danced before James's eyes. He did not grudge them the money, but
he grudged terribly the risk which the spending of that money might bring on
them; *he grudged the diminution of security.* And now that Cicely had
married, she might be having children too. He didn't know–couldn't tell!
Nobody thought of anything but spending money in these days, and racing
about, and having what they called a 'good time'. A motor-car went past the
window. Ugly great lumbering thing, making all that racket! But there it was,
the country rattling to the dogs! People in such a hurry that they couldn't even
care for style–a neat turn-out like his barouche and bays was worth all those
new-fangled things. And Consols at 116! There must be a lot of money in the
country. And now there was this old Kruger! They had tried to keep old
Kruger from him. But he knew better; there would be a pretty kettle of fish out
there! He had known how it would be when that fellow Gladstone–dead now,
thank God!–made such a mess of it after that dreadful business at Majuba. He
shouldn't wonder if the Empire split up and went to pot. And this vision of the
Empire going to pot filled a full quarter of an hour with qualms of the most
serious character. He had eaten a poor lunch because of them. But it was after

lunch that the real disaster to his nerves occurred. He had been dozing when he became aware of voices–low voices. Ah! they never told him anything! Winifred's and her mother's. 'Monty!' That fellow Dartie–always that fellow Dartie! The voices had receded; and James had been left alone, with his ears standing up like a hare's, and fear creeping about his inwards. Why did they leave him alone? Why didn't they come and tell him? And an awful thought, which through long years had haunted him, concreted again swiftly in his brain. Dartie had gone bankrupt–fraudulently bankrupt, and to save Winifred and the children, he–James–would have to pay! Could he–could Soames turn him into a limited company? No, he couldn't! There it was! With every minute before Emily came back the spectre fiercened. Why, it might be forgery! With eyes fixed on the doubted Turner in the centre of the wall, James suffered tortures. He saw Dartie in the dock, his grandchildren in the gutter, and himself in bed. He saw the doubted Turner being sold at Jobson's, and all the majestic edifice of property in rags. He saw in fancy Winifred unfashionably dressed, and heard in fancy Emily's voice saying: 'Now, don't fuss, James!' She was always saying: 'Don't fuss!' She had no nerves; he ought never to have married a woman eighteen years younger than himself. Then Emily's real voice said:

'Have you had a nice nap, James?'

Nap! He was in torment, and she asked him that!

'What's this about Dartie?' he said, and his eyes glared at her.

Emily's self-possession never deserted her.

'What have you been hearing?' she asked blandly.

'What's this about Dartie?' repeated James. 'He's gone bankrupt.'

'Fiddle!'

James made a great effort, and rose to the full height of his stork-like figure.

'You never tell me anything,' he said; 'he's gone bankrupt.'

The destruction of that fixed idea seemed to Emily all that mattered at the moment.

'He has not,' she answered firmly. 'He's gone to Buenos Aires.'

If she had said 'He's gone to Mars' she could not have dealt James a more stunning blow; his imagination, invested entirely in British securities, could as little grasp one place as the other.

'What's he gone there for?' he said. 'He's got no money. What did he take?'

Agitated within by Winifred's news, and goaded by the constant reiteration of this jeremiad, Emily said calmly:

'He took Winifred's pearls and a dancer.'

'What!' said James, and sat down.

His sudden collapse alarmed her, and smoothing his forehead, she said:

'Now, don't fuss, James!'

A dusky red had spread over James's cheeks and forehead.

'I paid for them,' he said tremblingly; 'he's a thief! I–I knew how it would be. He'll be the death of me; he–' Words failed him and he sat quite still. Emily, who thought she knew him so well, was alarmed, and went towards the sideboard where she kept some sal volatile. She could not see the tenacious Forsyte spirit working in that thin, tremulous shape against the extravagance of the emotion called up by this outrage on Forsyte principles–the Forsyte spirit deep in there, saying: 'You mustn't get into a fantod, it'll never do. You won't digest your lunch. You'll have a fit!' All unseen by her, it was doing better work in James than sal volatile.

'Drink this,' she said.

James waved it aside.

'What was Winifred about,' he said, 'to let him take her pearls?' Emily perceived the crisis past.

'She can have mine,' she said comfortably. 'I never wear them. She'd better get a divorce.'

'There you go!' said James. 'Divorce! We've never had a divorce in the family. Where's Soames?'

'He'll be in directly.'

'No, he won't,' said James, almost fiercely; 'he's at the funeral. You think I know nothing.'

'Well,' said Emily with calm, 'you shouldn't get into such fusses when we tell you things.' And plumping up his cushions, and putting the sal volatile beside him, she left the room.

But James sat there seeing visions—of Winifred in the Divorce Court, and the family name in the papers; of the earth falling on Roger's coffin; of Val taking after his father, of the pearls he had paid for and would never see again; of money back at four per cent., and the country going to the dogs; and, as the afternoon wore into evening, and tea-time passed, and dinner-time, those visions became more and more mixed and menacing—of being told nothing, till he had nothing left of all his wealth, and they told him nothing of it. Where was Soames? Why didn't he come in? . . . His hand grasped the glass of negus, he raised it to drink, and saw his son standing there looking at him. A little sigh of relief escaped his lips, and putting the glass down, he said:

'There you are! Dartie's gone to Buenos Aires!'

Soames nodded. 'That's all right,' he said; 'good riddance.'

A wave of assuagement passed over James's brain. Soames knew. Soames was the only one of them all who had sense. Why couldn't he come and live at home? He had no son of his own. And he said plaintively:

'At my age I get nervous. I wish you were more at home, my boy.'

Again Soames nodded; the mask of his countenance betrayed no understanding, but he went closer, and as if by accident touched his father's shoulder.

'They sent their love to you at Timothy's,' he said. 'It went off all right. I've been to see Winifred. I'm going to take steps.' And he thought: 'Yes, and you mustn't hear of them.'

James looked up; his long white whiskers quivered, his thin throat between the points of his collar looked very gristly and naked.

'I've been very poorly all day,' he said; 'they never tell me anything.'

Soames's heart twitched.

'Well, it's all right. There's nothing to worry about. Will you come up now?' and he put his hand under his father's arm.

James obediently and tremulously raised himself, and together they went slowly across the room, which had a rich look in the firelight, and out to the stairs. Very slowly they ascended.

'Good-night, my boy,' said James at his bedroom door.

'Good-night, father,' answered Soames. His hand stroked down the sleeve beneath the shawl; it seemed to have almost nothing in it, so thin was the arm. And, turning away from the light in the opening doorway, he went up the extra flight to his own bedroom.

'I want a son,' he thought, sitting on the edge of his bed; '*I want a son.*'

6

NO-LONGER-YOUNG JOLYON AT HOME

Trees take little account of Time, and the old oak on the upper lawn at Robin Hill looked no day older than when Bosinney sprawled under it and said to Soames: 'Forstye, I've found the very place for your house.' Since then Swithin had dreamed, and old Jolyon died, beneath its branches. And now, close to the swing, no-longer-young Jolyon often painted there. Of all spots in the world it was perhaps the most sacred to him, for he had loved his father.

Contemplating its great girth—crinkled and a little mossed, but not yet hollow—he would speculate on the passage of time. That tree had seen, perhaps, all real English history; it dated, he shouldn't wonder, from the days of Elizabeth at least. His own fifty years were as nothing to its wood. When the house behind it, which he now owned, was three hundred years of age instead of twelve, that tree might still be standing there, vast and hollow—for who would commit such sacrilege as to cut it down? A Forsyte might perhaps still be living in that house, to guard it jealously. And Jolyon would wonder what the house would look like coated with such age. Wistaria was already about its walls—the new look had gone. Would it hold its own and keep the dignity Bosinney had bestowed on it, or would the giant London have lapped it round and made it into an asylum in the midst of a jerry-built wilderness? Often, within and without of it, he was persuaded that Bosinney had been moved by the spirit when he built. He had put his heart into that house, indeed! It might even become one of the 'homes of England'—a rare achievement for a house in these degenerate days of building. And the æsthetic spirit, moving hand in hand with his Forsyte sense of possessive continuity, dwelt with pride and pleasure on his ownership thereof. There was the smack of reverence and ancestor-worship (if only for one ancestor) in his desire to hand this house down to his son and his son's son. His father had loved the house, had loved the view, the grounds, that tree; his last years had been happy there, and no one had lived there before him. These last eleven years at Robin Hill had formed in Jolyon's life, as a painter, the important period of success. He was now in the very van of water-colour art, hanging on the line everywhere. His drawings fetched high prices. Specialising in that one medium with the tenacity of his breed, he had 'arrived'—rather late, but not too late for a member of the family which made a point of living for ever. His art had really deepened and improved. In conformity with his position he had grown a short fair beard, which was just beginning to grizzle, and hid his Forsyte chin; his brown face had lost the warped expression of his ostracised period—he looked, if anything, younger. The loss of his wife in 1894 had been one of those domestic tragedies which turn out in the end for the good of all. He had, indeed, loved her to the last, for his was an affectionate spirit, but she had become increasingly difficult: jealous of her step-daughter June, jealous even of her own little daughter Holly, and making ceaseless plaint that he could not love her, ill as she was, and 'useless to everyone, and better dead'. He had mourned her sincerely, but his face had looked younger since she died. If she could only have believed that she made him happy, how much happier would the twenty years of their companionship have been!

June had never really got on well with her, who had reprehensibly taken her own mother's place; and ever since old Jolyon died she had been established in a sort of studio in London. But she had come back to Robin Hill on her stepmother's death, and gathered the reins there into her small decided hands. Jolly was then at Harrow; Holly still learning from Mademoiselle Beauce. There had been nothing to keep Jolyon at home, and he had removed his grief and his paint-box abroad. There he had wandered, for the most part in Brittany, and at last had fetched up in Paris. He had stayed there several months, and come back with the younger face and the short fair beard. Essentially a man who merely lodged in any house, it had suited him perfectly that June should reign at Robin Hill, so that he was free to go off with his easel where and when he liked. She was inclined, it is true, to regard the house rather as an asylum for her *protégés*; but his own outcast days had filled Jolyon for ever with sympathy towards an outcast, and June's 'lame ducks' about the place did not annoy him. By all means let her have them down and feed them up; and though his slightly cynical humour perceived that they ministered to his daughter's love of domination as well as moved her warm heart, he never ceased to admire her for having so many ducks. He fell, indeed, year by year into a more and more detached and brotherly attitude towards his own son and daughters, treating them with a sort of whimsical equality. When he went down to Harrow to see Jolly, he never quite knew which of them was the elder, and would sit eating cherries with him out of one paper bag, with an affectionate and ironical smile twisting up an eyebrow and curling his lips a little. And he was always careful to have money in his pocket, and to be modish in his dress, so that his son need not blush for him. They were perfect friends, but never seemed to have occasion for verbal confidences, both having the competitive self-consciousness of Forsytes. They knew they would stand by each other in scrapes, but there was no need to talk about it. Jolyon had a striking horror—partly original sin, but partly the result of his early immorality—of the moral attitude. The most he could ever have said to his son would have been:

'Look here, old man, don't forget you're a gentleman'; and then have wondered whimsically whether that was not a snobbish sentiment. The great cricket match was perhaps the most searching and awkward time they annually went through together, for Jolyon had been at Eton. They would be particularly careful during that match, continually saying: 'Hooray! Oh! hard luck, old man!' or 'Hooray! Oh! bad luck, Dad!' to each other, when some disaster at which their hearts bounded happened to the opposing school. And Jolyon would wear a grey top hat, instead of his usual soft one, to save his son's feelings, for a black top hat he could not stomach. When Jolly went up to Oxford, Jolyon went up with him, amused, humble, and a little anxious not to discredit his boy amongst all these youths who seemed so much more assured and old than himself. He often thought: 'Glad I'm a painter'—for he had long dropped under-writing at Lloyds—'it's so innocuous. You can't look down on a painter—you can't take him seriously enough.' For Jolly, who had a sort of natural lordliness, had passed at once into a very small set, who secretly amused his father. The boy had fair hair which curled a little, and his grandfather's deep-set iron-grey eyes. He was well-built, and very upright and always pleased Jolyon's æsthetic sense, so that he was a tiny bit afraid of him, as artists ever are of those of their own sex whom they admire physically. On that occasion, however, he actually did screw up his courage to give his son advice, and this was it:

'Look here, old man, you're bound to get into debt; mind you come to me at once. Of course, I'll always pay them. But you might remember that one respects oneself more afterwards if one pays one's own way. And don't ever borrow, except from me, will you?'

And Jolly had said:

'All right, Dad, I won't,' and he never had.

'And there's just one other thing. I don't know much about morality and that, but there is this: It's always worth while before you do anything to consider whether it's going to hurt another person more than is absolutely necessary.'

Jolly had looked thoughtful and nodded, and presently had squeezed his father's hand. And Jolyon had thought: 'I wonder if I had the right to say that?' He always had a sort of dread of losing the dumb confidence they had in each other; remembering how for long years he had lost his own father's, so that there had been nothing between them but love at a great distance. He under-estimated, no doubt, the change in the spirit of the age since he himself went up to Cambridge in '66; and perhaps he under-estimated, too, his boy's power of understanding that he was tolerant to the very bone. It was that tolerance of his, and possibly his scepticism, which ever made his relations towards June so queerly defensive. She was such a decided mortal, knew her own mind so terribly well; wanted things so inexorably until she got them—and then, indeed, often dropped them like a hot potato. Her mother had been like that, whence had come all those tears. Not that his incompatibility with his daughter was anything like what it had been with the first Mrs Young Jolyon. One could be amused where a daughter was concerned; in a wife's case one could not be amused. To see June set her heart and jaw on a thing until she got it was all right, because it was never anything which interfered fundamentally with Jolyon's liberty—the one thing on which his jaw was also obsolutely rigid, a considerable jaw, under that short grizzling beard. Nor was there ever any necessity for real heart-to-heart encounters. One could break away into irony—as indeed he often had to. But the real trouble with June was that she had never appealed to his æsthetic sense, though she might well have, with her red-gold hair and her viking-coloured eyes, and that touch of the Berserker in her spirit. It was very different with Holly, soft and quiet, shy and affectionate, with a playful imp in her somewhere. He watched this younger daughter of his through the duckling stage with extraordinary interest. Would she come out a swan? With her sallow oval face and her grey wistful eyes and those long dark lashes, she might, or she might not. Only this last year had he been able to guess. Yes, she would be a swan—rather a dark one, always a shy one, but an authentic swan. She was eighteen now, and Mademoiselle Beauce was gone—the excellent lady had removed, after eleven years, haunted by her continuous reminiscences of the 'well-brrred little Tayleurs', to another family whose bosom would now be agitated by her reminiscences of the 'well-brrred little Forsytes'. She had taught Holly to speak French like herself.

Portraiture was not Jolyon's forte, but he had already drawn his younger daughter three times, and was drawing her a fourth, on the afternoon of October 4th, 1899, when a card was brought to him which caused his eyebrows to go up:

MR SOAMES FORSYTE

The Shelter, Connoisseurs' Club,
Mapledurham. St James's.

But here the Forsyte Saga must digress again. . . .

To return from a long travel in Spain to a darkened house, to a little daughter bewildered with tears, to the sight of a loved father lying peaceful in his last sleep, had never been, was never likely to be, forgotten by so impressionable and warm-hearted a man as Jolyon. A sense as of mystery, too, clung to that sad day, and about the end of one whose life had been so well ordered, balanced, and above-board. It seemed incredible that his father could thus have vanished without, as it were, announcing his intention, without last words to his son, and due farewells. And those incoherent allusions of little Holly to 'the lady in grey', of Mademoiselle Beauce to a Madame Errant (as it sounded) involved all things in a mist, lifted a little when he read his father's will and the codicil thereto. It had been his duty as executor of that will and codicil to inform Irene, wife of his cousin Soames, of her life interest in fifteen thousand pounds. He had called on her to explain that the existing investments in India Stock, ear-marked to meet the charge, would produce for her the interesting net sum of £430 odd a year, clear of income tax. This was but the third time he had seen his cousin Soames's wife—if indeed she was still his wife, of which he was not quite sure. He remembered having seen her sitting in the Botanical Gardens waiting for Bosinney—a passive, fascinating figure, reminding him of Titian's 'Heavenly Love', and again, when, charged by his father, he had gone to Montpelier Square on the afternoon when Bosinney's death was known. He still recalled vividly her sudden appearance in the drawing-room doorway on that occasion—her beautiful face, passing from wild eagerness of hope to stony despair; remembered the compassion he had felt, Soames's snarling smile, his words: 'We are not at home', and the slam of the front door.

This third time he saw a face and form more beautiful—freed from that warp of wild hope and despair. Looking at her, he thought: 'Yes, you are just what the dad would have admired!' And the strange story of his father's Indian summer became slowly clear to him. She spoke of old Jolyon with reverence and tears in her eyes. 'He was so wonderfully kind to me; I don't know why. He looked so beautiful and peaceful sitting in that chair under the tree; it was I who first came on him sitting there, you know. Such a lovely day. I don't think an end could have been happier. We should all like to go out like that.'

'Quite right!' he had thought. 'We should all like to go out in full summer with beauty stepping towards us across a lawn.'

And looking round the little, almost empty drawing-room, he had asked her what she was going to do now. 'I am going to live again a little, Cousin Jolyon. It's wonderful to have money of one's own. I've never had any. I shall keep this flat, I think; I'm used to it; but I shall be able to go to Italy.'

'Exactly!' Jolyon had murmured, looking at her faintly smiling lips; and he had gone away thinking: 'A fascinating woman! What a waste! I'm glad the dad left her that money. He had not seen her again, but every quarter he had signed her cheque, forwarding it to her bank, with a note to the Chelsea flat to say that he had done so; and always he had received a note in acknowledgment, generally from the flat, but sometimes from Italy; so that her personality had become embodied in slightly scented grey paper, an upright fine handwriting, and the words: 'Dear Cousin Jolyon'. Man of property that he now was, the slender cheque he signed often gave rise to the thought: 'Well, I suppose she just manages'; sliding into a vague wonder how she was faring otherwise in a world of men not wont to let beauty go unpossessed. At first Holly had spoken of her sometimes, but 'ladies in grey' soon fade from children's memories; and the tightening of June's lips in those first weeks after her grandfather's death whenever her former friend's name was mentioned, had discouraged allusion. Only once, indeed, had June spoken definitely: 'I've forgiven her. I'm frightfully glad she's independent now. . . . '

On receiving Soames's card, Jolyon said to the maid—for he could not abide butlers—'Show him into the study, please, and say I'll be there in a minute'; and then he looked at Holly and asked:

'Do you remember 'the lady in grey', who used to give you music-lessons?'

'Oh yes, why? Has she come?'

Jolyon shook his head and, changing his holland blouse for a coat, was silent, perceiving suddenly that such history was not for those young ears. His face, in fact, became whimsical perplexity incarnate while he journeyed towards the study.

Standing by the french window, looking out across the terrace at the oak tree, were two figures, middle-aged and young, and he thought: 'Who's that boy? Surely they never had a child.'

The elder figure turned. The meeting of those two Forsytes of the second generation, so much more sophisticated than the first, in the house built for the one and owned and occupied by the other, was marked by subtle defensiveness beneath distinct attempt at cordiality. 'Has he come about his wife?' Jolyon was thinking; and Soames, 'How shall I begin?' while Val, brought to break the ice, stood negligently scrutinising this 'bearded pard' from under his dark, thick eyelashes.

'This is Val Dartie,' said Soames, 'my sister's son. He's just going up to Oxford. I thought I'd like him to know your boy.'

'Ah! I'm sorry Jolly's away. What college?'

'B.N.C.,' replied Val.

'Jolly's at the "House", but he'll be delighted to look you up.'

'Thanks awfully.'

'Holly's in—if you could put up with a female relation, she'd show you round. You'll find her in the hall if you go through the curtains. I was just painting her.'

With another 'Thanks, awfully!' Val vanished, leaving the two cousins with the ice unbroken.

'I see you've some drawings at the "Water Colours",' said Soames.

Jolyon winced. He had been out of touch with the Forsyte family at large for twenty-six years, but they were connected in his mind with Frith's 'Derby Day' and Landseer prints. He had heard from June that Soames was a connoisseur, which made it worse. He had become aware, too, of a curious sensation of repugnance.

'I haven't seen you for a long time,' he said.

'No,' answered Soames between close lips, 'not since—as a matter of fact, it's about that I've come. You're her trustee, I'm told.'

Jolyon nodded.

'Twelve years is a long time,' said Soames rapidly: 'I—I'm tired of it.'

Jolyon found no more appropriate answer than:

'Won't you smoke?'

'No, thanks.'

Jolyon himself lit a cigarette.

'I wish to be free,' said Soames abruptly.

'I don't see her,' murmured Jolyon through the fume of his cigarette.

'But you know where she lives, I suppose!'

Jolyon nodded. He did not mean to give her address without permission. Soames seemed to divine his thought.

'I don't want her address,' he said; 'I know it.'

'What exactly do you want?'

'She deserted me. I want a divorce.'

'Rather late in the day, isn't it?'

'Yes,' said Soames. And there was a silence'

'I don't know much about these things—at least, I've forgotten,' said Jolyon with a wry smile. He himself had had to wait for death to grant him a divorce from the first Mrs Jolyon. 'Do you wish me to see her about it?'

Soames raised his eyes to his cousin's face.

'I suppose there's someone,' he said.

A shrug moved Jolyon's shoulders.

'I don't know at all. I imagine you may have both lived as if the other were dead. It's usual in these cases.'

Soames turned to the window. A few early fallen oak leaves strewed the terrace already, and were rolling round in the wind. Jolyon saw the figures of Holly and Val Dartie moving across the lawn towards the stables. 'I'm not going to run with the hare and hunt with the hounds,' he thought. 'I must act for her. The dad would have wished that.' And for a swift moment he seemed to see his father's figure in the old arm-chair, just beyond Soames, sitting with knees crossed, *The Times* in his hand. It vanished.

'My father was fond of her,' he said quietly.

'Why he should have been, I don't know,' Soames answered without looking round. 'She brought trouble to your daughter June; she brought trouble to everyone. I gave her all she wanted. I would have given her even— forgiveness—but she chose to leave me.'

In Jolyon compassion was checked by the tone of that close voice. What was there in the fellow that made it so difficult to be sorry for him?

'I can go and see her, if you like,' he said. 'I suppose she might be glad of a divorce, but I know nothing.'

Soames nodded.

'Yes, please go. As I say, I know her address; but I've no wish to see her.' His tongue was busy with his lips, as if they were very dry.

'You'll have some tea?' said Jolyon, stifling the words: 'And see the house.' And he led the way into the hall. When he had rung a bell and ordered tea, he went to his easel to turn his drawing to the wall. He could not bear, somehow, that his work should be seen by Soames, who was standing there in the middle of the great room which had been designed expressly to afford wall space for his own pictures. In his cousin's face, with its unseizable family likeness to himself, and its chinny, narrow, concentrated look, Jolyon saw that which moved him to the thought: 'That chap could never forget anything—nor ever give himself away. He's pathetic!'

7

THE COLT AND THE FILLY

When young Val left the presence of the last generation he was thinking: 'This is jolly dull! Uncle Soames does take the bun. I wonder what this filly's like?' He anticipated no pleasure from her society; and suddenly he saw her standing there looking at him. Why, she was pretty! What luck!

'I'm afraid you don't know me,' he said. 'My name's Val Dartie–I'm once removed, second cousin, something like that, you know. My mother's name was Forsyte.'

Holly, whose slim brown hand remained in his because she was too shy to withdraw it, said:

'I don't know any of my relations. Are there many?'

'Tons. They're awful–most of them. At least, I don't know–some of them. One's relations always are, aren't they?'

'I expect they think one awful too,' said Holly.

'I don't know why they should. No one could think *you* awful, of course.'

Holly looked at him–the wistful candour of those grey eyes gave young Val a sudden feeling that he must protect her.

'I mean there are people and people,' he added astutely. 'Your dad looks awfully decent, for instance.'

'Oh yes!' said Holly fervently; 'he is.'

A flush mounted in Val's cheeks–that scene in the Pandemonium promenade–the dark man with the pink carnation developing into his own father! 'But you know what the Forsytes are,' he said almost viciously. 'Oh! I forgot; you don't.'

'What are they?'

'Oh! fearfully careful; not sportsmen a bit. Look at Uncle Soames!'

'I'd like to,' said Holly.

Val resisted a desire to run his arm through hers. 'Oh no,' he said, 'let's go out. You'll see him quite soon enough. What's your brother like?'

Holly led the way on to the terrace and down to the lawn without answering. How describe Jolly, who, ever since she remembered anything, had been her lord, master, and ideal?

'Does he sit on you?' said Val shrewdly. 'I shall be knowing him at Oxford. Have you got any horses?'

Holly nodded. 'Would you like to see the stables?'

'Rather!'

They passed under the oak tree, through a thin shrubbery, into the stable-yard. There under a clock tower lay a fluffy brown-and-white dog, so old that he did not get up, but faintly waved the tail curled over his back.

'That's Balthasar,' said Holly; 'he's so old–awfully old, nearly as old as I am. Poor old boy! He's devoted to dad.'

'Balthasar! That's a rum name. He isn't pure-bred, you know.'

'No! but he's a darling,' and she bent down to stroke the dog. Gentle and supple, with dark uncovered head and slim browned neck and hands, she seemed to Val strange and sweet, like a thing slipped between him and all previous knowledge.

'When grandfather died,' she said, 'he wouldn't eat for two days. He saw him die, you know.'

'Was that old Uncle Jolyon? Mother always says he was a topper.'

'He was,' said Holly simply, and opened the stable door.

In a loose-box stood a silver roan of about fifteen hands, with a long black tail and mane. 'This is mine – Fairy.'

'Ah!' said Val, 'she's a jolly palfrey. But you ought to bang her tail. She'd look much smarter.' Then catching her wondering look, he thought suddenly: 'I don't know – anything she likes!' And he took a long sniff of the stable air. 'Horses are ripping, aren't they? My dad –' he stopped.

'Yes?' said Holly.

An impulse to unbosom himself almost overcame him – but not quite. 'Oh! I don't know – he's often gone a mucker over them. I'm jolly keen on them too – riding and hunting. I like racing awfully, as well; I should like to be a gentleman rider.' And oblivious of the fact that he had but one more day in town, with two engagements, he plumped out:

'I say, if I hire a gee to-morrow, will you come and ride in Richmond Park?' Holly clasped her hands.

'Oh yes! I simply love riding. But there's Jolly's horse; why don't you ride him? Here he is. We could go after tea.'

Val looked doubtfully at his trousered legs. He had imagined them immaculate before her eyes in high brown boots and Bedford cords.

'I don't much like riding his horse,' he said. 'He mightn't like it. Besides, Uncle Soames wants to get back, I expect. Not that I believe in buckling under to him; you know. You haven't got an uncle, have you? This is rather a good beast,' he added, scrutinising Jolly's horse, a dark brown, which was showing the whites of its eyes. 'You haven't got any hunting here, I suppose?'

'No; I don't know that I want to hunt. It must be awfully exciting, of course; but it's cruel, isn't it? June says so.'

'Cruel?' ejaculated Val. 'Oh! that's all rot. Who's June?'

'My sister – my half-sister, you know – much older than me.' She had put her hands up to both cheeks of Jolly's horse, and was rubbing her nose against its nose with a gentle snuffling noise which seemed to have an hypnotic effect on the animal. Val contemplated her cheek resting against the horse's nose, and her eyes gleaming round at him. 'She's really a duck,' he thought.

They returned to the house less talkative, followed this time by the dog Balthasar, walking more slowly than anything on earth, and clearly expecting them not to exceed his speed limit.

'This is a ripping place,' said Val from under the oak tree, where they had paused to allow the dog Balthasar to come up.

'Yes,' said Holly, and sighed. 'Of course I want to go everywhere. I wish I were a gipsy.'

'Yes, gipsies are jolly,' replied Val, with a conviction which had just come to him; 'you're rather like one, you know.'

Holly's face shone suddenly and deeply, like dark leaves gilded by the sun.

'To go mad-rabbiting everywhere and see everything, and live in the open – oh! wouldn't it be fun?'

'Let's do it,' said Val.

'Oh yes, let's!'

'It'd be grand sport, just you and I.'

Then Holly perceived the quaintness and flushed.

'Well, we've got to do it,' said Val obstinately, but reddening too. 'I believe in doing things you want to do. What's down there?'

'The kitchen-garden, and the pond and the coppice, and the farm.'

'Let's go down!'

Holly glanced back at the house.

'It's tea-time, I expect; there's dad beckoning.'

Val, uttering a growly sound, followed her towards the house.

When they re-entered the hall gallery the sight of two middle-aged Forsytes drinking tea together had its magical effect, and they became quite silent. It was, indeed, an impressive spectacle. The two were seated side by side on an arrangement in marqueterie which looked like three silvery pink chairs made one, with a low tea-table in front of them. They seemed to have taken up that position, as far apart as the seat would permit, so that they need not look at each other too much; and they were eating and drinking rather than talking—Soames with his air of despising the teacake as it disappeared, Jolyon of finding himself slightly amusing. To the casual eye neither would have seemed greedy, but both were getting through a good deal of sustenance. The two young ones having been supplied with food, the process went on silent and absorbative, till, with the advent of cigarettes, Jolyon said to Soames:

'And how's Uncle James?'

'Thanks, very shaky.'

'We're a wonderful family, aren't we? The other day I was calculating the average age of the ten old Forsytes from my father's family Bible. I make it eighty-four already, and five still living. They ought to beat the record;' and looking whimsically at Soames, he added:

'We aren't the men they were, you know.'

Soames smiled. 'Do you really think I shall admit that I'm not their equal,' he seemed to be saying, 'or that I've got to give up anything, especially life?'

'We may live to their age, perhaps,' pursued Jolyon, 'but self-consciousness is a handicap, you know, and that's the difference between us. We've lost conviction. How and when self-consciousness was born I never can make out. My father had a little, but I don't believe any other of the old Forsytes ever had a scrap. Never to see yourself as others see you, it's a wonderful preservative. The whole history of the last century is in the difference between us. And between us and you,' he added, gazing through a ring of smoke at Val and Holly, uncomfortable under his quizzical regard, 'there'll be—another difference. I wonder what.'

Soames took out his watch.

'We must go,' he said, 'if we're to catch our train.'

'Uncle Soames never misses a train,' muttered Val, with his mouth full.

'Why should I?' Soames answered simply.

'Oh! I don't know,' grumbled Val, 'other people do.'

At the front door he gave Holly's slim brown hand a long and surreptitious squeeze.

'Look out for me to-morrow,' he whispered; 'three o'clock. I'll wait for you in the road; it'll save time. We'll have a ripping ride.' He gazed back at her from the lodge gate, and, but for the principles of a man about town, would have waved his hand. He felt in no mood to tolerate his uncle's conversation. But he was not in danger. Soames preserved a perfect muteness, busy with far-away thoughts.

The yellow leaves came down about those two walking the mile and a half which Soames had traversed so often in those long-ago days when he came down to watch with secret pride the building of the house—that house which was to have been the home of him and her from whom he was now going to seek release. He looked back once, up that endless vista of autumn lane between the yellowing hedges. What an age ago! 'I don't want to see her,' he had said to Jolyon. Was that true? 'I may have to,' he thought; and he shivered, seized by one of those queer shudderings that they say mean footsteps on one's grave. A chilly world! A queer world! And glancing sidelong at his nephew, he thought: 'Wish I were his age! I wonder what she's like now!'

8

JOLYON PROSECUTES TRUSTEESHIP

When those two were gone Jolyon did not return to his painting, for daylight was failing, but went to the study, craving unconsciously a revival of that momentary vision of his father sitting in the old brown leather chair with his knees crossed and his straight eyes gazing up from under the dome of his massive brow. Often in this little room, cosiest in the house, Jolyon would catch a moment of communion with his father. Not, indeed, that he had definitely any faith in the persistence of the human spirit—the feeling was not so logical—it was, rather, an atmospheric impact, like a scent, or one of those strong animistic impressions from forms, or effects of light, to which those with the artist's eye are especially prone. Here only—in this little unchanged room where his father had spent the most of his waking hours—could be retrieved the feeling that he was not quite gone, that the steady counsel of that old spirit and the warmth of his masterful lovability endured.

What would his father be advising now, in this sudden recrudescence of an old tragedy—what would he say to this menace against her to whom he had taken such a fancy in the last weeks of his life? 'I must do my best for her,' thought Jolyon; 'he left her to me in his will. But what *is* the best?'

And as if seeking to regain the sapience, the balance and shrewd common sense of that old Forsyte, he sat down in the ancient chair and crossed his knees. But he felt a mere shadow sitting there; nor did any inspiration come, while the fingers of the wind tapped on the darkening panes of the french window.

'Go and see her?' he thought, 'or ask her to come down here? What's her life been? What is it now, I wonder? Beastly to rake up things at this time of day.' Again the figure of his cousin standing with a hand on a front door of a fine olive-green leaped out, vivid, like one of those figures from old-fashioned clocks when the hour strikes; and his words sounded in Jolyon's ears clearer than any chime: 'I manage my own affairs. I've told you once, I tell you again: We are not at home.' The repugnance he had then felt for Soames—for his flat-cheeked, shaken face full of spiritual bulldoggedness, for his spare, square, sleek figure slightly crouched, as it were, over the bone he could not digest—came now again, fresh as ever, nay, with an odd increase. 'I dislike him,' he thought, 'I dislike him to the very roots of me. And that's lucky; it'll make it easier for me to back his wife.' Half artist and half Forsyte, Jolyon was constitutionally averse from what he termed 'ructions'; unless angered, he conformed deeply to that classic description of the she-dog, 'Er'd rather run than fight.' A little smile became settled in his beard. Ironical that Soames should come down here—to this house, built for himself! How he had gazed and gaped at this ruin of his past intention; furtively nosing at the walls and stairway, appraising everything! And intuitively Jolyon thought: 'I believe the fellow even now would like to be living here. He could never leave off longing for what he once owned! Well, I must act somehow or other; but it's a bore—a great bore.'

Late that evening he wrote to the Chelsea flat, asking if Irene would see him.

The old century which had seen the plant of individualism flower so wonderfully was setting in a sky orange with coming storms. Rumours of war added to the briskness of a London turbulent at the close of the summer holidays. And the streets to Jolyon, who was not often up in town, had a feverish look, due to these new motor-cars and cabs, of which he disapproved æsthetically. He counted these vehicles from his hansom, and made the proportion of them one in twenty. 'They were one in thirty about a year ago,' he thought; 'they've come to stay. Just so much more rattling round of wheels and general stink'—for he was one of those rather rare Liberals who object to anything new when it takes a material form; and he instructed his driver to get down to the river quickly, out of the traffic, desiring to look at the water through the mellowing screen of plane trees. At the little block of flats which stood back some fifty yards from the Embankment, he told the cabman to wait, and went up to the first floor.

Yes, Mrs Heron was at home!

The effect of a settled if very modest income was at once apparent to him, remembering the threadbare refinement in that tiny flat eight years ago when he announced her good fortune. Everything was now fresh, dainty, and smelled of flowers. The general effect was silvery with touches of black, hydrangea colour, and gold. 'A woman of great taste,' he thought. Time had dealt gently with Jolyon, for he was a Forsyte. But with Irene Time hardly seemed to deal at all—or such was his impression. She appeared to him not a day older, standing there in mole-coloured velvet corduroy, with soft dark eyes and dark gold hair, with outstretched hand and a little smile.

'Won't you sit down?'

He had probably never occupied a chair with a fuller sense of embarrassment.

'You look absolutely unchanged,' he said.

'And you look younger, Cousin Jolyon.'

Jolyon ran his hands through his hair, whose thickness was still a comfort to him.

'I'm ancient, but I don't feel it. That's one thing about painting, it keeps you young. Titian lived to ninety-nine, and had to have plague to kill him off. Do you know, the first time I ever saw you I thought of a picture by him?'

'When did you see me for the first time?'

'In the Botanical Gardens.'

'How did you know me, if you'd never seen me before?'

'By someone who came up to you.' He was looking at her hardily, but her face did not change; and she said quietly:

'Yes; many lives ago.'

'What is *your* recipe for youth, Irene?'

'People who don't *live* are wonderfully preserved.'

H'm! A bitter little saying! People who don't live! But an opening, and he took it. 'You remember my Cousin Soames?'

He saw her smile faintly at that whimsicality, and at once went on: 'He came to see me the day before yesterday! He wants a divorce. Do you?'

'I?' The word seemed startled out of her. 'After twelve years? It's rather late. Won't it be difficult?'

Jolyon looked hard into her face. 'Unless—' he said.

'Unless I have a lover now. But I have never had one since.'

What did he feel at the simplicity and candour of those words? Relief, surprise, pity! Venus for twelve years without a lover!

'And yet,' he said, 'I suppose you would give a good deal to be free, too?'

'I don't know. What does it matter now?'

'But if you were to love again?'

'I should love.' In that simple answer she seemed to sum up the whole philosophy of one on whom the world had turned its back.

'Well! Is there anything you would like me to say to him?'

'Only that I'm sorry he's not free. He had his chance once. I don't know why he didn't take it.'

'Because he was a Forsyte; we never part with things, you know, unless we want something in their place; and not always then.'

Irene smiled. 'Don't you, Cousin Jolyon?—I think you do.'

'Of course, I'm a bit of a mongrel—not quite a pure Forsyte. I never take the halfpennies off my cheques, I put them on,' said Jolyon uneasily.

'Well, what does Soames want in place of me now?'

'I don't know; perhaps children.'

She was silent for a little, looking down.

'Yes,' she murmured; 'it's hard. I would help him to be free if I could.'

Jolyon gazed into his hat, his embarrassment was increasing fast; so was his admiration, his wonder, and his pity. She was so lovely, and so lonely; and altogether it was such a coil!

'Well,' he said, 'I shall have to see Soames. If there's anything I can do for you I'm always at your service. You must think of me as a wretched substitute for my father. At all events, I'll let you know what happens when I speak to Soames. He may supply the material himself.'

She shook her head.

'You see, he has a lot to lose; and I have nothing. I should like him to be free; but I don't see what I can do.'

'Nor I at the moment,' said Jolyon, and soon after took his leave. He went down to his hansom. Half-past three! Soames would be at his office still.

'To the Poultry,' he called through the trap. In front of the Houses of Parliament and in Whitehall, newsvendors were calling: 'Grave situation in the Transvaal!' but the cries hardly roused him, absorbed in recollection of that very beautiful figure, of her soft dark glance, and the words: 'I have never had one since.' What on earth did such a woman do with her life, back-watered like this? Solitary, unprotected, with every man's hand against her or rather—reaching out to grasp her at the least sign. And year after year she went on like that!

The word 'Poultry' above the passing citizens brought him back to reality.

'Forsyte, Bustard and Forsyte,' in black letters on a ground the colour of pea-soup, spurred him to a sort of vigour, and he went up the stone stairs muttering: 'Fusty musty ownerships! Well, we couldn't do without them!'

'I want Mr Soames Forsyte,' he said to the boy who opened the door.

'What name?'

'Mr Jolyon Forsyte.'

The youth looked at him curiously, never having seen a Forsyte with a beard, and vanished.

The offices of 'Forsyte, Bustard and Forsyte' had slowly absorbed the offices of 'Tooting and Bowles', and occupied the whole of the first floor. The firm consisted now of nothing but Soames and a number of managing and articled clerks. The complete retirement of James some six years ago had accelerated business, to which the final touch of speed had been imparted when Bustard dropped off, worn out, as many believed, by the suit of 'Fryer *versus* Forsyte', more in Chancery than ever and less likely to benefit its beneficiaries. Soames, with his saner grasp of actualities, had never permitted it to worry him; on the contrary, he had long perceived that Providence had presented him therein with £200 a year net in perpetuity, and – why not?

When Jolyon entered, his cousin was drawing out a list of holdings in Consols, which in view of the rumours of war he was going to advise his companies to put on the market at once, before other companies did the same. He looked round, sidelong, and said:

'How are you? Just one minute. Sit down, won't you?' And having entered three amounts, and set a ruler to keep his place, he turned towards Jolyon, biting the side of his flat forefinger.

'Yes?' he said.

'I have seen her.'

Soames frowned.

'Well?'

'She has remained faithful to memory.'

Having said that Jolyon was ashamed. His cousin had flushed a dusky yellowish red. What had made him tease the poor brute! 'I was to tell you she is sorry you are not free. Twelve years is a long time. You know your law better than I do, and what chance it gives you.' Soames uttered a curious little grunt, and the two remained a full minute without speaking. 'Like wax?' thought Jolyon, watching that close face, where the flush was fast subsiding. 'He'll never give me a sign of what he's thinking, or going to do. Like wax!' And he transferred his gaze to a plan of that flourishing town, 'By-Street on Set', the future existence of which lay exposed on the wall to the possessive instincts of the firm's clients. The whimsical thought flashed through him: 'I wonder if I shall get a bill of costs for this–'To attending Mr Jolyon Forsyte in the matter of my divorce, to receiving his account of his visit to my wife, and to advising him to go and see her again, sixteen and eightpence.'

Suddenly Soames said: 'I can't go on like this. I tell you, I can't go on like this.' His eyes were shifting from side to side, like an animal's when it looks for way of escape. 'He really suffers, thought Jolyon; 'I've no business to forget that, just because I don't like him.'

'Surely,' he said gently, 'it lies with yourself. A man can always put these things through if he'll take it on himself.'

Soames turned square to him, with a sound which seemed to come from somewhere very deep.

'Why should I suffer more than I've suffered already? Why should I?'

Jolyon could only shrug his shoulders. His reason agreed, his instinct rebelled; he could not have said why.

'Your father,' went on Soames, 'took an interest in her—why, goodness knows! And I suppose you do too?' He gave Jolyon a sharp look. 'It seems to me that one only has to do another person a wrong to get all the sympathy. I don't know in what way I was to blame—I've never known. I always treated her well. I gave her everything she could wish for. I wanted her.'

Again Jolyon's reason nodded; again his instinct shook its head. 'What is it?' he thought; 'there must be something wrong in me. Yet if there is, I'd rather be wrong than right.'

'After all,' said Soames, with a sort of glum fierceness, 'she was my wife.'

In a flash the thought went through his listener: 'There it is! Ownerships! Well, we all own things. But—human beings! Pah!'

'You have to look at facts,' he said dryly, 'or rather the want of them.'

Soames gave him another quick suspicious look.

'The want of them?' he said. 'Yes, but I am not so sure.'

'I beg your pardon,' replied Jolyon; 'I've told you what she said. It was explicit.'

'My experience has not been one to promote blind confidence in her word. We shall see.'

Jolyon got up.

'Good-bye,' he said curtly.

'Good-bye,' returned Soames; and Jolyon went out trying to understand the look, half startled, half menacing, on his cousin's face. He sought Waterloo Station in a disturbed frame of mind, as though the skin of his moral being had been scraped; and all the way down in the train he thought of Irene in her lonely flat, and of Soames in his lonely office, and of the strange paralysis of life that lay on them both. 'In chancery!' he thought. 'Both their necks in chancery—and hers so pretty!'

9

VAL HEARS THE NEWS

The keeping of engagements had not as yet been a conspicuous feature in the life of young Val Dartie, so that when he broke two and kept one, it was the latter event which caused him, if anything, the greater surprise, while jogging back to town from Robin Hill after his ride with Holly. She had been even prettier than he had thought her yesterday, on her silver-roan, long-tailed 'palfrey'; and it seemed to him, self-critical in the brumous October gloaming and the outskirts of London, that only his boots had shone throughout their two-hour companionship. He took out his new gold 'hunter'—present from James—and looked not at the time, but at sections of his face in the glittering back of its opened case. He had a temporary spot over one eyebrow, and it displeased him, for it must have displeased her. Crum never had any spots. Together with Crum rose the scene in the promenade of the Pandemonium.

To-day he had not had the faintest desire to unbosom himself to Holly about his father. His father lacked poetry, the stirrings of which he was feeling for the first time in his nineteen years. The Liberty, with Cynthia Dark, that almost mythical embodiment of rapture; the Pandemonium, with the woman of uncertain age—both seemed to Val completely 'off', fresh from communion with this new, shy, dark-haired young cousin of his. She rode 'jolly well', too, so that it had been all the more flattering that she had let him lead her where he would in the long gallops of Richmond Park, though she knew them so much better than he did. Looking back on it all, he was mystified by the barrenness of his speech; he felt that he could say 'an awful lot of fetching things' if he had but the chance again, and the thought that he must go back to Littlehampton on the morrow, and to Oxford on the twelfth—'to that beastly exam, too'—without the faintest chance of first seeing her again, caused darkness to settle on his spirit even more quickly than on the evening. He should write to her, however, and she had promised to answer. Perhaps, too, she would come up to Oxford to see her brother. That thought was like the first star, which came out as he rode into Padwick's livery stables in the purlieus of Sloane Square. He got off and stretched himself luxuriously, for he had ridden some twenty-five good miles. The Dartie within him made him chaffer for five minutes with young Padwick concerning the favourite for the Cambridgeshire; then with the words, 'Put the gee down to my account,' he walked away, a little wide at the knees, and flipping his boots with his knotty little cane. 'I don't feel a bit inclined to go out,' he thought. 'I wonder if mother will stand fizz for my last night!' With 'fizz' and recollection, he could well pass a domestic evening.

When he came down, speckless after his bath, he found his mother scrupulous in a low evening dress, and, to his annoyance, his Uncle Soames. They stopped talking when he came in; then his uncle said:

'He'd better be told.'

At those words, which meant something about his father, of course, Val's first thought was of Holly. Was it anything beastly? His mother began speaking.

'Your father,' she said in her fashionably appointed voice, while her fingers plucked rather pitifully at sea-green brocade, 'your father, my dear boy, has—is not at Newmarket; he's on his way to South America. He—he's left us.'

Val looked from her to Soames. Left them! Was he sorry? Was he fond of his father? It seemed to him that he did not know. Then, suddenly—as at a whiff of gardenias and cigars—his heart twitched within him, and he *was* sorry. One's father belonged to one, could not go off in this fashion—it was not done! Nor had he always been the 'bounder' of the Pandemonium promenade. There were precious memories of tailors' shops and horses, tips at school, and general lavish kindness, when in luck.

'But why?' he said. Then, as a sportsman himself, was sorry he had asked. The mask of his mother's face was all disturbed; and he burst out:

'All right, Mother, don't tell me! Only, what does it mean?'

'A divorce, Val, I'm afraid.'

Val uttered a queer little grunt and looked quickly at his uncle—that uncle whom he had been taught to look on as a guarantee against the consequences of having a father, even against the Dartie blood in his own veins. The flat-cheeked visage seemed to wince, and this upset him.

'It won't be public, will it?'

So vividly before him had come recollection of his own eyes glued to the unsavoury details of many a divorce suit in the public Press.

'Can't it be done quietly somehow? It's so disgusting for–for mother, and–and everybody.'

'Everything will be done as quietly as it can, you may be sure.'

'Yes–but, why is it necessary at all? Mother doesn't want to marry again.'

Himself, the girls, their name tarnished in the sight of his school-fellows and of Crum, of the men at Oxford, of–Holly! Unbearable. What was to be gained by it?

'Do you, Mother?' he said sharply.

Thus brought face to face with so much of her own feeling by the one she loved best in the world, Winifred rose from the Empire chair in which she had been sitting. She saw that her son would be against her unless he was told everything; and yet, how could she tell him? Thus, still plucking at the green brocade, she stared at Soames. Val, too, stared at Soames. Surely this embodiment of respectability and the sense of property could not wish to bring such a slur on his own sister!

Soames slowly passed a little inlaid paper-knife over the smooth surface of a marqueterie table; then, without looking at his nephew, he began:

'You don't understand what your mother has had to put up with these twenty years. This is only the last straw, Val.' And glancing up sideways at Winifred, he added:

'Shall I tell him?'

Winifred was silent. If he were not told, he would be against her! Yet, how dreadful to be told such things of his own father! Clenching her lips, she nodded.

Soames spoke in a rapid, even voice:

'He has always been a burden round your mother's neck. She has paid his debts over and over again; he has often been drunk, abused and threatened her; and now he is gone to Buenos Aires with a dancer.' And, as if distrusting the efficacy of those words on the boy, he went on quickly:

'He took your mother's pearls to give to her.'

Val jerked up his hand then. At that signal of distress Winifred cried out:

'That'll do, Soames–stop!'

In the boy, the Dartie and the Forsyte were struggling. For debts, drink, dancers, he had a certain sympathy; but the pearls–no! That was too much! And suddenly he found his mother's hand squeezing his.

'You see,' he heard Soames say, 'we can't have it all begin over again. There's a limit; we must strike while the iron's hot.'

Val freed his hand.

'But–you're never going to bring out that about the pearls! I couldn't stand that–I simply couldn't!'

Winifred cried out:

'No, no, Val–oh no! That's only to show you how impossible your father is!' And his uncle nodded. Somewhat assuaged, Val took out a cigarette. His father had bought him that thin curved case. Oh! it was unbearable–just as he was going up to Oxford!

'Can't mother be protected without?' he said. 'I could look after her. It could always be done later if it was really necessary.'

A smile played for a moment round Soames's lips, and became bitter.

'You don't know what you're talking of; nothing's so fatal as delay in such matters.'

'Why?'

'I tell you, boy, nothing's so fatal. I know from experience.'

His voice had the ring of exasperation. Val regarded him round-eyed, never having known his uncle express any sort of feeling. Oh! Yes–he remembered now–there had been an Aunt Irene, and something had happened–something which people kept dark; he had heard his father once use an unmentionable word of her.

'I don't want to speak ill of your father,' Soames went on doggedly, 'but I know him well enough to be sure that he'll be back on your mother's hands before a year's over. You can imagine what that will mean to her and to all of you after this. The only thing is to cut the knot for good.'

In spite of himself, Val was impressed; and, happening to look at his mother's face, he got what was perhaps his first real insight into the fact that his own feelings were not always what mattered most.

'All right, Mother,' he said; 'we'll back you up. Only, I'd like to know when it'll be. It's my first term, you know. I don't want to be up there when it comes off.'

'Oh! my dear boy,' murmured Winifred, 'it *is* a bore for you.' So, by habit, she phrased what, from the expression of her face, was the most poignant regret. 'When will it be, Soames?'

'Can't tell–not for months. We must get restitution first.'

'What the deuce is that?' thought Val. 'What silly brutes lawyers are! Not for months! I know one thing: I'm not going to dine in!' And he said:

'Awfully sorry, Mother, I've got to go out to dinner now.'

Though it was his last night, Winifred nodded almost gratefully; they both felt that they had gone quite far enough in the expression of feeling.

Val sought the misty freedom of Green Street, reckless and depressed. And not till he reached Piccadilly did he discover that he had only eighteen-pence. One couldn't dine off eighteen-pence, and he was very hungry. He looked longingly at the windows of the Iseeum Club, where he had often eaten of the best with his father! Those pearls! There was no getting over them! But the more he brooded and the farther he walked the hungrier he naturally became. Short of trailing home, there were only two places where he could go: his grandfather's in Park Lane, and Timothy's in the Bayswater Road. Which was the less deplorable? At his grandfather's he would probably get a better dinner on the spur of the moment. At Timothy's they gave you a jolly good feed when they expected you, not otherwise. He decided on Park Lane, not unmoved by the thought that to go up to Oxford without affording his grandfather a chance to tip him was hardly fair to either of them. His mother would hear he had been there, of course, and might think it funny; but he couldn't help that. He rang the bell.

'Hullo, Warmson, any dinner for me, d'you think?'

'They're just going in, Master Val. Mr Forsyte will be very glad to see you. He was saying at lunch that he never saw you nowadays.'

Val grinned.

'Well, here I am. Kill the fatted calf, Warmson, let's have fizz.'

Warmson smiled faintly–in his opinion Val was a young limb.

'I will ask Mrs Forsyte, Master Val.'

'I say,' Val grumbled, taking off his overcoat, 'I'm not at school any more, you know.'

Warmson, not without a sense of humour, opened the door beyond the stag's horn coat-stand, with the words:

'Mr Valerus, ma'am.'

'Confound him!' thought Val, entering.

A warm embrace, a 'Well, Val!' from Emily, and a rather quavery 'So there you are at last!' from James, restored his sense of dignity.

'Why didn't you let us know? There's only saddle of mutton. Champagne, Warmson,' said Emily. And they went in.

At the great dining-table, shortened to its utmost, under which so many fashionable legs had rested, James sat at one end, Emily at the other, Val half-way between them; and something of the loneliness of his grandparents, now that all their four children were flown, reached the boy's spirit. 'I hope I shall kick the bucket long before I'm as old as grandfather,' he thought. 'Poor old chap, he's as thin as a rail!' And lowering his voice while his grandfather and Warmson were in discussion about sugar in the soup, he said to Emily:

'It's pretty brutal at home, Granny. I suppose you know.'

'Yes, dear boy.'

'Uncle Soames was there when I left. I say, isn't there anything to be done to prevent a divorce? Why is he so beastly keen on it?'

'Hush, my dear,' murmured Emily; 'we're keeping it from your grandfather.'

James's voice sounded from the other end.

'What's that? What are you talking about?'

'About Val's college,' returned Emily. 'Young Pariser was there, James; you remember—he nearly broke the Bank at Monte Carlo afterwards.'

James muttered that he did not know—Val must look after himself up there, or he'd get into bad ways. And he looked at his grandson with gloom, out of which affection distrustfully glimmered.

'What I'm afraid of,' said Val to his plate, 'is of being hard up, you know.'

By instinct he knew that the weak spot in that old man was fear of insecurity for his grandchildren.

'Well,' said James, and the soup in his spoon dribbled over, 'you'll have a good allowance; but you must keep within it.'

'Of course,' murmured Val; 'if it is good. How much will it be, Grandfather?'

'Three hundred and fifty; it's too much. I had next to nothing at your age.'

Val sighed. He had hoped for four, and been afraid of three. 'I don't know what your young cousin has,' said James; 'he's up there. His father's a rich man.'

'Aren't you?' asked Val hardily.

'I?' replied James, flustered. 'I've got so many expenses. Your father—' and he was silent.

'Cousin Jolyon's got an awfully jolly place. I went down there with Uncle Soames—ripping stables.'

'Ah!' murmured James profoundly. 'That house—I knew how it would be!' And he lapsed into gloomy meditation over his fishbones. His son's tragedy, and the deep cleavage it had caused in the Forsyte family, had still the power to draw him down into a whirlpool of doubts and misgivings. Val, who hankered to talk of Robin Hill, because Robin Hill meant Holly, turned to Emily and said:

'Was that the house built for Uncle Soames?' And, receiving her nod, went on: 'I wish you'd tell me about him, Granny. What became of Aunt Irene? Is she still going? He seems awfully worked-up about something to-night.'

Emily laid her finger on her lips, but the word Irene had caught James's ear.

'What's that?' he said, staying a piece of mutton close to his lips. 'Who's been seeing her? I knew we hadn't heard the last of that.'

'Now, James,' said Emily, 'eat your dinner. Nobody's been seeing anybody.'

James put down his fork.

'There you go,' he said. 'I might die before you'd tell me of it. Is Soames getting a divorce?'

'Nonsense,' said Emily, with incomparable aplomb; 'Soames is much too sensible.'

James had sought his own throat, gathering the long white whiskers together on the skin and bone of it.

'She—she was always—' he said, and with that enigmatic remark the conversation lapsed, for Warmson had returned. But later, when the saddle of mutton had been succeeded by sweet, savoury, and dessert, and Val had received a cheque for twenty pounds, and his grandfather's kiss—like no other kiss in the world from lips pushed out with a sort of fearful suddenness, as if yielding to weakness—he returned to the charge in the hall.

'Tell us about Uncle Soames, Granny. Why is he so keen on mother's getting a divorce?'

'Your Uncle Soames,' said Emily, and her voice had in it an exaggerated assurance, 'is a lawyer, my dear boy. He's sure to know best.'

'Is he?' muttered Val. 'But what did become of Aunt Irene? I remember she was jolly good-looking.'

'She—er—' said Emily, 'behaved very badly. We don't talk about it.'

'Well, I don't want everybody at Oxford to know about our affairs,' ejaculated Val; 'it's a brutal idea. Why couldn't father be prevented without its being made public?'

Emily sighed. She had always lived rather in an atmosphere of divorce, owing to her fashionable proclivities—so many of those whose legs had been under her table having gained a certain notoriety. When, however, it touched her own family, she liked it no better than other people. But she was eminently practical, and a woman of courage, who never pursued a shadow in preference to its substance.

'Your mother,' she said, 'will be happier if she's quite free, Val. Good-night, my dear boy; and don't wear loud waistcoats up at Oxford, they're not the thing just now. Here's a little present.'

With another five pounds in his hand, and a little warmth in his heart, for he was fond of his grandmother, he went out into Park Lane. A wind had cleared the mist, the autumn leaves were rustling and the stars were shining. With all that money in his pocket an impulse to 'see life' beset him; but he had not gone forty yards in the direction of Piccadilly when Holly's shy face, and her eyes with an imp dancing in their gravity, came up before him, and his hand seemed to be tingling again from the pressure of her warm gloved hand. 'No, dash it!' he thought. 'I'm going home!'

IO

SOAMES ENTERTAINS THE FUTURE

It was full late for the river, but the weather was lovely, and summer lingered below the yellowing leaves. Soames took many looks at the day from his riverside garden near Mapledurham that Sunday morning. With his own hands he put flowers about his little house-boat, and equipped the punt, in which, after lunch, he proposed to take them on the river. Placing those Chinese-looking cushions, he could not tell whether or no he wished to take Annette alone. She was so very pretty—could he trust himself not to say irrevocable words, passing beyond the limits of discretion? Roses on the veranda were still in bloom, and the hedges evergreen, so that there was almost nothing of middle-aged autumn to chill the mood; yet was he nervous, fidgety, strangely distrustful of his powers to steer just the right course. This visit had been planned to produce in Annette and her mother a due sense of his possessions, so that they should be ready to receive with respect any overture he might later be disposed to make. He dressed with great care, making himself neither too young nor too old, very thankful that his hair was still thick and smooth and had no grey in it. Three times he went up to his picture-gallery. If they had any knowledge at all, they must see at once that his collection alone was worth at least thirty thousand pounds. He minutely inspected, too, the pretty bedroom overlooking the river where they would take off their hats. It would be her bedroom if—if the matter went through, and she became his wife. Going up to the dressing-table he passed his hand over the lilac-coloured pin-cushion, into which were stuck all kinds of pins; a bowl of pot-pourri exhaled a scent that made his head turn just a little. His wife! If only the whole thing could be settled out of hand, and there was not the nightmare of this divorce to be gone through first; and with gloom puckered on his forehead, he looked out at the river shining beyond the roses and the lawn. Madame Lamotte would never resist this prospect for her child; Annette would never resist her mother. If only he were free! He drove to the station to meet them. What taste Frenchwomen had! Madame Lamotte was in black with touches of lilac colour, Annette in greyish lilac linen, with cream-coloured gloves and hat. Rather pale she looked, and Londony; and her blue eyes were demure. Waiting for them to come down to lunch, Soames stood in the open french window of the dining-room moved by that sensuous delight in sunshine and flowers and trees which only came to the full when youth and beauty were there to share it with one. He had ordered the lunch with intense consideration; the wine was a very special Sauterne, the whole appointments of the meal perfect, the coffee served on the veranda super-excellent. Madame Lamotte accepted *crème de menthe*; Annette refused. Her manners were charming, with just a suspicion of 'the conscious beauty' creeping into them. 'Yes,' thought Soames, 'another year of London and that sort of life, and she'll be spoiled.'

Madame was in sedate French raptures. '*Adorable! Le soleil est si bon!*' How everything is *chic*, is it not, Annette? Monsieur is a real Monte Cristo.' Annette murmured assent, with a look up at Soames which he could not read. He proposed a turn on the river. But to punt two persons when one of them looked so ravishing on those Chinese cushions was merely to suffer from a sense of lost opportunity; so they went but a short way towards Pangbourne, drifting slowly back, with every now and then an autumn leaf dropping on Annette or on her mother's black amplitude. And Soames was not happy, worried by the thought: 'How–when–where–can I say–what?' They did not yet even know that he was married. To tell them he was married might jeopardise his every chance; yet, if he did not definitely make them understand that he wished for Annette's hand, it would be dropping into some other clutch before he was free to claim it.

At tea, which they both took with lemon, Soames spoke of the Transvaal.

'There'll be war,' he said.

Madame Lamotte lamented.

'*Ces pauvres gens bergers!*' Could they not be left to themselves?

Soames smiled–the question seemed to him absurd. Surely as a woman of business she understood that the British could not abandon their legitimate commercial interests.

'Ah! that!' But Madame Lamotte found that the English were a little hypocrite. They were talking of justice and the Uitlanders, not of business. Monsieur was the first who had spoken to her of that.

'The Boers are only half civilised,' remarked Soames; 'they stand in the way of progress. It will never do to let our suzerainty go.'

'What does that mean to say? Suzerainty! What a strange word!' Soames became eloquent, roused by these threats to the principle of possession, and stimulated by Annette's eyes fixed on him. He was delighted when presently she said:

'I think Monsieur is right. They should be taught a lesson.' She was sensible!

'Of course,' he said, 'we must act with moderation. I'm no jingo. We must be firm without bullying. Will you come up and see my pictures?' Moving from one to another of these treasures, he soon perceived that they knew nothing. They passed his last Mauve, that remarkable study of a 'Hay-cart going Home', as if it were a lithograph. he waited almost with awe to see how they would view the jewel of his collection–an Israels whose price he had watched ascending till he was now almost certain it had reached top value, and would be better on the market again. They did not view it at all. This was a shock; and yet to have in Annette a virgin taste to form would be better than to have the silly, half-baked predilections of the English middle-class to deal with. At the end of the gallery was a Meissonier of which he was rather ashamed–Meissonier was so steadily going down. Madame Lamotte stopped before it.

'Meissonier! Ah! What a jewel!' She had heard the name; Soames took advantage of that moment. Very gently touching Annette's arm, he said:

'How do you like my place, Annette?'

She did not shrink, did not respond; she looked at him full, looked down, and murmured:

'Who would not like it? It is so beautiful!'

'Perhaps some day–' Soames said, and stopped.

So pretty she was, so self-possessed–she frightened him. Those cornflower-blue eyes, the turn of that creamy neck, her delicate curves–she was a standing temptation to indiscretion! No! No! One must be sure of one's ground–much surer! 'If I hold off,' he thought, 'it will tantalise her.' And he crossed over to

Madame Lamotte, who was still in front of the Meissonier.

'Yes, that's quite a good example of his later work. You must come again, madame, and see them lighted up. You must both come and spend a night.'

Enchanted, would it not be beautiful to see them lighted? By moonlight too, the river must be ravishing!

Annette murmured:

'Thou art sentimental, *Maman!*'

Sentimental! That black-robed, comely, substantial French woman of the world! And suddenly he was certain as he could be that there was no sentiment in either of them. All the better. Of what use sentiment? And yet–!

He drove to the station with them, and saw them into the train. To the tightened pressure of his hand it seemed that Annette's fingers responded just a little; her face smiled at him through the dark.

He went back to the carriage, brooding. 'Go on home, Jordan,' he said to the coachman; 'I'll walk.' And he strode out into the darkening lanes, caution and the desire of possession playing see-saw within him. *'Bon soir, monsieur!'* How softly she had said it. To know what was in her mind! The French–they were like cats–one could tell nothing! But–how pretty! What a perfect young thing to hold in one's arms! What a mother for his heir! And he thought, with a smile, of his family and their surprise at a French wife, and their curiosity, and of the way he would play with it and buffet it–confound them! The poplars sighed in the darkness; an owl hooted. Shadows deepened in the water. 'I will and must be free,' he thought. 'I won't hang about any longer. I'll go and see Irene. If you want things done, do them yourself. I must live again–live and move and have my being.' And in echo to that queer biblicality church-bells chimed the call to evening prayer.

II

AND VISITS THE PAST

On a Tuesday evening after dining at his club Soames set out to do what required more courage and perhaps less delicacy than anything he had yet undertaken in his life–save perhaps his birth, and one other action. He chose the evening, indeed, partly because Irene was more likely to be in, but mainly because he had failed to find sufficient resolution by daylight, had needed wine to give him extra daring.

He left his hansom on the Embankment and walked up to the Old Church, uncertain of the block of flats where he knew she lived. He found it hiding behind a much larger mansion; and having read the name, 'Mrs Irene Heron'–Heron, forsooth! Her maiden name: so she used that again, did she?–he stepped back into the road to look up at the windows of the first floor. Light was coming through in the corner flat, and he could hear a piano being played. He had never had a love of music, had secretly borne it a grudge in the old days when so often she had turned to her piano, making of it a refuge place into which she knew he could not enter. Repulse! The long repulse, at first restrained and secret, at last open! Bitter memory came with that sound. It must be she playing, and thus almost assured of seeing her, he stood more undecided than ever. Shivers of anticipation ran through him; his tongue felt dry, his heart beat fast. '*I* have no cause to be afraid,' he thought. And then the lawyer stirred within him. Was he doing a foolish thing? Ought he not to have arranged a formal meeting in the presence of her trustee? No! Not before that fellow Jolyon, who sympathised with her! Never! He crossed back into the doorway, and, slowly, to keep down the beating of his heart, mounted the single flight of stairs and rang the bell. When the door was opened to him his sensations were regulated by the scent which came—that perfume—from away back in the past, bringing muffled rememberance: fragrance of a drawing-room he used to enter, of a house he used to own—perfume of dried rose-leaves and honey!

'Say, Mr Forsyte,' he said, 'your mistress will see me, I know.' He had thought this out; she would think it was Jolyon.

When the maid was gone and he was alone in the tiny hall, where the light was dim from one pearly-shaded sconce, and walls, carpet, everything was silvery, making the walled-in space all ghostly, he could only think ridiculously: 'Shall I go in with my overcoat on, or take it off?' The music ceased, the maid said from the doorway:

'Will you walk in, sir?'

Soames walked in. He noted mechanically that all was still silvery, and that the upright piano was of satinwood. She had risen and stood recoiled against it; her hand, placed on the keys as if groping for support, had struck a sudden discord, held for a moment, and released. The light from the shaded piano-candle fell on her neck, leaving her face rather in shadow. She was in a black evening dress, with a sort of mantilla over her shoulders—he did not remember ever having seen her in black, and the thought passed through him: 'She dresses even when she's alone.'

'You!' he heard her whisper.

Many times Soames had rehearsed this scene in fancy. Rehearsal served him not at all. He simply could not speak. He had never thought that the sight of this woman whom he had once so passionately desired, so completely owned, and whom he had not seen for twelve years, could affect him in this way. He had imagined himself speaking and acting, half as man of business, half as judge. And now it was as if he were in the presence not of a mere woman and erring wife, but of some force, subtle and elusive as atmosphere itself, within him and outside. A kind of defensive irony welled up in him.

'Yes, it's a queer visit! I hope you're well.'

'Thank you. Will you sit down?'

She had moved away from the piano and gone over to a window-seat, sinking on to it, with her hands clasped in her lap. Light fell on her there, so that Soames could see her face, eyes, hair, strangely as he remembered them, strangely beautiful.

He sat down on the edge of a satinwood chair, upholstered with silver-coloured stuff, close to where he was standing.

'You have not changed,' he said.

'No? What have you come for?'

'To discuss things.'

'I have heard what you want from your cousin.'

'Well?'

'I am willing. I have always been.'

The sound of her voice, reserved and close, the sight of her figure watchfully poised, defensive, was helping him now. A thousand memories of her, ever on the watch against him, stirred, and he said bitterly:

'Perhaps you will be good enough, then, to give me information on which I can act. The law must be complied with.'

'I have none to give you that you don't know of.'

'Twelve years! Do you suppose I can believe that?'

'I don't suppose you will believe anything I say; but it's the truth.'

Soames looked at her hard. He had said that she had not changed; now he perceived that she had. Not in face, except that it was more beautiful; not in form, except that it was a little fuller–no! She had changed spiritually. There was more of her, as it were, something of activity and daring, where there had been sheer passive resistance. 'Ah!' he thought, 'that's her independent income! Confound Uncle Jolyon?'

'I suppose you're comfortably off now?' he said.

'Thank you, yes.'

'Why didn't you let me provide for you? I would have, in spite of everything.'

A faint smile came on her lips; but she did not answer.

'You are still my wife,' said Soames. Why he said that, what he meant by it, he knew neither when he spoke nor after. It was a truism almost preposterous, but its effect was startling. She rose from the window-seat and stood for a moment perfectly still, looking at him. He could see her bosom heaving. Then she turned to the window and threw it open.

'Why do that?' he said sharply. 'You'll catch cold in that dress. I'm not dangerous.' And he uttered a little sad laugh.

She echoed it–faintly, bitterly.

'It was–habit.'

'Rather odd habit,' said Soames as bitterly. 'Shut the window!'

She shut it and sat down again. She had developed power, this woman–this–wife of his! He felt it issuing from her as she sat there, in a sort of armour. And almost unconsciously he rose and moved nearer; he wanted to see the expression on her face. Her eyes met his unflinching. Heavens! how clear they were, and what a dark brown against that white skin, and that burnt-amber hair! And how white her shoulders! Funny sensation this! He ought to hate her.

'You had better tell me,' he said; 'it's to your advantage to be free as well as to mine. That old matter is too old.'

'I *have* told you.'

'Do you mean to tell me there has been nothing–nobody?'

'Nobody. You must go to your own life.'

Stung by that retort, Soames moved towards the piano and back to the hearth, to and fro, as he had been wont in the old days in their drawing-room when his feelings were too much for him.'

'That won't do,' he said. 'You deserted me. In common justice it's for you–'

He saw her shrug those white shoulders, heard her murmur:

'Yes. Why didn't you divorce me then? Should I have cared?'

He stopped and looked at her intently with a sort of curiosity. What on earth did she do with herself, if she really lived quite alone? And why had he not divorced her? The old feeling that she had never understood him, never done him justice, bit him while he stared at her.

'Why couldn't you have made me a good wife?' he said.

'Yes; it was a crime to marry you. I have paid for it. You will find some way perhaps. You needn't mind my name, I have none to lose. Now I think you had better go.'

A sense of defeat—of being defrauded of his self-justification, and of something else beyond power of explanation to himself, beset Soames like the breath of a cold fog. Mechanically he reached up, took from the mantel-shelf a little china bowl, reversed it, and said:

'Lowestoft. Where did you get this? I bought its fellow at Jobson's.' And, visited by the sudden memory of how, those many years ago, he and she had bought china together, he remained staring at the little bowl, as if it contained all the past. Her voice roused him.

'Take it. I don't want it.'

Soames put it back on the shelf.

'Will you shake hands?' he said.

A faint smile curved her lips. She held out her hand. It was cold to his rather feverish touch. 'She's made of ice,' he thought—'she was always made of ice!' But even as that thought darted through him, his senses were assailed by the perfume of her dress and body, as though the warmth within her, which had never been for him, were struggling to show its presence. And he turned on his heel. He walked out and away, as if someone with a whip were after him, not even looking for a cab, glad of the empty Embankment and the cold river, and the thick-strewn shadows of the plane tree leaves—confused, flurried, sore at heart, and vaguely disturbed, as though he had made some deep mistake whose consequences he could not foresee. And the fantastic thought suddenly assailed him: if instead of: 'I think you had better go,' she had said, 'I think you had better stay'! What should he have felt, what would he have done? That cursed attraction of her was there for him even now, after all these years of estrangement and bitter thoughts. It was there, ready to mount to his head at a sign, a touch. 'I was a fool to go!' he muttered. 'I've advanced nothing. Who could imagine? I never thought—!' Memory, flown back to the first years of his marriage, played him torturing tricks. She had not deserved to keep her beauty—the beauty he had owned and known so well. And a kind of bitterness at the tenacity of his own admiration welled up in him. Most men would have hated the sight of her, as she had deserved. She had spoiled his life, wounded his pride to death, defrauded him of a son. And yet the mere sight of her, cold and resisting as ever, had this power to upset him utterly! It was some damned magnetism she had! And no wonder if, as she asserted, she had lived untouched these last twelve years. So Bosinney—cursed be his memory!—had lived on all this time with her! Soames could not tell whether he was glad of that knowledge or no.

Nearing his club at last he stopped to buy a paper. A headline ran: 'Boers reported to repudiate suzerainty!' Suzerainty! 'Just like her!' he thought: 'she always did. Suzerainty! I still have it by rights. She must be awfully lonely in that wretched little flat!'

12

ON FORSYTE 'CHANGE

Soames belonged to two clubs, 'The Connoisseurs', which he put on his cards and seldom visited, and 'The Remove', which he did not put on his cards and frequented. He had joined this Liberal institution five years ago, having made sure that its members were now nearly all sound Conservatives in heart and pocket, if not in principle. Uncle Nicholas had put him up. The fine reading-room was decorated in the Adam style.

On entering that evening he glanced at the tape for any news about the Transvaal, and noted that Consols were down seven-sixteenths since the morning. He was turning away to seek the reading-room when a voice behind him said:

'Well, Soames, that went off all right.'

It was Uncle Nicholas, in a frock-coat and his special cut-away collar, with a black tie passed through a ring. Heavens! How young and dapper he looked at eighty-two!

'I think Roger'd have been pleased,' his uncle went on. 'The thing was very well done. Blackley's? I'll make a note of them. Buxton's done me no good. These Boers are upsetting me—that fellow Chamberlain's driving the country into war. What do you think?'

'Bound to come,' murmured Soames.

Nicholas passed his hand over his thin, clean-shaven cheeks, very rosy after his summer cure; a slight pout had gathered on his lips. This business had revived all his Liberal principles.

'I mistrust that chap; he's a stormy petrel. House property will go down if there's war. You'll have trouble with Roger's estate. I often told him he ought to get out of some of his houses. He was an opinionated beggar.'

'There was a pair of you!' thought Soames. But he never argued with an uncle, in that way preserving their opinion of him as 'a long-headed chap', and the legal care of their property.

'They tell me at Timothy's,' said Nicholas, lowering his voice, 'that Dartie has gone off at last. That'll be a relief to your father. He was a rotten egg.'

Again Soames nodded. If there was a subject on which the Forsytes really agreed, it was the character of Montague Dartie.

'You take care,' said Nicholas, 'or he'll turn up again. Winifred had better have the tooth out, I should say. No use preserving what's gone bad.'

Soames looked at him sideways. His nerves, exacerbated by the interview he had just come through, disposed him to see a personal allusion in those words.

'I'm advising her,' he said shortly.

'Well,' said Nicholas, 'the brougham's waiting; I must get home. I'm very poorly. Remember me to your father.'

And having thus reconsecrated the ties of blood, he passed down the steps at his youthful gait and was wrapped into his fur coat by the junior porter.

'I've never know Uncle Nicholas other than "very poorly",' mused Soames, 'or seen him look other than everlasting. What a family! Judging by him, I've got thirty-eight years of health before me. Well, I'm not going to waste them.' And going over to a mirror he stood looking at his face. Except for a line or two, and three or four grey hairs in his little dark moustache, had he aged any more than Irene? The prime of life—he and she in the very prime of life! And a fantastic thought shot into his mind. Absurd! Idiotic! But again it came. And genuinely alarmed by the recurrence, as one is by the second fit of shivering which presages a feverish cold, he sat down on the weighing machine. Eleven stone! He had not varied two pounds in twenty years. What age was she? Nearly thirty-seven—not too old to have a child—not at all! Thirty-seven on the ninth of next month. He remembered her birthday well—he had always observed it religiously, even that last birthday so soon before she left him, when he was almost certain she was faithless. Four birthdays in his house. He had looked forward to them, because his gifts had meant a semblance of gratitude, a certain attempt at warmth. Except, indeed, that last birthday—which had tempted him to be too religious! And he shied away in thought. Memory heaps dead leaves on corpse-like deeds, from under which they do but vaguely offend the sense. And then he thought suddenly: 'I could send her a present for her birthday. After all, we're Christians! Couldn't I—couldn't we join up again!' And he uttered a deep sigh sitting there. Annette! Ah! but between him and Annette was the need for that wretched divorce suit! And how?

'A man can always work these things, if he'll take it on himself.' Jolyon had said.

But why should he take the scandal on himself with his whole career as a pillar of the law at stake? It was not fair! It was quixotic! Twelve years' separation in which he had taken no steps to free himself put out of court the possibility of using her conduct with Bosinney as a ground for divorcing her. By doing nothing to secure relief he had acquiesced, even if the evidence could now be gathered, which was more than doubtful. Besides, his own pride would never let him use that old incident, he had suffered from it too much. No! Nothing but fresh misconduct on her part—but she had denied it; and— almost—he had believed her. Hung up! Utterly hung up!

He rose from the scooped-out red velvet seat with a feeling of constriction about his vitals. He would never sleep with this going on in him! And, taking coat and hat again, he went out, moving eastward. In Trafalgar Square he became aware of some special commotion travelling towards him out of the mouth of the Strand. It materialised in newspaper-men calling out so loudly that no words whatever could be heard. He stopped to listen, and one came by.

'Payper! Special! Ultimatium by Krooger! Declaration of war!' Soames bought the paper. There it was in the stop press! His first thought was: 'The Boers are committing suicide.' His second: 'Is there anything still I ought to sell?' If so he had missed the chance—there would certainly be a slump in the City to-morrow. He swallowed this thought with a nod of defiance. That ultimatum was insolent—sooner than let it pass he was prepared to lose money. They wanted a lesson, and they would get it; but it would take three months at least to bring them to heel. There weren't the troops out there; always behind time, the Government! Confound those newspaper rats! What was the use of waking everybody up? Breakfast to-morrow was quite soon enough. And he thought with alarm of his father. They would cry it down Park Lane. Hailing a hansom, he got in and told the man to drive there.

James and Emily had just gone up to bed, and after communicating the news to Warmson, Soames prepared to follow. He paused by after-thought to say:

'What do you think of it, Warmson?'

The butler ceased passing a hat-brush over the silk hat Soames had taken off and, inclining his face a little forward, said in a low voice:

'Well, sir, they 'aven't a chance, of course; but I'm told they're very good shots. I've got a son in the Inniskillings.'

'You, Warmson? Why, I didn't know you were married.'

'No, sir. I don't talk of it. I expect he'll be going out.'

The slighter shock Soames had felt on discovering that he knew so little of one whom he thought he knew so well was lost in the slight shock of discovering that the war might touch one personally. Born in the year of the Crimean War, he had only come to consciousness by the time the Indian Mutiny was over; since then the many little wars of the British Empire had been entirely professional, quite unconnected with the Forsytes and all they stood for in the body politic. This war would surely be no exception. But his mind ran hastily over his family. Two of the Haymans, he had heard, were in some Yeomanry or other—it had always been a pleasant thought, there was a certain distinction about the Yeomanry; they wore, or used to wear, a blue uniform with silver about it, and rode horses. And Archibald, he remembered, had once on a time joined the Militia, but had given it up because his father, Nicholas, had made such a fuss about his 'wasting his time peacocking about in a uniform'. Recently he had heard somewhere that young Nicholas's eldest, very young Nicholas, had become a Volunteer. 'No,' thought Soames, mounting the stairs slowly, 'there's nothing in that!'

He stood on the landing outside his parents' bed- and dressing-rooms debating whether or not to put his nose in and say a reassuring word. Opening the landing window, he listened. The rumble from Piccadilly was all the sound he heard, and with the thought, 'If these motor-cars increase, it'll affect house property' he was about to pass on up to the room always kept ready for him when he heard, distant as yet, the hoarse, rushing call of a newsvendor. There it was, and coming past the house! He knocked on his mother's door and went in.

His father was sitting up in bed, with his ears pricked under the white hair which Emily kept so beautifully cut. He looked pink, and extraordinarily clean, in his setting of white sheet and pillow, out of which the points of his high, thin, night-gowned shoulders emerged in small peaks. His eyes alone, grey and distrustful under their withered lids, were moving from the window to Emily, who in a wrapper was walking up and down, squeezing a rubber ball attached to a scent bottle. The room reeked faintly of the eau-de-Cologne she was spraying.

'All right!' said Soames, 'it's not a fire. The Boers have declared war—that's all.'

Emily stopped her spraying.

'Oh!' was all she said, and looked at James.

Soames, too, looked at his father. He was taking it differently from their expectation, as if some thought, strange to them, were working in him.

'H'm!' he muttered suddenly, 'I shan't live to see the end of this.'

'Nonsense, James! It'll be over by Christmas.'

'What do you know about it?' James answered her with asperity. 'It's a pretty mess—at this time of night, too!' He lapsed into silence, and his wife and son, as if hypnotised, waited for him to say: 'I can't tell—I don't know; I knew how it would be!' But he did not. The grey eyes shifted, evidently seeing nothing in the room; then movement occurred under the bedclothes, and the knees were drawn up suddenly to a great height.

'They ought to send out Roberts. It all comes from that fellow Gladstone and his Majuba.'

The two listeners noted something beyond the usual in his voice, something of real anxiety. It was as if he had said: 'I shall never see the old country peaceful and safe again. I shall have to die before I know she's won.' And in spite of the feeling that James must not be encouraged to be fussy, they were touched. Soames went up to the bedside and stroked his father's hand which had emerged from under the bedclothes, long and wrinkled with veins.

'Mark my words!' said James, 'Consols will go to par. For all I know, Val may go and enlist.'

'Oh, come, James!' cried Emily, 'you talk as if there were danger.'

Her comfortable voice seemed to soothe James for once.

'Well,' he muttered, 'I told you how it would be. I don't know, I'm sure—nobody tells me anything. Are you sleeping here, my boy?'

The crisis was past, he would now compose himself to his normal degree of anxiety: and, assuring his father that he was sleeping in the house, Soames pressed his hand and went up to his room.

The following afternoon witnessed the greatest crowd Timothy's had known for many a year. On national occasions, such as this, it was, indeed, almost impossible to avoid going there. Not that there was any danger, or rather only just enough to make it necessary to assure each other that there was none.

Nicholas was there early. He had seen Soames the night before—Soames had said it was bound to come. This old Kruger was in his dotage—why, he must be seventy-five if he was a day! (Nicholas was eighty-two.) What had Timothy said? He had had a fit after Majuba. These Boers were a grasping lot! The dark-haired Francie, who had arrived on his heels, with the contradictious touch which became the free spirit of a daughter of Roger, chimed in:

'Kettle and pot! Uncle Nicholas. What price the Uitlanders?' What price, indeed! A new expression, and believed to be due to her brother George.

Aunt Juley thought Francie ought not to say such a thing. Dear Mrs MacAnder's boy, Charlie MacAnder, was one, and no one could call him grasping. At this Francie uttered one of her *mots*, scandalising, and so frequently repeated:

'Well, his father's a Scotchman, and his mother's a cat.'

Aunt Juley covered her ears, too late, but Aunt Hester smiled; as for Nicholas, he pouted—witticism of which he was not the author was hardly to his taste. Just then Marian Tweetyman arrived, followed almost immediately by young Nicholas. On seeing his son, Nicholas rose.

'Well, I must be going,' he said, 'Nick here will tell you what'll win the race.' And with this hit at his eldest, who, as a pillar of accountancy and director of an insurance company, was no more addicted to sport than his father had even been, he departed. Dear Nicholas! What race was that? Or was it only one of his jokes? He was a wonderful man for his age! How many lumps would dear Marian take? And how were Giles and Jesse? Aunt Juley supposed their Yeo-manry would be very busy now guarding the coast, though of course the Boers had no ships. But one never knew what the French might do if they had the chance, especially since that dreadful Fashoda scare, which had upset Timothy so terribly that he had made no investments for months afterwards. It was the ingratitude of the Boers that was so dreadful, after everything had been done for them—Dr Jameson imprisoned, and he was so nice, Mrs MacAnder had always said. And Sir Alfred Milner sent out to talk to them—such a clever man! She didn't know what they wanted.

But at this moment occurred one of those sensations—so precious at Timothy's—which great occasions sometimes bring forth:

'Miss June Forsyte.'

Aunts Juley and Hester were on their feet at once, trembling from smothered resentment, and old affection bubbling up, and pride at the return of a prodigal June! Well, this *was* a surprise! Dear June—after all these years! And how well she was looking! Not changed at all! It was almost on their lips to add, 'And how is your dear grandfather?' forgetting in that giddy moment that poor dear Jolyon had been in his grave for seven years now.

Ever the most courageous and downright of all the Forsytes, June, with her decided chin and her spirited eyes and her hair like flames, sat down, slight and short, on a gilt chair with a bead-worked seat, for all the world as if ten years had not elapsed since she had been to see them—ten years of travel and independence and devotion to lame ducks. Those ducks of late had been all definitely painters, etchers, or sculptors, so that her impatience with the Forsytes and their hopelessly inartistic outlook had become intense. Indeed, she had almost ceased to believe that her family existed, and looked round her now with a sort of challenging directness which brought exquisite discomfort to the roomful. She had not expected to meet any of them but 'the poor old things'; and why she had come to see *them* she hardly knew, except that, while on her way from Oxford Street to a studio in Latimer Road, she had suddenly remembered them with compunction as two long-neglected old lame ducks.

Aunt Juley broke the hush again: 'We've just been saying, dear, how dreadful it is about these Boers! And what an impudent thing of that old Kruger!'

'Impudent!' said June. 'I think he's quite right. What business have we to meddle with them? If he turned out all those wretched Uitlanders it would serve them right. They're only after money.'

The silence of sensation was broken by Francie saying:

'What? Are you a pro-Boer?' (undoubtedly the first use of that expression).

'Well! Why can't we leave them alone?' said June, just as, in the open doorway, the maid said: 'Mr Soames Forsyte.' Sensation on sensation! Greeting was almost held up by curiosity to see how June and he would take this encounter, for it was shrewdly suspected, if not quite known, that they had not met since that old and lamentable affair of her fiancé Bosinney with Soames's wife. They were seen to just touch each other's hands and look each at the other's left eye only. Aunt Juley came at once to the rescue:

'Dear June is so original. Fancy, Soames, she thinks the Boers are not to blame.'

'They only want their independence,' said June; 'and why shouldn't they have it?'

'Because,' answered Soames, with his smile a little on one side, 'they happen to have agreed to our suzerainty.'

'Suzerainty!' repeated June scornfully; 'we shouldn't like anyone's suzerainty over us.'

'They got advantages in payment,' replied Soames; 'a contract is a contract.'

'Contracts are not always just,' flamed June, 'and when they're not, they ought to be broken. The Boers are much the weaker. We could afford to be generous.'

Soames sniffed. 'That's mere sentiment,' he said.

Aunt Hester, to whom nothing was more awful than any kind of disagreement, here leaned forward and remarked decisively:

'What lovely weather it has been for the time of year?'

But June was not to be diverted.

'I don't know why sentiment should be sneered at. It's the best thing in the world.' She looked defiantly round, and Aunt Juley had to intervene again:

'Have you bought any pictures lately, Soames?'

Her incomparable instinct for the wrong subject had not failed her. Soames flushed. To disclose the name of his latest purchases would be like walking into the jaws of disdain. For somehow they all knew of June's predilection for 'genius' not yet on its legs, and her contempt for 'success' unless she had had a finger in securing it.'

'One or two,' he muttered.

But June's face had changed; the Forsyte within her was seeing its chance. Why should not Soames buy some of the pictures of Eric Cobbley—her last lame duck? And she promptly opened her attack: Did Soames know his work? It was so wonderful. He was the coming man.

Oh yes, Soames knew his work. It was in his view 'splashy', and would never get hold of the public.

June blazed up.

'Of course it won't; that's the last thing one would wish for. I thought you were a connoisseur, not a picture-dealer.'

'Of course Soames is a connoisseur,' Aunt Juley said hastily; 'he has wonderful taste—he can always tell beforehand what's going to be successful.'

'Oh!' gasped June, and sprang up from the bead-covered chair, 'I hate that standard of success. Why can't people buy things because they like them?'

'You mean,' said Francie, 'because *you* like them.'

And in the slight pause young Nicholas was heard saying gently that Violet (his fourth) was taking lessons in pastel, he didn't know if they were any use.

'Well, good-bye, Auntie,' said June; 'I must get on,' and kissing her aunts, she looked defiantly round the room, said 'Good-bye' again, and went. A breeze seemed to pass out with her, as if everyone had sighed.

The third sensation came before anyone had time to speak:

'Mr James Forsyte.'

James came in using his stick slightly and wrapped in a fur coat which gave him a fictitious bulk.

Everyone stood up. James was so old; and he had not been at Timothy's for nearly two years.

'It's hot in here,' he said.

Soames divested him of his coat, and as he did so could not help admiring the glossy way his father was turned out. James sat down, all knees, elbows, frock-coat, and long white whiskers.

'What's the meaning of that?' he said.

Though there was no apparent sense in his words, they all knew that he was referring to June. His eyes searched his son's face.

'I thought I'd come and see for myself. What have they answered Kruger?'

Soames took out an evening paper and read the headline.

' "Instant action by our Government—state of war existing!" '

'Ah!' said James, and sighed. 'I was afraid they'd cut and run like old Gladstone. We shall finish with them this time.'

All stared at him. James! Always fussy, nervous, anxious! James with his continual, 'I told you how it would be!' and his pessimism, and his cautious investments. There was something uncanny about such resolution in this the oldest living Forsyte.

'Where's Timothy?' said James. 'He ought to pay attention to this.'

Aunt Juley said she didn't know; Timothy had not said much at lunch to-day. Aunt Hester rose and threaded her way out of the room, and Francie said rather maliciously:

'The Boers are a hard nut to crack, Uncle James.'

'H'm!' muttered James. 'Where do you get your information? Nobody tells me.'

Young Nicholas remarked in his mild voice that Nick (his eldest) was now going to drill regularly.

'Ah!' muttered James, and stared before him—his thoughts were on Val. 'He's got to look after his mother,' he said, 'he's got no time for drilling and that, with that father of his.' This cryptic saying produced silence, until he spoke again.

'What did June want here?' And his eyes rested with suspicion on all of them in turn. 'Her father's a rich man now.' The conversation turned on Jolyon, and when he had been seen last. It was supposed that he went abroad and saw all sorts of people now that his wife was dead; his water-colours were on the line, and he was a successful man. Francie went so far as to say:

'I should like to see him again; he was rather a dear.'

Aunt Juley recalled how he had gone to sleep on the sofa one day, where James was sitting. He had always been very amiable; what did Soames think?

Knowing that Jolyon was Irene's trustee, all felt the delicacy of this question, and looked at Soames with interest. A faint pink had come up in his cheeks.

'He's going grey,' he said.

Indeed! Had Soames seen him? Soames nodded, and the pink vanished.

James said suddenly: 'Well—I don't know, I can't tell.'

It so exactly expressed the sentiment of everybody present that there was something behind everything, that nobody responded. But at this moment Aunt Hester returned.

'Timothy,' she said in a low voice, 'Timothy has bought a map, and he's put in—he's put in three flags.'

Timothy had—! A sigh went round the company.

If Timothy had indeed put in three flags already, well!—it showed what the nation could do when it was roused. The war was as good as over.

13

JOLYON FINDS OUT WHERE HE IS

Jolyon stood at the window in Holly's old night nursery, converted into a studio, not because it had a north light, but for its view over the prospect away to the Grand Stand at Epsom. He shifted to the side window which overlooked the stable-yard, and whistled down to the dog Balthasar, who lay for ever under the clock tower. The old dog looked up and wagged his tail. 'Poor old boy!' thought Jolyon, shifting back to the other window.

He had been restless all this week, since his attempt to prosecute trusteeship, uneasy in his conscience which was ever acute, disturbed in his sense of compassion which was easily excited, and with a queer sensation as if his feeling for beauty had received some definite embodiment. Autumn was getting hold of the old oak tree, its leaves were browning. Sunshine had been plentiful and hot this summer. As with trees, so with men's lives! '*I* ought to live long,' thought Jolyon; 'I'm getting mildewed for want of heat. If I can't work, I shall be off to Paris.' But memory of Paris gave him no pleasure. Besides, how could he go? He must stay and see what Soames was going to do. 'I'm her trustee. I can't leave her unprotected,' he thought. It had been striking him as curious how very clearly he could still see Irene in her little drawing-room which he had only twice entered. Her beauty must have a sort of poignant harmony! No literal portrait would ever do her justice; the essence of her was—ah! yes, what? ... The noise of hoofs called him back to the other window. Holly was riding into the yard on her long-tailed 'palfrey'. She looked up and he waved to her. She had been rather silent lately; getting old, he supposed, beginning to want her future, as they all did—youngsters! Time was certainly the devil! And with the feeling that to waste this swift-travelling commodity was unforgivable folly, he took up his brush. But it was no use; he could not concentrate his eye—besides, the light was going. 'I'll go up to town,' he thought. In the hall a servant met him.

'A lady to see you, sir; Mrs Heron.'

Extraordinary coincidence! Passing into the picture-gallery, as it was still called, he saw Irene standing over by the window.

She came towards him saying:

'I've been trespassing; I came up through the coppice and garden. I always used to come that way to see Uncle Jolyon.'

'You couldn't trespass here,' replied Jolyon; 'history makes that impossible. I was just thinking of you.'

Irene smiled. And it was as if something shone through; not merely spirituality—serener, completer, more alluring.

'History!' she murmured. 'I once told Uncle Jolyon that love was for ever. Well, it isn't. Only aversion lasts.'

Jolyon stared at her. Had she got over Bosinney at last?

'Yes!' he said, 'aversion's deeper than love or hate because it's a natural product of the nerves, and we don't change them.'

'I came to tell you that Soames has been to see me. He said a thing that frightened me. He said: "You are still my wife!"'

'What!' ejaculated Jolyon. 'You ought not to live alone.' And he continued to stare at her, afflicted by the thought that where Beauty was, nothing ever ran quite straight, which, no doubt, was why so many people looked on it as immoral.

'What more?'

'He asked me to shake hands.'

'Did you?'

'Yes. When he came in I'm sure he didn't want to; he changed while he was there.'

'Ah! you certainly ought not to go on living there alone.'

'I know no woman I could ask; and I can't take a lover to order, Cousin Jolyon.'

'Heaven forbid!' said Jolyon. 'What a damnable position! Will you stay to dinner? No? Well, let me see you back to town; I wanted to go up this evening.'

'Truly?'

'Truly. I'll be ready in five minutes.'

On that walk to the station they talked of pictures and music, contrasting the English and French characters and the difference in their attitude to Art. But to Jolyon the colours in the hedges of the long straight lane, the twittering of chaffinches who kept pace with them, the perfume of weeds being already burned, the turn of her neck, the fascination of those dark eyes bent on him now and then, the lure of her whole figure, made a deeper impression than the remarks they exchanged. Unconsciously he held himself straighter, walked with a more elastic step.

In the train he put her through a sort of catechism as to what she did with her days.

Made her dresses, shopped, visited a hospital, played her piano, translated from the French. She had regular work from a publisher, it seemed, which supplemented her income a little. She seldom went out in the evening. 'I've been living alone so long, you see, that I don't mind it a bit. I believe I'm naturally solitary.'

'I don't believe that,' said Jolyon. 'Do you know many people?'

'Very few.'

At Waterloo they took a hansom, and he drove with her to the door of her mansions. Squeezing her hand at parting, he said:

'You know, you could always come to us at Robin Hill; you must let me know everything that happens. Good-bye, Irene.'

'Good-bye,' she answered softly.

Jolyon climbed back into his cab, wondering why he had not asked her to dine and go to the theatre with him. Solitary, starved, hung-up life that she had! 'Hotch Potch Club,' he said through the trap-door. As his hansom debouched on to the Embankment, a man in top-hat and overcoat passed, walking quickly, so close to the wall that he seemed to be scraping it.

'By Jove!' thought Jolyon; 'Soames himself! What's *he* up to now!' And, stopping the cab round the corner, he got out and retraced his steps to where he could see the entrance to the mansions. Soames had halted in front of them, and was looking up at the light in her windows. 'If he goes in,' thought Jolyon, 'what shall I do? What have I the right to do?' What the fellow had said was

true. She was still his wife, absolutely without protection from annoyance!
'Well, if he goes in,' he thought, 'I follow.' And he began moving towards the
mansions. Again Soames advanced; he was in the very entrance now. But
suddenly he stopped, spun round on his heel, and came back towards the river.
'What now?' thought Jolyon. 'In a dozen steps he'll recognise me.' And he
turned tail. His cousin's footsteps kept pace with his own. But he reached his
cab and got in before Soames had turned the corner. 'Go on!' he said through
the trap. Soames's figure ranged up alongside.

'Hansom!' he said. 'Engaged? Hallo!'

'Hallo!' answered Jolyon. 'You?'

The quick suspicion on his cousin's face, white in the lamplight, decided
him.

'I can give you a lift,' he said, 'if you're going West.'

'Thanks,' answered Soames, and got in.

'I've been seeing Irene,' said Jolyon when the cab had started.

'Indeed!'

'You went to see her yesterday yourself, I understand.'

'I did,' said Soames; 'she's my wife, you know.'

The tone, the half-lifted sneering lip, roused sudden anger in Jolyon; but he
subdued it.

'You ought to know best,' he said, 'but if you want a divorce it's not very wise
to go seeing her, is it? One can't run with the hare and hunt with the hounds.'

'You're very good to warn me,' said Soames, 'but I have not made up my
mind.'

'*She* has,' said Jolyon, looking straight before him; 'you can't take things up,
you know, as they were twelve years ago.'

'That remains to be seen.'

'Look here!' said Jolyon, 'she's in a damnable position, and I am the only
person with any legal say in her affairs.'

'Except myself,' retorted Soames, 'who am also in a damnable position. Hers
is what she made for herself; mine what she made for me. I am not at all sure
that in her own interests I shan't require her to return to me.'

'What!' exclaimed Jolyon; and a shiver went through his whole body.

'I don't know what you may mean by "what",' answered Soames coldly;
'your say in her affairs is confined to paying out her income; please bear that in
mind. In choosing not to disgrace her by a divorce, I retained my rights, and, as
I say, I am not at all sure that I shan't require to exercise them.'

'My God!' ejaculated Jolyon, and he uttered a short laugh.

'Yes,' said Soames, and there was a deadly quality in his voice. 'I've not
forgotten the nickname your father gave me, "The man of property"! I'm not
called names for nothing.'

'This is fantastic,' murmured Jolyon. Well, the fellow couldn't force his wife
to live with him. Those days were past, anyway! And he looked round at
Soames with the thought: 'Is he real, this man?' But Soames looked very real,
sitting square yet almost elegant with the clipped moustache on his pale face,
and a tooth showing where a lip was lifted in a fixed smile. There was a long
silence while Jolyon thought: 'Instead of helping her, I've made things worse.'
Suddenly Soames said:

'It would be the best thing that could happen to her in many ways.'

At those words such a turmoil began taking place in Jolyon that he could
barely sit still in the cab. It was as if he were boxed up with hundreds of

thousands of his countrymen, boxed up with that something in the national character which had always been to him revolting, something which he knew to be extremely natural and yet which seemed to him inexplicable–their intense belief in contracts and vested rights, their complacent sense of virtue in the exaction of those rights. Here beside him in the cab was the very embodiment, the corporeal sum, as it were, of the possessive instinct–his own kinsman, too! It was uncanny and intolerable! 'But there's something more in it than that!' he thought, with a sick feeling. 'The dog, they say, returns to his vomit! The sight of her has reawakened something. Beauty! The devil's in it!'

'As I say,' said Soames, 'I have not made up my mind. I shall be obliged if you will kindly leave her quite alone.'

Jolyon bit his lips; he who had always hated rows almost welcomed the thought of one now.

'I can give you no such promise,' he said shortly.

'Very well,' said Soames, 'then we know where we are. I'll get down here.' And stopping the cab he got out without word or sign of farewell. Jolyon travelled on to his club.

The first news of the war was being called in the streets, but he paid no attention. What could he do to help her? If only his father were alive! *He* could have done so much! But why could he not do all that his father could have done? Was he not old enough?–turned fifty and twice married, with grown-up daughters and a son. 'Queer,' he thought. 'If she were plain I shouldn't be thinking twice about it. Beauty is the devil, when you're sensitive to it!' And into the club reading-room he went with a disturbed heart. In that very room he and Bosinney had talked one summer afternoon; he well remembered even now the disguised and secret lecture he had given that young man in the interests of June, the diagnosis of the Forsytes he had hazarded; and how he had wondered what sort of woman it was he was warning him against. And now! He was almost in want of a warning himself. 'It's deuced funny!' he thought, 'really deuced funny!'

14

SOAMES DISCOVERS WHAT HE WANTS

It is so much easier to say, 'Then we know where we are,' than to mean anything particular by the words. And in saying them Soames did but vent the jealous rankling of his instincts. He got out of the cab in a state of wary anger–with himself for not having seen Irene, with Jolyon for having seen her; and now with his inability to tell exactly what he wanted.

He had abandoned the cab because he could not bear to remain seated beside his cousin, and walking briskly eastwards he thought: 'I wouldn't trust that fellow Jolyon a yard. Once outcast, always outcast!' The chap had a natural sympathy with–with–laxity (he had shied at the word 'sin' because it was too melodramatic for use by a Forsyte).

Indecision in desire was to him a new feeling. He was like a child between a promised toy and an old one which had been taken away from him; and he was astonished at himself. Only last Sunday desire had seemed simple–just his freedom and Annette. 'I'll go and dine there,' he thought. To see her might bring back his singleness of intention, calm his exasperation, clear his mind.

The restaurant was fairly full–a good many foreigners and folk whom, from their appearance, he took to be literary or artistic. Scraps of conversation came his way through the clatter of plates and glasses. He distinctly heard the Boers sympathised with, the British Government blamed. 'Don't think much of their clientèle,' he thought. He went stolidly through his dinner and special coffee without making his presence known, and when at last he had finished, was careful not to be seen going towards the sanctum of Madame Lamotte. They were, as he expected, having supper–such a much nicer-looking supper than the dinner he had eaten that he felt a kind of grief–and they greeted him with a surprise so seemingly genuine that he thought with sudden suspicion: 'I believe they knew I was here all the time.' He gave Annette a look furtive and searching. So pretty, seemingly so candid; could she be angling for him? He turned to Madame Lamotte and said:

'I've been dining here.'

Really! If she had only known! There were dishes she could have recommended; what a pity! Soames was confirmed in his suspicion. 'I must look out what I'm doing!' he thought sharply.

'Another little cup of very special coffee, *monsieur*; a liqueur, Grand Marnier?' and Madame Lamotte rose to order these delicacies.

Alone with Annette, Soames said: 'Well, Annette?' with a defensive little smile about his lips.

The girl blushed. This, which last Sunday would have set his nerves tingling, now gave him much the same feeling a man has when a dog that he owns wriggles and looks at him. He had a curious sense of power, as if he could have said to her: 'Come and kiss me,' and she would have come. And yet–it was strange–but there seemed another face and form in the room too; and the itch in his nerves, was it for that–or for this? He jerked his head towards the restaurant and said: 'You have some queer customers. Do you like this life?'

Annette looked up at him for a moment, looked down, and played with her fork.

'No,' she said, 'I do not like it.'

'I've got her,' thought Soames, 'if I want her. But do I want her?' She was graceful, she was pretty–very pretty; she was fresh, she had taste of a kind. His eyes travelled round the little room; but the eyes of his mind went another journey–a half-light, and silvery walls, a satinwood piano, a woman standing against it, reined back, as it were, from him–a woman with white shoulders that he knew, and dark eyes that he had sought to know, and hair like dull dark amber. And as in an artist who strives for the unrealisable and is ever thirsty, so there rose in him at that moment the thirst of the old passion he had never satisfied.

'Well,' he said calmly, 'you're young. There's everything before *you*.'

Annette shook her head.

'I think sometimes there is nothing before me but hard work. I am not so in love with work as mother.'

'Your mother is a wonder,' said Soames, faintly mocking; 'she will never let failure lodge in her house.'

Annette sighed. 'It must be wonderful to be rich.'

'Oh! You'll be rich some day,' answered Soames, still with that faint mockery; 'don't be afraid.'

Annette shrugged her shoulders. '*Monsieur* is very kind.' And between her pouting lips she put a chocolate.

'Yes, my dear,' thought Soames, 'they're very pretty.'

Madame Lamotte, with coffee and liqueur, put an end to that colloquy. Soames did not stay long.

Outside in the streets of Soho, which always gave him such a feeling of property improperly owned, he mused. If only Irene had given him a son, he wouldn't now be squirming after women! The thought had jumped out of its little dark sentry-box in his inner consciousness. A son—something to look forward to, something to make the rest of life worth while, something to leave himself to, some perpetuity of self. 'If I had a son,' he thought bitterly, 'a proper legal son, I could make shift to go on as I used. One woman's much the same as another, after all.' But as he walked he shook his head. No! One woman was not the same as another. Many a time had he tried to think that in the old days of his thwarted married life; and he had always failed. He was failing now. He was trying to think Annette the same as that other. But she was not, she had not the lure of that old passion. 'And Irene's my wife,' he thought, 'my legal wife. I have done nothing to put her away from me. Why shouldn't she come back to me? It's the right thing, the lawful thing. It makes no scandal, no disturbance. If it's disagreeable to her—but why *should* it be? I'm not a leper, and she—she's no longer in love!' Why should he be put to the shifts and the sordid disgraces and the lurking defeats of the Divorce Court, when there she was like an empty house only waiting to be retaken into use and possessed by him who legally owned her? To one so secretive as Soames the thought of re-entry into quiet possession of his own property with nothing given away to the world was intensely alluring. 'No,' he mused, 'I'm glad I went to see that girl. I know now what I want most. If only Irene will come back I'll be as considerate as she wishes; she could live her own life; but perhaps—perhaps she would come round to me.' There was a lump in his throat. And doggedly along by the railings of the Green Park, towards his father's house, he went, trying to tread on his shadow walking before him in the brilliant moonlight.

PART II

I

THE THIRD GENERATION

Jolly Forsyte was strolling down High Street, Oxford, on a November afternoon; Val Dartie was strolling up. Jolly had just changed out of boating flannels and was on his way to the 'Frying-pan', to which he had recently been elected. Val had just changed out of riding clothes and was on his way to the fire—a bookmaker's in Cornmarket.

'Hallo!' said Jolly.

'Hallo!' replied Val.

The cousins had met but twice, Jolly, the second-year man, having invited the freshman to breakfast; and last evening they had seen each other again under somewhat exotic circumstances.

Over a tailor's in the Cornmarket resided one of those privileged young beings called minors, whose inheritances are large, whose parents are dead, whose guardians are remote, and whose instincts are vicious. At nineteen he had commenced one of these careers attractive and inexplicable to ordinary mortals for whom a single bankruptcy is good as a feast. Already famous for having the only roulette-table then to be found in Oxford, he was anticipating his expectations at a dazzling rate. He out-crummed Crum, though of a sanguine and rather beefy type which lacked the latter's fascinating languor. For Val it had been in the nature of baptism to be taken there to play roulette; in the nature of confirmation to get back into college, after hours, through a window whose bars were deceptive. Once, during that evening of delight, glancing up from the seductive green before him, he had caught sight, through a cloud of smoke, of his cousin standing opposite. '*Rouge gagne, impair, et manque!*' He had not seen him again.

'Come into the Frying-pan and have tea,' said Jolly, and they went in.

A stranger, seeing them together, would have noticed an unseizable resemblance between these second cousins of the third generation of Forsytes; the same bone formation in face, though Jolly's eyes were darker grey, his hair lighter and more wavy.

'Tea and buttered buns, waiter, please,' said Jolly.

'Have one of my cigarettes?' said Val. 'I saw you last night. How did you do?'

'I didn't play.'

'I won fifteen quid.'

Though desirous of repeating a whimsical comment on gambling he had once heard his father make—'When you're fleeced you're sick, and when you fleece you're sorry'—Jolly contented himself with:

'Rotten game, I think; I was at school with that chap. He's an awful fool.'

'Oh! I don't know,' said Val, as one might speak in defence of a disparaged god; 'he's a pretty good sport.'

They exchanged whiffs in silence.

'You met my people, didn't you?' said Jolly. 'They're coming up tomorrow.'

Val grew a little red.

'Really! I can give you a rare good tip for the Manchester November Handicap.'

'Thanks, I only take interest in the classic races.'

'You can't make any money over them,' said Val.

'I hate the ring,' said Jolly; 'there's such a row and stink. I like the paddock.'

'I like to back my judgment,' answered Val.

Jolly smiled; his smile was like his father's. 'I haven't got any. I always lose money if I bet.'

'You have to buy experience, of course.'

'Yes, but it's all messed-up with doing people in the eye.'

'Of course, or they'll do you—that's the excitement.'

Jolly looked a little scornful.

'What do you do with yourself! Row?'

'No—ride, and drive about. I'm going to play polo next term, if I can get my granddad to stump up.'

'That's old Uncle James, isn't it. What's he like?'

'Older than forty hills,' said Val, 'and always thinking he's going to be ruined.'

'I suppose my granddad and he were brothers.'

'I don't believe any of that old lot were sportsmen,' said Val; 'they must have worshipped money.'

'Mine didn't!' said Jolly warmly.

Val flipped the ash off his cigarette.

'Money's only fit to spend,' he said; 'I wish the deuce I had more.'

Jolly gave him that direct upward look of judgment which he had inherited from old Jolyon: One didn't talk about money! And again there was silence, while they drank tea and ate the buttered buns.

'Where are your people going to stay?' asked Val, elaborately casual.

'"Rainbow." What do you think of the war?'

'Rotten, so far. The Boers aren't sports a bit. Why don't they come out into the open?'

'Why should they? They've got everything against them except their way of fighting. I rather admire them.'

'They can ride and shoot,' admitted Val, 'but they're a lousy lot. Do you know Crum?'

'Of Merton? Only by sight. He's in that fast set too, isn't he? Rather La-di-da and Brummagem.'

Val said fixedly: 'He's a friend of mine.'

'Oh! Sorry!' And they sat awkwardly staring past each other, having pitched on their pet points of snobbery. For Jolly was forming himself unconsciously on a set whose motto was: 'We defy you to bore us. Life isn't half long enough, and we're going to talk faster and more crisply, do more and know more, and dwell less on any subject than you can possibly imagine. We are "the best"—made of wire and whipcord.' And Val was unconsciously forming

himself on a set whose motto was: 'We defy you to interest or excite us. We have
had every sensation, or if we haven't, we pretend we have. We are so exhausted
with living that no hours are too small for us. We will lose our shirts with
equanimity. We have flown fast and are past everything. All is cigarette smoke.
Bismillah!' Competitive spirit, bone-deep in the English, was obliging those
two young Forsytes to have ideals; and at the close of a century ideals are mixed.
The aristocracy had already in the main adopted the 'jumping-jesus' principle;
though here and there one like Crum–who was an honourable–stood starkly
languid for that gambler's Nirvana which had been the *summum bonum* of the
old 'dandies' and of 'the mashers' in the eighties. And round Crum were still
gathered a forlorn hope of blue-bloods with a plutocratic following.

But there was between the cousins another far less obvious
antipathy–coming from the unseizable family resemblance, which each
perhaps resented; or from some half-consciousness of that old feud persisting
still between their branches of the clan, formed within them by odd words or
half-hints dropped by their elders. And Jolly, tinkling his teaspoon, was
musing: 'His tie-pin and his waistcoat and his drawl and his betting–good
Lord!'

And Val, finishing his bun, was thinking: 'He's rather a young beast!'

'I suppose you'll be meeting your people?' he said, getting up. 'I wish you'd
tell them I should like tó show them over B.N.C.–not that there's anything
much there–if they'd care to come.'

'Thanks, I'll ask them.'

'Would they lunch? I've got rather a decent scout.'

Jolly doubted if they would have time.

'You'll ask them, though?'

'Very good of you,' said Jolly, fully meaning that they should not go; but,
instinctively polite, he added: 'You'd better come and have dinner with us to-
morrow.'

'Rather. What time?'

'Seven-thirty.'

'Dress?'

'No.' And they parted, a subtle antagonism alive within them.

Holly and her father arrived by a midday train. It was her first visit to the city
of spires and dreams, and she was very silent, looking almost shyly at the
brother who was part of this wonderful place. After lunch she wandered,
examining his household gods with intense curiosity. Jolly's sitting-room was
panelled, and Art represented by a set of Bartolozzi prints which had belonged
to old Jolyon, and by college photographs–of young men, live young men, a
little heroic, and to be compared with her memories of Val. Jolyon also
scrutinised with care that evidence of his boy's character and tastes.

Jolly was anxious that they should see him rowing, so they set forth to the
river. Holly, between her brother and her father, felt elated when heads were
turned and eyes rested on her. That they might see him to the best advantage
they left him at the Barge and crossed the river to the towing-path. Slight in
build–for of all the Forsytes only old Swithin and George were beefy–Jolly
was rowing 'Two' in a trial eight. He looked very earnest and strenuous. With
pride Jolyon thought him the best-looking boy of the lot; Holly, as became a
sister, was more struck by one or two of the others, but would not have said so
for the world. The river was bright that afternoon, the meadows lush, the trees
still beautiful with colour. Distinguished peace clung around the old city;

Jolyon promised himself a day's sketching if the weather held. The Eight passed a second time, spurting home along the Barges–Jolly's face was very set, so as not to show that he was blown. They returned across the river and waited for him.

'Oh!' said Jolly in the Christ Church meadows, 'I had to ask that chap Val Dartie to dine with us to-night. He wanted to give you lunch and show you B.N.C., so I thought I'd better; then you needn't go. I don't like him much.'

Holly's rather sallow face had become suffused with pink.

'Why not?'

'Oh! I don't know. He seems to me rather showy and bad form. What are his people like, Dad? He's only a second cousin, isn't he?'

Jolyon took refuge in a smile.

'Ask Holly,' he said; 'she saw his uncle.'

'I *liked* Val,' Holly answered, staring at the ground before her; 'his uncle looked–awfully different.' She stole a glance at Jolly from under her lashes.

'Did you ever,' said Jolyon, with whimsical intention, 'hear our family history, my dears? It's quite a fairy-tale. The first Jolyon Forsyte–at all events, the first we know anything of, and that would be your great-great-grandfather–dwelt in the land of Dorset on the edge of the sea, being by profession an agriculturalist, as your great-aunt put it, and the son of an agriculturist–farmers, in fact; your grandfather used to call them, "Very small beer."' He looked at Jolly to see how his lordiness was standing it, and with the other eye noted Holly's malicious pleasure in the slight drop of her brother's face.

'We may suppose him thick and sturdy, standing for England as it was before the Industrial Era began. The second Jolyon Forsyte–your great-grandfather, Jolly; better known as Superior Dosset Forsyte–built houses, so the chronicle runs, begat ten children, and migrated to London town. It is known that he drank Madeira. We may suppose him representing the England of Napoleon's wars and general unrest. The eldest of his six sons was the third Jolyon, your grandfather, my dears–tea merchant and chairman of companies, one of the soundest Englishmen who ever lived–and to me the dearest.' Jolyon's voice had lost its irony, and his son and daughter gazed at him solemnly. 'He was just and tenacious, tender and young at heart. You remember him, and I remember him. Pass to the others! Your great-uncle James, that's young Val's grandfather, had a son called Soames–whereby hangs a tale of no love lost, and I don't think I'll tell it you. James and the other eight children of "Superior Dosset", of whom there are still five alive, may be said to have represented Victorian England, with its principles of trade and individualism at five per cent and your money back–if you know what that means. At all events, they've turned thirty thousand pounds into a cool million between them in the course of their long lives. They never did a wild thing–unless it was your great-uncle Swithin, who I believe was once swindled at thimble-rig, and was called "Four-in-hand Forsyte" because he drove a pair. Their day is passing, and their type, not altogether for the advantage of the country. They were pedestrian, but they, too, were sound. I am the fourth Jolyon Forsyte–a poor holder of the name–'

'No, Dad,' said Jolly, and Holly squeezed his hand.

'Yes,' repeated Jolyon, 'a poor specimen, representing, I'm afraid, nothing but the end of the century, unearned income, amateurism, and individual liberty–a different thing from individualism, Jolly. You are the fifth Jolyon

Forsyte, old man, and you open the ball of the new century.'

As he spoke they turned in through the college gates, and Holly said: 'It's fascinating, Dad.'

None of them quite knew what she meant. Jolly was grave.

The Rainbow, distinguished, as only an Oxford hostel can be, for lack of modernity, provided one small oak-panelled private sitting-room, in which Holly sat to receive, white-frocked, shy, and alone, when the only guest arrived.

Rather as one would touch a moth, Val took her hand. And wouldn't she wear this 'measly flower'? It would look ripping in her hair. He removed a gardenia from his coat.

'Oh! No, thank you—I couldn't!' But she took it and pinned it at her neck, having suddenly remembered that word 'showy'! Val's buttonhole would give offence; and she so much wanted Jolly to like him. Did she realise that Val was at his best and quietest in her presence, and was that, perhaps, half the secret of his attraction for her?

'I never said anything about our ride, Val.'

'Rather not! It's just between us.'

By the uneasiness of his hands and the fidgeting of his feet he was giving her a sense of power very delicious; a soft feeling too—the wish to make him happy.

'Do tell me about Oxford. It must be ever so lovely.'

Val admitted that it was frightfully decent to do what you liked; the lectures were nothing; and there were some very good chaps. 'Only,' he added, 'of course I wish I was in town, and could come down and see you.'

Holly moved one hand shyly on her knee, and her glance dropped.

'You haven't forgotten,' he said, suddenly gathering courage, 'that we're going madrabbiting together?'

Holly smiled.

'Oh! That was only make-believe. One can't do that sort of thing after one's grown up, you know.'

'Dash it! Cousins can,' said Val. 'Next Long Vac—it begins in June, you know, and goes on for ever—we'll watch our chance.'

But, though the thrill of conspiracy ran through her veins, Holly shook her head. 'It won't come off,' she murmured.

'Won't it!' said Val fervently; 'who's going to stop it? Not your father or your brother.'

At this moment Jolyon and Jolly came in; and romance fled into Val's patent leather and Holly's white satin toes, where it itched and tingled during an evening not conspicuous for open-heartedness.

Sensitive to atmosphere, Jolyon soon felt the latent antagonism between the boys, and was puzzled by Holly; so he became unconsciously ironical, which is fatal to the expansiveness of youth. A letter, handed to him after dinner, reduced him to a silence hardly broken till Jolly and Val rose to go. He went out with them, smoking his cigar, and walked with his son to the gates of Christ Church. Turning back, he took out the letter and read it again beneath a lamp.

DEAR JOLYON,

Soames came again to-night—my thirty-seventh birthday. You were right, I mustn't stay here. I'm going to-morrow to the Piedmont Hotel, but I won't go abroad without seeing you. I feel lonely and down-hearted.

Yours affectionately,

IRENE.

He folded the letter back into his pocket and walked on, astonished at the violence of his feelings. What had the fellow said or done?

He turned into High Street, down the Turl, and on among a maze of spires and domes and long college fronts and walls, bright or dark-shadowed in the strong moonlight. In this very heart of England's gentility it was difficult to realise that a lonely woman could be importuned or hunted, but what else could her letter mean? Soames must have been pressing her to go back to him again, with public opinion and the law on his side, too! 'Eighteen-ninety-nine!' he thought, gazing at the broken glass shining on the top of a villa garden wall; 'but when it comes to property we're still a heathen people! I'll go up to-morrow morning. I dare say it'll be best for her to go abroad.' Yet the thought displeased him. Why should Soames hunt her out of England! Besides, he might follow, and out there she would be still more helpless against the attentions of her own husband! 'I must tread warily,' he thought; 'that fellow could make himself very nasty. I didn't like his manner in the cab the other night.' His thoughts turned to his daughter June. Could she help? Once on a time Irene had been her greatest friend, and now she was a 'lame duck', such as must appeal to June's nature! He determined to wire to his daughter to meet him at Paddington Station. Retracing his steps towards the Rainbow he questioned his own sensations. Would he be upsetting himself over every woman in like case? No! he would not. The candour of this conclusion discomfited him; and finding that Holly had gone up to bed, he sought his own room. But he could not sleep, and sat for a long time at his window, huddled in an overcoat, watching the moonlight on the roofs.

Next door Holly, too, was awake, thinking of the lashes above and below Val's eyes, especially below; and of what she could do to make Jolly like him better. The scent of the gardenia was strong in her little bedroom, and pleasant to her.

And Val, leaning out of his first-floor window in B.N.C., was gazing at a moonlit quadrangle without seeing it at all, seeing instead Holly, slim and white-frocked, as she sat beside the fire when he first went in.

But Jolly, in his bedroom narrow as a ghost, lay with a hand beneath his cheek and dreamed he was with Val in one boat, rowing a race against him, while his father was calling from the towpath: 'Two! Get your hands away there, bless you!'

2

SOAMES PUTS IT TO THE TOUCH

Of all those radiant firms which emblazon with their windows the West End of London, Gaves and Cortegal were considered by Soames the most 'attractive'— word just coming into fashion. He had never had his Uncle Swithin's taste in precious stones, and the abandonment by Irene when she left his house in 1889 of all the glittering things he had given her had disgusted him with this form of investment. But he still knew a diamond when he saw one, and during the week before her birthday he had taken occasion, on his way into the Poultry or his way out therefrom, to dally a little before the greater jewellers where one got, if not one's money's worth, at least a certain cachet with the goods.

Constant cogitation since his cab drive with Jolyon had convinced him more and more of the supreme importance of this moment in his life, the supreme need for taking steps and those not wrong. And, alongside the dry and reasoned sense that it was now or never with his self-preservation, now or never if he were to range himself and found a family, went the secret urge of his senses roused by the sight of her who had once been a passionately desired wife, and the conviction that it was a sin against common sense and the decent secrecy of Forsyte to waste the wife he had.

In an opinion on Winifred's case, Dreamer, Q.C.–he would much have preferred Waterbuck, but they had made him a judge (so late in the day as to rouse the usual suspicion of a political job)–had advised that they should go forward and obtain restitution of conjugal rights, a point which to Soames had never been in doubt. When they had obtained a decree to that effect they must wait to see if it was obeyed. If not, it would constitute legal desertion, and they should obtain evidence of misconduct and file their petition for divorce. All of which Soames knew perfectly well. They had marked him ten and one. This simplicity in his sister's case only made him the more desperate about the difficulty in his own. Everything, in fact, was driving towards the simple solution of Irene's return. If it were still against the grain with her, had *he* not feelings to subdue, injury to forgive, pain to forget? He at least had never injured her, and this was a world of compromise! He could offer her so much more than she had now. He would be prepared to make a liberal settlement on her which would not be upset. He often scrutinised his image in these days. He had never been a peacock like that fellow Dartie, or fancied himself a woman's man, but he had a certain belief in his own appearance–not unjustly, for it was well-coupled and preserved, neat, healthy, pale, unblemished by drink or excess of any kind. The Forsyte jaw and the concentration of his face were, in his eyes, virtues. So far as he could tell, there was no feature of him which need inspire dislike.

Thoughts and yearnings, with which one lives daily, become natural, even if far-fetched in their inception. If he could only give tangible proof enough of his determination to let bygones be bygones, and to do all in his power to please her, why should she not come back to him.

He entered Gaves and Cortegal's, therefore, on the morning of November the 9th, to buy a certain diamond brooch. 'Four twenty-five and dirt cheap, sir, at the money. It's a lady's brooch.' There was that in his mood which made him accept without demur. And he went on into the Poultry with the flat green morocco case in his breast pocket. Several times that day he opened it to look at the seven soft shining stones in their velvet oval nest.

'If the lady doesn't like it, sir, happy to exchange it any time. But there's no fear of that.' If only there were not! He got through a vast amount of work, only soother of the nerves he knew. A cable came in while he was in the office with details from the agent in Buenos Aires, and the name and address of a stewardess who would be prepared to swear to what was necessary. It was a timely spur to Soames's intense and rooted distaste for the washing of dirty linen in public. And when he set forth by Underground to Victoria Station he received a fresh impetus towards the renewal of his married life from the account in his evening paper of a fashionable divorce suit. The homing instinct of all true Forsytes in anxiety and trouble, the corporate tendency which kept them strong and solid, made him choose to dine at Park Lane. He neither could nor would breathe a word to his people of his intention—too reticent and proud—but the thought that at least they would be glad if they knew, and wish him luck, was heartening.

James was in lugubrious mood, for the fire which the impudence of Kruger's ultimatum had lit in him had been cold-watered by the poor success of the last month, and the exhortations to effort in *The Times*. He didn't know where it would end. Soames sought to cheer him by the continual use of the word 'Buller'. But James couldn't tell! There was Colley—and he got stuck on that hill, and this Ladysmith was down in a hollow, and altogether it looked to him a 'pretty kettle of fish'; he thought they ought to be sending the sailors—they were the chaps, they did a lot of good in the Crimea. Soames shifted the ground of consolation. Winifred had heard from Val that there had been a 'rag' and a bonfire on Guy Fawkes day at Oxford, and that he had escaped detection by blacking his face.

'Ah!' James muttered, 'he's a clever little chap.' But he shook his head shortly afterwards, and remarked that he didn't know what would become of him, and looking wistfully at his son, murmured on that Soames had never had a boy. He would have liked a grandson of his own name. And now—well, there it was!

Soames flinched. He had not expected such a challenge to disclose the secret in his heart. And Emily, who saw him wince, said:

'Nonsense, James; don't talk like that!'

But James, not looking anyone in the face, muttered on. There were Roger and Nicholas and Jolyon; they all had grandsons. And Swithin and Timothy had never married. He had done his best; but he would soon be gone now. And, as though he had uttered words of profound consolation, he was silent, eating brains with a fork and a piece of bread, and swallowing the bread.

Soames excused himself directly after dinner. It was not really cold, but he put on his fur coat, which served to fortify him against the fits of nervous shivering he had been subject to all day. Subconsciously he knew that he looked better thus than in an ordinary black overcoat. Then, feeling the morocco case flat against his heart, he sallied forth. He was no smoker, but he lit a cigarette, and smoked it gingerly as he walked along. He moved slowly down the Row towards Knightsbridge, timing himself to get to Chelsea at nine-fifteen. What did she do with herself evening after evening in that little hole? How mysterious women were! One lived alongside and knew nothing of them. What could she have seen in that fellow Bosinney to send her mad? For there was madness, after all, in what she had done—crazy moonstruck madness, in which all sense of values had been lost, and her life and his life ruined! And for a moment he was filled with a sort of exaltation, as though he were a man read of in a story who, possessed by the Christian spirit, would restore to her all the prizes of existence, forgiving and forgetting, and becoming the good fairy of her future. Under a tree opposite Knightsbridge Barracks, where the moonlight struck down clear and white, he took out once more the morocco case, and let the beams draw colour from those stones. Yes, they were of the first water! But, at the hard-closing snap of the case, another cold shiver ran through his nerves; and he walked on faster, clenching his gloved hands in the pockets of his coat, almost hoping she would not be in. The thought of how mysterious she was again beset him. Dining alone there night after night—in an evening dress, too, as if she were making believe to be in society! Playing the piano—to herself! Not

even a dog or cat, so far as he had seen. And that reminded him suddenly of the
mare he kept for station work at Mapledurham. If ever he went to the stable,
there she was quite alone, half asleep, and yet, on her home journeys going
more freely than on her way out, as if longing to be back and lonely in her stable!
'I would treat her well.' he thought incoherently. 'I would be very careful.' And
all that capacity for home life of which a mocking Fate seemed for ever to have
deprived him swelled suddenly in Soames, so that he dreamed dreams opposite
South Kensington Station. In the King's Road a man came slithering out of a
public-house playing a concertina. Soames watched him for a moment dance
crazily on the pavement to his own drawling jagged sounds, then crossed over
to avoid contact with this piece of drunken foolery. A night in the lock-up!
What asses people were! But the man had noticed his movement of avoidance,
and streams of genial blasphemy followed him across the street. 'I hope they'll
run him in,' thought Soames viciously. 'To have ruffians like that about, with
women out alone!' A woman's figure in front had induced this thought. Her
walk seemed oddly familiar, and when she turned the corner for which he was
bound, his heart began to beat. He hastened on to the corner to make certain.
Yes! It was Irene; he could not mistake her walk in that little drab street. She
threaded two more turnings, and from the last corner he saw her enter her block
of flats. To make sure of her now, he ran those few paces, hurried up the stairs,
and caught her standing at her door. He heard the latchkey in the lock, and
reached her side just as she turned round, startled, in the open doorway.

'Don't be alarmed,' he said, breathless, 'I happened to see you. Let me come
in a minute.'

She had put her hand up to her breast, her face was colourless, her eyes
widened by alarm. Then seeming to master herself, she inclined her head and
said: 'Very well.'

Soames closed the door. He, too, had need to recover, and when she had
passed into the sitting-room, waited a full minute, taking deep breaths to still
the beating of his heart. At this moment, so fraught with the future, to take out
that morocco case seemed crude. Yet, not to take it out left him there before her
with no preliminary excuse for coming. And in this dilemma he was seized with
impatience at all this paraphernalia of excuse and justification. This was a
scene—it could be nothing else, and he must face it! He heard her voice,
uncomfortably, pathetically soft:

'Why have you come again? Didn't you understand that I would rather you
did not?'

He noticed her clothes—a dark brown velvet corduroy, a sable boa, a small
round toque of the same. They suited her admirably. She had money to spare
for dress, evidently! He said abruptly:

'It's your birthday. I brought you this.' and he held out to her the green
morocco case.

'Oh! No—no!'

Soames pressed the clasp; the seven stones gleamed out on the pale grey
velvet.

'Why not?' he said. 'Just as a sign that you don't bear me ill-feeling any
longer.'

'I couldn't.'

Soames took it out of the case.

'Let me just see how it looks.'

She shrank back.

He followed, thrusting his hand with the brooch in it against the front of her dress. She shrank again.

Soames dropped his hand.

'Irene,' he said, 'let bygones be bygones. If *I* can, surely you might. Let's begin again, as if nothing had been. Won't you?' His voice was wistful, and his eyes, resting on her face, had in them a sort of supplication.

She, who was standing literally with her back against the wall, gave a little gulp, and that was all her answer. Soames went on:

'Can you really want to live all your days half-dead in this little hole? Come back to me, and I'll give you all you want. You shall live your own life; I swear it.'

He saw her face quiver ironically.

'Yes,' he repeated, 'but I mean it this time. I'll only ask one thing. I just want—I just want a son. Don't look like that! I want one. It's hard.' His voice had grown hurried, so that he hardly knew it for his own, and twice he jerked his head back as if struggling for breath. It was the sight of her eyes fixed on him, dark with a sort of fascinated fright, which pulled him together and changed that painful incoherence to anger.

'Is it so very unnatural?' he said between his teeth. 'Is it unnatural to want a child from one's own wife? You wrecked our life and put this blight on everything. We go on only half alive, and without any future. Is it so very unflattering to you that in spite of everything I—I still want you for my wife? Speak, for goodness' sake! do speak.'

Irene seemed to try, but did not succeed.

'I don't want to frighten you,' said Soames more gently, 'Heaven knows. I only want you to see that I can't go on like this. I want you back. I want you.'

Irene raised one hand and covered the lower part of her face, but her eyes never moved from his, as though she trusted in them to keep him at bay. And all those years, barren and bitter, since—ah! when?—almost since he had first known her, surged up in one great wave of recollection in Soames; and a spasm that for his life he could not control constricted his face.

'It's not too late!,' he said; 'it's not—if you'll only believe it.'

Irene uncovered her lips and both her hands made a writhing gesture in front of her breast. Soames seized them.

'Don't!' she said under her breath. But he stood holding on to them, trying to stare into her eyes which did not waver. Then she said quietly:

'I am alone here. You won't behave again as you once behaved.'

Dropping her hands as though they had been hot irons, he turned away. Was it possible that there could be such relentless unforgiveness! Could that one act of violent possession be still alive within her? Did it bar him thus utterly? And doggedly he said, without looking up:

'I am not going till you've answered me. I am offering what few men would bring themselves to offer, I want a—a reasonable answer.'

And almost with surprise he heard her say:

'You can't have a reasonable answer. Reason has nothing to do with it. You can only have the brutal truth: I would rather die.'

Soames stared at her.

'Oh!' he said. And there intervened in him a sort of paralysis of speech and movement, the kind of quivering which comes when a man has received a deadly insult, and does not yet know how he is going to take it, or rather what it is going to do with him.

'Oh!' he said again, 'as bad as that? Indeed! You would rather die. That's pretty!'

'I am sorry. You wanted me to answer. I can't help the truth, can I?'

At that queer spiritual appeal Soames turned for relief to actuality. He snapped the brooch back into its case and put it in his pocket.

'The truth!' he said, 'there's no such thing with women. It's nerves—nerves.'

He heard the whisper:

'Yes; nerves don't lie. Haven't you discovered that?' He was silent, obsessed by the thought: 'I *will* hate this woman. I *will* hate her.' That was the trouble! If only he could! He shot a glance at her, who stood unmoving against the wall with her head up and her hands clasped, for all the world as if she were going to be shot. And he said quickly:

'I don't believe a word of it. You have a lover. If you hadn't, you wouldn't be such a—such a little idiot.' He was conscious, before the expression in her eyes, that he had uttered something of a non-sequitur, and dropped back too abruptly into the verbal freedom of his connubial days. He turned away to the door. But he could not go out. Something within him—that most deep and secret Forsyte quality, the impossibility of letting go, the impossibility of seeing the fantastic and forlorn nature of his own tenacity—prevented him. He turned about again, and there stood, with his back against the door, as hers was against the wall opposite, quite unconscious of anything ridiculous in this separation by the whole width of the room.

'Do you ever think of anybody but yourself?' he said.

Irene's lips quivered; then she answered slowly:

'Do you ever think that I found out my mistake—my hopeless, terrible mistake—the very first week of our marriage; that I went on trying three years—you know I went on trying! Was it for myself?'

Soames gritted his teeth. 'God knows what it was. I've never understood you; I shall never understand you. You had everything you wanted; and you can have it again, and more. What's the matter with me? I ask you a plain question: What is it?' Unconscious of the pathos in that enquiry, he went on passionately: 'I'm not lame, I'm not loathsome, I'm not a boor, I'm not a fool. What is it? What's the mystery about me?'

Her answer was a long sigh.

He clasped his hands with a gesture that for him was strangely full of expression. 'When I came here to-night I was—I hoped—I meant everything that I could to do away with the past and start fair again. And you meet me with "nerves", and silence, and sighs. There's nothing tangible. It's like—it's like a spider's web.'

'Yes.'

That whisper from across the room maddened Soames afresh.

'Well, I don't choose to be in a spider's web. I'll cut it.' He walked straight up to her. 'Now!' What he had gone up to her to do he really did not know. But when he was close, the old familiar scent of her clothes suddenly affected him. He put his hands on her shoulders and bent forward to kiss her. He kissed not her lips, but a little hard line where the lips had been drawn in; then his face was pressed away by her hands; he heard her say: 'Oh! No!' Shame, compunction, sense of futility flooded his whole being, he turned on his heel and went straight out.

3

VISIT TO IRENE

Jolyon found June waiting on the platform at Paddington. She had received his telegram while at breakfast. Her abode—a studio and two bedrooms in a St John's Wood garden—had been selected by her for the complete independence which it guaranteed. Unwatched by Mrs Grundy, unhindered by permanent domestics, she could receive lame ducks at any hour of day or night, and not seldom had a duck without studio of its own made use of June's. She enjoyed her freedom, and possessed herself with a sort of virginal passion; the warmth which she would have lavished on Bosinney, and of which—given her Forsyte tenacity—he must surely have tired, she now expended in championship of the underdogs and budding 'geniuses' of the artistic world. She lived, in fact, to turn ducks into the swans she believed they were. The very fervour of her protections warped her judgments. But she was loyal and liberal; her small eager hand was ever against the oppressions of academic and commercial opinion, and though her income was considerable, her bank balance was often a minus quantity.

She had come to Paddington Station heated in her soul by a visit to Eric Cobbley. A miserable Gallery had refused to let that straight-haired genius have his one-man show after all. Its impudent manager, after visiting his studio, had expressed the opinion that it would only be a 'one-horse show from the selling point of view'. This crowning example of commercial cowardice towards her favourite lame duck—and he so hard up, with a wife and two children, that he had caused her account to be overdrawn—was still making the blood glow in her small, resolute face, and her red-gold hair to shine more than ever. She gave her father a hug, and got into a cab with him, having as many fish to fry with him as he with her. It became at once a question which would fry them first.

Jolyon had reached the words: 'My dear, I want you to come with me,' when, glancing at her face, he perceived by her blue eyes moving from side to side—like the tail of a preoccupied cat—that she was not attending.

'Dad, is it true that I absolutely can't get at any of my money?'

'Only the income, fortunately, my love.'

'How perfectly beastly! Can't it be done somehow? There must be a way. I know I could buy a small Gallery for ten thousand pounds.'

'A small Gallery,' murmured Jolyon, 'seems a modest desire. But your grandfather forsaw it.'

'I think,' cried June vigorously, 'that all this care about money is awful, when there's so much genius in the world simply crushed out for want of a little. I shall never marry and have children; why shouldn't I be able to do some good instead of having it all tied up in case of things which will never come off?'

'Our name is Forsyte, my dear,' replied Jolyon in the ironical voice to which his impetuous daughter had never quite grown accustomed; 'and Forsytes, you know, are people who so settle their property that their grandchildren, in case they should die before their parents, have to make wills leaving the property that will only come to themselves when their parents die. Do you follow that? Nor do I, but it's a fact, anyway; we live by the principle that so long as there is a possibility of keeping wealth in the family it must not go out; if you die unmarried, your money goes to Jolly and Holly and their children if they marry. Isn't it pleasant to know that whatever you do you can none of you be destitute?'

'But can't I borrow the money?'

Jolyon shook his head. 'You can rent a Gallery, no doubt, if you could manage it out of your income.'

June uttered a contemptuous sound.

'Yes; and have no income left to help anybody with.'

'My dear child,' murmured Jolyon, 'wouldn't it come to the same thing?'

'No,' said June shrewdly. 'I could buy for ten thousand; that would only be four hundred a year. But I should have to pay a thousand a year rent, and that would only leave me five hundred. If I had that Gallery, Dad, think what I could do. I could make Eric Cobbley's name in no time, and ever so many others.'

'Names worth making make themselves in time.'

'When they're dead.'

'Did you ever know anybody living, my dear, improved by having his name made?'

'Yes, you,' said June, pressing his arm.

Jolyon started. 'I?' he thought. 'Oh! Ah! Now's she's going to ask me to do something. We take it out, we Forsytes, each in our different ways.'

June came closer to him in the cab.

'Darling,' she said, '*you* buy the Gallery, and I'll pay you four hundred a year for it. Then neither of us will be any the worse off. Besides, it's a splendid investment.'

Jolyon wriggled. 'Don't you think,' he said, 'that for an artist to buy a Gallery is a bit dubious? Besides, ten thousand pounds is a lump, and I'm not a commercial character.'

June looked at him with admiring appraisement.

'Of course you're not, but you're awfully business-like. And I'm sure we could make it pay. It'll be a perfect way of scoring off those wretched dealers and people.' And again she squeezed her father's arm.

Jolyon's face expressed quizzical despair.

'Where is this desirable Gallery? Splendidly situated, I suppose?'

'Just off Cork Street.'

'Ah!' thought Jolyon, 'I knew it was just off somewhere. Now for what I want out of *her*!'

'Well, I'll think of it, but not just now. You remember Irene? I want you to come with me and see her. Soames is after her again. She might be safer if we could give her asylum somewhere.'

The word 'asylum', which he had used by chance, was of all most calculated to rouse June's interest.

'Irene! I haven't seen her since—! Of course! I'd love to help her.'

It was Jolyon's turn to squeeze her arm, in warm admiration for this spirited, generous-hearted little creature of his begetting.

'Irene is proud,' he said, with a sidelong glance, in sudden doubt of June's discretion; 'she's difficult to help. We must tread gently. This is the place. I wired her to expect us. Let's send up our cards.'

'I can't bear Soames,' said June as she got up; 'he sneers at everything that isn't successful.'

Irene was in what was called the 'Ladies' drawing-room' of the Piedmont Hotel.

Nothing if not morally courageous, June walked straight up to her former friend, kissed her cheek, and the two settled down on a sofa never sat on since the hotel's foundation. Jolyon could see that Irene was deeply affected by this simple forgiveness.

'So Soames has been worrying you?' he said.

'I had a visit from him last night; he wants me to go back to him.'

'You're not, of course?' cried June.

Irene smiled faintly and shook her head. 'But his position is horrible,' she murmured.

'It's his own fault; he ought to have divorced you when he could.'

Jolyon remembered how fervently in the old days June had hoped that no divorce would smirch her dead and faithless lover's name.

'Let us hear what Irene *is* going to do,' he said.

Irene's lips quivered, but she spoke calmly.

'I'd better give him fresh excuse to get rid of me.'

'How horrible!' cried June.

'What else can I do?'

'Out of the question,' said Jolyon very quietly, '*sans amour.*'

He thought she was going to cry; but, getting up quickly, she half turned her back on them, and stood regaining control of herself.

June said suddenly:

'Well, I shall go to Soames and tell him he must leave you alone. What does he want at his age?'

'A child. It's not unnatural.'

'A child!' cried June scornfully. 'Of course! To leave his money to. If he wants one badly enough, let him take somebody and have one; then you can divorce him, and he can marry her.'

Jolyon perceived suddenly that he had made a mistake to bring June—her violent partisanship was fighting Soames's battle.

'It would be best for Irene to come quietly to us at Robin Hill, and see how things shape.'

'Of course,' said June; 'only—'

Irene looked full at Jolyon—in all his many attempts afterwards to analyse that glance he never could succeed.

'No! I should only bring trouble on you all. I will go abroad.'

He knew from her voice that this was final. The irrelevant thought flashed through him: 'Well, I could see her there.' But he said:

'Don't you think you would be more helpless abroad, in case he followed?'

'I don't know. I can but try.'

June sprang up and paced the room. 'It's all horrible,' she said. 'Why should people be tortured and kept miserable and helpless year after year by this disgusting sanctimonious law?' But someone had come into the room, and June came to a standstill. Jolyon went up to Irene:

'Do you want money?'

'No.'

'And would you like me to let your flat?'

'Yes, Jolyon, please.'

'When shall you be going?'

'To-morrow.'

'You won't go back there in the meantime, will you?' This he said with an anxiety strange to himself.

'No; I've got all I want here.'

'You'll send me your address?'

She put out her hand to him. 'I feel you're a rock.'

'Built on sand,' answered Jolyon, pressing her hand hard; 'but it's a pleasure to do anything, at any time, remember that. And if you change your mind–! Come along, June; say good-bye.'

June came from the window and flung her arms round Irene.

'Don't think of him,' she said under her breath; 'enjoy yourself, and bless you!'

With a memory of tears in Irene's eyes, and of a smile on her lips, they went away extremely silent, passing the lady who had interrupted the interview and was turning over the papers on the table.

Opposite the National Gallery June exclaimed:

'Of all undignified beasts and horrible laws!

But Jolyon did not respond. He had something of his father's balance, and could see things impartially even when his emotions were roused. Irene was right; Soames's position was as bad or worse than her own. As for the law–it catered for a human nature of which it took a naturally low view. And, feeling that if he stayed in his daughter's company he would in one way or another commit an indiscretion, he told her he must catch his train back to Oxford; and hailing a cab, left her to Turner's water-colours, with the promise that he would think over that Gallery.

But he thought over Irene instead. Pity, they said, was akin to love! If so he was certainly in danger of loving her, for he pitied her profoundly. To think of her drifting about Europe so handicapped and lonely! 'I hope to goodness she'll keep her head!' he thought; 'she might easily grow desperate.' In fact, now that she had cut loose from her poor threads of occupation, he couldn't imagine how she would go on–so beautiful a creature, hopeless, and fair game for anyone! In his exasperation was more than a little fear and jealousy. Women did strange things when they were driven into corners. 'I wonder what Soames will do now!' he thought. 'A rotten, idiotic state of things! And I suppose they would say it was her own fault.' Very preoccupied and sore at heart, he got into his train, mislaid his ticket, and on the platform at Oxford took his hat off to a lady whose face he seemed to remember without being able to put a name to her, not even when he saw her having tea at the Rainbow.

4

WHERE FORSYTES FEAR TO TREAD

Quivering from the defeat of his hopes, with the green morocco case still flat against his heart, Soames revolved thoughts bitter as death. A spider's web! Walking fast, and noting nothing in the moonlight, he brooded over the scene he had been through, over the memory of her figure rigid in his grasp. And the more he brooded, the more certain he became that she had a lover—her words, 'I would sooner die!' were ridiculous if she had not. Even if she had never loved him, she had made no fuss until Bosinney came on the scene. No; she was in love again, or she would not have made that melodramatic answer to his proposal, which in all the circumstances was reasonable! Very well! That simplified matters.

'I'll take steps to know where I am,' he thought; 'I'll go to Polteed's the first thing to-morrow morning.'

But even in forming that resolution, he knew he would have trouble with himself. He had employed Polteed's agency several times in the routine of his profession, even quite lately over Dartie's case, but he had never thought it possible to employ them to watch his own wife.

It was too insulting to himself!

He slept over that project and his wounded pride—or rather, kept vigil. Only while shaving did he suddenly remember that she called herself by her maiden name of Heron. Polteed would not know, at first at all events, whose wife she was, would not look at him obsequiously and leer behind his back. She would just be the wife of one of his clients. And that would be true—for was he not his own solicitor?

He was literally afraid not to put his design into execution at the first possible moment, lest, after all, he might fail himself. And making Warmson bring him an early cup of coffee, he stole out of the house before the hour of breakfast. He walked rapidly to one of those small West End streets where Polteed's and other firms ministered to the virtues of the wealthier classes. Hitherto he had always had Polteed to see him in the Poultry; but he well knew their address, and reached it at the opening hour. In the outer office, a room furnished so cosily that it might have been a moneylender's, he was attended by a lady who might have been a schoolmistress.

'I wish to see Mr Claud Polteed. He knows me—never mind my name.'

To keep everybody from knowing that he, Soames Forsyte, was reduced to having his wife spied on, was the overpowering consideration.

Mr Claud Polteed—so different from Mr Lewis Polteed—was one of those men with dark hair, slightly curved noses, and quick brown eyes who might be taken for Jews but are really Phœnicians; he received Soames in a room hushed by thickness of carpet and curtains. It was, in fact, confidentially furnished, without trace of document anywhere to be seen. Greeting Soames deferentially, he turned the key in the only door with a certain ostentation.

'If a client sends for me,' he was in the habit of saying, 'he takes what precaution he likes. If he comes here, we convince him that we have no leakages. I may safely say we lead in security, if in nothing else. . . .' 'Now, sir, what can I do for you?'

Soames's gorge had risen so that he could hardly speak. It was absolutely necessary to hide from this man that he had any but professional interest in the matter; and, mechanically, his face assumed its sideway smile.

'I've come to you early like this because there's not an hour to lose'—if he lost an hour he might fail himself yet! 'Have you a really trustworthy woman free?'

Mr Polteed unlocked a drawer, produced a memorandum, ran his eyes over it, and locked the drawer up again.

'Yes,' he said; 'the very woman.'

Soames had seated himself and crossed his legs—nothing but a faint flush, which might have been his normal complexion, betrayed him.

'Send her off at once, then, to watch a Mrs Irene Heron of Flat D, Truro Mansions, Chelsea, till further notice.'

'Precisely,' said Mr Polteed; 'divorce, I presume?' and he blew into a speaking-tube. 'Mrs Blanch in? I shall want to speak to her in ten minutes.'

'Deal with any reports yourself,' resumed Soames, 'and send them to me personally, marked confidential, sealed and registered. My client exacts the utmost secrecy.'

Mr Polteed smiled, as though saying: 'You are teaching your grandmother, my dear sir'; and his eyes slid over Soames's face for one unprofessional instant.

'Make his mind perfectly easy,' he said. 'Do you smoke?'

'No,' said Soames. 'Understand me: Nothing may come of this. If a name gets out, or the watching is suspected, it may have very serious consequences.'

Mr Polteed nodded. 'I can put it into the cipher category. Under that system a name is never mentioned; we work by numbers.'

He unlocked another drawer and took out two slips of paper, wrote on them, and handed one to Soames.

'Keep that, sir; it's your key. I retain this duplicate. The case we'll call 7x. The party watched will be 17; the watcher 19; the Mansions 25; yourself—I should say, your firm—31; my firm 32; myself 2. In case you should have to mention your client in writing, I have called him 43; any person we suspect will be 47; a second person 51. Any special hint or instruction while we're about it?'

'No,' said Soames; 'that is—every consideration compatible.'

Again Mr Polteed nodded. 'Expense?'

Soames shrugged. 'In reason,' he answered curtly, and got up. 'Keep it entirely in your own hands.'

'Entirely,' said Mr Polteed, appearing suddenly between him and the door. 'I shall be seeing you in that other case before long. Good-morning, sir.' His eyes slid unprofessionally over Soames once more, and he unlocked the door.

'Good-morning,' said Soames, looking neither to right nor left.

Out in the street he swore deeply, quietly, to himself. A spider's web, and to cut it he must use this spidery, secret, unclean method, so utterly repugnant to one who regarded his private life as his most sacred piece of property. But the die was cast, he could not go back. And he went on into the Poultry, and locked away the green morocco case and the key to that cipher destined to make crystal-clear his domestic bankruptcy.

Odd that one whose life was spent in bringing to the public eye all the private coils of property, the domestic disagreements of others, should dread so utterly the public eye turned on his own; and yet not odd, for who should know so well as he the whole unfeeling process of legal regulation?

He worked hard all day. Winifred was due at four o'clock; he was to take her down to a conference in the Temple with Dreamer, Q.C., and waiting for her he re-read the letter he had caused her to write the day of Dartie's departure, requiring him to return.

DEAR MONTAGUE,

I have received your letter with the news that you have left me for ever and are on your way to Buenos Aires. It has naturally been a great shock. I am taking this earliest opportunity of writing to tell you that I am prepared to let bygones be bygones if you will return to me at once. I beg you to do so. I am very much upset, and will not say any more now. I am sending this letter registered to the address you left at your club. Please cable to me.

Your still affectionate wife,
WINIFRED DARTIE.

Ugh! What bitter humbug! He remembered leaning over Winifred while she copied what he had pencilled, and how she had said, laying down her pen: 'Suppose he comes, Soames!' in such a strange tone of voice, as if she did not know her own mind. 'He won't come,' he had answered, 'till he's spent his money. That's why we must act at once.' Annexed to the copy of that letter was the original of Dartie's drunken scrawl from the Iseeum Club. Soames could have wished it had not been so manifestly penned in liquor. Just the sort of thing the court would pitch on. He seemed to hear the Judge's voice say: 'You took this seriously! Seriously enough to write him as you did? Do you think he meant it?' Never mind! The fact was clear that Dartie had sailed and had not returned. Annexed also was his cabled answer: 'Impossible return. Dartie.' Soames shook his head. If the whole thing were not disposed of within the next few months the fellow would turn up again like a bad penny. It saved a thousand a year at least to get rid of him, besides all the worry to Winifred and his father. 'I must stiffen Dreamer's back,' he thought; 'we must push it on.'

Winifred, who had adopted a kind of half-mourning which became her fair hair and tall figure very well, arrived in James's barouche drawn by James's pair. Soames had not seen it in the City since his father retired from business five years ago, and its incongruity gave him a shock. 'Times are changing,' he thought; 'one doesn't know what'll go next!' Top hats even were scarcer. He enquired after Val. Val, said Winifred, wrote that he was going to play polo next term. She thought he was in a very good set. She added with fashionably disguised anxiety: 'Will there be much publicity about my affair, Soames? *Must* it be in the papers? It's so bad for him, and the girls.'

With his own calamity all raw within him, Soames answered:

'The papers are a pushing lot; it's very difficult to keep things out. They pretend to be guarding the public's morals, and they corrupt them with their beastly reports. But we haven't got to that yet. We're only seeing Dreamer to-day on the restitution question. Of course he understands that it's to lead to divorce; but you must seem genuinely anxious to get Dartie back–you might practise that attitude to-day.'

Winifred sighed.

'Oh! What a clown Monty's been!' she said.

Soames gave her a sharp look. It was clear to him that she could not take her Dartie seriously, and would go back on the whole thing if given half a chance. His own instinct had been firm in this matter from the first. To save a little

scandal now would only bring on his sister and her children real disgrace and
perhaps ruin later on if Dartie were allowed to hang on to them, going downhill
and spending the money James would leave his daughter. Though it *was* all tied
up, that fellow would milk the settlements somehow, and make his family pay
through the nose to keep him out of bankruptcy or even perhaps gaol! They left
the shining carriage, with the shining horses and the shining-hatted servants on
the Embankment and walked up to Dreamer Q.C.'s Chambers in Crown Office
Row.

'Mr Bellby is here, sir,' said the clerk; 'Mr Dreamer will be ten minutes.'

Mr Bellby, the junior–not as junior as he might have been, for Soames only
employed barristers of established reputation; it was, indeed, something of a
mystery to him how barristers ever managed to establish that which made him
employ them–Mr Bellby was seated, taking a final glance through his papers.
He had come from Court, and was in wig and gown, which suited a nose jutting
out like the handle of a tiny pump, his small shrewd blue eyes, and rather
protruding lower lip–no better man to supplement and stiffen Dreamer.

The introduction to Winifred accomplished, they leaped the weather and
spoke of the war. Soames interjected suddenly:

'If he doesn't comply we can't bring proceedings for six months. I want to
get on with the matter, Bellby.'

Mr Bellby, who had the ghost of an Irish brogue, smiled at Winifred and
murmured: 'The Law's delays, Mrs Dartie.'

'Six months!' repeated Soames; 'it'll drive it up to June! We shan't get the
suit on till after the long vacation. We must put the screw on, Bellby'–he would
have all his work cut out to keep Winifred up to the scratch.

'Mr Dreamer will see you now, sir.'

They filed in, Mr Bellby going first, and Soames escorting Winifred after an
interval of one minute by his watch.

Dreamer Q.C., in a gown but divested of wig, was standing before the fire, as
if this conference were in the nature of a treat; he had the leathery, rather oily
complexion which goes with great learning, a considerable nose with glasses
perched on it, and little greyish whiskers; he luxuriated in the perpetual
cocking of one eye, and the concealment of his lower with his upper lip, which
gave a smothered turn to his speech. He had a way, too, of coming suddenly
round the corner on the person he was talking to; this, with a disconcerting tone
of voice and a habit of growling before he began to speak, had secured a
reputation second in Probate and Divorce to very few. Having listened, eye
cocked, to Mr Bellby's breezy recapitulation of the facts, he growled, and said:

'I know all that;' and coming round the corner at Winifred, smothered the
words:

'We want to get him back, don't we, Mrs Dartie?'

Soames interposed sharply:

'My sister's position, of course, is intolerable.'

Dreamer growled. 'Exactly. Now, can we rely on the cabled refusal, or must
we wait till after Christmas to give him a chance to have written–that's the
point, isn't it?'

'The sooner–' Soames began.

'What do you say, Bellby?' said Dreamer, coming round his corner.

Mr Bellby seemed to sniff the air like a hound.

'We won't be on till the middle of December. We've no need to give um more
rope than that.'

'No,' said Soames, 'why should my sister be incommoded by his choosing to go–'

'To Jericho!' said Dreamer, again coming round his corner; 'quite so. People oughtn't to go to Jericho, ought they, Mrs Dartie?' And he raised his gown into a sort of fantail. 'I agree. We can go forward. Is there anything more?'

'Nothing at present,' said Soames meaningly; 'I wanted you to see my sister.'

Dreamer growled softly: 'Delighted. Good-evening!' And let fall the protection of his gown.

They filed out. Winifred went down the stairs. Soames lingered. In spite of himself, he was impressed by Dreamer.

'The evidence is all right, I think,' he said to Bellby. 'Between ourselves, if we don't get the thing through quick, we never may. Do you think *he* understands that?'

'I'll make um,' said Bellby. 'Good man though–good man.'

Soames nodded and hastened after his sister. He found her in a draught, biting her lips behind her veil, and at once said:

'The evidence of the stewardess will be very complete.'

Winifred's face hardened; she drew herself up, and they walked to the carriage. And, all through that silent drive back to Green Street, the souls of both of them revolved a single thought: 'Why, oh! why should I have to expose my misfortune to the public like this? Why have to employ spies to peer into my private troubles? They were not of my making.'

5

JOLLY SITS IN JUDGMENT

The possessive instinct, which, so determinedly balked, was animating two members of the Forsyte family towards riddance of what they could no longer possess, was hardening daily in the British body politic. Nicholas, originally so doubtful concerning a war which must affect property, had been heard to say that these Boers were a pig-headed lot; they were causing a lot of expense, and the sooner they had their lesson the better. *He* would send out Wolseley! Seeing always a little farther than other people–whence the most considerable fortune of all the Forsytes–he had perceived already that Buller was not the man–'a bull of a chap, who just went butting, and if they didn't look out Ladysmith would fall.' This was early in December, so that when Black Week came, he was enabled to say to everybody: 'I told you so.' During that week of gloom such as no Forsyte could remember, very young Nicholas attended so many drills in his corps, 'The Devil's Own', that young Nicholas consulted the family physician about his son's health, and was alarmed to find that he was perfectly sound. The boy had only just eaten his dinners and been called to the Bar, at some expense, and it was in a way a nightmare to his father and mother that he should be playing with military efficiency at a time when military efficiency in the civilian population might conceivably be wanted. His grandfather, of course, pooh-poohed the notion, too thoroughly educated in the feeling that no British war could be other than little and professional, and profoundly distrustful of Imperial commitments, by which, moreover, he stood to lose, for he owned De

Beers, now going down fast, more than a sufficient sacrifice on the part of his grandson.

At Oxford, however, rather different sentiments prevailed. The inherent effervescence of conglomerate youth had, during the two months of the term before Black Week, been gradually crystallising out into vivid oppositions. Normal adolescence, ever in England of a conservative tendency, though not taking things too seriously, was vehement for a fight to a finish and a good licking for the Boers. Of this larger faction Val Dartie was naturally a member. Radical youth, on the other hand, a small but perhaps more vocal body, was for stopping the war and giving the Boers autonomy. Until Black Week, however, the groups were amorphous, without sharp edges, and argument remained but academic. Jolly was one of those who knew not where he stood. A streak of his grandfather old Jolyon's love of justice prevented him from seeing one side only. Moreover, in his set of 'the best' there was a 'jumping-jesus' of extremely advanced opinions and some personal magnetism. Jolly wavered. His father, too, seemed doubtful in his views. And though, as was proper at the age of twenty, he kept a sharp eye on his father, watchful for defects which might still be remedied, still that father had an 'air' which gave a sort of glamour to his creed of ironic tolerance. Artists, of course, were notoriously Hamlet-like, and to this extent one must discount for one's father, even if one loved him. But Jolyon's original view, that to 'put your nose in where you aren't wanted' (as the Uitlanders had done), 'and then work the oracle till you get on top is not being quite the clean potato', had, whether founded in fact or no, a certain attraction for his son, who thought a deal about gentility. On the other hand, Jolly could not abide such as his set called 'cranks', and Val's set called 'smugs', so that he was still balancing when the clock of Black Week struck. One–two–three, came those ominous repulses at Stormberg, Magersfontein, Colenso. The sturdy English soul reacting after the first cried, 'Ah! but Methuen!' after the second: 'Ah! but Buller!' then, in inspissated gloom, hardened. And Jolly said to himself: 'No, damn it! We've got to lick the beggars now; I don't care whether we're right or wrong.' And, if he had known it, his father was thinking the same thought.

That next Sunday, last of the term, Jolly was bidden to wine with 'one of the best'. After the second toast, 'Buller and damnation to the Boers', drunk–no heel taps–in the college Burgundy, he noticed that Val Dartie, also a guest, was looking at him with a grin and saying something to his neighbour. He was sure it was disparaging. The last boy in the world to make himself conspicuous or cause public disturbance, Jolly grew rather red and shut his lips. The queer hostility he had always felt towards his second-cousin was strongly and suddenly reinforced. 'All right!' he said to himself; 'you wait, my friend!' More wine than was good for him, as the custom was, helped him to remember, when they all trooped forth to a secluded spot, to touch Val on the arm.

'What did you say about me in there?'

'Mayn't I say what I like?'

'No.'

'Well, I said you were a pro-Boer–and so you are!'

'You're a liar!'

'D'you want a row?'

'Of course, but not here; in the garden.'

'All right. Come on.'

They went, eyeing each other askance, unsteady, and unflinching; they climbed the garden railings. The spikes on the top slightly ripped Val's sleeve, and occupied his mind. Jolly's mind was occupied by the thought that they were going to fight in the precincts of a college foreign to them both. It was not the thing, but never mind–the young beast!

They passed over the grass into very nearly darkness and took off their coats.

'You're not screwed, are you?' said Jolly suddenly. 'I can't fight you if you're screwed.'

'No more than you.'

'All right then.'

Without shaking hands, they put themselves at once into postures of defence. They had drunk too much for science, and so were especially careful to assume correct attitudes, until Jolly smote Val almost accidentally on the nose. After that it was all a dark and ugly scrimmage in the deep shadow of the old trees, with no one to call 'time', till, battered and blown, they unclinched and staggered back from each other, as a voice said:

'Your names, young gentlemen?'

At this bland query spoken from under the lamp at the garden gate, like some demand of a god, their nerves gave way, and snatching up their coats, they ran at the railings, shinned up them, and made for the secluded spot whence they had issued to the fight. Here, in dim light, they mopped their faces, and without a word walked, ten paces apart, to the college gate. They went out silently, Val going towards the Broad along the Brewery, Jolly down the lane towards the High. His head, still fumed, was busy with regret that he had not displayed more science, passing in review the counters and knock-out blows which he had not delivered. His mind strayed on to an imagined combat, infinitely unlike that which he had just been through, infinitely gallant, with sash and sword, with thrust and parry, as if he were in the pages of his beloved Dumas. He fancied himself La Mole, and Aramis, Bussy, Chicot, and D'Artagnan rolled into one, but he quite failed to envisage Val as Coconnas, Brissac, or Rochefort. The fellow was just a confounded cousin who didn't come up to Cocker. Never mind. He had given him one or two. 'Pro-Boer!' The word still rankled, and thoughts of enlisting jostled his aching head; of riding over the veldt, firing gallantly, while the Boers rolled over like rabbits. And, turning up his smarting eyes, he saw the stars shining between the house-tops of the High, and himself lying out on the Karoo (whatever that was) rolled in a blanket, with his rifle ready and his gaze fixed on a glittering heaven.

He had a fearful 'head' next morning, which he doctored, as became one of 'the best', by soaking it in cold water, brewing strong coffee which he could not drink, and only sipping a little hock at lunch. The legend that 'some fool' had run into him round a corner accounted for a bruise on his cheek. He would on no account have mentioned the fight, for, on second thoughts, it fell far short of his standards.

The next day he went 'down', and travelled through to Robin Hill. Nobody was there but June and Holly, for his father had gone to Paris. He spent a restless and unsettled vacation, quite out of touch with either of his sisters. June, indeed, was occupied with lame ducks, whom, as a rule, Jolly could not stand, especially that Eric Cobbley and his family, 'hopeless outsiders', who were always littering up the house in the vacation. And between Holly and himself there was a strange division, as if she were unnecessary. He punched viciously at a ball, rode furiously but alone in Richmond Park, making a point of jumping the stiff, high hurdles put up to close certain worn avenues of grass–keeping his nerve in, he called it. Jolly was more afraid of being afraid than most boys are. He bought a rifle, too, and put a range up in the home field, shooting across the pond into the kitchen-garden wall, to the peril of gardeners, with the thought that some day, perhaps, he would enlist and save South Africa for his country. In fact, now that they were appealing for Yeomanry recruits the boy was thoroughly upset. Ought he to go? None of 'the best', so far as he knew–and he was in correspondence with several–were thinking of joining. If they *had* been making a move he would have gone at once–very competitive, and with a strong sense of form, he could not bear to be left behind in anything–but to do it off his own bat might look like 'swagger'; because of course it wasn't really necessary. Besides, he did not want to go, for the other side of this young Forsyte recoiled from leaping before he looked. It was altogether mixed pickles within him, hot and sickly pickles, and he became quite unlike his serene and rather lordly self.

And then one day he saw that which moved him to uneasy wrath–two riders, in a glade of the Park close to the Ham Gate, of whom she on the left hand was most assuredly Holly on her silver roan, and he on the right hand as assuredly that 'squirt' Val Dartie. His first impulse was to urge on his own horse and demand the meaning of this portent, tell the fellow to 'bunk', and take Holly home. His second–to feel that he would look a fool if they refused. He reined his horse in behind a tree, then perceived that it was equally impossible to spy on them. Nothing for it but to go home and await her coming! Sneaking out with that young bounder! He could not consult with June, because she had gone up that morning in the train of Eric Cobbley and his lot. And his father was still in 'that rotten Paris'. He felt that this was emphatically one of those moments for which he had trained himself, assiduously, at school, where he and a boy called Brent had frequently set fire to newspapers and placed them in the centre of their studies to accustom them to coolness in moments of danger. He did not feel at all cool waiting in the stable-yard, idly stroking the dog Balthasar, who, queasy as an old fat monk, and sad in the absence of his master, turned up his face, panting with gratitude for this attention. It was half an hour before Holly came, flushed and ever so much prettier than she had any right to look. He saw her look at him quickly–guiltily of course–then followed her in and, taking her arm, conducted her into what had been their grandfather's study. The room, not much used now, was still vaguely haunted for them both by a presence with which they associated tenderness, large drooping white moustaches, the scent of cigar smoke, and laughter. Here Jolly, in the prime of his youth, before he went to school at all, had been wont to wrestle with his grandfather, who even at eighty had an irresistible habit of crooking his leg. Here Holly, perched on the arm of the great leather chair, had stroked hair curving silvery over an ear into which she would whisper secrets. Through that window they had all three sallied times without number to cricket on the lawn, and a mysterious game called 'Wopsy-doozle', not to be understood by outsiders, which made old Jolyon very hot. Here once on a warm night Holly had appeared in her 'nighty', having had a bad dream, to have the clutch of it released. And here Jolly, having begun the day badly by introducing fizzy magnesia into Mademoiselle Beauce's new-laid egg, and gone on to worse, had been sent down (in the absence of his father) to the ensuing dialogue.

'Now, my boy, you mustn't go on like this.'

'Well, she boxed my ears, Gran, so I only boxed hers, and then she boxed mine again.'

'Strike a lady? That'll never do! Have you begged her pardon?'

'Not yet.'

'Then you must go and do it at once. Come along.'

'But she began it, Gran; and she had two to my one.'

'My dear, it was an outrageous thing to do.'

'Well, she lost her temper; and I didn't lose mine.'

'Come along.'

'You come too, then, Gran.'

'Well–this time only.'

And they had gone hand in hand.

Here–where the Waverley novels and Byron's works and Gibbon's *Roman Empire* and Humboldt's *Cosmos*, and the bronzes on the mantelpiece, and that masterpiece of the oily school, 'Dutch Fishing Boats at Sunset', were fixed as fate, and for all sign of change old Jolyon might have been sitting there still, with legs crossed, in the arm-chair, and domed forehead and deep eyes grave above *The Times*–here they came, those two grandchildren. And Jolly said:

'I saw you and that fellow in the Park.'

The sight of blood rushing into her cheeks gave him some satisfaction; she *ought* to be ashamed!

'Well?' she said.

Jolly was surprised; he had expected more, or less.

'Do you know,' he said weightily, 'that he called me a pro-Boer last term? And I had to fight him.'

'Who won?'

Jolly wished to answer: 'I should have,' but it seemed beneath him.

'Look here!' he said, 'what's the meaning of it? Without telling anybody!'

'Why should I? Dad isn't here; why shouldn't I ride with him?'

'You've got me to ride with. I think he's an awful young rotter.'

Holly went pale with anger.

'He isn't. It's your own fault for not liking him.'

And slipping past her brother she went out, leaving him staring at the bronze Venus sitting on a tortoise, which had been shielded from him so far by his sister's dark head under her soft felt riding-hat. He felt queerly disturbed, shaken to his young foundations. A lifelong domination lay shattered round his feet. He went up to the Venus and mechanically inspected the tortoise. Why didn't he like Val Dartie? He could not tell. Ignorant of family history, barely aware of that vague feud which had started thirteen years before with Bosinney's defection from June in favour of Soames's wife, knowing really almost nothing about Val, he was at sea. He just *did* dislike him. The question, however, was: What should he do? Val Dartie, it was true, was a second-cousin, but it was not the thing for Holly to go about with him. And yet to 'tell' of what he had chanced on was against his creed. In this dilemma he went and sat in the old leather chair and crossed his legs. It grew dark while he sat there staring out through the long window at the old oak tree, ample yet bare of leaves, becoming slowly just a shape of deeper dark printed on the dusk.

'Grandfather!' he thought without sequence, and took out his watch. He could not see the hands, but he set the repeater going. 'Five o'clock!' His grandfather's first gold hunter watch, butter-smooth with age–all the milling worn from it, and dented with the mark of many a fall. The chime was like a little voice from out of that golden age, when they first came from St John's Wood, London, to this house–came driving with grandfather in his carriage, and almost instantly took to the trees. Trees to climb, and grandfather watering the geranium-beds below! What was to be done? Tell Dad he must come home? Confide in June?—only she was so–so sudden! Do nothing and trust to luck? After all, the vac. would soon be over. Go up and see Val and warn him off?' But how, get his address? Holly wouldn't give it him! A maze of paths, a cloud of possibilities! He lit a cigarette. When he had smoked it half-way through his brow relaxed, almost as if some thin old hand had been passed gently over it; and in his ear something seemed to whisper: 'Do nothing; be nice to Holly, be nice to her, my dear!' And Jolly heaved a sigh of contentment, blowing smoke through his nostrils. . . .

But up in her room, divested of her habit, Holly was still frowning. 'He is *not*–he is *not!*' were the words which kept forming on her lips.

6

JOLYON IN TWO MINDS

A little private hotel over a well-known restaurant near the Gare St Lazare was Jolyon's haunt in Paris. He hated his fellow Forsytes abroad–vapid as fish out of water in their well-trodden runs the Opera, Rue de Rivoli, and Moulin Rouge. Their air of having come because they wanted to be somewhere else as soon as possible annoyed him. But no other Forsytes came near this haunt, where he had a wood fire in his bedroom and the coffee was excellent. Paris was always to him more attractive in winter. The acrid savour from wood-smoke and chestnut-roasting braziers, the sharpness of the wintry sunshine on bright days, the open cafés defying keen-aired winter, the self-contained brisk boulevard crowds, all informed him that in winter Paris possessed a soul which, like a migrant bird, in high summer flew away.

He spoke French well, had some friends, knew little places where pleasant dishes could be met with, queer types observed. He felt philosophic in Paris, the edge of irony sharpened; life took on a subtle, purposeless meaning, became a bunch of flavours tasted, a darkness shot with shifting gleams of light.

When in the first week of December he decided to go to Paris, he was far from admitting that Irene's presence was influencing him. He had not been there two days before he owned that the wish to see her had been more than half the reason. In England one did not admit what was natural. He had thought it might be well to speak to her about the letting of her flat and other matters, but in Paris he at once knew better. There was a glamour over the city. On the third day he wrote to her, and received an answer which procured him a pleasurable shiver of the nerves:

My dear Jolyon,
It will be a happiness for me to see you.

IRENE.

He took his way to her hotel on a bright day with a feeling such as he had often had going to visit an adored picture. No woman, so far as he remembered, had ever inspired in him this special sensuous and yet impersonal sensation. He was going to sit and feast his eyes, and come away knowing her no better, but ready to go and feast his eyes again to-morrow. Such was his feeling, when in the tarnished and ornate little lounge of a quiet hotel near the river she came to him preceded by a small page-boy who uttered the word '*Madame*.' and vanished. Her face, her smile, the poise of her figure, were just as he had pictured, and the expression of her face said plainly: 'A friend!'

'Well,' he said, 'what news, poor exile?'

'None.'

'Nothing from Soames?'

'Nothing.'

'I have let the flat for you, and like a good steward I bring you some money. How do you like Paris?'

While he put her through this catechism, it seemed to him that he had never seen lips so fine and sensitive, the lower lip curving just a little upwards, the upper touched at one corner by the least conceivable dimple. It was like discovering a woman in what had hitherto been a sort of soft and breathed-on statue, almost impersonally admired. She owned that to be alone in Paris was a little difficult; and yet, Paris was so full of its own life that it was often, she confessed, as innocuous as a desert. Besides, the English were not liked just now!

'That will hardly be your case,' said Jolyon; 'you should appeal to the French.'

'It has its disadvantages.'

Jolyon nodded.

'Well, you must let *me* take you about while I'm here. We'll start to-morrow. Come and dine at my pet restaurant; and we'll go to the Opéra-Comique.'

It was the beginning of daily meetings.

Jolyon soon found that for those who desired a static condition of the affections, Paris was at once the first and last place in which to be friendly with a pretty woman. Revelation was alighting like a bird in his heart, singing: '*Elle est ton rêve! Elle est ton rêve!*' Sometimes this seemed natural, sometimes ludicrous—a bad case of elderly rapture. Having once been ostracised by Society, he had never since had any real regard for conventional morality; but the idea of a love which she could never return—and how could she at his age?—hardly mounted beyond his subconscious mind. He was full, too, of resentment, at the waste and loneliness of her life. Aware of being some comfort to her, and of the pleasure she clearly took in their many little outings, he was amiably desirous of doing and saying nothing to destroy that pleasure. It was like watching a starved plant draw up water, to see her drink in his companionship. So far as they could tell, no one knew her address except himself; she was unknown in Paris, and he but little known, so that discretion seemed unnecessary in those walks, talks, visits to concerts, picture-galleries, theatres, little dinners, expeditions to Versailles, St Cloud, even Fontaine-bleau. And time fled—one of those full months without past to it or future. What in his youth would certainly have been headlong passion was now per-haps as deep a feeling, but far gentler, tempered to protective companionship by admiration, hopelessness, and a sense of chivalry—arrested in his veins at least so long as she was there, smiling and happy in their friendship, and always to him more beautiful and spiritually responsive: for her philosophy of life seemed to march in admirable step with his own, conditioned by emotion more than by reason, ironically mistrustful, susceptible to beauty, almost passionately humane and tolerant, yet subject to instinctive rigidities of which as a mere man he was less capable. And during all this companionable month he never quite lost that feeling with which he had set out on the first day as if to visit an adored work of art, a well-nigh impersonal desire. The future—inexorable pendant to the present—he took care not to face, for fear of breaking up his untroubled manner; but he made plans to renew this time in places still more delightful, where the sun was hot and there were strange things to see and paint. The end came swiftly on the 20th of January with a telegram:

Have enlisted in Imperial Yeomanry.—JOLLY.

Jolyon received it just as he was setting out to meet her at the Louvre. It brought him up with a round turn. While he was lotus-eating here, his boy, whose philosopher and guide he ought to be, had taken this great step towards danger, hardship, perhaps even death. He felt disturbed to the soul, realising suddenly how Irene had twined herself round the roots of his being. Thus threatened with severance, the tie between them—for it had become a kind of tie—no longer had impersonal quality. The tranquil enjoyment of things in common, Jolyon perceived, was gone for ever. He saw his feeling as it was, in the nature of an infatuation. Ridiculous, perhaps, but so real that sooner or later it must disclose itself. And now, as it seemed to him, he could not, must not, make any such disclosure. The news of Jolly stood inexorably in the way. He was proud of this enlistment; proud of his boy for going off to fight for the country; for on Jolyon's pro-Boerism, too, Black Week had left its mark. And so the end was reached before the beginning! Well, luckily he had never made a sign!

When he came into the Gallery she was standing before the 'Virgin of the Rocks', graceful, absorbed, smiling and unconscious. 'Have I to give up seeing *that*?' he thought. 'It's unnatural, so long as she's willing that I should see her.' He stood, unnoticed, watching her, storing up the image of her figure, envying the picture on which she was bending that long scrutiny. Twice she turned her head towards the entrance, and he thought: 'That's for me!' At last he went forward.

'Look!' he said.

She read the telegram, and he heard her sigh.

That sigh, too, was for him! His position was really cruel! To be loyal to his son he must just shake her hand and go. To be loyal to the feeling in his heart he must at least tell her what that feeling was. Could she, would she understand the silence in which he was gazing at that picture?

'I'm afraid I must go home at once,' he said at last. 'I shall miss all this awfully.'

'So shall I; but, of course, you must go.'

'Well!' said Jolyon, holding out his hand.

Meeting her eyes, a flood of feeling nearly mastered him.

'Such is life!' he said. 'Take care of yourself, my dear!'

He had a stumbling sensation in his legs and feet, as if his brain refused to steer him away from her. From the doorway he saw her lift her hand and touch its finger with her lips. He raised his hat solemnly, and did not look back again.

7

DARTIE *VERSUS* DARTIE

The suit—Dartie *versus* Dartie—for restitution of those conjugal rights concerning which Winifred was at heart so deeply undecided, followed the laws of subtraction towards day of judgment. This was not reached before the Courts rose for Christmas, but the case was third on the list when they sat again. Winifred spent the Christmas holidays a thought more fashionably than usual, with the matter locked up in her low-cut bosom. James was particularly liberal to her that Christmas, expressing thereby his sympathy, and relief, at the approaching dissolution of her marriage with that 'precious rascal', which his old heart felt but his old lips could not utter.

The disappearance of Dartie made the fall in Consols a comparatively small matter; and as to the scandal—the real animus he felt against that fellow, and the increasing lead which property was attaining over reputation in a true Forsyte about to leave this world, served to drug a mind from which all allusions to the matter (except his own) were studiously kept. What worried him as a lawyer and a parent was the fear that Dartie might suddenly turn up and obey the Order of the Court when made. That would be a pretty how-de-do! The fear preyed on him in fact so much that, in presenting Winifred with a large Christmas cheque, he said: 'It's chiefly for that chap out there; to keep him from coming back.' It was, of course, to pitch away good money, but all in the nature of insurance against that bankruptcy which would no longer hang over him if only the divorce went through; and he questioned Winifred rigorously until she could assure him that the money had been sent. Poor woman!—it cost her many a pang to send what must find its way into the vanity-bag of 'that creature'! Soames, hearing of it, shook his head. They were not dealing with a Forsyte, reasonably tenacious of his purpose. It was very risky without knowing how the land lay out there. Still, it would look well with the Court; and he would see that Dreamer brought it out. 'I wonder,' he said suddenly, 'where that ballet goes after the Argentine'; never omitting a chance of reminder; for he knew that Winifred still had a weakness, if not for Dartie, at least for not laundering him in public. Though not good at showing admiration, he admitted that she was behaving extremely well, with all her children at home gaping like young birds for news of their father—Imogen just on the point of coming out, and Val very restive about the whole thing. He felt that Val was the real heart of the matter to Winifred, who certainly loved him beyond her other children. The boy could spoke the wheel of this divorce yet if he set his mind to it. And Soames was very careful to keep the proximity of the preliminary proceedings from his nephew's ears. He did more. He asked him to dine at the Remove, and over Val's cigar introduced the subject which he knew to be nearest to his heart.

'I hear,' he said, 'that you want to play polo up at Oxford.'

Val became less recumbent in his chair.

'Rather!' he said.

'Well,' continued Soames, 'that's a very expensive business. Your grandfather isn't likely to consent to it unless he can make sure that he's not got any other drain on him.' And he paused to see whether the boy understood his meaning.

Val's dark, thick lashes concealed his eyes, but a slight grimace appeared on his wide mouth, and he muttered:

'I suppose you mean my dad!'

'Yes,' said Soames; 'I'm afraid it depends on whether he continues to be a drag or not;' and said no more, letting the boy dream it over.

But Val was also dreaming in those days of a silver-roan palfrey and a girl riding it. Though Crum was in town and an introduction to Cynthia Dark to be had for the asking, Val did not ask, indeed, he shunned Crum and lived a life strange even to himself, except in so far as accounts with tailor and livery stable were concerned. To his mother, his sisters, his young brother, he seemed to spend this vacation in 'seeing fellows', and his evenings sleepily at home. They could not propose anything in daylight that did not meet with the one response: 'Sorry; I've got to see a fellow'; and he was put to extraordinary shifts to get in and out of the house unobserved in riding clothes; until, being made a member of the Goat's Club, he was able to transport them there, where he could change unregarded and slip off on his hack to Richmond Park. He kept his growing sentiment religiously to himself. Not for a world would he breathe to the 'fellows', who he was not 'seeing', anything so ridiculous from the point of view of their creed and his. But he could not help its destroying his other appetites. It was coming between him and the legitimate pleasures of youth at last on its own in a way which must, he knew, make him a milk-sop in the eyes of Crum. All he cared for was to dress in his last-created riding togs, and steal away to the Robin Hood Gate, where presently the silver-roan would come demurely sidling with its slim and dark-haired rider, and in the glades bare of leaves they would go off side by side, not talking very much, riding races sometimes, and sometimes holding hands. More than once of an evening, in a moment of expansion, he had been tempted to tell his mother how this shy, sweet cousin had stolen in upon him and wrecked his 'life'. But bitter experience, that all persons above thirty-five were spoil-sports, prevented him. After all, he supposed he would have to go through with college, and she would have to 'come out' before they could be married; so why complicate things, so long as he could see her? Sisters were teasing and unsympathetic beings, a brother worse, so there was no one to confide in; besides, this beastly divorce business! Ah! what a misfortune to have a name which other people hadn't! If only he had been called Gordon or Scott or Howard or something fairly common! But Dartie—there wasn't another in the directory! One might as well have been named Morkin for all the covert it afforded! So matters went on, till one day in the middle of January the silver-roan palfrey and its rider were missing at the tryst. Lingering in the cold, he debated whether he should ride on to the house. But Jolly might be there, and the memory of their dark encounter was still fresh within him. One could not be always fighting with her brother! So he returned dismally to town and spent an evening plunged in gloom. At breakfast next day he noticed that his mother had on an unfamiliar dress and was wearing her hat. The dress was black with a glimpse of peacock blue, the hat black and large—she looked exceptionally well. But when after breakfast she said to him, 'Come in here, Val,' and led the way to the drawing-room, he was at once beset by qualms. Winifred carefully shut the door and passed her handkerchief over her lips; inhaling the violette de Parme with which it had been soaked, Val thought: 'Has she found out about Holly?'

Her voice interrupted:

'Are you going to be nice to me, dear boy?'

Val grinned doubtfully.

'Will you come with me this morning–'

'I've got to see–' began Val, but something in her face stopped him. 'I say,' he said, 'you don't mean–'

'Yes, I have to go to the Court this morning.'

Already!–that d—d business which he had almost succeeded in forgetting, since nobody ever mentioned it. In self-commiseration he stood picking little bits of skin off his fingers. Then noticing that his mother's lips were all awry, he said impulsively: 'All right, mother; I'll come. The brutes!' What brutes he did not know, but the expression exactly summed up their joint feeling, and restored a measure of equanimity.

'I suppose I'd better change into a "shooter",' he muttered, escaping to his room. He put on the 'shooter', a higher collar, a pearl pin, and his neatest grey spats, to a somewhat blasphemous accompaniment. Looking at himself in the glass, he said: 'Well, I'm damned if I'm going to show anything!' and went down. He found his grandfather's carriage at the door, and his mother in furs, with the appearance of one going to a Mansion House Assembly. They seated themselves side by side in the closed barouche, and all the way to the Courts of Justice Val made but one allusion to the business in hand. 'There'll be nothing about those pearls, will there?'

The little tufted white tails of Winifred's muff began to shiver.

'Oh no,' she said, 'it'll be quite harmless to-day. Your grandmother wanted to come too, but I wouldn't let her. I thought you could take care of me. You look so nice, Val. Just pull your coat-collar up a little more at the back–that's right.'

'If they bully you–' began Val.

'Oh! they won't. I shall be very cool. It's the only way.'

'They won't want me to give evidence or anything?'

'No, dear; it's all arranged.' And she patted his hand. The determined front she was putting on it stayed the turmoil in Val's chest, and he busied himself in drawing his gloves off and on. He had taken what he now saw was the wrong pair to go with his spats; they should have been grey, but were deerskin of a dark tan; whether to keep them on or not he could not decide. They arrived soon after ten. It was his first visit to the Law Courts, and the building struck him at once.

'By Jove!' he said as they passed into the hall, 'this'd make four or five jolly good racket courts.'

Soames was awaiting them at the foot of some stairs.

'Here you are!' he said, without shaking hands, as if the event had made them too familiar for such formalities. 'It's Happerly Browne, Court I. We shall be on first.'

A sensation such as he had known when going in to bat was playing now in the top of Val's chest, but he followed his mother and uncle doggedly, looking at no more than he could help, and thinking that the place smelled 'fuggy'. People seemed to be lurking everywhere, and he plucked Soames by the sleeve.

'I say, Uncle, you're not going to let those beastly papers in, are you?'

Soames gave him the sideway look which had reduced many to silence in its time.

'In here,' he said. 'You needn't take off your furs, Winifred.'

Val entered behind them, nettled and with his head up. In this confounded hole everybody—and there were a good many of them—seemed sitting on everybody else's knee, though really divided from each other by pews; and Val had a feeling that they might all slip down together into the well. This, however, was but a momentary vision—of mahogany, and black gowns, and white blobs of wigs and faces and papers, all rather secret and whispery—before he was sitting next to his mother in the front row, with his back to it all, glad of her violette de Parme, and taking off his gloves for the last time. His mother was looking at him; he was suddenly conscious that she had really wanted him there next to her, and that he counted for something in this business. All right! He would show them! Squaring his shoulders, he crossed his legs and gazed inscrutably at his spats. But just then an 'old Johnny' in a gown and long wig, looking awfully like a funny raddled woman, came through a door into the high pew opposite, and he had to uncross his legs hastily and stand up with everybody else.

'Dartie *versus* Dartie!'

It seemed to Val unspeakably disgusting to have one's name called out like this in public! And, suddenly conscious that someone nearly behind him had begun talking about his family, he screwed his face round to see an old be-wigged buffer, who spoke as if he were eating his own words—queer-looking old cuss, the sort of man he had seen once or twice dining at Park Lane and punishing the port; he knew now where they 'dug them up'. All the same, he found the old buffer fascinating, and would have continued to stare if his mother had not touched his arm. Reduced to gazing before him, he fixed his eyes on the Judge's face instead. Why should that old 'sportsman' with his sarcastic mouth and his quick-moving eyes have the power to meddle with their private affairs—hadn't he affairs of his own, just as many, and probably just as nasty? And there moved in Val, like an illness, all the deep-seated individualism of his breed. The voice behind him droned along: 'Differences about money matters—extravagance of the respondent' (What a word! Was that his father?)—'strained situation—frequent absences on the part of Mr Dartie. My client, very rightly, your Ludship will agree, was anxious to check a course—but lead to ruin—remonstrated—gambling at cards and on the race-course—' ('That's right!' thought Val, 'pile it on!') 'Crisis early in October, when the respondent wrote her this letter from his club.' Val sat up and his ears burned. 'I propose to read it with the emendations necessary to the epistle of a gentleman who has been—shall we say dining, me Lud?'

'Old brute!' thought Val, flushing deeper; 'you're not paid to make jokes!'

'"You will not get the chance to insult me again in my own house. I am leaving the country to-morrow. It's played out"—an expression, your Ludship, not unknown in the mouths of those who have not met with conspicuous success.'

'Sniggering owls!' thought Val, and his flush deepened.

'"I am tired of being insulted by you." My client will tell your Ludship that these so-called insults consisted in her calling him "the limit"—a very mild expression, I venture to suggest, in all the circumstances.'

Val glanced sideways at his mother's impassive face; it had a hunted look in the eyes. 'Poor mother,' he thought, and touched her arm with his own. The voice behind droned on:

'"I am going to live a new life.–M.D."'

'And next day, me Lud, the respondent left by the steamship *Tuscarora* for Buenos Aires. Since then we have nothing from him but a cabled refusal in answer to the letter which my client wrote the following day in great distress, begging him to return to her. With your Ludship's permission, I shall now put Mrs Dartie in the box.'

When his mother rose, Val had a tremendous impulse to rise too and say: 'Look here! I'm going to see you jolly well treat her decently.' He subdued it, however; heard her saying, 'the truth, the whole truth, and nothing but the truth', and looked up. She made a rich figure of it, in her furs and large hat, with a slight flush on her cheek-bones, calm, matter-of-fact; and he felt proud of her thus confronting all these 'confounded lawyers'. The examination began. Knowing that this was only the preliminary to divorce, Val followed with a certain glee the questions framed so as to give the impression that she really wanted his father back. It seemed to him that they were 'foxing Old Bagwigs finely'. And he had a most unpleasant jar when the Judge said suddenly:

'Now, why did your husband leave you–not because you called him "the limit", you know?'

Val saw his uncle lift his eyes to the witness-box, without moving his face; heard a shuffle of papers behind him; and instinct told him that the issue was in peril. Had Uncle Soames and the old buffer behind made a mess of it? His mother was speaking with a slight drawl.

'No, my lord, but it had gone on a long time.'

'What had gone on?'

'Our differences about money.'

'But you supplied the money. Do you suggest that he left you to better his position?'

'The brute! The old brute, and nothing but the brute!' thought Val suddenly. 'He smells a rat–he's trying to get at the pastry!' And his heart stood still. If–if he did, then, of course, he would know that his mother didn't really want his father back. His mother spoke again, a thought more fashionably.

'No, my Lord, but you see, I had refused to give him any more money. It took him a long time to believe that, but he did at last–and when he did–'

'I see, you had refused. But you've sent him some since.'

'My Lord, I wanted him back.'

'And you thought that would bring him?'

'I don't know, my Lord, I acted on my father's advice.'

Something in the Judge's face, in the sound of the papers behind him, in the sudden crossing of his uncle's legs, told Val that she had made just the right answer. 'Crafty!' he thought; 'by Jove, what humbug it all is!'

The Judge was speaking:

'Just one more question, Mrs Dartie. Are you still fond of your husband?'

Val's hands, slack behind him, became fists. What business had that Judge to make things human suddenly? To make his mother speak out of her heart, and say what, perhaps, she didn't know herself, before all these people! It wasn't decent. His mother answered, rather low: 'Yes, my Lord.' Val saw the Judge nod. 'Wish I could take a cock-shy at your head!' he thought irreverently, as his mother came back to her seat beside him. Witnesses to his father's departure and continued absence followed–one of their own maids even, which struck Val as particularly beastly; there was more talking, all humbug; and then the Judge pronounced the decree for restitution, and they got up to go. Val walked

out behind his mother, chin squared, eyelids drooped, doing his level best to
despise everybody. His mother's voice in the corridor roused him from an
angry trance

'You behaved beautifully, dear. It was such a comfort to have you. Your
uncle and I are going to lunch.'

'All right,' said Val; 'I shall have time to go and see that fellow.' And, parting
from them abruptly, he ran down the stairs and out into the air. He bolted into a
hansom, and drove to the Goat's Club. His thoughts were on Holly and what he
must do before her brother showed her this thing in to-morrow's paper.

When Val had left them Soames and Winifred made their way to the Cheshire
Cheese. He had suggested it as a meeting-place with Mr Bellby. At that early
hour of noon they would have it to themselves, and Winifred had thought it
would be 'amusing' to see this far-famed hostelry. Having ordered a light
repast, to the consternation of the waiter, they awaited its arrival together with
that of Mr Bellby, in silent reaction after the hour and a half's suspense on the
tenterhooks of publicity. Mr Bellby entered presently, preceded by his nose,
as cheerful as they were glum. Well! they had got the decree of restitution, and
what was the matter with that!

'Quite,' said Soames in a suitably low voice, 'but we shall have to begin again
to get evidence. He'll probably try the divorce—it will look fishy if it comes out
that we knew of misconduct from the start. His questions showed well enough
that he doesn't like this restitution dodge.'

'Pho!' said Mr Bellby cheerily, 'he'll forget! Why, man, he'll have tried a
hundred cases between now and then. Besides, he's bound by precedent to give
ye your divorce, if the evidence is satisfactory. We won't let um know that Mrs
Dartie had knowledge of the facts. Dreamer did it very nicely—he's got a
fatherly touch about um!'

Soames nodded.

'And I compliment ye, Mrs Dartie,' went on Mr Bellby; 'ye've a natural gift
for giving evidence. Steady as a rock.'

Here the waiter arrived with three plates balanced on one arm, and the
remark: 'I 'urried up the pudden, sir. You'll find plenty o' lark in it to-day.'

Mr Bellby applauded his forethought with a dip of his nose. But Soames and
Winifred looked with dismay at their light lunch of gravified brown masses,
touching them gingerly with their forks in the hope of distinguishing the bodies
of the tasty little song-givers. Having begun, however, they found they were
hungrier than they thought, and finished the lot, with a glass of port apiece.
Conversation turned on the war. Soames thought Ladysmith would fall, and it
might last a year. Bellby thought it would be over by the summer. Both agreed
that they wanted more men. There was nothing for it but complete victory,
since it was now a question of prestige. Winifred brought things back to more
solid ground by saying that she did not want the divorce suit to come on till
after the summer holidays had begun at Oxford, then the boys would have
forgotten about it before Val had to go up again; the London season, too, would
be over. The lawyers reassured her, an interval of six months was
necessary—after that the earlier the better. People were now beginning to come
in, and they parted—Soames to the city, Bellby to his chambers, Winifred in a
hansom to Park Lane to let her mother know how she had fared. The issue had
been so satisfactory on the whole that it was considered advisable to tell James,
who never failed to say day after day that he didn't know about Winifred's

affair, he couldn't tell. As his sands ran out, the importance of mundane matters became increasingly grave to him, as if he were feeling: 'I must make the most of it, and worry well; I shall soon have nothing to worry about.'

He received the report grudgingly. It was a new-fangled way of going about things, and he didn't know! But he gave Winifred a cheque, saying:

'I expect you'll have a lot of expense. That's a new hat you've got on. Why doesn't Val come and see us?'

Winifred promised to bring him to dinner soon. And, going home, she sought her bedroom where she could be alone. Now that her husband had been ordered back into her custody with a view to putting him away from her for ever, she would try once more to find out from her sore and lonely heart what she really wanted.

8

THE CHALLENGE

The morning had been misty, verging on frost, but the sun came out while Val was jogging towards the Roehampton Gate, whence he would canter on to the usual tryst. His spirits were rising rapidly. There had been nothing so very terrible in the morning's proceedings beyond the general disgrace of violated privacy. 'If we were engaged!' he thought, 'what happens wouldn't matter.' He felt, indeed, like human society, which kicks and clamours at the results of matrimony, and hastens to get married. And he galloped over the winter-dried grass of Richmond Park, fearing to be late. But again he was alone at the trysting spot, and this second defection on the part of Holly upset him dreadfully. He could not go back without seeing her to-day! Emerging from the Park, he proceeded towards Robin Hill. He could not make up his mind for whom to ask. Suppose her father were back, or her sister or brother were in! He decided to gamble, and ask for them all first, so that if he were in luck and they were not there, it would be quite natural in the end to ask for Holly; while if any of them *were* in—an 'excuse for a ride' must be his saving grace.

'Only Miss Holly is in, sir.'

'Oh! thanks. Might I take my horse round to the stables? And would you say—her cousin, Mr Val Dartie.'

When he returned she was in the hall, very flushed and shy. She led him to the far end, and they sat down on a wide window-seat.

'I've been awfully anxious,' said Val in a low voice. 'What's the matter?'

'Jolly knows about our riding.'

'Is he in?'

'No; but I expect he will be soon.'

'Then–!' cried Val, and diving forward, he seized her hand. She tried to withdraw it, failed, gave up the attempt, and looked at him wistfully.

'First of all,' he said, 'I want to tell you something about my family. My dad, you know, isn't altogether–I mean, he's left my mother and they're trying to divorce him; so they've ordered him to come back, you see. You'll see that in the paper to-morrow.'

Her eyes deepened in colour and fearful interest; her hand squeezed his. But the gambler in Val was roused now, and he hurried on:

'Of course, there's nothing very much at present, but there will be, I expect, before it's over; divorce suits are beastly, you know. I wanted to tell you, because—because—you ought to know—if—' and he began to stammer, gazing at her troubled eyes, 'if—if you're going to be a darling and love me, Holly. I love you—ever so; and I want to be engaged.' He had done it in a manner so inadequate that he could have punched his own head; and, dropping on his knees, he tried to get nearer to that soft, troubled face. 'You do love me—don't you? If you don't, I—' There was a moment of silence and suspense, so awful that he could hear the sound of a mowing machine far out on the lawn pretending there was grass to cut. Then she swayed forward; her free hand touched his hair, and he gasped: 'Oh, Holly!'

Her answer was very soft: 'Oh, Val!'

He had dreamed of this moment, but always in an imperative mood, as the masterful young lover, and now he felt humble, touched, trembly. He was afraid to stir off his knees lest he should break the spell; lest, if he did, she should shrink and deny her own surrender—so tremulous was she in his grasp, with her eyelids closed and his lips nearing them. Her eyes opened, seemed to swim a little; he pressed his lips to hers. Suddenly he sprang up, there had been footsteps, a sort of startled grunt. He looked round. No one! But the long curtains which barred off the outer hall were quivering.

'My God! Who was that?'

Holly, too, was on her feet.

'Jolly, I expect,' she whispered.

Val clenched fists and resolution.

'All right!' he said, 'I don't care a bit now we're engaged,' and striding towards the curtains, he drew them aside. There at the fireplace in the hall stood Jolly, with his back elaborately turned. Val went forward. Jolly faced round on him.

'I beg your pardon for hearing,' he said.

With the best intentions in the world, Val could not help admiring him at that moment; his face was clear, his voice quiet, he looked somehow distinguished, as if acting up to principle.

'Well!' Val said abruptly, 'it's nothing to you.'

'Oh!' said Jolly; 'you come this way,' and he crossed the hall. Val followed. At the study door he felt a touch on his arm; Holly's voice said:

'I'm coming too.'

'No,' said Jolly.

'Yes,' said Holly.

Jolly opened the door, and they all three went in. Once in the little room, they stood in a sort of triangle on three corners of the worn Turkey carpet; awkwardly upright, not looking at each other, quite incapable of seeing any humour in the situation.

Val broke the silence.

'Holly and I are engaged.'

Jolly stepped back and leaned against the lintel of the window.

'This is our house,' he said; 'I'm not going to insult you in it. But my father's away. I'm in charge of my sister. You've taken advantage of me.'

'I didn't mean to,' said Val hotly.

'I think you did,' said Jolly. 'If you hadn't meant to, you'd have spoken to me, or waited for my father to come back.'

'There were reasons,' said Val.

'What reasons?'

'About my family—I've just told her. I wanted her to know before things happen.'

Jolly suddenly became less distinguished.

'You're kids,' he said, 'and you know you are.'

'I am *not* a kid,' said Val.

'You are—you're not twenty.'

'Well, what are you?'

'I *am* twenty,' said Jolly.

'Only just; anyway, I'm as good a man as you.'

Jolly's face crimsoned, then clouded. Some struggle was evidently taking place in him; and Val and Holly stared at him, so clearly was that struggle marked; they could even hear him breathing. Then his face cleared up and became oddly resolute.

'We'll see that,' he said. 'I dare you to do what I'm going to do.'

'Dare me?'

Jolly smiled. 'Yes,' he said, 'dare you; and I know very well you won't.'

A stab of misgiving shot through Val; this was riding very blind.

'I haven't forgotten that you're a fire-eater,' said Jolly slowly, 'and I think that's about all you are; or that you called me a pro-Boer.'

Val heard a gasp above the sound of his own hard breathing, and saw Holly's face poked a little forward, very pale, with big eyes.

'Yes,' went on Jolly, with a sort of smile, 'we shall soon see. I'm going to join the Imperial Yeomanry, and I dare you to do the same, Mr Val Dartie.'

Val's head jerked on its stem. It was like a blow between the eyes, so utterly unthought of, so extreme and ugly in the midst of his dreaming; and he looked at Holly with eyes grown suddenly, touchingly haggard.

'Sit down!' said Jolly. 'Take your time! Think it over well.' And he himself sat down on the arm of his grandfather's chair.

Val did not sit down; he stood with hands thrust deep into his breeches' pockets—hands clenched and quivering. The full awfulness of this decision one way or the other knocked at his mind with double knocks as of an angry postman. If he did not take that 'dare' he was disgraced in Holly's eyes, and in the eyes of that young enemy, her brute of a brother. Yet if he took it, ah! then all would vanish—her face, her eyes, her hair, her kisses just begun!

'Take your time,' said Jolly again; 'I don't want to be unfair.'

And they both looked at Holly. She had recoiled against the bookshelves reaching to the ceiling; her dark head leaned against Gibbon's *Roman Empire*, her eyes in a sort of soft grey agony were fixed on Val. And he, who had not much gift of insight, had suddenly a gleam of vision. She would be proud of her brother—that enemy! She would be ashamed of him! His hands came out of his pockets as if lifted by a spring.

'All right!' he said. 'Done!'

Holly's face—oh! it was queer! He saw her flush, start forward. He had done the right thing—her face was shining with wistful admiration. Jolly stood up and made a little bow as who should say: 'You've passed.'

'To-morrow, then,' he said, 'we'll go together.'

Recovering from the impetus which had carried him to that decision, Val looked at him maliciously from under his lashes. 'All right,' he thought, 'one to you. I shall have to join—but I'll get back on you somehow.' And he said with dignity: 'I shall be ready.'

'We'll meet at the main Recruiting Office, then,' said Jolly, 'at twelve o'clock.' And, opening the window, he went out on to the terrace, conforming to the creed which had made him retire when he surprised them in the hall.

The confusion in the mind of Val thus left alone with her for whom he had paid this sudden price was extreme. The mood of 'showing-off' was still, however, uppermost. One must do the wretched thing with an air!

'We shall get plenty of riding and shooting, anyway,' he said; 'that's one comfort.' And it gave him a sort of grim pleasure to hear the sigh which seemed to come from the bottom of her heart.

'Oh! the war'll soon be over,' he said; 'perhaps we shan't even have to go out. I don't care, except for you.' He would be out of the way of that beastly divorce. It was an ill-wind! He felt her warm hand slip into his. Jolly thought he had stopped their loving each other, did he? He held her tightly round the waist, looking at her softly through his lashes, smiling to cheer her up, promising to come down and see her soon, feeling somehow six inches taller and much more in command of her than he had ever dared feel before. Many times he kissed her before he mounted and rode back to town. So, swiftly, on the least provocation, does the possessive instinct flourish and grow.

9

DINNER AT JAMES'S

Dinner parties were not now given at James's in Park Lane—to every house the moment comes when master or mistress is no longer 'up to it'; no more can nine courses be served to twenty mouths above twenty fine white expanses; nor does the household cat any longer wonder why she is suddenly shut up.

So with something like excitement, Emily—who at seventy would still have liked a little feast and fashion now and then—ordered dinner for six instead of two, herself wrote a number of foreign words on cards, and arranged the flowers—mimosa from the Riviera, and white Roman hyacinths not from Rome. There would only be, of course, James and herself, Soames, Winifred, Val, and Imogen—but she liked to pretend a little and dally in imagination with the glory of the past. She so dressed herself that James remarked:

'What are you putting on that thing for? You'll catch cold.'

But Emily knew that the necks of women are protected by love of shining, unto four-score years, and she only answered:

'Let me put you on one of those dickies I got you, James; then you'll only have to change your trousers and put on your velvet coat, and there you'll be. Val likes you to look nice.'

'Dicky!' said James. 'You're always wasting your money on something.'

But he suffered the change to be made till his neck also shone, murmuring vaguely:

'He's an extravagant chap, I'm afraid.'

A little brighter in the eye, with rather more colour than usual in his cheeks, he took his seat in the drawing-room to wait for the sound of the front-door bell.

'I've made it a proper dinner-party,' Emily said comfortably; 'I thought it would be good practise for Imogen—she must get used to it now she's coming out.'

James uttered an indeterminate sound, thinking of Imogen as she used to climb about his knee or pull Christmas crackers with him.

'She'll be pretty,' he muttered, 'I shouldn't wonder.'

'She *is* pretty,' said Emily; 'she ought to make a good match.'

'There you go,' murmured James. 'She'd much better stay at home and look after her mother.' A second Dartie carrying off his pretty grand-daughter would finish him! He had never quite forgiven Emily for having been as much taken in by Montague Dartie as he himself had been.

'Where's Warmson?' he said suddenly. 'I should like a glass of Madeira to-night.'

'There's champagne, James.'

James shook his head. 'No body,' he said; 'I can't get any good out of it.'

Emily reached forward on her side of the fire and rang the bell.

'Your master would like a bottle of Madeira opened, Warmson.'

'No, no!' said James, the tips of his ears quivering with vehemence, and his eyes fixed on an object seen by him alone. 'Look here, Warmson, you go to the inner cellar, and on the middle shelf of the end bin on the left you'll see seven bottles; take the one in the centre, and don't shake it. It's the last of the Madeira I had from Mr Jolyon when we came in here—never been moved; it ought to be in prime condition still; but I don't know, I can't tell.'

'Very good, sir,' responded the withdrawing Warmson.

'I was keeping it for our golden wedding,' said James suddenly, 'but I shan't live three years at my age.'

'Nonsense, James,' said Emily, 'don't talk like that.'

'I ought to have got it up myself,' murmured James, 'he'll shake it as likely as not.' And he sank into silent recollection of long moments among the open gas-jets, the cobwebs and the good smell of wine-soaked corks, which had been appetiser to so many feasts. In the wine from that cellar was written the history of the forty-odd years since he had come to the Park Lane house with his young bride, and of the many generations of friends and acquaintances who had passed into the unknown; its depleted bins preserved the record of family festivity—all the marriages, births, deaths of his kith and kin. And when he was gone there it would be, and he didn't know what would become of it. It'd be drunk or spoiled, he shouldn't wonder!

From that deep reverie the entrance of his son dragged him, followed very soon by that of Winifred and her two eldest.

They went down arm-in-arm—James with Imogen, the débutante, because his pretty grandchild cheered him; Soames with Winifred; Emily with Val, whose eyes lighting on the oysters brightened. This was to be a proper full 'blow-out' with 'fizz' and port! And he felt in need of it, after what he had done that day, as yet undivulged. After the first glass or two it became pleasant to have this bomb-shell up his sleeve, this piece of sensational patriotism, or example, rather, of personal daring, to display—for his pleasure in what he had done for his Queen and Country was so far entirely personal. He was now a 'blood', indissolubly connected with guns and horses; he had a right to swagger—not, of course, that he was going to. He should just announce it quietly when there was a pause. And, glancing down the menu, he determined on *Bombe aux fraises* as the proper moment; there would be a certain solemnity while they were eating that. Once or twice before they reached that rosy summit of the dinner he was attacked by remembrance that his grandfather was never told anything! Still, the old boy was drinking Madeira, and looking jolly fit! Besides, he ought to be pleased at this set-off to the disgrace of the divorce. The sight of his uncle opposite, too, was a sharp incentive. He was so far from being a sportsman that it would be worth a lot to see his face. Besides, better to tell his mother in this way than privately, which might upset them both! He was sorry for her, but, after all, one couldn't be expected to feel much for others when one had to part from Holly.

His grandfather's voice travelled to him thinly.

'Val, try a little of the Madeira with your ice. You won't get that up at college.'

Val watched the slow liquid filling his glass, the essential oil of the old wine glazing the surface; inhaled its aroma, and thought: 'Now for it!' It was a rich moment. He sipped, and a gentle glow spread in his veins, already heated. With a rapid look round, he said: 'I joined the Imperial Yeomanry to-day, Granny,' and emptied his glass as though drinking the health of his own act.

'What!' It was his mother's desolate little word.

'Young Jolly Forsyte and I went down there together.'

'You didn't sign!' from Uncle Soames.

'Rather! We go into camp on Monday.'

'I *say!*' cried Imogen.

All looked at James. He was leaning forward with his hand behind his ear.

'What's that?' he said. 'What's he saying? I can't hear.'

Emily reached forward to pat Val's hand.

'It's only that Val has joined the Yeomanry, James; it's very nice of him. He'll look his best in uniform.'

'Joined the–rubbish!' came from James, tremulously loud. 'You can't see two yards before your nose. He–he'll have to go out there. Why! he'll be fighting before he knows where he is.'

Val saw Imogen's eyes admiring him, and his mother still and fashionable with her handkerchief before her lips.

Suddenly his uncle spoke.

'You're under age.'

'I thought of that,' smiled Val; 'I gave my age as twenty-one.'

He heard his grandmother's admiring: 'Well, Val, that *was* plucky of you'; was conscious of Warmson deferentially filling his champagne glass; and of his grandfather's voice moaning: '*I* don't know what'll become of you if you go on like this.'

Imogen was patting his shoulder, his uncle looking at him sidelong; only his mother was unmoving, till, affected by her stillness, Val said:

'It's all right, you know; we shall soon have them on the run. I only hope I shall come in for something.'

He felt elated, sorry, tremendously important all at once. This would show Uncle Soames, and all the Forsytes, how to be sportsmen. He had certainly done something heroic and exceptional in giving his age as twenty-one.

Emily's voice brought him back to earth.

'You mustn't have a second glass, James. Warmson!'

'Won't they be astonished at Timothy's!' burst out Imogen. 'I'd give anything to see their faces. Do you have a sword, Val, or only a pop-gun?'

'What made you?'

His uncle's voice produced a slight chill in the pit of Val's stomach. Made him? How answer that? He was grateful for his grandmother's comfortable:

'Well, I think it's very plucky of Val. I'm sure he'll make a splendid soldier; he's just the figure for it. We shall all be proud of him.'

'What had young Jolly Forsyte to do with it? Why did you go together?' pursued Soames, uncannily relentless. 'I thought you weren't friendly with him?'

'I'm not,' mumbled Val, 'but I wasn't going to be beaten by *him*.' He saw his uncle look at him quite differently, as if approving. His grandfather was nodding too, his grandmother tossing her head. They all approved of his not being beaten by that cousin of his. There must be a reason! Val was dimly conscious of some disturbing point outside his range of vision; as it might be, the unlocated centre of a cyclone. And, staring at his uncle's face, he had a quite unaccountable vision of a woman with dark eyes, gold hair, and a white neck, who smelt nice, and had pretty silken clothes which he had liked feeling when he was quite small. By Jove! yes! Aunt Irene! She used to kiss him, and he had bitten her arm once, playfully, because he liked it—so soft. His grandfather was speaking:

'What's his father doing?'

'He's away in Paris,' Val said, staring at the very queer expression on his uncle's face, like—like that of a snarling dog.

'Artists!' said James. The word coming from the very bottom of his soul, broke up the dinner.

Opposite his mother in the cab going home, Val tasted the after-fruits of heroism, like medlars over-ripe.

She only said, indeed, that he must go to his tailor's at once and have his uniform properly made, and not just put up with what they gave him. But he could feel that she was very much upset. It was on his lips to console her with the spoken thought that he would be out of the way of that beastly divorce, but the presence of Imogen, and the knowledge that his mother would *not* be out of the way, restrained him. He felt aggrieved that she did not seem more proud of him. When Imogen had gone to bed, he risked the emotional.

'I'm awfully sorry to have to leave you, Mother.'

'Well, I must make the best of it. We must try and get you a commission as soon as we can; then you won't have to rough it so. Do you know any drill, Val?'

'Not a scrap.'

'I hope they won't worry you much. I must take you about to get the things to-morrow. Good-night; kiss me.'

With that kiss, soft and hot, between his eyes, and those words, 'I hope they won't worry you much,' in his ears, he sat down to a cigarette, before a dying fire. The heat was out of him—the glow of cutting a dash. It was all a damned heart-aching bore. 'I'll be even with that chap Jolly,' he thought, trailing up the stairs, past the room where his mother was biting her pillow to smother a sense of desolation which was trying to make her sob.

And soon only one of the diners at James's was awake—Soames, in his bedroom above his father's.

So that fellow Jolyon was in Paris—what was he doing there? Hanging round Irene! The last report from Polteed had hinted that there might be something soon. Could it be this? That fellow, with his beard and his cursed amused way of speaking—son of the old man who had given him the nickname 'Man of Property', and bought the fatal house from him. Soames had ever resented having had to sell the house at Robin Hill; never forgiven his uncle for having bought it, or his cousin for living in it.

Reckless of the cold, he threw his window up and gazed out across the Park. Bleak and dark the January night; little sound of traffic; a frost coming; bare trees; a star or two. 'I'll see Polteed to-morrow,' he thought. 'By God! I'm mad, I think, to want her still. That fellow! If–? Um! No!'

IO

DEATH OF THE DOG BALTHASAR

Jolyon, who had crossed from Calais by night, arrived at Robin Hill on Sunday morning. He had sent no word beforehand, so walked up from the station, entering his domain by the coppice gate. Coming to the log seat fashioned out of an old fallen trunk, he sat down, first laying his overcoat on it. 'Lumbago!' he thought; 'that's what love ends in at my time of life!' And suddenly Irene seemed very near, just as she had been that day of rambling at Fontainebleau when they sat on a log to eat their lunch. Hauntingly near! Odour drawn out of fallen leaves by the pale filtering sunlight soaked his nostrils. 'I'm glad it isn't spring,' he thought. With the scent of sap, and the song of birds, and the bursting of the blossoms, it would have been unbearable! 'I hope I shall be over it by then, old fool that I am!' And picking up his coat, he walked on into the field. He passed the pond and mounted the hill slowly. Near the top a hoarse barking greeted him. Up on the lawn above the fernery he could see his old dog Balthasar. The animal, whose dim eyes took his master for a stranger, was warning the world against him. Jolyon gave his special whistle. Even at that distance of a hundred yards and more he could see the dawning recognition in the obese brown-white body. The old dog got off his haunches, and his tail, close-curled over his back, began a feeble, excited fluttering; he came waddling forward, gathered momentum, and disappeared over the edge of the fernery. Jolyon expected to meet him at the wicket gate, but Balthasar was not there, and, rather alarmed, he turned into the fernery. On his fat side, looking up with eyes already glazing, the old dog lay.

'What is it, my poor old man?' cried Joylon. Balthasar's curled and fluffy tail just moved; his filming eyes seemed saying: 'I can't get up, master, but I'm glad to see you.'

Jolyon knelt down; his eyes, very dimmed, could hardly see the slowly ceasing heave of the dog's side. He raised the head a little–very heavy.

'What is it, dear man? Where are you hurt?' The tail fluttered once; the eyes lost the look of life. Jolyon passed his hands all over the inert warm bulk. There was nothing–the heart had simply failed in that obese body from the emotion of his master's return. Jolyon could feel the muzzle, where a few whitish bristles grew, cooling already against his lips. He stayed for some minutes kneeling, with his hand beneath the stiffening head. The body was very heavy when he bore it to the top of the field; leaves had drifted there, and he strewed it with a covering of them; there was no wind, and they would keep him from curious eyes until the afternoon. 'I'll bury him myself,' he thought. Eighteen years had gone since he first went into the St John's Wood house with that tiny puppy in his pocket. Strange that the old dog should die just now! Was it an omen? He turned at the gate to look back at that russet mound, then went slowly towards the house, very choky in the throat.

June was at home; she had come down hot-foot on hearing the news of Jolly's enlistment. His patriotism had conquered her feeling for the Boers. The atmosphere of his house was strange and pocketty when Jolyon came in and told them of the dog Balthasar's death. The news had a unifying effect. A link with the past had snapped—the dog Balthasar! Two of them could remember nothing before his day; to June he represented the last years of her grandfather; to Jolyon that life of domestic stress and æsthetic struggle before he came again into the kingdom of his father's love and wealth! And he was gone!

In the afternoon he and Jolly took picks and spades and went out to the field. They chose a spot close to the russet mound, so that they need not carry him far, and, carefully cutting off the surface turf, began to dig. They dug in silence for ten minutes, and then rested.

'Well, old man,' said Jolyon, 'so you thought you ought?'

'Yes,' answered Jolly; 'I don't want to a bit, of course.'

How exactly those words represented Jolyon's own state of mind!

'I admire you for it, old boy. I don't believe I should have done it at your age—too much of a Forsyte, I'm afraid. But I suppose the type gets thinner with each generation. Your son, if you have one, may be a pure altruist; who knows?'

'He won't be like me, then, Dad; I'm beastly selfish.'

'No, my dear, that you clearly are not.' Jolly shook his head, and they dug again.

'Strange life a dog's,' said Jolyon suddenly; 'the only four-footer with rudiments of altruism and a sense of God!'

Jolly looked at his father.

'Do you believe in God, Dad? I've never known.'

At so searching a question from one to whom it was impossible to make a light reply, Jolyon stood for a moment, feeling his back tried by the digging.

'What do you mean by God?' he said; 'there are two irreconcilable ideas of God. There's the Unknowable Creative Principle—one believes in That. And there's the Sum of altruism in man—naturally one believes in That.'

'I see. That leaves out Christ, doesn't it?'

Jolyon stared. Christ, the link between those two ideas! Out of the mouths of babes! Here was orthodoxy scientifically explained at last! The sublime poem of the Christ life was man's attempt to join those two irreconcilable conceptions of God. And since the Sum of human altruism was as much a part of the Unknowable Creative Principle as anything else in Nature and the Universe, a worse link might have been chosen after all. Funny—how one went through life without seeing it in that sort of way!

'What do *you* think, old man?' he said.

Jolly frowned. 'Of course, my first year we talked a good bit about that sort of thing. But in the second year one gives it up; I don't know why—it's awfully interesting.'

Jolyon remembered that he also had talked a good deal about it in his first year at Cambridge, and given it up in his second.

'I suppose,' said Jolly, 'it's the second God, you mean, that old Balthasar had a sense of.'

'Yes, or he would never have burst his poor old heart because of something outside himself.'

'But wasn't that just selfish emotion, really?'

Jolyon shook his head. 'No, dogs are not pure Forsytes, they love something outside themselves.'

Jolly smiled.

'Well, I think I'm one,' he said. 'You know, I only enlisted because I dared Val Dartie to.'

'But why?'

'We bar each other,' said Jolly shortly.

'Ah!' muttered Jolyon. So the feud went on unto the third generation—this modern feud which had no overt expression!

'Shall I tell the boy about it?' he thought. But to what end—if he had to stop short of his own part?

And Jolly thought: 'It's for Holly to let him know about that chap. If she doesn't, it means she doesn't want him told, and I should be sneaking. Anyway, I've stopped it. I'd better leave well alone!'

So they dug on in silence, till Jolyon said:

'Now, old man, I think it's big enough.' And, resting on their spades, they gazed down into the hole where a few leaves had drifted already on a sunset wind.

'I can't bear this part of it,' said Jolyon suddenly.

'Let me do it, Dad. He never cared much for me.'

Jolyon shook his head.

'We'll lift him very gently, leaves and all. I'd rather not see him again. I'll take his head. Now!'

With extreme care they raised the old dog's body, whose faded tan and white showed here and there under the leaves stirred by the wind. They laid it, heavy, cold, and unresponsive, in the grave, and Jolly spread more leaves over it, while Jolyon, deeply afraid to show emotion before his son, began quickly shovelling the earth on to that still shape. There went the past! If only there were a joyful future to look forward to! It was like stamping down earth on one's own life. They replaced the turf carefully on the smooth little mound and, grateful that they had spared each other's feelings, returned to the house arm-in-arm.

I I

TIMOTHY STAYS THE ROT

On Forsyte 'Change news of the enlistment spread fast, together with the report that June, not to be outdone, was going to become a Red Cross nurse. These events were so extreme, so subversive of pure Forsyteism, as to have a binding effect upon the family, and Timothy's was thronged next Sunday afternoon by members trying to find out what they thought about it all, and exchange with each other a sense of family credit. Giles and Jesse Hayman would no longer defend the coast, but go to South Africa quite soon; Jolly and Val would be following in April; as to June—well, you never knew what she would really do!

The retirement from Spion Kop and the absence of any good news from the seat of war imparted an air of reality to all this, clinched in startling fashion by

Timothy. The youngest of the old Forsytes–scarcely eighty, in fact–popularly supposed to resemble their father, 'Superior Dosset', even in his best-known characteristic of drinking Madeira–had been invisible for so many years that he was almost mythical. A long generation had elapsed since the risks of a publisher's business had worked on his nerves at the age of forty, so that he had got out with a mere thirty-five thousand pounds in the world, and started to make his living by careful investment. Putting by every year, at compound interest, he had doubled his capital in forty years without having once known what it was like to shake in his shoes over money matters. He was now putting aside some two thousand a year, and, with the care he was taking of himself, expected, so Aunt Hester said, to double his capital again before he died. What he would do with it then, with his sisters dead and himself dead, was often mockingly queried by free spirits such as Francie, Euphemia, or young Nicholas's second, Christopher, whose spirit was so free that he had actually said he was going on the stage. All admitted, however, that this was best known to Timothy himself, and possibly to Soames, who never divulged a secret.

Those few Forsytes who had seen him reported a man of thick and robust appearance, not very tall, with a brown-red complexion, grey hair, and little of the refinement of feature with which most of the Forsytes had been endowed by 'Superior Dosset's' wife, a woman of some beauty and a gentle temperament. It was known that he had taken surprising interest in the war, sticking flags into a map ever since it began, and there was uneasiness as to what would happen if the English were driven into the sea, when it would be almost impossible for him to put the flags in the right places. As to his knowledge of family movements or his views about them, little was known, save that Aunt Hester was always declaring that he was very upset. It was, then, in the nature of a portent when Forsytes, arriving on the Sunday after the evacuation of Spion Kop, became conscious, one after the other, of a presence seated in the only really comfortable arm-chair, back to the light, concealing the lower part of his face with a large hand, and were greeted by the awed voice of Aunt Hester:

'Your Uncle Timothy, my dear,'

Timothy's greeting to them all was somewhat identical; and rather, as it were, passed over by him than expressed:

'How de do? How de do? 'Xcuse me gettin' up!'

Francie was present, and Eustace had come in his car; Winifred had brought Imogen, breaking the ice of the restitution proceedings with the warmth of family appreciation at Val's enlistment; and Marian Tweetyman with the last news of Giles and Jesse. These, with Aunts Juley and Hester, young Nicholas, Euphemia, and–of all people!–George, who had come with Eustace in the car, constituted an assembly worthy of the family's palmiest days. There was not one chair vacant in the whole of the little drawing-room, and anxiety was felt lest someone else should arrive.

The constraint caused by Timothy's presence having worn off a little, conversation took a military turn. George asked Aunt Juley when she was going out with the Red Cross, almost reducing her to a state of anxiety; whereon he turned to Nicholas and said:

'Young Nick's a warrior bold, isn't he? When's he going to don the wild khaki?'

Young Nicholas, smiling with a sort of sweet deprecation, intimated that of course his mother was very anxious.

'The Dromios are off, I hear,' said George, turning to Marian Tweetyman;

'we shall all be there soon. *En avant*, the Forsytes! Roll, bowl, or pitch! Who's for a cooler?'

Aunt Juley gurgled, George was so droll! Should Hester get Timothy's map? Then he could show them all where they were.

At a sound from Timothy, interpreted as assent. Aunt Hester left the room.

George pursued his image of the Forsyte advance, addressing Timothy as Field Marshal; and Imogen, whom he had noted at once for 'a pretty filly'–as Vivandière; and holding his top-hat between his knees, he began to beat it with imaginary drumsticks. The reception accorded to this fantasy was mixed. All laughed–George was licensed; but all felt that the family was being 'rotted'; and this seemed to them unnatural, now that it was going to give five of its members to the service of the Queen. George might go too far; and there was relief when he got up, offered his arm to Aunt Juley, marched up to Timothy, saluted him, kissed his aunt with mock passion, said, 'Oh! what a treat, dear papa! Come on, Eustace!' and walked out, followed by the grave and fastidious Eustace, who had never smiled. Aunt Juley's bewildered, 'Fancy not waiting for the map! You mustn't mind him, Timothy. He's *so* droll!' broke the hush, and Timothy removed the hand from his mouth.

'I don't know what things are comin' to,' he was heard to say. 'What's all this about goin' out there? That's not the way to beat those Boers.'

Francie alone had the hardihood to observe:

'What is, then, Uncle Timothy?'

'All this new-fangled volunteerin' and expense–lettin' money out of the country.'

Just then Aunt Hester brought in the map, handling it like a baby with eruptions. With the assistance of Euphemia it was laid on the piano, a small Colwood grand, last played on, it was believed, the summer before Aunt Ann died, thirteen years ago. Timothy rose. He walked over to the piano and stood looking at his map while they all gathered round.

'There you are,' he said; 'that's the position up to date; and very poor it is. H'm!'

'Yes,' said Francie, greatly daring, 'but how are you going to alter it, Uncle Timothy, without more men?'

'Men!' said Timothy; 'you don't want men–wastin' the country's money. You want a Napoleon, he'd settle it in a month.'

'But if you haven't got him, Uncle Timothy?'

'That's their business,' replied Timothy. 'What have we kept the Army up for–to eat their heads off in time of peace! They ought to be ashamed of themselves, comin' on the country to help them like this! Let every man stick to his business, and we shall get on.'

And looking round him, he added almost angrily:

'Volunteerin', indeed! Throwin' good money after bad! We must save! Conserve energy–that's the only way.' And with a prolonged sound, not quite a sniff and not quite a snort, he trod on Euphemia's toe, and went out, leaving a sensation and a faint scent of barley-sugar behind him.

The effect of something said with conviction by one who has evidently made a sacrifice to say it is ever considerable. And the eight Forsytes left behind, all women except young Nicholas, were silent for a moment round the map. Then Francie said:

'Really, I think he's right, you know. After all, what is the Army for? They ought to have known. It's only encouraging them.'

'My dear!' cried Aunt Juley, 'but they've been so progressive. Think of their giving up their scarlet. They were always so proud of it. And now they all look like convicts. Hester and I were saying only yesterday we were sure they must feel it very much. Fancy what the Iron Duke would have said!'

'The new colour's very smart,' said Winifred; 'Val looks quite nice in his.'

Aunt Juley sighed.

'I do so wonder what Jolyon's boy is like. To think we've never seen him! His father must be so proud of him.'

'His father's in Paris,' said Winifred.

Aunt Hester's shoulder was seen to mount suddenly, as if to ward off her sister's next remark, for Juley's crumpled cheeks had flushed.

'We had dear little Mrs MacAnder here yesterday, just back from Paris. And whom d'you think she saw there in the street? You'll never guess.'

'We shan't try, Auntie,' said Euphemia.

'Irene! Imagine! After all this time; walking with a fair beard—'

'Auntie! you'll kill me! A fair beard—'

'I was going to say,' said Aunt Juley severely, 'a fair-bearded gentleman. And not a day older; she was always so pretty,' she added, with a sort of lingering apology.

'Oh! tell us about her, Auntie,' cried Imogen; 'I can just remember her. She's the skeleton in the family cupboard, isn't she? And they're such fun.'

Aunt Hester sat down. Really, Juley had done it now!

'She wasn't much of a skeleton as I remember her,' murmured Euphemia, 'extremely well-covered.'

'My dear!' said Aunt Juley, 'what a peculiar way of putting it—not very nice.'

'No, but what *was* she like?' persisted Imogen.

'I'll tell you, my child,' said Francie; 'a kind of modern Venus, very well-dressed.'

Euphemia said sharply: 'Venus was never dressed, and she had blue eyes of melting sapphire.'

At this juncture Nicholas took his leave.

'Mrs Nick is awfully strict,' said Francie with a laugh.

'She has six children,' said Aunt Juley; 'it's very proper she should be careful.'

'Was Uncle Soames awfully fond of her?' pursued the inexorable Imogen, moving her dark luscious eyes from face to face.

Aunt Hester made a gesture of despair, just as Aunt Juley answered: 'Yes, your Uncle Soames was very much attached to her.'

'I suppose she ran off with someone?'

'No, certainly not; that is—not precisely.'

'What did she do, then, Auntie?'

'Come along, Imogen,' said Winifred, 'we must be getting back.'

But Aunt Juley interjected resolutely: 'She—she didn't behave at all well.'

'Oh, bother!' cried Imogen; 'that's as far as I ever get.'

'Well, my dear,' said Francie, 'she had a love affair which ended with the young man's death; and then she left your uncle. I always rather liked her.'

'She used to give me chocolates,' murmured Imogen, 'and smell nice.'

'Of course!' remarked Euphemia.

'Not of course at all!' replied Francie, who used a particularly expensive essence of gilly-flower herself.

'I can't think what we are about,' said Aunt Juley, raising her hands, 'talking of such things!'

'Was she divorced?' asked Imogen from the door.

'Certainly not,' cried Aunt Juley; 'that is—certainly not.'

A sound was heard over by the far door. Timothy had re-entered the back drawing-room. 'I've come for my map,' he said. 'Who's been divorced?'

'No one, Uncle,' replied Francie with perfect truth.

Timothy took his map off the piano.

'Don't let's have anything of that sort in the family,' he said. 'All this enlistin's bad enough. The country's breakin' up; I don't know what we're comin' to.' He shook a thick finger at the room: 'Too many women nowadays, and they don't know what they want.'

So saying, he grasped the map firmly with both hands, and went out as if afraid of being answered.

The seven women whom he had addressed broke into a subdued murmur, out of which emerged Francie's, 'Really, the Forsytes—!' and Aunt Juley's: 'He must have his feet in mustard and hot water to-night, Hester; will you tell Jane? The blood has gone to his head again, I'm afraid.' . . .

That evening, when she and Hester were sitting alone after dinner, she dropped a stitch in her crochet, and looked up.

'Hester, I can't think where I've heard that dear Soames wants Irene to come back to him again. Who was it told us that George had made a funny drawing of him with the words, "He won't be happy till he gets it"?'

'Eustace,' answered Aunt Hester from behind *The Times*; 'he had it in his pocket, but he wouldn't show it us.'

Aunt Juley was silent, ruminating. The clock ticked, *The Times* crackled, the fire sent forth its rustling purr. Aunt Juley dropped another stitch.

'Hester,' she said, 'I have had such a dreadful thought.'

'Then don't tell me,' said Aunt Hester quickly.

'Oh! but I must. You can't think how dreadful!' Her voice sank to a whisper. 'Jolyon—Jolyon, they say, has a—has a fair beard, now.'

12

PROGRESS OF THE CHASE

Two days after the dinner at James's, Mr Polteed provided Soames with food for thought.

'A gentleman,' he said, consulting the key concealed in his left hand, '47 as we say, has been paying marked attention to 17 during the last month in Paris. But at present there seems to have been nothing very conclusive. The meetings have all been in public places, without concealment—restaurants, the Opera, the Comique, the Louvre, Luxembourg Gardens, lounge of the hotel, and so forth. She has not been traced to his rooms, nor *vice versa*. They went to Fontainebleau—but nothing of value. In short, the situation is promising, but requires patience.' And looking up suddenly, he added:

'One rather curious point—47 has the same name as—er—31!'

'The fellow knows I'm her husband,' thought Soames.

'Christian name—an odd one—Jolyon,' continued Mr Polteed. 'We know his address in Paris and his residence here. We don't wish, of course, to be running a wrong hare.'

'Go on with it, but be careful,' said Soames doggedly.

Instinctive certainty that this detective fellow had fathomed his secret made him all the more reticent.

'Excuse me,' said Mr Polteed, 'I'll just see if there's anything fresh in.'

He returned with some letters. Re-locking the door, he glanced at the envelopes.

'Yes, here's a personal one from 19 to myself.'

'Well?' said Soames.

'Um!' said Mr Polteed, 'she says: "47 left for England to-day. Address on his baggage: Robin Hill. Parted from 17 in Louvre Gallery at 3.30; nothing very striking. Thought it best to stay and continue observation of 17. You will deal with 47 in England if you think desirable, no doubt." ' And Mr Polteed lifted an unprofessional glance on Soames, as though he might be storing material for a book on human nature after he had gone out of business. 'Very intelligent woman, 19, and a wonderful make-up. Not cheap, but earns her money well. There's no suspicion of being shadowed so far. But after a time, as you know, sensitive people are liable to get the feeling of it, without anything definite to go on. I should rather advise letting-up on 17, and keeping an eye on 47. We can't get at correspondence without great risk. I hardly advise that at this stage. But you can tell your client that it's looking up very well.' And again his narrowed eyes gleamed at his taciturn customer.

'No,' said Soames suddenly, 'I prefer that you should keep the watch going discreetly in Paris, and not concern yourself with this end.'

'Very well,' replied Mr Polteed, 'we can do it.'

'What—what is the manner between them?'

'I'll read you what she says,' said Mr Polteed, unlocking a bureau drawer and taking out a file of papers, 'she sums it up somewhere confidentially. Yes, here it is! "17 very attractive—conclude 47, longer in the tooth" (slang for age, you know)—"distinctly gone—waiting his time—17 perhaps holding off for terms, impossible to say without knowing more. But inclined to think on the whole—doesn't know her mind—likely to act on impulse some day. Both have style." '

'What does that mean?' said Soames between close lips.

'Well,' murmured Mr Polteed with a smile, showing many white teeth, 'an expression we use. In other words, it's not likely to be a week-end business—they'll come together seriously or not at all.'

'H'm!' muttered Soames, 'that's all, is it?'

'Yes,' said Mr Polteed, 'but quite promising.'

'Spider!' thought Soames. 'Good-day!'

He walked into the Green Park that he might cross to Victoria Station and take the Underground into the City. For so late in January it was warm; sunlight, through the haze, sparkled on the frosty grass—an illumined cobweb of a day.

Little spiders—and great spiders! And the greatest spinner of all, his own tenacity, for ever wrapping its cocoon of threads round any clear way out. What was that fellow hanging round Irene for? Was it really as Polteed suggested? Or was Jolyon but taking compassion on her loneliness, as he would call it—sentimental radical chap that he had always been! If it were, indeed, as Polteed hinted! Soames stood still. It could not be! The fellow was seven years older than himself, no better looking! No richer! What attraction had he?

'Besides, he's come back,' he thought; 'that doesn't look–I'll go and see him!' and, taking out a card, he wrote:

If you can spare half an hour some afternoon this week, I shall be at the Connoisseurs' any day between 5.30 and 6, or I could come to the Hotch Potch if you prefer it. I want to see you.–S. F.

He walked up St James's Street and confided it to the porter at the Hotch Potch.

'Give Mr Jolyon Forsyte this as soon as he comes in,' he said, and took one of the new motor cabs into the City. . . .

Jolyon received that card the same afternoon, and turned his face towards the Connoisseurs'. What did Soames want now? Had he got wind of Paris? And stepping across St James's Street, he determined to make no secret of his visit. 'But it won't do,' he thought, 'to let him know *she's* there, unless he knows already.' In this complicated state of mind he was conducted to where Soames was drinking tea in a small bay-window.

'No tea, thanks,' said Jolyon, 'but I'll go on smoking if I may.'

The curtains were not yet drawn, though the lamps outside were lighted; the two cousins sat waiting on each other.

'You've been in Paris, I hear,' said Soames at last.

'Yes; just back.'

'Young Val told me; he and your boy are going off, then?'

Jolyon nodded.

'You didn't happen to see Irene, I suppose. It appears she's abroad somewhere.'

Jolyon wreathed himself in smoke before he answered: 'Yes, I saw her.'

'How was she?'

'Very well.'

There was another silence; then Soames roused himself in his chair.

'When I saw you last,' he said, 'I was in two minds. We talked, and you expressed your opinion. I don't wish to re-open that discussion. I only wanted to say this: My position with her is extremely difficult. I don't want you to go using your influence against me. What happened is a very long time ago. I'm going to ask her to let bygones be bygones.'

'You have asked her, you know,' murmured Jolyon.

'The idea was new to her then; it came as a shock. But the more she thinks of it, the more she must see that it's the only way out for both of us.'

'That's not my impression of her state of mind,' said Jolyon with particular calm. 'And, forgive my saying, you misconceive the matter if you think reason comes into it at all.'

He saw his cousin's pale face grow paler–he had used, without knowing it, Irene's own words.

'Thanks,' muttered Soames, 'but I see things perhaps more plainly than you think. I only want to be sure that you won't try to influence her against me.'

'I don't know what makes you think I have any influence,' said Jolyon; 'but if I have I'm bound to use it in the direction of what I think is her happiness. I am what they call a "feminist", I believe.'

'Feminist!' repeated Soames, as if seeking to gain time. 'Does that mean that you're against me?'

'Bluntly,' said Jolyon, 'I'm against any woman living with any man whom she definitely dislikes. It appears to me rotten.'

'And I suppose each time you see her you put your opinions into her mind.'

'I am not likely to be seeing her.'

'Not going back to Paris?'

'Not so far as I know,' said Jolyon, conscious of the intent watchfulness in Soames's face.

'Well, that's all I had to say. Anyone who comes between man and wife, you know, incurs heavy responsibility.'

Jolyon rose and made a slight bow.

'Good-bye,' he said, and, without offering to shake hands, moved away, leaving Soames staring after him. 'We Forsytes,' thought Jolyon, hailing a cab, 'are very civilised. With simpler folk that might have come to a row. If it weren't for my boy going to the war–' The war! A gust of his old doubt swept over him. A precious war! Domination of peoples or of women! Attempts to master and possess those who did not want you! The negation of gentle decency! Possession, vested rights; and anyone 'agin' 'em—outcast! 'Thank Heaven!' he thought, '*I always* felt "agin" 'em, anyway!' Yes! Even before his first disastrous marriage he could remember fuming over the bludgeoning of Ireland, or the matrimonial suits of women trying to be free of men they loathed. Parsons would have it that freedom of soul and body were quite different things! Pernicious doctrine, that! Body and soul could not thus be separated. Free will was the strength of any tie, and not its weakness. 'I ought to have told Soames,' he thought, 'that I think him comic. Ah! but he's tragic, too!'

Was there anything, indeed, more tragic in the world than a man enslaved by his own possessive instinct, who couldn't see the sky for it, or even enter fully into what another person felt! 'I must write and warn her,' he thought; 'he's going to have another try.' And all the way home to Robin Hill he rebelled at the strength of that duty to his son which prevented him from posting back to Paris. . . .

But Soames sat long in his chair, the prey of a no less gnawing ache–a jealous ache, as if it had been revealed to him that this fellow held precedence of himself, and had spun fresh threads of resistance to his way out. 'Does that mean that you're against me?' he had got nothing out of that disingenuous question. Feminist! Phrasey fellow! 'I mustn't rush things,' he thought. 'I have some breathing space; he's not going back to Paris, unless he was lying. I'll let the spring come!' Though how the spring could serve him, save by adding to his ache, he could not tell. And gazing down into the street, where figures were passing from pool to pool of light from the high lamps, he thought: 'Nothing seems any good–nothing seems worth while. I'm lonely–that's the trouble.'

He closed his eyes; and at once he seemed to see Irene, in a dark street below a church–passing, turning her neck so that he caught the gleam of her eyes and her white forehead under a little dark hat, which had gold spangles on it and a veil hanging down behind. He opened his eyes–so vividly he had seen her! A woman *was* passing below, but not she! Oh no, there was nothing there!

13

Imogen's frocks for her first season exercised the judgment of her mother and the purse of her grandfather all through the month of March. With Forsyte tenacity Winifred quested for perfection. It took her mind off the slowly approaching rite which would give her a freedom but doubtfully desired; took her mind, too, off her boy and his fast approaching departure for a war from which the news remained disquieting. Like bees busy on summer flowers, or bright gadflies hovering and darting over spiky autumn blossoms, she and her 'little daughter', tall nearly as herself and with a bust measurement not far inferior, hovered in the shops of Regent Street, the establishments of Hanover Square and of Bond Street, lost in consideration and the feel of fabrics. Dozens of young women of striking deportment and peculiar gait paraded before Winifred and Imogen, draped in 'creations'. The models–'Very new, modom; quite the latest thing–' which those two reluctantly turned down, would have filled a museum; the models which they were obliged to have nearly emptied James's bank. It was no good doing things by halves, Winifred felt, in view of the need for making this first and sole untarnished season a conspicuous success. Their patience in trying the patience of those impersonal creatures who swam about before them could alone have been displayed by such as were moved by faith. It was for Winifred a long prostration before her dear goddess Fashion, fervent as a Catholic might make before the Virgin; for Imogen an experience by no means too unpleasant–she often looked so nice, and flattery was implicit everywhere: in a word it was 'amusing'.

On the afternoon of the 20th of March, having, as it were, gutted Skyward's, they had sought refreshment over the way at Caramel and Baker's, and, stored with chocolate frothed at the top with cream, turned homewards through Berkeley Square of an evening touched with spring. Opening the door–freshly painted a light olive-green; nothing neglected that year to give Imogen a good send-off–Winifred passed towards the silver basket to see if anyone had called, and suddenly her nostrils twitched. What was that scent?

Imogen had taken up a novel sent from the library, and stood absorbed. Rather sharply, because of the queer feeling in her breast, Winifred said:

'Take that up, dear, and have a rest before dinner.'

Imogen, still reading, passed up the stairs. Winifred heard the door of her room slammed to, and drew a long savouring breath. Was it spring tickling her senses–whipping up nostalgia for her 'clown', against all wisdom and outraged virtue? A male scent! A faint reek of cigars and lavender-water not smelt since that early autumn night six months ago, when she had called him 'the limit'. Whence came it, or was it ghost of scent–sheer emanation from memory? She looked round her. Nothing–not a thing, no tiniest disturbance of her hall, nor of the dining-room. A little day-dream of a scent–illusory, saddening, silly! In the silver basket were new cards, two with 'Mr and Mrs Polegate Thom', and one with 'Mr Polegate Thom' thereon; she sniffed them, but they smelled severe. 'I must be tired,' she thought, 'I'll go and lie down.' Upstairs the drawing-room was darkened, waiting for some hand to give it evening light; and she passed on up to her bedroom. This, too, was half-curtained and dim, for it was six o'clock. Winifred threw off her coat–that scent again!–then stood, as if shot, transfixed against the bedrail. Something dark had risen from the sofa in the far corner. A word of–horror–in her family escaped her: 'God!'

'It's I–Monty,' said a voice.

Clutching the bedrail, Winifred reached up and turned the switch of the light hanging above her dressing-table. He appeared just on the rim of the light's circumference, emblazoned from the absence of his watch-chain down to boots neat and sooty brown, but–yes!–split at the toecap. His chest and face were shadowy. Surely he was thin–or was it a trick of the light? He advanced, lighted now from toe-cap to the top of his dark head–surely a little grizzled! His complexion had darkened, sallowed; his black moustache had lost boldness, become sardonic; there were lines which she did not know about his face. There was no pin in his tie. His suit–ah!–she knew that–but how unpressed, unglossy! She stared again at the toe-cap of his boot. Something big and relentless had been 'at him', had turned and twisted, raked and scraped him. And she stayed, not speaking, motionless, staring at that crack across the toe.

'Well!' he said, 'I got the letter. I'm back.'

Winifred's bosom began to heave. The nostalgia for her husband which had rushed up with that scent was struggling with a deeper jealousy than any she had felt yet. There he was–a dark, and as if harried, shadow of his sleek and brazen self! What force had done this to him–squeezed him like an orange to its dry rind! That woman!

'I'm back, he said again. 'I've had a beastly time. By God! I came steerage. I've got nothing but what I stand up in, and that bag.'

'And who has the rest?' cried Winifred, suddenly alive. 'How dared you come? You knew it was just for divorce that you got that letter to come back. Don't touch me!'

They held each to the rail of the big bed where they had spent so many years of nights together. Many times, yes–many times she had wanted him back. But now that he had come she was filled with this cold and deadly resentment. He put up his hand to his moustache; but did not frizz and twist it in the old familiar way, he just pulled it downwards.

'Gad!' he said: 'If you knew the time I've had!'

'I'm glad I don't!'

'Are the kids all right?'

Winifred nodded. 'How did you get in?'

'With my key.'

'Then the maids don't know. You can't stay here, Monty.'

He uttered a little sardonic laugh.

'Where then?'

'Anywhere.'

'Well, look at me! That–that damned–'

'If you mention *her*,' cried Winifred, 'I go straight out to Park Lane and I don't come back.'

Suddenly he did a simple thing, but so uncharacteristic that it moved her. He shut his eyes. It was as if he had said: 'All right! I'm dead to the world!'

'You can have a room for the night,' she said; 'your things are still here. Only

Imogen is at home.'

He leaned back against the bedrail. 'Well, it's in your hands,' and his own made a writhing movement. 'I've been through it. You needn't hit too hard – it isn't worth while. I've been frightened; I've been frightened, Freddie.'

That old pet name, disused for years and years, sent a shiver through Winifred.

'What am I to do with him?' she thought. 'What in God's name am I to do with him?'

'Got a cigarette?'

She gave him one from a little box she kept up there for when she couldn't sleep at night, and lighted it. With that action the matter-of-fact side of her nature came to life again.

'Go and have a hot bath. I'll put some clothes out for you in the dressing-room. We can talk later.'

He nodded, and fixed his eyes on her – they looked half-dead, or was it that the folds in the lids had become heavier?

'He's not the same,' she thought. He would never be quite the same again! But what would he be?

'All right!' he said, and went towards the door. He even moved differently, like a man who has lost illusion and doubts whether it is worth while to move at all.

When he was gone, and she heard the water in the bath running, she put out a complete set of garments on the bed in his dressing-room, then went downstairs and fetched up the biscuit box and whisky. Putting on her coat again, and listening for a moment at the bathroom door, she went down and out. In the street she hesitated. Past seven o'clock! Would Soames be at his club or at Park Lane? She turned towards the latter. Back! Soames had always feared it – she had sometimes hoped it. Back! So like him – clown that he was – with this: 'Here we are again!' to make fools of them all – of the Law, of Soames, of herself! Yet to have done with the Law, not to have that murky cloud hanging over her and the children! What a relief! Ah! but how to accept his return? That 'woman' had ravaged him, taken from him passion such as he had never bestowed on herself, such as she had not thought him capable of. There was the sting! That selfish, blatant 'clown' of hers, whom she herself had never really stirred had been swept and ungarnished by another woman! Insulting! Too insulting! Not right, not decent to take him back! And yet she had asked for him; the Law perhaps would make her now! He was as much her husband as ever – she had put herself out of court! And all he wanted, no doubt, was money – to keep him in cigars and lavender-water! That scent! 'After all, I'm not old,' she thought, 'not old yet!' But that woman who had reduced him to those words: 'I've been through it. I've been frightened – frightened, Freddie!' She neared her father's house, driven this way and that, while all the time the Forsyte undertow was drawing her to deep conclusion that after all he was her property, to be held against a robbing world. And so she came to James's.

'Mr Soames? In his room? I'll go up; don't say I'm here.'

Her brother was dressing. She found him before a mirror, tying a black bow with an air of despising its ends.

'Hullo!' he said, contemplating her in the glass; 'what's wrong?'

'Monty!' said Winifred stonily.

Soames spun round. 'What!'

'Back!'

'Hoist,' muttered Soames, 'with our own petard. Why the deuce didn't you let me try cruelty? I always knew it was too much risk this way.'

'Oh! Don't talk about that! What shall I do?'

Soames answered, with a deep, deep sound.

'Well?' said Winifred impatiently.

'What has he to say for himself?'

'Nothing. One of his boots is split across the toe.'

Soames stared at her.

'Ah!' he said, 'of course! On his beam ends. So—it begins again! This'll about finish father.'

'Can't we keep it from him?'

'Impossible. He has an uncanny flair for anything that's worrying.'

And he brooded, with fingers hooked into his blue silk braces. 'There ought to be some way in law,' he muttered, 'to make him safe.'

'No,' cried Winifred, 'I won't be made a fool of again; I'd sooner put up with him.'

The two stared at each other. Their hearts were full of feeling, but they could give it no expression—Forsytes that they were.

'Where did you leave him?'

'In the bath,' and Winifred gave a little bitter laugh. 'The only thing he's brought back is lavender-water.'

'Steady!' said Soames; 'you're thoroughly upset. I'll go back with you.'

'What's the use?'

'We ought to make terms with him.'

'Terms! It'll always be the same. When he recovers—cards and betting, drink and—!' She was silent, remembering the look on her husband's face. The burnt child—the burnt child! Perhaps—!

'Recovers?' replied Soames: 'Is he ill?'

'No; burnt out; that's all.'

Soames took his waistcoat from a chair and put it on, he took his coat and got into it, he scented his handkerchief with eau-de-Cologne, threaded his watch-chain, and said: 'We haven't any luck.'

And in the midst of her own trouble Winifred was sorry for him, as if in that little saying he had revealed deep trouble of his own.

'I'd like to see mother,' she said.

'She'll be with father in their room. Come down quietly to the study. I'll get her.'

Winifred stole down to the little dark study, chiefly remarkable for a Canaletto too doubtful to be placed elsewhere, and a fine collection of Law Reports unopened for many years. Here she stood, with her back to maroon-coloured curtains close-drawn, staring at the empty grate, till her mother came in followed by Soames.

'Oh! my poor dear!' said Emily. 'How miserable you look in here! This is too bad of him, really!'

As a family they had so guarded themselves from the expression of all unfashionable emotion that it was impossible to go up and give her daughter a good hug. But there was comfort in her cushioned voice, and her still dimpled shoulders under some rare black lace. Summoning pride and the desire not to distress her mother, Winifred said in her most off-hand voice:

'It's all right, Mother; no good fussing.'

'I don't see,' said Emily, looking at Soames, 'why Winifred shouldn't tell him that she'll prosecute him if he doesn't keep off the premises. He took her pearls; and if he's not brought them back, that's quite enough.'

Winifred smiled. They would all plunge about with suggestions of this and that, but she knew already what she would be doing, and that was—nothing. The feeling that, after all, she had won a sort of victory, retained her property, was every moment gaining ground in her. No! if she wanted to punish him, she could do it at home without the world knowing.

'Well,' said Emily, 'come into the dining-room comfortably—you must stay and have dinner with us. Leave it to me to tell your father.' And, as Winifred moved towards the door, she turned out the light. Not till then did they see the disaster in the corridor.

There, attracted by light from a room never lighted, James was standing with his dun-coloured camel-hair shawl folded about him, so that his arms were not free and his silvered head looked cut off from his fashionably trousered legs as if by an expanse of desert. He stood, inimitably stork-like, with an expression as if he saw before him a frog too large to swallow.

'What's all this?' he said. 'Tell your father! You never tell me anything.'

The moment found Emily without reply. It was Winifred who went up to him, and, laying one hand on each of his swathed, helpless arms, said:

'Monty's not gone bankrupt, Father. He's only come back.'

They all three expected something serious to happen, and were glad she had kept that grip of his arms, but they did not know the depth of root in that shadowy old Forsyte. Something wry occurred about his shaven mouth and chin, something scratchy between those long silvery whiskers. Then he said with a sort of dignity: 'He'll be the death of me. I knew how it would be.'

'You mustn't worry, Father,' said Winifred calmly. 'I mean to make him behave.'

'Ah!' said James. 'Here, take this thing off, I'm hot.' They unwound the shawl. He turned, and walked firmly to the dining-room.

'I don't want any soup,' he said to Warmson, and sat down in his chair. They all sat down too, Winifred still in her hat, while Warmson laid the fourth place. When he left the room, James said: 'What's he brought back?'

'Nothing, Father.'

James concentrated his eyes on his own image in a tablespoon. 'Divorce!' he muttered; 'rubbish! What was I about! I ought to have paid him an allowance to stay out of England. Soames! you go and propose it to him.'

It seemed so right and simple a suggestion that even Winifred was surprised when she said: 'No, I'll keep him now he's back; he must just behave—that's all.'

They all looked at her. It had always been known that Winifred had pluck.

'Out there!' said James elliptically, 'who knows what cut-throats! You look for his revolver! Don't go to bed without. You ought to have Warmson to sleep in the house. I'll see him myself to-morrow.'

They were touched by this declaration, and Emily said comfortably: 'That's right, James, we won't have any nonsense.'

'Ah!' muttered James darkly, 'I can't tell.'

The advent of Warmson with fish diverted conversation.

When, directly after dinner, Winifred went over to kiss her father good-night, he looked up with eyes so full of question and distress that she put all the comfort she could into her voice.

'It's all right, Daddy dear; don't worry. I shan't need anyone—he's quite bland. I shall only be upset if you worry. Good-night, bless you!'

James repeated the words, 'Bless you!' as if he did not quite know what they meant, and his eyes followed her to the door.

She reached home before nine, and went straight upstairs.

Dartie was lying on the bed in his dressing-room, fully re-dressed in a blue serge suit and pumps; his arms were crossed behind his head, and an extinct cigarette drooped from his mouth.

Winifred remembered ridiculously the flowers in her window-boxes after a blazing summer day; the way they lay, or rather stood–parched, yet rested by the sun's retreat. It was as if a little dew had come already on her burnt-up husband.

He said apathetically: 'I suppose you've been to Park Lane. How's the old man?'

Winifred could not help the bitter answer: 'Not dead.'

He winced, actually he winced.

'Understand, Monty,' she said, 'I will *not* have him worried. If you aren't going to behave yourself, you may go back, you may go anywhere. Have you had dinner?'

'No.'

'Would you like some?'

He shrugged his shoulders.

'Imogen offered me some. I didn't want any.'

Imogen! In the plentitude of emotion Winifred had forgotten her.

'So you've seen her? What did she say?'

'She gave me a kiss.'

With mortification Winifred saw his dark sardonic face relaxed. 'Yes!' she thought, 'he cares for her, not for me a bit.'

Dartie's eyes were moving from side to side.

'Does she know about me?' he said.

It flashed through Winifred that here was the weapon she needed. *He minded their knowing!*

'No. Val knows. The others don't; they only know you went away.'

She heard him sigh with relief.

'But they *shall* know,' she said firmly, 'if you give me cause.'

'All right!' he muttered, 'hit me! I'm down!'

Winifred went up to the bed. 'Look here, Monty! I don't want to hit you. I don't want to hurt you. I shan't allude to anything. I'm not going to worry. What's the use?' She was silent a moment. 'I can't stand any more, though, and I won't! You'd better know. You've made me suffer. But I used to be fond of you. For the sake of that–' She met the heavy-lidded gaze of his brown eyes with the downward stare of her green-grey eyes, touched his hand suddenly, turned her back, and went into her room.

She sat there a long time before her glass, fingering her rings, thinking of this subdued dark man, almost a stranger to her, on the bed in the other room; resolutely not 'worrying', but gnawed by jealousy of what he had been through, and now and again just visited by pity.

14

OUTLANDISH NIGHT

Soames doggedly let the spring come–no easy task for one conscious that time was flying, his birds in the bush no nearer the hand, no issue from the web anywhere visible. Mr Polteed reported nothing, except that his watch went on–costing a lot of money. Val and his cousin were gone to the war, whence came news more favourable; Dartie was behaving himself so far; James had retained his health; business prospered almost terribly–there was nothing to worry Soames except that he was 'held up', could take no step in any direction.

He did not exactly avoid Soho, for he could not afford to let them think that he had 'piped off', as James would have put it–he might want to 'pipe on' again at any minute. But he had to be so restrained and cautious that he would often pass the door of the Restaurant Bretagne without going in, and wander out of the purlieus of that region which always gave him the feeling of having been possessively irregular.

He wandered thus one May night into Regent Street and the most amazing crowd he had ever seen: a shrieking, whistling, dancing, jostling, grotesque and formidably jovial crowd, with false noses and mouth-organs, penny whistles and long feathers, every appanage of idiocy, as it seemed to him. Mafeking! Of course, it had been relieved! Good! But was that an excuse? Who were these people, what were they, where had they come from into the West End? His face was tickled, his ears whistled into. Girls cried: 'Keep your hair on, stucco!' A youth so knocked off his top-hat that he recovered it with difficulty. Crackers were exploding beneath his nose, between his feet. He was bewildered, exasperated, offended. This stream of people came from every quarter, as if impulse had unlocked flood-gates, let flow waters of whose existence he had heard, perhaps, but believed in never. This, then, was the populace, the innumerable living negation of gentility and Forsyteism. This was–egad!–Democracy! It stank, yelled, was hideous! In the East End, or even Soho, perhaps–but here in Regent Street, in Piccadilly! What were the police about! In 1900, Soames, with his Forsyte thousands, had never seen the cauldron with the lid off; and now looking into it, could hardly believe his scorching eyes. The whole thing was unspeakable! These people had no restraint, they seemed to think him funny; such swarms of them, rude, coarse, laughing–and what laughter! Nothing sacred to them! He shouldn't be surprised if they began to break windows. In Pall Mall, past those august dwellings, to enter which people paid sixty pounds, this shrieking, whistling, dancing dervish of a crowd was swarming. From the club windows his own kind were looking out on them with regulated amusement. They didn't realise! Why, this was serious–might come to anything! The crowd was cheerful, but some day they would come in different mood! He remembered there had been a mob in the late 'eighties, when he was at Brighton; they had smashed things and made speeches. But more than dread, he felt a deep surprise. They were hysterical–it wasn't English! And all about the relief of a little town as big as–Watford, six thousand miles away. Restraint, reserve! Those qualities to him more dear almost than life, those indispensable attributes of property and culture, where were they? It wasn't English! No, it wasn't English! So Soames brooded, threading his way on. It was as if he had suddenly caught sight of someone cutting the covenant 'for quiet possession' out of his legal documents; or of a monster lurking and stalking out in the future, casting its shadow before. Their want of stolidity, their want of reverence! It was like discovering that nine-tenths of the people of England were foreigners. And if that were so–then anything might happen!

At Hyde Park Corner he ran into George Forsyte, very sunburnt from racing, holding a false nose in his hand.

'Hallo, Soames!' he said; 'have a nose!'

Soames responded with a pale smile.

'Got this from one of these sportsmen,' went on George, who had evidently been dining; 'had to lay him out–for trying to bash my hat. I say, one of these days we shall have to fight these chaps, they're getting so damned cheeky–all radicals and socialists. They want our goods. You tell Uncle James that, it'll make him sleep.'

'*In vino veritas*,' thought Soames, but he only nodded and passed on up Hamilton Place. There was but a trickle of roysterers in Park Lane, not very noisy. And looking up at the houses, he thought: 'After all, we're the backbone of the country. They won't upset us easily. Possession's nine points of the law.'

But, as he closed the door of his father's house behind him, all that queer outlandish nightmare in the streets passed out of his mind almost as completely as if, having dreamed it, he had awakened in the warm, clean morning comfort of his spring-mattressed bed.

Walking into the centre of the great empty drawing-room, he stood still.

A wife! Somebody to talk things over with. One had a right! Damn it! One had a right!

PART III

I

SOAMES IN PARIS

Soames had travelled little. Aged nineteen, he had made the 'petty tour' with his father, mother, and Winifred–Brussels, the Rhine, Switzerland, and home by way of Paris. Aged twenty-seven, just when he began to take interest in pictures, he had spent five hot weeks in Italy, looking into the Renaissance–not so much in it as he had been led to expect–and a fortnight in Paris on his way back, looking into himself, as became a Forsyte surrounded by people so strongly self-centred and 'foreign' as the French. His knowledge of their language being derived from his public school, he did not understand them when they spoke. Silence he had found better for all parties; one did not make a fool of oneself. He had disliked the look of the men's clothes, the closed-in cabs, the theatres which looked like beehives, the Galleries which smelled of beeswax. He was too cautious and shy to explore that side of Paris supposed by Forsytes to constitute its attraction under the rose; and as for a collector's bargain–not one to be had! As Nicholas might have put it–they were a grasping lot. He had come back uneasy, saying Paris was overrated.

When, therefore, in June of 1900, he went to Paris, it was but his third attempt on the centre of civilisation. This time, however, the mountain was going to Mahomet; for he felt by now more deeply civilised than Paris, and perhaps he really was. Moreover, he had a definite objective. This was no mere genuflexion to a shrine of taste and immorality, but the prosecution of his own legitimate affairs. He went, indeed, because things were getting past a joke. The watch went on and on, and–nothing–nothing! Jolyon had never returned to Paris, and no one else was 'suspect'! Busy with new and very confidential matters, Soames was realising more than ever how essential reputation is to a solicitor. But at night and in his leisure moments he was ravaged by the thought that time was always flying and money flowing in, and his own future as much 'in irons' as ever. Since Mafeking night he had become aware that a 'young fool of a doctor' was hanging round Annette. Twice he had come across him–a cheerful young fool, not more than thirty. Nothing annoyed Soames as much as cheerfulness–an indecent, extravagant sort of quality, which had no relation to facts. The mixture of his desires and hopes was, in a word, becoming torture; and lately the thought had come to him that perhaps Irene knew she was being shadowed. It was this which finally decided him to go and see for himself; to go and once more try to break down her repugnance, her refusal to make her own and his path comparatively smooth once more. If he failed again–well, he would see what she did with herself, anyway!

He went to an hotel in the Rue Caumartin, highly recommended to Forsytes, where practically nobody spoke French. He had formed no plan. He did not want to startle her; yet must contrive that she had no chance to evade him by flight. And next morning he set out in bright weather.

Paris had an air of gaiety, a sparkle over its star-shape which almost annoyed Soames. He stepped gravely, his nose lifted a little sideways in real curiosity. He desired now to understand things French. Was not Annette French? There was much to be got out of his visit, if he could only get it. In this laudable mood and the Place de la Concorde he was nearly run down three times. He came on the 'Cours la Reine', where Irene's hotel was situated, almost too suddenly, for he had not yet fixed on his procedure. Crossing over to the river side, he noted the building, white and cheerful-looking, with green sun-blinds, seen through a screen of plane tree leaves. And, conscious that it would be far better to meet her casually in some open place than to risk a call, he sat down on a bench whence he could watch the entrance. It was not quite eleven o'clock, and improbable that she had yet gone out. Some pigeons were strutting and preening their feathers in the pools of sunlight between the shadows of the plane trees. A workman in a blue blouse passed and threw them crumbs from the paper which contained his dinner. A *'bonne'* coiffed with ribbon shepherded two little girls with pigtails and frilled drawers. A cab meandered by, whose *cocher* wore a blue coat and a black-glazed hat. To Soames a kind of affectation seemed to cling about it all, a sort of picturesque which was out of date. A theatrical people, the French! He lit one of his rare cigarettes, with a sense of injury that Fate should be casting his life into outlandish waters. He shouldn't wonder if Irene quite enjoyed this foreign life; she had never been properly English–even to look at! And he began considering which of those windows could be hers under the green sun-blinds. How could he word what he had come to say so that it might pierce the defence of her proud obstinacy? He threw the fag-end of his cigarette at a pigeon, with the thought: 'I can't stay here for ever twiddling my thumbs. Better give it up and call on her in the late afternoon.' But he still sat on, heard twelve strike, and then half-past. 'I'll wait till one,' he thought, 'while I'm about it.' But just then he started up, and shrinkingly sat down again. A woman had come out in a cream-coloured frock, and was moving away under a fawn-coloured parasol. Irene herself! He waited till she was too far away to recognise him, then set out after her. She was strolling as though she had no particular objective; moving, if he remembered rightly, towards the Bois de Boulogne. For half an hour at least he kept his distance on the far side of the way till she had passed into the Bois itself. Was she going to meet someone after all? Some confounded Frenchman–one of those 'Bel Ami' chaps, perhaps, who had nothing to do but hang about women–for he had read that book with difficulty and a sort of disgusted fascination. He followed doggedly along a shady alley, losing sight of her now and then when the path curved. And it came back to him how, long ago, one night in Hyde Park he had slid and sneaked from tree to tree, from seat to seat, hunting blindly, ridiculously, in burning jealousy for her and young Bosinney. The path bent sharply, and, hurrying, he came on her sitting in front of a small fountain–a little green-bronze Niobe veiled in hair to her slender hips, gazing at the pool she had wept. He came on her so suddenly that he was past before he could turn and take off his hat. She did not start up. She had always had great self-command–it was one of the things he most admired in her, one of his greatest grievances against her, because he had never been able to tell what she was thinking. Had she realised that he was following? Her self-possession made him angry; and, disdaining to explain his presence, he pointed to the mournful little Niobe, and said:

'That's rather a good thing.'

He could see, then, that she was struggling to preserve her composure.

'I didn't want to startle you; is this one of your haunts?'

'Yes.'

'A little lonely.' As he spoke, a lady, strolling by, paused to look at the fountain and passed on.

Irene's eyes followed her.

'No,' she said, prodding the ground with her parasol, 'never lonely. One has always one's shadow.'

Soames understood; and, looking at her hard, he exclaimed:

'Well, it's your own fault. You can be free of it at any moment. Irene, come back to me and be free.'

Irene laughed.

'Don't!' cried Soames, stamping his foot; 'it's inhuman. Listen! Is there *any* condition I can make which will bring you back to me? If I promise you a separate house—and just a visit now and then?'

Irene rose, something wild suddenly in her face and figure.

'None! None! None! You may hunt me to the grave. I will not come.'

Outraged and on edge, Soames recoiled.

'Don't make a scene!' he said sharply. And they both stood motionless, staring at the little Niobe, whose greenish flesh the sunlight was burnishing.

'That's your last word, then,' muttered Soames, clenching his hands; 'you condemn us both.'

Irene bent her head. 'I can't come back. Good-bye!'

A feeling of monstrous injustice flared up in Soames.

'Stop!' he said, 'and listen to me a moment. You gave me a sacred vow—you came to me without a penny. You had all I could give you. You broke that vow without cause, you made me a by-word; you refused me a child; you've left me in prison; you—you still move me so that I want you—I want you. Well, what do you think of yourself?'

Irene turned, her face was deadly pale, her eyes burning dark.

'God made me as I am,' she said; 'wicked if you like—but not so wicked that I'll give myself again to a man I hate.'

The sunlight gleamed on her hair as she moved away, and seemed to lay a caress all down her clinging cream-coloured frock.

Soames could neither speak nor move. That word 'hate'—so extreme, so primitive—made all the Forsyte in him tremble. With a deep imprecation he strode away from where she had vanished, and ran almost into the arms of the lady sauntering back—the fool, the shadowing fool!

He was soon dripping with perspiration, in the depths of the Bois.

'Well,' he thought, 'I need have no consideration for her now; she has not a grain of it for me. I'll show her this very day that she's my wife still.'

But on the way home to his hotel, he was forced to the conclusion that he did not know what he meant. One could not make scenes in public, and short of scenes in public, what was there he could do? He almost cursed his own thin-skinnedness. She might deserve no consideration; but he—alas! deserved some at his own hands. And sitting lunchless in the hall of his hotel, with tourists passing every moment, Baedeker in hand, he was visited by black dejection. In irons! His whole life, with every natural instinct and every decent yearning gagged and fettered, and all because Fate had driven him seventeen years ago to set his heart upon this woman – so utterly that even now he had no real heart to set on any other! Cursed was the day he had met her, and his eyes for seeing in her anything but the cruel Venus she was! And yet, still seeing her with the sunlight on the clinging China crêpe of her gown, he uttered a little groan, so that a tourist who was passing, thought: 'Man in pain! Let's see! what did I have for lunch?'

Later, in front of a café near the Opera, over a glass of cold tea with lemon and a straw in it, he took the malicious resolution to go and dine at her hotel. If she were there, he would speak to her; if she were not, he would leave a note. He dressed carefully, and wrote as follows:

> Your idyll with that fellow Jolyon Forsyte is known to me at all events. If you pursue it, understand that I will leave no stone unturned to make things unbearable for him.
>
> S.F.

He sealed this note but did not address it, refusing to write the maiden name which she had impudently resumed, or to put the word 'Forsyte' on the envelope lest she should tear it up unread. Then he went out and made his way through the glowing streets, abandoned to evening pleasure-seekers. Entering her hotel, he took his seat in a far corner of the dining-room whence he could see all entrances and exits. She was not there. He ate little, quickly, watchfully. She did not come. He lingered in the lounge over his coffee, drank two liqueurs of brandy. But still she did not come. He went over to the key-board and examined the names. Number twelve, on the first floor! And he determined to take the note up himself. He mounted red-carpeted stairs, past a little salon; eight – ten – twelve! Should he knock, push the note under, or – ? He looked furtively round and turned the handle. The door opened, but into a little space leading to another door; he knocked on that – no answer. The door was locked. It fitted very closely to the floor; the note would not go under. He thrust it back into his pocket, and stood a moment listening. He felt somehow certain that she was not there. And suddenly he came away, passing the little salon down the stairs. He stopped at the bureau and said:

'Will you kindly see that Mrs Heron has this note?'

'Madame Heron left to-day, Monsieur – suddenly, about three o'clock. There was illness in her family.'

Soames compressed his lips. 'Oh!' he said; 'do you know her address?'

'*Non, Monsieur*. England, I think.'

Soames put the note into his pocket and went out. He hailed an open horse-cab which was passing.

'Drive me anywhere!'

The man, who, obviously, did not understand, smiled, and waved his whip. And Soames was borne along in that little yellow-wheeled Victoria all over star-shaped Paris, with here and there a pause, and the question: '*C'est par ici, Monsieur?*' 'No, go on,' till the man gave it up in despair, and the yellow-wheeled chariot continued to roll between the tall, flat-fronted shuttered houses and plane tree avenues – a little Flying Dutchman of a cab.

'Like my life,' thought Soames, 'without object, on and on!'

2

IN THE WEB

Soames returned to England the following day, and on the third morning received a visit from Mr Polteed, who wore a flower and carried a brown billycock hat. Soames motioned him to a seat.

'The news from the war is not so bad, is it?' said Mr Polteed. 'I hope I see you well, sir.'

'Thanks! quite.'

Mr Polteed leaned forward, smiled, opened his hand, looked into it, and said softly:

'I think we've done your business for you at last.'

'What?' ejaculated Soames.

'Nineteen reports quite suddenly what I think we shall be justified in calling conclusive evidence,' and Mr Polteed paused.

'Well?'

'On the 10th instant, after witnessing an interview between 17 and a party, earlier in the day, 19 can swear to having seen him coming out of her bedroom in the hotel about ten o'clock in the evening. With a little care in the giving of the evidence that will be enough, especially as 17 has left Paris—no doubt with the party in question. In fact, they both slipped off, and we haven't got on to them again yet; but we shall—we shall. She's worked hard under very difficult circumstances, and I'm glad she's brought it off at last.' Mr Polteed took out a cigarette, tapped its end against the table, looked at Soames, and put it back. The expression on his client's face was not encouraging.

'Who is this new person?' said Soames abruptly.

'That we don't know. She'll swear to the fact, and she's got his appearance pat.'

Mr Polteed took out a letter and began reading:

'"Middle-aged, medium height, blue dittoes in afternoon, evening dress at night, pale, dark hair, small dark moustache, flat cheeks, good chin, grey eyes, small feet, guilty look—"'

Soames rose and went to the window. He stood there in sardonic fury. Congenital idiot—spidery congenital idiot! Seven months at fifteen pounds a week—to be tracked down as his own wife's lover! Guilty look! He threw the window open.

'It's hot,' he said, and came back to his seat. Crossing his knees, he bent a supercilious glance on Mr Polteed.

'I doubt if that's quite good enough,' he said, drawling the words, 'with no name or address. I think you may let that lady have a rest, and take up our friend 47 at this end.' Whether Polteed had spotted him he could not tell; but he had a mental vision of him in the midst of his cronies dissolved in inextinguishable laughter. 'Guilty look!' Damnation!

Mr Polteed said in a tone of urgency, almost of pathos: 'I assure you we have put it through sometimes on less than that. It's Paris, you know. Attractive woman living alone. Why not risk it, sir? We might screw it up a peg.'

Soames had sudden insight. The fellow's professional zeal was stirred: 'Greatest triumph of my career; got a man his divorce through a visit to his own wife's bedroom! Something to talk of there, when I retire!' And for one wild moment he thought: 'Why not?' After all, hundreds of men of medium height had small feet and a guilty look!

'I'm not authorised to take any risk!' he said shortly.

Mr Polteed looked up.

'Pity,' he said, 'quite a pity! That other affair seemed very costive.'

Soames rose.

'Never mind that. Please watch 47, and take care not to find a mare's nest. Good-morning!'

Mr Polteed's eye glinted at the words 'mare's nest'!

'Very good. You shall be kept informed.'

And Soames was alone again. The spidery, dirty, ridiculous business! Laying his arms on the table, he leaned his forehead on them. Full ten minutes he rested thus, till a managing clerk roused him with the draft prospectus of a new issue of shares, very desirable, in Manifold and Topping's. That afternoon he left work early and made his way to the Restaurant Bretagne. Only Madame Lamotte was in. Would *monsieur* have tea with her?

Soames bowed.

When they were seated at right angles to each other in the little room, he said abruptly:

'I want a talk with you, *madame*.'

The quick lift of her clear brown eyes told him that she had long expected such words.

'I have to ask you something first: That young doctor—what's his name? Is there anything between him and Annette?'

Her whole personality had become, as it were, like jet—clear-cut, black, hard, shining.

'Annette is young,' she said; 'so is *monsieur le docteur*. Between young people things move quickly; but Annette is a good daughter. Ah! what a jewel of a nature!'

The least little smile twisted Soames's lips.

'Nothing definite, then?'

'But definite—no, indeed! The young man is veree nice, but—what would you? There is no money at present.'

She raised her willow-patterned tea-cup; Soames did the same. Their eyes met.

'I am a married man,' he said, 'living apart from my wife for many years. I am seeking to divorce her.'

Madame Lamotte put down her cup. Indeed! What tragic things there were! The entire absence of sentiment in her inspired a queer species of contempt in Soames.

'I am a rich man,' he added, fully conscious that the remark was not in good taste. 'It is useless to say more at present, but I think you understand.'

Madame's eyes, so open that the whites showed above them, looked at him very straight.

'Ah! *ça—mais nous avons le temps!*' was all she said. 'Another little cup' Soames refused and, taking his leave, walked westward.

He had got that off his mind; she would not let Annette commit herself with that cheerful young ass until–! But what chance of his ever being able to say: 'I'm free.' What chance? The future had lost all semblance of reality. He felt like a fly entangled in cobweb filaments, watching the desirable freedom of the air with pitiful eyes.

He was short of exercise and wandered on to Kensington Gardens and down Queen's Gate towards Chelsea. Perhaps she had gone back to her flat. That at all events he could find out. For since that last and most ignominious repulse his wounded self-respect had taken refuge again in the feeling that she must have a lover. He arrived before the little Mansions at the dinner-hour. No need to enquire! A grey-haired lady was watering the flower-boxes in her window. It was evidently let. And he walked slowly past again, along the river–an evening of clear, quiet beauty, all harmony and comfort, except within his heart.

3

RICHMOND PARK

On the afternoon that Soames crossed to France a cablegram was received by Jolyon at Robin Hill.

> Your son down with enteric no immediate danger will cable again.

It reached a household already agitated by the imminent departure of June, whose berth was booked for the following day. She was, indeed, in the act of confiding Eric Cobbley and his family to her father's care when the message arrived.

The resolution to become a Red Cross nurse, taken under stimulus of Jolly's enlistment, had been loyally fulfilled with the irritation and regret which all Forsytes feel at what curtails their individual liberties. Enthusiastic at first about the 'wonderfulness' of the work, she had begun after a month to feel that she could train herself so much better than others could train her. And if Holly had not insisted on following her example and being trained too, she must inevitably have 'cried off'. The departure of Jolly and Val with their troop in April had further stiffened her failing resolve. But now, on the point of departure, the thought of leaving Eric Cobbley, with a wife and two children, adrift in the cold waters of an unappreciative world weighed on her so that she was still in danger of backing out. The reading of that cablegram, with its disquieting reality, clinched the matter. She saw herself already nursing Jolly–for of course they would let her nurse her own brother! Jolyon–ever wide and doubtful–had no such hope. Poor June! Could any Forsyte of her generation grasp how rude and brutal life was? Ever since he knew of his boy's arrival at Cape Town the thought of him had been a kind of recurrent sickness in Jolyon. He could not get reconciled to the feeling that Jolly was in danger all the time. The cablegram, grave though it was, was almost a relief. He was now safe from bullets, anyway. And yet–this enteric was a virulent disease! *The Times* was full of deaths therefrom. Why could *he* not be lying out there in that up-country hospital, and his boy safe at home? The un-Forsytean self-sacrifice of his three children, indeed, had quite bewildered Jolyon. He would eagerly change places with Jolly, because he loved his boy; but no such personal motive was influencing *them*. He could only think that it marked the decline of the Forsyte type.

Late that afternoon Holly came out to him under the old oak tree. She had grown up very much during these last months of hospital training away from home. And, seeing her approach, he thought: 'She has more sense than June, child though she is; more wisdom. Thank God *she* isn't going out.' She had seated herself in the swing, very silent and still. 'She feels this,' thought Jolyon, 'as much as I.' And, seeing her eyes fixed on him, he said: 'Don't take it to heart too much, my child. If he weren't ill, he might be in much greater danger.'

Holly got out of the swing.

'I want to tell you something, Dad. It was through me that Jolly enlisted and went out.'

'How's that?'

'When you were away in Paris, Val Dartie and I fell in love. We used to ride in Richmond Park; we got engaged. Jolly found it out, and thought he ought to stop it; so he dared Val to enlist. It was all my fault, Dad; and I want to go out too. Because if anything happens to either of them I should feel awful. Besides, I'm just as much trained as June.'

Jolyon gazed at her in a stupefaction that was tinged with irony. So this was the answer to the riddle he had been asking himself; and his three children were Forsytes after all. Surely Holly might have told him all this before! But he smothered the sarcastic sayings on his lips. Tenderness to the young was perhaps the most sacred article of his belief. He had got, no doubt, what he deserved. Engaged! So this was why he had so lost touch with her! And to young Val Dartie—nephew of Soames—in the other camp! It was all terribly distasteful. He closed his easel and set his drawing against the tree.

'Have you told June?'

'Yes; she says she'll get me into her cabin somehow. It's a single cabin; but one of us could sleep on the floor. If you consent, she'll go up now and get permission.'

'Consent?' thought Jolyon. 'Rather late in the day to ask for that!' But again he checked himself.

'You're too young, my dear; they won't let you.'

'June knows some people that she helped to go to Cape Town. If they won't let me nurse yet, I could stay with them and go on training there. Let me go, Dad!'

Jolyon smiled because he could have cried.

'I never stop anyone from doing anything,' he said.

Holly flung her arms round his neck.

'Oh! Dad, you are the best in the world.'

'That means the worst,' thought Jolyon. If he had ever doubted his creed of tolerance he did so then.

'I'm not friendly with Val's family,' he said, 'and I don't know Val, but Jolly didn't like him.'

Holly looked at the distance and said:

'I love him.'

'That settles it,' said Jolyon dryly, then catching the expression on her face, he kissed her, with the thought: 'Is anything more pathetic than the faith of the young?' Unless he actually forbade her going it was obvious that he must make the best of it, so he went up to town with June. Whether due to her persistence, or the fact that the official they saw was an old school friend of Jolyon's, they obtained permission for Holly to share the single cabin. He took them to Surbiton station the following evening, and they duly slid away from him, provided with money, invalid foods, and those letters of credit without which Forsytes do not travel.

He drove back to Robin Hill under a brilliant sky to his late dinner, served with an added care by servants trying to show him that they sympathised, eaten with an added scrupulousness to show them that he appreciated that sympathy. But it was a real relief to get to his cigar on the terrace of flagstones—cunningly chosen by young Bosinney for shape and colour—with night closing in around him, so beautiful a night, hardly whispering in the trees, and smelling so sweet that it made him ache. The grass was drenched with dew, and he kept to those flagstones, up and down, till presently it began to seem to him that he was one of three, not wheeling, but turning right about at each end, so that his father was always nearest to the house, and his son always nearest to the terrace edge. Each had an arm lightly within his arm; he dared not lift his hand to his cigar lest he should disturb them, and it burned away, dripping ash on him, till it dropped from his lips, at last, which were getting hot. They left him then, and his arms felt chilly. Three Jolyons in one Jolyon they had walked!

He stood still, counting the sounds—a carriage passing on the high road, a distant train, the dog at Gage's farm, the whispering trees, the groom playing on his penny whistle. A multitude of stars up there—bright and silent, so far off! No moon as yet! just enough light to show him the dark flags and swords of the iris flowers along the terrace edge—his favourite flower that had the night's own colour on its curving crumpled petals. He turned round to the house. Big, unlighted, not a soul beside himself to live in all that part of it. Stark loneliness! He could not go on living here alone. And yet, so long as there was beauty, why should a man feel lonely? The answer—as to some idiot's riddle—was: Because he did. The greater the beauty, the greater the loneliness, for at the back of beauty was harmony, and at the back of harmony was—union. Beauty could not comfort if the soul were out of it. The night, maddeningly lovely, with bloom of grapes on it in starshine, and the breath of grass and honey coming from it, he could not enjoy, while she who was to him the life of beauty, its embodiment and essence, was cut off from him, utterly cut off now, he felt, by honourable decency.

He made a poor fist of sleeping, striving too hard after that resignation which Forsytes find difficult to reach, bred to their own way and left so comfortably off by their fathers. But after dawn he dozed off, and soon was dreaming a strange dream.

He was on a stage with immensely high rich curtains—high as the very stars—stretching in a semi-circle from footlights to footlights. He himself was very small, a little black restless figure roaming up and down; and the odd thing was that he was not altogether himself, but Soames as well, so that he was not only experiencing but watching. This figure of himself and Soames was trying to find a way out through the curtains, which, heavy and dark, kept him in. Several times he had crossed in front of them before he saw with delight a sudden narrow rift—a tall chink of beauty the colour of iris flowers, like a glimpse of Paradise, remote, ineffable. Stepping quickly forward to pass into it, he found the curtains closing before him. Bitterly disappointed he—or was it Soames?—moved on, and there was the chink again through the parted curtains, which again closed too soon. This went on and on and he never got through till he woke with the word 'Irene' on his lips. The dream disturbed him badly, especially that identification of himself with Soames.

Next morning, finding it impossible to work, he spent hours riding Jolly's horse in search of fatigue. And on the second day he made up his mind to move to London and see if he could not get permission to follow his daughters to South Africa. He had just begun to pack the following morning when he received this letter:

GREEN HOTEL,
RICHMOND.
June 13.

MY DEAR JOLYON,
   You will be surprised to see how near I am to you. Paris became impossible–and I have come here to be within reach of your advice. I would so love to see you again. Since you left Paris I don't think I have met anyone I could really talk to. Is all well with you and with your boy? No one knows, I think, that I am here at present.

Always your friend,
IRENE.

Irene within three miles of him!–and again in flight! He stood with a very queer smile on his lips. This was more than he had bargained for!

About noon he set out on foot across Richmond Park, and as he went along, he thought: 'Richmond Park! By Jove, it suits us Forsytes!' Not that Forsytes lived there–nobody lived there save royalty, rangers, and the deer–but in Richmond Park Nature was allowed to go so far and no farther, putting up a brave show of being natural, seeming to say: 'Look at my instincts–they are almost passions, very nearly out of hand, but not quite, of course; the very hub of possession is to possess oneself.' Yes! Richmond Park possessed itself, even on that bright day of June, with arrowy cuckoos shifting the tree-points of their calls, and the wood doves announcing high summer.

The Green Hotel, which Jolyon entered at one o'clock, stood nearly opposite that more famous hostelry, the Crown and Sceptre; it was modest, highly respectable, never out of cold beef, gooseberry tart, and a dowager or two, so that a carriage and pair was almost always standing before the door.

In a room draped in chintz so slippery as to forbid all emotion, Irene was sitting on a piano stool covered with crewel work, playing 'Hansel and Gretel' out of an old score. Above her on a wall, not yet Morris-papered, was a print of the Queen on a pony, amongst deer-hounds, Scotch caps, and slain stags; beside her in a pot on the window-sill was a white and rosy fuchsia. The Victorianism of the room almost talked; and in her clinging frock Irene seemed to Jolyon like Venus emerging from the shell of the past century.

'If the proprietor had eyes,' he said, 'he would show you the door; you have broken through his decorations.' Thus lightly he smothered up an emotional moment. Having eaten cold beef, pickled walnut, gooseberry tart, and drunk stone-bottle ginger-beer, they walked into the Park, and light talk was succeeded by the silence Jolyon had dreaded.

'You haven't told me about Paris,' he said at last.

'No. I've been shadowed for a long time; one gets used to that. But then Soames came. By the little Niobe–the same story; would I go back to him?'

'Incredible!'

She had spoken without raising her eyes, but she looked up now. Those dark eyes clinging to his said as no words could have: 'I have come to an end; if you want me, here I am.'

For sheer emotional intensity had he ever—old as he was—passed through such a moment?

The words: 'Irene, I adore you!' almost escaped him. Then, with a clearness of which he would not have believed mental vision capable, he saw Jolly lying with a white face turned to a white wall.

'My boy is very ill out there,' he said quietly.

Irene slipped her arm through his.

'Let's walk on; I understand.'

No miserable explanation to attempt! She had understood! And they walked on among the bracken, knee-high already, between the rabbit-holes and the oak trees, talking of Jolly. He left her two hours later at the Richmond Hill Gate, and turned towards home.

'She knows of my feeling for her, then,' he thought. Of course! One could not keep knowledge of that from such a woman!

4

OVER THE RIVER

Jolly was tired to death of dreams. They had left him now too wan and weak to dream again; left him to lie torpid, faintly remembering far-off things; just able to turn his eyes and gaze through the window near his cot at the trickle of river running by in the sands, at the straggling milk-bush of the Karoo beyond. He knew what the Karoo was now, even if he had not seen a Boer roll over like a rabbit, or heard the whiffle of flying bullets. This pestilence had sneaked on him before he had smelled powder. A thirsty day and a rash drink, or perhaps a tainted fruit—who knew? Not he, who had not even strength left to grudge the evil thing its victory—just enough to know that there were many lying here with him, that he was sore with frenzied dreaming; just enough to watch that thread of river and be able to remember faintly those far-away things. . . .

The sun was nearly down. It would be cooler soon. He would have liked to know the time—to feel his old watch, so butter-smooth, to hear the repeater strike. It would have been friendly, home-like. He had not even strength to remember that the old watch was last wound the day he began to lie here. The pulse of his brain beat so feebly that faces which came and went, nurse's, doctor's, orderly's, were indistinguishable, just one indifferent face; and the words spoken about him meant all the same thing, and that almost nothing. Those things he used to do, though far and faint, were more distinct—walking past the foot of the old steps at Harrow 'bill'—'Here, sir! Here, sir!'—wrapping boots in the *Westminster Gazette*, greenish paper, shining boots—grandfather coming from somewhere dark—a smell of earth—the mushroom house! Robin Hill! Burying poor old Balthasar in the leaves! Dad! Home. . . .

Consciousness came again with noticing that the river had no water in it—someone was speaking too. Want anything? No. What could one want? Too weak to want—only to hear his watch strike. . . .

Holly! She wouldn't bowl properly. Oh! Pitch them up! Not sneaks! . . . 'Back her, Two and Bow!' He was Two! . . . Consciousness came once more with a sense of the violet dusk outside, and a rising blood-red crescent moon. His eyes rested on it fascinated; in the long minutes of brain-nothingness it went moving up and up. . . .

'He's going, doctor!' Not pack boots again? Never? 'Mind your form, Two!' Don't cry! Go quietly—over the river—sleep! . . . Dark? If somebody would—strike—his—watch! . . .

———
5
———

SOAMES ACTS

A sealed letter in the handwriting of Mr Polteed remained unopened in Soames's pocket throughout two hours of sustained attention to the affairs of the 'New Colliery Company', which, declining almost from the moment of old Jolyon's retirement from the Chairmanship, had lately run down so fast that there was now nothing for it but a 'winding-up'. He took the letter out to lunch at his City club, sacred to him for the meals he had eaten there with his father in the early seventies, when James used to like him to come and see for himself the nature of his future life.

Here in a remote corner before a plate of roast mutton and mashed potato, he read:

DEAR SIR,
   In accordance with your suggestion we have duly taken the matter up at the other end with gratifying results. Observation of 47 has enabled us to locate 17 at the Green Hotel, Richmond. The two have been observed to meet daily during the past week in Richmond Park. Nothing absolutely crucial has so far been notified. But in conjunction with what we had from Paris at the beginning of the year, I am confident we could now satisfy the Court. We shall, of course, continue to watch the matter until we hear from you.

Very faithfully yours,
CLAUD POLTEED.

Soames read it through twice and beckoned to the waiter.
'Take this away; it's cold.'
'Shall I bring you some more, sir?'
'No. Get me some coffee in the other room.'
And, paying for what he had not eaten, he went out, passing two acquaintances without sign of recognition.

'Satisfy the Court!' he thought, sitting at a little round marble table with the coffee before him. That fellow Jolyon! He poured out his coffee, sweetened and drank it. He would disgrace him in the eyes of his own children! And rising, with that resolution hot within him, he found for the first time the inconvenience of being his own solicitor. He could not treat this scandalous matter in his own office. He must commit the soul of his private dignity to a stranger, some other professional dealer in family dishonour. Who was there he could go to? Linkman and Laver in Budge Row, perhaps—reliable, not too conspicuous, only nodding acquaintances. But before he saw them he must see Polteed again. But at this thought Soames had a moment of sheer weakness. To part with his secret? How find the words? How subject himself to contempt and secret laughter? Yet, after all, the fellow knew already—oh yes, he knew! And, feeling that he must finish with it now, he took a cab into the West End.

In this hot weather the window of Mr Polteed's room was positively open, and the only precaution was a wire gauze, preventing the intrusion of flies. Two or three had tried to come in, and been caught, so that they seemed to be clinging there with the intention of being devoured presently. Mr Polteed, following the direction of his client's eye, rose apologetically and closed the window.

'Posing ass!' thought Soames. Like all who fundamentally believe in themselves, he was rising to the occasion, and, with his little sideway smile, he said, 'I've had your letter. I'm going to act. I suppose you know who the lady you've been watching really is?'

Mr Polteed's expression at that moment was a masterpiece. It so clearly said: 'Well, what do you think? But mere professional knowledge, I assure you–pray forgive it!' He made a little half airy movement with his hand, as who should say: 'Such things–such things will happen to us!'

'Very well, then,' said Soames, moistening his lips, 'there's no need to say more. I'm instructing Linkman and Laver of Budge Row to act for me. I don't want to hear your evidence, but kindly make your report to them at five o'clock, and continue to observe the utmost secrecy.'

Mr Polteed half closed his eyes, as if to comply at once. 'My dear sir,' he said.

'Are you convinced,' asked Soames with sudden energy, 'that there is enough?'

The faintest movement occurred to Mr Polteed's shoulders.

'You can risk it,' he murmured; 'with what we have, and human nature, you can risk it.'

Soames rose. 'You will ask for Mr Linkman. Thanks; don't get up.' He could not bear Mr Polteed to slide as usual between him and the door. In the sunlight of Piccadilly he wiped his forehead. This had been the worst of it–he could stand the strangers better. And he went back into the City to do what still lay before him.

That evening in Park Lane, watching his father dine, he was overwhelmed by his old longing for a son–a son, to watch *him* eat as he went down the years, to be taken on *his* knee as James on a time had been wont to take him; a son of his own begetting, who could understand him because he was the same flesh and blood–understand, and comfort him, and become more rich and cultured than himself because he would start even better off. To get old–like that thin, grey, wiry-frail figure sitting there–and be quite alone with possessions heaping up around him; to take no interest in anything because it had no future and must pass away from him to hands and mouths and eyes for whom he cared no jot! No! He would force it through now, and be free to marry, and have a son to care for him before he grew to be like the old old man his father, wistfully watching now his sweetbread, now his son.

In that mood he went up to bed. But, lying warm between those fine linen sheets of Emily's providing, he was visited by memories and torture. Visions of Irene, almost the solid feeling of her body, beset him. Why had he ever been fool enough to see her again, and let this flood back on him so that it was pain to think of her with that fellow–that stealing fellow!

6

A SUMMER DAY

His boy was seldom absent from Jolyon's mind in the days which followed the first walk with Irene in Richmond Park. No further news had come; enquiries at the War Office elicited nothing; nor could he expect to hear from June and Holly for three weeks at least. In these days he felt how insufficient were his memories of Jolly, and what an amateur of a father he had been. There was not a single memory in which anger played a part; not one reconciliation, because there had never been a rupture; nor one heart-to-heart confidence, not even when Jolly's mother died. Nothing but half-ironical affection. He had been too afraid of committing himself in any direction, for fear of losing his liberty, or interfering with that of his boy.

Only in Irene's presence had he relief, highly complicated by the ever-growing perception of how divided he was between her and his son. With Jolly was bound up all that sense of continuity and social creed of which he had drunk deeply in his youth and again during his boy's public school and varsity life—all that sense of not going back on what father and son expected of each other. With Irene was bound up all his delight in beauty and in Nature. And he seemed to know less and less which was the stronger within him. From such sentimental paralysis he was rudely awakened, however, one afternoon, just as he was starting off to Richmond, by a young man with a bicycle, and a face oddly familiar, who came forward faintly smiling.

'Mr Jolyon Forsyte? Thank you!' Placing an envelope in Jolyon's hand he wheeled off the path and rode away. Bewildered, Jolyon opened it.

'Admiralty Probate and Divorce, Forsyte *v.* Forsyte and Forsyte!' A sensation of shame and disgust was followed by the instant reaction: 'Why, here's the very thing you want, and you don't like it!' But she must have one too; and he must go to her at once. He turned things over as he went along. It was an ironical business. For, whatever the Scriptures said about the heart, it took more than mere longings to satisfy the law. They could perfectly well defend this suit, or at least in good faith try to. But the idea of doing so revolted Jolyon. If not her lover in deed he was in desire, and he knew that she was ready to come to him. Her face had told him so. Not that he exaggerated her feeling for him. She had had her grand passion, and he could not expect another from her at his age. But she had trust in him, affection for him; and must feel that he would be a refuge. Surely she would not ask him to defend the suit, knowing that he adored her! Thank heaven she had not that maddening British conscientiousness which refused happiness for the sake of refusing! She must rejoice at this chance of being free—after seventeen years of death in life! As to publicity, the fat was in the fire! To defend the suit would not take away the slur. Jolyon had all the proper feeling of a Forsyte whose privacy is threatened. If he was to be hung by the Law, by all means let it be for a sheep! Moreover the notion of standing in a witness box and swearing to the truth that no gesture, not even a word of love had passed between them seemed to him more degrading than to take the tacit stigma of being an adulterer—more truly degrading, considering the feeling in his heart, and just as bad and painful for his children. The thought of explaining away, if he could, before a judge and twelve average Englishmen, their meetings in Paris, and the walks in Richmond Park, horrified him. The brutality and hypocritical censoriousness of the whole process; the probability that they would not be believed—the mere vision of her, whom he looked on as the embodiment of Nature and of Beauty, standing there before all those suspicious, gloating eyes was hideous to him. No, no! To defend a suit only made a London holiday, and sold the newspapers. A thousand times better accept what Soames and the gods had sent!

'Besides,' he thought honestly, 'who knows whether, even for my boy's sake, I could have stood this state of things much longer? Anyway, her neck will be out of chancery at last!' Thus absorbed, he was hardly conscious of the heavy heat. The sky had become overcast, purplish, with little streaks of white. A heavy heat-drop plashed a little star pattern in the dust of the road as he entered the Park. 'Phew!' he thought, 'thunder! I hope she's not come to meet me; there's a ducking up there!' But at that very minute he saw Irene coming towards the Gate. 'We must scuttle back to Robin Hill,' he thought.

The storm had passed over the Poultry at four o'clock, bringing welcome distraction to the clerks in every office. Soames was drinking a cup of tea when a note was brought in to him:

DEAR SIR,
Forsyte v. Forsyte and Forsyte
In accordance with your instructions, we beg to inform you that we personally served the respondent and co-respondent in this suit to-day, at Richmond, and Robin Hill, respectively.

Faithfully yours,
LINKMAN AND LAVER.

For some minutes Soames stared at that note. Ever since he had given those instructions he had been tempted to annul them. It was so scandalous, such a general disgrace! The evidence, too, what he had heard of it, had never seemed to him conclusive; somehow, he believed less and less that those two had gone all lengths. But this, of course, would drive them to it; and he suffered from the thought. That fellow to have her love, where he had failed! Was it too late? Now that they had been brought up sharp by service of this petition, had he not a lever with which he could force them apart? 'But if I don't act at once,' he thought, 'it will be too late, now they've had this thing. I'll go and see him; I'll go down!'

And, sick with nervous anxiety, he sent out for one of the 'new-fangled' motor-cabs. It might take a long time to run that fellow to ground, and Goodness knew what decision they might come to after such a shock! 'If I were a theatrical ass,' he thought, 'I suppose I should be taking a horse-whip or a pistol or something!' He took instead a bundle of papers in the case of 'Magentie versus Wake', intending to read them on the way down. He did not even open them, but sat quite still, jolted and jarred, unconscious of the draught down the back of his neck, or the smell of petrol. He must be guided by the fellow's attitude; the great thing was to keep his head!

London had already begun to disgorge its workers as he neared Putney Bridge; the ant-heap was on the move outwards. What a lot of ants, all with a living to get, holding on by their eyelids in the great scramble! Perhaps for the first time in his life Soames thought: '*I* could let go if I liked! Nothing could touch me; I could snap my fingers, live as I wished–enjoy myself!' No! One could not live as he had and just drop it all–settle down in Capua, to spend the money and reputation he had made. A man's life was what he possessed, and sought to possess. Only fools thought otherwise–fools, and socialists, and libertines!

The cab was passing villas now, going a great pace. 'Fifteen miles an hour, I should think!' he mused; 'this'll take people out of town to live!' and he thought of its bearing on the portions of London owned by his father–he himself had never taken to that form of investment, the gambler in him having all the outlet needed in his pictures. And the cab sped on, down the hill past Wimbledon Common. This interview! Surely a man of fifty-two with grown-up children, and hung on the line, would not be reckless. 'He won't want to disgrace the family,' he thought; 'he was as fond of his father as I am of mine, and they were brothers. That woman brings destruction–what is it in her? I've never known.' The cab branched off, along the side of a wood, and he heard a late cuckoo calling, almost the first he had heard that year. He was now almost opposite the site he had originally chosen for his house, and which had been so unceremoniously rejected by Bosinney in favour of his own choice. He began passing his handkerchief over his face and hands, taking deep breaths to give him steadiness. 'Keep one's head,' he thought, 'keep one's head!'

The cab turned in at the drive which might have been his own, and the sound of music met him. He had forgotten the fellow's daughters.

'I may be out again directly,' he said to the driver, 'or I may be kept some time;' and he rang the bell.

Following the maid through the curtains into the inner hall, he felt relieved that the impact of this meeting would be broken by June or Holly, whichever was playing in there, so that with complete surprise he saw Irene at the piano, and Jolyon sitting in an armchair listening. They both stood up. Blood surged into Soames's brain, and all his resolution to be guided by this or that left him utterly. The look of his farmer forbears–dogged Forsytes down by the sea, from 'Superior Dosset' back–grinned out of his face.

'Very pretty!' he said.

He heard the fellow murmur:

'This is hardly the place–we'll go to the study, if you don't mind.' And they both passed him through the curtain opening. In the little room to which he followed them, Irene stood by the open window, and the 'fellow' close to her by a big chair. Soames pulled the door to behind him with a slam; the sound carried him back all those years to the day when he had shut out Jolyon–shut him out for meddling with his affairs.

'Well,' he said, 'what have you to say for yourselves?'

The fellow had the effrontery to smile.

'What we have received to-day has taken away your right to ask. I should imagine you will be glad to have your neck out of chancery.'

'Oh!' said Soames, 'you think so! I came to tell you that I'll divorce her with every circumstance of disgrace to you both, unless you swear to keep clear of each other from now on.'

He was astonished at his fluency, because his mind was stammering and his hands twitching. Neither of them answered; but their faces seemed to him as if contemptuous.

'Well,' he said; 'you–Irene?'

Her lips moved, but Jolyon laid his hand on her arm.

'Let her alone!' said Soames furiously. 'Irene, will you swear it?'

'No.'

'Oh! and you?'

'Still less.'

'So then you're guilty, are you?'

'Yes, guilty.' It was Irene speaking in that serene voice, with that unreached air which had maddened him so often; and, carried beyond himself, he cried:

'*You* are a devil.'

'Go out! Leave this house, or I'll do you an injury.' That fellow to talk of injuries! Did he know how near his throat was to being scragged?

'A trustee,' he said, 'embezzling trust property! A thief, stealing his cousin's wife.'

'Call me what you like. You have chosen your part, we have chosen ours. Go out!'

If he had brought a weapon Soames might have used it at that moment.

'I'll make you pay!' he said.

'I shall be very happy.'

At that deadly turning of the meaning of his speech by the son of him who had nicknamed him 'the man of property', Soames stood glaring. It was ridiculous!

There they were, kept from violence by some secret force. No blow possible, no words to meet the case. But he could not, did not know how to turn and go away. His eyes fastened on Irene's face–the last time he would ever see that fatal face–the last time, no doubt!

'You,' he said suddenly, 'I hope you'll treat him as you treated me–that's all.'

He saw her wince, and with a sensation not quite triumph, not quite relief, he wrenched open the door, passed out through the hall, and got into his cab. He lolled against the cushions with his eyes shut. Never in his life had he been so near to murderous violence, never so thrown away the restraint whach was his second nature. He had a stripped and naked feeling, as if all virtue had gone out of him–life meaningless, mind striking work. Sunlight streamed in on him, but he felt cold. The scene he had passed through had gone from him already, what was before him would not materialise, he could catch on to nothing, and he felt frightened, as if he had been hanging over the edge of a precipice, as if with another turn of the screw sanity would have failed him. 'I'm not fit for it,' he thought; 'I mustn't–I'm not fit for it.' The cab sped on, and in mechanical procession trees, houses, people passed, but had no significance. 'I feel very queer,' he thought; 'I'll take a Turkish bath. I–I've been very near to something. It won't do.' The cab whirred its way back over the bridge, up the Fulham Road, along the Park.

'To the Hammam,' said Soames.

Curious that on so warm a summer day, heat should be so comforting! Crossing into the hot room he met George Forsyte coming out, red and glistening.

'Hallo!' said George; 'what are you training for? You've not got much superfluous.'

Buffoon! Soames passed him with his sideway smile. Lying back, rubbing his skin uneasily for the first signs of perspiration, he thought: 'Let them laugh! I *won't* feel anything! I can't stand violence! It's not good for me!'

7

A SUMMER NIGHT

Soames left dead silence in the little study.

'Thank you for that good lie,' said Jolyon suddenly. 'Come out—the air in here is not what it was!'

In front of a long high southerly wall on which were trained peach trees, the two walked up and down in silence. Old Jolyon had planted some cypressus trees, at intervals, between this grassy terrace and the dipping meadow full of buttercups and ox-eyed daisies; for twelve years they had flourished, till their dark spiral shapes had quite a look of Italy. Birds fluttered softly in the wet shrubbery; the swallows swooped past, with a steel-blue sheen on their swift little bodies; the grass felt springy beneath the feet, its green refreshed; and butterflies chased each other. After that painful scene the quiet of Nature was wonderfully poignant. Under the sun-soaked wall ran a narrow strip of garden-bed full of mignonette and pansies, and from the bees came a low hum in which all other sounds were set—the mooing of a cow deprived of her calf, the calling of a cuckoo from an elm tree at the bottom of the meadow. Who would have thought that behind them, within ten miles, London began—that London of the Forsytes, with its wealth, its misery; its dirt and noise; its jumbled stone isles of beauty, its grey sea of hideous brick and stucco? That London which had seen Irene's early tragedy, and Jolyon's own hard days; that web; that princely work-house of the possessive instinct!

And while they walked Jolyon pondered those words: 'I hope you'll treat him as you treated me.' That would depend on himself. Could he trust himself? Did Nature permit a Forsyte not to make a slave of what he adored? Could beauty be confided to him? Or should she not be just a visitor, coming when she would, possessed for moments which passed, to return only at her own choosing? 'We are a breed of spoilers!' thought Jolyon, 'close and greedy; the bloom of life is not safe with us. Let her come to me as she will, when she will, not at all if she will not. Let me be just her stand-by, her perching-place; never—never her cage!'

She was the chink of beauty in his dream. Was he to pass through the curtains now and reach her? Was the rich stuff of many possessions, the close encircling fabric of the possessive instinct walling in that little black figure of himself, and Soames—was it to be rent so that he could pass through into his vision, find there something not of the senses only? 'Let me,' he thought, 'ah! let me only know how not to grasp and destroy!'

But at dinner there were plans to be made. To-night she would go back to the hotel, but to-morrow he would take her up to London. He must instruct his solicitor—Jack Herring. Not a finger must be raised to hinder the process of the Law. Damages exemplary, judicial strictures, costs, what they liked—let it go through at the first moment, so that her neck might be out of chancery at last! To-morrow he would see Herring—they would go and see him together. And then—abroad, leaving no doubt, no difficulty about evidence, making the lie she had told into the truth. He looked round at her; and it seemed to his adoring eyes that more than a woman was sitting there. The spirit of universal beauty, deep, mysterious, which the old painters, Titian, Giorgione, Botticelli, had known how to capture and transfer to the faces of their women—this flying beauty seemed to him imprinted on her brow, her hair, her lips, and in her eyes.

'And this is to be mine!' he thought. 'It frightens me!'

After dinner they went out on to the terrace to have coffee. They sat there long, the evening was so lovely, watching the summer night come very slowly on. It was still warm and the air smelled of lime blossom—early this summer. Two bats were flighting with the faint mysterious little noise they make. He had placed the chairs in front of the study window, and moths flew past to visit the discreet light in there. There was no wind, and not a whisper in the old oak tree twenty yards away! The moon rose from behind the copse, nearly full; and the two lights struggled, till moonlight conquered, changing the colour and quality of all the garden, stealing along the flagstones, reaching their feet, climbing up, changing their faces.

'Well,' said Jolyon at last, 'you'll be so tired; we'd better start. The maid will show you to Holly's room,' and he rang the study bell. The maid who came handed him a telegram. Watching her take Irene away, he thought: 'This must have come an hour or two ago, and she didn't bring it out to us! That shows! Well, we'll be hung for a sheep soon!' And, opening the telegram, he read:

JOLYON FORSYTE, Robin Hill.—Your son passed painlessly away on June 20th. Deep sympathy—some name unknown to him.

He dropped it, spun round, stood motionless. The moon shone in on him; a moth flew in his face. The first day of all that he had not thought almost ceaselessly of Jolly. He went blindly towards the window, struck against the old armchair—his father's—and sank down on to the arm of it. He sat there huddled forward, staring into the night. Gone out like a candle flame; far from home, from love, all by himself, in the dark! His boy! From a little chap always so good to him—so friendly! Twenty years old, and cut down like grass—to have no life at all! 'I didn't really know him,' he thought, 'and he didn't know me; but we loved each other. It's only love that matters.'

To die out there—lonely—wanting them—wanting home! This seemed to his Forsyte heart more painful, more pitiful than death itself. No shelter, no protection, no love at the last! And all the deeply rooted clanship in him, the family feeling and essential clinging to his own flesh and blood which had been so strong in old Jolyon—was so strong in all the Forsytes—felt outraged, cut, and torn by his boy's lonely passing. Better far if he had died in battle, without time to long for them to come to him, to call out for them, perhaps, in his delirium!

The moon had passed behind the oak tree now, endowing it with uncanny life, so that it seemed watching him—the oak tree his boy had been so fond of climbing, out of which he had once fallen and hurt himself, and hadn't cried!

The door creaked. He saw Irene come in, pick up the telegram and read it. He heard the faint rustle of her dress. She sank on her knees close to him, and he forced himself to smile at her. She stretched up her arms and drew his head down on her shoulder. The perfume and warmth of her encircled him; her presence gained slowly his whole being.

8

JAMES IN WAITING

Sweated to serenity, Soames dined at the Remove and turned his face towards Park Lane. His father had been unwell lately. This would have to be kept from him! Never till that moment had he realised how much the dread of bringing James's grey hairs down with sorrow to the grave had counted with him; how intimately it was bound up with his own shrinking from scandal. His affection for his father, always deep, had increased of late years with the knowledge that James looked on him as the real prop of his decline. It seemed pitiful that one who had been so careful all his life and done so much for the family name—so that it was almost a byword for solid, wealthy respectability—should at his last gasp have to see it in all the newspapers. This was like lending a hand to Death, that final enemy of Forsytes. 'I must tell mother,' he thought, 'and when it comes on, we must keep the papers from him somehow. He sees hardly anyone.' Letting himself in with his latchkey, he was beginning to ascend the stairs when he became conscious of commotion on the second-floor landing. His mother's voice was saying:

'Now, James, you'll catch cold. Why can't you wait quietly?'

His father's answering:

'Wait? I'm always waiting. Why doesn't he come in?'

'You can speak to him to-morrow morning, instead of making a guy of yourself on the landing.'

'He'll go up to bed, I shouldn't wonder. I shan't sleep.'

'Now come back to bed, James.'

'Um! I might die before to-morrow morning for all you can tell.'

'You shan't have to wait till to-morrow morning; I'll go down and bring him up. Don't fuss!'

'There you go—always so cock-a-hoop. He mayn't come in at all.'

'Well, if he doesn't come in you won't catch him by standing out there in your dressing-gown.'

Soames rounded the last bend and came in sight of his father's tall figure wrapped in a brown silk quilted gown, stooping over the balustrade above. Light fell on his silvery hair and whiskers, investing his head with a sort of halo.

'Here he is!' he heard him say in a voice which sounded injured, and his mother's comfortable answer from the bedroom door:

'That's all right. Come in, and I'll brush your hair.' James extended a thin, crooked finger, oddly like the beckoning of a skeleton, and passed through the doorway of his bedroom.

'What is it?' thought Soames. 'What has he got hold of now?'

His father was sitting before the dressing-table sideways to the mirror, while Emily slowly passed two silver-backed brushes through and through his hair. She would do this several times a day, for it had on him something of the effect produced on a cat by scratching between its ears.

'There you are!' he said. 'I've been waiting.'

Soames stroked his shoulder, and, taking up a silver button hook, examined the mark on it.

'Well,' he said, 'you're looking better.'

James shook his head.

'I want to say something. Your mother hasn't heard.' He announced Emily's ignorance of what he hadn't told her as if it were a grievance.

'Your father's been in a great state all the evening. I'm sure I don't know what about.' The faint 'whish-whish' of the brushes continued the soothing of her voice.

'No! *you* know nothing,' said James. 'Soames can tell me.' And, fixing his grey eyes, in which there was a look of strain, uncomfortable to watch, on his son, he muttered:

'I'm getting on, Soames. At my age, I can't tell. I might die at any time. There'll be a lot of money. There's Rachel and Cicely got no children; and Val's out there—that chap his father will get hold of all he can. And somebody'll pick up Imogen, I shouldn't wonder.'

Soames listened vaguely—he had heard all this before. Whish-whish! went the brushes.

'If that's all—!' said Emily.

'All!' cried James; 'it's nothing. I'm coming to that.' And again his eyes strained pitifully at Soames.

'It's you, my boy,' he said suddenly; 'you ought to get a divorce.'

That word, from those of all lips, was almost too much for Soames's composure. His eyes reconcentrated themselves quickly on the buttonhook, and as if in apology James hurried on:

'I don't know what's become of her—they say she's abroad. Your Uncle Swithin used to admire her—he was a funny fellow.' (So he always alluded to his dead twin—'The Stout and the Lean of it', they had been called.) 'She wouldn't be alone, I should say.' And with that summing-up of the effect of beauty on human nature, he was silent, watching his son with eyes doubting as a bird's. Soames, too, was silent. Whish-whish! went the brushes.

'Come, James! Soames knows best. It's his business.'

'Ah!' said James, and the word came from deep down; 'but there's all my money, and there's his—who's it to go to? And when he dies the name goes out.'

Soames replaced the buttonhook on the lace and pink silk of the dressing-table coverlet.

'The name?' said Emily, 'there are all the other Forsytes.'

'As if that helped *me*,' muttered James. 'I shall be in my grave, and there'll be nobody, unless he marries again.'

'You're quite right,' said Soames quietly; 'I'm getting a divorce.'

James's eyes almost started from his head.

'What?' he cried. 'There! nobody tells me anything.'

'Well,' said Emily, 'who would have imagined you wanted it? My dear boy, that *is* a surprise, after all these years.'

'It'll be a scandal,' muttered James, as if to himself; 'but I can't help that. Don't brush so hard. When'll it come on?'

'Before the Long Vacation; it's not defended.'

James's lips moved in secret calculation. 'I shan't live to see my grandson,' he muttered.

Emily ceased brushing. 'Of course you will, James. Soames will be as quick as he can.'

There was a long silence, till James reached out his arm.

'Here! let's have the eau-de-Cologne,' and, putting it to his nose, he moved his forehead in the direction of his son. Soames bent over and kissed that brow just where the hair began. A relaxing quiver passed over James's face, as though the wheels of anxiety within were running down.

'I'll get to bed,' he said; 'I shan't want to see the papers when that comes. They're a morbid lot; but I can't pay attention to them, I'm too old.'

Queerly affected, Soames went to the door; he heard his father say:

'Here, I'm tired. I'll say a prayer in bed.'

And his mother answering:

'That's right, James; it'll be ever so much more comfy.'

9

OUT OF THE WEB

On Forsyte 'Change the announcement of Jolly's death, among a batch of troopers, caused mixed sensation. Strange to read that Jolyon Forsyte (fifth of the name in direct descent) had died of disease in the service of his country, and not be able to feel it personally. It revived the old grudge against his father for having estranged himself. For such was still the prestige of old Jolyon that the other Forsytes could never quite feel, as might have been expected, that it was they who had cut off his descendants for irregularity. The news increased, of course, the interest and anxiety about Val; but then Val's name was Dartie, and even if he were killed in battle or got the Victoria Cross it would not be at all the same as if his name were Forsyte. Not even casualty or glory to the Haymans would be really satisfactory. Family pride felt defrauded.

How the rumour arose, then, that 'something very dreadful, my dear', was pending, no one, least of all Soames, could tell, secret as he kept everything. Possibly some eye had seen 'Forsyte *v.* Forsyte and Forsyte' in the cause list; and had added it to 'Irene in Paris with a fair beard'. Possibly some wall at Park Lane had ears. The fact remained that it *was* known—whispered among the old, discussed among the young—that family pride must soon receive a blow.

Soames, paying one of his Sunday visits to Timothy's—paying it with the feeling that after the suit came on he would be paying no more—felt knowledge in the air as he came in. Nobody, of course, dared speak of it before him, but each of the four other Forsytes present held their breath, aware that nothing could prevent Aunt Juley from making them all uncomfortable. She looked so piteously at Soames, she checked herself on the point of speech so often that Aunt Hester excused herself and said she must go and bathe Timothy's eye—he had a sty coming. Soames impassive, slightly supercilious, did not stay long. He went out with a curse stifled behind his pale, just smiling lips.

Fortunately for the peace of his mind, cruelly tortured by the coming scandal, he was kept busy day and night with plans for his retirement—for he had come to that grim conclusion. To go on seeing all those people who had known him as a 'long-headed chap', an astute adviser—after *that*—no! The fastidiousness and pride which was so strangely, so inextricably blended in him with possessive obtuseness, revolted against the thought. He would retire, live privately, go on buying pictures, make a great name as a collector–after all, his heart was more in that than it had ever been in Law. In pursuance of this now fixed resolve, he had to get ready to amalgamate his business with another firm without letting people know, for that would excite curiosity and make humiliation cast its shadow before. He had pitched on the firm of Cuthcott, Holliday and Kingson, two of whom were dead. The full name after the amalgamation would therefore be Cuthcott, Holliday, Kingson, Forsyte, Bustard and Forsyte. But after debate as to which of the dead still had any influence with the living, it was decided to reduce the title to Cuthcott, Kingson and Forsyte, of whom Kingson would be the active and Soames the sleeping partner. For leaving his name, prestige, and clients behind him, Soames would receive considerable value.

One night, as befitted a man who had arrived at so important a stage of his career, he made a calculation of what he was worth, and after writing off liberally for depreciation by the war, found his value to be some hundred and thirty thousand pounds. At his father's death, which could not, alas, be delayed much longer, he must come into at least another fifty thousand, and his yearly expenditure at present just reached two. Standing among his pictures, he saw before him a future full of bargains earned by the trained faculty of knowing better than other people. Selling what was about to decline, keeping what was still going up, and exercising judicious insight into future taste, he would make a unique collection, which at his death would pass to the nation under the title 'Forsyte Bequest'.

If the divorce went through, he had determined on his line with Madame Lamotte. She had, he knew, but one real ambition–to live on her *'rentes'* in Paris near her grandchildren. He would buy the goodwill of the Restaurant Bretagne at a fancy price. Madame would live like a queen-mother in Paris on the interest, invested as she would know how. (Incidentally Soames meant to put a capable manager in her place, and make the restaurant pay good interest on his money. There were great possibilities in Soho.) On Annette he would promise to settle fifteen thousand pounds (whether designedly or not), precisely the sum old Jolyon had settled on 'that woman'.

A letter from Jolyon's solicitor to his own had disclosed the fact that 'those two' were in Italy. And an opportunity had been duly given for noting that they had first stayed at an hotel in London. The matter was clear as daylight, and would be disposed of in half an hour or so; but during that half-hour he, Soames, would go down to hell; and after that half-hour all bearers of the Forsyte name would feel the bloom was off the rose. He had no illusions like Shakespeare that roses by any other name would smell as sweet. The name was a possession, a concrete, unstained piece of property, the value of which would be reduced some twenty per cent. at least. Unless it were Roger, who had once refused to stand for Parliament, and–oh, irony!–Jolyon hung on the line, there had never been a distinguished Forsyte. But that very lack of distinction was the name's greatest asset. It was a private name, intensely individual, and his own property; it had never been exploited for good or evil by intrusive report. He and each member of his family owned it wholly, sanely, secretly, without any more interference from the public than had been necessitated by their births, their marriages, their deaths. And during these weeks of waiting and preparing to drop the Law, he conceived for that Law a bitter distaste, so deeply did he resent its coming violation of his name, forced on him by the need he felt to perpetuate that name in a lawful manner. The monstrous injustice of the whole thing excited in him a perpetual suppressed fury. He had asked no better than to live in spotless domesticity, and now he must go into the witness-box, after all these futile, barren years, and proclaim his failure to keep his wife–incur the pity, the amusement, the contempt of his kind. I was all upside down. She and that fellow ought to be the sufferers, and they–were in Italy! In these weeks the Law he had served so faithfully, looked on so reverently as the guardian of all property, seemed to him quite pitiful. What could be more insane than to tell a man that he owned his wife, and punish him when someone unlawfully took her away from him? Did the Law not know that a man's name was to him the apple of his eye, that it was far harder to be regarded as cuckold than as seducer? He actually envied Jolyon the reputation of succeeding where he, Soames, had failed. The question of damages worried him, too. He wanted to make that fellow suffer, but he remembered his cousin's words, 'I shall be very happy,' with the uneasy feeling that to claim damages would make not Jolyon but himself suffer; he felt uncannily that Jolyon would rather like to pay them–the chap was so loose. Besides, to claim damages was not the thing to do. The claim, indeed, had been made almost mechanically; and as the hour drew near Soames saw in it just another dodge of this insensitive and topsy-turvy Law to make him ridiculous; so that people might sneer and say: 'Oh yes, he got quite a good price for her!' And he gave instructions that his counsel should state that the money would be given to a Home for Fallen Women. He was a long time hitting off exactly the right charity; but, having pitched on it, he used to wake up in the night and think: 'It won't do, too lurid; it'll draw attention. Something quieter–better taste.' He did not care for dogs, or he would have named them; and it was in desperation at last–for his knowledge of charities was limited–that he decided on the blind. That could not be inappropriate, and it would make the Jury assess the damages high.

A good many suits were dropping out of the list, which happened to be exceptionally thin that summer, so that his case would be reached before August. As the day grew nearer, Winifred was his only comfort. She showed the fellow-feeling of one who had been through the mill, and was the 'feme-sole' in whom he confided, well knowing that she would not let Dartie into her confidence. That ruffian would be only too rejoiced! At the end of July, on the afternoon before the case, he went in to see her. They had not yet been able to leave town, because Dartie had already spent their summer holiday, and Winifred dared not go to her father for more money while he was waiting not to be told anything about this affair of Soames.

Soames found her with a letter in her hand.

'That from Val?' he asked gloomily. 'What does he say?'

'He says he's married,' said Winifred.

'Whom to, for goodness' sake?'

Winifred looked up at him.

'To Holly Forsyte, Jolyon's daughter.'

'What?'

'He got leave and did it. I didn't even know he knew her. Awkward, isn't it?'

Soames uttered a short laugh at that characteristic minimisation.

'Awkward! Well, I don't suppose they'll hear about this till they come back. They'd better stay out there. That fellow will give her money.'

'But I want Val back,' said Winifred almost piteously; 'I miss him, he helps me to get on.'

'I know,' murmured Soames. 'How's Dartie behaving now?'

'It might be worse; but it's always money. Would you like me to come down to the Court to-morrow Soames?'

Soames stretched out his hand for hers. The gesture so betrayed the loneliness in him that she pressed it between her two.

'Never mind, old boy. You'll feel ever so much better when it's all over.'

'I don't know what I've done,' said Soames huskily; 'I never have. It's all upside down. I was fond of her; I've always been.'

Winifred saw a drop of blood ooze out of his lip, and the sight stirred her profoundly.

'Of course,' she said, 'it's been *too* bad of her all along! But what shall I do about this marriage of Val's, Soames? I don't know how to write to him, with this coming on. You've seen that child. Is she pretty?'

'Yes, she's pretty,' said Soames. 'Dark–lady-like enough.'

'That doesn't sound so bad,' thought Winifred. 'Jolyon had style.'

'It *is* a coil,' she said. 'What will father say?'

'Mustn't be told,' said Soames. 'The war'll soon be over now, you'd better let Val take to farming out there.'

It was tantamount to saying that his nephew was lost.

'I haven't told Monty,' Winifred murmured desolately.

The case was reached before noon next day, and was over in little more than half an hour. Soames–pale, spruce, sad-eyed in the witness-box–had suffered so much beforehand that he took it all like one dead. The moment the decree nisi was pronounced he left the Courts of Justice.

Four hours until he became public property! 'Solicitor's divorce suit!' A surly, dogged anger replaced that dead feeling within him. 'Damn them all!' he thought; 'I won't run away. I'll act as if nothing had happened.' And in the sweltering heat of Fleet Street and Ludgate Hill he walked all the way to his City club, lunched, and went back to his office. He worked there stolidly throughout the afternoon.

On his way out he saw that his clerks knew, and answered their involuntary glances with a look so sardonic that they were immediately withdrawn. In front of St Paul's, he stopped to buy the most gentlemanly of the evening papers. Yes! there he was! 'Well-known solicitor's divorce. Cousin co-respondent. Damages given to the blind'–so, they had got that in! At every other face, he thought: 'I wonder if you know!' And suddenly he felt queer, as if something were racing round in his head.

What was this? He was letting it get hold of him! He mustn't! He would be ill. He mustn't think! He would get down to the river and row about, and fish. 'I'm not going to be laid up,' he thought.

It flashed across him that he had something of importance to do before he went out of town. Madame Lamotte! He must explain the Law. Another six months before he was really free! Only he did not want to see Annette! And he passed his hand over the top of his head–it was very hot.

He branched off through Covent Garden. On this sultry day of late July the garbage-tainted air of the old market offended him, and Soho seemed more than ever the disenchanted home of rapscallionism. Alone, the Restaurant Bretagne, neat, daintily painted, with its blue tubs and the dwarf trees therein, retained an aloof and Frenchified self-respect. It was the slack hour, and pale trim waitresses were preparing the little tables for dinner. Soames went through into the private part. To his discomfiture Annette answered his knock. She, too, looked pale and dragged down by the heat.

'You are quite a stranger,' she said languidly.

Soames smiled.

'I haven't wished to be; I've been busy. Where's your mother, Annette? I've got some news for her.'

'Mother is not in.'

It seemed to Soames that she looked at him in a queer way. What did she know? How much had her mother told her? The worry of trying to make that out gave him an alarming feeling in the head. He gripped the edge of the table, and dizzily saw Annette come forward, her eyes clear with surprise. He shut his own and said:

'It's all right. I've had a touch of the sun, I think.' The sun! What he had was a touch of darkness! Annette's voice, French and composed, said:

'Sit down, it will pass, then.' Her hand pressed his shoulder, and Soames sank into a chair. When the dark feeling dispersed and he opened his eyes, she was looking down at him. What an inscrutable and odd expression for a girl of twenty!

'Do you feel better?'

'It's nothing,' said Soames. Instinct told him that to be feeble before her was not helping him–age was enough handicap without that. Will-power was his fortune with Annette; he had lost ground these latter months from indecision–he could not afford to lose any more. He got up and said:

'I'll write to your mother. I'm going down to my river house for a long holiday. I want you both to come there presently and stay. It's just at its best. You will, won't you?'

'It will be veree nice.' A pretty little roll of that 'r', but no enthusiasm. And rather sadly he added:

'You're feeling the heat, too, aren't you, Annette? It'll do you good to be on the river. Good-night.' Annette swayed forward. There was a sort of compunction in the movement.

'Are you fit to go? Shall I give you some coffee?'

'No,' said Soames firmly. 'Give me your hand.'

She held out her hand, and Soames raised it to his lips. When he looked up, her face wore again that strange expression. 'I can't tell,' he thought as he went out; 'but I mustn't think–I mustn't worry.'

But worry he did, walking towards Pall Mall. English, not of her religion, middle-aged, scarred, as it were, by domestic tragedy, what had he to give her? Only wealth, social position, leisure, admiration! It was much, but was it enough for a beautiful girl of twenty? He felt so ignorant about Annette. He had, too, a curious fear of the French nature of her mother and herself. They knew so well what they wanted. They were almost Forsytes. They would never grasp a shadow and miss a substance!

The tremendous effort it was to write a simple note to Madame Lamotte when he reached his club warned him still further that he was at the end of his tether.

MY DEAR MADAME (he said),

You will see by the enclosed newspaper cutting that I obtained my decree of divorce to-day. By the English law I shall not, however, be free to marry again till the decree is confirmed six months hence. In the meanwhile I have the honour to ask to be considered a formal suitor for the hand of your daughter. I shall write again in a few days and beg you both to come and stay at my river house.

I am, dear Madame,
Sincerely yours,
SOAMES FORSYTE.

Having sealed and posted this letter, he went into the dining-room. Three mouthfuls of soup convinced him that he could not eat; and, causing a cab to be summoned, he drove to Paddington Station and took the first train to Reading. He reached his house just as the sun went down, and wandered out on to the lawn. The air was drenched with the scent of pinks and picotees in his flower borders. A stealing coolness came off the river.

Rest—peace! Let a poor fellow rest! Let not worry and shame and anger chase like evil night-birds in his head! Like those doves perched half sleeping on their dovecot, like the furry creatures in the woods on the far side, and the simple folk in their cottages, like the trees and the river itself, whitening fast in twilight, like the darkening cornflower-blue sky where stars were coming up—let him cease *from himself*, and rest!

IO

PASSING OF AN AGE

The marriage of Soames with Annette took place in Paris on the last day of January, 1901, with such privacy that not even Emily was told until it was accomplished. The day after the wedding he brought her to one of those quiet hotels in London where greater expense can be incurred for less result than anywhere else under heaven. Her beauty in the best Parisian frocks was giving him more satisfaction than if he had collected a perfect bit of china, or a jewel of a picture; he looked forward to the moment when he would exhibit her in Park Lane, in Green Street, and at Timothy's.

If someone had asked him in those days, 'In confidence—are you in love with this girl?' he would have replied: 'In love? What is love? If you mean do I feel to her as I did towards Irene in those old days when I first met her and she would not have me; when I sighed and starved after her and couldn't rest a minute until she yielded—no! If you mean do I admire her youth and prettiness, do my senses ache a little when I see her moving about—yes! Do I think she will keep me straight, make me a creditable wife and a good mother for my children?—again yes! What more do I need?—and what more do three-quarters of the women who are married get from the men who marry them?' And if the enquirer had pursued his query, 'And do you think it was fair to have tempted this girl to give herself to you for life unless you have really touched her heart?' he would have answered: 'The French see these things differently from us. They look at marriage from the point of view of establishments and children; and, from my own experience, I am not at all sure that theirs is not the sensible view. I shall not expect this time more than I can get, or she can give. Years hence I shouldn't be surprised if I have trouble with her; but I shall be getting old, I shall have children by then. I shall shut my eyes. I have had my great passion; hers is perhaps to come—I don't suppose it will be for me. I offer her a great deal, and I don't expect much in return, except children, or at least a son. But one thing I am sure of—she has very good sense!'

And if, insatiate, the enquirer had gone on, 'You do not look, then, for spiritual union in this marriage?' Soames would have lifted his sideway smile and rejoined: 'That's as it may be. If I get satisfaction for my senses, perpetuation of myself, good taste and good humour in the house, it is all I can expect at my age. I am not likely to be going out of my way towards any far-fetched sentimentalism.' Whereon, the enquirer must in good taste have ceased enquiry.

The Queen was dead, and the air of the greatest city upon earth grey with unshed tears. Fur-coated and top-hatted, with Annette beside him in dark furs, Soames crossed Park Lane on the morning of the funeral procession, to the rails in Hyde Park. Little moved though he ever was by public matters, this event, supremely symbolical, this summing-up of a long rich period, impressed his fancy. In '37, when she came to the throne, 'Superior Dosset' was still building houses to make London hideous; and James, a stripling of twenty-six, just laying the foundations of his practice in the Law. Coaches still ran; men wore stocks, shaved their upper lips, ate oysters out of barrels; 'tigers' swung behind cabriolets; women said 'La!' and owned no property; there were manners in the land, and pigsties for the poor; unhappy devils were hanged for little crimes, and Dickens had but just begun to write. Well-nigh two generations had slipped by–of steamboats, railways, telegraphs, bicycles, electric light, telephones, and now these motor-cars–of such accumulated wealth that eight per cent. had become three, and Forsytes were numbered by the thousand! Morals had changed, manners had changed, men had become monkeys twice-removed, God had become Mammon–Mammon so respectable as to deceive himself. Sixty-four years that favoured property, and had made the upper middle-class; buttressed, chiselled, polished it, till it was almost indistinguishable in manners, morals, speech, appearance, habit, and soul from the nobility. An epoch which had gilded individual liberty so that if a man had money, he was free in law and fact, and if he had not money he was free in law and not in fact. An era which had canonised hypocrisy, so that to seem to be respectable was to be. A great Age, whose transmuting influence nothing had escaped save the nature of man and the nature of the Universe.

And to witness the passing of this Age, London–its pet and fancy–was pouring forth her citizens through every gate into Hyde Park, hub of Victorianism, happy hunting-ground of Forsytes. Under the grey heavens, whose drizzle just kept off, the dark concourse gathered to see the show. The 'good old' Queen, full of years and virtue, had emerged from her seclusion for the last time to make a London holiday. From Houndsditch, Acton, Ealing, Hampstead, Battersea, and Fulham; and from those green pastures where Forsytes flourish–Mayfair and Kensington, St James's and Belgravia, Bayswater and Chelsea and the Regent's Park, the people swarmed down on to the roads where death would presently pass with dusky pomp and pageantry. Never again would a queen reign so long, or people have a chance to see so much history buried for their money. A pity the war dragged on, and that the Wreath of Victory could not be laid upon her coffin! All else would be there to follow and commemorate–soldiers, sailors, foreign princes, half-masted bunting, tolling bells, and above all the surging, great, dark-coated crowd, with perhaps a simple sadness here and there deep in hearts beneath black clothes put on by regulation. After all, more than a queen was going to her rest, a woman who had braved sorrow, lived well and wisely according to her lights.

Out in the crowd against the railings, with his arm hooked in Annette's, Soames waited. Yes! the Age was passing! What with this Trade Unionism and Labour fellows in the House of Commons, with Continental fiction, and something in the general feel of everything, not to be expressed in words,

things were very different; he recalled the crowd on Mafeking night, and
George Forsyte saying: 'They're all Socialists, they want our goods.' Like
James, Soames didn't know, he couldn't tell—with Edward on the throne!
Things would never be as safe again as under good old Viccy! Convulsively he
pressed his young wife's arm. There, at any rate, was something substantially
his own, domestically certain again at last; something which made property
worth while—a real thing once more. Pressed close against her and trying to
ward others off, Soames was content. The crowd swayed round them, ate
sandwiches and dropped crumbs; boys who had climbed the plane trees
chattered above like monkeys, threw twigs and orange-peel. It was past time;
they should be coming soon! And, suddenly, a little behind them to the left, he
saw a tallish man with a soft hat and short grizzling beard, and a tallish woman
in a little round fur cap and veil. Jolyon and Irene talking, smiling at each other,
close together like Annette and himself! They had not seen him; and stealthily,
with a very queer feeling in his heart, Soames watched those two. They looked
happy! What had they come here for—inherently illicit creatures, rebels from
the Victorian ideal? What business had they in this crowd? Each of them twice
exiled by morality—making a boast, as it were, of love and laxity! He watched
them fascinated; admitting grudgingly even with his arm thrust through
Annette's—that—that she—Irene—. No! he would *not* admit it; and he turned his
eyes away. He would *not* see them, and let the old bitterness, the old longing
rise up within him! And then Annette turned to him and said; 'Those two
people, Soames; they know you, I am sure. Who are they?'

Soames nosed sideways.

'What people?'

'There, you see them; just turning away. They know you.'

'No,' Soames answered; 'a mistake, my dear.'

'A lovely face! And how she walk! *Elle est très distinguée!*'

Soames looked then. Into his life, out of his life she had walked like
that—swaying and erect, remote, unseizable; ever eluding the contact of his
soul! He turned abruptly from that receding vision of the past.

'You'd better attend,' he said, 'they're coming now!'

But while he stood, grasping her arm, seemingly intent on the head of the
procession, he was quivering with the sense of always missing something, with
instinctive regret that he had not got them both.

Slow came the music and the march, till, in silence, the long line wound in
through the Park Gate. He heard Annette whisper: 'How sad it is and
beautiful!' felt the clutch of her hand as she stood up on tiptoe; and the crowd's
emotion gripped him. There it was—the bier of the Queen, coffin of the Age
slow passing! And as it went by there came a murmuring groan from all the long
line of those who watched, a sound such as Soames had never heard, so
unconscious, primitive, deep and wild, that neither he nor any knew whether
they had joined in uttering it. Strange sound, indeed! Tribute of an age to its
own death. . . . Ah! Ah! . . . The hold on life had slipped. That which had
seemed eternal was gone! The Queen—God bless her!

It moved on with the bier, that travelling groan, as a fire moves on over grass
in a thin line; it kept step, and marched alongside down the dense crowds mile
after mile. It was a human sound, and yet inhuman, pushed out by animal
subconsciousness, by intimate knowledge of universal death and change. None
of us—none of us can hold on for ever!

It left silence for a little—a very little time, till tongues began, eager to retrieve interest in the show. Soames lingered just long enough to gratify Annette, then took her out of the Park to lunch at his father's in Park Lane. . . .

James had spent the morning gazing out of his bedroom window. The last show he would see – last of so many! So she was gone! Well, she was getting an old woman. Swithin and he had seen her crowned – slim slip of a girl, not so old as Imogen! She had got very stout of late. Jolyon and he had seen her married to that German chap, her husband – he had turned out all right before he died, and left her with that son of his. And he remembered the many evenings he and his brothers and their cronies had wagged their heads over their wine and walnuts and that fellow in his salad days. And now he had come to the throne. They said he had steadied down – he didn't know – couldn't tell! He'd make the money fly still, he shouldn't wonder. What a lot of people out there! It didn't seem so very long since he and Swithin stood in the crowd outside Westminster Abbey when she was crowned, and Swithin had taken him to Cremorne afterwards – racketty chap, Swithin; no, it didn't seem much longer ago than Jubilee Year, when he had joined with Roger in renting a balcony in Piccadilly. Jolyon, Swithin, Roger all gone, and he would be ninety in August! And there was Soames married again to a French girl. The French were a queer lot, but they made good mothers, he had heard. Things changed! They said this German Emperor was here for the funeral, his telegram to old Kruger had been in shocking taste. He shouldn't be surprised if that chap made trouble some day. Change! H'm! Well, they must look after themselves when he was gone: he didn't know where he'd be! And now Emily had asked Dartie to lunch, with Winifred and Imogen, to meet Soames's wife – she was always doing something. And there was Irene living with that fellow Jolyon, they said. He'd marry her now, he supposed.

'My brother Jolyon,' he thought, 'what would he have said to it all?' And somehow the utter impossibility of knowing what his elder brother, once so looked up to, would have said, so worried James that he got up from his chair by the window and began slowly, feebly to pace the room.

'She was a pretty thing, too,' he thought; 'I was fond of her. Perhaps Soames didn't suit her – I don't know – I can't tell. We never had any trouble with *our* wives.' Women had changed – everything had changed! And now the Queen was dead – well, there it was! A movement in the crowd brought him to a standstill at the window, his nose touching the pane and whitening from the chill of it. They had got her as far as Hyde Park Corner – they were passing now! Why didn't Emily come up here where she could see, instead of fussing about lunch. He missed her at that moment – missed her! Through the bare branches of the plane trees he could just see the procession, could see the hats coming off the people's heads – a lot of them would catch colds, he shouldn't wonder! A voice behind him said:

'You've got a capital view here, James!'

'*There* you are!' muttered James; 'why didn't you come before? You might have missed it!'

And he was silent, staring with all his might.

'What's that noise?' he asked suddenly.

'There's no noise,' returned Emily; 'what are you thinking of? – they wouldn't cheer.'

'I can hear it.'

'Nonsense, James!'

No sound came through those double panes; what James heard was the groaning in his own heart at the sight of his Age passing.

'Don't you ever tell me where I'm buried,' he said suddenly. 'I shan't want to know.' And he turned from the window. There she went, the old Queen; she'd had a lot of anxiety—she'd be glad to be out of it, he should think!

Emily took up the hair-brushes.

'There'll be just time to brush your head,' she said, 'before they come. You must look your best, James.'

'Ah!' muttered James; 'they say she's pretty.'

The meeting with his new daughter-in-law took place in the dining-room. James was seated by the fire when she was brought in. He placed his hands on the arms of the chair and slowly raised himself. Stooping and immaculate in his frock-coat, thin as a line in Euclid, he received Annette's hand in his; and the anxious eyes of his furrowed face, which had lost its colour now, doubted above her. A little warmth came into them and into his cheeks, refracted from her bloom.

'How are you?' he said. 'You've been to see the Queen, I suppose? Did you have a good crossing?' In this way he greeted her from whom he hoped for a grandson of his name.

Gazing at him, so old, thin, white, and spotless, Annette murmured something in French which James did not understand.

'Yes, yes,' he said, 'you want your lunch, I expect. Soames, ring the bell; we won't wait for that chap Dartie.' But just then they arrived. Dartie had refused to go out of his way to see 'the old girl'. With an early cocktail beside him, he had taken a 'squint' from the smoking-room of the Iseeum, so that Winifred and Imogen had been obliged to come back from the Park to fetch him thence. His brown eyes rested on Annette with a stare of almost startled satisfaction. The second beauty that fellow Soames had picked up! What women could see in him! Well, she would play him the same trick as the other, no doubt; but in the meantime, he was a lucky devil! And he brushed up his moustache, having in nine months of Green Street domesticity regained almost all his flesh and his assurance. Despite the comfortable efforts of Emily, Winifred's composure, Imogen's enquiring friendliness, Dartie's showing-off, and James's solicitude about her food, it was not, Soames felt, a successful lunch for his bride. He took her away soon.

'That Monsieur Dartie,' said Annette in the cab, '*je n'aime pas ce type-là!*'

'No, by George!' said Soames.

'Your sister is veree amiable, and the girl is pretty. Your father is veree old. I think your mother has trouble with him; I should not like to be her.'

Soames nodded at the shrewdness, the clear hard judgment in his young wife; but it disquieted him a little. The thought may have just flashed through him, too: 'When I'm eighty she'll be fifty-five, having trouble with me!'

'There's just one other house of my relations I must take you to,' he said; 'you'll find it funny, but we must get it over; and then we'll dine and go to the theatre.'

In this way he prepared her for Timothy's. But Timothy's was different. They were *delighted* to see dear Soames after this long time; and so this was Annette!

'You are *so* pretty, my dear; almost too young and pretty for dear Soames, aren't you? But he's very attentive and careful—such a good husb—' Aunt Juley checked herself, and placed her lips just under each of Annette's eyes—she afterwards described them to Francie, who dropped in, as: 'Cornflower-blue, so pretty, I quite wanted to kiss them. I must say dear Soames is a perfect connoisseur. In her French way, and not so very French either, I think she's as pretty–though not so distinguished, not so alluring–as Irene. Because she *was* alluring, wasn't she? with that white skin and those dark eyes, and that hair, *couleur de*–what was it? I always forget.'

'*Feuille morte*,' Francie prompted.

'Of course, dead leaves–so strange. I remember when I was a girl, before we came to London, we had a foxhound puppy–to "walk" it was called then; it had a tan top to its head and a white chest, and beautiful dark brown eyes, and it was a lady.'

'Yes, Auntie,' said Francie, 'but I don't see the connection.'

'Oh!' replied Aunt Juley, rather flustered, 'it was so alluring, and her eyes and hair, you know–' She was silent, as if surprised in some indelicacy. '*Feuille morte*,' she added suddenly; 'Hester–do remember that!' . . .

Considerable debate took place between the two sisters whether Timothy should or should not be summoned to see Annette.

'Oh, don't bother!' said Soames.

'But it's no trouble, only of course Annette's being French might upset him a little. He was so scared about Fashoda. I think perhaps we had better not run the risk, Hester. It's nice to have her all to ourselves, isn't it? And how are you, Soames? Have you quite got over your–'

Hester interposed hurriedly:

'What do you think of London, Annette?'

Soames, disquieted, awaited the reply. It came, sensible, composed: 'Oh! I know London, I have visited before.'

He had never ventured to speak to her on the subject of the restaurant. The French had different notions about gentility, and to shrink from connection with it might seem to her ridiculous; he had waited to be married before mentioning it; and now he wished he hadn't.

'And what part do you know best?' asked Aunt Juley.

'Soho,' said Annette simply.

Soames snapped his jaw.

'Soho?' repeated Aunt Juley; 'Soho?'

'That'll go round the family,' thought Soames.

'It's very French, and interesting,' he said.

'Yes,' murmured Aunt Juley, 'your Uncle Roger had some houses there once; he was always having to turn the tenants out, I remember.'

Soames changed the subject to Mapledurham.

'Of course,' said Aunt Juley, 'you will be going down there soon to settle in. We are all so looking forward to the time when Annette has a dear little–'

'Juley!' cried Aunt Hester desperately, 'ring for tea!'

Soames dared not wait for tea, and took Annette away.

'I shouldn't mention Soho if I were you,' he said in the cab. 'It's rather a shady part of London; and you're altogether above that restaurant business now; I mean,' he added, 'I want you to know nice people, and the English are fearful snobs.'

Annette's clear eyes opened; a little smile came on her lips.

'Yes?' she said.

'H'm!' thought Soames, 'that's meant for me!' and he looked at her hard. 'She's got good business instincts,' he thought. 'I must make her grasp it once for all!'

'Look here, Annette! it's very simple, only it wants understanding. Our professional and leisured classes still think themselves a cut above our business classes, except, of course, the very rich. It may be stupid, but there it is, you see. It isn't advisable in England to let people know that you ran a restaurant or kept a shop or were in any kind of trade. It may have been extremely creditable, but it puts a sort of label on you; you don't have such a good time or meet such nice people—that's all.'

'I see,' said Annette; 'it is the same in France.'

'Oh!' murmured Soames, at once relieved and taken aback. 'Of course, class is everything, really.'

'Yes,' said Annette; '*comme vous êtes sage.*'

'That's all right,' thought Soames, watching her lips, 'only she's pretty cynical.' His knowledge of French was not yet such as to make him grieve that she had not said '*tu*'. He slipped his arm round her and murmured with an effort:

'*Et vous êtes ma belle femme.*'

Annette went off into a little fit of laughter.

'*Oh, non!*' she said. '*Oh, non! ne parlez pas français*, Soames. What is that old lady, your aunt, looking forward to?'

Soames bit his lip. 'God knows!' he said; 'she's always saying something;' but he knew better than God.

II

SUSPENDED ANIMATION

The war dragged on. Nicholas had been heard to say that it would cost three hundred millions if it cost a penny before they'd done with it! The income-tax was seriously threatened. Still, there would be South Africa for their money, once for all. And though the possessive instinct felt badly shaken at three o'clock in the morning, it recovered by breakfast-time with the recollection that one gets nothing in this world without paying for it. So, on the whole, people went about their business much as if there were no war, no concentration camps, no slippery de Wet, no feeling on the Continent, no anything unpleasant. Indeed, the attitude of the nation was typified by Timothy's map, whose animation was suspended—for Timothy no longer moved the flags, and they could not move themselves, not even backwards and forwards as they should have done.

Suspended animation went further; it invaded Forsyte 'Change and produced a general uncertainty as to what was going to happen next. The announcement in the marriage column of *The Times*, 'Jolyon Forsyte to Irene, only daughter of the late Professor Heron', had occasioned doubt whether Irene had been justly described. And yet, on the whole, relief was felt that she had not been entered as, 'Irene, late the wife', or 'the divorced wife', of 'Soames Forsyte'. Altogether, there had been a kind of sublimity from the first about the way the family had taken that 'affair'. As James had phrased it: 'There it was!' No use to fuss! Nothing to be had out of admitting that it had been a 'nasty jar'—in the phraseology of the day.

But what would happen now that both Soames and Jolyon were married again! That was very intriguing. George was known to have laid Eustace six to four on a little Jolyon before a little Soames. George was so droll! It was rumoured, too, that he and Dartie had a bet as to whether James would attain the age of ninety, though which of them had backed James no one knew.

Early in May, Winifred came round to say that Val had been wounded in the leg by a spent bullet, and was to be discharged. His wife was nursing him. He would have a little limp–nothing to speak of. He wanted his grandfather to buy him a farm out there where he could breed horses. Her father was giving Holly eight hundred a year, so they could be quite comfortable, because his grandfather would give Val five, he had said; but as to the farm, he didn't know–couldn't tell: he didn't want Val to go throwing away his money.

'But, you know,' said Winifred, 'he must do something.'

Aunt Hester thought that perhaps his dear grandfather was wise, because if he didn't buy a farm it couldn't turn out badly.

'But Val loves horses,' said Winifred. 'It'd be such an occupation for him.'

Aunt Juley thought that horses were very uncertain, had not Montague found them so?

'Val's different,' said Winifred; 'he takes after me.'

Aunt Juley was sure that dear Val was very clever. 'I always remember,' she added, 'how he gave his bad penny to a beggar. His dear grandfather was so pleased. He thought it showed such presence of mind. I remember his saying that he ought to go into the navy.'

Aunt Hester chimed in: Did not Winifred think that it was much better for the young people to be secure and not run any risk at their age?

'Well,' said Winifred, 'if they were in London, perhaps; in London it's amusing to do nothing. But out there, of course, he'll simply get bored to death.'

Aunt Hester thought that it would be nice for him to work, if he were quite sure not to lose by it. It was not as if they had no money. Timothy, of course, had done well by retiring. Aunt Juley wanted to know what Montague had said.

Winifred did not tell her, for Montague had merely remarked: 'Wait till the old man dies.'

At this moment Francie was announced. Her eyes were brimming with a smile.

'Well,' she said, 'what do you think of it?'

'Of what, dear?'

'In *The Times* this morning.'

'We haven't seen it, we always read it after dinner; Timothy has it till then.'

Francie rolled her eyes.

'Do you think you *ought* to tell us?' said Aunt Juley. 'What *was* it?'

'Irene's had a son at Robin Hill.'

Aunt Juley drew in her breath. 'But,' she said, 'they were only married in March!'

'Yes, Auntie; isn't it interesting?'

'Well,' said Winifred, 'I'm glad. I was sorry for Jolyon losing his boy. It might have been Val.'

Aunt Juley seemed to go into a sort of dream.

'I wonder,' she murmured, 'what dear Soames will think? He has so wanted to have a son himself. A little bird has always told me that.'

'Well,' said Winifred, 'he's going to–bar accidents.'

Gladness trickled out of Aunt Juley's eyes.

'How delightful!' she said. 'When?'

'November.'

Such a lucky month! But she did wish it could be sooner. It was a long time for James to wait, at his age!

To wait! They dreaded it for James, but they were used to it themselves. Indeed, it was their great distraction. To wait! For *The Times* to read; for one or other of their nieces or nephews to come in and cheer them up; for news of Nicholas's health; for that decision of Christopher's about going on the stage; for information concerning the mine of Mrs MacAnder's nephew; for the doctor to come about Hester's inclination to wake up early in the morning; for books from the library which were always out; for Timothy to have a cold; for a nice quiet warm day, not too hot, when they could take a turn in Kensington Gardens. To wait, one on each side of the hearth in the drawing-room, for the clock between them to strike; their thin, veined, knuckled hands plying knitting-needles and crochet-hooks, their hair ordered to stop–like Canute's waves–from any further advance in colour. To wait in their black silks or satins for the Court to say that Hester might wear her dark green, and Juley her darker maroon. To wait, slowly turning over and over in their old minds the little joys and sorrows, events and expectancies, of their little family world, as cows chew patient cuds in a familiar field. And this new event was so well worth waiting for. Soames had always been their pet, with his tendency to give them pictures, and his almost weekly visits which they missed so much, and his need for their sympathy evoked by the wreck of his first marriage. This new event–the birth of an heir to Soames–was so important for him, and for his dear father, too, that James might not have to die without some certainty about things. James did so dislike uncertainty; and with Montague, of course, he could not feel really satisfied to leave no grandchildren but the young Darties. After all, one's own name did count! And as James's ninetieth birthday neared they wondered what precautions he was taking. He would be the first of the Forsytes to reach that age, and set, as it were, a new standard in holding on to life. That was so important, they felt, at their ages, eighty-seven and eighty-five; though they did not want to think of themselves when they had Timothy, who was not yet eighty-two, to think of. There was, of course, a better world. 'In my Father's house are many mansions' was one of Aunt Juley's favourite sayings–it always comforted her, with its suggestion of house property, which had made the fortune of dear Roger. The Bible was indeed a great resource, and on *very* fine Sundays there was church in the morning; and sometimes Juley would steal into Timothy's study when she was sure he was out, and just put an open New Testament casually among the books on his little table–he was a great reader, of course, having been a publisher. But she had noticed that Timothy was always cross at dinner afterwards. And Smither had told her more than once that she had picked books off the floor in doing the room. Still, with all that, they did feel that heaven could not be quite so cosy as the rooms in which they and Timothy had been waiting so long. Aunt Hester, especially, could not bear the thought of the exertion. Any change, or rather the thought of a change–for there never *was* any–always upset her very much. Aunt Juley, who had more spirit, sometimes thought it would be quite exciting: she had so enjoyed that visit to Brighton the year dear Susan died. But then Brighton one knew was nice, and it was so difficult to tell what heaven would be like, so on the whole she was more than content to wait.

On the morning of James's birthday, August the 5th, they felt extraordinary animation, and little notes passed between them by the hand of Smither while they were having breakfast in their beds. Smither must go round and take their love and little presents and find out how Mr James was, and whether he had passed a good night with all the excitement. And on the way back would Smither call in at Green Street—it was a little out of her way, but she could take the bus up Bond Street afterwards; it would be a nice little change for her—and ask dear Mrs Dartie to be sure and look in before she went out of town.

All this Smither did—an undeniable servant trained thirty years ago under Aunt Ann to a perfection not now procurable. Mr James, so Mrs James said, had passed an excellent night, he sent his love; Mrs James had said he was very funny and had complained that he didn't know what all the fuss was about. Oh! and Mrs Dartie sent her love, and she would come to tea.

Aunts Juley and Hester, rather hurt that their presents had not received special mention—they forgot every year that James could not bear to receive presents, 'throwing away their money on him', as he always called it—were 'delighted'; it showed that James was in good spirits, and that was so important for him. And they began to wait for Winifred. She came at four, bringing Imogen and Maud, just back from school, and 'getting such a pretty girl, too', so that it was extremely difficult to ask for news about Annette. Aunt Juley, however, summoned courage to enquire whether Winifred had heard anything, and if Soames was anxious.

'Uncle Soames is always anxious, Auntie,' interrupted Imogen; 'he can't be happy now he's got it.'

The words struck familiarly on Aunt Juley's ears. Ah! yes; that funny drawing of George's, which had *not* been shown them! But what did Imogen mean? That her uncle always wanted more than he could have? It was not at all nice to think like that.

Imogen's voice rose clear and clipped:

'Imagine! Annette's only two years older than me; it must be awful for her, married to Uncle Soames.'

Aunt Juley lifted her hands in horror.

'My dear,' she said, 'you don't know what you're talking about. Your Uncle Soames is a match for anybody. He's a very clever man, and good-looking and wealthy, and most considerate and careful, and not at all old, considering everything.'

Imogen, turning her luscious glance from one to the other of the 'old dears', only smiled.

'I hope,' said Aunt Juley quite severely, 'that *you* will marry as good a man.'

'*I* shan't marry a good man, Auntie,' murmured Imogen; 'they're dull.'

'If you go on like this,' replied Aunt Juley, still very much upset, 'you won't marry anybody. We'd better not pursue the subject; and turning to Winifred, she said: 'How is Montague?'

That evening, while they were waiting for dinner, she murmured:

'I've told Smither to get up half a bottle of the sweet champagne, Hester. I think we ought to drink dear James's health, and—and the health of Soames's wife; only let's keep that quite secret. I'll just say like this, "And *you know*, Hester!" and then we'll drink. It might upset Timothy.'

'It's more likely to upset us,' said Aunt Hester. 'But we must, I suppose; for such an occasion.'

'Yes,' said Aunt Juley rapturously, 'it *is* an occasion! Only fancy if he has a dear little boy, to carry the family on! I do feel it so important, now that Irene has had a son. Winifred says George is calling Jolyon 'The Three-Decker', because of his three families, you know! George *is* droll. And fancy! Irene is living after all in the house Soames had built for them both. It does seem hard on dear Soames, and he's always been so regular.'

That night in bed, excited and a little flushed still by her glass of wine and the secrecy of the second toast, she lay with her prayer-book opened flat, and her eyes fixed on a ceiling yellowed by the light from her reading-lamp. Young things! It was so nice for them all! And she would be so happy if she could see dear Soames happy. But, of course, he must be now, in spite of what Imogen had said. He would have all that he wanted: property, and wife, and children! And he would live to a green old age, like his dear father, and forget all about Irene and that dreadful case. If only she herself could be here to buy his children their first rocking-horse! Smither should choose it for her at the stores, nice and dappled. Ah! how Roger used to rock her until she fell off? Oh dear! that was a long time ago! It *was*! 'In my Father's house are many mansions—' A little scrattling noise caught her ear—'but no mice!' she thought mechanically. The noise increased. There! it *was* a mouse! How naughty of Smither to say there wasn't! It would be eating through the wainscot before they knew where they were, and they would have to have the builders in. They were such destructive things! And she lay, with her eyes just moving, following in her mind that little scrattling sound, and waiting for sleep to release her from it.

12

BIRTH OF A FORSYTE

Soames walked out of the garden door, crossed the lawn, stood on the path above the river, turned round and walked back to the garden door, without having realised that he had moved. The sound of wheels crunching the drive convinced him that time had passed and the doctor gone. What, exactly, had he said?

'This is the position, Mr Forsyte. I can make pretty certain of her life if I operate, but the baby will be born dead. If I don't operate, the baby will most probably be born alive, but it's a great risk for the mother—a great risk. In either case, I don't think she can ever have another child. In her state she obviously can't decide for herself, and we can't wait for her mother. It's for you to make the decision, while I'm getting what's necessary. I shall be back within the hour.'

The decision! What a decision! No time to get a specialist down! No time for anything!

The sound of wheels died away, but Soames still stood intent; then, suddenly covering his ears, he walked back to the river. To come before its time like this, with no chance to foresee anything, not even to get her mother here! It was for her mother to make that decision, and she couldn't arrive from Paris till to-night! If only he could have understood the doctor's jargon, the medical niceties, so as to be sure he was weighing the chances properly; but they were Greek to him—like a legal problem to a layman. And yet he *must* decide! He brought his hand away from his brow wet, though the air was chilly. These sounds which came from her room! To go back there would only make it more difficult. He must be calm, clear. On the one hand life, nearly certain, of his young wife, death quite certain, of his child; and—no more children afterwards! On the other, death *perhaps* of his wife, nearly certain life for the child; and—no more children afterwards! Which to choose? ... It had rained this last fortnight—the river was very full, and in the water, collected round the little houseboat moored by his landing-stage, were many leaves from the woods above, brought off by a frost. Leaves fell, lives drifted down! Death! To decide about death! And no one to give him a hand. Life lost was lost for good. Let nothing go that you could keep; for, if it went, you couldn't get it back. It left you bare, like those trees when they lost their leaves; barer and barer until you, too, withered and came down. And, by a queer somersault of thought, he seemed to see not Annette lying up there behind that window-pane on which the sun was shining, but Irene lying in their bedroom in Montpelier Square, as it might conceivably have been her fate to lie, sixteen years ago. Would he have hesitated then. Not a moment! Operate, operate! Make certain of her life! No decision—a mere instinctive cry for help, in spite of his knowledge, even then, that she did not love him! But this! Ah! there was nothing overmastering in his feeling for Annette! Many times these last months, especially since she had been growing frightened, he had wondered. She had a will of her own, was selfish in her French way. And yet—so pretty! What would she wish—to take the risk? 'I know she wants the child,' he thought. 'If it's born dead, and no more chance afterwards—it'll upset her terribly. No more chance! All for nothing! Married life with her for years and years without a child. Nothing to steady her! She's too young. Nothing to look forward to, for her—for me! *For me!*' He struck his hands against his chest! Why couldn't he think without bringing himself in—get out of himself and see what he ought to do? The thought hurt him, then lost edge, as if it had come in contact with a breastplate. Out of oneself! Impossible! Out into soundless, scentless, touchless, sightless space! The very idea was ghastly, futile! And touching there the bed-rock of reality, the bottom of his Forsyte spirit, Soames rested for a moment. When one ceased, all ceased; it might go on, but there'd be nothing in it!

He looked at his watch. In half an hour the doctor would be back. He *must* decide! If against the operation and she died, how face her mother and the doctor afterwards? How face his own conscience? It was *his* child that she was having. If for the operation—then he condemned them both to childlessness. And for what else had he married her but to have a lawful heir? And his father—at death's door, waiting for the news! 'It's cruel!' he thought; 'I ought never to have such a thing to settle! It's cruel!' He turned towards the house. Some deep, simple way of deciding! He took out a coin, and put it back. If he spun it, he knew he would not abide by what came up! He went into the dining-room, farthest away from that room whence the sounds issued. The doctor had said there was a chance. In here that chance seemed greater; the river did not flow, nor the leaves fall. A fire was burning. Soames unlocked the tantalus. He hardly ever touched spirits, but now he poured himself out some whisky and drank it neat, craving a faster flow of blood. 'That fellow Jolyon,' he thought; 'he had children already. He has the woman I really loved; and now a son by her! And I—I'm asked to destroy my only child! Annette *can't* die; it's not possible. She's strong!'

He was still standing sullenly at the sideboard when he heard the doctor's carriage, and went out to him. He had to wait for him to come downstairs.

'Well, doctor?'

'The situation's the same. Have you decided?'

'Yes,' said Soames; 'don't operate?'

'Not? You understand—the risk's great?'

In Soames's set face nothing moved but his lips.

'You said there was a chance?'

'A chance, yes; not much of one.'

'You say the baby *must* be born dead if you do?'

'Yes.'

'Do you still think that in any case she can't have another?'

'One can't be absolutely sure, but it's most unlikely.'

'She's strong,' said Soames; 'we'll take the risk.'

The doctor looked at him very gravely. 'It's on your shoulders.' he said; 'with my own wife, I couldn't.'

Soames's chin jerked up as if someone had hit him.

'Am I of any use up there?' he asked.

'No; keep away.'

'I shall be in my picture-gallery, then; you know where.'

The doctor nodded and went upstairs.

Soames continued to stand, listening. 'By this time to-morrow,' he thought, 'I may have her death on my hands.' No! it was unfair—monstrous, to put it that way! Sullenness dropped on him again, and he went up to the gallery. He stood at the window. The wind was in the north; it was cold, clear; very blue sky, heavy ragged white clouds chasing across; the river blue, too, through the screen of goldening trees; the woods all rich with colour, glowing, burnished—an early autumn. If it were his own life, would he be taking that risk? 'But *she'd* take the risk of losing me,' he thought, 'sooner than lose her child! She doesn't really love me!' What could one expect—a girl and French? The one thing really vital to them both, vital to their marriage and their futures, was a child! 'I've been through a lot for this,' he thought, 'I'll hold on—hold on. There's a chance of keeping both—a chance!' One kept till things were taken—one naturally kept! He began walking round the gallery. He had made one purchase lately which he knew was a fortune in itself, and he halted before it—a girl with dull gold hair which looked like filaments of metal gazing at a little golden monster she was holding in her hand. Even at this tortured moment he could just feel the extraordinary nature of the bargain he had made—admire the quality of the table, the floor, the chair, the girl's figure, the absorbed expression on her face, the dull gold filaments of her hair, the bright gold of the little monster. Collecting pictures; growing richer, richer! What use, if—! He turned his back abruptly on the picture and went to the window. Some of his doves had flown up from their perches round the dovecot, and were stretching their wings in the wind. In the clear sharp sunlight their whiteness almost flashed. They flew far, making a flung-up hieroglyphic against the sky. Annette fed the doves; it was pretty to see her. They took it out of her hand; they knew she was matter-of-fact. A choking sensation came into his throat. She would not—could not die! She was too—too sensible; and she was strong, really strong, like her mother, in spite of her fair prettiness!

It was already growing dark when at last he opened the door, and stood listening. Not a sound! A milky twilight crept about the stairway and the landings below. He had turned back when a sound caught his ear. Peering down, he saw a black shape moving, and his heart stood still. What was it? Death? The shape of Death coming from her door? No! only a maid without cap or apron. She came to the foot of his flight of stairs and said breathlessly:

'The doctor wants to see you, sir.'

He ran down. She stood flat against the wall to let him pass, and said:

'Oh, sir! it's over.'

'Over?' said Soames, with a sort of menace; 'what d'you mean?'

'It's born, sir.'

He dashed up the four steps in front of him and came suddenly on the doctor in the dim passage. The man was wiping his brow.

'Well?' he said; 'quick!'

'Both living, it's all right, I think.'

Soames stood quite still, covering his eyes.

'I congratulate you,' he heard the doctor say; 'it was touch and go.'

Soames let fall the hand which was covering his face.

'Thanks,' he said; 'thanks very much. What is it?'

'Daughter—luckily; a son would have killed her—the head.'

A daughter!

'The utmost care of both,' he heard the doctor say, 'and we shall do. When does the mother come?'

'To-night, between nine and ten, I hope.'

'I'll stay till then. Do you want to see them?'

'Not now,' said Soames; 'before you go. I'll have dinner sent up to you.' And he went downstairs.

Relief unspeakable, and yet—a daughter! It seemed to him unfair. To have taken that risk—to have been through this agony—and what agony!—for a daughter! He stood before the blazing fire of wood logs in the hall, touching it with his toe and trying to readjust himself. 'My father!' he thought. A bitter disappointment, no disguising it! One never got all one wanted in this life! And there was no other—at least, if there was, it was no use!

While he was standing there, a telegram was brought him.

Come up at once, your father sinking fast.—MOTHER.

He read it with a choking sensation. One would have thought he couldn't feel anything after these last hours, but he felt this. Half-past seven, a train from Reading at nine, and madame's train, if she had caught it, came in at eight-forty—he would meet that and go on. He ordered the carriage, ate some dinner mechanically, and went upstairs. The doctor came out to him.

'They're sleeping.'

'I won't go in,' said Soames with relief. 'My father's dying; I have to go up. Is it all right?'

The doctor's face expressed a kind of doubting admiration. 'If they were all as unemotional!' he might have been saying.

'Yes, I think you may go with an easy mind. You'll be down soon?'

'To-morrow,' said Soames. 'Here's the address.'

The doctor seemed to hover on the verge of sympathy.

'Good-night!' said Soames abruptly, and turned away. He put on his fur coat. Death! It was a chilly business. He smoked a cigarette in the carriage—one of his rare cigarettes. The night was windy and flew on black wings; the carriage lights had to search out the way. His father! That old, old man! A comfortless night—to die!

The London train came in just as he reached the station, and Madame Lamotte, substantial, dark-clothed, very yellow in the lamplight, came towards the exit with a dressing-bag.

'This all you have?' asked Soames.

'But yes; I had not the time. How is my little one?'

'Doing well–both. A girl!'

'A girl! What joy! I had a frightful crossing!'

Her black bulk, solid, unreduced by the frightful crossing, climbed into the brougham.

'And you, *mon cher*?'

'My father's dying,' said Soames between his teeth. 'I'm going up. Give my love to Annette.'

'*Tiens!*' murmured Madame Lamotte; '*quel malheur!*'

Soames took his hat off and moved towards his train. 'The French!' he thought.

13

JAMES IS TOLD

A simple cold, caught in the room with double windows, where the air and the people who saw him were filtered, as it were, the room he had not left since the middle of September–and James was in deep waters. A little cold, passing his little strength and flying quickly to his lungs. 'He mustn't catch cold,' the doctor had declared, and he had gone and caught it. When he first felt it in his throat, he had said to his nurse–for he had one now–'There, I knew how it would be, airing the room like that!' For a whole day he was highly nervous about himself and went in advance of all precautions and remedies; drawing every breath with extreme care and having his temperature taken ever hour. Emily was not alarmed.

But next morning when she went in the nurse whispered: 'He won't have his temperature taken.'

Emily crossed to the side of the bed where he was lying, and said softly: 'How do you feel, James?' holding the thermometer to his lips. James looked up at her.

'What's the good of that?' he murmured huskily; 'I don't want to know.'

Then she *was* alarmed. He breathed with difficulty, he looked terribly frail, white, with faint red discolorations. She had 'had trouble' with him, goodness knew; but he was James, had been James for nearly fifty years; she couldn't remember or imagine life without James–James, behind all his fussiness, his pessimism, his crusty shell, deeply affectionate, really kind and generous to them all!

All that day and the next he hardly uttered a word, but there was in his eyes a noticing of everything done for him, a look on his face which told her he was fighting; and she did not lose hope. His very stillness, the way he conserved every little scrap of energy, showed the tenacity with which he was fighting. It touched her deeply; and though her face was composed and comfortable in the sick-room, tears ran down her cheeks when she was out of it.

About tea-time on the third day–she had just changed her dress, keeping her appearance so as not to alarm him, because he noticed everything–she saw a difference. 'It's no use; I'm tired,' was written plainly across that white face, and when she went up to him, he muttered: 'Send for Soames.'

'Yes, James,' she said comfortably; 'all right–at once.' And she kissed his forehead. A tear dropped there, and as she wiped it off she saw that his eyes looked grateful. Much upset, and without hope now, she sent Soames the telegram.

When he entered out of the black windy night, the big house was still as a grave. Warmson's broad face looked almost narrow; he took the fur coat with a sort of added care, saying:

'Will you have a glass of wine, sir?'

Soames shook his head, and his eyebrows made enquiry.

Warmson's lips twitched. 'He's asking for you, sir;' and suddenly he blew his nose. 'It's a long time, sir,' he said, 'that I've been with Mr Forsyte–a long time.'

Soames left him folding the coat and began to mount the stairs. This house, where he had been born and sheltered, had never seemed to him so warm, and rich, and cosy, as during this last pilgrimage to his father's room. It was not his taste; but in its own substantial, lincrusta way it was the acme of comfort and security. And the night was so dark and windy; the grave so cold and lonely!

He paused outside the door. No sound came from within. He turned the handle softly and was in the room before he was perceived. The light was shaded. His mother and Winifred were sitting on the far side of the bed; the nurse was moving away from the near side where was an empty chair. 'For me!' thought Soames. As he moved from the door his mother and sister rose, but he signed with his hand and they sat down again. He went up to the chair and stood looking at his father. James's breathing was as if strangled; his eyes were closed. And in Soames, looking on his father so worn and white and wasted, listening to his strangled breathing, there rose a passionate vehemence of anger against Nature, cruel, inexorable Nature, kneeling on the chest of that wisp of a body, slowly pressing out the breath, pressing out the life of the being who was dearest to him in the world. His father, of all men, had lived a careful life, moderate, abstemious, and this was his reward–to have life slowly, painfully squeezed out of him! And, without knowing that he spoke, he said: 'It's cruel.'

He saw his mother cover her eyes and Winifred bow her face towards the bed. Women! They put up with things so much better than men. He took a step nearer to his father. For three days James had not been shaved, and his lips and chin were covered with hair, hardly more snowy than his forehead. It softened his face, gave it a queer look already not of this world. His eyes opened. Soames went quite close and bent over. The lips moved.

'Here I am, Father.'

'Um–what–what news? They never tell–' the voice died and a flood of emotion made Soames's face work so that he could not speak. Tell him?–yes. But what? He made a great effort, got his lips together and said:

'Good news, dear, good–Annette, a son.'

'Ah!' It was the queerest sound, ugly, relieved, pitiful, triumphant–like the noise a baby makes getting what it wants. The eyes closed, and that strangled sound of breathing began again. Soames recoiled to the chair and stonily sat down. The lie he had told, based, as it were, on some deep, temperamental instinct that after death James would not know the truth, had taken away all power of feeling for the moment. His arm brushed against something. It was his father's naked foot. In the struggle to breathe he had pushed it out from under the clothes. Soames took it in his hand, a cold foot, light and thin, white, very cold. What use to put it back, to wrap up that which must be colder soon! He warmed it mechanically with his hand, listening to his father's laboured breathing; while the power of feeling rose again within him. A little sob, quickly smothered, came from Winifred, but his mother sat unmoving with her eyes fixed on James. Soames signed to the nurse.

'Where's the doctor?' he whispered.

'He's been sent for.'

'Can't you do anything to ease his breathing?'

'Only an injection; and he can't stand it. The doctor said, while he was fighting—'

'He's not fighting,' whispered Soames, 'he's being slowly smothered. It's awful.'

James stirred uneasily, as if he knew what they were saying. Soames rose and bent over him. James feebly moved his two hands and Soames took them.

'He wants to be pulled up,' whispered the nurse.

Soames pulled. He thought he pulled gently, but a look almost of anger passed over James's face. The nurse plumped the pillows. Soames laid the hands down, and bending over kissed his father's forehead. As he was raising himself again, James's eyes bent on him a look which seemed to come from the very depths of what was left within. 'I'm done, my boy,' it seemed to say, 'take care of them, take care of yourself; take care—I leave it all to you.'

'Yes, yes,' Soames whispered, 'yes, yes.'

Behind him the nurse did he knew not what, for his father made a tiny movement of repulsion as if resenting that interference; and almost at once his breathing eased away, became quiet; he lay very still. The strained expression on his face passed, a curious white tranquillity took its place. His eyelids quivered, rested; the whole face rested, at ease. Only by the faint puffing of his lips could they tell that he was breathing. Soames sank back on his chair and fell to cherishing the foot again. He heard the nurse quietly crying over there by the fire; curious that she, a stranger, should be the only one of them who cried! He heard the quiet lick and flutter of the fire flames. One more old Forsyte going to his long rest—wonderful, they were!—wonderful how he had held on! His mother and Winifred were leaning forward, hanging on the sight of James's lips. But Soames bent sideways over the feet, warming them both; they gave him comfort, colder and colder though they grew. Suddenly he started up; a sound, a dreadful sound such as he had never heard, was coming from his father's lips, as if an outraged heart had broken with a long moan. What a strong heart, to have uttered that farewell! It ceased. Soames looked into the face. No motion; no breath! Dead! He kissed the brow, turned round and went out of the room. He ran upstairs to the bedroom, his old bedroom, still kept for him, flung himself face down on the bed, and broke into sobs which he stifled with the pillow. . . .

A little later he went downstairs and passed into the room. James lay alone, wonderfully calm, free from shadow and anxiety, with the gravity on his ravaged face which underlies great age, the worn fine gravity of old coins.

Soames looked steadily at that face, at the fire, at all the room with windows thrown open to the London night.

'Good-bye!' he whispered, and went out.

14

He had much to see to, that night and all next day. A telegram at breakfast reassured him about Annette, and he only caught the last train back to Reading, with Emily's kiss on his forehead and in his ears her words:

'I don't know what I should have done without you, my dear boy.'

He reached his house at midnight. The weather had changed, was mild again, as though, having finished its work and sent a Forsyte to his last account, it could relax. A second telegram, received at dinner-time, had confirmed the good news of Annette, and, instead of going in, Soames passed down through the garden in the moonlight to his houseboat. He could sleep there quite well. Bitterly tired, he lay down on the sofa in his fur coat and fell asleep. He woke soon after dawn and went on deck. He stood against the rail, looking west where the river swept round in a wide curve under the woods. In Soames, appreciation of natural beauty was curiously like that of his farmer ancestors, a sense of grievance if it wasn't there, sharpened, no doubt, and civilised, by his researches among landscape painting. But dawn has power to fertilise the most matter-of-fact vision, and he was stirred. It was another world from the river he knew, under that remote cool light; a world into which man had not entered, an unreal world, like some strange shore sighted by discovery. Its colour was not the colour of convention, was hardly colour at all; its shapes were brooding yet distinct; its silence stunning; it had no scent. Why it should move him he could not tell, unless it were that he felt so alone in it, bare of all relationship and all possessions. Into such a world his father might be voyaging, for all resemblance it had to the world he had left. And Soames took refuge from it in wondering what painter could have done it justice. The white-grey water was like–like the belly of a fish! Was it possible that this world on which he looked was all private property, except the water–and even that was tapped! No tree, no shrub, not a blade of grass, not a bird or beast, not even a fish that was not owned. And once on a time all this was jungle and marsh and water, and weird creatures roamed and sported without human cognisance to give them names; rotting luxuriance had rioted where those tall, carefully planted woods came down to the water, and marsh-misted reeds on that far side had covered all the pasture. Well! they had got it under, kennelled it all up, labelled it, and stowed it in lawyers' offices. And a good thing too! But once in a way, as now, the ghost of the past came out to haunt and brood and whisper to any human who chanced to be awake: 'Out of my unowned loneliness you all came, into it some day you will all return.'

And Soames, who felt the chill and the eeriness of that world–new to him and so very old: the world, unmoved, visiting the scene of its past–went down and made himself tea on a spirit-lamp. When he had drunk it, he took out writing materials and wrote two paragraphs:

'On the 20th instant at his residence in Park Lane, James Forsyte, in his ninety-first year. Funeral at noon on the 24th at Highgate. No flowers by request.'

'On the 20th instant at The Shelter, Mapledurham, Annette, wife of Soames Forsyte, of a daughter.' And underneath on the blotting-paper he traced the word 'son'.

It was eight o'clock in an ordinary autumn world when he went across to the house. Bushes across the river stood round and bright-coloured out of a milky haze; the wood-smoke went up blue and straight; and his doves cooed, preening their feathers in the sunlight.

He stole up to his dressing-room, bathed, shaved, put on fresh linen and dark clothes.

Madame Lamotte was beginning her breakfast when he went down.

She looked at his clothes, said, 'Don't tell me!' and pressed his hand. 'Annette is prettee well. But the doctor say she can never have no more children. You knew that?' Soames nodded. 'It is a pity. *Mais la petite est adorable. Du café?*'

Soames got away from her as soon as he could. She offended him—solid, matter-of-fact, quick, clear—*French*. He could not bear her vowels, her 'r's'; he resented the way she had looked at him, as if it were his fault that Annette could never bear him a son! His fault! He even resented her cheap adoration of the daughter he had not yet seen.

Curious how he jibbed away from sight of his wife and child!

One would have thought he must have rushed up at the first moment. On the contrary, he had a sort of physical shrinking from it—fastidious possessor that he was. He was afraid of what Annette was thinking of him, author of her agonies, afraid of the look of the baby, afraid of showing his disappointment with the present and—the future.

He spent an hour walking up and down the drawing-room before he could screw his courage up to mount the stairs and knock on the door of their room.

Madame Lamotte opened it.

'Ah! At last you come! *Elle vous attend!*' She passed him, and Soames went in with his noiseless step, his jaw firmly set, his eyes furtive.

Annette was very pale and very pretty lying there. The baby was hidden away somewhere; he could not see it. He went up to the bed, and with sudden emotion bent and kissed her forehead.

'Here you are then, Soames,' she said. 'I am not so bad now. But I suffered terribly, terribly. I am glad I cannot have any more. Oh! how I suffered!'

Soames stood silent, stroking her hand; words of endearment, of sympathy, absolutely would not come; the thought passed through him: 'An English girl wouldn't have said that!' At this moment he knew with certainty that he would never be near to her in spirit and in truth, nor she to him. He had collected her—that was all! And Jolyon's words came rushing into his mind: 'I should imagine you will be glad to have your neck out of chancery.' Well, he had got it out! Had he got it in again?

'We must feed you up,' he said, 'you'll soon be strong.'

'Don't you want to see the baby, Soames? She is asleep.'

'Of course,' said Soames, 'very much.'

He passed round the foot of the bed to the other side and stood staring. For the first moment what he saw was much what he had expected to see—a baby. But as he stared and the baby breathed and made little sleeping movements with its tiny features, it seemed to assume an individual shape, grew to be like a picture, a thing he would know again; not repulsive, strangely bud-like and touching. It had dark hair. He touched it with his finger, he wanted to see its eyes. They opened, they were dark—whether blue or brown he could not tell. The eyes winked, stared, they had a sort of sleepy depth in them. And suddenly his heart felt queer, warm, as if elated.

'*Ma petite fleur!*' Annette said softly.

'Fleur,' repeated Soames: 'Fleur! we'll call her that.'

The sense of triumph and renewed possession swelled within him.

By God! this—this thing was *his*!

BOOK III
To Let

TO LET

'From out the fatal loins of those two foes
A pair of star-crossed lovers take their life.'

Romeo and Juliet

TO CHARLES SCRIBNER

PART I

I

ENCOUNTER

Soames Forsyte emerged from the Knightsbridge Hotel, where he was staying, in the afternoon of the 12th of May, 1920, with the intention of visiting a collection of pictures in a Gallery off Cork Street, and looking into the Future. He walked. Since the war, he never took a cab if he could help it. Their drivers were, in his view, an uncivil lot, though now that the war was over and supply beginning to exceed demand again, getting more civil in accordance with the custom of human nature. Still, he had not forgiven them, deeply identifying them with gloomy memories and now, dimly, like all members of their class, with revolution. The considerable anxiety he had passed through during the war, and the more considerable anxiety he had since undergone in the peace, had produced psychological consequences in a tenacious nature. He had, mentally, so frequently experienced ruin that he had ceased to believe in its material probability. Paying away four thousand a year in income and super tax, one could not very well be worse off! A fortune of a quarter of a million, encumbered only by a wife and one daughter, and very diversely invested, afforded substantial guarantee even against that 'wildcat notion'—a levy on capital. And as to confiscation of war profits, he was entirely in favour of it, for he had none, and 'serve the beggars right'! The price of pictures, moreover, had, if anything, gone up, and he had done better with his collection since the war began than ever before. Air-raids, also, had acted beneficially on a spirit congenitally cautious, and hardened a character already dogged. To be in danger of being entirely dispersed inclined one to be less apprehensive of the more partial dispersions involved in levies and taxation, while the habit of condemning the impudence of the Germans had led naturally to condemning that of Labour, if not openly at least in the sanctuary of his soul.

He walked. There was, moreover, time to spare, for Fleur was to meet him at the Gallery at four o'clock, and it was as yet but half-past two. It was good for him to walk—his liver was a little constricted, and his nerves rather on edge. His wife was always out when she was in Town, and his daughter *would* flibberty-gibbet all over the place like most young women since the war. Still, he must be thankful that she had been too young to do anything in that war itself. Not, of course, that he had not supported the war from its inception, with all his soul, but between that and supporting it with the bodies of his wife and daughter, there had been a gap fixed by something old-fashioned within him which abhorred emotional extravagance. He had, for instance, strongly objected to Annette, so attractive, and in 1914 only thirty-four, going to her native France, her '*chère patrie*' as, under the stimulus of war, she had begun to call it, to nurse her '*braves poilus*', forsooth! Ruining her health and her looks! As if she were really a nurse! He had put a stopper on it. Let her do needlework for them at home, or knit! She had not gone, therefore, and had never been quite the same woman since. A bad tendency of hers to mock at him, not openly, but in continual little ways, had grown. As for Fleur, the war had resolved the vexed problem whether or not she should go to school. She was better away from her mother in her war mood, from the chance of air-raids, and the impetus to do extravagant things; so he had placed her in a seminary as far West as had seemed to him compatible with excellence, and had missed her horribly. Fleur! He had never regretted the somewhat outlandish name by which at her birth he had decided so suddenly to call her—marked concession though it had been to the French. Fleur! A pretty name—a pretty child! But restless—too restless; and wilful! Knowing her power, too, over her father! Soames often reflected on the mistake it was to dote on his daughter. To get old and dote! Sixty-five! He was getting on; but he didn't feel it, for, fortunately, perhaps, considering Annette's youth and good looks, his second marriage had turned out a cool affair. He had known but one real passion in his life—for that first wife of his—Irene. Yes, and that fellow, his cousin Jolyon, who had gone off with her, was looking very shaky, they said. No wonder, at seventy-two, after twenty years of a third marriage!

Soames paused a moment in his march to lean over the railings of the Row. A suitable spot for reminiscence, half-way between that house in Park Lane which had seen his birth and his parents' deaths, and the little house in Montpelier Square where thirty-five years ago he had enjoyed his first edition of matrimony. Now, after twenty years of his second edition, that old tragedy seemed to him like a previous existence—which had ended when Fleur was born in place of the son he had hoped for. For many years he had ceased regretting, even vaguely, the son who had not been born; Fleur filled the bill in his heart. After all, she bore his name, and he was not looking forward at all to the time when she would change it. Indeed, if he ever thought of such a calamity, it was seasoned by the vague feeling that he could make her rich enough to purchase perhaps and extinguish the name of the fellow who married her—why not, since, as it seemed, women were equal to men nowadays? And Soames, secretly convinced that they were not, passed his curved hand over his face vigorously till it reached the comfort of his chin. Thanks to abstemious habits, he had not grown fat and flabby; his nose was pale and thin, his grey moustache close-clipped, his eyesight unimpaired. A slight stoop closened and corrected the expansion given to his face by the heightening of his forehead in the recession of his grey hair. Little change had Time wrought in the 'warmest' of the young Forsytes, as the last of the old Forsytes—Timothy—now in his hundred and first year, would have phrased it.

The shade from the plane trees fell on his neat Homburg hat; he had given up top hats—it was no use attracting attention to wealth in days like these. Plane trees! His thoughts travelled sharply to Madrid—the Easter before the war, when, having to make up his mind about that Goya picture, he had taken a voyage of discovery to study the painter on his spot. The fellow had impressed him—great range, real genius! Highly as the chap ranked, he would rank even higher before they had finished with him. The second Goya craze would be greater even than the first; oh, yes! And he had bought. On that visit he had—as never before—commissioned a copy of a fresco painting called 'La Vendimia', wherein was the figure of a girl with an arm akimbo, who had reminded him of his daughter. He had it now in the Gallery at Mapledurham, and rather poor it was–you couldn't copy Goya. He would still look at it, however, if his daughter were not there, for the sake of something irresistibly reminiscent in the light, erect balance of the figure, the width between the arching eyebrows, the eager dreaming of the dark eyes. Curious that Fleur should have dark eyes, when his own were grey–no pure Forsyte had brown eyes–and her mother's blue! But of course her grandmother Lamotte's eyes were dark as treacle!

He began to walk on again towards Hyde Park Corner. No greater change in all England than in the Row! Born almost within hail of it, he could remember it from 1860 on. Brought there as a child between the crinolines to stare at tight-trousered dandies in whiskers, riding with a cavalry seat; to watch the doffing of curly-brimmed and white top hats; the leisurely air of it all, and the little bow-legged man in a long red waistcoat who used to come among the fashion with dogs on several strings and try to sell one to his mother: King Charles spaniels, Italian greyhounds, affectionate to her crinoline–you never saw them now. You saw no quality of any sort, indeed, just working people sitting in dull rows with nothing to stare at but a few young bouncing females in pot hats, riding astride, or desultory Colonials charging up and down on dismal-looking hacks; with, here and there, little girls on ponies, or old gentlemen jogging their livers, or an orderly trying a great galumphing cavalry horse; no thoroughbreds, no grooms, no bowing, no scraping, no gossip–nothing; only the trees the same–the trees indifferent to the generations and declensions of mankind. A democratic England–dishevelled, hurried, noisy, and seemingly without an apex. And that something fastidious in the soul of Soames turned over within him. Gone forever, the close borough of rank and polish! Wealth there was–oh, yes! wealth–he himself was a richer man than his father had ever been; but manners, flavour, quality, all gone, engulfed in one vast, ugly, shoulder-rubbing, petrol-smelling Cheerio. Little half-beaten pockets of gentility and caste lurking here and there, dispersed and *chétif*, as Annette would say; but nothing ever again firm and coherent to look up to. And into this new hurly-burly of bad manners and loose morals his daughter–flower of his life–was flung! And when those Labour chaps got power–if they ever did–the worst was yet to come!

He passed out under the archway, at last no longer–thank goodness!–disfigured by the gun-grey of its searchlight. 'They'd better put a searchlight on to where they're all going,' he thought, 'and light up their precious democracy!' And he directed his steps along the club fronts of Piccadilly. George Forsyte, of course, would be sitting in the bay window of the Iseeum. The chap was so big now that he was there nearly all his time, like some immovable, sardonic, humorous eye noting the decline of men and things. And Soames hurried, ever constitutionally uneasy beneath his cousin's glance. George, who, as he had heard, had written a letter signed 'Patriot' in the middle of the War, complaining of the Government's hysteria in docking the oats of race-horses. Yes, there he was, tall, ponderous, neat, clean-shaven, with his smooth hair, hardly thinned, smelling, no doubt, of the best hair-wash, and a pink paper in his hand. Well, *he* didn't change! And for perhaps the first time in his life Soames felt a kind of sympathy tapping in his waistcoat for that sardonic kinsman. With his weight, his perfectly parted hair, and bull-like gaze, he was a guarantee that the old order would take some shifting yet. He saw George move the pink paper as if inviting him to ascend–the chap must want to ask something about his property. It was still under Soames's control; for in the adoption of a sleeping partnership at that painful period twenty years back when he had divorced Irene, Soames had found himself almost insensibly retaining control of all purely Forsyte affairs.

Hesitating for just a moment, he nodded and went in. Since the death of his brother-in-law Montague Dartie, in Paris, which no one had quite known what to make of, except that it was certainly not suicide—the Iseeum Club had seemed more respectable to Soames. George, too, he knew, had sown the last of his wild oats, and was committed definitely to the joys of the table, eating only of the very best so as to keep his weight down, and owning, as he said, 'just one or two old screws to give me an interest in life.' He joined his cousin, therefore, in the bay window without the embarrassing sense of indiscretion he had been used to feel up there. George put out a well-kept hand.

'Haven't seen you since the War,' he said. 'How's your wife?'

'Thanks,' said Soames coldly, 'well enough.'

Some hidden jest curved, for a moment, George's fleshy face, and gloated from his eye.

'That Belgian chap, Profond,' he said, 'is a member here now. He's a rum customer.'

'Quite!' muttered Soames. 'What did you want to see me about?'

'Old Timothy; he might go off the hooks at any moment. I suppose he's made his Will.'

'Yes.'

'Well, you or somebody ought to give him a look up—last of the old lot; he's a hundred, you know. They say he's like a mummy. Where are you goin' to put him? He ought to have a pyramid by rights.'

Soames shook his head. 'Highgate, the family vault.'

'Well, I suppose the old girls would miss him, if he was anywhere else. They say he still takes an interest in food. He might last on, you know. Don't we *get* anything for the old Forsytes? Ten of them—average age eighty-eight—I worked it out. That ought to be equal to triplets.'

'Is that all?' said Soames. 'I must be getting on.'

'You unsociable devil,' George's eyes seemed to answer. 'Yes, that's all: Look him up in his mausoleum—the old chap might want to prophesy.' The grin died on the rich curves of his face, and he added: 'Haven't you attorneys invented a way yet of dodging this damned income tax? It hits the fixed inherited income like the very deuce. I used to have two thousand five hundred a year; now I've got a beggarly fifteen hundred, and the price of living doubled.'

'Ah!' murmured Soames, 'the turf's in danger.'

Over George's face moved a gleam of sardonic self-defence.

'Well,' he said, 'they brought me up to do nothing, and here I am in the sere and yellow, getting poorer every day. These Labour chaps mean to have the lot before they've done. What are you going to do for a living when it comes? I shall work a six-hour day teaching politicians how to see a joke. Take my tip, Soames; go into Parliament, make sure of your four hundred—and employ me.'

And, as Soames retired, he resumed his seat in the bay window.

Soames moved along Piccadilly deep in reflections excited by his cousin's words. He himself had always been a worker and a saver, George always a drone and a spender; and yet, if confiscation once began, it was he—the worker and the saver—who would be looted! That was the negation of all virtue, the overturning of all Forsyte principles. Could civilisation be built on any other?

He did not think so. Well, they wouldn't confiscate his pictures, for they wouldn't know their worth. But what would they be worth, if these maniacs once began to milk capital? A drug on the market. 'I don't care about myself,' he thought; 'I could live on five hundred a year, and never know the difference, at my age.' But Fleur! This fortune, so wisely invested, these treasures so carefully chosen and amassed, were all for her. And if it should turn out that he couldn't give or leave them to her—well, life had no meaning, and what was the use of going in to look at this crazy, futuristic stuff with the view of seeing whether it had any future?

Arriving at the Gallery off Cork Street, however, he paid his shilling, picked up a catalogue, and entered. Some ten persons were prowling round. Soames took steps and came on what looked to him like a lamp-post bent by collision with a motor omnibus. It was advanced some three paces from the wall, and was described in his catalogue as 'Jupiter'. He examined it with curiosity, having recently turned some of his attention to sculpture. 'If that's Jupiter,' he thought, 'I wonder what Juno's like.' And suddenly he saw her, opposite. She appeared to him like nothing so much as a pump with two handles, lightly clad in snow. He was still gazing at her, when two of the prowlers halted on his left. '*Epatant!*' he heard one say.

'Jargon!' growled Soames to himself.

The other's boyish voice replied:

'Missed it, old bean; he's pulling your leg. When Jove and Juno created he them, he was saying: "I'll see how much these fools will swallow." And they've lapped up the lot.'

'You young duffer! Vospovitch is an innovator. Don't you see that he's brought satire into sculpture? The future of plastic art, of music, painting, and even architecture, has set in satiric. It was bound to. People are tired—the bottom's tumbled out of sentiment.'

'Well, I'm quite equal to taking a little interest in beauty. I was through the War. You've dropped your handkerchief, sir.'

Soames saw a handkerchief held out in front of him. He took it with some natural suspicion, and approached it to his nose. It had the right scent—of distant eau-de-Cologne—and his initials in a corner. Slightly reassured he raised his eyes to the young man's face. It had rather fawn-like ears, a laughing mouth, with half a toothbrush growing out of it on each side, and small lively eyes, above a normally dressed appearance.

'Thank you,' he said; and moved by a sort of irritation, added: 'Glad to hear you like beauty; that's rare, nowadays.'

'I dote on it,' said the young man; 'but you and I are the last of the old guard, sir.'

Soames smiled.

'If you really care for pictures,' he said, 'here's my card. I can show you some quite good ones any Sunday, if you're down the river and care to look in.'

'Awfully nice of you, sir. I'll drop in like a bird. My name's Mont—Michael.' And he took off his hat.

Soames, already regretting his impulse, raised his own slightly in response, with a downward look at the young man's companion, who had a purple tie, dreadful little slug-like whiskers, and a scornful look—as if he were a poet!

It was the first indiscretion he had committed for so long that he went and sat down in an alcove. What had possessed him to give his card to a rackety young fellow, who went about with a thing like that? And Fleur, always at the back of his thoughts, started out like a filigree figure from a clock when the hour strikes. On the screen opposite the alcove was a large canvas with a great many square tomato-coloured blobs on it, and nothing else, so far as Soames could see from where he sat. He looked at his catalogue:

'No. 32–"The Future Town"–Paul Post.' 'I suppose that's satiric too,' he thought. 'What a thing!' But his second impulse was more cautious. It did not do to condemn hurriedly. There had been those stripey, streaky creations of Monet's, which had turned out such trumps; and then the stippled school; and Gauguin. Why, even since the Post-Impressionists there had been one or two painters not to be sneezed at. During the thirty-eight years of his connoisseur's life, indeed, he had marked so many 'movements', seen the tides of taste and technique so ebb and flow, that there was really no telling anything except that there was money to be made out of every change of fashion. This too might quite well be a case where one must subdue primordial instinct, or lose the market. He got up and stood before the picture, trying hard to see it with the eyes of other people. Above the tomato blobs was what he took to be a sunset, till someone passing said: 'He's got the airplanes wonderfully, don't you think?' Below the tomato blobs was a band of white with vertical black stripes, to which he could assign no meaning whatever, till someone else came by, murmuring: 'What expression he gets with his foreground!' Expression! Of what? Soames went back to his seat. The thing was 'rich', as his father would have said, and he wouldn't give a damn for it. Expression! Ah! they were all Expressionists now, he had heard, on the Continent. So it was coming here too, was it? He remembered the first wave of influenza in 1887–or 8–hatched in China, so they said. He wondered where this–this Expressionism–had been hatched. The thing was a regular disease!

He had become conscious of a woman and a youth standing between him and the 'Future Town'. Their backs were turned; but very suddenly Soames put his catalogue before his face, and drawing his hat forward, gazed through the slit between. No mistaking that back, elegant as ever though the hair above had gone grey. Irene! His divorced wife–Irene! And this, no doubt, was her son–by that fellow Jolyon Forsyte–their boy, six months older than his own girl! And mumbling over in his mind the bitter days of his divorce, he rose to get out of sight, but quickly sat down again. She had turned her head to speak to her boy; her profile was still so youthful that it made her grey hair seem powdery, as if fancy-dressed; and her lips were smiling as Soames, first possessor of them, had never seen them smile. Grudgingly he admitted her still beautiful, and in figure almost as young as ever. And how that boy smiled back at her! Emotion squeezed Soames's heart. The sight infringed his sense of justice. He grudged her that boy's smile–it went beyond what Fleur gave him, and it was undeserved. Their son might have been his son; Fleur might have been her daughter, if she had kept straight! He lowered his catalogue. If she saw him, all the better! A reminder of her conduct in the presence of her son, who probably knew nothing of it, would be a salutary touch from the finger of that Nemesis which surely must soon or late visit her! Then, half-conscious that such a thought was extravagant for a Forsyte of his age, Soames took out his watch. Past four! Fleur was late. She had gone to his niece Imogen Cardigan's, and there they would keep her smoking cigarettes and gossiping, and that. He heard the boy laugh, and say eagerly: 'I say, Mum, is this by one of Auntie June's lame ducks?'

'Paul Post–I believe it is, darling.'

The word produced a little shock in Soames; he had never heard her use it. And then she saw him. His eyes must have had in them something of George Forsyte's sardonic look; for her gloved hand crisped the folds of her frock, her eyebrows rose, her face went stony. She moved on.

'It *is* a caution,' said the boy, catching her arm again.

Soames stared after them. That boy was good-looking, with a Forsyte chin, and eyes deep-grey, deep in; but with something sunny, like a glass of old sherry spilled over him; his smile perhaps, his hair. Better than they deserved–those two! They passed from his view into the next room, and Soames continued to regard the Future Town, but saw it not. A little smile snarled up his lips. He was despising the vehemence of his own feelings after all these years. Ghosts! And yet as one grew old–was there anything but what was ghost-like left? Yes, there was Fleur! He fixed his eyes on the entrance. She was due; but she would keep him waiting, of course! And suddenly he became aware of a sort of human breeze–a short, slight form clad in a sea-green djibbah with a metal belt and a fillet binding unruly red-gold hair all streaked with grey. She was talking to the Gallery attendants, and something familiar riveted his gaze–in her eyes, her chin, her hair, her spirit–something which suggested a thin Skye terrier just before its dinner. Surely June Forsyte! His cousin June–and coming straight to his recess! She sat down beside him, deep in thought, took out a tablet, and made a pencil note. Soames sat unmoving. A confounded thing cousinship! 'Disgusting!' he heard her murmur; then, as if resenting the presence of an overhearing stranger, she looked at him. The worst had happened.

'Soames!'

Soames turned his head a very little.

'How are *you*?' he said. 'Haven't seen you for twenty years.'

'No. Whatever made *you* come here?'

'My sins,' said Soames. 'What stuff!'

'Stuff? Oh, yes–of course; it hasn't *arrived* yet.'

'It never will,' said Soames; 'it must be making a dead loss.'

'Of course it is.'

'How d'you know?'

'It's my Gallery.'

Soames sniffed from sheer surprise.

'Yours? What on earth makes you run a show like this?'

'*I* don't treat Art as if it were grocery.'

Soames pointed to the Future Town. 'Look at that! Who's going to live in a town like that, or with it on his walls!'

June contemplated the picture for a moment. 'It's a vision,' she said.

'The deuce!'

There was silence, then June rose. 'Crazy-looking creature!' he thought.

'Well,' he said, 'you'll find your young stepbrother here with a woman I used to know. If you take my advice, you'll close this exhibition.'

June looked back at him. 'Oh! You Forsyte!' she said, and moved on. About her light, fly-away figure, passing so suddenly away, was a look of dangerous decisions. Forsyte! Of course he was a Forsyte! And so was she! But from the time when, as a mere girl, she brought Bosinney into his life to wreck it, he had never hit it off with June–and never would! And here she was, unmarried to this day, owning a Gallery! . . . And suddenly it came to Soames how little he knew now of his own family. The old aunts at Timothy's had been dead so many years; there was no clearing-house for news. What had they all done in the War? Young Roger's boy had been wounded, St John Hayman's second son killed; young Nicholas's eldest had got an O.B.E., or whatever they gave them. They had all joined up somehow, he believed. That boy of Jolyon's and Irene's, he supposed, had been too young; his own generation, of course, too old, though Giles Hayman had driven a car for the Red Cross–and Jesse Hayman been a special constable–those 'Dromios' had always been of a sporting type! As for himself, he had given a motor ambulance, read the papers till he was sick of them, passed through much anxiety, bought no clothes, lost seven pounds in weight; he didn't know what more he could have done at his age. Indeed, thinking it over, it struck him that he and his family had taken this war very differently to that affair with the Boers, which had been supposed to tax all the resources of the Empire. In that old war, of course, his nephew Val Dartie had been wounded, that fellow Jolyon's first son had died of enteric, 'the Dromios' had gone out on horses, and June had been a nurse; but all that had seemed in the nature of a portent, while in *this* war everybody had done 'their bit', so far as he could make out, as a matter of course. It seemed to show the growth of something or other–or perhaps the decline of something else. Had the Forsytes become less individual, or more Imperial, or less provincial? Or was it simply that one hated Germans? . . . Why didn't Fleur come, so that he could get away? He saw those three return together from the other room and pass back along the far side of the screen. The boy was standing before the Juno now. And, suddenly, on the other side of her, Soames saw–his daughter, with eyebrows raised, as well they might be. He could see her eyes glint sideways at the boy, and the boy look back at her. Then Irene slipped her hand through his arm, and drew him on. Soames saw him glancing round, and Fleur looking after them as the three went out.

A voice said cheerfully: 'Bit thick, isn't it?'

The young man who had handed him his handkerchief was again passing. Soames nodded.

'I don't know what we're coming to.'

'Oh! That's all right, sir,' answered the young man cheerfully; 'they don't either.'

Fleur's voice said: 'Hullo, Father! Here you are!' precisely as if he had been keeping her waiting.

The young man, snatching off his hat, passed on.

'Well,' said Soames, looking her up and down, 'you're a punctual sort of young woman!'

This treasured possession of his life was of medium height and colour, with short, dark-chestnut hair; her wide-apart brown eyes were set in whites so clear that they glinted when they moved, and yet in repose were almost dreamy under very white, black-lashed lids, held over them in a sort of suspense. She had a charming profile, and nothing of her father in her face save a decided chin. Aware that his expression was softening as he looked at her, Soames frowned to preserve the unemotionalism proper to a Forsyte. He knew she was only too inclined to take advantage of his weakness.

Slipping her hand under his arm, she said:

'Who was that?'

'He picked up my handkerchief. We talked about the pictures.'

'You're not going to buy *that*, Father?'

'No,' said Soames grimly; 'nor that Juno you've been looking at.'

Fleur dragged at his arm. 'Oh! Let's go! It's a ghastly show.'

In the doorway they passed the young man called Mont and his partner. But Soames had hung out a board marked 'Trespassers will be prosecuted', and he barely acknowledged the young fellow's salute.

'Well,' he said in the street, 'whom did you meet at Imogen's?'

'Aunt Winifred, and that Monsieur Profond.'

'Oh!' muttered Soames; 'that chap! What does your aunt see in him?'

'I don't know. He looks pretty deep–mother says she likes him.'

Soames grunted.

'Cousin Val and his wife were there, too.'

'What!' said Soames. 'I thought they were back in South Africa.'

'Oh, no! They've sold their farm. Cousin Val is going to train race-horses on the Sussex Downs. They've got a jolly old manorhouse; they asked me down there.'

Soames coughed: the news was distasteful to him. 'What's his wife like now?'

'Very quiet, but nice, I think.'

Soames coughed again. 'He's a rackety chap, your Cousin Val.'

'Oh! no, Father; they're awfully devoted. I promised to go–Saturday to Wednesday next.'

'Training race-horses!' said Soames. It was bad enough, but not the reason for his distaste. Why the deuce couldn't his nephew have stayed out in South Africa? His own divorce had been bad enough, without his nephew's marriage to the daughter of the co-respondent; a half-sister too of June, and of that boy whom Fleur had just been looking at from under the pump-handle. If he didn't look out, she would come to know all about that old disgrace! Unpleasant things! They were round him this afternoon like a swarm of bees!

'I don't like it!' he said.

'I want to see the race-horses,' murmured Fleur; 'and they've promised I shall ride. Cousin Val can't walk much, you know; but he can ride perfectly. He's going to show me their gallops.'

'Racing!' said Soames. 'It's a pity the War didn't knock that on the head. He's taking after his father, I'm afraid.'

'I don't know anything about his father.'

'No,' said Soames, grimly. 'He took an interest in horses and broke his neck in Paris, walking downstairs. Good riddance for your aunt.' He frowned, recollecting the inquiry into those stairs which he had attended in Paris six years ago, because Montague Dartie could not attend it himself–perfectly normal stairs in a house where they played baccarat. Either his winnings or the way he had celebrated them had gone to his brother-in-law's head. The French procedure had been very loose; he had had a lot of trouble with it.

A sound from Fleur distracted his attention. 'Look! The people who were in the Gallery with us.'

'What people?' muttered Soames, who knew perfectly well.

'I think that woman's beautiful.'

'Come into this pastry-cook's,' said Soames abruptly, and tightening his grip on her arm he turned into a confectioner's. It was–for him–a surprising thing to do, and he said rather anxiously: 'What will you have?'

'Oh! I don't want anything. I had a cocktail and a tremendous lunch.'

'We *must* have something now we're here,' muttered Soames, keeping hold of her arm.

'Two teas,' he said; 'and two of those nougat things.'

But no sooner was his body seated than his soul sprang up. Those three – those three were coming in! He heard Irene say something to her boy, and his answer:

'Oh! no, Mum; this place is all right. My stunt.' And the three sat down.

At that moment, most awkward of his existence, crowded with ghosts and shadows from his past, in presence of the only two women he had ever loved – his divorced wife and his daughter by her successor – Soames was not so much afraid of *them* as of his cousin June. She might make a scene – she might introduce those two children – she was capable of anything. He bit too hastily at the nougat, and it stuck to his plate. Working at it with his finger, he glanced at Fleur. She was masticating dreamily, but her eyes were on the boy. The Forsyte in him said: 'Think, feel, and you're done for!' And he wiggled his finger desperately. Plate! Did Jolyon wear a plate? Did that woman wear a plate? Time had been when he had seen her wearing nothing! That was something, anyway, which had never been stolen from him. And she knew it, though she might sit there calm and self-possessed, as if she had never been his wife. An acid humour stirred in his Forsyte blood; a subtle pain divided by hair's-breadth from pleasure. If only June did not suddenly bring her hornets about his ears! The boy was talking.

'Of course, Auntie June' – so he called his half-sister 'Auntie' did he? – well, she must be fifty, if she was a day! – 'it's jolly good of you to encourage them. Only – hang it all!' Soames stole a glance. Irene's startled eyes were bent watchfully on her boy. She – she had these devotions – for Bosinney – for that boy's father – for this boy! He touched Fleur's arm, and said:

'Well, have you had enough?'

'One more, Father, please.'

She would be sick! He went to the counter to pay. When he turned round again he saw Fleur standing near the door, holding a handkerchief which the boy had evidently just handed to her.

'F.F.,' he heard her say. 'Fleur Forsyte – it's mine all right. Thank you ever so.'

Good God! She had caught the trick from what he'd told her in the Gallery – monkey!

'Forsyte? Why – that's my name too. Perhaps we're cousins.'

'Really! We must be. There aren't any others. I live at Mapledurham; where do you?'

'Robin Hill.'

Question and answer had been so rapid that all was over before he could lift a finger. He saw Irene's face alive with startled feeling, gave the slightest shake of his head, and slipped his arm through Fleur's.

'Come along!' he said.

She did not move.

'Didn't you hear, Father? Isn't it queer – our name's the same. Are we cousins?'

'What's that?' he said. 'Forsyte? Distant perhaps.'

'My name's Jolyon, sir. Jon, for short.'

'Oh! Ah!' said Soames. 'Yes. Distant. How are you? Very good of you. Good-bye!'

He moved on.

'Thanks awfully,' Fleur was saying. '*Au revoir!*'

'*Au revoir!*' he heard the boy reply.

2

FINE FLEUR FORSYTE

Emerging from the 'pastry-cook's', Soames's first impulse was to vent his nerves by saying to his daughter: 'Dropping your handkerchief!' to which her reply might well be: 'I picked that up from you!' His second impulse therefore was to let sleeping dogs lie. But she would surely question him. He gave her a sidelong look, and found she was giving him the same. She said softly:

'Why don't you like those cousins, Father?'

Soames lifted the corner of his lip.

'What made you think that?'

'*Cela se voit.*'

'That sees itself!' What a way of putting it!'

After twenty years of a French wife Soames had still little sympathy with her language; a theatrical affair and connected in his mind with all the refinements of domestic irony.

'How?' he asked.

'You *must* know them; and you didn't make a sign. I saw them looking at you.'

'I've never seen the boy in my life,' replied Soames with perfect truth.

'No; but you've seen the others, dear.'

Soames gave her another look. What had she picked up? Had her Aunt Winifred, or Imogen, or Val Dartie and his wife, been talking? Every breath of the old scandal had been carefully kept from her at home, and Winifred warned many times that he wouldn't have a whisper of it reach her for the world. So far as she ought to know, he had never been married before. But her dark eyes, whose southern glint and clearness often almost frightened him, met his with perfect innocence.

'Well,' he said, 'your grandfather and his brother had a quarrel. The two families don't know each other.'

'How romantic!'

'Now, what does she mean by that?' he thought. The word was to him extravagant and dangerous – it was as if she had said: 'How jolly!'

'And they'll continue not to know each other,' he added, but instantly regretted the challenge in those words. Fleur was smiling. In this age, when young people prided themselves on going their own ways and paying no attention to any sort of decent prejudice, he had said the very thing to excite her wilfulness. Then, recollecting the expression on Irene's face, he breathed again.

'What sort of a quarrel?' he heard Fleur say.

'About a house. It's ancient history for you. Your grandfather died the day you were born. He was ninety.'

'Ninety? Are there many Forsytes besides those in the Red Book?'

'I don't know,' said Soames. 'They're all dispersed now. The old ones are dead, except Timothy.'

Fleur clasped her hands.

'Timothy? Isn't that delicious?'

'Not at all,' said Soames. It offended him that she should think 'Timothy' delicious—a kind of insult to his breed. This new generation mocked at anything solid and tenacious. 'You go and see the old boy. He might want to prophesy.' Ah! If Timothy could see the disquiet England of his greatnephews and greatnieces, he would certainly give tongue. And involuntarily he glanced up at the Iseeum; yes—George was still in the window, with the same pink paper in his hand.

'Where is Robin Hill, Father?'

Robin Hill! Robin Hill, round which all that tragedy had centred! What did she want to know for?

'In Surrey,' he muttered; 'not far from Richmond. Why?'

'Is the house there?'

'What house?'

'That they quarrelled about.'

'Yes. But what's all that to do with you? We're going home to-morrow—you'd better be thinking about your frocks.'

'Bless you. They're all thought about. A family feud? It's like the Bible or Mark Twain—awfully exciting. What did *you* do in the feud, Father?'

'Never you mind.'

'Oh! But if I'm to keep it up!'

'Who said you were to keep it up?'

'You, darling.'

'I? I said it had nothing to do with you.'

'Just what *I* think, you know; so that's all right.'

She was too sharp for him; *fine*, as Annette sometimes called her. Nothing for it but to distract her attention.

'There's a bit of rosaline point in there,' he said, stopping before a shop, 'that I thought you might like.'

When he had paid for it and they had resumed their progress, Fleur said:

'Don't you think that boy's mother is the most beautiful woman of her age you've ever seen?'

Soames shivered. Uncanny, the way she stuck to it!

'I don't know that I noticed her.'

'Dear, I saw the corner of your eye.'

'You see everything—and a great deal more, it seems to me!'

'What's her husband like? He must be your first cousin, if your fathers were brothers.'

'Dead, for all I know,' said Soames, with sudden vehemence. 'I haven't seen him for twenty years.'

'What was he?'

'A painter.'

'That's quite jolly.'

The words: 'If you want to please me you'll put those people out of your head,' sprang to Soames's lips, but he choked them back—he must *not* let her see his feelings.

'He once insulted me,' he said.

Her quick eyes rested on his face.

'I see! You didn't avenge it, and it rankles. Poor Father! You let me have a go!'

It was really like lying in the dark with a mosquito hovering above his face. Such pertinacity in Fleur was new to him, and, as they reached the hotel, he said grimly:

'I did my best. And that's enough about these people. I'm going up till dinner.'

'I shall sit here.'

With a parting look at her extended in a chair–a look half-resentful, half-adoring–Soames moved into the lift and was transported to their suite on the fourth floor. He stood by the window of the sitting-room which gave view over Hyde Park, and drummed a finger on its pane. His feelings were confused, techy, troubled. The throb of that old wound, scarred over by Time and new interests, was mingled with displeasure and anxiety, and a slight pain in his chest where that nougat stuff had disagreed. Had Annette come in? Not that she was any good to him in such a difficulty. Whenever she had questioned him about his first marriage, he had always shut her up; she knew nothing of it, save that it had been the great passion of his life, and his marriage with herself but domestic makeshift. She had always kept the grudge of that up her sleeve, as it were, and used it commercially. He listened. A sound–the vague murmur of a woman's movements–was coming through the door. She *was* in. He tapped.

'Who?'

'I,' said Soames.

She had been changing her frock, and was still imperfectly clothed; a striking figure before her glass. There was a certain magnificence about her arms, shoulders, hair, which had darkened since he first knew her, about the turn of her neck, the silkiness of her garments, her dark-lashed, grey-blue eyes–she was certainly as handsome at forty as she had ever been. A fine possession, an excellent housekeeper, a sensible and affectionate enough mother. If only she weren't always so frankly cynical about the relations between them! Soames, who had no more real affection for her than she had for him, suffered from a kind of English grievance in that she had never dropped even the thinnest veil of sentiment over their partnership. Like most of his countrymen and women, he held the view that marriage should be based on mutual love, but that when from a marriage love had disappeared, or been found never to have really existed–so that it was manifestly not based on love–you must not admit it. There it was, and the love was not–but there you were, and must continue to be! Thus you had it both ways, and were not tarred with cynicism, realism and immorality like the French. Moreover, it was necessary in the interests of property. He knew that she knew that they both knew there was no love between them, but he still expected her not to admit in words or conduct such a thing, and he could never understand what she meant when she talked of the hypocrisy of the English. He said:

'Whom have you got at "The Shelter" next week?'

Annette went on touching her lips delicately with salve–he always wished she wouldn't do that.'

'Your sister Winifred, and the Car-r-digans–' she took up a tiny stick of black–'and Prosper Profond.'

'That Belgian chap? Why him?'

Annette turned her neck lazily, touched one eyelash, and said:

'He amuses Winifred.'

'I want someone to amuse Fleur; she's restive.'

'R-restive?' repeated Annette. 'Is it the first time you see that, my friend?

She was born r-restive, as you call it.'

Would she never get that affected roll out of her r's?

He touched the dress she had taken off, and asked:

'What have you been doing?'

Annette looked at him, reflected in her glass. Her just-brightened lips smiled, rather full, rather ironical.

'Enjoying myself,' she said.

'Oh!' answered Soames glumly. 'Ribbandry, I suppose.'

It was his word for all that incomprehensible running in and out of shops that women went in for. 'Has Fleur got her summer dresses?'

'You don't ask if I have mine.'

'You don't care whether I do or not.'

'Quite right. Well, she has; and I have mine–terribly expensive.'

'H'm!' said Soames. 'What does that chap Profond do in England?'

Annette raised her eyebrows she had just finished.

'He yachts.'

'Ah!' said Soames; 'he's a sleepy chap.'

'Sometimes,' answered Annette, and her face had a sort of quiet enjoyment. 'But sometimes very amusing.'

'He's got a touch of the tar-brush about him.'

Annette stretched herself.

'Tar-brush?' she said. 'What is that? His mother was *Arménienne*.'

'That's it, then,' muttered Soames. 'Does he know anything about pictures?'

'He knows about everything–a man of the world.'

'Well, get someone for Fleur. I want to distract her. She's going off on Saturday to Val Dartie and his wife: I don't like it.'

'Why not?'

Since the reason could not be explained without going into family history, Soames merely answered:

'Racketing about. There's too much of it.'

'I like that little Mrs Val; she is very quiet and clever.'

'I know nothing of her except–. This thing's new.' And Soames took up a creation from the bed.

Annette received it from him.

'Would you hook me?' she said.

Soames hooked. Glancing once over her shoulder into the glass, he saw the expression on her face, faintly amused, faintly contemptuous, as much as to say: 'Thanks! You will never learn!' No, thank God, he wasn't a Frenchman! He finished with a jerk, and the words: 'It's too low here.' And he went to the door, with the wish to get away from her and go down to Fleur again.

Annette stayed a powder-puff, and said with startling suddenness:

'*Que tu es grossier!*'

He knew the expression–he had reason to. The first time she had used it he had thought it meant 'What a grocer you are!' and had not known whether to be relieved or not when better informed. He resented the word–he was *not* coarse! If he was coarse, what was that chap in the room beyond his, who made those horrible noises in the morning when he cleared his throat, or those people in the Lounge who thought it well-bred to say nothing but what the whole world could hear at the top of their voices–quacking inanity! Coarse, because he had said her dress was low! Well, so it was. He went out without reply.

Coming into the Lounge from the far end, he at once saw Fleur where he had left her. She sat with crossed knees, slowly balancing a foot in silk stocking and grey shoe, sure sign that she was dreaming. Her eyes showed it too–they went off like that sometimes. And then, in a moment, she would come to life, and be as quick and restless as a monkey. And she knew so much, so self-assured, and not yet nineteen. What was that odious word? Flapper! Dreadful young creatures–squealing and squawking and showing their legs! The worst of them bad dreams, the best of them powdered angels! Fleur was *not* a flapper, *not* one of those slangy, ill-bred young females. And yet she was frighteningly self-willed, and full of life, and determined to enjoy it. Enjoy! The word brought no puritan terror to Soames; but it brought the terror suited to his temperament. He had always been afraid to enjoy to-day for fear he might not enjoy to-morrow so much. And it was terrifying to feel that his daughter was divested of that safeguard. The very way she sat in that chair showed it–lost in her dream. He had never been lost in a dream himself–there was nothing to be had out of it; and where she got it from he did not know! Certainly not from Annette! And yet Annette, as a young girl, when he was hanging about her, had once had a flowery look. Well, she had lost it now!

Fleur rose from her chair–swiftly, restlessly, and flung herself down at a writing-table. Seizing ink and writing-paper, she began to write as if she had not time to breathe before she got her letter written. And suddenly she saw him. The air of desperate absorption vanished, she smiled, waved a kiss, made a pretty face as if she were a little puzzled and a little bored.

Ah! she was '*fine*'–'*fine!*'

3

AT ROBIN HILL

Jolyon Forsyte had spent his boy's nineteenth birthday at Robin Hill, quietly going into his affairs. He did everything quietly now, because his heart was in a poor way, and, like all his family, he disliked the idea of dying. He had never realised how much till one day, two years ago, he had gone to his doctor about certain symptoms, and been told:

'At any moment, on any overstrain.'

He had taken it with a smile–the natural Forsyte reaction against an unpleasant truth. But with an increase of symptoms in the train on the way home, he had realised to the full the sentence hanging over him. To leave Irene, his boy, his home, his work–though he did little enough work now! To leave them for unknown darkness, for the unimaginable state, for such nothingness that he would not even be conscious of wind stirring leaves above his grave, nor of the scent of earth and grass. Of such nothingness that, however hard he might try to conceive it, he never could, and must still hover on the hope that he might see again those he loved! To realise this was to endure very poignant spiritual anguish. Before he reached home that day he had determined to keep it from Irene. He would have to be more careful than man had ever been, for the least thing would give it away and make her as wretched as himself, almost. His doctor had passed him sound in other respects, and seventy was nothing of an age–he would last a long time yet, *if he could!*

Such a conclusion, followed out for nearly two years, develops to the full the subtler side of character. Naturally not abrupt, except when nervously excited, Jolyon had become control incarnate. The sad patience of old people who cannot exert themselves was masked by a smile which his lips preserved even in private. He devised continually all manner of cover to conceal his enforced lack of exertion.

Mocking himself for so doing, he counterfeited conversion to the Simple Life; gave up wine and cigars, drank a special kind of coffee with no coffee in it. In short, he made himself as safe as a Forsyte in his condition could, under the rose of his mild irony. Secure from discovery, since his wife and son had gone up to Town, he had spent the fine May day quietly arranging his papers, that he might die to-morrow without inconveniencing anyone, giving in fact a final polish to his terrestrial state. Having docketed and enclosed it in his father's old Chinese cabinet, he put the key into an envelope, wrote the words outside: 'Key of the Chinese cabinet, wherein will be found the exact state of me. J.F.', and put it in his breast-pocket, where it would be, always about him, in case of accident. Then, ringing for tea, he went out to have it under the old oak tree.

All are under sentence of death; Jolyon, whose sentence was but a little more precise and pressing, had become so used to it that he thought habitually, like other people, of other things. He thought of his son now.

Jon was nineteen that day, and Jon had come of late to a decision. Educated neither at Eton like his father, nor at Harrow, like his dead half-brother, but at one of those establishments which, designed to avoid the evil and contain the good of the Public School system, may or may not contain the evil and avoid the good, Jon had left in April perfectly ignorant of what he wanted to become. The War, which had promised to go on for ever, had ended just as he was about to join the Army, six months before his time. It had taken him ever since to get used to the idea that he could now choose for himself. He had held with his father several discussions, from which, under a cheery show of being ready for anything–except, of course, the Church, Army, Law, Stage, Stock Exchange, Medicine, Business, and Engineering–Jolyon had gathered rather clearly that Jon wanted to go in for nothing. He himself felt exactly like that at the same age. With him that pleasant vacuity had soon been ended by an early marriage, and its unhappy consequences. Forced to become an underwriter at Lloyd's, he had regained prosperity before his artistic talent had outcropped. But having–as the simple say–'learned' his boy to draw pigs and other animals, he knew that Jon would never be a painter, and inclined to the conclusion that his aversion from everything else meant that he was going to be a writer. Holding, however, the view that experience was necessary even for that profession, there seemed to Jolyon nothing in the meantime, for Jon, but University, travel, and perhaps the eating of dinners for the Bar. After that one would see, or more probably one would not. In face of these proffered allurements, however, Jon had remained undecided.

Such discussions with his son had confirmed in Jolyon a doubt whether the world had really changed. People said that it was a new age. With the profundity of one not too long for any age, Jolyon perceived that under slightly different surfaces the era was precisely what it had been. Mankind was still divided into two species: The few who had 'speculation' in their souls, and the many who had none, with a belt of hybrids like himself in the middle. Jon appeared to have speculation; it seemed to his father a bad lookout.

With something deeper, therefore, than his usual smile, he had heard the boy say, a fortnight ago: 'I should like to try farming, Dad; if it won't cost you too much. It seems to be about the only sort of life that doesn't hurt anybody; except art, and of course that's out of the question for me.'

Jolyon subdued his smile, and answered:

'All right; you shall skip back to where we were under the first Jolyon in 1760. It'll prove the cycle theory, and incidentally, no doubt, you may grow a better turnip than he did.'

A little dashed, Jon had answered:

'But don't you think it's a good scheme, Dad?'

''Twill serve, my dear; and if you should really take to it, you'll do more good than most men, which is little enough.'

To himself, however, he had said: 'But he won't take to it. I give him four years. Still, it's healthy, and harmless.'

After turning the matter over and consulting with Irene, he wrote to his daughter Mrs Val Dartie, asking if they knew of a farmer near them on the Downs who would take Jon as an apprentice. Holly's answer had been enthusiastic. There was an excellent man quite close; she and Val would love Jon to live with them.

The boy was due to go to-morrow.

Sipping weak tea with lemon in it, Jolyon gazed through the leaves of the old oak tree at that view which had appeared to him desirable for thirty-two years. The tree beneath which he sat seemed not a day older! So young, the little leaves of brownish gold; so old, the whitey-grey-green of its thick rough trunk. A tree of memories, which would live on hundreds of years yet, unless some barbarian cut it down—would see old England out at the pace things were going! He remembered a night three years before, when looking from his window, with his arm close round Irene, he had watched a German aeroplane hovering, it seemed, right over the old tree. Next day they had found a bomb hole in a field on Gage's farm. That was before he knew that he was under sentence of death. He could almost have wished the bomb had finished him. It would have saved a lot of hanging about, many hours of cold fear in the pit of his stomach. He had counted on living to the normal Forsyte age of eighty-five or more, when Irene would be seventy. As it was, she would miss him. Still there was Jon, more important in her life than himself; Jon, who adored his mother.

Under that tree, where old Jolyon—waiting for Irene to come to him across the lawn—had breathed his last, Jolyon wondered, whimsically, whether, having put everything in such perfect order, he had not better close his own eyes and drift away. There was something undignified in parasitically clinging on to the effortless close of a life wherein he regretted two things only—the long division between his father and himself when he was young, and the lateness of his union with Irene.

From where he sat he could see a cluster of apple trees in blossom. Nothing in Nature moved him so much as fruit trees in blossom; and his heart ached suddenly because he might never see them flower again. Spring! Decidedly no man ought to have to die while his heart was still young enough to love beauty! Blackbirds sang recklessly in the shrubbery, swallows were flying high, the leaves above him glistened; and over the fields was every imaginable tint of early foliage, burnished by the level sunlight, away to where the distant 'smoke-bush' blue was trailed along the horizon. Irene's flowers in their narrow beds had startling individuality that evening, little deep assertions of gay life. Only Chinese and Japanese painters, and perhaps Leonardo, had known how to get that startling little ego into each painted flower, and bird, and beast–the ego, yet the sense of species, the universality of life as well. They were the fellows! 'I've made nothing that will live!' thought Jolyon; 'I've been an amateur–a mere lover, not a creator. Still, I shall leave Jon behind me when I go.' What luck that the boy had not been caught by that ghastly war! He might so easily have been killed, like poor Jolly twenty years ago out in the Transvaal. Jon would do something some day–if the Age didn't spoil him–an imaginative chap! His whim to take up farming was but a bit of sentiment, and about as likely to last. And just then he saw them coming up the field: Irene and the boy, walking from the station, with their arms linked. And getting up, he strolled down through the new rose garden to meet them. . . .

Irene came into his room that night and sat down by the window. She sat there without speaking till he said:

'What is it, my love?'

'We had an encounter to-day.'

'With whom?'

'Soames.'

Soames! He had kept that name out of his thoughts these last two years; conscious that it was bad for him. And, now, his heart moved in a disconcerting manner, as if it had side-slipped within his chest.

Irene went on quietly:

'He and his daughter were in the Gallery, and afterwards at the confectioner's where we had tea.'

Jolyon went over and put his hand on her shoulder.

'How did he look?'

'Grey; but otherwise much the same.'

'And the daughter?'

'Pretty. At least, Jon thought so.'

Jolyon's heart side-slipped again. His wife's face had a strained and puzzled look.

'You didn't–?' he began.

'No; but Jon knows their name. The girl dropped her handkerchief and he picked it up.'

Jolyon sat down on his bed. An evil chance!

'June was with you. Did she put her foot into it?'

'No; but it was all very queer and strained, and Jon could see it was.'

Jolyon drew a long breath, and said:

'I've often wondered whether we've been right to keep it from him. He'll find out some day.'

'The later the better, Jolyon; the young have such cheap, hard judgment. When you were nineteen what would you have thought of *your* mother if she had done what I have?'

Yes! There it was! Jon worshipped his mother; and knew nothing of the tragedies, the inexorable necessities of life, nothing of the prisoned grief in an unhappy marriage, nothing of jealousy, or passion–knew nothing at all, as yet!

'What have you told him?' he said at last.

'That they were relations, but we didn't know them; that you had never cared much for your family, or they for you. I expect he will be asking *you*.'

Jolyon smiled. 'This promises to take the place of air-raids,' he said. 'After all, one misses them.'

Irene looked up at him.

'We've known it would come some day.'

He answered her with sudden energy:

'I could never stand seeing Jon blame you. He shan't do that, even in thought. He has imagination; and he'll understand if it's put to him properly. I think I had better tell him before he gets to know otherwise.'

'Not yet, Jolyon.'

That was like her—she had no foresight, and never went to meet trouble. Still—who knew?—she might be right. It was ill going against a mother's instinct. It might be well to let the boy go on, if possible, till experience had given him some touchstone by which he could judge the values of that old tragedy; till love, jealousy, longing, had deepened his charity. All the same, one must take precautions—every precaution possible! And, long after Irene had left him, he lay awake turning over those precautions. He must write to Holly, telling her that Jon knew nothing as yet of family history. Holly was discreet, she would make sure of her husband, she would see to it! Jon would take the letter with him when he went to-morrow.

And so the day on which he had put the polish on his material estate died out with the chiming of the stable clock; and another began for Jolyon in the shadow of a spiritual disorder which could not be so rounded off and polished.

But Jon, whose room had once been his day nursery, lay awake too, the prey of a sensation disputed by those who have never known it, 'love at first sight!' He had felt it beginning in him with the glint of those dark eyes gazing into his athwart the Juno—a conviction that this was his 'dream'; so that what followed had seemed to him at once natural and miraculous. Fleur! Her name alone was almost enough for one who was terribly susceptible to the charm of words. In a homœopathic age, when boys and girls were co-educated, and mixed up in early life till sex was almost abolished, Jon was singularly old-fashioned. His modern school took boys only, and his holidays had been spent at Robin Hill with boy friends, or his parents alone. He had never, therefore, been inoculated against the germs of love by small doses of the poison. And now in the dark his temperature was mounting fast. He lay awake, featuring Fleur—as they called it—recalling her words, especially that '*Au revoir!*' so soft and sprightly.

He was still so wide awake at dawn that he got up, slipped on tennis shoes, trousers, and a sweater, and in silence crept downstairs and out through the study window. It was just light; there was a smell of grass. 'Fleur!' he thought; 'Fleur!' It was mysteriously white out of doors, with nothing awake except the birds just beginning to chirp. 'I'll go down into the coppice,' he thought. He ran down through the fields, reached the pond just as the sun rose, and passed into the coppice. Bluebells carpeted the ground there; among the larch trees there was mystery—the air, as it were, composed of that romantic quality. Jon sniffed its freshness, and stared at the bluebells in the sharpening light. Fleur! It rhymed with her! And she lived at Mapledurham—a jolly name, too, on the river somewhere. He could find it in the atlas presently. He would write to her. But would she answer? Oh! She must. She had said '*Au revoir!*' Not good-bye! What luck that she had dropped her handkerchief! He would never have known her but for that. And the more he thought of that handkerchief, the more amazing his luck seemed. Fleur! It certainly rhymed with her! Rhythm thronged his head; words jostled to be joined together; he was on the verge of a poem.

Jon remained in this condition for more than half an hour, then returned to the house, and getting a ladder, climbed in at his bedroom window out of sheer exhilaration. Then, remembering that the study window was open, he went down and shut it, first removing the ladder, so as to obliterate all traces of his feeling. The thing was too deep to be revealed to mortal soul—even to his mother.

4

THE MAUSOLEUM

There are houses whose souls have passed into the limbo of Time, leaving their bodies in the limbo of London. Such was not quite the condition of 'Timothy's' on the Bayswater Road, for Timothy's soul still had one foot in Timothy Forsyte's body, and Smither kept the atmosphere unchanging, of camphor and port wine and house whose windows are only opened to air it twice a day.

To Forsyte imagination that house was now a sort of Chinese pill-box, a series of layers in the last of which was Timothy. One did not reach him, or so it was reported by members of the family who, out of old-time habit or absent-mindedness, would drive up once in a blue moon and ask after their surviving uncle. Such were Francie, now quite emancipated from God (she frankly avowed atheism), Euphemia, emancipated from old Nicholas, and Winifred Dartie from her 'man of the world'. But after all, everybody was emancipated now, or said they were—perhaps not quite the same thing!

When Soames, therefore, took it in on his way to Paddington Station on the morning after that encounter, it was hardly with the expectation of seeing Timothy in the flesh. His heart made a faint demonstration within him while he stood in full south sunlight on the newly whitened doorsteps of that little house where four Forsytes had once lived, and now but one dwelt on like a winter fly; the house into which Soames had come and out of which he had gone times without number, divested of, or burdened with, fardels of family gossip; the house of the 'old people' of another century, another age.

The sight of Smither—still corseted up to the armpits because the new fashion which came in as they were going out about 1903 had never been considered 'nice' by Aunts Juley and Hester—brought a pale friendliness to Soames's lips; Smither, still faithfully arranged to old pattern in every detail, an invaluable servant—none such left—smiling back at him, with the words: 'Why, it's Mr Soames, after all this time! And how are *you*, sir? Mr Timothy will be so pleased to know you've been.'

'How is he?'

'Oh! he keeps fairly bobbish for his age, sir; but of course he's a wonderful man. As I said to Mrs Dartie when she was here last: It *would* please Miss Forsyte and Mrs Juley and Miss Hester to see how he relishes a baked apple still. But he's quite deaf. And a mercy, I always think. For what we should have done with him in the air-raids, I don't know.'

'Ah!' said Soames. 'What *did* you do with him?'

'We just left him in his bed, and had the bell run down into the cellar, so that Cook and I could hear him if he rang. It would never have done to let him know there was a war on. As I said to Cook, 'If Mr Timothy rings, they may do what they like–I'm going up. My dear mistresses would have a fit if they could see him ringing and nobody going to him.' But he slept through them all beautiful. And the one in the daytime he was having his bath. It *was* a mercy, because he might have noticed the people in the street all looking up–he often looks out of the window.'

'Quite!' murmured Soames. Smither was getting garrulous! 'I just want to look round and see if there's anything to be done.'

'Yes, sir. I don't think there's anything except a smell of mice in the dining-room that we don't know how to get rid of. It's funny they should be there, and not a crumb, since Mr Timothy took to not coming down, just before the War. But they're nasty little things; you never know where they'll take you next.'

'Does he leave his bed?'

'Oh! yes, sir; he takes nice exercise between his bed and the window in the morning, not to risk a change of air. And he's quite comfortable in himself; has his Will out every day regular. It's a great consolation to him–that.'

'Well, Smither, I want to see him, if I can; in case he has anything to say to me.'

Smither coloured up above her corsets.

'It *will* be an occasion!' she said. 'Shall I take you round the house, sir, while I send Cook to break it to him?'

'No, you go to him,' said Soames. 'I can go round the house by myself.'

One could not confess to sentiment before another, and Soames felt that he was going to be sentimental nosing round those rooms so saturated with the past. When Smither, creaking with excitement, had left him, Soames entered the dining-room and sniffed. In his opinion it wasn't mice, but incipient wood-rot, and he examined the panelling. Whether it was worth a coat of paint, at Timothy's age, he was not sure. The room had always been the most modern in the house; and only a faint smile curled Soames's lips and nostrils. Walls of a rich green surmounted the oak dado; a heavy metal chandelier hung by a chain from a ceiling divided by imitation beams. The pictures had been bought by Timothy, a bargain, one day at Jobson's sixty years ago–three Snyder 'still lifes', two faintly coloured drawings of a boy and a girl, rather charming, which bore the initials 'J.R.'–Timothy had always believed they might turn out to be Joshua Reynolds, but Soames, who admired them, had discovered that they were only John Robinson; and a doubtful Morland of a white pony being shod. Deep-red plush curtains, ten high-backed dark mahogany chairs with deep-red plush seats, a Turkey carpet, and a mahogany dining-table as large as the room was small, such was an apartment which Soames could remember unchanged in soul or body since he was four years old. He looked especially at the two drawings, and thought: 'I shall buy those at the sale.'

From the dining-room he passed into Timothy's study. He did not remember ever having been in that room. It was lined from floor to ceiling with volumes, and he looked at them with curiosity. One wall seemed devoted to educational books, which Timothy's firm had published two generations back–sometimes as many as twenty copies of one book. Soames read their titles and shuddered. The middle wall had precisely the same books as used to be in the library at his own father's in Park Lane, from which he deduced the fancy that James and his youngest brother had gone out together one day and bought a brace of small libraries. The third wall he approached with more excitement. Here, surely, Timothy's own taste would be found. It was. The books were dummies. The fourth wall was all heavily curtained window. And turned toward it was a large chair with a mahogany reading-stand attached, on which a yellowish and folded copy of *The Times*, dated July 6, 1914, the day Timothy first failed to come down, as if in preparation for the War, seemed waiting for him still. In a corner stood a large globe of that world never visited by Timothy, deeply convinced of the unreality of everything but England, and permanently upset by the sea, on which he had been very sick one Sunday afternoon in 1836, out of a pleasure boat off the pier at Brighton, with Juley and Hester, Swithin and Hatty Chessman; all due to Swithin, who was always taking things into his head, and who, thank goodness, had been sick too. Soames knew all about it, having heard the tale fifty times at least from one or other of them. He went up to the globe, and gave it a spin; it emitted a faint creak and moved about an inch, bringing into his purview a daddy-long-legs which had died on it in latitude 44.

'Mausoleum!' he thought. 'George was right!' And he went out and up the stairs. On the half landing he stopped before the case of stuffed humming-birds which had delighted his childhood. They looked not a day older suspended on wires above pampas-grass. If the case were opened the birds would not begin to hum, but the whole thing would crumble, he suspected. It wouldn't be worth putting that into the sale! And suddenly he was caught by a memory of Aunt Ann—dear old Aunt Ann—holding him by the hand in front of that case and saying: 'Look, Soamey! Aren't they bright and pretty, dear little humming-birds!' Soames remembered his own answer: 'They don't hum, Auntie.' He must have been six, in a black velveteen suit with a light-blue collar—he remembered that suit well! Aunt Ann with her ringlets, and her spidery kind hands, and her grave old aquiline smile—a fine old lady, Aunt Ann! He moved on up to the drawing-room door. There on each side of it were the groups of miniatures. Those he would certainly buy in! The miniatures of his four aunts, one of his Uncle Swithin adolescent, and one of his Uncle Nicholas as a boy. They had all been painted by a young lady friend of the family at a time, 1830, about when miniatures were considered very genteel, and lasting too, painted as they were on ivory. Many a time had he heard the tale of that young lady: 'Very talented, my dear; she had quite a weakness for Swithin, and very soon after she went into a consumption and died: so like Keats—we often spoke of it.'

Well, there they were! Ann, Juley, Hester, Susan—quite a small child; Swithin, with sky-blue eyes, pink cheeks, yellow curls, white waistcoat—large as life; and Nicholas, like Cupid with an eye on heaven. Now he came to think of it, Uncle Nick had always been rather like that—a wonderful man to the last. Yes, she must have had talent, and miniatures always had a certain back-watered cachet of their own, little subject to the currents of competition on æsthetic Change. Soames opened the drawing-room door. The room was dusted, the furniture uncovered, the curtains drawn back, precisely as if his aunts still dwelt there patiently waiting. And a thought came to him: When Timothy died—why not? Would it not be almost a duty to preserve this house—like Carlyle's—and put up a tablet, and show it? 'Specimen of mid-Victorian abode—entrance, one shilling, with catalogue.' After all, it was the completest thing, and perhaps the deadest in the London of to-day. Perfect in its special taste and culture, if, that is, he took down and carried over to his own collection the four Barbizon pictures he had given them. The still sky-blue walls, the green curtains patterned with red flowers and ferns; the crewel-worked fire-screen before the cast-iron grate; the mahogany cupboard with glass windows, full of little knick-knacks; the beaded footstools; Keats,

Shelley, Southey, Cowper, Coleridge Byron's Corsair (but nothing else), and the Victorian poets in a bookshelf row; the marqueterie cabinet lined with dim red plush, full of family relics; Hester's first fan; the buckles of their mother's father's shoes; three bottled scorpions; and one very yellow elephant's tusk, sent home from India by Great-uncle Edgar Forsyte, who had been in jute; a yellow bit of paper propped up, with spidery writing on it, recording God knew what! And the pictures crowding on the walls—all water-colours save those four Barbizons looking like the foreigners they were, and doubtful customers at that—pictures bright and illustrative, 'Telling the Bees', 'Hey for the Ferry!' and two in the style of Frith, all thimblerig and crinolines, given them by Swithin. Oh! many, many pictures at which Soames had gazed a thousand times in supercilious fascination; a marvellous collection of bright, smooth gilt frames.

And the boudoir-grand piano, beautifully dusted, hermetically sealed as ever; and Aunt Juley's album of pressed seaweed on it. And the gilt-legged chairs, stronger than they looked. And on one side of the fireplace the sofa of crimson silk, where Aunt Ann, and after her Aunt Juley, had been wont to sit, facing the light and bolt upright. And on the other side of the fire the one really easy chair, back to the light, for Aunt Hester. Soames screwed up his eyes; he seemed to see them sitting there. Ah! and the atmosphere—even now, of too many stuffs and washed lace curtains, lavender in bags, and dried bees' wings. 'No,' he thought, 'there's nothing like it left; it ought to be preserved.' And, by George, they might laugh at it, but for a standard of gentle life never departed from, for fastidiousness of skin and eye and nose and feeling, it beat to-day hollow—to-day with its Tubes and cars, its perpetual smoking, its cross-legged, bare-necked girls visible up to the knees and down to the waist if you took the trouble (agreeable to the satyr within each Forsyte but hardly his idea of a lady), with their feet, too, screwed round the legs of their chairs while they ate, and their 'So longs', and their 'Old Beans', and their laughter—girls who gave him the shudders whenever he thought of Fleur in contact with them; and the hard-eyed, capable, older women who managed life and gave him the shudders too. No! his old aunts, if they never opened their minds, their eyes, or very much their windows, at least had manners, and a standard, and reverence for past and future.

With rather a choky feeling he closed the door and went tip-toeing upstairs. He looked in at a place on the way: H'm! in perfect order of the 'eighties, with a sort of yellow oilskin paper on the walls. At the top of the stairs he hesitated between four doors. Which of them was Timothy's? And he listened. A sound, as of a child slowly dragging a hobby-horse about, came to his ears. That must be Timothy! He tapped, and a door was opened by Smither, very red in the face.

Mr Timothy was taking his walk, and she had not been able to get him to attend. If Mr Soames would come into the back-room, he could see him through the door.

Soames went into the back-room and stood watching.

The last of the old Forsytes was on his feet, moving with the most impressive slowness, and an air of perfect concentration on his own affairs, backward and forward between the foot of his bed and the window, a distance of some twelve feet. The lower part of his square face, no longer clean-shaven, was covered with snowy beard clipped as short as it could be, and his chin looked as broad as his brow where the hair was also quite white, while nose and cheeks and brow were a good yellow. One hand held a stout stick, and the other grasped the skirt of his Jaeger dressing-gown, from under which could be seen his bed-socked ankles and feet thrust into Jaeger slippers. The expression on his face was that of a crossed child, intent on something that he has not got. Each time he turned he stumped the stick, and then dragged it, as if to show that he could do without it.

'He still looks strong,' said Soames under his breath.

'Oh! yes, sir. You should see him take his bath—it's wonderful; he does enjoy it so.'

Those quite loud words gave Soames an insight. Timothy had resumed his babyhood.

'Does he take any interest in things generally?' he said, also aloud.

'Oh! yes, sir; his food and his Will. It's quite a sight to see him turn it over and over, not to read it, of course; and every now and then he asks the price of Consols, and I write it on a slate for him—very large. Of course, I always write the same, what they were when he last took notice, in 1914. We got the doctor to forbid him to read the paper when the war broke out. Oh! he did take on about that at first. But he soon came round, because he knew it tired him; and he's a wonder to conserve energy as he used to call it when my dear mistresses were alive, bless their hearts! How he did go on at them about that; they were always so active, if you remember, Mr Soames.'

'What would happen if I were to go in?' asked Soames. 'Would he remember me? I made his Will, you know, after Miss Hester died in 1907.'

'Oh! that, sir,' replied Smither doubtfully, 'I couldn't take on me to say. I think he might; he really is a wonderful man for his age.'

Soames moved into the doorway, and waiting for Timothy to turn, said in a loud voice: 'Uncle Timothy!'

Timothy trailed back half-way, and halted.

'Eh?' he said.

'Soames,' cried Soames at the top of his voice, holding out his hand, 'Soames Forsyte!'

'No!' said Timothy, and stumping his stick loudly on the floor, he continued his walk.

'It doesn't seem to work,' said Soames.

'No, sir,' replied Smither, rather crestfallen; 'you see, he hasn't finished his walk. It always was one thing at a time with him. I expect he'll ask me this afternoon if you came about the gas, and a pretty job I shall have to make him understand.'

'Do you think he ought to have a man about him?'

Smither held up her hands. 'A man! Oh! no. Cook and me can manage perfectly. A strange man about would send him crazy in no time. And my mistresses wouldn't like the idea of a man in the house. Besides, we're so proud of him.'

'I suppose the doctor comes?'

'Every morning. He makes special terms for such a quantity, and Mr Timothy's so used, he doesn't take a bit of notice, except to put out his tongue.'

'Well,' said Soames, turning away, 'it's rather sad and painful to me.'

'Oh! sir,' returned Smither anxiously, 'you mustn't think that. Now that he can't worry about things, he quite enjoys his life, really he does. As I say to Cook, Mr Timothy is more of a man than he ever was. You see, when he's not walkin', or takin' his bath, he's eatin', and when he's not eatin', he's sleepin';

and there it is. There isn't an ache or a care about him, anywhere.'

'Well,' said Soames, 'there's something in that. I'll go down. By the way, let me see his Will.'

'I should have to take my time about that, sir; he keeps it under his pillow, and he'd see me, while he's active.'

'I only want to know if it's the one I made,' said Soames; 'you take a look at its date some time, and let me know.'

'Yes, sir; but I'm sure it's the same, because me and Cook witnessed, you remember, and there's our names on it still, and we've only done it once.'

'Quite,' said Soames. He did remember. Smither and Jane had been proper witnesses, having been left nothing in the Will that they might have no interest in Timothy's death. It had been—he fully admitted—an almost improper precaution, but Timothy had wished it, and, after all, Aunt Hester had provided for them amply.

'Very well,' he said; 'good-bye, Smither. Look after him, and if he should say anything at any time, put it down, and let me know.'

'Oh! yes, Mr Soames; I'll be sure to do that. It's been such a pleasant change to see you. Cook will be quite excited when I tell her.'

Soames shook her hand and went downstairs. He stood for fully two minutes by the hat-stand whereon he had hung his hat so many times. 'So it all passes,' he was thinking; 'passes and begins again. Poor old chap!' And he listened, if perchance the sound of Timothy trailing his hobby-horse might come down the well of the stairs; or some ghost of an old face show over the banisters, and an old voice say: 'Why, it's dear Soames and we were only saying that we hadn't seen him for a week!'

Nothing—nothing! Just the scent of camphor, and dust-motes in a sunbeam through the fanlight over the door. The little old house! A mausoleum! And, turning on his heel, he went out, and caught his train.

5

THE NATIVE HEATH

His foot's upon his native heath,
His name's—*Val Dartie*.

With some such feeling did Val Dartie, in the fortieth year of his age, set out that same Thursday morning very early from the old manor-house he had taken on the north side of the Sussex Downs. His destination was Newmarket, and he had not been there since the autumn of 1899, when he stole over from Oxford for the Cambridgeshire. He paused at the door to give his wife a kiss, and put a flask of port into his pocket.

'Don't overtire your leg, Val, and don't bet too much.'

With the pressure of her chest against his own, and her eyes looking into his, Val felt both leg and pocket safe. He should be moderate; Holly was always right—she had a natural aptitude. It did not seem so remarkable to him perhaps, as it might to others, that—half Dartie as he was—he should have been perfectly faithful to his young first cousin during the twenty years since he married her romantically out in the Boer War; and faithful without any feeling of sacrifice or boredom–she was so quick, so slyly always a little in front of his mood. Being cousins they had decided, or rather Holly had, to have no children; and, though a little sallower, she had kept her looks, her slimness, and the colour of her dark hair. Val particularly admired the life of her own she carried on, besides carrying on his, and riding better every year. She kept up her music, she read an awful lot–novels, poetry, all sorts of stuff. Out on their farm in Cape colony she had looked after all the 'nigger' babies and women in a miraculous manner. She was, in fact, clever; yet made no fuss about it, and had no 'side'. Though not remarkable for humility, Val had come to have the feeling that she was his superior, and he did not grudge it–a great tribute. It might be noted that he never looked at Holly without her knowing of it, but that she looked at him sometimes unawares.

He had kissed her in the porch because he should not be doing so on the platform, though she was going to the station with him, to drive the car back. Tanned and wrinkled by Colonial weather and the wiles inseparable from horses, and handicapped by the leg which, weakened in the Boer War, had probably saved his life in the War just past, Val was still much as he had been in the days of his courtship; his smile as wide and charming, his eyelashes, if anything, thicker and darker, his eyes screwed up under them, as bright a grey, his freckles deeper, his hair a little grizzled at the sides. He gave the impression of one who has lived actively *with horses* in a sunny climate.

Twisting the car sharp round at the gate, he said:

'When is young Jon coming?'

'To-day.'

'Is there anything you want for him? I could bring it down on Saturday.'

'No; but you might come by the same train as Fleur–one-forty.'

Val gave the Ford full rein; he still drove like a man in a new country on bad roads, who refuses to compromise and expects heaven at every hole.

'That's a young woman who knows her way about,' he said. 'I say, has it struck you?'

'Yes,' said Holly.

'Uncle Soames and your Dad–bit awkward, isn't it?'

'She won't know, and he won't know, and nothing must be said, of course. It's only for five days, Val.'

'Stable secret! Righto!' If Holly thought it safe, it was. Glancing slyly round at him, she said: 'Did you notice how beautifully she asked herself?'

'No!'

'Well, she did. What do you think of her, Val?'

'Pretty, and clever; but she might run out at any corner if she got her monkey up, I should say.'

'I'm wondering,' Holly murmured, 'whether she is the modern young woman. One feels at sea coming home into all this.'

'You! You get the hang of things so quick.'

Holly slid her hand into his coat-pocket.

'You keep one in the know,' said Val, encouraged. 'What do you think of that Belgian fellow, Profond?'

'I thin' e's rather "a good devil".'

Val grinned.

'He seems to me a queer fish for a friend of our family. In fact, our family is in pretty queer waters, with Uncle Soames marrying a Frenchwoman, and your

Dad marrying Soames's first. Our grandfathers would have had fits!'

'So would anybody's, my dear.'

'This car,' Val said suddenly, 'wants rousing; she doesn't get her hind legs under her uphill. I shall have to give her her head on the slope if I'm to catch that train.'

There was that about horses which had prevented him from ever really sympathising with a car, and the running of the Ford under his guidance compared with its running under that of Holly was always noticeable. He caught the train.

'Take care going home; she'll throw you down if she can. Good-bye, darling.'

'Good-bye,' called Holly, and kissed her hand.

In the train, after a quarter of an hour's indecision between thoughts of Holly, his morning paper, the look of the bright day, and his dim memory of Newmarket, Val plunged into the recesses of a small square book, all names, pedigrees, tap-roots, and notes about the make and shape of horses. The Forsyte in him was bent on the acquisition of a certain strain of blood, and he was subduing resolutely as yet the Dartie hankering for a flutter. On getting back to England, after the profitable sale of his South African farm and stud, and observing that the sun seldom shone, Val had said to himself: 'I've absolutely got to have an interest in life, or this country will give me the blues. Hunting's not enough, I'll breed and I'll train.' With just that extra pinch of shrewdness and decision imparted by long residence in a new country, Val had seen the weak point of modern breeding. They were all hypnotised by fashion and high prices. He should buy for looks, and let names go hang! And here he was already, hypnotised by the prestige of a certain strain of blood! Half-consciously, he thought: 'There's something in this damned climate which makes me go round in a ring. All the same, I must have a strain of Mayfly blood.'

In this mood he reached the Mecca of his hopes. It was one of those quiet meetings favourable to such as wish to look into horses, rather than into the mouths of bookmakers; and Val clung to the paddock. His twenty years of Colonial life, divesting him of the dandyism in which he had been bred, had left him the essential neatness of the horseman, and given him a queer and rather blighting eye over what he called 'the silly haw-haw' of some Englishmen, the 'flapping cockatoory' of some Englishwoman–Holly had none of that and Holly was his model. Observant, quick, resourceful, Val went straight to the heart of a transaction, a horse, a drink; and he was on his way to the heart of a Mayfly filly, when a slow voice said at his elbow:

'Mr Val Dartie? How's Mrs Val Dartie? She's well, I hope.' And he saw beside him the Belgian he had met at his sister Imogen's.

'Prosper Profond–I met you at lunch,' said the voice.

'How are you?' murmured Val.

'I'm very well,' replied Monsieur Profond, smiling with a certain inimitable slowness. 'A good devil!' Holly had called him. Well! He looked a little like a devil, with his dark, clipped, pointed beard; a sleepy one though, and good-humoured, with fine eyes, unexpectedly intelligent.

'Here's a gentleman wants to know you–cousin of yours–Mr George Forsyte.'

Val saw a large form, and a face clean-shaven, bull-like, a little lowering, with sardonic humour bubbling behind a full grey eye; he remembered it dimly from old days when he would dine with his father at the Iseeum Club.

'I used to go racing with your father,' George was saying. 'How's the stud? Like to buy one of my screws?'

Val grinned, to hide the sudden feeling that the bottom had fallen out of breeding. They believed in nothing over here, not even in horses. George Forsyte, Prosper Profond! The devil himself was not more disillusioned than those two.

'Didn't know you were a racing man,' he said to Monsieur Profond.

'I'm not. I don' care for it. I'm a yachtin' man. I don' care for yachtin' either, but I like to see my friends. I've got some lunch, Mr Val Dartie, just a small lunch, if you'd like to 'ave some; not much—just a small one—in my car.'

'Thanks,' said Val; 'very good of you. I'll come along in about quarter of an hour.'

'Over there. Mr Forsyde's comin',' and Monsieur Profond 'poinded' with a yellow-gloved finger; 'small car, with a small lunch'; he moved on, groomed, sleepy, and remote, George Forsyte following, neat, huge, and with his jesting air.

Val remained gazing at the Mayfly filly. George Forsyte, of course, was an old chap, but this Profond might be about his own age; Val felt extremely young, as if the Mayfly filly were a toy at which those two had laughed. The animal had lost reality.

'That "small" mare'—he seemed to hear the voice of Monsieur Profond—'what do you see in her?—we must all die!'

And George Forsyte, crony of his father, racing still! The Mayfly strain—was it any better than any other? He might just as well have a flutter with his money instead.

'No, by gum!' he muttered suddenly, 'if it's no good breeding horses, it's no good doing anything. What did I come for? I'll buy her.'

He stood back and watched the ebb of the paddock visitors towards the stand. Natty old chips, shrewd portly fellows, Jews, trainers looking as if they had never been guilty of seeing a horse in their lives; tall, flapping, languid women, or brisk, loud-voiced women; young men with an air as if trying to take it seriously—two or three of them with only one arm!

'Life over here's a game!' thought Val. 'Muffin bell rings, horses run, money changes hands; ring again, run again, money changes back.'

But, alarmed at his own philosophy, he went to the paddock gate to watch the Mayfly filly canter down. She moved well; and he made his way over to the 'small' car. The 'small' lunch was the sort a man dreams of but seldom gets; and when it was concluded Monsieur Profond walked back with him to the paddock.

'Your wife's a nice woman,' was his surprising remark.

'Nicest woman I know,' returned Val dryly.

'Yes,' said Monsieur Profond; 'she has a nice face. I admire nice woman.'

Val looked at him suspiciously, but something kindly and direct in the heavy diabolism of his companion disarmed him for the moment.

'Any time you like to come on my yacht, I'll give her a small cruise.'

'Thanks,' said Val, in arms again, 'she hates the sea.'

'So do I,' said Monsieur Profond.

'Then why do you yacht?'

The Belgian's eyes smiled. 'Oh! I don' know. I've done everything; it's the last thing I'm doin'.'

'It must be d—d expensive. I should want more reason than that.'

Monsieur Prosper Profond raised his eyebrows, and puffed out a heavy lower lip.

'I'm an easy-goin' man,' he said.

'Were you in the War?' asked Val.

'Ye-es. I've done that too. I was gassed; it was a small bit unpleasant.' He smiled with a deep and sleepy air of prosperity, as if he had caught it from his name. Whether his saying 'small' when he ought to have said 'little' was genuine mistake or affectation Val could not decide; the fellow was evidently capable of anything. Among the ring of buyers round the Mayfly filly who had won her race, Monsieur Profond said:

'You goin' to bid?'

Val nodded. With this sleepy Satan at his elbow, he felt in need of faith. Though placed above the ultimate blows of Providence by the forethought of a grandfather who had tied him up a thousand a year to which was added the thousand a year tied up for Holly by *her* grandfather, Val was not flush of capital that he could touch, having spent most of what he had realised from his South African farm on his establishment in Sussex. And very soon he was thinking: 'Dash it! she's going beyond me!' His limit–six hundred–was exceeded; he dropped out of the bidding. The Mayfly filly passed under the hammer at seven hundred and fifty guineas. He was turning away vexed when the slow voice of Monsieur Profond said in his ear:

'Well, I've bought that small filly, but I don't want her; you take her and give her to your wife.'

Val looked at the fellow with renewed suspicion, but the good humour in his eyes was such that he really could not take offence.

'I made a small lot of money in the War,' began Monsieur Profond in answer to that look. 'I 'ad armament shares. I like to give it away. I'm always makin' money. I want very small lot myself. I like my friends to 'ave it.'

'I'll buy her off you at the price you gave,' said Val with sudden resolution.

'No,' said Monsieur Profond. 'You take her. I don't want her.'

'Hang it! one doesn't–'

'Why not?' smiled Monsieur Profond. 'I'm a friend of your family.'

'Seven hundred and fifty guineas is not a box of cigars,' said Val impatiently.

'All right; you keep her for me till I want her, and do what you like with her.'

'So long as she's yours,' said Val. 'I don't mind that.'

'That's all right,' murmured Monsieur Profond, and moved away.

Val watched; he might be 'a good devil', but then again he might not. He saw him rejoin George Forsyte, and thereafter saw him no more.

He spent those nights after racing at his mother's house in Green Street.

Winifred Dartie at sixty-two was marvellously preserved, considering the three-and-thirty years during which she had put up with Montague Dartie, till almost happily released by a French staircase. It was to her a vehement satisfaction to have her favourite son back from South Africa after all this time, to feel him so little changed, and to have taken a fancy to his wife. Winifred, who in the late seventies, before her marriage, had been in the vanguard of freedom, pleasure, and fashion, confessed her youth outclassed by the donzellas of the day. They seemed, for instance, to regard marriage as an incident, and Winifred sometimes regretted that she had not done the same; a second, third, fourth incident might have secured her a partner of less dazzling inebriety; though, after all he had left her Val, Imogen, Maud, Benedict (almost a colonel and unharmed by the war)–none of whom had been divorced as yet. The steadiness of her children often amazed one who remembered their father; but, as she was fond of believing, they were really all Forsytes, favouring herself, with the exception, perhaps, of Imogen. Her brother's 'little girl' Fleur frankly puzzled Winifred. The child was as restless as any of these modern young women–'She's a small flame in a draught,' Prosper Profond had said one day after dinner–but she did not flop, or talk at the top of her voice. The steady Forsyteism in Winifred's own character instinctively resented the feeling in the air, the modern girl's habits and her motto: 'All's much of a muchness! Spend, to-morrow we shall be poor!' She found it a saving grace in Fleur that having set her heart on a thing, she had no change of heart until she got it–though what happened after, Fleur was, of course, too young to have made evident. The child was a 'very pretty little thing', too, and quite a credit to take about, with her mother's French taste and gift for wearing clothes; everybody turned to look at Fleur–great consideration to Winifred, a lover of the style and distinction which had so cruelly deceived her in the case of Montague Dartie.

In discussing her with Val, at breakfast on Saturday morning, Winifred dwelt on the family skeleton.

'That little affair of your father-in-law and your Aunt Irene, Val–it's old as the hills, of course, Fleur need know nothing about it–making a fuss. Your Uncle Soames is very particular about that. So you'll be careful.'

'Yes! But it's dashed awkward–Holly's young half-brother is coming to live with us while he learns farming. He's there already.'

'Oh!' said Winifred. 'That is a gaff! What is he like?'

'Only saw him once–at Robin Hill, when we were home in 1909; he was naked and painted blue and yellow in stripes–a jolly little chap.'

Winifred thought that 'rather nice', and added comfortably: 'Well, Holly's sensible; she'll know how to deal with it. I shan't tell your uncle. It'll only bother him. It's a great comfort to have you back, my dear boy, now that I'm getting on.'

'Getting on! Why! you're as young as ever. That chap Profond, Mother, is he all right?'

'Prosper Profond! Oh! the most amusing man I know.'

Val grunted, and recounted the story of the Mayfly filly.

'That's *so* like him,' murmured Winifred. 'He does all sorts of things.'

'Well,' said Val shrewdly, 'our family haven't been too lucky with that kind of cattle; they're too light-hearted for us.'

It was true, and Winifred's blue study lasted a full minute before she answered:

'Oh! well! He's a foreigner, Val: one must make allowances.'

'All right, I'll use his filly and make it up to him, somehow.'

And soon after he gave her his blessing, received a kiss, and left her for his bookmaker's, the Iseeum Club, and Victoria station.

6

JON

Mrs Val Dartie, after twenty years of South Africa, had fallen deeply in love, fortunately with something of her own, for the object of her passion was the prospect in front of her windows, the cool clear light on the green Downs. It was England again, at last! England more beautiful than she had dreamed. Chance had, in fact, guided the Val Darties to a spot where the South Downs had real charm when the sun shone. Holly had enough of her father's eye to apprehend the rare quality of their outlines and chalky radiance; to go up there by the ravine-like lane and wander along toward Chanctonbury or Amberley, was still a delight which she hardly attempted to share with Val, whose admiration of Nature was confused by a Forsyte's instinct for getting something out of it, such as the condition of the turf for his horses' exercise.

Driving the Ford home with a certain humouring smoothness, she promised herself that the first use she would make of Jon would be to take him up there, and show him 'the view' under this May-day sky.

She was looking forward to her young half-brother with a motherliness not exhausted by Val. A three-day visit to Robin Hill, soon after their arrival home, had yielded no sight of him–he was still at school; so that her recollection, like Val's, was of a little sunny-haired boy, striped blue and yellow, down by the pond.

Those three days at Robin Hill had been exciting, sad, embarrassing. Memories of her dead brother, memories of Val's courtship; the ageing of her father, not seen for twenty years, something funereal in his ironic gentleness which did not escape one who had much subtle instinct; above all, the presence of her stepmother, whom she could still vaguely remember as the 'lady in grey' of days when she was little and grandfather alive and Mademoiselle Beauce so cross because that intruder gave her music lessons–all these confused and tantalised a spirit which had longed to find Robin Hill untroubled. But Holly was adept at keeping things to herself, and all had seemed to go quite well.

Her father had kissed her when she left him, with lips which she was sure had trembled.

'Well, my dear,' he said, 'the War hasn't changed Robin Hill, has it? If only you could have brought Jolly back with you! I say, can you stand this spiritualistic racket? When the oak tree dies, it dies, I'm afraid.'

From the warmth of her embrace he probably divined that he had let the cat out of the bag, for he rode off at once on irony.

'Spiritualism–queer word, when the more they manifest the more they prove that they've got hold of matter.'

'How?' said Holly.

'Why! Look at their photographs of auric presences. You must have something material for light and shade to fall on before you can take a photograph. No, it'll end in our calling all matter spirit, or all spirit matter–I don't know which.'

'But don't you believe in survival, Dad?'

Jolyon had looked at her, and the sad whimsicality of his face impressed her deeply.

'Well, my dear, I should like to get something out of death. I've been looking into it a bit. But for the life of me I can't find anything that telepathy, sub-consciousness, and emanation from the storehouse of this world can't account for just as well. Wish I could! Wishes father thoughts but they don't breed evidence.'

Holly had pressed her lips again to his forehead with the feeling that it confirmed his theory that all matter was becoming spirit–his brow felt, somehow, so insubstantial.

But the most poignant memory of that little visit had been watching, unobserved, her stepmother reading to herself a letter from Jon. It was–she decided–the prettiest sight she had ever seen. Irene, lost as it were in the letter of her boy, stood at a window where the light fell on her face and her fine grey hair; her lips were moving, smiling, her dark eyes laughing, dancing, and the hand which did not hold the letter was pressed against her breast. Holly withdrew as from a vision of perfect love, convinced that Jon must be nice.

When she saw him coming out of the station with a kitbag in either hand, she was confirmed in her predisposition. He was a little like Jolly, that long-lost idol of her childhood, but eager-looking and less formal, with deeper eyes and brighter-coloured hair, for he wore no hat; altogether a very interesting 'little' brother!

His tentative politeness charmed one who was accustomed to assurance in the youthful manner; he was disturbed because she was to drive him home, instead of his driving her. Shouldn't he have a shot? They hadn't a car at Robin Hill since the War, of course, and he had only driven once, and landed up a bank, so she oughtn't to mind his trying. His laugh, soft and infectious, was very attractive, though that word, she had heard, was now quite old-fashioned. When they reached the house he pulled out a crumpled letter which she read while he was washing–a quite short letter, which must have cost her father many a pang to write.

MY DEAR,

You and Val will not forget, I trust, that Jon knows nothing of family history. His mother and I think he is too young at present. The boy is very dear, and the apple of her eye. Verbum sapientibus.

Your loving father,
J.F.

That was all; but it renewed in Holly an uneasy regret that Fleur was coming.

After tea she fulfilled that promise to herself and took Jon up the hill. They had a long talk, sitting above an old chalk-pit grown over with brambles and goosepenny. Milkwort and liverwort starred the green slope, the larks sang, and thrushes in the brake, and now and then a gull flighting inland would wheel very white against the paling sky, where the vague moon was coming up. Delicious fragrance came to them, as if little invisible creatures were running and treading scent out of the blades of grass.

Jon, who had fallen silent, said rather suddenly:

'I say; this is wonderful! There's no fat on it at all. Gull's flight and sheep-bells–'

'"Gull's flight and sheep-bells"! You're a poet, my dear!'

Jon sighed.

'Oh, Golly! No go!'

'Try! I used to at your age.'

'Did you? Mother says "try" too; but I'm so rotten. Have you any of yours for me to see?'

'My dear,' Holly murmured, 'I've been married nineteen years. I only wrote verses when I wanted to be.'

'Oh!' said Jon, and turned over on to his face: the one cheek she could see was a charming colour. Was Jon 'touched in the wind', then, as Val would have called it? Already? But, if so, all the better, he would take no notice of young Fleur. Besides, on Monday he would begin his farming. And she smiled. Was it Burns who followed the plough, or only Piers Plowman? Nearly every young man and most young women seemed to be poets nowadays, from the number of their books she had read out in South Africa, importing them from Hatchus and Bumphards; and quite good–oh! quite; much better than she had been herself! But then poetry had only really come in since her day–with motor-cars. Another long talk after dinner over a wood fire in the low hall, and there seemed little left to know about Jon except anything of real importance. Holly parted from him at his bedroom door, having seen twice over that he had everything, with the conviction that she would love him, and Val would like him. He was eager, but did not gush; he was a splendid listener, sympathetic, reticent about himself. He evidently loved their father, and adored his mother. He liked riding, rowing, and fencing better than games. He saved moths from candles, and couldn't bear spiders, but put them out of doors in screws of paper sooner than kill them. In a word, he was amiable. She went to sleep, thinking that he would suffer horribly if anybody hurt him; but who would hurt him?

Jon, on the other hand, sat awake at his window with a bit of paper and a pencil, writing his first 'real poem' by the light of a candle because there was not enough moon to see by, only enough to make the night seem fluttery and as if engraved on silver. Just the night for Fleur to walk, and turn her eyes, and lead on–over the hills and far away. And Jon, deeply furrowed in his ingenuous brow, made marks on the paper and rubbed them out and wrote them in again, and did all that was necessary for the completion of a work of art; and he had a feeling such as the winds of Spring must have, trying their first songs among the coming blossom. Jon was one of those boys (not many) in whom a home-trained love of beauty had survived school life. He had had to keep it to himself, of course, so that not even the drawing-master knew of it; but it was there, fastidious and clean within him. And his poem seemed to him as lame and stilted as the night was winged. But he kept it, all the same. It was a 'beast', but better than nothing as an expression of the inexpressible. And he thought with a sort of discomfiture: 'I shan't be able to show it to Mother.' He slept terribly well, when he did sleep, overwhelmed by novelty.

7

FLEUR

To avoid the awkwardness of questions which could not be answered, all that had been told Jon was:

'There's a girl coming down with Val for the week-end.'

For the same reason, all that had been told Fleur was: 'We've got a youngster staying with us.'

The two yearlings, as Val called them in his thoughts, met therefore in a manner which for unpreparedness left nothing to be desired. They were thus introduced by Holly:

'This is Jon, my little brother; Fleur's a cousin of ours, Jon.'

Jon, who was coming in through a french window out of strong sunlight, was so confounded by the providential nature of this miracle, that he had time to hear Fleur say calmly: 'Oh, how do you do?' as if he had never seen her, and to understand dimly from the quickest imaginable little movement of her head that he never *had* seen her. He bowed therefore over her hand in an intoxicated manner, and became more silent than the grave. He knew better than to speak. Once in his early life, surprised reading by a night-light, he had said fatuously: 'I was just turning over the leaves, Mum,' and his mother had replied: 'Jon, never tell stories, because of your face–nobody will ever believe them.'

The saying had permanently undermined the confidence necessary to the success of spoken untruth. He listened therefore to Fleur's swift and rapt allusions to the jolliness of everything, plied her with scones and jam, and got away as soon as might be. They say that in delirium tremens you see a fixed object, preferably dark, which suddenly changes shape and position. Jon saw the fixed object; it had dark eyes and passably dark hair, and changed its position, but never its shape. The knowledge that between him and that object there was already a secret understanding (however impossible to understand) thrilled him so that he waited feverishly, and began to copy out his poem–which of course he would never dare to show her–till the sound of horses' hoofs roused him, and, leaning from his window, he saw her riding forth with Val. It was clear that she wasted no time; but the sight filled him with grief. He wasted his. If he had not bolted, in his fearful ecstasy, he might have been asked to go too. And from his window he sat and watched them disappear, appear again in the chine of the road, vanish, and emerge once more for a minute clear on the outline of the Down. 'Silly brute!' he thought; 'I always miss my chances.'

Why couldn't he be self-confident and ready? And, leaning his chin on his hands, he imagined the ride he might have had with her. A week-end was but a week-end, and he had missed three hours of it. Did he know anyone except himself who would have been such a flat? He did not.

He dressed for dinner early, and was first down. He would miss no more. But he missed Fleur, who came down last. He sat opposite her at dinner, and it was terrible—impossible to say anything for fear of saying the wrong thing, impossible to keep his eyes fixed on her in the only natural way; in sum, impossible to treat normally one with whom in fancy he had already been over the hills and far away; conscious, too, all the time, that he must seem to her, to all of them, a dumb gawk. Yes, it was terrible! And she was talking so well—swooping with swift wing this way and that. Wonderful how she had learned an art which he found so disgustingly difficult. She must think him hopeless indeed!

His sister's eyes, fixed on him with a certain astonishment, obliged him at last to look at Fleur; but instantly her eyes, very wide and eager, seeming to say, 'Oh! for goodness' sake!' obliged him to look at Val, where a grin obliged him to look at his cutlet—that, at least, had no eyes, and no grin, and he ate it hastily.

'Jon is going to be a farmer,' he heard Holly say; 'a farmer and a poet.'

He glanced up reproachfully, caught the comic lift of her eyebrow just like their father's, laughed, and felt better.

Val recounted the incident of Monsieur Prosper Profond; nothing could have been more favourable, for, in relating it, he regarded Holly, who in turn regarded him, while Fleur seemed to be regarding with a slight frown some thought of her own, and Jon was really free to look at her at last. She had on a white frock, very simple and well made; her arms were bare, and her hair had a white rose in it. In just that swift moment of free vision, after such intense discomfort, Jon saw her sublimated, as one sees in the dark a slender white fruit tree; caught her like a verse of poetry flashed before the eyes of the mind, or a tune which floats out in the distance and dies.

He wondered giddily how old she was—she seemed so much more self-possessed and experienced than himself. Why mustn't he say they had met? He remembered suddenly his mother's face; puzzled, hurt-looking, when she answered: 'Yes, they're relations, but we don't know them.' Impossible that his mother, who loved beauty, should not admire Fleur if she did know her!

Alone with Val after dinner, he sipped port deferentially and answered the advances of his new-found brother-in-law. As to riding (always the first consideration with Val) he could have the young chestnut, saddle and unsaddle it himself, and generally look after it when he brought it in. Jon said he was accustomed to all that at home, and saw that he had gone up one in his host's estimation.

'Fleur,' said Val, 'can't ride much yet, but she's keen. Of course her father doesn't know a horse from a cartwheel. Does your dad ride?'

'He used to; but now he's—you know, he's—' He stopped, so hating the word 'old'. His father was old, and yet not old; no—never!

'Quite,' muttered Val. 'I used to know your brother up at Oxford, ages ago, the one who died in the Boer War. We had a fight in New College Gardens. That was a queer business,' he added, musing; 'a good deal came out of it.'

Jon's eyes opened wide; all was pushing him toward historical research, when his sister's voice said gently from the doorway:

'Come along, you two,' and he rose, his heart pushing him toward something far more modern.

Fleur having declared that it was 'simply too wonderful to stay indoors,' they all went out. Moonlight was frosting the dew, and an old sun-dial threw a long shadow. Two box hedges at right angles, dark and square, barred off the orchard. Fleur turned through that angled opening.

'Come on!' she called. Jon glanced at the others, and followed. She was running about the trees like a ghost. All was lovely and foamlike above her, and there was a scent of old trunks, and of nettles. She vanished. He thought he had lost her, then almost ran into her standing quite still.

'Isn't it jolly?' she cried, and Jon answered:

'Rather!'

She reached up, twisted off a blossom and, twirling it in her fingers, said:

'I suppose I can call you Jon?'

'I should think so just.'

'All right. But you know there's a feud between our families?'

Jon stammered: 'Feud? Why?'

'It's ever so romantic and silly. That's why I pretended we hadn't met. Shall we get up early to-morrow morning and go for a walk before breakfast and have it out? I hate being slow about things, don't you?'

Jon murmured a rapturous assent.

'Six o'clock, then. I think your mother's beautiful.'

Jon said fervently: 'Yes, she is.'

'I love all kinds of beauty,' went on Fleur, 'when it's exciting. I don't like Greek things a bit.'

'What! Not Euripides?'

'Euripides? Oh! no, I can't bear Greek plays; they're so long. I think beauty's always swift. I like to look at *one* picture, for instance, and then run off. I can't bear a lot of things together. Look!' She held up her blossom in the moonlight. 'That's better than all the orchard, I think.

And, suddenly, with her other hand she caught Jon's.

'Of all things in the world, don't you think caution's the most awful? Smell the moonlight!'

She thrust the blossom against his face; Jon agreed giddily that of all things in the world caution was the worst, and bending over, kissed the hand which held his.

'That's nice and old-fashioned,' said Fleur calmly. 'You're frightfully silent, Jon. Still I like silence when it's swift.' She let go his hand. 'Did you think I dropped my handkerchief on purpose?'

'No!' cried Jon, intensely shocked.

'Well, I did, of course. Let's get back, or they'll think we're doing this on purpose too.' And again she ran like a ghost among the trees. Jon followed, with love in his heart, Spring in his heart, and over all the moonlit white unearthly blossom. They came out where they had gone in, Fleur walking demurely.

'It's quite wonderful in there,' she said dreamily to Holly.

Jon preserved silence, hoping against hope that she might be thinking it swift.

She bade him a casual and demure good-night, which made him think he had been dreaming. . . .

In her bedroom Fleur had flung off her gown, and, wrapped in a shapeless garment, with the white flower still in her hair, she looked like a mousmé, sitting cross-legged on her bed, writing by candlelight.

DEAREST CHERRY

I believe I'm in love. I've got it in the neck, only the feeling is really lower down. He's a second cousin—such a child, about six months older and ten years younger than I am. Boys always fall in love with their seniors, and girls with their juniors or with old men of forty. Don't laugh, but his eyes are the truest things I ever saw; and he's quite divinely silent! We had a most romantic first meeting in London under the Vospovitch Juno. And now he's sleeping in the next room and the moonlight's on the blossom; and to-morrow morning, before anybody's awake, we're going to walk off into Down fairyland. There's a feud between our families, which makes it really exciting. Yes! and I may have to use subterfuge and come on you for invitations—if so, you'll know why! My father doesn't want us to know each other, but I can't help that. Life's too short. He's got the most beautiful mother, with lovely silvery hair and a young face with dark eyes, I'm staying with his sister—who married my cousin; it's all mixed up, but I mean to pump her to-morrow. We've often talked about love being a spoil-sport; well, that's all tosh, it's the beginning of sport, and the sooner you feel it, my dear, the better for you.

Jon (not simplified spelling, but short for Jolyon, which is a name in my family, they say) is the sort that lights up and goes out; about five feet ten, still growing, and I believe he's going to be a poet. If you laugh at me I've done with you forever. I perceive all sorts of difficulties, but you know when I really want a thing I get it. One of the chief effects of love is that you see the air sort of inhabited, like seeing a face in the moon; and you feel—you feel dancey and soft at the same time, with a funny sensation—like a continual first sniff of orange-blossom—just above your stays. This is my first, and I feel as if it were going to be my last, which is absurd, of course, by all the laws of Nature and morality. If you mock me I will smite you, and if you tell anybody I will never forgive you. So much so, that I almost don't think I'll send this letter. Anyway, I'll sleep over it. So good-night, my Cherry-oh!

YOUR FLEUR.

8

IDYLL ON GRASS

When those two young Forsytes emerged from the chine lane, and set their faces east toward the sun, there was not a cloud in heaven, and the Downs were dewy. They had come at a good bat up the slope and were a little out of breath; if they had anything to say they did not say it, but marched in the early awkwardness of unbreakfasted morning under the songs of the larks. The stealing out had been fun, but with the freedom of the tops the sense of conspiracy ceased, and gave place to dumbness.

'We've made one blooming error,' said Fleur, when they had gone half a mile. 'I'm hungry.'

Jon produced a stick of chocolate. They shared it and their tongues were loosened. They discussed the nature of their homes and previous existences, which had a kind of fascinating unreality up on that lonely height. There remained but one thing solid in Jon's past—his mother; but one thing solid in Fleur's—her father; and of these figures, as though seen in the distance with disapproving faces, they spoke little.

The Down dipped and rose again toward Chanctonbury Ring; a sparkle of far sea came into view, a sparrow-hawk hovered in the sun's eye so that the blood-nourished brown of his wings gleamed nearly red. Jon had a passion for birds, and an aptitude for sitting very still to watch them; keen-sighted, and with a memory for what interested him, on birds he was almost worth listening to. But in Chanctonbury Ring there were none—its great beech temple was empty of life, and almost chilly at this early hour; they came out willingly again into the sun on the far side. It was Fleur's turn now. She spoke of dogs, and the way people treated them. It was wicked to keep them on chains! She would like to flog people who did that. Jon was astonished to find her so humanitarian. She knew a dog, it seemed, which some farmer near her home kept chained up at the end of his chicken run, in all weathers, till it had almost lost its voice from barking!

'And the misery is,' she said vehemently, 'that if the poor thing didn't bark at every one who passes it wouldn't be kept there. I do think men are cunning brutes. I've let it go twice, on the sly; it's nearly bitten me both times, and then it goes simply mad with joy; but it always runs back home at last, and they chain it up again. If I had my way, I'd chain that man up.' Jon saw her teeth and her eyes gleam. 'I'd brand him on his forehead with the word "Brute"; that would teach him!'

Jon agreed that it would be a good remedy.

'It's their sense of property,' he said, 'which makes people chain things. The last generation thought of nothing but property, and that's why there was the War.'

'Oh!' said Fleur, 'I never thought of that. Your people and mine quarrelled about property. And anyway we've all got it—at least, I suppose your people have.'

'Oh! yes, luckily; I don't suppose I shall be any good at making money.'

'If you were, I don't believe I should like you.'

Jon slipped his hand tremulously under her arm.

Fleur looked straight before her and chanted:

> 'Jon, Jon, the farmer's son,
> Stole a pig, and away he run!'

Jon's arm crept round her waist.

'This is rather sudden,' said Fleur calmly; 'do you often do it!'

Jon dropped his arm. But when she laughed, his arm stole back again; and Fleur began to sing:

> 'O who will o'er the downs so free,
> O who will with me ride?
> O who will up and follow me—'

'Sing, Jon!'

Jon sang. The larks joined in, sheep-bells, and an early morning church far away over in Steyning. They went on from tune to tune, till Fleur said:

'My God! I am hungry now!'

'Oh! I *am* sorry!'

She looked round into his face.

'Jon, you're rather a darling.'

And she pressed his hand against her waist. Jon almost reeled from happiness. A yellow and white dog coursing a hare startled them apart. They watched the two vanish down the slope, till Fleur said with a sigh: 'He'll never catch it, thank goodness! What's the time? Mine's stopped. I never wound it.'

Jon looked at his watch. 'By Jove!' he said, 'mine's stopped, too.'

They walked on again, but only hand in hand.

'If the grass is dry,' said Fleur, 'let's sit down for half a minute.'

Jon took off his coat, and they shared it.

'Smell! Actually wild thyme!'

With his arm round her waist again, they sat some minutes in silence.

'We are goats!' cried Fleur, jumping up; 'we shall be most fearfully late, and look so silly, and put them on their guard. Look here, Jon! We only came out to get an appetite for breakfast, and lost our way. See?'

'Yes,' said Jon.

'It's serious; there'll be a stopper put on us. Are you a good liar?'

'I believe not very; but I can try.'

Fleur frowned.

'You know,' she said, 'I realise that they don't mean us to be friends.'

'Why not?'

'I told you why.'

'But that's silly.'

'Yes; but you don't know my father!'

'I suppose he's fearfully fond of you.'

'You see, I'm an only child. And so are you–of your mother. Isn't it a bore? There's so much expected of one. By the time they've done expecting, one's as good as dead.'

'Yes,' muttered Jon, 'life's beastly short. One wants to live forever, and know everything.'

'And love everybody!'

'No,' cried Jon; 'I only want to love once–you.'

'Indeed! You're coming on! Oh! Look! There's the chalk-pit; we can't be very far now. Let's run.'

Jon followed, wondering fearfully if he had offended her.

The chalk-pit was full of sunshine and the murmuration of bees. Fleur flung back her hair.

'Well,' she said, 'in case of accidents, you may give me one kiss, Jon.' and she pushed her cheek forward. With ecstasy he kissed that hot soft cheek.

'Now, remember! We lost our way; and leave it to me as much as you can. I'm going to be rather beastly to you; it's safer; try and be beastly to me!'

Jon shook his head. 'That's impossible.'

'Just to please me; till five o'clock, at all events.'

'Anybody will be able to see through it,' said Jon gloomily.

'Well, do your best. Look! There they are! Wave your hat! Oh! you haven't got one. Well, I'll cooee! Get a little away from me, and look sulky.'

Five minutes later, entering the house and doing his utmost to look sulky, Jon heard her clear voice in the dining-room:

'Oh! I'm simply *ravenous*! He's going to be a farmer–and he loses his way! The boy's an idiot!'

9

GOYA

Lunch was over and Soames mounted to the picture-gallery in his house near Mapledurham. He had what Annette called 'a grief'. Fleur was not yet home. She had been expected on Wednesday; had wired that it would be Friday; and again on Friday that it would be Sunday afternoon; and here was her aunt, and her cousins the Cardigans, and this fellow Profond, and everything flat as a pancake for the want of her. He stood before his Gauguin–sorest point of his collection. He had bought the ugly great thing with two early Matisses before the War, because there was such a fuss about those Post-Impressionists chaps. He was wondering whether Profond would take them off his hands–the fellow seemed not to know what to do with his money–when he heard his sister's voice say: 'I think that's a horrid thing, Soames,' and saw that Winifred had followed him up.

'Oh! you *do*?' he said dryly; 'I gave five hundred for it.'

'Fancy! Women aren't made like that even if they are black.'

Soames uttered a glum laugh. 'You didn't come up to tell me that.'

'No. Do you know that Jolyon's boy is staying with Val and his wife?'

Soames spun round.

'What?'

'Yes,' drawled Winifred; 'he's gone to live with them there while he learns farming.'

Soames had turned away, but her voice pursued him as he walked up and down. 'I warned Val that neither of them was to be spoken to about old matters.'

'Why didn't you tell me before?'

Winifred shrugged her substantial shoulders.

'Fleur does what she likes. You've always spoiled her. Besides, my dear boy, what's the harm?'

'The harm!' muttered Soames. 'Why, she–' he checked himself. The Juno, the handkerchief, Fleur's eyes, her questions, and now this delay in her return–the symptoms seemed to him so sinister that, faithful to his nature, he could not part with them.

'I think you take too much care,' said Winifred. 'If I were you, I should tell her of that old matter. It's no good thinking that girls in these days are as they used to be. Where they pick up their knowledge I can't tell, but they seem to know everything.'

Over Soames's face, closely composed, passed a sort of spasm, and Winifred added hastily:

'If you don't like to speak of it, I could for you.'

Soames shook his head. Unless there was absolute necessity the thought that his adored daughter should learn of that old scandal hurt his pride too much.

'No,' he said, 'not yet. Never if I can help it.'

'Nonsense, my dear. Think what people are!'

'Twenty years is a long time,' muttered Soames. 'Outside our family, who's likely to remember?'

Winifred was silenced. She inclined more and more to that peace and quietness of which Montague Dartie had deprived her in her youth. And, since pictures always depressed her, she soon went down again.

Soames passed into the corner where, side by side, hung his real Goya and the copy of the fesco 'La Vendimia.' His acquisition of the real Goya rather beautifully illustrated the cobweb of vested interests and passions which mesh the bright-winged fly of human life. The real Goya's noble owner's ancestor had come into possession of it during some Spanish war–it was in a word loot. The noble owner had remained in ignorance of its value until in the nineties an enterprising critic discovered that a Spanish painter named Goya was a genius. It was only a fair Goya, but almost unique in England, and the noble owner became a marked man. Having many possessions and that aristocratic culture which, independent of mere sensuous enjoyment, is founded on the sounder principle that one must know everything and be fearfully interested in life, he had fully intended to keep an article which contributed to his reputation while he was alive, and to leave it to the nation after he was dead. Fortunately for Soames, the House of Lords was violently attacked in 1909, and the noble owner became alarmed and angry. 'If,' he said to himself, 'they think they can have it both ways they are very much mistaken. So long as they leave me in quiet enjoyment the nation can have some of my pictures at my death. But if the nation is going to bait me, and rob me like this, I'm damned if I won't sell the–lot. They can't have my private property and my public spirit–both.' He brooded in this fashion for several months till one morning, after reading the speech of a certain statesman, he telegraphed to his agent to come down and bring Bodkin. On going over the collection Bodkin, than whose opinion on market values none was more sought, pronounced that with a free hand to sell to America, Germany, and other places where there was an interest in art, a lot more money could be made than by selling in England. The noble owner's public spirit–he said–was well known but the pictures were unique. The noble owner put this opinion in his pipe and smoked it for a year. At the end of that time he read another speech by the same statesman, and telegraphed to his agents; 'Give Bodkin a free hand.' It was at this juncture that Bodkin conceived the idea which salved the goya and two other unique pictures for the native country of the noble owner. With one hand Bodkin proffered the pictures to the foreign market, with the other he formed a list of private British collectors. Having obtained what he considered the highest possible bids from across the seas, he submitted pictures and bids to the private British collectors, and invited them, of their public spirit, to outbid. In three instances (including the Goya) out of twenty-one he was successful. And why? One of the private collectors made buttons–he had made so many that he desired that his wife should be called Lady 'Buttons'. He therefore bought a unique picture at great cost, and gave it to the nation. It was 'part,' his friends said, 'of his general game.' The second of the private collectors was an Americophobe, and bought a unique picture to 'spite the damned Yanks.' The third of the private collectors was Soames, who–more sober than either of the others–bought after a visit to Madrid, because he was certain that Goya was still on the up grade. Goya was not booming at the moment, but he would come again; and, looking at that portrait, Hogarthian, Manetesque in its directness, but with its own queer sharp beauty of paint, he was perfectly satisfied still that he had made no error, heavy though the price had been–heaviest he had ever paid. And next to it was hanging the copy of 'La Vendimia'. There she was–the little wretch–looking back at him in her dreamy mood, the mood he loved best because he felt so much safer when she looked like that.

He was still gazing when the scent of a cigar impinged on his nostrils, and a voice said:

'Well, Mr Forsyde, what you goin' to do with this small lot?'

That Belgian chap, whose mother–as if Flemish blood were not enough–had been Armenian! Subduing a natural irritation, he said:

'Are you a judge of pictures?'

'Well, I've got a few myself.'

'Any Post-Impressionists?'

'Ye-es, I rather like them.'

'What do you think of this?' said Soames, pointing to the Gauguin.

Monsieur Profond protruded his lower lip and short pointed beard.

'Rather fine, I think,' he said; 'do you want to sell it?'

Soames checked his instinctive. 'Not particularly'–he would not chaffer with this alien.

'Yes,' he said.

'What do you want for it?'

'What I gave.'

'All right,' said Monsieur Profond. 'I'll be glad to take that small picture. Post-Impressionists–they're awful dead, but they're amusin'. I don't care for pictures much, but I've got some, just a small lot.'

'What *do* you care for?'

Monsieur Profond shrugged his shoulders.

'Life's awful like a lot of monkeys scrambling for empty nuts.'

'You're young,' said Soames. If the fellow must make a generalisation, he needn't suggest that the forms of property lacked solidity!

'I don't worry,' replied Monsieur Profond smiling; 'we're born, and we die. Half the world's starvin'. I feed a small lot of babies out in my mother's country; but what's the use? Might as well throw my money in the river.'

Soames looked at him, and turned back toward his Goya. He didn't know what the fellow wanted.

'What shall I make my cheque for?' pursued Monsieur Profond.

'Five hundred,' said Soames shortly; 'but I don't want you to take it if you don't care for it more than that.'

'That's all right,' said Monsieur Profond; 'I'll be 'appy to 'ave that picture.'

He wrote a cheque with a fountain-pen heavily chased with gold. Soames watched the process uneasily. How on earth had the fellow known that he wanted to sell that picture? Monsieur Profond held out the cheque.

'The English are awful funny about pictures,' he said. 'So are the French, so are people. They're all awful funny.'

'I don't understand you,' said Soames stiffly.

'It's like hats,' said Monsieur Profond enigmatically, 'small or large, turnin' up or down–just the fashion. Awful funny.' And, smiling, he drifted out of the gallery again blue and solid like the smoke of his excellent cigar.

Soames had taken the cheque, feeling as if the intrinsic value of ownership had been called in question. 'He's a cosmopolitan,' he thought, watching Profond emerge from under the verandah with Annette, and saunter down the lawn toward the river. What his wife saw in the fellow he didn't know, unless it was that he could speak her language; and there passed in Soames what Monsieur Profond would have called a 'small doubt' whether Annette was not too handsome to be walking with any one so 'cosmopolitan'. Even at that distance he could see the blue fumes from Profond's cigar wreathe out in the quiet sunlight; and his grey buckskin shoes, and his grey hat–the fellow was a dandy! And he could see the quick turn of his wife's head, so very straight on her desirable neck and shoulders. That turn of her neck always seemed to him a little too showy, and in the 'Queen of all I survey' manner–not quite distinguished. He watched them walk along the path at the bottom of the garden. A young man in flannels joined them down there–a Sunday caller no doubt, from up the river. He went back to his Goya. He was still staring at that replica of Fleur, and worrying over Winifred's news, when his wife's voice said:

'Mr Michael Mont, Soames. You invited him to see your pictures.'

There was the cheerful young man of the Gallery off Cork Street!

'Turned up, you see, sir; I live only four miles from Pangbourne. Jolly day, isn't it?'

Confronted with the results of his expansiveness, Soames scrutinised his visitor. The young man's mouth was excessively large and curly–he seemed always grinning. Why didn't he grow the rest of those idiotic little moustaches, which made him look like a music-hall buffoon? What on earth were young men about, deliberately lowering their class with these tooth-brushes, or little slug whiskers? Ugh! Affected young idiots! In other respects he was presentable, and his flannels very clean.

'Happy to see you!' he said.

The young man, who had been turning his head from side to side, became transfixed. 'I say!' he said, '"some" picture!'

Soames saw, with mixed sensations, that he had addressed the remark to the Goya copy.

'Yes,' he said dryly, 'that's not a Goya. It's a copy. I had it painted because it reminded me of my daughter.'

'By Jove! I thought I knew the face, sir. Is she here?'

The frankness of his interest almost disarmed Soames.

'She'll be in after tea,' he said. 'Shall we go round the pictures?'

And Soames began that round which never tired him. He had not anticipated much intelligence from one who had mistaken a copy for an original, but as they passed from section to section, period to period, he was startled by the young man's frank and relevant remarks. Natively shrewd himself, and even sensuous beneath his mask. Soames had not spent thirty-eight years over his one hobby without knowing something more about pictures than their market values. He was, as it were, the missing link between artist and the commercial public. Art for art's sake and all that, of course, was cant. But æsthetics and good taste were necessary. This appreciation of enough persons of good taste was what gave a work of art its permanent market value, or in other words made it 'a work of art'. There was no real cleavage. And he was sufficiently accustomed to sheep-like and unseeing visitors, to be intrigued by one who did not hesitate to say of Mauve: 'Good old haystacks!' or of James Maris: 'Didn't he just paint and paper 'em! Mathew was the real swell, sir; you could dig into his surfaces!' It was after the young man had whistled before a Whistler, with the words, 'D'you think he ever really saw a naked woman, sir?' that Soames remarked:

'What *are* you, Mr Mont, if I may ask?'

'I, sir? I was going to be a painter, but the War knocked that. Then in the trenches, you know, I used to dream of the Stock Exchange, snug and warm and just noisy enough. But the Peace knocked that; shares seem off, don't they? I've only been demobbed about a year. What do you recommend, sir?'

'Have you got money?'

'Well,' answered the young man, 'I've got a father; I kept him alive during the War, so he's bound to keep me alive now. Though, of course, there's the question whether he ought to be allowed to hang on to his property. What do you think about that, sir?'

Soames, pale and defensive, smiled.

'The old man has fits when I tell him he may have to work yet. He's got land, you know; it's a fatal disease.'

'This is my real Goya,' said Soames dryly.

'By George! He *was* a swell. I saw a Goya in Munich once that bowled me middle stump. A most evil-looking old woman in the most gorgeous lace. *He* made no compromise with the public taste. That old boy was 'some' explosive; he must have smashed up a lot of convention in his day. Couldn't he just paint! He makes Velasquez stiff, don't you think?'

'I have no Velasquez,' said Soames.

The young man stared. 'No,' he said; 'only nations or profiteers can afford him, I suppose. I say, why shouldn't all the bankrupt nations sell their Velasquez and Titians and other swells to the profiteers by force, and then pass a law that anyone who holds a picture by an Old Master–see schedule–must hang it in a public gallery! There seems something in that.'

'Shall we go down to tea?' said Soames.

The young man's ears seemed to droop on his skull. 'He's not dense,' thought Soames, following him off the premises.

Goya, with his satiric and surpassing precision, his original 'line', and the daring of light and shade, could have reproduced to admiration the group assembled round Annette's tea-tray in the ingle-nook below. He alone, perhaps, of painters would have done justice to the sunlight filtering through a screen of creeper, to the lovely pallor of brass, the old cut glasses, the thin slices of lemon in pale amber tea; justice to Annette in her black lacey dress; there was something of the fair Spaniard in her beauty, though it lacked the spirituality of that rare type; to Winifred's grey-haired, corseted solidity; to Soames, of a certain grey and flat-cheeked distinction; to the vivacious Michael Mont, pointed in ear and eye; to Imogen, dark, luscious of glance, growing a little stout; to Prosper Profond, with his expression as who should say, 'Well, Mr Goya, what's the use of paintin' this small party?' finally, to Jack Cardigan, with his shining stare and tanned sanguinity betraying the moving principle: 'I'm English, and I live to be fit.'

Curious, by the way, that Imogen, who as a girl had declared solemnly one day at Timothy's that she would never marry a good man–they were so dull–should have married Jack Cardigan, in whom health had so destroyed all traces of original sin, that she might have retired to rest with ten thousand other Englishmen without knowing the difference from the one she had chosen to repose beside. 'Oh!' she would say of him, in her 'amusing' way, 'Jack keeps himself so fearfully fit; he's never had a day's illness in his life. He went right through the War without a finger-ache. You really can't imagine how fit he is!' Indeed, he was so 'fit' that he couldn't see when she was flirting, which was such a comfort in a way. All the same she was quite fond of him, so far as one could be of a sports-machine, and of the two little Cardigans made after his pattern. Her eyes just then were comparing him maliciously with Prosper Profond. There was no 'small' sport or game which Monsieur Profond had not played at too, it seemed, from skittles to tarpon-fishing, and worn out everyone. Imogen would sometimes wish that they had worn out Jack, who continued to play at them and talk of them with the simple zeal of a schoolgirl learning hockey; at the age of Great-uncle Timothy she well knew that Jack would be playing carpet-golf in her bedroom, and 'wiping somebody's eye'.

He was telling them now how he had 'pipped the pro–a charmin' fellow, playin' a very good game,' at the last hole this morning; and how he had pulled down to Caversham since lunch, and trying to incite Prosper Profond to play him a set of tennis after tea–do him good–'keep him fit.'

'But what's the use of keepin' fit?' said Monsieur Profond.

'Yes, sir,' murmured Michael Mont, 'what do you keep fit for?'

'Jack,' cried Imogen, enchanted, 'what *do* you keep fit for?'

Jack Cardigan stared with all his health. The questions were like the buzz of a mosquito, and he put up his hand to wipe them away. During the War, of course, he had kept fit to kill Germans; now that it was over he either did not know, or shrank in delicacy from explanation of his moving principle.

'But he's right,' said Monsieur Profond unexpectedly, 'there's nothin' left but keepin' fit.'

The saying, too deep for Sunday afternoon, would have passed unanswered, but for the mercurial nature of young Mont.

'Good!' he cried. 'That's the great discovery of the War. We all thought we were progressing–now we know we're only changing.'

'For the worse,' said Monsieur Profond genially.

'How you are cheerful, Prosper!' murmured Annette.

'You come and play tennis!' said Jack Cardigan; 'you've got the hump. We'll soon take that down. D'you play, Mr Mont?'

'I hit the ball about, sir.'

At this juncture Soames rose, ruffled in that deep instinct of preparation for the future which guided his existence.

'When Fleur comes–' he heard Jack Cardigan say.

Ah! and why didn't she come? He passed through drawing-room, hall, and porch out on to the drive, and stood there listening for the car. All was still and Sundayfied; the lilacs in full flower scented the air. There were white clouds, like the feathers of ducks gilded by the sunlight. Memory of the day when Fleur was born, and he had waited in such agony with her life and her mother's balanced in his hands, came to him sharply. He had saved her then, to be the flower of his life. And now! Was she going to give him trouble–pain–give him trouble? He did not like the look of things! A blackbird broke in on his reverie with an evening song–a great big fellow up in that acacia tree. Soames had taken quite an interest in his birds of late years: he and Fleur would walk round and watch them; her eyes were sharp as needles, and she knew every nest. He saw her dog, a retriever, lying on the drive in a patch of sunlight, and called to him. 'Hallo, old fellow–waiting for her too?' The dog came slowly with a grudging tail, and Soames mechanically laid a pat on his head. The dog, the bird, the lilac, all were part of Fleur for him; no more, no less. 'Too fond of her!' he thought, 'too fond!' He was like a man uninsured, with his ships at sea. Uninsured again–as in that other time, so long ago, when he would wander dumb and jealous in the wilderness of London, longing for that woman–his first wife–the mother of this infernal boy. Ah! There was the car at last! It drew up, it had luggage, but no Fleur.

'Miss Fleur is walking up, sir, by the towing-path.'

Walking all those miles? Soames stared. The man's face had the beginning of a smile on it. What was he grinning at? And very quickly he turned saying, 'All right, Sims!' and went into the house. He mounted to the picture-gallery once more. He had from there a view of the river bank and stood with his eyes fixed on it, oblivious of the fact that it would be an hour at least before her figure showed there. Walking up! And that fellow's grin. The boy–! He turned abruptly from the window. He couldn't spy on her. If she wanted to keep things from him–she must; he could not spy on her. His heart felt empty, and bitterness mounted from it into his very mouth. The staccato shouts of Jack Cardigan pursuing the ball, the laugh of young Mont rose in the stillness and came in. He hoped they were making that chap Profond run. And the girl in 'La Vendimia' stood with her arm akimbo and her dreamy eyes looking past him 'I've done all I could for you,' he thought, 'since you were no higher than my knee. You aren't going to–to–hurt me, are you?'

But the Goya copy answered not, brilliant in colour just beginning to tone down. 'There's no real life in it,' thought Soames. 'Why doesn't she come?'

10

TRIO

Among those four Forsytes of the third, and, as one might say, fourth generation, at Wansdon under the Downs, a week-end prolonged into the ninth day had stretched the crossing threads of tenacity almost to snapping-point. Never had Fleur been so '*fine*', Holly so watchful, Val so stable-secretive, Jon so silent and disturbed. What he learned of farming in that week might have been balanced on the point of a penknife and puffed off. He, whose nature was essentially averse from intrigue, and whose adoration of Fleur disposed him to think that any need for concealing it was 'skittles', chafed and fretted, yet obeyed, taking what relief he could in the few moments when they were alone. On Thursday, while they were standing in the bay window of the drawing-room, dressed for dinner, she said to him:

'Jon, I'm going home on Sunday by the 3.40 from Paddington; if you were to go home on *Saturday* you could come up on Sunday and take me down, and just get back here by the last train, after. You *were* going home anyway, weren't you?'

Jon nodded.

'Anything to be with you,' he said; 'only why need I pretend—'

Fleur slipped her little finger into his palm:

'You have no instinct, Jon; you *must* leave things to me. It's serious about our people. We've simply got to be secret at present, if we want to be together.' The door was opened, and she added loudly: 'You *are* a duffer, Jon.'

Something turned over within Jon; he could not bear this subterfuge about a feeling so natural, so overwhelming, and so sweet.

On Friday night about eleven he had packed his bag, and was leaning out of his window, half miserable, and half lost in a dream of Paddington station, when he heard a tiny sound, as of a finger-nail tapping on his door. He rushed to it and listened. Again the sound. It *was* a nail. He opened. Oh! What a lovely thing came in!

'I wanted to show you my fancy dress,' it said, and struck an attitude at the foot of his bed.

Jon drew a long breath and leaned against the door. The apparition wore white muslin on its head, a fichu round its bare neck over a wine-coloured dress, fulled out below its slender waist. It held one arm akimbo, and the other raised, right-angled, holding a fan which touched its head.

'This ought to be a basket of grapes,' it whispered, 'but I haven't got it here. It's my Goya dress. And this is the attitude in the picture. Do you like it?'

'It's a dream.'

The apparition pirouetted. 'Touch it, and see.'

Jon knelt down and took the skirt reverently.

'Grape colour,' came the whisper, 'all grapes—La Vendimia—the vintage.'

Jon's fingers scarcely touched each side of the waist; he looked up, with adoring eyes.

'Oh! Jon,' it whispered; bent, kissed his forehead, pirouetted again, and, gliding out, was gone.

Jon stayed on his knees, and his head fell forward against the bed. How long he stayed like that he did not know. The little noises of the tapping nail, the feet, the skirts rustling–as in a dream–went on about him; and before his closed eyes the figure stood and smiled and whispered, a faint perfume of narcissus lingering in the air. And his forehead where it had been kissed had a little cool place between the brows, like the imprint of a flower. Love filled his soul, that love of boy for girl which knows so little, hopes so much, would not brush the down off for the world, and must become in time a fragrant memory–a searing passion–a humdrum mateship–or, once in many times, vintage full and sweet with sunset colour on the grapes.

Enough has been said about Jon Forsyte here and in another place to show what long marches lay between him and his great-great-grandfather, the first Jolyon, in Dorset down by the sea. Jon was sensitive as a girl, more sensitive than nine out of ten girls of the day; imaginative as one of his half-sister June's 'lame duck' painters; affectionate as a son of his father and his mother naturally would be. And yet, in his inner tissue, there was something of the old founder of his family, a secret tenacity of soul, a dread of showing his feelings, a determination not to know when he was beaten. Sensitive, imaginative, affectionate boys get a bad time at school, but Jon had instinctively kept his nature dark, and been but normally unhappy there. Only with his mother had he, up till then, been absolutely frank and natural; and when he went home to Robin Hill that Saturday his heart was heavy because Fleur had said that he must not be frank and natural with her from whom he had never yet kept anything, must not even tell her that they had met again, unless he found that she knew already. So intolerable did this seem to him that he was very near to telegraphing an excuse and staying up in London. And the first thing his mother said to him was:

'So you've had our little friend of the confectioner's there, Jon. What is she like on second thoughts?'

With relief, and a high colour, Jon answered:

'Oh! awfully jolly, Mum.'

Her arm pressed his.

Jon had never loved her so much as in that minute which seemed to falsify Fleur's fears and to release his soul. He turned to look at her, but something in her smiling face–something which only he perhaps would have caught–stopped the words bubbling up in him. Could fear go with a smile? If so, there was fear in her face. And out of Jon tumbled quite other words, about farming, Holly, and the Downs. Talking fast, he waited for her to come back to Fleur. But she did not. Nor did his father mention her, though of course, he too, must know. What deprivation, and killing of reality was in this silence about Fleur–when he was so full of her; when his mother was so full of Jon, and his father so full of his mother! And so the trio spent the evening of that Saturday.

After dinner his mother played; she seemed to play all the things he liked best, and he sat with one knee clasped, and his hair standing up where his fingers had run through it. He gazed at his mother while she played, but he saw Fleur–Fleur in the moonlit orchard, Fleur in the sunlit gravel-pit, Fleur in that fancy dress, swaying, whispering, stooping, kissing his forehead. Once, while he listened, he forgot himself and glanced at his father in that other easy chair.

What was Dad looking like that for? The expression on his face was so sad and puzzling. It filled him with a sort of remorse, so that he got up and went and sat on the arm of his father's chair. From there he could not see his face; and again he saw Fleur—in his mother's hands, slim and white on the keys, in the profile of her face and her powdery hair; and down the long room in the open window where the May night walked outside.

When he went up to his bed his mother came into his room. She stood at the window, and said:

'Those cypresses your grandfather planted down there have done wonderfully. I always think they look beautiful under a dropping moon. I wish you had known your grandfather, Jon.'

'Were you married to father when he was alive?' asked Jon suddenly.

'No, dear; he died in '92—very old—eighty-five, I think.'

'Is Father like him?'

'A little, but more subtle, and not quite so solid.'

'I know, from grandfather's portrait; who painted that?'

'One of June's 'lame ducks'. But it's quite good.'

Jon slipped his hand through his mother's arm. 'Tell me about the family quarrel, Mum.'

He felt her arm quivering. 'No, dear; that's for your father some day, if he thinks fit.'

'Then it *was* serious,' said Jon, with a catch in his breath.

'Yes.' And there was a silence, during which neither knew whether the arm or the hand within it were quivering most.

'Some people,' said Irene softly, 'think the moon on her back is evil; to me she's always lovely. Look at those cypress shadows! Jon, Father says we may go to Italy, you and I, for two months. Would you like?'

Jon took his hand from under her arm: his sensation was so sharp and so confused. Italy with his mother! A fortnight ago it would have been perfection; now it filled him with dismay; he felt that the sudden suggestion had to do with Fleur. He stammered out:

'Oh! yes; only—I don't know. Ought I—now I've just begun? I'd like to think it over.'

Her voice answered, cool and gentle:

'Yes, dear; think it over. But better now than when you've begun farming seriously. Italy with you—! It would be nice!'

Jon put his arm round her waist, still slim and firm as a girl's.

'Do you think you ought to leave Father?' he said feebly, feeling very mean.

'Father suggested it; he thinks you ought to see Italy at least before you settle down to anything.'

The sense of meanness died in Jon; he knew, yes—he knew—that his father and his mother were not speaking frankly, no more than he himself. They wanted to keep him from Fleur. His heart hardened. And, as if she felt that process going on, his mother said:

'Good-night darling. Have a good sleep and think it over. But it would be lovely!'

She pressed him to her so quickly that he did not see her face. Jon stood feeling exactly as he used to when he was a naughty little boy; sore because he was not loving, and because he was justified in his own eyes.

But Irene, after she had stood a moment in her own room, passed through the dressing-room between it and her husband's.

'Well?'

'He will think it over, Jolyon.'

Watching her lips that wore a little drawn smile, Jolyon said quietly:

'You had better let me tell him, and have done with it. After all, Jon has the instincts of a gentleman. He has only to understand–'

'Only! He can't understand; that's impossible.'

'I believe I could have at his age.'

Irene caught his hand. 'You were always more of a realist than Jon; and never so innocent.'

'That's true,' said Jolyon. 'It's queer, isn't it? You and I would tell our story to the world without a particle of shame; but our own boy stumps us.'

'We've never cared whether the world approves or not.'

'Jon would not disapprove of *us*!'

'Oh! Jolyon, yes. He's in love, I feel he's in love. And he'd say: "My mother once married *without love*! How could she have!" It'll seem to him a crime! And so it was!'

Jolyon took her hand, and said with a wry smile:

'Ah! why on earth are we born young? Now, if only we were born old and grew younger year by year, we should understand how things happen, and drop all our cursed intolerance. But you know if the boy is really in love, he won't forget, even if he goes to Italy. We're a tenacious breed; and he'll know by instinct why he's being sent. Nothing will really cure him but the shock of being told.'

'Let me try, anyway.'

Jolyon stood a moment without speaking. Between this devil and this deep sea–the pain of a dreaded disclosure and the grief of losing his wife for two months–he secretly hoped for the devil; yet if she wished for the deep sea he must put up with it. After all, it would be training for that departure from which there would be no return. And, taking her in his arms, he kissed her eyes, and said:

'As you will, my love.'

I I

DUET

That 'small' emotion, love, grows amazingly when threatened with extinction. Jon reached Paddington station half an hour before his time and a full week after, as it seemed to him. He stood at the appointed book-stall, amid a crowd of Sunday travellers, in a Harris tweed suit exhaling, as it were, the emotion of his thumping heart. He read the names of the novels on the book-stall, and bought one at last, to avoid being regarded with suspicion by the book-stall clerk. It was called *The Heart of the Trail* which must mean something, though it did not seem to. He also bought *The Lady's Mirror* and *The Landsman*. Every minute was an hour long, and full of horrid imaginings. After nineteen had passed, he saw her with a bag and a porter wheeling her luggage. She came swiftly; she came cool. She greeted him as if he were a brother.

'First class,' she said to the porter, 'corner seats; opposite.'

Jon admired her frightful self-possession.

'Can't we get a carriage to ourselves?' he whispered.

'No good; it's a stopping train. After Maidenhead perhaps. Look natural, Jon.'

Jon screwed his features into a scowl. They got in—with two other beasts!–oh! heaven! He tipped the porter unnaturally, in his confusion. The brute deserved nothing for putting them in there, and looking as if he knew all about it into the bargain.

Fleur hid herself behind *The Lady's Mirror*. Jon imitated her behind *The Landsman*. The train started. Fleur let *The Lady's Mirror* fall and leaned forward.

'Well?' she said.

'It's seemed about fifteen days.'

She nodded, and Jon's face lighted up at once.

'Look natural,' murmured Fleur, and went off into a bubble of laughter. It hurt him. How could he look natural with Italy hanging over him? He had meant to break it to her gently, but now he blurted it out.

'They want me to go to Italy with Mother for two months.'

Fleur drooped her eyelids, turned a little pale, and bit her lips.

'Oh!' she said. It was all, but it was much.

That 'Oh!' was like the quick drawback of the wrist in fencing ready for riposte. It came.

'You must go!'

'Go?' said Jon in a strangled voice.

'Of course.'

'But—two months—it's ghastly.'

'No,' said Fleur, 'six weeks. You'll have forgotten me by then. We'll meet in the National Gallery the day after you get back.'

Jon laughed.

'But suppose you've forgotten *me*,' he muttered into the noise of the train.

Fleur shook her head.

'Some other beast–' murmured Jon.

Her foot touched his.

'No other beast,' she said, lifting the *Lady's Mirror*.

The train stopped; two passengers got out, and one got in.

'I shall die,' thought Jon, 'if we're not alone at all.'

The train went on; and again Fleur leaned forward.

'I never let go,' she said; 'do you?'

Jon shook his head vehemently.

'Never!' he said. 'Will you write to me?'

'No; but *you* can–to my club.'

She had a club, she was wonderful!

'Did you pump Holly?' he muttered.

'Yes, but I got nothing. I didn't dare pump hard.'

'What can it be?' cried Jon.

'I shall find out all right.'

A long silence followed till Fleur said: 'This is Maidenhead; stand by, Jon!'

The train stopped. The remaining passenger got out. Fleur drew down her blind.

'Quick!' she cried. 'Hang out! Look as much of a beast as you can.'

Jon blew his nose, and scowled; never in all his life had he scowled like that!

An old lady recoiled, a young one tried the handle. It turned, but the door would not open. The train moved, the young lady darted to another carriage.

'What luck!' cried Jon. 'It jammed.'

'Yes,' said Fleur; 'I was holding it.'

The train moved out, and Jon fell on his knees.

'Look out for the corridor,' she whispered; 'and–quick!'

Her lips met his. And though their kiss only lasted perhaps ten seconds Jon's soul left his body and went so far beyond, that, when he was again sitting opposite that demure figure, he was pale as death. He heard her sigh, and the sound seemed to him the most precious he had ever heard–an exquisite declaration that he meant something to her.

'Six weeks isn't really long,' she said; 'and you can easily make it six if you keep your head out there, and never seem to think of me.'

Jon gasped.

'This is just what's really wanted, Jon, to convince them, don't you see? If we're just as bad when you come back they'll stop being ridiculous about it. Only, I'm sorry it's not Spain; there's a girl in a Goya picture at Madrid who's like me, Father says. Only she isn't–we've got a copy of her.'

It was to Jon like a ray of sunshine piercing through a fog. 'I'll make it Spain,' he said, 'Mother won't mind; she's never been there. And my father thinks a lot of Goya.'

'Oh! yes, he's a painter–isn't he?'

'Only water-colour,' said Jon, with honesty.

'When we come to Reading, Jon, get out first and go down to Caversham lock and wait for me. I'll send the car home and we'll walk by the towing-path.'

Jon seized her hand in gratitude, and they sat silent, with the world well lost, and one eye on the corridor. But the train seemed to run twice as fast now, and its sound was almost lost in that of Jon's sighing.

'We're getting near,' said Fleur; 'the towing-path's awfully exposed. One more! Oh! Jon, don't forget me.'

Jon answered with his kiss. And very soon, a flushed, distracted-looking youth could have been seen–as they say–leaping from the train and hurrying along the platform, searching his pockets for his ticket.

When at last she rejoined him on the towing-path a little beyond Caversham lock he had made an effort, and regained some measure of equanimity. If they had to part, he would not make a scene! A breeze by the bright river threw the white side of the willow leaves up into the sunlight, and followed those two with its faint rustle.

'I told our chauffeur that I was train-giddy,' said Fleur. 'Did you look pretty natural as you went out?'

'I don't know. What is natural?'

'It's natural to you to look seriously happy. When I first saw you I thought you weren't a bit like other people.'

'Exactly what I thought when I saw you. I knew at once I should never love anybody else.'

Fleur laughed.

'We're absurdly young. And love's young dream is out of date, Jon. Besides, it's awfully wasteful. Think of all the fun you might have. You haven't begun, even; it's a shame, really. And there's me. I wonder!'

Confusion came on Jon's spirit. How could she say such things just as they were going to part?

'If you feel like that,' he said, 'I can't go. I shall tell Mother that I ought to try and work. There's always the condition of the world!'

'The condition of the world!'

Jon thrust his hands deep into his pockets.

'But there is,' he said; 'think of the people starving!'

Fleur shook her head. 'No, no, I never, never will make myself miserable for nothing.'

'Nothing! But there's an awful state of things, and of course one ought to help.'

'Oh! yes, I know all that. But you can't help people, Jon; they're hopeless. When you pull them out they only get into another hole. Look at them, still fighting and plotting and struggling, though they're dying in heaps all the time. Idiots!'

'Aren't you sorry for them?'

'Oh! sorry–yes, but I'm not going to make myself unhappy about it; that's no good.'

And they were silent, disturbed by this first glimpse of each other's natures.

'I think people are brutes and idiots,' said Fleur stubbornly.

'I think they're poor wretches,' said Jon. It was as if they had quarrelled–and at this supreme and awful moment, with parting visible out there in that last gap of the willows!

'Well, go and help your poor wretches, and don't think of me.'

Jon stood still. Sweat broke out on his forehead, and his limbs trembled. Fleur too had stopped and was frowning at the river.

'I *must* believe in things,' said Jon with a sort of agony; 'we're all meant to enjoy life.'

Fleur laughed. 'Yes; and that's what you won't do, if you don't take care. But perhaps your idea of enjoyment is to make yourself wretched. There are lots of people like that, of course.'

She was pale, her eyes had darkened, her lips had thinned. Was it Fleur thus staring at the water? Jon had an unreal feeling as if he were passing through the scene in a book where the lover has to choose between love and duty. But just then she looked round at him. Never was anything so intoxicating as that vivacious look. It acted on him exactly as the tug of a chain acts on a dog–brought him up to her with his tail wagging and his tongue out.

'Don't let's be silly,' she said, 'time's too short. Look, Jon, you can just see where I've got to cross the river. There, round the bend, where the woods begin.'

Jon saw a gable, a chimney or two, a patch of wall through the trees–and felt his heart sink.

'I mustn't dawdle any more. It's no good going beyond the next hedge, it gets all open. Let's get on to it and say good-bye.'

They went side by side, hand in hand, silently toward the hedge, where the may-flower, both pink and white, was in full bloom.

'My club's the Talisman', Stratton Street, Piccadilly. Letters there will be quite safe, and I'm almost up once a week.'

Jon nodded. His face had become extremely set, his eyes stared straight before him.

'To-day's the twenty-third of May,' said Fleur; 'on the ninth of July I shall be in front of the "Bacchus and Ariadne" at three o'clock; will you?'

'I will.'

'If you feel as bad as I it's all right. Let those people pass!'

A man and woman airing their children went by strung out in Sunday fashion.

The last of them passed the wicket gate.

'Domesticity!' said Fleur, and blotted herself against the hawthorn hedge. The blossom sprayed out above her head, and one pink cluster brushed her cheek. Jon put up his hand jealously to keep it off.

'Good-bye, Jon.' For a second they stood with hands hard clasped. Then their lips met for the third time, and when they parted Fleur broke away and fled through the wicket gate. Jon stood where she had left him, with his forehead against that pink cluster. Gone! For an eternity–for seven weeks all but two days! And here he was, wasting the last sight of her! He rushed to the gate. She was walking swiftly on the heels of the straggling children. She turned her head, he saw her hand make a little flitting gesture; then she sped on, and the trailing family blotted her out from his view.

The words of a comic song–

> 'Paddington groan–worst ever known–
> He gave a sepulchral Paddington groan–'

came into his head, and he sped incontinently back to Reading station. All the way up to London and down to Wansdon he sat with the *Heart of the Trail* open on his knee, knitting in his head a poem so full of feeling that it would not rhyme.

I 2

CAPRICE

Fleur sped on. She had need of rapid motion; she was late, and wanted all her wits about her when she got in. She passed the islands, the station, and hotel, and was about to take the ferry, when she saw a skiff with a young man standing up in it, and holding to the bushes.

'Miss Forsyte,' he said; 'let me put you across. I've come on purpose.'

She looked at him in blank amazement.

'It's all right, I've been having tea with your people. I thought I'd save you the last bit. It's on my way, I'm just off back to Pangbourne. My name's Mont. I saw you at the picture-gallery–you remember–when your father invited me to see his pictures.'

'Oh!' said Fleur; 'yes–the handkerchief.'

To this young man she owed Jon; and, taking his hand, she stepped down into the skiff. Still emotional, and a little out of breath, she sat silent; not so the young man. She had never heard anyone say so much in so short a time. He told her his age, twenty-four; his weight, ten stone eleven; his place of residence, not far away; described his sensations under fire, and what it felt like to be gassed; criticised the Juno, mentioned his own conception of that goddess; commented on the Goya copy, said Fleur was not too awfully like it; sketched in rapidly the condition of England, spoke of Monsieur Profond–or whatever his name was–as 'an awful sport'; thought her father had some 'ripping' pictures and some rather 'dug-up'; hoped he might row down again and take her on the river because he was quite trustworthy; inquired her opinion of Tchekov, gave her his own; wished they could go to the Russian ballet together some time–considered the name Fleur Forsyte simply topping; cursed his people for giving him the name of Michael on the top of Mont; outlined his father, and said that if she wanted a good book she should read 'Job'; his father was rather like Job while Job still had land.

'But Job didn't have land,' Fleur murmured; 'he only had flocks and herds and moved on.'

'Ah!' answered Michael Mont, 'I wish my gov'nor would move on. Not that I want his land. Land's an awful bore these days, don't you think?'

'We never have it in my family,' said Fleur. 'We have everything else. I believe one of my great-uncles once had a sentimental farm in Dorset, because we came from there originally, but it cost him more than it made him happy.'

'Did he sell it?'

'No; he kept it.'

'Why?'

'Because nobody would buy it.'

'Good for the old boy!'

'No, it wasn't good for him. Father says it soured him. His name was Swithin.'

'What a corking name!'

'Do you know that we're getting farther off, not nearer? This river flows.'

'Splendid!' cried Mont, dipping his sculls vaguely; 'it's good to meet a girl who's got wit.'

'But better to meet a young man who's got it in the plural.'

Young Mont raised a hand to tear his hair.

'Look out!' cried Fleur. 'Your scull!'

'All right! It's thick enough to bear a scratch.'

'Do you mind *sculling*?' said Fleur severely. 'I want to get in.'

'Ah!' said Mont; 'but when we get in, you see, I shan't see you any more to-day. *Fini*, as the French girl said when she jumped on her bed after saying her prayers. Don't you bless the day that gave you a French mother, and a name like yours?'

'I like my name, but Father gave it me. Mother wanted me called Marguerite.'

'Which is absurd. Do you mind calling me M. M. and letting me call you F. F.? It's in the spirit of the age.'

'I don't mind anything, so long as I get in.'

Mont caught a little crab, and answered: 'That was a nasty one!'

'Please row.'

'I am.' And he did for several strokes, looking at her with rueful eagerness. 'Of course, you know,' he ejaculated, pausing, 'that I came to see you, not your father's pictures.'

Fleur rose.

'If you don't row, I shall get out and swim.'

'Really and truly? Then I could come in after you.'

'Mr Mont, I'm late and tired; please put me on shore at once.'

When she stepped out on to the garden landing-stage he rose, and grasping his hair with both hands, looked at her.

Fleur smiled.

'Don't!' cried the irrepressible Mont. 'I know you're going to say: "Out, damnèd hair!"'

Fleur whisked round, threw him a wave of her hand. 'Good-bye, Mr M. M.!' she called, and was gone among the rose trees. She looked at her wrist-watch and the windows of the house. It struck her as curiously uninhabited. Past six! The pigeons were just gathering to roost, and sunlight slanted on the dove-cot, on their snowy feathers, and beyond in a shower on the top boughs of the woods. The click of billiard-balls came from the ingle-nook—Jack Cardigan, no doubt; a faint rustling, too, from a eucalyptus tree, startling Southerner in this old English garden. She reached the verandah and was passing in, but stopped at the sound of voices from the drawing-room to her left. Mother! Monsieur Profond! From behind the verandah screen which fenced the ingle-nook she heard these words:

'I don't, Annette.'

Did Father know that he called her mother 'Annette'? Always on the side of her father—as children are ever on one side or the other in houses where relations are a little strained—she stood, uncertain. Her mother was speaking in her low, pleasing, slightly metallic voice—one word she caught: '*Demain.*' And Profond's answer: 'All right.' Fleur frowned. A little sound came out into the stillness. Then Profond's voice: 'I'm taking a small stroll.'

Fleur darted through the window into the morning-room. There he came—from the drawing-room, crossing the verandah, down the lawn; and the click of billiard-balls which, in listening for other sounds, she had ceased to hear, began again. She shook herself, passed into the hall, and opened the drawing-room door. Her mother was sitting on the sofa between the windows, her knees crossed, her head resting on a cushion, her lips half parted, her eyes half closed. She looked extraordinarily handsome.

'Ah! Here you are, Fleur! Your father is beginning to fuss.'

'Where is he?'

'In the picture-gallery. Go up!'

'What are you going to do to-morrow, Mother?'

'To-morrow? I go up to London with your aunt.'

'I thought you might be. Will you get me a quite plain parasol?'

'What colour?'

'Green. They're all going back, I suppose.'

'Yes, all; you will console your father. Kiss me, then.'

Fleur crossed the room, stooped, received a kiss on the forehead, and went out past the impress of a form on the sofa-cushions in the other corner. She ran upstairs.

Fleur was by no means the old-fashioned daughter who demands the regulation of her parents' lives in accordance with the standard imposed upon herself. She claimed to regulate her own life, not those of others; besides, an unerring instinct for what was likely to advantage her own case was already at work. In a disturbed domestic atmosphere the heart she had set on Jon would have a better chance. None the less was she offended, as a flower by a crisping wind. If that man had really been kissing her mother it was—serious, and her father ought to know. '*Demain!*' 'All right!' And her mother going up to Town! She turned into her bedroom and hung out of the window to cool her face, which had suddenly grown very hot. Jon must be at the station by now! What did her father know about Jon? Probably everything—pretty nearly!

She changed her dress, so as to look as if she had been in some time, and ran up to the gallery.

Soames was standing stubbornly still before his Alfred Stevens–the picture he loved best. He did not turn at the sound of the door, but she knew he had heard, and she knew he was hurt. She came up softly behind him, put her arms round his neck, and poked her face over his shoulder till her cheek lay against his. It was an advance which had never yet failed, but it failed her now, and she augured the worst.

'Well,' he said stonily, 'so you've come!'

'Is that all,' murmured Fleur, 'from a bad parent?' And she rubbed her cheek against his.

Soames shook his head so far as that was possible.

'Why do you keep me on tenterhooks like this, putting me off and off?'

'Darling, it was very harmless.'

'Harmless! Much you know what's harmless and what isn't.'

Fleur dropped her arms.

'Well, then, dear, suppose you tell me; and be quite frank about it.'

And she went over to the window-seat.

Her father had turned from his picture, and was staring at his feet. He looked very grey. 'He has nice small feet,' she thought, catching his eye, at once averted from her.

'You're my only comfort,' said Soames suddenly, 'and you go on like that.'

Fleur's heart began to beat.

'Like what, dear?'

Again Soames gave her a look which, but for the affection in it, might have been called furtive.

'You know what I told you,' he said. 'I don't choose to have anything to do with that branch of the family.'

'Yes, ducky, but I don't know why *I* shouldn't.'

Soames turned on his heel.

'I'm not going into the reasons,' he said; 'you ought to trust me, Fleur!'

The way he spoke those words affected Fleur, but she thought of Jon, and was silent, tapping her foot against the wainscot. Unconsciously she had assumed a modern attitude, with one leg twisted in and out of the other, with her chin on one bent wrist, her other arm across her chest, and its hand hugging her elbow; there was not a line of her that was not involuted, and yet–in spite of all–she retained a certain grace.

'You knew my wishes,' Soames went on, 'and yet you stayed on there four days. And I suppose that boy came with you to-day.'

Fleur kept her eyes on him.

'I don't ask you anything,' said Soames; 'I make no inquisition where you're concerned.'

Fleur suddenly stood up, leaning out of the window with her chin on her hands. The sun had sunk behind trees, the pigeons were perched, quite still, on the edge of the dove-cot; the click of the billiard-balls mounted, and a faint radiance shone out below where Jack Cardigan had turned the light up.

'Will it make you any happier,' she said suddenly, 'if I promise you not to see him for say–the next six weeks?' She was not prepared for a sort of tremble in the blankness of his voice.

'Six weeks? Six years–sixty years more like. Don't delude yourself, Fleur; don't delude yourself!'

Fleur turned in alarm.

'Father, what is it?'

Soames came close enough to see her face.

'Don't tell me,' he said, 'that you're foolish enough to have any feeling beyond caprice. That would be too much!' And he laughed.

Fleur, who had never heard him laugh like that, thought: 'Then it *is* deep! Oh! what is it?' And putting her hand through his arm she said lightly:

'No, of course, caprice. Only, I like my caprices and I don't like yours, dear.'

'Mine!' said Soames bitterly, and turned away.

The light outside had chilled, and threw a chalky whiteness on the river. The trees had lost all gaiety of colour. She felt a sudden hunger for Jon's face, for his hands, and the feel of his lips again on hers. And pressing her arm tight across her breast she forced out a little laugh.

'*O la! la!* What a small fuss! as Profond would say. Father, I don't like that man.'

She saw him stop, and take something out of his breast pocket.

'You don't?' he said. 'Why?'

'Nothing,' murmured Fleur; 'just caprice!'

'No,' said Soames; 'not caprice!' And he tore what was in his hands across. 'You're right. *I* don't like him either!'

'Look!' said Fleur softly. 'There he goes! I hate his shoes: they don't make any noise.'

Down in the failing light Prosper Profond moved, his hands in his side pockets, whistling softly in his beard; he stopped, and glanced up at the sky, as if saying: 'I don't think much of that small moon.'

Fleur drew back. 'Isn't he a great cat?' she whispered; and the sharp click of the billiard-balls rose, as if Jack Cardigan had capped the cat, the moon, caprice, and tragedy with: 'In off the red!'

Monsieur Profond had resumed his strolling, to a teasing little tune in his beard. What was it? Oh! yes, from 'Rigoletto': '*Donna é mobile*'. Just what he *would* think! She squeezed her father's arm.

'Prowling!' she muttered, as he turned the corner of the house. It was past that disillusioned moment which divides the day and night–still and lingering and warm, with hawthorn scent and lilac scent clinging on the riverside air. A blackbird suddenly burst out. Jon would be in London by now; in the Park, perhaps, crossing the Serpentine, thinking of her! A little sound beside her made her turn her eyes; her father was again tearing the paper in his hands. Fleur saw it was a cheque.

'I shan't sell him my Gauguin,' he said. 'I don't know what your aunt and Imogen see in him.'

'Or Mother.'

'Your mother!' said Soames.

'Poor Father!' she thought. 'He never looks happy–not really happy. I don't want to make him worse, but of course I shall have to, when Jon comes back. Oh! well, sufficient unto the night!'

'I'm going to dress,' she said.

In her room she had a fancy to put on her 'freak' dress. It was of gold tissue with little trousers of the same, tightly drawn in at the ankles, a page's cap slung from the shoulders, little gold shoes, and a gold-winged Mercury helmet; and all over her were tiny gold bells, especially on the helmet; so that if she shook her head she pealed. When she was dressed she felt quite sick because Jon could not see her; it even seemed a pity that the sprightly young man Michael Mont would not have a view. But the gong had sounded, and she went down.

She made a sensation in the drawing-room. Winifred thought it 'Most amusing.' Imogen was enraptured. Jack Cardigan called it 'stunning', 'ripping', 'topping', and 'corking'. Monsieur Profond, smiling with his eyes, said: 'That's a nice small dress!' Her mother, very handsome in black, sat looking at her, and said nothing. It remained for her father to apply the test of common sense. 'What did you put on that thing for? You're not going to dance.'

Fleur spun round, and the bells pealed.

'Caprice!'

Soames stared at her, and, turning away, gave his arm to Winifred. Jack Cardigan took her mother. Prosper Profond took Imogen. Fleur went in by herself, with her bells jingling. . . .

The 'small' moon had soon dropped down, and May night had fallen soft and warm, enwrapping with its grape-bloom, colour and its scents the billion caprices, intrigues, passions, longings, and regrets of men and women. Happy was Jack Cardigan who snored into Imogen's white shoulder fit as a flea; or Timothy in his 'mausoleum', too old for anything but baby's slumber. For so many lay awake, or dreamed, teased by the criss-cross of the world.

The dew fell and the flowers closed; cattle grazed on in the river meadows, feeling with their tongues for the grass they could not see; and the sheep on the Downs lay quiet as stones. Pheasants in the tall trees of the Pangbourne woods, larks on their grassy nests above the gravel-pit at Wansdon, swallows in the eaves at Robin Hill, and the sparrows of Mayfair, all made a dreamless night of it soothed by the lack of wind. The Mayfly filly, hardly accustomed to her new quarters, scraped at her straw a little; and the few night-flitting things—bats, moths, owls—were vigorous in the warm darkness; but the peace of night lay in the brain of all day-time Nature, colourless and still. Men and women, alone, riding the hobby-horses of anxiety or love, burned their wavering tapers of dream and thought into the lonely hours.

Fleur, leaning out of her window, heard the hall clock's muffled chime of twelve, the tiny splash of a fish, the sudden shaking of an aspen's leaves in the puffs of breeze that rose along the river, the distant rumble of a night train, and time and again the sounds which none can put a name to in the darkness, soft obscure expressions of uncatalogued emotions from man and beast, bird and machine, or, maybe, from departed Forsytes, Darties, Cardigans, taking night strolls back into a world which had once suited their embodied spirits. But Fleur heeded not these sounds; her spirit, far from disembodied, fled with swift wing from railway-carriage to flowery hedge, straining after Jon, tenacious of his forbidden image, and the sound of his voice which was taboo. And she crinkled her nose, retrieving from the perfume of the riverside night that moment when his hand slipped between the may-flowers and her cheek. Long she leaned out in her freak dress, keen to burn her wings at life's candle; while the moths brushed her cheeks on their pilgrimage to the lamp on her dressing-table, ignorant that in a Forsyte's house there is no open flame. But at last even she felt sleepy, and, forgetting her bells, drew quickly in.

Through the open window of his room, alongside Annette's, Soames, wakeful too, heard their thin faint tinkle, as it might be shaken from stars, or the dewdrops falling from a flower, if one could hear such sounds.

'Caprice!' he thought. 'I can't tell. She's wilful. What shall I do? Fleur!'

And long into the 'small' night he brooded.

PART II

I

MOTHER AND SON

To say that Jon Forsyte accompanied his mother to Spain unwillingly would scarcely have been adequate. He went as a well-natured dog goes for a walk with its mistress, leaving a choice mutton-bone on the lawn. He went looking back at it. Forsytes deprived of their mutton-bones are wont to sulk. But Jon had little sulkiness in his composition. He adored his mother, and it was his first travel. Spain had become Italy by his simply saying: 'I'd rather go to Spain, Mum; you've been to Italy so many times; I'd like it new to both of us.'

The fellow was subtle besides naïve. He never forgot that he was going to shorten the proposed two months into six weeks, and must therefore show no sign of wishing to do so. For one with so enticing a mutton-bone and so fixed an idea, he made a good enough travelling companion, indifferent to where or when he arrived, superior to food, and thoroughly appreciative of a country strange to the most travelled Englishman. Fleur's wisdom in refusing to write to him was profound, for he reached each new place entirely without hope or fever, and could concentrate immediate attention on the donkeys and tumbling bells, the priests, patios, beggars, children, crowing cocks, sombreros, cactus hedges, old high white villages, goats, olive-trees, greening plains, singing birds in tiny cages, water-sellers, sunsets, melons, mules, great churches, pictures, and swimming grey brown mountains of a fascinating land.

It was already hot, and they enjoyed an absence of their compatriots. Jon, who, so far as he knew, had no blood in him which was not English, was often innately unhappy in the presence of his own countrymen. He felt they had no nonsense about them, and took a more practical view of things than himself. He confided to his mother that he must be an unsociable beast—it was jolly to be away from everybody who could talk about the things people did talk about. To which Irene had replied simply:

'Yes, Jon, I know.'

In this isolation he had unparalleled opportunities of appreciating what few sons can apprehend, the wholeheartedness of a mother's love. Knowledge of something kept from her made him, no doubt, unduly sensitive; and a Southern people stimulated his admiration for her type of beauty, which he had been accustomed to hear called Spanish, but which he now perceived to be no such thing. Her beauty was neither English, French, Spanish, nor Italian—it was special! He appreciated, too, as never before, his mothers subtlety of instinct. He could not tell, for instance, whether she had noticed his absorption in that Goya picture, 'La Vendimia', or whether she knew that he had slipped back there after lunch and again next morning, to stand before it full half an hour, a second and third time. It was not Fleur, of course, but like enough to give him heartache–so dear to lovers–remembering her standing at the foot of his bed with her hand held above her head. To keep a postcard reproduction of this picture in his pocket and slip it out to look at became for Jon one of those bad habits which soon or late disclose themselves to eyes sharpened by love, fear, or jealousy. And his mother's were sharpened by all three. In Granada he was fairly caught, sitting on a sun-warmed stone bench in a little battlemented garden on the Alhambra hill, whence he ought to have been looking at the view. His mother, he had thought, was examining the potted stocks between the polled acacias, when her voice said:

'Is that your favourite Goya, Jon?'

He checked, too late, a movement such as he might have made at school to conceal some surreptitious document, and answered: 'Yes.'

'It certainly is most charming; but I think I prefer the "Quitasol". Your father would go crazy about Goya; I don't believe he saw them when he was in Spain in '92.'

In '92–nine years before he had been born! What had been the previous existences of his father and his mother! If they had a right to share in his future, surely he had a right to share in their pasts. He looked up at her. But something in her face–a look of life hard-lived, the mysterious impress of emotions, experience, and suffering–seemed, with its incalculable depth, its purchased sanctity, to make curiosity impertinent. His mother must have had a wonderfully interesting life; she was so beautiful, and so–so–but he could not frame what he felt about her. He got up, and stood gazing down at the town, at the plain all green with crops, and the ring of mountains glamorous in sinking sunlight. Her life was like the past of this old Moorish city, full, deep, remote–his own life as yet such a baby of a thing, hopelessly ignorant and innocent! They said that in those mountains to the West, which rose sheer from the blue green plain, as if out of a sea, Phœnicians had dwelt–a dark, strange, secret race, above the land! His mother's life was as unknown to him, as secret, as that Phœnician past was to the town down there, whose cocks crowed and whose children played and clamoured so gaily, day in, day out. He felt aggrieved that she should know all about him and he nothing about her except that she loved him and his father, and was beautiful. His callow ignorance–he had not even had the advantage of the War, like nearly everybody else–made him small in his own eyes.

That night, from the balcony of his bedroom, he gazed down on the roof of the town–as if inlaid with honeycomb of jet, ivory, and gold; and, long after, he lay awake, listening to the cry of the sentry as the hours struck, and forming in his head these lines:

> 'Voice in the night crying, down in the old sleeping
> Spanish city darkened under her white stars!
>
> What says the voice–its clear–lingering anguish?
> Just the watchman, telling his dateless tale of safety?
> Just a road-man, flinging to the moon his song?
>
> No! 'Tis one deprived, whose lover's heart is weeping
> Just his cry: "How long?"'

The word 'deprived' seemed to him cold and unsatisfactory, but 'bereaved' was too final, and no other word of two syllables short-long came to him, which would enable him to keep 'whose lover's heart is weeping'. It was past two by the time he had finished it, and past three before he went to sleep, having said it over to himself at least twenty-four times. Next day he wrote it out and enclosed it in one of those letters to Fleur which he always finished before he went down, so as to have his mind free and companionable.

About noon that same day, on the tiled terrace of their hotel, he felt a sudden dull pain in the back of his head, a queer sensation in the eyes, and sickness. The sun had touched him too affectionately. The next three days were passed in semi-darkness, and a dulled, aching indifference to all except the feel of ice on his forehead and his mother's smile. She never moved from his room, never relaxed her noiseless vigilance, which seemed to Jon angelic. But there were moments when he was extremely sorry for himself, and wished terribly that Fleur could see him. Several times he took a poignant imaginary leave of her and of the earth, tears oozing out of his eyes. He even prepared the message he would send to her by his mother–who would regret to her dying day that she had ever sought to separate them–his poor mother! He was not slow, however, in perceiving that he had now his excuse for going home.

Toward half-past six each evening came a 'gasgacha' of bells–a cascade of tumbling chimes, mounting from the city below and falling back chime on chime. After listening to them on the fourth day he said suddenly:

'I'd like to be back in England, Mum, the sun's too hot.'

'Very well, darling. As soon as you're fit to travel.' And at once he felt better, and–meaner.

They had been out five weeks when they turned toward home. Jon's head was restored to its pristine clarity, but he was confined to a hat lined by his mother with many layers of orange and green silk and he still walked from choice in the shade. As the long struggle of discretion between them drew to its close, he wondered more and more whether she could see his eagerness to get back to that which she had brought him away from. Condemned by Spanish Providence to spend a day in Madrid between their trains, it was but natural to go again to the Prado. Jon was elaborately casual this time before his Goya girl. Now that he was going back to her, he could afford a lesser scrutiny. It was his mother who lingered before the picture, saying:

'The face and the figure of the girl are exquisite.'

Jon heard her uneasily. Did she understand? But he felt once more that he was no match for her in self-control and subtlety. She could, in some supersensitive way, of which he had not the secret, feel the pulse of his thought; she knew by instinct what he hoped and feared and wished. It made him terribly uncomfortable and guilty, having, beyond most boys, a conscience. He wished she would be frank with him, he almost hoped for an open struggle. But none came, and steadily, silently, they travelled north. Thus did he first learn how much better than men women play a waiting game. In Paris they had again to pause for a day. Jon was grieved because it lasted two, owing to certain matters in connection with a dressmaker; as if his mother, who looked beautiful in anything, had any need of dresses! The happiest moment of his travel was that when he stepped on to the Folkestone boat.

Standing by the bulwark rail, with her arm in his, she said:

'I'm afraid you haven't enjoyed it much, Jon. But you've been very sweet to me.'

Jon squeezed her arm.

'Oh! yes, I've enjoyed it awfully–except for my head lately.'

And now that the end had come, he really had, feeling a sort of glamour over the past weeks–a kind of painful pleasure, such as he had tried to screw into those lines about the voice in the night crying: a feeling such as he had known as a small boy listening avidly to Chopin, yet wanting to cry. And he wondered why it was that he couldn't say to her quite simply what she had said to him: 'You were very sweet to me.' Odd–one never could be nice and natural like that! He substituted the words: 'I expect we shall be sick.'

They were, and reached London somewhat attenuated, having been away six weeks and two days, without a single allusion to the subject which had hardly ever ceased to occupy their minds.

2

FATHERS AND DAUGHTERS

Deprived of his wife and son by the Spanish adventure, Jolyon found the solitude at Robin Hill intolerable. A philosopher when he has all that he wants is different from a philosopher when he has not. Accustomed, however, to the idea, if not to the reality of resignation, he would perhaps have faced it out but for his daughter June. He was a 'lame duck' now, and on her conscience. Having achieved–momentarily–the rescue of an etcher in low circumstances, which she happened to have in hand, she appeared at Robin Hill a fortnight after Irene and Jon had gone. The little lady was living now in a tiny house with a big studio at Chiswick. A Forsyte of the best period, so far as the lack of responsibility was concerned, she had overcome the difficulty of a reduced income in a manner satisfactory to herself and her father. The rent of the Gallery off Cork Street which he had bought for her and her increased income tax happening to balance, it had been quite simple–she no longer paid him the rent. The Gallery might be expected now at any time, after eighteen years of barren usufruct, to pay its way, so that she was sure her father would not feel it. Through this device she still had twelve hundred a year, and by reducing what she ate, and in place of two Belgians in a poor way, employing one Austrian in a poorer, practically the same surplus for the relief of genius. After three days at Robin Hill she carried her father back with her to Town. In those three days she had stumbled on the secret he had kept for two years, and had instantly decided to cure him. She knew, in fact, the very man. He had done wonders with Paul Post–that painter a little in advance of Futurism; and she was impatient with her father because his eyebrows would go up, and because he had heard of neither. Of course, if he hadn't 'faith' he would never get well! It was absurd not to have faith in the man who had healed Paul Post so that he had only just relapsed, from having overworked, or overlived, himself again. The great thing about this healer was that he relied on Nature. He had made a special study of the symptoms of Nature–when his patient failed in any natural symptom he supplied the poison which caused it–and there you were! She was extremely hopeful. Her father had clearly not been living a natural life at Robin Hill, and she intended to provide the symptoms. He was–she felt–out of touch with the times, which was not natural; his heart wanted stimulating. In the little Chiswick house she and the Austrian–a grateful soul, so devoted to June for rescuing her that she was in danger of decease from overwork–stimulated

Jolyon in all sorts of ways, preparing him for his cure. But they could not keep his eyebrows down; as, for example, when the Austrian woke him at eight o'clock just as he was going to sleep, or June took *The Times* away from him, because it was unnatural to read 'that stuff' when he ought to be taking an interest in 'life'. He never failed, indeed, to be astonished at her resource, especially in the evenings. For his benefit, as she declared, though he suspected that she also got something out of it, she assembled the Age so far as it was satellite to genius; and with some solemnity it would move up and down the studio before him in the foxtrot, and that more mental form of dancing–the one-step–which so pulled against the music, that Jolyon's eyebrows would be almost in his hair from wonder at the strain it must impose on the dancers' will-power. Aware that, hung on the line in the Water Colour Society, he was a back number to those with any pretension to be called artists, he would sit in the darkest corner he could find, and wonder about rhythm, on which so long ago he had been raised. And when June brought some girl or young man up to him, he would rise humbly to their level so far as was possible, and think: 'Dear me! This is very dull for them!' Having his father's perennial sympathy with Youth, he used to get very tired from entering into their points of view. But it was all stimulating, and he never failed in admiration of his daughter's indomitable spirit. Even genius itself attended these gatherings now and then, with its nose on one side; and June always introduced it to her father. This she felt, was exceptionally good for him, for genius was a natural symptom he had never had–fond as she was of him.

Certain as a man can be that she was his own daughter, he often wondered whence she got herself–her red-gold hair, now greyed into a special colour; her direct, spirited face, so different from his own rather folded and subtilized countenance, her little light figure, when he and most of the Forsytes were tall. And he would dwell on the origin of species, and debate whether she might be Danish or Celtic, he thought, from her pugnacity, and her taste in fillets and djibbahs. It was not too much to say that he preferred her to the Age with which she was surrounded, youthful though, for the greater part, it was. She took, however, too much interest in his teeth, for he still had some of those natural symptoms. Her dentist at once found 'Staphylococcus aureus present in pure culture' (which might cause boils, of course), and wanted to take out all the teeth he had and supply him with two complete sets of unnatural symptoms. Jolyon's native tenacity was roused, and in the studio that evening he developed his objections. He had never had any boils, and his own teeth would last his time. Of course–June admitted–they would last his time if he didn't have them out! But if he had more teeth he would have a better heart and his time would be longer. His recalcitrance–she said–was a symptom of his whole attitude; he was taking it lying down. He ought to be fighting. When was he going to see the man who had cured Paul Post? Jolyon was very sorry, but the fact was he was not going to see him. June chafed, Pondridge–she said–the healer was such a fine man, and he had such difficulty in making two ends meet, and getting his theories recognised. It was just such indifference and prejudice as her father manifested which was keeping him back. It would be so splendid for both of them!

'I perceive,' said Jolyon, 'that you are trying to kill two birds with one stone.'

'To cure, you mean!' cried June.

'My dear, it's the same thing.'

June protested. It was unfair to say that without a trial.

Jolyon thought he might not have the chance of saying it after.

'Dad!' cried June, 'you're hopeless.'

'That,' said Jolyon, 'is a fact, but I wish to remain hopeless as long as possible. I shall let sleeping dogs lie, my child. They are quiet at present.'

'That's not giving science a chance,' cried June. 'You've no idea how devoted Pondridge is. He puts his science before everything.'

'Just,' replied Jolyon, puffing the mild cigarette to which he was reduced, 'as Mr Paul Post puts his art, eh? Art for Art's sake – Science for the sake of Science. I know those enthusiastic egomaniac gentry. They vivisect you without blinking. I'm enough of a Forsyte to give them the go-by, June.'

'Dad,' said June, 'if you only knew how old-fashioned that sounds! Nobody can afford to be half-hearted nowadays.'

'I'm afraid,' murmured Jolyon, with his smile, 'that's the only natural symptom with which Mr Pondridge need not supply me. We are born to be extreme or to be moderate, my dear; though, if you'll forgive my saying so, half the people nowadays who believe they're extreme are really very moderate. I'm getting on as well as I can expect, and I must leave it at that.'

June was silent, having experienced in her time the inexorable character of her father's amiable obstinacy so far as his own freedom of action was concerned.

How he came to let her know why Irene had taken Jon to Spain puzzled Jolyon, for he had little confidence in her discretion. After she had brooded on the news, it brought a rather sharp discussion, during which he perceived to the full the fundamental opposition between her active temperament and his wife's passivity. He even gathered that a little soreness still remained from that generation-old struggle between them over the body of Philip Bosinney, in which the passive had so signally triumphed over the active principle.

According to June, it was foolish and even cowardly to hide the past from Jon. Sheer opportunism, she called it.

'Which,' Jolyon put in mildly, 'is the working principle of real life, my dear.'

'Oh!' cried June, '*you* don't really defend her for not telling Jon, Dad. If it were left to you, you would.'

'I might, but simply because I know he must find out, which will be worse than if we told him.'

'Then why *don't* you tell him? It's just sleeping dogs again.'

'My dear,' said Jolyon, 'I wouldn't for the world go against Irene's instinct. He's her boy.'

'Yours too,' cried June.

'What is a man's instinct compared with a mother's?'

'Well, I think it's very weak of you.'

'I dare say,' said Jolyon, 'I dare say.'

And that was all she got from him; but the matter rankled in her brain. She could not bear sleeping dogs. And there stirred in her a tortuous impulse to push the matter toward decision. Jon ought to be told, so that either his feeling might be nipped in the bud, or, flowering in spite of the past, come to fruition. And she determined to see Fleur, and judge for herself. When June determined on anything, delicacy became a somewhat minor consideration. After all, she was Soames's cousin, and they were both interested in pictures. She would go and tell him that he ought to buy a Paul Post, or perhaps a piece of sculpture by Boris Strumolowski, and of course she would say nothing to her father. She went on the following Sunday, looking so determined that she had some difficulty in getting a cab at Reading station. The river country was lovely in those days of her own month, and June ached at its loveliness. She who had passed through this life without knowing what union was had a love of natural beauty which was almost madness. And when she came to that choice spot where Soames had pitched his tent, she dismissed her cab, because, business over, she wanted to revel in the bright water and the woods. She appeared at his front door, therefore, as a mere pedestrian, and sent in her card. It was in June's character to know that when her nerves were fluttering she was doing something worth while. If one's nerves did not flutter, she was taking the line of least resistance, and knew that nobleness was not obliging her. She was conducted to a drawing-room, which, though not in her style, showed every mark of fastidious elegance. Thinking, 'Too much taste—too many knick-knacks,' she saw in an old lacquer-framed mirror the figure of a girl coming in from the verandah. Clothed in white, and holding some white roses in her hand, she had, reflected in that silvery-grey pool of glass, a vision-like appearance, as if a pretty ghost had come out of the green garden.

'How do you do?' said June, turning round. 'I'm a cousin of your father's.'

'Oh, yes; I saw you in that confectioner's.'

'With my young stepbrother. Is your father in?'

'He will be directly. He's only gone for a little walk.'

June slightly narrowed her blue eyes, and lifted her decided chin.

'Your name's Fleur, isn't it? I've heard of you from Holly. What do you think of Jon?'

The girl lifted the roses in her hand, looked at them, and answered calmly:

'He's quite a nice boy.'

'Not a bit like Holly or me, is he?'

'Not a bit.'

'She's cool,' thought June.

And suddenly the girl said, 'I wish you'd tell me why our families don't get on?'

Confronted with the question she had advised her father to answer, June was silent; whether because this girl was trying to get something out of her, or simply because what one would do theoretically is not always what one will do when it comes to the point.

'You know,' said the girl, 'the surest way to make people find out the worst is to keep them ignorant. My father's told me it was a quarrel about property. But I don't believe it; we've both got heaps. They wouldn't have been so *bourgeois* as all that.'

June flushed. The word applied to her grandfather and father offended her.

'My grandfather,' she said, 'was very generous, and my father is, too; neither of them was in the least *bourgeois*.'

'Well, what was it then?' repeated the girl. Conscious that this young Forsyte meant having what she wanted, June at once determined to prevent her, and to get something for herself instead.

'Why do you want to know?'

The girl smelled at her roses. 'I only want to know because they won't tell me.'

'Well, it *was* about property, but there's more than one kind.'

'That makes it worse. Now I really *must* know.'

June's small and resolute face quivered. She was wearing a round cap, and her hair had fluffed out under it. She looked quite young at that moment, rejuvenated by encounter.

'You know,' she said, 'I saw you drop your handkerchief. Is there anything between you and Jon? Because, if so, you'd better drop that too.'

The girl grew paler, but she smiled.

'If there were, that isn't the way to make me.'

At the gallantry of that reply, June held out her hand.

'I like you; but I don't like your father; I never have. We may as well be frank.'

'Did you come down to tell him that?'

June laughed. 'No; I came down to see you.'

'How delightful of you!'

This girl could fence.

'I'm two and a half times your age,' said June, 'but I quite sympathise. It's horrid not to have one's own way.'

The girl smiled again. 'I really think you might tell me.'

How the child stuck to her point!

'It's not my secret. But I'll see what I can do, because I think both you and Jon *ought* to be told. And now I'll say good-bye.'

'Won't you wait and see Father?'

June shook her head. 'How can I get over to the other side?'

'I'll row you across.'

'Look!' said June impulsively, 'next time you're in London, come and see me. This is where I live. I generally have young people in the evening. But I shouldn't tell your father that you're coming.'

The girl nodded.

Watching her scull the skiff across, June thought: 'She's awfully pretty and well made. I never thought Soames would have a daughter as pretty as this. She and Jon would make a lovely couple.'

The instinct to couple, starved within herself, was always at work in June. She stood watching Fleur row back; the girl took her hand off a scull to wave farewell, and June walked languidly on between the meadows and the river, with an ache in her heart. Youth to youth, like the dragonflies chasing each other, and love like the sun warming them through and through. Her youth! So long ago–when Phil and she–. And since? Nothing–no one had been quite what she had wanted. And so she had missed it all. But what a coil was round those two young things, if they really were in love, as Holly would have it–as her father, and Irene, and Soames himself seemed to dread. What a coil, and what a barrier! And the itch for the future, the contempt, as it were, for what was over, past, which forms the active principle, moved in the heart of one who ever believed that what one wanted was more important than what other people did not want. From the bank, awhile, in the warm summer stillness, she watched the water-lily plants and willow leaves, the fishes rising; sniffed the scent of grass and meadow-sweet, wondering how she could force everybody to be happy. Jon and Fleur! Two little lame ducks–charming callow yellow little ducks! A great pity! Surely something could be done! One must not take such situations lying down. She walked on, and reached a station, hot and cross.

That evening, faithful to the impulse toward direct action, which made many people avoid her, she said to her father:

'Dad, I've been down to see young Fleur. I think she's very attractive. It's no good hiding our heads under our wings, is it?'

The startled Jolyon set down his barley-water, and began crumbling his bread.

'It's what you appear to be doing,' he said. 'Do you realise whose daughter she is?'

'Can't the dead past bury its dead?'

Jolyon rose.

'Certain things can never be buried.'

'I disagree,' said June. 'It's that which stands in the way of all happiness and progress. You don't understand the Age, Dad. It's got no use for outgrown things. Why do you think it matters so terribly that Jon should know about his mother? Who pays any attention to that sort of thing now? The marriage laws are just as they were when Soames and Irene couldn't get a divorce, and you had to come in. We've moved, and they haven't. So nobody cares. Marriage without a decent chance of relief is only a sort of slave-owning; people oughtn't to own each other. Everybody sees that now. If Irene broke such laws, what does it matter?'

'It's not for me to disagree there,' said Jolyon; 'but that's all quite beside the mark. This is a matter of human feeling.'

'Of course it is,' cried June, 'the human feeling of those two young things.'

'My dear,' said Jolyon with gentle exasperation, 'you're talking nonsense.'

'I'm not. If they prove to be really fond of each other, why should they be made unhappy because of the past?'

'*You* haven't lived that past. I have–through the feelings of my wife; through my own nerves and my imagination, as only one who is devoted can.'

June, too, rose, and began to wander restlessly.

'If,' she said suddenly, 'she were the daughter of Phil Bosinney, I could understand you better. Irene loved him, she never loved Soames.'

Jolyon uttered a deep sound–the sort of noise an Italian peasant woman utters to her mule. His heart had begun beating furiously, but he paid no attention to it, quite carried away by his feelings.

'That shows how little you understand. Neither I nor Jon, if I know him, would mind a love-past. It's the brutality of a union without love. This girl is the daughter of the man who once owned Jon's mother as a negro slave was owned. You can't lay that ghost; don't try to, June! It's asking us to see Jon joined to the flesh and blood of the man who possessed Jon's mother against her will. It's no good mincing words; I want it clear once for all. And now I mustn't talk any more, or I shall have to sit up with this all night.' And, putting his hand over his heart, Jolyon turned his back on his daughter and stood looking at the River Thames.

June, who by her nature never saw a hornet's nest until she had put her hand into it, was seriously alarmed. She came and slipped her arm through his. Not convinced that he was right, and she herself was wrong, because that was not natural to her, she was yet profoundly impressed by the obvious fact that the subject was very bad for him. She rubbed her cheek against his shoulder, and said nothing.

After taking her elderly cousin across, Fleur did not land at once, but pulled in among the reeds, into the sunshine. The peaceful beauty of the afternoon seduced for a little one not much given to the vague and poetic. In the field beyond the bank where her skiff lay up, a machine drawn by a grey horse was turning an early field of hay. She watched the grass cascading over and behind the light wheels with fascination–it looked so cool and fresh. The click and swish blended with the rustle of the willows and the poplars, and the cooing of a wood-pigeon, in a true river song. Alongside, in the deep green water, weeds, like yellow snakes, were writhing and nosing with the current; pied cattle on the farther side stood in the shade lazily swishing their tails. It was an afternoon to dream. And she took out Jon's letters—not flowery effusions, but haunted in their recital of things seen and done by a longing very agreeable to her, and all ending 'Your devoted J'. Fleur was not sentimental, her desires were ever concrete and concentrated, but what poetry there was in the daughter of Soames and Annette had certainly in those weeks of waiting gathered round her memories of Jon. They all belonged to grass and blossom, flowers and running water. She enjoyed him in the scents absorbed by her crinkling nose. The stars could persuade her that she was standing beside him in the centre of the map of Spain; and of an early morning the dewy cobwebs, the hazy sparkle and promise of the day down in the garden, were Jon personified to her.

Two white swans came majestically by, while she was reading his letters, followed by their brood of six young swans in a line, with just so much water between each tail and head, a flotilla of grey destroyers. Fleur thrust her letters back, got out her sculls, and pulled up to the landing-stage. Crossing the lawn, she wondered whether she should tell her father of June's visit. If he learned of it from the butler, he might think it odd if she did not. It gave her, too, another chance to startle out of him the reason of the feud. She went, therefore, up the road to meet him.

Soames had gone to look at a patch of ground on which the Local Authorities were proposing to erect a Sanatorium for people with weak lungs. Faithful to his native individualism, he took no part in local affairs, content to pay the rates which were always going up. He could not, however, remain indifferent to this new and dangerous scheme. The site was not half a mile from his own house. He was quite of opinion that the country should stamp out tuberculosis; but this was not the place. It should be done farther away. He took, indeed, an attitude common to all true Forsytes, that disability of any sort in other people was not his affair, and the State should do its business without prejudicing in any way the natural advantages which he had acquired or inherited. Francie, the most free-spirited Forsyte of his generation (except perhaps that fellow Jolyon), had once asked him in her malicious way: 'Did you ever see the name Forsyte in a subscription list, Soames?' That was as it might be, but a Sanatorium would depreciate the neighbourhood, and he should certainly sign the petition which was being got up against it. Returning with this decision fresh within him, he saw Fleur coming.

She was showing him more affection of late, and the quiet time down here with her in this summer weather had been making him feel quite young; Annette was always running up to Town for one thing or another, so that he had Fleur to himself almost as much as he could wish. To be sure, young Mont had formed a habit of appearing on his motor-cycle almost every other day. Thank goodness, the young fellow had shaved off his half-toothbrushes, and no longer looked like a mountebank! With a girl friend of Fleur's who was staying in the house, and a neighbouring youth or so, they made two couples after dinner, in the hall, to the music of the electric pianola, which performed foxtrots unassisted, with a surprised shine on its expressive surface. Annette, even, now and then passed gracefully up and down in the arms of one or other of the young men. And Soames, coming to the drawing-room door, would lift his nose a little sideways, and watch them, waiting to catch a smile from Fleur; then move back to his chair by the drawing-room hearth, to peruse *The Times* or some other collector's price list. To his ever-anxious eyes Fleur showed no signs of remembering that caprice of hers.

When she reached him on the dusty road, he slipped his hand within her arm. 'Who, do you think, has been to see you, Dad? She couldn't wait! Guess!'

'I never guess,' said Soames uneasily. 'Who?'

'Your cousin, June Forsyte.'

Quite unconsciously Soames gripped her arm. 'What did *she* want?'

'I don't know. But it was rather breaking through the feud, wasn't it?'

'Feud? What feud?'

'The one that exists in your imagination, dear.'

Soames dropped her arm. Was she mocking, or trying to draw him on?

'I suppose she wanted me to buy a picture,' he said at last.

'I don't think so. Perhaps it was just family affection.'

'She's only a first cousin once removed,' muttered Soames.

'And the daughter of your enemy.'

'What d'you mean by that?'

'I beg your pardon, dear; I thought he was.'

'Enemy!' repeated Soames. 'It's ancient history. I don't know where you get your notions.'

'From June Forsyte.'

It had come to her as an inspiration that if he thought she knew, or were on the edge of knowledge, he would tell her.

Soames was startled, but she had underrated his caution and tenacity.

'If you know,' he said coldly, 'why do you plague me?'

Fleur saw that she had overreached herself.

'I don't want to plague you, darling. As you say, why want to know more? Why want to know anything of that 'small' mystery–*Je m'en fiche*, as Profond says?'

'That chap!' said Soames profoundly.

That chap, indeed, played a considerable, if invisible, part this summer–for he had not turned up again. Ever since the Sunday when Fleur had drawn attention to him prowling on the lawn, Soames had thought of him a good deal, and always in connection with Annette, for no reason, except that she was looking handsomer than for some time past. His possessive instinct, subtler, less formal, more elastic since the War, kept all misgiving underground. As one looks on some American river, quiet and pleasant, knowing that an alligator perhaps is lying in the mud with his snout just raised and indistinguishable from a snag of wood–so Soames looked on the river of his own existence, subconscious of Monsieur Profond, refusing to see more than the suspicion of his snout. He had at this epoch in his life practically all he wanted, and was as nearly happy as his nature would permit. His senses were at rest; his affections found all the vent they needed in his daughter; his collection was well known, his money well invested; his health excellent, save for a touch of liver now and again; he had not yet begun to worry seriously about what would happen after death, inclining to think that nothing would happen. He resembled one of his own gilt-edged securities, and to knock the gilt off by seeing anything he could avoid seeing would be, he felt instinctively, perverse and retrogressive. Those two crumpled rose-leaves, Fleur's caprice and Monsieur Profond's snout, would level away if he lay on them industriously.

That evening Chance, which visits the lives of even the best-invested Forsytes, put a clue into Fleur's hands. Her father came down to dinner without a handkerchief, and had occasion to blow his nose.

'I'll get you one, dear,' she had said, and ran upstairs. In the sachet where she sought for it—an old sachet of very faded silk—there were two compartments: one held handkerchiefs; the other was buttoned, and contained something flat and hard. By some childish impulse Fleur unbuttoned it. There was a frame and in it a photograph of herself as a little girl. She gazed at it, fascinated, as one is by one's own presentment. It slipped under her fidgeting thumb, and she saw that another photograph was behind. She pressed her own down farther, and perceived a face, which she seemed to know, of a young woman, very good-looking, in a very old style of evening dress. Slipping her own photograph up over it again, she took out a handkerchief and went down. Only on the stairs did she identify that face. Surely—surely Jon's mother! The conviction came as a shock. And she stood still in a flurry of thought. Why, of course! Jon's father had married the woman her father had wanted to marry, had cheated him out of her, perhaps. Then, afraid of showing by her manner that she had lighted on his secret, she refused to think further, and, shaking out the silk handkerchief, entered the dining-room.

'I chose the softest, Father.'

'H'm!' said Soames; 'I only use those after a cold. Never mind!'

That evening passed for Fleur in putting two and two together; recalling the look on her father's face in the confectioner's shop—a look strange and coldly intimate, a queer look. He must have loved that woman very much to have kept her photograph all this time, in spite of having lost her. Unsparing and matter-of-fact, her mind darted to his relations with her own mother. Had he ever really loved *her*? She thought not. Jon was the son of the woman he had really loved. Surely, then, he ought not to mind his daughter loving him; it only wanted getting used to. And a sigh of sheer relief was caught in the folds of her nightgown slipping over her head.

3

MEETINGS

Youth only recognises Age by fits and starts. Jon, for one, had never really seen his father's age till he came back from Spain. The face of the fourth Jolyon, worn by waiting, gave him quite a shock—it looked so wan and old. His father's mask had been forced awry by the emotion of the meeting, so that the boy suddenly realised how much he must have felt their absence. He summoned to his aid the thought: 'Well, I didn't want to go!' It was out of date for Youth to defer to Age. But Jon was by no means typically modern. His father had always been 'so jolly' to him, and to feel that one meant to begin again at once the conduct which his father had suffered six weeks' loneliness to cure was not agreeable.

At the question, 'Well, old man, how did the great Goya strike you?' his conscience pricked him badly. The great Goya only excited because he had created a face which resembled Fleur's.

On the night of their return, he went to bed full of compunction; but awoke full of anticipation. It was only the fifth of July, and no meeting was fixed with

Fleur until the ninth. He was to have three days at home before going back to farm. Somehow he must contrive to see her!

In the lives of men an inexorable rhythm, caused by the need for trousers, not even the fondest parents can deny. On the second day, therefore, Jon went to Town, and having satisfied his conscience by ordering what was indispensable in Conduit Street, turned his face toward Piccadilly. Stratton Street, where her club was, adjoined Devonshire House. It would be the merest chance that she should be at her club. But he dawdled down Bond Street with a beating heart, noticing the superiority of all other young men to himself. They wore their clothes with such an air; they had assurance; they were *old*. He was suddenly overwhelmed by the conviction that Fleur must have forgotten him. Absorbed in his own feeling for her all these weeks, he had mislaid that possibility. The corners of his mouth drooped, his hands felt clammy. Fleur with the pick of youth at the beck of her smile – Fleur incomparable! It was an evil moment. Jon, however, had a great idea that one must be able to face anything. And he braced himself with that dour reflection in front of a bric-à-brac shop. At this high-water mark of what was once the London season, there was nothing to mark it out from any other except a grey top hat or two, and the sun. Jon moved on, and turning the corner into Piccadilly, ran into Val Dartie moving toward the Iseeum Club, to which he had just been elected.

'Hallo! young man! Where are you off to?'

Jon flushed. 'I've just been to my tailor's.'

Val looked him up and down. 'That's good! I'm going in here to order some cigarettes; then come and have some lunch.'

Jon thanked him. He might get news of *her* from Val!

The condition of England, that nightmare of its Press and Public men, was seen in different perspective within the tobacconist's which they now entered.

'Yes, sir; precisely the cigarette I used to supply your father with. Bless me! Mr Montague Dartie was a customer here from – let me see – the year Melton won the Derby. One of my very best customers he was.' A faint smile illumined the tobacconist's face. 'Many's the tip he's given me, to be sure! I suppose he took a couple of hundred of these every week, year in, year out, and never changed his cigarette. Very affable gentleman, brought me a lot of custom. I was sorry he met with that accident. One misses an old customer like him.'

Val smiled. His father's decease had closed an account which had been running longer, probably, than any other; and in a ring of smoke puffed out from that time-honoured cigarette he seemed to see again his father's face, dark, good-looking, moustachioed, a little puffy, in the only halo it had earned. His father had his fame here, anyway – a man who smoked two hundred cigarettes a week, who could give tips, and run accounts for ever! To his tobacconist a hero! Even that was some distinction to inherit!

'I pay cash,' he said; 'how much?'

'To his son, sir, and cash – ten and six. I shall never forget Mr Montague Dartie. I've known him stand talkin' to me half an hour. We don't get many like him now, with everybody in such a hurry. The War was bad for manners, sir – it was bad for manners. You were in it, I see.'

'No,' said Val, tapping his knee, 'I got this in the war before. Saved my life, I expect. Do you want any cigarettes, Jon?'

Rather ashamed, Jon murmured: 'I don't smoke, you know,' and saw the tobacconist's lips twisted, as if uncertain whether to say 'Good God!' or 'Now's your chance, sir!'

'That's right,' said Val; 'keep off it while you can. You'll want it when you take a knock. This is really the same tobacco, then?'

'Identical, sir; a little dearer, that's all. Wonderful staying power – the British Empire, I always say.'

'Send me down a hundred a week to this address, and invoice it monthly. Come on, Jon.'

Jon entered the Iseeum with curiosity. Except to lunch now and then at the Hotch-Potch with his father he had never been in a London club. The Iseeum, comfortable and unpretentious, did not move, could not, so long as George Forsyte sat on its committee, where his culinary acumen was almost the controlling force. The club had made a stand against the newly rich, and it had taken all George Forsyte's prestige, and praise of him as a 'good sportsman', to bring in Prosper Profond.

The two were lunching together when the half-brothers-in-law entered the dining-room, and attracted by George's forefinger, sat down at their table, Val with his shrewd eyes and charming smile, Jon with solemn lips and an attractive shyness in his glance. There was an air of privilege around that corner table, as though past masters were eating there. Jon was fascinated by the hypnotic atmosphere. The waiter, lean in the chaps, pervaded with such free-masonical deference. He seemed to hang on George Forsyte's lips, to watch the gloat in his eye with a kind of sympathy, to follow the movements of the heavy club-marked silver fondly. His liveried arm and confidential voice alarmed Jon, they came so secretly over his shoulder.

Except for George's, 'Your grandfather tipped me once; he was a deuced good judge of a cigar!' neither he nor the other past master took any notice of him, and he was grateful for this. The talk was all about breeding, points, and prices of horses, and he listened to it vaguely at first, wondering how it was possible to retain so much knowledge in a head. He could not take his eyes off the dark past master – what he said was so deliberate and discouraging – such heavy, queer, smiled-out words. Jon was thinking of butterflies, when he heard him say:

'I want to see Mr Soames Forsyde take an interest in 'orses.'

'Old Soames! He's too dry a file!'

With all his might Jon tried not to grow red, while the dark past master went on.

'His daughter's an attractive small girl. Mr Soames Forsyde is a bit old-fashioned. I want to see him have a pleasure some day.'

George Forsyte grinned.

'Don't you worry; he's not so miserable as he looks. He'll never show he's enjoying anything – they might try and take it from him. Old Soames! Once bit, twice shy!'

'Well, Jon,' said Val hastily, 'if you've finished, we'll go and have coffee.'

'Who were those?' Jon asked, on the stairs. 'I didn't quite –'

'Old George Forsyte is a first cousin of your father's and of my Uncle Soames. He's always been here. The other chap, Profond, is a queer fish. I think he's hanging round Soames's wife, if you ask me!'

Jon looked at him, startled. 'But that's awful,' he said: 'I mean – for Fleur.'

'Don't suppose Fleur cares very much; she's very up to date.'

'Her mother!'

'You're very green, Jon.'

Jon grew red. 'Mothers,' he stammered angrily, 'are different.'

'You're right,' said Val suddenly; 'but things aren't what they were when I was your age. There's a "To-morrow we die" feeling. That's what old George means about my Uncle Soames. *He* doesn't mean to die to-morrow.'

Jon said, quickly: 'What's the matter between him and my father?'

'Stable secret, Jon. Take my advice, and bottle up. You'll do no good by knowing. Have a liqueur?'

Jon shook his head.

'I hate the way people keep things from one,' he muttered, 'and then sneer at one for being green.'

'Well, you can ask Holly. If *she* won't tell you, you'll believe it's for your own good, I suppose.'

Jon got up. 'I must go now; thanks awfully for the lunch.'

Val smiled up at him half-sorry, and yet amused. The boy looked so upset.

'All right! See you on Friday.'

'I don't know,' murmured Jon.

And he did not. This conspiracy of silence made him desperate. It was humiliating to be treated like a child! He retraced his moody steps to Stratton Street. But he would go to her club now, and find out the worst! To his enquiry the reply was that Miss Forsyte was not in the club. She might be in perhaps later. She was often in on Monday–they could not say. Jon said he would call again, and, crossing into the Green Park, flung himself down under a tree. The sun was bright and a breeze fluttered the leaves of the young lime tree beneath which he lay; but his heart ached. Such darkness seemed gathered round his happiness. He heard Big Ben chime 'Three' above the traffic. The sound moved something in him, and, taking out a piece of paper, he began to scribble on it with a pencil. He had jotted a stanza, and was searching the grass for another verse, when something hard touched his shoulder–a green parasol. There above him stood Fleur!

'They told me you'd been, and were coming back. So I thought you might be out here, and you are–it's rather wonderful!'

'Oh, Fleur! I thought you'd have forgotten me.'

'When I told you I shouldn't!'

Jon seized her arm.

'It's too much luck! Let's get away from this side.' He almost dragged her on through that too thoughtfully regulated Park, to find some cover where they could sit and hold each other's hands.

'Hasn't anybody cut in?' he said, gazing round at her lashes, in suspense above her cheeks.

'There *is* a young idiot, but he doesn't count.'

Jon felt a twitch of compassion for the–young idiot.

'You know I've had sunstroke; I didn't tell you.'

'Really! Was it interesting?'

'No. Mother was an angel. Has anything happened to *you*?'

'Nothing. Except that I think I've found out what's wrong between our families, Jon.'

His heart began beating very fast.

'I believe my father wanted to marry your mother, and your father got her instead.'

'Oh!'

'I came on a photo of her; it was in a frame behind a photo of me. Of course, if he was very fond of her, that would have made him pretty mad, wouldn't it?'

Jon thought for a minute. 'Not if she loved my father best.'

'But suppose they were engaged?'

'If we were engaged, and you found you loved somebody better, I might go cracked, but I shouldn't grudge it you.'

'I should. You mustn't ever do that with me, Jon.'

'My God! Not much!'

'I don't believe that he's ever really cared for my mother.'

Jon was silent. Val's words, the two past masters in the club!

'You see, we don't know,' went on Fleur; 'it may have been a great shock. She may have behaved badly to him. People do.'

'My mother wouldn't.'

Fleur shrugged her shoulders. 'I don't think we know much about our fathers and mothers. We just see them in the light of the way they treat *us*; but they've treated other people, you know, before we were born—plenty, I expect. You see, they're both old. Look at your father, with three separate families!'

'Isn't there any place,' cried Jon, 'in all this beastly London where we can be alone?'

'Only a taxi.'

'Let's get one, then.'

When they were installed, Fleur asked suddenly: 'Are you going back to Robin Hill? I should like to see where you live, Jon. I'm staying with my aunt for the night, but I could get back in time for dinner. I wouldn't come to the house, of course.'

Jon gazed at her enraptured.

'Splendid! I can show you it from the copse, we shan't meet anybody. There's a train at four.'

The god of property and his Forsytes great and small, leisured, official, commercial, or professional, like the working classes, still worked their seven hours a day, so that those two of the fourth generation travelled down to Robin Hill in an empty first-class carriage, dusty and sun-warmed, of that too early train. They travelled in blissful silence, holding each other's hands.

At the station they saw no one except porters, and a villager or two unknown to Jon, and walked out up the lane, which smelled of dust and honeysuckle.

For Jon—sure of her now, and without separation before him—it was a miraculous dawdle, more wonderful than those on the Downs, or along the River Thames. It was love-in-a-mist—one of those illumined pages of Life, where every word and smile, and every light touch they gave each other were as little gold and red and blue butterflies and flowers and birds scrolled in among the text—a happy communing, without afterthought, which lasted thirty-seven minutes. They reached the coppice at the milking hour. Jon would not take her as far as the farmyard; only to where she could see the field leading up to the gardens, and the house beyond. They turned in among the larches, and suddenly, at the winding of the path, came on Irene, sitting on an old log seat.

There are various kinds of shocks: to the vertebræ; to the nerves; to moral sensibility; and, more potent and permanent, to personal dignity. This last was the shock Jon received, coming thus on his mother. He became suddenly conscious that he was doing an indelicate thing. To have brought Fleur down openly—yes! But to sneak her in like this! Consumed with shame, he put on a front as brazen as his nature would permit.

Fleur was smiling, a little defiantly; his mother's startled face was changing quickly to the impersonal and gracious. It was she who uttered the first words:

'I'm very glad to see you. It was nice of Jon to think of bringing you down to us.'

'We weren't coming to the house,' Jon blurted out. 'I just wanted Fleur to see where I lived.'

His mother said quietly:

'Won't you come up and have tea?'

Feeling that he had but aggravated his breach of breeding, he heard Fleur answer:

'Thanks very much; I have to get back to dinner. I met Jon by accident, and we thought it would be rather jolly just to see his home.'

How self-possessed she was!

'Of course; but you *must* have tea. We'll send you down to the station. My husband will enjoy seeing you.'

The expression of his mother's eyes, resting on him for a moment, cast Jon down level with the ground–a true worm. Then she led on, and Fleur followed her. He felt like a child, trailing after those two, who were talking so easily about Spain and Wansdon, and the house up there beyond the trees and the grassy slope. He watched the fencing of their eyes, taking each other in–the two beings he loved most in the world.

He could see his father sitting under the oak tree; and suffered in advance all the loss of caste he must go through in the eyes of that tranquil figure, with his knees crossed, thin, old, and elegant; already he could feel the faint irony which would come into his voice and smile.

'This is Fleur Forsyte, Jolyon; Jon brought her down to see the house. Let's have tea at once–she has to catch a train. Jon, tell them, dear, and telephone to the Dragon for a car.'

To leave her alone with them was strange, and yet, as no doubt his mother had foreseen, the least of evils at the moment; so he ran up into the house. Now he would not see Fleur alone again–not for a minute, and they had arranged no further meeting! When he returned under cover of the maids and teapots, there was not a trace of awkwardness beneath the tree; it was all within himself, but not the less for that. They were talking of the Gallery off Cork Street.

'We back numbers,' his father was saying, 'are awfully anxious to find out why we can't appreciate the new stuff; you and Jon must tell us.'

'It's supposed to be satiric, isn't it?' said Fleur.

He saw his father's smile.

'Satiric? Oh! I think it's more than that. What do you say, Jon?'

'I don't know at all,' stammmered Jon. His father's face had a sudden grimness.

'The young are tired of us, our gods and our ideals. Off with their heads, they say–smash their idols! And let's get back to–nothing! And, by Jove, they've done it! Jon's a poet. He'll be going in, too, and stamping on what's left of us. Property, beauty, sentiment–all smoke. We mustn't own anything nowadays, not even our feelings. They stand in the way of–Nothing.'

Jon listened, bewildered, almost outraged by his father's words, behind which he felt a meaning that he could not reach. He didn't want to stamp on anything!

'Nothing's the god of to-day,' continued Jolyon, 'we're back where the Russians were sixty years ago, when they started Nihilism.'

'No, Dad,' cried Jon suddenly, 'we only want to *live*, and we don't know how, because of the Past–that's all!'

'By George!' said Jolyon, 'that's profound, Jon. Is it your own? The Past! Old ownerships, old passions, and their aftermath. Let's have cigarettes.'

Conscious that his mother had lifted her hand to her lips, quickly, as if to hush something, Jon handed the cigarettes. He lighted his father's and Fleur's, then one for himself. Had he taken the knock that Val had spoken of? The smoke was blue when he had not puffed, grey when he had; he liked the sensation in his nose, and the sense of equality it gave him. He was glad no one said 'So you've begun!' He felt less young.

Fleur looked at her watch, and rose. His mother went with her into the house. Jon stayed with his father, puffing at the cigarette.

'See her into the car, old man,' said Jolyon; 'and when she's gone, ask your mother to come back to me.'

Jon went. He waited in the hall. He saw her into the car. There was no chance for any word; hardly for a pressure of the hand. He waited all that evening for something to be said to him. Nothing was said. Nothing might have happened. He went up to bed, and in the mirror on his dressing-table met himself. He did not speak, nor did the image; but both looked as if they thought the more.

4

IN GREEN STREET

Uncertain, whether the impression that Prosper Profond was dangerous should be traced to his attempt to give Val the Mayfly filly; to a remark of Fleur's: 'He's like the hosts of Midian—he prowls and prowls around'; to his preposterous inquiry of Jack Cardigan: 'What's the use of keepin' fit?' or, more simply, to the fact that he was a foreigner, or alien as it was now called. Certain, that Annette was looking particularly handsome, and that Soames had sold him a Gauguin and then torn up the cheque, so that Monsieur Profond himself had said: 'I didn't get that small picture I bought from Mr Forsyde.'

However suspiciously regarded, he still frequented Winifred's evergreen little house in Green Street, with a good-natured obtuseness which no one mistook for naïveté, a word hardly applicable to Monsieur Prosper Profond. Winifred still found him 'amusing', and would write him little notes saying: 'Come and have a "jolly" with us'—it was breath of life to her to keep up with the phrases of the day.

The mystery, with which all felt him to be surrounded, was due to his having done, seen, heard, and known everything, and found nothing in it—which was unnatural. The English type of disillusionment was familiar enough to Winifred, who had always moved in fashionable circles. It gave a certain cachet or distinction, so that one got something out of it. But to see nothing in anything, not as a pose, but because there *was* nothing in anything, was not English; and that which was not English one could not help secretly feeling dangerous, if not precisely bad form. It was like having the mood which the War had left, seated—dark, heavy, smiling, indifferent—in your Empire chair; it was like listening to that mood talking through thick pink lips above a little diabolic beard. It was, as Jack Cardigan expressed it—for the English character at large—'a bit too thick'—for if nothing was really worth getting excited about, there were always games, and one could make it so! Even Winifred, ever a Forsyte at heart, felt that there was nothing to be had out of such a mood of disillusionment, so that it really ought not to be there. Monsieur Profond, in fact, made the mood too plain in a country which decently veiled such realities.

When Fleur, after her hurried return from Robin Hill, came down to dinner that evening, the mood was standing at the window of Winifred's little drawing-room, looking out into Green Street, with an air of seeing nothing in it. And Fleur gazed promptly into the fireplace with an air of seeing a fire which was not there.

Monsieur Profond came from the window. He was in full fig, with a white waistcoat and a white flower in his buttonhole.

'Well, Miss Forsyde,' he said, 'I'm awful pleased to see you. Mr Forsyde well? I was sayin' to-day I want to see him have some pleasure. He worries.'

'You think so?' said Fleur shortly.

'Worries,' repeated Monsieur Profond burring the r's.

Fleur spun round. 'Shall I tell you,' she said, 'what would give him pleasure?' But the words, 'To hear that you had cleared out,' died at the expression on his face. All his fine white teeth were showing.

'I was hearin'' at the club to-day about his old trouble.'

Fleur opened her eyes. 'What do you mean?'

Monsieur Profond moved his sleek head as if to minimise his statement.

'Before you were born,' he said; 'that small business.'

Though conscious that he had cleverly diverted her from his own share in her father's worry, Fleur was unable to withstand a rush of nervous curiosity. 'Tell me what you heard.'

'Why!' murmured Monsieur Profond, 'you know all that.'

'I expect I do. But I should like to know that you haven't heard it all wrong.'

'His first wife,' murmured Monsieur Profond.

Choking back the words, 'He was never married before,' she said: 'Well, what about her?'

'Mr George Forsyte was tellin'' me about your father's first wife marryin' his cousin Jolyon afterward. It was a small bit unpleasant, I should think. I saw their boy—nice boy!'

Fleur looked up. Monsieur Profond was swimming, heavily diabolical, before her. That—the reason! With the most heroic effort of her life so far, she managed to arrest that swimming figure. She could not tell whether he had noticed. And just then Winifred came in.

'Oh! here you both are already! Imogen and I have had the most amusing afternoon at the Babies' bazaar.'

'What babies?' said Fleur mechanically.

'The "Save the Babies". I got such a bargain, my dear. A piece of old Armenian work—from before the Flood. I want your opinion on it, Prosper.'

'Auntie,' whispered Fleur suddenly.

At the tone in the girl's voice Winifred closed in on her.

'What's the matter? Aren't you well?'

Monsieur Profond had withdrawn into the window, where he was practically out of hearing.

'Auntie, he—he told me that father has been married before. Is it true that he divorced her, and she married Jon Forsyte's father?'

Never in all the life of the mother of four little Darties had Winifred felt more seriously embarrassed. Her niece's face was so pale, her eyes so dark, her voice so whispery and strained.

'Your father didn't wish you to hear,' she said, with all the aplomb she could muster. 'These things will happen. I've often told him he ought to let you know.'

'Oh!' said Fleur, and that was all, but it made Winifred pat her shoulder–a firm little shoulder, nice and white! She never could help an appraising eye and touch in the matter of her niece, who would have to be married, of course–though not to that boy Jon.

'We've forgotten all about it years and years ago,' she said comfortably. 'Come and have dinner!'

'No, Auntie. I don't feel very well. May I go upstairs?'

'My dear!' murmured Winifred, concerned, 'you're not taking this to heart? Why, you haven't properly come out yet! That boy's a child!'

'What boy? I've only got a headache. But I can't stand that man to-night.'

'Well, well,' said Winifred, 'go and lie down. I'll send you some bromide, and I shall talk to Prosper Profond. What business had he to gossip? Though I must say I think it's much better you should know.'

Fleur smiled. 'Yes,' she said, and slipped from the room.

She went up with her head whirling, a dry sensation in her throat, a fluttered, frightened feeling in her breast. Never in her life as yet had she suffered from even a momentary fear that she would not get what she had set her heart on. The sensations of the afternoon had been full and poignant, and this gruesome discovery coming on the top of them had really made her head ache. No wonder her father had hidden that photograph so secretly behind her own–ashamed of having kept it! But could he hate Jon's mother and yet keep her photograph! She pressed her hands over her forehead, trying to see things clearly. Had they told Jon–had her visit to Robin Hill forced them to tell him? Everything now turned on that! She knew, they all knew, except–perhaps–Jon!

She walked up and down, biting her lip and thinking desperately hard. Jon loved his mother. If they had told him, what would he do? She could not tell. But if they had not told him, should she not–could she not get him for herself–get married to him, before he knew? She searched her memories of Robin Hill. His mother's face so passive–with its dark eyes and as if powdered hair, its reserve, its smile–baffled her; and his father's–kindly, sunken, ironic. Instinctively she felt they would shrink from telling Jon, even now, shrink from hurting him–for of course it would hurt him awfully to know!

Her aunt must be made not to tell her father that she knew. So long as neither she herself nor Jon were supposed to know, there was still a chance–freedom to cover one's tracks, and get what her heart was set on. But she was almost overwhelmed by her isolation. Everyone's hand was against her–everyone's! It was as Jon had said–he and she just wanted to live and the past was in their way, a past they hadn't shared in, and didn't understand. Oh! What a shame! And suddenly she thought of June. Would she help them? For somehow June had left on her the impression that she would be sympathetic with their love, impatient of obstacle. Then, instinctively, she thought: 'I won't give any-thing away, though, even to her. I daren't! I mean to have Jon; against them all.'

Soup was brought up to her, and one of Winifred's pet headache cachets. She swallowed both. Then Winifred herself appeared. Fleur opened her campaign with the words:

'You know, Auntie, I do wish people wouldn't think I'm in love with that boy. Why, I've hardly seen him!'

Winifred, though experienced, was not '*fine*'. She accepted the remark with considerable relief. Of course, it was not pleasant for the girl to hear of the family scandal, and she set herself to minimise the matter, a task for which she was eminently qualified, 'raised' fashionably under a comfortable mother and a father whose nerves might not be shaken, and for many years the wife of Montague Dartie. Her description was a masterpiece of understatement. Fleur's father's first wife had been very foolish. There had been a young man who had got run over, and she had left Fleur's father. Then, years after, when it might all have come right again, she had taken up with their cousin Jolyon; and, of course, her father had been obliged to have a divorce. Nobody remembered anything of it now, except just the family. And, perhaps, it had all turned out for the best; her father had Fleur; and Jolyon and Irene had been quite happy, they said, and their boy was a nice boy. 'Val having Holly, too, is a sort of plaster, don't you know?' With these soothing words, Winifred patted her niece's shoulder; thought: 'She's a nice, plump little thing!' and went back to Prosper Profond, who, in spite of his indiscretion, was very 'amusing' this evening.

For some minutes after her aunt had gone Fleur remained under influence of bromide material and spiritual. But then reality came back. Her aunt had left out all that mattered—all the feeling, the hate, the love, the unforgiveness of passionate hearts. She, who knew so little of life, and had touched only the fringe of love, was yet aware by instinct that words have as little relation to fact and feeling as coin to the bread it buys. 'Poor Father!' she thought. 'Poor me! Poor Jon! But I don't care, I mean to have him!' From the window of her darkened room she saw 'that man' issue from the door below and 'prowl' away. If he and her mother—how would that affect her chance? Surely it must make her father cling to her more closely, so that he would consent in the end to anything she wanted, or become reconciled the sooner to what she did without his knowledge.

She took some earth from the flower-box in the window, and with all her might flung it after that disappearing figure. It fell short, but the action did her good.

And a little puff of air came up from Green Street, smelling of petrol, not sweet.

5

PURELY FORSYTE AFFAIRS

Soames, coming up to the City, with the intention of calling in at Green Street at the end of the day and taking Fleur back home with him, suffered from rumination. Sleeping partner that he was, he seldom visited the City now, but he still had a room of his own at Cuthcott Kingson and Forsyte's, and one special clerk and a half assigned to the management of purely Forsyte affairs. They were somewhat in flux just now—an auspicious moment for the disposal of house property. And Soames was unloading the estates of his father and

Uncle Roger, and to some extent of his Uncle Nicholas. His shrewd and matter-of-course probity in all money concerns had made him something of an autocrat in connection with these trusts. If Soames thought this or thought that, one had better save oneself the bother of thinking too. He guaranteed, as it were, irresponsibility to numerous Forsytes of the third and fourth generations. His fellow trustees, such as his cousins Roger or Nicholas, his cousins-in-law Tweetyman and Spender, or his sister Cicely's husband, all trusted him; he signed first, and where he signed first they signed after, and nobody was a penny the worse. Just now they were all a good many pennies the better, and Soames was beginning to see the close of certain trusts, except for distribution of the income from securities as gilt-edged as was compatible with the period.

Passing the more feverish parts of the City toward the most perfect backwater in London, he ruminated. Money was extraordinary tight; and morality extraordinary loose! The War had done it. Banks were not lending; people breaking contracts all over the place. There was a feeling in the air and a look on faces that he did not like. The country seemed in for a spell of gambling and bankruptcies. There was satisfaction in the thought that neither he nor his trusts had an investment which could be affected by anything less maniacal than national repudiation or a levy on capital. If Soames had faith it was in what he called 'English common sense'—or the power to have things, if not one way then another. He might—like his father James before him—say he didn't know what things were coming to, but he never in his heart believed they were. If it rested with him, they wouldn't—and, after all, he was only an Englishman like any other, so quietly tenacious of what he had that he knew he would never really part with it without something more or less equivalent in exchange. His mind was essentially equilibristic in material matters, and his way of putting the national situation difficult to refute in a world composed of human beings. Take his own case, for example! He was well off. Did that do anybody harm? He did not eat ten meals a day; he ate no more than, perhaps not so much as, a poor man. He spent no money on vice; breathed no more air, used no more water to speak of than the mechanic or the porter. He certainly had pretty things about him, but they had given employment in the making, and somebody must use them. He bought pictures, but Art must be encouraged. He was, in fact, an accidental channel through which money flowed, employing labour. What was there objectionable in that? In his charge money was in quicker and more useful flux than it would be in charge of the State and a lot of slow-fly money-sucking officials. And as to what he saved each year—it was just as much in flux as what he didn't save, going into Water Board or Council Stocks, or something sound and useful. The State paid him no salary for being trustee of his own or other people's money—*he did all that for nothing*. Therein lay the whole case against nationalisation—owners of private property were unpaid, and yet had every incentive to quicken up the flux. Under nationalisation—just the opposite! In a country smarting from officialism he felt that he had a strong case.

It particularly annoyed him, entering that backwater of perfect peace, to think that a lot of unscrupulous Trusts and Combinations had been cornering the market in goods of all kinds, and keeping prices at an artificial height. Such abusers of the individualistic system were the ruffians who caused all the trouble, and it was some satisfaction to see them getting into a stew at last lest the whole thing might come down with a run—and land them in the soup.

The offices of Cuthcott Kingson and Forsyte occupied the ground and first floors of a house on the right-hand side; and, ascending to his room, Soames thought: 'Time we had a coat of paint '

His old clerk Gradman was seated, where he always was, at a huge bureau with countless pigeonholes. Half-the-clerk stood beside him, with a broker's note recording investment of the proceeds from sale of the Bryanston Square house, in Roger Forsyte's estate. Soames took it, and said:

'Vancouver City Stock. H'm. It's down to-day!'

With a sort of grating ingratiation old Gradman answered him:

'Yes-es; but everything's down, Mr Soames.' And half-the-clerk withdrew.

Soames skewered the document on to a number of other papers and hung up his hat.

'I want to look at my Will and Marriage Settlement, Gradman.'

Old Gradman, moving to the limit of his swivel chair, drew out two drafts from the bottom left-hand drawer. Recovering his body, he raised his grizzle-haired face, very red from stooping.

'Copies, sir.'

Soames took them. It struck him suddenly how like Gradman was to the stout brindled yard dog they had been wont to keep on his chain at The Shelter, till one day Fleur had come and insisted it should be let loose, so that it had at once bitten the cook and been destroyed. If you let Gradman off his chain, would he bite the cook?

Checking this frivolous fancy, Soames unfolded his Marriage Settlement. He had not looked at it for over eighteen years, not since he remade his Will when his father died and Fleur was born. He wanted to see whether the words 'during coverture' were in. Yes, they were—odd expression, when you thought of it, and derived perhaps from horse-breeding! Interest on fifteen thousand pounds (which he paid her without deducting income tax) so long as she remained his wife, and afterwards during widowhood 'dum casta'—old-fashioned and rather pointed words, put in to insure the conduct of Fleur's mother. His will made it up to an annuity of a thousand under the same conditions. All right! He returned the copies to Gradman, who took them without looking up, swung the chair, restored the papers to their drawer, and went on casting up.

'Gradman! I don't like the condition of the country; there are a lot of people about without any common sense. I want to find a way by which I can safeguard Miss Fleur against anything which might arise.'

Gradman wrote the figure '2' on his blotting-paper.

'Yes-es,' he said; 'there's a nahsty spirit.'

'The ordinary restraint against anticipation doesn't meet the case.'

'Nao,' said Gradman.

'Suppose those Labour fellows come in, or worse! It's these people with fixed ideas who are the danger. Look at Ireland!'

'Ah!' said Gradman.

'Suppose I were to make a settlement on her at once with myself as beneficiary for life, they couldn't take anything but the interest from me, unless of course they alter the law.'

Gradman moved his head and smiled.

'Aoh!' he said, 'they wouldn't do tha-at!'

'I don't know,' muttered Soames; 'I don't trust them.'

'It'll take two years, sir, to be valid against death duties.'

Soames sniffed. Two years! He was only sixty-five!

'That's not the point. Draw a form of settlement that passes all my property to Miss Fleur's children in equal shares, with antecedent life-interests first to myself and then to her without power of anticipation, and add a clause that in the event of anything happening to divert her life-interest, that interest passes to the trustees, to apply for her benefit, in their absolute discretion.'

Gradman grated: 'Rather extreme at your age, sir; you lose control.'

'That's my business,' said Soames, sharply.

Gradman wrote on a piece of paper: 'Life-interest–anticipation–divert interest–absolute discretion . . .' and said:

'What trustees? There's young Mr Kingson; he's a nice steady young fellow.'

'Yes, he might do for one. I must have three. There isn't a Forsyte now who appeals to me.'

'Not young Mr Nicholas? He's at the Bar. We've given 'im briefs.'

'He'll never set the Thames on fire,' said Soames.

A smile oozed out on Gradman's face, greasy with countless mutton-chops, the smile of a man who sits all day.

'You can't expect it, at his age, Mr Soames.'

'Why? What is he? Forty?'

'Ye-es, quite a young fellow.'

'Well, put him in; but I want somebody who'll take a personal interest. There's no one that I can see.'

'What about Mr Valerius, now he's come home?'

'Val Dartie? With that father?'

'We-ell,' murmured Gradman, 'he's been dead seven years–the Statute runs against him.'

'No,' said Soames. 'I don't like the connection.' He rose. Gradman said suddenly:

'If they were making a levy on capital, they could come on the trustees, sir. So there you'd be just the same. I'd think it over, if I were you.'

'That's true,' said Soames, 'I will. What have you done about that dilapidation notice in Vere Street?'

'I 'aven't served it yet. The party's very old. She won't want to go out at her age.'

'I don't know. This spirit of unrest touches every one.'

'Still, I'm lookin' at things broadly, sir. She's eighty-one.'

'Better serve it,' said Soames, 'and see what she says. Oh! and Mr Timothy? Is everything in order in case of–'

'I've got the inventory of his estate all ready; had the furniture and pictures valued so that we know what reserves to put on. I shall be sorry when he goes, though. Dear me! It is a time since I first saw Mr Timothy!'

'We can't live for ever,' said Soames, taking down his hat.

'Nao,' said Gradman; 'but it'll be a pity–the last of the old family! Shall I take up the matter of that nuisance in Old Compton Street? Those organs–they're nahsty things.'

'Do. I must call for Miss Fleur and catch the four o'clock. Good-day, Gradman.'

'Good-day, Mr Soames. I hope Miss Fleur–'

'Well enough, but gads about too much.'

'Ye-es,' grated Gradman; 'she's young.'

Soames went out, musing: 'Old Gradman! If he were younger I'd put him in the trust. There's nobody I can depend on to take a real interest.'

Leaving the bilious and mathematical exactitude, the preposterous peace of that backwater, he thought suddenly: 'During coverture! Why can't they exclude fellows like Profond, instead of a lot of hard-working Germans?' and was surprised at the depth of uneasiness which could provoke so unpatriotic a thought. But there it was! One never got a moment of real peace. There was always something at the back of everything! And he made his way toward Green Street.

Two hours later by his watch, Thomas Gradman, stirring in his swivel chair, closed the last drawer of his bureau, and putting into his waistcoat pocket a bunch of keys so fat that they gave him a protuberance on the liver side, brushed his old top hat with his sleeve, took his umbrella, and descended. Thick, short, and buttoned closely into his old frock coat, he walked toward Covent Garden market. He never missed that daily promenade to the Tube for Highgate, and seldom some critical transaction on the way in connection with vegetables and fruit. Generations might be born, and hats might change, wars be fought, and Forsytes fade away, but Thomas Gradman, faithful and grey, would take his daily walk and buy his daily vegetable. Times were not what they were, and his son had lost a leg, and they never gave him those nice little plaited baskets to carry the stuff in now, and these Tubes were convenient things—still he mustn't complain; his health was good considering his time of life, and after fifty-four years in the Law he was getting a round eight hundred a year and a little worried of late, because it was mostly collector's commission on the rents, and with all this conversion of Forsyte property going on, it looked like drying up, and the price of living still so high; but it was no good worrying—'The good God made us all'—as he was in the habit of saying; still, house property in London—he didn't know what Mr Roger or Mr James would say if they could see it being sold like this—seemed to show a lack of faith; but Mr Soames—he worried. Life and lives in being and twenty-one years after—beyond that you couldn't go; still, he kept his health wonderfully—and Miss Forsyte was a pretty little thing—she was; she'd marry; but lots of people had no children nowadays—he had his first child at twenty-two; and Mr Jolyon, married while he was at Cambridge, had his child the same year—gracious Peter! That was back in '69, a long time before old Mr Jolyon—fine judge of property—had taken his Will away from Mr James—dear, yes! Those were the days when they were buyin' property right and left, and none of this khaki and fallin' over one another to get out of things; and cucumbers at twopence; and a melon—the old melons, that made your mouth water! Fifty years since he went into Mr James's office, and Mr James had said to him: 'Now, Gradman, you're only a shaver—you pay attention, and you'll made your five hundred a year before you've done.' And he had, and feared God, and served the Forsytes, and kept a vegetable diet at night. And, buying a copy of *John Bull*—not that he approved of it, an extravagant affair—he entered the Tube elevator with his mere brown-paper parcel, and was borne down into the bowels of the earth.

6

SOAMES'S PRIVATE LIFE

On his way to Green Street it occured to Soames that he ought to go into Dumetrius's in Suffolk Street about the possibility of the Bolderby Old Crome. Almost worth while to have fought the war to have Bolderby Old Crome, as it were, in flux! Old Bolderby had died, his son and grandson had been killed–a cousin was coming into the estate, who meant to sell it, some said because of the condition of England, others said because he had asthma.

If Dumetrius once got hold of it the price would become prohibitive; it was necessary for Soames to find out whether Dumetrius had got it, before he tried to get it himself. He therefore confined himself to discussing with Dumetrius whether Monticellis would come again now that it was the fashion for a picture to be anything except a picture; and the future of Johns, with a side-slip into Buxton Knights. It was only when leaving that he added: 'So they're not selling the Bolderby Old Crome, after all?' In sheer pride of racial superiority, as he had calculated would be the case, Dumetrius replied:

'Oh! I shall get it, Mr Forsyte, sir!'

The flutter of his eyelids fortified Soames in a resolution to write direct to the new Bolderby, suggesting that the only dignified way of dealing with an Old Crome was to avoid dealers. He therefore said, 'Well, good-day! and went, leaving Dumetrius the wiser.

At Green Street he found that Fleur was out and would be all the evening; she was staying one more night in London. He cabbed on dejectedly, and caught his train.

He reached his house about six o'clock. The air was heavy, midges biting, thunder about. Taking his letters he went up to his dressing-room to cleanse himself of London.

An uninteresting post. A receipt, a bill for purchases on behalf of Fleur. A circular about an exhibition of etchings. A letter beginning:

SIR,
I feel it my duty–

That would be an appeal or something unpleasant. He looked at once for the signature. There was none! Incredulously he turned the page over and examined each corner. Not being a public man, Soames had never yet had an anonymous letter, and his first impulse was to tear it up, as a dangerous thing; his second to read it, as a thing still more dangerous.

SIR,
I feel it my duty to inform you that having no interest in the matter your lady is carrying on with a foreigner–

Reaching that word Soames stopped mechanically and examined the postmark. So far as he could pierce the impenetrable disguise in which the Post

Office had wrapped it, there was something with a 'sea' at the end and a 't' in it. Chelsea? No! Battersea? Perhaps! He read on.

These foreigners are all the same. Sack the lot. This one meets your lady twice a week. I know it of my own knowledge – and to see an Englishman put on goes against the grain. You watch it and see if what I say isn't true. I shouldn't meddle if it wasn't a dirty foreigner that's in it. Yours obedient.

The sensation with which Soames dropped the letter was similar to that he would have had entering his bedroom and finding it full of black-beetles. The meanness of anonymity gave a shuddering obscenity to the moment. And the worst of it was that this shadow had been at the back of his mind ever since the Sunday evening when Fleur had pointed down at Prosper Profond strolling on the lawn, and said: 'Prowling cat!' Had he not in connection therewith, this very day, perused his Will and Marriage Settlement? And now this anonymous ruffian, with nothing to gain, apparently, save the venting of his spite against foreigners, had wrenched it out of the obscurity in which he had hoped and wished it would remain. To have such knowledge forced on him, at his time of life, about Fleur's mother! He picked the letter up from the carpet, tore it across, and then, when it hung together by just the fold at the back, stopped tearing, and re-read it. He was taking at that moment one of the decisive resolutions of his life. He would *not* be forced into another scandal. No! However he decided to deal with this matter – and it required the most far-sighted and careful consideration – he would do nothing that might injure Fleur. That resolution taken, his mind answered the helm again, and he made his ablutions. His hands trembled as he dried them. Scandal he would not have, but something must be done to stop this sort of thing! He went into his wife's room and stood looking round him. The idea of searching for anything which would incriminate, and entitle him to hold a menace over her, did not even come to him. There would be nothing – she was much too practical. The idea of having her watched had been dismissed before it came – too well he remembered his previous experience of that. No! He had nothing but this torn-up letter from some anonymous ruffian, whose impudent intrusion into his private life he so violently resented. It was repugnant to him to make use of it, but he might have to. What a mercy Fleur was not at home to-night! A tap on the door broke up his painful cogitations.

'Mr Michael Mont, sir, is in the drawing-room. Will you see him?'

'No,' said Soames; 'yes. I'll come down.'

Anything that would take his mind off for a few minutes!

Michael Mont in flannels stood on the verandah, smoking a cigarette. He threw it away as Soames came up, and ran his hand through his hair.

Soames's feeling toward this young man was singular. He was no doubt a rackety, irresponsible young fellow according to old standards, yet somehow likeable, with his extraordinary cheerful way of blurting out his opinions.

'Come in,' he said; 'have you had tea?'

Mont came in.

'I thought Fleur would have been back, sir; but I'm glad she isn't. The fact is, I – I'm fearfully gone on her; so fearfully gone that I thought you'd better know. It's old-fashioned, of course, coming to fathers first, but I thought you'd forgive that. I went to my own Dad, and he says if I settle down he'll see me through. He rather cottons to the idea, in fact. I told him about your Goya.'

'Oh!' said Soames, inexpressibly dry. 'He rather cottons?'

'Yes, sir; do you?'

Soames smiled faintly.

'You see,' resumed Mont, twiddling his straw hat, while his hair, ears, eyebrows, all seemed to stand up from excitement, 'when you've been through the War you can't help being in a hurry.'

'To get married, and unmarried afterwards,' said Soames slowly.

'Not from Fleur, sir. Imagine, if you were me!'

Soames cleared his throat. That way of putting it was forcible enough.

'Fleur's too young,' he said.

'Oh! no, sir. We're awfully old nowadays. My Dad seems to me a perfect babe; his thinking apparatus hasn't turned a hair. But he's a Baronight, of course; that keeps him back.'

'Baronight,' repeated Soames; 'what may that be?'

'Bart, sir. I shall be a Bart some day. But I shall live it down, you know.'

'Go away and live this down,' said Soames.

Young Mont said imploringly: 'Oh! no, sir. I simply must hang around, or I shouldn't have a dog's chance. You'll let Fleur do what she likes, I suppose, anyway. Madame passes me.'

'Indeed!' said Soames frigidly.

'You don't really bar me, do you?' and the young man looked so doleful that Soames smiled.

'You may think you're very old,' he said; 'but you strike me as extremely young. To rattle ahead of everything is not a proof of maturity.'

'All right, sir; I give in to you on age. But to show you I mean business—I've got a job.'

'Glad to hear it.'

'Joined a publisher; my governor is putting up the stakes.'

Soames put his hand over his mouth—he had so very nearly said: 'God help the publisher!' His grey eyes scrutinised the agitated young man.

'I don't dislike you, Mr Mont, but Fleur is everything to me. Everything—do you understand?'

'Yes, sir, I know; but so she is to me.'

'That's as may be. I'm glad you've told me, however. And now I think there's nothing more to be said.'

'I know it rests with her, sir.'

'It will rest with her a long time, I hope.'

'You aren't cheering,' said Mont suddenly.

'No,' said Soames, 'my experience of life has not made me anxious to couple people in a hurry. Good-night, Mr Mont. I shan't tell Fleur what you've said.'

'Oh!' murmured Mont blankly; 'I really could knock my brains out for want of her. She knows that perfectly well.'

'I dare say.' And Soames held out his hand. A distracted squeeze, a heavy sigh, and soon after sounds from the young man's motor-cycle called up visions of flying dust and broken bones.

'The younger generation!' he thought heavily, and went out on to the lawn. The gardeners had been mowing, and there was still the smell of fresh-cut grass—the thundery air kept all scents close to earth. The sky was of a purplish hue—the poplars black. Two or three boats passed on the river, scuttling, as it were, for shelter before the storm. 'Three days' fine weather,' thought Soames, 'and then a storm!' Where was Annette? With that chap, for all he knew—she was a young woman! Impressed with the queer charity of that thought, he entered the summer-house and sat down. The fact was—and he admitted it–Fleur was so much to him that his wife was very little–very little; French–had never been much more than a mistress, and he was getting indifferent to that side of things! It was odd how, with all this ingrained care for moderation and secure investment, Soames ever put his emotional eggs into one basket. First Irene–now Fleur. He was dimly conscious of it, sitting there, conscious of its old dangerousness. It had brought him to wreck and scandal once, but now–now it should save him! He cared so much for Fleur that he would have no further scandal. If only he could get at that anonymous letter-writer, he would teach him not to meddle and stir up mud at the bottom of water which he wished should remain stagnant! ... A distant flash, a low rumble, and large drops of rain spattered on the thatch above him. He remained indifferent, tracing a pattern with his finger on the dusty surface of a little rustic table. Fleur's future! 'I want fair sailing for her,' he thought. 'Nothing else matters at my time of life.' A lonely business–life! What you had you never could keep to yourself! As you warned one off, you let another in. One could make sure of nothing! He reached up and pulled a red rambler rose from a cluster which blocked the window. Flowers grew and dropped–Nature was a queer thing! The thunder rumbled and crashed, travelling east along the river, the paling flashes flicked his eyes; the poplar tops showed sharp and dense against the sky, a heavy shower rustled and rattled and veiled in the little house wherein he sat, indifferent, thinking.

When the storm was over, he left his retreat and went down the wet path to the river bank.

Two swans had come, sheltering in among the reeds. He knew the birds well, and stood watching the dignity in the curve of those white necks and formidable snake-like heads. 'Not dignified–what I have to do!' he thought. And yet it must be tackled, lest worse befell. Annette must be back by now from wherever she had gone, for it was nearly dinner-time, and as the moment for seeing her approached, the difficulty of knowing what to say and how to say it had increased. A new and scaring thought occured to him. Suppose she wanted her liberty to marry this fellow! Well, if she did, she couldn't have it. He had not married her for that. The image of Prosper Profond dawdled before him reassuringly. Not a marrying man! No, no! Anger replaced that momentary scare. 'He had better not come my way,' he thought. The mongrel represented–! But what did Prosper Profond represent? Nothing that mattered surely. And yet something real enough in the world–unmorality let off its chain, disillusionment on the prowl! That expression Annette had caught from him: *'Je m'en fiche!'* A fatalistic chap! A continental–a cosmopolitan–a product of the age! If there were condemnation more complete, Soames felt that he did not know it.

The swans had turned their heads, and were looking past him into some distance of their own. One of them uttered a little hiss, wagged its tail, turned as if answering to a rudder, and swam away. The other followed. Their white bodies, their stately necks, passed out of his sight, and he went toward the house.

Annette was in the drawing-room, dressed for dinner, and he thought as he went upstairs: 'Handsome is as handsome does.' Handsome! Except for remarks about the curtains in the drawing-room, and the storm, there was practically no conversation during a meal distinguished by exactitude of quantity and perfection of quality. Soames drank nothing. He followed her into the drawing-room afterward, and found her smoking a cigarette on the sofa between the two french windows. She was leaning back, almost upright, in a low black frock, with her knees crossed and her blue eyes half-closed; grey-blue smoke issued from her red, rather full lips, a fillet bound her chestnut hair, she wore the thinnest silk stockings, and shoes with very high heels showing off her instep. A fine piece in any room! Soames, who held that torn letter in a hand thrust deep into the side-pocket of his dinner-jacket, said:

'I'm going to shut the window; the damp's lifting in.'

He did so, and stood looking at a David Cox adorning the cream-panelled wall close by.

What was she thinking of? He had never understood a woman in his life–except Fleur–and Fleur not always. His heart beat fast. But if he meant to do it, now was the moment. Turning from the David Cox, he took out the torn letter.

'I've had this.'

Her eyes widened, stared at him, and hardened.

Soames handed her the letter.

'It's torn, but you can read it.' And he turned back to the David Cox–a sea-piece, of good tone–but without movement enough. 'I wonder what that chap's doing at this moment?' he thought. 'I'll astonish him yet.' Out of the corner of his eye he saw Annette holding the letter rigidly; her eyes moved from side to side under her darkened lashes and frowning, darkened eyebrows. She dropped the letter, gave a little shiver, smiled, and said:

'Dirrty!'

'I quite agree,' said Soames; 'degrading. Is it true?'

A tooth fastened on her red lower lip. 'And what if it were?'

She was brazen!

'Is that all you have to say?'

'No.'

'Well, speak out!'

'What is the good of talking?'

Soames said icily: 'So you admit it?'

'I admit nothing. You are a fool to ask. A man like you should not ask. It is dangerous.'

Soames made a tour of the room, to subdue his rising anger.

'Do you remember,' he said, halting in front of her, 'what you were when I married you? Working at accounts in a restaurant.'

'Do you remember that I was not half your age?'

Soames broke off the hard encounter of their eyes, and went back to the David Cox.

'I am not going to bandy words. I require you to give up this–friendship. I think of the matter entirely as it affects Fleur.'

'Ah!–Fleur!'

'Yes,' said Soames stubbornly; 'Fleur. She is your child as well as mine.'

'It is kind to admit that!'

'Are you going to do what I say?'

'I refuse to tell you.'

'Then I must make you.'

Annette smiled.

'No, Soames,' she said. 'You are helpless. Do not say things that you will regret.'

Anger swelled the veins on his forehead. He opened his mouth to vent that emotion, and–could not. Annette went on:

'There shall be no more such letters, I promise you. That is enough.'

Soames writhed. He had a sense of being treated like a child by this woman who had deserved he did not know what.

'When two people have married, and lived like us, Soames, they had better be quiet about each other. There are things one does not drag up into the light for people to laugh at. You will be quiet, then; not for my sake–for your own. You are getting old; I am not, yet. You have made me ver-ry practical.'

Soames, who had passed through all the sensations of being choked, repeated dully:

'I require you to give up this friendship.'

'And if I do not?'

'Then–then I will cut you out of my Will.'

Somehow it did not seem to meet the case. Annette laughed.

'You will live a long time, Soames.'

'You–you are a bad woman,' said Soames suddenly.

Annette shrugged her shoulders.

'I do not think so. Living with you has killed things in me, it is true; but I am not a bad woman. I am sensible–that is all. And so will you be when you have thought it over.'

'I shall see this man,' said Soames sullenly, 'and warn him off.'

'*Mon cher*, you are funny. You do not want me, you have as much of me as you want; and you wish the rest of me to be dead. I admit nothing, but I am not going to be dead, Soames, at my age; so you had better be quiet, I tell you. I myself will make no scandal; none. Now, I am not saying any more, whatever you do.'

She reached out, took a French novel off a little table, and opened it. Soames watched her, silenced by the tumult of his feelings. The thought of that man was almost making him want her, and this was a revelation of their relationship, startling to one little given to introspective philosophy. Without saying another word he went out and up to the picture-gallery. This came of marrying a Frenchwoman! And yet, without her there would have been no Fleur! She had served her purpose.

'She's right,' he thought; 'I can do nothing. I don't even *know* that there's anything in it.' The instinct of self-preservation warned him to batten down his hatches, to smother the fire with want of air. Unless one believed there was something in a thing, there wasn't.

That night he went into her room. She received him in the most matter-of-fact way, as if there had been no scene between them. And he returned to his own room with a curious sense of peace. If one didn't choose to see, one needn't. And he did not choose–in future he did not choose. There was nothing to be gained by it–nothing! Opening the drawer he took from the sachet a handkerchief, and the framed photograph of Fleur. When he had looked at it a little he slipped it down, and there was that other one–that old one of Irene. An owl hooted while he stood in his window gazing at it. The owl hooted, the red climbing roses seemed to deepen in colour, there came a scent of lime-blossom. God! That had been a different thing! Passion–Memory! Dust!

7

JUNE TAKES A HAND

One who was a sculptor, a Slav, a sometime resident in New York, an egoist, and impecunious, was to be found of an evening in June Forsyte's studio on the bank of the Thames at Chiswick. On the evening of July 6, Boris Strumolowski—several of whose works were on show there because they were as yet too advanced to be on show anywhere else—had begun well, with that aloof and rather Christ-like silence which admirably suited his youthful, round, broad cheek-boned countenance framed in bright hair banged like a girl's. June had known him three weeks, and he still seemed to her the principal embodiment of genius, and hope of the future; a sort of Star of the East which had strayed into an unappreciative West. Until that evening he had conversationally confined himself to recording his impressions of the United States, whose dust he had just shaken from off his feet—a country, in his opinion, so barbarous in every way that he had sold practically nothing there, and become an object of suspicion to the police; a country, as he said, without a race of its own, without liberty, equality, or fraternity, without principles, traditions, taste, without—in a word—a soul. He had left it for his own good, and come to the only other country where he could live well. June had dwelt unhappily on him in her lonely moments, standing before his creations—frightening, but powerful and symbolic once they had been explained! That he, haloed by bright hair like an early Italian painting, and absorbed in his genius to the exclusion of all else—the only sign of course by which real genius could be told—should still be a 'lame duck' agitated her warm heart almost to the exclusion of Paul Post. And she had begun to take steps to clear her Gallery, in order to fill it with Strumolowski masterpieces. She had at once encountered trouble. Paul Post had kicked; Vospovitch had stung. With all the emphasis of a genius which she did not as yet deny them, they had demanded another six weeks at least of her Gallery. The American stream, still flowing in, would soon be flowing out. The American stream was their right, their only hope, their salvation—since nobody in this 'beastly' country cared for Art. June had yielded to the demonstration. After all Boris would not mind them having the full benefit of an American stream, which he himself so violently despised.

This evening she had put that to Boris with nobody else present, except Hannah Hobdey, the medieval black-and-whitist, and Jimmy Portugal, editor of the *Neo-Artist*. She had put it to him with that sudden confidence which continual contact with the neo-artistic world had never been able to dry up in her warm and generous nature. He had not broken his Christ-like silence, however, for more than two minutes before she began to move her blue eyes from side to side, as a cat moves its tail. This—he said—was characteristic of England, the most selfish country in the world; the country which sucked the blood of other countries; destroyed the brains and hearts of Irishmen, Hindus,

Egyptians, Boers, and Burmese, all the finest races in the world; bullying, hypocritical England! This was what he had expected, coming to such a country, where the climate was all fog, and the people all tradesmen perfectly blind to Art, and sunk in profiteering and the grossest materialism. Conscious that Hannah Hobdey was murmuring, 'Hear, hear!' and Jimmy Portugal sniggering, June grew crimson, and suddenly rapped out:

'Then why did you ever come? We didn't ask you.'

The remark was so singularly at variance with all that she had led him to expect from her, that Strumolowski stretched out his hand and took a cigarette.

'England never wants an idealist,' he said.

But in June something primitively English was thoroughly upset; old Jolyon's sense of justice had risen, as it were, from bed. 'You come and sponge on us,' she said, 'and then abuse us. If you think that's playing the game, I don't.'

She now discovered that which others had discovered before her–the thickness of hide beneath which the sensibility of genius is sometimes veiled. Strumolowski's young and ingenuous face became the incarnation of a sneer.

'Sponge, one does not sponge, one takes what is owing–a tenth part of what is owing. You will repent to say that, Miss Forsyte.'

'Oh, no,' said June, 'I shan't.'

'Ah! We know very well, we artists–you take us to get what you can out of us. I want nothing from you'–and he blew out a cloud of June's smoke.

Decision rose in an icy puff from the turmoil of insulted shame within her. 'Very well, then, you can take your things away.'

And, almost in the same moment, she thought: 'Poor boy! He's only got a garret, and probably not a taxi fare. In front of these people, too; it's positively disgusting!'

Young Strumolowski shook his head violently; his hair, thick, smooth, close as a golden plate, did not fall off.

'I can live on nothing,' he said shrilly. 'I have often had to for the sake of my Art. It is you bourgeois who force us to spend money.'

The words hit June like a pebble, in the ribs. After all she had done for Art, all her identification with its troubles and lame ducks. She was struggling for adequate words when the door was opened, and her Austrian murmured:

'A young lady, *gnädiges Fräulein*.'

'Where?'

'In the little meal-room.'

With a glance at Boris Strumolowski, at Hannah Hobdey, at Jimmy Portugal, June said nothing, and went out, devoid of equanimity. Entering the 'little meal-room', she perceived the young lady to be Fleur–looking very pretty, if pale. At this disenchanted moment a little lame duck of her own breed was welcome to June, so homœopathic by instinct.

The girl must have come, of course, because of Jon; or, if not, at least to get something out of her. And June felt just then that to assist somebody was the only bearable thing.

'So you've remembered to come,' she said.

'Yes. What a jolly little duck of a house! But please don't let me bother you, if you've got people.'

'Not at all,' said June. 'I want to let them stew in their own juice for a bit. Have you come about Jon?'

'You said you thought we ought to be told. Well, I've found out.'

'Oh!' said June blankly. 'Not nice, is it?'

They were standing one on each side of the little bare table at which June took her meals. A vase on it was full of Iceland poppies; the girl raised her hand and touched them with a gloved finger. To her new-fangled dress, frilly about the hips and tight below the knees, June took a sudden liking–a charming colour, flax-blue.

'She makes a picture,' thought June. Her little room with its whitewashed walls, its floor and hearth of old pink brick, its black paint, and latticed window athwart which the last of the sunlight was shining, had never looked so charming, set off by this young figure, with the creamy, slightly frowning face. She remembered with sudden vividness how nice she herself had looked in those old days when *her* heart was set on Philip Bosinney, that dead lover, who had broken from her to destroy for ever Irene's allegiance to this girl's father. Did Fleur know of that, too?'

'Well,' she said, 'what are you going to do?'

It was some seconds before Fleur answered.

'I don't want Jon to suffer. I must see him once more to put an end to it.'

'You're going to put an end to it!'

'What else is there to do?'

The girl seemed to June, suddenly, intolerably spiritless.

'I suppose you're right,' she muttered. 'I know my father thinks so; but–I should never have done it myself. I can't take things lying down.'

How poised and watchful that girl looked; how unemotional her voice sounded!

'People *will* assume that I'm in love.'

'Well, aren't you?'

Fleur shrugged her shoulders. 'I might have known it,' thought June; 'she's Soames's daughter–fish! And yet–he!'

'What do you want *me* to do then?' she said with a sort of disgust.

'Could I see Jon here to-morrow on his way down to Holly's? He'd come if you sent him a line to-night. And perhaps afterward you'd let them know quietly at Robin Hill that it's all over, and that they needn't tell Jon about his mother.'

'All right!' said June abruptly. 'I'll write now, and you can post it. Half-past two to-morrow. I shan't be in, myself.'

She sat down at the tiny bureau which filled one corner. When she looked round with the finished note Fleur was still touching the poppies with her gloved finger.

June licked a stamp. 'Well, here it is. If you're not in love, of course, there's no more to be said. Jon's lucky.'

Fleur took the note. 'Thanks awfully!'

'Cold-blooded little baggage!' thought June. Jon, son of her father, to love, and not be loved by the daughter of–Soames! It was humiliating!

'Is that all?'

Fleur nodded; her frills shook and trembled as she swayed toward the door.

'Good-bye!'

'Good-bye! ... Little piece of fashion!' muttered June, closing the door. 'That family!' And she marched back toward her studio. Boris Strumolowski had regained his Christ-like silence, and Jimmy Portugal was damning everybody, except the group on whose behalf he ran the *Neo-Artist*. Among the condemned were Eric Cobbley, and several other 'lame-duck' genii who at one time or another held first place in the repertoire of June's aid and adoration. She experienced a sense of futility and disgust, and went to the window to let the river-wind blow those squeaky words away.

But when at length Jimmy Portugal had finished, and gone with Hannah Hobdey, she sat down and mothered young Strumolowski for half an hour, promising him a month, at least, of the American stream; so that he went away with his halo in perfect order. 'In spite of all,' June thought, 'Boris *is* wonderful.'

8

THE BIT BETWEEN THE TEETH

To know that your hand is against every one's is—for some natures—to experience a sense of moral release. Fleur felt no remorse when she left June's house. Reading condamnatory resentment in her little kinswoman's blue eyes—she was glad that she had fooled her, despising June because that elderly idealist had not seen what she was after.

End it, forsooth! She would soon show them all that she was only just beginning. And she smiled to herself on the top of the bus which carried her back to Mayfair. But the smile died, squeezed out by spasms of anticipation and anxiety. Would she be able to manage Jon? She had taken the bit between her teeth, but could she make him take it too? She knew the truth and the real danger of delay—he knew neither; therein lay all the difference in the world.

'Suppose I tell him,' she thought; 'wouldn't it really be safer?' This hideous luck had no right to spoil their love; he must see that! They could not let it! People always accepted an accomplished fact in time! From that piece of philosophy—profound enough at her age—she passed to another consideration less philosophic. If she persuaded Jon to a quick and secret marriage, and he found out afterward that she had known the truth. What then? Jon hated subterfuge. Again, then, would it not be better to tell him? But the memory of his mother's face kept intruding on that impulse. Fleur was afraid. His mother had power over him; more power perhaps than she herself. Who could tell? It was too great a risk. Deep-sunk in those instinctive calculations she was carried on past Green Street as far as Ritz Hotel. She got down there, and walked back on the Green Park side. The storm had washed every tree; they still dripped. Heavy drops fell on to her frills, and to avoid them she crossed over under the eyes of the Iseeum Club. Chancing to look up she saw Monsieur Profond with a tall stout man in the bay window. Turning into Green Street she heard her name called, and saw 'that prowler' coming up. He took off his hat—a glossy 'bowler' such as she particularly detested.

'Good evenin'! Miss Forsyde. Isn't there a small thing I can do for you?'

'Yes, pass by on the other side.'

'I say! Why do you dislike me?'

'Do I?'

'It looks like it.'

'Well, then, because you make me feel life isn't worth living.'

Monsieur Profond smiled.

'Look here, Miss Forsyde, don't worry. It'll be all right. Nothing lasts.'

'Things do last,' cried Fleur; 'with me anyhow—especially likes and dislikes.'

'Well, that makes me a bit un'appy.'

'I should have thought nothing could ever make you happy or unhappy.'

'I don't like to annoy other people. I'm goin' on my yacht.'

Fleur looked at him, startled.

'Where?'

'Small voyage to the South Seas or somewhere,' said Monsieur Profond.

Fleur suffered relief and a sense of insult. Clearly he meant to convey that he was breaking with her mother. How dared he have anything to break, and yet how dared he break it?

'Good-night, Miss Forsyde! Remember me to Mrs Dartie. I'm not so bad really. Good-night!' Fleur left him standing there with his hat raised. Stealing a look round, she saw him stroll—immaculate and heavy—back toward his club.

'He can't even love with conviction,' she thought. 'What will Mother do?'

Her dreams that night were endless and uneasy; she rose heavy and unrested, and went at once to the study of Whitaker's Almanack. A Forsyte is instinctively aware that facts are the real crux of any situation. She might conquer Jon's prejudice, but without exact machinery to complete their desperate resolve, nothing would happen. From the invaluable tome she learned that they must each be twenty-one; or someone's consent would be necessary, which of course was unobtainable; then she became lost in directions concerning licences, certificates, notices, districts, coming finally to the word 'perjury'. But that was nonsense! Who would really mind their giving wrong ages in order to be married for love! She ate hardly any breakfast, and went back to Whitaker. The more she studied the less sure she became; till, idly turning the pages, she came to Scotland. People could be married there without any of this nonsense. She had only to go and stay there twenty-one days, then Jon could come, and in front of two people they could declare themselves married. And what was more—they would be! It was far the best way; and at once she ran over her schoolfellows. There was Mary Lambe who lived in Edinburgh and was 'quite a sport'! She had a brother too. She could stay with Mary Lambe, who with her brother would serve for witnesses. She well knew that some girls would think all this unnecessary, and that all she and Jon need do was to go away together for a week-end and then say to their people: 'We are married by Nature, we must now be married by Law.' But Fleur was Forsyte enough to feel such a proceeding dubious, and to dread her father's face when he heard of it. Besides, she did not believe that Jon would do it; he had an opinion of her such as she could not bear to diminish. No! Mary Lambe was preferable, and it was just the time of year to go to Scotland. More at ease now, she packed, avoided her aunt, and took a bus to Chiswick. She was too early, and went on to Kew Gardens. She found no peace among the flower-beds, labelled trees, and broad green spaces, and having lunched off anchovy-paste sandwiches and coffee, returned to Chiswick and rang June's bell. The Austrian admitted her to the 'little meal-room'. Now that she knew what she and Jon were up against, her longing for him had increased tenfold, as if he were a toy with sharp edges or dangerous paint such as they had tried to take from her as a child. If she could not have her way, and get Jon for good and all, she felt like dying of privation. By hook or crook she must and would get him! A round dim mirror of very old glass hung over the pink brick hearth. She stood looking at herself reflected in it, pale, and rather dark under the eyes; little shudders kept passing through her nerves. Then she heard the bell ring, and, stealing to the window, saw him standing on the doorstep smoothing his hair and lips, as if he too were trying to subdue the fluttering of his nerves.

She was sitting on one of the two rush-seated chairs with her back to the door, when he came in, and she said at once:

'Sit down, Jon, I want to talk seriously.'

Jon sat on the table by her side, and without looking at him she went on:

'If you don't want to lose me, we must get married.'

Jon gasped.

'Why? Is there anything new?'

'No, but I felt it at Robin Hill, and among my people.'

'But–' stammered Jon, 'at Robin Hill–it was all smooth–and they've said nothing to me.'

'But they mean to stop us. Your mother's face was enough. And my father's.'

'Have you seen him since?'

Fleur nodded. What mattered a few supplementary lies?

'But,' said Jon eagerly, 'I can't see how they can feel like that after all these years.'

Fleur looked up at him.

'Perhaps you don't love me enough.'

'Not love you enough! Why–I–'

'Then make sure of me.'

'Without telling them?'

'Not till after.'

Jon was silent. How much older he looked than on that day, barely two months ago, when she first saw him–quite two years older!

'It would hurt Mother awfully,' he said.

Fleur drew her hand away.

'You've got to choose.'

Jon slid off the table on to his knees.

'But why not tell them? They can't really stop us, Fleur!'

'They can! I tell you, they can.'

'How?'

'We're utterly dependent–by putting money pressure, and all sorts of other pressure. I'm not patient, Jon.'

'But it's deceiving them.'

Fleur got up.

'You can't really love me, or you wouldn't hesitate. "He either fears his fate too much–!"'

Lifting his hands to her waist, Jon forced her to sit down again. She hurried on:

'I've planned it all out. We've only to go to Scotland. When we're married they'll soon come round. People always come round to facts. Don't you *see*, Jon?'

'But to hurt them so awfully!'

So he would rather hurt her than those people of his! 'All right, then; let me go!'

Jon got up and put his back against the door.

'I expect you're right,' he said slowly; 'but I want to think it over.'

She could see that he was seething with feelings he wanted to express; but she did not mean to help him. She hated herself at this moment, and almost hated him. Why had she to do all the work to secure their love? It wasn't fair. And then she saw his eyes, adoring and distressed.

'Don't look like that! I only don't want to lose you, Jon.'

'You can't lose me so long as you want me.'

'Oh, yes, I can.'

Jon put his hands on her shoulders.

'Fleur, do you know anything you haven't told me?'

It was the point-blank question she had dreaded. She looked straight at him, and answered: 'No.' She had burnt her boats; but what did it matter, if she got him? He would forgive her. And throwing her arms round his neck, she kissed him on the lips. She was winning! She felt it in the beating of his heart against her, in the closing of his eyes. 'I want to make sure! I want to make sure!' she whispered. 'Promise!'

Jon did not answer. His face had the stillness of extreme trouble. At last he said:

'It's like hitting them. I must think a little, Fleur. I really must.'

Fleur slipped out of his arms.

'Oh! Very well!' And suddenly she burst into tears of disappointment, shame, and overstrain. Followed five minutes of acute misery. Jon's remorse and tenderness knew no bounds; but he did not promise. Despite her will to cry, 'Very well, then, if you don't love me enough–good-bye!' she dared not. From birth accustomed to her own way, this check from one so young, so tender, so devoted, baffled and surprised her. She wanted to push him away from her, to try what anger and coldness would do, and again she dared not. The knowledge that she was scheming to rush him blindfold into the irrevocable weakened everything–weakened the sincerity of pique, and the sincerity of passion; even her kisses had not the lure she wished for them. That stormy little meeting ended inconclusively.

'Will you some tea, *gnädiges Fräulein*?'

Pushing Jon from her, she cried out:

'No–no, thank you! I'm just going.'

And before he could prevent her she was gone.

She went stealthily, mopping her flushed, stained cheeks, frightened, angry, very miserable. She had stirred Jon up so fearfully, yet nothing definite was promised or arranged! But the more uncertain and hazardous the future, the more 'the will to have' worked its tentacles into the flesh of her heart–like some burrowing tick!

No one was at Green Street. Winifred had gone with Imogen to see a play which some said was allegorical, and others 'very exciting, don't you know.' It was because of what others said that Winifred and Imogen had gone. Fleur went on to Paddington. Through the carriage the air from the brick-kilns of West Drayton and the late hayfields fanned her still flushed cheeks. Flowers had seemed to be had for the plucking; now they were all thorned and prickled. But the golden flower within the crown of spikes seemed to her tenacious spirit all the fairer and more desirable.

9

THE FAT IN THE FIRE

On reaching home Fleur found an atmosphere so peculiar that it penetrated even the perplexed aura of her own private life. Her mother was inaccessibly entrenched in a brown study; her father contemplating fate in the vinery. Neither of them had a word to throw to a dog. 'Is it because of me?' thought Fleur. 'Or because of Profond?' To her mother she said:

'What's the matter with Father?'

Her mother answered with a shrug of her shoulders.

To her father:

'What's the matter with Mother?'

Her father answered:

'Matter? What should be the matter?' and gave her a sharp look.

'By the way,' murmured Fleur, 'Monsieur Profond is going a 'small' voyage on his yacht, to the South Seas.'

Soames examined a branch on which no grapes were growing.

'This vine's a failure,' he said. 'I've had young Mont here. He asked me something about you.'

'Oh! How do you like him, Father?'

'He–he's a product–like all these young people.'

'What were you at his age, dear?'

Soames smiled grimly.

'We went to work, and didn't play about–flying and motoring, and making love.'

'Didn't you ever make love?'

She avoided looking at him while she said that, but she saw him well enough. His pale face had reddened, his eyebrows, where darkness was still mingled with the grey, had come close together.

'I had no time or inclination to philander.'

'Perhaps you had a grand passion.'

Soames looked at her intently.

'Yes–if you want to know–and much good it did me.' He moved away, along by the hot-water pipes. Fleur tiptoed silently after him.

'Tell me about it, Father!'

Soames became very still.

'What should you want to know about such things, at your age?'

'Is she alive?'

He nodded.

'And married?'

'Yes.'

'It's Jon Forsyte's mother, isn't it? And she was your wife first.'

It was said in a flash of intuition. Surely his opposition came from his anxiety that she should not know of that old wound to his pride. But she was startled.

To see someone so old and calm wince as if struck, to hear so sharp a note of pain in his voice!

'Who told you that? If your aunt–! I can't bear the affair talked of.'

'But, darling,' said Fleur, softly, 'it's so long ago.'

'Long ago or not, I–'

Fleur stood stroking his arm.

'I've tried to forget,' he said suddenly; 'I don't wish to be reminded.' And then, as if venting some long and secret irritation, he added: 'In these days people don't understand. Grand passion, indeed! No one knows what it is.'

'I do,' said Fleur, almost in a whisper.

Soames, who had turned his back on her, spun round.

'What are you talking of–a child like you!'

'Perhaps I've inherited it, Father.'

'What?'

'For her son, you see.'

He was pale as a sheet, and she knew that she was as bad. They stood staring at each other in the steamy heat, redolent of the mushy scent of earth, of potted geranium, and of vines coming along fast.

'This is crazy,' said Soames at last, between dry lips.

Scarcely moving her own, she murmured:

'Don't be angry, Father. I can't help it.'

But she could see he wasn't angry; only scared, deeply scared.

'I thought that foolishness,' he stammered, 'was all forgotten.'

'Oh, no! It's ten times what it was.'

Soames kicked at the hot-water pipe. The hapless movement touched her, who had no fear of her father–none.

'Dearest!' she said. 'What must be, must, you know.'

'Must!' repeated Soames. 'You don't know what you're talking of. Has that boy been told?'

The blood rushed into her cheeks.

'Not yet.'

He had turned from her again, and, with one shoulder a little raised, stood staring fixedly at a joint in the pipes.

'It's most distasteful to me,' he said suddenly; 'nothing could be more so. Son of that fellow! It's–it's–perverse!'

She had noted, almost unconsciously, that he did not say 'son of that woman', and again her intuition began working.

Did the ghost of that grand passion linger in some corner of his heart?

She slipped her hand under his arm.

'Jon's father is quite ill and old; I saw him.'

'You–?'

'Yes, I went there with Jon; I saw them both.'

'Well, and what did they say to you?'

'Nothing. They were very polite.'

'They would be.' He resumed his contemplation of the pipe-joint, and then said suddenly:

'I must think this over–I'll speak to you again to-night.'

She knew this was final for the moment, and stole away leaving him still looking at the pipe-joint. She wandered into the fruit-garden, among the raspberry and currant bushes, without impetus to pick and eat. Two months ago–she was light-hearted! Even two days ago–light-hearted, before Prosper

Profond told her. Now she felt tangled in a web–of passions, vested rights, oppressions and revolts, the ties of love and hate. At this dark moment of discouragement there seemed, even to her hold-fast nature, no way out. How deal with it–how sway and bend things to her will, and get her heart's desire? And, suddenly, round the corner of the high box hedge, she came plump on her mother, walking swiftly, with an open letter in her hand. Her bosom was heaving, her eyes dilated, her cheeks flushed. Instantly Fleur thought: 'The yacht! Poor Mother!'

Annette gave her a wide startled look, and said:

'*J'ai la migraine.*'

'I'm awfully sorry, Mother.'

'Oh, yes! you and your father–sorry!'

'But, Mother–I am. I know what it feels like.'

Annette's startled eyes grew wide, till the whites showed above them. 'Poor innocent!' she said.

Her mother–so self-possessed, and common-sensical–to look and speak like this! It was all frightening! Her father, her mother, herself! And only two months back they had seemed to have everything they wanted in this world.

Annette crumpled the letter in her hand. Fleur knew that she must ignore the sight.

'Can't I do anything for your head, Mother?'

Annette shook her head and walked on, swaying her hips.

'It's cruel,' thought Fleur, 'and I was glad! That man! What do men come prowling for, disturbing everything! I suppose he's tired of her. What business has he to be tired of my mother? What business!' And at that thought, so natural and so peculiar, she uttered a little choked laugh.

She ought, of course, to be delighted, but what was there to be delighted at? Her father didn't really care! Her mother did, perhaps? She entered the orchard, and sat down under a cherry tree. A breeze sighed in the higher boughs; the sky seen through their green was very blue and very white in cloud–those heavy white clouds almost always present in river landscape. Bees, sheltering out of the wind, hummed softly, and over the lush green fell the thick shade from those fruit trees planted by her father five-and-twenty years ago. Birds were almost silent, the cuckoos had ceased to sing, but wood-pigeons were cooing. The breath and drone and cooing of high summer were not for long a sedative to her excited nerves. Crouched over her knees she began to scheme. Her father must be made to back her up. Why should he mind so long as she was happy? She had not lived for nearly nineteen years without knowing that her future was all he really cared about. She had, then, only to convince him that her future could not be happy without Jon. He thought it a mad fancy. How foolish the old were, thinking they could tell what the young felt! Had not he confessed that he–when young–had loved with a grand passion? He ought to understand! 'He piles up his money for me,' she thought; 'but what's the use, if I'm not going to be happy!' Money, and all it bought, did not bring happiness. Love only brought that. The ox-eyed daisies in this orchard, which gave it such a moony look sometimes, grew wild and happy, and had their hour. 'They oughtn't to have called me Fleur,' she mused, 'if they didn't mean me to have my hour, and be happy while it lasts.' Nothing real stood in the way, like poverty, or disease–sentiment only, a ghost from the unhappy past! Jon was right. They wouldn't let you live, these old people! They made mistakes, committed crimes, and wanted their children to go on

paying! The breeze died away; midges began to bite. She got up, plucked a
piece of honeysuckle, and went in.

It was hot that night. Both she and her mother had put on thin, pale low
frocks. The dinner flowers were pale. Fleur was struck with the pale look of
everything; her father's face, her mother's shoulders; the pale panelled walls,
the pale grey velvety carpet, the lamp-shade, even the soup was pale. There was
not one spot of colour in the room, not even wine in the pale glasses, for no one
drank it. What was not pale was black—her father's clothes, the butler's clothes,
her retriever stretched out exhausted in the window, the curtains black with a
creamed pattern. A moth came in, and that was pale. And silent was that half-
mourning dinner in the heat.

Her father called her back as she was following her mother out.

She sat down beside him at the table, and, unpinning the pale honeysuckle,
put it to her nose.

'I've been thinking,' he said.

'Yes, dear?'

'It's extremely painful for me to talk, but there's no help for it. I don't know
if you understand how much you are to me—I've never spoken of it, I didn't
think it necessary; but—but you're everything. Your mother—' he paused,
staring at his finger-bowl of Venetian glass.

'Yes?'

'I've only you to look to. I've never had—never wanted anything else, since
you were born.'

'I know,' Fleur murmured.

Soames moistened his lips.

'You may think this a matter I can smooth over and arrange for you. You're
mistaken. I—I'm helpless.'

Fleur did not speak.

'Quite apart from my own feelings,' went on Soames with more resolution,
'those two are not amenable to anything I can say. They—they hate me, as
people always hate those whom they have injured.'

'But he—Jon—'

'He's their flesh and blood, her only child. Probably he means to her what
you mean to me. It's a deadlock.'

'No,' cried Fleur, 'no, Father!'

Soames leaned back, the image of pale patience, as if resolved on the betrayal
of no emotion.

'Listen!' he said. 'You're putting the feelings of two months—two
months—against the feelings of thirty-five years! What chance do you think you
have? Two months—your very first love affair, a matter of half a dozen
meetings, a few walks and talks, a few kisses—against, against what you can't
imagine, what no one could who hasn't been through it. Come, be reasonable,
Fleur! It's mid-summer madness!'

Fleur tore the honeysuckle into little, slow bits.

'The madness is in letting the past spoil it all. What do we care about the
past? It's our lives, not yours.'

Soames raised his hand to his forehead, where suddenly she saw moisture
shining.

'Whose child are you?' he said. 'Whose child is he? The present is linked with
the past, the future with both. There's no getting away from that.'

She had never heard philosophy pass those lips before. Impressed even in her agitation, she leaned her elbows on the table, her chin on her hands.

'But, Father, consider it practically. We want each other. There's ever so much money, and nothing whatever in the way but sentiment. Let's bury the past, Father.'

His answer was a sigh.

'Besides,' said Fleur gently, 'you can't prevent us.'

'I don't suppose,' said Soames, 'that if left to myself I should try to prevent you; I must put up with things, I know, to keep your affection. But it's not I who control this matter. That's what I want you to realise before it's too late. If you go on thinking you can get your way, and encourage this feeling, the blow will be much heavier when you find you can't.'

'Oh!' cried Fleur, 'help me, Father; you *can* help me, you know.'

Soames made a startled movement of negation.

'I?' he said bitterly. 'Help? I am the impediment–the just cause and impediment–isn't that the jargon? You have my blood in your veins.'

He rose.

'Well, the fat's in the fire. If you persist in your wilfulness you'll have yourself to blame. Come! Don't be foolish, my child–my only child!'

Fleur laid her forehead against his shoulder.

All was in such turmoil within her. But no good to show it! No good at all! She broke away from him, and went out into the twilight, distraught, but unconvinced. All was indeterminate and vague within her, like the shapes and shadows in the garden, except–her will to have. A poplar pierced up into the dark-blue sky and touched a white star there. The dew wetted her shoes, and chilled her bare shoulders. She went down to the river bank, and stood gazing at a moonstreak on the darkening water. Suddenly she smelled tobacco smoke, and a white figure emerged as if created by the moon. It was young Mont in flannels, standing in his boat. She heard the tiny hiss of his cigarette extinguished in the water.

'Fleur,' came his voice, 'don't be hard on a poor devil! I've been waiting hours.'

'For what?'

'Come in my boat!'

'Not I.'

'Why not?'

'I'm not a water-nymph.'

'Haven't you *any* romance in you? Don't be modern Fleur!'

He appeared on the path within a yard of her.

'Go away!'

'Fleur, I love you. Fleur!'

Fleur uttered a short laugh.

'Come again,' she said, 'when I haven't got my wish.'

'What is your wish?'

'Ask another.'

'Fleur,' said Mont, and his voice sounded strange, 'don't mock me! Even vivisected dogs are wo. th decent treatment before they're cut up for good.'

Fleur shook her head, but her lips were trembling.

'Well, you shouldn't make me jump. Give me a cigarette.'

Mont gave her one, lighted it, and another for himself.

'I don't want to talk rot,' he said, 'but please imagine all the rot that all the lovers that ever were have talked, and all my special rot thrown in.'

'Thank you, I have imagined it. Good-night!'

They stood for a moment facing each other in the shadow of an acacia tree with very moonlit blossoms, and the smoke from their cigarettes mingled in the air between them.

'Also ran: "Michael Mont"?' he said. Fleur turned abruptly toward the house. On the lawn she stopped to look back. Michael Mont was whirling his arms above him; she could see them dashing at his head; then waving at the moonlit blossoms of the acacia. His voice just reached her. 'Jolly-jolly!' Fleur shook herself. She couldn't help him, she had too much trouble of her own! On the verandah she stopped very suddenly again. Her mother was sitting in the drawing-room at her writing bureau, quite alone. There was nothing remarkable in the expression of her face except its utter immobility. But she looked desolate! Fleur went upstairs. At the door of her room she paused. She could hear her father walking up and down, up and down the picture-gallery.

'Yes,' she thought, 'jolly! Oh, Jon!'

10

DECISION

When Fleur left him Jon stared at the Austrian. She was a thin woman with a dark face and the concerned expression of one who has watched every little good that life once had slip from her, one by one.

'No tea?' she said.

Susceptible to the disappointment in her voice, Jon murmured:

'No, really; thanks.'

'A lil cup—it ready. A lil cup and cigarette.'

Fleur was gone. Hours of remorse and indecision lay before him! And with a heavy sense of disproportion he smiled, and said:

'Well—thank you!'

She brought in a little pot of tea with two little cups, and a silver box of cigarettes on a little tray.

'Sugar? Miss Forsyte has much sugar—she buy my sugar, my friend's sugar also. Miss Forsyte is a veree kind lady. I am happy to serve her. You her brother?'

'Yes,' said Jon, beginning to puff the second cigarette of his life.

'Very young brother,' said the Austrian, with a little anxious smile, which reminded him of the wag of a dog's tail.

'May I give you some?' he said. 'And won't you sit down, please?'

The Austrian shook her head.

'Your father is a very nice old man—the most nice old man I ever see. Miss Forsyte tell me all about him. Is he better?'

Her words fell on Jon like a reproach. 'Oh! Yes, I think he's all right.'

'I like to see him again,' said the Austrian, putting a hand on her heart; 'he have veree kind heart.'

'Yes,' said Jon. And again her words seemed to him a reproach.

'He never give no trouble to no one, and smile so gentle.'

'Yes, doesn't he?'

'He look at Miss Forsyte so funny sometimes. I tell him all my story; he so sympátisch. Your mother–she nice and well?'

'Yes, very.'

'He have her photograph on his dressing-table. Veree beautiful.'

Jon gulped down his tea. This woman, with her concerned face and her reminding words, was like the first and second murderers.

'Thank you,' he said: 'I must go now. May–may I leave this with you?'

He put a ten-shilling note on the tray with a doubting hand and gained the door. He heard the Austrian gasp, and hurried out. He had just time to catch his train, and all the way to Victoria looked at every face that passed, as lovers will, hoping against hope. On reaching Worthing he put his luggage into the local train, and set out across the Downs for Wansdon, trying to walk off his aching irresolution. So long as he went full bat, he could enjoy the beauty of those green slopes, stopping now and again to sprawl on the grass, admire the perfection of a wild rose or listen to a lark's song. But the war of motives within him was but postponed–the longing for Fleur, and the hatred of deception. He came to the old chalk-pit above Wansdon with his mind no more made up than when he started. To see both sides of a question vigorously was at once Jon's strength and weakness. He tramped in, just as the first dinner-bell rang. His things had already been brought up. He had a hurried bath and came down to find Holly alone–Val had gone to Town and would not be back till the last train.

Since Val's advice to him to ask his sister what was the matter between the two families, so much had happened–Fleur's disclosure in the Green Park, her visit to Robin Hill, to-day's meeting–that there seemed nothing to ask. He talked of Spain, his sunstroke, Val's horses, their father's health. Holly startled him by saying that she thought their father not at all well. She had been twice to Robin Hill for the week-end. He had seemed fearfully languid, sometimes even in pain, but had always refused to talk about himself.

'He's awfully dear and unselfish–don't you think, Jon?'

Feeling far from dear and unselfish himself, Jon answered: 'Rather!'

'I think, he's been a simply perfect father, so long as I can remember.'

'Yes,' answered Jon, very subdued.

'He's never interfered, and he's always seemed to understand. I shall never forget his letting me go to South Africa in the Boer War when I was in love with Val.'

'That was before he married Mother, wasn't it?' said Jon suddenly.

'Yes. Why?'

'Oh! nothing. Only, wasn't she engaged to Fleur's father first?'

Holly put down the spoon she was using, and raised her eyes. Her stare was circumspect. What did the boy know? Enough to make it better to tell him? She could not decide. He looked strained and worried, altogether older, but that might be the sunstroke.

'There *was* something,' she said. 'Of course we were out there, and got no news of anything.' She could not take the risk. It was not her secret. Besides, she was in the dark about his feelings now. Before Spain she had made sure he was in love; but boys were boys; that was seven weeks ago, and all Spain between.

She saw that he knew she was putting him off, and added:

'Have you heard anything of Fleur?'

'Yes.'

His face told her, then, more than the most elaborate explanations. So he had not forgotten!

She said very quietly: 'Fleur is awfully attractive, Jon, but you know—Val and I don't really like her very much.'

'Why?'

'We think she's got rather a "having" nature.'

'"Having"? I don't know what you mean. She—she—' he pushed his dessert plate away, got up, and went to the window.

Holly, too, got up, and put her arm round his waist.

'Don't be angry, Jon, dear. We can't all see people in the same light, can we? You know, I believe each of us only has about one or two people who can see the best that's in us, and bring it out. For you I think it's your mother. I once saw her looking at a letter of yours; it was wonderful to see her face. I think she's the most beautiful woman I ever saw—Age doesn't seem to touch her.'

Jon's face softened; then again became tense. Everybody—everybody was against him and Fleur! It all strengthened the appeal of her words: 'Make sure of me—marry me, Jon!'

Here, where he had passed that wonderful week with her—the tug of her enchantment, the ache in his heart increased with every minute that she was not there to make the room, the garden, the very air magical. Would he ever be able to live down here, not seeing her? And he closed up utterly, going early to bed. It would not make him healthy, wealthy, and wise, but it closeted him with memory of Fleur in her fancy frock. He heard Val's arrival—the Ford discharging cargo, then the stillness of the summer night stole back—with only the bleating of very distant sheep, and a night-jar's harsh purring. He leaned far out. Cold moon—warm air—the Downs like silver! Small wings, a stream bubbling, the rambler roses! God—how empty all of it without her! In the Bible it was written: Thou shalt leave father and mother and cleave to—Fleur!

Let him have pluck, and go and tell them! They couldn't stop him marrying her—they wouldn't want to stop him when they knew how he felt. Yes! He would go! Bold and open—Fleur was wrong!

The night-jar ceased, the sheep were silent; the only sound in the darkness was the bubbling of the stream. And Jon in his bed slept, freed from the worst of life's evils—indecision.

II

TIMOTHY PROPHESIES

On the day of the cancelled meeting at the National Gallery began the second anniversary of the resurrection of England's pride and glory—or, more shortly, the top hat. 'Lord's'—that festival which the War had driven from the field—raised its light and dark blue flags for the second time, displaying almost every feature of a glorious past. Here, in the luncheon interval, were all species of female and one species of male hat, protecting the multiple types of face associated with 'the classes'. The observing Forsyte might discern in the free or unconsidered seats a certain number of the squash-hatted, but they hardly ventured on the grass; the old school—or schools—could still rejoice that the proletariat was not yet paying the necessary half-crown. Here was still a close borough, the only one left on a large scale–for the papers were about to estimate the attendance at ten thousand. And the ten thousand, all animated by one hope, were asking each other one question: 'Where are you lunching?' Something wonderfully uplifting and reassuring in the query and the sight of so many people like themselves voicing it! What reserve power in the British realm–enough pigeons, lobsters, lamb, salmon mayonnaise, strawberries, and bottles of champagne to feed the lot! No miracle in prospect–no case of seven loaves and a few fishes–faith rested on surer foundations. Six thousand top hats; four thousand parasols would be doffed and furled, ten thousand mouths all speaking the same English would be filled. There was life in the old dog yet! Tradition! And again Tradition! How strong and how elastic! Wars might rage, taxation prey, Trades Unions take toll, and Europe perish of starvation; but the ten thousand would be fed; and, within their ring fence, stroll upon green turf, wear their top hats, and meet–themselves. The heart was sound, the pulse still regular. E-ton! E-ton! Har-r-o-o-o-w!

Among the many Forsytes, present on a hunting-ground theirs, by personal prescriptive right, or proxy, was Soames with his wife and daughter. He had not been at either school, he took no interest in cricket, but he wanted Fleur to show her frock, and he wanted to wear his top hat–parade it again in peace and plenty among his peers. He walked sedately with Fleur between him and Annette. No woman equalled them so far as he could see. They could walk, and hold themselves up; there was substance in their good looks; the modern woman had no build, no chest, no anything! He remembered suddenly with what intoxication of pride he had walked round with Irene in the first years of his first marriage. And how they used to lunch on the drag which his mother *would* make his father have, because it was so 'chic'–all drags and carriages in those days, not these lumbering great Stands! And how consistently Montague Dartie had drunk too much. He supposed that people drank too much still, but there was not the scope for it there used to be. He remembered George Forsyte–whose brothers Roger and Eustace had been at Harrow and Eton–towering up on the top of the drag waving a light blue flag with one hand and a dark blue flag with the other, and shouting, 'Etroow–Harrton!' just when everybody was silent, like the buffoon he had always been; and Eustace got up to the nines below, too dandified to wear any colour or take any notice. H'm! Old days, and Irene in grey silk shot with palest green. He looked, sideways, at Fleur's face. Rather colourless–no light, no eagerness! That love affair was preying on her–a bad business! He looked beyond, at his wife's face, rather more touched up than usual, a little disdainful–not that she had any business to disdain, so far as he could see. She was taking Profond's defection with curious quietude; or was his 'small' voyage just a blind? If so, he should refuse to see it! Having promenaded round the pitch and in front of the pavillion they sought Winifred's table in the Bedouin Club tent. This Club–a new 'cock and hen'–had been founded in the interests of travel, and of a gentleman with an old Scottish name, whose father had somewhat strangely been called Levi. Winifred had joined, not because she had travelled, but because instinct told her that a Club with such a name and such a founder was bound to go far; if one didn't join at once one might never have the chance. Its tent, with a text from the Koran on an orange ground, and a small green camel embroidered over the entrance, was the most striking on the ground. Outside it they found Jack Cardigan in a dark blue tie (he had once played for Harrow), batting with a

Malacca cane to show how that fellow ought to have hit that ball. He piloted them in. Assembled in Winifred's corner were Imogen, Benedict with his young wife, Val Dartie without Holly, Maud and her husband, and, after Soames and his two were seated, one empty place.

'I'm expecting Prosper,' said Winifred, 'but he's so busy with his yacht.'

Soames stole a glance. No movement in his wife's face! Whether that fellow were coming or not, she evidently knew all about it. It did not escape him that Fleur, too, looked at her mother. If Annette didn't respect his feelings, she might think of Fleur's! The conversation, very desultory, was syncopated by Jack Cardigan talking about 'mid-off'. He cited all the 'great mid-offs' from the beginning of time, as if they had been a definite racial entity in the composition of the British people. Soames had finished his lobster, and was beginning on pigeon-pie, when he heard the words, 'I'm a small bit late, Mrs Dartie,' and saw that there was no longer any empty place. *That fellow* was sitting between Annette and Imogen. Soames ate steadily on, with an occasional word to Maud and Winifred. Conversation buzzed around him. He heard the voice of Profond say:

'I think you're mistaken, Mrs Forsyde; I'll–I'll bet Miss Forsyde agrees with me.'

'In what?' came Fleur's clear voice across the table.

'I was sayin', young gurls are much the same as they always were–there's very small difference.'

'Do you know so much about them?'

That sharp reply caught the ears of all, and Soames moved uneasily on his thin green chair.

'Well, I don't know, I think they want their own small way, and I think they always did.'

'Indeed!'

'Oh, but–Prosper,' Winifred interjected comfortably, 'the girls in the streets–the girls who've been in munitions, the little flappers in the shops; their manners now really quite hit you in the eye.'

At the word 'hit' Jack Cardigan stopped his disquisition; and in the silence Monsieur Profond said:

'It was inside before, now it's outside; that's all.'

'But their morals!' cried Imogen.

'Just as moral as they were, Mrs Cardigan, but they've got more opportunity.'

The saying, so cryptically cynical, received a little laugh from Imogen, a slight opening of Jack Cardigan's mouth, and a creak from Soames's chair.

Winifred said: 'That's too bad, Prosper.'

'What do you say, Mrs Forsyde; don't you think human nature's always the same?'

Soames subdued a sudden longing to get up and kick the fellow. He heard his wife reply:

'Human nature is not the same in England as anywhere else.' That was her confounded mockery!

'Well, I don't know much about this small country'–"No, thank God!" thought Soames–'but I should say the pot was boilin' under the lid everywhere. We all want pleasure, and we always did.'

Damn the fellow! His cynicism was–was outrageous!

When lunch was over they broke up into couples for the digestive promenade. Too proud to notice, Soames knew perfectly that Annette and that fellow had gone prowling round together. Fleur was with Val; she had chosen him, no doubt, because he knew that boy. He himself had Winifred for partner. They walked in the bright, circling stream, a little flushed and sated, for some minutes, till Winifred sighed:

'I wish we were back forty years, old boy!'

Before the eyes of her spirit an interminable procession of her own 'Lord's' frocks was passing, paid for with the money of her father, to save a recurrent crisis. 'It's been very amusing, after all. Sometimes I even wish Monty was back. What do you think of people nowadays, Soames?'

'Precious little style. The thing began to go to pieces with bicycles and motor-cars; the War has finished it.'

'I wonder what's coming?' said Winifred in a voice dreamy from pigeon-pie. 'I'm not at all sure we shan't go back to crinolines and pegtops. Look at that dress!'

Soames shook his head.

'There's money, but no faith in things. We don't lay by for the future. These youngsters–it's all a short life and a merry one with them.'

'There's a hat!' said Winifred. 'I don't know–when you come to think of the people killed and all that in the War, it's rather wonderful, I think. There's no other country–Prosper says the rest are all bankrupt, except America; and of course her men always took their style in dress from us.'

'Is that chap,' said Soames, 'really going to the South Seas?'

'Oh! one never knows where Prosper's going!'

'*He's* a sign of the times,' muttered Soames, 'if you like.'

Winifred's hand gripped his arm.

'Don't turn your head,' she said in a low voice, 'but look to your right in the front row of the Stand.'

Soames looked as best he could under that limitation. A man in a grey top hat, grey-bearded, with thin brown, folded cheeks, and a certain elegance of posture, sat there with a woman in a lawn-coloured frock, whose dark eyes were fixed on himself. Soames looked quickly at his feet. How funnily feet moved, one after the other like that! Winifred's voice said in his ear:

'Jolyon looks very ill, but he always had style. *She* doesn't change–except her hair.'

'Why did you tell Fleur about that business?'

'I didn't; she picked it up. I always knew she would.'

'Well, it's a mess. She's set her heart upon their boy.'

'The little wretch,' murmured Winifred. 'She tried to take me in about that. What shall you do, Soames?'

'Be guided by events.'

They moved on, silent, in the almost solid crowd.

'Really,' said Winifred suddenly; 'it almost seems like Fate. Only that's so old-fashioned. Look! There are George and Eustace!'

George Forsyte's lofty bulk had halted before them.

'Hallo, Soames!' he said. 'Just met Profond and your wife. You'll catch 'em if you put on a pace. Did you ever go to see old Timothy?'

Soames nodded, and the streams forced them apart.

'I always liked old George,' said Winifred. 'He's so droll.'

'I never did,' said Soames. 'Where's your seat? I shall go to mine. Fleur may be back there.'

Having seen Winifred to her seat, he regained his own, conscious of small, white, distant figures running, the click of the bat, the cheers and counter-cheers. No Fleur, and no Annette! You could expect nothing of women nowadays! They had the vote. They were 'emancipated,' and much good it was doing them! So Winifred would go back, would she, and put up with Dartie all over again? To have the past once more—to be sitting here as he had sat in '83 and '84, before he was certain that his marriage with Irene had gone all wrong, before her antagonism had become so glaring that with the best will in the world he could not overlook it. The sight of her with that fellow had brought all memory back. Even now he could not understand why she had been so impracticable. She could love other men; she had it in her! To himself, the one person she ought to have loved, she had chosen to refuse her heart. It seemed to him, fantastically, as he looked back, that all this modern relaxation of marriage—though its forms and laws were the same as when he married her—that all this modern looseness had come out of her revolt; it seemed to him, fantastically, that she had started it, till all decent ownership of anything had gone, or was on the point of going. All came from her! And now—a pretty state of things! Homes! How could you have them without mutual ownership? Not that he had ever had a real home! But had that been his fault? He had done his best. And his rewards were—those two sitting in the Stand, and this affair of Fleur's!

And overcome by loneliness he thought: 'Shan't wait any longer! They must find their own way back to the hotel—if they mean to come!' Hailing a cab outside the ground, he said:

'Drive me to the Bayswater Road.' His old aunts had never failed him. To them he had meant an ever-welcome visitor. Though they were gone, there, still, was Timothy!

Smither was standing in the open doorway.

'Mr Soames! I was just taking the air. Cook will be so pleased.'

'How is Mr Timothy?'

'Not himself at all these last few days, sir; he's been talking a great deal. Only this morning he was saying: "My brother James, he's getting old." His mind wanders, Mr Soames, and then he will talk of them. He troubles about their investments. The other day he said: "There's my brother Jolyon won't look at Consols"—he seemed quite down about it. Come in, Mr Soames, come in! It's such a pleasant change!'

'Well,' said Soames, 'just for a few minutes.'

'No,' murmured Smither in the hall, where the air had the singular freshness of the outside day, 'we haven't been very satisfied with him, not all this week. He's always been one to leave a titbit to the end; but ever since Monday he's been eating it first. If you notice a dog, Mr Soames, at its dinner, it eats the meat first. We've always thought it such a good sign of Mr Timothy at his age to leave it to the last, but now he seems to have lost all his self-control; and, of course, it makes him leave the rest. The doctor doesn't make anything of it, but'—Smither shook her head—'he seems to think he's got to eat it first, in case he shouldn't get to it. That and his talking makes us anxious.'

'Has he said anything important?'

'I shouldn't like to say that, Mr Soames; but he's turned against his Will. He gets quite pettish—and after having had it out every morning for years, it does seem funny. He said the other day: "They want my money." It gave me such a turn, because, as I said to him, nobody wants his money, I'm sure. And it does seem a pity he should be thinking about money at his time of life. I took my courage in my 'ands. "You know, Mr Timothy," I said, "my dear mistress"–that's Miss Forsyte, Mr Soames, Miss Ann that trained me–"*she* never thought about money," I said, "it was all *character* with her." He looked at me, I can't tell you how funny, and he said quite dry: "Nobody wants my character." Think of his saying a thing like that! But sometimes he'll say something as sharp and sensible as anything.'

Soames, who had been staring at an old print by the hat-rack, thinking. 'That's got value!' murmured: 'I'll go up and see him, Smither.'

'Cook's with him,' answered Smither above her corsets; 'she will be pleased to see you.'

He mounted slowly, with the thought: 'Shan't care to live to be that age.'

On the second floor, he paused, and tapped. The door was opened, and he saw the round homely face of a woman about sixty.

'Mr Soames!' she said: 'Why! Mr Soames!'

Soames nodded. 'All right, Cook!' and entered.

Timothy was propped up in bed, with his hands joined before his chest, and his eyes fixed on the ceiling, where a fly was standing upside-down. Soames stood at the foot of the bed, facing him.

'Uncle Timothy,' he said, raising his voice, 'Uncle Timothy!'

Timothy's eyes left the fly, and levelled themselves on his visitor. Soames could see his pale tongue passing over his darkish lips.

'Uncle Timothy,' he said again, 'is there anything I can do for you? Is there anything you'd like to say?'

'Ha!' said Timothy.

'I've come to look you up and see that everything's all right.'

Timothy nodded. He seemed trying to get used to the apparition before him.

'Have you got everything you want?'

'No,' said Timothy.

'Can I get you anything?'

'No,' said Timothy.

'I'm Soames, you know; your nephew, Soames Forsyte. Your brother James's son.'

Timothy nodded.

'I shall be delighted to do anything I can for you.'

Timothy beckoned. Soames went close to him.

'You–' said Timothy in a voice which seemed to have outlived tone, 'you tell them all from me–you tell them all–' and his finger tapped on Soames's arm, 'to hold on–hold on–Consols are goin' up,' and he nodded thrice.

'All right!' said Soames; 'I will.'

'Yes,' said Timothy, and, fixing his eyes again on the ceiling he added: 'That fly!'

Strangely moved, Soames looked at the Cook's pleasant fattish face, all little puckers from staring at fires.

'That'll do him a world of good, sir,' she said.

A mutter came from Timothy, but he was clearly speaking to himself, and Soames went out with the cook.

'I wish I could make you a pink cream, Mr Soames, like in old days: you did so relish them. Good-bye, sir; it *has* been a pleasure.'

'Take care of him, Cook, he *is* old.'

And, shaking her crumpled hand, he went downstairs. Smither was still taking the air in the doorway.

'What do you think of him, Mr Soames?'

'H'm!' Soames murmured: 'He's lost touch.'

'Yes,' said Smither, 'I was afraid you'd think that coming fresh out of the world to see him like.'

'Smither,' said Soames, 'we're all indebted to you.'

'Oh, no, Mr Soames, don't say that! It's a pleasure–he's such a wonderful man.'

'Well, good-bye!' said Soames, and got into his taxi.

'Going up!' he thought; 'going up!'

Reaching the hotel at Knightsbridge he went to their sitting-room, and rang for tea. Neither of them was in. And again that sense of loneliness came over him. These hotels! What monstrous great places they were now! He could remember when there was nothing bigger than Long's or Brown's, Morley's or the Tavistock, and the heads that were shaken over the Langham and the Grand. Hotels and clubs–clubs and hotels; no end to them now! And Soames, who had just been watching at Lord's a miracle of tradition and continuity, fell into reverie over the changes in that London where he had been born five-and-sixty years before. Whether Consols were going up or not, London had become a terrific property. No such property in the world, unless it were New York! There was a lot of hysteria in the papers nowadays; but anyone who, like himself, could remember London sixty years ago, and see it now, realised the fecundity and elasticity of wealth. They had only to keep their heads, and go at it steadily. Why! he remembered cobblestones, and stinking straw on the floor of your cab. And old Timothy–what could *he* not tell them, if he had kept his memory! Things were unsettled, people in a funk or in a hurry, but here were London and the Thames, and out there the British Empire, and the ends of the earth. 'Consols are goin' up?' He shouldn't be a bit surprised. It was that breed that counted. And all that was bull-dogged in Soames stared for a moment out of his grey eyes, till diverted by the print of a Victorian picture on the walls. The hotel had bought three dozen of that little lot! The old hunting or 'Rake's Progress' prints in the old inns were worth looking at–but this sentimental stuff–well, Victorianism had gone! 'Tell them to hold on!' old Timothy had said. But to what were they to hold on in this modern welter of the 'democratic principle'? Why, even privacy was threatened! And at the thought that privacy might perish, Soames pushed back his teacup and went to the window. Fancy owning no more of Nature than the crowd out there owned of the flowers and trees and waters of Hyde Park! No, no! Private possession underlay everything worth having. The world had slipped its sanity a bit, as dogs now and again at full moon slipped theirs and went off for a night's rabbiting; but the world, like the dog, knew where its bread was buttered and its bed warm, and would come back sure enough to the only home worth having–to private ownership. The world was in its second childhood for the moment, like old Timothy–eating its titbit first!

He heard a sound behind him, and saw that his wife and daughter had come in.

'So you're back!' he said.

Fleur did not answer; she stood for a moment looking at him and her mother, then passed into her bedroom. Annette poured herself out a cup of tea.

'I am going to Paris, to my mother, Soames.'

'Oh! To your mother?'

'Yes.'

'For how long?'

'I do not know.'

'And when are you going?'

'On Monday.'

Was she really going to her mother? Odd, how indifferent he felt! Odd, how clearly she had perceived the indifference he would feel so long as there was no scandal. And suddenly between her and himself he saw distinctly the face he had seen that afternoon—Irene's.

'Will you want money?'

'Thank you; I have enough.'

'Very well. Let us know when you are coming back.'

Annette put down the cake she was fingering, and, looking up through darkened lashes, said:

'Shall I give *Maman* any message?'

'My regards.'

Annette stretched herself, her hands on her waist, and said in French:

'What luck that you have never loved me, Soames!' Then rising, she too left the room. Soames was glad she had spoken it in French—it seemed to require no dealing with. Again that other face—pale, dark-eyed, beautiful still! And there stirred far down within him the ghost of warmth, as from sparks lingering beneath a mound of flaky ash. And Fleur infatuated with *her* boy! Queer chance! Yet, was there such a thing as chance? A man went down a street, a brick fell on his head. Ah! that was chance, no doubt. But this! 'Inherited,' his girl had said. She—she was 'holding on'!

PART III

I

OLD JOLYON WALKS

Twofold impulse had made Jolyon say to his wife at breakfast: 'Let's go up to Lord's!'

'Wanted'–something to abate the anxiety in which those two had lived during the sixty hours since Jon had brought Fleur down. 'Wanted'–too, that which might assuage the pangs of memory in one who knew he might lose them any day!

Fifty-eight years ago Jolyon had become an Eton boy, for old Jolyon's whim had been that he should be canonised at the greatest possible expense. Year after year he had gone to Lord's from Stanhope Gate with a father whose youth in the eighteen-twenties had been passed without polish in the game of cricket. Old Jolyon would speak quite openly of swipes, full tosses, half and three-quarter balls; and young Jolyon with the guileless snobbery of youth had trembled lest his sire should be overheard. Only in this supreme matter of cricket he had been nervous, for his father–in Crimean whiskers then–had ever impressed him as the beau ideal. Though never canonised himself, old Jolyon's natural fastidiousness and balance had saved him from the errors of the vulgar. How delicious, after howling in a top hat and a sweltering heat, to go home with his father in a hansom cab, bathe, dress, and forth to the 'Disunion' Club, to dine off whitebait, cutlets, and a tart, and go–two 'swells', old and young, in lavender kid gloves–to the opera or play. And on Sunday, when the match was over, and his top hat duly broken, down with his father in a special hansom to the 'Crown and Sceptre', and the terrace above the river–the golden sixties when the world was simple, dandies glamorous, Democracy not born, and the books of Whyte Melville coming thick and fast.

A generation later, with his own boy, Jolly, Harrow-buttonholed with cornflowers–by old Jolyon's whim his grandson had been canonised at a trifle less expense–again Jolyon had experienced the heat and counter-passions of the day, and come back to the cool and the strawberry beds of Robin Hill, and billiards after dinner, his boy making the most heart-breaking flukes and trying to seem languid and grown-up. Those two days each year he and his son had been alone together in the world, one on each side–and Democracy just born!

And so, he had unearthed a grey top hat, borrowed a tiny bit of light-blue ribbon from Irene, and gingerly, keeping cool, by car and train and taxi had reached Lord's Ground. There, beside her in a lawn-coloured frock with narrow black edges, he had watched the game, and felt the old thrill stir within him.

When Soames passed, the day was spoiled. Irene's face was distorted by compression of the lips. No good to go on sitting here with Soames or perhaps his daughter recurring in front of them, like decimals. And he said:

'Well, dear, if you've had enough–let's go!'

That evening Jolyon felt exhausted. Not wanting her to see him thus, he waited till she had begun to play, and stole off to the little study. He opened the long window for air, and the door, that he might still hear her music drifting in; and, settled in his father's old armchair, closed his eyes, with his head against the worn brown leather. Like that passage of the César Franck sonata–so had been his life with her, a divine third movement. And now this business of Jon's–this bad business! Drifted to the edge of consciousness, he hardly knew if it were in sleep that he smelled the scent of a cigar, and seemed to see his father in the blackness before his closed eyes. That shape formed, went, and formed again; as if in the very chair where he himself was sitting, he saw his father, black-coated, with knees crossed, glasses balanced between thumb and finger; saw the big white moustaches, and the deep eyes looking up below a dome of forehead and seeming to search his own, seeming to speak. 'Are you facing it, Jo? It's for you to decide. She's only a woman!' Ah! how well he knew his father in that phrase; how all the Victorian Age came up with it! And his answer 'No, I've funked it–funked hurting her and Jon and myself. I've got a heart; I've funked it.' But the old eyes, so much older, so much younger than his own, kept at it: 'It's your wife, your son; your past. Tackle it, my boy!' Was it a message from walking spirit; or but the instinct of his sire living on within him? And again came that scent of cigar smoke–from the old saturated leather. Well! he would tackle it, write to Jon, and put the whole thing down in black and white! And suddenly he breathed with difficulty, with a sense of suffocation, as if his heart were swollen. He got up and went out into the air. The stars were very bright. He passed along the terrace round the corner of the house, till, through the window of the music-room, he could see Irene at the piano, with lamp-light falling on her powdery hair; withdrawn into herself she seemed, her dark eyes staring straight before her, her hands idle. Jolyon saw her raise those hands and clasp them over her breast. 'It's Jon, with her,' he thought; 'all Jon! I'm dying out of her–it's natural!'

And, careful not to be seen, he stole back.

Next day, after a bad night, he sat down to his task. He wrote with difficulty and many erasures.

MY DEAREST BOY,

You are old enough to understand how very difficult it is for elders to give themselves away to their young. Especially when–like your mother and myself, though I shall never think of her as anything but young–their hearts are altogether set on him to whom they must confess. I cannot say we are conscious of having sinned exactly–people in real life very seldom are, I believe–but most persons would say we had, and at all events our conduct, righteous or not, has found us out. The truth is, my dear, we both have pasts, which it is now my task to make known to you, because they so grievously and deeply affect your future. Many, very many years ago, as far back indeed as 1883, when she was only twenty, your mother had the great and lasting misfortune to make an unhappy marriage–no, not with me, Jon. Without money of her own, and with only a stepmother–closely related to Jezebel–she was very unhappy in her home life. It was Fleur's father that she married, my cousin Soames Forsyte. He had pursued her very tenaciously and to do him justice was deeply in love with her. Within a week she knew the fearful mistake she had made. It was not his fault; it was her error of judgment–her misfortune.

So far Jolyon had kept some semblance of irony, but now his subject carried him away.

Jon, I want to explain to you if I can – and it's very hard – how it is that an unhappy marriage such as this can so easily come about. You will of course say: 'If she didn't really love him how could she ever have married him?' You would be right if it were not for one or two rather terrible considerations. From this initial mistake of hers all the subsequent trouble, sorrow, and tragedy have come, and so I must make it clear to you if I can. You see, Jon, in those days and even to this day – indeed, I don't see, for all the talk of enlightenment, how it can well be otherwise – most girls are married ignorant of the sexual side of life. Even if they know what it means they have not *experienced* it. That's the crux. It is this actual lack of experience, whatever verbal knowledge they have, which makes all the difference and all the trouble. In a vast number of marriages – and your mother's was one – girls are not and *cannot* be certain whether they love the man they marry or not; they do not know until after that act of union which makes the reality of marriage. Now, in many, perhaps in most doubtful cases, this act cements and strengthens the attachment, but in other cases, and your mother's was one, it is a revelation of mistake, a destruction of such attraction as there was. There is nothing more tragic in a woman's life than such a revelation, growing daily, nightly clearer. Coarse-grained and unthinking people are apt to laugh at such a mistake, and say, 'What a fuss about nothing?' Narrow and self-righteous people, only capable of judging the lives of others by their own, are apt to condemn those who make this tragic error, to condemn them for life to the dungeons they have made for themselves. You know the expression: 'She has made her bed, she must lie on it!' It is a hard-mouthed saying, quite unworthy of a gentleman or lady in the best sense of those words; and I can use no stronger condemnation. I have not been what is called a moral man, but I wish to use no words to you, my dear, which will make you think lightly of ties or contracts into which you enter. Heaven forbid! But with the experience of a life behind me I do say that those who condemn the victims of these tragic mistakes, condemn them and hold out no hands to help them, are inhuman, or rather they would be if they had the understanding to know what they are doing. But they haven't! Let them go! They are as much anathema to me as I, no doubt, am to them. I have had to say all this, because I am going to put you into a position to judge your mother, and you are very young, without experience of what life is. To go on with the story. After three years of effort to subdue her shrinking – I was going to say her loathing and it's not too strong a word, for shrinking soon becomes loathing under such circumstances – three years of what to a sensitive, beauty-loving nature like your mother's, Jon, was torment, she met a young man who fell in love with her. He was the architect of this very house that we live in now, he was building it for her and Fleur's father to live in, a new prison to hold her, in place of the one she inhabited with him in London. Perhaps that fact played some part in what came of it. But in any case she, too, fell in love with him. I know it's not necessary to explain to you that one does not precisely choose with whom one will fall in love. It comes! Very well! It came. I can imagine – though she never said much to me about it – the struggle that then took place in her, because, Jon, she was brought up strictly and was not light in her ideas – not at all. However, this was an overwhelming feeling, and it came to pass that they loved in deed as well as in thought. Then came a fearful tragedy. I must tell you of it because if I don't you will never understand the real situation that you now have to face. The man whom she had married – Soames Forsyte, the father of Fleur – one night, at the height of her passion for this young man, forcibly reasserted his rights over her. The next day she met her lover and told him of it. Whether he committed suicide or whether he was accidentally run over in his distraction, we never knew; but so it was. Think of your mother as she was that evening when she heard of his death. I happened to see her. Your grandfather sent me to help her if I could. I only just saw her, before the door was shut against me by her husband. But I have never forgotten her face, I can see it now. I was not in love with her then, not for twelve years after, but I have never forgotten. My dear boy – it is not easy to write like this. But you see, I must. Your mother is wrapped up in you, utterly, devotedly. I don't wish to write harshly of Soames Forsyte. I don't think harshly of him. I have long been sorry for him; perhaps I was sorry even then. As the world judges she was in error, he within his rights. He loved her – in his way. *She was his property.* That is the view he holds of life – of human feelings and hearts – property. It's not his fault – so was he born. To me it is a view that has always been abhorrent – so was I born! Knowing you as I do, I feel it cannot be otherwise than abhorrent to you. Let me go on with the story. Your mother fled from his house that night; for twelve years she lived quietly alone without companionship of any sort, until in 1899 her husband – you see, he was still her husband, for he did not attempt to divorce her, and she of course had no right to divorce him – became conscious, it seems, of the want of children, and commenced a long attempt to induce her to go back to him and give him a child. I was her trustee then, under your grandfather's Will, and I watched this going on. While watching, I became attached to her, devotedly attached. His pressure increased, till one day she came to me here and practically put herself under my protection. Her husband, who was kept informed of all her movements, attempted to force us apart by bringing a divorce suit, or possibly he really meant it, I don't know; but anyway our names were publicly joined. That decided us, and we became united in fact. She was divorced, married me, and you were born. We have lived in perfect happiness, at least I have, and I believe your mother also. Soames, soon after the divorce, married Fleur's mother, and she was born. That is the story. Jon. I have told it you, because by the affection which we see you have formed for this man's daughter you are blindly moving toward what must utterly destroy your mother's happiness, if not your own. I don't wish to speak of myself, because at my age there's no use supposing I shall cumber the ground much longer, besides, what I should suffer would be mainly on her account, and on yours. But what I want you to realise is that feelings of horror and aversion such as those can never be buried or forgotten. They are alive in her to-day. Only yesterday at Lord's we happened to see Soames Forsyte. Her face, if you had seen it, would have convinced you. The idea that you should marry his daughter is a nightmare to me, Jon. I have nothing to say against Fleur save that she *is* his daughter. But your children, if you married her, would be the grandchildren of Soames, as much as of your mother, of a man who once owned your mother as a man might own a slave. Think what that would mean. By such a marriage you enter the camp which held your mother prisoner and wherein she ate her heart out. You are just on the threshold of life, you have only known this girl two months, and however deeply you think you love her, I appeal to you to break it off at once. Don't give your mother this rankling pain and humiliation during the rest of her life. Young though she will always seem to be, she is fifty-seven. Except for us two she has no one in the world. She will soon have only you. Pluck up your spirit, Jon, and break away. Don't put this cloud and barrier between you. Don't break her heart! Bless you, my dear boy, and again forgive me for all the pain this letter must bring you—we tried to spare it you, but Spain—it seems—was no good.

> Ever your devoted father
> JOLYON FORSYTE.

Having finished his confession, Jolyon sat with a thin cheek on his hand, re-reading. There were things in it which hurt him so much, when he thought of Jon reading them, that he nearly tore the letter up. To speak of such things at all to a boy—his own boy—to speak of them in relation to his own wife and the boy's own mother, seemed dreadful to the reticence of his Forsyte soul. And yet without speaking of them how make Jon understand the reality, the deep cleavage, the ineffaceable scar? Without them, how justify this stifling of the boy's love? He might just as well not write at all!

He folded the confession, and put it in his pocket. It was—thank Heaven!—Saturday; he had till Sunday evening to think it over; for even if posted now it could not reach Jon till Monday. He felt a curious relief at this delay, and at the fact that, whether sent or not, it was written.

In the rose garden, which had taken the place of the old fernery, he could see Irene snipping and pruning, with a little basket on her arm. She was never idle, it seemed to him, and he envied her now that he himself was idle nearly all his time. He went down to her. She held up a stained glove and smiled. A piece of lace tied under her chin concealed her hair, and her oval face with its still dark brows looked very young.

'The green fly are awful this year, and yet it's cold. You look tired, Jolyon.'

Jolyon took the confession from his pocket. 'I've been writing this. I think you ought to see it.'

'To Jon?' Her whole face had changed in that instant, becoming almost haggard.

'Yes; the murder's out.'

He gave it to her, and walked away among the roses. Presently, seeing that she had finished reading and was standing quite still with the sheets of the letter against her skirt, he came back to her.

'Well?'

'It's wonderfully put. I don't see how it could be put better. Thank you, dear.'

'Is there anything you would like left out?'

She shook her head.

'No! he must know all, if he's to understand.'

'That's what I thought, but–I hate it!'

He had the feeling that he hated it more than she–to him sex was so much easier to mention between man and woman than between man and man; and she had always been more natural and frank, not deeply secretive like his Forsyte self.

'I wonder if he will understand, even now, Jolyon? He's so young; and he shrinks from the physical.'

'He gets that shrinking from my father, he was as fastidious as a girl in all such matters. Would it be better to rewrite the whole thing, and just say you hated Soames?'

Irene shook her head.

'Hate's only a word. It conveys nothing. No, better as it is.'

'Very well. It shall go to-morrow.'

She raised her face to his, and in sight of the big house's many creepered windows, he kissed her.

2

CONFESSION

Late that same afternoon, Jolyon had a nap in the old armchair. Face down on his knee was *La Rôtisserie de la Reine Pédauque*, and just before he fell asleep he had been thinking: 'As a people shall we ever really like the French? Will they ever really like us!' He himself had always liked the French, feeling at home with their wit, their taste, their cooking. Irene and he had paid many visits to France before the War, when Jon had been at his private school. His romance with her had begun in Paris–his last and most enduring romance. But the French–no Englishman could like them who could not see them in some sort with the detached æsthetic eye! And with that melancholy conclusion he had nodded off.

When he woke he saw Jon standing between him and the window. The boy had evidently come in from the garden and was waiting for him to wake. Jolyon smiled, still half asleep. How nice the chap looked–sensitive, affectionate, straight! Then his heart gave a nasty jump; and a quaking sensation overcame him. Jon! That confession! He controlled himself with an effort. 'Why, Jon, where did you spring from?'

Jon bent over and kissed his forehead.

Only then he noticed the look on the boy's face.

'I came home to tell you something, Dad.'

With all his might Jolyon tried to get the better of the jumping, gurgling sensations within his chest.

'Well, sit down, old man. Have you seen your mother?'

'No,' The boy's flushed look gave place to pallor; he sat down on the arm of the old chair, as, in old days, Jolyon himself used to sit beside his own father, installed in its recesses. Right up to the time of the rupture in their relations he had been wont to perch there–had he now reached such a moment with his own son? All his life he had hated scenes like poison, avoided rows, gone on his own way quietly and let others go on theirs. But now–it seemed–at the very end of things, he had a scene before him more painful than any he had avoided. He drew a visor down over his emotion, and waited for his son to speak.

'Father,' said Jon slowly, 'Fleur and I are engaged.'

'Exactly!' thought Jolyon, breathing with difficulty.

'I know that you and Mother don't like the idea. Fleur says that Mother was engaged to her father before you married her. Of course I don't know what happened, but it must be ages ago. I'm devoted to her, Dad, and she says she is to me.'

Jolyon uttered a queer sound, half laugh, half groan.

'You are nineteen, Jon, and I am seventy-two. How are we to understand each other in a matter like this, eh?'

'You love Mother, Dad; you must know what we feel. It isn't fair to us to let old things spoil our happiness, is it?'

Brought face to face with his confession, Jolyon resolved to do without it if by any means he could. He laid his hands on the boy's arm.

'Look, Jon! I might put you off with talk about your both being too young and not knowing your own minds, and all that, but you wouldn't listen, besides, it doesn't meet the case–Youth, unfortunately, cures itself. You talk lightly about 'old things like that', knowing nothing–as you say truly–of what happened. Now, have I ever given you reason to doubt my love for you, or my word?'

At a less anxious moment he might have been amused by the conflict his words aroused–the boy's eager clasp, to reassure him on these points, the dread on his face of what that reassurance would bring forth; but he could only feel grateful for the squeeze.

'Very well, you can believe what I tell you. If you don't give up this love affair, you will make Mother wretched to the end of her days. Believe me, my dear, the past, whatever it was, can't be buried–it can't indeed.'

Jon got off the arm of the chair.

'The girl'–thought Jolyon–'there she goes–starting up before him–life itself–eager, pretty, loving!'

'I can't, Father, how can I–just because you say that? Of course I can't!'

'Jon, if you knew the story you would give this up without hesitation; you would have to! Can't you believe me?'

'How can you tell what I should think? Father, I love her better than anything in the world.'

Jolyon's face twitched, and he said with painful slowness:

'Better than your mother, Jon?'

From the boy's face, and his clenched fists Jolyon realised the stress and struggle he was going through.

'I don't know,' he burst out, 'I don't know! But to give Fleur up for nothing–for something I don't understand, for something that I don't believe can really matter half so much, will make me–make me–'

'Make you feel us unjust, put a barrier–yes. But that's better than going on with this.'

'I can't. Fleur loves me, and I love her. You want me to trust you, why don't you trust *me*, Father? We wouldn't want to know anything–we wouldn't let it make any difference. It'll only make us both love you and Mother all the more.'

Jolyon put his hand into his breast pocket, but brought it out again empty, and sat, clucking his tongue against his teeth.

'Think what your mother's been to you, Jon! She has nothing but you; I shan't last much longer.'

'Why not? It isn't fair to—Why not?'

'Well,' said Jolyon, rather coldly, 'because the doctors tell me I shan't; that's all.'

'Oh! Dad!' cried Jon, and burst into tears.

This downbreak of his son, whom he had not seen cry since he was ten, moved Jolyon terribly. He recognised to the full how fearfully soft the boy's heart was, how much he would suffer in this business, and in life generally. And he reached out his hand helplessly—not wishing, indeed not daring to get up.

'Dear man,' he said, 'don't—or you'll make me!'

Jon smothered down his paroxysm, and stood with face averted, very still.

'What now?' thought Jolyon. 'What can I say to move him?'

'By the way, don't speak of that to Mother,' he said; 'she has enough to frighten her with this affair of yours. I know how you feel. But, Jon, you know her and me well enough to be sure we wouldn't wish to spoil your happiness lightly. Why, my dear boy, we don't care for anything but your happiness—at least, with me it's just yours and Mother's and with her just yours. It's all the future for you both that's at stake.'

Jon turned. His face was deadly pale; his eyes, deep in his head, seemed to burn.

'What is it? *What is it?* Don't keep me like this!'

Jolyon, who knew that he was beaten, thrust his hand again into his breast pocket, and sat for a full minute, breathing with difficulty, his eyes closed. The thought passed through his mind: 'I've had a good long innings—some pretty bitter moments—this is the worst!' Then he brought his hand out with the letter, and said with a sort of fatigue: 'Well, Jon, if you hadn't come to-day, I was going to send you this. I wanted to spare you—I wanted to spare your mother and myself, but I see it's no good. Read it, and I think I'll go into the garden.' He reached forward to get up.

Jon, who had taken the letter, said quickly: 'No, I'll go;' and was gone.

Jolyon sank back in his chair. A blue-bottle chose that moment to come buzzing round him with a sort of fury; the sound was homely, better than nothing. ... Where had the boy gone to read his letter? The wretched letter—the wretched story! A cruel business—cruel to her—to Soames—to those two children—to himself! ... His heart thumped and pained him. Life—its loves—its work—its beauty—its aching, and—its end! A good time; a fine time in spite of all; until—you regretted that you had ever been born. Life—it wore you down, yet did not make you want to die—that was the cunning evil! Mistake to have a heart! Again the blue-bottle came buzzing—bringing in all the heat and hum and scent of summer—yes, even the scent—as of ripe fruits, dried grasses, sappy shrubs, and the vanilla breath of cows. And out there somewhere in the fragrance Jon would be reading that letter, turning and twisting its pages in his trouble, his bewilderment and trouble—breaking his heart about it! The thought made Jolyon acutely miserable. Jon was such a tender-hearted chap, affectionate to his bones, and conscientious, too—it was so unfair, so damned unfair! He remembered Irene saying to him once: 'Never was anyone born more loving and lovable than Jon.' Poor little Jon! His world gone up the spout, all of a summer afternoon! Youth took things so hard! And stirred, tormented by that vision of Youth taking things hard, Jolyon got out of his chair, and went to the window. The boy was nowhere visible. And he passed out. If one could take any help to him now—one must!

He traversed the shrubbery, glanced into the walled garden—no Jon! Nor where the peaches and the apricots were beginning to swell and colour. He passed the cypressus trees, dark and spiral, into the meadow. Where had the boy got to? Had he rushed down to the coppice—his old hunting-ground? Jolyon crossed the rows of hay. They would cock it on Monday and be carrying the day after, if rain held off. Often they had crossed this field together—hand in hand, when Jon was a little chap. Dash it! The golden age was over by the time one was ten! He came to the pond, where flies and gnats were dancing over a bright reedy surface; and on into the coppice. It was cool there, fragrant of larches. Still no Jon! He called. No answer! On the log seat he sat down, nervous, anxious, forgetting his own physical sensations. He had been wrong to let the boy get away with that letter; he ought to have kept him under his eye from the start! Greatly troubled, he got up to retrace his steps. At the farm buildings he called again, and looked into the dark cow-house. There in the cool, and the scent of vanilla and ammonia, away from flies, the three Alderneys were chewing the quiet cud; just milked, waiting for evening, to be turned out again into the lower field. One turned a lazy head, a lustrous eye; Jolyon could see the slobber on its grey lower lip. He saw everything with passionate clearness, in the agitation of her nerves—all that in his time he had adored and tried to paint—wonder of light and shade and colour. No wonder the legend put Christ into a manger—what more devotional than the eyes and moonwhite horns of a chewing cow in the warm dusk! He called again. No answer! And he hurried away out of the coppice, past the pond, up the hill. Oddly ironical—now he came to think of it—if Jon had taken the gruel of his discovery down in the coppice where his mother and Bosinney in those old days had made the plunge of acknowledging their love. Where he himself, on the log seat the Sunday morning he came from Paris, had realised to the full that Irene had become the world to him. That would have been the place for Irony to tear the veil from before the eyes of Irene's boy! But he was not here! Where had he got to? One must find the poor chap!

A gleam of sun had come, sharpening to his hurrying senses all the beauty of the afternoon, of the tall trees and lengthening shadows, of the blue, and the white clouds, the scent of the hay, and the cooing of the pigeons; and the flower shapes standing tall. He came to the rosery, and the beauty of the roses in that sudden sunlight seemed to him unearthly. 'Rose, you Spaniard!' Wonderful three words! There she had stood by that bush of dark red roses; had stood to read and decide that Jon must know it all! He knew all now! Had she chosen wrong? He bent and sniffed a rose, its petals brushed his nose and trembling lips; nothing so soft as a rose-leaf's velvet, except her neck—Irene! On across the lawn he went, up the slope, to the oak tree. Its top alone was glistening, for the sudden sun was away over the house; the lower shade was thick, blessedly cool—he was greatly overheated. He paused a minute with his hand on the rope of the swing—Jolly, Holly—Jon! The old swing! And suddenly, he felt horribly—deadly ill! 'I've overdone it!' he thought: 'by Jove! I've overdone it—after all!' He staggered up toward the terrace, dragged himself up the steps, and fell against the wall of the house. He leaned there gasping, his face buried in the honeysuckle that he and she had taken such trouble with that it might sweeten the air which drifted in. Its fragrance mingled with awful pain. 'My love!' he thought; 'the boy!' And with a great effort he tottered in through the long window, and sank into old Jolyon's chair. The book was there, a pencil in it; he caught it up, scribbled a word on the open page. . . . His hand dropped. . . . So it was like this—was it? . . .

There was a great wrench; and darkness. . . .

———

3

———

IRENE!

When Jon rushed away with the letter in his hand, he ran along the terrace and round the corner of the house, in fear and confusion. Leaning against the creepered wall he tore open the letter. It was long—very long! This added to his fear, and he began reading. When he came to the words: 'It was Fleur's father that she married,' everything seemed to spin before him. He was close to a window, and entering by it, he passed, through music-room and hall, up to his bedroom. Dipping his face in cold water, he sat on his bed, and went on reading, dropping each finished page on the bed beside him. His father's writing was easy to read—he knew it so well, though he had never had a letter from him one quarter so long. He read with a dull feeling—imagination only half at work. He best grasped, on that first reading, the pain his father must have had in writing such a letter. He let the last sheet fall, and in a sort of mental, moral helplessness began to read the first again. It all seemed to him disgusting—dead and disgusting. Then, suddenly, a hot wave of horrified emotion tingled through him. He buried his face in his hands. His mother! Fleur's father! He took up the letter again, and read on mechanically. And again came the feeling that it was all dead and disgusting; his own love so different! This letter said his mother—and her father! An awful letter!

Property! Could there be men who looked on women as their property? Faces seen in street and countryside came thronging up before him—red, stock-fish faces; hard, dull faces; prim, dry faces; violent faces; hundreds, thousands of them! How could he know what men who had such faces thought and did? He held his head in his hands and groaned. His mother! He caught up the letter and read on again: 'horror and aversion—alive in her today . . . your children . . . grandchildren . . . of a man who once owned your mother as a man might own a slave. . . .' He got up from his bed. This cruel shadowy past, lurking there to murder his love and Fleur's, was true, or his father could never have written it. 'Why didn't they tell me the first thing,' he thought, 'the day I first saw Fleur? They knew I'd seen her. They were afraid, and—now—I've—got it!' Overcome by misery too acute for thought or reason, he crept into a dusky corner of the room and sat down on the floor. He sat there, like some unhappy little animal. There was comfort in dusk, and the floor—as if he were back in those days when he played his battles sprawling all over it. He sat there huddled, his hair ruffled, his hands clasped round his knees, for how long he did not know. He was wrenched from his blank wretchedness by the sound of the door opening from his mother's room. The blinds were down over the windows of his room, shut up in his absence, and from where he sat he could only hear a rustle, her footsteps crossing, till beyond the bed he saw her standing before his dressing-table. She had something in her hand. He hardly breathed, hoping she would not see him, and go away. He saw her touch things on the table as if they had some virtue in them, then face the window—grey from head to foot like a ghost. The least turn of her head, and she must see him! Her lips moved: 'Oh, Jon!' She was speaking to herself; the tone of her voice troubled Jon's heart. He saw in her hand a little photograph. She held it towards the light, looking at it—very small. He knew it—one of himself as a tiny boy, which she always kept in her bag. His heart beat fast. And, suddenly as if she had heard it, she turned her eyes and saw him. At the gasp she gave, and the movement of her hands pressing the photograph against her breast, he said:

'Yes, it's me.'

She moved over to the bed, and sat down on it, quite close to him, her hands still clasping her breast, her feet among the sheets of the letter which had slipped to the floor. She saw them, and her hands grasped the edge of the bed. She sat very upright, her dark eyes fixed on him. At last she spoke.

'Well, Jon, you know, I see.'

'Yes.'

'You've seen Father?'

'Yes.'

There was a long silence, till she said:

'Oh! my darling!'

'It's all right.' The emotions in him were so violent and so mixed that he dared not move—resentment, despair, and yet a strange yearning for the comfort of her hand on his forehead.

'What are you going to do?'

'I don't know.'

There was another long silence, then she got up. She stood a moment, very still, made a little movement with her hand, and said: 'My darling boy, my most darling boy, don't think of me—think of yourself,' and, passing round the foot of the bed, went back into her room.

Jon turned—curled into a sort of ball, as might a hedgehog—into the corner made by the two walls.

He must have been twenty minutes there before a cry roused him. It came from the terrace below. He got up, scared. Again came the cry: 'Jon!' His mother was calling! He ran out and down the stairs, through the empty dining-room into the study. She was kneeling before the old armchair, and his father was lying back quite white, his head on his breast, one of his hands resting on an open book, with a pencil clutched in it—more strangely still than anything he had ever seen. She looked round wildly, and said:

'Oh! Jon—he's dead—he's dead!'

Jon flung himself down, and reaching over the arm of the chair, where he had lately been sitting, put his lips to the forehead. Icy cold! How could—how could Dad be dead, when only an hour ago—! His mother's arms were round the knees; pressing her breast against them. 'Why—why wasn't I with him?' he heard her whisper. Then he saw the tottering word 'Irene' pencilled on the open page and broke down himself. It was his first sight of human death, and its unutterable stillness blotted from him all other emotion; all else, then, was but preliminary to this! All love and life, and joy, anxiety, and sorrow, all movement, light and beauty, but a beginning to this terrible white stillness. It made a dreadful mark on him; all seemed suddenly little, futile, short. He mastered himself at last, got up, and raised her.

'Mother! don't cry—Mother!'

Some hours later, when all was done that had to be, and his mother was lying down, he saw his father alone, on the bed, covered with a white sheet. He stood for a long time gazing at that face which had never looked angry—always whimsical, and kind. 'To be kind and keep your end up—there's nothing else in it,' he had once heard his father say. How wonderfully Dad had acted up to that philosophy! He understood now that his father had known for a long time past that this would come suddenly—known, and not said a word. He gazed with an awe and passionate reverence. The loneliness of it—just to spare his mother and himself! His own trouble seemed small while he was looking at that face. The word scribbled on the page! The farewell word! Now his mother had no one but himself! He went up close to the dead face—not changed at all, and yet completely changed. He had heard his father say once that he did not believe in consciousness surviving death, or that if it did it might be just survival till the natural age limit of the body had been reached—the natural term of its inherent vitality; so that if the body were broken by accident, excess, violent disease, consciousness might still persist till, in the course of Nature uninterfered with, it would naturally have faded out. It had struck him because he had never heard anyone else suggest it. When the heart failed like this—surely it was not quite natural! Perhaps his father's consciousness was in the room with him. Above the bed hung a picture of his father's father. Perhaps *his* consciousness, too, was still alive; and his brother's—his half-brother, who had died in the Transvaal. Were they all gathered round this bed? Jon kissed the forehead, and stole back to his own room. The door between it and his mother's was ajar; she had evidently been in—everything was ready for him, even some biscuits and hot milk, and the letter no longer on the floor. He ate and drank, watching the last light fade. He did not try to see into the future—just stared at the dark branches of the oak tree, level with his window, and felt as if life had stopped. Once in the night, turning in his heavy sleep, he was conscious of something white and still beside his bed, and started up.

His mother's voice said:

'It's only I, Jon dear!' Her hand pressed his forehead gently back; her white figure disappeared.

Alone! He fell heavily asleep again, and dreamed he saw his mother's name crawling on his bed.

4

SOAMES COGITATES

The announcement in *The Times* of his cousin Jolyon's death affected Soames quite simply. So that chap was gone! There had never been a time in their two lives when love had not been lost between them. That quick-blooded sentiment hatred had run its course long since in Soames's heart, and he had refused to allow any recrudescence, but he considered this early decease a piece of poetic justice. For twenty years the fellow had enjoyed the reversion of his wife and house, and—he was dead! The obituary notice, which appeared a little later, paid Jolyon—he thought—too much attention. It spoke of that 'diligent and agreeable painter whose work we have come to look on as typical of the best late-Victorian water-colour art.' Soames, who had almost mechanically preferred Mole, Morpin, and Caswell Baye, and had always sniffed quite audibly when he came to one of his cousin's on the line, turned *The Times* with a crackle.

He had to go up to Town that morning on Forsyte affairs, and was fully conscious of Gradman's glance side-long over his spectacles. The old clerk had about him an aura of regretful congratulation. He smelled, as it were, of old days. One could almost hear him thinking: 'Mr Jolyon, ye-es—just my age, and gone—dear, dear! I dare say she feels it. She was a naice-lookin' woman. Flesh is flesh! They've given 'im a notice in the papers. Fancy!' His atmosphere in fact caused Soames to handle certain leases and conversions with exceptional swiftness.

'About that settlement on Miss Fleur, Mr Soames!'

'I've thought better of that,' answered Soames shortly.

'Aoh! I'm glad of that. I thought you were a little hasty. The times do change.'

How this death would affect Fleur had begun to trouble Soames. He was not certain that she knew of it—she seldom looked at the paper, never at the births, marriages, and deaths.

He pressed matters on, and made his way to Green Street for lunch. Winifred was almost doleful. Jack Cardigan had broken a splashboard, so far as one could make out, and would not be 'fit' for some time. She could not get used to the idea.

'Did Profond ever get off?' he said suddenly.

'He got off,' replied Winifred, 'but where—I don't know.'

Yes, there it was—impossible to tell anything?! Not that he wanted to know. Letters from Annette were coming from Dieppe, where she and her mother were staying.

'You saw that fellow's death, I suppose?'

'Yes,' said Winifred. 'I'm sorry for—for his children. He was very amiable.' Soames uttered a rather queer sound. A suspicion of the old deep truth—that men were judged in this world rather by what they *were*, than by what they *did*—crept and knocked resentfully at the back doors of his mind.

'I know there was a superstition to that effect,' he muttered.

'One must do him justice now he's dead.'

'I should like to have done him justice before,' said Soames; 'but I never had the chance. Have you got a 'Baronetage' here?'

'Yes; in that bottom row.'

Soames took out a fat red book, and ran over the leaves.

'Mont—Sir Lawrence, 9th Bt., cr. 1620, e.s. of Geoffrey, 8th Bt., and Lavinia, daur. of Sir Charles Muskham, Bt., of Muskham Hall, Shrops: marr. 1890 Emily. daur. of Conway Charwell, esq., of Condaford Grange, co. Oxon; 1 son, heir Michael Conway, b. 1895, 2 daurs. Residence: Lippinghall Manor, Folwell, Bucks. Clubs: Snooks': Coffee House: Aeroplane. See Bidlicott.'

'H'm!' he said. 'Did you ever know a publisher?'

'Uncle Timothy.'

'Alive I mean.'

'Monty knew one at his Club. He brought him here to dinner once. Monty was always thinking of writing a book, you know, about how to make money on the turf. He tried to interest that man.'

'Well?'

'He put him on to a horse—for the Two Thousand. We didn't see him again. He was rather smart, if I remember.'

'Did it win?'

'No; it ran last, I think. You know Monty really was quite clever in his way.'

'Was he?' said Soames. 'Can you see any connection between a sucking baronet and publishing?'

'People do all sorts of things nowadays,' replied Winifred. 'The great stunt seems not to be idle—so different from our time. To do nothing was the thing then. But I suppose it'll come again.'

'This young Mont that I'm speaking of is very sweet on Fleur. If it would put an end to that other affair, I might encourage it.'

'Has he got style?' asked Winifred.

'He's no beauty; pleasant enough, with some scattered brains. There's a good deal of land, I believe. He seems genuinely attached. But I don't know.'

'No,' murmured Winifred; 'it's very difficult. I always found it best to do nothing. It *is* such a bore about Jack; now we shan't get away till after Bank Holiday. Well, the people are always amusing, I shall go into the Park and watch them.'

'If I were you,' said Soames, 'I should have a country cottage, and be out of the way of holidays and strikes when you want.'

'The country bores me,' answered Winifred, 'and I found the railway strike quite exciting.'

Winifred had always been noted for sang-froid.

Soames took his leave. All the way down to Reading he debated whether he should tell Fleur of that boy's father's death. It did not alter the situation except that he would be independent now, and only have his mother's opposition to encounter. He would come into a lot of money, no doubt, and perhaps the house—the house built for Irene and himself—the house whose architect had wrought his domestic ruin. His daughter—mistress of that house! That would be poetic justice! Soames uttered a little mirthless laugh. He had designed that house to re-establish his failing union, meant it for the seat of his descendants, if he could have induced Irene to give him one! Her son and Fleur! Their children would be, in some sort, offspring of the union between himself and her!

The theatricality in that thought was repulsive to his sober sense. And yet—it would be the easiest and wealthiest way out of the impasse, now that Jolyon was gone. The juncture of two Forsyte fortunes had a kind of conservative charm. And she—Irene—would be linked to him once more. Nonsense! Absurd! He put the notion from his head.

On arriving home he heard the click of billiard-balls and through the window saw young Mont sprawling over the table. Fleur, with her cue akimbo, was watching with a smile. How pretty she looked! No wonder that young fellow was out of his mind about her. A title—land! There was little enough in land, these days; perhaps less in a title. The old Forsytes had always had a kind of contempt for titles, rather remote and artificial things—not worth the money they cost, and having to do with the Court. They had all had that feeling in differing measure—Soames remembered. Swithin, indeed, in his most expansive days had once attended a Levee. He had come away saying he shouldn't go again—'all that small fry.' It was suspected that he had looked too big in knee-breeches. Soames remembered how his own mother had wished to be presented because of the fashionable nature of the performance, and how his father had put his foot down with unwonted decision. What did she want with that peacocking–wasting time and money; there was nothing in it!

The instinct which had made and kept the British Commons the chief power in the State, a feeling that their own world was good enough and a little better than any other because it was *their* world, had kept the old Forsytes singularly free of 'flummery', as Nicholas had been wont to call it when he had the gout. Soames's generation, more selfconscious and ironical, had been saved by a sense of Swithin in knee-breeches. While the third and the fourth generation, as it seemed to him, laughed at everything.

However, there was no harm in the young fellow's being heir to a title and estate–a thing one couldn't help. He entered quietly, as Mont missed his shot. He noted the young man's eyes, fixed on Fleur bending over in her turn; and the adoration in them almost touched him.

She paused with the cue poised on the bridge of her slim hand, and shook her crop of short dark chestnut hair.

'I shall never do it.'

'"Nothing venture."'

'All right.' The cue struck, the ball rolled. 'There!'

'Bad luck! Never mind!'

Then they saw him, and Soames said:

'I'll mark for you.'

He sat down on the raised seat beneath the marker, trim and tired, furtively studying those two young faces. When the game was over Mont came up to him.

'I've started in, sir. Rum game, business, isn't it? I suppose you saw a lot of human nature as a solicitor.'

'I did.'

'Shall I tell you what I've noticed: People are quite on the wrong track in offering less than they can afford to give; they ought to offer more, and work backward.'

Soames raised his eyebrows.

'Suppose the more is accepted?'

'That doesn't matter a little bit,' said Mont; 'it's much more paying to abate a price than to increase it. For instance, say we offer an author good terms–he naturally takes them. Then we go into it, find we can't publish at a decent profit and tell him so. He's got confidence in us because we've been generous to him, and he comes down like a lamb, and bears us no malice. But if we offer him poor terms at the start, he doesn't take them, so we have to advance them to get him, and he thinks us damned screws into the bargain.'

'Try buying pictures on that system,' said Soames; 'an offer accepted is a contract–haven't you learned that?'

Young Mont turned his head to where Fleur was standing in the window.

'No,' he said, 'I wish I had. Then there's another thing. Always let a man off a bargain if he wants to be let off.'

'As advertisement?' said Soames dryly.

'Of course it *is*; but I meant on principle.'

'Does your firm work on those lines?'

'Not yet,' said Mont, 'but it'll come.'

'And they will go.'

'No, really sir. I'm making any number of observations, and they all confirm my theory. Human nature is consistently underrated in business, people do themselves out of an awful lot of pleasure and profit by that. Of course, you must be perfectly genuine and open, but that's easy if you feel it. The more human and generous you are the better chance you've got in business.'

Soames rose.

'Are you a partner?'

'Not for six months, yet.'

'The rest of the firm had better make haste and retire.'

Mont laughed.

'You'll see,' he said. 'There's going to be a big change. The possessive principle has got its shutters up.'

'What?' said Soames.

'The house is to let! Good-bye, sir; I'm off now.'

Soames watched his daughter give her hand, saw her wince at the squeeze it received, and distinctly heard the young man's sigh as he passed out. Then she came from the window, trailing her finger along the mahogany edge of the billiard-table. Watching her, Soames knew that she was going to ask him something. Her finger felt round the last pocket, and she looked up.

'Have you done anything to stop Jon writing to me, Father?'

Soames shook his head.

'You haven't seen, then?' he said. 'His father died just a week ago to-day.'

'Oh!'

In her startled, frowning face he saw the instant struggle to apprehend what this would mean.

'Poor Jon! Why didn't you tell me, Father?'

'I never know!' said Soames slowly; 'you don't confide in me.'

'I would, if you'd help me, dear.'

'Perhaps I shall.'

Fleur clasped her hands. 'Oh! darling–when one wants a thing fearfully, one doesn't think of other people. Don't be angry with me.'

Soames put out his hand, as if pushing away an aspersion.

'I'm cogitating,' he said. What on earth had made him use a word like that! 'Has young Mont been bothering you again?'

Fleur smiled. 'Oh, Michael. He's always bothering; but he's such a good sort–I don't mind him.'

'Well,' said Soames, 'I'm tired; I shall go and have a nap before dinner.'

He went up to his picture-gallery, lay down on the couch there, and closed his eyes. A terrible responsibility this girl of his–whose mother was–ah! what was she? A terrible responsibility! Help her–how could he help her? He could not alter the fact that he was her father. Or that Irene–! What was it young Mont had said–some nonsense about the possessive instinct–shutters up–. To let? Silly!

The sultry air, charged with a scent of meadow-sweet, of river and roses, closed on his senses, drowsing them.

5

THE FIXED IDEA

'The fixed idea', which has outrun more constables than any other form of human disorder, has never more speed and stamina than when it takes the avid guise of love. To hedges and ditches, and doors, to humans without ideas fixed or otherwise, to perambulators and the contents sucking their fixed ideas, even to the other sufferers from this fast malady—the fixed idea of love pays no attention. It runs with eyes turned inward to its own light, oblivious of all other stars. Those with the fixed ideas that human happiness depends on their art, on vivisecting dogs, on hating foreigners, on paying supertax, on remaining Ministers, on making wheels go round, on preventing their neighbours from being divorced, on conscientious objection, Greek roots, Church dogma, paradox and superiority to everybody else, with other forms of ego-mania—all are unstable compared with him or her whose fixed idea is the possession of some of her or him. And though Fleur, those chilly summer days, pursued the scattered life of a little Forsyte whose frocks are paid for, and whose business is pleasure, she was—as Winifred would have said in the latest fashion of speech—'honest to God' indifferent to it all. She wished and wished for the moon, which sailed in cold skies above the river or the Green Park when she went to Town. She even kept Jon's letters, covered with pink silk, on her heart, than which in days when corsets were so low, sentiment so despised, and chests so out of fashion, there could, perhaps, have been no greater proof of the fixity of her idea.

After hearing of his father's death, she wrote to Jon, and received his answer three days later on her return from a river picnic. It was his first letter since their meeting at June's. She opened it with misgiving, and read it with dismay.

'Since I saw you I've heard everything about the past. I won't tell it you—I think you knew when we met at June's. She says you did. If you did, Fleur, you ought to have told me. I expect you only heard your father's side of it. I have heard my mother's. It's dreadful. Now that she's so sad I can't do anything to hurt her more. Of course, I long for you all day, but I don't believe now that we shall ever come together—there's something too strong pulling us apart.'

So! Her deception had found her out. But Jon—she felt—had forgiven that. It was what he said of his mother which caused the fluttering in her heart and the weak sensation in her legs.

Her first impulse was to reply—her second, not to reply. These impulses were constantly renewed in the days which followed, while desperation grew within her. She was not her father's child for nothing. The tenacity which had at once made and undone Soames was her backbone, too, frilled and embroidered by French grace and quickness. Instinctively she conjugated the verb 'to have' always with the pronoun 'I'. She concealed, however, all signs of her growing desperation, and pursued such river pleasures as the winds and rain of a disagreeable July permitted, as if she had no care in the world; nor did any 'sucking baronet' ever neglect the business of a publisher more consistently than her attendant spirit, Michael Mont.

To Soames she was a puzzle. He was almost deceived by this careless gaiety. Almost—because he did not fail to mark her eyes often fixed on nothing, and the film of light shining from her bedroom window late at night. What was she thinking and brooding over into small hours when she ought to have been asleep? But he dared not ask what was in her mind; and, since that one little talk in the billiard-room, she said nothing to him.

In this taciturn condition of affairs it chanced that Winifred invited them to lunch and to go afterward to 'a most amusing little play, "The Beggar's Opera",' and would they bring a man to make four? Soames, whose attitude toward theatres was to go to nothing, accepted, because Fleur's attitude was to go to everything. They motored up, taking Michael Mont, who, being in his seventh heaven, was found by Winifred 'very amusing'. 'The Beggar's Opera' puzzled Soames. The people were very unpleasant, the whole thing very cynical. Winifred was 'intrigued'–by the dresses. The music, too, did not displease her. At the Opera, the night before, she had arrived too early for the Russian Ballet, and found the stage occupied by singers, for a whole hour pale or apoplectic from terror lest by some dreadful inadvertence they might drop into a tune. Michael Mont was enraptured with the whole thing. And all three wondered what Fleur was thinking of it. But Fleur was not thinking of it. Her fixed idea stood on the stage and sang with Polly Peachum, mimed with Filch, danced with Jenny Diver, postured with Lucy Lockit, kissed, trolled, and cuddled with Macheath. Her lips might smile, her hands applaud, but the comic old masterpiece made no more impression on her than if it had been pathetic, like a modern 'Revue'. When they embarked in the car to return, she ached because Jon was not sitting next to her instead of Michael Mont. When, at some jolt, the young man's arm touched hers as if by accident, she only thought: 'If that were Jon's arm!' When his cheerful voice, tempered by her proximity, murmured above the sound of the car's progress, she smiled and answered, thinking: 'If that were Jon's voice!' and when once he said, 'Fleur, you look a perfect angel in that dress!' she answered, 'Oh, do you like it?' thinking, 'If only Jon could see it!'

During this drive she took a resolution. She would go to Robin Hill and see him–alone; she would take the car, without word beforehand to him or to her father. It was nine days since his letter, and she could wait no longer. On Monday she would go! The decision made her well disposed toward young Mont. With something to look forward to she could afford to tolerate and respond. He might stay to dinner; propose to her as usual; dance with her, press her hand, sigh–do what he liked. He was only a nuisance when he interferred with her fixed idea. She was even sorry for him so far as it was possible to be sorry for anybody but herself just now. At dinner he seemed to talk more wildly than usual about what he called 'the death of the close borough' –she paid little attention, but her father seemed paying a good deal, with the smile on his face which meant opposition, if not anger.

'The younger generation doesn't think as you do, sir; does it, Fleur?'

Fleur shrugged her shoulders–the younger generation was just Jon, and she did not know what he was thinking.

'Young people will think as I do when they're my age, Mr Mont. Human nature doesn't change.'

'I admit, that, sir; but the forms of thought change with the times. The pursuit of self-interest is a form of thought that's going out.'

'Indeed! To mind one's own business is not a form of thought, Mr Mont, it's an instinct.'

Yes, when Jon was the business!

'But what is one's business, sir? That's the point. *Everybody's* business is going to be one's business. Isn't it, Fleur?'

Fleur only smiled.

'If not,' added young Mont, 'there'll be blood.'

'People have talked like that from time immemorial.'

'But you'll admit, sir, that the sense of property is dying out?'

'I should say increasing among those who have none.'

'Well, look at me! I'm heir to an entailed estate. I don't want the thing; I'd cut the entail to-morrow.'

'You're not married, and you don't know what you're talking about.'

Fleur saw the young man's eyes turn rather piteously upon her.

'Do you really mean that marriage–?' he began.

'Society is built on marriage,' came from between her father's close lips; 'marriage and its consequences. Do you want to do away with it?'

Young Mont made a distracted gesture. Silence brooded over the dinner table, covered with spoons bearing the Forsyte crest–a pheasant proper–under the electric light in an alabaster globe. And outside, the river evening darkened, charged with heavy moisture and sweet scents.

'Monday,' thought Fleur; 'Monday!'

6

DESPERATE

The weeks which followed the death of his father were sad and empty to the only Jolyon Forsyte left. The necessary forms and ceremonies–the reading of the Will, valuation of the estate, distribution of the legacies–were enacted over the head, as it were, of one not yet of age. Jolyon was cremated. By his special wish no one attended that ceremony, or wore black for him. The succession of his property, controlled to some extent by old Jolyon's Will, left his widow in possession of Robin Hill, with two thousand five hundred pounds a year for life. Apart from this the two Wills worked together in some complicated way to insure that each of Jolyon's three children should have an equal share in their grandfather's property in the future as in the present, save only that Jon, by virtue of his sex, would have control of his capital when he was twenty-one, while June and Holly would only have the spirit of theirs, in order that their children might have the body after them. If they had no children, it would all come to Jon if he outlived them; and since June was fifty, and Holly nearly forty, it was considered in Lincoln's Inn Fields that but for the cruelty of income tax, young Jon would be as warm a man as his grandfather when he died. All this was nothing to Jon, and little enough to his mother. It was June who did everything needful for one who had left his affairs in perfect order. When she had gone, and those two were alone again in the great house, alone with death drawing them together, and love driving them apart, Jon passed very painful days secretly disgusted and disappointed with himself. His mother would look at him with such a patient sadness which yet had in it an instinctive pride, as if she were reserving her defence. If she smiled he was angry that his answering smile should be so grudging and unnatural. He did not judge or condemn her; that was all too remote–indeed, the idea of doing so had never come to him. No! he was grudging and unnatural because he couldn't have what he wanted because of her. There was one alleviation–much to do in connection with his father's career, which could not be safely entrusted to June, though she had offered to undertake it. Both Jon and his mother had felt that if she took his portfolios, unexhibited drawings and unfinished matter, away with her, the work would encounter such icy blasts from Paul Post and other frequenters of her studio, that it would soon be frozen out even of her warm heart. On its old-fashioned plane and of its kind the work was good, and they could not bear the thought of its subjection to ridicule. A one-man exhibition of his work was the least testimony they could pay to one they had loved; and on preparation for this they spent many hours together. Jon came to have a curiously increased respect for his father. The quiet tenacity with which he had converted a mediocre talent into something really individual was disclosed by these researches. There was a great mass of work with a rare continuity of growth in depth and reach of vision. Nothing certainly went very deep, or reached very high–but such as the work was, it was thorough, conscientious, and complete. And, remembering his father's utter absence of 'side' or self-assertion, the chaffing humility with which he had always spoken of his own efforts, ever calling himself 'an amateur', Jon could not help feeling that he had never really known his father. To take himself seriously, yet never bore others by letting them know that he did so, seemed to have been his ruling principle. There was something in this which appealed to the boy, and made him heartily endorse his mother's comment: 'He had true refinement; he couldn't help thinking of others, whatever he did. And when he took a resolution which went counter, he did it with the minimum of defiance–not like the Age, is it? Twice in his life he had to go against everything; and yet it never made him bitter.' Jon saw tears running down her face, which she at once turned away from him. She was so quiet about her loss that sometimes he had thought she didn't feel it much. Now, as he looked at her, he felt how far he fell short of the reserve power and dignity in both his father and his mother. And, stealing up to her, he put his arm round her waist. She kissed him swiftly, but with a sort of passion, and went out of the room.

The studio, where they had been sorting and labelling, had once been Holly's schoolroom, devoted to her silkworms, dried lavender, music, and other forms of instruction. Now at the end of July, despite its northern and eastern aspects, a warm and slumberous air came in between the long-faded lilac linen curtains. To redeem a little the departed glory, as of a field that is golden and gone, clinging to a room which its master has left, Irene had placed on the paint-stained table a bowl of red roses. This, and Jolyon's favourite cat, who still clung to the deserted habitat, were the pleasant spots in that dishevelled, sad workroom. Jon, at the north window, sniffing air mysteriously scented with warm strawberries, heard a car drive up. The lawyers again about some nonsense! Why did that scent so make one ache? And where did it come from–there were no strawberry beds on this side of the house. Instinctively he took a crumpled sheet of paper from his pocket, and wrote down some broken words. A warmth began spreading in his chest; he rubbed the palms of his hands together. Presently he had jotted this:

'If I could make a little song—
A little song to soothe my heart!
I'd make it all of little things—
The plash of water, rub of wings,
The puffing-off of dandie's crown,
The hiss of raindrop spilling down,
The purr of cat, the trill of bird,
And ev'ry whispering I've heard
From willy wind in leaves and grass,
And all the distant drones that pass
A song as tender and as light
As flower, or butterfly in flight;
And when I saw it opening,
   I'd let it fly and sing!'

He was still muttering it over to himself at the window, when he heard his name called, and, turning round, saw Fleur. At that amazing apparition, he made at first no movement and no sound, while her clear vivid glance ravished his heart. Then he went forward to the table, saying: 'How nice of you to come!' and saw her flinch as if he had thrown something at her.

'I asked for you,' she said, 'and they showed me up here. But I can go away again.'

Jon clutched the paint-stained table. Her face and figure in its frilly frock photographed itself with such startling vividness upon his eyes, that if she had sunk through the floor he must still have seen her.

'I know I told you a lie, Jon. But I told it out of love.'

'Yes, oh! yes! That's nothing!'

'I didn't answer your letter. What was the use—there wasn't anything to answer. I wanted to see you instead.' She held out both her hands, and Jon grasped them across the table. He tried to say something, but all his attention was given to trying not to hurt her hands. His own felt so hard and hers so soft. She said almost defiantly.

'That old story—was it so very dreadful?'

'Yes.' In his voice, too, there was a note of defiance.

She dragged her hands away. 'I didn't think in these days boys were tied to their mothers' apron-strings.'

Jon's chin went up as if he had been struck.

'Oh! I didn't mean it, Jon. What a horrible thing to say!' Swiftly she came close to him. 'Jon, dear; I didn't mean it.'

'All right.'

She had put her two hands on his shoulder, and her forehead down on them; the brim of her hat touched his neck, and he felt it quivering. But, in a sort of paralysis, he made no response. She let go of his shoulder and drew away.

'Well, I'll go, if you don't want me. But I never thought you'd have given me up.'

'I *haven't*,' cried Jon, coming suddenly to life. 'I can't. I'll try again.'

Her eyes gleamed, she swayed toward him. 'Jon—I love you! Don't give me up! If you do, I don't know what—I feel so desperate. What does it matter—all that past—compared with *this*?'

She clung to him. He kissed her eyes, her cheeks, her lips. But while he kissed her he saw the sheets of that letter fallen down on the floor of his bedroom—his father's white dead face—his mother kneeling before it. Fleur's whisper, 'Make her! Promise! Oh! Jon, try!' seemed childish in his ear. He felt curiously old.

'I promise!' he muttered. 'Only, you don't understand.'

'She wants to spoil our lives, just because—'

'Yes, of what?'

Again that challenge in his voice, and she did not answer. Her arms tightened round him, and he returned her kisses; but even while he yielded, the poison worked in him, the poison of the letter. Fleur did not know, she did not understand—she misjudged his mother; she came from the enemy's camp! So lovely, and he loved her so—yet, even in her embrace, he could not help the memory of Holly's words: 'I think she has a "having" nature,' and his mother's, 'My darling boy, don't think of me—think of yourself!'

When she was gone like a passionate dream, leaving her image on his eyes, her kisses on his lips, such an ache in his heart, Jon leaned in the window, listening to the car bearing away. Still the scent as of warm strawberries, still the little summer sounds that should make his song; still all the promise of youth and happiness in sighing, floating, fluttering July—and his heart torn; yearning strong in him; hope high in him yet with its eyes cast down, as if ashamed. The miserable task before him! If Fleur was desperate, so was he—watching the poplars swaying, the white clouds passing, the sunlight on the grass.

He waited till evening, till after their almost silent dinner, till his mother had played to him—and still he waited, feeling that she knew what he was waiting to say. She kissed him and went upstairs, and still he lingered, watching the moonlight and the moths, and that unreality of colouring which steals along and stains a summer night. And he would have given anything to be back again in the past—barely three months back; or away forward, years, in the future. The present with this dark cruelty of a decision, one way or the other, seemed impossible. He realised now so much more keenly what his mother felt than he had at first; as if the story in that letter had been a poisonous germ producing a kind of fever of partisanship, so that he really felt there were two camps, his mother's and his—Fleur's and her father's. It might be a dead thing, that old tragic ownership and enmity, but dead things were poisonous till time had cleaned them away. Even his love felt tainted, less illusioned, more of the earth, and with a treacherous lurking doubt less Fleur, like her father, might want to *own;* not articulate, just a stealing haunt, horribly unworthy, which crept in and about the ardour of his memories, touched with its tarnishing breath the vividness and grace of that charmed face and figure—a doubt, not real enough to convince him of its presence, just real enough to deflower a perfect faith. And perfect faith, to Jon, not yet twenty, was essential. He still had Youth's eagerness to give with both hands, to take with neither—to give lovingly to one who had his own impulsive generosity. Surely she had! He got up from the window-seat and roamed in the big grey ghostly room, whose walls were hung with silvered canvas. This house—his father said in that death-bed letter—had been built for his mother to live in—with Fleur's father! He put out his hand in the half-dark, as if to grasp the shadowy hand of the dead. He clenched, trying to feel the thin vanished fingers of his father; to squeeze them, and reassure him that he—he was on his father's side. Tears, prisoned within him, made his eyes feel dry and hot. He went back to the window. It was warmer, not so eerie, more comforting outside, where the moon hung golden, three days off full; the freedom of the night was comforting. If only Fleur and he had met on some desert island without a past—and Nature for their house! Jon had still his high regard for desert islands, where breadfruit grew, and the water was blue above the coral. The night was deep, was free—there was enticement in it; a lure, a promise, a refuge from entanglement, and love! Milksop tied to his mother's—! His cheeks burned. He shut the window, drew curtains over it, switched off the lighted sconce, and went upstairs.

The door of his room was open, the light turned up, his mother, still in her evening gown, was standing at the window. She turned and said:

'Sit down, Jon; let's talk.' She sat down on the window-seat, Jon on his bed. She had her profile turned to him, and the beauty and grace of her figure, the delicate line of the brow, the nose, the neck, the strange and as it were remote refinement of her, moved him. His mother never belonged to her surroundings. She came into them from somewhere—as it were! What was she going to say to him, who had in his heart such things to say to her?

'I know Fleur came to-day. I'm not surprised.' It was as though she had added: 'She is her father's daughter!' And Jon's heart hardened. Irene went on quietly:

'I have Father's letter. I picked it up that night and kept it. Would you like it back, dear?'

Jon shook his head.

'I had read it, of course, before he gave it to you. It didn't quite do justice to my criminality.'

'Mother!' burst from Jon's lips.

'He put it very sweetly, but I know that in marrying Fleur's father without love I did a dreadful thing. An unhappy marriage, Jon, can play such havoc with other lives besides one's own. You are fearfully young, my darling, and fearfully loving. Do you think you can possibly be happy with this girl?'

Staring at her dark eyes, darker now from pain, Jon answered:

'Yes; oh! yes—if *you* could be.'

Irene smiled.

'Admiration of beauty and longing for possession are not love. If yours were another case like mine, Jon—where the deepest things are stifled; the flesh joined, and the spirit at war!'

'Why should it, Mother? You think she must be like her father, but she's not. I've seen him.'

Again the smile came on Irene's lips and in Jon something wavered; there was such irony and experience in that smile.

'You are a giver, Jon; she is a taker.'

That unworthy doubt, that haunting uncertainty again. He said with vehemence:

'She isn't—she isn't. It's only because I can't bear to make you unhappy, Mother, now that Father—' He thrust his fists against his forehead.

Irene got up.

'I told you that night, dear, not to mind me. I meant it. Think of yourself and your own happiness! I can stand what's left—I've brought it on myself.'

Again the word 'Mother!' burst from Jon's lips.

She came over to him and put her hands over his.

'Do you feel your head, darling?'

Jon shook it. What he felt was in his chest—a sort of tearing asunder of the tissue there, by the two loves.

'I shall always love you just the same, Jon, whatever you do. You won't lose anything.' She smoothed his hair gently, and walked away.

He heard the door shut; and, rolling over on the bed, lay, stifling his breath, with an awful held-up feeling within him.

7

EMBASSY

Enquiring for her at tea time Soames learned that Fleur had been out in the car since two. Three hours! Where had she gone? Up to London without a word to him? He had never become quite reconciled with cars. He had embraced them in principle—like the born empiricist, or Forsyte, that he was—adopting each symptom of progress as it came along with: 'Well, we couldn't do without them now.' But in fact he found them tearing, great, smelly things. Obliged by Annette to have one—a Rollhard with pearl-grey cushions, electric light, little mirrors, trays for the ashes of cigarettes, flower vases—all smelling of petrol and stephanotis—he regarded it much as he used to regard his brother-in-law, Montague Dartie. The thing typified all that was fast, insecure, and subcutaneously oily in modern life. As modern life became faster, looser, younger, Soames was becoming older, slower, tighter, more and more in thought and language like his father James before him. He was almost aware of it himself. Pace and progress pleased him less and less; there was an ostentation, too, about a car which he considered provocative in the prevailing mood of Labour. On one occasion that fellow Sims had driven over the only vested interest of a working man. Soames had not forgotten the behaviour of its master, when not many people would have stopped to put up with it. He had been sorry for the dog, and quite prepared to take its part against the car, if that ruffian hadn't been so outrageous. With four hours fast becoming five, and still no Fleur all the old car-wise feelings he had experienced in person and by proxy balled within him, and shaking sensations troubled the pit of his stomach. At seven he telephoned to Winifred by trunk call. No! Fleur had not been to Green Street. Then where was she? Visions of his beloved daughter rolled up in her pretty frills, all blood and dust-stained, in some hideous catastrophe, began to haunt him. He went to her room and spied among her things. She had taken nothing—no dressing-case, no jewellery. And this, a relief in one sense, increased his fears of an accident. Terrible to be helpless when his loved one was missing, especially when he couldn't bear fuss or publicity of any kind! What should he do if she were not back by night-fall?

At a quarter to eight he heard the car. A great weight lifted from off his heart; he hurried down. She was getting out—pale and tired-looking, but nothing wrong. He met her in the hall.

'You've frightened me. Where have you been?'

'To Robin Hill. I'm sorry, dear. I had to go; I'll tell you afterwards.' And, with a flying kiss, she ran upstairs.

Soames waited in the drawing-room. To Robin Hill! What did that portend?

It was not a subject they could discuss at dinner—consecrated to the susceptibilities of the butler. The agony of nerves Soames had been through, the relief he felt at her safety, softened his power to condemn what she had done, or resist what she was going to do; he waited in a relaxed stupor for her revelation. Life was a queer business. There he was at sixty-five and no more in command of things than if he had not spent forty years in building up security—always something one couldn't get on terms with! In the pocket of his dinner-jacket was a letter from Annette. She was coming back in a fortnight. He knew nothing of what she had been doing out there. And he was glad that he did not. Her absence had been a relief. Out of sight was out of mind! And now she was coming back. Another worry! And the Bolderby Old Crome was gone—Dumetrius had got it—all because that anonymous letter had put it out of his thoughts. He furtively remarked the strained look on his daughter's face, as if she too were gazing at a picture that she couldn't buy. He almost wished the War back. Worries didn't seem, then, quite so worrying. From the caress in her voice, the look on her face, he became certain that she wanted something from him, uncertain whether it would be wise of him to give it her. He pushed his savoury away uneaten, and even joined her in a cigarette.

After dinner she set the electric piano-player going. And he augured the worst when she sat down on a cushion footstool at his knee, and put her hand on his.

'Darling, be nice to me. I had to see Jon—he wrote to me. He's going to try what he can do with his mother. But I've been thinking. It's really in *your* hands, Father. If you'd persuade her that it doesn't mean renewing the past in any way! That I shall stay yours, and Jon will stay hers; that you need never see him or her, and she need never see you or me! Only you could persuade her, dear, because only you could promise. One can't promise for other people. Surely it wouldn't be too awkward for you to see her just this once—now that Jon's father is dead?'

'Too awkward?' Soames repeated. 'The whole thing's preposterous.'

'You know,' said Fleur, without looking up, 'you wouldn't mind seeing her, really.'

Soames was silent. Her words had expressed a truth too deep for him to admit. She slipped her fingers between his own—hot, slim, eager, they clung there. This child of his would corkscrew her way into a brick wall!

'What am I to do if you won't, Father?' she said very softly.

'I'll do anything for your happiness,' said Soames; 'but this isn't for your happiness.'

'Oh! it is; it is!'

'It'll only stir things up,' he said grimly.

'But they are stirred up. The thing is to quiet them. To make her feel that this is just *our* lives, and has nothing to do with yours or hers. You can do it, Father, I know you can.'

'You know a great deal, then,' was Soames's glum answer.

'If you will, Jon and I will wait a year—two years if you like.'

'It seems to me,' murmured Soames, 'that you care nothing about what *I* feel.'

Fleur pressed his hand against her cheek.

'I do, darling. But you wouldn't like me to be awfully miserable.' How she wheedled to get her ends! And trying with all his might to think she really cared for him—he was not sure—not sure. All she cared for was this boy! Why should he help her get this boy, who was killing her affection for himself? Why should he? By the laws of the Forsytes it was foolish! There was nothing to be had out of it–nothing! To give her to that boy! To pass her into the enemy's camp, under the influence of the woman who had injured him so deeply! Slowly–inevitably–he would lose this flower of his life! And suddenly he was conscious that his hand was wet. His heart gave a little painful jump. He couldn't bear her to cry. He put his other hand quickly over hers, and a tear dropped on that, too. He couldn't go on like this! 'Well, well,' he said, 'I'll think it over, and do what I can. Come, come!' If she must have it for her happiness–she must; he couldn't refuse to help her. And lest she should begin to thank him he got out of his chair and went up to the piano-player–making that noise! It ran down, as he reached it, with a faint buzz. That musical box of his nursery days: 'The Harmonious Blacksmith', 'Glorious Port'–the thing had always made him miserable when his mother set it going on Sunday afternoons. Here it was again–the same thing, only larger, more expensive, and now it played 'The Wild, Wild Women', and 'The Policeman's Holiday', and he was no longer in black velvet with a sky blue collar. 'Profond's right,' he thought, 'there's nothing in it! We're all progressing to the grave!' And with that surprising mental comment he walked out.

He did not see Fleur again that night. But, at breakfast, her eyes followed him about with an appeal he could not escape–not that he intended to try. No! He had made up his mind to the nerve-racking business. He would go to Robin Hill–to that house of memories. Pleasant memory–the last! Of going down to keep that boy's father and Irene apart by threatening divorce. He had often thought since, that it had clinched their union. And, now, he was going to clinch the union of that boy with his girl. 'I don't know what I've done,' he thought, 'to have such things thrust on me!' He went up by train and down by train, and from the station walked by the long rising lane, still very much as he remembered it over thirty years ago. Funny–so near London! Someone evidently was holding on to the land there. This speculation soothed him, moving between the high hedges slowly, so as not to get overheated, though the day was chill enough. After all was said and done there was something real about land, it didn't shift. Land, and good pictures! The values might fluctuate a bit, but on the whole they were always going up–worth holding on to, in a world where there was such a lot of unreality, cheap building, changing fashions, such a 'Here to-day and gone to-morrow' spirit. The French were right, perhaps, with their peasant proprietorship, though he had no opinion of the French. One's bit of land! Something solid in it! He had heard peasant proprietors described as a pig-headed lot; had heard young Mont call his father a pig-headed *Morning Poster*–disrespectful young devil. Well, there were worse things than being pig-headed or reading the *Morning Post*. There was Profond and his tribe, and all these Labour chaps, and loud-mouthed politicians, and 'wild, wild women'! A lot of worse things! And, suddenly, Soames became conscious of feeling weak, and hot, and shaky. Sheer nerves at the meeting before him! As Aunt Juley might have said–quoting 'Superior Dosset'–his nerves were 'in a proper fantigue'. He could see the house now among its trees, the house he had watched being built, intending it for himself and this woman, who, by such strange fate, had lived in it with another after all! He began to think of Dumetrius, Local Loans, and other forms of investment. He could not afford to meet her with his nerves all shaking; he who represented the Day of Judgment for her on earth as it was in heaven; he, legal ownership, personified, meeting lawless beauty, incarnate. His dignity demanded impassivity during this embassy designed to link their offspring, who, if she had behaved herself, would have been brother and sister. That wretched tune, 'The Wild, Wild Women', kept running in his head, perversely, for tunes did not run as a rule. Passing the poplars in front of the house, he thought: 'How they've grown; I had them planted!'

A maid answered his ring.

'Will you say–Mr Forsyte, on a very special matter.'

If she realised who he was, quite probably she would not see him. 'By George!' he thought, hardening as the tug came. 'It's a topsy-turvy affair!'

The maid came back. 'Would the gentleman state his business, please?'

'Say it concerns Mr Jon,' said Soames.

And once more he was alone in that hall with the pool of grey-white marble designed by her first lover. Ah! she had been a bad lot–had loved two men, and not himself! He must remember that when he came face to face with her once more. And suddenly he saw her in the opening chink between the long heavy purple curtains, swaying, as if in hesitation; the old perfect poise and line, the old startled dark-eyed gravity, the old calm defensive voice: 'Will you come in, please?'

He passed through that opening. As in the picture-gallery and the confectioner's shop, she seemed to him still beautiful. And this was the first time–the very first–since he married her six-and-thirty years ago, that he was speaking to her without the legal right to call her his. She was not wearing black–one of that fellow's radical notions, he supposed.

'I apologise for coming,' he said glumly; 'but this business must be settled one way or the other.'

'Won't you sit down?'

'No, thank you.'

Anger at his false position, impatience of ceremony between them, mastered him, and words came tumbling out:

'It's an infernal mischance; I've done my best to discourage it. I consider my daughter crazy, but I've got into the habit of indulging her; that's why I'm here. I suppose you're fond of your son.'

'Devotedly.'

'Well?'

'It rests with him.'

He had a sense of being met and baffled. Always–always she had baffled him, even in those old first married days.

'It's a mad notion,' he said.

'It is.'

'If you had only–! Well–they might have been–' he did not finish that sentence 'brother and sister and all this saved', but he saw her shudder as if he had, and stung by the sight he crossed over to the window. Out *there* the trees had not grown–they couldn't, they were old!

'So far as I'm concerned,' he said, 'you may make your mind easy. I desire to see neither you nor your son if this marriage comes about. Young people in these days are–are unaccountable. But I can't bear to see my daughter unhappy. What am I to say to her when I go back?'

'Please say to her as I said to you, that it rests with Jon.'

'You don't oppose it?'

'With all my heart; not with my lips.'

Soames stood, biting his finger.

'I remember an evening–' he said suddenly; and was silent. What was there–what was there in this woman that would not fit into the four corners of his hate or condemnation. 'Where is he–your son?'

'Up in his father's studio, I think.'

'Perhaps you'd have him down.'

He watched her ring the bell, he watched the maid come in.

'Please tell Mr Jon that I want him.'

'If it rests with him,' said Soames hurriedly, when the maid was gone, 'I suppose I may take it for granted that this unnatural marriage will take place; in that case there'll be formalities. Whom do I deal with–Herring's?'

Irene nodded.

'You don't propose to live with them?'

Irene shook her head.

'What happens to this house?'

'It will be as Jon wishes.'

'This house,' said Soames suddenly: 'I had hopes when I began it. If *they* live in it–their children! They say there's such a thing as Nemesis. Do you believe in it?'

'Yes.'

'Oh! You do!'

He had come back from the window, and was standing close to her, who, in the curve of her grand piano, was, as it were, embayed.

'I'm not likely to see you again,' he said slowly. 'Will you shake hands'–his lip quivered, the words came out jerkily–'and let the past die.' He held out his hand. Her pale face grew paler, her eyes so dark, rested immovably on his, her hands remained clasped in front of her. He heard a sound and turned. That boy was standing in the opening of the curtains. Very queer he looked, hardly recognisable as the young fellow he had seen in the Gallery off Cork Street–very queer; much older, no youth in the face at all–haggard, rigid, his hair ruffled, his eyes deep in his head. Soames made an effort, and said with a lift of his lip, not quite a smile, nor quite a sneer.

'Well, young man! I'm here for my daughter; it rests with you, it seems–this matter. Your mother leaves it in your hands.'

The boy continued staring at his mother's face, and made no answer.

'For my daughter's sake I've brought myself to come,' said Soames. 'What am I to say to her when I go back?'

Still looking at his mother, the boy said, quietly:

'Tell Fleur that it's no good, please; I must do as my father wished before he died.'

'Jon!'

'It's all right, Mother.'

In a kind of stupefaction Soames looked from one to the other, then, taking up hat and umbrella which he had put down on a chair, he walked toward the curtains. The boy stood aside for him to go by. He passed through and heard the grate of the rings as the curtains were drawn behind him. The sound liberated something in his chest.

'So that's that!' he thought, and passed out of the front door.

8

THE DARK TUNE

As Soames walked away from the house at Robin Hill the sun broke through the grey of the chill afternoon, in smoky radiance. So absorbed in landscape painting that he seldom looked seriously for effects of Nature out of doors – he was struck by that moody effulgence – it mounted with a triumph suited to his own feeling. Victory in defeat! His embassy had come to naught. But he was rid of those people, had regained his daughter at the expense of – her happiness. What would Fleur say to him? Would she believe he had done his best? And under that sunlight flaring on the elms, hazels, hollies of the lane and those unexploited fields, Soames felt dread. She would be terribly upset! He must appeal to her pride. That boy had given her up, declared part and lot with the woman who so long ago had given her father up! Soames clenched his hands. Given him up, and why? What had been wrong with him? And once more he felt the *malaise* of one who contemplates himself as seen by another – like a dog who chances on his reflection in a mirror and is intrigued and anxious at the unseizable thing.

Not in a hurry to get home, he dined in town at the Connoisseurs. While eating a pear it suddenly occurred to him that, if he had not gone down to Robin Hill, the boy might not have so decided. He remembered the expression on his face while his mother was refusing the hand he had held out. A strange, an awkward thought! Had Fleur cooked her own goose by trying to make too sure?

He reached home at half-past nine. While the car was passing in at one drive gate he heard the grinding sputter of a motor-cycle passing out by the other. Young Mont, no doubt, so Fleur had not been lonely. But he went in with a sinking heart. In the cream-panelled drawing-room she was sitting with her elbows on her knees, and her chin on her clasped hands, in front of a white camellia plant which filled the fireplace. That glance at her before she saw him renewed his dread. What was she seeing among those white camellias?

'Well, Father!'

Soames shook his head. His tongue failed him. This was murderous work! He saw her eyes dilate, her lips quivering.

'What? What? Quick, Father!'

'My dear,' said Soames, 'I – I did my best, but –' And again he shook his head.

Fleur ran to him, and put a hand on each of his shoulders.

'She?'

'No,' muttered Soames; 'he. I was to tell you that it was no use; he must do what his father wished before he died.' He caught her by the waist. 'Come, child, don't let them hurt you. They're not worth your little finger.'

Fleur tore herself from his grasp.

'You didn't – you couldn't have tried. You – you betrayed me, Father!'

Bitterly wounded, Soames gazed at her passionate figure writhing there in front of him.

'You didn't try–you didn't–I was a fool–I won't believe he could–he ever could! Only yesterday he–! Oh! why did I ask you?'

'Yes,' said Soames, quietly, 'why did you? I swallowed my feelings; I did my best for you, against my judgment–and this is my reward. Good-night!'

With every nerve in his body twitching he went toward the door.

Fleur darted after him.

'He gives me up? You mean that? Father!'

Soames turned and forced himself to answer:

'Yes.'

'Oh!' cried Fleur. 'What did you–what could you have done in those old days?'

The breathless sense of really monstrous injustice cut the power of speech in Soames's throat. What had *he* done! What had they done to him! And with quite unconscious dignity he put his hand on his breast, and looked at her.

'It's a shame!' cried Fleur passionately.

Soames went out. He mounted, slow and icy, to his picture-gallery, and paced among his treasures. Outrageous! Oh! Outrageous! She was spoiled! Ah! and who had spoiled her? He stood still before his Goya copy. Accustomed to her own way in everything. Flower of his life! And now that she couldn't have it! He turned to the window for some air. Daylight was dying, the moon rising, gold behind the poplars! What sound was that? Why! That piano thing! A dark tune, with a thrum and a throb! She had set it going–what comfort could she get from that? His eyes caught movement down there beyond the lawn, under the trellis of rambler roses and young acacia trees, where the moonlight fell. There she was, roaming up and down. His heart gave a little sickening jump. What would she do under this blow? How could he tell? What did he know of her–he had only loved her all his life–looked on her as the apple of his eye! He knew nothing–had no notion. There she was–and that dark tune–and the river gleaming in the moonlight!

'I must go out,' he thought.

He hastened down to the drawing-room, lighted just as he had left it, with the piano thrumming out that waltz, or foxtrot, or whatever they called it these days, and passed through on to the verandah.

Where could he watch, without her seeing him? And he stole down through the fruit garden to the boat-house. He was between her and the river now, and his heart felt lighter. She was his daughter, and Annette's–she wouldn't do anything foolish; but there it was–he didn't know! From the boat-house window he could see the last acacia and the spin of her skirt when she turned in her restless march. That tune had run down at last–thank goodness! He crossed the floor and looked through the farther window at the water slow–flowing past the lilies. It made little bubbles against them, bright where a moon-streak fell. He remembered suddenly that early morning when he had slept on the house-boat after his father died, and she had just been born–nearly nineteen years ago! Even now he recalled the unaccustomed world when he woke up, the strange feeling it had given him. That day the second passion of his life began–for this girl of his, roaming under the acacias. What a comfort she had been to him! And all the soreness and sense of outrage left him. If he could make her happy again, he didn't care! An owl flew, queeking, queeking; a bat flitted by; the moonlight brightened and broadened on the water. How long was she going to roam about like this! He went back to the window, and suddenly saw her coming down the bank. She stood quite close, on the landing-stage. And Soames watched, clenching his hands. Should he speak to her? His excitement was intense. The stillness of her figure, its youth, its absorption in despair, in longing, in–itself. He would always remember it, moonlit like that; and the faint sweet reek of the river and the shivering of the willow leaves. She had everything in the world that he could give her except the one thing that she could not have because of him! The perversity of things hurt him at that moment, as might a fish-bone in his throat.

Then, with an infinite relief, he saw her turn back toward the house. What could he give her to make amends? Pearls, travel, horses, other young men–anything she wanted–that he might lose the memory of her young figure lonely by the water! There! She had set that tune going again! Why–it was a mania! Dark, thrumming, faint, travelling from the house. It was as though she had said: 'If I can't have something to keep me going, I shall die of this!' Soames dimly understood. Well, if it helped her, let her keep it thrumming on all night! And, mousing back through the fruit garden, he regained the verandah. Though he meant to go in and speak to her now, he still hesitated, not knowing what to say, trying hard to recall how it felt to be thwarted in love. He ought to know, ought to remember–and he could not! Gone–all real recollection; except that it had hurt him horribly. In this blankness he stood passing his handkerchief over hands and lips, which were very dry. By craning his head he could just see Fleur, standing with her back to that piano still grinding out its tune, her arms tight crossed on her breast, a lighted cigarette between her lips, whose smoke half veiled her face. The expression on it was strange to Soames, the eyes shone and stared, and every feature was alive with a sort of wretched scorn and anger. Once or twice he had seen Annette look like that–the face was too vivid, too naked, not *his* daughter's at that moment. And he dared not go in, realising the futility of any attempt at consolation. He sat down in the shadow of the ingle-nook.

Monstrous trick, that Fate had played him! Nemesis! That old unhappy marriage! And in God's name–why? How was he to know, when he wanted Irene so violently, and she consented to be his, that she would never love him? The tune died and was renewed, and died again, and still Soames sat in the shadow, waiting for he knew not what. The fag of Fleur's cigarette, flung through the window, fell on the grass; he watched it glowing, burning itself out. The moon had freed herself above the poplars, and poured her unreality on the garden. Comfortless light, mysterious, withdrawn–like the beauty of that woman who had never loved him–dappling the nemesias and the stocks with a vesture not of earth. Flowers! And his flower so unhappy! Ah! Why could one not put happiness into Local Loans, gild its edges, insure it against going down?

Light had ceased to flow out now from the drawing-room window. All was silent and dark in there. Had she gone up? He rose, and, tiptoeing, peered in. It seemed so! He entered. The verandah kept the moonlight out; and at first he could see nothing but the outlines of furniture blacker than the darkness. He groped toward the farther window to shut it. His foot struck a chair, and he heard a gasp. There she was, curled and crushed into the corner of the sofa! His hand lowered. Did she want his consolation? He stood, gazing at that ball of crushed frills and hair and graceful youth, trying to burrow its way out of sorrow. How leave her there? At last he touched her hair and said:

'Come, darling, better go to bed. I'll make it up to you, somehow.' How fatuous! But what could he have said?

9

UNDER THE OAK TREE

When their visitor had disappeared Jon and his mother stood without speaking, till he said suddenly:

'I ought to have seen him out.'

But Soames was already walking down the drive, and Jon went upstairs to his father's studio, not trusting himself to go back.

The expression on his mother's face confronting the man she had once been married to, had sealed a resolution growing within him ever since she left him the night before. It had put the finishing touch of reality. To marry Fleur would be to hit his mother in the face; to betray his dead father! It was no good! Jon had the least resentful of natures. He bore his parents no grudge in this hour of his distress. For one so young there was a rather strange power in him of seeing things in some sort of proportion. It was worse for Fleur, worse for his mother even, than it was for him. Harder than to give up was to be given up, or to be the cause of someone you loved giving up for you. He must not, would not behave grudgingly! While he stood watching the tardy sunlight, he had again that sudden vision of the world which had come to him the night before. Sea on sea, country on country, millions on millions of people, all with their own lives, energies, joys, griefs, and suffering—all with things they had to give up, and separate struggles for existence. Even though he might be willing to give up all else for the one thing he couldn't have, he would be a fool to think his feelings mattered much in so vast a world and to behave like a cry-baby or a cad. He pictured the people who had nothing— the millions who had given up life in the War, the millions whom the War had left with life and little else; the hungry children he had read of, the shattered men; people in prison, every kind of unfortunate. And—they did not help him much. If one had to miss a meal, what comfort in the knowledge that many others had to miss it too? There was more distraction in the thought of getting away out into this vast world of which he knew nothing yet. He could not go on staying here, walled in and sheltered, with everything so slick and comfortable, and nothing to do but brood and think what might have been. He could not go back to Wansdon, and the memories of Fleur. If he saw her again he could not trust himself; and if he stayed here or went back there, he would surely see her. While they were within reach of each other that must happen. To go far away and quickly was the only thing to do. But, however much he loved his mother, he did not want to go away with her. Then feeling that he was brutal, he made up his mind desperately to propose that they should go to Italy. For two hours in that melancholy room he tried to master himself, then dressed solemnly for dinner.

His mother had done the same. They ate little, at some length, and talked of his father's catalogue. The show was arranged for October, and beyond clerical detail there was nothing more to do.

After dinner she put on a cloak and they went out; walked a little, talked a little, till they were standing silent as last beneath the oak tree. Ruled by the thought: 'If I show anything, I show all,' Jon put his arm through hers and said quite casually:

'Mother, let's go to Italy.'

Irene pressed his arm, and said as casually:

'It would be very nice; but I've been thinking you ought to see and do more than you would if I were with you.'

'But then you'd be alone.'

'I was once alone for more than twelve years. Besides, I should like to be here for the opening of Father's show.'

Jon's grip tightened round her arm; he was not deceived.

'You couldn't stay here all by yourself; it's too big.'

'Not here, perhaps. In London, and I might go to Paris, after the show opens. You ought to have a year at least, Jon, and see the world.'

'Yes, I'd like to see the world and rough it. But I don't want to leave you all alone.'

'My dear, I owe you that at least. If it's for your good, it'll be for mine. Why not start to-morrow? You've got your passport.'

'Yes; if I'm going it had better be at once. Only–Mother–if–if I wanted to stay out somewhere–America or anywhere, would you mind coming presently?'

'Wherever and whenever you send for me. But don't send until you really want me.'

Jon drew a deep breath.

'I feel England's choky.'

They stood a few minutes longer under the oak tree–looking out to where the grandstand at Epsom was veiled in evening. The branches kept the moonlight from them, so that it only fell everywhere else–over the fields and far away, and on the windows of the creepered house behind, which soon would be to let.

10

FLEUR'S WEDDING

The October paragraphs describing the wedding of Fleur Forsyte to Michael Mont hardly conveyed the symbolic significance of this event. In the union of the great-granddaughter of 'Superior Dosset' with the heir of a ninth baronet was the outward and visible sign of that merger of class in class which buttresses the political stability of a realm. The time had come when the Forsytes might resign their natural resentment against a 'flummery' not theirs by birth, and accept it as the still more natural due of their possessive instincts. Besides, they had to mount to make room for all those so much more newly rich. In that quiet but tasteful ceremony in Hanover Square, and afterward among the furniture in Green Street, it had been impossible for those not in the know to distinguish the Forsyte troop from the Mont contingent–so far away was 'Superior Dosset' now. Was there, in the crease of his trousers, the expression of his moustache, his accent, or the shine on his top-hat, a pin to choose between Soames and the ninth baronet himself? Was not Fleur as self-possessed, quick, glancing, pretty, and hard as the likeliest Muskham, Mont, or Charwell filly present? If anything, the Forsytes had it in dress and looks and manners. They had become 'upper class' and now their name would be formally recorded in the Stud Book, their money joined to land. Whether this was a little late in the day, and those rewards of the possessive instinct, lands and money destined for the melting-pot—was still a question so moot that it was not mooted. After all, Timothy had said Consols were goin' up. Timothy, the last, the missing link; Timothy, *in extremis* on the Bayswater Road—so Francie had reported. It was whispered, too, that this young Mont was a sort of socialist—strangely wise of him, and in the nature of insurance, considering the days they lived in. There was no uneasiness on that score. The landed classes produced that sort of amiable foolishness at times, turned to safe uses and confined to theory. As George remarked to his sister Francie: 'They'll soon be having puppies—that'll give him pause.'

The church with white flowers and something blue in the middle of the East window looked extremely chaste, as though endeavouring to counteract the somewhat lurid phraseology of a Service calculated to keep the thoughts of all on puppies. Forsytes, Haymans, Tweetymans, sat in the left aisle; Monts, Charwells, Muskhams in the right; while a sprinkling of Fleur's fellow-sufferers at school, and of Mont's fellow-sufferers in the War, gaped indiscriminately from either side, and three maiden ladies, who had dropped in on their way from Skyward's, brought up the rear, together with two Mont retainers and Fleur's old nurse. In the unsettled state of the country as full a house as could be expected.

Mrs Val Dartie, who sat with her husband in the third row, squeezed his hand more than once during the performance. To her, who knew the plot of this tragi-comedy, its most dramatic moment was wellnigh painful. 'I wonder if Jon knows by instinct,' she thought—Jon, out in British Columbia. She had received a letter from him only that morning which had made her smile and say:

'Jon's in British Columbia, Val, because he wants to be in California. He thinks it's too nice there.'

'Oh!' said Val, 'so he's beginning to see a joke again.'

'He's bought some land and sent for his mother.'

'What on earth will she do out there?'

'All she cares about is Jon. Do you still think it a happy release?'

Val's shrewd eyes narrowed to grey pin-points between their dark lashes.

'Fleur wouldn't have suited him a bit. She's not bred right.'

'Poor little Fleur!' sighed Holly. Ah! it was strange—this marriage. The young man, Mont, had caught her on the rebound, of course, in the reckless mood of one whose ship has just gone down. Such a plunge could not but be—as Val put it—an outside chance. There was little to be told from the back view of her young cousin's veil, and Holly's eyes reviewed the general aspect of this Christian wedding. She, who had made a love-match which had been successful, had a horror of unhappy marriages. This might not be one in the end—but it was clearly a toss-up; and to consecrate a toss-up in this fashion with manufactured unction before a crowd of fashionable free-thinkers—for who thought otherwise than freely, or not at all, when they were 'dolled' up—seemed to her as near a sin as one could find in an age which had abolished them. Her eyes wandered from the prelate in his robes (a Charwell—the Forsytes had not as yet produced a prelate) to Val, beside her, thinking—she was certain—of the Mayfly filly at fifteen to one for the Cambridgeshire. They passed on and caught the profile of the ninth baronet, in counterfeitment of the kneeling process. She could just see the neat ruck above his knees where he had pulled his trousers up, and thought: 'Val's forgotten to pull up his!' Her eyes passed to the pew in front of her, where Winifred's substantial form was gowned with passion and on again to Soames and Annette kneeling side by side. A little smile came on her lips–Prosper Profond, back from the South Seas of the Channel, would be kneeling too, about six rows behind. Yes! This was a funny 'small' business, however it turned out; still it was in a proper church and would be in the proper papers to-morrow morning.

They had begun a hymn; she could hear the ninth baronet across the aisle, singing of the hosts of Midian. Her little finger touched Val's thumb–they were holding the same hymn-book–and a tiny thrill passed through her, preserved from twenty years ago. He stooped and whispered:

'I say, d'you remember the rat?' The rat at their wedding in Cape Colony, which had cleaned its whiskers behind the table at the Registrar's! And between her little and third finger she squeezed his thumb hard.

The hymn was over, the prelate had begun to deliver his discourse. He told them of the dangerous times they lived in, and the awful conduct of the House of Lords in connection with divorce. They were all soldiers–he said–in the trenches under the poisonous gas of the Prince of Darkness, and must be manful. The purpose of marriage was children, not mere sinful happiness.

An imp danced in Holly's eyes–Val's eyelashes were meeting. Whatever happened, he must *not* snore. Her finger and thumb closed on his thigh till he stirred uneasily.

The discourse was over, the danger past. They were signing in the vestry; and general relaxation had set in.

A voice behind her said:

'Will she stay the course?'

'Who's that?' she whispered.

'Old George Forsyte!'

Holly demurely scrutinised one of whom she had often heard. Fresh from South Africa, and ignorant of her kith and kin, she never saw one without an almost childish curiosity. He was very big, and very dapper; his eyes gave her a funny feeling of having no particular clothes.

'They're off!' she heard him say.

They came, stepping from the chancel. Holly looked first in young Mont's face. His lips and ears were twitching, his eyes, shifting from his feet to the hand within his arm, stared suddenly before them as if to face a firing party. He gave Holly the feeling that he was spiritually intoxicated. But Fleur! Ah! That was different. The girl was perfectly composed, prettier than ever, in her white robes and veil over her banged dark chestnut hair; her eyelids hovered demure over her dark hazel eyes. Outwardly, she seemed all there. But inwardly, where was she? As those two passed, Fleur raised her eyelids–the restless glint of those clear whites remained on Holly's vision as might the flutter of a caged bird's wings.

In Green Street Winifred stood to receive, just a little less composed than usual. Soames's request for the use of her house had come on her at a deeply psychological moment. Under the influence of a remark of Prosper Profond, she had begun to exchange her Empire for Expressionistic furniture. There were the most amusing arrangements, with violet, green, and orange blobs and scriggles, to be had at Mealard's. Another month and the change would have been complete. Just now, the very 'intriguing' recruits she had enlisted, did not march too well with the old guard. It was as if her regiment were half in khaki, half in scarlet and bearskins. But her strong and comfortable character made the best of it in a drawing-room which typified, perhaps, more perfectly than she imagined, the semi-bolshevized imperialism of her country. After all, this was a day of merger, and you couldn't have too much of it! Her eyes travelled indulgently among her guests. Soames had gripped the back of a buhl chair; young Mont was behind that 'awfully amusing' screen, which no one as yet had been able to explain to her. The ninth baronet had shied violently at a round scarlet table, inlaid under glass with blue Australian butterflies' wings, and was clinging to her Louis-Quinze cabinet; Francie Forsyte had seized the new mantel-board, finely carved with little purple grotesques on an ebony ground; George, over by the old spinet, was holding a little sky-blue book as if about to enter bets; Prosper Profond was twiddling the knob of the open door, black with peacock-blue panels; and Annette's hands, close by, were grasping her own waist; two Muskhams clung to the balcony among the plants, as if feeling ill; Lady Mont, thin and brave-looking, had taken up her long-handled glasses and was gazing at the central light shade, of ivory and orange dashed with deep magenta, as if the heavens had opened. Everybody, in fact, seemed holding on to something. Only Fleur, still in her bridal dress, was detached from all support, flinging her words and glances to left and right.

The room was full of the bubble and the squeak of conversation. Nobody could hear anything that anybody said; which seemed of little consequence, since no one waited for anything so slow as an answer. Modern conversation seemed to Winifred so different from the days of her prime, when a drawl was all the vogue. Still it was 'amusing', which, of course, was all that mattered. Even the Forsytes were talking with extreme rapidity – Fleur and Christopher, and Imogen, and young Nicholas's youngest, Patrick. Soames, of course, was silent; but George, by the spinet, kept up a running commentary, and Francie, by her mantel-shelf. Winifred drew nearer to the ninth baronet. He seemed to promise a certain repose; his nose was fine and drooped a little, his grey moustaches too; and she said, drawling through her smile:

'It's rather nice, isn't it?'

His reply shot out of his smile like a snipped bread pellet:

'D'you remember, in Frazer, the tribe that buries the bride up to the waist?'

He spoke as fast as anybody! He had dark lively little eyes, too, all crinkled round like a Catholic priest's. Winifred felt suddenly he might say things she would regret.

'They're always so amusing – weddings,' she murmured, and moved on to Soames. He was curiously still, and Winifred saw at once what was dictating his immobility. To his right was George Forsyte, to his left Annette and Prosper Profond. He could not move without either seeing those two together, or the reflection of them in George Forsyte's japing eyes. He was quite right not to be taking notice.

'They say Timothy's sinking,' he said glumly.

'Where will you put him, Soames?'

'Highgate.' He counted on his fingers. 'It'll make twelve of them there, including wives. How do you think Fleur looks?'

'Remarkably well.'

Soames nodded. He had never seen her look prettier, yet he could not rid himself of the impression that this business was unnatural–remembering still that crushed figure burrowing into the corner of the sofa. From that night to this day he had received from her no confidences. He knew from his chauffeur that she had made one more attempt on Robin Hill and drawn blank–an empty house, no one at home. He knew that she had received a letter, but not what was in it, except that it had made her hide herself and cry. He had remarked that she looked at him sometimes when she thought he wasn't noticing, as if she were wondering still what he had done–forsooth–to make those people hate him so. Well, there it was! Annette had come back, and things had worn on through the summer–very miserable, till suddenly Fleur had said she was going to marry young Mont. She had shown him a little more affection when she told him that. And he had yielded–what was the good of opposing it? God knew that he had never wished to thwart her in anything! And the young man seemed quite delirious about her. No doubt she was in a reckless mood, and she was young, absurdly young. But if he opposed her, he didn't know what she would do; for all he could tell she might want to take up a profession, become a doctor or solicitor, some nonsense. She had no aptitude for painting, writing, music, in his view the legitimate occupations of unmarried women, if they must do something in these days. On the whole, she was safer married, for he could see too well how feverish and restless she was at home. Annette, too, had been in favour of it–Annette, from behind the veil of his refusal to know what she was about, if she was about anything. Annette had said: 'Let her marry this young man. He is a nice boy–not so highty-flighty as he seems.' Where she got her expressions, he didn't know–but her opinion soothed his doubts. His wife, whatever her conduct, had clear eyes and an almost depressing amount of common sense. He had settled fifty thousand on Fleur, taking care that there was no cross settlement in case it didn't turn out well. Could it turn out well? She had not got over that other boy–he knew. They were to go to Spain for the honeymoon. He would be even lonelier when she was gone. But later, perhaps, she would forget, and turn to him again!

Winifred's voice broke on his reverie.

'Why? Of all wonders–June!'

There, in a djibbah–what things she wore!–with her hair straying from under a fillet, Soames saw his cousin, and Fleur going forward to greet her. The two passed from their view out on to the stairway.

'Really,' said Winifred, 'she does the most impossible things! Fancy *her* coming!'

What made you ask her?' muttered Soames.

'Because I thought she wouldn't accept, of course.'

Winifred had forgotten that behind conduct lies the main trend of character; or, in other words, omitted to remember that Fleur was now a 'lame duck'.

On receiving her invitation, June had first thought, 'I wouldn't go near them for the world!' and then, one morning, had awakened from a dream of Fleur waving to her from a boat with a wild unhappy gesture. And she had changed her mind.

When Fleur came forward and said to her, 'Do come up while I'm changing my dress,' she had followed up the stairs. The girl led the way into Imogen's old bedroom, set ready for her toilet.

June sat down on the bed, thin and upright, like a little spirit in the sear and yellow. Fleur locked the door.

The girl stood before her divested of her wedding-dress. What a pretty thing she was!

'I suppose you think me a fool,' she said, with quivering lips, 'when it was to have been Jon. But what does it matter? Michael wants me and I don't care. It'll get me away from home.' Diving her hand into the frills on her breast, she brought out a letter. 'Jon wrote me this.'

June read: 'Lake Okanagan, British Columbia. I'm not coming back to England. Bless you always.–Jon.'

'She's made safe, you see,' said Fleur.

June handed back the letter.

'That's not fair to Irene,' she said; 'she always told Jon he could do as he wished.'

Fleur smiled bitterly. 'Tell me, didn't she spoil your life too?'

June looked up. 'Nobody can spoil a life, my dear. That's nonsense. Things happen, but we bob up.'

With a sort of terror she saw the girl sink on her knees and bury her face in the djibbah. A strangled sob mounted to June's ears.

'It's all right–all right,' she murmured. 'Don't! There, there!'

But the point of the girl's chin was pressed ever closer into her thigh, and the sound was dreadful of her sobbing.

Well, well! It had to come. She would feel better afterward! June stroked the short hair of that shapely head; and all the scattered mother-sense in her focused itself and passed through the tips of her fingers into the girl's brain.

'Don't sit down under it, my dear,' she said at last. 'We can't control life, but we can fight it. Make the best of things. I've had to. I held on, like you; and I cried, as you're crying now. And look at me!'

Fleur raised her head; a sob merged suddenly into a little choked laugh. In truth it was a thin and rather wild and wasted spirit she was looking at, but it had brave eyes.

'All right!' she said. 'I'm sorry. I shall forget him, I suppose, if I fly fast and far enough.'

And scrambling to her feet she went over to the wash-stand.

June watched her removing with cold water the traces of emotion. Save for a little becoming pinkness there was nothing left when she stood before the mirror. June got off the bed and took a pin-cushion in her hand. To put two pins into the wrong places was all the vent she found for sympathy.

'Give me a kiss,' she said when Fleur was ready, and dug her chin into the girl's warm cheek.

'I want a whiff,' said Fleur; 'don't wait.'

June left her, sitting on the bed with a cigarette between her lips and her eyes half closed, and went downstairs. In the doorway of the dressing-room stood Soames as if unquiet at his daughter's tardiness. June tossed her head and passed down on to the half-landing. Her cousin Francie was standing there.

'Look!' said June, pointing with her chin at Soames. 'That man's fatal!'

'How do you mean,' said Francie, 'Fatal?'

June did not answer her. 'I shan't wait to see them off,' she said. 'Good-bye!'

'Good-bye!' said Francie, and her eyes, of a Celtic grey, goggled. That old feud! Really, it was quite romantic!

Soames, moving to the well of the staircase, saw June go, and drew a breath of satisfaction. Why didn't Fleur come? They would miss their train. That train would bear her away from him, yet he could not help fidgeting at the thought that they would lose it. And then she did come, running down in her tan-coloured frock and black velvet cap, and passed him into the drawing-room. He saw her kiss her mother, her aunt, Val's wife, Imogen, and then come forth, quick and pretty as ever. How would she treat him at this last moment of her girlhood? He couldn't hope for much!

Her lips pressed the middle of his cheek.

'Daddy!' she said, and was past and gone. Daddy! She hadn't called him that for years. He drew a long breath and followed slowly down. There was all the folly with that confetti stuff and the rest of it to go through with, yet. But he would like just to catch her smile, if she leaned out, though they would hit her in the eye with the shoe, if they didn't take care. Young Mont's voice said fervently in his ear:

'Good-bye, sir; and thank you! I'm so fearfully bucked.'

'Good-bye,' he said; 'don't miss your train.'

He stood on the bottom step but three, whence he could see above the heads—the silly hats and heads. They were in the car now; and there was that stuff, showering, and there went the shoe. A flood of something welled up in Soames, and—he didn't know—he couldn't see!

I I

THE LAST OF THE OLD FORSYTES

When they came to prepare that terrific symbol Timothy Forsyte—the one pure individualist left, the only man who hadn't heard of the Great War—they found him wonderful—not even death had undermined his soundness.

To Smither and Cook that preparation came like final evidence of what they had never believed possible—the end of the old Forsyte family on earth. Poor Mr Timothy must now take a harp and sing in the company of Miss Forsyte, Mrs Julia, Miss Hester; with Mr Jolyon, Mr Swithin, Mr James, Mr Roger and Mr Nicholas of the party. Whether Mrs Hayman would be there was more doubtful, seeing that she had been cremated. Secretly Cook thought that Mr Timothy would be upset—he had always been so set against barrel organs. How many times had she not said: 'Drat the thing! There it is again! Smither, you'd better run up and see what you can do.' And in her heart she would so have enjoyed the tunes, if she hadn't known that Mr Timothy would ring the bell in a minute and say: 'Here, take him a halfpenny and tell him to move on.' Often they had been obliged to add threepence of their own before the man would go—Timothy had ever underrated the value of emotion. Luckily he had taken the organs for blue-bottles in his last years, which had been a comfort, and they had been able to enjoy the tunes. But a harp! Cook wondered. It *was* a change! And Mr Timothy had never liked change. But she did not speak of this to Smither, who did so take a line of her own in regard to heaven that it quite put one about sometimes.

She cried while Timothy was being prepared, and they all had sherry afterward out of the yearly Christmas bottle, which would not be needed now. Ah! dear! She had been there five-and-forty years and Smither three-and-forty! And now they would be going to a tiny house in Tooting, to live on their

savings and what Miss Hester had so kindly left them–for to take fresh service
after the glorious past–No! But they *would* like just to see Mr Soames again,
and Mrs Dartie, and Miss Francie, and Miss Euphemia. And even if they had
to take their own cab, they felt they must go to the funeral. For six years Mr
Timothy had been their baby, getting younger and younger every day, till at
last he had been too young to live.

They spent the regulation hours of waiting in polishing and dusting, in
catching the one mouse left, and asphyxiating the last beetle so as to leave it
nice, discussing with each other what they would buy at the sale. Miss Ann's
work-box; Miss Juley's (that is Mrs Julia's) seaweed album; the fire-screen
Miss Hester had crewelled; and Mr Timothy's hair–little golden curls, glued
into a black frame. Oh! they must have those–only the price of things had gone
up so!

It fell to Soames to issue invitations for the funeral. He had them drawn up
by Gradman in his office–only blood relations, and no flowers. Six carriages
were ordered. The Will would be read afterwards at the house.

He arrived at eleven o'clock to see that all was ready. At a quarter past old
Gradman came in black gloves and crape on his hat. He and Soames stood in
the drawing-room waiting. At half-past eleven the carriages drew up in a long
row. But no one else appeared. Gradman said:

'It surprises me, Mr Soames. I posted them myself.'

'I don't know,' said Soames; 'he'd lost touch with the family.'

Soames had often noticed in old days how much more neighbourly his family
were to the dead than to the living. But, now, the way they had flocked to
Fleur's wedding and abstained from Timothy's funeral, seemed to show some
vital change. There might, of course, be another reason; for Soames felt that if
he had not known the contents of Timothy's Will, he might have stayed away
himself through delicacy. Timothy had left a lot of money, with nobody in
particular to leave it to. They mightn't like to seem to expect something.

At twelve o'clock the procession left the door; Timothy alone in the first
carriage under glass. Then Soames alone; then Gradman alone; then Cook and
Smither together. They started at a walk, but were soon trotting under a bright
sky. At the entrance to Highgate Cemetery they were delayed by service in the
Chapel. Soames would have liked to stay outside in the sunshine. He didn't
believe a word of it; on the other hand, it was a form of insurance which could
not safely be neglected, in case there might be something in it after all.

They walked up two and two–he and Gradman, Cook and Smither–to the
family vault. It was not very distinguished for the funeral of the last old
Forsyte.

He took Gradman into his carriage on the way back to the Bayswater Road
with a certain glow in his heart. He had a surprise in pickle for the old chap who
had served the Forsytes four-and-fifty years–a treat that was entirely his doing.
How well he remembered saying to Timothy the day after Aunt Hester's
funeral: 'Well, Uncle Timothy, there's Gradman. He's taken a lot of trouble for
the family. What do you say to leaving him five thousand?' and his surprise,
seeing the difficulty there had been in getting Timothy to leave anything, when
Timothy had nodded. And now the old chap would be as pleased as Punch, for
Mrs Gradman, he knew, had a weak heart, and their son had lost a leg in the
War. It was extraordinarily gratifying to Soames to have left him five thousand
pounds of Timothy's money. They sat down together in the little drawing-
room, whose walls–like a vision of heaven–were sky-blue and gold with every

picture-frame unnaturally bright, and every speck of dust removed from every piece of furniture, to read that little masterpiece–the Will of Timothy. With his back to the light in Aunt Hester's chair, Soames faced Gradman with his face to the light on Aunt Ann's sofa; and, crossing his legs, began:

'This is the last Will and Testament of me Timothy Forsyte of The Bower Bayswater Road London I appoint my nephew Soames Forsyte of The Shelter Mapledurham and Thomas Gradman of 159 Folly Road Highgate (hereinafter called my Trustees) to be the trustees and executors of this my Will. To the said Soames Forsyte I leave the sum of one thousand pounds free of legacy duty and to the said Thomas Gradman I leave the sum of five thousand pounds free of legacy duty.'

Soames paused. Old Gradman was leaning forward, convulsively gripping a stout black knee with each of this thick hands; his mouth had fallen open so that the gold fillings of three teeth gleamed; his eyes were blinking, two tears rolled slowly out of them. Soames read hastily on.

'All the rest of my property of whatsoever description I bequeath to my Trustees upon Trust to convert and hold the same upon the following trusts namely. To pay thereout all my debts funeral expenses and outgoings of any kind in connection with my Will and to hold the residue thereof in trust for that male lineal descendant of my father Jolyon Forsyte by his marriage with Ann Pierce who after the decease of all lineal descendants whether male or female of my said father by his said marriage in being at the time of my death shall last attain the age of twenty-one years absolutely it being my desire that my property shall be nursed to the extreme limit permitted by the laws of England for the benefit of such male lineal descendant as aforesaid.'

Soames read the investment and attestation clauses, and ceasing, looked at Gradman. The old fellow was wiping his brow with a large handkerchief, whose brilliant colour supplied a sudden festive tinge to the proceedings.

'My word, Mr Soames!' he said, and it was clear that the lawyer in him had utterly wiped out the man: 'My word! Why, there are two babies now, and some quite young children–if one of them lives to be eighty–it's not a great age–and add twenty-one–that's a hundred years; and Mr Timothy worth a hundred and fifty thousand pound nett if he's worth a penny. Compound interest at five per cent. doubles you in fourteen years. In fourteen years three hundred thousand–six hundred thousand in twenty-eight–twelve hundred thousand in forty-two–twenty-four hundred thousand in fifty-six–four million eight hundred thousand in seventy–nine million six hundred thousand in eighty-four–. Why, in a hundred years it'll be twenty million! And we shan't live to see it! It *is* a Will!'

Soames said dryly: 'Anything may happen. The State might take the lot; they're capable of anything in these days.'

'And carry five,' said Gradman to himself. 'I forgot–Mr Timothy's in Consols; we shan't get more than two per cent. with this income tax. To be on the safe side, say eight million. Still, that's a pretty penny.'

Soames rose and handed him the Will. 'You're going into the City. Take care of that, and do what's necessary. Advertise; but there are no debts. When's the sale?'

'Tuesday week,' said Gradman. 'Life or lives in bein' and twenty-one years afterward–it's a long way off. But I'm glad he's left it in the family. . . .'

The sale–not at Jobson's, in view of the Victorian nature of the effects–was far more freely attended than the funeral, though not by Cook and Smither, for

Soames had taken it on himself to give them their heart's desires. Winifred was present, Euphemia, and Francie, and Eustace had come in his car. The miniatures, Barbizons, and J. R. drawings had been bought in by Soames; and relics of no marketable value were set aside in an off-room for members of the family who cared to have mementoes. These were the only restrictions upon bidding characterised by an almost tragic langour. Not one piece of furniture, no picture or porcelain figure appealed to modern taste. The humming-birds had fallen like autumn leaves when taken from where they had not hummed for sixty years. It was painful to Soames to see the chairs his aunts had sat on, the little grand piano they had practically never played, the books whose outsides they had gazed at, the china they had dusted, the curtains they had drawn, the hearth-rug which had warmed their feet; above all, the beds they had lain and died in—sold to little dealers, and the housewives of Fulham. And yet—what could one do? Buy them and stick them in a lumber-room? No; they had to go the way of all flesh and furniture, and be worn out. But when they put up Aunt Ann's sofa and were going to knock it down for thirty shillings, he cried out, suddenly: 'Five pounds!' The sensation was considerable, and the sofa his.

When that little sale was over in the fusty sale-room, and those Victorian ashes scattered, he went out into the misty October sunshine feeling as if cosiness had died out of the world, and the board 'To Let' was up, indeed. Revolutions on the horizon; Fleur in Spain, no comfort in Annette; no Timothy's on the Bayswater Road. In the irritable desolation of his soul he went into the Goupenor Gallery. That chap Jolyon's water-colours were on view there. He went in to look down his nose at them—it might give him some faint satisfaction. The news had trickled through from June to Val's wife, from her to Val, from Val to his mother, from her to Soames, that the house—the fatal house at Robin Hill—was for sale, and Irene going to join her boy out in British Columbia, or some such place. For one wild moment the thought had come to Soames: 'Why shouldn't I buy it back? I meant it for my—!' No sooner come than gone. Too lugubrious a triumph; with too many humiliating memories for himself and Fleur. She would never live there after what had happened. No, the place must go its way to some peer or profiteer. It had been a bone of contention from the first, the shell of the feud; and with the woman gone, it was an empty shell. 'For Sale or To Let'. With his mind's eye he could see that board raised high above the ivied wall which he had built.

He passed through the first of the two rooms in the Gallery. There was certainly a body of work! And now that the fellow was dead it did not seem so trivial. The drawings were pleasing enough, with quite a sense of atmosphere, and something individual in the brush work. 'His father and my father; he and I; his child and mine!' thought Soames. So it had gone on! And all about that woman! Softened by the events of the past week, affected by the melancholy beauty of the autumn day, Soames came nearer than he had ever been to realisation of that truth—passing the understanding of a Forsyte pure—that the body of Beauty has a spiritual essence, uncapturable save by a devotion which thinks not of self. After all, he was near that truth in his devotion to his daughter; perhaps that made him understand a little how he had missed the prize. And there, among the drawings of his kinsman, who had attained to that which he had found beyond his reach, he thought of him and her with a tolerance which surprised him. But he did not buy a drawing.

Just as he passed the seat of custom on his return to the outer air he met with a contingency which had not been entirely absent from his mind when he went into the Gallery—Irene, herself, coming in. So she had not gone yet, and was still paying farewell visits to that fellow's remains! He subdued the little involuntary leap of his subconsciousness, the mechanical reaction of his senses to the charm of this once-owned woman, and passed her with averted eyes. But when he had gone by he could not for the life of him help looking back. This, then, was finality—the heat and stress of his life, the madness and the longing thereof, the only defeat he had known, would be over when she faded from his view this time; even such memories had their own queer aching value. She, too, was looking back. Suddenly she lifted her gloved hand, her lips smiled faintly, her dark eyes seemed to speak. It was the turn of Soames to make no answer to that smile and that little farewell wave; he went out into the fashionable street quivering from head to foot. He knew what she had meant to say: 'Now that I am going for ever out of the reach of you and yours—forgive me; I wish you well.' That was the meaning; last sign of that terrible reality—passing morality, duty, common sense—her aversion from him who had owned her body, but had never touched her spirit or her heart. It hurt; yes—more than if she had kept her mask unmoved, her hand unlifted.

Three days later, in that fast-yellowing October, Soames took a taxi-cab to Highgate Cemetery and mounted through its white forest to the Forsyte vault. Close to the cedar, above catacombs and columbaria, tall, ugly, and individual, it looked like an apex of the competitive system. He could remember a discussion wherein Swithin had advocated the addition to its face of the pheasant proper. The proposal had been rejected in favour of a wreath in stone, above the stark words: 'The family vault of Jolyon Forsyte: 1850'. It was in good order. All trace of the recent interment had been removed, and its sober grey gloomed reposefully in the sunshine. The whole family lay there now, except old Jolyon's wife, who had gone back under a contract to her own family vault in Suffolk; old Jolyon himself lying at Robin Hill; and Susan Hayman, cremated so that none might know where she might be. Soames gazed at it with satisfaction—massive, needing little attention; and this was important, for he was well aware that no one would attend to it when he himself was gone, and he would have to be looking out for lodgings soon. He might have twenty years before him, but one never knew. Twenty years without an aunt or uncle, with a wife of whom one had better not know anything, with a daughter gone from home. His mood inclined to melancholy and retrospection.

This cemetery was full, they said—of people with extraordinary names, buried in extraordinary taste. Still, they had a fine view up here, right over London. Annette had once given him a story to read by that Frenchman, Maupassant—a most lugubrious concern, where all the skeletons emerged from their graves one night, and all the pious inscriptions on the stones were altered to descriptions of their sins. Not a true story at all. He didn't know about the French, but there was not much real harm in English people except their teeth and their taste, which were certainly deplorable. 'The family vault of Jolyon Forsyte: 1850'. A lot of people had been buried here since then—a lot of English life crumbled to mould and dust! The boom of an airplane passing under the gold-tinted clouds caused him to lift his eyes. The deuce of a lot of expansion had gone on. But it all came back to a cemetery—to a name and a date on a tomb. And he thought with a curious pride that he and his family had done little or nothing to help this feverish expansion. Good solid middlemen, they had gone to work with dignity to manage and possess. 'Superior Dosset', indeed, had built in a dreadful, and Jolyon painted in a doubtful, period, but so far as he remembered not another of them all had soiled his hands by creating anything–unless you counted Val Dartie and his horse-breeding. Collectors, solicitors, barristers, merchants, publishers, accountants, directors, land agents, even soldiers–there they had been! The country had expanded, as it were, in spite of them. They had checked, controlled, defended, and taken advantage of the process–and when you considered how 'Superior Dosset' had begun life with next to nothing, and his lineal descendants already owned what old Gradman estimated at between a million and a million and a half, it was not so bad! And yet he sometimes felt as if the family bolt was shot, their possessive instinct dying out. They seemed unable to make money–this fourth generation; they were going into art, literature, farming, or the army; or just living on what was left them–they had no push and no tenacity. They would die out if they didn't take care.

Soames turned from the vault and faced toward the breeze. The air up here would be delicious if only he could rid his nerves of the feeling that mortality was in it. He gazed restlessly at the crosses and the urns, the angels, the 'immortelles', the flowers, gaudy or withering, and suddenly he noticed a spot which seemed so different from anything else up there that he was obliged to walk the few necessary yards and look at it. A sober corner, with a massive queer-shaped cross of grey rough-hewn granite, guarded by four dark yew trees. The spot was free from the pressure of the other graves, having a little box-hedged garden on the far side, and in front, a goldening birch tree. This oasis in the desert of conventional graves appealed to the æsthetic sense of Soames, and he sat down there in the sunshine. Through those trembling gold birch leaves he gazed out at London, and yielded to the waves of memory. He thought of Irene in Montpelier Square, when her hair was rusty golden and her white shoulders his–Irene, the prize of his love-passion, resistant to his ownership. He saw Bosinney's body lying in that white mortuary, and Irene sitting on the sofa looking at space with the eyes of a dying bird. Again he thought of her by the little green Niobe in the Bois de Boulogne, once more rejecting him. His fancy took him on beside his drifting river on the November day when Fleur was to be born, took him to the dead leaves floating on the green-tinged water and the snake-headed weed for ever swaying and nosing, sinuous, blind, tethered. And on again to the window opened to the cold starry night above Hyde Park, with his father lying dead. His fancy darted to that picture of 'the future town', to that boy's and Fleur's first meeting; to the bluish trail of Prosper Profond's cigar, and Fleur in the window pointing down to where the fellow prowled. To the sight of Irene and that dead fellow sitting side by side in the stand at Lord's. To her and that boy at Robin Hill. To the sofa, where Fleur lay crushed up in the corner; to her lips pressed into his cheek, and her farewell 'Daddy'. And suddenly he saw again Irene's grey-gloved hand waving its last gesture of release.

He sat there a long time dreaming his career, faithful to the scut of his possessive instinct, warming himself even with its failures.

'To Let'–the Forsyte age and way of life, when a man owned his soul, his investments, and his woman, without check or question. And now the State had, or would have, his investments, his woman had herself, and God knew who had his soul. 'To Let'–that sane and simple creed!

The waters of change were foaming in, carrying the promise of new forms only when their destructive flood should have passed its full. He sat there, subconscious of them, but with his thoughts resolutely set on the past—as a man might ride into a wild night with his face to the tail of his galloping horse. Athwart the Victorian dykes the waters were rolling on property, manners, and morals, on melody and the old forms of art—waters bringing to his mouth a salt taste as of blood, lapping to the foot of this Highgate Hill where Victorianism lay buried. And sitting there, high up on its most individual spot, Soames—like a figure of Investment—refused their restless sounds. Instinctively he would not fight them—there was in him too much primeval wisdom, of Man the possessive animal. They would quiet down when they had fulfilled their tidal fever of dispossessing and destroying; when the creations and the properties of others were sufficiently broken and dejected—they would lapse and ebb, and fresh forms would rise based on an instinct older than the fever of change—the instinct of Home.

'*Je m'en fiche*,' said Prosper Profond. Soames did not say '*Je m'en fiche*'—it was French, and the fellow was a thorn in his side—but deep down he knew that change was only the interval of death between two forms of life, destruction necessary to make room for fresher property. What though the board was up, and cosiness to let?—someone would come along and take it again some day.

And only one thing really troubled him, sitting there—the melancholy craving in his heart—because the sun was like enchantment on his face and on the clouds and on the golden birch leaves, and the wind's rustle was so gentle, and the yew tree green so dark, and the sickle of a moon pale in the sky.

He might wish and wish and never get it—the beauty and the loving in the world!

A Modern Comedy

BOOK I

The White Monkey

A MODERN COMEDY

To my wife

without whom I know not what
could have been written,
this second trilogy of
the Forsyte chronicles
is
dedicated

THE WHITE MONKEY

'No retreat, no retreat
They must conquer or die
Who have no retreat!'

Mr Gay

TO MAX BEERBOHM

PART I

I

PROMENADE

Coming down the steps of 'Snooks' Club, so nicknamed by George Forsyte in the late 'eighties, on that momentous mid-October afternoon of 1922, Sir Lawrence Mont, ninth baronet, set his fine nose towards the east wind, and moved his thin legs with speed. Political by birth rather than by nature, he reviewed the revolution which had restored his Party to power with a detachment not devoid of humour. Passing the Remove Club, he thought. 'Some sweating into shoes, there! No more confectioned dishes. A woodcock–without trimmings, for a change!'

The captains and the kings had departed from 'Snooks' before he entered it, for he was not of 'that catch-penny-crew, now paid off, no sir; fellows who turned their tails on the land the moment the war was over. Pah!' But for an hour he had listened to echoes, and his lively twisting mind, embedded in deposits of the past, sceptical of the present and of all political protestations and pronouncements, had recorded with amusement the confusion of patriotism and personalities left behind by the fateful gathering. Like most landowners, he distrusted doctrine. If he had a political belief, it was a tax on wheat; and so far as he could see, he was now alone in it–but then he was not seeking election; in other words, his principle was not in danger of extinction from the votes of those who had to pay for bread. Principles–he mused–*au fond* were pocket; and he wished the deuce people wouldn't pretend they weren't! Pocket, in the deep sense of that word, of course, self-interest as member of a definite community. And how the devil was this definite community, the English nation, to exist, when all its land was going out of cultivation, and all its ships and docks in danger of destruction by aeroplanes? He had listened that hour past for a single mention of the land. Not one! It was not practical politics! Confound the fellows! They had to wear their breeches out–keeping seats or getting them. No connection between posteriors and posterity! No, by George! Thus reminded of posterity, it occurred to him rather suddenly that his son's wife showed no signs as yet. Two years! Time they were thinking about children. It was dangerous to get into the habit of not having them, when a title and estate depended. A smile twisted his lips and eyebrows which resembled spinneys of dark pothooks. A pretty young creature, most taking; and knew it, too! Whom was she not getting to know? Lions and tigers, monkeys and cats–her house was becoming quite a menagerie of more or less celebrities. There was a certain unreality about that sort of thing! And opposite a British lion in Trafalgar Square Sir Lawrence thought: 'She'll be getting these to her house next! She's got the collecting habit. Michael must look out—in a collector's house there's always a lumber-room for old junk, and husbands are liable to get into it. That reminds me: I promised her a Chinese Minister. Well, she must wait now till after the General Election.'

Down Whitehall, under the grey easterly sky, the towers of Westminster came for a second into view. 'A certain unreality in that, too,' he thought. 'Michael and his fads! Well, it's the fashion—Socialistic principles and a rich wife. Sacrifice with safety! Peace with plenty! Nostrums—ten a penny!'

Passing the newspaper hubbub of Charing Cross, frenzied by the political crisis, he turned up to the left towards Danby and Winter, publishers, where his son was junior partner. A new theme for a book had just begun to bend a mind which had already produced a 'Life of Montrose, Far Cathay', that work of Eastern travel, and a fanciful conversation between the shades of Gladstone, and Disraeli—entitled 'A Duet'. With every step taken, from 'Snooks' eastward, his erect thin figure in astrakhan-collared coat, his thin grey-moustached face, and tortoise-shell rimmed monocle under the lively dark eyebrow, had seemed more rare. It became almost a phenomenon in this dingy back street, where carts stuck like winter flies, and persons went by with books under their arms, as if educated.

He had nearly reached the door of Danby's when he encountered two young men. One of them was clearly his son, better dressed since his marriage, and smoking a cigar—thank goodness—instead of those eternal cigarettes; the other—ah! yes—Michael's sucking poet and best man, head in air, rather a sleek head under a velour hat! He said:

'Ha, Michael!'

'*Hallo*, Bart! You know my governor, Wilfrid! Wilfrid Desert. "Copper Coin"—some poet, Bart, I tell you. You must read him. We're going home. Come along!'

Sir Lawrence went along.

'What happened at "Snooks"?'

'*Le roi est mort*. Labour can start lying, Michael—election next month.'

'Bart was brought up, Wilfrid, in days that knew not Demos.'

'Well, Mr Desert, do *you* find reality in politics now?'

'Do you find reality in anything, sir?'

'In income tax, perhaps.'

Michael grinned.

'Above knighthood,' he said, 'there's no such thing as simple faith.'

'Suppose your friends came into power, Michael—in some ways not a bad thing, help 'em to grow up—what could they do, eh? Could they raise national taste? Abolish the cinema? Teach English people to cook? Prevent other countries from threatening war? Make us grow our own food? Stop the increase of town life? Would they hang dabblers in poison gas? Could they prevent flying in war-time? Could they weaken the possessive instinct—anywhere? Or do anything, in fact, but alter the incidence of possession a little? All party politics are top dressing. We're ruled by the inventors, and human nature; and we live in Queer Street, Mr Desert.'

'Much my sentiments, sir.'

Michael flourished his cigar.

'Bad old men, you two!'

And removing their hats, they passed the Cenotaph.

'Curiously symptomatic—that thing,' said Sir Lawrence; 'monument to the dread of swank–most characteristic. And the dread of swank–'

'Go on, Bart,' said Michael.

'The fine, the large, the florid–all off! No far-sighted views, no big schemes, no great principles, no great religion, or great art–aestheticism in cliques and backwaters, small men in small hats.'

'As panteth the heart after Byron, Wilberforce, and the Nelson Monument. My poor old Bart! What about it, Wilfrid?'

'Yes, Mr Desert–what about it?'

Desert's dark face contracted.

'It's an age of paradox,' he said. 'We all kick up for freedom, and the only institutions gaining strength are Socialism and the Roman Catholic Church. We're frightfully self-conscious about art–and the only art development is the cinema. We're nuts on peace–and all we're doing about it is to perfect poison gas.'

Sir Lawrence glanced sideways at a young man so bitter.

'And how's publishing, Michael?'

'Well, "Copper Coin" is selling like hot cakes; and there's quite a movement in "A Duet". What about this for a new ad.: "A Duet, by Sir Lawrence Mont, Bart. The most distinguished Conversation ever held between the Dead." That ought to get the psychic. Wilfrid suggested "G.O.M. and Dizzy–broadcasted from Hell." Which do you like best?'

They had come, however, to a policeman holding up his hand against the nose of a van horse, so that everything marked time. The engines of the cars whirred idly, their drivers' faces set towards the space withheld from them; a girl on a bicycle looked vacantly about her, grasping the back of the van, where a youth sat sideways with his legs stretched out towards her. Sir Lawrence glanced again at young Desert. A thin, pale-dark face, good-looking, but a hitch in it, as if not properly timed; nothing *outré* in dress or manner, and yet socially at large; less vivacious than that lively rascal, his own son, but as anchorless, and more sceptical–might feel things pretty deeply, though! The policeman lowered his arm.

'You were in the war, Mr Desert?'

'Oh, yes.'

'Air service?'

'And line. Bit of both.'

'Hard on a poet.'

'Not at all. Poetry's only possible when you may be blown up at any moment, or when you live in Putney.'

Sir Lawrence's eyebrow rose. 'Yes?'

'Tennyson, Browning, Wordsworth, Swinburne–they could turn it out; *ils vivaient, mais si peu.*'

'Is there not a third condition favourable?'

'And that, sir?'

'How shall I express it–a certain cerebral agitation in connection with women?'

Desert's face twitched, and seemed to darken.

Michael put his latchkey into the lock of his front door.

2

HOME

The house in South Square, Westminster, to which the young Monts had come after their Spanish honeymoon two years before, might have been called 'emancipated'. It was the work of an architect whose dream was a new house perfectly old, and an old house perfectly new. It followed, therefore, no recognised style or tradition, and was devoid of structural prejudice; but it soaked up the smuts of the metropolis with such special rapidity that its stone already respectably resembled that of Wren. Its windows and doors had gently rounded tops. The high-sloping roof, of a fine sooty pink, was almost Danish, and two 'ducky little windows' looked out of it, giving an impression that very tall servants lived up there. There were rooms on each side of the front door, which was wide and set off by bay trees in black and gold bindings. The house was thick through, and the staircase, of a broad chastity, began at the far end of a hall which had room for quite a number of hats and coats and cards. There were four bathrooms; and not even a cellar underneath. The Forsyte instinct for a house had co-operated in its acquisiton. Soames had picked it up for his daughter, undecorated, at that psychological moment when the bubble of inflation was pricked, and the air escaping from the balloon of the world's trade. Fleur, however, had established immediate contact with the architect–an element which Soames himself had never quite got over–and decided not to have more than three styles in her house: Chinese, Spanish, and her own. The room to the left of the front door, running the breadth of the house, was Chinese, with ivory panels, a copper floor, central heating, and cut-glass lustres. It contained four pictures–all Chinese–the only school in which her father had not yet dabbled. The fireplace, wide and open, had Chinese dogs with Chinese tiles for them to stand on. The silk was chiefly of jade green. There were two wonderful old black tea-chests, picked up with Soames's money at Jobson's–not a bargain. There was no piano, partly because pianos were too uncompromisingly occidental, and partly because it would have taken up much room. Fleur aimed at space–collecting people rather than furniture or *bibelots*. The light, admitted by windows at both ends, was unfortunately not Chinese. She would stand sometimes in the centre of this room, thinking–how to 'bunch' her guests, how to make her room more Chinese without making it uncomfortable; how to seem to know all about literature and politics; how to accept everything her father gave her, without making him aware that his taste had no sense of the future; how to keep hold of Sibley Swan, the new literary star, and to get hold of Gurdon Minho, the old; of how Wilfrid Desert was getting too fond of her; of what was really her style in dress; of why Michael had such funny ears; and sometimes she stood not thinking at all–just aching a little.

When those three came in she was sitting before a red lacquer tea-table, finishing a very good tea. She always had tea brought in rather early, so that she could have a good quiet preliminary 'tuck-in' all by herself, because she was not quite twenty-one, and this was her hour for remembering her youth. By her side Ting-a-ling was standing on his hind feet, his tawny forepaws on a Chinese foot-stool, his snubbed black and tawny muzzle turned up towards the fruits of his philosophy.

'That'll do, Ting. No more, ducky! *No more!*'

The expression of Ting-a-ling answered:

'Well, then, stop, too! Don't subject me to torture!'

A year and three months old, he had been bought by Michael out of a Bond Street shop window on Fleur's twentieth birthday, eleven months ago.

Two years of married life had not lengthened her short dark chestnut hair; had added a little more decision to her quick lips, a little more allurement to her white-lidded, dark-lashed hazel eyes, a little more poise and swing to her carriage, a little more chest and hip measurement; had taken a little from waist and calf measurement, a little colour from cheeks a little less round, and a little sweetness from a voice a little more caressing.

She stood up behind the tray, holding out her white round arms without a word. She avoided unnecessary greetings or farewells. She would have had to say them so often, and their purpose was better served by look, pressure, and slight inclination of head to one side.

With circular movement of her squeezed hand, she said:

'Draw up. Cream, sir? Sugar, Wilfrid? Ting has had too much—don't feed him. Hand things, Michael. I've heard all about the meeting at "Snooks". You're not going to canvass for Labour, Michael—canvassing's so silly. If anyone canvassed me, I should vote the other way at once.'

'Yes, darling; but you're not the average elector.'

Fleur looked at him. Very sweetly put! Conscious of Wilfrid biting his lips, of Sir Lawrence taking that in, of the amount of silk leg she was showing, of her black and cream teacups, she adjusted these matters. A flutter of her white lids—Desert ceased to bite his lips; a movement of her silk legs—Sir Lawrence ceased to look at him. Holding out her cups, she said:

'I suppose I'm not modern enough?'

Desert, moving a bright little spoon round in his magpie cup, said without looking up:

'As much more modern than the moderns, as you are more ancient.'

''Ware poetry!' said Michael.

But when he had taken his father to see the new cartoons by Aubrey Greene, she said:

'Kindly tell me what you meant, Wilfrid.'

Desert's voice seemed to leap from restraint.

'What does it matter? I don't want to waste time with that.'

'But I want to know. It sounded like a sneer.'

'A sneer? From me? Fleur!'

'Then tell me.'

'I meant that you have all their restlessness and practical get-thereness; but you have what they haven't, Fleur—power to turn one's head. And mine is turned. You know it.'

'How would Michael like that—from *you*, his best man?'

Desert moved quickly to the windows.

Fleur took Ting-a-ling on her lap. Such things had been said to her before; but from Wilfrid it was serious. Nice to think she had his heart, of course! Only, where on earth could she put it, where it wouldn't be seen except by her? He was incalculable—did strange things! She was a little afraid—not of him, but of that quality in him. He came back to the hearth, and said:

'Ugly, isn't it? Put that damn' dog down, Fleur; I can't see your face. If you were really fond of Michael—I swear I wouldn't; but you're not, you know.'

Fleur said coldly:

'You know very little; I *am* fond of Michael.'

Desert gave his little jerky laugh.

'Oh yes; not the sort that counts.'

Fleur looked up.

'It counts quite enough to make one safe.'

'A flower that I can't pick.'

Fleur nodded.

'Quite sure, Fleur? Quite, quite sure?'

Fleur stared; her eyes softened a little, her eyelids, so excessively white, drooped over them; she nodded. Desert said slowly:

'The moment I believe that, I shall go East.'

'East?'

'Not so stale as going West, but much the same—you don't come back.'

Fleur thought: 'The East? I should love to know the East! Pity one can't manage that, too. Pity!'

'You won't keep me in your Zoo, my dear. I shan't hang around and feed on crumbs. You know what I feel—it means a smash of some sort.'

'It hasn't been my fault, has it?'

'Yes; you've collected me, as you collect everybody that comes near you.'

'I don't know what you mean.'

Desert bent down, and dragged her hand to his lips.

'Don't be riled with me; I'm too unhappy.'

Fleur let her hand stay against his hot lips.

'Sorry, Wilfrid.'

'All right, dear. I'll go.'

'But you're coming to dinner to-morrow?'

Desert said violently:

'*To-morrow?* Good God—no! What d'you think I'm made of?'

He flung her hand away.

'I don't like violence, Wilfrid.'

'Well, good-bye; I'd better go.'

The words 'And you'd better not come again' trembled up to her lips, but were not spoken. Part from Wilfrid—life would lose a little warmth! She waved her hand. He was gone. She heard the door closing. Poor Wilfrid?—nice to think of a flame at which to warm her hands! Nice but rather dreadful! And suddenly, dropping Ting-a-ling, she got up and began to walk about the room. To-morrow! Second anniversary of her wedding-day! Still an ache when she thought of what it had not been. But there was little time to think—and she made less. What good in thinking? Only one life, full of people, of things to do and have, of things wanted—a life only void of—one thing, and that—well, if people had it, they never had it long! On her lids two tears, which had gathered, dried without falling. Sentimentalism! No! The last thing in the world—the unforgivable offence! Whom should she put next to whom to-morrow? And whom should she get in place of Wilfrid, if Wilfrid wouldn't come—silly boy! One day—one night—what difference? Who should sit on her right, and who on

her left? Was Aubrey Greene more distinguished, or Sibley Swan? Were they
either as distinguished as Walter Nazing or Charles Upshire? Dinner of twelve,
exclusively literary and artistic, except for Michael and Alison Charwell. Ah!
Could Alison get her Gurdon Minho—just one writer of the old school, one
glass of old wine to mellow effervescence? He didn't publish with Danby and
Winter; but he fed out of Alison's hand. She went quickly to one of the old tea-
chests, and opened it. Inside was a telephone.

'Can I speak to Lady Alison—Mrs Michael Mont ... Yes ... That you,
Alison? ... Fleur speaking. Wilfrid has fallen through to-morrow night ... Is
there any chance of your bringing Gurdon Minho? I don't know him, of course;
but he might be interested. You'll try? ... That'll be ever so delightful. Isn't
the "Snooks" Club meeting rather exciting? Bart says they'll eat each other
now they've split ... About Mr Minho. Could you let me know to-night?
Thanks—thanks awfully! ... Good-bye!'

Failing Minho, whom? Her mind hovered over the names in her address
book. At so late a minute it must be someone who didn't stand on ceremony;
but except Alison, none of Michael's relations would be safe from Sibley Swan
or Nesta Gorse, and their subversive shafts; as to the Forsytes—out of the
question; they had their own sub-acid humour (some of them), but they were
not modern, not really modern. Besides, she saw as little of them as she
could—they dated, belonged to the dramatic period, had no sense of life without
beginning or end. No! If Gurdon Minho was a frost, it would have to be a
musician, whose works were hieroglyphical with a dash of surgery; or, better,
perhaps, a psychoanalyst. Her fingers turned the pages till she came to those
two categories. Hugo Solstis? A possibility; but suppose he wanted to play
them something recent? There was only Michael's upright Grand, and that
would mean going to his study. Better Gerald Hanks—he and Nesta Gorse
would get off together on dreams; still, if they did, there would be no actual loss
of life. Yes, failing Gurdon Minho, Gerald Hanks; he would be free—and put
him between Alison and Nesta. She closed the book, and, going back to her
jade-green settee, sat gazing at Ting-a-ling. The little dog's prominent round
eyes gazed back; bright, black, very old. Fleur thought: 'I *don't* want Wilfrid to
drop off.' Among all the crowd who came and went, here, there and
everywhere, she cared for nobody. Keep up with them, keep up with
everything, of course! It was all frightfully amusing, frightfully necessary!
Only—only—what?

Voices! Michael and Bart coming back. Bart had noticed Wilfrid. He *was* a
noticing old Bart. She was never very comfortable when he was about—lively
and twisting, but with something settled and ancestral in him; a little like Ting-
a-ling—something judgmatic, ever telling her that she was fluttering and new.
He was anchored, could only move to the length of his old-fashioned cord, but
he could drop on to things disconcertingly. Still, he admired her, she felt—oh!
yes.

Well! What had he thought of the cartoons? Ought Michael to publish them,
and with letterpress or without? Didn't he think the cubic called 'Still Life'—of
the Government—too frightfully funny, especially the 'old bean' representing
the Prime? For answer she was conscious of a twisting, rapid noise; Sir
Lawrence was telling her of his father's collection of electioneering cartoons.
She did wish Bart would not tell her about his father; he had been so
distinguished, and he must have been so dull, paying all his calls on horseback,
with trousers strapped under his boots. He and Lord Charles Cariboo and the

Marquis of Forfar had been the last three 'callers' of that sort. If only they hadn't, they'd have been clean forgot. She had that dress to try, and fourteen things to see to, and Hugo's concert began at eight-fifteen! Why did people of the last generation always have so much time? And, suddenly, she looked down. Ting-a-ling was licking the copper floor. She took him up: 'Not that, darling; nasty!' Ah! the spell was broken! Bart was going, reminiscent to the last. She waited at the foot of the stairs till Michael shut the door on him, then flew. Reaching her room, she turned on all the lights. Here was her own style–a bed which did not look like one, and many mirrors. The couch of Ting-a-ling occupied a corner, whence he could see himself in three. She put him down, and said: 'Keep quiet, now!' His attitude to the other dogs in the room had long become indifferent; though of his own breed and precisely his colouring, they had no smell and no licking power in their tongues–nothing to be done with them, imitative creatures, incredibly unresponsive.

Stripping off her dress, Fleur held the new frock under her chin.

'May I kiss you?' said a voice, and there was Michael's image behind her own reflection in the glass.

'My dear boy, there isn't time! Help me with this.' She slipped the frock over her head. 'Do those three top hooks. How do you like it? Oh! and–Michael! Gurdon Minho may be coming to dinner to-morrow–Wilfrid can't. Have you read his things? Sit down and tell me something about them. All novels, aren't they? What sort?'

'Well, he's always had something to say. And his cats are good. He's a bit romantic, of course.'

'Oh! Have I made a gaff?'

'Not a bit; jolly good shot. The vice of our lot is, they say it pretty well, but they've nothing to say. They won't last.'

'But that's just why they will last. They won't date.'

'Won't they? My gum!'

'Wilfrid will last.'

'Ah! Wilfrid has emotions, hates, pities, wants; at least sometimes; when he has, his stuff is jolly good. Otherwise, he just makes a song about nothing–like the rest.'

Fleur tucked in the top of her undergarment.

'But, Michael, if that's so, we–I've got the wrong lot.'

Michael grinned.

'My dear child! The lot of the hour is always right; only you've got to watch it, and change it quick enough.'

'But d'you mean to say that Sibley isn't going to live?'

'Sib? Lord, no!'

'But he's so perfectly sure that almost everybody else is dead or dying. Surely he has critical genius!'

'If I hadn't more judgment than Sib, I'd go out of publishing to-morrow.'

'You–more than Sibley Swan?'

'Of course, I've more judgment than Sib. Why! Sib's judgment is just his opinion of Sib–common or garden impatience of anyone else. He doesn't even read them. He'll read one specimen of every author and say: 'Oh! that fellow! He's dull, or he's moral, or he's sentimental, or he dates, or he drivels'–I've heard him dozens of times. That's if they're alive. Of course, if they're dead, it's different. He's always digging up and canonising the dead; that's how he's got his name. There's always a Sib in literature. He's a standing example of how people can get taken at their own valuation. But as to lasting–of course he won't; he's never creative, even by mistake.'

Fleur had lost the thread. Yes! It suited her–quite a nice line! Off with it! Must write those three notes before she dressed.

Michael had begun again.

'Take my tip, Fleur. The really big people don't talk–and don't bunch–they paddle their own canoes in what seem backwaters. But it's the backwaters that make the main stream. By Jove, that's a *mot*, or is it a bull; and are bulls *mots* or *mots* bulls?'

'Michael, if you were me, would you tell Frederic Wilmer that he'll be meeting Hubert Marsland at lunch next week? Would it bring him or would it put him off?'

'Marsland's rather an old duck, Wilmer's rather an old goose–I don't know.'

'Oh! do be serious, Michael–you never give me any help in arranging–No! Don't maul my shoulders please.'

'Well, darling, I *don't* know. I've no genius for such things, like you. Marsland paints windmills, cliffs and things–I doubt if he's heard of the future. He's almost a Mathew Maris for keeping out of the swim. If you think he'd like to meet a Vertiginist–'

'I didn't ask you if he'd like to meet Wilmer; I asked you if Wilmer would like to meet him.'

'Wilmer will just say: "I like little Mrs Mont, she gives deuced good grub"–and so you do, ducky. A Vertiginist wants nourishing, you know, or it wouldn't go to his head.'

Fleur's pen resumed its swift strokes, already become slightly illegible. She murmured:

'I think Wilfrid would help–you won't be there; one–two–three. What women?'

'Four painters–pretty and plump; no intellect.'

Fleur said crossly:

'I can't get them plump; they don't go about now.' And her pen flowed on:

'DEAR WILFRID,–Wednesday–lunch; Wilmer, Hubert Marsland, two other women. Do help me live it down.

'Yours ever,
'FLEUR.'

'Michael, your chin is like a bootbrush.'

'Sorry, old thing; your shoulders shouldn't be so smooth. Bart gave Wilfrid a tip as we were coming along.'

Fleur stopped writing. 'Oh!'

'Reminded him that the state of love was a good stunt for poets.'

'Apropos of what?'

'Wilfrid was complaining that he couldn't turn it out now.'

'Nonsense! His last things are his best.'

'Well, that's what I think. Perhaps he's forestalled the tip. Has he, d'you know?'

Fleur turned her eyes towards the face behind her shoulder. No, it had its native look–frank, irresponsible, slightly fawn-like, with its pointed ears, quick lips, and nostrils.

She said slowly,

'If *you* don't know, nobody does.'

A snuffle interrupted Michael's answer. Ting-a-ling, long, low, slightly higher at both ends, was standing between them, with black muzzle upturned. 'My pedigree is long,' he seemed to say: 'but my legs are short—what about it?'

3

MUSICAL

According to a great and guiding principle, Fleur and Michael Mont attended the Hugo Solstis concert, not because they anticipated pleasure, but because they knew Hugo. They felt, besides, that Solstis, an Englishman of Russo-Dutch extraction, was one of those who were restoring English music, giving to it a wide and spacious freedom from melody and rhythm, while investing it with literary and mathematical charms. And one never could go to a concert given by any of this school without using the word 'interesting' as one was coming away. To sleep to this restored English music, too, was impossible. Fleur, a sound sleeper, had never even tried. Michael had, and complained afterwards that it had been like a nap in Liège railway station. On this occasion they occupied those gangway seats in the front row of the dress circle of which Fleur had a sort of natural monopoly. There Hugo and the rest could see her taking her place in the English restoration movement. It was easy, too, to escape into the corridor and exchange the word 'interesting' with side-whiskered cognoscenti; or, slipping out a cigarette from the little gold case, wedding present of Cousin Imogen Cardigan, get a whiff or two's repose. To speak quite honestly, Fleur had a natural sense of rhythm which caused her discomfort during those long and 'interesting' passages which evidenced, as it were, the composer's rise and fall from his bed of thorns. She secretly loved a tune, and the impossibility of ever confessing this without losing hold of Solstis, Baff, Birdigal, MacLewis, Clorane, and other English restoration composers, sometimes taxed to its limits a nature which had its Spartan side. Even to Michael she would not 'confess'; and it was additionally trying when, with his native disrespect of persons, accentuated by life in the trenches and a publisher's office, he would mutter: 'Gad! Get on with it!' or: 'Cripes! Ain't he took bad!' especially as she knew that Michael was really putting up with it better than herself, having a more literary disposition, and a less dancing itch in his toes.

The first movement of the new Solstis composition—'Phantasmagoria Piémontesque'—to which they had come especially to listen, began with some drawn-out chords.

'What oh!' said Michael's voice in her ear: 'Three pieces of furniture moved simultaneously on a parquet floor!'

In Fleur's involuntary smile was the whole secret of why her marriage had not been intolerable. After all, Michael was a dear! Devotion and mercury—jesting and loyalty—combined, they piqued and touched even a heart given away before it was bestowed on him. 'Touch' without 'pique' would have bored; 'pique' without 'touch' would have irritated. At this moment he was at peculiar advantage! Holding on to his knees, with his ears standing up, eyes glassy from loyalty to Hugo, and tongue in cheek, he was listening to that opening in a way which evoked Fleur's admiration. The piece would be 'interesting'–she fell into the state of outer observation and inner calculation very usual with her nowadays. Over there was L.S.D., the greater dramatist; she didn't know him–yet. He looked rather frightening, his hair stood up so straight. And her eye began picturing him on her copper floor against a Chinese picture. And there–yes! Gurdon Minho! Imagine *his* coming to anything so modern! His profile *was* rather Roman–of the Aurelian period! Passing on from that antique, with the pleased thought that by this time to-morrow she might have collected it, she quartered the assembly face by face–she did not want to miss anyone important.

'The furniture' had come to a sudden standstill.

'Interesting!' said a voice over her shoulder. Aubrey Greene! Illusive, rather moonlit, with his silky fair hair brushed straight back, and his greenish eyes–his smile always made her feel that he was 'getting' at her. But, after all, he was a cartoonist!

'Yes, isn't it?'

He curled away. He might have stayed a little longer–there wouldn't be time for anyone else before those songs of Birdigal's! Here came the singer Charles Powls! How stout and efficient he looked, dragging little Birdigal to the piano.

Charming accompaniment–rippling, melodious!

The stout, efficient man began to sing. How different from the accompaniment. The song hit every note just off the solar plexus, it mathematically prevented her from feeling pleasure. Birdigal must have written it in horror of someone calling it 'vocal'. Vocal! Fleur knew how catching the word was; it would run like a measle round the ring, and Birdigal would be no more! Poor Birdigal! But this was 'interesting'. Only, as Michael was saying: 'O, my Gawd!'

Three songs! Powls was wonderful–so loyal! Never one note hit so that it rang out like music! Her mind fluttered off to Wilfrid. To him, of all the younger poets, people accorded the right to say something; it gave him such a position–made him seem to come out of life, instead of literature. Besides, he had done things in the war, was a son of Lord Mullyon, would get the Mercer Prize probably for 'Copper Coin'. If Wilfrid abandoned her, a star would fall from the firmament above her copper floor. He had no right to leave her in the lurch. He must learn not to be violent–not to think physically. No! she couldn't let Wilfrid slip away; nor could she have any more sob-stuff in her life, searing passions, culs-de-sac, aftermaths. She had tasted of that; a dulled ache still warned her.

Birdigal was bowing, Michael saying: 'Come out for a whiff! The next thing's a dud!' Oh! ah! Beethoven. Poor old Beethoven! So out of date–one did *rather* enjoy him!

The corridor, and refectory beyond, were swarming with the restoration movement. Young men and women·with faces and heads of lively and distorted character, were exchanging the word 'interesting'. Men of more massive type, resembling sedentary matadors, blocked all circulation. Fleur and Michael passed a little way along, stood against the wall, and lighted cigarettes. Fleur smoked hers delicately–a very little one in a tiny amber holder. She had the air of admiring blue smoke rather than of making it; there were spheres to consider beyond this sort of crowd–one never knew who might be about!–the sphere, for instance, in which Alison Charwell moved, politico-literary, catholic in taste, but, as Michael always put it: 'Convinced, like a sanitary system, that it's the only sphere in the world; look at the way they all write books of reminiscence about each other!' They might, she always felt, disapprove of women smoking in public halls. Consorting delicately with iconoclasm. Fleur never forgot that her feet were in two worlds at least. Standing there, observant of all to left and right, she noted against the wall one whose face was screened by his programme. 'Wilfrid,' she thought, 'and doesn't mean to see me!' Mortified, as a child from whom a sixpence is filched, she said:

'There's Wilfrid! Fetch him, Michael!'

Michael crossed, and touched his best man's sleeve; Desert's face emerged, frowning. She saw him shrug his shoulders, turn and walk into the throng. Michael came back.

'Wilfrid's got the hump to-night; says he's not fit for human society–queer old son!'

How obtuse men were! Because Wilfrid was his pal, Michael did not see; and that was lucky! So Wilfrid really meant to avoid her! Well, she would see! And she said:

'I'm tired, Michael; let's go home.'

His hand slid round her arm.

'Sorry, old thing; come along!'

They stood a moment in a neglected doorway, watching Woomans, the conductor, launched towards his orchestra.

'Look at him,' said Michael; 'guy hung out of an Italian window, legs and arms all stuffed and flying! And look at the Frapka and her piano–that's a turbulent union!'

There was a strange sound.

'Melody, by George!' said Michael.

An attendant muttered in their ears: 'Now, sir, I'm going to shut the door.' Fleur had a fleeting view of L.S.D. sitting upright as his hair, with closed eyes. The door was shut–they were outside in the hall.

'Wait here, darling; I'll nick a rickshaw.'

Fleur huddled her chin in her fur. It was easterly and cold.

A voice behind her said:

'Well, Fleur, am I going East?'

Wilfrid! His collar up to his ears, a cigarette between his lips, hands in pockets, eyes devouring.

'You're very silly, Wilfrid!'

'Anything you like; am I going East?'

'No; Sunday morning–eleven o'clock at the Tate. We'll talk it out.'

'*Convenu!*' And he was gone.

Alone suddenly, like that, Fleur felt the first shock of reality. Was Wilfrid truly going to be unmanageable? A taxi-cab ground up; Michael beckoned; Fleur stepped in.

Passing a passionately lighted oasis of young ladies displaying to the interested Londoner the acme of Parisian undress, she felt Michael incline towards her. If she were going to keep Wilfrid, she must be nice to Michael. Only:

'You needn't kiss me in Piccadilly Circus, Michael!'

'Sorry, ducky! It's a little previous–I meant to get you opposite the Partheneum.'

Fleur remembered how he had slept on a Spanish sofa for the first fortnight of their honeymoon; how he always insisted that she must not spend anything on him, but must always let him give her what he liked, though she had three thousand a year and he twelve hundred; how jumpy he was when she had a cold–and how he always came home to tea. Yes, he was a dear! But would she break her heart if he went East or West to-morrow?

Snuggled against him, she was surprised at her own cynicism.

A telephone message written out, in the hall, ran: 'Please tell Mrs Mont I've got Mr Gurding Minner. Lady Alisson.'

It was restful. A real antique! She turned on the lights in her room, and stood for a moment admiring it. Truly pretty! A slight snuffle from the corner–Ting-a-ling, tan on a black cushion, lay like a Chinese lion in miniature; pure, remote, fresh from evening communion with the Square railings.

'I see you,' said Fleur.

Ting-a-ling did not stir; his round black eyes watched his mistress undress. When she returned from the bathroom he was curled into a ball. Fleur thought: 'Queer! How does he know Michael won't be coming?' And slipping into her well-warmed bed, she too curled herself up and slept.

But in the night, contrary to her custom, she awoke. A cry–long, weird, trailing, from somewhere–the river–the slums at the back–rousing memory–poignant, aching–of her honeymoon–Granada, its roofs below, jet, ivory, gold; the watchman's cry, the lines in Jon's letter:

> 'Voice in the night crying, down in the old sleeping
> Spanish City darkened under her white stars.
> What says the voice–its clear, lingering anguish?
> Just the watchman, telling his dateless tale of safety?
> Just a road-man, flinging to the moon his song?
> No! 'Tis one deprived, whose lover's heart is weeping,
> Just his cry: "How long?"'

A cry, or had she dreamed it? Jon, Wilfrid, Michael! No use to have a heart!

4

DINING

Lady Alison Charwell, born Heathfield, daughter of the first Earl of Campden, and wife to Lionel Charwell, K.C., Michael's somewhat young uncle, was a delightful Englishwoman brought up in a set accepted as the soul of society. Full of brains, energy, taste, money, and tinctured in its politico-legal ancestry by blue blood, this set was linked to, but apart from 'Snooks' and the duller haunts of birth and privilege. It was gay, charming, free-and-easy, and, according to Michael, 'Snobbish, old thing, aesthetically and intellectually, but they'll never see it. They think they're the top notch–quick, healthy, up-to-date, well-bred, intelligent; they simply can't imagine their equals. But you see their imagination is deficient. Their really creative energy would go into a pint pot. Look at their books–they're always *on* something–philosophy, spiritualism, poetry, fishing, themselves; why, even their sonnets dry up before they're twenty-five. They know everything–except mankind outside their own set. Oh! they work–they run the show–they have to; there's no one else with their brains, and energy, and taste. But they run it round and round in their own blooming circle. It's the world to them—and it might be worse. They've patented their own golden age; but it's a trifle fly-blown since the war.'

Alison Charwell—in and of this world, so spryly soulful, debonnaire, free, and cosy—lived within a stone's throw of Fleur, in a house pleasant, architecturally, as any in London. Forty years old, she had three children and considerable beauty, wearing a little fine from mental and bodily activity. Something of an enthusiast, she was fond of Michael, in spite of his strange criticisms, so that his matrimonial venture had piqued her from the start. Fleur was dainty, had quick natural intelligence—this new niece was worth cultivation. But, though adaptable and assimilative, Fleur had remained curiously unassimilated; she continued to whet the curiosity of Lady Alison, accustomed to the close borough of choice spirits, and finding a certain poignancy in contact with the New Age on Fleur's copper floor. She met with an irreverence there, which, not taken too seriously, flipped her mind. On that floor she almost felt a back number. It was stimulating.

Receiving Fleur's telephonic enquiry about Gurdon Minho, she had rung up the novelist. She knew him, if not well. Nobody seemed to know him well; amiable, polite, silent, rather dull and austere; but with a disconcerting smile, sometimes ironical, sometimes friendly. His books were now caustic, now sentimental. On both counts it was rather the fashion to run him down, though he still seemed to exist.

She rang him up. Would he come to a dinner to-morrow at her young nephew, Michael Mont's, and meet the younger generation? His answer came, rather high-pitched:

'Rather! Full fig, or dinner jacket?'

'How awfully nice of you! They'll be ever so pleased. Full fig, I believe. It's the second anniversary of their wedding.' She hung up the receiver with the thought: 'He must be writing a book about them!'

Conscious of responsibility, she arrived early.

It was a grand night at her husband's Inn, so that she brought nothing with her but the feeling of adventure, pleasant after a day spent in fluttering over the decision at 'Snooks'. She was received only by Ting-a-ling, who had his back to the fire, and took no notice beyond a stare. Sitting down on the jade green settee, she said:

'Well, you funny little creature, don't you know me after all this time?'

Ting-a-ling's black shiny gaze seemed saying: 'You recur here, I know; most things recur. There is nothing new about the future.'

Lady Alison fell into a train of thought: The new generation! Did she want her own girls to be of it! She would like to talk to Mr Minho about that—they had had a very nice talk down at Beechgroves before the war. Nine years ago—Sybil only six, Joan only four then! Time went, things changed! A new generation! And what was the difference! 'I think we had more tradition!' she said to herself softly.

A slight sound drew her eyes up from contemplation of her feet. Ting-a-ling was moving his tail from side to side on the hearthrug, as if applauding. Fleur's voice, behind her, said:

'Well, darling, I'm awfully late. It *was* good of you to get me Mr Minho. I do hope they'll all behave. He'll be between you and me, anyway; I'm sticking him at the top, and Michael at the bottom, between Pauline Upshire and Amabel Nazing. You'll have Sibley on your left, and I'll have Aubrey on my right, then

Nesta Gorse and Walter Nazing; opposite them Linda Frewe and Charles Upshire. Twelve. You know them all. Oh! and you mustn't mind if the Nazings and Nesta smoke between the courses. Amabel will do it. She comes from Virginia–it's the reaction. I do hope she'll have some clothes on; Michael always says it's a mistake when she has; but having Mr Minho makes one a little nervous. Did you see Nesta's skit in "The Bouquet"? Oh, too frightfully amusing–clearly meant for L.S.D.! Ting, my Ting, are you going to stay and see all these people? Well, then, get up here or you'll be trodden on. Isn't he Chinese? He does so round off the room.'

Ting-a-ling laid his nose on his paws, in the centre of a jade green cushion.

'Mr Girding Minner!'

The well-known novelist looked pale and composed. Shaking the two extended hands, he gazed at Ting-a-ling, and said:

'How nice! How are *you*, my little man?'

Ting-a-ling did not stir. 'You take me for a common English dog, sir!' his silence seemed to say.

'Mr and Mrs Walter Nazon, Miss Lenda Frow.'

Amabel Nazing came first, clear alabaster from her fair hair down to the six inches of gleaming back above her waist-line, shrouded alabaster from four inches below the knee to the gleaming toes of her shoes; the eminent novelist mechanically ceased to commune with Ting-a-ling.

Walter Nazing, who followed a long way up above his wife, had a tiny line of collar emergent from swathes of black, and a face, cut a hundred years ago, that slightly resembled Shelley's. His literary productions were sometimes felt to be like the poetry of that bard, and sometimes like the prose of Marcel Proust. 'What oh!' as Michael said.

Linda Frewe, whom Fleur at once introduced to Gurdon Minho, was one about whose work no two people in her drawing-room ever agreed. Her works 'Trifles' and 'The Furious Don' had quite divided all opinion. Genius according to some, drivel according to others, those books always roused an interesting debate whether a slight madness enhanced or diminished the value of art. She herself paid little attention to criticism–she produced.

'*The* Mr Minho? How interesting! I've never read anything of yours.'

Fleur gave a little gasp.

'What–don't you know Mr Minho's cats? But they're wonderful. Mr Minho, I do want Mrs Walter Nazing to know you. Amabel–Mr Gurdon Minho.'

'Oh! Mr Minho–how perfectly lovely! I've wanted to know you ever since my cradle.'

Fleur heard the novelist say quietly:

'I could wish it had been longer;' and passed on in doubt to greet Nesta Gorse and Sibley Swan, who came in, as if they lived together, quarrelling over L.S.D., Nesta upholding him because of his 'panache', Sibley maintaining that wit had died with the Restoration; this fellow was alive!

Michael followed with the Upshires and Aubrey Greene, whom he had encountered in the hall. The party was complete.

Fleur loved perfection, and that evening was something of a nightmare. Was it a success? Minho was so clearly the least brilliant person there; even Alison talked better. And yet he had such a fine skull. She did hope he would not go away early. Someone would be almost sure to say 'Dug up!' or 'Thick and bald!' before the door closed behind him. He was pathetically agreeable, as if trying to be liked, or, at least, not despised too much. And there must, of course, be more in him than met the sense of hearing. After the crab soufflé he did seem to be talking to Alison, and all about youth. Fleur listened with one ear.

'Youth feels . . . main stream of life . . . not giving it what it wants. Past and future getting haloes . . . Quite! Contemporary life no earthly just now . . . No . . . Only comfort for us—we'll be antiquated, some day, like Congreve, Sterne, Defoe . . . have our chance again . . . *Why?* What *is* driving them out of the main current? Oh! Probably surfeit . . . newspapers . . . photographs. Don't see life itself, only reports . . . reproductions of it; all seems shoddy, lurid, commercial . . . Youth says: "Away with it, let's have the past or the future!" '

He took some salted almonds, and Fleur saw his eyes stray to the upper part of Amabel Nazing. Down there the conversation was like Association football—no one kept the ball for more than one kick. It shot from head to head. And after every set of passes someone would reach out and take a cigarette, and blow a blue cloud across the unclothed refectory table. Fleur enjoyed the glow of her Spanish room—its tiled floor, richly coloured fruits in porcelain, its tooled leather, copper articles, and Soames's Goya above a Moorish divan. She headed the ball promptly when it came her way, but initiated nothing. Her gift was to be aware of everything at once. 'Mrs Michael Mont presented' the brilliant irrelevances of Linda Frewe, the pricks and stimulations of Nesta Gorse, the moonlit sliding innuendoes of Aubrey Greene, the upturning strokes of Sibley Swan, Amabel Nazing's little cool American audacities, Charles Upshire's curious bits of lore, Walter Nazing's subversive contradictions, the critical intricacies of Pauline Upshire; Michael's happy-go-lucky slings and arrows, even Alison's knowledgeable quickness, and Gurdon Minho's silences—she presented them all, showed them off, keeping her eyes and ears on the ball of talk lest it should touch earth and rest. Brilliant evening; but—a success?

On the jade green settee, when the last of them had gone and Michael was seeing Alison home, she thought of Minho's 'Youth—not getting what it wants.' No! Things didn't fit. 'They don't fit, do they, Ting!' But Ting-a-ling was tired, only the tip of one ear quivered. Fleur leaned back and sighed. Ting-a-ling uncurled himself, and putting his forepaws on her thigh, looked up in her face. 'Look at me,' he seemed to say, 'I'm all right. I get what I want, and I want what I get. At present I want to go to bed.'

'But I don't,' said Fleur, without moving.

'Just take me up!' said Ting-a-ling.

'Well,' said Fleur, 'I suppose–. It's a nice person, but not the right person, Ting.'

Ting-a-ling settled himself on her bare arms.

'It's all right,' he seemed to say. 'There's a great deal too much sentiment and all that, out of China. Come on!'

5

EVE

The Honourable Wilfrid Desert's rooms were opposite a picture gallery off Cork Street. The only male member of the aristocracy writing verse that anyone would print, he had chosen them for seclusion rather than for comfort. His 'junk', however, was not devoid of the taste and luxury which overflows from the greater houses of England. Furniture from the Hampshire seat of the Cornish nobleman, Lord Mullyon, had oozed into two vans, when Wilfrid settled in. He was seldom to be found, however, in his nest, and was felt to be a rare bird, owing his rather unique position among the younger writers partly to his migratory reputation. He himself hardly, perhaps, knew where he spent his time, or did his work, having a sort of mental claustrophobia, a dread of being hemmed in by people. When the war broke out he had just left Eton; when the war was over he was twenty-three, as old a young man as ever turned a stave. His friendship with Michael, begun in hospital, had languished and renewed itself suddenly, when in 1920 Michael joined Danby and Winter, publishers, of Blake Street, Covent Garden. The scattery enthusiasm of the sucking publisher had been roused by Wilfrid's verse. Hob-nobbing lunches over the poems of one in need of literary anchorage had been capped by the firm's surrender to Michael's insistence. The mutual intoxication of the first book Wilfrid had written and the first book Michael had sponsored was crowned at Michael's wedding. Best man! Since then, so far as Desert could be tied to anything, he had been tied to those two; nor, to do him justice, had he realised till a month ago that the attraction was not Michael, but Fleur. Desert never spoke of the war, it was not possible to learn from his own mouth an effect which he might have summed up thus: 'I lived so long with horror and death; I saw men so in the raw; I put hope of anything out of my mind so utterly, that I can never more have the faintest respect for theories, promises, conventions, moralities, and principles. I have hated too much the men who wallowed in them while I was wallowing in mud and blood. Illusion is off. No religion and no philosophy will satisfy me—words, all words. I have still my senses—no thanks to them; am still capable—I find—of passion; can still grit my teeth and grin; have still some feeling of trench loyalty, but whether real or just a complex, I don't yet know. I am dangerous, but not so dangerous as those who trade in words, principles, theories, and all manner of fanatical idiocy to be worked out in the blood and sweat of other men. The war's done one thing for me—converted life to comedy. Laugh at it—there's nothing else to do!'

Leaving the concert hall on the Friday night, he had walked straight home to his rooms. And lying down full length on a monk's seat of the fifteenth century, restored with down cushions and silk of the twentieth, he crossed his hands behind his head and delivered himself to these thoughts: 'I am not going on like this. She has bewitched me. It doesn't mean anything to her. But it means hell to me. I'll finish with it on Sunday—Persia's a good place. Arabia's a good

place–plenty of blood and sand! She's incapable of giving anything up. How
has she hooked herself into me? By trick of eyes, and hair, by her walk, by the
sound of her voice–by trick of warmth, scent, colour. Fling her cap over the
windmill–not she! What then? Am I to hang about her Chinese fireside and her
little Chinese dog; and have this ache and this fever because I can't be kissing
her? I'd rather be flying again in the middle of Boche whiz-bangs! Sunday!
How women like to drag out agonies! It'll be just this afternoon all over again.
'How unkind of you to go, when your friendship is so precious to me! Stay, and
be my tame cat, Wilfrid!' No, my dear, for once you're up against it! And–so
am I, by the Lord! . . .'

When in that gallery which extends asylum to British art, those two young
people met so accidentally on Sunday morning in front of Eve smelling at the
flowers of the Garden of Eden, there were present also six mechanics in various
stages of decomposition, a custodian and a couple from the provinces, none of
whom seemed capable of observing anything whatever. And, indeed, that
meeting was inexpressive. Two young people, of the disillusioned class,
exchanging condemnations of the past. Desert with his off-hand speech, his
smile, his well-tailored informality, suggested no aching heart. Of the two
Fleur was the paler and more interesting. Desert kept saying to himself: 'No
melodrama–that's all it would be!' And Fleur was thinking: 'If I can keep him
ordinary like this, I shan't lose him, because he'll never go away without a
proper outburst.'

It was not until they found themselves a second time before the Eve, that he
said:

'I don't know why you asked me to come, Fleur. It's playing the goat for no
earthly reason. I quite understand your feeling. I'm a bit of "Ming" that you
don't want to lose. But it's not good enough, my dear; and that's all about it.'

'How horrible of you, Wilfrid!'

'Well! Here we part! Give us your flipper.'

His eyes–rather beautiful–looked dark and tragic above the smile on his lips,
and she said stammering:

'Wilfrid–I–I don't know. I want time. I can't bear you to be unhappy. Don't
go away! Perhaps I–I shall be unhappy, too; I–I don't know.'

Through Desert passed the bitter thought: 'She *can't* let go–she doesn't
know how.' But he said quite softly: 'Cheer up, my child; you'll be over all that
in a fortnight. I'll send you something to make up. Why shouldn't I make it
China–one place is as good as another? I'll send you a bit of real "Ming", of a
better period than this.'

Fleur said passionately:

'You're insulting! Don't!'

'I beg your pardon. I don't want to leave you angry.'

'What is it you want of me?'

'Oh! no–come! This is going over it twice. Besides, since Friday I've been
thinking. I want nothing, Fleur, except a blessing and your hand. Give it me!
Come on!'

Fleur put her hand behind her back. It was too mortifying! He took her for a
cold-blooded, collecting little cat–clutching and playing with mice that she
didn't want to eat!

'You think I'm made of ice,' she said, and her teeth caught her upper lip:
'Well, I'm not!'

Desert looked at her; his eyes were very wretched. 'I didn't mean to play up your pride,' he said. 'Let's drop it, Fleur. It isn't any good.'

Fleur turned and fixed her eyes on the Eve–rumbustious-looking female, care-free, avid, taking her fill of flower perfume! Why not be care-free, take anything that came along? Not so much love in the world that one could afford to pass, leaving it unsmelled, unplucked. Run away! Go to the East! Of course, she couldn't do anything extravagant like that! But, perhaps–What did it matter? One man or another, when neither did you really love!

From under her drooped, white, dark-lashed eyelids she saw the expression on his face, and that he was standing stiller than the statues. And suddenly she said: 'You will be a fool to go. Wait!' And without another word or look, she walked away, leaving Desert breathless before the avid Eve.

6

'OLD FORSYTE' AND 'OLD MONT'

Moving away, in the confusion of her mood, Fleur almost trod on the toes of a too-familiar figure standing before an Alma Tadema with a sort of grey anxiety, as if lost in the mutability of market values.

'Father! *You* up in town? Come along to lunch, I have to get home quick.'

Hooking his arm and keeping between him and Eve, she guided him away, thinking: 'Did he see us? Could he have seen us?'

'Have you got enough on?' muttered Soames.

'Heaps!'

'That's what you women always say. East wind, and your neck like that! Well, I don't know.'

'No, dear, but I do.'

The grey eyes appraised her from head to foot.

'What are you doing here?' he said. And Fleur thought: 'Thank God he didn't see. He'd never have asked if he had.' And she answered:

'I take an interest in art, darling, as well as you.'

'Well, I'm staying with your aunt in Green Street. This east wind has touched my liver. How's your–how's Michael?'

'Oh, he's all right–a little cheap. We had a dinner last night.'

Anniversary! The realism of a Forsyte stirred in him, and he looked under her eyes. Thrusting his hand into his overcoat pocket, he said:

'I was bringing you this.'

Fleur saw a flat substance wrapped in pink tissue paper.

'Darling, what is it?'

Soames put it back into his pocket.

'We'll see later. Anybody to lunch?'

'Only Bart.'

'Old Mont! Oh, Lord!'

'Don't you like Bart, dear?'

'Like him? He and I have nothing in common.'

'I thought you fraternised rather over the state of things.'

'He's a reactionary,' said Soames.

'And what are you, ducky?'

'I? What should *I* be?' With these words he affirmed that policy of non-commitment which, the older he grew, the more he perceived to be the only attitude for a sensible man.

'How is Mother?'

'Looks well. I see nothing of her—she's got her own mother down—they go gadding about.'

He never alluded to Madame Lamotte as Fleur's grandmother—the less his daughter had to do with her French side, the better.

'Oh!' said Fleur. 'There's Ting and a cat!' Ting-a-ling, out for a breath of air, and tethered by a lead in the hands of a maid, was snuffling horribly and trying to climb a railing whereon was perched a black cat, all hunch and eyes.

'Give him to me, Ellen. Come with Mother, darling!'

Ting-a-ling came, indeed, but only because he couldn't go, bristling and snuffling and turning his head back.

'I like to see him natural,' said Fleur.

'Waste of money, a dog like that,' Soames commented. 'You should have had a bulldog and let him sleep in the hall. No end of burglaries. Your aunt had her knocker stolen.'

'I wouldn't part with Ting for a hundred knockers.'

'One of these days you'll be having *him* stolen—fashionable breed.'

Fleur opened her front door. 'Oh!' she said, 'Bart's here, already!'

A shiny hat was reposing on a marble coffer, present from Soames, intended to hold coats and discourage moth. Placing his hat alongside the other, Soames looked at them. They were too similar for words, tall, high, shiny, and with the same name inside. He had resumed the 'tall hat' habit after the failure of the general and coal strikes in 1921, his instinct having told him that revolution would be at a discount for some considerable period.

'About this thing,' he said, taking out the pink parcel, 'I don't know what you'll do with it, but here it is.'

It was a curiously carved and coloured bit of opal in a ring of tiny brilliants.

'Oh!' Fleur cried: 'What a delicious thing!'

'Venus floating on the waves, or something,' murmured Soames. 'Uncommon. You want a strong light on it.'

'But it's lovely. I shall put it on at once.'

Venus? If Dad had known! She put her arms round his neck to disguise her sense of *à propos*. Soames received the rub of her cheek against his own well-shaved face with his usual stillness. Why demonstrate when they were both aware that his affection was double hers?

'Put it on then,' he said, 'and let's see.'

Fleur pinned it at her neck before an old lacquered mirror. 'It's a jewel. Thank you, darling! Yes, your tie is straight. I like that white piping. You ought always to wear it with black. Now, come along!' And she drew him into her Chinese room. It was empty.

'Bart must be up with Michael, talking about his new book.'

'Writing at his age?' said Soames.

'Well, ducky, he's a year younger than you.'

'I don't write. Not such a fool. Got any more new-fangled friends?'

'Just one—Gurdon Minho, the novelist.'

'Another of the new school?'

'Oh, no dear! Surely you've heard of Gurdon Minho; he's older than the hills.'

'They're all alike to me,' muttered Soames. 'Is he well thought of?'

'I should think his income is larger than yours. He's almost a classic–only waiting to die.'

'I'll get one of his books and read it. What name did you say?'

'Get "Big and Little Fishes," by Gurdon Minho. You can remember that, can't you? Oh! here they are! Michael, look at what Father's given me.'

Taking his hand, she put it up to the opal at her neck. 'Let them both see,' she thought, 'what good terms we're on.' Though her father had not seen her with Wilfrid in the gallery, her conscience still said: 'Strengthen your respectability, you don't quite know how much support you'll need for it in future.'

And out of the corner of her eye she watched those two. The meetings between 'Old Mont' and 'Old Forsyte'–as she knew Bart called her father when speaking of him to Michael–always made her want to laugh, but she never quite knew why. Bart knew everything, but his knowledge was beautifully bound, strictly edited by a mind tethered to the 'eighteenth century'. Her father only knew what was of advantage to him, but the knowledge was unbound, and subject to no editorship. If he *was* late Victorian, he was not above profiting if necessary by even later periods. 'Old Mont' had faith in tradition; 'Old Forsyte' none. Fleur's acuteness had long perceived a difference which favoured her father. Yet 'Old Mont's' talk was so much more up-to-date, rapid, glancing, garrulous, redolent of precise information; and 'Old Forsyte's' was constricted, matter-of-fact. Really impossible to tell which of the two was the better museum specimen; and both so well-preserved!

They did not precisely shake hands; but Soames mentioned the weather. And almost at once they all four sought that Sunday food which by a sustained effort of will Fleur had at last deprived of reference to the British character. They partook, in fact, of lobster cocktails, and a mere risotto of chickens' livers, an omelette *au rhum*, and dessert trying to look as Spanish as it could.

'I've been in the Tate,' Fleur said; 'I do think it's touching.'

'Touching?' queried Soames with a sniff.

'Fleur means, sir, that to see so much old English art together is like looking at a baby show.'

'I don't follow,' said Soames stiffly. 'There's some very good work there.'

'But not grown-up, sir.'

'Ah! You young people mistake all this crazy cleverness for maturity.'

'That's not what Michael means, Father. It's quite true that English painting has no wisdom teeth. You can see the difference in a moment, between it and any Continental painting.'

'And thank God for it!' broke in Sir Lawrence. 'The beauty of this country's art is its innocence. We're the oldest country in the world politically, and the youngest aesthetically. What do you say, Forsyte?'

'Turner is old and wise enough for me,' said Soames curtly. 'Are you coming to the P.P.R.S. Board on Tuesday?'

'Tuesday? We were going to shoot the spinneys, weren't we, Michael?'

Soames grunted. 'I should let them wait,' he said. 'We settle the report.'

It was through 'Old Mont's' influence that he had received a seat on the board of that flourishing concern, the Providential Premium Reassurance Society, and, truth to tell, he was not sitting very easily in it. Though the law of averages was, perhaps, the most reliable thing in the world, there were circumstances which had begun to cause him disquietude. He looked round his nose. Light weight, this narrow-headed, twisting-eyebrowed baronet of a chap–like his son before him! And he added suddenly: 'I'm not easy. If I'd realised how that chap Elderson ruled the roost, I doubt if I should have come on to that board.'

One side of 'Old Mont's' face seemed to try to leave the other.

'Elderson!' he said. 'His grandfather was my grandfather's parliamentary agent at the time of the Reform Bill; he put him through the most corrupt election ever fought–bought every vote–used to kiss all the farmers' wives. Great days, Forsyte, great days!'

'And over,' said Soames. 'I don't believe in trusting a man's judgment as far as we trust Elderson's; I don't like this foreign insurance.'

'My dear Forsyte–first-rate head, Elderson; I've known him all my life, we were at Winchester together.'

Soames uttered a deep sound. In that answer of 'Old Mont's' lay much of the reason for his disquietude. On the Board they had all, as it were, been at Winchester together! It was the very deuce! They were all so honourable that they dared not scrutinise each other, or even their own collective policy. Worse than their dread of mistake or fraud was their dread of seeming to distrust each other. And this was natural, for to distrust each other was an immediate evil. And, as Soames knew, immediate evils are those which one avoids. Indeed, only that tendency, inherited from his father, James, to lie awake between the hours of two and four, when the chrysalis of faint misgiving becomes so readily the butterfly of panic, had developed his uneasiness. The P.P.R.S. was so imposing a concern, and he had been connected with it so short a time, that it seemed presumptuous to smell a rat; especially as he would have to leave the Board and the thousand a year he earned on it if he raised smell of rat without rat or reason. But what if there were a rat? That was the trouble! And here sat 'Old Mont' talking of his spinneys and his grandfather. The fellow's head was too small! And visited by the cheerless thought: 'There's nobody here, not even my own daughter, capable of taking a thing seriously,' he kept silence. A sound at his elbow roused him. That marmoset of a dog, on a chair between him and his daughter, was sitting up! Did it expect him to give it something? Its eyes would drop out one of these days. And he said: 'Well, what do *you* want?' The way the little beast stared with those boot-buttons! 'Here,' he said, offering it a salted almond. 'You don't eat these.'

Ting-a-ling did.

'He has a passion for them, Dad. Haven't you, darling?'

Ting-a-ling turned his eyes up at Soames, through whom a queer sensation passed. 'Believe the little brute likes me,' he thought, 'he's always looking at me.' He touched the dog's nose with the tip of his finger. Ting-a-ling gave it a slight lick with his curly blackish tongue.

'Poor fellow!' muttered Soames involuntarily, and turned to 'Old Mont'.

'Don't mention what I said.'

'My dear Forsyte, what was that?'

Good heavens! And he was on a Board with a man like this! What had made him come on, when he didn't want the money, or any more worries–goodness knew. As soon as he had become a director, Winifred and others of his family had begun to acquire shares to neutralise their income tax–seven per cent preference–nine per cent ordinary– instead of the steady five they ought to be content with. There it was, he couldn't move without people following him. He had always been so safe, so perfect a guide in the money maze! To be worried at his time of life! His eyes sought comfort from the opal at his daughter's

neck—pretty thing, pretty neck! Well! She seemed happy enough—had
forgotten her infatuation of two years ago! That was something to be thankful
for. What she wanted now was a child to steady her in all this modern
scrimmage of twopenny-ha'penny writers and painters and musicians. A loose
lot, but she had a good little head on her. If she had a child, he would put
another twenty thousand into her settlement. That was one thing about her
mother—steady in money matters, good French method. And Fleur—so far as
he knew—cut her coat according to her cloth. What was that? The word 'Goya'
had caught his ear. New life of him coming out? H'm! That confirmed his
slowly growing conviction that Goya had reached top point again.

'Think I shall part with that,' he said, pointing to the picture. 'There's an
Argentine over here.'

'Sell your Goya, sir?' It was Michael speaking. 'Think of the envy with
which you're now regarded!'

'One can't have everything,' said Soames.

'That reproduction we've got for "The New Life" has turned out first-rate.
"Property of Soames Forsyte, Esquire." Let's get the book out first, sir,
anyway.'

'Shadow or substance, eh, Forsyte?'

Narrow-headed baronet chap—was he mocking?

'*I've* no family place,' he said.

'No, but we have sir,' murmured Michael; 'you could leave it to Fleur, you
know.'

'Well,' said Soames, 'we shall see if that's worth while.' And he looked at his
daughter.

Fleur seldom blushed, but she picked up Ting-a-ling and rose from the
Spanish table. Michael followed suit. 'Coffee in the other room,' he said. 'Old
Forsyte' and 'Old Mont' stood up, wiping their moustaches.

7

'OLD MONT' AND 'OLD FORSYTE'

The offices of the P.P.R.S. were not far from the College of Arms. Soames, who
knew that 'three dexter buckles on a sable ground gules' and a 'pheasant
proper' had been obtained there at some expense by his Uncle Swithin in the
'sixties of the last century, had always pooh-poohed the building, until, about a
year ago, he had been struck by the name Golding in a book which he had
absently taken up at the Connoisseurs' Club. The affair purported to prove that
William Shakespeare was really Edward de Vere, Earl of Oxford. The mother
of the earl was a Golding—so was the mother of Soames! The coincidence struck
him; and he went on reading. The tome left him with judgment suspended over
the main issue, but a distinct curiosity as to whether he was not of the same
blood as Shakespeare. Even if the earl were not the bard, he felt that the
connection could only be creditable, though, so far as he could make out,
Oxford was a shady fellow. Recently appointed on the board of the P.P.R.S., so
that he passed the college every other Tuesday, he had thought: 'Shan't go
spending a lot of money on it, but might look in one day.' Having looked in, it

was astonishing how taken he had been by the whole thing. Tracing his mother had been quite like a criminal investigation, nearly as ramified and fully as expensive. Having begun, the tenacity of a Forsyte could hardly bear to leave him short of the mother of Shakespeare de Vere, even though she would be collateral; unfortunately, he could not get past a certain William Gouldyng, Ingerer—whatever that might be, and he was almost afraid to enquire—of the time of Oliver Cromwell. There were still four generations to be unravelled, and he was losing money and the hope of getting anything for it. This it was which caused him to gaze askance at the retired building while passing it on his way to the Board on the Tuesday after the lunch at Fleur's. Two more wakeful early mornings had screwed him to the pitch of bringing his doubts to a head and knowing where he stood in the matter of the P.P.R.S.; and this sudden reminder that he was spending money here, there and everywhere, when there was a possibility, however remote, of financial liability somewhere else, sharpened the edge of a nerve already stropped by misgivings. Neglecting the lift and walking slowly up the two flights of stairs, he 'went over' his fellow-directors for the fifteenth time. Old Lord Fontenoy was there for his name, of course; seldom attended, and was what they called 'a dud'–h'm!–nowadays; the chairman, Sir Luke Sharman, seemed always to be occupied in not being taken for a Jew. His nose was straight, but his eyelids gave cause for doubt. His surname was impeccable, but his Christian dubious; his voice was reassuringly roughened, but his clothes had a suspicious tendency towards gloss. Altogether a man who, though shrewd, could not be trusted–Soames felt–to be giving his whole mind to other business. As for 'Old Mont'–what was the good of a ninth baronet on a Board? Guy Meyricke, King's Counsel, last of the three who had been 'together', was a good man in court, no doubt, but with no time for business and no real sense of it! Remained that converted Quaker, old Cuthbert Mothergill–whose family name had been a byword for successful integrity throughout the last century, so that people still put Mothergills on to boards almost mechanically–rather deaf, nice clean old chap, and quite bland, but nothing more. A perfectly honest lot, no doubt, but perfunctory. None of them really giving their minds to the thing! In Elderson's pocket, too, except perhaps Sharman, and he on the wobble. And Elderson himself–clever chap, bit of an artist, perhaps; managing director from the start, with everything at his finger-tips! Yes! That was the mischief! Prestige of superior knowledge, and years of success–they all kow-towed to him, and no wonder! Trouble with a man like that was that if he once admitted to having made a mistake he destroyed the legend of his infallibility. Soames had enough infallibility of his own to realise how powerful was its impetus towards admitting nothing. Ten months ago, when he had come on to the Board, everything had seemed in full sail; exchanges had reached bottom, so they all thought–the 'reassurance of foreign contracts' policy, which Elderson had initiated about a year before, had seemed, with rising exchanges, perhaps the brightest feather in the cap of possibility. And now, a twelvemonth later, Soames suspected darkly that they did not know where they were–and the general meeting only six weeks off! Probably not even Elderson knew; or, if he did, he was keeping knowledge which ought to belong to the whole directorate severely to himself.

He entered the board-room without a smile. All there—even Lord Fontenoy and 'Old Mont'–given up his spinneys, had he! Soames took his seat at the end on the fireside. Staring at Elderson, he saw, with sudden clearness, the strength of the fellow's position; and, with equal clearness, the weakness of the P.P.R.S.

With this rising and falling currency, they could never know exactly their liability–they were just gambling. Listening to the minutes and other routine business, with his chin clasped in his hand, he let his eyes move from face to face–old Mothergill, Elderson, Mont opposite; Sharman at the head; Fontenoy, Meyricke, back to himself–decisive board of the year. He could not, must not, be placed in any dubious position! At his first general meeting on this concern, he must not face the shareholders without knowing exactly where he stood. He looked again at Elderson–sweetish face, bald head rather like Julius Caesar's, nothing to suggest irregularity or excessive optimism–in fact, somewhat resembling that of old Uncle Nicholas Forsyte, whose affairs had been such an example to the last generation but one. The managing director having completed his exposition, Soames directed his gaze at the pink face of dozy old Mothergill, and said:

'I'm not satisfied that these accounts disclose our true position. I want the Board adjourned to this day week, Mr Chairman, and during the week I want every member of the Board furnished with exact details of the foreign contract commitments which do *not* mature during the present financial year. I notice that those are lumped under a general estimate of liability. I am not satisfied with that. They ought to be separately treated.' Shifting his gaze past Elderson to the face of 'Old Mont', he went on: 'Unless there's a material change for the better on the Continent, which I don't anticipate (quite the contrary), I fully expect those commitments will put us in Queer Street next year.'

The scraping of feet, shifting of legs, clearing of throats which accompany a slight sense of outrage greeted the words 'Queer Street'; and a sort of satisfaction swelled in Soames; he had rattled their complacency, made them feel a touch of the misgiving from which he himself was suffering.

'We have always treated our commitments under one general estimate, Mr Forsyte.'

Plausible chap!

'And to my mind wrongly. This foreign contract business is a new policy. For all I can tell, instead of paying a dividend, we ought to be setting this year's profits against a certain loss next year.'

Again that scrape and rustle.

'My dear sir, absurd!'

The bulldog in Soames snuffled.

'So you say!' he said. 'Am I to have those details?'

'The Board can have what details it likes, of course. But permit me to remark on the general question that it *can* only be a matter of estimate. A conservative basis has always been adopted.'

'That is a matter of opinion,' said Soames; 'and in my view it should be the Board's opinion after very careful discussion of the actual figures.'

'Old Mont' was speaking.

'My dear Forsyte, to go into every contract would take us a week, and then get us no further; we can but average it out.'

'What we have not got in these accounts,' said Soames, 'is the relative proportion of foreign risk to home risk–in the present state of things a vital matter.'

The chairman spoke.

'There will be no difficulty about that, I imagine, Elderson! But in any case, Mr Forsyte, we should hardly be justified in penalising the present year for the sake of eventualities which we hope will not arise.'

'I don't know,' said Soames. 'We are here to decide policy according to our common sense, and we must have the fullest opportunity of exercising it. That is my point. We have not enough information.'

That 'plausible chap' was speaking again:

'Mr Forsyte seems to be indicating a lack of confidence in the management.' Taking the bull by the horns—was he?

'Am I to have that information?'

The voice of old Mothergill rose cosy in the silence.

'The Board could be adjourned, perhaps, Mr Chairman; I could come up myself at a pinch. Possibly we could all attend. The times are very peculiar—we mustn't take any unnecessary risks. The policy of foreign contracts is undoubtedly somewhat new to us. We have no reason so far to complain of the results. And I am sure we have the utmost confidence in the judgment of our managing director. Still, as Mr Forsyte has asked for this information, I think perhaps we ought to have it. What do you say, my lord?'

'I can't come up next week. I agree with the chairman that on these accounts we couldn't burke this year's dividend. No good getting the wind up before we must. When do the accounts go out, Elderson?'

'Normally at the end of this week.'

'These are not normal times,' said Soames. 'To be quite plain, unless I have that information I must tender my resignation.' He saw very well what was passing in their minds. A newcomer making himself a nuisance—they would take his resignation readily—only it would look awkward just before a general meeting unless they could announce 'wife's ill-health' or something satisfactory, which he would take very good care they didn't.

The chairman said coldly:

'Well, we will adjourn the Board to this day week; you will be able to get us those figures, Elderson?'

'Certainly.'

Into Soames's mind flashed the thought: 'Ought to ask for an independent scrutiny.' But he looked round. Going too far—perhaps—if he intended to remain on the Board—and he had no wish to resign—after all, it was a big thing, and a thousand a year! No! Mustn't overdo it!

Walking away, he savoured his triumph doubtfully, by no means sure that he had done any good. His attitude had only closed the 'all together' attitude round Elderson. The weakness of his position was that he had nothing to go on, save an uneasiness, which when examined was found to be simply a feeling that he hadn't enough control himself. And yet, there couldn't be two managers—you must trust your manager!

A voice behind him tittupped: 'Well, Forsyte, you gave us quite a shock with your alternative. First time I remember anything of the sort on that Board.'

'Sleepy hollow,' said Soames.

'Yes, I generally have a nap. It gets very hot in there. Wish I'd stuck to my spinneys. They come high, even as early as this.'

Incurably frivolous, this tittupping baronet!

'By the way, Forsyte, I wanted to say: With all this modern birth control and the rest of it, one gets uneasy. We're not the royal family; but don't you feel with me it's time there was a movement in heirs?'

Soames did, but he was not going to confess to anything so indelicate about his own daughter.

'Plenty of time,' he muttered.

'I don't like that dog, Forsyte.'

Soames stared.

'Dog!' he said. 'What's that to do with it?'

'I like a baby to come before a dog. Dogs and poets distract young women. My grandmother had five babies before she was twenty-seven. She was a Montjoy; wonderful breeders, you remember them–the seven Montjoy sisters–all pretty. Old Montjoy had forty-seven grandchildren. You don't get it nowadays, Forsyte.'

'Country's over-populated,' said Soames grimly.

'By the wrong sort–less of them, more of ourselves. It's almost a matter for legislation.'

'Talk to your son,' said Soames.

'Ah! but they think us fogies, you know. If we could only point to a reason for existence. But it's difficult, Forsyte, it's difficult.'

'They've got everything they want,' said Soames.

'Not enough, my dear Forsyte, not enough; the condition of the world is on the nerves of the young. England's dished, they say, Europe's dished. Heaven's dished, and so is Hell! No future in anything but the air. You can't breed in the air; at least, I doubt it–the difficulties are considerable.'

Soames sniffed.

'If only the journalists would hold their confounded pens,' he said; for, more and more of late, with the decrescendo of scare in the daily Press, he was regaining the old sound Forsyte feeling of security. 'We've only to keep clear of Europe,' he added.

'Keep clear and keep the ring! Forsyte, I believe you've hit it. Good friendly terms with Scandinavia, Holland, Spain, Italy, Turkey–all the outlying countries that we can get at by sea. And let the others dree their weirds. It's an idea!' How the chap rattled on!

'I'm no politician,' said Soames.

'Keep the ring! The new formula. It's what we've been coming to unconsciously! And as to trade–to say we can't do without trading with this country or with that–bunkum, my dear Forsyte. The world's large–we can.'

'I don't know anything about that,' said Soames. 'I only know we must drop this foreign contract assurance.'

'Why not confine it to the ring countries? Instead of "balance of power", "keep the ring"! Really, it's an inspiration!'

Thus charged with inspiration, Soames said hastily:

'I leave you here, I'm going to my daughter's.'

'Ah! I'm going to my son's. Look at these poor devils!'

Down by the Embankment at Blackfriars a band of unemployed were trailing dismally with money-boxes.

'Revolution in the bud! There's one thing that's always forgotten, Forsyte, it's a great pity.'

'What's that?' said Soames, with gloom. The fellow would tittup all the way to Fleur's!

'Wash the working-class, put them in clean, pleasant-coloured jeans, teach 'em to speak like you and me, and there'd be an end of class feeling. It's all a matter of the senses. Wouldn't you rather share a bedroom with a clean, neat-clothed plumber's assistant who spoke and smelled like you than with a profiteer who dropped his aitches and reeked of opoponax? Of course you would.'

'Never tried,' said Soames, 'so don't know.'

'Pragmatist! But believe me, Forsyte–if the working-class would concentrate on baths and accent instead of on their political and economic tosh,
equality would be here in no time.'

'I don't want equality,' said Soames, taking his ticket to Westminster.

The 'tittupping' voice pursued him entering the tube lift.

'Aesthetic equality, Forsyte, if we had it, would remove the wish for any
other. Did you ever catch an impecunious professor wishing he was the King?'

'No,' said Soames, opening his paper.

8

BICKET

Beneath its veneer of cheerful irresponsibility, the character of Michael Mont
had deepened during two years of anchorage and continuity. He had been
obliged to think of others; and his time was occupied. Conscious, from the fall
of the flag, that he was on sufferance with Fleur, admitting as whole the half-
truth: '*Il y a toujours un qui baise, et l'autre qui tend la joue*,' he had developed
real powers of domestic consideration; and yet he did not seem to redress the
balance in his public or publishing existence. He found the human side of his
business too strong for the monetary. Danby and Winter, however, were
bearing up against him, and showed, so far, no signs of the bankruptcy
prophesied for them by Soames on being told of the principles which his son-
in-law intended to introduce. No more in publishing than in any other walk of
life was Michael finding it possible to work too much on principle. The field of
action was so strewn with facts–human, vegetable and mineral.

On this same Tuesday afternoon, having long tussled with the price of those
vegetable facts, paper and linen, he was listening with his pointed ears to the
plaint of a packer discovered with five copies of 'Copper Coin' in his overcoat
pocket, and the too obvious intention of converting them to his own use.

Mr Danby had 'given him the sack'–he didn't deny that he was going to sell
them, but what would Mr Mont have done? He owed rent–and his wife wanted
nourishing after pneumonia–wanted it bad. 'Dash it!' thought Michael, 'I'd
snoop an edition to nourish Fleur after pneumonia!'

'And I can't live on my wages with prices what they are. I can't Mr Mont, so
help me!'

Michael swivelled. 'But look here, Bicket, if we let you snoop copies, all the
packers will snoop copies; and if they do, where are Danby and Winter? In the
cart. And, if they're in the cart, where are all of you? In the street. It's better
that one of you should be in the street than that all of you should, isn't it?'

'Yes, sir, I quite see your point–it's reason; but I can't live on reason, the
least thing knocks you out, when you're on the bread line. Ask Mr Danby to
give me another chance.'

'Mr Danby always says that a packer's work is particularly confidential,
because it's almost impossible to keep a check on it.'

'Yes, sir, I should feel that in future; but with all this unemployment and no
reference, I'll never get another job. What about my wife?'

To Michael it was as if he had said: 'What about Fleur?' He began to pace the room; and the young man Bicket looked at him with large dolorous eyes. Presently he came to a standstill, with his hands deep plunged into his pockets and his shoulders hunched.

'I'll ask him,' he said; 'but I don't believe he will; he'll say it isn't fair on the others. You had five copies; it's pretty stiff, you know—means you've had 'em before, doesn't it? What?'

'Well, Mr Mont, anything that'll give me a chance, I don't mind confessin'. I have 'ad a few previous, and it's just about kept my wife alive. You've no idea what that pneumonia's like for poor people.'

Michael pushed his fingers through his hair.

'How old's your wife?'

'Only a girl—twenty.'

Twenty! Just Fleur's age!

'I'll tell you what I'll do, Bicket; I'll put it up to Mr Desert; if he speaks for you, perhaps it may move Mr Danby.'

'Well, Mr Mont, thank you—you're a gentleman, we all sy that.'

'Oh! hang it! But look here, Bicket, you were reckoning on those five copies. Take this to make up, and get your wife what's necessary. Only for goodness' sake don't tell Mr Danby.'

'Mr Mont, I wouldn't deceive you for the world—I won't sy a word, sir. And my wife—well!'

A sniff, a shuffle—Michael was alone, with his hands plunged deeper, his shoulders hunched higher. And suddenly he laughed. Pity! Pity was pop! It was all dam' funny. Here he was rewarding Bicket for snooping 'Copper Coin'! A sudden longing possessed him to follow the little packer and see what he did with the two pounds—see whether 'the pneumonia' was real or a figment of the brain behind those dolorous eyes. Impossible, though! Instead he must ring up Wilfrid and ask him to put in a word with old Danby. His own word was no earthly. He had put it in too often! Bicket! Little one knew of anybody, life was deep and dark, and upside down! What was honesty? Pressure of life versus power of resistance—the result of that fight, when the latter won, was honesty! But why resist? Love thy neighbour as thyself—but not more! And wasn't it a darned sight harder for Bicket on two pounds a week to love him, than for him on twenty-four pounds a week to love Bicket? . . .

'Hallo! . . . That you, Wilfrid? . . . Michael speaking. . . . One of our packers has been sneaking copies of "Copper Coin". He's "got the sack"—poor devil! I wondered if you'd mind putting in a word for him—old Dan won't listen to me . . . yes, got a wife—Fleur's age; pneumonia, so he says. Won't do it again with yours anyway, insurance by common gratitude—what! . . . Thanks, old man, awfully good of you—will you bob in, then? We can go round home together . . . Oh! Well! You'll bob in anyway. Aurev!'

Good chap, old Wilfrid! Real good chap—underneath! Underneath—what?

Replacing the receiver, Michael saw a sudden great cloud of sights and scents and sounds, so foreign to the principles of his firm that he was in the habit of rejecting instantaneously every manuscript which dealt with them. The war might be 'off'; but it was still 'on' within Wilfrid, and himself. Taking up a tube, he spoke:

'Mr Danby in his room? Right! If he shows any signs of flitting, let me know at once. . . .'

Between Michael and his senior partner a gulf was fixed, not less deep than that between two epochs, though partially filled in by Winter's middle-age and accommodating temperament. Michael had almost nothing against Mr Danby except that he was always right–Philip Norman Danby, of Sky House, Campden Hill, a man of sixty and some family, with a tall forehead, a preponderance of body to leg, and an expression both steady and reflective. His eyes were perhaps rather close together, and his nose rather thin, but he looked a handsome piece in his well-proportioned room. He glanced up from the formation of a correct judgment on a matter of advertisement when Wilfrid Desert came in.

'Well, Mr Desert, what can I do for you? Sit down!'

Desert did not sit down, but looked at the engravings, at his fingers, at Mr Danby, and said:

'Fact is, I want you to let that packer chap off, Mr Danby.'

'Packer chap. Oh! Ah! Bicket. Mont told you, I suppose?'

'Yes; he's got a young wife down with pneumonia.'

'They all go to our friend Mont with some tale or other, Mr Desert–he has a very soft heart. But I'm afraid I can't keep this man. It's a most insidious thing. We've been trying to trace a leak for some time.'

Desert leaned against the mantelpiece and stared into the fire.

'Well, Mr Danby,' he said, 'your generation may like the soft in literature, but you're precious hard in life. Ours won't look at softness in literature, but we're a deuced sight less hard in life.'

'I don't think it's hard,' said Mr Danby, 'only just.'

'Are you a judge of justice?'

'I hope so.'

'Try four years' hell, and have another go.'

'I really don't see the connection. The experience you've been through, Mr Desert, was bound to be warping.'

Wilfrid turned and started at him.

'Forgive my saying so, but sitting here and being just is much more warping. Life is pretty good purgatory, to all except about thirty per cent of grown-up people.'

Mr Danby smiled.

'We simply couldn't conduct our business, my dear young man, without scrupulous honesty in everybody. To make no distinction between honesty and dishonesty would be quite unfair. You know that perfectly well.'

'I don't know anything perfectly well, Mr Danby; and I mistrust those who say they do.'

'Well, let us put it that there are rules of the game which must be observed, if society is to function at all.'

Desert smiled, too: 'Oh! hang rules! Do it as a favour to me. I wrote the rotten book.'

No trace of struggle showed in Mr Danby's face; but his deep-set, close-together eyes shone a little.

'I should be only too glad, but it's a matter–well, of conscience, if you like. I'm not prosecuting the man. He must leave–that's all.'

Desert shrugged his shoulders.

'Well, good-bye!' and he went out.

On the mat was Michael in two minds.

'Well?'

'No go. The old blighter's too just.'

Michael stivered his hair.

'Wait in my room five minutes while I let the poor beggar know, then I'll come along.'

'No,' said Desert, 'I'm going the other way.'

Not the fact that Wilfrid was going the other way—he almost always was—but something in the tone of his voice and the look on his face obsessed Michael's imagination while he went downstairs to seek Bicket. Wilfrid was a rum chap—he went 'dark' so suddenly!

In the nether regions he asked:

'Bicket gone?'

'No, sir, there he is.'

There he was, in his shabby overcoat, with his pale narrow face, and his disproportionately large eyes, and his sloping shoulders.

'Sorry, Bicket, Mr Desert has been in, but it's no go.'

'No, sir?'

'Keep your pecker up, you'll get something.'

'I'm afryde not, sir. Well, I thank you very 'eartily; and I thank Mr Desert. Good-night, sir; and good-bye!'

Michael watched him down the corridor, saw him waver into the dusky street.

'Jolly!' he said, and laughed. . . .

The natural suspicions of Michael and his senior partner that a tale was being pitched were not in fact justified. Neither the wife nor the pneumonia had been exaggerated; and wavering away in the direction of Blackfriars Bridge, Bicket thought not of his turpitude nor of how just Mr Danby had been, but of what he should say to her. He should not, of course, tell her that he had been detected in stealing; he must say he had 'got the sack for cheeking the foreman'; but what would she think of him for doing that, when everything as it were depended on his not cheeking the foreman? This was one of those melancholy cases of such affection that he had been coming to his work day after day feeling as if he had 'left half his guts' behind him in the room where she lay, and when at last the doctor said to him:

'She'll get on now, but it's left her very run down—you must feed her up,' his anxiety had hardened into a resolution to have no more. In the next three weeks he had 'pinched' eighteen 'Copper Coins', including the five found in his overcoat. He had only 'pitched on' Mr Desert's books because it was 'easy sold', and he was sorry now that he hadn't pitched on someone else's. Mr Desert had been very decent. He stopped at the corner of the Strand, and went over his money. With the two pounds given him by Michael and his wages he had seventy-five shillings in the world, and going into the Stores he bought a meat jelly and a tin of Benger's food that could be made with water. With pockets bulging he took a bus, which dropped him at the corner of his little street on the Surrey side. His wife and he occupied the two ground-floor rooms, at eight shillings a week, and he owed for three weeks. 'Py that!' he thought, 'and have a roof until she's well.' It would help him over the news, too, to show her a receipt for the rent and some good food. How lucky they had been careful to have no baby! He sought the basement. His landlady was doing the week's washing. She paused, in sheer surprise at such full and voluntary payment, and inquired after his wife.

'Doing nicely, thank you.'

'Well, I'm glad of that, it must be a relief to your mind.'

'It is,' said Bicket.

The landlady thought: 'He's a thread-paper—reminds me of a shrimp before you bile it, with those eyes.'

'Here's your receipt, and thank you. Sorry to 'ave seemed nervous about it, but times are 'ard.'

'They are,' said Bicket. 'So long!'

With the receipt and the meat jelly in his left hand, he opened the door of his front room.

His wife was sitting before a very little fire. Her bobbed black hair, crinkly towards the ends, had grown during her illness; it shook when she turned her head and smiled. To Bicket—not for the first time—that smile seemed queer, 'pathetic-like', mysterious—as if she saw things that one didn't see oneself. Her name was Victorine, and he said: 'Well, Vic? This jelly's a bit of all right, and I've pyde the rent.' He sat on the arm of the chair and she put her hand on his knee—her thin arm emerging blue-white from the dark dressing-gown.

'Well, Tony?'

Her face—thin and pale with those large dark eyes and beautifully formed eyebrows—was one that 'looked at you from somewhere; and when it looked at you—well! it got you right inside!'

It got him now and he said: 'How've you been breathin'?'

'All right—much better. I'll soon be out now.'

Bicket twisted himself round and joined his lips to hers. The kiss lasted some time, because all the feelings which he had not been able to express during the past three weeks to her or to anybody got into it. He sat up again, 'sort of exhausted,' staring at the fire, and said: 'News isn't bright—lost my job, Vic.'

'Oh! Tony! Why?'

Bicket swallowed.

'Fact is, things are slack, and they're reducin'.'

There had surged into his mind the certainty that sooner than tell her the truth he would put his head under the gas!

'Oh! dear! What shall we do, then?'

Bicket's voice hardened.

'Don't you worry—I'll get something'; and he whistled.

'But you liked that job.'

'Did I! I liked some o' the fellers; but as for the job—why, what was it? Wrappin' books up in a bysement all dy long. Let's have something to eat and get to bed early—I feel as if I could sleep for a week, now I'm shut of it.'

Getting their supper ready with her help, he carefully did not look at her face for fear it might 'get him agyne inside!' They had only been married a year, having made acquaintance on a tram, and Bicket often wondered what had made her take to him, eight years her senior and C3 during the war! And yet she must be fond of him, or she'd never look at him as she did.

'Sit down and try this jelly.'

He himself ate bread and margarine and drank cocoa, he seldom had any particular appetite.

'Shall I tell you what I'd like?' he said; 'I'd like Central Austrylia. We had a book in there about it; they sy there's quite a movement. I'd like some sun. I believe if we 'ad sun we'd both be twice the size we are. I'd like to see colour in your cheeks, Vic.'

'How much does it cost to get out there?'

'A lot more than we can ly hands on, that's the trouble. But I've been thinkin'. England's about done. There's too many like me.'

'No,' said Victorine. 'There aren't enough.'

Bicket looked at her face, then quickly at his plate.

'What myde you take a fancy to me?'

'Because you don't think first of yourself, that's why.'

'Used to before I knew you. But I'd do anything for you, Vic.'

'Have some of this jelly, then, it's awful good.'

Bicket shook his head.

'If we could wyke up in Central Austrylia,' he said. 'But there's only one thing certain, we'll wyke up in this blighted little room. Never mind, I'll get a job and earn the money yet.'

'Could we win it on a race?'

'Well, I've only got forty-seven bob all told, and if we lose it, where'll you be? You've got to feed up, you know. No, I must get a job.'

'They'll give you a good recommend, won't they?'

Bicket rose and stacked his plate and cup.

'They would, but that job's off–overstocked.'

Tell her the truth? Never! So help him!

In their bed, one of those just too wide for one and just not wide enough for two, he lay, with her hair almost in his mouth, thinking what to say to his Union, and how to go to work to get a job. And in his thoughts as the hours drew on he burned his boats. To draw his unemployment money he would have to tell his Union what the trouble was. Blow the Union! He wasn't going to be accountable to them! *He* knew why he'd pinched the books; but it was nobody else's business, nobody else could understand his feelings, watching her so breathless, pale and thin. Strike out for himself! And a million and a half out o' work! Well, he had a fortnight's keep, and something would turn up–and he might risk a bob or two and win some money, you never knew. She turned in her sleep. 'Yes,' he thought, 'I'd do it agyne. . . .'

Next day, after some hours on foot, he stood under the grey easterly sky in the grey street, before a plate-glass window protecting an assortment of fruits and sheaves of corn, lumps of metal, and brilliant blue butterflies, in the carefully golden light of advertised Australia. To Bicket, who had never been out of England, not often out of London, it was like standing outside Paradise. The atmosphere within the office itself was not so golden, and the money required considerable; but it brought Paradise nearer to take away pamphlets which almost burned his hands, they were so warm.

Later, he and she, sitting in the one armchair–advantage of being thin–pored over these alchemised pages and inhaled their glamour.

'D'you think it's true, Tony?'

'If it's thirty per cent true it's good enough for me. We just must get there somehow. Kiss me.'

From around the corner in the main road the rumbling of the trams and carts, and the rattling of their window-pane in the draughty dry easterly wind increased their feeling of escape into a gas-lit Paradise.

9

CONFUSION

Two hours behind Bicket, Michael wavered towards home. Old Danby was right as usual–if you couldn't trust your packers, you might shut up shop! Away from Bicket's eyes, he doubted. Perhaps the chap hadn't a wife at all! Then Wilfrid's manner usurped the place of Bicket's morals. Old Wilfrid had been abrupt and queer the last three times of meeting. Was he boiling-up for verse?

He found Ting-a-ling at the foot of the stairs in a conservative attitude. 'I am not going up,' he seemed saying, 'until someone carries me–at the same time it is later than usual!'

'Where's your mistress, you heraldic little beast?'

Ting-a-ling snuffled. 'I could put up with it,' he implied, 'if *you* carried me–these stairs are laborious!'

Michael took him up. 'Let's go and find her.'

Squeezed under an arm harder than his mistress', Ting-a-ling stared as if with black-glass eyes; and the plume of his emergent tail quivered.

In the bedroom Michael dropped him so absent-mindedly that he went to his corner plume pendent, and crouched there in dudgeon.

Nearly dinner time and Fleur not in! Michael went over his sketchy recollection of her plans. To-day she had been having Hubert Marsland and that Vertiginist–what was his name?–to lunch. There would have been fumes to clear off. Vertiginists–like milk–made carbonic acid gas in the lungs! Still! half-past seven! What was happening to-night? Weren't they going to that play of L.S.D.'s? No–that was to-morrow! Was there conceivably nothing? If so, of course she would shorten her unoccupied time as much as possible. He made that reflection humbly. Michael had no illusions, he knew himself to be commonplace, with only a certain redeeming liveliness, and, of course, his affection for her. He even recognised that his affection was a weakness, tempting him to fussy anxieties, which on principle he restrained. To enquire, for instance, of Coaker or Philps–their man and their maid–when she had gone out, would be thoroughly against that principle. The condition of the world was such that Michael constantly wondered if his own affairs were worth paying attention to; but then the condition of the world was also such that sometimes one's own affairs seemed all that were worth paying attention to. And yet his affairs were, practically speaking, Fleur; and if he paid too much attention to them, he was afraid of annoying her.

He went into his dressing-room and undid his waistcoat.

'But no!' he thought; 'if she finds me "dressed" already, it'll put too much point on it.' So he did up his waistcoat and went downstairs again. Coaker was in the hall.

'Mr Forsyte and Sir Lawrence looked in about six, sir. Mrs Mont was out. What time shall I serve dinner?'

'Oh! about a quarter-past eight. I don't think we're going out.'

He went into the drawing-room and passing down its Chinese emptiness, drew aside the curtain. The square looked cold and dark and draughty; and he thought: 'Bicket–pneumonia–I hope she's got her fur coat.' He took out a cigarette and put it back. If she saw him at the window she would think him fussy; and he went up again to see if she had put on her fur!

Ting-a-ling, still couchant, greeted him plume dansetti arrested as at disappointment. Michael opened a wardrobe. She had! Good! He was taking a sniff round, when Ting-a-ling passed him trottant, and her voice said: 'Well, my darling!' Wishing that he was, Michael emerged from behind the wardrobe door. Heaven! She looked pretty, coloured by the wind! He stood rather wistfully silent.

'Hallo, Michael! I'm rather late. Been to the Club and walked home.'

Michael had a quite unaccountable feeling that there was suppression in that statement. He also suppressed, and said: 'I was just looking to see that you'd got your fur, it's beastly cold. Your dad and Bart have been and went away fasting.'

Fleur shed her coat and dropped into a chair. 'I'm tired. Your ears are sticking up so nicely to-night, Michael.'

Michael went on his knees and joined his hands behind her waist. Her eyes had a strange look, a scrutiny which held him in suspense, a little startled.

'If *you* got pneumonia,' he said, 'I should go clean out of curl.'

'Why on earth should I?'

'You don't know the connection–never mind, it wouldn't interest you. We're not going out, are we?'

'Of course we are. It's Alison's monthly.'

'Oh! Lord! If you're tired we could cut that.'

'My dear! Impos.! She's got all sorts of people coming.'

Stifling a disparagement, he sighed out: 'Right-o! War-paint?'

'Yes, white waistcoat. I like you in white waistcoats.'

Cunning little wretch? He squeezed her waist and rose. Fleur laid a light stroke on his hand, and he went into his dressing-room comforted. . . .

But Fleur sat still for at least five minutes–not precisely 'a prey to conflicting emotions,' but the victim of very considerable confusion. *Two* men within the last hour had done this thing–knelt at her knees and joined their fingers behind her waist. Undoubtedly she had been rash to go to Wilfrid's rooms. The moment she got there she had perceived how entirely unprepared she really was to commit herself to what was physical. True he had done no more than Michael. But–Goodness!–she had seen the fire she was playing with, realised what torment he was in. She had strictly forbidden him to say a word to Michael, but intuitively she knew that in his struggle between loyalties she could rely on nothing. Confused, startled, touched, she could not help a pleasant warmth in being so much loved by two men at once, nor an itch of curiosity about the upshot. And she sighed. She had added to her collection of experiences–but how to add further without breaking up the collection, and even perhaps the collector, she could not see.

After her words to Wilfrid before the Eve: 'You will be a fool to go–wait!' she had known he would expect something before long. Often he had asked her to come and pass judgment on his 'junk'. A month, even a week, ago she would have gone without thinking more than twice about it, and discussed his 'junk' with Michael afterwards! But now she thought it over many times, and but for the fumes of lunch, and the feeling, engendered by the society of the

'Vertiginist', of Amabel Nazing, of Linda Frewe, that scruples of any kind were 'stuffy', sensations of all sorts 'the thing', she would probably still have been thinking it over now. When they departed, she had taken a deep breath and her telephone receiver from the Chinese tea-chest.

If Wilfrid were going to be in at half-past five, she would come and see his 'junk'.

His answer: 'My God! Will you?' almost gave her pause. But dismissing hesitation with the thought: 'I will be Parisian–Proust!' she had started for her Club. Three-quarters of an hour, with no more stimulant than three cups of China tea, three back numbers of the 'Glass of Fashion', three back views of country members 'dead in chairs', had sent her forth a careful quarter of an hour behind her time.

On the top floor Wilfrid was standing in his open doorway, pale as a soul in purgatory. He took her hand gently, and drew her in. Fleur thought with a little thrill: 'Is this what it's like? *Du côté de chez Swann!*' Freeing her hand, she began at once to flutter round the 'junk', clinging to it piece by piece.

Old English 'junk' rather manorial, with here and there an Eastern or First Empire bit, collected by some bygone Desert, nomadic, or attached to the French court. She was afraid to sit down, for fear that he might begin to follow the authorities; nor did she want to resume the intense talk of the Tate Gallery. 'Junk' was safe, and she only looked at him in those brief intervals when he was not looking at her. She knew she was not playing the game according to 'La Garçonne' and Amabel Nazing; that, indeed, she was in danger of going away without having added to her sensations. And she couldn't help being sorry for Wilfrid; his eyes yearned after her, his lips were bitter to look at. When at last from sheer exhaustion of 'junk' she sat down, he had flung himself at her feet. Half hypnotised, with her knees against his chest, as safe as she could hope for, she really felt the tragedy of it–his horror of himself, his passion for herself. It was painful, deep; it did not fit in with what she had been led to expect; it was not in the period, and how–how was she to get away without more pain to him and to herself? When she *had* got away, with one kiss received but not answered, she realised that she had passed through a quarter of an hour of real life, and was not at all sure that she liked it. . . . But now, safe in her own room, undressing for Alison's monthly, she felt curious as to what she would have been feeling if things had gone as far as was proper according to the authorities. Surely she had not experienced one-tenth of the thoughts or sensations that would have been assigned to her in any advanced piece of literature! It had been disillusioning, or else she was deficient, and Fleur could not bear to feel deficient. And, lightly powdering her shoulders, she bent her thoughts towards Alison's monthly.

Though Lady Alison enjoyed an occasional encounter with the younger generation, the Aubrey Greenes and Linda Frewes of this life were not conspicuous by their presence at her gatherings. Nesta Gorse, indeed, had once attended, but one legal and two literary politicos who had been in contact with her, had complained of it afterwards. She had, it seemed, rent little spiked holes in the garments of their self-esteem. Sibley Swan would have been welcome, for his championship of the past, but he seemed, so far, to have turned up his nose and looked down it. So it was not the intelligentsia, but just intellectual society, which was gathered there when Fleur and Michael entered, and the conversation had all the sparkle and all the *savoir-faire* incidental to talk about art and letters by those who—as Michael put it—'fortunately had not to *faire*.'

'All the same, these are the guys,' he muttered in Fleur's ear, 'who make the names of artists and writers. What's the stunt, to-night?'

It appeared to be the London début of a lady who sang Balkan folk songs. But in a refuge to the right were four tables set out for bridge. They were already filled. Among those who still stood listening, were, here and there, a Gurdon Minho, a society painter and his wife, a sculptor looking for a job. Fleur, wedged between Lady Feynte, the painter's wife, and Gurdon Minho himself, began planning an evasion. There—yes, there was Mr Chalfont! At Lady Alison's, Fleur, an excellent judge of milieu, never wasted her time on artists and writers—she could meet *them* anywhere. Here she intuitively picked out the biggest 'bug', politico-literary, and waited to pin him. Absorbed in the idea of pinning Mr Chalfont, she overlooked a piece of drama passing without.

Michael had clung to the top of the stairway, in no mood for talk and skirmish; and, leaning against the balustrade, wasp-thin in his long white waistcoat, with hands deep thrust into his trousers' pockets, he watched the turns and twists of Fleur's white neck, and listened to the Balkan songs, with a sort of blankness in his brain. The word: 'Mont!' startled him. Wilfrid was standing just below. Mont? He had not been that to Wilfrid for two years!

'Come down here.'

On that half-landing was a bust of Lionel Charwell, K.C., by Boris Strumolowski, in the genre he had cynically adopted when June Forsyte gave up supporting his authentic but unrewarded genius. It had been almost indistinguishable from any of the other busts in that year's Academy, and was used by the young Charwells to chalk moustaches on.

Beside this object Desert leaned against the wall with his eyes closed. His face was a study to Michael.

'What's wrong, Wilfrid?'

Desert did not move. 'You've got to know—I'm in love with Fleur.'

'What!'

'I'm not going to play the snake. You're up against me. Sorry, but there it is! You can let fly!' His face was death-pale, and its muscles twitched. In Michael, it was the mind, the heart that twitched. What a very horrible, strange, 'too beastly' moment! His best friend—his best man! Instinctively he dived for his cigarette-case—instinctively handed it to Desert. Instinctively they both took cigarettes, and lighted each other's. Then Michael said:

'Fleur—knows?'

Desert nodded: 'She doesn't know I'm telling you—wouldn't have let me. You've nothing against her—yet.' And, still with closed eyes, he added: 'I couldn't help it.'

It was Michael's own subconscious thought! Natural! Natural! Fool not to see how natural! Then something shut-to within him, and he said: 'Decent of you to tell me; but—aren't you going to clear out?'

Desert's shoulders writhed against the wall.

'I thought so; but it seems not.'

'Seems? I don't understand.'

'If I knew for certain I'd no chance—but I don't,' and he suddenly looked at Michael: 'Look here, it's no good keeping gloves on. I'm desperate, and I'll take her from you if I can.'

'Good God!' said Michael. 'It's the limit!'

'Yes! Rub it in! But, I tell you, when I think of you going home with her, and of myself,' he gave a dreadful little laugh, 'I advise you *not* to rub it in.'

'Well,' said Michael, 'as this isn't a Dostoevsky novel, I suppose there's no more to be said.'

Desert moved from the wall and laid his hand on the bust of Lionel Charwell.

'You realise, at least, that I've gone out of my way—perhaps dished myself—by telling you. I've not bombed without declaring war.'

'No,' said Michael dully.

'You can chuck my books over to some other publisher.' Michael shrugged.

'Good-night, then,' said Desert. 'Sorry for being so primitive.'

Michael looked straight into his 'best man's' face. There was no mistaking its expression of bitter despair. He made a half-movement with his hand, uttered half the word 'Wilfrid,' and, as Desert went down, he went upstairs.

Back in his place against the balustrade, he tried to realise that life was a laughing matter, and couldn't. His position required a serpent's cunning, a lion's courage, a dove's gentleness: he was not conscious of possessing such proverbial qualities. If Fleur had loved him as he loved her, he would have had for Wilfrid a real compassion. It was so natural to fall in love with Fleur! But she didn't—oh! no, she didn't! Michael had one virtue—if virtue it be—a moderate opinion of himself, a disposition to think highly of his friends. He had thought highly of Desert; and—odd! he still did not think lowly of him. Here was his friend trying to do him mortal injury, to alienate the affection—more honestly, the toleration—of his wife; and yet he did not think him a cad. Such leniency, he knew, was hopeless; but the doctrines of free-will, and free contract, were not to him mere literary conceptions, they were part of his nature. To apply duress, however desirable, would not be on his cards. And something like despair ravaged the heart of him, watching Fleur's ingratiating little tricks with the great Gerald Chalfont. If she left him for Wilfrid! But surely—no—her father, her house, her dog, her friends, her—her collection of—of—she would not—could not give *them* up? But suppose she kept everything, Wilfrid included! No, no! She wouldn't! Only for a second did that possibility blur the natural loyalty of his mind.

Well, what to do? Tell her—talk the thing out? Or wait and watch? For what? Without deliberate spying, he could not watch. Desert would come to their house no more. No! Either complete frankness; or complete ignoring—and that meant living with the sword of Damocles above his head! No! Complete frankness! And not do anything that seemed like laying a trap! He passed his hand across a forehead that was wet. If only they were at home, away from that squalling and these cultivated jackanapes! Could he go in and hook her out? Impossible without some reason! Only his brain-storm for a reason! He must just bite on it. The singing ceased. Fleur was looking round. Now she would beckon! On the contrary, she came towards him. He could not help the cynical thought: 'She's hooked old Chalfont!' He loved her, but he knew her little weaknesses. She came up and took hold of his sleeve.

'I've had enough, Michael, let's slip off; d'you mind?'

'Quick!' he said, 'before they spot us!'

In the cold air outside he thought: 'Now? Or in her room?'

'I think,' said Fleur, 'that Mr Chalfont is overrated—he's nothing but a mental yawn. He's coming to lunch to-morrow week.'

Not now—in her room!

'Whom do you think to meet him, besides Alison?'

'Nothing jazzy.'

'Of course not; but it must be somebody intriguing, Michael. Bother! sometimes I think it isn't worth it.'

Michael's heart stood still. Was that a portent–sign of 'the primitive' rising within his adored practitioner of social arts? An hour ago he would have said:

'You're right, my child; it jolly well isn't!' But now–any sign of change was ominous! He slipped his arm in hers.

'Don't worry, we'll snare the just-right cuckoos, somehow.'

'A Chinese Minister would be perfect,' mused Fleur, 'with Minho and Bart–four men–two women–cosy. I'll talk to Bart.'

Michael had opened their front door. She passed him; he lingered to see the stars, the plane trees, a man's figure motionless, collared to the eyes, hatted down to them. 'Wilfrid!' he thought: 'Spain! Why Spain? And all poor devils who are in distress–the heart–oh! darn the heart!' He closed the door.

But soon he had another to open, and never with less enthusiasm. Fleur was sitting on the arm of a chair, in the dim lavender pyjamas she sometimes wore just to keep in with things, staring at the fire. Michael stood, looking at her and at his own reflection beyond in one of the five mirrors–white and black, the pierrot pyjamas she had bought him. 'Figures in a play,' he thought, 'figures in a play! Is it real?' He moved forward and sat on the chair's other arm.

'Hang it!' he muttered. 'Wish I were Antinous!' And he slipped from the arm into the chair, to be behind her face, if she wanted to hide it from him.

'Wilfrid's been telling me,' he said quietly.

Off his chest! What now? He saw the blood come flushing into her neck and cheek.

'Oh! What business–how do you mean "telling you"?'

'Just that he's in love with you–nothing more–there's nothing more to tell, is there?' And drawing his feet up on to the chair, he clasped his hands hard round his knees. Already–already he had asked a question! Bite on it! Bite on it! And he shut his eyes.

'Of course,' said Fleur, very slowly, 'there's nothing more. If Wilfrid chooses to be so silly.'

Chooses! The word seemed unjust to one whose own 'silliness' was so recent–so enduring! And–curious! his heart wouldn't bound. Surely it ought to have bounded at her words!

'Is that the end of Wilfrid, then?'

'The end? I don't know.'

Ah! Who knew anything–when passion was about?

'Well,' he said, holding himself hard together, 'don't forget I love you awfully!'

He saw her eyelids flicker, her shoulders shrugging.

'Am I likely to?'

Bitter, cordial, simple–which? Suddenly her hands came round and took him by the ears. Holding them fast she looked down at him, and laughed. And again his heart *would* not bound. If she did not lead him by the nose, she–! But he clutched her to him in the chair. Lavender and white and black confused– she returned his kiss. But from the heart? Who knew? Not Michael.

10

PASSING OF A SPORTSMAN

Soames, disappointed of his daughter, said: 'I'll wait,' and took his seat in the centre of the jade green settee, oblivious of Ting-a-ling before the fire, sleeping off the attentions of Amabel Nazing, who had found him 'just too cunning'. Grey and composed, with one knee over the other, and a line between his eyes, he thought of Elderson and the condition of the world, and of how there was always something. And the more he thought, the more he wondered why he had ever been such a flat as to go on to a Board which had anything to do with foreign contracts. All the old wisdom that in the nineteenth century had consolidated British wealth, all the Forsyte philosophy of attending to one's own business, and taking no risks, the close-fibred national individualism which refused to commit the country to chasing this wild goose or that, held within him silent demonstration. Britain was on the wrong tack politically to try and influence the Continent, and the P.P.R.S. on the wrong tack monetarily to insure business outside Britain. The special instinct of his breed yearned for resumption of the straight and private path. Never meddle with what you couldn't control! 'Old Mont' had said: 'Keep the ring!' Nothing of the sort: Mind one's own business! That was the real 'formula'. He became conscious of his calf—Ting-a-ling was sniffing at his trousers.

'Oh!' said Soames. 'It's you!'

Placing his forepaws against the settee, Ting-a-ling licked the air.

'Pick you up?' said Soames. 'You're too long.' And again he felt that faint warmth of being liked.

'There's something about me that appeals to him,' he thought, taking him by the scruff and lifting him on to a cushion. 'You and I,' the little dog seemed saying with his stare—Chinese little object! The Chinese knew what they were about, they had minded their own business for five thousand years!

'I shall resign,' thought Soames. But what about Winifred, and Imogen, and some of the Rogers and Nicholases who had been putting money into this thing because he was a director? He wished they wouldn't follow him like a lot of sheep! He rose from the settee. It was no good waiting, he would walk on to Green Street and talk to Winifred at once. She would have to sell again, though the shares had dropped a bit. And without taking leave of Ting-a-ling, he went out.

All this last year he had almost enjoyed life. Having somewhere to come and sit and receive a certain sympathy once at least a week, as in old days at Timothy's, was of incalculable advantage to his spirit. In going from home Fleur had taken most of his heart with her; but Soames had found it almost an advantage to visit his heart once a week rather than to have it always about. There were other reasons conducing to light-heartedness. That diabolical foreign chap, Prosper Profond, had long been gone he didn't know where, and his wife had been decidedly less restive and sarcastic ever since. She had taken up a thing they called Coué, and grown stouter. She used the car a great deal.

Altogether she was more domestic. Then, too, he had become reconciled to Gauguin–a little slump in that painter had convinced him that he was still worth attention, and he had bought three more. Gauguin would rise again! Soames almost regretted his intuition of that second coming, for he had quite taken to the chap. His colour, once you got used to it, was very attractive. One picture, especially, which meant nothing so far as he could see, had a way of making you keep your eyes on it. He even felt uneasy when he thought of having to part with the thing at an enhanced price. But, most of all, he had been feeling so well, enjoying a recrudescence of youth in regard to Annette, taking more pleasure in what he ate, while his mind dwelt almost complacently on the state of money. The pound going up in value; Labour quiet! And now they had got rid of that Jack-o'-lantern, they might look for some years of solid Conservative administration. And to think, as he did, stepping across St James's park towards Green Street, that he had gone and put his foot into a concern which he could not control, made him feel–well, as if the devil had been in it!

In Piccadilly he moused along on the Park side, taking his customary look up at the 'Iseeum' Club. The curtains were drawn, and chinks of light glowed, long and cosy. And that reminded him–someone had said George Forsyte was ill. Certainly he had not seen him in the bay window for months past. Well, George had always eaten and drunk too much. He crossed over and passed beneath the Club; and a sudden feeling–he didn't know what–a longing for his own past, a sort of nostalgia–made him stop and mount the steps.

'Mr George Forsyte in the Club?'

The janitor stared, a grey-haired, long-faced chap, whom he had known from away back in the 'eighties.

'Mr Forsyte, sir,' he said, 'is very ill indeed. They say he won't recover, sir.'

'What?' said Soames. 'Nobody told me that.'

'He's very bad–*very* bad indeed. It's the heart.'

'The heart! Where is he?'

'At his rooms, sir; just round the corner. They say the doctors have given him up. He *will* be missed here. Forty years I've known him. One of the old school, and a wonderful judge of wine and horses. We none of us last for ever, they say, but I never thought to see him out. Bit too full-blooded, sir, and that's a fact.'

With a slight shock Soames realised that he had never known where George lived, so utterly anchored had he seemed to that bay window above.

'Just give me the number of his rooms,' he said.

'Belville Row–No. 11, sir; I'm sure I hope you'll find him better. I shall miss his jokes–I shall, indeed.'

Turning the corner into Belville Row, Soames made a rapid calculation. George was sixty-one, only one year younger than himself! If George was really *in extremis* it would be quite unnatural! 'Comes of not leading a careful life,' he thought; 'always rackety–George! When was it I made his will?' So far as he remembered, George had left his money to his brothers and sisters–no one else to leave it to. The feeling of kinship stirred in Soames, the instinct of family adjustment. George and he had never got on–opposite poles of temperament–still he would have to be buried, and who would see to it if not Soames, who had seen to so many Forsyte burials in his time? He recalled the nickname George had once given him, 'the undertaker'! H'm! Here was poetical justice! Belville Row! Ah! No. 11–regular bachelor-looking place! And

putting his hand up to the bell, he thought: 'Women!' What had George done
about women all his life?

His ring was answered by a man in a black cut-away coat with a certain
speechless reticence.

'My cousin, Mr George Forsyte? How is he?'

The man compressed his lips.

'Not expected to last the night, sir.'

Soames felt a little clutch beneath his Jaeger vest.

'Conscious?'

'Yes, sir.'

'Could you show him my card? He might possibly like to see me.'

'Will you wait in here, sir?' Soames passed into a low room panelled
up to the level of a man's chest, and above that line decorated with
prints. George–a collector! Soames had never supposed he had it in him!
On those walls, wherever the eye roved, were prints coloured and uncoloured,
old and new, depicting the sports of racing and prize-fighting! Hardly an
inch of the red wall space visible! About to examine them for marks of
value, Soames saw that he was not alone. A woman–age uncertain in the shaded
light–was sitting in a very high-backed chair before the fire with her elbow on
the arm of it, and a handkerchief held to her face. Soames looked at her, and his
nostrils moved in a stealthy sniff. 'Not a lady,' he thought. 'Ten to one but
there'll be complications.' The muffled voice of the cut-away man said:

'I'm to take you in, sir.' Soames passed his hand over his face and followed.

The bedroom he now entered was in curious contrast. The whole of one wall
was occupied by an immense piece of furniture, all cupboards and drawers.
Otherwise there was nothing in the room but a dressing-table with silver
accoutrements, an electric radiator alight in the fireplace, and a bed opposite.
Over the fireplace was a single picture, at which Soames glanced mechanically.
What! Chinese! A large whitish sidelong monkey, holding the rind of a
squeezed fruit in its outstretched paw. Its whiskered face looked back at him
with brown, almost human eyes. What on earth had made his inartistic cousin
buy a thing like that and put it up to face his bed? He turned and looked at the
bed's occupant. 'The only sportsman of the lot,' as Montague Dartie in his
prime had called him, lay with his swollen form outlined beneath a thin quilt. It
gave Soames quite a turn to see that familiar beef-coloured face pale and puffy
as a moon, with dark corrugated circles round eyes which still had their japing
stare. A voice, hoarse and subdued, but with the old Forsyte timbre, said:

'Hallo, Soames! Come to measure me for my coffin?'

Soames put the suggestion away with a movement of his hand; he felt queer
looking at that travesty of George. They had never got on, but–!

And in his flat, unemotional voice he said:

'Well, George! You'll pick up yet. You're no age. Is there anything I can do
for you?'

A grin twitched George's pallid lips.

'Make me a codicil. You'll find paper in the dressing-table drawer.'

Soames took out a sheet of 'Iseeum' Club notepaper. Standing at the table,
he inscribed the opening words of a codicil with his stylographic pen, and
looked round at George. The words came with a hoarse relish.

'My three screws to young Val Dartie, because he's the only Forsyte that
knows a horse from a donkey.' A throaty chuckle sounded ghastly in the ears of
Soames. 'What have you said?'

Soames read: 'I hereby leave my three racehorses to my kinsman, Valerius Dartie, of Wansdon, Sussex, because he has special knowledge of horses.'

Again the throaty chuckle. 'You're a dry file, Soames. Go on. To Milly Moyle, of 12, Claremont Grove, twelve thousand pounds, free of legacy duty.'

Soames paused on the verge of a whistle.

The woman in the next room!

The japing in George's eyes had turned to brooding gloom.

'It's a lot of money,' Soames could not help saying.

George made a faint choleric sound.

'Write it down, or I'll leave her the lot.'

Soames wrote. 'Is that all?'

'Yes. Read it!'

Soames read. Again he heard that throaty chuckle.

'That's a pill. You won't let *that* into the papers. Get that chap in, and you and he can witness.'

Before Soames reached the door, it was opened and the man himself came in.

'The—er—vicar, sir,' he said in a deprecating voice, 'has called. He wants to know if you would like to see him.'

George turned his face, his fleshy grey eyes rolled.

'Give him my compliments,' he said, 'and say I'll see him at the funeral.'

With a bow the man went out, and there was silence.

'Now,' said George, 'get him in again. I don't know when the flag'll fall.'

Soames beckoned the man in. When the codicil was signed and the man gone, George spoke:

'Take it, and see she gets it. I can trust you, that's one thing about you, Soames.'

Soames pocketed the codicil with a very queer sensation.

'Would you like to see her again?' he said.

George stared up at him a long time before he answered.

'No. What's the good? Give me a cigar from that drawer.'

Soames opened the drawer.

'Ought you?' he said.

George grinned. 'Never in my life done what I ought; not going to begin now. Cut it for me.'

Soames nipped the end of the cigar. 'Shan't give him a match,' he thought. 'Can't take the responsibility.' But George did not ask for a match. He lay quite still, the unlighted cigar between his pale lips, the curved lids down over his eyes.

'Good-bye,' he said. 'I'm going to have a snooze.'

'Good-bye,' said Soames. 'I—I hope—you—you'll soon—'

George reopened his eyes—fixed, sad, jesting, they seemed to quench the shams of hope and consolation. Soames turned hastily and went out. He felt bad, and almost unconsciously turned again into the sitting-room. The woman was still in the same attitude; the same florid scent was in the air. Soames took up the umbrella he had left there, and went out.

'This is my telephone number,' he said to the servant waiting in the corridor; 'let me know.'

The man bowed.

Soames turned out of Belville Row. Never had he left George's presence without the sense of being laughed at. Had he been laughed at now? Was that codicil George's last joke? If he had not gone in this afternoon, would George ever have made it, leaving a third of his property away from his family to that florid woman in the high-backed chair? Soames was beset by a sense of mystery. How could a man joke at death's door? It was, in a way, heroic. Where would he be buried? Somebody would know—Francie or Eustace. And what would they think when they came to know about that woman in the chair—twelve thousand pounds! 'If I can get hold of that white monkey, I will,' he thought suddenly. 'It's a good thing.' The monkey's eyes, the squeezed-out fruit—was life all a bitter jest and George deeper than himself? He rang the Green Street bell.

Mrs Dartie was very sorry, but Mrs Cardigan had called for her to dine and make a fourth at the play.

Soames went in to dinner alone. At the polished board below which Montague Dartie had now and again slipped, if not quite slept, he dined and brooded. 'I can trust you, that's one thing about you, Soames.' The words flattered and yet stung him. The depths of that sardonic joke! To give him a family shock and trust him to carry the shock out! George had never cared twelve thousand pounds for a woman who smelled of patchouli. No! It was a final gibe at his family, the Forsytes, at Soames himself! Well! one by one those who had injured or gibed at him—Irene, Bosinney, old and young Jolyon, and now George, had met their fates. Dead, dying, or in British Columbia! He saw again his cousin's eyes above that unlighted cigar, fixed, sad, jesting—poor devil! He got up from the table, and nervously drew aside the curtains. The night was fine and cold. What happened to one—after? George used to say that he had been Charles the Second's cook in a former existence! But reincarnation was all nonsense, weak-minded theorising! Still, one would be glad to hold on if one could, after one was gone. Hold on, and be near Fleur! What noise was that? Gramophone going in the kitchen! When the cat was away, the mice—! People were all alike—take what they could get, and give as little as they could for it. Well! he would smoke a cigarette. Lighting it at a candle—Winifred dined by candle-light, it was the 'mode' again—he thought: 'Has he still got that cigar between his teeth?' A funny fellow, George—all his days a funny fellow! He watched a ring of smoke he had made without intending to—very blue, he never inhaled! Yes! George had lived too fast, or he would not have been dying twenty years before his time—too fast! Well, there it was, and he wished he had a cat to talk to! He took a little monster off the mantelboard. Picked up by his nephew Benedict in an Eastern bazaar the year after the War, it had green eyes—'Not emeralds,' thought Soames, 'some cheap stone!'

'The telephone for you, sir.'

He went into the hall and took up the receiver.

'Yes?'

'Mr Forsyte has passed away, sir—in his sleep, the doctor says.'

'Oh!' said Soames: 'Had he a cig–? Many thanks.' He hung up the receiver.

Passed away! And, with a nervous movement, he felt for the codicil in his breast pocket.

I I

VENTURE

For a week Bicket had seen 'the job', slippery as an eel, evasive as a swallow, for ever passing out of reach. A pound for keep, and three shillings invested on a horse, and he was down to twenty-four bob. The weather had turned sou'-westerly and Victorine had gone out for the first time. That was something off his mind, but the cramp of the unemployed sensation, that fearful craving for the means of mere existence, a protesting, agonising anxiety, was biting into the very flesh of his spirit. If he didn't get a job within a week or two, there would be nothing for it but the work-house, or the gas. 'The gas,' thought Bicket, 'if she will. I will. I'm fed up. After all, what is it? In her arms I wouldn't mind.' Instinct, however, that it was not so easy as all that to put one's head under the gas, gave him a brain-wave that Monday night. Balloons—that chap in Oxford Street to-day! Why not? He still had the capital for a flutter in them, and no hawker's licence needed. His brain, working like a squirrel in the small hours, grasped the great, the incalculable advantage of coloured balloons over all other forms of commerce. You couldn't miss the man who sold them—there he was for every eye to see, with his many radiant circumferences dangling in front of him! Not much profit in them, he had gathered—a penny on a sixpenny globe of coloured air, a penny on every three small twopenny globes; still their salesman was alive, and probably had pitched him a poor tale for fear of making his profession seem too attractive. Over the Bridge, just where the traffic—no, up by St Paul's! He knew a passage where he could stand back a yard or two, like that chap in Oxford Street! But to the girl sleeping beside him he said nothing. No word to her till he had thrown the die. It meant gambling with his last penny. For a bare living he would have to sell—why, three dozen big and four dozen small balloons a day would only be twenty-six shillings a week profit, unless that chap was kidding. Not much towards 'Austrylia' out of that! And not a career—Victorine would have a shock! But it was neck or nothing now—he must try it, and in off hours go on looking for a job.

Our thin capitalist, then, with four dozen big and seven dozen small on a tray, two shillings in his pocket, and little in his stomach, took his stand off St Paul's at two o'clock next day. Slowly he blew up and tied the necks of two large and three small, magenta, green and blue, till they dangled before him. Then with the smell of rubber in his nostrils, and protruding eyes, he stood back on the kerb and watched the stream go by. It gratified him to see that most people turned to look at him. But the first person to address him was a policeman, with:

'I'm not sure you can stand there.'

Bicket did not answer, his throat felt too dry. He had heard of the police. Had he gone the wrong way to work? Suddenly he gulped, and said: 'Give us a chance, constable; I'm right on my bones. If I'm in the way, I'll stand anywhere you like. This is new to me, and two bob's all I've got left in the world besides a wife.'

The constable, a big man, looked him up and down. 'Well, we'll see. I shan't make trouble for you if no one objects.'

Bicket's gaze deepened thankfully.

'I'm much obliged,' he said; 'tyke one for your little girl–to please me.'

'I'll buy one,' said the policeman, 'and give you a start. I go off duty in an hour, you 'ave it ready–a big one, magenta.'

He moved away. Bicket could see him watching. Edging into the gutter, he stood quite still; his large eyes clung to every face that passed; and, now and then, his thin fingers nervously touched his wares. If Victorine could see him! All the spirit within him mounted. By Golly! he would get out of this somehow into the sun, into a life that was a life!

He had been standing there nearly two hours, shifting from foot to unaccustomed foot, and had sold four big and five small–sixpenny worth of profit–when Soames, who had changed his route to spite those fellows who couldn't get past William Gouldyng, Ingerer, came by on his way to the P.P.R.S. board. Startled by a timid murmur: 'Balloon, sir, best quality,' he looked round from that contemplation of St Paul's which had been his lifelong habit, and stopped in sheer surprise.

'Balloon!' he said. 'What should I want with a balloon?'

Bicket smiled. Between those green and blue and orange globes and Soames's grey self-containment there was incongruity which even he could appreciate.

'Children like 'em–no weight, sir, waistcoat pocket.'

'I dare say,' said Soames, 'but I've no children.'

'Grandchildren, sir.'

'Nor any grandchildren.'

'Thank you, sir.'

Soames gave him one of those rapid glances with which he was accustomed to gauge the character of the impecunious. 'A poor, harmless little rat!' he thought. 'Here, give me two–how much?'

'A shilling, sir, and much obliged.'

'You can keep the change,' said Soames hurriedly, and passed on, astonished. Why on earth he had bought the things, and for more than double their price, he could not conceive. He did not recollect such a thing having happened to him before. Extremely peculiar! And suddenly he realised why. The fellow had been humble, mild–to be encouraged, in these days of Communistic bravura. After all, the little chap was–was on the side of Capital, had invested in those balloons! Trade! And, raising his eyes towards St Paul's again, he stuffed the nasty-feeling things down into his overcoat pocket. Somebody would be taking them out, and wondering what was the matter with him! Well, he had other things to think of! . . .

Bicket, however, stared after him, elated. Two hundred and fifty odd per cent profit on those two–that was something like. The feeling, that not enough women were passing him here, became less poignant–after all, women knew the value of money, no extra shillings out of them! If only some more of these shiny-hatted old millionaires would come along!

At six o'clock, with a profit of three and eightpence, to which Soames had contributed just half, he began to add the sighs of deflating balloons to his own; untying them with passionate care he watched his coloured hopes one by one collapse, and stored them in the drawer of his tray. Taking it under his arm, he moved his tired legs in the direction of the Bridge. In a full day he might make four to five shillings – Well, it would just keep them alive, and something might turn up! He was his own master, anyway, accountable neither to employer nor to union. That knowledge gave him a curious lightness inside, together with the fact that he had eaten nothing since breakfast.

'Wonder if he was an alderman,' he thought; 'they say those aldermen live on turtle soup.' Nearing home, he considered nervously what to do with the tray? How prevent Victorine from knowing that he had joined the ranks of Capital, and spent his day in the gutter? Ill luck! She was at the window! He must put a good face on it. And he went in whistling.

'What's that, Tony?' she said, pointing to the tray.

'Ah! ha! Great stunt – this! Look 'ere!'

Taking a balloon out from the tray, he blew. He blew with a desperation he had not yet put into the process. They said the things would swell to five feet in circumference. He felt somehow that if he could get it to attain those proportions, it would soften everything. Under his breath the thing blotted out Victorine, and the room, till there was just the globe of coloured air. Nipping its neck between thumb and finger, he held it up, and said:

'There you are; not bad value for sixpence, old girl!' and he peered round it. Lord, she was crying! He let the 'blymed' thing go; it floated down, the air slowly evaporating till a little crinkled wreck rested on the dingy carpet. Clasping her heaving shoulders, he said desperately:

'Cheerio, my dear, don't quarrel with bread and butter. I shall get a job, this is just to tide us over. I'd do a lot worse than that for you. Come on, and get my tea, I'm hungry, blowin' up those things.'

She stopped crying, looked up, said nothing – mysterious with those big eyes! You'd say she had thoughts! But what they were Bicket could not tell. Under the stimulus of tea, he achieved a certain bravado about his new profession. To be your own master! Go out when you liked, come home when you liked – lie in bed with Vic if he jolly well pleased. A lot in that! And there rose in Bicket something truly national, something free and happy-go-lucky, resenting regular work, enjoying a spurt, and a laze-off, craving independence – something that accounted for the national life, the crowds of little shops, of middlemen, casual workers, tramps, owning their own souls in their own good time, and damning the consequences – something inherent in the land, the race, before the Saxons and their conscience and their industry came in – something that believed in swelling and collapsing coloured air, demanded pickles and high flavours without nourishment – yes, all that something exulted above Bicket's kipper and his tea, good and strong. He would rather sell balloons than be a packer any day, and don't let Vic forget it! And when she was able to take a job, they would get on fine, and not be long before they'd saved enough to get out of it to where those blue butterflies came from. And he spoke of Soames. A few more aldermen without children – say two a day, fifteen bob a week outside legitimate trade. Why, in under a year they'd have the money! And once away, Vic would blow out like one of those balloons; she'd be twice the size, and a colour in her cheeks to lay over that orange and magenta. Bicket became full of air. And the girl, his wife, watched with her large eyes and spoke little; but she did not cry again, or, indeed, throw any water, warm or cold, on him who sold balloons.

12

FIGURES AND FACTS

With the exception of old Fontenoy–in absence as in presence ornamental–the Board was again full; Soames, conscious of special ingratiation in the manner of 'that chap' Elderson, prepared himself for the worst. The figures were before them; a somewhat colourless show, appearing to disclose a state of things which would pass muster, if within the next six months there were no further violent disturbances of currency exchange. The proportion of foreign business to home business was duly expressed in terms of two to seven; German business, which constituted the bulk of the foreign, had been lumped–Soames noted–in the middle section, of countries only half bankrupt, and taken at what might be called a conservative estimate.

During the silence which reigned while each member of the Board digested the figures, Soames perceived more clearly than ever the quandary he was in. Certainly, these figures would hardly justify the foregoing of the dividend earned on the past year's business. But suppose there were another Continental crash and they became liable on the great bulk of their foreign business, it might swamp all profits on home business next year, and more besides. And then his uneasiness about Elderson himself–founded he could not tell on what, intuitive, perhaps silly.

'Well, Mr Forsyte,' the chairman was speaking; 'there are the figures. Are you satisfied?'

Soames looked up; he had taken a resolution.

'I will agree to this year's dividend on condition that we drop this foreign business in future, lock, stock and barrel.' The manager's eyes, hard and bright, met his, then turned towards the chairman.

'That appears to savour of the panicky,' he said; 'the foreign business is responsible for a good third of our profit this year.'

The chairman seemed to garner the expressions of his fellow-directors, before he said:

'There is nothing in the foreign situation at the moment, Mr Forsyte, which gives particular cause for alarm. I admit that we should watch it closely–'

'You can't,' interjected Soames. 'Here we are four years from the Armistice, and we know no more where we stand than we did then. If I'd realised our commitment to this policy, I should never have come on the Board. We must drop it.'

'Rather an extreme view. And hardly a matter we can decide in a moment.'

The murmur of assent, the expression, faintly ironical, of 'that chap's' lips, jolted the tenacity in Soames.

'Very well! Unless you're prepared to tell the shareholders in the report that we are dropping foreign business, you drop me. I must be free to raise the question myself at the general meeting.' He did not miss the shift and blink in the manager's eyes. That shot had gone home!

The chairman said:

'You put a pistol to our heads.'

'I am responsible to the shareholders,' said Soames, 'and I shall do my duty by them.'

'So we all are, Mr Forsyte; and I hope we shall all do our duty.'

'Why not confine the foreign business to the small countries–their currency is safe enough?'

'Old Mont', and his precious 'ring'!

'No,' said Soames, 'we must go back to safety.'

'Splendid isolation, Forsyte?'

'Meddling was all very well in the war, but in peace–politics or business–this half-and-half interference is no good. We can't control the foreign situation.'

He looked around him, and was instantly conscious that with those words he had struck a chord. 'I'm going through with this!' he thought.

'I should be glad, Mr Chairman'–the manager was speaking–'if I might say a word. The policy was of my initiation, and I think I may claim that it has been of substantial benefit to the Society so far. When, however, a member of the Board takes so strong a view against its continuance, I certainly don't press the Board to continue it. The times *are* uncertain, and a risk, of course, is involved, however conservative our estimates.'

'Now why?' thought Soames. 'What's he ratting for?'

'That's very handsome of you, Elderson; Mr Chairman, I think we may say that is very handsome of our manager.'

Old Dosey Cosey! Handsome! The old woman!

The chairman's rather harsh voice broke a silence.

'This is a very serious point of policy. I should have been glad to have Lord Fontenoy present.'

'If I am to endorse the report,' said Soames shortly, 'it must be decided to-day. I have made up my mind. But please yourselves.'

He threw in those last three words from a sort of fellow feeling–it was unpleasant to be dragooned! A moment's silence, and then discussion assumed that random volubility which softens a decision already forced on one. A quarter of an hour thus passed before the chairman said:

'We are agreed then, gentlemen, that the report shall contain the announcement that, in view of Continental uncertainty, we are abandoning foreign risks for the present.'

Soames had won. Relieved and puzzled, he walked away alone.

He had shown character; their respect for him had gone up, he could see; their liking for him down, if they'd ever had any–he didn't know! But why had Elderson veered round? He recalled the shift and blink of the fellow's steely eyes at the idea of the question being raised at the general meeting.

That had done it! But why? Were the figures faked? Surely not! That would be too difficult, in the face of the accountants. If Soames had faith, it was in chartered accountants. Sandis and Jevon were tip-top people. It couldn't be that! He glanced up from the pavement. The dome of St Paul's was dim already in the evening sky–nothing to be had out of it! He felt badly in need of someone to talk to; but there was nobody; and he quickened his pace among the hurrying crowd. His hand, driven deep into his overcoat pocket, came into sudden contact with some foreign sticky substance. 'Gracious!' he thought: 'those things!' Should he drop them in the gutter? If only there were a child he could take them home to! He must get Annette to speak to Fleur. He knew what came of bad habits from his own experience of long ago. Why shouldn't he speak to her himself? He was staying the night there! But there came on him a helpless sense of ignorance. These young people! What did they really think and feel? Was old Mont right? Had they given up interest in everything except the moment, abandoned all belief in continuity, and progress? True enough that Europe was in Queer Street. But look at the state of things after the Napoleonic Wars. He couldn't remember his grandfather 'Superior Dosset', the old chap had died five years before he was born, but he perfectly remembered how Aunt Ann, born in 1799, used to talk about 'that dreadful Bonaparte—we used to call him Boney, my dear;' of how her father could get eight or ten per cent for his money; and of what an impression 'those Chartists' had made on Aunts Juley and Hester, and that was long afterwards. Yet, in spite of all that, look at the Victorian era—a golden age, things worth collecting, children worth having! Why not again! Consols had risen almost continuously since Timothy died. Even if Heaven and Hell had gone, they couldn't be the reason; none of his uncles had believed in either, and yet had all made fortunes, and all had families, except Timothy and Swithin. No! It couldn't be the want of Heaven and Hell! What, then, was the reason of the change—if change there really were? And suddenly it was revealed to Soames. They talked too much—too much and too fast! They got to the end of interest in this and that and the other. They ate life and threw away the rind, and—and—By the way, he must buy that picture of George's! . . . Had these young folk more mind than his own generation? And if so—why? Was it diet? That lobster cocktail Fleur had given him the Sunday before last. He had eaten the thing—very nasty! But it hadn't made him want to talk. No! He didn't think it could be diet. Besides—Mind! Where were the minds now that equalled the Victorians—Darwin, Huxley, Dickens, Disraeli, even old Gladstone? Why, he remembered judges and advocates who seemed giants compared with those of the present day, just as he remembered that the judges of James his father's youth had seemed giants to James compared with those of Soames's prime. According to that, mind was steadily declining. It must be something else. There was a thing they called psycho-analysis, which so far as he could understand attributed people's action not to what they ate at breakfast, or the leg they got out of bed with, as in the good old days, but to some shock they had received in the remote past and entirely forgotten. The subconscious mind! Fads! Fads and microbes! The fact was this generation had no digestion. His father and his uncles had all complained of liver, but they had never had anything the matter with them—no need of any of these vitamins, false teeth, mental healing, newspapers, psycho-analysis, spiritualism, birth control, osteopathy, broadcasting, and what not. 'Machines!' thought Soames. 'That's it—I shouldn't wonder!' How could you believe in anything when everything was going round so fast? When you couldn't count your chickens—they ran about so? But Fleur had got a good little head on her! 'Yes,' he mused, 'and French teeth, she can digest anything. Two years! I'll speak to her before she gets the habit confirmed. Her mother was quick enough about it!' And perceiving the Connoisseurs' Club in front of him, he went in.

The hall porter came out of his box. A gentleman was waiting.

'What gentleman?' said Soames, sidelong.

'I think he's your nephew, sir, Mr Dartie.'

'Val Dartie! H'm! Where?'

'In the little room, sir.'

The little room—all the accommodation considered worthy of such as were not Connoisseurs—was at the end of a passage, and in no taste at all, as if the Club were saying: 'See what it is not to be one of us!' Soames entered it, and saw Val Dartie smoking a cigarette and gazing with absorption at the only object of interest, his own reflection in the glass above the fire.

He never saw his nephew without wondering when he would say: 'Look here, Uncle Soames, I'm up a stump.' Breeding race-horses! There could only be one end to that!'

'Well?' he said, 'how are *you*?'

The face in the glass turned round, and became the back of a clipped sandyish head.

'Oh! bobbish, thanks! *You* look all right, Uncle Soames. I just wanted to ask you: Must I take these screws of old George Forsyte's? They're dashed bad.'

'Gift horse in the mouth?' said Soames.

'Well,' said Val, 'but they're *so* dashed bad; by the time I've paid legacy duty, boxed them to a sale, and sold them, there won't be a sixpence. One of them falls down when you look at it. And the other two are broken-winded. The poor old boy kept them, because he couldn't get rid of them. They're about five hundred years old.'

'Thought you were fond of horses,' said Soames. 'Can't you turn them out?'

'Yes,' said Val, drily; 'but I've got my living to make. I haven't told my wife, for fear she should suggest that. I'm afraid I might see them in my dreams if I sold them. They're only fit for the kennels. Can I write to the executors and say I'm not rich enough to take them?'

'You can,' said Soames, and the words: 'How's your wife?' died unspoken on his lips. She was the daughter of his enemy, young Jolyon. That fellow was dead, but the fact remained.

'I will, then,' said Val. 'How did his funeral go off?'

'Very simple affair—I had nothing to do with it.' The days of funerals were over. No flowers, no horses, no plumes—a motor hearse, a couple of cars or so, was all the attention paid nowadays to the dead. Another sign of the times!

'I'm staying the night at Green Street,' said Val. 'I suppose you're not there, are you?'

'No,' said Soames, and did not miss the relief in his nephew's countenance.

'Oh! by the way, Uncle Soames—do you advise me to buy P.P.R.S. shares?'

'On the contrary. I'm going to advise your mother to sell. Tell her I'm coming in to-morrow.'

'Why? I thought—'

'Never mind my reasons!' said Soames shortly.

'So long, then!'

Exchanging a chilly hand-shake, he watched his nephew withdraw.

So long! An expression, old as the Boer war, that he had never got used to—meant nothing so far as he could see! He entered the reading-room. A number of Connoisseurs were sitting and standing about, and Soames, least clubbable of men, sought the solitude of an embrasured window. He sat there polishing the nail of one forefinger against the back of the other, and chewing the cud of life. After all, what was the point of anything? There was George! He had had an easy life—never done any work! And here was himself, who had done a lot of work! And sooner or later they would bury him too, with a motor hearse probably! And there was his son-in-law, young Mont, full of talk about good-ness knew what—and that thin-cheeked chap who had sold him the balloons this afternoon. And old Fontenoy, and that waiter over there; and the out-of-works and the in-works; and those chaps in Parliament, and the parsons in their pulpits–what were they all for? There was the old gardener down at Mapledurham pushing his roller over and over the lawn, week after week, and if he didn't, what would the lawn be like? That was life–gardener rolling lawn! Put it that there was another life–he didn't believe it, but for the sake of argument–that life must be just the same. Rolling lawn–to keep it lawn! What point in lawn? Conscious of pessimism, he rose. He had better be getting back to Fleur's–they dressed for dinner! He supposed there was something in dressing for dinner, but it was like lawn–you came unrolled–undressed again, and so it went on! Over and over and over to keep up to a pitch, that was–ah! what *was* the pitch for?

Turning into South Square, he cannoned into a young man, whose head was craned back as if looking after someone he had parted from. Uncertain whether to apologise or to wait for an apology, Soames stood still.

The young man said abruptly: 'Sorry, sir,' and moved on; dark, neat-looking chap with a hungry look obviously unconnected with his stomach. Murmuring: 'Not at all!' Soames moved forward and rang his daughter's bell. She opened to him herself. She was in hat and furs–just in. The young man recurred to Soames. Had he left her there? What a pretty face it was! He should certainly speak to her. If she once took to gadding about!

He put it off, however, till he was about to say 'Good-night'–Michael having gone to the political meeting of a Labour candidate, as if he couldn't find something better to do!

'Now you've been married two years, my child, I suppose you'll be looking towards the future. There's a great deal of nonsense talked about children. The whole thing's much simpler. I hope you feel that.'

Fleur was leaning back among the cushions of the settee, swinging her foot. Her eyes became a little restless, but her colour did not change.

'Of course!' she said; 'only there's no hurry, Dad.'

'Well, I don't know,' Soames murmured. 'The French and the royal family have a very sound habit of getting it over early. There's many a slip and it keeps them out of mischief. You're very attractive, my child–I don't want to see you take too much to gad-about ways. You've got all sorts of friends.'

'Yes,' said Fleur.

'You get on well with Michael, don't you?'

'Oh! yes.'

'Well, then, why not? You must remember that your son will be a what-you-call-it.'

In those words he compromised with his instinctive dislike of titles and flummery of that nature.

'It mightn't be a son,' said Fleur.

'At your age that's easily remedied.'

'Oh, I don't want a lot, Dad. One, perhaps, or two.'

'Well,' said Soames, 'I should almost prefer a daughter, something like–well, something like you.'

Her softened eyes flew, restive, from his face to her foot, to the dog, all over the room.

'I don't know, it's a tie–like digging your own grave in a way.'

'I shouldn't put it as high as that,' murmured Soames, persuasively.

'No man would, Dad.'

'Your mother wouldn't have got on at all without you,' and recollection of how her mother had been to not getting on at all with her – of how, but for him, she would have made a mess of it, reduced him to silent contemplation of the restive foot.

'Well,' he said, at last, 'I thought I'd mention it. I – I've got your happiness at heart.'

Fleur rose and kissed his forehead.

'I know, Dad,' she said, 'I'm a selfish pig. I'll think about it. In fact, I – I have thought about it.'

'That's right,' said Soames; 'that's right! You've a good head on you – it's a great consolation to me. Good-night, my dear!'

And he went up to his bed. If there was point in anything, it was in perpetuation of oneself, though, of course, that begged the question. 'Wonder,' he thought, 'if I ought to have asked her whether that young man –!' But young people were best left alone. The fact was, he didn't understand them. His eye lighted on the paper bag containing those – those things he had bought. He had brought them up from his overcoat to get rid of them – but how? Put into the fire, they would make a smell. he stood at his dressing-table, took one up and looked at it. Good Lord! And, suddenly, rubbing the mouthpiece with his handkerchief, he began to blow the thing up. He blew until his cheeks were tired, and then, nipping the aperture, took a bit of the dental cotton he used on his teeth every night and tied it up. There the thing was! With a pettish gesture he batted the balloon. Off it flew – purple and extravagant, alighting on his bed. H'm! He took up the other, and did the same to it. Purple and green! The deuce! If anyone came in and saw! He threw up the window, batted them, balloon after balloon, into the night, and shut the window down. There they'd be in the dark, floating about. His lips contracted in a nervous grin. People would see them in the morning. Well! What else could you do with things like that?

13

TENTERHOOKS

Michael had gone to the Labour candidate's meeting partly because he wanted to, and partly out of fellow feeling for 'old Forsyte', whom he was always conscious of having robbed. His father-in-law had been very decent about Fleur, and he liked the 'old man' to have her to himself when he could.

In a constituency which had much casual and no trades-union labour to speak of, the meeting would be one of those which enabled the intellectuals of the Party to get it 'off their chests'. Sentiment being 'slop', and championship mere condescension, one might look for sound economic speeches which left out discredited factors, such as human nature. Michael was accustomed to hearing people disparaged for deprecating change because human nature was constant; he was accustomed to hearing people despised for feeling compassion; he knew that one ought to be purely economic. And anyway that kind of speech was preferable to the tub-thumpings of the North or of the Park, which provoked a nasty underlying class spirit in himself.

The meeting was in full swing when he arrived, the candidate pitilessly exposing the fallacies of a capitalism which, in his view, had brought on the war. For fear that it should bring on another, it must be changed for a system which would ensure that nations should not want anything too much. The individual–said the candidate–was in every respect superior to the nation of which he formed a part; and the problem before them was to secure an economic condition which would enable the individual to function freely in his native superiority. In that way alone, he said, would they lose those mass movements and emotions which imperilled the sanity of the world. He spoke well. Michael listened, purring almost audibly, till he found that he was thinking of himself, Wilfrid and Fleur. Would he ever function so freely in a native superiority that he did not want Fleur too much? And did he wish to? He did not. That seemed to introduce human nature into the speaker's argument. Didn't everybody want something too much? Wasn't it natural? And if so, wouldn't there always be a collective wanting too much–pooling of primary desire, such as the desire of keeping your own head above water? The candidate's argument seemed to him suddenly to leave out heat, to omit friction, to be that of a man in an armchair after a poor lunch. He looked attentively at the speaker's shrewd, dry, doubting face. 'No juice!' he thought. And when 'the chap' sat down, he got up and left the hall.

This Wilfrid business had upset him horribly. Try as he had to put it out of his mind, try as he would to laugh it off, it continued to eat into his sense of security and happiness. Wife and best friend! A hundred times a day he assured himself that he trusted Fleur. Only, Wilfred was so much more attractive than himself, and Fleur deserved the best of everything. Besides, Wilfrid was going through torture, and it was not a pleasant thought! How end the thing, restore peace of mind to himself, to him, to her? She had told him nothing; and it simply was impossible to ask. No way even of showing his anxiety! The whole thing was just 'dark', and, so far as he could see, would have to stay so; nothing to be done but screw the lid on tighter, be as nice as he could to her, try not to feel bitter about him. Hades!

He turned down Chelsea Embankment. Here the sky was dark and wide and streaming with stars. The river wide, dark and gleaming with oily rays from the Embankment lamps. The width of it all gave him relief. Dash the dumps! A jolly, queer, muddled, sweet and bitter world; an immensely intriguing game of chance, no matter how the cards were falling at the moment! In the trenches he had thought: 'Get out of this, and I'll never mind anything again!' How seldom now he remembered thinking that! The human body renewed itself–they said–in seven years. In three years' time his body would not be the body of the trenches, but a whole-time peace body with a fading complex. If only Fleur would tell him quite openly what she felt, what she was doing about Wilfrid, for she must be doing something! And Wilfrid's verse? Would his confounded passion–as Bart suggested–flow in poetry? And if so, who would publish it? A miserable business! Well the night was beautiful, and the great thing not to be a pig. Beauty and not being a pig! Nothing much else to it–except laughter–the comic side! Keep one's sense of humour, anyway! And Michael searched, while he strode beneath plane trees half-stripped of leaves and plume-like in the dark, for the fun in his position. He failed to find it. There seemed absolutely nothing funny about love. Possibly he might fall out of love again some day, but not so long as she kept him on her tenterhooks. Did she do it on purpose? Never! Fleur simply could not be like those women who kept their husbands hungry and fed them when they wanted dresses, furs, jewels. Revolting!

He came in sight of Westminster. Only half-past ten! Suppose he took a cab to Wilfrid's rooms, and tried to have it out with him. It would be like trying to make the hands of a clock move backwards to its ticking. What use in saying: 'You love Fleur–well, don't!' or in Wilfrid saying it to him. 'After all, I was first with Fleur,' he thought. Pure chance, perhaps, but fact! Ah! And wasn't that just the danger? He was no longer a novelty to her–nothing unexpected about him now! And he and she had agreed times without number that novelty was the salt of life, the essence of interest and drama. Novelty now lay with Wilfrid! Lord! Lord! Possession appeared far from being nine points of the law! He rounded-in from the Embankment towards home–jolly part of London, jolly Square; everything jolly except just this infernal complication. Something, soft as a large leaf, tapped twice against his ear. He turned, astonished; he was in empty space, no tree near. Floating in the darkness, a round thing–he grabbed, it bobbed. What? A child's balloon! He secured it between his hands, took it beneath a lamp-post–green, he judged. Queer! He looked up. Two windows lighted, one of them Fleur's! Was this the bubble of his own happiness expelled? Morbid! Silly ass! Some gust of wind–a child's plaything lodged and loosened! He held the balloon gingerly. He would take it in and show it to her. He put his latch-key in the door. Dark in the hall–gone up! He mounted, swinging the balloon on his finger. Fleur was standing before a mirror.

'What on earth's that?' she said.

The blood returned to Michael's heart. Curious how he had dreaded its having anything to do with her!

'Don't know, darling; fell on my hat–must belong to heaven.' And he batted it.

The balloon floated, dropped, bounded twice, wobbled and came to rest.

'You *are* a baby, Michael. I believe you bought it.'

Michael came closer, and stood quite still.

'My hat! What a misfortune to be in love!'

'You think so!'

'*Il y a toujours un qui baise, et l'autre qui ne tend pas la joue.*'

'But I do.'

'Fleur!'

Fleur smiled.

'*Baise* away.'

Embracing her, Michael thought: 'She holds me–does with me what she likes; I know nothing of her!'

And there arose a small sound–from Ting-a-ling smelling the balloon.

PART II

I

THE MARK FALLS

The state of the world had been getting more and more on Soames's nerves ever since the general meeting of the P.P.R.S. It had gone off with that fatuity long associated by him with such gatherings—a watertight rigmarole from the chairman; butter from two reliable shareholders; vinegar from shareholders not so reliable; and the usual 'gup' over the dividend. He had gone there glum, come away glummer. From a notion once taken into his head Soames parted more slowly than a cheese parts from its mites. Two-sevenths of foreign business, nearly all German! And the mark falling! It had begun to fall from the moment that he decided to support the dividend. And why? What was in the wind? Contrary to his custom, he had taken to sniffing closely the political columns of his paper. The French—he had always mistrusted them, especially since his second marriage—the French were going to play old Harry, if he was not greatly mistaken! Their papers, he noticed, never lost a chance of having a dab at English policy; seemed to think they could always call the tune for England to pipe to! And the mark and the franc, and every other sort of money, falling. And, though in Soames was that which rejoiced in the thought that one of his country's bits of paper could buy a great quantity of other countries' bits of paper, there was also that which felt the whole thing silly and unreal, with an ever-growing consciousness that the P.P.R.S. would pay no dividend next year. The P.P.R.S. was a big concern; no dividend would be a sign, no small one, of bad management. Assurance was one of the few things on God's earth which could and should be conducted without real risk. But for that he would never have gone to the Board. And to find assurance had not been so conducted and that by himself, was—well! He had caused Winifred to sell, anyway, though the shares had already fallen slightly. 'I thought it was such a good thing, Soames,' she had said plaintively: 'it's rather a bore, losin' money on these shares.' He had answered without mercy: 'If you don't sell, you'll lose more.' And she had done it. If the Rogers and Nicholases who had followed him into it hadn't sold too—well, it was their look-out! He had made Winifred warn them. As for himself, he had nothing but his qualifying shares, and the missing of a dividend or two would not hurt one whose director's fees more than compensated. It was not, therefore, private uneasiness so much as resentment at a state of things connected with foreigners and the slur on his infallibility.

Christmas had gone off quietly at Mapledurham. He abominated Christmas, and only observed it because his wife was French, and her national festival New Year's Day. One could not go so far as to observe that, encouraging a foreign notion. But Christmas with no child about—he still remembered the holly and snapdragons of Park Lane in his own childhood—the family parties; and how disgusted he had been if he got anything symbolic—the thimble, or the ring—instead of the shilling. They had never gone in for Santa Claus at Park Lane, partly because they could see through the old gentleman, and partly because he was not at all a late thing. Emily, his mother, had seen to that. Yes; and, by the way, that William Gouldyng, Ingerer, had so stumped those fellows at the Heralds' College, that Soames had dropped the enquiry—it was just encouraging them to spend his money for a sentimental satisfaction which did not materlialise. That narrow-headed chap, 'Old Mont', peacocked about his ancestry; all the more reason for having no ancestry to peacock about. The Forsytes and the Goldings were good English country stock—that was what mattered. And if Fleur and her child, if one came, had French blood in them—well, he couldn't help it now.

In regard to the coming of a grandchild, Soames knew no more than in October. Fleur had spent Christmas with the Monts; she was promised to him, however, before long, and her mother must ask her a question or two!

The weather was extremely mild; Soames had even been out in a punt fishing. In a heavy coat he trailed a line for perch and dace, and caught now and then a roach—precious little good, the servants wouldn't eat them, nowadays! His grey eyes would brood over the grey water under the grey sky; and in his mind the mark would fall. It fell with a bump on that eleventh of January when the French went and occupied the Ruhr. He said to Annette at breakfast: 'Your country's cracked! Look at the mark now!'

'What do I care about the mark?' she had answered over her coffee. 'I care that they shall not come again into my country. I hope they will suffer a little what we have suffered.'

'You,' said Soames; 'you never suffered anything.'

Annette put her hand where Soames sometimes doubted the existence of a heart.

'I have suffered here,' she said.

'I didn't notice it. You never went without butter. What do you suppose Europe's going to be like now for the next thirty years! How about British trade?'

'We French see before our noses,' said Annette with warmth. 'We see that the beaten must be kept the beaten, or he will take revenge. You English are so sloppy.'

'Sloppy, are we?' said Soames. 'You're talking like a child. Could a sloppy people ever have reached our position in the world?'

'That is your selfishness. You are cold and selfish.'

'Cold, selfish and sloppy—they don't go together. Try again.'

'Your slop is in your thought and your talk; it is your instinct that gives you your success, and your English instinct is cold and selfish, Soames. You are a mixture, all of you, of hypocrisy, stupidity and egoism.'

Soames took some marmalade.

'Well,' he said, 'and what are the French?—cynical, avaricious and revengeful. And the Germans are sentimental, heady and brutal. We can all abuse each other. There's nothing for it but to keep clear. And that's what you French won't do.'

Annette's handsome person stiffened.

'When you are tied to a person, as I am tied to you, Soames, or as we French are tied to the Germans, it is necessary to be top dog, or to be bottom dog.'

Soames stayed his toast.

'Do you suppose yourself top dog in this house?'

'Yes, Soames.'

'Oh! Then you can go back to France to-morrow.'

Annette's eyebrows rose quizzically.

'I would wait a little longer, my friend; you are still too young.'

But Soames had already regretted his remark; he did not wish any disturbance at his time of life, and he said more calmly:

'Compromise is the essence of any reasonable existence between individuals or nations. We can't have the fat thrown into the fire every few years.'

'That is so English,' murmured Annette. 'We others never know what you English will do. You always wait to see which way the cat jumps.'

However deeply sympathetic with such a reasonable characteristic, Soames would have denied it at any ordinary moment–to confess to temporising was not, as it were, done. But, with the mark falling like a cartload of bricks, he was heated to the point of standing by his nature.

'And why shouldn't we? Rushing into things that you'll have to rush out of! I don't want to argue. French and English never did get on, and never will.'

Annette rose. 'You speak the truth, my friend. *Entente, mais pas cordiale.* What are you doing to-day?'

'Going up to town,' said Soames glumly. 'Your precious Government has put business into Queer Street with a vengeance.'

'Do you stay the night?'

'I don't know.'

'*Adieu*, then, *jusqu'au revoir!*' And she got up.

Soames remained brooding above his marmalade–with the mark falling in his mind–glad to see the last of her handsome figure, having no patience at the moment for French tantrums. An irritable longing to say to somebody 'I told you so' possessed him. He would have to wait, however, till he found somebody to say it to.

A beautiful day, quite warm; and, taking his umbrella as an assurance against change, he set out for the station.

In the carriage going up they were talking about the Ruhr. Averse from discussion in public, Soames listened from behind his paper. The general sentiment was surprisingly like his own. In so far as it was unpleasant for the Huns–all right; in so far as it was unpleasant for British trade–all wrong; in so far as love of British trade was active and hate of Huns now passive–more wrong than right. A Francophil remark that the French were justified in making themselves safe at all cost, was coldly received. At Maidenhead a man got in whom Soames connected automatically with disturbance. He had much grey hair, a sanguine face, lively eyes, twisting eyebrows, and within five minutes had asked in a breezy voice whether anyone had heard of the League of Nations. Confirmed in his estimate, Soames looked round the corner of his paper. Yes, that chap would get off on some hobby-horse or other! And there he went! The question–said the newcomer–was not whether the Germans should get one in the eye, the British one in the pocket, or the French one in the heart, but whether the world should get peace and goodwill. Soames lowered his paper. If–this fellow said–they wanted peace, they must sink their individual interests, and think in terms of collective interest. The good of all was the good of one! Soames saw the flaw at once; that might be, but the good of one was not the good of all. He felt that if he did not take care he would be pointing this out. The man was a perfect stranger to him, and no good ever came of argument. Unfortunately his silence amid the general opinion that the League of Nations was 'no earthly', seemed to cause the newcomer to regard him as a sympathiser; the fellow kept on throwing his eyebrows at him! To put up his paper again seemed too pointed, and his position was getting more and more false when the train ran in at Paddington. He hastened to a cab. A voice behind him said:

'Hopeless lot, sir, eh! Glad to see *you* saw my point.'

'Quite!' said Soames. 'Taxi!'

'Unless the League of Nations functions, we're all for Gehenna.'

Soames turned the handle of the cab door.

'Quite!' he said again. 'Poultry!' and got in. He was not going to be drawn. The fellow was clearly a firebrand!

In the cab the measure of his disturbance was revealed. He had said 'Poultry', an address that 'Forsyte, Bustard and Forsyte' had abandoned two-and-twenty years ago when, merged with 'Cuthcott, Holliday and Kingson,' they became 'Cuthcott, Kingson and Forsyte'. Rectifying the error, he sat forward, brooding. Fall of the mark! The country was sound about it, yes—but when they failed to pay the next dividend, could they rely on resentment against the French instead of against the directors? Doubtful! The directors ought to have seen it coming! That might be said of the other directors, but not of himself—here was a policy that he personally never would have touched. If only he could discuss the whole thing with someone—but old Gradman would be out of his depth in a matter of this sort. And, on arrival at his office, he gazed with a certain impatience at that changeless old fellow, sitting in his swivel chair.

'Ah! Mr Soames, I was hopin' you might come in this morning. There's a young man been round to see you from the P.P.R.S. Wouldn't give his business, said he wanted to see you privately. Left his number on the phone.'

'Oh!' said Soames.

'Quite a young feller—in the office.'

'What did he look like?'

'Nice, clean young man. I was quite favourably impressed—name of Butterfield.'

'Well, ring him up, and let him know I'm here.' And going over to the window, he stood looking out on to a perfectly blank wall.

Suited to a sleeping partner, his room was at the back, free from disturbance. Young man! The call was somewhat singular! And he said over his shoulder: 'Don't go when he comes, Gradman, I know nothing of him.'

The world changed, people died off, the mark fell, but Gradman was there—embodiment, faithful and grey, of service and integrity—an anchor.

Gradman's voice, grating, ingratiating, rose.

'This French news—it's not nice, Mr Soames. They're a hasty lot. I remember your father, Mr James, coming into the office the morning the Franco-Prussian war was declared—quite in his prime then, hardly more than sixty, I should say. Why, I recall his very words: "There," he said, "I told them so." And here they are—at it still. The fact is, they're cat and dog.'

Soames, who had half turned, resumed his contemplation of a void. Poor old Gradman dated! What would he say when he heard that they had been insuring foreign business? Stimulated by the old-time quality of Gradman's presence, his mind ranged with sudden freedom. He himself had another twenty years, perhaps. What would he see in that time? Where would old England be at the end of it? 'In spite of the papers, we're not such fools as we look,' he thought. 'If only we can steer clear of flibberty-gibberting, and pay our way!'

'Mr Butterfield, sir.' H'm! The young man had been very spry. Covered by Gradman's bluff and greasy greeting, he 'took a lunar,' as his Uncle Roger used to call it. The young fellow, in a neat suit, a turndown collar, with his hat in his hand, was a medium modest-looking chap. Soames nodded.

'You want to see me?'

'Alone if I might, sir.'

'Mr Gradman here is my right-hand man.'

Gradman's voice purred gratingly: 'You can state your business. Nothing goes outside these walls, young man.'

'I'm in the office of the P.P.R.S., sir. The fact is, accident has just put some information in my hands, and I'm not easy in my mind. Knowing you to be a solicitor, sir, I preferred to come to you, rather than go to the chairman. As a lawyer, would you tell me: Is my first duty to the Society, being in their employ?'

'Certainly,' said Soames.

'I don't like this job, sir, and I hope you'll understand that I'm not here for any personal motive–it's just because I feel I ought to.'

Soames regarded him steadily. Though large and rather swimming, the young man's eyes impressed him by their resemblance to a dog's. 'What's it all about?' he said.

The young man moistened his lips.

'The insurance of our German business, sir.'

Soames pricked his ears, already slightly pointed by Nature.

'It's a very serious matter,' the young man went on, 'and I don't know how it'll affect me, but the fact is, this morning I overhead a private conversation.'

'Oh!' said Soames.

'Yes, sir. I quite understand your tone, but the very first words did it. I simply couldn't make myself known after hearing them. I think you'll agree, sir.'

'Who were the speakers?'

'The manager, and a man called Smith–I fancy by his accent his name's a bit more foreign–who's done most of the agenting for the German business.'

'What were the words?' said Soames.

'Well, sir, the manager was speaking, and then this Smith said: "Quite so, Mr Elderson, but we haven't paid you a commission on all this business for nothing; if the mark goes absolutely phut, you will have to see that your Society makes it good for us!"'

The intense longing, which at that moment came on Soames to emit a whistle, was checked by sight of Gradman's face. The old fellow's mouth had opened in the nest of his grizzly short beard; his eyes stared puglike, he uttered a prolonged: 'A-ow!'

'Yes,' said the young man, 'it was a knock-out!'

'Where were you?' asked Soames, sharply.

'In the lobby between the manager's room and the board-room. I'd just come from sorting some papers in the board-room, and the manager's door was open an inch or so. Of course I know the voices well.'

'What after?'

'I heard Mr Elderson say: "H'ssh! Don't talk like that!" and I slipped back into the board-room. I'd had more than enough, sir, I assure you.'

Suspicion and surmise clogged Soames's thinking apparatus. Was this young fellow speaking the truth? A man like Elderson–the risk was monstrous! And, if true, what was the directors' responsibility? But proof–proof? He stared at the young man, who looked upset and pale enough, but whose eyes did not waver. Shake him if he could! And he said sharply:

'Now mind what you're saying! This is most serious!'

'I know that, sir. If I'd consulted my own interest, I'd never have come here. I'm not a sneak.'

The words rang true, but Soames did not drop his caution.

'Ever had any trouble in the office?'

'No, sir, you can make enquiry. I've nothing against Mr Elderson, and he's nothing against me.'

Soames thought suddenly: 'Good heavens! He's shifted it on to me, and in the presence of a witness. And I supplied the witness!'

'Have you any reason to suppose,' he said, 'that they became aware of your being there?'

'They couldn't have, I think.'

The implications of this news seemed every second more alarming. It was as if Fate, kept at bay all his life by clever wrist-work, had suddenly slipped a thrust under his guard. No good to get rattled, however–must think it out at leisure!

'Are you prepared, if necessary, to repeat this to the Board?'

The young man pressed his hands together.

'Well, sir, I'd much rather have held my tongue; but if you decide it's got to be taken up, I suppose I must go through with it now. I'm sure I hope you'll decide to leave it alone; perhaps it isn't true–only why didn't Mr Elderson say: "You ruddy liar!"?'

Exactly! Why didn't he? Soames gave a grunt of intense discomfort.

'Anything more?' he said.

'No, sir.'

'Very well. You've not told anyone?'

'No, sir.'

'Then don't, and leave it to me.'

'I'll be only too happy to, sir. Good-morning!'

'Good-morning!'

No–very bad morning! No satisfaction whatever in this sudden fulfilment of his prophetic feeling about Elderson. None!

'What d'you think of that young fellow, Gradman? Is he lying?'

Thus summoned, as it were, from stupor, Gradman thoughtfully rubbed a nose both thick and shining.

'It's one word against another, Mr Soames, unless you get more evidence. But I can't see what the young man has to gain by it.'

'Nor I; but you never know. The trouble will be to get more evidence. Can I act without it?'

'It's delicate,' said Gradman. And Soames knew that he was thrown back on himself. When Gradman said a thing was delicate, it meant that it was the sort of matter on which he was accustomed to wait for orders–presumptuous even to hold opinion! But had he got one? Well, one would never know! The old chap would sit and rub his nose over it till Kingdom Come.

'I shan't act in a hurry,' he said, almost angrily: 'I can't see to the end of this.'

Every hour confirmed that statement. At lunch the tape of his city club

showed the mark still falling–to unheard-of depths! How they could talk of
golf, with this business on his mind, he could not imagine!

'I must go and see that fellow,' he said to himself. 'I shall be guarded. He may
throw some light.' He waited until three o'clock and repaired to the P.P.R.S.

Reaching the office, he sought the board-room. The chairman was there in
conference with the manager. Soames sat down quietly to listen; and while he
listened he watched that fellow's face. It told him nothing. What nonsense
people talked when they said you could tell character from faces! Only a perfect
idiot's face could be read like that. And here was a man of experience and culture, one who knew every rope of business life and polite society. The hairless,
neat features exhibited no more concern than the natural mortification of one
whose policy had met with such a nasty knock. The drop of the mark had
already wiped out any possible profit on the next half-year. Unless the
wretched thing recovered, they would be carrying a practically dead load of
German insurance. Really it was criminal that no limit of liability had been
fixed! How on earth could he ever have overlooked that when he came on the
Board? But he had only known of it afterwards. And who could have foreseen
anything so mad as this Ruhr business, or realised the slack confidence of his
colleagues in this confounded fellow? The words 'gross negligence' appeared
'close up' before his eyes. What if an action lay against the Board! Gross negligence! At his age and with his reputation! Why! The thing was plain as a pike-
staff; for omitting a limit of liability this chap had got his commission! Ten
per cent probably, on all that business–he must have netted thousands! A man
must be in Queer Street indeed to take a risk like that! But conscious that his
fancy was running on, Soames rose, and turned his back. The action suggested
another. Simulate anger, draw some sign from that fellow's self-control! He
turned again, and said pettishly: 'What on earth were you about, Mr Manager,
when you allowed these contracts to go through without limit of liability? A
man of your experience! What was your motive?'

A slight narrowing of the eyes, a slight compression of the lips. He had relied
on the word 'motive', but the fellow passed it by.

'For such high premiums as we have been getting, Mr Forsyte, a limited
liability was not possible. This is a most outrageous development, and I'm
afraid it must be considered just bad luck.'

'Unfortunately,' said Soames, 'there's no such thing as luck in properly
regulated assurance, as we shall find, or I'm much mistaken. I shouldn't be
surprised if an action lay against the Board for gross negligence!'

That had got the chairman's goat!–Got his goat? What expressions they used
nowadays! Or did it mean the opposite? One never knew! But as for Elderson–
he seemed to Soames to be merely counterfeiting a certain flusteration. Futile
to attempt to spring anything out of a chap like that. If the thing were true, the
fellow must be entirely desperate, prepared for anything and everything. And
since from Soames the desperate side of life–the real holes, the impossible positions which demand a gambler's throw–had always been carefully barred by
the habits of a prudent nature, he found it now impossible to imagine Elderson's state of mind, or his line of conduct if he were guilty. For all he could tell,
the chap might be carrying poison about with him; might be sitting on a revolver
like a fellow on the film. The whole thing was too unpleasant, too worrying for
words. And without saying any more he went away, taking nothing with him
but the knowledge that their total liability on this German business, with the
mark valueless, was over two hundred thousand pounds. He hastily reviewed

the fortunes of his co-directors. Old Fontenoy was always in low water; the chairman a dark horse; Mont was in land, land right down in value, and mortgaged at that; old Cosey Mothergill had nothing but his name and his director's fees; Meyricke must have a large income, but light come, light go, like most of those big counsel with irons in many fires and the certainty of a judgeship. Not a really substantial man among the lot, except himself! He ploughed his way along, head down. Public companies! Preposterous system! You had to trust somebody, and there you were! It was appalling!

'Balloons, sir—beautiful colours, five feet circumference. Take one, gentleman!'

'Good gad!' said Soames. As if the pricked bubble of German business were not enough!

2

VICTORINE

All through December ballooons had been slack—hardly any movement about them, even in Christmas week, and from the Bickets Central Australia was as far ever. The girl Victorine, restored to comparative health, had not regained her position in the blouse department of Messrs Boney Blayds & Co. They had given her some odd sewing, but not of late, and she had spent much time trying to get work less uncertain. Her trouble was—had always been—her face. It was unusual. People did not know what to make of a girl who looked like that. Why employ one who without qualification of wealth, rank, fashion, or ability (so far as they knew) made them feel ordinary? For—however essential to such as Fleur and Michael—dramatic interest was not primary in the manufacture or sale of blouses, in the fitting-on of shoes, the addressing of envelopes, making-up of funeral wreaths, or the other ambitions of Victorine. Behind those large dark eyes and silent lips, what went on? It worried Boney Blayds & Co., and the more wholesale firms of commerce. The lurid professions—film-super, or mannequin—did not occur to one, of self-deprecating nature, born in Putney.

When Bicket had gone out of a morning with his tray and his balloons not yet blown up, she would stand biting her finger, as though to gnaw her way to some escape from this hand-to-mouth existence which kept her husband thin as a rail, tired as a rook, shabby as a tailless sparrow, and, at the expense of all caste feeling, brought them in no more than just enough to keep them living under a roof. It had long been clear to them both that there was no future in balloons, just a cadging present. And there smouldered in the silent, passive Victorine a fierce resentment. She wanted better things for herself, for him, chiefly for him.

On the morning when the mark was bumping down, she was putting on her velveteen jacket and toque (best remaining items of her wardrobe), having taken a resolve. Bicket never mentioned his old job, and his wife had subtly divined some cause beyond the ordinary for his loss of it. Why not see if she could get him taken back? He had often said: 'Mr Mont's a gent and a sort o' Socialist; been through the war, too; no high-and-mighty about *him*.' If she could 'get at' this phenomenon! With the flush of hope and daring in her sallow cheeks, she took stock of her appearance from the window-glasses of the

Strand. Her velveteen of jade-green always pleased one who had an eye for colour, but her black skirt–well, perhaps the wear and tear of it wouldn't show if she kept behind the counter. Had she brass enough to say that she came about a manuscript? And she rehearsed with silent lips, pinching her accent: 'Would you ask Mr Mont, please, if I could see him; it's about a manuscript.' Yes! and then would come the question: 'What name, please?' 'Mrs Bicket?' Never! 'Miss Victorine Collins?' All authoresses had maiden names. Victorine–yes! But Collins! It didn't sound like. And no one would know what her maiden name had been. Why not choose one? They often chose. And she searched. Something Italian, like–like–Hadn't their landlady said to them when they came in: 'Is your wife Eyetalian?' Ah! Manuelli! That was certainly Italian–the ice-cream man in Little Ditch Street had it! She walked on practising beneath her breath. If only she could get to see this Mr Mont!

She entered, trembling. All went exactly as foreseen, even to the pinching of her accent, till she stood waiting for them to bring an answer from the speaking-tube, concealing her hands in their very old gloves. Had Miss Manuelli an appointment? There was no manuscript.

'No,' said Victorine, 'I haven't sent it yet. I wanted to see him first.' The young man at the counter was looking at her hard. He went again to the tube, then spoke.

'Will you wait a minute, please–Mr Mont's lady secretary is coming down.'

Victorine inclined her head towards her sinking heart. A lady secretary! She would never get there now! And there came on her the sudden dread of false pretences. But the thought of Tony standing at his corner, ballooned up to the eyes, as she had spied out more than once, fortified her desperation.

A girl's voice said: 'Miss Manuelli? Mr Mont's secretary, perhaps you could give me a message.'

A fresh-faced young woman's eyes were travelling up and down her. Pinching her accent hard, she said: 'Oh! I'm afraid I couldn't do that.'

The travelling gaze stopped at her face. 'If you'll come with me, I'll see if he can see you.'

Alone in a small waiting-room, Victorine sat without movement, till she saw a young man's face poked through the doorway, and heard the words:

'Will you come in?'

She took a deep breath, and went. Once in the presence, she looked from Michael to his secretary and back again, subtly daring his youth, his chivalry, his sportsmanship, to refuse her a private interview. Through Michael passed at once the thought: 'Money, I suppose. But what an interesting face!' The secretary drew down the corners of her mouth and left the room.

'Well, Miss–er–Manuelli?'

'Not Manuelli, please–Mrs Bicket; my husband used to be here.'

'What!' The chap that had snooped 'Copper Coin'! Phew! Bicket's yarn–his wife–pneumonia! She looked as if she might have had it.

'He often spoke of you, sir. And, please, he hasn't any work. Couldn't you find room for him again, sir?'

Michael stood silent. Did this terribly interesting-looking girl know about the snooping?

'He just sells balloons in the street now; I can't bear to see him. Over by St Paul's he stands, and there's no money in it; and we do so want to get out to Australia. I know he's very nervy, and gets wrong with people. But if you *could* take him back here. . . .'

No! she did not know!

'Very sorry, Mrs Bicket. I remember your husband well, but we haven't a place for him. Are *you* all right again?'

'Oh! yes. Except that I can't get work again either.'

What a face for wrappers! Sort of Mona Lisa-ish! Storbert's novel! Ha!

'Well, I'll have a talk with your husband. I suppose you wouldn't like to sit to an artist for a book-wrapper? It might lead to work in that line if you want it. You're just the type for a friend of mine. Do you know Aubrey Greene's work?'

'No, sir.'

'It's pretty good–in fact, very good in a decadent way. You wouldn't mind sitting?'

'I wouldn't mind anything to save some money. But I'd rather you didn't tell my husband I'd been to see you. He might take it amiss.'

'All right! I'll see him by accident. Near St Paul's, you said? But there's no chance here, Mrs Bicket. Besides, he couldn't make two ends meet on this job, he told me.'

'When I was ill, sir.'

'Of course, that makes a difference.'

'Yes, sir.'

'Well, let me write you a note to Mr Greene. Will you sit down a minute?'

He stole a look at her while she sat waiting. Really, her sallow, large-eyed face, with its dead-black, bobbed, frizzy-ended hair, was extraordinarily interesting–a little too refined and anaemic for the public; but, dash it all! the public couldn't always have its Reckitt's blue eyes, corn-coloured hair, and poppy cheeks. 'She's not a peach,' he wrote, 'on the main tree of taste; but so striking in her way that she really might become a type, like Beardsley's or Dana's.'

When she had taken the note and gone, he rang for his secretary.

'No, Miss Perren, she didn't take anything off me. But some type, eh?'

'I thought you'd like to see her. She wasn't an authoress, was she?'

'Far from it.'

'Well, I hope she got what she wanted.'

Michael grinned. 'Partly, Miss Perren–partly. You think I'm an awful fool, don't you?'

'I'm sure I don't; but I think you're too soft-hearted.'

Michael ran his fingers through his hair.

'Would it surprise you to hear that I've done a stroke of business?'

'Yes, Mr Mont.'

'Then I won't tell you what it is. When you've done pouting, go on with that letter to my father about "Duet": "We are sorry to say that in the present state of the trade we should not be justified in reprinting the dialogue between those two old blighters; we have already lost money by it!" You must translate, of course. Now can we say something to cheer the old boy up? How about this? "When the French have recovered their wits, and the birds begin to sing–in short, when spring comes–we hope to reconsider the matter in the light of–of–"–er–what, Miss Perren?'

'"The experience we shall have gained." Shall I leave out about the French and the birds?'

'Excellent! "Yours faithfully, Danby and Winter." Don't you think it was a scandalous piece of nepotism bringing the book here at all, Miss Perren?'

'What is "nepotism"?'

'Taking advantage of your son. He's never made a sixpence by any of his books.'

'He's a very distinguished writer, Mr Mont.'

'And we pay for the distinction. Well, he's a good old Bart. That's all before lunch, and mind you have a good one. That girl's figure wasn't usual either, was it? She's thin, but she stands up straight. There's a question I always want to ask, Miss Perren: Why do modern girls walk in a curve with their heads poked forward? They can't all be built like that.'

The secretary's cheeks brightened.

'There *is* a reason, Mr Mont.'

'Good! What is it?'

The secretary's cheeks continued to brighten. 'I don't really know whether I can–'

'Oh! sorry. I'll ask my wife. Only she's quite straight herself.'

'Well, Mr Mont, it's this, you see: They aren't supposed to have anything be–behind, and, of course, they have, and they can't get the proper effect unless they curve their chests in and poke their heads forward. It's the fashion-plates and mannequins that do it.'

'I see,' said Michael; 'thank you, Miss Perren; awfully good of you. It's the limit, isn't it?'

'Yes, I don't hold with it, myself.'

'No, quite!'

The secretary lowered her eyelids and withdrew.

Michael sat down and drew a face on his blotting-paper. It was not Victorine's. . . .

Armed with the note to Aubrey Greene, Victorine had her usual lunch, a cup of coffee and a bit of heavy cake, and took the tube towards Chelsea. She had not succeeded, but the gentleman had been friendly and she felt cheered.

At the studio door was a young man inserting a key–very elegant in smoke-grey Harris tweeds, a sliding young man with no hat, beautifully brushed-back bright hair, and a soft voice.

'Model?' he said.

'Yes, sir, please. I have a note for you from Mr Mont.'

'Michael? Come in.'

Victorine followed him in. It was 'not half' sea-green in there; a high room with rafters and a top light, and lots of pictures and drawings on the walls, and as if they had slipped off on to the floor. A picture on an easel of two ladies with their clothes sliding down troubled Victorine. She became conscious of the gentleman's eyes, sea-green like the walls, sliding up and down her.

'Will you sit for anything?' he asked.

Victorine answered mechanically: 'Yes, sir.'

'Do you mind taking your hat off?'

Victorine took off the toque, and shook out her hair.

'Ah!' said the gentleman. 'I wonder.'

Victorine wondered what.

'Just sit down on the dais, will you?'

Victorine looked about her, uncertain. A smile seemed to fly up his forehead and over his slippery bright hair.

'This is your first shot, then?'

'Yes, sir.'

'All the better.' And he pointed to a small platform.

Victorine sat down on it in a black oak chair.

'You look cold.'

'Yes, sir.'

He went to a cupboard and returned with two small glasses of a brown fluid.

'Have a Grand Marnier?'

She noticed that he tossed his off in one gulp, and did the same. It was sweet, strong, very nice, and made her gasp.

'Take a cigarette.'

Victorine took one from a case he handed, and put it between her lips. He lit it. And again a smile slid up away over the top of his head.

'You draw it in,' he said. 'Where were you born?'

'In Putney, sir.'

'That's very interesting. Just sit still a minute. It's not as bad as having a tooth out, but it takes longer. The great thing is to keep awake.'

'Yes, sir.'

He took a large piece of paper and a bit of dark stuff, and began to draw.

'Tell me,' he said, 'Miss—'

'Collins, sir—Victorine Collins.' Some instinct made her give her maiden name. It seemed somehow more professional.

'Are you at large?' He paused, and again the smile slid up over his bright hair: 'Or have you any other occupation?'

'Not at present, sir. I'm married, but nothing else.'

For some time after that the gentleman was silent. It was interesting to see him, taking a look, making a stroke on the paper, taking another look. Hundreds of looks, hundreds of strokes. At last he said: 'All right! Now we'll have a rest. Heaven sent you here, Miss Collins. Come and get warm.'

Victorine approached the fire.

'Do you know anything about expressionism?'

'No, sir.'

'Well, it means not troubling about the outside except in so far as it expresses the inside. Does that convey anything to you?'

'No, sir.'

'Quite! I think you said you'd sit for the—er—altogether?'

Victorine regarded the bright and sliding gentleman. She did not know what he meant, but she felt that he meant something out of the ordinary.

'Altogether what, sir?'

'Nude.'

'Oh!' She cast her eyes down, then raised them to the sliding clothes of the two ladies. 'Like that?'

'No, I shouldn't be treating you cubistically.'

A slow flush was burning out the sallow in her cheeks. She said slowly:

'Does it mean more money?'

'Yes, half as much again—more perhaps. I don't want you to if you'd rather not. You can think it over and let me know next time.'

She raised her eyes again, and said: 'Thank you, sir.'

'Righto! Only please don't "sir" me.'

Victorine smiled. It was the first time she had achieved this functional disturbance, and it seemed to have a strange effect. He said hurriedly: 'By George! When you smile, Miss Collins, I see you *im*pressionistically. If you've rested, sit up there again.'

Victorine went back.

The gentleman took a fresh piece of paper.

'Can you think of anything that will keep you smiling?'

She shook her head. That was a fact.

'Nothing comic at all? I suppose you're not in love with your husband, for instance?'

'Oh! yes.'

'Well, try that.'

Victorine tried that, but she could only see Tony selling his balloons.

'That won't do,' said the gentleman. 'Don't think of him! Did you ever see "*L'après-midi d'un Faune*"?'

'No, sir.'

'Well, I've got an idea. "*L'après-midi d'une Dryade.*" About the nude you really needn't mind. It's quite impersonal. Think of art, and fifteen bob a day. Shades of Nijinsky, I see the whole thing!'

All the time that he was talking his eyes were sliding off and on to her, and his pencil off and on to the paper. A sort of infection began to ferment within Victorine. Fifteen shillings a day! Blue butterflies!

There was a profound silence. His eyes and hand slid off and on. A faint smile had come on Victorine's face–she was adding up the money she might earn.

At last his eyes and hand ceased moving, and he stood looking at the paper.

'That's all for to-day, Miss Collins. I've got to think it out. Will you give me your address?'

Victorine thought rapidly.

'Please, sir, will you write to me at the post office. I don't want my husband to know that I'm–I'm–'

'Affiliated to art? Well! Name of post office?'

Victorine gave it and resumed her hat.

'An hour and a half, five shillings, thank you. And to-morrow, at half-past two, Miss Collins–not "sir".'

'Yes, s–, thank you.'

Waiting for her bus in the cold January air, the altogether appeared to Victorine improbable. To sit in front of a strange gentleman in her skin! If Tony knew! The slow flush again burned up the sallow in her cheeks. She climbed into the bus. But fifteen shillings! Six days a week–why, it would be four pound ten! In four months she could earn their passage out. Judging by the pictures in there, lots must be doing it. Tony must know nothing, not even that she was sitting for her face. He was all nerves, and that fond of her! He would imagine things; she had heard him say those artists were just like cats. But that gentleman had been very nice, though he did seem as if he were laughing at everything. She wished he had shown her the drawing. Perhaps she would see herself in an exhibition some day. But without–oh! And suddenly she thought: 'If I ate a bit more, I'd look nice like that, too!' And as if to escape from the daring of that thought, she stared up into the face opposite. It had two chins, was calm and smooth and pink, with light eyes staring back at her. People had thoughts, but you couldn't tell what they were! And the smile which Aubrey Greene desired crept out on his model's face.

3

MICHAEL WALKS AND TALKS

The face Michael drew began by being Victorine's, and ended by being Fleur's. If physically Fleur stood up straight, was she morally as erect? This was the speculation for which he continually called himself a cad. He saw no change in her movements, and loyally refrained from enquiring into the movements he could not see. But his aroused attention made him more and more aware of a certain cynicism, as if she were continually registering the belief that all values were equal and none of much value.

Wilfrid, though still in London, was neither visible nor spoken of. 'Out of sight and hearing, out of mind,' seemed to be the motto. It did not work with Michael—Wilfrid was constantly in his mind. If Wilfrid were not seeing Fleur, how could he bear to stay within such tantalising reach of her? If Fleur did not want Wilfrid to stay, why had she not sent him away? He was finding it difficult, too, to conceal from others the fact that Desert and he were no longer pals. Often the impetus to go and have it out with him surged up and was beaten back. Either there was nothing beyond what he already knew, or there was something—and Wilfrid would say there wasn't. Michael accepted that without cavil; one did not give a woman away! But he wanted to hear no lies from a war comrade. Between Fleur and himself no word had passed; for words, he felt, would add no knowledge, merely imperil a hold weak enough already. Christmas at the ancestral manor of the Monts had been passed in covert-shooting. Fleur had come and stood with him at the last drive on the second day, holding Ting-a-ling on a lead. The Chinese dog had been extraordinarily excited, climbing the air every time a bird fell, and quite unaffected by the noise of guns. Michael, waiting to miss his birds—he was a poor shot—had watched her eager face emerging from grey fur, her form braced back against Ting-a-ling. Shooting was new to her; and under the stimulus of novelty she was always at her best. He had loved even her 'Oh, Michaels!' when he missed. She had been the success of the gathering, which meant seeing almost nothing of her except a sleepy head on a pillow; but, at least, down there he had not suffered from lurking uneasiness.

Putting a last touch to the bobbed hair on the blotting-paper, he got up. St Paul's, that girl had said. He might stroll up and have a squint at Bicket. Something might occur to him. Tightening the belt of his blue overcoat round his waist, he sallied forth, thin and sprightly, with a little ache in his heart.

Walking east, on that bright, cheerful day, nothing struck him so much as the fact that he was alive, well, and in work. So very many were dead, ill, or out of a job. He entered Covent Garden. Amazing place! A human nature which, decade after decade, could put up with Covent Garden was not in danger of extinction from its many ills. A comforting place—one needn't take anything too seriously after walking through it. On this square island were the vegetables of the earth and the fruits of the world, bounded on the west by publishing, on the east by opera, on the north and south by rivers of mankind. Among discharging carts and litter of paper, straw and men out of drawing, Michael walked and sniffed. Smell of its own, Covent Garden, earthy and just not rotten! He had never seen–even in the war–any place that so utterly lacked form. Extraordinarily English! Nobody looked as if they had anything to do with the soil–drivers, hangers-on, packers, and the salesmen inside the covered markets, seemed equally devoid of acquaintanceship with sun, wind, water, earth or air–town types all! And–Golly!–how their faces jutted, sloped, sagged and swelled, in every kind of featural disharmony. What was the English type amongst all this infinite variety of disproportion? There just wasn't one! He came on the fruits, glowing piles, still and bright–foreigners from the land of the sun–globes all the same size and colour. They made Michael's mouth water. 'Something in the sun,' he thought; 'there really is.' Look at Italy, at the Arabs, at Australia–the Australians came from England, and see the type now! Nevertheless–a Cockney for good temper! The more regular a person's form and features, the more selfish they were! Those grape-fruit looked horribly self-satisfied, compared with the potatoes!

He emerged still thinking about the English. Well! They were now one of the plainest and most distorted races of the world; and yet was there any race to compare with them for good temper and for 'guts'? And they needed those in their smoky towns, and their climate–remarkable instance of adaptation to environment, the modern English character! 'I could pick out an Englishman anywhere,' he thought, 'and yet, physically, there's no general type now!' Astounding people! So ugly in the mass, yet growing such flowers of beauty, and such strange sprigs–like that little Mrs Bicket; so unimaginative in bulk, yet with such a blooming lot of poets! How would old Danby like it, by the way, when Wilfrid took his next volume to some other firm; or rather what should he–Wilfrid's particular friend!–say to old Danby? Aha! He knew what he should say:

'Yes, sir, but you should have let that poor blighter off who snooped the "Copper Coins". Desert hasn't forgotten your refusal.' One for old Danby and his eternal in-the-rightness! 'Copper Coin' had done uncommonly well. Its successor would probably do uncommonly better. The book was a proof of what he–Michael–was always saying: The 'cockyolly-bird period' was passing. People wanted life again. Sibley, Walter Nazing, Linda–all those who had nothing to say except that they were superior to such as had–were already measured for their coffins. Not that they would know when they were in them; not blooming likely! They would continue to wave their noses and look down them!

'*I'm* fed-up with them,' thought Michael. 'If only Fleur would see that looking down your nose is a sure sign of inferiority!' And, suddenly, it came to him that she probably did. Wilfrid was the only one of the whole lot she had ever been thick with; the others were there because–well, because she was Fleur, and had the latest things about her. When, very soon, they were no longer the latest things, she would drop them. But Wilfrid she would not drop. No, he felt sure that she had not dropped, and would not drop Wilfrid.

He looked up. Ludgate Hill! 'Near St Paul's–sells balloons?' And there–sure enough–the poor beggar was!

Bicket was deflating with a view to going off his stand for a cup of cocoa. Remembering that he had come on him by accident, Michael stood for a moment preparing the tones of surprise. Pity the poor chap couldn't blow himself into one of those coloured shapes and float over St Paul's to Peter. Mournful little cuss he looked, squeezing out the air! Memory tapped sharply on his mind. Balloon–in the square–November the first–joyful night! Special! Fleur! Perhaps they brought luck. He moved and said in an astounded voice: '*You*, Bicket? Is this your stunt now?'

The large eyes of Bicket regarded him over a puce-coloured sixpennyworth.

'Mr Mont! Often thought I'd like to see you again, sir.'

'Same here, Bicket. If you're not doing anything, come and have some lunch.'

Bicket completed the globe's collapse, and, closing his tray-lid, said: 'Reelly, sir?'

'Rather! I was just going into a fish place.'

Bicket detached his tray.

'I'll leave this with the crossing-sweeper.' He did so, and followed at Michael's side.

'Any money in it, Bicket?'

'Bare livin', sir.'

'How about this place? We'll have oysters.'

A little saliva at the corner of Bicket's mouth was removed by a pale tongue.

At a small table decorated with white oilcloth and a cruet stand, Michael sat down.

'Two dozen oysters, and all that; then two good soles, and a bottle of Chablis. Hurry up, please.'

When the white-aproned fellow had gone about it, Bicket said simply: 'My Gawd!'

'Yes, it's a funny world, Bicket.'

'It *is*, and that's a fact. This lunch'll cost you a pound, I shouldn't wonder. If I take twenty-five bob a week, it's all I do.'

'You touch it there, Bicket. I eat my conscience every day.'

Bicket shook his head.

'No, sir, if you've got money, spend it. I would. Be 'appy if you can–there yn't too many that are.'

The white-aproned fellow began blessing them with oysters. He brought them fresh-opened, three at a time. Michael bearded them; Bicket swallowed them whole. Presently above twelve empty shells, he said:

'That's where the Socialists myke their mistyke, sir. Nothing keeps me going but the sight of other people spendin' money. It's what we might all come to with a bit of luck. Reduce the world to a level of a pound a dy–and it won't even run to that, they sy! It's not good enough, sir. I'd rather 'ave less with the 'ope of more. Take awy the gamble, and life's a frost. Here's luck!'

'Almost thou persuadest me to be a capitalist, Bicket.'

A glow had come up in the thin and large-eyed face behind the greenish Chablis glass.

'I wish to Gawd I had my wife here, sir. I told you about her and the pneumonia. She's all right agyne now, only thin. She's the prize I drew. I don't want a world where you can't draw prizes. If it were all bloomin' conscientious an' accordin' to merit, I'd never have got her. See?'

'Me, too,' thought Michael, mentally drawing that face again.

'We've all got our dreams; mine's blue butterflies–Central Austrylia. The Socialists won't 'elp me to get there. Their ideas of 'eaven don't run beyond Europe.'

'Cripes!' said Michael. 'Melted butter, Bicket?'

'Thank you, sir.'

Silence was not broken for some time, but the soles were.

'What made you think of balloons, Bicket?'

'You don't 'ave to advertise, they do it for you.'

'Saw too much of advertising with us, eh?'

'Well, sir, I did use to read the wrappers. Astonished me, I will sy–the number of gryte books.'

Michael ran his hands through his hair.

'Wrappers! The same young woman being kissed by the same young man with the same clean-cut jaw. But what can you do, Bicket? They *will have it*. I tried to make a break only this morning–I shall see what comes of it.' 'And I hope *you* won't!' he thought: 'Fancy coming on Fleur outside a novel!'

'I did notice a tendency just before I left,' said Bicket, 'to 'ave cliffs or landskips and two sort of dolls sittin' on the sand or in the grass lookin' as if they didn't know what to do with each other.'

'Yes,' murmured Michael, 'we tried that. It was supposed not to be vulgar. But we soon exhausted the public's capacity. What'll you have now–cheese?'

'Thank you, sir; I've had too much already, but I won't say "No".'

'Two Stiltons,' said Michael.

'How's Mr Desert, sir?'

Michael reddened.

'Oh! He's all right.'

Bicket had reddened also.

'I wish–I wish you'd let him know that it was quite a–an accident my pitchin' on his book. I've always regretted it.'

'It's usually an accident, I think,' said Michael slowly, 'when we snoop other people's goods. We never *want* to.'

Bicket looked up.

'No, sir, I don't agree. 'Alf mankind's predytory–only, I'm not that sort, meself.'

In Michael loyalty tried to stammer 'Nor is he.' He handed his cigarette-case to Bicket.

'Thank you, sir, I'm sure.'

His eyes were swimming, and Michael thought: 'Dash it! This is sentimental. Kiss me good-bye and go!' He beckoned up the white-aproned fellow.

'Give us your address, Bicket. If integuments are any good to you, I might have some spare slops.'

Bicket backed the bill with his address and said, hesitating: 'I suppose, sir, Mrs Mont wouldn't 'ave anything to spare. My wife's about my height.'

'I expect she would. We'll send them along.' He saw the 'little snipe's' lips quivering, and reached for his overcoat. 'If anything blows in, I'll remember you. Good-bye, Bicket, and good luck.'

Going east, because Bicket was going west, he repeated to himself the maxim: 'Pity is tripe–pity is tripe!' Then getting on a bus, he was borne back past St Paul's. Cautiously 'taking a lunar'–as old Forsyte put it–he saw Bicket inflating a balloon; little was visible of his face or figure behind that rosy circumference. Nearing Blake Street, he developed an invincible repugnance to work, and was carried on to Trafalgar Square. Bicket had stirred him up. The world was sometimes almost unbearably jolly. Bicket, Wilfrid, and the

Ruhr! 'Feeling is tosh! Pity is tripe!' He descended from his bus, and passed the lions towards Pall Mall. Should he go into 'Snooks' and ask for Bart? No use—he would not find Fleur there. That was what he really wanted—to see Fleur in the daytime. But—where? She was everywhere to be found, and that was nowhere.

She was restless. Was that his fault? If he had been Wilfrid—would she be restless? 'Yes,' he thought stoutly, 'Wilfrid's restless, too.' They were all restless—all the people he knew. At least all the young ones—in life and in letters. Look at their novels! Hardly one in twenty had any repose, any of that quality which made one turn back to a book as a corner of refuge. They dashed and sputtered and skidded and rushed by like motor-cycles—violent, oh! and clever. How tired he was of cleverness! Sometimes he would take a manuscript home to Fleur for her opinion. He remembered her saying once: 'This is exactly like life, Michael, it just rushes—it doesn't dwell on anything long enough to mean anything anywhere. Of course the author didn't mean it for satire, but if you publish it, I advice you to put: "This awful satire on modern life" outside the cover.' And they had. At least, they had put: 'This wonderful satire on modern life.' Fleur *was* like that! She could see the hurry, but, like the author of the wonderful satire, she didn't know that she herself veered and hurried, or—did she know? Was she conscious of kicking at life, like a flame at air?

He had reached Piccadilly, and suddenly he remembered that he had not called on her aunt for ages. That was a possible draw. He bent his steps towards Green Street.

'Mrs Dartie at home?'

'Yes, sir.'

Michael moved his nostrils. Fleur used—but he could catch no scent, except incense. Winifred burnt joss-sticks when she remembered what a distinguished atmosphere they produced.

'What name?'

'Mr Mont. My wife's not here, I suppose?'

'No, sir. Only Mrs Val Dartie.'

Mrs Val Dartie! Yes, he remembered, nice woman—but not a substitute for Fleur! Committed, however, he followed the maid.

In the drawing-room Michael found three people, one of them his father-in-law, who had a grey and brooding aspect, and, from an Empire chair, was staring at blue Australian butterflies' wings under a glass on a round scarlet table. Winifred had jazzed the Empire foundations of her room with a superstructure more suitable to the age. She greeted Michael with fashionable warmth. It was good of him to come when he was so busy with all these young poets. 'I thought "Copper Coin",' she said—'what a *nice* title!—such an intriguing little book. I do think Mr Desert is clever! What is he doing now?'

Michael said: 'I don't know,' and dropped on to a settee beside Mrs Val. Ignorant of the Forsyte family feud, he was unable to appreciate the relief he had brought in with him. Soames said something about the French, got up, and went to the window; Winifred joined him—their voices sounded confidential.

'How is Fleur?' said Michael's neighbour.

'Thanks, awfully well.'

'Do you like your house?'

'Oh, fearfully. Won't you come and see it?'

'I don't know whether Fleur would—?'

'Why not?'

'Oh! Well!'

'She's frightfully accessible.'

She seemed to be looking at him with more interest than he deserved, to be trying to make something out from his face, and he added:

'You're a relation–by blood as well as marriage, aren't you?'

'Yes.'

'Then what's the skeleton?'

'Oh! nothing. I'll certainly come. Only–she has so many friends.'

Michael thought: 'I like this woman!' 'As a matter of fact,' he said, 'I came here this afternoon thinking I might find Fleur. I should like her to know you. With all the jazz there is about, she'd appreciate somebody restful.'

'Thank you.'

'You've never lived in London?'

'Not since I was six.'

'I wish she could get a rest–pity there isn't a d-desert handy.' He had stuttered; the word was not pronounced the same–still! He glanced, disconcerted, at the butterflies. 'I've just been talking to a little Cockney whose S.O.S. is "Central Austrylia". But what do you say–Have we got souls to save?'

'I used to think so, but now I'm not so sure–something's struck me lately.'

'What was that?'

'Well, I notice that anyone at all out of proportion, or whose nose is on one side, or whose eyes jut out, or even have a special shining look, always believes in the soul; people who are in proportion, and have no prominent physical features, don't seem to be really interested.'

Michael's ears moved.

'By Jove!' he said; 'some thought! Fleur's beautifully proportioned–*she* doesn't seem to worry. I'm not–and I certainly do. The people in Covent Garden must have lots of soul. You think "the soul's" the result of loose-gearing in the organism–sort of special consciousness from not working in one piece.'

'Yes, rather like that–what's called psychic power is, I'm almost sure.'

'I say, is your life safe? According to your theory, though, we're in a mighty soulful era. I must think over my family. How about yours?'

'The Forsytes! Oh, they're quite too well-proportioned.'

'I agree, they haven't any special juts so far as I've seen. The French, too, are awfully close-knit. It really is an idea, only, of course, most people see it the other way. They'd say the soul produces the disproportion, makes the eyes shine, bends the nose, and all that; where the soul is small, it's not trying to get out of the body, whence the barber's block. I'll think about it. Thanks for the tip. Well, do come and see us. Good-bye! I don't think I'll disturb them in the window. Would you mind saying I had to scoot?' Squeezing a slim, gloved hand, receiving and returning a smiling look, he slid out, thinking: 'Dash the soul, where's her body?'

4

FLEUR'S BODY

Fleur's body, indeed, was at the moment in one of those difficult positions which continually threaten the spirit of compromise. It was in fact in Wilfrid's arms; sufficiently, at least, to make her say:

'No, Wilfrid—you promised to be good.'

It was a really remarkable tribute to her powers of skating on thin ice that the word 'good' should still have significance. For eleven weeks exactly this young man had danced on the edge of fulfilment, and was even now divided from her by two clenched hands pressed firmly against his chest, and the word 'good'; and this after not having seen her for a fortnight.

When she said it, he let her go, with a sort of violence, and sat down on a piece of junk. Only the sense of damnable iteration prevented him from saying: 'It can't go on, Fleur.' She knew that! And yet it did! This was what perpetually amazed him. How a poor brute could hang on week after week saying to her and to himself: 'Now or never!' when it wasn't either? Subconsciousness, that, until the word 'now' had been reached, Fleur would not know her own mind, alone had kept him dancing. His own feelings were so intense that he almost hated her for indecision. And he was unjust. It was not exactly indecision. Fleur wanted the added richness and excitement which Wilfrid's affection gave to life, but without danger and without loss. How natural! His frightful passionateness was making all the trouble. Neither by her wish, nor through her fault, was he passionate! And yet—it was both nice and proper to inspire passion; and, of course, she had the lurking sense that she was not 'in the mode' to cavil at a lover, especially since life owed her one.

Released, she smoothed herself and said: 'Talk of something sensible; what have you been writing?'

'This.'

Fleur read. Flushing and biting her lips, she said:

'It's frightfully bitter.'

'It's frightfully true. Does *he* ever ask you now whether you see me?'

'Never.'

'Why?'

'I don't know.'

'What would you answer if he did?'

Fleur shrugged her shoulders.

Desert said quietly: 'Yes, that's your attitude. It can't last, Fleur.' He was standing by the window. She put the sheets down on his desk and moved towards him. Poor Wilfrid! Now that he was quiet she was sorry.

He said suddenly: 'Stop! Don't move! *He's* down there in the street.'

Recoiling, she gasped: 'Michael! Oh! But how—how could he have known?'

Desert said grimly: 'Do you only know him as little as that? Do you suppose he'd be there if he knew you were here?'

Fleur winced.

'Why *is* he there, then?'

'He probably wants to see me. He looks as if he couldn't make up his mind. Don't get the wind up, he won't be let in.'

Fleur sat down; she felt weak in the legs. The ice seemed suddenly of an appalling thinness – the water appallingly cold.

'Has he seen you?' she said.

'No.'

The thought flashed through him: 'If I were a blackguard, I could force her hand, by moving one step and crooking my finger.' Pity one wasn't a blackguard – at all events, not to that point – things would be so much simpler!

'Where is he now?' asked Fleur.

'Going away.'

In profound relief, she sighed out:

'But it's queer, isn't it, Wilfrid?'

'You don't suppose he's easy in his mind, do you?'

Fleur bit her lips. He was jeering, because she didn't or couldn't really love either of them. It was unjust. She *could* have loved – she *had* loved! Wilfrid and Michael – they might go to the deuce!

'I wish I had never come here,' she said suddenly: 'and I'll never come again!'

He went to the door, and held it open.

'You are right.'

Fleur stood quite still, her chin on the collar of her fur, her clear-glancing eyes fixed on his face, her lips set and mutinous.

'You think I'm a heartless beast,' she said slowly. 'So I am – now. Good-bye!'

He neither took her hand nor spoke, he only bowed. His eyes were very tragic. Trembling with mortification, Fleur went out. She heard the door closed, while she was going down the stairs. At the bottom she stood uncertain. Suppose Michael had come back! Almost opposite was that gallery where she had first met him and – Jon. Slip across in there! If he were still hovering round the entrance of the little street, she could tell him with a good conscience where she had been. She peeped. Not in sight! Swiftly she slid across into the doorway opposite. They would be closing in a minute – just on four o'clock! She put down a shilling and slipped in. She must see – in case! She stood revolving – one-man show, the man – Claud Brains! She put down another shilling for a catalogue, and read as she went out. 'No. 7. Woman getting the wind up.' It told her everything; and with a lighter heart she skimmed along, and took a taxi. Get home before Michael! She felt relieved, almost exhilarated. So much for skating on thin ice! It wasn't good enough. Wilfrid must go. Poor Wilfrid! Well, he shouldn't have sneered – what did he know of her? Nobody knew anything of her! She was alone in the world. She slipped her latchkey into the hall door. No Michael. She sat down in the drawing-room before the fire, and took up Walter Nazing's last. She read a page three times. It meant no more with every reading – it meant less; he was the kind of author who must be read at a gallop, and given away lest a first impression of wind in the hair be lost in a sensation of wind lower down; but Wilfrid's eyes came between her and the words. Pity! Nobody pitied her; why, then, should she pity them? Besides, pity was 'pop', as Amabel would say. The situation demanded cast-iron sense. But Wilfrid's eyes! Well – she wouldn't be seeing them again! Beautiful eyes when they smiled or when – so much more often – they looked at her with longing, as now between her and the sentence: 'Solemnly and with a delicious egoism he more than awfully desired her who snug and rosy in the pink shell of her involuted and so petulant social periphrasis–' Poor Wilfrid! Pity was 'pop', but there was pride! Did she choose that he should go away thinking that she had 'played him up' just out of vanity, as Walter Nazing said American women did? Did she? Would it not be more in the mode, really dramatic–if one 'went over the deep end', as they said, just once? Would that not be something they could both look back on–he in the East he was always talking of, she in this West? The proposition had a momentary popularity in that organism called Fleur too finely proportioned for a soul according to the theory which Michael was thinking over. Like all popularities, it did not last. First: Would she like it? She did not think she would; one man, without love, was quite enough. Then there was the danger of passing into Wilfrid's power. He was a gentleman, but he was passionate; the cup once sipped, would he consent to put it down? But more than all was a physical doubt of the last two or three weeks which awaited verification, and which made her feel solemn. She stood up and passed her hands all over her, with a definite recoil from the thought of Wilfrid's hands doing the same. No! To have his friendship, his admiration, but not at that price. She viewed him suddenly, as a bomb set on her copper floor; and in fancy ran and seized and flung him out into the Square–poor Wilfrid! Pity was 'pop'! But one might be sorry for *oneself*, losing him; losing too that ideal of modern womanhood expounded to her one evening by Majorie Ferrar, pet of the 'panjoys', whose red-gold hair excited so much admiration: 'My ambition–old thing–is to be the perfect wife of one man, the perfect mistress of another, and the perfect mother of a third, all at once. It's perfectly possible–they do it in France.'

But was it really so perfectly possible–even if pity *was* posh? How be perfect to Michael, when the slightest slip might reveal to him that she was being perfect to Wilfrid; how be perfect to Wilfrid, when every time she was perfect to Michael would be a dagger in Wilfrid's heart? And if–if her physical doubt should mature into certainty, how be perfect mother to the certainty, when she was either torturing two men, or lying to them like a trooperess? Not so perfectly possible as all that! 'If only I were all French!' thought Fleur. . . .

The clicking door startled her–the reason that she was not all French was coming in. He looked very grey, as if he had been thinking too much. He kissed her, and sat down moodily before the fire.

'Have you come for the night, Dad?'

'If I may,' murmured Soames. 'Business.'

'Anything unpleasant, ducky?'

Soames looked up as if startled.

'Unpleasant? Why should it be unpleasant?'

'I only thought from your face.'

Soames grunted. 'This Ruhr!' he said. 'I've brought you a picture. Chinese!'

'Oh, Dad! How jolly!'

'It isn't,' said Soames; 'it's a monkey eating fruit.'

'But that's perfect! Where is it–in the hall?'

Soames nodded.

Stripping the coverings off the picture, Fleur brought it in, and setting it up on the jade-green settee, stood away and looked at it. The large white monkey with its brown haunting eyes, as if she had suddenly wrested its interest from the orange-like fruit in its crisped paw, the grey background, the empty rinds all round—bright splashes in a general ghostliness of colour, impressed her at once.

'But, Dad, it's a masterpiece—I'm sure it's of a frightfully good period.'

'I don't know,' said Soames. 'I must look up the Chinese.'

'But you oughtn't to give it to me, it must be worth any amount. You ought to have it in your collection.'

'They didn't know its value,' said Soames, and a faint smile illumined his features. 'I gave three hundred for it. It'll be safer here.'

'Of course it'll be safe. Only why safer?'

Soames turned towards the picture.

'I can't tell. Anything may come of this.'

'Of what, dear?'

'Is "old Mont" coming in to-night?'

'No, he's at Lippinghall still.'

'Well, it doesn't matter—he's no good.'

Fleur took his hand and gave it a squeeze.

'Tell me!'

Soames's tickled heart quivered. Fancy her wanting to know what was troubling him! But his sense of the becoming, and his fear of giving away his own alarm, forbade response.

'Nothing you'd understand,' he said. 'Where are you going to hang it?'

'There, I think; but we must wait for Michael.'

Soames grumbled out:

'I saw him just now at your aunt's. Is that the way he attends to business?'

'Perhaps,' thought Fleur, 'he was only on his way back to the office. Cork Street *is* more or less between! If he passed the end of it, he would think of Wilfrid, he might have been wanting to see him about books.'

'Oh, here's Ting! Well, darling!'

The Chinese dog, let in, as it were, by Providence, seeing Soames, sat down suddenly with snub upturned eyes brilliant. 'The expression of your face,' he seemed to say, 'pleases me. We belong to the past and could sing hymns together, old man.'

'Funny little chap,' said Soames: 'he always knows me.'

Fleur lifted him. 'Come and see the new monkey, ducky.'

'Don't let him lick it.'

Held rather firmly by his jade-green collar and confronted by an inexplicable piece of silk smelling of the past, Ting-a-ling raised his head higher and higher to correspond with the action of his nostrils, and his little tongue appeared, tentatively savouring the emanation of his country.

'It's a nice monkey, isn't it, darling?'

'No,' said Ting-a-ling, rather clearly. 'Put me down!'

Restored to the floor, he sought a patch where the copper came through between two rugs, and licked it quietly.

'Mr Aubrey Greene, ma'am!'

'H'm!' said Soames.

The painter came gliding and glowing in; his bright hair slipping back, his green eyes sliding off.

'Ah!' he said, pointing to the floor. 'That's what I've come about.'

Fleur followed his finger in amazement.

'Ting!' she said severely, 'stop it! He will lick the copper, Aubrey.'

'But how perfectly Chinese! They do everything we don't.'

'Dad–Aubrey Greene. My father's just brought me this picture, Aubrey–isn't it a gem?'

The painter stood quite still, his eyes ceased sliding off, his hair ceased slipping back.

'Phew!' he said.

Soames rose. He had waited for the flippant; but he recognised in the tone something reverential, if not aghast.

'By George,' said Aubrey Greene, 'those eyes! Where did you pick it up, sir?'

'It belonged to a cousin of mine–a racing man. It was his only picture.'

'Good for him! He must have had taste.'

Soames stared. The idea that George should have had taste almost appalled him.

'No,' he said, with a flash of inspiration: 'What he liked about it was that it makes you feel uncomfortable.'

'Same thing! I don't know where I've seen a more pungent satire on human life.'

'I don't follow,' said Soames dryly.

'Why, it's a perfect allegory, sir! Eat the fruits of life, scatter the rinds, and get copped doing it. When they're still, a monkey's eyes are the human tragedy incarnate. Look at them! He thinks there's something beyond, and he's sad or angry because he can't get at it. That picture ought to be in the British Museum, sir, with the label: "Civilisation, caught out".'

'Well, it won't be,' said Fleur. 'It'll be here, labelled "The White Monkey."'

'Same thing.'

'Cynicism,' said Soames abruptly, 'gets you nowhere. If you'd said "*Modernity* caught out"–'

'I do, sir; but why be narrow? You don't seriously suppose this age is worse than any other?'

'Don't I?' said Soames. 'In my belief the world reached its highest point in the 'eighties, and will never reach it again.'

The painter stared.

'That's frightfully interesting. I wasn't born, and I suppose you were about my age then, sir. You believed in God and drove in *diligences*.'

Diligences! The word awakened in Soames a memory which somehow seemed appropriate.

'Yes,' he said, 'and I can tell you a story of those days that you can't match in these. When I was a youngster in Switzerland with my people, two of my sisters had some black cherries. When they'd eaten about half a dozen they discovered that they all had little maggots in them. An English climber there saw how upset they were, and ate the whole of the rest of the cherries–about two pounds–maggots, stones and all, just to show them. That was the sort of men they were then.'

'Oh! Father!'

'Gee! He must have been gone on them.'

'No,' said Soames, 'not particularly. His name was Powley; he wore side whiskers.'

'Talking of God and diligences: I saw a hansom yesterday.'

'More to the point if you'd seen God,' thought Soames, but he did not say so; indeed, the thought surprised him, it was not the sort of thing he had ever seen himself.

'You mayn't know it, sir, but there's more belief now than there was before the war–they've discovered that we're not all body.'

'Oh!' said Fleur. 'That reminds me, Aubrey. Do you know any mediums? Could I get one to come here? On our floor, with Michael outside the door, one would know there couldn't be any hanky. Do the dark seance people ever go out?–they're much more thrilling, they say.'

'Spiritualism!' said Soames. 'H'mph!' He could not in half an hour have expressed himself more clearly.

Aubrey Greene's eyes slid off to Ting-a-ling. 'I'll see what I can do, if you'll lend me your Peke for an hour or so to-morrow afternoon. I'd bring him back on a lead, and give him every luxury.'

'What do you want him for?'

'Michael sent me a most topping little model to-day. But, you see, she can't smile.'

'Michael?'

'Yes. Something quite new; and I've got a scheme. Her smile's like sunlight going off an Italian valley; but when you tell her to, she can't. I thought your Peke could make her, perhaps.'

'May I come and see?' said Fleur.

'Yes, bring him to-morrow; but, if I can persuade her, it'll be in the "altogether".'

'Oh! Will you get a seance, if I lend you Ting?'

'I will.'

'H'mph!' said Soames again. Seances, Italian sunlight, the 'altogether'! It was time he got back to Elderson, and what was to be done now, and left this fiddling while Rome burned.

'Good-bye, Mr Greene,' he said; 'I've got no time.'

'Quite, sir,' said Aubrey Greene.

'Quite!' mimicked Soames to himself, going out.

Aubrey Greene took his departure a few minutes later, crossing a lady in the hall who was delivering her name to the manservant.

Alone with her body, Fleur again passed her hands all over it. The 'altogether'–was a reminder of the dangers of dramatic conduct.

5

FLEUR'S SOUL

'Mrs Val Dartie, ma'am.'

A name which could not be distorted even by Coaker affected her like a finger applied suddenly to the head of the sciatic nerve. Holly! Not seen since the day when she did not marry Jon. Holly! A flood of remembrance–Wansdon, the Downs, the gravel pit, the apple orchard, the river, the copse at Robin Hill! No! it was not a pleasant sensation–to see Holly, and she said: 'How awfully nice of you to come!'

'I met your husband this afternoon at Green Street; he asked me. What a lovely room!'

'Ting! Come and be introduced! This is Ting-a-ling; isn't he perfect? He'a a little upset because of the new monkey. How's Val, and dear Wansdon? It was too wonderfully peaceful.'

'It's a nice backwater. I don't get tired of it.'

'And–' said Fleur, with a little laugh, 'Jon?'

'He's growing peaches in North Carolina. British Columbia didn't do.'

'Oh! Is he married?'

'No.'

'I suppose he'll marry an American.'

'He isn't twenty-two, you know.'

'Good Lord!' said Fleur: 'Am I only twenty-one? I feel forty-eight.'

'That's living in the middle of things and seeing so many people–'

'And getting to know none.'

'But don't you?'

'No, it isn't done. I mean we all call each other by our Christian names; but *après*–'

'I like your husband very much.'

'Oh! yes, Michael's a dear. How's June?'

'I saw her yesterday–she's got a new painter, of course–Claud Brains. I believe he's what they call a Vertiginist.'

Fleur bit her lip.

'Yes, they're quite common. I suppose June thinks he's the only one.'

'Well, she thinks he's a genius.'

'She's wonderful.'

'Yes,' said Holly, 'the most loyal creature in the world while it lasts. It's like poultry farming–once they're hatched. You never saw Boris Strumolowski?'

'No.'

'Well, don't.'

'I know his bust of Michael's uncle. It's rather sane.'

'Yes. June thought it a pot-boiler, and he never forgave her. Of course it was. As soon as her swan makes money, she looks round for another. She's a darling.'

'Yes,' murmured Fleur; 'I liked June.'

Another flood of remembrance–from a tea-shop, from the river, from June's little dining-room, from where in Green Street she had changed her wedding dress under the upward gaze of June's blue eyes. She seized the monkey and held it up.

'Isn't it a picture of "life"?' Would she have said that if Aubrey Greene hadn't? Still it seemed very true at the moment.

'Poor monkey!' said Holly. 'I'm always frightfully sorry for monkeys. But it's marvellous, I think.'

'Yes. I'm going to hang it here. If I can get one more I shall have done in this room; only people have so got on to Chinese things. This was luck–somebody died–George Forsyte, you know, the racing one.'

'Oh!' said Holly softly. She saw again her old kinsman's japing eyes in the church when Fleur was being married, heard his throaty whisper: 'Will she stay the course?' And was she staying it, this pretty filly? 'Wish she could get a rest. If only there were a desert handy!' Well, one couldn't ask a question so personal, and Holly took refuge in a general remark.

'What do all you smart young people feel about life, nowadays, Fleur? When one's not of it and has lived twenty years in South Africa, one still feels out of it.'

'Life! Oh! well, we know it's supposed to be a riddle, but we've given it up. We just want to have a good time because we don't believe anything can last.

But I don't think we know how to have it. We just fly on, and hope for it. Of course, there's art, but most of us aren't artists; besides, expressionism– Michael says it's got no inside. We gas about it, but I suppose it hasn't. I see a frightful lot of writers and painters, you know; they're supposed to be amusing.'

Holly listened, amazed. Who would have thought that this girl *saw*? She might be seeing wrong, but anyway she saw!

'Surely,' she said, 'you enjoy yourselves?'

'Well, I like getting hold of nice things, and interesting people; I like seeing everything that's new and worth while, or seems so at the moment. But that's just how it is–nothing lasts. You see, I'm not of the "Pan-joys", nor of the "new-faithfuls".'

'The new-faithfuls?'

'Oh! don't you know–it's a sort of faith-healing done on oneself, not exactly the old "God-good, good-God!" sort; but a kind of mixture of will-power, psycho-analysis, and belief that everything will be all right on the night if you say it will. You must have come across them. They're frightfully in earnest.'

'I know,' said Holly; 'their eyes shine.'

'I dare say. I don't believe in them–I don't believe in anyone; or anything–much. How can one?'

'How about simple people, and hard work?'

Fleur sighed. 'I dare say. I will say for Michael–*he's* not spoiled. Let's have tea? Tea, Ting?' and, turning up the lights, she rang the bell.

When her unexpected visitor had gone, she sat very still before the fire. To-day, when she had been so very nearly Wilfrid's! So Jon was not married! Not that it made any odds! Things did not come round as they were expected to in books. And anyway sentiment was swosh! Cut it out! She tossed back her hair; and, getting hammer and nail, proceeded to hang the white monkey. Between the two tea-chests with their coloured pearl-shell figures, he would look his best. Since she couldn't have Jon, what did it matter–Wilfrid or Michael, or both, or neither? Eat the orange in her hand, and throw away the rind! And suddenly she became aware that Michael was in the room. He had come in very quietly and was standing before the fire behind her. She gave him a quick look and said:

'I've had Aubrey Greene here about a model you sent him, and Holly–Mrs Val Dartie–she said she's seen you. Oh! and father's brought us this. Isn't it perfect?'

Michael did not speak.

'Anything the matter, Michael?'

'No, nothing.' He went up to the monkey. From behind him now Fleur searched his profile. Instinct told her of a change. Had he, after all, seen her going to Wilfrid's–coming away?

'Some monkey!' he said. 'By the way, have you any spare clothes you could give the wife of a poor snipe–nothing too swell?'

She answered mechanically: 'Yes, of course!' while her brain worked furiously.

'Would you put them out, then? I'm going to make up a bunch for him myself–they could go together.'

Yes! He was quite unlike himself, as if the spring in him had run down. A sort of *malaise* overcame her. Michael not cheerful! It was like the fire going out on a cold day. And, perhaps for the first time, she was conscious that his cheerfulness was of real importance to her. She watched him pick up Ting-a-ling and sit down. And going up behind him, she bent over till her hair was against his cheek. Instead of rubbing his cheek on hers, he sat quite still, and her heart misgave her.

'What is it?' she said, coaxing.

'Nothing!'

She took hold of his ears.

'But there is. I suppose you know somehow that I went to see Wilfrid.'

He said stonily: 'Why not?'

She let go, and stood up straight.

'It was only to tell him that I couldn't see him again.'

That half-truth seemed to her the whole.

He suddenly looked up, a quiver went over his face; he took her hand.

'It's all right, Fleur. You must do what you like, you know. That's only fair. I had too much lunch.'

Fleur withdrew to the middle of the room.

'You're rather an angel,' she said slowly, and went out.

Upstairs she looked out garments, confused in her soul.

6

MICHAEL GETS 'WHAT-FOR'

After his Green Street quest Michael had wavered back down Piccadilly, and, obeying one of those impulses which make people hang around the centres of disturbance, on to Cork Street. He stood for a minute at the mouth of Wilfrid's backwater.

'No,' he thought at last, 'ten to one he isn't in; and if he is, twenty to one that I get any change except bad change!'

He was moving slowly on to Bond Street, when a little light lady, coming from the backwater, and reading as she went, ran into him from behind.

'Why don't you look where you're going! Oh! You? Aren't you the young man who married Fleur Forsyte? I'm her cousin, June. I thought I saw her just now.' She waved a hand which held a catalogue with a gesture like the flirt of a bird's wing. 'Opposite my gallery. She went into a house, or I should have spoken to her–I'd like to have seen her again.'

Into a house! Michael dived for his cigarette-case. Hard-grasping it, he looked up. The little lady's blue eyes were sweeping from side to side of his face with a searching candour.

'Are you happy together?' she said.

A cold sweat broke out on his forehead. A sense of general derangement afflicted him–hers, and his own.

'I beg your pardon?' he gasped.

'I hope you are. She ought to have married my little brother–but I hope you are. She's a pretty child.'

In the midst of a dull sense of stunning blows, it staggered him that she seemed quite unconscious of inflicting them. He heard his teeth gritting, and said dully: 'Your little brother, who was he?'

'What! Jon–didn't you know Jon? He was too young, of course, and so was she. But they were head over–the family feud stopped that. Well! it's all past. I was at your wedding. I hope you're happy. Have you seen the Claud Brains show at my gallery? He's a genius. I was going to have a bun in here; will you join me? You ought to know his work.'

She had paused at the door of a confectioner's. Michael put his hand on his chest.

'Thank you,' he said, 'I have just had a bun–two, in fact. Excuse me!'

The little lady grasped his other hand.

'Well, good-bye, young man! Glad to have met you. You're not a beauty, but I like your face. Remember me to that child. You should go and see Claud Brains. He's a real genius.'

Stock-still before the door, he watched her turn and enter, with a scattered motion, as of flying, and a disturbance among those seated in the pastry-cook's. Then he moved on, the cigarette unlighted in his mouth, dazed, as a boxer from a blow which knocks him sideways, and another which knocks him straight again.

Fleur visiting Wilfrid–at this moment in his rooms up there–in his arms, perhaps! He groaned. A well-fed young man in a new hat skipped at the sound. Never! He could never stick that! He would have to clear out! He had believed Fleur honest! A double life! The night before last she had smiled on him. Oh! God! He dashed across into Green Park. Why hadn't he stood still and let something go over him? And that lunatic's little brother–John–family feud? Himself–a *pis aller*, then–taken without love at all–a makeshift! He remembered now her saying one night at Mapledurham: 'Come again when I know I can't get my wish.' So that was the wish she couldn't get! A makeshift! 'Jolly,' he thought: 'Oh! jolly!' No wonder, then! What could she care? One man or another! Poor little devil! She had never let him know–never breathed a word! Was that decent of her–or was it treachery? 'No,' he thought, 'if she *had* told me, it wouldn't have made any difference–I'd have taken her at any price. It was decent of her not to tell me.' But how was it he hadn't heard from someone? Family feud? The Forsytes! Except 'Old Forsyte', he never saw them; and 'Old Forsyte' was closer than a fish. Well! he had got what-for! And again he groaned, in the twilight spaces of the Park. Buckingham Palace loomed up unlighted, huge and dreary. Conscious of his cigarette, at last, he stopped to strike a match, and drew the smoke deep into his lungs with the first faint sense of comfort.

'You couldn't spare us a cigarette, Mister?'

A shadowy figure with a decent sad face stood beside the statue of Australia, so depressingly abundant!

'Of course!' said Michael; 'take the lot.' He emptied the case into the man's hand. 'Take the case too–"present from Westminster"–you'll get thirty bob for it. Good luck!' He hurried on. A faint: 'Hi, Mister!' pursued him unavailingly. Pity was pulp! Sentiment was bilge! Was he going home to wait till Fleur had–finished and come back? Not he! He turned towards Chelsea, batting along as hard as he could stride. Lighted shops, gloomy great Eton Square, Chester Square, Sloane Square, the King's Road–along, along! Worse than the trenches–far worse–this whipped and scorpioned sexual jealousy! Yes, and he would have felt even worse, but for that second blow. It made it less painful to know that Fleur had been in love with that cousin, and Wilfrid, too, perhaps, nothing to her. Poor little wretch! 'Well, what's the game now?' he thought. The game of life–in bad weather, in stress? What was it? In the war–what had a fellow done? Somehow managed to feel himself not so dashed important; reached a condition of acquiescence, fatalism, 'Who dies if England live' sort of sob-stuff state. The game of life? Was it different? 'Bloody but unbowed' might be tripe; still–get up when you were knocked down! The whole was big, oneself was little! Passion, jealousy, ought they properly to destroy one's sportsmanship, as Nazing and Sibley and Linda Frewe would have it? Was the word 'gentleman' a dud? Was it? Did one keep one's form, or get down to squealing and kicking in the stomach?

'I don't know,' he thought, 'I don't know what I shall do when I see her–I simply don't know.' Steel-blue of the fallen evening, bare plane trees, wide river, frosty air! He turned towards home. He opened his front door, trembling, and trembling, went into the drawing-room. . . .

When Fleur had gone upstairs and left him with Ting-a-ling he didn't know whether he believed her or not. If she had kept that other thing from him all this time, she could keep anything! Had she understood his words: 'You must do as you like, that's only fair?' He had said them almost mechanically, but they were reasonable. If she had never loved him, even a little, he had never had any right to expect anything; he had been all the time in the position of one to whom she was giving alms. Nothing compelled a person to go on giving alms. And nothing compelled one to go on taking them–except–the ache of want, the ache, the ache!

'You little Djinn! You lucky little toad! Give me some of your complacency–you Chinese atom!' Ting-a-ling turned up his boot-buttons. 'When you have been civilised as long as I,' they seemed to say: 'In the meantime, scratch my chest.'

And scrattling in that yellow fur Michael thought: 'Pull yourself together! Man at the South Pole with the first blizzard doesn't sing: "Want to go home! Want to go home!"–he sticks it. Come, get going!' He placed Ting-a-ling on the floor, and made for his study. Here were manuscripts of which the readers to Danby and Winter had already said: 'No money in this, but a genuine piece of work meriting consideration.' It was Michael's business to give the consideration; Danby's to turn the affair down with the words: 'Write him (or her) a civil letter, say we were greatly interested, regret we do not see our way–hope to have the privilege of considering next effort, and so forth. What!'

He turned up his reading-lamp and pulled out a manuscript he had already begun.

> 'No retreat, no retreat; they must conquer or die who have no retreat;
> No retreat, no retreat; they must conquer or die who have no retreat!'

The black footmen's refrain from 'Polly' was all that happened in his mind. Dash it! He must read the thing! Somehow he finished the chapter. He remembered now. The manuscript was all about a man who, when he was a boy, had been so greatly impressed by the sight of a maidservant changing her clothes in a room over the way, that his married life was a continual struggle not to be unfaithful with his wife's maids. They had just discovered his complex, and he was going to have it out. The rest of the manuscript no doubt would show how that was done. It went most conscientiously into all those precise bodily details which it was now so timorous and Victorian to leave out. Genuine piece of work, and waste of time to go on with it! Old Danby–Freud bored him stiff; and for once Michael did not mind old Danby being in the right. He put the thing back into the drawer. Seven o'clock! Tell Fleur what he had been told about that cousin? Why? Nothing could mend *that*! If only she were speaking the truth about Wilfrid! He went to the window–stars above, and stripes below, stripes of courtyard and back garden. 'No retreat, no retreat; they must conquer or die who have no retreat!'

A voice said:

'When will your father be up?'

Old Forsyte! Lord! Lord!

'To-morrow, I believe, sir. Come in! You don't know my den, I think.'

'No,' said Soames. 'Snug! Caricatures. You go in for them–poor stuff!'

'But not modern, sir–a revived art.'

'Queering your neighbours–I never cared for them. They only flourish when the world's in a mess and people have given up looking straight before them.'

'By Jove!' said Michael; 'that's good. Won't you sit down, sir?'

Soames sat down, crossing his knees in his accustomed manner. Slim, grey, close–a sealed book, neatly bound! What was *his* complex? Whatever it was, he had never had it out. One could not even imagine the operation.

'I shan't take away my Goya,' he said very unexpectedly; 'consider it Fleur's. In fact, if I only knew you were interested in the future, I should make more provision. In my opinion death duties will be prohibitive in a few years' time.'

Michael frowned. 'I'd like you to know, sir, once for all, that what you do for Fleur, you do for Fleur. I can be Epicurus whenever I like–bread, and on feast days a little bit of cheese.'

Soames looked up with shrewdness in his glance. 'I know that,' he said, 'I always knew it.'

Michael bowed.

'With this land depression your father's hard hit, I should think.'

'Well, he talks of being on the look-out for soap or cars; but I shouldn't be surprised if he mortgages again and lingers on.'

'A title without a place,' said Soames, 'is not natural. He'd better wait for me to go, if I leave anything, that is. But listen to me: I've been thinking. Aren't you happy together, you two, that you don't have children?'

Michael hesitated.

'I don't think,' he said slowly, 'that we have ever had a scrap, or anything like it. I have been–I am–terribly fond of her, but you have known better than I that I only picked up the pieces.'

'Who told you that?'

'To-day–Miss June Forsyte.'

'*That* woman!' said Soames. 'She can't keep her foot out of anything. A boy and girl affair–over months before you married.'

'But deep, sir,' said Michael gently.

'Deep–who knows at that age? Deep?' Soames paused: 'You're a good fellow–I always knew. Be patient–take a long view.'

'Yes, sir,' said Michael, very still in his chair, 'if I can.'

'She's everything to me,' muttered Soames abruptly.

'And to me–which doesn't make it easier.'

The line between Soames's brows deepened.

'Perhaps not. But hold on! As gently as you like, but hold on! She's young. She'll flutter about; there's nothing in it.'

'Does he know about the other thing?' thought Michael.

'I have my own worries,' went on Soames, 'but they're nothing to what I should feel if anything went wrong with her.'

Michael felt a twinge of sympathy, unusual towards that self-contained grey figure.

'I shall try my best,' he said quietly; 'but I'm not naturally Solomon at six stone seven.'

'I'm not so sure,' said Soames, 'I'm not so sure. Anyway, a child—well, a child would be—a—sort of insur—' He baulked, the word was not precisely—!

Michael froze.

'As to that, I can't say anything.'

Soames got up.

'No,' he said wistfully, 'I suppose not. It's time to dress.'

To dress—to dine, and if to dine, to sleep—to sleep, to dream! And then what dreams might come!

On the way to his dressing-room Michael encountered Coaker; the man's face was long.

'What's up, Coaker?'

'The little dog, sir, has been sick in the drawing-room.'

'The deuce he has!'

'Yes, sir; it appears that someone left him there alone. He makes himself felt, sir. I always say: He's an important little dog. . . .'

During dinner, as if visited by remorse for having given them advice and two pictures worth some thousands of pounds, Soames pitched a tale like those of James in his palmy days. He spoke of the French—the fall of the mark—the rise in Consols—the obstinacy of Dumetrius, the picture-dealer, over a Constable skyscape which Soames wanted and Dumetrius did not, but to which the fellow held on just for the sake of a price which Soames did not mean to pay. He spoke of the trouble which he foresaw with the United States over their precious Prohibition. They were a headstrong lot. They took up a thing and ran their heads against a stone wall. He himself had never drunk anything to speak of, but he liked to feel that he could. The Americans liked to feel that he couldn't, that was tyranny. They were overbearing. He shouldn't be surprised if everybody took to drinking over there. As to the League of Nations, a man that morning had palavered it up. That cock wouldn't fight—spend money, and arrange things which would have arranged themselves, but as for anything important, such as abolishing Bolshevism, or poison gas, they never would, and to pretend it was all-me-eye-and-Betty-Martin. It was almost a record for one habitually taciturn, and deeply useful to two young people only anxious that he should continue to talk, so that they might think of other things. The conduct of Ting-a-ling was the sole other subject of consideration. Fleur thought it due to the copper floor. Soames that he must have picked up something in the Square—dogs were always picking things up. Michael suggested that it was just Chinese—a protest against there being nobody to watch his self-sufficiency. In China there were four hundred million people to watch each other being self-sufficient. What would one expect of a Chinaman suddenly placed in the Gobi Desert? He would certainly be sick.

'No retreat, no retreat; they must conquer or die who have no retreat!'

When Fleur left them, both felt that they could not so soon again bear each other's company, and Soames said:

'I've got some figures to attend to—I'll go to my room.'

Michael stood up. 'Wouldn't you like my den, sir?'

'No,' said Soames, 'I must concentrate. Say good-night to Fleur for me.'

Michael remained smoking above the porcelain effigies of Spanish fruits. That white monkey couldn't eat those and throw away the rinds! Would the fruits of his life be porcelain in future? Live in the same house with Fleur, estranged? Live with Fleur as now, feeling a stranger, even an unwelcome stranger? Clear out, and join the Air Force, or the 'Save the Children' corps? Which of the three courses was least to be deplored? The ash of his cigar grew long, dropped incontinent, and grew again; the porcelain fruits mocked him with their sheen and glow; Coaker put his head in and took it away again. (The Governor had got the hump—good sort, the Governor!) Decision waited for him, somewhere, somewhen—Fleur's, not his own. His mind was too miserable and disconcerted to be known; but she would know hers. She had the information which alone made decision possible about Wilfrid, that cousin, her own actions and feelings. Yes, decision would come, and would it matter in a world where pity was punk and only a Chinese philosophy of any use?

But not be sick in the drawing-room, try and keep one's end up, even if there were no one to see one being important! . . .

He had been asleep and it was dark, or all but, in his bed-dressing-room. Something white by his bed. A fragrant faint warmth close to him; a voice saying low: 'It's only me. Let me come in your bed, Michael.' Like a child—like a child! Michael reached out his arms. The whiteness and the warmth came into them. Curls smothered his mouth, the voice in his ear: 'I wouldn't have come, would I, if there'd—if there'd been anything?' Michael's heart, wild, confused, beat against hers.

7

'THE ALTOGETHER'

Tony Bicket, replete, was in vein that fine afternoon; his balloons left him freely, and he started for home in the mood of a conqueror.

Victorine, too, had colour in her cheeks. She requited the story of his afternoon with the story of hers. A false tale for a true—no word of Danby and Winter, the gentleman with the sliding smile, of the Grand Marnier, or 'the altogether'. She had no compunction. It was her secret, her surprise; if, by sitting in or out of 'the altogether', not yet decided, she could make their passage money—well, she should tell him she had won it on a horse. That night she asked:

'Am I so very thin, Tony?' more than once. 'I do so want to get fat.'

Bicket, still troubled that she had not shared that lunch, patted her tenderly, and said he would soon have her as fat as butter—he did not explain how.

They dreamed together of blue butterflies, and awoke to chilly gaslight and a breakfast of cocoa and bread-and-butter. Fog! Bicket was swallowed up before the eyes of Victorine ten yards from the door. She returned to the bedroom with anger in her heart. Who would buy balloons in a fog? She would do anything rather than let Tony go on standing out there all the choking days! Undressing again, she washed herself intensively, in case—! She had not long finished when her landlady announced the presence of a messenger boy. He bore an enormous parcel entitled 'Mr Bicket.'

There was a note inside. She read:

DEAR BICKET,–Here are the togs. Hope they'll be useful.–Yours, MICHAEL MONT.

In a voice that trembled she said to the boy:

'Thank you, it's O.K. Here's twopence.'

When his rich whistle was heard writhing into the fog, she flung herself down before the 'togs' in ecstasy. The sexes were divided by tissue paper. A blue suit, a velour hat, some brown shoes, three pairs of socks with two holes in them, four shirts only a little frayed at the cuffs, two black-and-white ties, six collars, not too new, some handkerchiefs, two vests beautifully thick, two pairs of pants, and a brown overcoat with a belt and just two or three nice little stains. She held the blue suit up against her arms and legs, the trousers and sleeves would only need taking-in about two inches. She piled them in a pyramid, and turned with awe to the spoil beneath the tissue paper. A brown knitted frock with little clear yellow buttons–unsoiled, uncreased. How could anybody spare a thing like that! A brown velvet toque with a little tuft of goldeny-brown feathers. She put it on. A pair of pink stays ever so little faded, with only three inches of bone above the waist, and five inches of bone below, pink silk ribbons, and suspenders–a perfect dream. She could not resist putting them on also. Two pairs of brown stockings; brown shoes; two combinations, a knitted camisole. A white silk jumper with a hole in one sleeve, a skirt of lilac linen that had gone a little in the wash; a pair of pallid pink silk pants; and underneath them all an almost black-brown coat, long and warm and cosy, with great jet buttons, and in the pocket six small handkerchiefs. She took a deep breath of sweetness–geranium!

Her mind leaped forward. Clothed, trousseaued, fitted out–blue butterflies–the sun! Only the money for the tickets wanting. And suddenly she saw herself with nothing on standing before the gentleman with sliding eyes. Who cared! The money!

For the rest of the morning she worked feverishly, shortening Tony, mending the holes in his socks, turning the fray of his cuffs. She ate a biscuit, drank another cup of cocoa–it was fattening, and went for the hole in the white silk jumper. One o'clock. In panic she stripped once more, put on a new combination, pair of stockings, and the stays, then paused in superstition. No! Her own dress and hat–like yesterday! Keep the rest until–! She hastened to her bus, overcome alternately by heat and cold. Perhaps he would give her another glass of that lovely stuff. If only she could go swimmy and not care for anything!

She reached the studio as two o'clock was striking, and knocked. It was lovely and warm in there, much warmer than yesterday, and the significance of this struck her suddenly. In front of the fire was a lady with a little dog.

'Miss Collins–Mrs Michael Mont; she's lending us her Peke, Miss Collins.'

The lady–only her own age, and ever so pretty–held out her hand. Geranium! This, then, was she whose clothes–!

She took the hand, but could not speak. If this lady was going to stay, it would be utterly impossible. Before her–so pretty, so beautifully covered–oh! no!

'Now, Ting, be good, and as amusing as you can. Good-bye, Aubrey! Good luck to the picture! Good-bye, Miss Collins; it ought to be wonderful.'

Gone! The scent of geranium fading; the little dog snuffling at the door. The sliding gentleman had two glasses in his hands.

'Ah!' thought Victorine, and drank hers at a gulp.

'Now, Miss Collins, you don't mind, do you! You'll find everything in there. It's really nothing. I shall want you lying on your face just here with your elbows on the ground and your head up a little turned this way; your hair as loose as it can be, and your eyes looking at this bone. You must imagine that it's a faun or some other bit of all right. The dog'll help you when he settles down to it. F-a-u-n, you know, not f-a-w-n.'

'Yes,' said Victorine faintly.

'Have another little tot?'

'Oh! please.'

He brought it.

'I quite understand; but you know, really, it's absurd. You wouldn't mind with a doctor. That's right. Look here, I'll put this little cow-bell on the ground. When you're in position, give it a tinkle, and I'll come out. That'll help you.'

Victorine murmured:

'You *are* kind.'

'Not at all–it's natural. Now will you start in? The light won't last for ever. Fifteen bob a day, we said.'

Victorine saw him slide away behind a screen, and looked at the little cow-bell. Fifteen bob! And fifteen bob! And fifteen bob! Many, many, fifteen bobs before–! But not more times of sitting than of Tony's standing from foot to foot, offering balloons. And as if wound up by that thought, she moved like clockwork off the dais, into the model's room. Cosy in there, too; warm, a green silk garment thrown on a chair. She took off her dress. The beauty of the pink stays struck her afresh. Perhaps the gentleman would like–no, that would be even worse–! A noise reached her–from Ting-a-ling complaining of solitude. If she delayed, she never would–! Stripping hastily, she stood looking at herself in a glass. If only that slim, ivory-white image could move out on to the dais and she could stay here! Oh! It was awful–awful! She couldn't–no! she couldn't. She caught up her final garment again. Fifteen bob! But fifteen bob! Before her eyes, wild and mournful, came a vision: Of a huge dome, and a tiny Tony, with little, little balloons in a hand held out! Something cold and steely formed over her heart as icicles form on a window. If that was all they would do for him, she would do better! She dropped the garment; and, confused, numb, stepped forth in 'the altogether'. Ting-a-ling growled at her above his bone. She reached the cow-bell and lay down on her face as she had been told, with feet in the air, crossed. Resting her chin on one hand, she wagged the bell. It made a sound like no bell she had ever heard; and the little dog barked–he did look funny!

'Perfect, Miss Collins! Hold that!'

Fifteen bob! and fifteen bob!

'Just point those left toes a bit more. That's right! The flesh tone's perfect! My God, why must one walk before one runs! Drawing's a bore, Miss Collins; one ought to draw with a brush only; a sculptor draws with a chisel, at least when he's a Michelangelo. How old are you?'

'Twenty-one,' came from lips that seemed to Victorine quite far away.

'I'm thirty-two. They say our generation was born so old that it can never get any older. Without illusions. Well! I never had any beliefs that I can remember. Had you?'

Victorine's wits and senses were astray, but it did not matter, for he was rattling on:

'We don't even believe in our ancestors. All the same, we're beginning to copy them again. D'you know a book called 'The Sobbing Turtle' that's made such a fuss?–sheer Sterne, very well done; but sheer Sterne, and the author's tongue in his cheek. That's it in a nutshell, Miss Collins–our tongues are in our cheeks–bad sign. Never mind; I'm going to out-Piero Cosimo with this. Your head an inch higher, and that curl out of your eye, please. Thanks! Hold that! By the way, have you Italian blood? What was your mother's name, for instance?'

'Brown.'

'Ah! You can never tell with Browns. It may have been Brune–or Bruno–but very likely she was Iberian. Probably all the inhabitants of Britain left alive by the Saxons were called Brown. As a fact, that's all tosh, though. Going back to Edward the Confessor, Miss Collins–a mere thirty generations–we each of us have one thousand and seventy-four million, five hundred and seventy-three thousand, nine hundred and eighty-four ancestors, and the population of this island was then well under a million. We're as inbred as race-horses, but not so nice to look at, are we? I assure you, Miss Collins, you're something to be grateful for. So is Mrs Mont. Isn't she pretty? Look at that dog!'

Ting-a-ling, indeed, with forelegs braced, and wrinkled nose, was glaring, as if under the impression that Victorine was another bone.

'He's funny,' she said, and again her voice sounded far away. Would Mrs Mont lie here if he'd asked her? *She* would look pretty! But *she* didn't need the fifteen bob!

'Comfortable in that position?'

In alarm, she murmured:

'Oh! yes, thank you!'

'Warm enough?'

'Oh! yes, thank you!'

'That's good. Just a little higher with the head.'

Slowly in Victorine the sense of the dreadfully unusual faded. Tony should never know. If he never knew, he couldn't care. She could lie like this all day–fifteen bob, and fifteen bob! It was easy. She watched the quick, slim fingers moving, the blue smoke from the cigarette. She watched the little dog.

'Like a rest? You left your gown; I'll get it for you.'

In that green silk gown, beautifully padded, she sat up, with her feet on the floor over the dais edge.

'Cigarette? I'm going to make some Turkish coffee. You'd better walk about.'

Victorine obeyed.

'You're out of a dream, Miss Collins. I shall have to do a Mathew Maris of you in that gown.'

The coffee, like none she had ever tasted, gave her a sense of well-being. She said:

'It's not like coffee.'

Aubrey Greene threw up his hands.

'You have said it. The British are a great race–nothing will ever do them in. If they could be destroyed, they must long ago have perished of their coffee. Have some more?'

'Please,' said Victorine. There was such a little in the cup.

'Ready, again?'

She lay down, and let the gown drop off.

'That's right! Leave it there–you're lying in long grass, and the green helps me. Pity it's winter; I'd have hired a glade.'

Lying in long grass–flowers, too, perhaps. She did love flowers. As a little girl she used to lie in the grass, and make daisy-chains, in the field at the back of her grandmother's lodge at Norbiton. Her grandmother kept the lodge. Every year, for a fortnight, she had gone down there–she had liked the country ever so. Only she had always had something on. It would be nicer with nothing. Were there flowers in Central Australia? With butterflies there must be! In the sun–she and Tony–like the Garden of Eden! . . .

'Thank you, that's all for to-day. Half a day–ten bob. To-morrow morning at eleven. You're a first-rate sitter, Miss Collins.'

Putting on the pink stays, Victorine had a feeling of elation. She had done it! Tony should never know! The thought that he never would gave her pleasure. And once more divested of 'the altogether', she came forth.

Aubrey Greene was standing before his handiwork.

'Not yet, Miss Collins,' he said; 'I don't want to depress you. That hip-bone's too high. We'll put it right to-morrow. Forgive my hand, it's all chalk. *Au revoir!* Eleven o'clock. And we shan't need this chap. No, you don't!'

For Ting-a-ling was showing signs of accompanying the larger bone. Victorine passed out smiling.

8

SOAMES TAKES THE MATTER UP

Soames had concentrated, sitting before the fire in his bedroom till Big Ben struck twelve. His reflections sum-totalled in a decision to talk it over with 'old Mont' after all. Though light-brained, the fellow was a gentleman, and the matter delicate. He got into bed and slept, but awoke at half-past two. There it was! '*I won't* think of it,' he thought; and instantly began to. In a long life of dealings with money, he had never had such an experience. Perfectly straightforward conformity with the law–itself so often far from perfectly straightforward–had been the *sine qua non* of his career. Honesty, they said, was the best policy. But was it anything else? A normally honest man couldn't keep out of a perfectly penitentiary for a week. But then a perfect penitentiary had no relation to prison, or the Bankruptcy Court. The business of working honesty was to keep out of those two institutions. And so far he had never had any difficulty. What, besides the drawing of fees and the drinking of tea, were the duties of a director? That was the point. And how far, if he failed in them, was he liable? It was a director's duty to be perfectly straightforward. But if a director were perfectly straightforward, he couldn't be a director. That was clear. In the first place, he would have to tell his shareholders that he didn't anything like earn his fees. For what did he do on his Boards? Well, he sat and signed his name and talked a little, and passed that which the general trend of business decided must be passed. Did he initiate? Once in a blue moon. Did he calculate? No, he read calculations. Did he check payments out and in? No, the auditors did that. There was policy! A comforting word, but–to be perfectly straightforward–a director's chief business was to let the existing policy alone. Take his own case! If he had done his duty, he would have stopped this foreign insurance business–which he had instinctively distrusted the moment he heard of it–within a month of sitting on the Board, or, having failed in doing so, resigned his seat. But he had not. Things had been looking better! It was not the moment, and so forth! If he had done his duty as a perfectly straightforward director, indeed, he would never have become a director of the P.P.R.S., because he would have looked into the policy of the Society much more closely than he had before accepting a position on the Board. But what with the names, and the prestige, and not looking a gift horse too closely in the mouth–there it had been! To be perfectly straightforward, he ought now to be circularising the shareholders, saying: 'My *laissez-faire* has cost you two hundred odd thousand pounds. I have lodged this amount in the hands of trustees for your benefit, and am suing the rest of the directors for their quotas of the amount.' But he was not proposing to do so, because–well–because it wasn't done, and the other directors wouldn't like it. In sum: You waited till the shareholders found out the mess, and you hoped they wouldn't. In fact, just like a Government, you confused the issues, and made the best case you could for yourselves. With a sense of comfort Soames thought of Ireland: The late Government had let the country in for all that mess in Ireland, and at the end taken credit for putting an end to what need never have been! The Peace, too, and the Air Force, and Agriculture, and Egypt–the five most important issues they'd had to deal with–they had put the chestnuts into the fire in every case! But had they confessed to it? Not they. One didn't confess. One said: 'The question of policy made it imperative at the time.' Or, better still, one said nothing; and trusted to the British character. With his chin resting on the sheet, Soames felt a momentary relief. The late Government weren't sweating into *their* sheets–not they–he was convinced of it! Fixing his eyes on the dying embers in the grate, he reflected on the inequalities and injustices of existence. Look at the chaps in politics and business, whose whole lives were passed in skating on thin ice, and getting knighted for it. They never turned a hair. And look at himself, for the first time in forty years on thin ice, and suffering confoundedly. There was a perfect cult of hoodwinking the public, a perfect cult of avoiding the consequences of administrative acts; and here was he, a man of the world, a man of the law, ignorant of those cults, and–and glad of it. From engrained caution and a certain pride, which had in it a touch of the fine, Soames shrank from that coarse-grained standard of honesty which conducted the affairs of the British public. In anything that touched money he was, he always had been, stiff-necked, stiff-kneed. Money was money, a pound a pound, and there was no way of pretending it wasn't and keeping your self-respect. He got up, drank some water, took a number of deep breaths, and stamped his feet. Who was it said the other day that nothing had ever lost him five minutes' sleep? The fellow must have the circulation of an ox, or the gift of Baron Munchausen. He took up a book. But his mind would only turn over and over the realisable value of his resources. Apart from his pictures, he decided that he could not be worth less than two hundred and fifty thousand pounds, and there was only Fleur–and she already provided for more or less. His wife had her settlement, and could live on it perfectly well in France. As for himself–what did he care? A room at his club near Fleur–he would be just as happy, perhaps happier! And suddenly he found that he

had reached a way out of his disturbance and anxiety. By imagining the far-
fetched, by facing the loss of his wealth, he had exorcised the demon. The
book, 'The Sobbing Turtle', of which he had not read one word, dropped
from his hand; he slept. . . .

His meeting with 'Old Mont' took place at 'Snooks' directly after lunch. The
tape in the hall, at which he glanced on going in, recorded a further heavy drop
in the mark. Just as he thought: The thing was getting valueless!

Sitting there, sipping coffee, the baronet looked to Soames almost
offensively spry. Two to one he had realised nothing! 'Well!' thought Soames,
'as old Uncle Jolyon used to say, I shall astonish his weak nerves!'

And without preamble he began.

'How are you, Mont? This mark's valueless. You realise we've lost the
P.P.R.S. about a quarter of a million by that precious foreign policy of
Elderson's. I'm not sure an action won't lie against us for taking unjustifiable
risk. But what I've come to see you about is this.' He retailed the interview with
the clerk, Butterfield, watching the eyebrows of his listener, and finished with
the words: 'What do you say?'

Sir Lawrence, whose foot was jerking his whole body, fixed his monocle.

'Hallucination, my dear Forsyte! I've known Elderson all my life. We were at
Winchester together.'

Again! Again! Oh! Lord! Soames said slowly:

'You can't tell from that. A man who was at Marlborough with me ran away
with his mess fund and his colonel's wife, and made a fortune in Chili out of
canned tomatoes. The point is this: If the young man's story's true, we're in the
hands of a bad hat. It won't do, Mont. Will you tackle him, and see what he says
to it? You wouldn't like a story of that sort about yourself. Shall we both go?'

'Yes,' said Sir Lawrence, suddenly. 'You're right. We'll both go, Forsyte. I
don't like it, but we'll both go. He ought to hear it.'

'Now?'

'Now.'

With solemnity they assumed top hats, and issued.

'I think, Forsyte, we'll take a taxi.'

'Yes,' said Soames.

The cab ground its way slowly past the lions, then dashed on down to the
Embankment. Side by side its occupants held their noses steadily before them.

'He was shooting with me a month ago,' said Sir Lawrence. 'Do you know
the hymn "O God, our help in ages past"? It's very fine, Forsyte.'

Soames did not answer. The fellow was beginning to tittup!

'We had it that Sunday,' went on Sir Lawrence. 'Elderson used to have a fine
voice–sang solos. It's a foghorn now, but a good delivery still.' He gave his little
whinnying laugh.

'Is it possible,' thought Soames, 'for this chap to be serious?' and he said:

'If we find this is true of Elderson, and conceal it, we could all be put in the
dock.'

Sir Lawrence refixed his monocle. 'The deuce!' he said.

'Will you do the talking,' said Soames, 'or shall I?'

'I think you had better, Forsyte; ought we to have the young man in?'

'Wait and see,' said Soames.

They ascended to the offices of the P.P.R.S. and entered the board-room.
There was no fire, the long table was ungarnished; an old clerk, creeping about
like a fly on a pane, was filling ink-stands out of a magnum.

Soames addressed him:

'Ask the manager to be so kind as to come and see Sir Lawrence Mont and Mr Forsyte.'

The old clerk blinked, put down the magnum, and went out.

'Now,' said Soames in a low voice, 'we must keep our heads. He'll deny it, of course.'

'I should hope so, Forsyte; I should hope so. Elderson's a gentleman.'

'No liar like a gentleman,' muttered Soames, below his breath.

After that they stood in their overcoats before the empty grate, staring at their top hats placed side by side on the table.

'One minute!' said Soames, suddenly, and crossing the room, he opened a door opposite. There, as the young clerk had said, was a sort of lobby between board-room and Manager's Room, with a door at the end into the main corridor. He stepped back, closed the door, and, rejoining Sir Lawrence, resumed his contemplation of the hats.

'Geography correct,' he said with gloom.

The entrance of the manager was marked by Sir Lawrence's monocle dropping on to his coat-button with a tinkle. In cutaway black coat, clean-shaven, with grey eyes rather baggy underneath, a pink colour, every hair in place on a rather bald egg-shaped head, and lips alternately pouting, compressed, or smiling, the manager reminded Soames ridiculously of old Uncle Nicholas in his middle period. Uncle Nick was a clever fellow – 'cleverest man in London,' someone had called him – but none had ever impugned his honesty. A pang of doubt and disinclination went through Soames. This seemed a monstrous thing to have to put to a man of his own age and breeding. But young Butterfield's eyes – so honest and dog-like! Invent a thing like that – was it possible? He said abruptly:

'Is that door shut?'

'Yes; do you feel a draught?' said the manager. 'Would you like a fire?'

'No, thank you,' said Soames. 'The fact is, Mr Elderson, a young man in this office came to me yesterday with a very queer story. Mont and I think you should hear it.'

Accustomed to watching people's eyes, Soames had the impression of a film (such as passes over the eyes of parrots) passing over the eyes of the manager. It was gone at once, if, indeed, it had ever been.

'By all means.'

Steadily, with that power he had over his nerves when it came to a point, and almost word for word, Soames repeated a story which he had committed to heart in the watches of the night. He concluded with:

'You'd like him in, no doubt. His name is Butterfield.'

During the recital Sir Lawrence had done nothing but scrutinise his finger nails; he now said:

'You had to be told, Elderson.'

'Naturally.'

The manager was crossing to the bell. The pink in his cheeks looked harder; his teeth showed, they had a pouted look.

'Ask Mr Butterfield to come here.'

There followed a minute of elaborate inattention to each other. Then the young man came in, neat, commonplace, with his eyes on the manager's face. Soames had a moment of compunction. This young fellow held his life in his hands, as it were – one of the great army who made their living out of self-suppression and respectability, with a hundred ready to step into his shoes at his first slip. What was that old tag of the provincial actor's declamation–at which old Uncle Jolyon used to cackle so? 'Like a pale martyr with his shirt on fire.'

'So, Mr Butterfield, you have been good enough to exercise your imagination in my regard.'

'No, sir.'

'You stick to this fantastic story of eavesdropping?'

'Yes, sir.'

'We have no further use for your services then. Good-morning!'

The young man's eyes, dog-like, sought the face of Soames; a string twitched in his throat, his lips moved without a sound. He turned and went out.

'So much for that,' said the manager's voice; '*he'll* never get another job.'

The venom in those words affected Soames like the smell of Russian fat. At the same moment he had the feeling: This wants thinking out. Only if innocent, or guilty and utterly resolved, would Elderson have been so drastic. Which was he?

The manager went on:

'I thank you for drawing my attention to the matter, gentlemen. I have had my eye on that young man for some time. A bad hat all round.'

Soames said glumly:

'What do you make out he had to gain?'

'Foresaw dismissal, and thought he would get in first.'

'I see,' said Soames. But he did not. His mind was back in his own office with Gradman rubbing his nose, shaking his grey head, and Butterfield's: 'No, sir, I've nothing against Mr Elderson, and he's nothing against me.'

'I shall require to know more about that young man,' he thought.

The manager's voice again cut through.

'I've been thinking over what you said yesterday, Mr Forsyte, about an action lying against the Board for negligence. There's nothing in that; our policy has been fully disclosed to the shareholders at two general meetings, and has passed without comment. The shareholders are just as responsible as the Board.'

'H'm!' said Soames, and took up his hat. 'Are you coming, Mont?'

As if summoned from a long distance, Sir Lawrence galvanitically refixed his monocle.

'It's been very distasteful,' he said; 'you must forgive us, Elderson. You had to be told. I don't think that young man can be quite all there–he had a peculiar look; but we can't have this sort of thing, of course. Good-bye, Elderson.'

Placing their hats on their heads simultaneously the two walked out. They walked some way without speaking. Then Sir Lawrence said:

'Butterfield? My brother-in-law has a head gardener called Butterfield– quite a good fellow. Ought we to look into that young man, Forsyte?'

'Yes,' said Soames, 'leave him to me.'

'I shall be very glad to. The fact is, when one has been at school with a man, one has a feeling, don't you know.'

Soames gave vent to a sudden outburst.

'You can't trust anyone nowadays, it seems to me,' he said. 'It comes of–well, I don't know what it comes of. But I've not done with this matter yet.'

9

SLEUTH

The Hotch-potch Club went back to the eighteen-sixties. Founded by a posse of young sparks, social and political, as a convenient place in which to smoulder, while qualifying for the hearth of 'Snooks', The Remove, The Wayfarers, Burton's, Ostrich Feather, and other more permanent resorts, the club had, chiefly owing to a remarkable chef in its early days, acquired a stability and distinction of its own. It still, however, retained a certain resemblance to its name, and this was its attraction to Michael—all sorts of people belonged. From Walter Nazing, and young semi-writers and patrons of the stage, who went to Venice, and talked of being amorous in gondolas, or of how so-and-so ought to be made love to; from such to bottle-brushed demi-generals, who had sat on courts-martial and shot men out of hand for the momentary weaknesses of human nature; from Wilfrid Desert (who never came there now) to Maurice Elderson, in the card-room, he could meet them all, and take the temperature of modernity. He was doing this in the Hotch-potch smoking-room, the late afternoon but one after Fleur had come into his bed, when he was informed:

'A Mr Forsyte, sir, in the hall for you. Not the member we had here many years before he died; his cousin, I think.'

Conscious that his associates at the moment would not be his father-in-law's 'dream', nor he theirs, Michael went out, and found Soames on the weighing machine.

'I don't vary,' he said, looking up. 'How's Fleur?'

'Very well, thank you, sir.'

'I'm at Green Street. I stayed up about a young man. Have you any vacancy in your office for a clerk—used to figures. I want a job for him.'

'Come in here, sir,' said Michael, entering a small room.

Soames followed and looked round him.

'What do you call this?' he said.

'Well, we call it "the grave"; it's nice and quiet. Will you have a sherry?'

'Sherry!' repeated Soames. 'You young people think you've invented sherry; when I was a boy no one dreamed of dining without a glass of dry sherry with his soup, and a glass of fine old sherry with his sweet. Sherry!'

'I quite believe you, sir. There really is nothing new. Venice, for instance—wasn't that the fashion, too; and knitting, and royalties? It's all cyclic. Has your young man got the sack?'

Soames stared. 'Yes,' he said, 'he has. His name is Butterfield; he wants a job.'

'That's frightfully rife; we get applications every day. I don't want to be swanky, but ours is a rather specialised business. It has to do with books.'

'He strikes me as capable, orderly, and civil; I don't see what more you want in a clerk. He writes a good hand, and, so far as I can see, he tells the truth.'

'That's important, of course,' said Michael; 'but is he a good liar as well? I mean, there's more likely to be something in the travelling line; selling special editions, and that kind of thing. Could you open up about him a bit? Anything human is to the good–I don't say old Danby would appreciate that, but he needn't know.'

'H'm! Well–he–er–did his duty–quite against his interest–in fact, it's ruination for him. He seems to be married and to have two children.'

'Ho, ho! Jolly! If I got him a place, would he–would he be doing his duty again, do you think?'

'I am serious,' said Soames; 'the young man is on my mind.'

'Yes,' said Michael, ruminative, 'the first thing in such a case is to get him on to someone else's, sharp. Could I see him?'

'I told him to step round and see you to-night after dinner. I thought you'd prefer to look him over in private before considering him for your office.'

'Very thoughtful of you, sir! There's just one thing. Don't you think I ought to know the duty he did–in confidence? I don't see how I can avoid putting my foot into my mouth without, do you?'

Soames stared at his son-in-law's face, where the mouth was wide; for the *n*th time it inspired in him a certain liking and confidence; it looked so honest.

'Well,' he said, going to the door and ascertaining that it was opaque, 'this is matter for a criminal slander action, so for your own sake as well as mine you will keep it strictly to yourself;' and in a low voice he retailed the facts.

'As I expected,' he ended, 'the young man came to me again this morning. He is naturally upset. I want to keep my hand on him. Without knowing more, I can't make up my mind whether to go further or not. Besides–' Soames hesitated; to claim a good motive was repulsive to him: 'I–it seems hard on him. He's been getting three hundred and fifty.'

'Dashed hard!' said Michael. 'I say, Elderson's a member here.'

Soames looked with renewed suspicion at the door–it still seemed opaque, and he said: 'The deuce he is! Do you know him?'

'I've played bridge with him,' said Michael; 'he's taken some of the best off me–snorting good player.'

'Ah!' said Soames–he never played cards himself. 'I can't take this young man into my own firm for obvious reasons; but I can trust you.'

Michael touched his forelock.

'Frightfully bucked, sir. Protection of the poor–some sleuth, too. I'll see him to-night, and let you know what I can wangle.'

Soames nodded. 'Good Gad!' he thought; 'what jargon! . . .'

The interview served Michael the good turn of taking his thoughts off himself. Temperamentally he sided already with the young man Butterfield; and, lighting a cigarette, he went into the card-room. Sitting on the high fender, he was impressed–the room was square, and within it were three square card-tables, set askew to the walls, with three triangles of card players.

'If only,' thought Michael, 'the fourth player sat under the table, the pattern would be complete. It's having the odd player loose that spoils the cubes.' And with something of a thrill he saw that Elderson was a fourth player! Sharp and impassive, he was engaged in applying a knife to the end of a cigar. Gosh! what sealed books faces were! Each with pages and pages of private thoughts, interests, schemes, fancies, passions, hopes and fears; and down came death–splosh!–and a creature wiped out, like a fly on a wall, and nobody any more could see its little close mechanism working away for its own ends, in its own privacy and its own importance; nobody any more could speculate on whether it was a clean or a dirty little bit of work. Hard to tell! They ran in all shapes! Elderson, for instance—was he a nasty mess, or just a lamb of God who didn't look it? 'Somehow,' thought Michael, 'I feel he's a womaniser. Now why?' He spread his hands out behind him to the fire, rubbing them together like a fly that has been in treacle. If one couldn't tell what was passing in the mind of one's own wife in one's own house, how on earth could one tell anything from the face of a stranger, and he one of the closest bits of mechanism in the world—an English gentleman of business! If only life were like 'The Idiot' or 'The Brothers Karamazov', and everybody went about turning out their inmost hearts at the tops of their voices! If only club card-rooms had a dash of epilepsy in their composition! But—nothing! Nothing! The world was full of wonderful secrets which everybody kept to themselves without captions or close-ups to give them away!

A footman came in, looked at the fire, stood a moment expressionless as a stork, waiting for an order to ping out, staccato, through the hum, turned and went away.

Mechanism! Everywhere—mechanism! Devices for getting away from life so complete that there seemed no life to get away from.

'It's all,' he thought, 'awfully like a man sending a registered letter to himself. And perhaps it's just as well. Is "life" a good thing—is it? Do I want to see "life" raw again?'

Elderson was seated now, and Michael had a perfect view of the back of his head. It disclosed nothing.

'I'm no sleuth,' he thought; 'there ought to be something in the way he doesn't part his hair behind.' And, getting off the fender, he went home.

At dinner he caught one of his own looks at Fleur and didn't like it. Sleuth! And yet how not try to know what were the real thoughts and feelings of one who held his heart, like an accordion, and made it squeak and groan at pleasure!

'I saw the model you sent Aubrey yesterday,' she said. 'She didn't say anything about the clothes, but she looked ever so! What a face, Michael! Where did you come across her?'

Through Michael sped the thought: 'Could I make her jealous?' And he was shocked at it. A low-down thought—mean and ornery! 'She blew in,' he said. 'Wife of a little packer we had who took to snooping—er—books. He sells balloons now; they want money badly.'

'I see. Did you know that Aubrey's going to paint her in the nude?'

'Phew! No! I thought she'd look good on a wrapper. I say! Ought I to stop that?'

Fleur smiled. 'It's more money and her look-out. It doesn't matter to you, does it?'

Again that thought; again the recoil from it!

'Only,' he said, 'that her husband is a decent little snipe for a snooper, and I don't want to be more sorry for him.'

'She won't tell him, of course.'

She said it so naturally, so simply, that the words disclosed a whole attitude of mind. One didn't tell one's mate what would tease the poor brute! He saw by the flutter of her white eyelids that she also realised the give-away. Should he follow it up, tell her what June Forsyte had told him—have it all out—all out? But with what purpose—to what end? Would it change things, make her love him? Would it do anything but harass her a little more; and give him the sense that he had lost his wicket trying to drive her to the pavilion? No! Better adopt the principle of secrecy she had unwittingly declared her own, bite on it, and grin. He muttered:

'I'm afraid he'll find her rather thin.'

Her eyes were bright and steady; and again he was worried by that low-down thought: 'Could he make her–?'

'I've only seen her once,' he added, 'and then she was dressed.'

'I'm not jealous, Michael.'

'No,' he thought, 'I wish to heaven you were!'

The words: 'A young man called Butterfill to see you, sir,' were like the turning of a key in a cell door.

In the hall the young man 'called Butterfill' was engaged in staring at Ting-a-ling.

'Judging by his eyes,' thought Michael, 'he's more of a dog than that little Djinn!'

'Come up to my study,' he said, 'it's cold down here. My father-in-law tells me you want a job.'

'Yes, sir,' said the young man, following up the stairs.

'Take a pew,' said Michael; 'and a cigarette. Now then! I know all about the turmoil. From your moustache, you were in the war, I suppose, like me! As between fellow-sufferers: Is your story O.K.?'

'God's truth, sir; I only wish it wasn't. I'd nothing to gain and everything to lose. I'd have done better to hold my tongue. It's his word against mine, and here I am in the street. That was my first job since the war, so I can whistle for a reference.'

'Wife and two children, I think?'

'Yes, and I've put them in the cart for the sake of my conscience! It's the last time I'll do that, I know. What did it matter to me, whether the Society was cheated? My wife's quite right, I was a fool, sir.'

'Probably,' said Michael. 'Do you know anything about books?'

'Yes, sir; I'm a good book-keeper.'

'Holy Moses! *Our* job is getting rid of them. My firm are publishers. We were thinking of putting on an extra traveller. Is your tongue persuasive?'

The young man smiled wanly.

'I don't know, sir.'

'Well, look here,' said Michael, carried away by the look in his eyes, 'it's all a question of a certain patter. But, of course, that's got to be learned. I gather that you're not a reader.'

'Well, sir, not a great reader.'

'That, perhaps, is fortunate. What you would have to do is to impress on the poor brutes who sell books that every one of the books on your list–say about thirty-five–is necessary in large numbers to his business. It's lucky you've just chucked your conscience, because, as a matter of fact, most of them won't be. I'm afraid there's nowhere you could go to to get lessons in persuasion, but you can imagine the sort of thing, and if you like to come here for an hour or two this week, I'll put you wise about our authors, and ready you up to go before Peter.'

'Before Peter, sir?'

'The Johnny with the keys; luckily it's Mr Winter, not Mr Danby; I believe I could get him to let you in for a month's trial.'

'Sir, I'll try my very best. My wife knows about books, she could help me a lot. I can't tell you what I think of your kindness. The fact is, being out of a job has put the wind up me properly. I've not been able to save with two children; it's like the end of the world.'

'Right-o, then! Come here to-morrow evening at nine, and I'll stuff you. I believe you've got the face for the job, if you can get the patter. Only one book in twenty is a necessity really, the rest are luxuries. Your stunt will be to make them believe the nineteen are necessaries, and the twentieth a luxury that they need. It's like food or clothes, or anything else in civilisation.'

'Yes, sir, I quite understand.'

'All right, then. Good-night, and good luck!'

Michael stood up and held out his hand. The young man took it with a queer reverential little bow. A minute later he was out in the street; and Michael in the hall was thinking: 'Pity is tripe! Clean forgot I was a sleuth!'

IO

FACE

When Michael rose from the refectory table, Fleur had risen, too. Two days and more since she left Wilfrid's rooms, and she had not recovered zest. The rifling of the oyster Life, the garlanding of London's rarer flowers which kept colour in her cheeks, seemed stale, unprofitable. Those three hours, when from shock off Cork Street she came straight to shocks in her own drawing-room, had dislocated her so that she had settled to nothing since. The wound re-opened by Holly had nearly healed again. Dead lion beside live donkey cuts but dim figure. But she could not get hold again of–what? That was the trouble: What? For two whole days she had been trying. Michael was still strange, Wilfrid still lost, Jon still buried alive, and nothing seemed novel under the sun. The only object that gave her satisfaction during those two dreary, disillusioned days was the new white monkey. The more she looked at it, the more Chinese it seemed. It summed up the satirical truth of which she was perhaps subconscious, that all her little modern veerings and flutterings and rushings after the future showed that she believed in nothing but the past. The age had overdone it and must go back to ancestry for faith. Like a little bright fish out of a warm bay, making a splash in chill, strange waters, Fleur felt a subtle nostalgia.

In her Spanish room, alone with her own feelings, she stared at the porcelain fruits. They glowed, cold, uneatable! She took one up. Meant for a passion fruit? Alas! Poor passion! She dropped it with a dull clink on to the pyramid, and shuddered a little. Had she blinded Michael with her kisses? Blinded him to–what? To her incapacity for passion?

'But I'm not incapable,' she thought; 'I'm not. Some day I'll show him; I'll show them all.' She looked up at 'the Goya' hanging opposite. What gripping determination in the painting–what intensity of life in the black eyes of a rather raddled dame! *She* would know what she wanted, and get it, too! No compromise and uncertainty there–no capering round life, wondering what it meant, and whether it was worth while, nothing but hard living for the sake of living!

Fleur put her hands where her flesh ended, and her dress began. Wasn't she as warm and firm—yes, and ten times as pretty, as that fine and evil-looking Spanish dame, with the black eyes and the wonderful lace? And, turning her back on the picture, she went into the hall. Michael's voice and another's! They were coming down! She slipped across into the drawing-room and took up the manuscript of a book of poems, on which she was to give Michael her opinion. She sat, not reading, wondering if he were coming in. She heard the front door close. No! He had gone out! A relief, yet chilling! Michael not warm and cheerful in the house—if it were to go on, it would be wearing. She curled herself up and tried to read. Dreary poems—free verse, blank, introspective, all about the author's inside! No lift, no lilt! Duds! She seemed to have read them a dozen times before. She lay quite still—listening to the click and flutter of the burning logs! If the light were out she might go to sleep. She turned it off, and came back to the settee. She could see herself sitting there, a picture in the firelight; see how lonely she looked, pretty, pathetic, with everything she wished for, and—nothing! Her lip curled. She could even see her own spoiled-child ingratitude. And what was worse, she could see herself seeing it—a triple-distilled modern, so subtly arranged in life-tight compartments that she could not be submerged. If only something would blow in out of the unkempt cold, out of the waste and wilderness of a London whose flowers she plucked. The firelight—soft, uncertain—searched out spots and corners of her Chinese room, as on a stage in one of those scenes, seductive and mysterious, where one waited, to the sound of tambourines, for the next moment of the plot. She reached out and took a cigarette. She could see herself lighting it, blowing out the smoke—her own half-curled fingers, her parted lips, her white rounded arm. She was decorative! Well, and wasn't that all that mattered? To be decorative, and make little decorations; to be pretty in a world that wasn't pretty! In 'Copper Coin' there was a poem of a flicker-lit room, and a spoiled Columbine before the fire, and a Harlequin hovering without, like 'the spectre of the rose'. And suddenly, without warning, Fleur's heart ached. It ached definitely, rather horribly, and, slipping down on to the floor before the fire, she snuggled her face against Ting-a-ling. The Chinese dog raised his head—his black eyes lurid in the glow.

He licked her cheek, and turned his nose away. Huf! Powder! But Fleur lay like the dead. And she saw herself lying—the curve of her hip, the chestnut glow in her short hair; she heard the steady beat of her heart. Get up! Go out! Do something! But what—what was worth doing? What had any meaning in it? She saw herself doing—extravagant things; nursing sick women; tending pale babies; making a speech in Parliament; riding a steeplechase; hoeing turnips in knickerbockers—decorative. And she lay perfectly still, bound by the filaments of her self-vision. So long as she saw herself she would do nothing—she knew it—for nothing would be worth doing! And it seemed to her, lying there so still, that not to see herself would be worse than anything. And she felt that to feel this was to acknowledge herself caged for ever.

Ting-a-ling growled, turning his nose towards the windows. 'In here,' he seemed to say, 'we are cosy; we think of the past. We have no use for anything outside. Kindly go away—whoever it is out there!' And again he growled—a low, continuous sound.

'What is it, Ting?'

Ting-a-ling rose on his fore-legs, with muzzle pointed at the window.

'Do you want your walk?'

'No,' said the growl.

Fleur picked him up. 'Don't be so silly!' And she went to the window. The curtains were closely drawn; rich, Chinese lined, they excluded the night. Fleur made a chink with one hand, and started back. Against the pane was a face, the forehead pressed against the glass, the eyes closed, as if it had been there a long time. In the dark it seemed featureless, vaguely pale. She felt the dog's body stiffen under her arm—she felt his silence. Her heart pumped. It was ghastly—face without body.

Suddenly the forehead was withdrawn, the eyes opened. She saw—the face of Wilfrid. Could he see in—see her peering out from the darkened room? Quivering all over, she let the curtains fall to. Beckon? Let him in? Go out to him? Wave him away? Her heart beat furiously. How long had he been out there—like a ghost? What did he want of her? She dropped Ting-a-ling with a flump, and pressed her hands to her forehead, trying to clear confusion from her brain. And suddenly she stepped forward and flung the curtains apart. No face! Nothing! He was gone! The dark, draughty square—not a soul in it! Had he ever been—or was the face her fancy? But Ting-a-ling! Dogs had no fancies. He had gone back to the fire and settled down again.

'It's not my fault,' she thought passionately. 'It's not? I didn't want him to love me. I only wanted his—his—!' Again she sank down before the fire. 'Oh! Ting, have a feeling heart!' But the Chinese dog, mindful of the flump, made no response. . . .

I I

COCKED HAT

After missing his vocation with the young man Butterfield, Michael had hesitated in the hall. At last he had not gone upstairs again, but quietly out. He walked past the Houses of Parliament and up Whitehall. In Trafalgar Square, it occurred to him that he had a father. Bart might be at 'Snooks', The Coffee House, The Aeroplane; and, with the thought, 'He'd be restful,' he sought the most modern of the three.

'Yes, Sir Lawrence Mont is in the lounge, sir.'

He was sitting with knees crossed, and a cigar between his fingertips, waiting for someone to talk to.

'Ah! Michael! Can you tell me why I come here?'

'To wait for the end of the world, sir?'

Sir Lawrence sniggered. 'An idea,' he said. 'When the skies are wrecking civilisation, this will be the best-informed tape in London. The wish to be in at the death is perhaps the strongest of our passions, Michael. I should very much dislike being blown up, especially after dinner; but I should still more dislike missing the next show if it's to be a really good one. The air-raids were great fun, after all.'

Michael sighed.

'Yes,' he said, 'the war got us used to thinking of the millennium, and then it went and stopped, and left the millennium hanging over us. Now we shall never be happy till we get it. Can I take one of your cigars, sir?'

'My dear fellow! I've been reading Frazer again. Extraordinary how remote all superstition seems, now that we've reached the ultimate truth: That enlightenment never can prevail.'

Michael stopped the lighting of his cigar.

'Do you really think that, sir?'

'What else can one think? Who can have any reasonable doubt now that with the aid of mechanics the head-strong part of man must do him in? It's an unavoidable conclusion from all recent facts. "*Per ardua ad astra*", "Through hard knocks we shall see stars."'

'But it's always been like that, sir, and here we are alive?'

'They say so, but I doubt it. I fancy we're really dead, Michael. I fancy we're only living in the past. I don't think—no, I don't think we can be said to expect a future. We talk of it, but I hardly think we hope for one. Underneath our protestations we subconsciously deduce. From the mess we've made of it these last ten years, we can feel the far greater mess we shall make of it in the next thirty. Human nature can argue the hind legs off a donkey, but the donkey will be four-legged at the end of the discussion.'

Michael sat down suddenly and said:

'You're a bad, bold Bart.'

Sir Lawrence smiled.

'I should be glad to think that men really believed in humanity, and all that, but you know they don't—they believe in novelty and getting their own way. With rare exceptions they're still monkeys, especially the scientific variety; and when you put gunpowder and a lighted match into the paws of monkeys, they blow themselves up to see the fun. Monkeys are only safe when deprived of means to be otherwise.'

'Lively, that!' said Michael.

'Not livelier than the occasion warrants, my dear boy. I've been thinking. We've got a member here who knows a trick worth twenty of any played in the war—an extraordinarily valuable fellow. The Government have got their eye on him. He'll help the other valuable fellows in France and Germany and America and Russia to make history. Between them, they'll do something really proud—something that'll knock all the other achievements of man into a cocked hat. By the way, Michael, new device of "*Homo sapiens*"—the cocked hat.'

'Well,' said Michael, 'what are you going to do about it?'

Sir Lawrence's eyebrow sought his hair.

'Do, my dear fellow? What should I do? Can I go out and grab him and the Government by the slack of their breeches; yes, and all the valuable fellows and Governments of the other countries? No! All I can do is to smoke my cigar and say: "God rest you, merry gentlemen, let nothing you dismay!" By hook or crook, they will come into their own, Michael; but in the normal course of things I shall be dead before they do.'

'I shan't,' said Michael.

'No, my dear; but think of the explosions, the sights, the smells. By Jove, you've got something to live for, yet. Sometimes I wish I were your age. And sometimes,' Sir Lawrence relighted his cigar, 'I don't. Sometimes I think I've had enough of our pretences, and that there's nothing left but to die like gentlemen.'

'Some Jeremiad, Dad!'

'Well,' said Sir Lawrence, with a twirl of his little grizzled moustache, 'I hope I'm wrong. But we're driving fast to a condition of things when millions can be killed by the pressing of a few buttons. What reason is there to suppose that our bumps of benevolence will increase in time to stop our using these great new toys of destruction, Michael!'

'"Where you know little, place terrors."'

'Very nice; where did you get that?'

'Out of a life of Christopher Columbus.'

'Old C.C.! I could bring myself to wish sometimes that he hadn't been so deucedly inquisitive. We were snugger in the dark ages. There were something to be said for not discovering the Yanks.'

'Well,' said Michael, '*I* think we shall pedal through, yet. By the way, about this Elderson stunt: I've just seen the clerk—he doesn't look to me the sort that would have made that up.'

'Ah! That! But if Elderson could do such a thing, well—really, anything might happen. It's a complete stumper. He was such a pretty bat, always went in first wicket down. He and I put on fifty-four against Eton. I suppose old Forsyte told you?'

'Yes, he wanted me to find the chap a job.'

'Butterfield. Ask him if he's related to old Butterfield the gardener! It would be something to go on. D'you find old Forsyte rather trying?'

Loyal to Fleur, Michael concealed his lips. 'No, I get on very well with him.'

'He's straight, I admit that.'

'Yes,' said Michael, 'very straight.'

'But somewhat reticent.'

'Yes,' said Michael.

On this conclusion they were silent, as though terrors had been placed beyond it. And soon Michael rose.

'Past ten, I'd better go home.'

Returning the way he came, he could think of nothing but Wilfrid. What wouldn't he give to hear him say: 'It's all right, old man; I've got over it!'—to wring him by the hand again. Why should one catch this fatal disease called love? Why should one be driven half crazy by it? They said love was Nature's provision against Bart's terrors, against the valuable fellows. An insistent urge—lest the race die out. Prosaic, if true! Not that he cared whether Fleur had children. Queer how Nature camouflaged her schemes—leery old bird! But over-reaching herself a bit, wasn't she? Children might yet go clean out of fashion if Bart was right. A very little more would do it; who would have children for the mere pleasure of seeing them blown up, poisoned, starved to death? A few fanatics would hold on, the rest of the world go barren. The cocked hat! Instinctively Michael straightened his own, ready for crossing under Big Ben. He had reached the centre of Parliament Square, when a figure coming towards him swerved suddenly to its left and made in the direction of Victoria. Tall, with a swing in its walk. Wilfrid! Michael stood still. Coming from—South Square! And suddenly he gave chase. He did not run, but he walked his hardest. The blood beat in his temples, and he felt confused to a pitch past bearing. Wilfrid must have seen him, or he wouldn't have swerved, wouldn't be legging it away like a demon. Black!—black! He was not gaining, Wilfrid had the legs of him—to overtake him, he must run! But there rose in Michael a sort of exaltation. His best friend—his wife! There was a limit. One might be too proud to fight that. Let him go his ways! He stood still, watched the swift figure disappear, and slowly, head down under the now cocked hat, turned towards home. He walked quite quietly, and with a sense of finality. No use making a song about it! No fuss, but no retreat! In the few hundred yards before he reached his Square he was chiefly conscious of the tallness of houses, the shortness of men. Such midgets to have made this monstrous pile, lighted it so that it shone in an enormous glittering heap whose glow blurred the colour of the sky! What a vast business this midget activity! Absurd to think that his love for another midget mattered! He turned his key in the lock, took off his cocked hat and went into the drawing-room. Unlighted–empty? No. She and Ting-a-ling were on the floor before the fire! He sat down on the settee, and was abruptly conscious that he was trembling and sweating as if he had smoked a too strong cigar. Fleur had raised herself, cross-legged, and was staring up at him. He waited to get the better of his trembling. Why didn't she speak? Why was she sitting there, in the dark? 'She knows,' he thought: 'we both know this is the end. O God, let me at least be a sport!' He took a cushion, put it behind him, crossed his legs, and leaned back. His voice surprised him suddenly:

'May I ask you something, Fleur? And will you please answer me quite truly?'

'Yes.'

'It's this: I know you didn't love me when you married me. I don't think you love me now. Do you want me to clear out?'

A long time seemed to pass.

'No.'

'Do you mean that?'

'Yes.'

'Why?'

'Because I don't.'

Michael got up.

'Will you answer one thing more?'

'Yes.'

'Was Wilfrid here to-night?'

'Yes–no. That is–'

His hands clutched each other; he saw her eyes fix on them, and kept them still.

'Fleur, don't!'

'I'm not. He came to the window there. I saw his face–that's all. His face–it–Oh! Michael, don't be unkind to-night!'

Unkind! Unkind! Michael's heart swelled at that strange word.

'It's all right,' he stammered. 'So long as you tell me what it is you want.'

Fleur said, without moving:

'I want to be comforted.'

Ah! She knew exactly what to say, how to say it! And going on his knees, he began to comfort her.

12

GOING EAST

He had not been on his knees many minutes before they suffered from reaction. To kneel there comforting Fleur brought him a growing discomfort. He believed her to-night, as he had not believed her for months past. But what was Wilfrid doing? Where wandering? The face at the window–face without voice, without attempt to reach her! Michael ached in that illegitimate organ the heart. Withdrawing his arms, he stood up.

'Would you like me to have a look for him? If it's all over–he might–I might–'

Fleur, too, stood up. She was calm enough now.

'Yes, I'll go to bed.' With Ting-a-ling in her arms, she went to the door; her face, between the dog's chestnut fur and her own, was very pale, very still.

'By the way,' she said, 'this is my second no go, Michael; I suppose it means–'

Michael gasped. Currents of emotion, welling, ebbing, swirling, rendered him incapable of speech.

'The night of the balloon,' she said: 'Do you mind?'

'Mind? Good God! Mind!'

'That's all right, then. *I* don't. Good-night!'

She was gone. Without reason, Michael thought: 'In the beginning was the Word, and the Word was with God, and the Word was God.' And he stood, as if congealed, overcome by an uncontrollable sense of solidity. A child coming! It was as though the barque of his being, tossed and drifted, suddenly rode tethered–anchor down. He turned and tore at the curtains. Night of stars! Wonderful world! Jolly–jolly! And–Wilfrid! He flattened his face against the glass. Outside there Wilfrid's had been flattened. He could see it if he shut his eyes. Not fair! Dog lost–man lost! S.O.S. He went into the hall, and from the mothless marble coffer rived his thickest coat. He took the first taxi that came by.

'Cork Street! Get along!' Needle in bundle of hay! Quarter-past eleven by Big Ben! The intense relief of his whole being in that jolting cab seemed to him brutal. Salvation! It *was*–he had a strange certainty of that as though he saw Fleur suddenly 'close-up' in a very strong light, concrete beneath her graceful veerings. Family! Continuation! He had been unable to anchor her, for he was not of her! But her child could and would! And, perhaps, he would yet come in with the milk. Why did he love her so–it was not done! Wilfrid and he were donkeys–out of touch, out of tune with the times!

'Here you are, sir–what number?'

'All right! Cool your heels and wait for me! Have a cigarette!'

With one between his own lips which felt so dry, he went down the backwater.

A light in Wilfrid's rooms! He rang the bell. The door was opened, the face of Wilfrid's man looked forth.

'Yes, sir?'

'Mr Desert in?'

'No, sir. Mr Desert has just started for the East. His ship sails to-morrow.'

'Oh!' said Michael blankly. 'Where from?'

'Plymouth, sir. His train leaves Paddington at midnight. You might catch him yet.'

'It's very sudden,' said Michael, 'he never–'

'No, sir. Mr Desert is a sudden gentleman.'

'Well, thanks; I'll try and catch him.'

Back in the cab with the words: 'Paddington–flick her along!' he thought: 'A sudden gentleman!' Perfect! He remembered the utter suddenness of that little interview beside the bust of Lionel Charwell. Sudden their friendship, sudden its end–sudden even Wilfrid's poems–offspring of a sudden soul! Staring from window to window in that jolting, rattling cab, Michael suffered from St Vitus's dance. Was he a fool? Could he not let well alone? Pity was posh! And yet! With Wilfrid would go a bit of his heart, and in spite of all he would like him to know that. Upper Brook Street, Park Lane! Emptying streets, cold night, stark plane trees painted-up by the lamps against a bluish dark. And Michael thought: 'We wander! What's the end–the goal? To do one's bit, and not worry! But what is my bit? What's Wilfrid's? Where will he end up, now?'

The cab rattled down the station slope and drew up under cover. Ten minutes to twelve, and a long heavy train on platform one!

'What shall I do?' thought Michael: 'It's so darned crude! Must I go down–carriage by carriage? "Couldn't let you go, old man, without"–blurb!'

Bluejackets! If not drunk–as near as made no matter. Eight minutes still! He began slowly walking along the train. He had not passed four windows before he saw his quarry. Desert was sitting back to the engine in the near corner of an empty first. An unlighted cigarette was in his mouth, his fur collar turned up to his eyes, and his eyes fixed on an unopened paper on his lap. He sat without movement; Michael stood looking at him. His heart beat fast. He struck a match, took two steps, and said:

'Light, old boy?'

Desert stared up at him.

'Thanks,' he said, and took the match. By its flare his face was dark, thin, drawn; his eyes dark, deep, tired. Michael leaned in the window. Neither spoke.

'Take your seat, if you're going, sir.'

'I'm not,' said Michael. His whole inside seemed turning over.

'Where are you going, old man?' he said suddenly.

'Jericho.'

'God, Wilfrid, I'm sorry!'

Desert smiled.

'Cut it out!'

'Yes, I know! Shake hands?'

Desert held out his hand.

Michael squeezed it hard.

A whistle sounded.

Desert rose suddenly and turned to the rack above him. He took a parcel from a bag. 'Here,' he said, 'these wretched things! Publish them if you like.'

Something clicked in Michael's throat.

'Thanks, old man! That's great! Good-bye!'

A sort of beauty came into Desert's face.

'So long!' he said.

The train moved. Michael withdrew his elbows; quite still, he stared at the motionless figure slowly borne along, away. Carriage after carriage went by him, full of bluejackets leaning out, clamouring, singing, waving handkerchiefs and bottles. Guard's van now–the tail light–all spread–a crimson blur–setting East–going–going–gone!

And that was all–was it? He thrust the parcel into his coat pocket. Back to Fleur, now! Way of the world–one man's meat, another's poison! He passed his hand over his eyes. The dashed things were full of–blurb!

PART III

I

BANK HOLIDAY

Whitsuntide Bank Holiday was producing its seasonal invasion of Hampstead Heath, and among the ascending swarm were two who meant to make money in the morning and spend it in the afternoon.

Tony Bicket, with balloons and wife, embarked early on the Hampstead Tube.

'You'll see,' he said, 'I'll sell the bloomin' lot by twelve o'clock, and we'll go on the bust.'

Squeezing his arm, Victorine fingered, through her dress, a slight swelling just above her right knee. It was caused by fifty-four pounds fastened in the top of her stocking. She had little feeling, now, against balloons. They afforded temporary nourishment, till she had the few more pounds needful for their passage-money. Tony still believed he was going to screw salvation out of his blessed balloons: he was 'that hopeful–Tony', though their heads were only just above water on his takings. And she smiled. With her secret she could afford to be indifferent now to the stigma of gutter hawking. She had her story pat. From the evening paper, and from communion on buses with those interested in the national pastime, she had acquired the necessary information about racing. She even talked of it with Tony, who had street-corner knowledge. Already she had prepared chapter and verse of two imaginary coups; a sovereign made out of stitching imaginary blouses, invested on the winner of the Two Thousand Guineas, and the result on the dead-heater for the Jubilee at nice odds; this with a third winner, still to be selected, would bring her imaginary winnings up to the needed sixty pounds odd she would so soon have saved now out of 'the altogether'. This tale she would pitch to Tony in a week or two, reeling off by heart the wonderful luck she had kept from him until she had the whole of the money. She would slip her forehead against his eyes if he looked at her too hard, and kiss his lips till his head was no longer clear. And in the morning they would wake up and take their passages. Such was the plan of Victorine, with five ten-pound and four one-pound notes in her stocking, attached to the pink silk stays.

'Afternoon of a Dryad' had long been finished, and was on exhibition at the Dumetrius Gallery, with other works of Aubrey Greene. Victorine had paid a shilling to see it; had stood some furtive minutes gazing at that white body glimmering from among grass and spikey flowers, at the face, turned as if saying: 'I know a secret!'

'Bit of a genius, Aubrey Greene–that face is jolly good!' Scared, and hiding the face, Victorine had slipped away.

From the very day when she had stood shivering outside the studio of Aubrey Greene she had been in full work. He had painted her three times—always nice, always polite, quite the gentleman! And he had given her introductions. Some had painted her in clothes, some half-draped, some in that 'altogether', which no longer troubled her, with the money swelling her stocking and Tony without suspicion. Not everyone had been 'nice'; advances had been made to her, but she had nipped them in the bud. It would have meant the money quicker, but—Tony! In a fortnight now she could snap her fingers at it all. And often on the way home she stood by that plate-glass window, before the fruits, and the corn, and the blue butterflies. . . .

In the packed railway carriage they sat side by side, Bicket with tray on knee, debating where he had best stand.

'I favour the mokes,' he said at last, 'up by the pond. People'll have more money than when they get down among the swings and coconuts; and you can go and sit in a chair by the pond, like the seaside—I don't want you with me not till I've sold out.'

Victorine pressed his arm.

Along the top and over on to the heath to north and south the holiday swarms surged, in perfect humour, carrying paper bags. Round the pond children, with thin, grey-white, spindly legs, were paddling and shrilly chattering, too content to smile. Elderly couples crawled slowly by, with jutting stomachs, and faces discoloured by the unaccustomed climb. Girls and young men were few, for they were dispersed already on the heath, in search of a madder merriment. On benches, in chairs of green canvas or painted wood, hundreds were sitting, contemplating their feet, as if imagining the waves of the sea. Now and again three donkeys would start, urged from behind, and slowly tittup their burdens along the pond's margin. Hawkers cried goods. Fat dark women told fortunes. Policemen stood cynically near them. A man talked and talked and took his hat round.

Tony Bicket unslung his tray. His Cockney voice, wheedling and a little husky, offered his coloured airs without intermission. This was something like! It was brisk! And now and again he gazed through the throng away across the pond, to where Victorine would be seated in a canvas chair, looking different from everyone—he knew.

'Fine balloons—fine balloons! Six for a bob! Big one, Madam? Only sixpence. See the size! Buy, buy! Tyke one for the little boy!'

No 'aldermen' up here, but plenty in the mood to spend their money on a bit of brightness!

At five minutes before noon he snapped his tray to—not a bally balloon left! With six Bank Holidays a week he would make his fortune! Tray under arm, he began to tour the pond. The kiddies were all right, but—good Lord—how thin and pale! If he and Vic had a kid—but not they—not till they got out there! A fat brown kid, chysin' blue butterflies, and the sun oozin' out of him! Rounding the end of the pond, he walked slowly along the chairs. Lying back, elegant, with legs crossed, in brown stockings showing to the knees, and neat brown shoes with the flaps over—My! she looked a treat—in a world of her own, like that! Something caught Bicket by the throat. Gosh! He wanted things for her!

'Well, Vic! Penny!'

'I was thinkin' of Australia.'

'Ah! It's a gaudy long wait. Never mind—I've sold the bally lot. Which shall we do, go down among the trees, or get to the swings, at once?'

'The swings,' said Victorine.

The Vale of Health was in rhapsodic mood. The crowd flowed here in a slow, speechless stream, to the cries of the booth-keepers, and the owners of swings and coconuts. 'Roll–bowl–or pitch! Now for the milky ones! Penny a shy! . . . Who's for the swings? . . . Ices . . . Ices . . . Fine bananas!'

On the giant merry-go-round under its vast umbrella the thirty chain-hung seats were filled with girls and men. Round to the music–slowly–faster–whirling out to the full extent of the chain, bodies bent back, legs stuck forward, laughter and speech dying, faces solemn, a little lost, hands gripping the chains hard. Faster, faster; slowing, slowing to a standstill, and the music silent.

'My word!' murmured Victorine. 'Come on, Tony!'

They entered the enclosure and took their seats. Victorine, on the outside, locked her feet, instinctively, one over the other, and tightening her clasp on the chains, curved her body to the motion. Her lips parted:

'Lor, Tony!'

Faster, faster–every nerve and sense given to that motion! O-o-h! It *was* a feeling–flying round like that above the world! Faster–faster! Slower–slow, and the descent to earth.

'Tony–it's 'eaven!'

'Queer feelin' in yer inside, when you're swung right out!'

'I'd like it level with the top. Let's go once more!'

'Right-o!'

Twice more they went–half his profit on balloons! But who cared? He liked to see her face. After that, six shies at the milky ones without a hit, an ice apiece: then arm-in-arm to find a place to eat their lunch. That was the time Bicket enjoyed most, after the ginger-beer and sandwiches; smoking his fag, with his head on her lap, and the sky blue. A long time like that; till at last she stirred.

'Let's go and see the dancin'!'

In the grass enclosure ringed by the running path, some two dozen couples were jigging to a band.

Victorine pulled at his arm. 'I *would* love a turn!'

'Well, let's 'ave a go,' said Bicket. 'This one-legged bloke'll 'old my tray.'

They entered the ring.

'Hold me tighter, Tony!'

Bicket obeyed. Nothing he liked better; and slowly their feet moved–to this side and that. They made little way, revolving, keeping time, oblivious of appearances.

'You dance all right, Tony.'

'*You* dance a treat!' gasped Bicket.

In the intervals, panting, they watched over the one-legged man; then to it again, till the band ceased for good.

'My word!' said Victorine. 'They dance on board ship, Tony!'

Bicket squeezed her waist.

'I'll do the trick yet, if I 'ave to rob the Bank. There's nothin' I wouldn't do for you, Vic.'

But Victorine smiled. She had done the trick already.

The crowd with parti-coloured faces, tired, good-humoured, frowsily scented, strolled over a battlefield thick-strewn with paper bags, banana peel, and newspapers.

'Let's 'ave tea, and one more swing,' said Bicket; 'then we'll get over on the other side among the trees.'

Away over on the far side were many couples. The sun went very slowly down. Those two sat under a bush and watched it go. A faint breeze swung and rustled the birch leaves. There was little human sound out here. All seemed to have come for silence, to be waiting for darkness in the hush. Now and then some stealthy spy would pass and scrutinise.

'Foxes!' said Bicket. 'Gawd! I'd like to rub their noses in it!'

Victorine sighed, pressing closer to him.

Someone was playing on a banjo now; a voice singing. It grew dusk, but a moon was somewhere rising, for little shadows stole out along the ground.

They spoke in whispers. It seemed wrong to raise the voice, as though the grove were under a spell. Even their whisperings were scarce. Dew fell, but they paid no heed to it. With hands locked, and cheeks together, they sat very still. Bicket had a thought. This was poetry–this was! Darkness now, with a sort of faint and silvery glow, a sound of drunken singing on the Spaniard's Road, the whirr of belated cars returning from the north–and suddenly an owl hooted.

'My!' murmured Victorine, shivering. 'An owl! Fancy! I used to hear one at Norbiton. I 'ope it's not bad luck!'

Bicket rose and stretched himself.

'Come on!' he said: 'we've 'ad a dy. Don't you go catchin' cold!'

Arm-in-arm, slowly, through the darkness of the birch-grove, they made their way upwards–glad of the lamps, and the street, and the crowded station, as though they had taken an overdose of solitude.

Huddled in their carriage on the Tube, Bicket idly turned the pages of a derelict paper. But Victorine sat thinking of so much, that it was as if she thought of nothing. The swings and the grove in the darkness, and the money in her stocking. She wondered Tony hadn't noticed when it crackled–there wasn't a safe place to keep it in! What was he looking at, with his eyes so fixed? She peered, and read: '"Afternoon of a Dryad." The striking picture by Aubrey Greene, on exhibition at the Dumetrius Gallery.'

Her heart stopped beating.

'Cripes!' said Bicket. 'Ain't that like you?'

'Like me? No!'

Bicket held the paper closer. 'It *is*. It's like you all over. I'll cut that out. I'd like to see that picture.'

The colour came up in her cheeks, released from a heart beating too fast now.

''Tisn't decent,' she said.

'Dunno about that; but it's awful like you. It's even got your smile.'

Folding the paper, he began to tear the sheet. Victorine's little finger pressed the notes beneath her stocking.

'Funny,' she said slowly, 'to think there's people in the world so like each other.'

'I never thought there could be one like you. Charin' Cross; we gotta change.'

Hurrying along the rat-runs of the Tube, she slipped her hand into his pocket, and soon some scraps of torn paper fluttered down behind her following him in the crush. If only he didn't remember where the picture was!

Awake in the night, she thought:

'I don't care; I'm going to get the rest of the money–that's all about it.'

But her heart moved queerly within her, like that of one whose feet have trodden suddenly the quaking edge of a bog.

2

OFFICE WORK

Michael sat correcting the proofs of *Counterfeits*—the book left by Wilfrid behind him.

'Can you see Butterfield, sir?'

'I can.'

In Michael the word Butterfield excited an uneasy pride. The young man fulfilled with increasing success the function for which he had been engaged, on trial, four months ago. The head traveller had even called him 'a find'. Next to 'Copper Coin' he was the finest feather in Michael's cap. The Trade were not buying, yet Butterfield was selling books, or so it was reported; he appeared to have a natural gift of inspiring confidence where it was not justified. Danby and Winter had even entrusted to him the private marketing of the vellum-bound 'Limited' of 'A Duet', by which they were hoping to recoup their losses on the ordinary edition. He was now engaged in working through a list of names considered likely to patronise the little masterpiece. This method of private approach had been suggested by himself.

'You see, sir,' he had said to Michael: 'I know a bit about Coué. Well, you can't work that on the Trade—they've got no capacity for faith. What can you expect? Every day they buy all sorts of stuff, always basing themselves on past sales. You can't find one in twenty that'll back the future. But with private gentlemen, and especially private ladies, you can leave a thought with them like Coué does—put it into them again and again that day by day in every way the author's gettin' better and better; and ten to one when you go round next, it's got into their subconscious, especially if you take 'em just after lunch or dinner, when they're a bit drowsy. Let me take my own time, sir, and I'll put that edition over for you.'

'Well,' Michael had answered, 'if you can inspire confidence in the future of my governor, Butterfield, you'll deserve more than your ten per cent.'

'I can do it, sir; it's just a question of faith.'

'But you haven't any, have you?'

'Well, not, so to speak, in the author—but I've got faith that I can give *them* faith in him; that's the real point.'

'I see—the three-card stunt; inspire the faith you haven't got, that the card is there, and they'll take it. Well, the disillusion is not immediate—you'll probably always get out of the room in time. Go ahead, then!'

The young man Butterfield had smiled. . . .

The uneasy part of the pride inspired in Michael now by the name was due to old Forsyte's continually saying to him that he didn't know—he couldn't tell—there was that young man and his story about Elderson, and they got no further. . . .

'Good morning, sir. Can you spare me five minutes?'

'Come in, Butterfield. Bunkered with "Duet"?'

'No, sir. I've placed forty already. It's another matter.' Glancing at the shut door, the young man came closer.

'I'm working my list alphabetically. Yesterday I was in the E's.' His voice dropped. 'Mr Elderson.'

'Phew!' said Michael. 'You can give *him* the go-by.'

'As a fact, sir, I haven't.'

'What! Been over the top?'

'Yes, sir. Last night.'

'Good for you, Butterfield! What happened?'

'I didn't send my name in, sir—just the firm's card.'

Michael was conscious of a very human malice in the young man's voice and face.

'Well?'

'Mr Elderson, sir, was at his wine. I'd thought it out, and I began as if I'd never seen him before. What struck me was—he took my cue!'

'Didn't kick you out?'

'Far from it, sir. He said at once: "Put my name down for two copies."'

Michael grinned. 'You both had a nerve.'

'No, sir; that's just it. Mr Elderson got it between wind and water. He didn't like it a little bit.'

'I don't twig,' said Michael.

'My being in this firm's employ, sir. He knows you're a partner here, and Mr Forsyte's son-in-law, doesn't he?'

'He does.'

'Well, sir, you see the connection—two directors believing me—not *him*. That's why I didn't miss him out. I fancied it'd shake him up. I happened to see his face in the sideboard glass as I went out. *He's* got the wind up all right.'

Michael bit his forefinger, conscious of a twinge of sympathy with Elderson, as for a fly with the first strand of cobweb round his hind leg.

'Thank you, Butterfield,' he said.

When the young man was gone, he sat stabbing his blotting-paper with a paper-knife. What curious 'class' sensation was this? Or was it merely fellow-feeling with the hunted, a tremor at the way things found one out? For, surely, this was real evidence, and he would have to pass it on to his father, and 'Old Forsyte'. Elderson's nerve must have gone phut, or he'd have said: 'You impudent young scoundrel—get out of here!' That, clearly, was the only right greeting from an innocent, and the only advisable greeting from a guilty man. Well! Nerve did fail sometimes—even the best. Witness the very proof-sheet he had just corrected:

THE COURT MARTIAL

"'See 'ere! I'm myde o' nerves and blood
The syme as you, not meant to be
Froze stiff up to me ribs in mud.
You try it, like I 'ave, an' see!

"'Aye, you snug beauty brass hats, when
You stick what I stuck out that d'y,
An' keep yer ruddy 'earts up—then
You'll learn, maybe, the right to s'y:

"'Take aht an' shoot 'im in the snow,
Shoot 'im for cowardice! 'E who serves
His King and Country's got to know
There's no such bloody thing as nerves.'"

Good old Wilfrid!

'Yes, Miss Perren?'

'The letter to Sir James Foggart, Mr Mont; you told me to remind you. And will you see Miss Manuelli?'

'Miss Manu–Oh! Ah! Yes.'

Bicket's girl wife, whose face they had used on Storbert's novel, the model for Aubrey Greene's–. Michael rose, for the girl was in the room already.

'I remember that dress!' he thought: 'Fleur never liked it.'

'What can I do for you, Mrs Bicket? How's Bicket, by the way?'

'Fairly, sir, thank you.'

'Still in balloons?'

'Yes.'

'Well, we all are, Mrs Bicket.'

'Beg pardon?'

'In the air–don't you think? But you didn't come to tell me that?'

'No, sir.'

A slight flush in those sallow cheeks, fingers concerned with the tips of the worn gloves, lips uncertain; but the eyes steady–really an uncommon girl!

'You remember givin' me a note to Mr Greene, sir?'

'I do; and I've seen the result; it's topping, Mrs Bicket.'

'Yes. But it's got into the papers–my husband saw it there last night; and of course, he doesn't know about me.'

Phew! For what had he let this girl in?

'I've made a lot of money at it, sir–almost enough for our passage to Australia; but now I'm frightened. "Isn't it like you?" he said to me. I tore the paper up, but suppose he remembers the name of the Gallery and goes to see the picture! That's even much more like me! He might go on to Mr Greene. So would you mind, sir, speaking to Mr Greene, and beggin' him to say it was someone else, in case Tony did go?'

'Not a bit,' said Michael. 'But do you think Bicket would mind so very much, considering what it's done for you? It can be quite a respectable profession.'

Victorine's hands moved up to her breast.

'Yes,' she said, simply. 'I have been quite respectable. And I only did it because we do so want to get away, and I couldn't bear seein' him standin' in the gutter there sellin' those balloons in the fogs. But I'm ever so scared, sir, now.'

Michael stared.

'My God!' he said; 'money's an evil thing!'

Victorine smiled faintly. 'The want of it is, I know.'

'How much more do you need, Mrs Bicket?'

'Only another ten pound, about, sir.'

'I can let you have that.'

'Oh! thank you; but it's not that–I can easy earn it–I've got used to it; a few more days don't matter.'

'But how are you going to account for having the money?'

'Say I won it bettin'.'

'*Thin!*' said Michael. 'Look here! Say you came to me and I advanced it. If Bicket repays it from Australia, I can always put it to your credit again at a bank out there. I've got you into a hole, in a way, and I'd like to get you out of it.'

'Oh! no, sir; you did me a service. I don't want to put you about, telling falsehoods for me.'

'It won't worry me a bit, Mrs Bicket. I can lie to the umpteenth when there's no harm in it. The great thing for you is to get away sharp. Are there many other pictures of you?'

'Oh! yes, a lot–not that you'd recognise them, I think, they're so square and funny.'

'Ah! well–Aubrey Greene has got you to the life!'

'Yes; it's like me all over, Tony says.'

'Quite. Well, I'll speak to Aubrey, I shall be seeing him at lunch. Here's the ten pounds! That's agreed, then? You came to me to-day–see? Say you had a brain-wave. I quite understand the whole thing. You'd do a lot for him; and he'd do a lot for you. It's all right–don't cry!'

Victorine swallowed violently. Her hand in the worn glove returned his squeeze.

'I'd tell him to-night, if I were you,' said Michael, 'and I'll get ready.'

When she had gone he thought: 'Hope Bicket won't think I received value for that sixty pounds!' And, pressing his bell, he resumed the stabbing of his blotting-paper.

'Yes, Mr Mont?'

'Now let's get on with it, Miss Perren.'

'"Dear Sir James Foggart,–We have given the utmost consideration to your very interesting–er–production. While we are of opinion that the views so well expressed on the present condition of Britain in relation to the rest of the world are of great value to all–er–thinking persons, we do not feel that there are enough–er–thinking persons to make it possible to publish the book, except at a loss. The–er–thesis that Britain should now look for salvation through adjustment of markets, population, supply and demand, within the Empire, put with such exceedingly plain speech, will, we are afraid, get the goat of all the political parties; nor do we feel that your plan of emigrating boys and girls in large quantities before they are spoiled by British town life, can do otherwise than irritate a working-class which knows nothing of conditions outside its own country, and is notably averse to giving its children a chance in any other."'

'Am I to put that, Mr Mont?'

'Yes; but tone it in a bit. Er–'

'"Finally, your view that the land should be used to grow food is so very unusual in these days, that we feel your book would have a hostile Press except from the Old Guard and the Die-hard, and a few folk with vision."'

'Yes, Mr Mont?'

'"In a period of veering–er–transitions"–keep that, Miss Perren–"and the airy unreality of hopes that have gone up the spout"–almost keep that–"any scheme that looks forward and defers harvest for twenty years, must be extraordinarily unpopular. For all these reasons you will see how necessary it is for you to–er–seek another publisher. In short, we are not taking any.

'"With–er–" what you like–"dear Sir James Foggart,"

'"We are your obedient servants,

'"Danby and Winter."'

'When you've translated that, Miss Perren, bring it in, and I'll sign it.'

'Yes. Only, Mr Mont–I thought you were a Socialist. This almost seems–forgive my asking?'

'Miss Perren, it's struck me lately that labels are "off". How can a man be anything at a time when everything's in the air? Look at the Liberals. They can't see the situation whole because of Free Trade; nor can the Labour Party because of their Capital levy; nor can the Tories because of Protection; they're all hag-ridden by catch-words! Old Sir James Foggart's jolly well right, but nobody's going to listen to him. His book will be waste paper if anybody ever publishes it. The world's unreal just now, Miss Perren; and of all countries we're the most unreal.'

'Why, Mr Mont?'

'Why? Because with the most stickfast of all the national temperaments, we're holding on to what's gone more bust for us than for any other country. Anyway, Mr Danby shouldn't have left the letter to me, if he didn't mean me to enjoy myself. Oh! and while we're about it—I've got to refuse Harold Master's new book. It's a mistake, but they won't have it.'

'Why not, Mr Mont? "The Sobbing Turtle" was such a success!'

'Well, in this new thing Master's got hold of an idea which absolutely forces him to say something. Winter says those who hailed "The Sobbing Turtle" as such a work of art, are certain to be down on this for that; and Mr Danby calls the book an outrage on human nature. So there's nothing for it. Let's have a shot:

'"My Dear Master,—In the exhilaration of your subject it has obviously not occurred to you that you've bust up the show. In "The Sobbing Turtle" you were absolutely in tune with half the orchestra, and that—er—the noisiest half. You were charmingly archaic, and securely cold-blooded. But now, what have you gone and done? Taken the last Marquesan islander for your hero and put him down in London town! This thing's a searching satire, a real criticism of life. I'm sure you didn't mean to be contemporary, or want to burrow into reality; but your subject has run off with you. Cold acid and cold blood are very different things, you know, to say nothing of your having had to drop the archaic. Personally, of course, I think this new thing miles better than "The Sobbing Turtle", which was a nice little affair, but nothing to make a song about. But I'm not the public, and I'm not the critics. The young and thin will be aggrieved by your lack of modernity, they'll say you're moralising; the old and fat will call you bitter and destructive; and the ordinary public will take your Marquesan seriously, and resent your making him superior to themselves. The prospects, you see, are not gaudy. How d'you think we're going to "get away" with such a book? Well, we're not! Such is the fiat of the firm. I don't agree with it. I'd publish it to-morrow; but needs must when Danby and Winter drive. So, with every personal regret, I return what is really a masterpiece.

> '"Always yours,
> '"Michael Mont."'

'D'you know, Miss Perren, I don't think you need translate that?'

'I'm afraid it would be difficult.'

'Right-o, then; but do the other, please. I'm going to take my wife out to see a picture; back by four. Oh! and if a little chap called Bicket, that we used to have here, calls any time and asks to see me, he's to come up; but I want warning first. Will you let them know downstairs?'

'Yes, Mr Mont. Oh! didn't—wasn't that Miss Manuelli the model for the wrapper on Mr Storbert's novel?'

'She was, Miss Perren; alone I found her.'

'She's very interesting-looking, isn't she?'

'She's unique, I'm afraid.'

'She needn't mind that, I should think.'

'That depends,' said Michael; and stabbed his blotting-paper.

3

'AFTERNOON OF A DRYAD'

Fleur was still gracefully concealing most of what Michael called 'the eleventh baronet', now due in about two months' time. She seemed to be adapting herself, in mind and body, to the quiet and persistent collection of the heir. Michael knew that, from the first, following the instructions of her mother, she had been influencing his sex, repeating to herself, every evening before falling asleep, and every morning on waking the words: 'Day by day, in every way, he is getting more and more male,' to infect the subconscious which, everybody now said, controlled the course of events; and that she was abstaining from the words. 'I *will* have a boy,' for this, setting up a reaction, everybody said, was liable to produce a girl. Michael noted that she turned more and more to her mother, as if the French, or more naturalistic, side of her, had taken charge of a process which had to do with the body. She was frequently at Mapledurham, going down in Soames's car, and her mother was frequently in South Square. Annette's handsome presence, with its tendency to black lace was always pleasing to Michael, who had never forgotten her espousal of his suit in days when it was a forlorn hope. Though he still felt only on the threshold of Fleur's heart, and was preparing to play second fiddle to 'the eleventh baronet', he was infinitely easier in mind since Wilfrid had been gone. And he watched, with a sort of amused adoration, the way in which she focused her collecting powers on an object that had no epoch, a process that did not date.

Personally conducted by Aubrey Greene, the expedition to view his show at the Dumetrius Gallery left South Square after an early lunch.

'Your Dryad came to me this morning, Aubrey,' said Michael in the cab. 'She wanted me to ask you to put up a barrage if by any chance her husband blows round to accuse you of painting his wife. It seems he's seen a reproduction of the picture.'

'Umm!' murmured the painter: 'Shall I, Fleur?'

'Of course you must, Aubrey!'

Aubrey Greene's smile slid from her to Michael.

'Well, what's his name?'

'Bicket.'

Aubrey Greene fixed his eyes on space, and murmured slowly:

> 'An angry young husband called Bicket
> Said: "Turn yourself round and I'll kick it;
>   You have painted my wife
>   In the nude to the life.
> Do you think, Mr Greene, it was cricket?"'

'Oh! Aubrey!'

'Chuck it!' said Michael, 'I'm serious. She's a most plucky little creature. She's made the money they wanted, and remained respectable.'

'So far as I'm concerned, certainly.'

'Well, I should think so.'

'Why, Fleur?'

'You're not a vamp, Aubrey!'

'As a matter of fact, she excited my æsthetic sense.'

'Much that'd save her from some æsthetes!' muttered Michael.

'Also, she comes from Putney.'

'There you have a real reason. Then, you *will* put up a barrage if Bicket blows in?'

Aubrey Greene laid his hand on his heart. 'And there we are!'

For the convenience of the eleventh baronet Michael had chosen the hour when the proper patrons of Aubrey Greene would still be lunching. A shock-headed young man and three pale-green girls alone wandered among the pictures. The painter led the way at once to his masterpiece; and for some minutes they stood before it in a suitable paralysis. To speak too soon in praise would never do; to speak too late would be equally tactless; to speak too fulsomely would jar; to mutter coldly: 'Very nice–very nice indeed!' would blight. To say bluntly: 'Well, old man, to tell you the truth, I don't like it a little bit!' would get his goat.

At last Michael pinched Fleur gently, and she said:

'It really is charming, Aubrey; and awfully like–at least–'

'So far as one can tell. But really, old man, you've done it in once. I'm afraid Bicket will think so, anyway.'

'Dash that!' muttered the painter. 'How do you find the colour values?'

'Jolly fine; especially the flesh; don't you think so, Fleur?'

'Yes; only I should have liked that shadow down the side a little deeper.'

'Yes?' murmured the painter: 'Perhaps!'

'You've caught the spirit,' said Michael. 'But I tell you what, old man, you're for it–the thing's got meaning. I don't know what the critics will do to you.'

Aubrey Greene smiled. 'That was the worst of her. She led me on. To get an idea's fatal.'

'Personally, I don't agree to that; do you Fleur?'

'Of course not; only one doesn't say so.'

'Time we did, instead of kow-towing to the Café C'rillon. I say, the hair's all right, and so are the toes–they curl as you look at 'em.'

'And it *is* a relief not to get legs painted in streaky cubes. The asphodels rather reminds one of the flowers in Leonardo's "Virgin of the Rocks", Aubrey.'

'The whole thing's just a bit Leonardoish, old man. You'll have to live that down.'

'Oh! Aubrey, my father's seen it. I believe he's biting. Something you said impressed him–about our white monkey, d'you remember?'

Aubrey Greene threw up his hands. 'Ah! That white monkey–to have painted that! Eat the fruit and chuck the rinds around, and ask with your eyes what it's all about.'

'A moral!' said Michael: 'Take care, old man! Well! Our taxi's running up. Come along, Fleur; we'll leave Aubrey to his conscience.'

Once more in the cab, he took her arm.

'That poor little snipe, Bicket! Suppose I'd come on *you* as he'll come on his wife!'

'I shouldn't have looked so nice.'

'Oh! yes; much nicer; though she looks nice enough, I must say.'

'Then why should Bicket mind, in these days of emancipation?'

'Why? Good Lord, ducky! you don't suppose Bicket–! I mean, we emancipated people have got into the habit of thinking we're the world–well! we aren't; we're an excrescence, small, and noisy. We talk as if all the old values and prejudices had gone; but they've no more gone, really, you know, than the rows of villas and little grey houses.'

'Why this outburst, Michael?'

'Well, darling, I'm a bit fed-up with the attitude of our crowd. If emancipation were true, one could stick it; but it's not. There isn't ten per cent difference between now and thirty years ago.'

'How do you know? You weren't alive.'

'No; but I read the papers, and talk to the man in the street, and look at people's faces. Our lot think they're the tablecloth, but they're only the fringe. D'you know, only one hundred and fifty thousand people in this country have ever heard a Beethoven Symphony? How many, do you suppose, think old B. a back number? Five thousand, perhaps, out of forty-two millions. How's that for emancipation?'

He stopped, observing that her eyelids had drooped.

'I was thinking, Michael, that I should like to change my bedroom curtains to blue. I saw the exact colour yesterday at Harton's. They say blue has an effect on the mind–the present curtains really are too jazzy.'

The eleventh baronet!

'Anything you like, darling. Have a blue ceiling if it helps.'

'Oh, no! But I think I'll change the carpet, too; there's a lovely powder blue at Harton's.'

'Then get it. Would you like to go there now? I can take the Tube back to the office.'

'Yes, I think I'd better. I might miss it.'

Michael put his head out of the window. 'Harton's, please!' And, replacing his hat, he looked at her. Emancipated! Phew!

4

AFTERNOON OF A BICKET

Just about that moment Bicket re-entered his sitting-room and deposited his tray. All the morning under the shadow of St Paul's he had relived Bank Holiday. Exceptionally tired in feet and legs, he was also itching mentally. He had promised himself a refreshing look from time to time at what was almost like a photo of Vic herself. And he had lost the picture! Yet he had taken nothing out of his pockets–just hung his coat up. Had it jogged out in the crush at the station, or had he missed his pocket opening and dropped it in the carriage? And he had wanted to see the original, too. He remembered that the Gallery began with a 'D', and at lunch-time squandered a penny-halfpenny to look up the names. Foreign, he was sure–the picture being naked. 'Dumetrius?' Ah!

Back at his post, he had a bit of luck. 'That alderman', whom he had not seen for months, came by. Intuition made him say at once: 'Hope I see you well sir. Never forgotten your kindness.'

The 'alderman', who had been staring up as if he saw a magpie on the dome of St Paul's, stopped as though attacked by cramp.

'Kindness?' he said; 'what kindness? Oh! balloons! They were no good to me!'

'No, sir, I'm sure,' said Bicket humbly.

'Well, here you are!' muttered the 'alderman'; 'don't expect it again.'

Half a crown! A whole half-crown! Bicket's eyes pursued the hastening form. 'Good luck!' he said softly to himself, and began putting up his tray. 'I'll go home and rest my feet, and tyke Vic to see that picture. It'll be funny lookin' at it together.'

But she was not in. He sat down and smoked a fag. He felt aggrieved that she was out, this the first afternoon he had taken off. Of course she couldn't stay in all day! Still–! He waited twenty minutes, then put on Michael's suit and shoes.

'I'll go and see it alone,' he thought. 'It'll cost half as much. They charge you sixpence, I expect.'

They charged him a shilling–a shilling! One fourth of his day's earnings, to see a picture! He entered bashfully. There were ladies who smelled of scent and had drawling voices but not a patch on Vic for looks. One of them, behind him, said:

'See! There's Aubrey Greene himself! And that's the picture they're talking of–"Afternoon of a Dryad".'

They passed him and moved on. Bicket followed. At the end of the room, between their draperies and catalogues, he glimpsed the picture. A slight sweat broke out on his forehead. Almost life-size, among the flowers and spiky grasses, the face smiled round at him–very image of Vic! Could someone in the world be as like her as all that? The thought offended him, as a collector is offended finding the duplicate of a unique possession.

'It's a wonderful picture, Mr Greene. What a type!'

A young man without hat, and fair hair sliding back, answered:

'A find, wasn't she?'

'Oh! perfect! the very spirit of a wood-nymph; so mysterious!'

The word that belonged to Vic! It was unholy. There she lay for all to look at, just because some beastly woman was made like her! A kind of rage invaded Bicket's throat, caused his cheeks to burn; and with it came a queer physical jealousy. That painter! What business had he to paint a woman so like Vic as that–a woman that didn't mind lyin' like that! They and their talk about cahryscuro and paganism, and a bloke called Leneardo! Blast their drawling and their tricks! He tried to move away, and could not, fascinated by that effigy, so uncannily resembling what he had thought belonged to himself alone. Silly to feel so bad over a 'coincidence', but he felt like smashing the glass and cutting the body up into little bits. The ladies and the painter passed on, leaving him alone before the picture. Alone, he did not mind so much. The face was mournful-like, and lonely, and–and teasing, with its smile. It sort of haunted you–it did! 'Well!' thought Bicket, 'I'll get home to Vic. Glad I didn't bring her, after all, to see herself-like. If I was an alderman, I'd buy the blinkin' thing, and burn it!'

And there, in the entrance-lobby, talking to a 'dago', stood–his very own 'alderman'! Bicket paused in sheer amazement.

'It's a rithing name, Mr Forthyte,' he heard the Dago say: 'hith prithes are going up.'

'That's all very well, Dumetrius, but it's not everybody's money in these days—too highly-finished, altogether!'

'Well, Mr Forthyte, to *you* I take off ten per thent.'

'Take off twenty and I'll buy it.'

That Dago's shoulders mounted above his hairy ears—they did; and what a smile!

'Mithter Forthyte! Fifteen, thir!'

'Well, you're doing me; but send it round to my daughter's in South Square—you know the number. When do you close?'

'Day after to-morrow, thir.'

So! The counterfeit of Vic had gone to that 'alderman', had it? Bicket uttered a savage little sound, and slunk out.

He walked with a queer feeling. Had he got unnecessary wind up? After all, it wasn't her. But to know that another woman could smile that way, have frizzy-ended short black hair, and be all curved the same! And at every woman's passing face he looked—so different, so utterly unlike Vic's!

When he reached home she was standing in the middle of the room, with her lips to a balloon. All around her, on the floor, chairs, table, mantelpiece, were the blown-out shapes of his stock; one by one they had floated from her lips and selected their own resting-places: puce, green, orange, purple, blue, enlivening with their colour the dingy little space. All his balloons blown up! And there, in her best clothes, she stood, smiling, queer, excited.

'What in thunder!' said Bicket.

Raising her dress, she took some crackling notes from the top of her stocking, and held them out to him.

'See! Sixty-four pounds, Tony! I've got it all. We can go.'

'*What!*'

'I had a brain-wave—went to that Mr Mont who gave us the clothes, and he's advanced it. We can pay it back, some day. Isn't it a marvel?'

Bicket's eyes, startled like a rabbit's, took in her smile, her excited flush, and a strange feeling shot through all his body, as if *they* were taking *him* in! She wasn't like Vic! No! Suddenly he felt her arms round him, felt her moist lips on his. She clung so tight, he could not move. His head went round.

'At last! At last! Isn't it fine? Kiss me, Tony!'

Bicket kissed, his vertigo was real, but behind it, for the moment stifled, what sense of unreality! . . .

Was it before night, or in the night, that the doubt first came—ghostly, tapping, fluttering, haunting—then, in the dawn, jabbing through his soul, turning him rigid. The money—the picture—the lost paper—that sense of unreality! This story she had told him! Were such things possible? Why should Mr Mont advance that money? She had seen him—that was certain; the room, the secretary—you couldn't mistake her description of that Miss Perren. Why, then, feel this jabbing doubt? The money—such a lot of money! Not with Mr Mont—never—he was a gent! Oh! Swine that he was, to have a thought like that—of Vic! He turned his back to her and tried to sleep. But once you got a thought like that—sleep? No! Her face among the balloons the way she had smothered his eyes and turned his head—so that he couldn't think, couldn't go into it and ask her questions! A prey to dim doubts, achings, uncertainty, thrills of hope, and visions of 'Austrylia', Bicket arose haggard.

'Well,' he said, over their cocoa and margarined bread: 'I must see Mr Mont, that's certain.' And suddenly he added: 'Vic?' looking straight into her face.

She answered his look–straight, yes, straight. Oh! he was a proper swine! . . .

When he had left the house Victorine stood quite still, with hands pressed against her chest. She had slept less than he. Still as a mouse, she had turned and turned the thought: 'Did I take him in? Did I?' And if not–what? She took out the notes which had bought–or sold?–their happiness, and counted them once more. And the sense of injustice burned within her. Had she wanted to stand like that before men? Hadn't she been properly through it about that? Why, she could have had the sixty pounds three months ago from that sculptor, who was wild about her; or–so he said! But she had stuck it; yes, she had. Tony had nothing against her really–even if he knew it all. She had done it for him–. Well! mostly–for him selling those balloons day after day in all weathers! But for her, they would still be stuck, and another winter coming, and unemployment–so they said in the paper–to be worse and worse! Stuck in the fogs and the cold, again! Ugh! Her chest was still funny sometimes; and he always hoarse. And this poky little room, and the bed so small that she couldn't stir without waking him. Why should Tony doubt her? For he did–she had felt it, heard it in his 'Vic?' Would Mr Mont convince him? Tony was sharp! Her head drooped. The unfairness of it all. Some had everything to their hand, like that pretty wife of Mr Mont's! And if one tried to find a way and get out to a new chance–then–then–this! She flung her hair back. Tony *must* believe–he should! If he wouldn't, let him look out. She had done nothing to be ashamed of! No, indeed! And with the longing to go in front and lead her happiness along, she got out her old tin trunk, and began with careful method to put things into it.

5

MICHAEL GIVES ADVICE

Michael still sat, correcting the proofs of 'Counterfeits'. Save 'Jericho', there had been no address to send them to. The East was wide, and Wilfrid had made no sign. Did Fleur ever think of Wilfrid–well, probably he was forgetting her already. Even passion required a little sustenance.

'A Mr Forsyte to see you, sir.'

Apparition in bookland!

'Ah! Show him in.'

Soames entered with an air of suspicion.

'This your place?' he said. 'I've looked in to tell you that I've bought that picture of young Greene's. Have you anywhere to hang it?'

'I should think we had,' said Michael. 'Jolly good, sir, isn't it?'

'Well,' muttered Soames, 'for these days, yes. He'll make a name.'

'He's an intense admirer of that White Monkey you gave us.'

'Ah! I've been looking into the Chinese. If I go on buying–' Soames paused.

'They *are* a bit of an antidote, aren't they, sir? That 'Earthly Paradise'! And those geese–they don't seem to mind your counting their feathers, do they?'

Soames made no reply; he was evidently thinking: 'How on earth I missed those things when they first came on the market!' Then, raising his umbrella, and pointing it as if at the book trade, he asked:

'Young Butterfield–how's he doing?'

'Ah! I was going to let you know, sir. He came in yesterday and told me that he saw Elderson two days ago. He went to sell him a copy of my father's "Limited"; Elderson said nothing and bought two.'

'The deuce he did!'

'Butterfield got the impression that his visit put the wind up him. Elderson knows, of course, that I'm in this firm, and your son-in-law.'

Soames frowned. 'I'm not sure,' he said, 'that sleeping dogs–! Well, I'm on my way there now.'

'Mention the book, sir, and see how Elderson takes it. Would you like one yourself? You're on the list. E, F–Butterfield should be reaching you to-day. It'll save you a refusal. Here it is–nice get-up. One guinea.'

'"A Duet",' read Soames. 'What's it about? Musical?'

'Not precisely. A sort of cat-calling between the ghosts of the G.O.M. and Dizzy!'

'I'm not a reader,' said Soames. He pulled out a note. 'Why didn't you make it a pound? Here's the shilling.'

'Thanks awfully, sir; I'm sure my father'll be frightfully bucked to think you've got one.'

'Will he?' said Soames, with a faint smile. 'D'you ever do any *work* here?'

'Well, we try to turn a doubtful penny.'

'What d'you make at it?'

'Personally, about five hundred a year.'

'That all?'

'Yes, but I doubt if I'm worth more than three.'

'H'm! I thought you'd got over your Socialism.'

'I fancy I have, sir. It didn't seem to go with my position.'

'No,' said Soames. 'Fleur seems well.'

'Yes, she's splendid. She does the Coué stunt, you know.'

Soames stared. 'That's her mother,' he said; 'I can't tell. Good-bye! Oh! I want to know; what's the meaning of that expression "got his goat"?'

'"Got his goat"? Oh, raised his dander, if you know what that means, it was before my time.'

'I see,' said Soames; 'I had it right, then. Well!' He turned. His back was very neat and real. It vanished through the doorway, and with it seemed to go the sense of definition.

Michael took up the proofs, and read two poems. Bitter as quinine! The unrest in them–the yearning behind the words! Nothing Chinese there! After all, the ancients–like Old Forsyte, and his father in a very different way–had an anchor down. 'What is it?' thought Michael. 'What's wrong with us? We're quick, and clever, cocksure, and dissatisfied. If only something would enthuse us, or get *our* goats! We've chucked religion, tradition, property, pity; and in their place we put–what? Beauty? Gosh! See Walter Nazing, and the Café C'rillon! and yet–we must be after something! Better world? Doesn't look like it. Future life? Suppose I ought to "look into" spiritualism, as Old Forsyte would say. But–half in this world, half in that–deuced odd if spirits are less restive than we are!'

To what–to what, then, was it all moving?

'Dash it!' thought Michael, getting up, 'I'll try dictating an advertisement!'

'Will you come in, please, Miss Perren? For the new Desert volume–Trade Journals: "Danby and Winter will shortly issue 'Counterfeits', by the author of 'Copper Coin', the outstanding success of the last publishing season." I wonder how many publishers have claimed that, Miss Perren, for how many books this year? "These poems show all the brilliancy of mood, and more than the technical accomplishment of the young author's first volume." How's that?'

'Brilliancy of mood, Mr Mont? Do you think?'

'No. But what am I to say? "All the pangs and pessimism"?'

'Oh, no! But possibly: "All the brilliancy of diction. The strangeness and variety of mood."'

'Good. But it'll cost more. Say: "All the brilliant strangeness"; that'll ring their bells in once. We're nuts on "the strange", but we're not getting it–the *outré*, yes, but not the strange.'

'Surely Mr Desert gets–'

'Yes, sometimes; but hardly anyone else. To be strange, you've got to have guts, if you'll excuse the phrase, Miss Perren.'

'Certainly, Mr Mont. That young man Bicket is waiting to see you.'

'He is, is he?' said Michael, taking out a cigarette. 'Give me time to tighten my belt, Miss Perren, and ask him up.'

'The lie benevolent,' he thought; 'now for it!'

The entrance of Bicket into a room where his last appearance had been so painful, was accomplished with a certain stolidity. Michael stood, back to the hearth, smoking; Bicket, back to a pile of modern novels, with the words 'This great new novel' on it. Michael nodded.

'Hallo, Bicket!'

Bicket nodded.

'Hope you're keeping well, sir?'

'Frightfully well, thank you.' And there was silence.

'Well,' said Michael at last, 'I suppose you've come about that little advance to your wife. It's quite all right; no hurry whatever.'

While saying this he had become conscious that the 'little snipe' was dreadfully disturbed. His eyes had a most peculiar look, those large, shrimp-like eyes which seemed, as it were, in advance of the rest of him. He hastened on:

'I believe in Australia myself. I think you're perfectly right, Bicket, and the sooner you go, the better. She doesn't look too strong.'

Bicket swallowed.

'Sir,' he said, 'you've been a gent to me, and it's hard to say things.'

'Then don't.'

Bicket's cheeks became suffused with blood: queer effect in that pale, haggard face.

'It isn't what you think,' he said: 'I've come to ask you to tell me the truth.' Suddenly he whipped from his pocket what Michael perceived to be a crumpled novel-wrapper.

'I took this from a book on the counter as I came by, downstairs. There! Is that my wife?' He stretched it out.

Michael beheld with consternation the wrapper of Stobert's novel. One thing to tell the lie benevolent already determined on–quite another to deny this!

Bicket gave him little time.

'I see it is, from your face,' he said. 'What's it all mean? I want the truth–I must 'ave it! I'm gettin' wild over all this. If that's 'er fyce there, then that's 'er body in the Gallery–Aubrey Greene; it's the syme nyme. What's it all mean?'

His face had become almost formidable; his Cockney accent very broad. 'What gyme 'as she been plyin'? You gotta tell me before I go aht of 'ere.'

Michael's heels came together. He said quietly:

'Steady, Bicket.'

'Steady! You'd be steady if *your* wife–! All that money! *You* never advanced it–you never give it 'er–never! Don't tell me you did!'

Michael had taken his line. No lies!

'I lent her ten pounds to make a round sum of it–that's all; the rest she earned–honourably; and you ought to be proud of her.'

Bicket's mouth fell open.

'Proud? And how's she earned it? Proud! My Gawd!'

Michael said coldly:

'As a model. I myself gave her the introduction to my friend, Mr Greene, the day you had lunch with me. You've heard of models, I suppose?'

Bicket's hands tore the wrapper, and the pieces fell to the floor. 'Models!' he said: 'Pynters–yes, I've 'eard of 'em–Swines!'

'No more swine than you are, Bicket. Be kind enough not to insult my friend. Pull yourself together, man, and take a cigarette.'

Bicket dashed the proffered case aside.

'I–I–was stuck on her,' he said passionately, 'and she's put this up on me!' A sort of sob came out of his lungs.

'You were stuck on her,' said Michael; his voice had sting in it. 'And when she does her best for you, you turn her down–is that it? Do you suppose she liked it?'

Bicket covered his face suddenly.

'What should I know?' he muttered from behind his hands.

A wave of pity flooded up in Michael. Pity! Blurb!

He said dryly: 'When you've quite done, Bicket. D'you happen to remember what *you* did for *her*?'

Bicket uncovered his face and stared wildly. 'You've never told her that?'

'No; but I jolly well will if you don't pull yourself together.'

'What do I care if you do, now–lyin' like that, for all the men in the world! Sixty pounds! Honourably! D'you think I believe that?' His voice had desolation in it.

'Ah!' said Michael. 'You don't believe simply because you're ignorant, as ignorant as the swine you talk of. A girl can do what she did and be perfectly honest, as I haven't the faintest doubt she is. You've only to look at her, and hear the way she speaks of it. She did it because she couldn't bear to see you selling those balloons. She did it to get you out of the gutter, and give you both a chance. And now you've got the chance, you kick up like this. Dash it all, Bicket, be a sport! Suppose I tell her what you did for her–d'you think she's going to squirm and squeal? Not she! It was damned human of you, and it was damned human of her; and don't you forget it!'

Bicket swallowed violently again.

'It's all very well,' he said sullenly; 'it 'asn't 'appened to you.'

Michael was afflicted at once. No! It hadn't happened to him! And all his doubts of Fleur in the days of Wilfrid came hitting him.

'Look here, Bicket,' he said, 'do you doubt your wife's affection? The whole thing is there. I've only seen her twice, but I don't see how you can. If she weren't fond of you, why should she want to go to Australia, when she knows she can make good money here, and enjoy herself if she wants? I can vouch for my friend Greene. He's dashed decent, and I *know* he's played cricket.'

But searching Bicket's face, he wondered: Were all the others she had sat to as dashed decent?

'Look here, Bicket! We all get up against it sometimes; and that's the test of us. You've just *got* to believe in her; there's nothing else to it.'

'To myke a show of herself for all the world to see!' The words seemed to struggle from the skinny throat. 'I saw that picture bought yesterday by a ruddy alderman.'

Michael could not conceal a grin at this description of 'Old Forsyte'.

'As a matter of fact,' he said, 'it was bought by my own father-in-law as a present to us, to hang in our house. And, mind you, Bicket, it's a fine thing.'

'Ah!' cried Bicket, 'it *is* a fine thing! Money! It's money bought her. Money'll buy anything. It'll buy the 'eart out of your chest.'

And Michael thought: 'I can't get away with it a bit! What price emancipation? He's never heard of the Greeks! And if he had, they'd seem to him a lot of loose-living foreigners. I must quit.' And, suddenly, he saw tears come out of those shrimp's eyes, and trickle down the hollowed cheeks.

Very disturbed, he said hastily:

'When you get out there, you'll never think of it again. Hang it all, Bicket, be a man! She did it for the best. If I were you, I'd never let on to her that I knew. That's what she'd do if I told her how you snooped those "Copper Coins".'

Bicket clenched his fists–the action went curiously with the tears; then, without a word, he turned and shuffled out.

'Well,' thought Michael, 'giving advice is clearly not my stunt! Poor little snipe!'

6

QUITTANCE

Bicket stumbled, half-blind, along the Strand. Naturally good-tempered, such a nerve-storm made him feel ill, and bruised in the brain. Sunlight and motion slowly restored some power of thought. He had got the truth. But was it the whole and nothing but the truth? Could she have made all that money without–? If he could believe that, then, perhaps–out of this country where people could see her naked for a shilling–he might forget. But–all that money! And even if all earned 'honourable', as Mr Mont had put it, in how many days, exposed to the eyes of how many men? He groaned aloud in the street. The thought of going home to her–of a scene, of what he might learn if there *were* a scene, was just about unbearable. And yet–must do it, he supposed. He could have borne it better under St Paul's, standing in the gutter, offering his balloons. A man of leisure for the first time in his life, a blooming 'alderman' with nothing to do but step in and take a ticket to the ruddy butterflies! And he owed that leisure to what a man with nothing to take his thoughts off simply could not bear! He would rather have snaffled the money out of a shop till. Better that on his soul, than the jab of this dark fiendish sexual jealousy. 'Be a man!' Easy said! 'Pull yourself together! She did it for you!' He would a hundred times rather she had not. Blackfriars Bridge! A dive, and an end in the mud down there? But you had to rise three times; they would fish you out alive, and run you in for it–and nothing gained–not even the pleasure of thinking that Vic would see what she had done, when she came to identify the body. Dead was dead, anyway, and he would never know what she felt post-mortem! He trudged across the bridge, keeping his eyes before him. Little Ditch Street–how he used to scuttle down it, back to her, when she had pneumonia! Would he never feel like that again? He strode past the window, and went in.

Victorine was still bending over the brown tin trunk. She straightened herself, and on her face came a cold, tired look. 'Well,' she said, 'I see you know.'

Bicket had but two steps to take in that small room. He took them, and put his hands on her shoulders. His face was close, his eyes, so large and strained, searched hers.

'I know you've myde a show of yourself for all London to see; what I want to know is–the rest!'

Victorine stared back at him.

'The rest!' she said–it was not a question, just a repetition, in a voice that seemed to mean nothing.

'Ah!' said Bicket hoarsely; 'the rest–Well?'

'If you think there's a "rest", that's enough.'

Bicket jerked his hands away.

'Aoh! for the land's sake, daon't be mysterious. I'm 'alf orf me nut!'

'I see that,' said Victorine; 'and I see this: You aren't what I thought you. D'you think I liked doing it?' She raised her dress and took out the notes. 'There you are! You can go to Australia without me.'

Bicket cried hoarsely: 'And leave you to the blasted pynters?'

'And leave me to meself. Take them!'

But Bicket recoiled against the door, staring at the notes with horror. 'Not me!'

'Well, *I* can't keep 'em. I earned them to get you out of this.'

There was a long silence, while the notes lay between them on the table, still crisp if a little greasy–the long-desired, the dreamed-of means of release, of happiness together in the sunshine. There they lay; neither would take them! What then?

'Vic,' said Bicket at last, in a hoarse whisper, 'swear you never let 'em touch you!'

'Yes, I can swear that.'

And she could smile, too, saying it–that smile of hers! How believe her–living all these months, keeping it from him, telling him a lie about it in the end! He sank into a chair by the table and laid his head on his arms.

Victorine turned and began pulling an old cord round the trunk. He raised his head at the tiny sound. Then she really meant to go away! He saw his life devastated, empty as a coconut on Hampstead Heath; and all defence ran melted out of his Cockney spirit. Tears rolled from his eyes.

'When you were ill,' he said, 'I stole for you. I got the sack for it.'

She spun round. 'Tony–you never told me! What did you steal?'

'Books. All your extra feedin' was books.'

For a long minute she stood looking at him, then stretched out her hands without a word. Bicket seized them.

'I don't care about anything,' he gasped, 'so 'elp me, so long as you're fond of me, Vic!'

'And I don't neither. Oh! let's get out of this Tony! this awful little room, this awful country. Let's get out of it all!'

'Yes,' said Bicket; and put her hands to his eyes.

7

LOOKING INTO ELDERSON

Soames had left Danby and Winter divided in thought between Elderson and the White Monkey. As Fleur surmised, he had never forgotten Aubrey Greene's words concerning that bit of salvage from the wreck of George Forsyte. 'Eat the fruits of life, scatter the rinds, and get copped doing it.' His application of them tended towards the field of business.

The country was still living on its capital. With the collapse of the carrying trade and European markets, they were importing food they couldn't afford to pay for. In his opinion they would get copped doing it, and that before long. British credit was all very well, the wonder of the world and that, but you couldn't live indefinitely on wonder. With shipping idle, concerns making a loss all over the place, and the unemployed in swarms, it was a pretty pair of shoes! Even insurance must suffer before long. Perhaps that chap Elderson had foreseen this already, and was simply feathering his nest in time. If one was to be copped in any case, why bother to be honest? This was cynicism so patent, that all the Forsyte in Soames rejected it; and yet it would keep coming back. In a general bankruptcy, why trouble with thrift, far-sightedness, integrity? Even the Conservatives were refusing to call themselves Conservatives again, as if there were something ridiculous about the word, and they knew there was really nothing left to conserve. 'Eat the fruit, scatter the rinds, and get copped doing it.' That young painter had said a clever thing—yes, and his picture was clever, though Dumetrius had done one over the price—as usual! Where would Fleur hang it? In the hall, he shouldn't be surprised—good light there; and the sort of people they knew wouldn't jib at the nude. Curious—where all the nudes went to! You never saw a nude—no more than you saw the proverbial dead donkey! Soames had a momentary vision of dying donkeys laden with pictures of the nude, stepping off the edge of the world. Refusing its extravagance, he raised his eyes, just in time to see St Paul's, as large as life. That little beggar with his balloons wasn't there to-day! Well—he'd nothing for him! At a tangent his thoughts turned towards the object of his pilgrimage—the P.P.R.S. and its half-year's accounts. At his suggestion, they were writing off that German business wholesale—a dead loss of two hundred and thirty thousand pounds. There would be no interim dividend, and even then they would be carrying forward a debit towards the next half-year. Well! better have a rotten tooth out at once and done with; the shareholders would have six months to get used to the gap before the general meeting. He himself had got used to it already, and so would they in time. Shareholders were seldom nasty unless startled—a long-suffering lot!

In the board-room the old clerk was still filling his ink-pots from the magnum.

'Manager in?'

'Yes, sir.'

'Say I'm here, will you?'

The old clerk withdrew. Soames looked at the clock. Twelve! A little shaft of sunlight slanted down the wainscotting and floor. There was nothing else alive in the room save a bluebottle and the tick of the clock; not even a daily paper. Soames watched the bluebottle. He remembered how, as a boy, he had preferred bluebottles and greenbottles to the ordinary fly, because of their bright colour. It was a lesson. The showy things, the brilliant people, were the dangerous. Witness the Kaiser, and that precious Italian poet—what was his name! And this Jack-o'-lantern of their own! He shouldn't be surprised if Elderson were brilliant in private life. Why didn't the chap come? Was that encounter with young Butterfield giving him pause? The bluebottle crawled up the pane, buzzed down, crawled up again; the sunlight stole inward along the floor. All was vacuous in the board-room, as though embodying the principle of insurance: 'Keep things as they are.'

'Can't kick my heels here for ever,' thought Soames, and moved to the window. In that wide street leading to the river, sunshine illuminated a few pedestrians and a brewer's dray, but along the main artery at the end the traffic streamed and rattled. London! A monstrous place! And all insured! 'What'll it be like thirty years hence?' he thought. To think that there would be London, without himself to see it! He felt sorry for the place, sorry for himself. Even old Gradman would be gone. He supposed the insurance societies would look after it, but he didn't know. And suddenly he became aware of Elderson. The fellow looked quite jaunty, in a suit of dittoes and a carnation.

'Contemplating the future, Mr Forsyte?'

'No,' said Soames. How had the fellow guessed his thoughts?

'I'm glad you've come in. It gives me a chance to say how grateful I am for the interest you take in the concern. It's rare. A manager has a lonely job.'

Was he mocking? He seemed altogether very spry and uppish. Light-heartedness always made Soames suspicious—there was generally some reason for it.

'If every director were as conscientious as you, one would sleep in one's bed. I don't mind telling you that the amount of help I got from the Board before you came on it was—well—negligible.'

Flattery! The fellow must be leading up to something!

Elderson went on:

'I can say to you what I couldn't say to any of the others: I'm not at all happy about business, Mr Forsyte. England is just about to discover the state she's really in.'

Faced with this startling confirmation of his own thoughts, Soames reacted.

'No good crying out before we're hurt,' he said; 'the pound's still high. We're good stayers.'

'In the soup, I'm afraid. If something drastic isn't done—we *shall* stay there. And anything drastic, as you know, means disorganisation and lean years before you reap reward.'

How could the fellow talk like this, and look as bright and pink as a new penny? It confirmed the theory that he didn't care what happened. And, suddenly, Soames resolved to try a shot.

'Talking of lean years—I came in to say that I think we must call a meeting of the shareholders over this dead loss of the German business.' He said it to the floor, and looked quickly up. The result was disappointing. The manager's light-grey eyes met his without a blink.

'I've been expecting that from you,' he said.

'The deuce you have!' thought Soames, for it had but that moment come into his mind.

'By all means call one,' went on the manager; 'but I'm afraid the Board won't like it.'

Soames refrained from saying: 'Nor do I.'

'Nor the shareholders, Mr Forsyte. In a long experience I've found that the less you rub their noses in anything unpleasant, the better for everyone.'

'That may be,' said Soames, stiffening in contrariety; 'but it's all a part of the vice of not facing things.'

'I don't think, Mr Forsyte, that you will accuse *me* of not facing things, in the time to come.'

Time to come! Now, what on earth did the fellow mean by that?

'Well, I shall moot it at the next Board,' he said.

'Quite!' said the manager. 'Nothing like bringing things to a head, is there?'

Again that indefinable mockery, as if he had something up his sleeve. Soames looked mechanically at the fellow's cuffs–beautifully laundered, with a blue stripe; at his holland waistcoat, and his bird's-eye tie–a regular dandy. He would give him a second barrel!

'By the way,' he said, 'Mont's written a book. I've taken a copy.'

Not a blink! A little more show of teeth, perhaps–false, no doubt!

'I've taken two–poor, dear Mont!'

Soames had a sense of defeat. This chap was armoured like a crab, varnished like a Spanish table.

'Well,' he said, 'I must go.'

The manager held out his hand.

'Good-bye, Mr Forsyte. I'm so grateful to you.'

The fellow was actually squeezing his hand. Soames went out confused. To have his hand squeezed was so rare! It undermined him. And yet, it might be the crown of a consummate bit of acting. He couldn't tell. He had, however, less intention even than before of moving for a meeting of the shareholders. No, no! That had just been a shot to get a rise; and it had failed. But the Butterfield shot had gone home, surely! If innocent, Elderson must certainly have alluded to the impudence of the young man's call. And yet such a cool card was capable of failing to rise, just to tease you! No! nothing doing–as they said nowadays. He was as far as ever from a proof of guilt; and to speak truth, glad of it. Such a scandal could serve no purpose save that of blackening the whole concern, directors and all. People were so careless, they never stopped to think, or apportion blame where it was due. Keep a sharp eye open, and go on as they were! No good stirring hornets' nests! He had got so far in thought and progress, when a voice said:

'Well met, Forsyte! Are you going my way?'

'Old Mont', coming down the steps of 'Snooks'!

'I don't know,' said Soames.

'I'm off to the Aeroplane for lunch.'

'That new-fangled place?'

'Rising, you know, Forsyte–rising.'

'I've just been seeing Elderson. He's bought two copies of your book.'

'Dear me! Poor fellow!'

Soames smiled faintly. 'That's what he said of you! And who d'you think sold them to him? Young Butterfield.'

'Is he still alive?'

'He was this morning.'

Sir Lawrence's face took on a twist:

'I've been thinking, Forsyte. They tell me Elderson keeps two women.'

Soames stared. The idea was attractive; would account for everything.

'My wife says it's one too many, Forsyte. What do you say?'

'I?' said Soames. 'I only know the chap's as cool as a cucumber. I'm going in here. Good-bye!' One could get no help from that baronet fellow; he couldn't take anything seriously. Two women! At Elderson's age! What a life! There were always men like that, not content with one thing at a time–living dangerously. It was mysterious to him. You might look and look into chaps like that, and see nothing. And yet, there they were! He crossed the hall, and went into the room where connoisseurs were lunching. Taking down the menu at the service table, he ordered himself a dozen oysters; but, suddenly remembering that the month contained no 'r', changed them to a fried sole.

8

LEVANTED

'No, dear heart, Nature's "off"!'

'How d'you mean, Michael?'

'Well, look at the Nature novels we get. Sedulous stuff pitched on Cornish cliffs or Yorkshire moors–ever been on a Yorkshire moor?–it comes off on you; and the Dartmoor brand. Gosh! Dartmoor, where the passions come from–ever been on Dartmoor? Well, they don't, you know. And the South Sea bunch! Oh, la, la! And the poets, the splash-and-splutter school don't get within miles of Nature. The village idiot school is a bit better, certainly. After all, old Wordsworth made Nature, and she's a bromide. Of course, there's raw nature with the small "n"; but if you come up against that, it takes you all your time to keep alive–the Nature we gas about is licensed, nicely blended and bottled. She's not modern enough for contemporary style.'

'Oh! well, let's go on the river, anyway, Michael. We can have tea at "The Shelter".'

They were just reaching what Michael always called 'this desirable residence', when Fleur leaned forward, and, touching his knee, said:

'I'm not half as nice to you as you deserve, Michael.'

'Good Lord, darling! I thought you were.'

'I know I'm selfish; especially just now.'

'It's only the eleventh baronet.'

'Yes; it's a great responsibility. I only hope he'll be like you.'

Michael slid in to the landing-stage, shipped his sculls, and sat down beside her.

'If he's like me, I shall disown him. But sons take after their mothers.'

'I meant in character. I want him frightfully to be cheerful and not restless, and have the feeling that life's worth while.'

Michael stared at her lips–they were quivering; at her cheek, slightly browned by the afternoon's sunning; and, bending sideways, he put his own against it.

'He'll be a sunny little cuss, I'm certain.'

Fleur shook her head.

'I don't want him greedy and self-centred; it's in my blood, you know. I can see it's ugly, but I can't help it. How do you manage not to be?'

Michael ruffled his hair with his free hand.

'The sun isn't too hot for you, is it, ducky?'

'No. Seriously, Michael—how?'

'But I *am*. Look at the way I want you. Nothing will cure me of that.'

A slight pressure of her cheek on his own was heartening, and he said:

'Do you remember coming down the garden one night, and finding me in a boat just here? When you'd gone, I stood on my head, to cool it. I was on my uppers; I didn't think I'd got an earthly–' He stopped. No! He would not remind her, but that was the night when she said: 'Come again when I know I can't get my wish!' The unknown cousin!

Fleur said quietly:

'I was a pig to you, Michael, but I was awfully unhappy. That's gone. It's gone at last; there's nothing wrong now, except my own nature.'

Conscious that his feelings betrayed the period, Michael said:

'Oh! if that's all! What price tea?'

They went up the lawn arm-in-arm. Nobody was at home—Soames in London, Annette at a garden party.

'We'll have tea on the verandah, please,' said Fleur.

Sitting there, happier than he ever remembered being, Michael conceded a certain value to Nature, to the sunshine stealing down, the scent of pinks and roses, the sighing in the aspens. Annette's pet doves were cooing; and, beyond the quietly-flowing river, the spires of poplar trees rose along the further bank. But, after all, he was only enjoying them because of the girl beside him, whom he loved to touch and look at, and because, for the first time, he felt as if she did not want to get up and flutter off to someone or something else. Curious that there could be, outside oneself, a being who completely robbed the world of its importance, 'snooped', as it were, the whole 'bag of tricks'—and she one's own wife! Very curious, considering what one was! He heard her say:

'Of course, mother's a Catholic; only, living with father down here, she left off practising. She didn't even bother me much. I've been thinking, Michael—what shall we do about *him*?'

'Let him rip.'

'I don't know. He must be taught something, because of going to school. The Catholics, you know, really do get things out of their religion.'

'Yes; they go it blind; it's the only logical way now.'

'I think having no religion makes one feel that nothing matters.'

Michael suppressed the words: 'We could bring him up as a sun-worshipper,' and said, instead:

'It seems to me that whatever he's taught will only last till he can think for himself; then he'll settle down to what suits him.'

'But what do *you* think about things, Michael? You're as good as anyone I know.'

'Gosh!' murmured Michael, strangely flattered: 'Is that so?'

'What *do* you think? Be serious!'

'Well, darling, doctrinally nothing—which means, of course, that I haven't got religion. I believe one has to play the game—but that's ethics.'

'But surely it's a handicap not to be able to rely on anything but oneself? If there's something to be had out of any form of belief, one might as well have it.'

Michael smiled, but not on the surface.

'You're going to do just as you like about the eleventh baronet, and I'm going to abet you. But considering his breeding–I fancy he'll be a bit of a sceptic.'

'But I don't *want* him to be. I'd rather he were snug, and convinced and all that. Scepticism only makes one restless.'

'No white monkey in him? Ah! I wonder! It's in the air, I guess. The only thing will be to teach him a sense of other people, as young as possible, with a slipper, if necessary.'

Fleur gave him a clear look, and laughed.

'Yes,' she said: 'Mother used to try, but Father wouldn't let her.'

They did not reach home till past eight o'clock.

'Either your father's here, or mine,' said Michael, in the hall: 'there's a prehistoric hat.'

'It's Dad's. His is grey inside. Bart's is buff.'

In the Chinese room Soames indeed was discovered, with an opened letter, and Ting-a-ling at his feet. He held the letter out to Michael, without a word.

There was no date, and no address; Michael read:

DEAR MR FORSYTE.–Perhaps you will be good enough to tell the Board at the meeting on Tuesday that I am on my way to immunity from the consequences of any peccadillo I may have been guilty of. By the time you receive this, I shall be there. I have always held that the secret of life, no less than that of business, is to know when not to stop. It will be no use to proceed against me, for my person will not be attachable, as I believe you call it in the law, and I have left no property behind. If your object was to corner me, I cannot congratulate you on your tactics. If, on the other hand, you inspired that young man's visit as a warning that you were still pursuing the matter, I should like to add new thanks to those which I expressed when I saw you a few days ago.

Believe me, dear Mr Forsyte,

Faithfully yours,

ROBERT ELDERSON.

Michael said cheerfully:

'Happy release! Now you'll feel safer, sir.'

Soames passed his hand over his face, evidently wiping off its expression. 'We'll discuss it later,' he said. 'This dog's been keeping me company.'

Michael admired him at that moment. He was obviously swallowing his 'grief', to save Fleur.

'Fleur's a bit tired,' he said. 'We've been on the river, and had tea at 'The Shelter'; Madame wasn't in. Let's have dinner at once, Fleur.'

Fleur had picked up Ting-a-ling, and was holding her face out of reach of his avid tongue.

'Sorry you've had to wait, Dad,' she murmured, behind the yellow fur; 'I'm just going to wash; shan't change.'

When she had gone, Soames reached for the letter.

'A pretty kettle of fish!' he muttered. 'Where it'll end, I can't tell!'

'But isn't this the end, sir?'

Soames stared. These young people! Here he was, faced with a public scandal, which might lead to he didn't know what–the loss of his name in the city, the loss of his fortune, perhaps; and they took it as if–! They had no sense of responsibility–none! All his father's power of seeing the worst, all James' nervous pessimism, had come to the fore in him during the hour since, at the Connoisseurs' Club, he had been handed that letter. Only the extra 'form' of the generation that succeeded James saved him, now that Fleur was out of the room, from making an exhibition of his fears.

'Your father in town?'

'I believe so, sir.'

'Good!' Not that he felt relief. That baronet chap was just as irresponsible–
getting him to go on that Board! It all came of mixing with people brought
up in a sort of incurable levity, with no real feeling for money.

'Now that Elderson's levanted,' he said, 'the whole thing must come out.
Here's his confession in my hand–'

'Why not tear it up, sir, and say Elderson has developed consumption?'

The impossibility of getting anything serious from this young man afflicted
Soames like the eating of heavy pudding.

'You think that would be honourable?' he said grimly.

'Sorry, sir!' said Michael, sobered. 'Can I help at all?'

'Yes; by dropping your levity, and taking care to keep wind of this matter
away from Fleur.'

'I will,' said Michael earnestly: 'I promise you. I'll Dutch-oyster the whole
thing. What's your line going to be?'

'We shall have to call the shareholders together and explain this dicky-
dealing. They'll very likely take it in bad part.'

'I can't see why they should. How could you have helped it?'

Soames sniffed.

'There's no connection in life between reward and your deserts. If the war
hasn't taught you that, nothing will.'

'Well,' said Michael, 'Fleur will be down directly. If you'll excuse me a
minute; we'll continue it in our next.'

Their next did not occur till Fleur had gone to bed.

'Now, sir,' said Michael, 'I expect my governor's at the Aeroplane. He goes
there and meditates on the end of the world. Would you like me to ring him up,
if your Board meeting's to-morrow?'

Soames nodded. He himself would not sleep a wink–why should 'Old
Mont'?

Michael went to the Chinese tea-chest.

'Bart? This is Michael. Old For– my father-in-law is here; he's had a
pill. . . . No; Elderson. Could you blow in by any chance and hear? . . . He's
coming, sir. Shall we stay down, or go up to my study?'

'Down,' muttered Soames, whose eyes were fixed on the white monkey. 'I
don't know what we're all coming to,' he added, suddenly.

'If we did, sir, we should die of boredom.'

'Speak for yourself. All this unreliability! I can't tell where it's leading.'

'Perhaps there's somewhere, sir, that's neither heaven nor hell.'

'A man of *his* age!'

'Same age as my dad; it was a bad vintage, I expect. If you'd been in the war,
sir, it would have cheered you up no end.'

'Indeed!' said Soames.

'It took the linch-pins out of the cart–admitted; but, my Lord! it did give you
an idea of the grit there is about, when it comes to being up against it.'

Soames stared. Was this young fellow reading him a lesson against
pessimism?

'Look at young Butterfield, the other day,' Michael went on, 'going over the
top, to Elderson! Look at the girl who sat for "the altogether" in that picture
you bought us! She's the wife of a packer we had, who got hoofed for snooping
books. She made quite a lot of money by standing for the nude, and never lost

her wicket. They're going to Australia on it. Yes, and look at that little snooper himself; he snooped to keep her alive after pneumonia, and came down to selling balloons.'

'I don't know what you're talking about,' said Soames.

'Only grit, sir. You said you didn't know what we were coming to. Well, look at the unemployed! Is there a country in the world where they stick it as they do here? I get awfully bucked at being English every now and then. Don't you?'

The words stirred something deep in Soames; but far from giving it away, he continued to gaze at the white monkey. The restless, inhuman, and yet so human, angry sadness of the creature's eyes! 'No whites to them!' thought Soames: 'that's what does it, I expect!' And George had liked that picture to hang opposite his bed! Well, George had grit–joked with his last breath: very English, George! Very English, all the Forsytes! Old Uncle Jolyon, and his way with shareholders; Swithin, upright, puffy, huge in a too little armchair at Timothy's: 'All these small fry!' he seemed to hear the words again; and Uncle Nicholas, whom that chap Elderson reproduced as it were unworthily, spry and all-there, and pretty sensual, but quite above suspicion of dishonesty! And old Roger, with his crankiness, and German mutton! And his own father, James–how he had hung on, long and frail as a reed, hung on and on! And Timothy, preserved in Consols, dying at a hundred! Grit and body in those old English boys, in spite of their funny ways. And there stirred in Soames a sort of atavistic will-power. He would see, and they would see–and that was all about it!

The grinding of a taxi's wheels brought him back from reverie. Here came 'Old Mont', tittuppy, and light in the head as ever, no doubt. And, instead of his hand, Soames held out Elderson's letter.

'Your precious schoolfellow's levanted,' he said.

Sir Lawrence read it through, and whistled.

'What do you think, Forsyte–Constantinople?'

'More likely Monte Carlo,' said Soames gloomily. 'Secret commission–it's not an extraditable offence.'

The odd contortions of that baronet's face were giving him some pleasure–the fellow seemed to be feeling it, after all.

'I should think he's really gone to escape his women, Forsyte.'

The chap was incorrigible! Soames shrugged his shoulders almost violently.

'You'd better realise,' he said, 'that the fat is in the fire.'

'But surely, my dear Forsyte, it's been there ever since the French occupied the Ruhr. Elderson has cut his lucky; we appoint someone else. What more is there to it?'

Soames had the peculiar feeling of having overdone his own honesty. If an honourable man, a ninth baronet, couldn't see the implications of Elderson's confession, were they really there? Was any fuss and scandal necessary? Goodness knew, *he* didn't want it! He said heavily:

'We now have conclusive evidence of a fraud; we *know* Elderson was illegally paid for putting through business by which the shareholders have suffered a dead loss. How can we keep this knowledge from them?'

'But the mischief's done, Forsyte. How will the knowledge help them?'

Soames frowned.

'We're in a fiduciary position. I'm not prepared to run the risks of concealment. If we conceal, we're accessory after the fact. The thing might come out at any time.' If that was caution, not honesty, he couldn't help it.

'I should be glad to spare Elderson's name. We were at–'

'I'm aware of that,' said Soames, drily.

'But what risk is there of its coming out, Forsyte? Elderson won't mention it; nor young Butterfield, if you tell him not to. Those who paid the commission certainly won't. And beyond us three here, no one else knows. It's not as if we profited in any way.'

Soames was silent. The argument was specious. Entirely unjust, of course, that he should be penalised for what Elderson had done!

'No,' he said, suddenly, 'it won't do. Depart from the law, and you can't tell where it'll end. The shareholders have suffered this loss and they have the right to all the facts within the directors' knowledge. There might be some means of restitution they could avail themselves of. We can't judge. It may be they've a remedy against ourselves.'

'If that's so, Forsyte, I'm with you.'

Soames felt disgust. Mont had no business to put it with a sort of gallantry that didn't count the cost; when the cost, if cost there were, would fall, not on Mont, whose land was heavily mortgaged, but on himself, whose property was singularly realisable.

'Well,' he said, coldly, 'remember that to-morrow. I'm going to bed.'

At his open window upstairs he felt no sense of virtue, but he enjoyed a sort of peace. He had taken his line, and there it was!

9

SOAMES DOESN'T GIVE A DAMN

During the month following the receipt of Elderson's letter, Soames aged more than thirty days. He had forced his policy of disclosure on a doubting Board, the special meeting had been called, and, just as, twenty-three years ago, pursuing divorce from Irene, he had to face the public eye, so now he suffered day and night in dread of that undiscriminating optic. The French had a proverb: '*Les absents ont toujours tort!*' but Soames had grave doubts about it. Elderson would be absent from that meeting of the shareholders, but–unless he was much mistaken–he himself, who would be present, would come in for the blame. The French were not to be relied on. What with his anxiety about Fleur, and his misgiving about the public eye, he was sleeping badly, eating little, and feeling below par. Annette had recommended him to see a doctor. That was probably why he did not. Soames had faith in doctors for other people; but they had never–he would say–done anything for *him*, possibly because, so far, there had not been anything to do.

Failing in her suggestion, and finding him every day less sociable, Annette had given him a book on Coué. After running it through, he had meant to leave it in the train, but the theory, however extravagant, had somehow clung to him. After all, Fleur was doing it; and the thing cost you nothing: there might be something in it! There was. After telling himself that night twenty-five times that he was getting better and better, he slept so soundly that Annette, in the next room, hardly slept at all.

'Do you know, my friend,' she said at breakfast, 'you were snoring last night so that I could not hear the cock crow.'

'Why should you want to?' said Soames.

'Well, never mind–if you had a good night. Was it my little Coué who gave you that nice dream?'

Partly from fear of encouraging Coué, and partly from fear of encouraging her, Soames avoided a reply; but he had a curious sense of power, as if he did not care what people said of him.

'I'll do it again to-night,' he thought.

'You know,' Annette went on 'you are just the temperament for Coué, Soames. When you cure yourself of worrying, you will get quite fat.'

'Fat!' said Soames, looking at her curves. 'I'd as soon grow a beard.'

Fatness and beards were associated with the French. He would have to keep an eye on himself if he went on with this–er–what was one to call it? Tomfoolery was hardly the word to conciliate the process, even if it did require you to tie twenty-five knots in a bit of string: very French, that, like telling your beads! He himself had merely counted on his fingers. The sense of power lasted all the way up to London; he had the conviction that he could sit in a draught if he wanted to, that Fleur would have her boy all right; and as to the P.P.R.S.–ten to one he wouldn't be mentioned by name in any report of the proceedings.

After an early lunch and twenty-five more assurances over his coffee, he set out for the city.

This Board, held just a week before the special meeting of the shareholders, was in the nature of a dress rehearsal. The details of confrontation had to be arranged, and Soames was chiefly concerned with seeing that a certain impersonality should be preserved. He was entirely against disclosure of the fact that young Butterfield's story and Elderson's letter had been confided to himself. The phrase to be used should be a 'member of the Board.' He saw no need for anything further. As for explanations, they would fall, of course, to the chairman and the senior director, Lord Fontenoy. He found, however, that the Board thought he himself was the right person to bring the matter forward. No one else–they said–could supply the personal touch, the necessary conviction; the chairman should introduce the matter briefly, then call on Soames to give the evidence within his knowledge. Lord Fontenoy was emphatic.

'It's up to you, Mr Forsyte. If it hadn't been for you, Elderson would be sitting there to-day. From beginning to end you put the wind up him; and I wish the deuce you hadn't. The whole thing's a confounded nuisance. He was a very clever fellow, and we shall miss him. Our new man isn't a patch on him. If he did take a few thou. under the rose, he took 'em off the Huns.'

Old guinea-pig! Soames replied, acidly:

'And the quarter of a million he's lost the shareholders, for the sake of those few thou.? Bagatelle, I suppose?'

'Well, it might have turned out a winner; for the first year it did. We all back losers sometimes.'

Soames looked from face to face. They did not support this blatant attitude, but in them all, except perhaps 'Old Mont's', he felt a grudge against himself. Their expressions seemed to say: 'Nothing of this sort ever happened till you came on the Board.' He had disturbed their comfort, and they disliked him for it. They were an unjust lot! He said doggedly:

'You leave it to me, do you? Very well!'

What he meant to convey–or whether he meant to convey anything, he did not know; but even that 'old guinea-pig' was more civil afterwards. He came away from the Board, however, without any sense of power at all. There he would be on Tuesday next, bang in the public eye.

After calling to enquire after Fleur, who was lying down rather poorly, he returned home with a feeling of having been betrayed. It seemed that he could not rely, after all, on this fellow with his twenty-five knots. However much better he might become, his daughter, his reputation, and possibly his fortune, were not apparently at the disposition of his subconscious self. He was silent at dinner, and went up afterwards to his picture gallery, to think things over. For half an hour he stood at the open window, alone with the summer evening; and the longer he stood there, the more clearly he perceived that the three were really one. Except for his daughter's sake, what did he care for his reputation or his fortune? His reputation! Lot of fools—if they couldn't see that he was careful and honest so far as had lain within his reach—so much the worse for them! His fortune—well, he had better make another settlement on Fleur and her child at once, in case of accidents; another fifty thousand. Ah! if she were only through her trouble! It was time Annette went up to her for good; and there was a thing they called twilight sleep. To have her suffering was not to be thought of!

The evening lingered out; the sun went down behind familiar trees; Soames's hands, grasping the window-ledge, felt damp with dew; sweetness of grass and river stole up into his nostrils. The sky had paled, and now began to darken; a scatter of stars came out. He had lived here a long time, through all Fleur's childhood—best years of his life; still, it wouldn't break his heart to sell. His heart was up in London. Sell? That was to run before the hounds with a vengeance. No—no!—it wouldn't come to *that*! He left the window and, turning up the lights, began the thousand and first tour of his pictures. He had made some good purchases since Fleur's marriage, and without wasting his money on fashionable favourites. He had made some good sales, too. The pictures in this gallery, if he didn't mistake, were worth from seventy to a hundred thousand pounds; and, with the profits on his sales from time to time, they stood him in at no more than five-and-twenty thousand—not a bad result from a life's hobby, to say nothing of the pleasure! Of course, he might have taken up something—butterflies, photography, archæology, or first editions; some other sport in which you backed your judgment against the field, and collected the results; but he had never regretted choosing pictures. Not he! More to show for your money, more kudos, more profit, and more risk! The thought startled him a little; had he really taken to pictures because of the risk? A risk had never appealed to him; at least, he hadn't realised it, so far. Had his 'subconscious' some part in the matter? He suddenly sat down and closed his eyes. Try the thing once more; very pleasant feeling, that morning, of not 'giving a damn'; he never remembered having it before! He had always felt it necessary to worry—kind of insurance against the worst; but worry was wearing, no doubt about it, wearing. Turn out the light! They said in that book, you had to relax. In the now dim and shadowy room, with the starlight, through many windows, dusted over its reality, Soames, in his easy chair, sat very still. A faint drone rose on the words: 'fatter and fatter' through his moving lips. 'No, no,' he thought: 'that's wrong!' And he began the drone again. The tips of his fingers ticked it off; on and on—he would give it a good chance. If only one needn't worry! On and on—'better and better!' If only—! His lips stopped moving; his grey head fell forward into the subconscious. And the stealing starlight dusted over him, too, a little unreality.

10

BUT TAKES NO CHANCES

Michael knew nothing of the City; and, in the spirit of the old cartographers: 'Where you know nothing, place terrors,' made his way through the purlieus of the Poultry, towards that holy of holies, the offices of Cuthcott, Kingson and Forsyte. His mood was attuned to meditation, for he had been lunching with Sibley Swan at the Café C'rillon. He had known all the guests–seven chaps even more modern than old Sib–save only a Russian so modern that he knew no French and nobody could talk to him. Michael had watched them demolish everything, and the Russian closing his eyes, like a sick baby, at mention of any living name. . . . 'Carry on!' he thought, several of his favourites having gone down in the *mêlée*. 'Stab and bludge! Importance awaits you at the end of the alley.' But he had restrained his irreverence till the moment of departure.

'Sib,' he said, rising, 'all these chaps here are dead–ought they to be about in this hot weather?'

'What's that?' ejaculated Sibley Swan, amidst the almost painful silence of the chaps.

'I mean–they're alive–so they *must* be damned!' And avoiding a thrown chocolate which hit the Russian, he sought the door.

Outside, he mused: 'Good chaps, really! Not half so darned superior as they think they are. Quite a human touch–getting that Russian on the boko. Phew! It's hot!'

On that first day of the Eton and Harrow match all the forfeited heat of a chilly summer had gathered and shimmered over Michael, on the top of his Bank bus; shimmered over straw hats, and pale, perspiring faces, over endless other buses, business men, policemen, shopmen at their doors, sellers of newspapers, laces, jumping toys, endless carts and cabs, letterings and wires, all the confusion of the greatest conglomeration in the world–adjusted almost to a hair's-breadth, by an unseen instinct. Michael stared and doubted. Was it possible that, with everyone pursuing his own business, absorbed in his own job, the thing could work out? An ant-heap was not busier, or more seemingly confused. Live wires crossed and crossed and crossed–inextricable entanglement, you'd say; and yet, life, the order needful to life, somehow surviving! 'No slouch of a miracle!' he thought, 'modern town life!' And suddenly it seemed to cease, as if demolished by the ruthless dispensation of some super Sibley Swan; for he was staring down a *cul-de-sac*. On both sides, flat houses, recently re-buffed, extraordinarily alike; at the end, a flat buff house, even more alike, and down to it, grey virgin pavement, unstained by horses or petrol; no cars, cats, carts, policemen, hawkers, flies, or bees. No sign of human life, except the names of legal firms to right and left of each open doorway.

'"Cuthcott, Kingson and Forsyte, Commissioners for Oaths: First Floor."'

'Rule Britannia!' thought Michael, ascending wide stone steps.

Entering the room to which he had been ushered, he saw an old and pug-faced fellow with a round grizzled beard, a black alpaca coat, and a roomy holland waistcoat round his roomy middle, who rose from a swivel chair.

'Aoh!' he said, 'Mr Michael Mont, I think. I've been expecting you. We shan't be long about it, after Mr Forsyte comes. He's just stepped round the corner. Mrs Michael well, I hope?'

'Thanks; as well as—'

'Ye-es; it makes you anxious. Take a seat. Perhaps you'd like to read the draft?'

Thus prescribed for, Michael took some foolscap from a pudgy hand, and sat down opposite. With one eye on the old fellow, and the other on the foolscap, he read steadily.

'It seems to mean something,' he said at last.

He saw a gape, as a frog at a fly, settle in the beard; and hastened to repair his error.

'Calculating what's going to happen if something else doesn't, must be rather like being a bookmaker.'

He felt at once that he had not succeeded. There was a grumpy mutter:

'We don't waste our time 'ere. Excuse me, I'm busy.'

Michael sat, compunctious, watching him tick down a long page of entries. He was like one of those old dogs which lie outside front doors, keeping people off the premises, and notifying their fleas. After less than five minutes of that perfect silence Soames came in.

'You're here, then?' he said.

'Yes, sir; I thought it best to come at the time you mentioned. What a nice cool room!'

'Have you read this?' asked Soames, pointing to the draft.

Michael nodded.

'Did you understand it?'

'Up to a point, I think.'

'The interest on *this* fifty thousand,' said Soames, 'is Fleur's until her eldest child, if it's a boy, attains the age of twenty-one, when the capital becomes his absolutely. If it's a girl, Fleur retains half the income for life, the rest of the income becomes payable to the girl when she attains the age of twenty-one or marries, and the capital of that half goes to her child or children lawfully begotten, at majority or marriage, in equal shares. The other half of the capital falls into Fleur's estate, and is disposable by her will, or follows the laws of intestacy.'

'You make it wonderfully clear,' said Michael.

'Wait!' said Soames. 'If Fleur has no children—'

Michael started.

'Anything is possible,' said Soames gravely, 'and my experience is that the contingencies not provided for are those which happen. In such a case the income of the whole is hers for life, and the capital hers at death to do as she likes with. Failing that, it goes to the next of kin. There are provisions against anticipation and so forth.'

'Ought she to make a fresh will?' asked Michael, conscious of sweat on his forehead.

'Not unless she likes. Her present will covers it.'

'Have I to do anything?'

'No. I wanted you to understand the purport before I sign; that's all. Give me the deed, Gradman, and get Wickson in, will you?'

Michael saw the old chap produce from a drawer a fine piece of parchment covered with copper-plate writing and seals, look at it lovingly, and place it before Soames. When he had left the room, Soames said in a low voice:

'This meeting on Tuesday – I can't tell! But, whatever happens, so far as I can see, this ought to stand.'

'It's awfully good of you, sir.'

Soames nodded, testing a pen.

'I'm afraid I've got wrong with your old clerk,' said Michael; 'I like the look of him frightfully, but I accidentally compared him to a bookmaker.'

Soames smiled. 'Gradman,' he said, 'is a "character". There aren't many, nowadays.'

Michael was wondering: Could one be a 'character' under the age of sixty? – when the 'character' returned, with a pale man in dark clothes.

Lifting his nose sideways, Soames said at once:

'This is a post-nuptial settlement on my daughter. I deliver this as my act and deed.'

He wrote his name, and got up.

The pale person and Gradman wrote theirs, and the former left the room. There was a silence as of repletion.

'Do you want me any more?' asked Michael.

'Yes. I want you to see me deposit it at the bank with the marriage settlement. Shan't come back, Gradman!'

'Good-bye, Mr Gradman.'

Michael heard the old fellow mutter through his beard half buried in a drawer to which he was returning the draft, and followed Soames out.

'Here's where I used to be,' said Soames as they went along the Poultry; 'and my father before me.'

'More genial, perhaps,' said Michael.

'The trustees are meeting us at the bank; you remember them?'

'Cousins of Fleur's, weren't they, sir?'

'Second cousins; young Roger's eldest, and young Nicholas'. I chose them youngish. Very young Roger was wounded in the war – he does nothing. Very young Nicholas is at the Bar.'

Michael's ears stood up. 'What about the next lot, sir? Very, very young Roger would be almost insulting, wouldn't it?'

'There won't be one,' said Soames, 'with taxation where it is. He can't afford it; he's a steady chap. What are you going to call your boy, if it *is* one?'

'We think Christopher, because of St Paul's and Columbus. Fleur wants him solid, and I want him enquiring.'

'H'm. And if it's a girl?'

'Oh! – if it's a girl – Anne.'

'Yes,' said Soames: 'very neat. Here they are!'

They had reached the bank, and in the entrance Michael saw two Forsytes between thirty and forty, whose chinny faces he dimly remembered. Escorted by a man with bright buttons down his front, they all went to a room, where a man without buttons produced a japanned box. One of the Forsytes opened it with a key; Soames muttered an incantation, and deposited the deed. When he and the chinnier Forsyte had exchanged a few remarks with the manager on the question of the bank rate, they all went back to the lobby and parted with the words: 'Well, good-bye.'

'Now,' said Soames, in the din and hustle of the street, 'he's provided for, so far as I can see. When exactly do you expect it?'

'It should be just a fortnight.'

'Do you believe in this—this twilight sleep?'

'I should like to,' said Michael, conscious again of sweat on his forehead. 'Fleur's wonderfully calm; she does Coué night and morning.'

'That!' said Soames. He did not mention that he himself was doing it, thus giving away the state of his nerves. 'If you're going home, I'll come, too.'

'Good!'

He found Fleur lying down with Ting-a-ling on the foot of the sofa.

'Your father's here, darling. He's been anointing the future with another fifty thou. I expect he'd like to tell you all about it.'

Fleur moved restlessly.

'Presently. If it's going on as hot as this, it'll be rather a bore, Michael.'

'Oh! but it won't, ducky. Three days and a thunder-storm.'

Taking Ting-a-ling by the chin, he turned his face up.

'And how on earth is your nose going to be put out of joint, old man? There's no joint to put.'

'He knows there's something up.'

'He's a wise little brute, aren't you, old son?'

Ting-a-ling sniffed.

'Michael!'

'Yes, darling?'

'I don't seem to care about anything now—it's a funny feeling.'

'That's the heat.'

'No. I think it's because the whole business is too long. Everything's ready, and now it all seems rather stupid. One more person in the world or one more out of it—what does it matter?'

'Don't! It matters frightfully!'

'One more gnat to dance, one more ant to run about!'

Anguished, Michael said again:

'Don't, Fleur! That's just a mood.'

'Is Wilfrid's book out?'

'It comes out to-morrow.'

'I'm sorry I gave you such a bad time, there. I only didn't want to lose him.' Michael took her hand.

'Nor did I—goodness knows!' he said.

'He's never written, I suppose?'

'No.'

'Well, I expect he's all right by now. Nothing lasts.'

Michael put her hand to his cheek.

'*I* do, I'm afraid,' he said.

The hand slipped round over his lips.

'Give Dad my love, and tell him I'll be down to tea. Oh! I'm so hot!'

Michael hovered a moment, and went out. Damn the heat, upsetting her like this!

He found Soames standing in front of the white monkey.

'I should take this down, if I were you,' he muttered, 'until it's over.'

'Why, sir?' asked Michael, in surprise.

Soames frowned.

'Those eyes!'

Michael went up to the picture. Yes! He was a haunting kind of brute!
'But it's such top-hole work, sir.'
Soames nodded.
'Artistically, yes. But at such times you can't be too careful what she sees.'
'I believe you're right. Let's have him down.'
'I'll hold him,' said Soames, taking hold of the bottom of the picture.
'Got him tight? Right-o. Now!'
'You can say I wanted an opinion on his period,' said Soames, when the picture had been lowered to the floor.
'There can hardly be a doubt of that, sir–the present!'
Soames stared. 'What? Oh! You mean–? Ah! H'm! Don't let her know he's in the house.'
'No. I'll lock him up.' Michael lifted the picture. 'D'you mind opening the door, sir?'
'I'll come back at tea-time,' said Soames. 'That'll look as if I'd taken him off. You can hang him again later.'
'Yes. Poor brute!' said Michael, bearing the monkey off to limbo.

I I

WITH A SMALL 'n'

On the night of the Monday following, after Fleur had gone to bed, Michael and Soames sat listening to the mutter of London coming through the windows of the Chinese room opened to the brooding heat.
'They say the war killed sentiment,' said Soames suddenly: 'Is that true?'
'In a way, yes, sir. We had so much reality that we don't want any more.'
'I don't follow you.'
'I meant that only reality really makes you feel. So if you pretend there *is* no reality, you don't have to feel. It answers awfully well, up to a point.'
'Ah!' said Soames. 'Her mother comes up to-morrow morning, to stay. This P.P.R.S. meeting of mine is at half-past two. Goodnight!'
Michael, at the window, watched the heat gathered black over the Square. A few tepid drops fell on his outstretched hand. A cat stole by under a lamp-post, and vanished into shadow so thick that it seemed uncivilised.
Queer question of 'Old Forsyte's' about sentiment; odd that he should ask it! 'Up to a point! But don't we all get past that point?' he thought. Look at Wilfrid, and himself–after the war they had deemed it blasphemous to admit that anything mattered except eating and drinking, for to-morrow they died; even fellows like Nazing, and Master, who were never in the war, had felt like that ever since. Well, Wilfrid had got it in the neck; and he himself had got it in the wind; and he would bet that–barring one here and there whose blood was made of ink–they would all get it in the neck or wind soon or late. Why, he would cheerfully bear Fleur's pain and risk, instead of her! But if nothing mattered, why should he feel like that?
Turning from the window, he leaned against the lacquered back of the jade-green settee, and stared at the wall space between the Chinese tea-chests. Jolly thoughtful of the 'old man' to have that white monkey down! The brute was

potent–symbolic of the world's mood: beliefs cancelled, faiths withdrawn! And, dash it! not only the young–but the old–were in that temper! 'Old Forsyte', or he would never have been scared by that monkey's eyes; yes, and his own governor, and Elderson, and all the rest. Young and old–no real belief in anything! And yet–revolt sprang up in Michael, with a whirr, like a covey of partridges. It *did* matter that some person or some principle outside oneself should be more precious than oneself–it dashed well did! Sentiment, then, wasn't dead–nor faith, nor belief, which were the same things. They were only shedding shells, working through chrysalis, into–butterflies, perhaps. Faith, sentiment, belief, had gone underground, possibly, but they were there, even in 'Old Forsyte' and himself. He had a good mind to put the monkey up again. No use exaggerating his importance! . . . By George! Some flare! A jagged streak of vivid light had stripped darkness off the night. Michael crossed, to close the windows. A shattering peal of thunder blundered overhead; and down came the rain, slashing and sluicing. He saw a man running, black, like a shadow across a dark-blue screen; saw him by the light of another flash, suddenly made lurid and full of small meaning, with face of cheerful anxiety, as if he were saying: 'Hang it, I'm getting wet!' Another frantic crash!

'Fleur!' thought Michael; and clanging the last window down, he ran upstairs.

She was sitting up in bed, with a face all round, and young, and startled.

'Brutes!' he thought–guns and the heavens confounded in his mind: 'They've waked her up!'

'It's all right, darling! Just another little summer kick-up! Were you asleep?'

'I was dreaming!' He felt her hand clutching within his own, saw a sudden pinched look on her face, with a sort of rage. What infernal luck!

'Where's Ting?'

No dog was in the corner.

'Under the bed–you bet! Would you like him up?'

'No. Let him stay; he hates it.'

She put her head against his arm, and Michael curled his hand round her other ear.

'I never liked thunder much!' said Fleur, 'and now it–it hurts!'

High above her hair Michael's face underwent the contortions of an overwhelming tenderness. One of those crashes which seem just overhead sent her face burrowing against his chest, and, sitting on the bed, he gathered her in, close.

'I wish it were over,' came, smothered, from her lips.

'It will be directly, darling; it came on so suddenly!' But he knew she didn't mean the storm.

'If I come through, I'm going to be quite different to you, Michael.'

Anxiety was the natural accompaniment of such events, but the words: 'If I come through' turned Michael's heart right over. Incredible that one so young and pretty should be in even the remotest danger of extinction; incredibly painful that she should be in fear of it! He hadn't realised. She had been so calm, so matter-of-fact about it all.

'Don't!' he mumbled; 'of course you'll come through.'

'I'm afraid.'

The sound was small and smothered, but the words hurt horribly. Nature, with the small 'n', forcing fear into this girl he loved so awfully! Nature kicking up this godless din above her poor little head!

'Ducky, you'll have twilight sleep and know nothing about it; and be as right as rain in no time.'

Fleur freed her hand.

'Not if it's not good for him. Is it?'

'I expect so, sweetheart; I'll find out. What makes you think–?'

'Only that it's not natural. I want to do it properly. Hold my hand hard, Michael. I–I'm not going to be a fool. Oh! Someone's knocking–go and see.'

Michael opened the door a crack. Soames was there–unnatural–in a blue dressing-gown and scarlet slippers!

'Is she all right?' he whispered.

'Yes, yes.'

'In this bobbery she oughtn't to be left.'

'No, sir, of course not. I shall sleep on the sofa.'

'Call me, if anything's wanted.'

'I will.'

Soames's eyes slid past, peering into the room. A string worked in his throat, as if he had things to say which did not emerge. He shook his head, and turned. His slim figure, longer than usual, in its gown, receded down the corridor, past the Japanese prints which he had given them. Closing the door again, Michael stood looking at the bed. Fleur had settled down; her eyes were closed, her lips moving. He stole back on tiptoe. The thunder, travelling away south blundered and growled as if regretfully. Michael saw her eyelids quiver, her lips stop, then move again. 'Coué!' he thought.

He lay down on the sofa at the foot of the bed, whence, without sound, he could raise himself and see her. Many times he raised himself. She had dropped off, was breathing quietly. The thunder was faint now, the flashes imperceptible. Michael closed his eyes.

A faint last mutter roused him to look at her once more, high on her pillows by the carefully shaded light. Young–young! Colourless, like a flower in wax! No scheme in her brain, no dread–peaceful! If only she could stay like that and wake up with it all over! He looked away. And there she was at the far end, dim, reflected in a glass; and there to the right, again. She lay, as it were, all round him in the pretty room, the inhabiting spirit–of his heart.

It was quite still now. Through a chink in those powder-blue curtains he could see some stars. Big Ben chimed one.

He had slept, perhaps, dozed at least, dreamed a little. A small sound woke him. A very little dog, tail down, yellow, low and unimportant, was passing down the room, trailing across it to the far corner. 'Ah!' thought Michael, closing his eyes again: 'You!'

12

ORDEAL BY SHAREHOLDER

Repairing, next day, to the Aeroplane Club, where, notably spruce, Sir Lawrence was waiting in the lounge, Michael thought: 'Good old Bart! he's got himself up for the guillotine all right!'

'That white piping will show the blood!' he said. 'Old Forsyte's neat this morning, but not so gaudy.'

'Ah! How is "Old Forsyte"? In good heart?'

'One doesn't ask him, sir. How do you feel yourself?'

'Exactly as I used to before the Eton and Winchester match. I think I shall have shandy-gaff at lunch.'

When they had taken their seats, Sir Lawrence went on:

'I remember seeing a man tried for murder in Colombo; the poor fellow was positively blue. I think my favourite moment in the past, Michael, is Walter Raleigh asking for a second shirt. By the way, it's never been properly settled yet whether the courtiers of that day were lousy. What are you going to have, my dear fellow?'

'Cold beef, pickled walnuts, and gooseberry-tart.'

'Excellent for the character. I shall have curry; they give you a very good Bombay duck here. I rather fancy we shall be fired, Michael. '*Nous sommes trahis!*' used to be the prerogative of the French, but I'm afraid we're getting the attitude, too. The Yellow Press has made a difference.'

Michael shook his head.

'We say it, but we don't act on it; the climate's too uncertain.'

'That sounds deep. This looks very good curry–will you change your mind? Old Fontenoy sometimes comes in here; he has no inside. It'll be serious for him if we're shown the door.'

'Deuced rum,' said Michael suddenly, 'how titles still go down. There can't be any belief in their business capacity.'

'Character, my dear fellow–the good old English gentleman. After all, there's something in it.'

'I fancy, sir, it's more a case of complex in the shareholders. Their parents show them a lord when they're young.'

'Shareholders,' said Sir Lawrence; 'the world is comprehensive. Who are they, what are they, when are they?'

'This afternoon,' said Michael, 'and I shall have a good look at them.'

'They won't let you in, my dear.'

'No?'

'Certainly not.'

Michael frowned.

'What paper,' he said, 'is sure not to be represented?'

Sir Lawrence gave his whinnying laugh.

'*The Field*,' he said; '*The Horse and Hound*; *The Gardener's Weekly.*'

'I'll slide in on them.'

'You'll see us die game, I hope,' said Sir Lawrence, with sudden gravity.

They took a cab together to the meeting, but separated before reaching the door of the hotel.

Michael had thought better of the Press, and took up a position in the passage, whence he could watch for a chance. Stout men, in dark suits, with a palpable look of having lunched off turbot, joints, and cheese, kept passing him. He noticed that each handed the janitor a paper. 'I'll hand him a paper, too,' he thought, 'and scoot in.' Watching for some even stouter men, he took cover between two of them, and approached the door, with an announcement of 'Counterfeits' in his left hand. Handing it across a neighbouring importance, he was quickly into a seat. He saw the janitor's face poked round the door. 'No, my friend,' thought Michael, 'if you could tell duds from shareholders, you wouldn't be in that job!'

He found a report before him, and holding it up, looked at other things. The room seemed to him to have been got by a concert-hall out of a station waiting-room. It had a platform with a long table, behind which were seven empty chairs, and seven inkpots, with seven quill pens upright in them. 'Quills!' thought Michael; 'symbolic, I suppose—they'll all use fountain-pens!'

Back-centre of the platform was a door, and in front, below it, a table, where four men were sitting, fiddling with notebooks. 'Orchestra,' thought Michael. He turned his attention to the eight or ten rows of shareholders. They looked what they were, but he could not tell why. Their faces were cast in an infinity of moulds, but all had the air of waiting for something they knew they would not get. What sort of lives did they lead, or did their lives lead them? Nearly all wore moustaches. His neighbours to right and left were the same stout shareholders between whom he had slipped in; they both had thick lobes to their ears, and necks even broader than the straight broad backs of their heads. He was a good deal impressed. Dotted here and there he noticed a woman, or a parson. There was practically no conversation, from which he surmised that no one knew his neighbour. He had a feeling that a dog somewhere would have humanised the occasion. He was musing on the colour scheme of green picked out with chocolate and chased with gold, when the door behind the platform was thrown open, and seven men in black coats filed in, and with little bows took their seats behind the quills. They reminded him of people getting up on horses, or about to play the piano—full of small adjustments. That—on the Chairman's right—would be old Fontenoy, with a face entirely composed of features. Michael had an odd conceit: a little thing in a white top-hat sat inside the brain, driving the features eight-in-hand. Then came a face straight from a picture of Her Majesty's Government in 1850, round and pink, with a high nose, a small mouth, and little white whiskers; while at the end on the right was a countenance whose jaw and eyes seemed boring into a conundrum beyond the wall at Michael's back. 'Legal!' he thought. His scrutiny passed back to the Chairman. Chosen? Was he—or was he not? A bearded man, a little behind on the Chairman's left, was already reading from a book, in a rapid monotonous voice. That must be the secretary letting off his minute guns. And in front of him was clearly the new manager, on whose left Michael observed his own father. The dark pothooks over Sir Lawrence's right eye were slightly raised, and his mouth was puckered under the cut line of his small moustache. He looked almost Oriental, quick but still. His left hand held his tortoise-shell-rimmed monocle between thumb and finger. 'Not quite in the scene!' thought Michael; 'poor old Bart!' He had come now to the last of the row. 'Old Forsyte' was sitting precisely as if alone in the world; with one corner of his mouth just drawn down, and one nostril just drawn up, he seemed to Michael quite fascinatingly detached; and yet not out of the picture. Within that still neat figure, whereof only one patent-leather boot seemed with a slight movement to be living, was intense concentration, entire respect for the proceedings, and yet, a queer contempt for them; he was like a statue of reality, by one who had seen that there was precious little reality in it. 'He chills my soup,' thought Michael, 'but—dash it!—I can't help half admiring him!'

The Chairman had now risen. 'He *is*'—thought Michael; 'no, he isn't—yes—no—I can't tell!' He could hardly attend to what the Chairman said, for wondering whether he was chosen or not, though well aware that it did not matter at all. The Chairman kept steadily on. Distracted, Michael caught words and words: 'European situation—misguided policy—French—totally unexpected—position disclosed—manager—unfortunate circumstances shortly to be explained to you–future of this great concern–no reason to doubt–'

'Oil,' thought Michael, 'he is–and yet–!'

'I will now ask for one of your directors, Mr Forsyte, to give you at first hand an account of this painful matter.'

Michael saw Soames, pale and deliberate, take a piece of paper from his breast-pocket, and rise. Was it to the occasion?

'I will give you the facts shortly,' he said in a voice which reminded Michael of a dry, made-up wine. 'On the eleventh of January last I was visited by a clerk in the employ of the Society–'

Familiar with these details, Michael paid them little attention, watching the shareholders for signs of reaction. He saw none, and it was suddenly borne in on him why they wore moustaches: They could not trust their mouths! Character was in the mouth. Moustaches had come in when people no longer went about, like the old Duke saying: 'Think what you damned well like of my character!' Mouths had tried to come in again, of course, before the war; but what with majors, shareholders, and the working-classes, they now had little or no chance! He heard Soames say: 'In these circumstances we came to the conclusion that there was nothing for it but to wait and see.' Michael saw a sudden quiver pass over the moustaches, as might wind over grass.

'Wrong phrase,' he thought; 'we all do it, but we can't bear being reminded of it.'

'Six weeks ago, however,' he heard Soames intone, 'an accidental incident seems to have warned your late manager that Sir Lawrence and I still entertained suspicions, for I received a letter from him practically admitting that he had taken this secret commission on the German business, and asking me to inform the Board that he had gone abroad and left no property behind him. This statement we have been at pains to verify. In these circumstances we had no alternative but to call you together, and lay the facts before you.'

The voice, which had not varied an iota, ceased its recital; and Michael saw his father-in-law return to his detachment–stork on one leg, about to apply beak to parasite, could have inspired no greater sense of loneliness. 'Too like the first account of the battle of Jutland!' he thought: 'He mentioned all the losses, and never once struck the human note.'

A pause ensued, such as occurs before an awkward fence, till somebody has found a gate. Michael rapidly reviewed the faces of the Board. Only one showed any animation. It was concealed in a handkerchief. The sound of the blown nose broke the spell. Two shareholders rose to their feet at once–one of them Michael's neighbour on the right.

'Mr Sawdry,' said the Chairman, and the other shareholder sat down.

With a sonorous clearing of the throat, Michael's neighbour turned his blunt red face towards Soames.

'I wish to ask you, sir, why you didn't inform the Board when you first 'eard of this?'

Soames rose slightly.

'You are aware, I presume, that such an accusation, unless it can be fully substantiated, is a matter for criminal proceedings?'

'No; it would ha' been privileged.'

'As between members of the Board, perhaps; but any leakage would have rendered us liable. It was a mere case of word against word.'

'Perhaps Sir Lawrence Mont will give us 'is view of that?'

Michael's heart began to beat. There was an air of sprightliness about his father's standing figure.

'You must remember, sir,' he said, 'that Mr Elderson had enjoyed our complete confidence for many years; he was a gentleman, and, speaking for myself, an old school-fellow of his, I preferred, in common loyalty, to give his word preference, while–er–keeping the matter in mind.'

'Oh!' said Michael's neighbour: 'What's the Chairman got to say about bein' kept in the dark?'

'We are all perfectly satisfied, sir, with the attitude of our co-directors, in a very delicate situation. You will kindly note that the mischief was already done over this unfortunate assurance, so that there was no need for undue haste.'

Michael saw his neighbour's neck grow redder.

'I don't agree,' he said. '"Wait and see"–We might have 'ad that commission out of him, if he'd been tackled promptly.' And he sat down.

He had not reached mahogany before the thwarted shareholder had started up.

'Mr Botterill,' said the Chairman.

Michael saw a lean and narrow head, with two hollows in a hairy neck, above a back slightly bent forward, as of a doctor listening to a chest.

'I take it from you, then, sir,' he said, 'that these two directors represent the general attitude of the Board, and that the Board were content to allow a suspected person to remain manager. The gentleman on your extreme left–Mr Forsyte, I think–spoke of an accidental incident. But for that, apparently, we should still be in the hands of an unscrupulous individual. The symptoms in this case are very disquieting. There appears to have been gross over-confidence; a recent instance of the sort must be in all our minds. The policy of assuring foreign business was evidently initiated by the manager for his own ends. We have made a severe loss by it. And the question for us shareholders would seem to be whether a Board who placed confidence in such a person, and continued it after their suspicions were aroused, are the right people to direct this important concern.'

Throughout this speech Michael had grown very hot. '"Old Forsyte" was right,' he thought; 'they're on their uppers after all.'

There was a sudden creak from his neighbour on the left.

'Mr Tolby,' said the Chairman.

'It's a serious matter, this, gentlemen. I propose that the Board withdraw, an' leave us to discuss it.'

'I second that,' said Michael's neighbour on the right.

Searching the vista of the Board, Michael saw recognition gleam for a second in the lonely face at the end, and grinned a greeting.

The Chairman was speaking.

'If that is your wish, gentlemen, we shall be happy to comply with it. Will those who favour the motion hold up their hands?'

All hands were held up, with the exception of Michael's, of two women whose eager colloquy had not permitted them to hear the request, and of one shareholder, just in front of Michael, so motionless that he seemed to be dead.

'Carried,' said the Chairman, and rose from his seat.

Michael saw his father smiling, and speaking to 'Old Forsyte' as they both stood up. They all filed out, and the door was closed.

'Whatever happens,' Michael thought, 'I've got to keep my head shut, or I shall be dropping a brick.'

'Perhaps the Press will kindly withdraw, too,' he heard someone say.

With a general chinny movement, as if enquiring their rights of no one in particular, the four Pressmen could be seen to clasp their notebooks. When their pale reluctance had vanished, there was a stir among the shareholders, like that of ducks when a dog comes up behind. Michael saw why at once. They had their backs to each other. A shareholder said:

'Perhaps Mr Tolby, who proposed the withdrawal, will act as Chairman.'

Michael's left-hand neighbour began breathing heavily.

'Right-o!' he said. 'Anyone who wants to speak, kindly ketch my eye.'

Everyone now began talking to his neighbour, as though to get at once a quiet sense of proportion, before speaking. Mr Tolby was breathing so heavily that Michael felt a positive draught.

' 'Ere, gentlemen,' he said suddenly, 'this won't do! We don't want to be too formal, but we must preserve some order. I'll open the discussion myself. Now, I didn't want to 'urt the feelin's of the Board by plain speakin' in their presence. But, as Mr What's-'is-name there, said: The public 'as got to protect itself against sharpers, and against slackness. We all know what 'appened the other day, and what'll 'appen again in other concerns, unless we shareholders look after ourselves. In the first place, then, what I say is: They ought never to 'ave touched anything to do with the 'Uns. In the second place, I say they showed bad judgment. And in the third place I say they were too thick together. In my opinion, we should propose a vote of no confidence.'

Cries of: 'Hear, hear!' mixed with indeterminate sounds, were broken sharply by a loud: 'No!' from the shareholder who had seemed dead. Michael's heart went out to him, the more so as he still seemed dead. The negative was followed by the rising of a thin, polished-looking shareholder, with a small grey moustache.

'If you'll forgive my saying so, sir,' he began, 'your proposal seems to me very rough-and-ready justice. I should be interested to know how you would have handled such a situation if you had been on the Board. It is extremely easy to condemn other people!'

'Hear, hear!' said Michael, astonished at his own voice.

'It is all very well,' the polished shareholder went on, 'when anything of this sort happens, to blame a directorate, but, speaking as a director myself, I should be glad to know whom one is to trust, if not one's manager. As to the policy of foreign insurance, it has been before us at two general meetings; and we have pocketed the profit from it for nearly two years. Have we raised a voice against it?'

The dead shareholder uttered a 'No!' so loud that Michael almost patted his head.

The shareholder, whose neck and back were like a doctor's, rose to answer.

'I differ from the last speaker in his diagnosis of the case. Let us admit all he says, and look at the thing more widely. The proof of pudding is in the eating. When a Government makes a bad mistake of judgment, the electorate turns against it as soon as it feels the effects. This is a very sound check on administration; it may be rough and ready, but it is the less of two evils. A Board backs its judgment; when it loses, it should pay. I think, perhaps, Mr Tolby, being our informal Chairman, was out of order in proposing a vote of no confidence; if that be so, I should be happy to do so, myself.'

The dead shareholder's 'No!' was so resounding this time that there was a pause for him to speak; he remained, however, without motion. Both of

Michael's neighbours were on their feet. They bobbed at each other over Michael's head, and Mr Tolby sat down.

'Mr Sawdry,' he said.

'Look 'ere, gentlemen,' said Mr Sawdry, 'and ladies, this seems to me a case for compromise. The Directors that knew about the manager ought to go; but we might stop at that. The gentleman in front of me keeps on saying "No." Let 'im give us 'is views.'

'No,' said the dead shareholder, but less loudly.

'If a man can't give 'is views,' went on Mr Sawdry, nearly sitting down on Michael, ''e shouldn't interrupt, in my opinion.'

A shareholder in the front row now turned completely round so that he faced the meeting.

'I think,' he said, 'that to prolong this discussion is to waste time; we are evidently in two, if not three, minds. The whole of the business of this country is now conducted on a system of delegated trust; it may be good, it may be bad—but there it is. You've got to trust somebody. Now, as to this particular case, we've had no reason to distrust the Board, so far; and, as I take it, the Board had no previous reason to distrust the late manager. I think it's going too far, at present, to propose anything definite like a vote of no confidence; it seems to me that we should call the Board in and hear what assurances they have to give us against a repetition of anything of the sort in the future.'

The sounds which greeted this moderate speech were so inextricable that Michael could not get the sense of them. Not so with the speech which followed. It came from a shareholder on the right, with reddish hair, light eyelashes, a clipped moustache, and a scraped colour.

'I have no objection whatever to having the Board in,' he said in a rather jeering voice, 'and passing a vote of no confidence in their presence. There is a question, which no one has touched on, of how far, if we turn them out, we could make them liable for this loss. The matter is not clear, but there is a good sporting chance, if we like to take it. Whereas, if we don't turn them out, it's obvious we can't take it, even if we wish.'

The impression made by this speech was of quite a different order from any of the others. It was followed by a hush, as though something important had been said at last. Michael stared at Mr Tolby. The stout man's round, light, rather prominent eye was extraordinarily reflective. 'Trout must look like that,' thought Michael, 'when they see a mayfly.' Mr Tolby suddenly stood up.

'All right,' he said, ''ave 'em in!'

'Yes,' said the dead shareholder. There was no dissent. Michael saw someone rise and ascend the platform.

'Let the Press know!' said Mr Tolby.

13

SOAMES AT BAY

When the door had closed behind the departing directors, Soames sought a window as far as possible from the lunch eaten before the meeting.

'Funeral baked meats, eh, Forsyte?' said a voice in his ear. 'Our number's up, I think. Poor old Mothergill's looking very blue. I think he ought to ask for a second shirt!'

Soames's tenacity began wriggling within him.

'The thing wants tackling,' he grumbled; 'the Chairman's not the man for the job!' Shades of old Uncle Jolyon! He would have made short work of this! It wanted a masterful hand.

'Warning to us all, Forsyte, against loyalty! It's not in the period. Ah! Fontenoy!'

Soames became conscious of features rather above the level of his own.

'Well, Mr Forsyte, hope you're satisfied? A pretty damned mess! If I'd been the Chairman, I'd never have withdrawn. Always keep hounds under your eye, Mont. Take it off, and they'll go for you! Wish I could get among 'em with a whip; I'd give it those two heavy pug-faced chaps–they mean business! Unless you've got something up your sleeve, Mr Forsyte, we're dished.'

'What should I have up my sleeve?' said Soames coldly.

'Damn it, sir, you put the chestnuts in the fire, it's up to you to pull 'em out. I can't afford to lose these fees!'

Soames heard Sir Lawrence murmur: 'Crude, my dear Fontenoy!' and said with malice:

'You may lose more than your fees!'

'Can't! They may have Eaglescourt to-morrow, and take a loss off my hands.' A gleam of feeling burned up suddenly in the old eyes: 'The country drives you to the wall, skins you to the bone, and expects you to give 'em public service gratis. Can't be done, Mont–can't be done!'

Soames turned away; he had an utter disinclination for talk, like one standing before an open grave, watching a coffin slowly lowered. Here was his infallibility going–going! He had no illusions. It would all be in the papers, and his reputation for sound judgment gone for ever! Bitter! No more would the Forsytes say: 'Soames say–' No more would old Gradman follow him with eyes like an old dog's, grudging sometimes, but ever submitting to infallibility. It would be a nasty jar for the old fellow. His business acquaintances–after all, they were not many, now!–would no longer stare with envious respect. He wondered if the reverberations would reach Dumetrius, and the picture market! The sole comfort was: Fleur needn't know. Fleur! Ah! If only her business were safely over! For a moment his mind became empty of all else. Then with a rush the present filled it up again. Why were they all talking as if there were a corpse in the room? Well! There was–the corpse of his infallibility! As for monetary loss–that seemed secondary, remote, incredible–like a future life. Mont had said something about loyalty. He didn't know what loyalty had to do with it! But if they thought he was going to show any white feather, they were extremely mistaken. Acid courage welled up into his brain. Shareholders, directors—they might howl and shake their fists; he was not going to be dictated to. He heard a voice say:

'Will you come in, please, gentlemen?'

Taking his seat again before his unused quill, he noticed the silence—shareholders waiting for directors, directors for shareholders. 'Wish I could get among 'em with a whip!' Extravagant words of that 'old guinea-pig's,' but expressive, somehow!

At last the Chairman, whose voice always reminded Soames of a raw salad with oil poured over it, said ironically:

'Well, gentlemen, we await your pleasure.'

That stout, red-faced fellow, next to Michael, stood up, opening his pug's mouth.

'To put it shortly, Mr Chairman, we're not at all satisfied; but before we take any resolution, we want to 'ear what you've got to say.'

Just below Soames, someone jumped up and added:

'We'd like to know, sir, what assurances you can offer us against anything of this sort in the future.'

Soames saw the Chairman smile—no real backbone in that fellow!

'In the nature of things, sir,' he said, 'none whatever! You can hardly suppose that if we had known our manager was not worthy of our confidence, we should have continued him in the post for a moment!'

Soames thought: 'That won't do—he's gone back on himself!' Yes, and that other pug-faced chap had seen it!

'That's just the point, sir,' he was saying: 'Two of you *did* know, and yet, there the fellow was for months afterwards, playin' 'is own 'and and, cheatin' the Society for all he was worth, I shouldn't wonder.'

One after another, they were yelping now:

'What about your own words?'

'You admitted collective responsibility.'

'You said you were perfectly satisfied with the attitude of your co-directors in the matter.' Regular pack!

Soames saw the Chairman incline his head as if he wanted to shake it; old Fontenoy muttering, old Mothergill blowing his nose, Meyricke shrugged his sharp shoulders. Suddenly he was cut off from view of them—Sir Lawrence was standing up between.

'Allow me a word! Speaking for myself, I find it impossible to accept the generous attempt of the Chairman to shoulder a responsibility which clearly rests on me. If I made a mistake of judgment in not disclosing our suspicions, I must pay the penalty; and I think it will clear the—er—situation if I tender my resignation to the meeting.'

Soames saw him give a little bow, place his monocle in his eye, and sit down.

A murmur greeted the words—approval, surprise, deprecation, admiration? It had been gallantly done. Soames distrusted gallantry—there was always a dash of the peacock about it. He felt curiously savage.

'I, apparently,' he said, rising, 'am the other incriminated director. Very good! I am not conscious of having done anything but my duty from beginning to end of this affair. I am confident that I made no mistake of judgment. And I consider it entirely unjust that I should be penalised. I have had worry and anxiety enough, without being made a scapegoat by shareholders who accepted this policy without a murmur, before ever I came on the Board, and are now angry because they have lost by it. You owe it to me that the policy has been dropped: you owe it to me that you have no longer a fraudulent person for a manager. And you owe it to me that you were called together to-day to pass judgment on the matter. I have no intention whatever of singing small. But there is another aspect to this affair. I am not prepared to go on giving my services to people who don't value them. I have no patience with the attitude displayed this afternoon. If anyone here thinks he has a grievance against me, let him bring an action. I shall be happy to carry it to the House of Lords, if necessary. I have been familiar with the City all my life, and I have not been in the habit of meeting with suspicions and ingratitude. If this is an instance of present manners, I have been familiar with the City long enough. I do not tender my resignation to the meeting; I resign.'

Bowing to the Chairman, and pushing back his chair, he walked doggedly to the door, opened it and passed through.

He sought his hat. He had not the slightest doubt but that he had astonished their weak nerves! Those pug-faced fellows had their mouths open! He would have liked to see what he had left behind, but it was hardly consistent with dignity to open the door again. He took a sandwich instead, and began to eat it with his back to the door and his hat on. He felt better than he had for months. A voice said:

'"And the subsequent proceedings interested him no more!" I'd no idea, Forsyte, you were such an orator! You gave it 'em between the eyes! Never saw a meeting so knocked out! Well, you've saved the Board by focusing their resentment entirely on yourself. It was very gallant, Forsyte!'

Soames growled through his sandwich:

'Nothing of the sort! Are you out, too?'

'Yes. I pressed my resignation. That red-faced fellow was proposing a vote of confidence in the Board when I left–and they'll pass it, Forsyte–they'll pass it! Something was said about financial liability, by the way!'

'Was there?' said Soames, with a grim smile: 'That cock won't fight. Their only chance was to claim against the Board for initiating foreign assurance *ultra vires*; if they're reaffirming the Board, after the question's been raised in open meeting, they're dished. Nothing'll lie against you and me, for not disclosing our suspicions–that's certain.'

'A relief, I confess,' said Sir Lawrence, with a sigh. 'It was the speech of your life, Forsyte!'

Perfectly well aware of that, Soames shook his head. Apart from the horror of seeing himself in print, he was beginning to feel that he had been extravagant. It was always a mistake to lose your temper! A bitter little smile came on his lips. Nobody, not even Mont, would see how unjustly he had been treated.

'Well,' he said, 'I shall go.'

'I think I shall wait, Forsyte, and hear the upshot.'

'Upshot? They'll appoint two other fools, and slaver over each other. Shareholders! Good-bye!' He moved to the door.

Passing the Bank of England, he had a feeling of walking away from his own life. His acumen, his judgment, his manner of dealing with affairs–aspersed! They didn't like it; well–he would leave it! Catch him meddling, in future! It was all of a piece with the modern state of things. Hand to mouth, and the steady men pushed to the wall! The men to whom a pound was a pound, and not a mess of chance and paper. The men who knew that the good of the country was the strict, straight conduct of their own affairs. They were not wanted. One by one, they would get the go-by—as he had got it—in favour of Jack-o'-lanterns, revolutionaries, restless chaps, or clever, unscrupulous fellows, like Elderson. It was in the air. No amount of eating your cake and wanting to have it could take the place of common honesty.

He turned into the Poultry before he knew why he had come there. Well, he might as well tell Gradman at once that he must exercise his own judgment in the future. At the mouth of the backwater he paused for a second, as if to print its buffness on his brain. He would resign his trusts, private and all! He had no notion of being sneered at in the family. But a sudden wave of remembrance almost washed his heart into his boots. What a tale of trust deeds executed, leases renewed, houses sold, investments decided on—in that back room up there; what a mint of quiet satisfaction in estates well managed! Ah! well! He would continue to manage his own. As for the others, they must look out for themselves, now. And a precious time they'd have of it, in face of the spirit there was about!

He mounted the stone steps slowly.

In the repository of Forsyte affairs, he was faced by the unusual—not Gradman, but, on the large ripe table, a large ripe melon alongside a straw bag. Soames sniffed. The thing smelled delicious. He held it to the light. Its greeny yellow tinge, its network of threads—quite Chinese! Was old Gradman going to throw its rind about, like that white monkey?

He was still holding it when a voice said:

'Aoh! I wasn't expecting you to-day, Mr Soames. I was going early; my wife's got a little party.'

'So I see!' said Soames, restoring the melon to the table. 'There's nothing for you to do at the moment, but I came in to tell you to draw my resignation from the Forsyte trusts.'

The old chap's face was such a study that he could not help a smile.

'You can keep me in Timothy's; but the rest must go. Young Roger can attend to them. He's got nothing to do.'

A gruff and deprecating: 'Dear me! They won't like it!' irritated Soames.

'Then they must lump it! I want a rest.'

He did not mean to enter into the reason—Gradman could read it for himself in the *Financial News*, or whatever he took in.

'Then I shan't be seeing you so often, Mr Soames; there's never anything in Mr Timothy's. Dear me! I'm quite upset. Won't you keep your sister's?'

Soames looked at the old fellow, and compunction stirred within him—as ever, at any sign that he was appreciated.

'Well,' he said, 'keep me in hers; I shall be in about my own affairs, of course. Good afternoon, Gradman. That's a fine melon.'

He waited for no more words. The old chap! *He* couldn't last much longer, anyway, sturdy as he looked! Well, they would find it hard to match him!

On reaching the Poultry, he decided to go to Green Street and see Winifred—queerly and suddenly home-sick for the proximity of Park Lane, for the old secure days, the efflorescent privacy of his youth under the wings of James and Emily. Winifred alone represented for him now, the past; her solid nature never varied, however much she kept up with the fashions.

He found her, a little youthful in costume, drinking China tea, which she did not like—but what could one do, other teas were 'common'! She had taken to a parrot. Parrots were coming in again. The bird made a dreadful noise. Whether under its influence or that of the China tea–which, made in the English way, of a brand the Chinese grew for foreign stomachs, always upset him–he was soon telling her the whole story.

When he had finished, Winifred said comfortably:

'Well, Soames, I think you did splendidly; it serves them right!'

Conscious that his narrative must have presented the truth as it would not appear to the public, Soames muttered:

'That's all very well; you'll find a very different version in the financial papers.'

'Oh! but nobody reads them. I shouldn't worry. Do you do Coué? Such a comfortable little man, Soames; I went to hear him. It's rather a bore sometimes, but it's quite the latest thing.'

Soames became inaudible–he never confessed a weakness.

'And how,' asked Winifred, 'is Fleur's little affair?'

'"Little affair!"' echoed a voice above his head. That bird! It was clinging to the brocade curtains, moving its neck up and down.

'Polly!' said Winifred: 'don't be naughty!'

'Soames!' said the bird.

'I've taught him that. Isn't he rather sweet?'

'No,' said Soames. 'I should shut him up; he'll spoil your curtains.'

The vexation of the afternoon had revived within him suddenly. What was life, but parrotry? What did people see of the real truth? They just repeated each other, like a lot of shareholders, or got their precious sentiments out of *The Daily Liar*. For one person who took a line, a hundred followed on, like sheep!

'You'll stay and dine, dear boy!' said Winifred.

Yes! he would dine. Had she a melon, by any chance? He'd no inclination to go and sit opposite his wife at South Square. Ten to one Fleur would not be down. And as to young Michael–the fellow had been there that afternoon and witnessed the whole thing; he'd no wish to go over it again.

He was washing his hands for dinner, when a maid, outside, said:

'You're wanted on the phone, sir.'

Michael's voice came over the wire, strained and husky:

'That you, sir?'

'Yes. What is it?'

'Fleur. It began this afternoon at three. I've been trying to reach you.'

'What?' cried Soames. 'How? Quick!'

'They say it's all normal. But it's so awful. They say quite soon, now.' The voice broke off.

'My God!' said Soames. 'My hat!'

By the front door the maid was asking: 'Shall you be back to dinner, sir?'

'Dinner!' muttered Soames, and was gone.

He hurried along, almost running, his eyes searching for a cab. None to be had, of course! None to be had! Opposite the 'Iseeum' Club he got one, open in the fine weather after last night's storm. That storm! He might have known. Ten days before her time. Why on earth hadn't he gone straight back, or at least telephoned where he would be? All that he had been through that afternoon was gone like smoke. Poor child! Poor little thing! And what about twilight sleep? Why hadn't he been there? He might have–nature! Damn it! Nature–as if it couldn't leave even her alone!

'Get on!' he said, leaning out: 'Double fare!'

Past the Connoisseurs', and the Palace, and Whitehall; past all preserves whence nature was excluded, deep in the waters of primitive emotion Soames sat, grey, breathless. Past Big Ben—eight o'clock! Five hours! Five hours of it! 'Let it be over!' he muttered aloud: 'Let it be over, God!'

14

ON THE RACK

When his father-in-law bowed to the Chairman and withdrew, Michael had restrained a strong desire to shout: 'Bravo!' Who'd have thought the 'old man' could let fly like that? He had 'got their goats' with a vengeance. Quite an interval of fine mixed vociferation followed, before his neighbour, Mr Sawdry, made himself heard at last.

'Now that the director implicated has resigned, I shall 'ave pleasure in proposing a vote of confidence in the rest of the Board.'

Michael saw his father rise, a little finicky and smiling, and bow to the Chairman. 'I take my resignation as accepted also; if you permit me, I will join Mr Forsyte in retirement.'

Someone was saying:

'I shall be glad to second that vote of confidence.'

And brushing past the knees of Mr Sawdry, Michael sought the door. From there he could see that nearly every hand was raised in favour of the vote of confidence; and with the thought: 'Thrown to the shareholders!' he made his way out of the hotel. Delicacy prevented him from seeking out those two. They had saved their dignity; but the dogs had had the rest.

Hurrying west, he reflected on the rough ways of justice. The shareholders had a grievance, of course; and someone had to get it in the neck to satisfy their sense of equity. They had pitched on 'Old Forsyte', who, of all, was least to blame; for if Bart had only held his tongue, they would certainly have lumped him into the vote of confidence. All very natural and illogical; and four o'clock already!

'Counterfeits'! The old feeling for Wilfrid was strong in him this day of publication. One must do everything one could for his book—poor old son! There simply must not be a frost.

After calling in at two big booksellers, he made for his club, and closeted himself in the telephone booth. In old days they 'took cabs and went about'. Ringing-up was quicker—was it? With endless vexations, he tracked down Sibley, Nazing, Upshire, Master, and half a dozen others of the elect. He struck a considered note likely to move them. The book—he said—was bound to 'get the goat of the old guard and the duds generally'; it would want a bit of drumbeating from the cognoscenti. To each of them he appealed as the only one whose praise really mattered. 'If you haven't reviewed the book, old chap, will you? It's you who count, of course.' And to each he added: 'I don't care two straws whether it sells, but I do want old Wilfrid to get his due.' And he meant it. The publisher in Michael was dead during that hour in the telephone booth, the friend alive and kicking hard. He came out with sweat running down his forehead, quite exhausted; and it was half-past five.

'Cup of tea–and home!' he thought. He reached his door at six. Ting-a-ling, absolutely unimportant, was cowering in the far corner of the hall.

'What's the matter, old man?'

A sound from above, which made his blood run cold, answered–a long, low moaning.

'Oh, God!' he gasped, and ran upstairs.

Annette met him at the door. He was conscious of her speaking in French, of being called '*mon cher*,' of the words '*vers trois heures*. . . . The doctor says one must not worry–all goes for the best.' Again that moan, and the door shut in his face; she was gone. Michael remained standing on the rug with perfectly cold sweat oozing from him, and his nails dug deep into his palms.

'This is how one becomes a father!' he thought: 'This is how I became a son!' That moaning! He could not bear to stay there, and he could not bear to go away. It might be hours, yet! He kept repeating to himself: 'One must not worry–must not worry!' How easily said! How meaningless! His brain, his heart, ranging for relief, lighted on the strangest relief which could possibly have come to him. Suppose this child being born, had not been his–had been–been Wilfrid's; how would he have been feeling, here, outside this door? It might–it might so easily have been–since nothing was sacred, now! Nothing except–yes, just that which was dearer than oneself–just that which was in there, moaning. He could not bear it on the rug, and went downstairs. Across and across the copper floor, a cigar in his mouth, he strode in vague, rebellious agony. Why should birth be like this? And the answer was: It isn't–not in China! To have the creed that nothing mattered–and then run into it like this! Something born at such a cost, must matter, should matter. One must see to that! Speculation ceased in Michael's brain; he stood, listening terribly. Nothing! He could not bear it down there, and went up again. No sound at first, and then another moan! This time he fled into his study, and ranged round the room, looking at the cartoons of Aubrey Greene. He did not see a single one, and suddenly bethought him of 'Old Forsyte'. He ought to be told! He rang up the 'Connoisseurs', the 'Remove', and his own father's clubs, in case they might have gone there together after the meeting. He drew blank everywhere. It was half-past seven. How much longer was this going on? He went back to the bedroom door; could hear nothing. Then down again to the hall. Ting-a-ling was lying by the front door, now. 'Fed-up!' thought Michael, stroking his back, and mechanically clearing the letter-box. Just one letter–Wilfrid's writing! He took it to the foot of the stairs and read it with half his brain, the other half wondering–wandering up there.

DEAR MONT,–I start to-morrow to try and cross Arabia. I thought you might like a line in case Arabia crosses me. I have recovered my senses. The air here is too clear for sentiment of any kind; and passion in exile soon becomes sickly. I am sorry I made you so much disturbance. It was a mistake for me to go back to England after the war, and hang about writing drivel for smart young women and inky folk to read. Poor old England–she's in for a bad time. Give her my love; the same to yourselves.

Yours ever,
WILFRID DESERT.

P.S.–If you've published the things I left behind, send any royalties to me care of my governor.–W.D.

Half Michael's brain thought: 'Well, that's that! And the book coming out to-day!' Queer! Was Wilfrid right–was it all a blooming gaff–the inky stream? Was one just helping on England's sickness? Ought they all to get on camels and ride the sun down? And yet, in books were comfort and diversion; and they were wanted! England had to go on–go on! 'No retreat, no retreat, they must conquer or die who have no retreat!' . . . God! There it was again. Back he flew upstairs, with his ears covered and his eyes wild. The sounds ceased; Annette came out to him.

'Her father, *mon cher*; try to find her father!'

'I have–I can't' gasped Michael.

'Try Green Street–Mrs Dartie. *Courage!* All is normal–it will be quite soon, now.'

When he had rung up Green Street and been answered at last, he sat with the door of his study open, waiting for 'Old Forsyte' to come. Half his sight remarked a round hole burnt in his trouser leg–he hadn't even noticed the smell; hadn't even realised that he had been smoking. He must pull himself together for the 'old man'. He heard the bell ring, and ran down to open.

'Well?' said Soames.

'Not yet, sir. Come up to my study. It's nearer.'

They went up side by side. That trim grey head, with the deep furrow between the eyes, and those eyes staring as if at pain behind them, steadied Michael. Poor old chap! He was 'for it', too! They were both on 'their uppers'!

'Have a peg, sir? I've got brandy here.'

'Yes,' said Soames. 'Anything.'

With the brandies in their hands, half-raised, they listened–jerked their hands up, drank. They were automatic, like two doll figures worked by the same string.

'Cigarette, sir?' said Michael.

Soames nodded.

With the lighted cigarettes just not in their mouths, they listened, put them in, took them out, puffed smoke. Michael had his right arm across his chest. Soames his left. They formed a pattern, thus, side by side.

'Bad to stick, sir. Sorry!'

Soames nodded. His teeth were clenched. Suddenly his hand relaxed.

'Listen!' he said. Sounds–different–confused!

Michael's hand seized something, gripped it hard; it was cold, thin–the hand of Soames. They sat thus, hand in hand, staring at the doorway, for how long neither knew.

Suddenly that doorway darkened; a figure in grey stood there–Annette!

'It is all r-right! A son!'

15

CALM

On waking from deep sleep next morning, Michael's first thought was: 'Fleur is back!' He then remembered.

To his: 'O.K.?' whispered at her door, he received an emphatic nod from the nurse.

In the midst of excited expectation he retained enough modernity to think: 'No more blurb! Go and eat your breakfast quietly!'

In the dining-room Soames was despising the broken egg before him. He looked up as Michael entered, and buried his face in his cup. Michael understood perfectly; they had sat hand in hand! He saw, too, that the journal opened by his plate was of a financial nature.

'Anything about the meeting, sir? Your speech must read like one o'clock!'

With a queer little sound Soames held out the paper. The headlines ran: 'Stormy meeting–resignation of two directors–a vote of confidence.' Michael skimmed down till he came to:

'Mr Forsyte, the director involved, in a speech of some length, said he had no intention of singing small. He deprecated the behaviour of the shareholders; he had not been accustomed to meet with suspicions. He tendered his resignation.'

Michael dropped the sheet.

'By Jove!' he said–'"Involved–suspicions". They've given it a turn, as though–!'

'The papers!' said Soames, and resumed his egg.

Michael sat down, and stripped the skin off a banana. '"Nothing became him like his death",' he thought: 'Poor old boy!'

'Well, sir,' he said, 'I was there, and all I can say is: You and my father were the only two people who excited my respect.'

'That!' said Soames, putting down his spoon.

Michael perceived that he wished to be alone, and swallowing the banana, went to his study. Waiting for his summons, he rang up his father.

'None the worse for yesterday, sir?'

Sir Lawrence's voice came clear and thin, rather high.

'Poorer and wiser. What's the bulletin?'

'Top-hole.'

'Our love to both. Your mother wants to know if he has any hair?'

'Haven't seen him yet. I'm just going.'

Annette, indeed, was beckoning from the doorway.

'She wants you to bring the little dog, *mon cher*.'

With Ting-a-ling under his arm, and treading on tiptoe, Michael entered. The eleventh baronet! He did not seem to amount to much, beneath her head bent over him. And surely her hair was darker! He walked up to the bed, and touched it reverently.

Fleur raised her head, and revealed the baby sucking vigorously at her little finger. 'Isn't he a monkey?' said her faint voice.

Michael nodded. A monkey clearly–but whether white–that was the question!

'And you, sweetheart?'

'All right now, but it was–' She drew her breath in, and her eyes darkened: 'Ting, look!'

The Chinese dog, with nostrils delicately moving, drew backward under Michael's arm. His whole demeanour displayed a knowing criticism. 'Puppies,' he seemed to say, 'we do it in China. Judgment reserved!'

'What eyes!' said Michael: 'We needn't tell *him* that this was brought from Chelsea by the doctor.'

Fleur gave the tiniest laugh.

'Put him down, Michael.'

Michael put him down, and he went to his corner.

'I mustn't talk,' said Fleur, 'but I want to, frightfully; as if I'd been dumb for months.'

'Just as I felt,' thought Michael, 'she's been away, away somewhere, utterly away.'

'It was like being held down, Michael. Months of not being yourself.'

Michael said softly: 'Yes! the process *is* behind the times! Has he got any hair? My mother wants to know.'

Fleur revealed the head of the eleventh baronet, covered with dark down.

'Like my grandmother's; but it'll get lighter. His eyes are going to be grey. Oh! and, Michael, about godparents? Alison, of course–but men?'

Michael dwelled a little before answering:

'I had a letter from Wilfrid yesterday. Would you like him? He's still out there, but I could hold the sponge for him in church.'

'Is he all right again?'

'He says so.'

He could not read the expression of her eyes, but her lips were pouted slightly.

'Yes,' she said: 'and I think one's enough, don't you? Mine never gave me anything.'

'One of mine gave me a Bible, and the other gave me a wigging. Wilfrid, then.' And he bent over her.

Her eyes seemed to make him a little ironic apology. He kissed her hair, and moved hurriedly away.

By the door Soames was standing, awaiting his turn.

'Just a minute only, sir,' the nurse was saying.

Soames walked up to the bedside, and stood looking at his daughter.

'Dad, dear!' Michael heard her say.

Soames just touched her hand, nodded, as if implying approval of the baby, and came walking back, but, in a mirror, Michael saw his lips quivering.

On the ground floor once more, he had the most intense desire to sing. It would not do; and, entering the Chinese room, he stood staring out into the sunlit square. Gosh! It was good to be alive! Say what you liked, you couldn't beat it! They might turn their noses up at life, and look down them at it; they might bolster up the future and the past, but–give him the present!

'I'll have that white monkey up again!' he thought. 'I'll see the brute further before he shall depress me!'

He went out to a closet under the stairs, and, from beneath four pairs of curtains done up in moth-preserver and brown paper, took out the picture. He held it away from him in the dim light. The creature's eyes! It was all in those eyes!

'Never mind, old son!' he said: 'Up you go!' And he carried it into the Chinese room.

Soames was there.

'I'm going to put him up again, sir.'

Soames nodded.

'Would you hold him, while I hook the wire?'

Soames held the picture.

Returning to the copper floor, Michael said:

'All right, sir!' and stood back.

Soames joined him. Side by side they contemplated the white monkey.

'He won't be happy till he gets it,' said Michael at last: 'The only thing is, you see, he doesn't know what *it* is.'

BOOK II
The Silver Spoon

THE SILVER SPOON

'But O, the thorns we stand upon!'

Winter's Tale

TO JOHN FORTESCUE

PART I

I

A STRANGER

The young man who, at the end of September, 1924, dismounted from a taxicab in South Square, Westminster, was so unobtrusively American that his driver had some hesitation in asking for double his fare. The young man had no hesitation in refusing it.

'Are you unable to read?' he said softly. 'Here's four shillings.'

With that he turned his back and looked at the house before which he had descended. This, the first private English house he had ever proposed to enter, inspired him with a certain uneasiness, as of a man who expects to part with a family ghost. Comparing a letter with the number chased in pale brass on the door, he murmured: 'It surely is,' and rang the bell.

While waiting for the door to be opened, he was conscious of extreme quietude, broken by a clock chiming four as if with the voice of Time itself. When the last boom died, the door yawned inwards, and a man, almost hairless, said:

'Yes, sir?'

The young man removed a soft hat from a dark head.

'This is Mrs Michael Mont's house?'

'Correct, sir.'

'Will you give her my card, and this letter?'

'"Mr Francis Wilmot, Naseby, S.C." Will you wait in here, sir?'

Ushered through the doorway of a room on the right, Francis Wilmot was conscious of a commotion close to the ground, and some teeth grazing the calf of his leg.

'Dandie!' said the voice of the hairless man, 'you little devil! That dog is a proper little brute with strangers, sir. Stand still! I've known him bite clean through a lady's stockings.'

Francis Wilmot saw with interest a silver-grey dog nine inches high and nearly as broad, looking up at him with lustrous eyes above teeth of extreme beauty.

'It's the baby, sir,' said the hairless man, pointing to a sort of nest on the floor before the fireless hearth; 'he *will* go for people when he's with the baby. But once he gets to smelling your trousers, he's all right. Better not touch the baby, though. Mrs Mont was here a minute ago; I'll take your card up to her.'

Francis Wilmot sat down on a settee in the middle of the room; and the dog lay between him and the baby.

And while the young man sat he gazed around him. The room was painted in panels of a sub-golden hue, with a silver-coloured ceiling. A clavichord, little golden ghost of a piano, stood at one end. Glass lustres, pictures of flowers and of a silvery-necked lady swinging a skirt and her golden slippers, adorned the walls. The curtains were of gold and silver. The silver-coloured carpet felt wonderfully soft beneath his feet, the furniture was of a golden wood.

The young man felt suddenly quite home-sick. He was back in the living-room of an old 'Colonial' house in the bend of a lonely South Carolina river, reddish in hue. He was staring at the effigy of his high-collared, red-coated great-grandfather, Francis Wilmot, Royalist major in the War of Independence. They always said it was like the effigy he saw when shaving every morning; the smooth dark hair drooping across his right temple, the narrow nose and lips, the narrow dark hand on the sword-hilt or the razor, the slits of dark eyes gazing steadily out. Young Francis was seeing the darkies working in the cotton-fields under a sun that he did not seem to have seen since he came over here; he was walking with his setter along the swamp edge, where Florida moss festooned the tall dolorous trees; he was thinking of the Wilmot inheritance, ruined in the Civil War, still decayed yet precious, and whether to struggle on with it, or to sell it to the Yank who wanted a weekend run-to from his Charleston dock job, and would improve it out of recognition. It would be lonely there, now that Anne had married that young Britisher, Jon Forsyte, and gone away north, to Southern Pines. And he thought of his sister, thus lost to him, dark, pale, vivid, 'full of sand'. Yes! this room made him home-sick, with its perfection, such as he had never beheld, where the only object out of keeping was that dog, lying on its side now, and so thick through that all its little legs were in the air. Softly he said:

'It's the prettiest room I ever was in.'

'What a perfectly charming thing to overhear!'

A young woman, with crinkly chestnut hair above a creamy face, with smiling lips, a short straight nose, and very white dark-lashed eyelids active over dark hazel eyes, stood near the door. She came towards him, and held out her hand.

Francis Wilmot bowed over it, and said gravely:

'Mrs Michael Mont?'

'So Jon's married your sister. Is she pretty?'

'She is.'

'Very?'

'Yes, indeed.'

'I hope baby has been entertaining you.'

'He's just great.'

'He is, rather. I hear Dandie bit you?'

'I reckon he didn't break the cuticle.'

'Haven't you looked? But he's quite healthy. Sit down, and tell me all about your sister and Jon. Is it a marriage of true minds?'

Francis Wimot sat down.

'It certainly is. Young Jon is a pretty white man, and Anne–'

He heard a sigh.

'I'm very glad. He says in his letter that he's awfully happy. You must come and stay here. You can be as free as you like. Look on us as an hotel.'

The young man's dark eyes smiled.

'That's too good of you! I've never been on this side before. They got through the war too soon.'

Fleur took the baby out of its nest.

'*This* creature doesn't bite. Look–two teeth, but they don't antagonise–isn't that how you put it?'

'What is its name?'

'Kit–for Christopher. We agreed about its name luckily. Michael–my husband–will be in directly. He's in Parliament, you know. They're not sitting till Monday–Ireland, of course. We only came back for it from Italy yesterday. Italy's so wonderful–you must see it.'

'Pardon me, but is that the Parliament clock that chimes so loud?'

'Big Ben–yes. He marks time for them. Michael says Parliament is the best drag on Progress ever invented. With our first Labour Government, it's been specially interesting this year. Don't you think it's rather touching the way this dog watches my baby? He's got the most terrific jaw!'

'What kind of dog is he?'

'A Dandie Dinmont. We did have a Peke. It was a terrible tragedy. He *would* go after cats; and one day he struck a fighting Tom, and got clawed over both eyes–quite blinded–and so–'

The young man saw her eyes suddenly too bright. He made a soft noise, and said gently: 'That was too bad.'

'I had to change this room completely. It used to be Chinese. It reminded me too much.'

'This little fellow would chaw any cat.'

'Luckily he was brought up with kittens. We got him for his legs–they're so bowed in front that he can hardly run, so he just suits the pram. Dan, show your legs!'

The Dandie looked up with a negative sound.

'He's a terrible little "character". Do tell me, what's Jon like now? Is he still English?'

The young man was conscious that she had uttered at last something really in her mind.

'He is; but he's a dandy fellow.'

'And his mother? She used to be beautiful.'

'And is to this day.'

'She would be. Grey, I suppose, by now?'

'Yes. You don't like her?'

'Well, I hope she won't be jealous of your sister!'

'I think, perhaps, you're unjust.'

'I think, perhaps, I am.'

She sat very still, her face hard above the baby's. And the young man, aware of thoughts beyond his reach, got up.

'When you write to Jon,' she said suddenly, 'tell him that I'm awfully glad, and that I wish him luck. I shan't write to him myself. May I call you Francis?'

Francis Wilmot bowed. 'I shall be proud, ma'am.'

'Yes; but you must call me Fleur. We're sort of related, you know.'

The young man smiled, and touched the name with his lips.

'Fleur! It's a beautiful name!'

'Your room will be ready when you come back. You'll have a bathroom to yourself, of course.'

He put his lips to the hand held out.

'It's wonderful,' he said. 'I was feeling kind of homesick; I miss the sun over here.'

In going out, he looked back. Fleur had put her baby back in its nest, and was staring straight before her.

2

CHANGE

But more than the death of a dog had caused the regarnishing of Fleur's Chinese room. On the evening of her twenty-second birthday Michael had come home saying:

'Well, my child, I've chucked publishing. With old Danby always in the right—it isn't a career.'

'Oh! Michael, you'll be bored to death.'

'I'll go into Parliament. It's quite usual, and about the same screw.'

He had spoken in jest. Six days later it became apparent that she had listened in earnest.

'You were absolutely right, Michael. It's the very thing for you. You've got ideas.'

'Other people's.'

'And the gift of the gab. We're frightfully handy for the House, here.'

'It costs money, Fleur.'

'Yes, I've spoken to Father. It was rather funny—there's never been a Forsyte, you know, anywhere near Parliament. But he thinks it'll be good for me; and that it's all baronets are fit for.'

'One has to have a Seat, unfortunately.'

'Well, I've sounded your father, too. He'll speak to people. They want young men.'

'Ah! And what are my politics?'

'My dear boy, you must know—at thirty.'

'I'm not a Liberal. But am I Labour or Tory?'

'You can think it out before the next election!'

Next day, while he was shaving, and she was in her bath, he cut himself slightly and said:

'The land and this unemployment is what I really care about. I'm a Foggartist.'

'What?'

'Old Sir James Foggart's book. You read it.'

'No.'

'Well, you said so.'

'So did others.'

'Never mind—his eyes are fixed on 1944, and his policy's according. Safety in the Air, the Land and Child Emigration; adjustment of Supply and Demand within the Empire; cut our losses in Europe; and endure a worse Present for the sake of a better Future. Everything, in fact, that's unpopular, and said to be impossible.'

'Well, you could keep all that to yourself till you get in. You'll have to stand as a Tory.'

'How lovely you look!'

'If you get in, you can disagree with everybody. That'll give you a position from the start.'

'Some scheme!' murmured Michael.

'You can initiate this–this Foggartism. He isn't mad, is he?'

'No, only too sane, which is much the same thing, of course. You see we've got a higher wage-scale than any other country except America and the dominions; and it isn't coming down again; we really group in with the new countries. He's for growing as much of our food as we can, and pumping British town children, before they're spoiled, into the Colonies, till Colonial demand for goods equal our supply. It's no earthly, of course, without wholehearted co-operation between the Governments within the Empire.'

'It sounds very sensible.'

'We published him, you know, but at his own expense. It's a "faith and the mountain" stunt. He's got the faith all right, but the mountain shows no signs of moving.'

Fleur stood up. 'Well,' she said, 'that's settled. Your father says he can get you a nomination as a Tory, and you can keep your own views to yourself. You'll get in on the human touch, Michael.'

'Thank you ducky. Can I help dry you?' . . .

Before redecorating her Chinese room, however, Fleur had waited till after Michael was comfortably seated for a division which professed to be interested in agriculture. She chose a blend between Adam and Louis Quinze. Michael called it the 'bimetallic parlour'; and carried off 'The White Monkey' to his study. The creature's pessimism was not, he felt, suited to political life.

Fleur had initiated her 'salon' with a gathering in February. The soul of society had passed away since the Liberal *débâcle* and Lady Alison's politico-legal coterie no longer counted. Plainer people were in the ascendant. Her Wednesday evenings were youthful, with age represented by her father-in - law, two minor ambassadors, and Pevensey Blythe, editor of *The Outpost*. So unlike his literary style that he was usually mistaken for a Colonial Prime Minister, Blythe was a tall man with a beard, and grey bloodshot eyes, who expressed knowledge in paragraphs that few could really understand. 'What Blythe thinks to-day, the Conservative Party will not think to-morrow,' was said of him. He spoke in a small voice, and constantly used the impersonal pronoun.

'One is walking in one's sleep,' he would say of the political situation, 'and will wake up without any clothes on.'

A warm supporter of Sir James Foggart's book, characterising it as 'the masterpiece of a blind archangel,' he had a passion for listening to the clavichord, and was invaluable in Fleur's 'salon'.

Freed from poetry and modern music, from Sibley Swan, Walter Nazing and Hugo Solstis, Fleur was finding time for her son–the eleventh baronet. He represented for her the reality of things. Michael might have posthumous theories, and Labour predatory hopes, but for her the year 1944 would see the eleventh baronet come of age. That Kit should inherit an England worth living in was of more intrinsic importance than anything they proposed in the Commons and were unable to perform. All those houses they were going to build, for instance–very proper, but a little unnecessary if Kit still had Lippinghall Manor and South Square, Westminster, to dwell in. Not that Fleur voiced such cynical convictions, or admitted them even to herself. She did orthodox lip-service to the great god Progress.

The Peace of the world, Hygiene, Trade, and the End of Unemployment, preoccupied all, irrespective of Party, and Fleur was in the fashion; but instinct, rather than Michael and Sir James Foggart, told her that the time-honoured motto: 'Eat your cake and have it', which underlay the platforms of all Parties, was not 'too frightfully' sound. So long as Kit had cake, it was no good bothering too deeply about the rest; though, of course, one must seem to. Fluttering about her 'salon'–this to that person, and that to the other, and to all so pretty, she charmed by her grace, her common sense, her pliancy. Not infrequently she attended at the House, and sat, not listening too much to the speeches, yet picking up, as it were, by a sort of seventh sense (if women in Society all had six, surely Fleur had seven) what was necessary to the conduct of that 'salon'–the rise and fall of the Governmental barometer, the catchwords and clichés of policy; and, more valuable, impressions of personality, of the residuary man within the Member. She watched Michael's career, with the fostering eye of a godmother who has given her godchild a blue morocco prayer-book, in the hope that some day he may remember its existence. Although a sedulous attendant at the House all through the spring and summer, Michael had not yet opened his mouth, and so far she had approved of his silence, while nurturing his desire to know his own mind by listening to his wanderings in Foggartism. If it were indeed the only permanent cure for Unemployment, as he said, she too was a Foggartist; common sense assuring her that the only real danger to Kit's future lay in that national malady. Eliminate Unemployment, and nobody would have time to make a fuss. But her criticisms were often pertinent:

'My dear boy, does a country ever sacrifice the present for the sake of the future?' or: 'Do you really think country life is better than town life?' or: 'Can you imagine sending Kit out of England at fourteen to some God-forsaken end of the world?' or: 'Do you suppose the towns will have it?' And they roused Michael to such persistence and fluency that she felt he would really catch on in time–like old Sir Giles Snoreham, whom they would soon be making a peer, because he had always worn low-crowned hats and advocated a return to hansom cabs. Hats, buttonholes, an eye-glass–she turned over in her mind all such little realities as help a political career.

'Plain glass doesn't harm the sight; and it really has a focusing value, Michael.'

'My child, it's never done my Dad a bit of good; I doubt if it's sold three copies of any of his books. No! If I get on, it'll be by talking.'

But still she encouraged him to keep his mouth shut.

'It's no good starting wrong, Michael. These Labour people aren't going to last out the year.'

'Why not?'

'Their heads are swelling, and their tempers going. They're only on sufferance; people on sufferance have got to be pleasant or they won't be suffered. When they go out, the Tories will get in again and probably last. You'll have several years to be eccentric in, and by the time they're out again, you'll have your licence. Just go on working the human touch in your constituency; I'm sure it's a mistake to forget you've got constituents.'

Michael spent most week-ends that summer working the human touch in mid-Bucks; and Fleur spent most week-ends with the eleventh baronet at her father's house near Mapledurham.

Since wiping the dust of the city off his feet, after that affair of Elderson and the P.P.R.S., Soames had become almost too countrified for a Forsyte. He had bought the meadows on the far side of the river and several Jersey cows. Not that he was going in for farming or nonsense of that sort, but it gave him an interest to punt himself over and see them milked. He had put up a good deal of glass, too, and was laying down melons. The English melon was superior to any other, and every year's connection with a French wife made him more and more inclined to eat what he grew himself. After Michael was returned for Parliament, Fleur had sent him Sir James Foggart's book, 'The Parlous State of England'. When it came, he said to Annette:

'I don't know what she thinks I want with this great thing!'

'To read it, Soames, I suppose.'

Soames sniffed, turning the pages.

'I can't tell what it's all about.'

'I will sell it at my bazaar, Soames. It will do for some good man who can read English.'

From that moment Soames began almost unconsciously to read the book. He found it a peculiar affair, which gave most people some good hard knocks. He began to enjoy them, especially the chapter deprecating the workman's dislike of parting with his children at a reasonable age. Having never been outside Europe, he had a somewhat sketchy idea of places like South Africa, Australia, Canada, and New Zealand; but this old fellow Foggart, it appeared, had been there, and knew what he was talking about. What he said about their development seemed quite sensible. Children who went out there put on weight at once, and became owners of property at an age when in England they were still delivering parcels, popping in and out of jobs, hanging about street corners, and qualifying for unemployment and Communism. Get them out of England! There was a startling attraction in the idea for one who was English to a degree. He was in favour, too, of what was said about growing food and making England safe in the air. And then, slowly, he turned against it. The fellow was too much of a Jeremiah altogether. He complained to Fleur that the book dealt with nothing but birds in the bush; it was unpractical. What did 'Old Mont' say?'

'He won't read it; he says he knows old Foggart.'

'H'm!' said Soames, 'I shouldn't be surprised if there were something in it then.' That little-headed baronet was old-fashioned! 'Anyway, it shows that Michael's given up those Labour fellows.'

'Michael says Foggartism will be Labour's policy when they understand all it means.'

'How's that?'

'He thinks it's going to do them much more good than anybody else. He says one or two of their leaders are beginning to smell it out, and that the rest of the leaders are bound to follow in time.'

'In that case,' said Soames, 'it'll never go down with their rank and file.' And for two minutes he sat in a sort of trance. Had he said something profound, or had he not?

Fleur's presence at week-ends with the eleventh baronet was extremely agreeable to him. Though at first he had felt a sort of disappointment that his grandchild was not a girl—an eleventh baronet belonged too definitely to the Monts—he began, as the months wore on, to find him 'an engaging little chap', and, in any case, to have him down at Mapledurham kept him away from

Lippinghall. It tried him at times, of course, to see how the women hung about the baby–there was something very excessive about motherhood. He had noticed it with Annette; he noticed it now with Fleur. French–perhaps! He had not remembered his own mother making such a fuss; indeed, he could not remember anything that happened when he was one. A week-end, when Madame Lamotte, Annette and Fleur were all hanging over his grandson, three generations of maternity concentrated on that pudgy morsel, reduced him to a punt, fishing for what he felt sure nobody would eat.

By the time he had finished Sir James Foggart's book, the disagreeable summer of 1924 was over, and a more disagreeable September had set in. The mellow golden days that glow up out of a haze which stars with dewdrops every cobweb on a gate, simply did not come. It rained, and the river was so unnaturally full, that the newspapers were at first unnaturally empty–there was literally no news of drought; they filled up again slowly with reports of the wettest summer 'for thirty years'. Calm, greenish with weed and tree shadow, the river flowed unendingly between Soames's damp lawn and his damp meadows. There were no mushrooms. Blackberries tasted of rain. Soames made a point of eating one every year, and, by the flavour, could tell what sort of year it had been. There was a good deal of 'old-man's-beard'. In spite of all this, however, he was more cheerful than he had been for ages. Labour had been 'in', if not in real power, for months, and the heavens had only lowered. Forced by Labour-in-office to take some notice of politics, he would utter prophecies at the breakfast-table. They varied somewhat, according to the news; and, since he always forgot those which did not come true, he was constantly able to tell Annette that he had told her so. She took no interest, however, occupied, 'like a woman, with her bazaars and jam-making, running about in the car, shopping in London, attending garden-parties'; and, in spite of her tendency to put on flesh, still remarkably handsome. Jack Cardigan, his niece Imogen's husband, had made him a sixty-ninth-birthday present of a set of golf-clubs. This was more puzzling to Soames than anything that had ever happened to him. What on earth was he to do with them? Annette, with that French quickness which so often annoyed him, suggested that he should use them. She was uncomfortable! At his age–! And then, one week-end in May the fellow himself had come down with Imogen and, teeing a ball up on half a mole-hill, had driven it across the river.

'I'll bet you a box of cigars, Uncle Soames, that you don't do that before we leave on Monday.'

'I never bet,' said Soames, 'and I don't smoke.'

'Time you began both. Look here, we'll spend to-morrow learning to knock the ball!'

'Absurd!' said Soames.

But in his room that night he had stood in his pyjamas swinging his arms in imitation of Jack Cardigan. The next day he sent the women out in the car with their lunch; he was not going to have them grinning at him. He had seldom spent more annoying hours than those which followed. They culminated in a moment when at last he hit the ball, and it fell into the river three yards from the near bank. He was so stiff next morning in arms and ribs, that Annette had to rub him till he said:

'Look out! you're taking the skin off!'

He had, however, become infected. After destroying some further portions of his lawn, he joined the nearest golf club, and began to go round by himself during the luncheon-hour, accompanied by a little boy. He kept at it with characteristic tenacity, till by July he had attained a certain proficiency; and he began to say to Annette that it would do her all the good in the world to take it up, and keep her weight down.

'*Merci*, Soames,' she would reply; 'I have no wish to be the figure of your English Misses, flat as a board before and behind.' She was reactionary, 'like her nation'; and Soames, who at heart had a certain sympathy with curves, did not seriously press the point. He found that the exercise jogged both his liver and his temper. He began to have colour in his cheeks. The day after his first nine-hole round with Jack Cardigan, who had given him three strokes a hole and beaten him by nine holes, he received a package which, to his dismay, contained a box of cigars. What the fellow was about, he could not imagine! He only discovered when, one evening a few days later, sitting at the window of his picture gallery, he found that he had one in his mouth. Curiously enough, it did not make him sick. It produced rather something of the feeling he used to enjoy after 'doing Coué'–now comparatively out of fashion, since an American, so his sister Winifred said, had found a shorter cut. A suspicion, however, that the family had set Jack Cardigan on, prevented him from indulging his new sensation anywhere but in his picture gallery; so that cigars gathered the halo of a secret vice. He renewed his store stealthily. Only when he found that Annette, Fleur, and others had known for weeks, did he relax his rule, and say openly that the vice of the present day was cigarettes.

'My dear boy,' said Winifred, when she next saw him, 'everybody's saying you're a different man!'

Soames raised his eyebrows. He was not conscious of any change.

'That chap Cardigan,' he said, 'is a funny fellow! . . . I'm going to dine and sleep at Fleur's; they're just back from Italy. The House sits on Monday.'

'Yes,' said Winifred; 'very fussy of them–sitting in the Long Vacation.'

'Ireland!' said Soames deeply. 'A pretty pair of shoes again!' Always had been; always would be!

3

MICHAEL TAKES 'A LUNAR'

Michael had returned from Italy with the longing to 'get on with it', which results from Southern holidays. Countryman by upbringing, still deeply absorbed by the unemployment problem and committed to Foggartism, as its remedy, he had taken up no other hobby in the House, and was eating the country's bread, if somewhat unbuttered, and doing nothing for it. He desired, therefore, to know where he stood, and how long he was going to stand there.

Bent on 'taking this lunar'–as 'Old Forsyte' would call it–at his own position, he walked away from the House that same day, after dealing with an accumulated correspondence. He walked towards Pevensey Blythe, in the office of that self-sufficing weekly: *The Outpost*. Sunburnt from his Italian holiday and thinned by Italian cookery, he moved briskly, and thought of many things. Passing down on to the Embankment, where a number of unemployed birds on a number of trees were also wondering, it seemed, where they stood and how long they were going to stand there, he took a letter from his pocket to read a second time.

12 Sapper's Row,
Camden Town.

HONOURABLE SIR,

  Being young in 'Who's Who', you will not be hard, I think, to those in suffering. I am an Austrian woman who married a German eleven years ago. He was an actor on the English stage, for his father and mother, who are no more living, brought him to England quite young. Interned he was, and his health broken up. He has the neurasthenie very bad so he cannot be trusted for any work. Before the war he was always in a part, and we had some good money; but this went partly when I was left with my child alone, and the rest was taken by the P.T., and we got very little back, neither of us being English. What we did get has all been to the doctor, and for our debts, and for burying our little child, which died happily, for though I loved it much this life which we have is not fit for a child to live. We live on my needle, and that is not earning much, a pound a week and sometimes nothing. The managers will not look at my husband all these years, because he shakes suddenly, so they think he drinks, but, Sir, he has not the money to buy it. We do not know where to turn, or what to do. So I thought, dear Sir, whether you could do anything for us with the P.T.; they have been quite sympatical; but they say they administrate an order and cannot do more. Or if you could get my husband some work where he will be in open air—the doctor say that is what he want. We have nowhere to go in Germany or in Austria, our well-beloved families being no more alive. I think we are like many, but I cannot help asking you, Sir, because we want to keep living if we can, and now we are hardly having any food. Please to forgive me my writing, and to believe your very anxious and humble

ANNA BERGFELD.

'God help them!' thought Michael, under a plane tree close to Cleopatra's Needle, but without conviction. For in his view God was not so much interested in the fate of individual aliens as the Governor of the Bank of England in the fate of a pound of sugar bought with the fraction of a Bradbury; He would not arbitrarily interfere with a ripple of the tides set loose by His arrangement of the Spheres. God, to Michael, was a monarch strictly limited by His own Constitution. He restored the letter to his pocket. Poor creatures! But really, with 1,200,000 and more English unemployed, mostly due to that confounded Kaiser and his Navy stunt–! If that fellow and his gang had not started their naval rivalry in 1899, England would have been out of the whole mess, or, perhaps, there never would have been a mess!

He turned up from the Temple station towards the offices of *The Outpost*. He had 'taken' that weekly for some years now. It knew everything, and managed to convey a slight impression that nobody else knew anything; so that it seemed more weighty than any other weekly. Having no particular Party to patronise, it could patronise the lot. Without Imperial bias, it professed a special knowledge of the Empire. Not literary, it made a point of reducing the heads of literary men–Michael, in his publishing days, had enjoyed every opportunity of noticing that. Professing respect for Church and the Law, it was an adept at giving them 'what-for'. It fancied itself on Drama, striking a somewhat Irish attitude towards it. But, perhaps above all, it excelled in neat detraction from political reputations, keeping them in their place, and that place a little lower than *The Outpost*'s. Moreover, from its editorials emanated that 'holy ghost' of inspired knowledge in periods just a little beyond average comprehension, without which no such periodical had real importance.

Michael went up the stairs two at a time, and entered a large square room, where Mr Blythe, back to the door, was pointing with a ruler to a circle drawn on a map.

'This is a bee map,' said Mr Blythe to himself. 'Quite the bee-est map I ever saw.'

Michael could not contain a gurgle, and the eyes of Mr Blythe came round, prominent, epileptic, richly encircled by pouches.

'Hallo!' he said defiantly. 'You? The Colonial Office prepared this map specially to show the best spots for Settlement schemes. And they've left out Baggersfontein–the very hub.'

Michael seated himself on the table.

'I've come in to ask what you think of the situation? My wife says Labour will be out in no time.'

'Our charming little lady!' said Mr Blythe; 'Labour will survive Ireland; they will survive Russia; they will linger on in their precarious way. One hesitates to predict their decease. Fear of their Budget may bring them down in February. After the smell of Russian fat has died away–say in November, Mont–one may make a start.'

'This first speech,' said Michael, 'is a nightmare to me. How, exactly, am I to start Foggartism?'

'One will have achieved the impression of a body of opinion before then.'

'But will there be one?'

'No,' said Mr Blythe.

'Oh!' said Michael. 'And, by the way, what about Free Trade?'

'One will profess Free Trade, and put on duties.'

'God and Mammon.'

'Necessary in England, before any new departure, Mont. Witness Liberal-Unionism, Tory-Socialism, and–'

'Other ramps,' said Michael gently.

'One will glide, deprecate Protection till there is more Protection than Free Trade, then deprecate Free Trade. Foggartism is an end, not a means; Free Trade and Protection are means, not the ends politicians have made them.'

Roused by the word 'politician', Michael got off the table; he was coming to have a certain sympathy with those poor devils. They were supposed to have no feeling for the country, and to be wise only after the event. But, really, who could tell what was good for the country, among the mists of talk? Not even old Foggart, Michael sometimes thought.

'You know, Blythe,' he said, 'that we politicians don't think ahead, simply because we know it's no earthly. Every elector thinks his own immediate good is the good of the country. Only their own shoes pinching will change electors' views. If Foggartism means adding to the price of living now, and taking wage-earning children away from workmen's families for the sake of benefit–ten or twenty years hence–who's going to stand for it?'

'My dear young man,' said Mr Blythe, 'conversion is our job. At present our trade-unionists despise the outside world. They've never seen it. Their philosophy is bounded by their smoky little streets. But five million pounds spent on the organised travel of a hundred thousand working men would do the trick in five years. It would infect the working-class with a feverish desire for a place in the sun. The world is their children's for the taking. But who can blame them, when they know nothing of it?'

'Some thought!' said Michael. 'Only–what Government will think it? Can I take those maps? . . . By the way,' he said at the door, 'there are Societies, you know, for sending out children.'

Mr Blythe grunted. 'Yes. Excellent little affairs! A few hundred children doing well–concrete example of what might be. Multiply it a hundredfold, and you've got a beginning. You can't fill pails with a teaspoon. Good-bye!'

Out on the Embankment Michael wondered if one could love one's country with a passion for getting people to leave it. But this over-bloated town condition, with its blight and smoky ugliness; the children without a chance from birth; these swarms of poor devils without work, who dragged about and hadn't an earthly, and never would, on present lines; this unbalanced, hand-to-mouth, dependent state of things—surely that wasn't to be for ever the state of the country one loved! He stared at the towers of Westminster, with the setting sun behind them. And there started up before him the thousand familiars of his past—trees, fields and streams, towers, churches, bridges; the English breeds of beasts, the singing birds, the owls, the jays and rooks at Lippinghall, the little differences from foreign sorts in shrub, flower, lichen, and winged life; the English scents, the English haze, the English grass; the eggs and bacon; the slow good humour, the moderation and the pluck; the smell of rain; the apple-blossom, the heather, and the sea. His country, and his breed—unspoilable at heart! He passed the Clock Tower. The House looked lacey and imposing, more beautiful than fashion granted. Did they spin the web of England's future in that House? Or were they painting camouflage—a screen over old England?

A familiar voice said: 'This is a monstrous great thing!'

And Michael saw his father-in-law staring up at the Lincoln statue. 'What did they want to put it here for?' said Soames. 'It's not English.' He walked along at Michael's side. 'Fleur well?'

'Splendid. Italy suited her like everything.'

Soames sniffed. 'They're a theatrical lot,' he said. 'Did you see Milan cathedral?'

'Yes, sir. It's about the only thing we didn't take to.'

'H'm! Their cooking gave me the collywobbles in '82. I dare say it's better now. How's the boy?'

'A1, sir.'

Soames made a sound of gratification, and they turned the corner into South Square.

'What's this?' said Soames.

Outside the front door were two battered-looking trunks, a young man, grasping a bag, and ringing the bell, and a taxi-cab turning away.

'I can't tell you, sir,' murmured Michael. 'Unless it's the angel Gabriel.'

'He's got the wrong house,' said Soames, moving forward.

But just then the young man disappeared within.

Soames walked up to the trunks. 'Francis Wilmot,' he read out. '"S.S. Amphibian." There's some mistake!'

4

MERE CONVERSATION

When they came in, Fleur was returning downstairs from showing the young man to his room. Already fully dressed for the evening, she had but little on, and her hair was shingled. . . .

'My dear girl,' Michael had said, when shingling came in, 'to please me, don't! Your *nuque* will be too bristly for kisses.'

'My dear boy,' she had answered, 'as if one could help it! You're always the same with any new fashion!'

She had been one of the first twelve to shingle, and was just feeling that without care she would miss being one of the first twelve to grow some hair again. Marjorie Ferrar, 'the Pet of the Panjoys', as Michael called her, already had more than an inch. Somehow, one hated being distanced by Marjorie Ferrar. . . .

Advancing to her father, she said:

'I've asked a young American to stay, Dad; Jon Forsyte has married his sister, out there. You're quite brown, darling. How's mother?'

Soames only gazed at her.

And Fleur passed through one of those shamed moments, when the dumb quality of his love for her seemed accusing the glib quality of her love for him. It was not fair–she felt–that he should look at her like that; as if she had not suffered in that old business with Jon more than he; if she could take it lightly now, surely he could! As for Michael–not a word!–not even a joke! She bit her lips, shook her shingled head, and passed into the 'bimetallic parlour'.

Dinner began with soup and Soames deprecating his own cows for not being Herefords. He supposed that in America they had plenty of Herefords?

Francis Wilmot believed that they were going in for Holsteins now.

'Holsteins!' repeated Soames. 'They're new since my young days. What's their colour?'

'Parti-coloured,' said Francis Wilmot. 'The English grass is just wonderful.'

'Too damp, with us,' said Soames. 'We're on the river.'

'The river Thames? What size will that be, where it hasn't a tide?'

'Just there–not more than a hundred yards.'

'Will it have fish?'

'Plenty.'

'And it'll run clear–not red; our Southern rivers have a red colour. And your trees will be willows, and poplars, and elms.'

Soames was a good deal puzzled. He had never been in America. The inhabitants were human, of course, but peculiar and all alike, with more face than feature, heads fastened upright on their backs, and shoulders too square to be real. Their voices clanged in their mouths; they pronounced the words 'very' and 'America' in a way that he had tried to imitate without success; their dollar was too high, and they all had motor-cars; they despised Europe, came over in great quantities, and took back all they could; they talked all the time, and were not allowed to drink. This young man cut across all these preconceptions. He drank sherry and only spoke when he was spoken to. His shoulders looked natural; he had more feature than face; and his voice was soft. Perhaps, at least, he despised Europe.

'I suppose,' he said, 'you find England very small.'

'No, sir. I find London very large; and you certainly have the loveliest kind of a countryside.'

Soames looked down one side of his nose. 'Pretty enough!' he said.

Then came turbot and a silence, broken, low down, behind his chair.

'That dog!' said Soames, impaling a morsel of fish he had set aside as uneatable.

'No, no, Dad! He just wants to know you've seen him!'

Soames stretched down a finger, and the Dandie fell on his side.

'He never eats,' said Fleur; 'but he has to be noticed.'

A small covey of partridges came in, cooked.

'Is there any particular thing you want to see over here, Mr Wilmot?' said Michael. 'There's nothing very un-American left. You're just too late for Regent Street.'

'I want to see the Beefeaters; and Cruft's Dog Show; and your blood horses; and the Derby.'

'Darby!' Soames corrected. 'You can't stay for that—it's not till next June.'

'My cousin Val will show you race-horses,' said Fleur. 'He married Jon's sister, you know.'

A 'bombe' appeared. 'You have more of this in America, I believe,' said Soames.

'We don't have much ice-cream in the South, sir, but we have special cooking—very tasty.'

'I've heard of terrapin.'

'Well, *I* don't get frills like that. I live away back, and have to work pretty hard. My place is kind of homey; but I've got some mighty nice darkies that can cook fine—old folk that knew my grannies. The old-time darky is getting scarce, but he's the real thing.'

A Southerner!

Soames had been told that the Southerner was a gentleman. He remembered the 'Alabama', too; and his father, James, saying: 'I told you so' when the Government ate humble pie over that business.

In the savoury silence that accompanied soft roes on toast, the patter of the Dandie's feet on the parquet floor could be plainly heard.

'This is the only thing he likes,' said Fleur. 'Dan! go to your master. Give him a little bit, Michael.' And she stole a look at Michael, but he did not answer it.

On their Italian holiday, with Fleur in the throes of novelty, sun and wine warmed, disposed to junketing, amenable to his caresses, he had been having his real honeymoon, enjoying, for the first time since his marriage, a sense of being the chosen companion of his adored. And now had come this stranger, bringing reminder that one played but second fiddle to that young second cousin and first lover; and he couldn't help feeling the cup withdrawn again from his lips. She had invited this young man because he came from that past of hers whose tune one could not play. And, without looking up, he fed the Dandie with tid-bits of his favourite edible.

Soames broke the silence.

'Take some nutmeg, Mr Wilmot. Melon without nutmeg—'

When Fleur rose, Soames followed her to the drawing-room; while Michael led the young American to his study.

'You knew Jon?' said Francis Wilmot.

'No; I never met him.'

'He's a great little fellow; and some poet. He's growing dandy peaches.'

'Is he going on with that, now he's married?'

'Surely.'

'Not coming to England?'

'Not this year. They have a nice home—horses and dogs. They have some hunting there, too. Perhaps he'll bring my sister over for a trip, next fall.'

'Oh!' said Michael. 'And are you staying long, yourself?'

'Why! I'll go back for Christmas. I'd like to see Rome and Seville; and I want to visit the old home of my people, down in Worcestershire.'

'When did they go over?'

'William and Mary. Catholics–they were. Is it a nice part, Worcestershire?'

'Very; especially in the spring. It grows a lot of fruit.'

'Oh! You still grow things in this country?'

'Not many.'

'I thought that was so, coming on the cars, from Liverpool. I saw a lot of grass and one or two sheep, but I didn't see anybody working. The people all live in the towns, then?'

'Except a few unconsidered trifles. You must come down to my father's; they still grow a turnip or two thereabouts.'

'It's sad,' said Francis Wilmot.

'It is. We began to grow wheat again in the war; but they've let it all slip back–and worse.'

'Why was that?'

Michael shrugged his shoulders: 'No accounting for statesmanship. It lets the Land go to blazes when in office; and beats the drum of it when in opposition. At the end of the war we had the best air force in the world, and agriculture was well on its way to recovery. And what did they do? Dropped them both like hot potatoes. It was tragic. What do you grow in Carolina?'

'Just cotton, on my place. But it's mighty hard to make cotton pay nowadays. Labour's high.'

'High with you, too?'

'Yes, sir. Do they let strangers into your Parliament?'

'Rather. Would you like to hear the Irish debate? I can get you a seat in the Distinguished Strangers' gallery.'

'I thought the English were stiff; but it's wonderful the way you make me feel at home. Is that your father-in-law–the old gentleman?'

'Yes.'

'He seems kind of rarefied. Is he a banker?'

'No. But now you mention it–he ought to be.'

Francis Wilmot's eyes roved round the room and came to rest on 'The White Monkey'.

'Well, now,' he said, softly, 'that, surely, is a wonderful picture. Could I get a picture painted by that man, for Jon and my sister?'

'I'm afraid not,' said Michael. 'You see, he was a Chink–not quite of the best period; but he must have gone West five hundred years ago at least.'

'Ah! Well, he had a great sense of animals.'

'We think he had a great sense of human beings.'

Francis Wilmot stared.

There was something, Michael decided, in this young man unresponsive to satire.

'So you want to see Cruft's Dog Show?' he said. 'You're keen on dogs, then?'

'I'll be taking a bloodhound back for Jon, and two for myself. I want to raise bloodhounds.'

Michael leaned back, and blew out smoke. To Francis Wilmot, he felt, the world was young, and life running on good tyres to some desirable destination. In England–!

'What is it you Americans want of life?' he said abruptly.

'Well, I suppose you might say we want success–in the North at all events.'

'*We* wanted that in 1824,' said Michael.

'Oh! And nowadays?'

'We've had success, and now we're wondering whether it hasn't cooked our goose.'

'Well,' said Francis Wilmot, 'we're sort of thinly populated, compared with you.'

'That's it,' said Michael. 'Every seat here is booked in advance; and a good many sit on their own knees. Will you have another cigar, or shall we join the lady?'

5

SIDE-SLIPS

If Providence was completely satisfied with Sapper's Row, Camden Town, Michael was not. What could justify those twin dismal rows of three-storeyed houses, so begrimed that they might have been collars washed in Italy? What possible attention to business could make these little ground-floor shops do anything but lose money? From the thronged and tram-lined thoroughfare so pregnantly scented with fried fish, petrol, and old clothes, who would turn into this small backwater for sweetness or for profit. Even the children, made with heroic constancy on its second and third floors, sought the sweets of life outside its precincts; for in Sapper's Row they could neither be run over nor stare at the outside of cinemas. Hand-carts, bicycles, light vans which had lost their nerve and taxicabs which had lost their way, provided all the traffic; potted geraniums and spotted cats supplied all the beauty. Sapper's Row drooped and dithered.

Michael entered from its west end, and against his principles. Here was overcrowded England at its most dismal, and here was he, who advocated a reduction of its population, about to visit some broken-down aliens with the view of keeping them alive. He looked into three of the little shops. Not a soul! Which was worst! Such little shops frequented, or–deserted? He came to No. 12, and looking up, saw a face looking down. It was wax white, movingly listless, above a pair of hands sewing at a garment. 'That,' he thought, 'is my "obedient humble" and her needle.' He entered the shop below, a hairdresser's, containing a dirty basin below a dusty mirror, suspicious towels, bottles, and two dingy chairs. In his shirt-sleeves, astride one of them, reading *The Daily Mail*, sat a shadowy fellow with pale hollow cheeks, twisted moustache, lank hair, and the eyes, at once knowing and tragic, of a philosopher.

'Hair-cut, sir?'

Michael shook his head.

'Do Mr and Mrs Bergfeld live here?'

'Upstairs, top floor.'

'How do I get up?'

'Through there.'

Passing through a curtained aperture, Michael found a stairway, and at its top, stood, hesitating. His conscience was echoing Fleur's comment on Anna Bergfeld's letter: 'Yes, I dare say; but what's the good?' when the door was opened, and it seemed to him almost as if a corpse were standing there, with a face as though someone had come knocking on its grave, so eager and so white.

'Mrs Bergfeld? My name's Mont. You wrote to me.'

The woman trembled so, that Michael thought she was going to faint.

'Will you excuse me, sir, that I sit down?' And she dropped on to the end of the bed. The room was spotless, but, besides the bed, held only a small deal washstand, a pot of geranium, a tin trunk with a pair of trousers folded on it, a woman's hat on a peg, and a chair in the window covered with her sewing.

The woman stood up again. She seemed not more than thirty, thin but prettily formed; and her oval face, without colour except in her dark eyes, suggested Rafael rather than Sapper's Row.

'It is like seeing an angel,' she said. 'Excuse me, sir.'

'Queer angel, Mrs Bergfeld. Your husband not in?'

'No, sir. Fritz has gone to walk.'

'Tell me, Mrs Bergfeld. If I pay your passages to Germany, will you go?'

'We cannot get a passport now; Fritz has been here twenty years, and never back; he has lost his German nationality, sir; they do not want people like us, you know.'

Michael stivered up his hair.

'Where are you from yourself?'

'From Salzburg.'

'What about going back there?'

'I would like to, but what would we do? In Austria everyone is poor now, and I have no relative left. Here at least we have my sewing.'

'How much is that a week?'

'Sometimes a pound; sometimes fifteen shillings. It is bread and the rent.'

'Don't you get the dole?'

'No, sir. We are not registered.'

Michael took out a five-pound note and laid it with his card on the washstand. 'I've got to think this over, Mrs Bergfeld. Perhaps your husband will come and see me.' He went out quickly, for the ghostly woman had flushed pink.

Repassing through the curtained aperture, he caught the hairdresser wiping out the basin.

'Find 'em, sir?'

'The lady.'

'Ah! Seen better days, I should say. The 'usband's a queer customer; 'alf off his nut. Wanted to come in here with me, but I've got to give this job up.'

'Oh! How's that?'

'I've got to have fresh air – only got one lung, and that's not very gaudy. I'll have to find something else.'

'That's bad, in these days.'

The hairdresser shrugged his bony shoulders. 'Ah!' he said. 'I've been a hairdresser from a boy, except for the war. Funny place this, to fetch up in after where I've been. The war knocked me out.' He twisted his little thin moustache.

'No pension?' said Michael.

'Not a bob. What I want to keep me alive is something in the open.'

Michael took him in from head to foot. Shadowy, narrow-headed, with one lung.

'But do you know anything about country life?'

'Not a blessed thing. Still, I've got to find something, or peg out.'

His tragic and knowing eyes searched Michael's face.

'I'm awfully sorry,' said Michael. 'Good-bye!'

The hairdresser made a queer jerky little movement.

Emerging from Sapper's Row into the crowded, roaring thoroughfare, Michael thought of a speech in a play he had seen a year or two before. 'The condition of the people leaves much to be desired. I shall make a point of taking up the cudgels in the House. I shall move–!' The condition of the people! What a remote thing! The sportive nightmare of a few dreaming nights, the skeleton in a well-locked cupboard, the discomforting rare howl of a hungry dog! And probably no folk in England less disturbed by it than the gallant six hundred odd who sat with him in 'that House'. For to improve the condition of the people was their job, and that relieved them of a sense of nightmare. Since Oliver Cromwell some sixteen thousand, perhaps, had sat there before them, to the same end. And was the trick done–not precisely! Still *they* were really working for it, and other people were only looking on and telling them how to do it!

Thus was he thinking when a voice said:

'Not got a job about you, sir?'

Michael quickened his steps, then stood still. He saw that the man who had spoken, having cast his eyes down again, had missed this sign of weakness; and he went back to him. They were black eyes in a face round and pasty like a mince-pie. Decent and shabby, quiet and forlorn, he wore an ex-Serviceman's badge.

'You spoke to me?' said Michael.

'I'm sure I don't know why, sir; it just hopped out of me.'

'No work?'

'No; and pretty low.'

'Married?'

'Widower, sir; two children.'

'Dole?'

'Yes; and fair sick of it.'

'In the war, I see?'

'Yes, Mespot.'

'What sort of a job do you want?'

'Any mortal thing.'

'Give me your name and address.'

'Henry Boddick, 4 Waltham Buildings, Gunnersbury.'

Michael took it down.

'Can't promise anything,' he said.

'No, sir.'

'Good luck, anyway. Have a cigar?'

'Thank you, and good luck to *you*, sir.'

Michael saluted, and resumed his progress; once out of sight of Henry Boddick, he took a taxi. A little more of this, and he would lose the sweet reasonableness without which one could not sit in 'that House'!

'For Sale or to Let' recorded recurrently in Portland Place, somewhat restored his sense of balance.

That same afternoon he took Francis Wilmot with him to the House, and leaving him at the foot of the Distinguished Strangers' stairway, made his way on to the floor.

He had never been in Ireland, so that the debate had for him little relation to reality. It seemed to illustrate, however, the obstacles in the way of agreement on any mortal subject. Almost every speech emphasised the paramount need for a settlement, but declared the impossibility of 'going back' on this, that, or the other factor which precluded such settlement. Still, for a debate on Ireland it seemed good-tempered; and presently they would all go out and record the votes they had determined on before it all began. He remembered the thrill with which he had listened to the first debates after his election; the impression each speech had given him that somebody must certainly be converted to something and the reluctance with which he had discovered that nobody ever was. Some force was at work far stronger than any eloquence, however striking or sincere. The clothes were washed elsewhere; in here they were but aired before being put on. Still, until people put thoughts into words, they didn't know what they thought, and sometimes they didn't know afterwards. And for the hundredth time Michael was seized by a weak feeling in his legs. In a few weeks he himself must rise on them. Would the House accord him its 'customary indulgence'! or would it say: 'Young fellow–teaching your grandmother to suck eggs–shut up!'

He looked around him.

His fellow members were sitting in all shapes. Chosen of the people, they confirmed the doctrine that human nature did not change, or so slowly that one could not see the process–he had seen their prototypes in Roman statues, in mediæval pictures. ... 'Plain but pleasant,' he thought, unconsciously reproducing George Forsyte's description of himself in his palmy days. But did they take themselves seriously, as under Burke, as under Gladstone even?

The words 'customary indulgence' roused him from reverie; for they meant a maiden speech. Ha! yes! the member for Cornmarket. He composed himself to listen. Delivering himself with restraint and clarity, the speaker seemed suggesting that the doctrine 'Do unto others as you would they should do unto you' need not be entirely neglected, even in Ireland; but it was long–too long–Michael watched the House grow restive. 'Alas! poor brother!' he thought, as the speaker somewhat hastily sat down. A very handsome man rose in his place. He congratulated his honourable friend on his able and well-delivered effort, he only regretted that it had nothing to do with the business in hand. Exactly! Michael slipped out. Recovering his 'distinguished stranger', he walked away with him to South Square.

Francis Wilmot was in a state of some enthusiasm.

'That was fine,' he said. 'Who was the gentleman under the curtains?'

'The Speaker?'

'No; I mean the one who didn't speak.'

'Exactly; he's the dignity of the House.'

'They ought to feed him oxygen; it must be sleepy under there. I liked the delegate who spoke last. He would "go" in America; he had big ideas.'

'The idealism which keeps you out of the League of Nations, eh?' said Michael with a grin.

Francis Wilmot turned his head rather sharply.

'Well,' he said, 'we're like any other people when it comes to bed-rock.'

'Quite so,' said Michael, 'idealism is just a by-product of geography–it's the haze that lies in the middle distance. The farther you are from bed-rock, the less quick you need to be to see it. We're twenty sea-miles more idealistic about the European situation than the French are. And you're three thousand sea-miles more idealistic than we are. But when it's a matter of niggers, we're three thousand sea-miles more idealistic than you; isn't that so?'

Francis Wilmot narrowed his dark eyes.

'It is,' he said. 'The farther North we go in the States, the more idealistic we get about the negro. Anne and I've lived all our life with darkies, and never had trouble; we love them, and they love us; but I wouldn't trust myself not to join in lynching one that laid his hands on her. I've talked that over many times with Jon. He doesn't see it that way; he says a darky should be tried like a white man; but he doesn't know the real South. His mind is still three thousand sea-miles away.'

Michael was silent. Something within him always closed up at mention of a name which he still spelt mentally with an 'h'.

Francis Wilmot added ruminatively: 'There are a few saints in every country proof against your theory; but the rest of us, I reckon, aren't above human nature.'

'Talking of human nature,' said Michael, 'here's my father-in-law!'

6

SOAMES KEEPS HIS EYES OPEN

Soames, having prolonged his week-end visit, had been spending the afternoon at the Zoological Gardens, removing his great-nephews, the little Cardigans from the too close proximity of monkeys and cats. After standing them once more in Imogen's hall, he had roosted at his Club till, idly turning his evening paper, he had come on this paragraph, in the 'Chiff-chaff' column:

'A surprise for the coming Session is being confectioned at the Wednesday gatherings of a young hostess not a hundred yards from Westminster. Her husband, a prospective baronet lately connected with literature, is to be entrusted with the launching in Parliament of a policy which enjoys the peculiar label of Foggartism, derived from Sir James Foggart's book called *The Parlous State of England*. This amusing alarum is attributed to the somewhat fantastic brain which guides a well-known weekly. We shall see what comes of it. In the meantime the enterprising little lady in question is losing no chance of building up her "salon" on the curiosity which ever surrounds any buccaneering in politics.'

Soames rubbed his eyes; then read it again with rising anger. 'Enterprising little lady is losing no chance of building up her "salon".' Who had written that? He put the paper in his pocket—almost the first theft he had ever committed—and all the way across St James's Park in the gathering twilight he brooded on that anonymous paragraph. The allusion seemed to him unmistakable, and malicious into the bargain. 'Lion-hunter' would not have been plainer. Unfortunately, in a primary sense 'lion-hunter' was a compliment, and Soames doubted whether its secondary sense had ever been 'laid down' as libellous. He was still brooding deeply, when the young men ranged alongside.

'Well, sir?'

'Ah!' said Soames. 'I want to speak to you. You've got a traitor in the camp.' And without meaning to at all, he looked angrily at Francis Wilmot.

'Now, sir?' said Michael, when they were in his study.

Soames held out the folded paper.

Michael read the paragraph and made a face.

'Whoever wrote that comes to your evenings,' said Soames; 'that's clear. Who is he?'

'Very likely a she.'

'D'you mean to say they print such things by women?'

Michael did not answer. Old Forsyte was behind the times.

'Will they tell me who it is, if I go down to them?' asked Soames.

'No, fortunately.'

'How d'you mean "fortunately"?'

'Well, sir, the Press is a sensitive plant. I'm afraid you might make it curl up. Besides, it's always saying nice things that aren't deserved.'

'But this—' began Soames; he stopped in time, and substituted: 'Do you mean that we've got to sit down under it?'

'To lie down, I'm afraid.'

'Fleur has an evening to-morrow.'

'Yes.'

'I shall stay up for it, and keep my eyes open.'

Michael had a vision of his father-in-law, like a plain clothes man in the neighbourhood of wedding-presents.

But in spite of assumed levity, Michael had been hit. The knowledge that his adored one had the collector's habit, and flitted, alluring, among the profitable, had, so far, caused him only indulgent wonder. But now it seemed more than an amusing foible. The swiftness with which she turned her smile off and on as though controlled by a switch under her shingled hair; the quick turns of her neck, so charming and exposed; the clever roving, disguised so well but not quite well enough, of the pretty eyes; the droop and flutter of their white lids; the expressive hands grasping, if one could so call such slim and dainty apprehensions, her career—all this suddenly caused Michael pain. Still she was doing it for him and Kit! French women, they said, co-operated with their husbands in the family career. It was the French blood in her. Or perhaps just idealism, the desire to have and be the best of whatever bunch there was about! Thus Michael, loyally. But his uneasy eyes roved from face to face of the Wednesday gathering, trying to detect signs of quizzicality.

Soames followed another method. His mind, indeed, was uncomplicated by the currents awash in that of one who goes to bed with the object of his criticism. For him there was no reason why Fleur should not know as many aristocrats, Labour members, painters, ambassadors, young fools, even writing fellows, as might flutter her fancy. The higher up they were, the less likely, he thought with a certain naïveté, they would be to borrow money or get her into a mess. His daughter was as good or better than any of them, and his deep pride was stung to the quick by the notion that people should think she had to claw and scrape to get them round her. It was not she who was after them, but they who were after her! Standing under the Fragonard which he had given her, grizzled, neatly moustached, close-faced, chinny, with a gaze concentrated on nothing in particular, as of one who has looked over much and found little in it, he might have been one of her ambassadors.

A young woman, with red-gold hair, about an inch long on her de-shingled neck, came and stood with her back to him, beside a soft man, who kept washing his hands. Soames could hear every word of their talk.

'Isn't the little Mont amusing? Look at her now, with "Don Fernando"—

you'd think he was her only joy. Ah! There's young Bashly! Off she goes.
She's a born little snob. But that doesn't make this a "salon", as she thinks.
To found a "salon" you want personality, and wit, and the "don't care a
damn" spirit. She hasn't got a scrap. Besides, who is she?'

'Money?' said the soft man.

'Not so very much. Michael's such dead nuts on her that he's getting dull;
though it's partly Parliament, of course. Have you heard them talk this
Foggartism? All food, children, and the future–the very dregs of dullness.'

'Novelty,' purred the soft man, 'is the vice of our age.'

'One resents a nobody like her climbing in on piffle like this Foggartism. Did
you read the book?'

'Hardly. Did you?'

'No jolly fear! I'm sorry for Michael. He's being exploited by that little snob.'

Penned without an outlet, Soames had begun breathing hard. Feeling a
draught, perhaps, the young woman turned to encounter a pair of eyes so grey,
so cold, in a face so concentrated, that she moved away. 'Who was that old
buffer?' she asked of the soft man; 'he gave me "the jim-jams".'

The soft man thought it might be a poor relation–he didn't seem to know
anybody.

But Soames had already gone across to Michael.

'Who's the young woman with the red hair?'

'Marjorie Ferrar.'

'She's the traitress–turn her out!'

Michael stared.

'But we know her quite well–she's a daughter of Lord Charles Ferrar, and–'

'Turn her out!' said Soames again.

'How do you know that she's the traitress, sir?'

'I've just heard her use the very words of that paragraph, and worse.'

'But she's our guest.'

'Pretty guest!' growled Soames through his teeth.

'One can't turn a guest out. Besides, she's the granddaughter of a
marquess and the pet of the Panjoys–it would make the deuce of a scandal.'

'Make it, then!'

'We won't ask her again; but really, that's all one can do.'

'Is it?' said Soames; and walking past his son-in-law, he went towards the
object of his denunciation. Michael followed, much perturbed. He had never
yet seen his father-in-law with his teeth bared. He arrived in time to hear him
say in a low but quite audible voice:

'You were good enough, madam, to call my daughter a snob in her own
house.'

Michael saw the de-shingled neck turn and rear, the hard blue eyes stare with
a sort of outraged impudence; he heard her laugh, then Soames saying:

'You are a traitress; be so kind as to withdraw.'

Of the half-dozen people round, not a soul was missing it! Oh, hell! And he
the master of the house! Stepping forward, he put his arm through that of
Soames:

'That'll do, sir,' he said, quietly; 'this is not a Peace Conference.'

There was a horrid hush; and in all the group only the soft man's white
hands, washing each other, moved.

Marjorie Ferrar took a step towards the door.

'I don't know who this person is,' she said; 'but he's a liar.'

'I reckon not.'

At the edge of the little group was a dark young man. His eyes were fixed on Marjorie Ferrar's, whose eyes in turn were fixed on his.

And suddenly, Michael saw Fleur, very pale, standing just behind him. She must have heard it all! She smiled, waved her hand, and said:

'Madame Carelli's going to play.'

Marjorie Ferrar walked on towards the door, and the soft man followed her, still washing those hands, as if trying to rid them of the incident. Soames, like a slow dog making sure, walked after them; Michael walked after him. The words 'How amusing!' floated back, and a soft echoing snigger. Slam! Both outer door and incident were closed.

Michael wiped his forehead. One half of the brain behind admired his father-in-law; the other thought: 'Well, the old man *has* gone and done it!' He went back into the drawing-room. Fleur was standing near the clavichord, as if nothing had happened. But Michael could see her fingers crisping at her dress; and his heart felt sore. He waited, quivering, for the last chord.

Soames had gone upstairs. Before 'The White Monkey' in Michael's study, he reviewed his own conduct. He regretted nothing. Red-headed cat! 'Born snob!' 'Money? Not very much.' Ha! 'A nobody like her!' Granddaughter of a marquess, was she? Well, he had shown the insolent baggage the door. All that was sturdy in his fibre, all that was acrid in his blood, all that resented patronage and privilege, the inherited spirit of his forefathers, moved within him. Who were the aristocracy, to give themselves airs? Jackanapes! Half of 'em descendants of those who had got what they had by robbery or jobbery! That one should call his daughter, *his* daughter, a snob! He wouldn't lift a finger, wouldn't cross a road, to meet the Duke of Seven Dials himself! If Fleur like to amuse herself by having people round her, why shouldn't she? His blood ran suddenly a little cold. Would she say that he had spoiled her 'salon'? Well! He couldn't help it if she did; better to have had the thing out, and got rid of that cat, and know where they all were. 'I shan't wait up for her,' he thought. 'Storm in a tea-cup!'

The thin strumming of the clavichord came up to him out on the landing, waiting to climb to his room. He wondered if these evenings woke the baby. A gruff sound at his feet made him jump. That dog lying outside the baby's door! He wished the little beggar had been downstairs just now—he would have known how to put his teeth through that red-haired cat's nude stockings. He passed on up, looking at Francis Wilmot's door, which was opposite his own.

That young American chap must have overheard something too; but he shouldn't allude to the matter with him; not dignified. And, shutting his door on the strumming of the clavichord, Soames closed his eyes again as best he could.

7

SOUNDS IN THE NIGHT

Michael had never heard Fleur cry, and to see her, flung down across the bed, smothering her sobs in the quilt, gave him a feeling akin to panic. She stopped at his touch on her hair, and lay still.

'Buck up, darling!' he said gently. 'If you aren't one, what does it matter?'

She struggled up, and sat cross-legged, her flushed face smudged with tears, her hair disordered.

'Who cares what one is? It's what one's labelled.'

'Well, we've labelled her "Traitress".'

'As if that made it better! We all talk behind people's backs. Who minds that? But how can I go on when everybody is sniggering and thinking me a lion-hunting snob? She'll cry it all over London in revenge. How can I have any more evenings?'

Was it for her career, or his, that she was sorrowing? Michael went round to the other side of the bed and put his arms about her from behind.

'Never mind what people think, my child. Sooner or later one's got to face that, anyway.'

'It's you who aren't facing it. If I'm not thought nice, I can't *be* nice.'

'Only the people who really know one matter.'

'Nobody knows me,' said Fleur sullenly. 'The fonder they are, the less they know, and the less it matters what they think.'

Michael withdrew his arms.

She sat silent for so long that he went back to the other side of the bed to see if he could tell anything from her face resting moodily on her hands. The grace of her body thus cramped was such that his senses ached. And since caresses would only worry her, he ached the more.

'I hate her,' she said at last; 'and if I can hurt her, I will.'

He would have liked to hurt the 'pet of the Panjoys' himself, but it did not console him to hear Fleur utter that sentiment; it meant more from her than from himself, who, when it came to the point, was a poor hand at hurting people.

'Well, darling,' he said, 'shall we sleep on it?'

'I said I wouldn't have any more evenings; but I shall.'

'Good!' said Michael; 'that's the spirit.'

She laughed. It was a funny hard little sound in the night. And with it Michael had to remain discontented.

All through the house it was a wakeful night. Soames had the three o'clock tremors, which cigars and the fresh air wherein he was obliged to play his golf had subdued for some time past. He was disturbed, too, by that confounded great clock from hour to hour, and by a stealthy noise between three and four, as of someone at large in the house.

This was, in fact, Francis Wilmot. Ever since his impulsive denial that Soames was a liar, the young man had been in a peculiar state of mind. As Soames surmised, he too had overheard Marjorie Ferrar slandering her hostess; but in the very moment of his refutation, like Saul setting forth to attack the Christians, he had been smitten by blindness. Those blue eyes, pouring into his the light of defiance, had finished with a gleam which seemed to say: 'Young man, you please me!' And it haunted him. That lissome nymph—with her white skin and red-gold hair, her blue eyes full of insolence, her red lips full of joy, her white neck fragrant as a pinewood in sunshine—the vision was abiding. He had been watching her all through the evening; but it was uncanny the way she had left her image on his senses in that one long moment, so that now he got no sleep. Though he had not been introduced, he knew her name to be Marjorie Ferrar, and he thought it 'fine'. Countryman that he was and with little knowledge of women—she was unlike any woman he had known. And he had given her the lie direct! This made him so restless that he drank the contents of his water-bottle, put on his clothes, and stole downstairs. Passing the Dandie, who stirred as though muttering: 'Unusual! But I know those legs!' he reached the hall, where a milky glimmer came in through the fanlight. Lighting a cigarette, he sat down on the marble coat-sarcophagus. It cooled his anatomy, so that he got off it, turned up the light, saw a telephone directory resting beside him, and mechanically sought the letter 'F'. There she was! 'Ferrar, Marjorie, 3, River Studios, Wren Street.' Switching off the light, he slipped back the door-chain and stole out. He knew his way to the river, and went towards it.

It was the hour when sound, exhausted, has laid its head on the pillow, and one can hear a moth pass. London, in clear air, with no smoke going up, slept beneath the moon. Bridges, towers, water, all silvered, had a look as if withdrawn from man. Even the houses and the trees enjoyed their moony hour apart, and seemed to breathe out with Francis Wilmot a stanza from 'The Ancient Mariner':

> 'O Sleep, it is a gentle thing,
> Beloved from pole to pole!
> To Mary Queen the praise be given,
> She sent the gentle sleep from heaven
> That slid into my soul!'

He turned at random to the right along the river. Never in his life had he walked through a great city at the dead hour. Not a passion alive, nor a thought of gain; haste asleep, and terrors dreaming; here and there, no doubt, one turning on his bed; perhaps a soul passing. Down on the water lighters and barges lay shadowy and abandoned, with red lights burning; the lamps along the Embankment shone without purpose, as if they had been freed. Man was away. In the whole town only himself up and doing–what? Natively shrewd and resourceful in all active situations, the young Southerner had little power of diagnosis, and certainly did not consider himself ridiculous wandering about like this at night, not even when he suddenly felt that if he could 'locate' her windows, he could go home and sleep. He passed the Tate Gallery and saw a human being with moonlit buttons.

'Pardon me, officer,' he said, 'but where is Wren Street?'

'Straight on and fifth to the right.'

Francis Wilmot resumed his march. The 'moving' moon was heeling down, the stars were gaining light, the trees had begun to shiver. He found the fifth turning, walked down 'the block', and was no wiser; it was too dark to read names or numbers. He passed another buttoned human effigy and said:

'Pardon me, officer, but where are River Studios?'

'Comin' away from them; last house on the right.'

Francis Wilmot retraced his steps. There it was, then–by itself, back from the street. He stood before it and gazed at dark windows. She might be behind any one of them! Well! He had 'located' her, and, in the rising wind, he turned and walked home. He went upstairs stealthily as he had come down, past the Dandie, who again raised his head, muttered: 'Still more unusual, but the same legs!' entered his room, lay down, and fell asleep like a baby.

8

ROUND AND ABOUT

General reticence at breakfast concerning the incident of the night before, made little impression on Soames, because the young American was present, before whom, naturally, one would not discuss it; but he noted that Fleur was pale. In his early-morning vigil legal misgivings had assailed him. Could one call even a red-haired baggage 'traitress' in the hearing of some half-dozen persons with impunity? He went off to his sister Winifred's after breakfast, and told her the whole story.

'Quite right, my dear boy,' was her comment. 'They tell me that young woman is as fast as they're made. Her father, you know, owned the horse that didn't beat the French horse—I never can remember its name—in that race, the Something Stakes, at—dear me! what was the meeting?'

'I know nothing about racing,' said Soames.

But that afternoon at the Connoisseurs' Club a card was brought to him:

LORD CHARLES FERRAR

High Marshes,
Nr. Newmarket.   Burton's Club.

For a moment his knees felt a little weak; but the word 'snob' coming to his assistance, he said dryly: 'Show him into the strangers' room.' He was not going to hurry himself for this fellow, and finished his tea before repairing to that forlorn corner.

A tallish man was standing in the middle of the little room, thin and upright, with a moustache brushed arrogantly off his lips, and a single eye-glass which seemed to have grown over the right eye, so unaided was it. There were corrugations in his thin weathered cheeks, and in his thick hair flecked at the sides with grey. Soames had no difficulty in disliking him at sight.

'Mr Forsyte, I believe?'

Soames inclined his head.

'You made use of an insulting word to my daughter last night in the presence of several people.'

'Yes; it was richly deserved.'

'You were not drunk, then?'

'Not at all,' said Soames.

His dry precision seemed to disconcert the visitor, who twisted his moustache, frowned his eyeglass closer to his eye, and said:

'I have the names of those who overheard it. You will be good enough to write to each of them separately, withdrawing your expression unreservedly.'

'I shall do nothing of the kind.'

A moment's silence ensued.

'You are an attorney, I believe?'

'A solicitor.'

'Then you know the consequences of refusal.'

'If your daughter likes to go into Court, I shall be happy to meet her there.'

'You refuse to withdraw?'

'Absolutely.'

'Good-evening, then!'

'Good-evening!'

For two pins he would have walked round the fellow, the bristles rising on his back, but, instead, he stood a little to one side to let him out. Insolent brute! He could so easily hear again the voice of old Uncle Jolyon, characterising some person of the 'eighties as 'a pettifogging little attorney'. And he felt that, somehow or other, he must relieve his mind. 'Old Mont' would know about this fellow–he would go across and ask him.

At 'The Aeroplane' he found not only Sir Lawrence Mont, looking almost grave, but Michael, who had evidently been detailing to his father last evening's incident. This was a relief to Soames, who felt the insults to his daughter too bitterly to talk of them. Describing the visit he had just received, he ended with the words:

'This fellow–Ferrar–what's his standing?'

'Charlie Ferrar? He owes money everywhere, has some useful horses, and is a very good shot.'

'He didn't strike me as a gentleman,' said Soames.

Sir Lawrence cocked his eyebrow, as if debating whether he ought to answer this remark about one who had ancestors, from one who had none.

'And his daughter,' said Soames, 'isn't a lady.'

Sir Lawrence wagged his head.

'Single-minded, Forsyte, single-minded; but you're right; there's a queer streak in that blood. Old Shropshire's a dear old man; it skipped his generation, but it's there–it's there. His aunt–'

'He called me an attorney,' said Soames with a grim smile, 'and she called me a liar. I don't know which is worse.'

Sir Lawrence got up and looked into St James's Street. Soames had the feeling that the narrow head perched up on that straight thin back counted for more than his own, in this affair. One was dealing here with people who said and did what they liked and damned the consequences; this baronet chap had been brought up in that way himself, no doubt, he ought to know how their minds worked.

Sir Lawrence turned.

'She may bring an action, Forsyte; it was very public. What evidence have you?'

'My own ears.'

Sir Lawrence looked at the ears, as if to gauge their length.

'M'm! Anything else?'

'That paragraph.'

'She'll get at the paper. Yes?'

'The man she was talking to.'

Michael ejaculated: 'Philip Quinsey–put not your trust in Gath!'

'What more?'

'Well,' said Soames, 'there's what that young American overheard, whatever it was.'

'Ah!' said Sir Lawrence: 'Take care she doesn't get at *him*. Is that all?'

Soames nodded. It didn't seem much, now he came to think of it!

'You say she called you a liar. How would it be to take the offensive?'

There was a silence; then Soames said: 'Women? No!'

'Quite right, Forsyte! They have their privileges still. There's nothing for it but to wait and see how the cat jumps. Traitress! I suppose you know how much the word costs?'

'The cost,' said Soames, 'is nothing; it's the publicity!'

His imagination was playing streets ahead of him. He saw himself already in 'the box', retailing the spiteful purring of that cat, casting forth to the public and the papers the word 'snob', of his own daughter; for if he didn't, he would have no defence. Too painful!

'What does Fleur say?' he asked, suddenly, of Michael.

'War to the knife.'

Soames jumped in his chair.

'Ah!' he said: 'That's a woman all over—no imagination!'

'That's what I thought at first, sir, but I'm not so sure. She says if Marjorie Ferrar is not taken by the short hairs, she'll put it across everybody—and that the more public the thing is, the less harm she can do.'

'I think,' said Sir Lawrence, coming back to his chair, 'I'll go and see old Shropshire. My father and his shot woodcock together in Albania in 'fifty-four.'

Soames could not see the connection, but did not snub the proposal. A marquess was a sort of gone-off duke; even in this democratic age, he would have some influence, one supposed.

'He's eighty,' went on Sir Lawrence, 'and gets gout in the stomach, but he's as brisk as a bee.'

Soames could not be sure whether it was a comfort.

'The grass shall not grow, Forsyte. I'll go there now.'

They parted in the street, Sir Lawrence moving north—towards Mayfair.

The Marquess of Shropshire was dictating to his secretary a letter to his County Council, urging on them an item of his lifelong programme for the electrification of everything. One of the very first to take up electricity, he had remained faithful to it all his brisk and optimistic days. A short, bird-like old man, in shaggy Lovat tweeds, with a blue tie of knitted silk passed through a ring, bright cheeks and well-trimmed white beard and moustache, he was standing in his favourite attitude, with one foot on a chair, his elbow on his knee, and his chin on his hand.

'Ah! young Mont!' he said: 'Sit down.'

Sir Lawrence took a chair, crossed his knees, and threaded his finger-tips. He found it pleasing to be called 'young Mont', at sixty-six or so.

'Have you brought me another of your excellent books?'

'No, Marquess; I've come for your advice.'

'Ah! Go on, Mr Mersey: "In this way, gentlemen, you will save at least three thousand a year to your ratepayers; confer a blessing on the countryside by abolishing the smoke of four filthy chimneys; and make me your obliged servant,

SHROPSHIRE."

Thank you, Mr Mersey. Now, my dear young Mont?'

Having watched the back of the secretary till it vanished, and noted the old peer pivoting his bright eyes, with their expression of one who means to see more every day, on his visitor, Sir Lawrence took his eyeglass between thumb and finger, and said:

'Your granddaughter, sir, and my daughter-in-law want to fight like billy-o.'

'Marjorie?' said the old man, and his head fell to one side like a bird's. 'I draw the line–a charming young woman to look at, but I draw the line. What has she done now?'

'Called my daughter-in-law a snob and a lion-hunter; and my daughter-in-law's father has called your granddaughter a traitress to her face.'

'Bold man,' said the Marquess; 'bold man! Who is he?'

'His name is Forsyte.'

'Forsyte?' repeated the old peer; 'Forsyte? The name's familiar–now where would that be? Ah! Forsyte and Treffry–the big tea men. My father had his tea from them direct–real caravan; no such tea now. Is that the–?'

'Some relation, perhaps. This man is a solicitor–retired; chiefly renowned for his pictures. A man of some substance, and probity.'

'Indeed! And *is* his daughter a–a lion-hunter?'

Sir Lawrence smiled.

'She's a charmer. Likes to have people about her. Very pretty. Excellent little mother; some French blood.'

'Ah!' said the Marquess: 'the French! Better built round the middle than our people. What do you want me to do?'

'Speak to your son Charles.'

The old man took his foot off the chair, and stood nearly upright. His head moved sideways with a slight continuous motion.

'I never speak to Charlie,' he said gravely. 'We haven't spoken for six years.'

'I beg your pardon, sir. Didn't know. Sorry to have bothered you.'

'No, no; pleasure to see you. If I run across Marjorie, I'll see–I'll see. But, my dear Mont, what shall we do with these young women–no sense of service; no continuity; no hair; no figures? By the way, do you know this Power Scheme on the Severn?' He held up a pamphlet: 'I've been at them to do it for years. My Colliery among others could be made to pay with electricity; but they won't move. We want some Americans over here.'

Sir Lawrence had risen; the old man's sense of service had so clearly taken the bit between its teeth again. He held out his hand.

'Good-bye, Marquess; delighted to see you looking so well.'

'Good-bye, my dear young Mont; command me at any time, and let me have another of your nice books.'

They shook hands; and from the Lovat clothes was disengaged a strong whiff of peat. Sir Lawrence, looking back, saw the old man back in his favourite attitude, foot on chair and chin on hand, already reading the pamphlet. 'Some boy!' he thought; 'as Michael would say. But what has Charlie Ferrar done not be spoken to for six years? Old Forsyte ought to know. . . .'

In the meantime 'Old Forsyte' and Michael were walking homewards across St James's Park.

'That young American,' said Soames; 'what do you suppose made him put his oar in?'

'I don't know, sir; and I don't like to ask.'

'Exactly,' said Soames, glumly. There was, indeed, something repulsive to him in treating with an American over a matter of personal dignity.

'Do they use the word "snob" over there?'

'I'm not sure; but, in the States to hunt lions is a form of idealism. They want to associate with what they think better than themselves. It's rather fine.'

Soames did not agree; but found difficulty in explaining why. Not to recognise anyone as better than himself or his daughter had been a sort of guiding principle, and guiding principles were not talked about. In fact, it was so deep in him that he hadn't known of it.

'I shan't mention it,' he said, 'unless he does. What more can this young woman do? She's in a set, I suppose?'

'The Panjoys—'

'Panjoys!'

'Yes, sir; out for a good time at any cost—they don't really count, of course. But Marjorie Ferrar is frightfully in the limelight. She paints a bit; she's got some standing with the Press; she dances; she hunts; she's something of an actress; she goes everywhere week-ending. It's the week-ends that matter, where people have nothing to do but talk. Were you ever at a week-end party, sir?'

'I?' said Soames: 'Good Lord—no!'

Michael smiled—incongruity, indeed, could go no farther.

'We must get one up for you at Lippinghall.'

'No, thank you.'

'You're right, sir; nothing more boring. But they're the *coulisses* of politics. Fleur thinks they're good for me. And Marjorie Ferrar knows all the people we know, and lots more. It *is* awkward.'

'I should go on as if nothing had happened,' said Soames. 'But about that paper? They ought to be warned that this woman is venomous.'

Michael regarded his father-in-law quizzically.

On entering, they found the manservant in the hall.

'There's a man to see you, sir, by the name of Bugfill.'

'Oh! Ah! Where have you put him, Coaker?'

'Well, I didn't know what to make of him, sir, he shakes all over. I've stood him in the dining-room.'

'Excuse me, sir,' said Michael.

Soames passed into the 'parlour', where he found his daughter and Francis Wilmot.

'Mr Wilmot is leaving us, Father. You're just in time to say good-bye.'

If there were moments when Soames felt cordial, they were such as these. He had nothing against the young man; indeed, he rather liked the look of him; but to see the last of almost anybody was in a sense a relief; besides, there was this question of what he had overheard, and to have him about the place without knowing would be a continual temptation to compromise with one's dignity and ask him what it was.

'Good-bye, Mr Wilmot,' he said, 'if you're interested in pictures—' he paused, and, holding out his hand, added, 'you should look in at the British Museum.'

Francis Wilmot shook the hand deferentially.

'I will. It's been a privilege to know you, sir.'

Soames was wondering why, when the young man turned to Fleur.

'I'll be writing to Jon from Paris, and I'll surely send your love. You've been perfectly wonderful to me. I'll be glad to have you and Michael visit me at any time you come across to the States; and if you bring the little dog, why—I'll just be honoured to let him bite me again.'

He bowed over Fleur's hand, and was gone, leaving Soames staring at the back of his daughter's neck.

'That's rather sudden,' he said, when the door was closed; 'anything upset him?'

She turned on him, and said coldly:

'Why did you make that fuss last night, Father?'

The injustice of her attack was so palpable, that Soames bit his moustache in silence. As if he could help himself, when she was insulted in his hearing!

'What good do you think you've done?'

Soames, who had no notion, made no attempt to enlighten her. He only felt sore inside.

'You've made me feel as if I couldn't look anybody in the face. But I'm going to, all the same. If I'm a lion-hunter and a snob, I'll do it thoroughly. Only I do wish you wouldn't go on thinking I'm a child and can't defend myself.'

And still Soames was silent, sore to the soles of his boots.

Fleur flashed a look at him, and said:

'I'm sorry, but I can't help it; everything's queered;' and she too went out of the room.

Soames moved blindly to the window and stood looking out. He saw a cab with luggage drive away; saw some pigeons alight, peck at the pavement, and fly off again; he saw a man kissing a woman in the dusk; a policeman light his pipe and go off duty. He saw many human and interesting things; he heard Big Ben chime. Nothing in it all! He was staring at a silver spoon. He himself had put it in her mouth at birth.

9

POULTRY AND CATS

He who had been stood in the dining-room, under the name of Bugfill, was still upright. Rather older than Michael, with an inclination to side-whisker, darkish hair, and a pale face stamped with that look of schooled quickness common to so many actors but unfamiliar to Michael, he was grasping the edge of the dining-table with one hand, and a wide-brimmed black hat with the other. The expression of his large, dark-circled eyes was such that Michael smiled and said:

'It's all right, Mr Bergfeld, I'm not a manager. Do sit down, and smoke.'

The visitor silently took the proffered chair and cigarette with an attempt at a fixed smile. Michael sat on the table.

'I gather from Mrs Bergfeld that you're on the rocks.'

'Fast,' said the shaking lips.

'Your health, and your name, I suppose?'

'Yes.'

'You want an open-air job, I believe? I haven't been able to think of anything very gaudy, but an idea did strike me last night in the stilly watches. How about raising poultry–everybody's doing it.'

'If I had my savings.'

'Yes, Mrs Bergfeld told me about them. I can inquire but I'm afraid–'

'It's robbery.' The chattered sound let Michael at once into the confidence of the many managers who had refused to employ him who uttered it.

'I know,' he said, soothingly, 'robbing Peter to pay Paul. That clause in the Treaty was a bit of rank barbarism, of course, camouflage it as they like. Still, it's no good to let it prey on your mind, is it?'

But his visitor had risen. 'To take from civilian to pay civilian! Then why not take civilian life for civilian life? What is the difference? And England does it—the leading nation to respect the individual. It is abominable.'

Michael began to feel that he was overdoing it.

'You forget,' he said, 'that the war made us all into barbarians, for the time being; we haven't quite got over it yet. And *your* country dropped the spark into the powder magazine, you know. But what about this poultry stunt?'

Bergfeld seemed to make a violent effort to control himself.

'For my wife's sake,' he said, 'I will do anything; but unless I get my savings back, how can I start?'

'I can't promise; but perhaps I could start you. That hairdresser below you wants an open-air job, too. What's his name, by the way?'

'Swain.'

'How do you get on with him?'

'He is an opinionated man, but we are good friends enough.'

Michael got off the table. 'Well, leave it to me to think it out. We shall be able to do something, I hope;' and he held out his hand.

Bergfeld took it silently, and his eyes resumed the expression with which they had first looked at Michael.

'That man,' thought Michael, 'will be committing suicide some day, if he doesn't look out.' And he showed him to the door. He stood there some minutes gazing after the German actor's vanishing form, with a feeling as if the dust were formed out of the dark stories of such as he and the hairdresser and the man who had whispered to him to stand and deliver a job. Well, Bart must lend him that bit of land beyond the coppice at Lippinghall. He would buy a war hut if there were any left and some poultry stock, and start a colony—the Bergfelds, the hairdresser, and Henry Boddick. They could cut the timber in the coppice, and put up the fowl-houses for themselves. It would be growing food—a practical experiment in Foggartism! Fleur would laugh at him. But was there anything one could do nowadays that somebody couldn't laugh at? He turned back into the house. Fleur was in the hall.

'Francis Wilmot has gone,' she said.

'Why?'

'He's off to Paris.'

'What was it he overheard last night?'

'Do you suppose I asked?'

'Well, no,' said Michael, humbly. 'Let's go up and look at Kit, it's about his bath time.'

The eleventh baronet, indeed, was already in his bath.

'All right, nurse,' said Fleur, 'I'll finish him.'

'He's been in three minutes, ma'am.'

'Lightly boiled,' said Michael.

For one aged only fourteen months this naked infant had incredible vigour—from lips to feet he was all sound and motion. He seemed to lend a meaning to life. His vitality was absolute, not relative. His kicks and crows and splashings had the joy of a gnat's dance, or a jackdaw's gambols in the air. He gave thanks not for what he was about to receive, but for what he was receiving. White as a turtle-dove, with pink toes, darker in eyes and hair than he would be presently, he grabbed at the soap, at his mother, at the bath-towelling–he seemed only to need a tail. Michael watched him, musing. This manikin, born with all that he could possibly wish for within his reach–how were they to bring him up? Were they fit to bring him up, they who had been born–like all their generation in the richer classes–emancipated, to parents properly broken-in to worship the fetich–Liberty? Born to everything they wanted, so that they were at wits' end to invent something they could not get; driven to restive searching by having their own way? The war had deprived one of one's own way, but the war had overdone it, and left one grasping at licence. And for those, like Fleur, born a little late for the war, the tale of it had only lowered what respect they could have for anything. With veneration killed, and self-denial 'off', with atavism buried, sentiment derided, and the future in the air, hardly a wonder that modernity should be a dance of gnats, taking itself damned seriously! Such were the reflections of Michael, sitting there above the steam, and frowning at his progeny. Without faith was one fit to be a parent? Well, people were looking for faith again. Only they were bound to hatch the egg of it so hard that it would be addled long before it was a chicken. 'Too self-conscious!' he thought. 'That's our trouble!'

Fleur had finished drying the eleventh baronet, and was dabbing powder over him; her eyes seemed penetrating his skin, as if to gauge the state of health behind it. He watched her take the feet and hands one by one and examine each nail, lost in her scrutiny, unselfconscious in her momentary devotion! And oppressed by the difficulty, as a Member of Parliament, of being devoted, Michael snapped his fingers at the baby and left the nursery. He went to his study and took down a volume of the Encyclopædia Britannica containing the word Poultry. He read about Leghorns, Orpingtons, White Sussex, Bramaputras, and was little the wiser. He remembered that if you drew a chalk-line to the beak of a hen, the hen thought it was tied up. He wished somebody would draw a chalk-line to his beak. Was Foggartism a chalk-line? A voice said:

'Tell Fleur I'm going to her aunt's.'

'Leaving us, sir?'

'Yes, I'm not wanted.'

What had happened?

'You'll see her before you go, sir?'

'No,' said Soames.

Had somebody rubbed out the chalk-line to Old Forsyte's nose?

'Is there any money in poultry-farming, sir?'

'There's no money in anything nowadays.'

'And yet the Income Tax returns continue to rise.'

'Yes,' said Soames; 'there's something wrong there.'

'You don't think people make their incomes out more than they are?'

Soames blinked. Pessimistic though he felt at the moment, he could not take quite that low view of human nature.

'You'd better see that Fleur doesn't go about abusing that red-haired baggage,' he said. 'She was born with a silver spoon in her mouth; she thinks she can do what she likes.' And he shut Michael in again.

Silver spoon in her mouth. How *à propos*! . . .

After putting her baby into its cot Fleur had gone to the marqueterie bureau in the little sanctuary that would have been called a boudoir in old days. She sat there brooding. How could her father have made it all glaringly public!

Couldn't he have seen that it was nothing so long as it was not public, but everything the moment it was. She longed to pour out her heart, and tell people her opinion of Marjorie Ferrar.

She wrote three letters—one to Lady Alison, and two to women in the group who had overheard it all last night. She concluded her third letter with the words: 'A woman like that, who pretends to be a friend and sneaks into one's house to sting one behind one's back, is a snake of the first water. How Society can stick her, I can't think; she hasn't a moral about her nor a decent impulse. As for her charm—Good Lord!' Yes! And there was Francis Wilmot! She had not said all she wanted to say to him.

'My Dear Francis,' she wrote:
    'I am sorry you have to run away like this. I wanted to thank you for standing up for me last night. Marjorie Ferrar is just about the limit. But in London society one doesn't pay attention to backbiting. It has been so jolly to know you. Don't forget us; and do come and see me again when you come back from Paris.
                                'Your very good friend,
                                        'Fleur Mont.'

In future she would have nothing but men at her evenings! But would they come if there were no women? And men like Philip Quinsey were just as snake-like. Besides, it would look as if she were really hurt. No! She would have to go on as before, just dropping people who were 'catty'. But who wasn't? Except Alison, and heavyweights like Mr Blythe, the minor Ambassadors, and three or four earnest politicians, she couldn't be sure about any of them. It was the thing to be 'catty'. They all scratched other people's backs, and their faces too when they weren't looking. Who in Society was exempt from scratches and who didn't scratch? Not to scratch a little was so dreadfully dull. She could not imagine a scratchless life except perhaps in Italy. Those Fra Angelico frescoes in the San Marco monastery! There was a man who did not scratch. St Francis talking to his birds, among his little flowers, with the sun and the moon and the stars for near relations. St Claire! St Fleur—little sister of St Francis! To be unworldly and quite good! To be one who lived to make other people happy! How new! How exciting, even—for about a week; and how dull afterwards! She drew aside the curtains and looked out into the Square. Two cats were standing in the light of a lamp—narrow, marvellously graceful, with their heads turned towards each other. Suddenly they began uttering horrible noises, and became all claws. Fleur dropped the curtain.

10

FRANCIS WILMOT REVERSES

About that moment Francis Wilmot sat down in the lounge of the Cosmopolis Hotel, and as suddenly sat up. In the middle of the parquet floor, sliding and lunging, backing and filling, twisting and turning in the arms of a man with a face like a mask, was she, to avoid whom, out of loyalty to Fleur and Michael, he had decided to go to Paris! Fate! For he could hardly know that she came there most afternoons during the dancing hours. She and her partner were easily the show couple; and, fond of dancing, Francis Wilmot knew he was looking at something special. When they stopped, quite close to him, he said in his soft drawl:

'That was beautiful.'

'How do you do, Mr Wilmot?'

Why! She knew his name! This was the moment to exhibit loyalty! But she had sunk into a chair next his.

'And so you thought me a traitress last night?'

'I did.'

'Why?'

'Because I heard you call your hostess a snob.'

Marjorie Ferrar uttered an amused sound.

'My dear young man, if one never called one's friends anything worse than that−! I didn't mean you to hear, or that poptious old person in the chin!'

'He was her father,' said Francis Wilmot, gravely. 'It hurt him.'

'Well! I'm sorry!'

A hand without a glove, warm but dry, was put into his. When it was withdrawn the whole of his hand and arm were tingling.

'Do you dance?'

'Yes, indeed, but I wouldn't presume to dance with you.'

'Oh! but you must.'

Francis Wilmot's head went round, and his body began going round too.

'You dance better than an Englishman, unless he's professional,' said her lips six inches from his own.

'I'm proud to hear you say so, ma'am.'

'Don't you know my name? or do you always call women ma'am? It's ever so pretty.'

'Certainly I know your name and where you live. I wasn't six yards from you this morning at four o'clock.'

'What were you doing there?'

'I just thought I'd like to be near you.'

Marjorie Ferrar said, as if to herself:

'The prettiest speech I ever heard. Come and have tea with me there tomorrow.'

Reversing, side-stepping, doing all he knew, Francis Wilmot said, slowly:

'I have to be in Paris.'

'Don't be afraid, I won't hurt you.'

'I'm not afraid, but−'

'Well, I shall expect you.' And transferring herself again to her mask-faced partner, she looked back at him over her shoulder.

Francis Wilmot wiped his brow. An astonishing experience, another blow to his preconception of a stiff and formal race! If he had not known she was the daughter of a lord, he would have thought her an American. Would she ask him to dance with her again? But she left the lounge without another glance.

An up-to-date young man, a typical young man, would have felt the more jaunty. But he was neither. Six months' training for the Air Service in 1918, one visit to New York, and a few trips to Charleston and Savannah, had left him still a countryman, with a tradition of good manners, work, and simple living. Women, of whom he had known few, were to him worthy of considerable respect. He judged them by his sister, or by the friends of his dead mother, in

Savannah, who were all of a certain age. A Northern lady on the boat had told
him that Southern girls measured life by the number of men they could attract;
she had given him an amusing take-off of a Southern girl. It had been a surprise
to this young Southerner. Anne was not like that; she had never had the chance
to be, anyway, having married at nineteen the first young man who had asked
her!

By the morning's post he received Fleur's little letter. 'Limit!' Limit of what?
He felt indignant. He did not go to Paris, and at four o'clock he was at Wren
Street.

In her studio Marjorie Ferrar, clad in a flax-blue overall, was scraping at a
picture with a little knife. An hour later he was her slave. Cruft's Dog Show, the
Beefeaters, the Derby–he could not even remember his desire to see them; he
only desired to see one English thing–Marjorie Ferrar. He hardly remembered
which way the river flowed, and by mere accident walked East instead of West.
Her hair, her eyes, her voice–he 'had fallen for her'! He knew himself for a fool,
and did not mind; farther man cannot go. She passed him in a little open car,
driving it herself, on her way to a rehearsal. She waved her hand. Blood rushed
to his heart and rushed away; he trembled and went pale. And, as the car
vanished, he felt lost, as if in a world of shadow, grey and dreary! Ah! There was
Parliament! And, near-by, the one spot in London where he could go and talk
of Marjorie Ferrar, and that was where she had misbehaved herself!
He itched to defend her from the charge of being 'the limit'. He could perceive
the inappropriateness of going back there to talk to Fleur of her enemy, but
anything was better than not talking of her. So, turning into South Square, he
rang the bell.

Fleur was in her 'parlour', if not precisely eating bread and honey, at least
having tea.

'Not in Paris? How nice! Tea?'

'I've had it,' said Francis Wilmot, colouring. 'I had it with *her*.'

Fleur stared.

'Oh!' she said, with a laugh. 'How interesting! Where did she pick you up?'

Without taking in the implication of the words, Francis Wilmot was
conscious of something deadly in them.

'She was at the *thé dansant* at my hotel yesterday. She's a wonderful dancer. I
think she's a wonderful person altogether; I'd like to have you tell me what you
mean by calling her "the limit"?'

'I'd like to have you tell me why this *volte face* since Wednesday night?'

Francis Wilmot smiled: 'You people have been ever so kind to me, and I want
you to be friends with her again. I'm sure she didn't mean what she said that
night.'

'Indeed! Did she tell you that?'

'Why–not exactly! She said she didn't mean us to hear them.'

'No?'

He looked at her smiling face, conscious perhaps of deep waters, but
youthfully, Americanly, unconscious of serious obstacle to his desire to smooth
things out.

'I just hate to think you two are out after each other. Won't you come and
meet her at my hotel, and shake hands?'

Fleur's eyes moved slowly over him from head to toe.

'You look as if you might have some French blood in you. Have you?'

'Yes. My grandmother was of French stock.'

'Well, I have more. The French, you know, don't forgive easily. And they don't persuade themselves into believing what they want to.'

Francis Wilmot rose, and spoke with a kind of masterfulness.

'You're going to tell me what you meant in your letter.'

'Am I! My dear young man, the limit of perfection, of course. Aren't you a living proof?'

Aware that he was being mocked, and mixed in his feelings, Francis Wilmot made for the door.

'Good-bye!' he said. 'I suppose you'll have no use for me in future.'

'Good-bye!' said Fleur.

He went out rueful, puzzled, lonelier even than when he went in. He was guideless, with no one to 'put him wise'! No directness and simplicity in this town. People did not say what they meant; and his goddess—as enigmatic and twisting as the rest! More so—more so—for what did the rest matter?

I I

SOAMES VISITS THE PRESS

Soames had gone off to his sister's in Green Street thoroughly upset. That Fleur should have a declared enemy, powerful in Society, filled him with uneasiness; that she should hold him accountable for it, seemed the more unjust, because, in fact, he was.

An evening spent under the calming influence of Winifred Dartie's common sense, and Turkish coffee, which, though 'liverish stuff', he always drank with relish, restored in him something of the feeling that it was a storm in a tea-cup.

'But that paper paragraph,' he said, 'sticks in my gizzard.'

'Very tiresome, Soames, the whole thing; but I shouldn't bother. People skim those 'chiff-chaff' little notes and forget them the next moment. They're just put in for fun.'

'Pretty sort of fun! That paper says it has a million readers.'

'There's no name mentioned.'

'These political people and whipper-snappers in Society all know each other,' said Soames.

'Yes, my dear boy,' said Winifred in her comfortable voice, so cosy, and above disturbance, 'but nobody takes anything seriously nowadays.'

She was sensible. He went up to bed in more cheerful mood.

But retirement from affairs had effected in Soames a deeper change that he was at all aware of. Lacking professional issues to anchor the faculty for worrying he had inherited from James Forsyte, he was inclined to pet any trouble that came along. The more he thought of that paragraph, the more he felt inclined for a friendly talk with the editor. If he could go to Fleur and say: 'I've made it all right with those fellows, anyway. There'll be no more of that sort of thing,' he would wipe out her vexation. If you couldn't make people in private think well of your daughter, you could surely check public expression of the opposite opinion.

Except that he did not like to get into them, Soames took on the whole a favourable view of 'the papers'. He read *The Times*; his father had read it before him, and he had been brought up on its crackle. It had news—more news for his money than he could get through. He respected its leading articles; and if its great supplements had at times appeared to him too much of a good thing, still it was a gentleman's paper. Annette and Winifred took the *Morning Post*. That also was a gentleman's paper, but it had bees in its bonnet. Bees in bonnets were respectable things, but personally Soames did not care for them. He knew little of the other papers except that those he saw about had bigger headlines and seemed cut into little bits. Of the Press as a whole he took the English view: It was an institution. It had its virtues and its vices—anyway, you had to put up with it.

About eleven o'clock he was walking towards Fleet Street.

At the office of the *Evening Sun* he handed in his card and asked to see the editor. After a moment's inspection of his top-hat, he was taken down a corridor and deposited in a small room. It seemed a 'wandering great place'. Someone would see him, they said.

'Someone?' said Soames. 'I want the editor.'

'The editor was very busy; could he come again when the rush was over?'

'No,' said Soames.

Would he state his business? Soames wouldn't.

The attendant again looked at his top-hat and went away.

Soames waited a quarter of an hour, and was then taken to an even smaller room, where a cheery-looking man in eye-glasses was turning over a book of filed cuttings. He glanced up as Soames entered, took his card from the table, and read it:

'Mr Soames Forsyte? Yes?'

'Are you the editor?' asked Soames.

'One of them. Take a seat. What can I do for you?'

Impressed by a certain speed in the air, and desirous of making a good impression, Soames did not sit down, but took from his pocket-book the paragraph.

'I've come about this in your issue of last Thursday.'

The cheery man put it up to his eyes, seemed to chew the sense of it a little with his mouth, and said: 'Yes?'

'Would you kindly tell me who wrote it'

'We never disclose the names of correspondents, sir.'

'Well, as a matter of fact, I know.'

The cheery man's mouth opened, as if to emit the words: 'Then why did you ask?' but closed in a smile instead.

'You'll forgive me,' said Soames; 'it quite clearly refers to my daughter, Mrs Michael Mont, and her husband.'

'Indeed! You have the advantage of me; but what's the matter with it? Seems rather a harmless piece of gossip.'

Soames looked at him. He was too cheery!

'You think so?' he said dryly. 'May I ask if you like to have your daughter alluded to as an enterprising little lady?'

'Why not? It's quite a pleasant word. Besides, there's no name mentioned.'

'Do you put things in,' asked Soames shrewdly, 'in order that they may be Greek to all your readers?'

The cheery man laughed: 'Well,' he said, 'hardly. But really, sir, aren't you rather thin-skinned?'

This was an aspect of the affair that Soames had not foreseen. Before he could ask this editor chap not to repeat his offence, he had apparently to convince him that it *was* an offence; but to do that he must expose the real meaning of the paragraph.

'Well,' he said, 'if you can't see that the tone of the thing's unpleasant, I can't make you. But I beg you won't let any more such paragraphs appear. I happen to know that your correspondent is actuated by malevolence.'

The cheery man again ran his eye over the cutting.

'I shouldn't have judged that. People in politics are taking and giving knocks all the time–they're not mealy-mouthed. This seems perfectly innocuous as gossip goes.'

Thus back-handed by the words 'thin-skinned' and 'mealy-mouthed', Soames said testily:

'The whole thing's extremely petty.'

'Well, sir, you know, I rather agree. Good-morning!' and the cheery man blandly returned to his file.

The fellow was like an india-rubber ball! Soames clenched his top-hat. Now or never he must make him bound.

'If your correspondent thinks she can vent her spleen in print with impunity, she will find herself very much mistaken.' He waited for the effect. There was absolutely none. 'Good-morning!' he said, and turned on his heel.

Somehow it had not been so friendly as he had expected. Michael's words 'The Press is a sensitive plant' came into his mind. He shouldn't mention his visit.

Two days later, picking up the *Evening Sun* at the Connoisseurs', he saw the word 'Foggartism'. H'm! A leader!

'Of the panaceas rife among the young hopefuls in politics, perhaps the most absurd is one which goes by the name of Foggartism. We are in a position to explain the nature of this patent remedy for what is supposed to be the national ill-health before it has been put on the market. Based on Sir James Foggart's book, *The Parlous State of England*, the main article of faith in this crazy creed would appear to be the depletion of British man-power. According to its prophets, we are to despatch to the ends of the Empire hundreds of thousands of our boys and girls as soon as they leave school. Quite apart from the rank impossibility of absorbing them into the life of the slowly developing Dominions, we are to lose this vital stream of labour and defensive material, in order that twenty years hence the demand from our Dominions may equal the supplying power of Great Britain. A crazier proposition was never conceived in woolly brains. Well does the word Foggartism characterise such a proposition. Alongside this emigration 'stunt'–for there is no other term which suits its sensational character–rises a feeble back-to-the-land propaganda. The keystone of the whole professes to be the doctrine that the standard of British wages and living now preclude us from any attempt to rival German production, or to recover our trade with Europe. Such a turning of the tail on our industrial supremacy has probably never before been mooted in this country. The sooner these cheap-jack gerrymanders of British policy realise that the British voter will have nothing to do with so crack-brained a scheme, the sooner it will come to the still birth which is its inevitable fate.'

Whatever attention Soames had given to *The Parlous State of England*, he could not be accused of anything so rash as a faith in Foggartism. If Foggartism were killed to-morrow, he, with his inherent distrust of theories and ideas, his truly English pragmatism, could not help feeling that Michael would be well rid of a white elephant. What disquieted him, however, was the suspicion that he himself had inspired this article. Was this that too-cheery fellow's retort?

Decidedly, he should not mention his visit when he dined in South Square that evening.

The presence of a strange hat on the sarcophagus warned him of a fourth party. Mr Blythe, in fact, with a cocktail in his hand and an olive in his mouth, was talking to Fleur, who was curled up on a cushion by the fire.

'You know Mr Blythe, Dad?'

Another editor! Soames extended his hand with caution.

Mr Blythe swallowed the olive. 'It's of no importance,' he said.

'Well,' said Fleur. '*I* think you ought to put it all off, and let them feel they've made fools of themselves.'

'Does Michael think that, Mrs Mont?'

'No; Michael's got his shirt out!' And they all looked round at Michael, who was coming in.

He certainly had a somewhat headstrong air.

According to Michael, they must take it by the short hairs and give as good as they got, or they might as well put up the shutters. They were sent to Parliament to hold their own opinions, not those stuck into them by Fleet Street. If they genuinely believed the Foggart policy to be the only way to cure unemployment, and stem the steady drain into the towns, they must say so, and not be stampeded by every little newspaper attack that came along. Common sense was on their side, and common sense, if you aired it enough, won through in the end. The opposition to Foggartism was really based on an intention to force lower wages and longer hours on Labour, only they daren't say so in so many words. Let the papers jump through their hoops as much as they liked. He would bet that when Foggartism had been six months before the public, they would be eating half their words with an air of eating someone else's! And suddenly he turned to Soames:

'I suppose, sir, you didn't go down about that paragraph?'

Soames, privately, and as a business man, had always so conducted himself that, if cornered, he need never tell a direct untruth. Lies were not English, not even good form. Looking down his nose, he said slowly:

'Well, I let them know that I knew that woman's name.'

Fleur frowned; Mr Blythe reached out and took some salted almonds.

'What did I tell you, sir?' said Michael. 'They always get back on you. The Press has a tremendous sense of dignity; and corns on both feet; eh, Mr Blythe?'

Mr Blythe said weightily: 'It's a very human institution, young man. It prefers to criticise rather than to be criticised.'

'I thought,' said Fleur icily, 'that I was to be left to my own cudgels.'

The discussion broke back to Foggartism, but Soames sat brooding. He would never again interfere in what didn't concern himself. Then, like all who love, he perceived the bitterness of his fate. He had only meddled with what *did* concern himself–her name, her happiness; and she resented it. Basket in which were all his eggs, to the end of his days he must go on walking gingerly, balancing her so that she was not upset, spilling his only treasure.

She left them over the wine that only Mr Blythe was drinking. Soames heard an odd word now and then, gathered that this great frog-chap was going to burst next week in *The Outpost*, gathered that Michael was to get on to his hind legs in the House at the first opportunity. It was all a muzz of words to him. When they rose, he said to Michael:

'I'll take myself off.'

'We're going down to the House, sir: won't you stay with Fleur?'

'No,' said Soames; 'I must be getting back.'

Michael looked at him closely.

'I'll just tell her you're going.'

Soames had wrapped himself into his coat, and was opening the door when he smelled violet soap. A bare arm had come round his neck. He felt soft pressure against his back. 'Sorry, Dad, for being such a pig.'

Soames shook his head.

'No,' said her voice; 'you're not going like that.'

She slipped between him and the door. Her clear eye looked into his; her teeth gleamed, very white. 'Say you forgive me!'

'There's no end to it,' said Soames.

She thrust her lips against his nose. 'There! Good-night, ducky! I know I'm spoiled!'

Soames gave her body a convulsive little squeeze, opened the door and went out without a word.

Under Big Ben boys were calling—political news, he supposed. Those Labour chaps were going to fall—some editor had got them into trouble. He would! Well—one down, t'other come on! It was all remote to him. She alone—she alone mattered.

12

MICHAEL MUSES

Michael and Mr Blythe sought the Mother of Parliaments and found her in commotion. Liberalism had refused, and Labour was falling from its back. A considerable number of people were in Parliament Square contemplating Big Ben and hoping for sensation.

'I'm not going in,' said Michael. 'There won't be a division tonight. General Election's a foregone conclusion, now. I want to think.'

'One will go up for a bit,' said Mr Blythe; and they parted, Michael returning to the streets. The night was clear, and he had a longing to hear the voice of his country. But—where? For his countrymen would be discussing this pro and that con, would be mentioning each his personal 'grief'—here the Income Tax, there the dole, the names of leaders, the word Communism. Nowhere would he catch the echo of the uneasiness in the hearts of all. The Tories—as Fleur had predicted—would come in now. The country would catch at the anodyne of 'strong stable government'. But could strong stable government remove the inherent canker, the lack of balance in the top-heavy realm? Could it still the gnawing ache which everybody felt, and nobody would express?

'Spoiled,' thought Michael, 'by our past prosperity. We shall never admit it,' he thought, 'never! And yet in our bones we feel it!'

England with the silver spoon in her mouth and no longer the teeth to hold it there, or the will to part with it! And her very qualities—the latent 'grit', the power to take things smiling, the lack of nerves and imagination! Almost vices, now, perpetuating the rash belief that England could still 'muddle through' without special effort, although with every year there was less chance of recovering from shock, less time in which to exercise the British 'virtues'. 'Slow in the uptak',' thought Michael, 'it's a ghastly fault in 1924.'

Thus musing, he turned East. Mid-theatre-hour, and the 'Great Parasite'–as Sir James Foggart called it–was lying inert and bright. He walked the length of wakeful Fleet Street into the City so delirious by day, so dead by night. Here England's wealth was snoozing off the day's debauch. Here were all the frame and filaments of English credit. And based on–what? On food and raw material from which England, undefended in the air, might be cut off by a fresh war; on Labour, too big for European boots. And yet that credit stood high still, soothing all with its 'panache'–save, perhaps, receivers of the dole. With her promise to pay, England could still purchase anything, except a quiet heart.

And Michael walked on–through Whitechapel, busy still and coloured–into Mile End. The houses had become low, as if to give the dwellers a better view of stars they couldn't reach. He had crossed a frontier. Here was a different race almost; another England, but as happy-go-lucky and as hand-to-mouth as the England of Fleet Street and the City. Aye, and more! For the England in Mile End knew that whatever she felt could have no effect on policy. Mile on mile, without an end, the low grey streets stretched towards the ultimate deserted grass. Michael did not follow them, but coming to a cinema, turned in.

The show was far advanced. Bound and seated in front of the bad cowboy on a bronco, the heroine was crossing what Michael shrewdly suspected to be the film company's pet paddock. Every ten seconds she gave way to John T. Bronson, manager of the Tucsonville Copper Mine, devouring the road in his 60-h.p. Packard, to cut her off before she reached the Pima river. Michael contemplated his fellow gazers. Lapping it up! Strong stable government–not much! This was their anodyne and they could not have enough of it. He saw the bronco fall, dropped by a shot from John T. Bronson, and the screen disclose the words: 'Hairy Pete grows desperate. . . . "You shall not have her, Bronson."' Quite! He was throwing her into the river instead, to the words: 'John T. Bronson dives.' There he goes! He has her by her flowing hair! But Hairy Pete is kneeling on the bank. The bullets chip the water. Through the heroine's fair perforated shoulder the landscape is almost visible. What is that sound? Yes! John T. Bronson is setting his teeth! He lands, he drags her out. From his cap he takes his automatic. Still dry–thank God!

'Look to yourself, Hairy Pete!' A puff of smoke. Pete squirms and bites the sand–he seems almost to absorb the desert. 'Hairy Pete gets it for keeps!' Slow music, slower! John T. Bronson raises the reviving form. Upon the bank of the Pima river they stand embraced, and the sun sets. 'At last, my dinky love!'

'Pom, pom! that's the stuff!' thought Michael, returning to the light of night: 'Back to the Land! "Plough the fields and scatter"–when they can get this? Not much!' And he turned West again, taking a seat on the top of a bus beside a man with grease-stains on his clothes. They travelled in silence till Michael said:

'What do you make of the political situation, sir?'

The possible plumber replied, without turning his head:

'I should say they've over-reached theirselves.'

'Ought to have fought on Russia–oughtn't they?'

'Russia–that cock won't fight either. No–ought to 'ave 'eld on to the Spring, an' fought on a good stiff Budget.'

'Real class issue?'

'Yus!'

'But do you think class politics can wipe out unemployment?'

The man's mouth moved under his moustache as if mumbling a new idea.

'Ah! I'm fed up with politics; in work to-day and out to-morrow—what's the good of politics that can't give you a permanent job?'

'That's it.'

'Reparations,' said his neighbour; '*we're* not goin' to benefit by reparations. The workin' classes ought to stand together in every country.' And he looked at Michael to see how he liked *that*.

'A good many people thought so before the war; and see what happened.'

'Ah! said the man, 'and what good's it done us?'

'Have you thought of emigrating to the Dominions?'

The man shook his head.

'Don't like what I see of the Austrylians and Canydians.'

'Confirmed Englishman—like myself.'

'That's right,' said the man. 'So long, Mister,' and he got off.

Michael travelled till the bus put him down under Big Ben, and it was nearly twelve. Another election! Could he stand a second time without showing his true colours? Not the faintest hope of making Foggartism clear to a rural constituency in three weeks! If he spoke from now till the day of the election, they would merely think he held rather extreme views on Imperial Preference, which, by the way, he did. He could never tell the electorate that he thought England was on the wrong tack—one might just as well not stand. He could never buttonhole the ordinary voter, and say to him: 'Look here, you know, there's no earthly hope of any real improvement for another ten years; in the meantime we must face the music, and pay more for everything, so that twenty years hence we may be safe from possible starvation, and self-supporting within the Empire.' It wasn't done. Nor could he say to his Committee: 'My friends, I represent a policy that no one else does, so far.'

No! If he meant to stand again, he must just get the old wheezes off his chest. But did he mean to stand again? Few people had less conceit than Michael—he knew himself for a lightweight. But he had got this bee into his bonnet; the longer he lived the more it buzzed, the more its buzz seemed the voice of one crying in the wilderness, and that wilderness his country. To stop up that buzzing in his ears; to turn his back on old Blythe; to stifle his convictions, and yet remain in Parliament—he could not! It was like the war over again. Once in, you couldn't get out. And he was 'in'—committed to something deeper far than the top dressings of Party politics. Foggartism had a definite solution of England's troubles to work towards—an independent, balanced Empire; an England safe in the air, and free from unemployment—with Town and Country once more in some sort of due proportion! Was it such a hopeless dream? Apparently!

'Well,' thought Michael, putting his latch-key in his door, 'they may call me what kind of a bee fool they like—I shan't budge.' He went up to his dressing-room and, opening the window, leaned out.

The rumourous town still hummed; the sky was faintly coloured by reflection from its million lights. A spire was visible, some stars; the tree foliage in the Square hung flat, unstirred by wind. Peaceful and almost warm—the night. Michael remembered a certain evening—the last London air-raid of the war. From his convalescent hospital he had watched it for three hours.

'What fools we all are not to drop fighting in the air,' he thought. 'Well, if we don't, I shall go all out for a great air force—all hangs, for us, on safety from air attack. Even the wise can understand that.'

Two men had stopped beneath his window, talking. One was his next-door neighbour.

'Mark my words,' said his neighbour, 'the election'll see a big turnover.'

'Yes; and what are you going to do with it?' said the other.

'Let things alone; they'll right themselves. I'm sick of all this depressing twaddle. A shilling off the Income Tax, and you'll see.'

'How are you going to deal with the Land?'

'Oh! damn the Land! Leave it to itself, that's all the farmers really want. The more you touch it, the worse it gets.'

'Let the grass grow under your feet?'

The neighbour laughed. 'That's about it. Well, what else *can* you do—the Country won't have it. Good night!'

Sounds of a door, of footsteps. A car drove by; a moth flew in Michael's face. 'The Country won't have it!' Policies! What but mental yawns, long shrugs of the shoulders, trustings to Luck! What else could they be? *The Country wouldn't have it!* And Big Ben struck twelve.

13

INCEPTION OF THE CASE

There are people in every human hive born to focus talk; perhaps their magnetism draws the human tongue, or their lives are lived at an acute angle. Of such was Marjorie Ferrar—one of the most talked-of young women in London. Whatever happened to her was rumoured at once in that collection of the busy and the idle called Society. That she had been ejected from a drawing-room was swiftly known. Fleur's letters about her became current gossip. The reasons for ejectment varied from truth to a legend that she had lifted Michael from the arms of his wife.

The origins of lawsuits are seldom simple. And when Soames called it all 'a storm in a tea-cup', he might have been right if Lord Charles Ferrar had not been so heavily in debt that he had withdrawn his daughter's allowance; if, too, a Member for a Scottish borough, Sir Alexander MacGown, had not for some time past been pursuing her with the idea of marriage. Wealth made out of jute, a rising Parliamentary repute, powerful physique, and a determined character, had not advanced Sir Alexander's claims in twelve months so much as the withdrawal of her allowance advanced them in a single night. Marjorie Ferrar was, indeed, of those who can always get money at a pinch, but even to such come moments when they have seriously to consider what kind of pinch. In proportion to her age and sex, she was 'dipped' as badly as her father, and the withdrawal of her allowance was in the nature of a last straw. In a moment of discouragement she consented to an engagement, not yet to be made public. When the incident at Fleur's came to Sir Alexander's ears, he went to his betrothed flaming. What could he do?

'Nothing, of course; don't be silly, Alec! Who cares?'

'The thing's monstrous. Let me go and exact an apology from this old blackguard.'

'Father's been, and he wouldn't give it. He's got a chin you could hang a kettle on.'

'Now, look here, Marjorie, you've got to make our engagement public, and let me get to work on him. I won't have this story going about.'

Marjorie Ferrar shook her head.

'Oh! no, my dear. You're still on probation. I don't care a tuppenny ice about the story.'

'Well, I do, and I'm going to that fellow to-morrow.'

Marjorie Ferrar studied his face–its brown, burning eyes, its black, stiff hair, its jaw–shivered slightly, and had a brain-wave.

'You will do nothing of the kind, Alec, or you'll spill your ink. My father wants me to bring an action. He says I shall get swingeing damages.'

The Scotsman in MacGown applauded, the lover quailed.

'That may be very unpleasant for you,' he muttered, 'unless the brute settles out of Court.'

'Of course he'll settle. I've got all his evidence in my vanity-bag.'

MacGown gripped her by the shoulders and gave her a fierce kiss.

'If he doesn't, I'll break every bone in his body.'

'My dear! He's nearly seventy, I should think.'

'H'm! Isn't there a young man in the same boat with him?'

'Michael? Oh! Michael's a dear. I couldn't have his bones broken.'

'Indeed!' said MacGown. 'Wait till he launches this precious Foggartism they talk of–dreary rot! I'll eat him!'

'Poor little Michael!'

'I heard something about an American boy, too.'

'Oh!' said Marjorie Ferrar, releasing herself from his grip. 'A bird of passage–don't bother about him.'

'Have you got a lawyer?'

'Not yet.'

'I'll send you mine. He'll make them sit up!'

She remained pensive after he had left her, distrusting her own brain-wave. If only she weren't so hard up! She had learned during this month of secret engagement that 'Nothing for nothing and only fair value for sixpence' ruled North of the Tweed as well as South. He had taken a good many kisses and given her one trinket which she dared not take to 'her Uncle's'. It began to look as if she would have to marry him. The prospect was in some ways not repulsive–he was emphatically a man; her father would take care that she only married him on terms as liberal as his politics; and perhaps her motto 'Live dangerously' could be even better carried out with him than without. Resting inert in a long chair, she thought of Francis Wilmot. Hopeless as husband, he might be charming as lover, naïve, fresh, unknown in London, absurdly devoted, oddly attractive, with his lithe form, dark eyes, engaging smile. Too old-fashioned for words, he had made it clear already that he wanted to marry her. He was a baby. But until she was beyond his reach, she had begun to feel that he was beyond hers. After? Well, who knew? She lived in advance, dangerously, with Francis Wilmot. In the meantime this action for slander was a bore! And shaking the idea out of her head, she ordered her horse, changed her clothes, and repaired to the Row. After that she again changed her clothes, went to the Cosmopolis Hotel, and danced with her mask-faced partner and

Francis Wilmot. After that she changed her clothes once more, went to a first night, partook of supper afterwards with the principal actor and his party, and was in bed by two o'clock.

Like most reputations, that of Marjorie Ferrar received more than its deserts. If you avow a creed of indulgence, you will be indulged by the credulous. In truth she had only had two love-affairs passing the limits of decorum; had smoked opium once, and been sick over it; and had sniffed cocaine just to see what it was like. She gambled only with discretion, and chiefly on race-horses; drank with strict moderation and a good head; smoked of course, but the purest cigarettes she could get, and through a holder. If she had learned suggestive forms of dancing, she danced them but once in a blue moon. She rarely rode at a five-barred gate, and that only on horses whose powers she knew. To be in the know she read, of course, anything 'extreme', but would not go out of her way to do so. She had flown, but just to Paris. She drove a car well, and of course fast, but never to the danger of herself, and seldom to the real danger of the public. She had splendid health, and took care of it in private. She could always sleep at ten minutes' notice, and when she sat up half the night, slept half the day. She was 'in' with the advanced theatre, but took it as it came. Her book of poems, which had received praise because they emanated from one of a class supposed to be unpoetic, was remarkable not so much for irregularity of thought as for irregularity of metre. She was, in sum, credited with a too strict observance of her expressed creed: 'Take life in both hands, and eat it.'

This was why Sir Alexander MacGown's lawyer sat on the edge of his chair in her studio the following morning, and gazed at her intently. He knew her renown better than Sir Alexander. Messrs. Settlewhite and Stark liked to be on the right side of a matter before they took it up. How far would this young lady, with her very attractive appearance and her fast reputation, stand fire? For costs—they had Sir Alexander's guarantee and the word 'traitress' was a good enough beginning; but in cases of word against word, it was ill predicting.

Her physiognomy impressed Mr Settlewhite favourably. She would not 'get rattled' in Court, if he was any judge; nor had she the Aubrey Beardsley cast of feature he had been afraid of, that might alienate a jury. No! an upstanding young woman with a good blue eye and popular hair. She would do, if her story were all right.

Marjorie Ferrar, in turn, scrutinised one who looked as if he might take things out of her hands. Long-faced, with grey deep eyes under long dark lashes, all his hair, and good clothes, he was as well preserved a man of sixty as she had ever seen.

'What do you want me to tell you, Mr Settlewhite?'

'The truth.'

'Oh! but naturally. Well, I was just saying to Mr Quinsey that Mrs Mont was very eager for form a "salon", and had none of the right qualities, and the old person who overheard me thought I was insulting her—'

'That all?'

'Well, I may have said she was fond of lions; and so she is.'

'Yes; but why did he call you a traitress?'

'Because she was his daughter and my hostess, I suppose.'

'Will this Mr Quinsey confirm you?'

'Philip Quinsey?—oh! rather! He's in my pocket.'

'Did anybody else overhear you running her down?'

She hesitated a second. 'No.'

'First lie!' thought Mr Settlewhite, with his peculiar sweet-sarcastic smile. 'What about an American?'

Marjorie Ferrar laughed. 'He won't say so, anyway.'

'An admirer?'

'No. He's going back to America.'

'Second lie!' thought Mr Settlewhite. 'But she tells them well.'

'You want an apology you can show to those who overheard the insult; and what we can get, I suppose?'

'Yes. The more the better.'

'Speaking the truth there,' thought Mr Settlewhite. 'Are you hard up?'

'Couldn't well be harder.'

Mr Settlewhite put one hand on each knee, and reared his slim body.

'You don't want it to come into Court?'

'No; though I suppose it might be rather fun.'

Mr Settlewhite smiled again.

'That entirely depends on how many skeletons you have in your cupboard.'

Marjorie Ferrar also smiled.

'I shall put everything in your hands,' she said.

'Not the skeletons, my dear young lady. Well, we'll serve him and see how the cat jumps; but he's a man of means and a lawyer.'

'I think he'll hate having anything about his daughter brought out in Court.'

'Yes,' said Mr Settlewhite, drily. 'So should I.'

'And she *is* a little snob, you know.'

'Ah! Did you happen to use that word?'

'N-no; I'm pretty sure I didn't.'

'Third lie!' thought Mr Settlewhite: 'not so well told.'

'It makes a difference. Quite sure?'

'Not quite.'

'He says you did?'

'Well, I told him he was a liar.'

'Oh! did you? And they heard you?'

'Rather!'

'That may be important.'

'I don't believe he'll say I called her a snob, in Court, anyway.'

'That's very shrewd, Miss Ferrar,' said Mr Settlewhite. 'I think we shall do.'

And with a final look at her from under his long lashes, he stalked, thin and contained, to the door.

Three days later Soames received a legal letter. It demanded a formal apology, and concluded with the words 'failing it, action will be taken.' Twice in his life he had brought actions himself; once for breach of contract, once for divorce; and now to be sued for slander! In every case he had been the injured party, in his own opinion. He was certainly not going to apologise. Under the direct threat he felt much calmer. He had nothing to be ashamed of. He would call that 'baggage' a traitress to her face again to-morrow, and pay for the luxury, if need be. His mind roved back to when, in the early 'eighties, as a very young lawyer, he had handled his Uncle Swithin's defence against a fellow member of the Walpole Club. Swithin had called him in public 'a little touting whipper-snapper of a parson.' He remembered how he had whittled the charge down to the word 'whipper-snapper', by proving the plaintiff's height to be five feet four, his profession the church, his habit the collection of money for the purpose of small-clothing the Fiji islanders. The jury had assessed 'whipper-snapper' at ten pounds–Soames always believed the small clothes had done it. His Counsel had made great game of them–Bobstay, Q.C. There *were* Counsel in those days; the Q.C.'s had been better than the K.C.'s were. Bobstay would have gone clean through this 'baggage' and come out on the other side. Uncle Swithin had asked him to dinner afterwards and given him York ham with Madeira sauce, and his special Heidsieck. He had never given anybody anything else. Well! There must still be cross-examiners who could tear a reputation to tatters, especially if there wasn't one to tear. And one could always settle at the last moment if one wished. There was no possibility anyway of Fleur being dragged in as witness or anything of that sort.

He was thunder-struck, a week later, when Michael rang him up at Mapledurham to say that Fleur had been served with a writ for libel in letters containing among others the expression 'a snake of the first water' and 'she hasn't a moral about her.'

Soames went cold all over. 'I told you not to let her go about abusing that woman.'

'I know; but she doesn't consult me every time she writes a letter to a friend.'

'Pretty friend!' said Soames into the mouthpiece. 'This is a nice pair of shoes!'

'Yes, sir; I'm very worried. She's absolutely spoiling for a fight–won't hear of an apology.'

Soames grunted so deeply that Michael's ear tingled forty miles away.

'In the meantime, what shall we do?'

'Leave it to me,' said Soames. 'I'll come up to-night. Has she any evidence to support those words?'

'Well, she says–'

'No,' said Soames, abruptly, 'don't tell me over the phone.' And he rang off. He went out on to the lawn. Women! Petted and spoiled–thought they could say what they liked! And so they could till they came up against another woman. He stopped by the boat-house and gazed at the river. The water was nice and clean, and there it was–flowing down to London to get all dirty! That feverish, quarrelsome business up there! Now he would have to set to and rake up all he could against this Ferrar woman, and frighten her off. It was distasteful. But nothing else for it, if Fleur was to be kept out of Court! Terribly petty. Society lawsuits–who ever got anything out of them, save heart-burning and degradation? Like the war, you might win and regret it ever afterwards, or lose and regret it more. All temper! Jealousy and temper!

In the quiet autumn light, with the savour of smoke in his nostrils from his gardener's first leaf bonfire, Soames felt moral. Here was his son-in-law, wanting to do some useful work in Parliament, and make a name for the baby, and Fleur beginning to settle down and take a position; and now this had come along, and all the chatterers and busy mockers in Society would be gnashing on them with their teeth–if they had any! He looked at his shadow on the bank, grotesquely slanting towards the water as if wanting to drink. Everything was grotesque, if it came to that! In Society, England, Europe–shadows scrimmaging and sprawling, scuffling and posturing; the world just marking time before another Flood! H'm! He moved towards the river. There went his shadow, plunging in before him! They would all plunge into that mess of cold water if they didn't stop their squabblings. And, turning abruptly, he entered his kitchen-garden. Nothing unreal there, and most things running to seed–stalks, and so on! How to set about raking up the past of this young woman? Where was it? These young sparks and fly-by-nights! They all had pasts, no doubt; but the definite, the concrete bit of immorality alone was of use, and when it came to the point, was unobtainable, he shouldn't wonder. People didn't like giving chapter and verse! It was risky, and not the thing! Tales out of school!

And, among his artichokes, approving of those who did not tell tales, disapproving of anyone who wanted them told, Soames resolved grimly that told they must be. The leaf-fire smouldered, and the artichokes smelled rank, the sun went down behind the high brick wall mellowed by fifty years of weather; all was peaceful and chilly, except in his heart. Often now, morning or evening, he would walk among his vegetables–they were real and restful, and you could eat them. They had better flavour then the greengrocer's and saved his bill–middlemen's profiteering and all that. Perhaps they represented atavistic instincts in this great-grandson of 'Superior Dosset's' father, last of a long line of Forsyte 'agriculturists'. He set more and more store by vegetables the older he grew. When Fleur was a little bit of a thing, he would find her when he came back from the City, seated among the sunflowers or blackcurrants, nursing her doll. He had once taken a bee out of her hair, and the little brute had stung him. Best years he ever had, before she grew up and took to this gadabout Society business, associating with women who went behind her back. Apology! So she wouldn't hear of one? She was in the right. But to be in the right and have to go into Court because of it, was one of the most painful experiences that could be undergone. The Courts existed to penalise people who were in the right–in divorce, breach of promise, libel and the rest of it. Those who were in the wrong went to the South of France, or if they did appear, defaulted afterwards and left you to pay your costs. Had he not himself had to pay them in his action against Bosinney? And in his divorce suit had not Young Jolyon and Irene been in Italy when he brought it? And yet, he couldn't bear to think of Fleur eating humble-pie to that red-haired cat. Among the gathering shadows, his resolve hardened. Secure evidence that would frighten the baggage into dropping the whole thing like a hot potato–it was the only way!

I4

FURTHER CONSIDERATION

The Government had 'taken their toss' over the Editor–no one could say precisely why–and Michael sat down to compose his address. How say enough without saying anything? And having impetuously written: 'Electors of mid-Bucks,' he remained for many moments still as a man who has had too good a dinner. 'If' he traced words slowly–'if you again return me as your representative, I shall do my best for the country according to my lights. I consider the limitations of armaments, and, failing that, the security of Britain through the enlargement of our air defences; the development of home agriculture; the elimination of unemployment through increased emigration to the Dominions; and the improvement of the national health particularly through the abatement of slums and smoke, to be the most pressing and immediate concerns of British policy. If I am returned, I shall endeavour to foster these ends with determination and coherence; and try not to abuse those whose opinions differ from my own. At my meetings I shall seek to give you some concrete idea of what is in my mind, and submit myself to your questioning.'

Dared he leave it at that? Could one issue an address containing no disparagement of the other side, no panegyric of his own? Would his Committee allow it? Would the electors swallow it? Well, if his Committee didn't like it–they could turn it down, and himself with it; only–they wouldn't have time to get another candidate!

The Committee, indeed, did not like it, but they lumped it; and the address went out with an effigy on it of Michael, looking, as he said, like a hairdresser. Thereon he plunged into a fray, which, like every other, began in the general and ended in the particular.

During the first Sunday lull at Lippinghall, he developed his poultry scheme–by marking out sites, and deciding how water could be laid on. The bailiff was sulky. In his view it was throwing away money. 'Fellers like that!' Who was going to teach them the job? He had no time, himself. It would run into hundreds, and might just as well be poured down the gutter. 'The townsman's no mortal use on the land, Master Michael.'

'So everybody says. But, look here, Tutfield, here are three 'down and outs', two of them ex-Service, and you've got to help me put this through. You say yourself this land's all right for poultry–well, it's doing no good now. Bowman knows every last thing about chickens, set him on to it until these chaps get the hang. Be a good fellow and put your heart into it; you wouldn't like being 'down and out' yourself.'

The bailiff had a weakness for Michael, whom he had known from his bottle up. He knew the result, but if Master Michael liked to throw his father's money away, it was no business of his. He even went so far as to mention that he knew 'a feller' who had a hut for sale not ten miles away; and that there was 'plenty of wood in the copse for the cuttin'.'

On the Tuesday after the Government had fallen Michael went up to town and summoned a meeting of his 'down and outs'. They came at three the following day, and he placed them in chairs round the dining-table. Standing under the Goya, like a general about to detail a plan of attack which others would have to execute, he developed his proposal. The three faces expressed little, and that without conviction. Only Bergfeld had known anything of it, before, and his face was the most doubting.

'I don't know in the least,' went on Michael, 'what you think of it; but you all want jobs–two of you out of doors, and you, Boddick, don't mind what it is, I think.'

'That's right, sir,' said Boddick, 'I'm on.'

Michael instantly put him down as the best man of the three.

The other two were silent till Bergfeld said:

'If I had my savings–'

Michael interrupted quickly:

'I'm putting in the capital; you three put in the brains and labour. It's probably not more than a bare living, but I hope it'll be a healthy one. What do *you* say, Mr Swain?'

The hairdresser, more shadow-stricken than ever, in the glow of Fleur's Spanish room, smiled.

'I'm sure it's very kind of you. I don't mind havin' a try—only, who's goin' to boss the show?'

'Co-operation, Mr Swain.'

'Ah!' said the hairdresser; 'thought so. But I've seen a lot of tries at that, and it always ends in one bloke swallerin' the rest.'

'Very well,' said Michael, suddenly, 'I'll boss it. But if any of you crane at the job, say so at once, and have done with it. Otherwise I'll get that hut delivered and set up, and we'll start this day month.'

Boddick got up, and said: 'Right, sir. What about my children?'

'How old, Boddick?'

'Two little girls, four and five.'

'Oh! yes!' Michael had forgotten this item. 'We must see about that.'

Boddick touched his forelock, shook Michael's hand, went out. The other two remained standing.

'Good-bye, Mr Bergfeld; good-bye, Mr Swain!'

'If I might—'

'Could I speak to you for a minute?'

'Anything you have to say,' said Michael, astutely, 'had better be said in each other's presence.'

'I've always been used to hair.'

'Pity,' thought Michael, 'that Life didn't drop that "h" for him—poor beggar!' 'Well, we'll get you a breed of birds that can be shingled,' he said. The hairdresser smiled down one side of his face. 'Beggars can't be choosers,' he remarked.

'*I* wished to ask you,' said Bergfeld, 'what system we shall adopt?'

'That's got to be worked out. Here are two books on poultry-keeping; you'd better read one each, and swop.'

He noted that Bergfeld took both without remonstrance on the part of Swain.

Seeing them out into the Square, he thought: 'Rum team! It won't work, but they've got their chance.'

A young man who had been standing on the pavement came forward.

'Mr Michael Mont, M.P.?'

'Yes.'

'Mrs Michael Mont at home?'

'I think so. What do you want?'

'I must see her personally, please.'

'Who are you from?'

'Messrs Settlewhite and Stark—a suit.'

'Dressmakers?'

The young man smiled.

'Come in,' said Michael. 'I'll see if she's at home.'

Fleur was in the 'parlour'.

'A young man from some dressmaker's for you, dear.'

'Mrs Michael Mont? In the suit of Ferrar against Mont—libel. Good-day, madam.'

Between those hours of four and eight, when Soames arrived from Mapledurham, Michael suffered more than Fleur. To sit and see a legal operation performed on her with all the scientific skill of the British Bar, it was an appalling prospect; and there would be no satisfaction in Marjorie Ferrar's also being on the table, with her inside exposed to the gaze of all! He was only disconcerted, therefore, when Fleur said:

'All right; if she wants to be opened up, she shall be. I know she flew to Paris with Walter Nazing last November; and I've always been told she was Bertie Curfew's mistress for a year.'

A Society case–cream for all the cats in Society, muck for all the blowflies in the streets–and Fleur the hub of it! He waited for Soames with impatience. Though 'Old Forsyte's' indignation had started this, Michael turned to him now, as to an anchor let go off a lee shore. The 'old man' had experience, judgment, and a chin; he would know what, except bearing it with a grin, could be done. Gazing at a square foot of study wall which had escaped a framed caricature, he reflected on the underlying savagery of life. He would be eating a lobster to-night that had been slowly boiled alive! This study had been cleaned out by a charwoman whose mother was dying of cancer, whose son had lost a leg in the war, and who looked so jolly tired that he felt quite bad whenever he thought of her. The Bergfelds, Swains and Boddicks of the world–the Camden Towns, and Mile Ends–the devastated regions of France, the rock villages of Italy! Over it all what a thin crust of gentility! Members of Parliament and ladies of fashion, like himself and Fleur, simpering and sucking silver spoons, and now and then dropping spoons and simper, and going for each other like Kilkenny cats!

'What evidence has she got to support those words?' Michael racked his memory. This was going to be a game of bluff. That Walter Nazing and Marjorie Ferrar had flown to Paris together appeared to him of next to no importance. People could still fly in couples with impunity; and as to what had happened afterwards in the great rabbit-warren Outre Manche–Pff! The Bertie Curfew affair was different. Smoke of a year's duration probably had fire behind it. He knew Bertie Curfew, the enterprising director of the 'Ne Plus Ultra Play Society', whose device was a stork swallowing a frog–a long young man, with long young hair that shone and was brushed back, and a long record; a strange mixture of enthusiasm and contempt, from one to the other of which he passed with extreme suddenness. His sister, of whom he always spoke as 'Poor Norah,' in Michael's opinion was worth ten of him. She ran a Children's House in Bethnal Green, and had eyes from which meanness and evil shrank away.

Big Ben thumped out eight strokes; the Dandie barked, and Michael knew that Soames had come.

Very silent during dinner, Soames opened the discussion over a bottle of Lippinghall Madeira by asking to see the writ.

When Fleur had brought it, he seemed to go into a trance.

'The old boy,' thought Michael, 'is thinking of his past. Wish he'd come to!'

'Well, Father?' said Fleur at last.

As if from long scrutiny of a ghostly Court of Justice, Soames turned his eyes on his daughter's face.

'You won't eat your words, I suppose?'

Fleur tossed her now de-shingled head. 'Do you want me to?'

'Can you substantiate them? You mustn't rely on what was told you–that isn't evidence.'

'I know that Amabel Nazing came here and said that she didn't mind Walter flying to Paris with Marjorie Ferrar, but that she did object to not having been told beforehand, so that she herself could have flown to Paris with somebody else.'

'We could subpoena that young woman,' said Soames.

Fleur shook her head. 'She'd never give Walter away in Court.'

'H'm! What else about this Miss Ferrar?'

'Everybody knows of her relationship with Bertie Curfew.'

'Yes,' Michael put in, 'and between "everybody knows" and "somebody tells" is a great gap fixed.'

Soames nodded.

'She just wants money out of us,' cried Fleur; 'she's always hard up. As if she cared whether people thought her moral or not! She despises morality–all her set do.'

'Ah! Her view of morality!' said Soames, deeply; he was suddenly seeing a British jury confronted by a barrister describing the modern view of morals: 'No need, perhaps, to go into personal details.'

Michael started up.

'By Jove, sir, you've hit it! If you can get her to admit that she's read certain books, seen or acted in certain plays, danced certain dances, worn certain clothes–' He fell back again into his chair; what if the other side started asking Fleur the same questions? Was it not the fashion to keep abreast of certain things, however moral one might really be? Who could stand up and profess to be shocked, to-day?

'Well?' said Soames.

'Only that one's own point of view isn't quite a British jury's, sir. Even yours and ours, I expect, don't precisely tally.'

Soames looked at his daughter. He understood. Loose talk–afraid of being out of the fashion–evil communication corrupting all profession of good manners! Still, no jury could look at her face without–who could resist the sudden raising of those white lids? Besides, she was a mother, and the older woman wasn't; or if she was–she shouldn't be! No, he held to his idea. A clever fellow at the Bar could turn the whole thing into an indictment of the fast set and modern morality, and save all the invidiousness of exposing a woman's private life.

'You give me the names of her set and those books and plays and dancing clubs and things,' he said. 'I'll have the best man at the Bar.'

Michael rose from the little conference somewhat eased in mind. If the matter could be shifted from the particular to the general; if, instead of attacking Marjorie Ferrar's practice, the defence could attack her theory, it would not be so dreadful. Soames took him apart in the hall.

'I shall want all the information I can get about that young man and her.'

Michael's face fell.

'You can't get it from me, sir, I haven't got it.'

'She must be frightened,' said Soames. 'If I can frighten her, I can probably settle it out of Court without an apology.'

'I see; use the information out of Court, but not in.'

Soames nodded. 'I shall tell them that we shall justify. Give me the young man's address.'

'Macbeth Chambers, Bloomsbury. It's close to the British Museum. But do remember, sir, that to air Miss Ferrar's linen in Court will be as bad for us as for her.'

Again Soames nodded.

When Fleur and her father had gone up, Michael lit a cigarette, and passed back into the 'parlour'. He sat down at the clavichord. The instrument made very little noise–so he could strum on it without fear of waking the eleventh baronet. From a Spanish tune picked up three years ago on his honeymoon, whose savagery always soothed him, his fingers wandered on: 'I got a crown, you got a crown–all God's childern got a crown! Eb'ryone dat talk 'bout 'Eaben ain't goin' dere. All God's childern got a crown.'

Glass lustres on the wall gleamed out at him. As a child he had loved the colours of his aunt Pamela's glass chandeliers in the panelled rooms at Brook Street; but when he knew what was what, he and everyone had laughed at them. And now lustres had come in again; and Aunt Pamela had gone out! 'She had a crown–he had a crown–' Confound that tune! '*Auprès de ma blonde–il fait bon–fait bon–fait bon; Auprès de ma blonde, il fait bon dormir.*'

His 'blonde'–not so very blonde, either–would be in bed by now. Time to go up! But still he strummed on, and his mind wandered in and out–of poultry and politics, Old Forsyte, Fleur, Foggartism, and the Ferrar girl–like a man in a mælstrom whirling round with his head just above water. Who was it said the landing-place for modernity was a change of heart; the re-birth of a belief that life was worth while, and better life attainable? 'Better life?' Prerogative of priests? Not now. Humanity had got to save itself! To save itself–what was that, after all, but expression of 'the will to live'? But did humanity will to live as much as it used? That was the point. Michael stopped strumming and listened to the silence. Not even a clock ticking–time was inhospitable in 'parlours'; and England asleep outside. Was the English 'will to live' as strong as ever; or had they all become so spoiled, so sensitive to life, that they had weakened on it? Had they sucked their silver spoon so long that, threatened with a spoon of bone, they preferred to get down from table? 'I don't believe it,' thought Michael, 'I won't believe it. Only where are we going? Where am I going? Where are all God's children going?' To bed, it seemed!

And Big Ben struck: One.

PART II

I

MICHAEL MAKES HIS SPEECH

When in the new Parliament Michael rose to deliver his maiden effort towards the close of the debate on the King's Speech, he had some notes in his hand and not an idea in his head. His heart was beating and his knees felt weak. The policy he was charged to express, if not precisely new in concept, was in reach and method so much beyond current opinion that he awaited nothing but laughter. His would be a stray wind carrying the seed of a new herb into a garden, so serried and so full that no corner would welcome its growth. There was a plant called Chinese weed which having got hold never let go, and spread till it covered everything. Michael desired for Foggartism the career of Chinese weed; but all he expected was the like of what he had seen at Monterey on his tour round the world after the war. Chance had once brought to that Californian shore the seeds of the Japanese yew. In thick formation the little dark trees had fought their way inland to a distance of some miles. That battalion would never get farther now that native vegetation had been curiously roused against it; but its thicket stood—a curious and strong invader.

His first period had been so rehearsed that neither vacant mind nor dry mouth could quite prevent delivery. Straightening his waistcoat and jerking his head back, he regretted that the speech from the throne foreshadowed no coherent and substantial policy such as might hope to free the country from its present plague of under-employment and over-population. Economically speaking, any foreseeing interpretation of the course of affairs must now place Britain definitely in the orbit of the overseas world. . . . (*'Oh! oh!'*) Ironical laughter so soon and sudden cleared Michael's mind and relaxed his lips; and, with the grin that gave his face a certain charm, he resumed:

Speakers on all sides of the House, dwelling on the grave nature of the Unemployment problem, had pinned their faith to the full recapture of European trade, some in one way, some in another. August as they were, he wished very humbly to remark that they could not eat cake and have it. (*Laughter.*) Did they contend that wages in Britain must come down and working hours be lengthened; or did they assert that European wages must go up, and European working hours be shortened? No, they had not had the temerity. Britain, which was to rid itself of unemployment in the ways suggested, was the only important country in the world which had to buy about seven-tenths of its food, and of whose population well-nigh six-sevenths lived in towns. It employed those six-sevenths in producing articles in some cases too dearly for European countries to buy, and yet it had to sell a sufficient surplus above the normal exchanges of trade to pay for seven-tenths of the wherewithal to keep its producers alive. (*A laugh.*) If this was a joke, it was a grim one. (*A voice: 'You have forgotten the carrying trade.'*) He accepted the honourable Member's correction, and hoped that he felt happy about the future of that trade. It was, he feared, a somewhat shrinking asset.

At this moment in his speech Michael himself became a somewhat shrinking asset, overwhelmed by a sudden desire to drop Foggartism and sit down. The cool attention, the faint smiles, the expression on the face of a past Prime Minister, seemed conspiring towards his subsidence. 'How young–oh! how young you are!' they seemed to say. 'We sat here before you were breeched.' And he agreed with them completely. Still there was nothing for it but to go on–with Fleur in the Ladies' Gallery, old Blythe in the Distinguished Strangers'; yes, and something stubborn in his heart! Clenching the notes in his hand, therefore, he proceeded:

In spite of the war, and because of the war, the population of their island had increased by 2,000,000. Emigration had fallen from over 200,000 to 100,000. And this state of things was to be remedied by the mere process of recapturing to the full European trade which, quite obviously, had no intention of being so recaptured. What alternative, then, was there? Some honourable Members, he was afraid not many, would be familiar with the treatise of Sir James Foggart, entitled *The Parlous State of England.* (*'Hear, hear:' from a back Labour bench.*) He remembered to have read in a certain organ, or perhaps he should say harmonium, of the Press, for it was not a very deep-voiced instrument– (*laughter*)–that no such crack-brained policy had ever been devised for British consumption. (*'Hear, hear!'*) Certainly Foggartism was mad enough to look ahead, to be fundamental, and to ask the country to face its own position and the music into the bargain. . . .

About to go over 'the top'–with public confession of his faith trembling behind his lips–Michael was choked by the sudden thought: 'Is it all right–is it what I think it, or am I an ignorant fool?' He swallowed vigorously and staring straight before him, went on:

'Foggartism deprecates surface measures for a people in our position; it asks the country to fix its mind on a date–say twenty years hence–a minute in a nation's life–and to work steadily and coherently up to that date. It demands recognition of the need to make the British Empire, with its immense resources mostly latent, a self-sufficing unit. Imperialists will ask: What is there new in that? The novelty lies in degree and in method. Foggartism urges that the British people should be familiarised with the Empire by organised tours and propaganda on a great scale. It urges a vast increase–based on this familiarisation–of controlled and equipped emigration from these shores. But it has been found impossible, as honourable members well know, to send out suitable grown folk in any adequate quantity, because confirmed town-dwellers with their town tastes and habits, and their physique already impaired by town life, are of little use in the Dominions, while the few still on the English land cannot be spared. Foggartism, therefore, would send out boys and girls, between the ages of fifteen, or perhaps sixteen, and eighteen, in great numbers. The House is aware that experiments in this direction have already been made, with conspicuous success, but such experiments are but a drop in the bucket. This is a matter which can only be tackled in the way that things were tackled during the war. Development of child emigration is wanted, in fact, on the same scale and with the same energy as was manifested in Munitions after a certain most honourable Member had put his shoulder to that wheel–multiplication a hundredfold. Although the idea must naturally prove abortive without the utmost good-will and co-operating energy on the part of the Dominions, I submit that this co-operation is not beyond the bounds of hope. The present hostility of people in the Dominions towards British immigrants is due to their very reasonable distrust of the usefulness of adult immigrants from this country. Once they have malleable youth to deal with, that drawback vanishes. In fact, the opening up of these vast new countries is like the progress of a rolling snowball, each little bit of "all right"–I beg the House's pardon–picks up another little bit; and there is no limit to the cumulative possibilities if a start is made at the right end and the scheme pushed and controlled by the right people.' Someone behind him said: 'Talking through his hat.' Michael paused, disconcerted; then, snatching at his bitt, went on: 'A job of this sort half done is better left alone, but in the war, when something was found necessary, it *was* done, and men were always available for the doing of it. I put it to the House that the condition of our country now demands efforts almost as great as then.'

He could see that some members were actually listening to him with attention, and, taking a deep breath, he went on:

'Leaving out Ireland–' (*A voice: 'Why?'*) 'I prefer not to touch on anything that does not like to be touched–' (*laughter*) 'the present ratio of white population between Britain and the rest of the Empire is roughly in the nature of five to two. Child Emigration on a great scale will go far to equalise this ratio within twenty years; the British character of the British Empire will be established for ever, and supply and demand between the Mother Country and the Dominions will be levelled up.' (*A voice: 'The Dominions will then supply themselves.'*) 'The honourable Member will forgive me if I doubt that, for some time to come. We have the start in the machinery of manufacture. It may, of course, be five, seven, ten years before unemployment here comes down even to the pre-war rate, but can you point to any other plan which will really decrease it? I am all for good wages and moderate working hours. I believe the standard in Britain and the new countries, though so much higher than the European, is only a decent minimum, and in some cases does not reach it; I want better wages, even more moderate working hours; and the want is common among working men wherever the British flag flies.' (*'Hear, hear!'*) 'They are not going back on that want; and it is no good supposing that they are!' (*'Hear, hear!' 'Oh! oh!'*) 'The equalisation of demand and supply *within the Empire* is the only way of preserving and improving the standards of life, which are now recognised as necessary on British soil. The world has so changed that the old maxim 'buy in the cheapest, sell in the dearest market' is standing on its head so far as England is concerned. Free Trade was never a principle–' (*'Oh! oh!' 'Hear, hear!' and laughter.*) 'Oh! well, it was born twins with expediency, and the twins have got mixed, and are both looking uncommonly peeky.' (*Laughter.*) 'But I won't go into that. . . .' (*A voice: 'Better not!'*) Michael could see the mouth it came from below a clipped moustache in a red, black-haired face turned round at him from a Liberal bench. He could not put a name to it, but he did not like the unpolitical expression it wore. Where was he? Oh! yes. . . . 'There is another point in the Foggart programme: England as she now is, insufficiently protected in the air, and lamentably devoid of food-producing power, is an abiding temptation to the aggressive feelings of other nations. And here I must beg the House's pardon for a brief reference to Cinderella–in other words, the

Land. The speech from the throne gave no lead in reference to that vexed question, beyond implying that a conference of all interested will be called. Well, without a definite intention in the minds of all the political Parties to join in some fixed and long-lasting policy for rehabilitation, such a conference is bound to fail. Here again Foggartism–' ('*Ho! ho!*') 'Here again Foggartism steps in. Foggartism says: Lay down your Land policy *and don't change it.* Let it be as sacred as the Prohibition Law in America.' (*A voice: 'And as damned!'* *Laughter.*) 'The sacred and damned–it sounds like a novel by Dostoievski.' (*Laughter.*) 'Well, we shall get nowhere without this damned sanctity. On our Land policy depends, not only the prosperity of farmers, landlords, and labourers, desirable and important though that is, but the very existence of England, if unhappily there should come another war under the new conditions. Yes, and in a fixed land policy lies the only hope of preventing the permanent deterioration of the British type. Foggartism requires that we lay down our land policy, so that within ten years we may be growing up to seventy per cent of our food. Estimates made during the war showed that as much as eighty-two per cent could be grown at a pinch; and the measures then adopted went a long way to prove that this estimate was no more than truth. Why were those measures allowed to drop? Why was all that great improvement allowed to run to seed and grass? What is wanted is complete confidence in every branch of home agriculture; and nothing but a policy guaranteed over a long period can ever produce that confidence.' Michael paused. Close by, a member yawned; he heard a shuffle of feet; another old Prime Minister came in; several members were going out. There was nothing new about "the Land". Dared he tackle the air–that third plank in the Foggart programme? There was nothing new about the air either! Besides, he would have to preface it by a plea for the abolition of air fighting, or at least for the reduction of armaments. It would take too long! Better leave well alone! He hurried on:

'Emigration! The Land! Foggartism demands for both the same sweeping attention as was given to vital measures during the war. I feel honoured in having been permitted to draw the attention of all Parties to this–I will brave an honourable Member's disposition to say "Ho, ho!"–great treatise of Sir James Foggart. And I beg the House's pardon for having been so long in fulfilling my task.'

He sat down, after speaking for thirteen minutes. Off his chest! An honourable Member rose.

'I must congratulate the Member for mid-Bucks on what, despite its acquaintanceship with the clouds, and its Lewis Carrollian appeal for less bread, more taxes, we must all admit to be a lively and well-delivered first effort. The Member for Tyne and Tees, earlier in the Debate, made an allusion to the Party to which I have the honour to belong, which–er–'

'Exactly!' thought Michael, and after waiting for the next speech, which contained no allusion whatever to his own, he left the House.

2

RESULTS

He walked home, lighter in head and heart. That was the trouble—a light weight! No serious attention would be paid to him. He recollected the maiden speech of the Member for Cornmarket. At least he had stopped, to-day, as soon as the House began to fidget. He felt hot, and hungry. Opera-singers grew fat through their voices, Members of Parliament thin. He would have a bath.

He was half clothed again when Fleur came in.

'You did splendidly, Michael. That beast!'

'Which?'

'His name's MacGown.'

'Sir Alexander MacGown? What about him?'

'You'll see to-morrow. He insinuated that you were interested in the sale of the Foggart book, as one of its publishers.'

'That's rather the limit.'

'And all the rest of his speech was a cut-up; horrid tone about the whole thing. Do you know him?'

'MacGown? No. He's Member for some Scottish borough.'

'Well, he's an enemy. Blythe is awfully pleased with you, and wild about MacGown; and so is Bart. I've never seen him so angry. You'll have to write to *The Times* and explain that you've had no interest in Danby & Winter's since before you were elected. Bart and your mother are coming to dinner. Did you know she was with me?'

'Mother? She abhors politics.'

'All she said was: "I wish dear Michael would brush his hair back before speaking. I like to see his forehead." And when MacGown sat down, she said: "My dear, the back of that man's head is perfectly straight. D'you think he's a Prussian? And he's got thick lobes to his ears. I shouldn't like to be married to him!" She had her opera-glasses.'

Sir Lawrence and Lady Mont were already in the 'parlour' when they went down, standing opposite each other like two storks, if not precisely on one leg, still very distinguished. Pushing Michael's hair up, Lady Mont pecked his forehead, and her dove-like eyes gazed at the top of his head from under their arched brows. She was altogether a little Norman in her curves; she even arched her words. She was considered 'a deah; but not too frightfully all there'.

'How did you manage to stick it, Mother?'

'My dear boy, I was thrilled; except for that person in jute. I thought the shape of his head insufferable. Where did you get all that knowledge? It was so sensible.'

Michael grinned. 'How did it strike you, sir?'

Sir Lawrence grimaced.

'You played the *enfant terrible*, my dear. Half the party won't like it because they've never thought of it; and the other half won't like it because they *have*.

'What! Foggartists at heart?'

'Of course; but in Office. You mustn't support your real convictions in Office–it's not done.'

'This nice room,' murmured Lady Mont. 'When I was last here it was Chinese. And where's the monkey?'

'In Michael's study, Mother. We got tired of him. Would you like to see Kit before dinner?'

Left alone, Michael and his father stared at the same object, a Louis Quinze snuff-box picked up by Soames.

'Would you take any notice of MacGown's insinuation, Dad?'

'Is that his name–the hairy haberdasher! I should.'

'How?'

'Give him the lie.'

'In private, in the Press, or in the House?'

'All three. In private I should merely call him a liar. In the Press you should use the words: "Reckless disregard for truth." And in Parliament–that you regret he "should have been so misinformed." To complete the crescendo you might add that men's noses have been pulled for less.'

'But you don't suppose,' said Michael, 'that people would believe a thing like that?'

'They will believe anything, my dear, that suggests corruption in public life. It's one of the strongest traits in human nature. Anxiety about the integrity of public men would be admirable, if it wasn't so usually felt by those who have so little integrity themselves that they can't give others credit for it.' Sir Lawrence grimaced, thinking of the P.P.R.S. 'And talking of that–why wasn't Old Forsyte in the House to-day?'

'I offered him a seat, but he said: He hadn't been in the House since Gladstone moved the Home Rule Bill, and then only because he was afraid his father would have a fit.'

Sir Lawrence screwed his eye-glass in.

'That's not clear to me,' he said.

'His father had a pass, and didn't like to waste it.'

'I see. That was noble of Old Forsyte.'

'He said that Gladstone had been very windy.'

'Ah! They were even longer in those days. You covered your ground very quickly, Michael. I should say with practice you would do. I've a bit of news for Old Forsyte. Shropshire doesn't speak to Charlie Ferrar because the third time the old man paid his debts to prevent his being posted, he made that a condition, for fear of being asked again. It's not so lurid as I'd hoped. How's the action?'

'The last I heard was something about administering what they call interrogatories.'

'Ah! I know. They answer you in a way nobody can make head or tail of, and that without prejudice. Then they administer them to you, and you answer in the same way; it all helps the lawyers. What is there for dinner?'

'Fleur said we'd kill the fatted calf when I'd got my speech off.'

Sir Lawrence sighed.

'I'm glad. Your mother has Vitamins again rather badly; we eat little but carrots, generally raw. French blood in a family is an excellent thing–prevents faddiness about food. Ah! here they come! . . .'

It has often been remarked that the breakfast-tables of people who avow themselves indifferent to what the Press may say of them are garnished by all the newspapers on the morning when there is anything to say. In Michael's case this was a waste of almost a shilling. The only allusions to his speech were contained in four out of thirteen dailies. *The Times* reported it (including the laughter) with condensed and considered accuracy. The *Morning Post* picked out three imperial bits, prefaced by the words: 'In a promising speech.' The *Daily Telegraph* remarked: 'Among the other speakers were Mr Michael Mont.' And the *Manchester Guardian* observed: 'The Member for Mid-Bucks in a maiden speech advocated the introduction of children into the Dominions.'

Sir Alexander MacGown's speech received the added attention demanded by his extra years of Parliamentary service, but there was no allusion to the insinuation. Michael turned to Hansard. His own speech seemed more coherent than he had hoped. When Fleur came down he was still reading MacGown's.

'Give me some coffee, old thing.'

Fleur gave him the coffee and leaned over his shoulder.

'This MacGown is after Marjorie Ferrar,' she said; 'I remember now.'

Michael stirred his cup. 'Dash it all! The House is free from that sort of pettiness.'

'No. I remember Alison telling me–I didn't connect him up yesterday. Isn't it a disgusting speech?'

'Might be worse,' said Michael, with a grin.

'"As a member of the firm who published this singular production, he is doubtless interested in pressing it on the public, so that we may safely discount the enthusiasm displayed." Doesn't that make your blood boil?'

Michael shrugged his shoulders.

'Don't you ever feel angry, Michael?'

'My dear, I was through the war. Now for *The Times*. What shall I say?

'"Sir,

'"May I trespass upon your valuable space" (that's quite safe), "in the interests of public life–" (that keeps it impersonal) "to–" er–. Well?'

'To say that Sir Alexander MacGown in his speech yesterday told a lie when he suggested that I was interested in the sale of Sir James Foggart's book.'

'Straight,' said Michael, 'but they wouldn't put it in. How's this?'

'"To draw attention to a misstatement in Sir Alexander MacGown's speech of yesterday afternoon. As a matter of fact" (always useful) "I ceased to have any interest whatever in the firm which published Sir James Foggart's book, *The Parlous State of England*, even before I became a member of the late Parliament; and am therefore in no way interested, as Sir Alexander MacGown suggested, in pressing it on the public. I hesitate to assume that he meant to impugn my honour" (must get in "honour") "but his words might bear that construction. My interest in the book is simply my interest in what is truly the "parlous state of England".

"Faithfully, etc."

That do?'

'Much too mild. Besides, I shouldn't say that you really believe the state of England is parlous. It's all nonsense, you know. I mean it's exaggerated.'

'Very well,' said Michael, 'I'll put the state of the country instead. In the House I suppose I rise to a point of order. And in the Lobby to a point of disorder, probably. I wonder what the *Evening Sun* will say?'

The *Evening Sun*, which Michael bought on his way to the House, gave him a leader, headed: 'Foggartism again,' beginning as follows: 'Young Hopeful, in the person of the Member for Mid-Bucks, roused the laughter of the House yesterday by his championship of the insane policy called Foggartism, to which we have already alluded in these columns;' and so on for twenty lines of vivid disparagement. Michael gave it to the door-keeper.

In the House, after noting that MacGown was present, he rose at the first possible moment.

'Mr Speaker, I rise to correct a statement in yesterday's debate reflecting on my personal honour. The honourable member for Greengow, in his speech said–' He then read the paragraph from Hansard. 'It is true that I was a member of the firm which published Sir James Foggart's book in August, 1923, but I retired from all connection with that firm in October, 1923, before ever I entered this House. I have therefore no pecuniary or other interest whatever in pressing the claims of the book, beyond my great desire to see its principles adopted.'

He sat down to some applause; and Sir Alexander MacGown rose. Michael recognised the face with the unpolitical expression he had noticed during his speech.

'I believe,' he said, 'that the honourable Member for Mid-Bucks was not sufficiently interested in his own speech to be present when I made my reply to it yesterday. I cannot admit that my words bear the construction which he has put on them. I said, and I still say, that one of the publishers of a book must necessarily be interested in having the judgment which induced him to publish it vindicated by the public. The honourable Member has placed on his head a cap which I did not intend for it.' His face came round towards Michael, grim, red, provocative.

Michael rose again.

'I am glad the honourable Member has removed a construction which others beside myself had put on his words.'

A few minutes later, with a certain unanimity, both left the House.

The papers not infrequently contain accounts of how Mr Swash, the honourable Member for Topcliffe, called Mr Buckler, the honourable Member for Tooting, something unparliamentary. (*'Order!'*) And of how Mr Buckler retorted that Mr Swash was something worse. (*'Hear, hear!' and 'Order!'*) And of how Mr Swash waved his fists (*uproar*), and Mr Buckler threw himself upon the Chair, or threw some papers (*'Order! order! order!'*) And of how there was great confusion, and Mr Swash, or Mr Buckler, was suspended, and led vociferous out of the Mother of Parliaments by the Serjeant-at-Arms, with other edifying details. The little affair between Michael and Sir Alexander went off in other wise. With an instinct of common decency, they both made for the lavatory; nor till they reached those marble halls did either take the slightest notice of the other. In front of a roller towel Michael said:

'Now, sir, perhaps you'll tell me why you behaved like a dirty dog. You knew perfectly well the construction that would be placed on your words.'

Sir Alexander turned from a hair-brush.

'Take that!' he said, and gave Michael a swinging box on the ear. Staggering, Michael came up wildly with his right, and caught Sir Alexander on the nose. Their movements then became intensive. Michael was limber, Sir Alexander stocky; neither was over proficient with his fists. The affair was cut short by the honourable Member for Wasbaston, who had been in retirement. Coming hastily out of a door, he received simultaneously a black eye, and a blow on the diaphragm, which caused him to collapse. The speaker, now, was the Member for Wasbaston, in language stronger than those who knew the honourable gentleman would have supposed possible.

'I'm frightfully sorry, sir,' said Michael. 'It's always the innocent party who comes off worst.'

'I'll dam' well have you both suspended,' gasped the Member for Wasbaston.

Michael grinned, and Sir Alexander said: 'To hell!'

'You're a couple of brawling cads!' said the Member for Wasbaston. 'How the devil am I to speak this afternoon?'

'If you went in bandaged,' said Michael, dabbing the damaged eye with cold water, 'and apologised for a motor accident, you would get a special hearing, and a good Press. Shall I take the silver lining out of my tie for a bandage?'

'Leave my eye alone,' bellowed the Member for Wasbaston, 'and get out, before I lose my temper!'

Michael buttoned the top of his waistcoat loosened by Sir Alexander's grip, observed in the glass that his ear was very red, his cuff bloodstained, and his opponent still bleeding from the nose, and went out.

'Some scrap!' he thought, entering the fresher air of Westminster. 'Jolly lucky we were tucked away in there! I don't think I'll mention it!' His ear was singing and he felt rather sick, physically and mentally. The salvational splendour of Foggartism already reduced to a brawl in a lavatory! It made one doubt one's vocation. Not even the Member for Wasbaston, however, had come off with dignity, so that the affair was not likely to get into the papers.

Crossing the road towards home, he sighted Francis Wilmot walking west. 'Hallo!'

Francis Wilmot looked up, and seemed to hesitate. His face was thinner, his eyes deeper set; he had lost his smile.

'How is Mrs Mont?'

'Very well, thanks. And you?'

'Fine,' said Francis Wilmot. 'Will you tell her I've had a letter from her cousin Jon. They're in great shape. He was mighty glad to hear I'd seen her, and sent his love.'

'Thanks,' said Michael, drily. 'Come and have tea with us.'

The young man shook his head.

'Have you cut your hand?'

Michael laughed. 'No, somebody's nose,'

Francis Wilmot smiled wanly. 'I'm wanting to do that all the time. Whose was it?'

'A man called MacGown's.'

Francis Wilmot seized Michael's hand. 'It's the very nose!' Then, apparently disconcerted by his frankness, he turned on his heel and made off, leaving Michael putting one and one together.

Next morning's papers contained no allusion to the blood-letting of the day before, except a paragraph to the effect that the Member for Wasbaston was confined to his house by a bad cold. The Tory journals preserved a discreet silence about Foggartism; but in two organs—one Liberal and one Labour—were little leaders, which Michael read with some attention.

The Liberal screed ran thus: 'The debate on the King's speech produced one effort which at least merits passing notice. The policy alluded to by the Member for mid-Bucks under the label of Foggartism, because it emanates from that veteran Sir James Foggart, has a certain speciousness in these unsettled times, when everyone is looking for quack specifics. Nothing which departs so fundamentally from all that Liberalism stands for will command for a moment the support of any truly Liberal vote. The risk lies in its appeal to backwoodism in the Tory ranks. Loose thought and talk of a pessimistic nature always attracts a certain type of mind. The state of England is not really parlous. It in no way justifies any unsound or hysterical departure from our traditional policy. But there is no disguising the fact that certain so-called thinkers have been playing for some time past with the idea of reviving a 'splendid isolation', based (whether they admit it or not) on the destruction of Free Trade. The young Member for mid-Bucks in his speech handled for a moment that corner-stone of Liberalism, and then let it drop; perhaps he thought it too weighty for him. But reduced to its elements, Foggartism is a plea for the abandonment of Free Trade, and a blow in the face of the League of Nations.'

Michael sighed and turned to the Labour article, which was signed, and struck a more human note:

'And so we are to have our children carted off to the Antipodes as soon as they can read and write, in order that the capitalist class may be relieved of the menace lurking in Unemployment. I know nothing of Sir James Foggart, but if he was correctly quoted in Parliament yesterday by a member for an agricultural constituency, I smelled Prussianism about that old gentleman. I wonder what the working man is saying over his breakfast-table? I fear the words: 'To hell!' are not altogether absent from his discourse. No, Sir James Foggart, English Labour intends to call its own hand; and with all the old country's drawbacks, still prefers it for itself and its children. We are not taking any, Sir James Foggart.'

'There it is naked,' thought Michael. 'The policy ought never to have been entrusted to me. Blythe ought to have found a Labour townsman.'

Foggartism, whittled to a ghost by jealousy and class-hatred, by shibboleth, section and Party—he had a vision of it slinking through the purlieus of the House and the corridors of the Press, never admitted to the Presence, nor accepted as flesh and blood!

'Never mind,' he muttered; 'I'll stick it. If one's a fool, one may as well be a blazing fool. Eh, Dan?'

The Dandie, raising his head from his paws, gave him a lustrous glance.

3

MARJORIE FERRAR AT HOME

Francis Wilmot went on his way to Chelsea. He had a rendezvous with Life. Over head and ears in love, and old-fashioned to the point of marriage, he spent his days at the tail of a petticoat as often absent as not. His simple fervour had wrung from Marjorie Ferrar confession of her engagement. She had put it bluntly: She was in debt, she wanted shekels and she could not live in the backwoods.

He had promptly offered her all his shekels. She had refused them with the words:

'My poor dear, I'm not so far gone as that.'

Often on the point of saying 'Wait until I'm married,' the look on his face had always deterred her. He was primitive; would never understand her ideal: Perfection, as wife, mistress, and mother, all at once. She kept him only by dangling the hope that she would throw MacGown over; taking care to have him present when MacGown was absent, and absent when MacGown was present. She had failed to keep them apart on two occasions, painful and productive of more lying than she was at all accustomed to. For she was really taken with this young man; he was a new flavour. She 'loved' his dark 'slinky' eyes, his grace, the way his 'back-chat' grew, dark and fine, on his slim comely neck. She 'loved' his voice and his old-fashioned way of talking. And, rather oddly, she 'loved' his loyalty. Twice she had urged him to find out whether Fleur wasn't going to 'climb down' and 'pay up'. Twice he had refused, saying: 'They were mighty nice to me; and I'd never tell you what they said, even if I did go and find out.'

She was painting his portrait, so that a prepared canvas with a little paint on it chaperoned their almost daily interviews, which took place between three and four when the light had already failed. It was an hour devoted by MacGown to duty in the House. A low and open collar suited Francis Wilmot's looks. She liked him to sit lissom on a divan with his eyes following her; she liked to come close to him, and see the tremor of his fingers touching her skirt or sleeve, the glow in his eyes, the change in his face when she moved away. His faith in her was inconvenient. P's and Q's were letters she despised. And yet, to have to mind them before him gave her a sort of pleasure, made her feel good. One did not shock children!

That day, since she expected MacGown at five, she had become uneasy, before the young man came in saying:

'I met Michael Mont; his cuff was bloody. Guess whose blood!'

'Not Alec's?'

Francis Wilmot dropped her hands.

'Don't call that man "Alec" to me.'

'My dear child, you're too sensitive. I thought they'd have a row—I read their speeches. Hadn't Michael a black eye? No? Tt–tt! Al–er–"that man" will be awfully upset. Was the blood fresh?'

'Yes,' said Francis Wilmot, grimly.

'Then he won't come. Sit down, and let's do some serious work for once.'

But throwing himself on his knees, he clasped his hands behind her waist.

'Marjorie, Marjorie!'

Disciple of Joy, in the forefront of modern mockery, she was yet conscious of pity, for him and for herself. It was hard not to be able to tell him to run out, get licence and ring, or whatever he set store by, and have done with it! Not even that she was ready to have done with it without ring or licence! For one must keep one's head. She had watched one lover growing tired, kept her head, and dismissed him before he knew it; grown tired of another, kept her head, and gone on till he was tired too. She had watched favourites she had backed go down, kept her head and backed one that didn't; had seen cards turn against her, and left off playing before her pile was gone. Time and again she had earned the good mark of Modernity.

So she kissed the top of his head, unclasped his hands, and told him to be good; and, in murmuring it, felt that she had passed her prime.

'Amuse me while I paint,' she said. 'I feel rotten.'

And Francis Wilmot, like a dark ghost, amused her.

Some believe that a nose from which blood has been drawn by a blow swells less in the first hour than it does later. This was why Sir Alexander MacGown arrived at half-past four to say that he could not come at five. He had driven straight from the House with a little bag of ice held to it. Having been led to understand that the young American was 'now in Paris,' he stood stock still, staring at one whose tie was off and whose collar was unbuttoned. Francis Wilmot rose from the divan, no less silent. Marjorie Ferrar put a touch on the canvas.

'Come and look, Alec; it's only just begun.'

'No, thanks,' said MacGown.

Crumpling his tie into his pocket, Francis Wilmot bowed and moved towards the door.

'Won't you stay for tea, Mr Wilmot?'

'I believe not, thank you.'

When he was gone Marjorie Ferrar fixed her eyes on the nose of her betrothed. Strong and hard, it was, as yet, little differentiated from the normal.

'Now,' said MacGown, 'why did you lie about that young blighter? You said he was in Paris. Are you playing fast and loose with me, Marjorie?'

'Of course! Why not?'

MacGown advanced to within reach of her.

'Put down that brush.'

Marjorie Ferrar raised it; and suddenly it hit the wall opposite.

'You'll stop that picture, and you'll not see that fellow again; he's in love with you.'

He had taken her wrists.

Her face, quite as angry as his own, was reined back.

'Let go! I don't know if you call yourself a gentleman?'

'No, a plain man.'

'Strong and silent—out of a dull novel. Sit down, and don't be unpleasant.'

The dual of their eyes, brown and burning, blue and icy, endured for quite a minute. Then he did let go.

'Pick up that brush and give it to me.'

'I'm damned if I will!'

'Then our engagement is off. If you're old-fashioned, I'm not. You want a young woman who'll give you a whip for a wedding present.'

MacGown put his hands up to his head.

'I want you too badly to be sane.'

'Then pick up the brush.'

MacGown picked it up.

'What have you done to your nose?'

MacGown put his hand to it.

'Ran it against a door.'

Marjorie Ferrar laughed. 'Poor door!'

MacGown gazed at her in genuine astonishment.

'You're the hardest woman I ever came across; and why I love you, I don't know.'

'It hasn't improved your looks or your temper, my dear. You were rash to come here to-day.'

MacGown uttered a sort of groan. 'I can't keep away, and you know it.'

Marjorie Ferrar turned the canvas face to the wall, and leaned there beside it. 'I don't know what you think of the prospects of our happiness, Alec; but I think they're pretty poor. Will you have a whisky and soda? It's in that cupboard. Tea, then? Nothing? We'd better understand each other. If I marry you which is very doubtful, I'm not going into purdah. I shall have what friends I choose. And until I marry you, I shall even see them. If you don't like it, you can leave it.'

She watched his clenched hands, and her wrists tingled. To be perfect wife to him would 'take a bit of doing'! If only she knew of a real 'good thing' instead, and had a 'shirt to put on it'! If only Francis Wilmot had money and did not live where the cotton came from and darkies crooned in the fields; where rivers ran red, Florida moss festooned the swamps and the sun shone; where grapefruit grew—or didn't?—and mocking-birds sang sweeter than the nightingale. South Carolina, described to her with such enthusiasm by Francis Wilmot! A world that was not her world stared straight into the eyes of Marjorie Ferrar. South Carolina! Impossible! It was like being asked to be ancient!

MacGown came up to her. 'I'm sorry,' he said. 'Forgive me, Marjorie.'

On her shrugging shoulders he put his hands, kissed her lips, and went away.

And she sat down in her favourite chair, listless, swinging her foot. The sand had run out of her dolly—life was a bore! It was like driving tandem, when the leader would keep turning round; or the croquet party in 'Alice in Wonderland', read in the buttercup-fields at High Marshes not twenty years ago that felt like twenty centuries!

What did she want? Just a rest from men and bills? or that fluffy something called 'real love'? Whatever it was, she hadn't got it! And so! Dress, and go out, and dance; and later dress again, and go out and dine; and the dresses not paid for!

Well, nothing like an egg-nog for 'the hump'!

Ringing for the ingredients, she made one with plenty of brandy, capped it with nutmeg, and drank it down.

4

FONS ET ORIGO

Two mornings later Michael received two letters. The first, which bore an Australian post-mark, ran thus:

DEAR SIR,

I hope you are well and the lady. I thought perhaps you'd like to know how we are. Well, Sir, we're not much to speak of out here after a year and a half. I consider there's too much gilt on the ginger-bread as regards Australia. The climate's all right when it isn't too dry or too wet—it suits my wife fine, but Sir when they talk about making your fortune all I can say is tell it to the marines. The people here are a funny lot they don't seem to have any use for us and I don't seem to have any use for them. They call us Pommies and treat us as if we'd took a liberty in coming to their blooming country. You'd say they wanted a few more out here, but they don't seem to think so. I often wish I was back in the old Country. My wife says we're better off here, but I don't know. Anyway they tell a lot of lies as regards emigration.

Well, Sir, I've not forgotten your kindness. My wife says please to remember her to you and the lady.

Yours faithfully,
ANTHONY BICKET.

With that letter in his hand, Michael, like some psychometric medium, could see again the writer, his thin face, prominent eyes, large ears, a shadowy figure of the London streets behind his coloured balloons. Poor little snipe–square peg in round hole wherever he might be; and all those other pegs–thousands upon thousands, that would never fit in. Pommies! Well! He wasn't recommending emigration for them; he was recommending it for those who could be shaped before their wood had set. Surely they wouldn't put that stigma on to children! He opened the other letter.

Roll Manor,
Nr. Huntingdon.

My DEAR SIR,

The disappointment I have felt since the appearance of my book was somewhat mitigated by your kind allusions to it in Parliament, and your championship of its thesis. I am an old man, and do not come to London now, but it would give me pleasure to meet you. If you are ever in this neighbourhood, I should be happy if you would lunch with me, or stay the night, as suits you best.

With kind regards,

Faithfully yours,
JAS: FOGGART.

He showed it to Fleur.

'If you go, my dear, you'll be bored to tears.'

'I must go,' said Michael; *'Fons et Origo!'*

He wrote that he would come to lunch the following day.

He was met at the station by a horse drawing a vehicle of a shape he had never before beheld. The green-liveried man to whose side he climbed introduced it with the words: 'Sir James thought, sir, you'd like to see about you; so 'e sent the T cart.'

It was one of those grey late autumn days, very still, when the few leaves that are left hang listless, waiting to be windswept. The puddled road smelled of rain; rooks rose from the stubbles as if in surprise at the sound of horses' hoofs; and the turned earth of ploughed fields had the sheen that betokened clay. To the flat landscape poplars gave a certain spirituality; and the russet-tiled farmhouse roofs a certain homeliness.

'That's the manor, sir,' said the driver, pointing with his whip. Between an orchard and a group of elms, where was obviously a rookery, Michael saw a long low house of deeply weathered brick covered by Virginia creeper whose leaves had fallen. At a little distance were barns, out-houses, and the wall of a kitchen-garden. The T cart turned into an avenue of limes and came suddenly on the house unprotected by a gate. Michael pulled an old iron bell. Its lingering clang produced a lingering man, who, puckering his face, said: 'Mr Mont? Sir James is expecting you. This way, sir.'

Through an old low hall smelling pleasantly of wood-smoke, Michael reached a door which the puckered man closed in his face.

Sir James Foggart! Some gaitered old countryman with little grey whiskers, neat, weathered and firm-featured; or one of those short-necked John Bulls, still extant, square and weighty, with a flat top to his head, and a flat white topper on it?

The puckered man reopened the door, and said:

'Sir James will see you, sir.'

Before the fire in a large room with a large hearth and many books was a huge old man, grey-bearded and grey-locked, like a superannuated British lion, in an old velvet coat with whitened seams.

He appeared to be trying to rise.

'Please don't, sir,' said Michael.

'If you'll excuse me, I won't. Pleasant journey?'

'Very.'

'Sit down. Much touched by your speech. First speech, I think?'

Michael bowed.

'Not the last, I hope.'

The voice was deep and booming; the eyes looked up keenly, as if out of thickets, so bushy were the eyebrows, and the beard grew so high on the cheeks. The thick grey hair waved across the forehead and fell on to the coat collar. A primeval old man in a high state of cultivation. Michael was deeply impressed.

'I've looked forward to this honour, sir,' he said, 'ever since we published your book.'

'I'm a recluse–never get out now. Tell you the truth, don't want to–see too many things I dislike. I write, and smoke my pipe. Ring the bell, and we'll have lunch. Who's this Sir Alexander MacGown? His head wants punching!'

'No longer, sir,' said Michael.

Sir James Foggart leaned back and laughed. His laugh was long, deep, slightly hollow, like a laugh in a trombone.

'Capital! And how did those fellows take your speech? Used to know a lot of 'em at one time–fathers of these fellows, grandfathers, perhaps.'

'How do you know so well what England wants, sir,' said Michael, suavely, 'now that you never leave home?'

Sir James Foggart pointed with a large thin hand covered with hair to a table piled with books and magazines.

'Read,' he said; 'read everything–eyes as good as ever–seen a good deal in my day.' And he was silent, as if seeing it again.

'Are you following your book up?'

'M'm. Something for 'em to read when I'm gone. Eighty-four, you know.'

'I wonder,' said Michael, 'that you haven't had the Press down.'

'Have–had 'em yesterday; three by different trains; very polite young men; but I could see they couldn't make head or tail of the old creature–too far gone, eh?'

At this moment the door was opened, and the puckered man came in, followed by a maid and three cats. They put a tray on Sir James's knees and another on a small table before Michael. On each tray was a partridge with chipped potatoes, spinach and bread sauce. The puckered man filled Sir James's glass with barley-water, Michael's with claret, and retired. The three cats, all tortoise-shells, began rubbing themselves against Sir James's trousers, purring loudly.

'Don't mind cats, I hope? No fish to-day, pussies!'

Michael was hungry and finished his bird. Sir James gave most of his to the cats. They were then served with fruit salad, cheese, coffee and cigars, and everything removed except the cats, who lay replete before the fire curled up in a triangle.

Michael gazed through the smoke of two cigars at the fount and origin, eager, but in doubt whether it would stand pumping–it seemed so very old! Well! anyway, he must have a shot!

'You know Blythe, sir, of *The Outpost*? He's your great supporter; I'm only a mouthpiece.'

'Know his paper–best of the weeklies; but too clever by half.'

'Now that I've got the chance,' said Michael, 'would you mind if I asked you one or two questions?'

Sir James Foggart looked at the lighted end of his cigar. 'Fire ahead.'

'Well, sir, can England really stand apart from Europe?'

'Can she stand with Europe? Alliances based on promise of assistance that won't be forthcoming—worse than useless.'

'But suppose Belgium were invaded again, or Holland?'

'The one case, perhaps. Let that be understood. Knowledge in Europe, young man, of what England will or will not do in given cases is most important. And they've never had it. *Perfide Albion!* Heh! We always wait till the last moment to declare our policy. Great mistake. Gives the impression that we serve Time—which, with our democratic system, by the way, we generally do.'

'I like that, sir,' said Michael, who did not. 'About wheat? How would you stabilise the price so as to encourage our growth of it?'

'Ha! My pet lamb. We want a wheat loan, Mr Mont, and Government control. Every year the Government should buy in advance all the surplus we need and store it; then fix a price for the home farmers that gives them a good profit; and sell to the public at the average between the two prices. You'd soon see plenty of wheat grown here, and a general revival of agriculture.'

'But wouldn't it raise the price of bread, sir?'

'Not it.'

'And need an army of officials?'

'No. Use the present machinery properly organised.'

'State trading, sir?' said Michael, with diffidence.

Sir James Foggart's voice boomed out. 'Exceptional case—basic case—why not?'

'I quite agree,' said Michael, hastily. 'I never thought of it, but why not? . . . Now as to the opposition to child emigration in this country. Do you think it comes from the affection of parents for their children?'

'More from dislike of losing the children's wages.'

'Still, you know,' murmured Michael, 'one might well kick against losing one's children for good at fifteen!'

'One might; human nature's selfish, young man. Hang on to 'em and see 'em rot before one's eyes, or grow up to worse chances than one's own—as you say, that's human nature.'

Michael who had not said it, felt somewhat stunned.

'The child emigration scheme will want an awful lot of money, and organisation.'

Sir James stirred the cats with his slippered foot.

'Money! There's still a mint of money—misapplied. Another hundred million loan—four and a half millions a year in the Budget; and a hundred thousand children at least sent out every year. In five years we should save the lot in unemployment dole.' He waved his cigar, and its ash spattered on his velvet coat.

'Thought it would,' said Michael to himself, knocking his own off into a coffee-cup. 'But can children sent out wholesale like that be properly looked after, and given a real chance, sir?'

'Start gradually; where there's a will there's a way.'

'And won't they just swell the big towns out there?'

'Teach 'em to want land, and give it 'em.'

'I don't know if it's enough,' said Michael, boldly; 'the lure of the towns is terrific.'

Sir James nodded. 'A town's no bad thing till it's overdone, as they are here. Those that go to the towns will increase the demand for our supplies.'

'Well,' thought Michael, 'I'm getting on. What shall I ask him next?' And he contemplated the cats, who were stirring uneasily. A peculiar rumbling noise had taken possession of the silence. Michael looked up. Sir James Foggart was asleep! In repose he was more tremendous than ever–perhaps rather too tremendous; for his snoring seemed to shake the room. The cats tucked their heads farther in. There was a slight smell of burning. Michael picked a fallen cigar from the carpet. What should he do now? Wait for a revival, or clear out? Poor old boy! Foggartism had never seemed to Michael a more forlorn hope than in this sanctum of its founts and origin. Covering his ears, he sat quite still. One by one the cats got up. Michael looked at his watch. 'I shall lose my train,' he thought, and tiptoed to the door, behind a procession of deserting cats. It was as though Foggartism was snoring the little of its life away! 'Good-bye, sir!' he said softly, and went out. He walked to the station very thoughtful. Foggartism! That vast if simple programme seemed based on the supposition that human beings could see two inches before their noses. But was that supposition justified; if so would England be so town-ridden and over-populated? For one man capable of taking a far and comprehensive view and going to sleep on it, there were nine–if not nine-and-ninety–who could take near and partial views and remain wide awake. Practical politics! The answer to all wisdom however you might boom it out. 'Oh! Ah! Young Mont–not a practical politician!' It was public death to be so labelled. And Michael, in his railway carriage, with his eyes on the English grass, felt like a man on whom everyone was heaping earth. Had pelicans crying in the wilderness a sense of humour? If not, their time was poor. Grass, grass, grass! Grass and the towns! And, nestling his chin into his heavy coat, he was soon faster asleep than Sir James Foggart.

5

PROGRESS OF THE CASE

When Soames said 'Leave it to me,' he meant it, of course; but it was really very trying that whenever anything went wrong, he, and not somebody else, had to set it right!

To look more closely into the matter he was staying with his sister Winifred Dartie in Green Street. Finding his nephew Val at dinner there the first night, he took the opportunity of asking him whether he knew anything of Lord Charles Ferrar.

'What do you want to know, Uncle Soames?'

'Anything unsatisfactory. I'm told his father doesn't speak to him.'

'Well,' said Val, 'it's generally thought he'll win the Lincolnshire with a horse that didn't win the Cambridgeshire.'

'I don't see the connection.'

Val Dartie looked at him through his lashes. He was not going to enter for the slander stakes. 'Well, he's got to bring off a *coup* soon, or go under.'

'Is that all?'

'Except that he's one of those chaps who are pleasant to you when you can be of use, and unpleasant when you can't.'

'So I gathered from his looks,' said Soames. 'Have you had any business dealings with him?'

'Yes; I sold him a yearling by Torpedo out of Banshee.'

'Did he pay you?'

'Yes,' said Val, with a grin; 'and she turned out no good.'

'H'm! I suppose he was unpleasant afterwards? That all you know?'

Val nodded. He knew more, if gossip can be called 'more'; but what was puffed so freely with the smoke of racing-men's cigars was hardly suited to the ears of lawyers.

For so old a man of the world Soames was singularly unaware how in that desirable sphere, called Society, everyone is slandered daily, and no bones broken; slanderers and slandered dining and playing cards together with the utmost good feeling and the intentions of re-slandering each other the moment they are round the corner. Such genial and hair-raising reports reach no outside ears, and Soames really did not know where to begin investigation.

'Can you ask this Mr Curfew to tea?' he said to Fleur.

'What for, Father?'

'So that I can pump him.'

'I thought there were detectives for all that sort of thing.'

Soames went a special colour. Since his employment of Mr Polteed, who had caught him visiting his own wife's bedroom in Paris, at the beginning of the century, the word detective produced a pain in his diaphragm. He dropped the subject. And yet, without detectives, what was he to do?

One night, Winifred having gone to the theatre, he sat down with a cigar, to think. He had been provided by Michael with a list of 'advanced' books and plays which 'modern' people were reading, attending and discussing. He had even been supplied with one of the books: *Canthar*, by Perceval Calvin. He fetched it from his bedroom, and, turning up a lamp, opened the volume. After reading the first few pages, in which he could see nothing, he turned to the end and read backwards. In this way he could skip better, and each erotic passage, to which he very soon came, led him insensibly on to the one before it. He had reached the middle of the novel, before he had resort in wonder to the title-pages. How was it that the publisher and author were at large? Ah! The imprint was of a foreign nature. Soames breathed more freely. Though sixty-nine, and neither judge, juryman nor otherwise professionally compelled to be shocked, he was shaken. If women were reading this sort of thing, then there really was no distinction between men and women nowadays. He took up the book again, and read steadily on to the beginning. The erotic passages alone interested him. The rest seemed rambling, disconnected stuff. He rested again. What was this novel written for? To make money, of course. But was there another purpose? Was the author one of these 'artist' fellows who thought that to give you 'life'–wasn't that the phrase? they must put down every visit to a bedroom, and some besides? 'Art for Art's sake', 'realism'–what did they call it? In Soames's comparatively bleak experience 'life' did not consist wholly of visiting bedrooms, so that he was unable to admit that this book was life, the whole of life, and nothing but life. 'Calvin's a crank, sir,' Michael had said, when he handed him the novel. 'He thinks people can't become continent except through being excessively incontinent; so he shows his hero and heroine arriving gradually at continence.' 'At Bedlam,' thought Soames. They would see what a British jury had to say to that, anyway. But how elicit a confession that this woman and her set had read it with gusto? And then an idea occurred to him, so brilliant that he had to ponder deeply before he could feel any confidence in it. These 'advanced' young people had any amount of conceit; everyone who didn't share their views was a 'dud', or a 'grundy'. Suppose the book were attacked in the Press, wouldn't it draw their fire? And if their fire could be drawn in print, could it not be used afterwards as evidence of their views on morality? H'm! This would want very nice handling. And first of all, how was he to prove that Marjorie Ferrar had read this book? Thus casting about him, Soames was rewarded by another brilliant thought: Young Butterfield—who had helped him to prove the guilt of Elderson in that matter of the P.P.R.S. and owed his place at Danby & Winter's, the publishers, to Soames's recommendation! Why not make use of him? Michael always said the young man was grateful. And obscuring the title of the book against his flank, in case he should meet a servant, Soames sought his own bedroom.

His last thought that night was almost diagnostic.

'In my young days we read that sort of book if we could get hold of it, and didn't say so; now, it seems, they make a splash of reading it, and pretend it does them good!'

Next morning from the Connoisseurs' he telephoned to Danby & Winter's, and asked to speak to Mr. Butterfield.

'Yes?'

'Mr Forsyte speaking. Do you remember me?'

'Yes, indeed, sir.'

'Can you step round to the Connoisseurs' Club this morning some time?'

'Certainly, sir. Will twelve-thirty suit you?'

Secretive and fastidious in matters connected with sex, Soames very much disliked having to speak to a young man about an 'immoral' book. He saw no other way of it, however, and, on his visitor's arrival, shook hands and began at once.

'This is confidential, Mr Butterfield.'

Butterfield, whose dog-like eyes had glowed over the handshake, answered: 'Yes, sir. I've not forgotten what you did for me, sir.'

Soames held out the book.

'Do you know that novel?'

Butterfield smiled slightly.

'Yes, sir. It's printed in Brussels. They're paying five pounds a copy for it.'

'Have you read it?'

The young man shook his head. 'It's not come my way, sir.'

Soames was relieved. 'Well, don't! But just attend a moment. Can you buy ten copies of it, at my expense, and post them to ten people whose names I'll give you? They're all more or less connected with literature. You can put in slips to say the copies are complimentary, or whatever you call it. But mention no names.'

The young man Butterfield said deprecatingly:

'The price is rising all the time, sir. It'll cost you well on sixty pounds.'

'Never mind that.'

'You wish the book boomed, sir?'

'Good Gad—no! I have my reasons, but we needn't go into them.'

'I see, sir. And you want the copies to come–as if–as if from heaven?'

'That's it,' said Soames. 'I take it that publishers often send doubtful books to people they think will support them. There's just one other thing. Can you call a week later on one of the people to whom you've sent the books, and offer to sell another copy as if you were an agent for it? I want to make quite sure it's already reached that person, and been read. You won't give your name, of course. Will you do this for me?'

The eyes of the young man Butterfield again glowed.

'Yes, sir. I owe you a great deal, sir.'

Soames averted his eyes; he disliked all expression of gratitude.

'Here's the list of names, then, with their addresses. I've underlined the one you call on. I'll write you a cheque to go on with; and you can let me know later if there's anything more to pay.'

He sat down, while the young man Butterfield scrutinised the list.

'I see it's a lady, sir, that I'm to call on.'

'Yes; does that make any difference to you?'

'Not at all, sir. Advanced literature is written for ladies nowadays.'

'H'm!' said Soames. 'I hope you're doing well?'

'Splendidly, sir. I was very sorry that Mr Mont left us; we've been doing better ever since.'

Soames lifted an eyebrow. The statement confirmed many an old suspicion. When the young man had gone, he took *Canthar*. Was he capable of writing an attack on it in the Press, over the signature 'Paterfamilias'? He was not. The job required someone used to that sort of thing. Besides, a real signature would be needed to draw fire. It would not do to ask Michael to suggest one; but Old Mont might know some fogey at the 'Parthenæum' who carried metal. Sending for a bit of brown paper, he disguised the cover with it, put the volume in his overcoat pocket, and set out for 'Snooks'.

He found Sir Lawrence about to lunch, and they sat down together. Making sure that the waiter was not looking over his shoulder, Soames, who had brought the book in with him, pushed it over, and said:

'Have you read that?'

Sir Lawrence whinnied.

'My dear Forsyte, why this morbid curiosity? Everybody's reading it. They say the thing's unspeakable.'

'Then you haven't?' said Soames, keeping him to the point.

'Not yet, but if you'll lend it me, I will. I'm tired of people who've enjoyed it asking me if I've read 'that most disgusting book'. It's not fair, Forsyte. Did *you* enjoy it?'

'I skimmed it,' said Soames, looking round his nose. 'I had a reason. When you've read it, I'll tell you.'

Sir Lawrence brought it back to him at the Connoisseurs' two days later.

'Here you are, my dear Forsyte,' he said. 'I never was more glad to get rid of a book! I've been in a continual stew for fear of being overseen with it! Perceval Calvin–*quel sale Monsieur!*'

'Exactly!' said Soames. 'Now, I want to get that book attacked.'

'You! Is Saul also among the prophets? Why this sudden zest?'

'It's rather roundabout,' said Soames, sitting on the book. He detailed the reason, and ended with:

'Don't say anything to Michael, or Fleur.'

Sir Lawrence listened with his twisting smile.

'I see,' he said, 'I see. Very cunning, Forsyte. You want me to get someone whose name will act like a red rag. It musn't be a novelist, or they'll say he's jealous–which he probably is: the book's selling like hot cakes–I believe that's the expression. Ah! I think–I rather think, Forsyte, that I have the woman.'

'Woman!' said Soames. 'They won't pay any attention to that.'

Sir Lawrence cocked his eyebrow. 'I believe you're right–the only women they pay attention to nowadays are those who go one better than themselves. Shall I do it myself, and sign "Outraged Parent"?'

'I believe it wants a real name.'

'Again right, Forsyte; it does. I'll drop into the 'Parthenæum', and see if anyone's alive.'

Two days later Soames received a note.

The Parthenæum,
Friday.

MY DEAR FORSYTE,

I've got the man–the editor of the *Protagonist*; and he'll do it under his own name. What's more, I've put him on to the right line. We had a spirited argument. He wanted to treat it *de haut en bas* as the work of a dirty child. I said: 'No. This thing is symptomatic. Treat it seriously; show that it represents a school of thought, a deliberate literary attitude; and make it a plea for censorship.' Without the word censorship, Forsyte, they will never rise. So he's leaving his wife and taking it into the country for the week-end. I admire your conduct of the defence, my dear Forsyte; it's very subtle. But if you'll forgive me for saying so, it's more important to prevent the case coming into Court than to get a verdict if it does.

Sincerely yours,
LAWRENCE MONT.

With which sentiment Soames so entirely agreed, that he went down to Mapledurham, and spent the next two afternoons going round and round with a man he didn't like, hitting a ball, to quiet his mind.

6

MICHAEL VISITS BETHNAL GREEN

The feeling of depression with which Michael had come back from the fount and origin was somewhat mitigated by letters he was receiving from people of varying classes, nearly all young. They were so nice and earnest. They made him wonder whether after all practical politicians were not too light-hearted, like the managers of music-halls who protected the public carefully from their more tasteful selves. They made him feel that there might be a spirit in the country that was not really represented in the House, or even in the Press. Among these letters was one which ran:

Sunshine House,
Bethnal Green.

DEAR MR MONT,

I was so awfully glad to read your speech in *The Times.* I instantly got Sir James Foggart's book. I think the whole policy is simply splendid. You've no idea how heart-breaking it is for us who try to do things for children, to know that whatever we do is bound to be snowed under by the life they go to when school age ends. We have a good opportunity here of seeing the realities of child life in London. It's wonderful to see the fondness of the mothers for the little ones, in spite of their own hard lives–though not all, of course, by any means; but we often notice, and I think it's common experience, that when the children get beyond ten or twelve, the fondness for them begins to assume another form. I suppose it's really the commercial possibilities of the child making themselves felt. When money comes in at the door, disinterested love seems to move towards the window. I suppose it's natural, but it's awfully sad, because the commercial possibilities are generally so miserable; and the children's after-life is often half ruined for the sake of the few shillings they earn. I do fervently hope something will come of your appeal; only–things move so slowly, don't they? I wish you would come down and see our House here. The children are adorable, and we try to give them sunshine.

Sincerely yours,
NORAH CURFEW.

Bertie Curfew's sister! But surely that case would not really come to anything! Grateful for encouragement, and seeking light on Foggartism, he decided to go. Perhaps Norah Curfew would take the little Boddicks! He suggested to Fleur that she should accompany him, but she was afraid of picking up something unsuitable to the eleventh baronet, so he went alone.

The house, facing the wintry space called Bethnal Green, consisted of three small houses converted into one, with their three small back yards, trellised round and gravelled, for a playground. Over the door were the words: 'SUNSHINE HOUSE' in gold capitals. The walls were cream-coloured, the woodwork dark, and the curtains of gay chintz. Michael was received in the entrance-lobby by Norah Curfew herself. Tall, slim and straight, with dark hair brushed back from a pale face, she had brown eyes, clear, straight and glowing.

'Gosh!' thought Michael, as she wrung his hand. 'She *is* swept and garnished. No basement in her soul!'

'It *was* good of you to come, Mr. Mont. Let me take you over the house. This is the play-room.'

Michael entered a room of spotless character, which had evidently been formed from several knocked into one. Six small children dressed in blue linen were seated on the floor, playing games. They embraced the knees of Norah Curfew when she came within reach. With the exception of one little girl Michael thought them rather ugly.

'These are our residents. The others only come out of school hours. We have to limit them to fifty, and that's a pretty good squeeze. We want funds to take the next two houses.'

'How many of you are working here?'

'Six. Two of us do the cooking; one the accounts; and the rest washing, mending, games, singing, dancing and general chores. Two of us live in.'

'I don't see your harps and crowns.'

Norah Curfew smiled.

'Pawned,' she said.

'What do you do about religion?' asked Michael, thinking of the eleventh baronet's future.

'Well, on the whole we don't. You see, they're none of them more than twelve; and the religious age, when it begins at all, begins with sex about fourteen. We just try to teach kindness and cheerfulness. I had my brother down the other day. He's always laughed at me; but he's going to do a matinée for us, and give us the proceeds.'

'What play?'

'I think it's called "The Plain Dealer". He says he's always wanted to do it for a good object.'

Michael stared. 'Do you know "The Plain Dealer"?'

'No; it's by one of the Restoration people, isn't it?'

'Wycherley.'

'Oh! yes!' Her eyes remaining clearer than the dawn, Michael thought: 'Poor dear! It's not my business to queer the pitch of her money-getting; but Master Bertie likes his little joke!'

'I must bring my wife down here,' he said; 'she'd love your walls and curtains. And I wanted to ask you. You haven't room, have you, for two more little girls, if we pay for them? Their father's down and out, and I'm starting him in the country–no mother.'

Norah Curfew wrinkled her straight brows, and on her face came the look Michael always connected with haloes, an anxious longing to stretch good-will beyond power and pocket.

'Oh! we must!' she said. 'I'll manage somehow. What are their names?'

'Boddick–Christian, I don't know. I call them by their ages–Four and Five.'

'Give me the address. I'll go and see them myself; if they haven't got anything catching, they shall come.'

'You really are an angel,' said Michael simply.

Norah Curfew coloured, and opened a door. 'That's silly,' she said, still more simply. 'This is our mess-room.'

It was not large, and contained a girl working a typewriter, who stopped with her hands on the keys and looked round; another girl beating up eggs in a bowl, who stopped reading a book of poetry; and a third, who seemed practising a physical exercise, and stopped with her arms extended.

'This is Mr Mont,' said Norah Curfew, 'who made that splendid speech in the House. Miss Betts, Miss La Fontaine, Miss Beeston.'

The girls bowed, and the one who continued to beat the eggs, said: 'It was bully.'

Michael also bowed. 'Beating the air, I'm afraid.'

'Oh! but, Mr Mont, it must have an effect. It said what so many people are really thinking.'

'Ah!' said Michael, 'but their thoughts are so deep, you know.'

'Do sit down.'

Michael sat on the end of a peacock-blue divan.

'I was born in South Africa,' said the egg-beater, 'and I know what's waiting.'

'My father was in the House,' said the girl, whose arms had come down to her splendid sides. 'He was very much struck. Anyway, we're jolly grateful.'

Michael looked from one to the other.

'I suppose if you didn't all believe in things, you wouldn't be doing this? *You* don't think the shutters are up in England, anyway?'

'Good Lord, no!' said the girl at the typewriter; 'you've only to live among the poor to know that.'

'The poor haven't got every virtue, and the rich haven't got every vice–that's nonsense!' broke in the physical exerciser.

Michael murmured soothingly.

'I wasn't thinking of that. I was wondering whether something doesn't hang over our heads too much?'

'D'you mean poison-gas?'

'Partly; and town blight, and a feeling that Progress had been found out.'

'Well, I don't know,' replied the egg-beater, who was dark and pretty. 'I used to think so in the war. But Europe isn't the world. Europe isn't even very important, really. The sun hardly shines there, anyway.'

Michael nodded. 'After all, if the Millennium comes and we do blot each other out in Europe, it'll only mean another desert about the size of the Sahara, and the loss of a lot of people obviously too ill-conditioned to be fit to live. It'd be a jolly good lesson to the rest of the world, wouldn't it? Luckily the other continents are far off each other.'

'Cheerful!' exclaimed Norah Curfew.

Michael grinned.

'Well, one can't help catching the atmosphere of this place. I admire you all frightfully, you know, giving up everything, to come and do this.'

'That's tosh,' said the girl at the typewriter. 'What is there to give up–bunny-hugging? One got used to doing things in the war.'

'If it comes to that,' said the egg-beater, 'we admire you much more for not giving up Parliament.'

Again Michael grinned.

'Miss La Fontaine–wanted in the kitchen!'

The egg-beater went towards the door.

'Can you beat eggs? D'you mind–shan't be a minute.' Handing Michael the bowl and fork, she vanished.

'What a shame!' said Norah Curfew. 'Let me!'

'No,' said Michael; 'I can beat eggs with anybody. What do you all feel about cutting children adrift at fifteen?'

'Well, of course, it'll be bitterly opposed,' said the girl at the typewriter. 'They'll call it inhuman, and all that. It's much more inhuman really to keep them here.'

'The real trouble,' said Norah Curfew, 'apart from the shillings earned, is the class-interference idea. Besides, Imperialism isn't popular.'

'I should jolly well think it isn't,' muttered the physical exerciser.

'Ah!' said the typist, 'but this isn't Imperialism, is it, Mr Mont? It's all on the lines of making the Dominions the equal of the Mother Country.'

Michael nodded. 'Commonwealth.'

'That won't prevent their camouflaging their objection to losing the children's wages,' said the physical exerciser.

A close discussion ensued between the three young women as to the exact effect of children's wages on the working-class budget. Michael beat his eggs and listened. It was, he knew, a point of the utmost importance. The general conclusion seemed to be that children earned on the whole rather more than their keep, but that it was 'very shortsighted in the long run', because it fostered surplus population and unemployment, and a 'great shame' to spoil the children's chances for the sake of the parents.

The re-entrance of the egg-beater put a stop to it.

'They're beginning to come in, Norah.'

The physical exerciser slipped out, and Norah Curfew said:

'Now Mr Mont, would you like to see them?'

Michael followed her. He was thinking: 'I wish Fleur had come!' These girls seemed really to believe in things.

Downstairs the children were trickling in from school. He stood and watched them. They seemed a queer blend of anæmia and vitality, of effervescence and obedience. Unselfconscious as puppies, but old beyond their years; and yet looking as if they never thought ahead. Each movement, each action was as if it were their last. They were very quick. Most of them carried something to eat in a paper bag or a bit of grease-paper. They chattered, and didn't laugh. Their accent struck Michael as deplorable. Six or seven at most were nice to look at; but nearly all looked good-tempered, and none seemed to be selfish. Their movements were jerky. They mobbed Norah Curfew and the physical exerciser; obeyed without question, ate without appetite, and grabbed at the house cat. Michael was fascinated.

With them came four or five mothers, who had questions to ask, or bottles to fill. They too were on perfect terms with the young women. Class did not exist in this house; only personality was present. He noticed that the children responded to his grin, that the women didn't, though they smiled at Norah Curfew and the physical exerciser; he wondered if they would give him a bit of their minds if they knew of his speech.

Norah Curfew accompanied him to the door.

'Aren't they ducks?'

'I'm afraid if I saw much of them, I should give up Foggartism.'

'Oh! but why?'

'Well, you see, it designs to make them men and women of property.'

'You mean that would spoil them?'

Michael grinned. 'There's something dangerous about silver spoons. Here's my initiation fee.' He handed her all his money.

'Oh! Mr Mont, we didn't–!'

'Well, give me back sixpence, otherwise I shall have to walk home.'

'It's frightfully kind of you. Do come again; and please don't give up Foggartism.'

He walked to the train thinking of her eyes; and, on reaching home, said to Fleur:

'You absolutely must come and see that place. It's quite clean, and the spirit's topping. It's bucked me up like anything. Norah Curfew's perfectly splendid.'

Fleur looked at him between her lashes.

'Oh!' she said. 'I will.'

7

CONTRASTS

The land beyond the coppice at Lippinghall was a ten-acre bit of poor grass, chalk and gravel, fenced round to show that it was property. Except for one experiment with goats, abandoned because nobody would drink their milk in a country that did not demean itself by growing food, nothing had been done with it. By December this poor relation of Sir Lawrence Mont's estate was being actively exploited. Close to the coppice the hut had been erected, and at least an acre converted into a sea of mud. The coppice itself presented an incised and draggled appearance, owing to the ravages of Henry Boddick and another man, who had cut and stacked a quantity of timber, which a contractor was gradually rejecting for the fowl-house and granary. The incubator-house was at present in the nature of a prophecy. Progress, in fact, was somewhat slow, but it was hoped that fowls might be asked to begin their operations soon after the New Year. In the meantime Michael had decided that the colony had better get the worst over and go into residence. Scraping the Manor House for furniture, and sending in a store of groceries, oil-lamps, and soap, he installed Boddick on the left, earmarked the centre for the Bergfelds, and the right hand for Swain. He was present when the Manor car brought them from the station. The murky day was turning cold, the trees dripped, the car-wheels splashed up the surface water. From the doorway of the hut Michael watched them get out, and thought he had never seen three more untimely creatures. Bergfeld came first; having only one suit, he had put it on, and looked what he was–an actor out of a job. Mrs Bergfeld came second, and having no outdoor coat, looked what she was–nearly frozen. Swain came last. On his shadowy face was nothing quite so spirited as a sneer; but he gazed about him, and seemed to say: 'My hat!'

Boddick, with a sort of prescience, was absent in the coppice. 'He,' thought Michael, 'is my only joy!'

Taking them into the kitchen mess-room of the hut, he deployed a thermos of hot coffee, a cake, and a bottle of rum.

'Awfully sorry things look so dishevelled; but I think the hut's dry, and there are plenty of blankets. These oil-lamps smell rather. You were in the war, Mr Swain; you'll feel at home in no time. Mrs Bergfeld, you look so cold, do put some rum into your coffee; we always do when we go over the top.'

They all put rum into their coffee, which had a marked effect. Mrs Bergfeld's cheeks grew pink, and her eyes darkened. Swain remarked that the hut was a 'bit of all right'; Bergfeld began making a speech. Michael checked him. 'Boddick knows all the ropes. I'm afraid I've got to catch a train; I've only just time to show you round.'

While whirling back to town afterwards he felt that he had, indeed, abandoned his platoon just as it was going over the top. That night he would be dining in Society; there would be light and warmth, jewels and pictures, wine and talk; the dinner would cost the board of his 'down and outs' for a quarter at least; and nobody would give them and their like a thought. If he ventured to draw Fleur's attention to the contrast, she would say:

'My dear boy, that's like a book by Gurdon Minho; you're getting sentimental.' and he would feel a fool. Or would he? Would he not, perhaps, look at her small distinguished head and think: 'Too easy a way out, my dear; those who take it have little heads!' And, then, his eyes, straying farther down to that white throat and all the dainty loveliness below, would convey a warmth to his blood and a warning to his brain not to give way to blasphemy, lest it end by disturbing bliss. For what with Foggartism, poultry, and the rest of it, Michael had serious thoughts sometimes that Fleur had none; and with wisdom born of love, he knew that if she hadn't, she never would have, and he must get used to it. She was what she was, and could be converted only in popular fiction. Excellent business for the self-centred heroine to turn from interest in her own belongings to interest in people who had no belongings; but in life it wasn't done. Fleur at least camouflaged her self-concentration gracefully; and with Kit–! Ah! but Kit was herself!

So he did not mention his 'down and outs' on their way to dinner in Eaton Square. He took instead a lesson in the royal Personage named on their invitation card, and marvelled at Fleur's knowledge. 'She's interested in social matters. And do remember, Michael, not to sit down till she asks you to, and not to go away before her, and to say "ma'am".'

Michael grinned. 'I suppose they'll all be nobs, or sn—er—why the deuce did they ask us?'

But Fleur was silent, thinking of her curtsey.

Royalty was affable, the dinner short but superb, served and eaten off gold plate, at a rate which suited the impression that there really wasn't a moment to spare. Fleur took a mental note of this new necessity. She knew personally five of the twenty-four diners, and the rest as in an illustrated paper, darkly. She had seen them all there at one time or another, stepping hideously in paddocks, photographed with their offspring or their dogs, about to reply for the Colonies, or 'taking a lunar' at a flying grouse. Her quick instinct apprehended almost at once the reason why she and Michael had been invited. His speech! Like some new specimen at the Zoo, he was an object of curiosity, a stunt. She saw people nodding in the direction of him, seated opposite her between two ladies covered with flesh and pearls. Excited and very pretty, she flirted with the Admiral on her right, and defended Michael with spirit from the Under-Secretary on her left. The Admiral grew warm, the Under-Secretary, too young for emotion, cold.

'A little knowledge, Mrs Mont,' he said at the end of his short second innings, 'is a dangerous thing.'

'Now where have I heard that?' said Fleur. 'Is it in the Bible?'

The Under-Secretary tilted his chin.

'We who have to work departments know too much, perhaps; but your husband certainly doesn't know enough. Foggartism is an amusing idea, but there it stops.'

'We shall see!' said Fleur. 'What do you say, Admiral?'

'Foggartism! What's that—new kind of death ray? I saw a fellow yesterday, Mrs Mont—give you my word!—who's got a ray that goes through three bullocks, a nine-inch brick wall, and gives a shock to a donkey on the other side; and only at quarter strength.'

Fleur flashed a look round towards the Under-Secretary, who had turned his shoulder, and, leaning towards the Admiral, murmured:

'I wish you'd give a shock to the donkey on *my* other side; he wants it, and I'm not nine inches thick.'

But before the Admiral could shoot his death ray, Royalty had risen.

In the apartment to which Fleur was withdrawn, she had been saying little for some minutes, and noticing much, when her hostess came up and said:

'My dear, Her Royal Highness—'

Fleur followed, retaining every wit.

A frank and simple hand patted the sofa beside her. Fleur sat down. A frank and simple voice said:

'What an interesting speech your husband made! It was so refreshing, I thought.'

'Yes, ma'am,' said Fleur; 'but there it will stop, I am told.'

A faint smile curled lips guiltless of colouring matter.

'Well, perhaps. Has he been long in Parliament?'

'Only a year.'

'Ah! I liked his taking up the cudgels for the children.'

'Some people think he's proposing a new kind of child slavery.'

'Oh! really! Have you any children?'

'One,' said Fleur, and added honestly: 'And I must say I wouldn't part with him at fourteen.'

'Ah! And have you been long married?'

'Four years.'

At this moment the royal lady saw someone else she wished to speak to, and was compelled to break off the conversation, which she did very graciously, leaving Fleur with the feeling that she had been disappointed with the rate of production.

In the cab trailing its way home through the foggy night, she felt warm and excited, and as if Michael wasn't.

'What's the matter, Michael?'

His hand came down on her knee at once.

'Sorry, old thing! Only, really–when you think of it–eh?'

'Of what? You were quite a li–object of interest.'

'The whole thing's a game. Anything for novelty!'

'The Princess was very nice about you.'

'Ah! Poor thing! But I suppose you get used to anything!'

Fleur laughed. Michael went on:

'Any new idea gets seized and talked out of existence. It never gets farther than the brain, and the brain gets bored; and there it is already a back number!'

'That can't be true, Michael. What about Free Trade, or Woman Suffrage?'

Michael squeezed her knee. 'All the women say to me: 'But how interesting, Mr Mont; I think it's most thrilling!' And the men say: 'Good stunt, Mont! But not practical politics, of course.' And I've only one answer: 'Things as big got done in the war.' By George, it's foggy!'

They were going, indeed, at a snail's pace, and through the windows could see nothing but the faint glow of the street lamps emerging slowly, high up, one by one. Michael let down a window and leaned out.

'Where are we?'

'Gawd knows, sir.'

Michael coughed, put up the window again, and resumed his clutch of Fleur.

'By the way, Wastwater asked me if I'd read *Canthar*. He says there's a snorting cut-up of it in *The Protagonist*. It'll have the usual effect–sends sales up.'

'They say it's very clever.'

'Horribly out of drawing–not fit for children, and tells adults nothing they don't know. I don't see how it can be justified.'

'Genius, my dear. If it's attacked, it'll be defended.'

'Sib Swan won't have it–he says it's muck.'

'Oh! yes; but Sib's getting a back number.'

'That's very true,' said Michael, thoughtfully. 'By Jove! how fast things move, except in politics, and fog.'

Their cab had come to a standstill. Michael let down the window again.

'I'm fair lost, sir,' said the driver's hoarse voice. 'Ought to be near the Embankment, but for the life of me I can't find the turning.' Michael buttoned his coat, put up the window again, and got out on the near side.

The night was smothered, alive only with the continual hootings of creeping cars. The black vapour, acrid and cold, surged into Michael's lungs.

'I'll walk beside you; we're against the kerb; creep on till we strike the river, or a bobby.'

The cab crept on, and Michael walked beside it, feeling with his foot for the kerb.

The refined voice of an invisible man said: 'This is sanguinary!'

'It is,' said Michael. 'Where are we?'

'In the twentieth century, and the heart of civilisation.'

Michael laughed, and regretted it; the fog tasted of filth.

'Think of the police!' said the voice, 'having to be out in this all night!'

'Splendid force, the police!' replied Michael. 'Where are you, sir?'

'Here, sir. Where are you?'

It was the exact position. The blurred moon of a lamp glowed suddenly above Michael's head. The cab ceased to move.

'If I could only smell the 'Ouses of Parliament, said the cabman. 'They'll be 'avin' supper there be now.'

'Listen!' said Michael–Big Ben was striking. 'That was to our left.'

'At our back,' said the cabman.

'Can't be, or we should be in the river; unless you've turned right round!'

'Gawd knows where I've turned,' said the cabman, sneezing. 'Never saw such a night!'

'There's only one thing for it–drive on until we hit something. Gently does it.'

The cabman started the cab, and Michael, with his hand on it, continued to feel for the kerb with his foot.

'Steady!' he said, suddenly. 'Car in front.' There was a slight bump.

'Nah then!' said a voice. 'Where yer comin'? Cawn't yer see?'

Michael moved up alongside of what seemed to be another taxi.

'Comin' along at that pice!' said its driver; 'and full moon, too!'

'Awfully sorry,' said Michael. 'No harm done. You got any sense of direction left?'

'The pubs are all closed–worse luck! There's a bloomin' car in front o' me that I've hit three times, Can't make any impression on it. The driver's dead, I think. Would yer go and look, Guv'nor?'

Michael moved towards the loom in front. But at that moment it gave way to the more universal blackness. He ran four steps to hail the driver, stumbled off the kerb, fell, picked himself up and spun round. He moved along the kerb to his right, felt he was going wrong, stopped and called: 'Hallo!' A faint 'Hallo!' replied from–where? He moved what he thought was back, and called again. No answer! Fleur would be frightened. He shouted. Half a dozen faint hallos replied to him; and someone at his elbow said: 'Don't cher know where y'are?'

'No; do you?'

'What do you think? Lost anything?'

'Yes; my cab,'

'Left anything in it?'

'My wife.'

'Lawd! You won't get 'er back to-night.' A hoarse laugh, ghostly and obscene, floated by. A bit of darkness loomed for a moment, and faded out. Michael stood still. 'Keep your head!' he thought. 'Here's the kerb–either they're in front, or they're behind; or else I've turned a corner.' He stepped forward along the kerb. Nothing! He stepped back. Nothing! 'What the blazes have I done?' he muttered: 'or have they moved on!' Sweat poured down him in spite of the cold. Fleur would be really scared! And the words of his election address sprang from his lips: 'Chiefly by the elimination of smoke!'

'Ah!' said a voice, 'got a cigarette, Guv'nor?'

'I'll give you all I've got and half a crown, if you'll find a cab close by with a lady in it. What street's this?'

'Don't arst me! The streets 'ave gone mad, I think.'

'Listen!' said Michael sharply.

'That's right, "Someone callin' so sweet." '

'Hallo!' cried Michael. 'Fleur!'

'Here! Here!'

It sounded to his right, to his left, behind him, in front. Then came the steady blowing of a cab's horn.

'Now we've got 'em,' said the bit of darkness. 'This way, Guv'nor, step slow, and mind my corns!'

Michael yielded to a tugging at his coat.

'It's like no-man's-land in a smoke barrage!' said his guide.

'You're right. Hallo! Coming!'

The horn sounded a yard off. A voice said: 'Oh! Michael!'

His face touched Fleur's in the window of the cab.

'Just a second, darling. There you are, my friend, and thanks awfully! Hope you'll get home!'

'I've 'ad worse nights out than this. Thank you, Captain! Wish you and the lady luck.' There was a sound of shuffling on, and the fog sighed out: 'So long!'

'All right, sir,' said the hoarse voice of Michael's cabman. 'I know where I am now. First on the left, second on the right. I'll bump the kerb till I get there. Thought you was swallered up, sir!'

Michael got into the cab, and clasped Fleur close. She uttered a long sigh, and sat quite still.

'Nothing more scaring than a fog!' he said.

'I thought you'd been run over!'

Michael was profoundly touched.

'Awfully sorry, darling. And you've got all that beastly fog down your throat. We'll drown it out when we get in. That poor chap was an ex-service man. Wonderful the way the English keep their humour and don't lose their heads.'

'I lost mine!'

'Well, you've got it back,' said Michael, pressing it against his own to hide the emotion he was feeling. 'Fog's our sheet-anchor, after all. So long as we have fog, England will survive.' He felt Fleur's lips against his.

He belonged to her, and she couldn't afford to have him straying about in fogs or Foggartism! Was that the—? And then, he yielded to the thrill.

The cabman was standing by the opened door. 'Now, sir, I'm in your Square. P'r'aps you know your own 'ouse.'

Wrenched from the kiss, Michael stammered: 'Righto!' The fog was thinner here; he could consult the shape of the trees. 'On and to your right, third house.'

There it was—desirable—with its bay trees in its tubs and its fanlight shining. He put his latch-key in the door.

'A drink?' he said.

The cabman coughed: 'I won't say no, sir.'

Michael brought the drink.

'Far to go?'

'Near Putney Bridge. Your 'ealth, sir!'

Michael watched his pinched face drinking.

'Sorry you've got to plough into that again!'

The cabman handed back the glass.

'Thank'ee, sir; I shall be all right now; keep along the river, and down the

Fulham Road. Thought they couldn't lose me in London. Where I went wrong was trying for a short cut instead of takin' the straight road round. 'Ope the young lady's none the worse, sir. She was properly scared while you was out there in the dark. These fogs ain't fit for 'uman bein's. They ought to do somethin' about 'em in Parliament.'

'They ought!' said Michael, handing him a pound note. 'Goodnight, and good luck!'

'It's an ill wind!' said the cabman, starting his cab. 'Goodnight, sir, and thank you kindly.'

'Thank *you!*' said Michael.

The cab ground slowly away, and was lost to sight.

Michael went into the Spanish room. Fleur, beneath the Goya, was boiling a silver kettle, and burning pastilles. What a contrast to the world outside–its black malodorous cold reek, its risk and fear! In this pretty glowing room, with this pretty glowing woman, why think of its tangle, lost shapes, and straying cries?

Lighting his cigarette, he took his drink from her by its silver handle, and put it to his lips.

'I really think we ought to have a car, Michael!'

8

COLLECTING EVIDENCE

The editor of *The Protagonist* had so evidently enjoyed himself that he caused a number of other people to do the same.

'There's no more popular sight in the East, Forsyte,' said Sir Lawrence, 'than a boy being spanked; and the only difference between East and West is that in the East the boy at once offers himself again at so much a spank. I don't see Mr Perceval Calvin doing that.'

'If he defends himself,' said Soames, gloomily, 'other people won't.'

They waited, reading daily denunciations signed: 'A Mother of Three'; 'Roger: Northampton'; 'Victorian'; 'Alys St Maurice'; 'Plus Fours'; 'Arthur Whiffkin'; 'Sportsman if not Gentleman'; and 'Pro Patria'; which practically all contained the words: 'I cannot say that I have read the book through, but I have read enough to–'

It was five days before the defence fired a shot. But first came a letter above the signature: 'Swishing Block', which, after commenting on the fact that a whole school of so-called literature had been indicted by the editor of *The Protagonist* in his able letter of the 14th inst., noted with satisfaction that the said school had grace enough to takes its swishing without a murmur. Not even an anonymous squeak had been heard from the whole apostolic body.

'Forsyte,' said Sir Lawrence, handing it to Soames, 'that's my very own mite, and if it doesn't draw them–nothing will!'

But it did. The next issue of the interested journal in which the correspondence was appearing contained a letter from the greater novelist L. S. D. which restored everyone to his place. This book might or might not be Art, he hadn't read it; but the editor of *The Protagonist* wrote like a pedagogue, and there was an end of him. As to the claim that literature must always wear a flannel petticoat, it was 'piffle', and that was that. From under the skirts of this letter the defence, to what of exultation Soames ever permitted himself, moved out in force. Among the defenders were as many as four of the selected ten associates to whom young Butterfield had purveyed copies. They wrote over their own names that *Canthar* was distinctly LITERATURE; they were sorry for people who thought in these days that LITERATURE had any business with morals. The work must be approached æsthetically or not at all. ART was ART, and morality was morality, and never the twain could, would, or should meet. It was monstrous that a work of this sort should have to appear with a foreign imprint. When would England recognise genius when she saw it?

Soames cut the letters out one after the other, and pasted them in a book. He had got what he wanted, and the rest of the discussion interested him no more. He had received, too, a communication from young Butterfield.

SIR,

I called on the lady last Monday, and was fortunately able to see her in person. She seemed rather annoyed when I offered her the book. 'That book,' she said: 'I read it weeks ago.' 'It's exciting a great deal of interest, Madam,' I said. 'I know,' she said. 'Then you won't take a copy; the price is rising steadily, it'll be very valuable in time?' 'I've got one,' she said. That's what you told me to find out, sir; so I didn't pursue the matter. I hope I have done what you wanted. But if there is anything more, I shall be most happy. I consider that I owe my present position entirely to you.

Soames didn't know about that, but as to his future position—he might have to put the young man into the box. The question of a play remained. He consulted Michael.

'Does that young woman still act in the advanced theatre place you gave me the name of?'

Michael winced. 'I don't know, sir; but I could find out.'

Inquiry revealed that she was cast for the part of Olivia in Bertie Curfew's matinée of 'The Plain Dealer'.

'"The Plain Dealer"?' said Soames. 'Is that an advanced play?'

'Yes, sir, two hundred and fifty years old.'

'Ah!' said Soames; 'they were a coarse lot in those days. How is it she goes on there if she and the young man have split?'

'Oh! well, they're very cool hands. I do hope you're going to keep things out of Court, sir?'

'I can't tell. When's this performance?'

'January the seventh.'

Soames went to his club library and took down 'Wycherley'. He was disappointed with the early portions of 'The Plain Dealer', but it improved as it went on, and he spent some time making a list of what George Forsyte would have called the 'nubbly bits'. He understood that at that theatre they did not bowdlerise. Excellent! There were passages that would raise hair on any British jury. Between *Canthar* and this play, he felt as if he had a complete answer to any claim by the young woman and her set to having 'morals about them'. Old professional instincts were rising within him. He had retained Sir James Foskisson, K.C., not because he admired him personally, but because if he didn't, the other side might. As junior he was employing very young Nicholas Forsyte; he had no great option of him, but it was as well to keep the matter in the family, especially if it wasn't to come into Court.

A conversation with Fleur that evening contributed to his intention that it should not.

'What's happened to that young American?' he said.

Fleur smiled acidly. 'Francis Wilmot? Oh! he's "fallen for" Majorie Ferrar.'

'"Fallen for her"?' said Soames. 'What an expression!'

'Yes, dear; it's American.'

'"For" her? It means nothing, so far as I can see.'

'Let's hope not, for his sake! She's going to marry Sir Alexander MacGown, I'm told.'

'Oh!'

'Did Michael tell you that he hit him on the nose?'

'Which–who?' said Soames testily. 'Whose nose?'

'MacGown's dear; and it bled like anything.'

'Why on earth did he do that?'

'Didn't you read his speech about Michael?'

'Oh!' said Soames. 'Parliamentary fuss–that's nothing. They're always behaving like schoolboys, there. And so she's going to marry him. Has he been putting her up to all this?'

'No; *she's* been putting him.'

Soames discounted the information with a sniff; he scented the hostility of woman for woman. Still, chicken and egg–political feeling and social feeling, who could say which first promoted which? In any case, this made a difference. Going to be married–was she? He debated the matter for some time, and then decided that he would go and see Settlewhite and Stark. If they had been a firm of poor repute or the kind always employed in '*causes célèbres*', he wouldn't have dreamed of it; but, as a fact, they stood high, were solid family people, with an aristocratic connection and all that.

He did not write, but took his hat and went over from the Connoisseurs' to their offices in King Street, St James's. The journey recalled old days–to how many such negotiatory meetings had he not gone or caused his adversaries to come! He had never cared to take things into Court if they could be settled out of it. And always he had approached negotiation with the impersonality of one passionless about to meet another of the same kidney–two calculating machines, making their livings out of human nature. He did not feel like that to-day; and, aware of this handicap, stopped to stare into the print and picture shop next door. Ah! There were those first proofs of the Roussel engravings of the Prince Consort Exhibition of '51, that Old Mont had spoken of–he had an eye for an engraving, Old Mont. Ah! and there was a Fred Walker, quite a good one! Mason, and Walker–they weren't done for yet by any means. And the sensation that a man feels hearing a blackbird sing on a tree just coming into blossom, stirred beneath Soames's ribs. Long–long since he had bought a picture! Let him but get this confounded case out of the way, and he could enjoy himself again. Riving his glance from the window, he took a long breath, and walked into Settlewhite and Stark's.

The chief partner's room was on the first floor, and the chief partner standing where chief partners stand.

'How do you do, Mr Forsyte? I've not met you since "Bobbin against the L. & S. W." That must have been 1900!'

'1899,' said Soames. 'You were for the Company.'

Mr Settlewhite pointed to a chair.

Soames sat down and glanced up at the figure before the fire. H'm! a long-lipped, long-eyelashed, long-chinned face; a man of his own calibre, education, and probity! He need not beat about the bush.

'This action,' he said, 'is a very petty business. What can we do about it?'

Mr Settlewhite frowned.

'That depends, Mr Forsyte, on what you have to propose? My client has been very grossly libelled.'

Soames smiled sourly.

'She began it. And what is she relying on—private letters to personal friends of my daughter's, written in very natural anger! I'm surprised that a firm of your standing–'

Mr Settlewhite smiled.

'Don't trouble to compliment my firm? I'm surprised myself that you are acting for your daughter. You can hardly see all round the matter. Have you come to offer an apology?'

'That!' said Soames. 'I should have thought it was for your client to apologise.'

'If such is your view, I'm afraid it's no use continuing this discussion.'

Soames regarded him fixedly.

'How do you think you're going to prove damage? She belongs to the fast set.'

Mr Settlewhite continued to smile.

'I understand she's going to marry Sir Alexander MacGown,' said Soames.

Mr Settlewhite's lips tightened.

'Really, Mr Forsyte, if you have come to offer an apology and a substantial sum in settlement, we can talk. Otherwise–'

'As a sensible man,' said Soames, 'you know that these Society scandals are always dead sea fruit–nothing but costs and vexations, and a feast for all the gossips about town. I'm prepared to offer you a thousand pounds to settle the whole thing, but an apology I can't look at. A mutual expression of regret–perhaps; but an apology's out of the question.

'Fifteen hundred I might accept–the insults have had wide currency. But an apology is essential.'

Soames sat silent, chewing the injustice of it all. Fifteen hundred! Monstrous! Still he would pay even that to keep Fleur out of Court. But humble-pie! She wouldn't eat it, and he couldn't make her, and he didn't know that he wanted to. He got up.

'Look here, Mr Settlewhite, if you take this into Court, you will find yourself up against more than you think. But the whole thing is so offensive to me, that I'm prepared to meet you over the money, though I tell you frankly I don't believe a jury would award a penny piece. As to an apology, a "formula" could be found perhaps'–why the deuce was the fellow smiling?–'Something like this: "We regret that we have said hasty things about each other," to be signed by both parties.'

Mr Settlewhite caressed his chin.

'Well, I'll put your proposition before my client. I join with you in wishing to see the matter settled, not because I'm afraid of the result'–'Oh, no!'–thought Soames–'but because these cases, as you say, are not edifying.' He held out his hand.

Soames gave it a cold touch.

'You understand that this is entirely "without prejudice",' he said, and went out. 'She'll take it!' he thought. Fifteen hundred pounds of his money thrown away on that baggage, just because for once she had been labelled what she was; and all his trouble to get evidence wasted! For a moment he resented his devotion to Fleur. Really it was fatuous to be so fond as that! Then his heart rebounded. Thank God! He had settled it.

Christmas was at hand. It did not alarm him, therefore, that he received no answering communication. Fleur and Michael were at Lippinghall with the ninth and eleventh baronets. He and Annette had Winifred and the Cardigans down at 'The Shelter'. Not till the 6th of January did he receive a letter from Messrs. Settlewhite and Stark.

DEAR SIR,
In reference to your call of the 17th ultimo, your proposition was duly placed before our client, and we are instructed to say that she will accept the sum of £1,500—fifteen hundred pounds—and an apology, duly signed by your client, copy of which we enclose.
We are, dear Sir,
Faithfully yours,
SETTLEWHITE AND STARK.

Soames turned to the enclosure. It ran thus:

I, Mrs Michael Mont, withdraw the words concerning Miss Marjorie Ferrar contained in my letters to Mrs Ralph Ppynrryn and Mrs Edward Maltese of October 4th last, and hereby tender a full and free apology for having written them.

(Signed)

Pushing back the breakfast-table, so violently that it groaned, Soames got up.

'What is it, Soames?' said Annette. 'Have you broken your plate again? You should not bite so hard.'

'Read that!'

Annette read.

'You would give that woman fifteen hundred pounds? I think you are mad, Soames. I would not give her fifteen hundred pence! Pay this woman, and she tells her friends. That is fifteen hundred apologies in all their minds. Really, Soames— I am surprised. A man of business, a clever man! Do you not know the world better than that? With every pound you pay, Fleur eats her words!'

Soames flushed. It was so French, and yet somehow it was so true. He walked to the window. The French—they had no sense of compromise, and every sense of money!

'Well,' he said, 'that ends it anyway. She won't sign. And I shall withdraw my offer.'

'I should hope so. Fleur has a good head. She will look very pretty in Court. I think that woman will be sorry she ever lived! Why don't you have her what you call shadowed? It is no good to be delicate with women like that.'

In a weak moment he had told Annette about the book and the play; for, unable to speak of them to Fleur and Michael, he had really had to tell someone; indeed, he had shown her *Canthar*, with the words: 'I don't advise you to read it, it's very French.'

Annette had returned it to him two days later, saying: 'It is not French at all; it is disgusting. You English are so coarse. It has no wit. It is only nasty. A serious nasty book—that is the limit. You are so old-fashioned, Soames. Why do you say this book is French?'

Soames, who really didn't know why, had muttered:

'Well, they can't get it printed in England.' And with the words: 'Bruxelles, Bruxelles, you call Bruxelles–' buzzing about his ears, had left the room. He had never known any people so touchy as the French!

Her remark about 'shadowing', however, was not easily forgotten. Why be squeamish, when all depended on frightening this woman? And on arriving in London he visited an office that was not Mr Polteed's, and gave instructions for the shadowing of Marjorie Ferrar's past, present, and future.

His answer to Settlewhite and Stark, too, was brief, determined and written on the paper of his own firm.

Jan. 6th, 1925.

DEAR SIRS,

I have your letter of yesterday's date, and note that your client has rejected my proposition, which, as you know, was made entirely without prejudice, and is now withdrawn *in toto*.

Yours faithfully,
SOAMES FORSYTE.

If he did not mistake, they would be sorry. And he gazed at the words '*in toto*'; somehow they looked funny. *In toto*! And now for 'The Plain Dealer'!

The theatre of the 'Ne Plus Ultra' Play-Producing Society had a dingy exterior, a death-mask of Congreve in the hall, a peculiar smell, and an apron stage. There was no music. They hit something three times before the curtain went up. There were no footlights. The scenery was peculiar–Soames could not take his eyes off it till, in the first Entr'acte, its principle was revealed to him by the conversation of two people sitting just behind.

'The point of the scenery here is that no one need look at it, you see. They go farther than anything yet done.'

'They've gone farther in Moscow.'

'I believe not. Curfew went over there. He came back raving about the way they speak their lines.'

'Does he know Russian?'

'No. You don't need to. It's the timbre. I think he's doing pretty well here with that. You couldn't give a play like this if you took the words in.'

Soames, who had been trying to take the words in–it was, indeed, what he had come for–squinted round at the speakers. They were pale and young and went on with a strange unconcern.

'Curfew's doing great work. He's shaking them up.'

'I see they've got Marjorie Ferrar as Olivia.'

'Don't know why he keeps on an amateur like that.'

'Box office, dear boy; she brings the smart people. She's painful, I think.'

'She did one good thing–the dumb girl in that Russian play. But she can't speak for nuts; you're following the sense of her words all the time. She doesn't rhythmatise you a little bit.'

'She's got looks.'

'M'yes.'

At this moment the curtain went up again. Since Marjorie Ferrar had not yet appeared, Soames was obliged to keep awake; indeed, whether because she couldn't 'speak for nuts', or merely from duty, he was always awake while she was on the stage, and whenever she had anything outrageous to say he noted it carefully; otherwise he passed an excellent afternoon, and went away much rested. In his cab he mentally rehearsed Sir James Foskisson in the part of cross-examiner:

'I think, madam, you played Olivia in a production of "The Plain Dealer" by the "Ne Plus Ultra" Play-Producing Society? . . . Would it be correct to say that the part was that of a modest woman? . . . Precisely. And did it contain the following lines (Quotation of nubbly bits.) . . . Did that convey anything to your mind, madam? . . . I suppose that you would not say it was an immoral passage? . . . No? Nor calculated to offend the ears and debase the morals of a decent-minded audience? . . . No, In fact, you don't take the same view of morality that I, or, I venture to think, the jury do? . . . No. The dark scene—you did not remonstrate with the producer for not omitting that scene? . . . Quite. Mr Curfew, I think, was the producer? Yes. Are you on such terms with that gentleman, as would have made a remonstrance easy? . . . Ah! Now, madam, I put it to you that throughout 1923 you were seeing this gentleman nearly every day. . . . Well, say three or four times a week. And yet you say that you were not on such terms as would have made it possible for you to represent to him that no modest young woman should be asked to play a scene like that. . . . Indeed! They jury will form their own opinion of your answer. You are not a professional actress, dependent for your living on doing what you are told to do? . . .No. And yet you have the face to come here and ask for substantial damages because of the allegation in a private letter that you haven't a moral about you? . . .Have you? . . .' And so on, and so on. Oh! no. Damages! She wouldn't get a farthing.

9

VOLTE FACE

Keeping Sir Alexander MacGown and Francis Wilmot in the air, fulfilling her week-end and other engagements, playing much bridge in the hope of making her daily expenses, getting a day's hunting when she could, and rehearsing the part of Olivia, Marjorie Ferrar had almost forgotten the action, when the offer of fifteen hundred pounds and the formula were put before her by Messrs. Settlewhite and Stark. She almost jumped at it. The money would wipe out her more pressing debts; she would be able to breathe, and reconsider her future.

She received their letter on the Friday before Christmas, just as she was about to go down to her father's, near Newmarket, and wrote hastily to say she would call at their office on her way home on Monday. The following evening she consulted her father. Lord Charles was of the opinion that if this attorney fellow would go as far as fifteen hundred, he must be dead keen on settling, and she had only to press for the apology to get it. Anyway, she should let them stew in their juice for a bit. On Monday he wanted to show her his yearlings. She did not, therefore, return to Town till the 23rd, and found the office closed for Christmas. It had never occurred to her that solicitors had holidays. On Christmas Eve she herself went away for ten days; so that it was January the 4th before she was again able to call. Mr Settlewhite was still in the South of France, but Mr Stark would see her. Mr Stark knew little about the matter, but thought Lord Charles's advice probably sound; he proposed to write accepting the fifteen hundred pounds if a formal apology were tendered; they could fall back on the formula if necessary, but it was always wise to get as much as you could. With some misgiving Marjorie Ferrar agreed.

Returning from the matinée on January 7th, tired and elated by applause, by Bertie Curfew's words: 'You did quite well, darling,' and almost the old look on his face, she got into a hot bath, and was just out when her maid announced Mr Wilmot.

'Keep him, Fanny; say I'll be with him in twenty minutes.'

Feverish and soft, as if approaching a crisis, she dressed hastily, put essence of orange-blossom on her neck and hands, and went to the studio. She entered without noise. The young man, back to the door, in the centre of the room, evidently did not hear her. Approaching within a few feet, she waited for the effect on him of orange-blossom. He was standing like some Eastern donkey, that with drooped ears patiently awaits the fresh burdening of a sore back. And suddenly he spoke: 'I'm all in.'

'Francis!'

The young man turned.

'Oh! Marjorie!' he said, 'I never heard.' And taking her hands, he buried his face in them.

She was hampered at that moment. To convert his mouth from despairing kissing of her hands to triumphal flame upon her lips would have been so easy if he had been modern, if his old-fashioned love had not complimented her so subtly; if, too, she were not feeling for him something more–or was it less?–than passion. Was she to know at last the sensations of the simple–a young girl's idyll–something she had missed? She led him to the divan, sat down by his side, and looked into his eyes. Fabled sweetness, as of a spring morning–Francis and she, children in the wood, with the world well lost! She surrendered to the innocence of it; deliberately grasped something delicious, new. Poor boy! How delightful to feel him happy at last–to promise marriage and mean to perform it! When? Oh! when he liked–. Soon, quite soon; the sooner the better! Almost unconscious that she was 'playing' a young girl, she was carried away by his amazement and his joy. He was on fire, on air; yet he remained delicate–he was wonderful! For an hour they sat–a fragrant hour for memory to sniff–before she remembered that she was dining out at half-past eight. She put her lips to his, and closed her eyes. And thought ran riot. Should she spoil it, and make sure of him in modern fashion? What was his image of her but a phlizz, but a fraud? She saw his eyes grow troubled, felt his hands grow fevered. Something seemed drowning before her eyes. She stood up.

'Now, my darling, you must fly!'

When he had flown, she threw off her dress and brushed out her hair that in the mirror seemed to have more gold than red. . . . Some letters on her dressing-table caught her eye. The first was a bill, the second a bill; the third ran thus:

DEAR MADAM,

We regret to say that Cuthcott Kingson & Forsyte have refused to give the apology we asked for, and withdrawn their verbal offer *in toto*. We presume, therefore, that the action must go forward. We have every hope, however, that they may reconsider the matter before it comes into Court.

Your obedient servants,
SETTLEWHITE & STARK.

She dropped it and sat very still, staring at a little hard line on the right of her mouth and a little hard line on the left. . . .

Francis Wilmot, flying, thought of steamship-lines and state-rooms, of registrars and rings. An hour ago. he had despaired; now it seemed he had always known she was 'too fine not to give up this fellow whom she didn't love'. He would make her the queen of South Carolina–he surely would! But if she didn't like it out there, he would sell the 'old home', and they would go and live where she wished–in Venice; he had heard her say Venice was wonderful; or New York, or Sicily; with her he wouldn't care! And London in the cold dry wind seemed beautiful, no longer a grey maze of unreality and shadows, but a city where you could buy rings and steamship passages. The wind cut him like a knife and he did not feel it. That poor devil MacGown! He hated the sight, the thought of him, and yet felt sorry, thinking of him with the cup dashed from his lips. And all the days, weeks, months himself had spent circling round the flame, his wings scorched and drooping, seemed now but the natural progress of the soul towards Paradise. Twenty-four–his age and hers; an eternity of bliss before them! He pictured her on the porch at home. Horses! A better car than the old Ford! The darkies would adore her–kind of grand, and so white! To walk with her among the azaleas in the spring, that he could smell already; no–it was his hands where he had touched her! He shivered, and resumed his flight under the bare trees, well-nigh alone in the east wind; the stars of a bitter night shining.

A card was handed to him as he entered his hotel.

'Mr Wilmot, a gentleman to see you.'

Sir Alexander was seated in a corner of the lounge, with a crush hat in his hand. He rose and came towards Francis Wilmot, grim and square.

'I've been meaning to call on you for some time, Mr Wilmot.'

'Yes, sir. May I offer you a cocktail, or a glass of sherry?'

'No, thank you. You are aware of my engagement to Miss Ferrar?'

'I was, sir.'

This red aggressive face, with its stiff moustache and burning eyes, revived his hatred; so that he no longer felt sorry.

'You know that I very much object to your constant visits to that young lady. In this country it is not the part of a gentleman to pursue an engaged young woman.'

'That,' said Francis Wilmot coolly, 'is for Miss Ferrar herself to say.'

MacGown's face grew even redder.

'If you hadn't been an American, I should have warned you to keep clear a long time ago.'

Francis Wilmot bowed.

'Well! Are you going to?'

'Permit me to decline an answer.'

MacGown thrust forward his face.

'I've told you,' he said. 'If you trespass any more, look out for yourself.'

'Thank you; I will,' said Francis Wilmot softly.

MacGown stood for a moment swaying slightly. Was he going to hit out? Francis Wilmot put his hands into his trouser pockets.

'You've had your warning,' said MacGown, and turned on his heel.

'Good-night!' said Francis Wilmot to that square receding back. He had been gentle, he had been polite, but he hated the fellow, yes, indeed! Save for the triumphal glow within him, there might have been a fuss!

10

PHOTOGRAPHY

Summoned to the annual Christmas covert-shooting at Lippinghall, Michael found there two practical politicans and one member of the Government.

In the mullion-windowed smoking-room, where men retired, and women too sometimes, into chairs old, soft, leathery, the ball of talk was lightly tossed, and naught so devastating as Foggartism mentioned. But in odd minutes and half-hours Michael gained insight into political realities, and respect for practical politicians. Even on this holiday they sat up late, got up early, wrote letters, examined petitions, dipped into Blue Books. They were robust, ate heartily, took their liquor like men, never seemed fatigued. They shaved clean, looked healthy, and shot badly with enjoyment. The member of the Government played golf instead, and Fleur went round with him. Michael learned the lesson: Have so much on your mind that you have practically nothing in it; no time to pet your schemes, fancies, feelings. Carry on, and be careful that you don't know to what end.

As for Foggartism, they didn't–à la *Evening Sun*–pooh-pooh it; they merely asked, as Michael had often asked himself: 'Yes, but how are you going to work it? Your scheme might be very good, if it didn't hit people's pockets. Any addition to the price of living is out of the question–the country's taxed up to the hilt. Your Foggartism's going to need money in every direction. You may swear till you're blue in the face that ten or twenty years hence it'll bring fivefold return; nobody will listen. You may say: 'Without it we're all going to the devil'; but we're accustomed to that–some people think we're there already, and they resent its being said. Others, especially manufacturers, believe what they want to. They can't bear anyone who cries 'stinking fish', whatever his object. Talk about reviving trade, and less taxation, or offer more wages and talk of a capital levy, and, according to Party, we shall believe you've done the trick–until we find you haven't. But you're talking of less trade and more taxation in the present with a view to a better future. Great Scott! In politics you can shuffle the cards, but you mustn't add or subtract. People only react to immediate benefit, or, as in the war, to imminent danger. You must cut out sensationalism.'

In short, they were intelligent, and completely fatalistic.

After these quiet talks, Michael understood, much better than before, the profession of politics. He was greatly attracted by the member of the Government; his personality was modest, his manner pleasant, he had Departmental ideas, and was doing his best with his own job according to those ideas; if he had others he kept them to himself. He seemed to admire Fleur, and he listened better than the other two. He said, too, some things they hadn't. 'Of course, what we're able to do may be found so inadequate that there'll be a great journalistic outcry, and under cover of it we may bring in some sweeping measures that people will swallow before they know what they're in for.'

'The Press,' said Michael; 'I don't see them helping.'

'Well! It's the only voice there is. If you could get fast hold of the vociferous papers, you might even put your Foggartism over. What you're really up against is the slow town growth of the last hundred and fifty years, an ingrained state of mind which can only see England in terms of industrialism and the carrying trade. And in the town-mind, of course, hope springs eternal. They don't like calamity talk. Some genuinely think we can go on indefinitely on the old lines, and get more and more prosperous into the bargain. Personally, I don't. It's possible that much of what old Foggart advocates may be adopted bit by bit, even child emigration, from sheer practical necessity; but it won't be called Foggartism. Inventor's luck! *He'll* get no credit for being the first to see it. And,' added the Minister gloomily, 'by the time it's adopted, it'll probably be too late.'

Receiving the same day a request for an interview from a Press syndicate whose representative would come down to suit his convenience, Michael made the appointment, and prepared an elaborate exposition of his faith. The representative, however, turned out to be a camera, and a photograph entitled: 'The Member for mid-Bucks expounding Foggartism to our Representative,' became the only record of it. The camera was active. It took a family group in front of the porch: 'Right to left, Mr Michael Mont, M.P., Lady Mont, Mrs Michael Mont, Sir Lawrence Mont, Bt.' It took Fleur: 'Mrs Michael Mont, with Kit and Dandie.' It took the Jacobean wing. It took the Minister, with his pipe, 'enjoying a Christmas rest'. It took a corner of the walled garden: 'In the grounds.' It then had lunch. After lunch it took the whole house-party: 'At Sir Lawrence Mont's, Lippinghall Manor, Bucks'; with the Minister on Lady Mont's right and the Minister's wife on Sir Lawrence's left. This photograph would have turned out better if the Dandie, inadvertently left out, had not made a sudden onslaught on the camera legs. It took a photograph of Fleur alone: 'Mrs Michael Mont–a charming young Society hostess.' It understood that Michael was making an interesting practical experiment–could it take Foggartism in action? Michael grinned and said: 'Yes, if it would take a walk, too.'

They departed for the coppice. The colony was in its normal state–Boddick, with two of the contractor's men cheering him on, was working at the construction of the incubator-house; Swain, smoking a cigarette, was reading the *Daily Mail*; Bergfeld was sitting with his head in his hands, and Mrs Bergfeld was washing up.

The camera took three photographs. Michael, who had noted that Bergfeld had begun shaking, suggested to the camera that it would miss its train. It at once took a final photograph of Michael in front of the hut, two cups of tea at the Manor, and its departure.

As Michael was going upstairs that night, the butler came to him.

'The man Boddick's in the pantry, Mr Michael; I'm afraid something's happened, sir.'

'Oh!' said Michael blankly.

Where Michael had spent many happy hours, when he was young, was Boddick, his pale face running with sweat, and his dark eyes very alive.

'The German's gone, sir.'

'Gone?'

'Hanged hisself. The woman's in an awful state. I cut him down and sent Swain to the village.'

'Good God! Hanged! But why?'

'He's been very funny these last three days; and that camera upset him properly. Will you come, sir?'

They set out with a lantern, Boddick telling his tale.

'As soon as ever you was gone this afternoon he started to shake and carry on about having been made game of. I told 'im not to be a fool, and went out to get on with it. But when I came in to tea, he was still shakin', and talkin' about his honour and his savin's; Swain had got fed-up and was jeerin' at him, and Mrs Bergfeld was as white as a ghost in the corner. I told Swain to shut his head; and Fritz simmered down after a bit, and sat humped up as he does for hours together. Mrs Bergfeld got our tea. I had some chores to finish, so I went out after. When I come in at seven, they was at it again hammer and tongs, and Mrs Bergfeld cryin' fit to bust her heart. "Can't you see," I said, "how you're upsettin' your wife?" "Henry Boddick," he said, "I've nothing against *you*, you've always been decent to me. But this Swain," he said, "'is name is Swine!" and he took up the bread-knife. I got it away from him, and spoke him calm. "Ah!" he said, "but *you've* no pride." Swain was lookin' at him with that sort o' droop in his mouth he's got. "Pride," he says, "you silly blighter, what call 'ave *you* to 'ave any pride?" Well, I see that while we was there he wasn't goin' to get any better, so I took Swain off for a glass at the pub. When we came back at ten o'clock, Swain went straight to bed, and I went into the mess-room, where I found his wife alone. "Has he gone to bed?" I said. "No," she said, "he's gone out to cool his head. Oh! Henry Boddick," she said, "I don't know what to do with him!" We sat there a bit, she tellin' me about 'im brooding, and all that—nice woman she is, too; till suddenly she said: "Henry Boddick," she said, "I'm frightened. Why don't he come?" We went out to look for him, and where d'you think he was, sir? You know that big tree we're just goin' to have down? There's a ladder against it, and the guidin' rope all fixed. He'd climbed up that ladder in the moonlight, put the rope round his neck, and jumped off; and there he was, six feet from the ground, dead as a duck. I roused up Swain, and we got him in, and—Well, we 'ad a proper time! Poor woman, I'm sorry for her, sir—though really I think it's just as well he's gone—he couldn't get upsides with it, anyhow. That camera chap would have given something for a shot at what we saw there in the moonlight.'

'Foggartism in action!' thought Michael bitterly. 'So endeth the First Lesson!'

The hut looked lonely in the threading moonlight and the bitter wind. Inside, Mrs Bergfeld was kneeling beside the body placed on the deal table, with a handkerchief over its face. Michael put a hand on her shoulder. She gave him a wild look, bowed her head again, and her lips began moving. 'Prayer!' thought Michael. 'Catholic—of course!' He took Boddick aside. 'Don't let her see Swain. I'll talk to him.'

When the police and the doctor came in, he button-holed the hairdresser, whose shadowy face looked ghastly in the moonlight. He seemed much upset.

'You'd better come down to the house for the night, Swain.'

'All right, sir. I never meant to hurt the poor beggar. But he did carry on so, and I've got my own trouble. I couldn't stand 'im monopolisin' misfortune the way he does. When the inquest's over, I'm off. If I can't get some sun soon, I'll be as dead as 'im.'

Michael was relieved. Boddick would be left alone.

When at last he got back to the house with Swain, Fleur was asleep. He did not wake her to tell her the news, but lay a long time trying to get warm, and thinking of that great obstacle to all salvation–the human element. And, mingled with his visions of the woman beside that still, cold body, were longings for the warmth of the young body close to him.

The photographs were providential. For three days no paper could be taken up which did not contain some allusion, illustrated, to 'The Tragedy on a Buckinghamshire estate' 'German actor hangs himself''; 'The drama at Lippinghall'; 'Tragic end of an experiment'; 'Right to Left: Mr Michael Mont, Member for mid-Bucks; Bergfeld, the German actor who hanged himself; Mrs Bergfeld.'

The *Evening Sun* wrote more in sorrow than in anger:

'The suicide of a German actor on Sir Lawrence Mont's estate at Lippinghall has in it a touch of the grotesquely moral. The unfortunate man seems to have been one of three "out-of-works" selected by the young Member for mid-Bucks, recently conspicuous for his speech on "Foggartism", for a practical experiment in that peculiar movement. Why he should have chosen a German to assist the English people to return to the Land is not perhaps very clear; but, largely speaking, the incident illustrates the utter unsuitability of all amateur attempts to solve this problem, and the futility of pretending to deal with the unemployment crisis while we still tolerate among us aliens who take the bread out of the mouths of our own people.' The same issue contained a short leader entitled: 'The Alien in Our Midst.' The inquest was well attended. It was common knowledge that three men and one woman lived in the hut, and sensational developments were expected. A good deal of disappointment was felt that the evidence disclosed nothing at all of a sexual character.

Fleur, with the eleventh baronet, returned to town after it was over. Michael remained for the funeral–in a Catholic cemetery some miles away. He walked with Henry Boddick behind Mrs Bergfeld. A little sleet was drifting out of a sky the colour of the gravestones, and against that whitish sky the yew trees looked very stark. He had ordered a big wreath laid on the grave, and when he saw it thus offered up, he thought: 'First human beings, then rams, now flowers! Progress? I wonder!'

Having arranged that Norah Curfew should take Mrs Bergfeld as cook in Bethnal Green, he drove her up to London in the Manor car. During that long drive he experienced again feelings that he had not had since the war. Human hearts, dressed-up to the nines in circumstance, interests, manners, accents, race, and class, when stripped by grief, by love, by hate, by laughter were one and the same heart. But how seldom were they stripped! Life was a clothed affair! A good thing too, perhaps–the strain of nakedness was too considerable! He was, in fact, infinitely relieved to see the face of Norah Curfew, and hear her cheerful words to Mrs Bergfeld:

'Come in, my dear, and have some tea!' She was the sort who stripped to the heart without strain or shame.

Fleur was in the drawing-room when he got home, furred up to her cheeks, which were bright as if she had just come in from the cold.

'Been out, my child?'

'Yes. I–' She stopped, looked at him rather queerly, and said: 'Well, have you finished with that business?'

'Yes; thank God. I've dropped the poor creature on Norah Curfew.'

Fleur smiled. 'Ah! Yes, Norah Curfew! *She* lives for everybody but herself, doesn't she?'

'She does,' said Michael, rather sharply.

'The new woman. One's getting clean out of fashion.'

Michael took her cheeks between his hands.

'What's the matter, Fleur?'

'Nothing.'

'There is.'

'Well, one gets a bit fed up with being left out, as if one were fit for nothing but Kit, and looking appetising.'

Michael dropped his hands, hurt and puzzled. Certainly he had not consulted her about his 'down and outs'; had felt sure it would only bore or make her laugh— No future in it! And had there been?

'Any time you like to go shares in any mortal thing, Fleur, you've only to say so.'

'Oh! I don't want to poke into your affairs. I've got my own. Have you had tea?'

'Do tell me what's the matter?'

'My dear boy, you've already asked me that, and I've already told you—nothing.'

'Won't you kiss me?'

'Of course. And there's Kit's bath—would you like to go up?'

Each short stab went in a little farther. This was a spiritual crisis, and he did not know in the least how to handle it. Didn't she want him to admire her, to desire her? What did she want? Recognition that she was as interested as he in—in the state of the country? Of course! Only—was she?

'Well,' she said, '*I* want tea, anyway. Is the new woman dramatic?'

Jealousy? The notion was absurd. He said quietly:

'I don't quite follow you.'

Fleur looked up at him with very clear eyes.

'Good God!' said Michael, and left the room.

He went upstairs and sat down before 'The White Monkey'. In that strategic position he better perceived the core of his domestic moment. Fleur had to be first—had to take precedence. No object in her collection must live a life of its own! He was appalled by the bitterness of that thought. No, no! It was only that she had a complex—a silver spoon, and it had become natural in her mouth. She resented his having interests in which she was not first; or rather, perhaps, resented the fact that they were not her interests too. And that was to her credit, when you came to think of it. She was vexed with herself for being egocentric. Poor child! 'I've got to mind my eye,' thought Michael, 'or I shall make some modern-novel mess of this in three parts.' And his mind strayed naturally to the science of dishing up symptoms as if they were roots—ha! He remembered his nursery governess locking him in; he had dreaded being penned up ever since. The psycho-analysts would say that was due to the action of his governess. It wasn't—many small boys wouldn't have cared a hang; it was due to a nature that existed before that action. He took up the photograph of Fleur that stood on his desk. He loved the face, he would always love it. If she had limitations—well! So had he—lots! This was comedy, one mustn't make it into a tragedy! Surely she had a sense of humour, too! Had she? Had she not? And Michael searched the face he held in his hands. . . .

But, as is usual with husbands, he had diagnosed without knowledge of all the facts.

Fleur had been bored at Lippinghall, even collection of the Minister had tried her. She had concealed her boredom from Michael. But self-sacrifice takes its revenge. She reached home in a mood of definite antagonism to public affairs. Hoping to feel better if she bought a hat or two, she set out for Bond Street. At the corner of Burlington Street, a young man bared his head.

'Fleur!'

Wilfrid Desert! Very lean and very brown!

'You!'

'Yes. I'm just back. How's Michael?'

'Very well. Only he's in Parliament.'

'Great Scott! And how are you?'

'As you see. Did you have a good time?'

'Yes. I'm only perching. The East has got me!'

'Are you coming to see us?'

'I think not. The burnt child, you know.'

'Yes; you *are* brown!'

'Well, good-bye, Fleur! You look just the same, only more so. I'll see Michael somewhere.'

'Good-bye!' She walked on without looking back, and then regretted not having found out whether Wilfrid had done the same.

She had given Wilfrid up for–well, for Michael, who–who had forgotten it! Really she was too self-sacrificing!

And then at three o'clock a note was brought her:

'By hand, ma'am; answer waiting.'

She opened an envelope, stamped 'Cosmopolis Hotel.'

MADAM,

We apologise for troubling you, but are in some perplexity. Mr Francis Wilmot, a young American gentleman, who has been staying in this hotel since early October, has, we are sorry to say, contracted pneumonia. The doctor reports unfavourably on his condition. In these circumstances we thought it right to examine his effects, in order that we might communicate with his friends; but the only indication we can find is a card of yours. I venture to ask you if you can help us in the matter.

Believe me to be, Madam,
Your faithful servant,
(for the Management).

Fleur stared at an illegible signature, and her thoughts were bitter. Jon had dumped Francis on her as a herald of his happiness; her enemy had lifted him! Well, then, why didn't that Cat look after him herself? Oh! well, poor boy! Ill in a great hotel–without a soul!

'Call me a taxi, Coaker.'

On her way to the hotel she felt slight excitement of the 'ministering angel' order.

Giving her name at the bureau, she was taken up to Room 209. A chambermaid was there. The doctor, she said, had ordered a nurse, who had not yet come.

Francis Wilmot, very flushed, was lying back, propped up; his eyes were closed.

'How long has he been ill like this?'

'I've noticed him looking queer, ma'am; but we didn't know how bad he was until to-day. I think he's just neglected it. The doctor says he's got to be packed. Poor gentleman, it's very sad. You see, he's hardly there!'

Francis Wilmot's lips were moving; he was evidently on the verge of delirium.

'Go and make some lemon tea in a jug as weak and hot as you can; quick!'

When the maid had gone, she went up and put her cool hand to his forehead. 'It's all right, Francis. Much pain?'

Francis Wilmot's lips ceased to move; he looked up at her and his eyes seemed to burn.

'If you cure me,' he said, 'I'll hate you. I just want to get out, quick!'

She changed her hand on his forehead, whose heat seemed to scorch the skin of her palm. His lips resumed their almost soundless movement. The meaningless, meaningful whispering frightened her, but she stood her ground, constantly changing her hand, till the maid came back with the tea.

'The nurse has come, miss; she'll be up in a minute.'

'Pour out the tea. Now, Francis, drink!'

His lips sucked, chattered, sucked. Fleur handed back the cup, and stood away. His eyes had closed again.

'Oh! ma'am,' whispered the maid, 'he *is* bad! Such a nice young gentleman, too.'

'What was his temperature; do you know?'

'I did hear the doctor say nearly 105. Here is the nurse, ma'am.'

Fleur went to her in the doorway.

'It's not just ordinary, nurse—he *wants* to go. I think a love-affair's gone wrong. Shall I stop and help you pack him?'

When the pneumonia jacket had been put on, she lingered, looking down at him. His eyelashes lay close and dark against his cheeks, long and innocent, like a little boy's.

Outside the door, the maid touched her arm.

'I found this letter, ma'am; ought I to show it to the doctor?'

Fleur read:

MY POOR DEAR BOY,

We were crazy yesterday. It isn't any good, you know. Well, I haven't got a breakable heart; nor have you really, though you may think so when you get this. Just go back to your sunshine and your darkies, and put me out of your thoughts. I can't stay the course. I couldn't possibly stand being poor. I must just go through it with my Scotsman and travel the appointed road. What is the good of thinking we can play at children in the wood, when one of them is

Your miserable (at the moment)

MARJORIE.

I mean this—I mean it. Don't come and see me any more, and make it worse for yourself.   M.

'Exactly!' said Fleur. 'I've told the nurse. Keep it and give it him back if he gets well. If he doesn't, burn it. I shall come to-morrow.' And, looking at the maid with a faint smile, she added: '*I* am not that lady!'

'Oh! no, ma'am—miss—no, I'm sure! Poor young gentleman! Isn't there nothing to be done?'

'I don't know. I should think not. . . .'

She had kept all these facts from Michael with a sudden retaliatory feeling. He couldn't have private—or was it public—life all to himself!

After he had gone out with his 'Good God!' she went to the window. Queer to have seen Wilfrid again! Her heart had not fluttered, but it tantalised her not to know whether she could attract him back. Out in the Square it was as dark as when last she had seen him before he fled to the East—a face pressed to this window that she was touching with her fingers. 'The burnt child!' No! She did not want to reduce him to that state again; to copy Marjorie Ferrar, who had copied her. If, instead of going East, Wilfrid had chosen to have pneumonia like poor Francis! What would she have done? Let him die for want of her? And what ought she to do about Francis, having seen that letter? Tell Michael? No, he thought her frivolous and irresponsible. Well! She would show him! And that sister—who had married Jon? Ought she to be cabled to? But this would have a rapid crisis, the nurse had said, and to get over from America in time would be impossible! Fleur went back to the fire. What kind of girl was this wife of Jon's? Another in the new fashion—like Norah Curfew; or just one of those Americans out for her own way and the best of everything? But they would have the new fashion in America, too—even though it didn't come from Paris. Anne Forsyte!—Fleur gave a little shiver in front of the hot fire.

She went upstairs, took off her hat, and scrutinised her image. Her face was coloured and rounded, her eyes were clear, her brow unlined, her hair rather flattened. She fluffed it out, and went across into the nursery.

The eleventh baronet, asleep, was living his private life with a very determined expression on his face; at the foot of his cot lay the Dandie, with his chin pressed to the floor, and at the table the nurse was sewing. In front of her lay an illustrated paper with the photograph inscribed: 'Mrs Michael Mont, with Kit and Dandie.'

'What do you think of it, nurse?'

'I think it's horrible, ma'am; it makes Kit look as if he hadn't any sense—giving him a stare like that!'

Fleur took up the paper; her quick eyes had seen that it concealed another. There on the table was a second effigy of herself: 'Mrs Michael Mont, the pretty young London hostess, who, rumour says, will shortly be defendant in a Society lawsuit.' And, above, yet another effigy, inscribed: 'Miss Majorie Ferrar, the brilliant granddaughter of the Marquis of Shropshire, whose engagement to Sir Alexander MacGown, M.P., is announced.'

Fleur dropped paper back on paper.

II

SHADOWS

The dinner, which Marjorie Ferrar had so suddenly recollected, was MacGown's, and when she reached the appointed restaurant, he was waiting in the hall.

'Where are the others, Alec?'

'There are no others,' said MacGown.

Marjorie Ferrar reined back. 'I can't dine with you alone in a place like this!'

'I had the Ppynrryns, but they fell through.'

'Then I shall go to my club.'

'For God's sake, no, Marjorie. We'll have a private room. Go and wait in there, while I arrange it.'

With a shrug she passed into a little 'lounge'. A young woman whose face seemed familiar idled in, looked at her, and idled out again, the ormolu clock

ticked, the walls of striped pale grey stared blankly in the brilliant light, and
Marjorie Ferrar stared blankly back–she was still seeing Francis Wilmot's
ecstatic face.

'Now!' said MacGown. 'Up those stairs, and third on the right. I'll follow in
a minute.'

She had acted in a play, she had passed an emotional hour, and she was
hungry. At least she could dine before making the necessary scene. And while
she drank the best champagne MacGown could buy, she talked and watched
the burning eyes of her adorer. That red-brown visage, square, stiff-haired
head, and powerful frame–what a contrast to the pale, slim face and form of
Francis! This was a man, and when he liked, agreeable. With him she would
have everything she wanted except–what Francis could give her. And it was
one or the other–not both, as she had thought it might be. She had once crossed
the 'striding edge' on Helvellyn, with a precipice on one side and a precipice on
the other, and herself; doubting down which to fall, in the middle. She hadn't
fallen, and–she supposed–she wouldn't now! One didn't if one kept one's
head.

Coffee was brought; and she sat, smoking, on the sofa. Her knowledge of
private rooms taught her that she was now as alone with her betrothed as
money could make them. How would he behave?

He threw his cigar away, and sat down by her side. This was the moment to
rise and tell him that he was no longer her betrothed. His arm went round her,
his lips sought her face. 'Mind my dress; it's the only decent one I've got.'

And, suddenly, not because she heard a noise, but because her senses were
not absorbed like his, she perceived a figure in the open doorway. A woman's
voice said: 'Oh! I beg your pardon; I thought–' Gone!

Marjorie Ferrar started up.

'Did you see that young woman?'

'Yes. Damn her!'

'She's shadowing me.'

'What?'

'I don't know her, and yet I know her perfectly. She had a good look at me
downstairs, when I was waiting.'

MacGown dashed to the door and flung it open. Nobody was there! He shut
it, and came back.

'By heaven! Those people, I'll–! Well, that ends it! Marjorie, I shall send our
engagement to the papers to-morrow.'

Marjorie Ferrar, leaning her elbows on the mantelpiece, stared at her own
face in the glass above it. 'Not a moral about her!' What did it matter? If only
she could decide to marry Francis out of hand, slide away from them all–debts,
lawyers, Alec! And then the 'You be damned' spirit in her blood revolted. The
impudence of it! Shadowing her! No! She was not going to leave Miss Fleur
triumphant–the little snob; and that old party with the chin!

MacGown raised her hand to his lips; and somehow the caress touched her.

'Oh! well,' she said, 'I suppose you'd better.'

'Thank God!'

'Do you really think that to get me is a cause for gratitude?'

'I would go through Hell to get you.'

'And after? Well, as we're public property, let's go down and dance.'

For an hour she danced. She would not let him take her home, and in her cab
she cried. She wrote to Francis when she got in. She went out again to post it.

The bitter stars, the bitter wind, the bitter night! At the little slurred thump of her letter dropping, she laughed. To have played at children! It was too funny! So that was done with! 'On with the dance!'

Extraordinary, the effect of a little paragraph in the papers! Credit, like new-struck oil, spurted sky-high. Her post contained, not bills for dresses, but solicitations to feed, frizz, fur, flower, feather, furbelow, and photograph her. London offered itself. To escape that cynical avalanche she borrowed a hundred pounds and flew to Paris. There, every night, she went to the theatre. She had her hair done in a new style, she ordered dresses, ate at places known to the few–living up to Michael's nickname for her; and her heart was heavy.

She returned after a week, and burned the avalanche–fortunately all letters of congratulation contained the phrase 'of course you won't think of answering this.' She didn't. The weather was mild; she rode in the Row; she prepared to hunt. On the eve of departure, she received an anonymous communication.

'Francis Wilmot is very ill with pneumonia at the Cosmopolis Hotel. He is not expected to live.'

Her heart flurried round within her breast and flumped; her knees felt weak; her hand holding the note shook; only her head stayed steady. The handwriting was 'that little snob's'. Had Francis caused this message to be sent? Was it his appeal? Poor boy! And must she go and see him if he were going to die? She so hated death. Did this mean that it was up to her to save him? What did it mean? But indecision was not her strong point. In ten minutes she was in a cab, in twenty at the hotel. Handing her card, she said:

'You have a Mr Wilmot here–a relative of mine. I've just heard of his serious illness. Can I go up and see the nurse?'

The management looked at the card, inquisitively at her face, touched a bell, and said:

'Certainly, madam. . . . Here, you–take this lady up to room–er–209.'

Led by what poor Francis called a 'bell-boy' into the lift, she walked behind his buttons along a pale-grey river of corridor carpet, between pale-grey walls, past cream-coloured after cream-coloured door in the bright electric light, with her head a little down.

The 'bell-boy' knocked ruthlessly on a door.

It was opened and in the lobby of the suite stood Fleur. . . .

12

DEEPENING

However untypically American according to Soames, Francis Wilmot seemed to have the national passion for short cuts.

In two days from Fleur's first visit he had reached the crisis, hurrying towards it like a man to his bride. Yet, compared with the instinct to live, the human will is limited, so that he failed to die. Fleur, summoned by telephone, went home cheered by the doctor's words: 'He'll do now, if we can coax a little strength into him.' That, however, was the trouble. For three afternoons she watched his exhausted indifference seeming to increase. And she was haunted by cruel anxiety. On the fourth day she had been sitting for more than an hour when his eyes opened.

'Yes, Francis?'

'I'm going to quit all right, after all.'

'Don't talk like that—it's not American. Of course you're not going to quit.'
He smiled, and shut his eyes. She made up her mind then.

Next day he was about the same, more dead than alive. But her mind was at
rest; her messenger had brought back word that Miss Ferrar would be in at four
o'clock. She would have had the note by now; but would she come? How little
one knew of other people, even when they were enemies!

He was drowsing, white and strenghtless, when she heard the 'bell-boy's'
knock. Passing into the lobby, she closed the door softly behind her, and
opened the outer door. So she *had* come!

If this meeting of two declared enemies had in it something dramatic, neither
perceived it at the moment. It was just intensely unpleasant to them both. They
stood for a moment looking at each other's chins. Then Fleur said:

'He's extremely weak. Will you sit down while I tell him you're here?'

Having seen her settled where Francis Wilmot put his clothes out to be
valeted in days when he had worn them, Fleur passed back into the bedroom,
and again closed the door.

'Francis,' she said, 'someone is waiting to see you.'

Francis Wilmot did not stir, but his eyes opened and cleared strangely. To
Fleur they seemed suddenly the eyes she had known; as if all these days they
had been 'out', and someone had again put a match to them.

'You understand what I mean?'

The words came clear and feeble: 'Yes; but if I wasn't good enough for her
before, I surely am not now. Tell her I'm through with that fool business.'

A lump rose in Fleur's throat.

'Thank her for coming!' said Francis Wilmot, and closed his eyes again.

Fleur went back into the lobby. Marjorie Ferrar was standing against the
wall with an unlighted cigarette between her lips.

'He thanks you for coming; but he doesn't want to see you. I'm sorry I
brought you down.'

Marjorie Ferrar took out the cigarette. Fleur could see her lips quivering.
'Will he get well?'

'I don't know. I think so—now. He says he's 'through with that fool
business'.'

Marjorie Ferrar's lips tightened. She opened the outer door, turned
suddenly, and said:

'Will you make it up?'

'No,' said Fleur.

There was a moment of complete stillness: then Marjorie Ferrar gave a little
laugh, and slipped out.

Fleur went back. He was asleep. Next day he was stronger. Three days later
Fleur ceased her visits; he was on the road to recovery. She had become
conscious, moreover, that she had a little lamb which, wherever Mary went,
was sure to go. She was being shadowed! How amusing! And what a bore that
she couldn't tell Michael; because she had not yet begun again to tell him
anything.

On the day that she ceased her visits he came in while she was dressing for
dinner, with a 'weekly' in his hand.

'Listen to this,' he said:

FONDOUK

"When to God's fondouk the donkeys are taken—
    Donkeys of Africa, Sicily, Spain—
If peradventure the Deity waken,
    He shall not easily slumber again.

Where in the sweet of God's straw they have laid them
    Broken and dead of their burdens and sores,
He, for a change, shall remember He made them—
    One of the best of His numerous chores—

Order from someone a sigh of repentance—
    Donkeys of Araby, Syria, Greece—
Over the fondouk distemper the sentence:
    'God's own forsaken—the stable of peace.' "

'Who's that by? It sounds like Wilfrid.'

'It is by Wilfrid,' said Michael, and did not look at her. 'I met him at the Hotch-Potch.'

'And how is he?'

'Very fit.'

'Have you asked him here?'

'No. He's going East again soon.'

Was he fishing? Did he know that she had seen him? And she said:

'I'm going down to father's, Michael. He's written twice.'

Michael put her hand to his lips.

'All right, darling.'

Fleur reddened; her strangled confidence seemed knotted in her throat. She went next day with Kit and Dandie. The "little lamb" would hardly follow to "The Shelter".

Annette had gone with her mother to Cannes for a month; and Soames was alone with the English winter. He was paying little attention to it, for the "case" was in the List, and might be reached in a few weeks' time. Deprived of French influence, he was again wavering towards compromise. The announcement of Marjorie Ferrar's engagement to MacGown had materially changed the complexion of affairs. In the eyes of a British jury, the character of a fast young lady, and the character of the same young lady publicly engaged to a Member of Parliament, with wealth and a handle to his name, would not be at all the same thing. They were now virtually dealing with Lady MacGown, and nothing, Soames knew, was so fierce as a man about to be married. To libel his betrothed was like approaching a mad dog.

He looked very grave when Fleur told him of her "little lamb". It was precisely the retaliation he had feared; nor could he tell her that he had "told her so", because he hadn't. He had certainly urged her to come down to him, but delicacy had forbidden him to give her the reason. So far as he could tell through catechism, there had been nothing "suspect" in her movements since Lippinghall, except those visits to the Cosmopolis Hotel. But they were bad enough. Who was going to believe that she went to this sick young man out of pure kindness? Such a motive was not current in a Court of Law. He was staggered when she told him that Michael didn't know of them. Why not?

'I didn't feel like telling him.'

'Feel? Don't you see what a position you've put yourself in? Here you are, running to a young man's bedside, without your husband's knowledge.'

'Yes, darling; but he was terribly ill.'

'I dare say,' said Soames; 'so are lots of people.'

'Besides, he was over head and ears in love with *her*.'

'D'you think he's going to admit that, even if we could call him?'

Fleur was silent, thinking of Francis Wilmot's face.

'Oh! I don't know,' she said at last. 'How horrid it all is!'

'Of course it's horrid,' said Soames. 'Have you had a quarrel with Michael?'

'No; not a quarrel. Only he doesn't tell *me* things.'

'What things?'

'How should I know, dear?'

Soames grunted. 'Would he have minded your going?'

'Of course not. He'd have minded if I hadn't. He likes that boy.'

'Well, then,' said Soames, 'either you or he, or both, will have to tell a lie, and say that he did know. I shall go up and talk to him. Thank goodness we can prove the illness. If I catch anybody coming down here after you–!'

He went up the following afternoon. Parliament being in recess, he sought the Hotch-Potch Club. He did not like a place always connected in his mind with his dead cousin, that fellow young Jolyon, and said to Michael at once: 'Can we go somewhere else?'

'Yes, sir; where would you like?'

'To your place, if you can put me up for the night. I want to have a talk with you.'

Michael looked at him askance.

'Now,' said Soames, after dinner, 'what's this about Fleur–she says you don't tell her things?'

Michael gazed into his glass of port.

'Well, sir,' he said slowly, 'I'd be only too glad to, of course, but I don't think they really interest her. She doesn't feel that public things matter.'

'Public! I meant private.'

'There aren't any private things. D'you mean that she thinks there are?'

Soames dropped his scrutiny.

'I don't know–she said "things".'

'Well, you can put that out of your head, and hers.'

'H'm! Anyway, the result's been that she's been visiting that young American with pneumonia at the Cosmopolis Hotel, without letting you know. It's a mercy she hasn't picked it up.'

'Francis Wilmot?'

'Yes. He's out of the wood, now. That's not the point. She's been shadowed.'

'Good God!' said Michael.

'Exactly! This is what comes of not talking to your wife. Wives are funny–they don't like it.'

Michael grinned.

'Put yourself in my place, sir. It's my profession, now, to fuss about the state of the country, and all that; and you know how it is–one gets keen. But to Fleur, it's all a stunt. I quite understand that; but, you see, the keener I get, the more I'm afraid of boring her, and the less I feel I can talk to her about it. In a sort of way she's jealous.'

Soames rubbed his chin. The state of the country was a curious sort of co-respondent. He himself was often worried by the state of the country, but as a source of division between husband and wife it seemed to him cold-blooded; he had known other sources in his time!

'Well, you mustn't let it go on,' he said. 'It's trivial.'

Michael got up.

'Trivial! Well, sir, I don't know, but it seems to me very much the sort of thing that happened when the war came. Men had to leave their wives then.'

'Wives put up with that,' said Soames, 'the country was in danger.'

'Isn't it in danger now?'

With his inveterate distrust of words, it seemed to Soames almost indecent for a young man to talk like that. Michael was a politician, of course; but politicians were there to keep the country quiet, not to go raising scares and talking through their hats.

'When you've lived a little longer,' he said, 'you'll know that there's always something to fuss about if you like to fuss. There's nothing in it really; the pound's going up. Besides, it doesn't matter what you tell Fleur, so long as you tell her something.'

'She's intelligent, sir,' said Michael.

Soames was taken aback. He could not deny the fact, and answered:

'Well, national affairs are too remote; you can't expect a woman to be interested in them.'

'Quite a lot of women are.'

'Blue-stockings.'

'No, sir; they nearly all wear "nude".'

'H'm! Those! As to interest in national affairs—put a tax on stockings, and see what happens!'

Michael grinned.

'I'll suggest it, sir.'

'If you expect,' said Soames, 'that people—women or not—are going to put themselves out of the way for any scheme like this—this Foggartism of yours, you'll be very much disappointed.'

'So everybody tells me. It's just because I don't like cold water at home as well as abroad, that I've given up worrying Fleur.'

'Well, if you take my advice, you'll take up something practical—the state of the traffic, or penny postage. Drop pessimism; people who talk at large like that, never get trusted in this country. In any case you'll have to say you knew about her visits to that young man.'

'Certainly, sir, wife and husband are one. But you don't really mean to let them make a circus of it in Court?'

Soames was silent. He did not *mean* them to; but what if they did?

'I can't tell,' he said, at last. 'The fellow's a Scotchman. What did you go hitting him on the nose for?'

'He gave me a thick ear first. I know it was an excellent opportunity for turning the other cheek, but I didn't think of it in time.'

'You must have called him something.'

'Only a dirty dog. As you know, he suggested a low motive for my speech.'

Soames stared. In his opinion this young man was taking himself much too seriously.

'Your speech! You've got to get it out of your mind,' he said, 'that anything you can say or do will make any difference.'

'Then what's the good of my being in Parliament?'

'Well, you're in the same boat with everybody else. The country's like a tree; you can keep it in order, but you can't go taking it up by the roots to look at them.'

Michael looked at him, impressed.

'In public matters,' said Soames, 'the thing is to keep a level head, and do no more than you're obliged.'

'And what's to govern one's view of necessity?'

'Common sense. One can't have everything.'

And rising, he began scrutinising the Goya.

'Are you going to buy another Goya, sir?'

'No; if I buy any more pictures, I shall go back to the English School.'

'Patriotism?'

Soames gave him a sharp look.

'There's no patriotism,' he said, 'in fussing. And another thing you've got to remember is that foreigners like to hear that we've got troubles. It doesn't do to discuss our affairs out loud.'

Michael took these sayings to bed with him. He remembered, when he came out of the war, thinking: 'If there's another war, nothing will induce me to go.' But now, if one were to come, he knew he *would* be going again. So Old Forsyte thought he was just 'fussing'! Was he? Was Foggartism a phlizz? Ought he to come to heel, and take up the state of the traffic? Was everything unreal? Surely not his love for Fleur? Anyway he felt hungry for her lying there. And Wilfrid back, too! To risk his happiness with her for the sake of–what? *Punch* had taken a snap at him this week, grinning and groping at a surrounding fog. Old England, like Old Forsyte, had no use for theories. Self-conscious national efforts were just pomposity. Pompous! He? The thought was terribly disturbing. He got out of bed and went to the window. Foggy! In fog all were shadows; and he the merest shadow of them all, an unpractical politician, taking things to heart! One! Two! Big Ben! How many hearts had he turned to water! How many dreams spoiled, with his measured resonance! Line up with the top-dressers, and leave the country to suck its silver spoon!

PART III

I

'CIRCUSES'

In his early boyhood Soames had been given to the circus. He had outgrown it; 'Circuses' were now to him little short of an abomination. Jubilees and Pageants, that recurrent decimal, the Lord Mayor's Show, Earl's Court, Olympia, Wembley–all he disliked. He could not stand a lot of people with their mouths open. Dressing up was to him a symptom of weak-mindedness, and the collective excitement of a crowd an extravagance that offended his reticent individualism. Though not deeply versed in history, he had an idea, too, that nations who went in for "circuses" were decadent. Queen Victoria's funeral, indeed, had impressed him–there had been a feeling in the air that day; but, ever since, things had gone from bad to worse. They made everything into a 'circus' now! A man couldn't commit a murder without the whole paper-reading population–himself included–looking over each other's shoulders; and as to these football-matches, and rodeos–they interfered with the traffic and the normal course of conversation; people were so crazy about them!

Of course, 'circuses' had their use. They kept the people quiet. Violence by proxy, for instance, was obviously a political principle of some value. It was difficult to gape at the shedding of blood and shed it at the same time; the more people stood in rows to see others being hurt, the less trouble would they take to hurt others, and the sounder Soames could sleep by night. Still sensation-hunting had become a disease, in his opinion, and no one was being inoculated for it, so far as he could see!

As the weeks went on and the cases before it in the List went off, the 'circus' they were proposing to make of his daughter appeared to him more and more monstrous. He had an instinctive distrust of Scotchmen–they called themselves Scotsmen nowadays, as if it helped their character!–they never let go, and he could not approve in other people a quality native to himself. Besides, 'Scotchmen' were so–so exuberant–always either dour or else hearty–extravagant chaps! Towards the middle of March, with the case in the List for the following week, he took an extreme step and entered the lobby of the House of Commons. He had spoken to no one of his determination to make this last effort, for it seemed to him that all–Annette, Michael, Fleur herself–had done their best to spoil the chance of settlement.

Having sent in his card, he waited a long while in that lofty purlieu. 'Lobbying', he knew the phrase, but had never realised the waste of time involved in it. The statues consoled him somewhat. Sir Stafford Northcote–a steady chap; at old Forsyte dinner-parties in the 'eighties his character had been as much a standby as the saddle of mutton. He found even 'that fellow Gladstone' bearable in stucco, or whatever it was up there. You might dislike, but you couldn't sneeze at him, as at some of these modern chaps. He was sunk in coma before Lord Granville when at last he heard the words:

'Sir Alexander MacGown,' and saw a square man with a ruddy face, stiff black hair, and clipped moustache, coming between the railings, with a card in his hand.

'Mr Forsyte?'

'Yes. Can we go anywhere that's not quite so public?'

The 'Scotchman' nodded, and led him down a corridor to a small room. 'Well?'

Soames smoothed his hat. 'This affair,' he said, 'can't be any more agreeable to you than it is to me.'

'Are you the individual who was good enough to apply the word "traitress" to the lady I'm engaged to?'

'That is so.'

'Then I don't see how you have the impudence to come and speak to me.'

Soames bit his lips.

'I spoke under the provocation of hearing your fiancée call my daughter a snob, in her own house. Do you want this petty affair made public?'

'If you think that you and your daughter can get away with calling the lady I'm going to marry "a snake", "a traitress", "an immoral person", you're more mistaken than you ever were in your life. An unqualified apology that her Counsel can announce in Court is your only way out.'

'That you won't get; mutual regret is another thing. As to the question of damages—'

'Damn the damages!' said MacGown violently. And there was that in Soames which applauded.

'Well,' he said, 'I'm sorry for you and her.'

'What the devil do you mean, sir?'

'You will know by the end of next week, unless you revise your views in between. If it comes into Court, we shall justify.'

The 'Scotchman' went so red that for a moment Soames was really afraid he would have an apoplectic fit.

'You'd better look out what you say in Court.'

'We pay no attention to bullies in Court.'

MacGown clenched his fists.

'Yes,' said Soames, 'it's a pity I'm not your age. Good-evening!'

He passed the fellow and went out. He had noted his way in this 'rabbit warren', and was soon back among the passionless statues. Well! He had turned the last stone and could do no more, except make that overbearing fellow and his young woman sorry they'd ever been born. He came out into the chilly mist of Westminster. Pride and temper! Sooner than admit themselves in the wrong, people would turn themselves into an expensive 'circus' for the gaping and the sneers, the japing and the jeers of half the town! To vindicate her 'honour', that 'Scotchman' would have his young woman's past dragged out! And fairly faced by the question whether to drag it out or not, Soames stood still. If he didn't, she might get a verdict; if he did, and didn't convince the jury, the damages would be shockingly increased. They might run into thousands. He felt the need of definite decision. One had been drifting in the belief that the thing wouldn't come into Court! Four o'clock! Not too late, perhaps, to see Sir James Foskisson. He would telephone to very young Nicholas to arrange a conference at once, and if Michael was at South Square, he would take him down to it. . . .

In his study, Michael had been staring with lugubrious relish at Aubrey Green's cartoon of himself in a Society paper. On one leg, like Guy–or was it Slingsby?–in the Edward Lear 'Nonsense' book, he was depicted crying in the wilderness where a sardonic smile was rising on the horizon. Out of his mouth the word 'Foggartism' wreathed like the smoke of a cigar. Above a hole in the middle distance, a meercat's body supported the upturned face and applauding forepaws of Mr Blythe. The thing was devastating in treatment and design–not unkind, merely killing. Michael's face had been endowed with a sort of after-dinner rapture, as if he were enjoying the sound of his own voice. Ridicule! Not even a personal friend, an artist, could see that the wilderness was at least as deserving of ridicule as the pelican! The cartoon seemed to write the word 'futility' large across his page. It recalled to him Fleur's words at the outset: 'And by the time the Tories go out you'll have your licence.' She was a born realist! From the first she had foreseen for him the position of an eccentric, picturesquely beating a little private drum! A dashed good cartoon! And no one could appreciate it so deeply as its victim. But why did everyone smile at Foggartism? Why? Because among a people who naturally walked, it leaped like a grasshopper; to a nation that felt its way in fog, it seemed a will-o'-the-wisp. Yes, he was a fool for his pains! And–just then, Soames arrived.

'I've been to see that Scotchmen,' he said. 'He means to take it into Court.'

'Oh! Not really, sir! I always thought you'd keep it out.'

'Only an unqualified apology will do that. Fleur can't give it; she's in the right. Can you come down with me now and see Sir James Foskisson?'

They set out in a taxi for the Temple.

The chambers of very young Nicholas Forsyte were in Paper Buildings. Chinny, mild and nearly forty, he succeeded within ten minutes in presenting to them every possible doubt.

'He seems to enjoy the prospect of getting tonked,' murmured Michael while they were going over to Sir James.

'A poor thing,' Soames responded; 'but careful. Foskisson must attend to the case himself.'

After those necessary minutes during which the celebrated K.C. was regathering from very young Nicholas what it was all about, they were ushered into the presence of one with a large head garnished by small grey whiskers, and really obvious brains. Since selecting him, Soames had been keeping an eye on the great advocate; had watched him veiling his appeals to a jury with an air of scrupulous equity; very few–he was convinced–and those not on juries, could see Sir James Foskisson coming round a corner. Soames had specially remarked his success in cases concerned with morals or nationality–no one so apt at getting a co-respondent, a German, a Russian, or anybody at all bad, non-suited! At close quarters his whiskers seemed to give him an intensive respectability–difficult to imagine him dancing, dicing, or in bed. In spite of his practice, too, he enjoyed the reputation of being thorough; he might be relied on to know more than half the facts of any case by the time he went into Court, and to pick up the rest as he went along–or at least not to show that he hadn't. Very young Nicholas, knowing all the facts, had seemed quite unable to see what line could possibly be taken. Sir James, on the other hand, appeared to know only just enough. Sliding his light eyes from Soames to Michael, he retailed them, and said: 'Eminently a case for an amicable settlement.'

'Indeed!' said Soames.

Something in his voice seemed to bring Sir James to attention.

'Have you attempted that?'

'I have gone to the limit.'

'Excuse me, Mr Forsyte, but what do you regard as the limit?'

'Fifteen hundred pounds, and a mutual expression of regret. They'd accept the money, but they ask for an unqualified apology.'

The great lawyer rested his chin. 'Have you tried the unqualified apology without the money?'

'No.'

'I would almost be inclined. MacGown is a very rich man. The shadow and the substance, eh? The expressions in the letters are strong. What do you say, Mr Mont?'

'Not so strong as those she used of my wife.'

Sir James Foskisson looked at very young Nicholas.

'Let me see,' he said, 'those were—?'

'Lion-huntress and snob,' said Michael curtly.

Sir James wagged his head precisely as if it were a pair of scales.

'Immoral, snake, traitress, without charm—you think those weaker?'

'They don't make you snigger, sir, the others do. In Society it's the snigger that counts.'

Sir James smiled.

'The jury won't be in Society, Mr Mont.'

'My wife doesn't feel like making an apology, anyway, unless there's an expression of regret on the other side; and I don't see why she should.'

Sir James Foskisson seemed to breathe more freely.

'In that case,' he said, 'we have to consider whether to use the detective's evidence or not. If we do, we shall need to subpœna the hall porter and the servants at Mr—er—Curfew's flat.'

'Exactly,' said Soames; 'that's what we're here to decide.' It was as if he had said: 'The conference is now opened.'

Sir James perused the detective's evidence for five silent minutes.

'If this is confirmed, even partially,' he said at last, 'we win.'

Michael had gone to the window. The trees in the garden had tiny buds; some pigeons were strutting on the grass below. He heard Soames say:

'I ought to tell you that they've been shadowing my daughter. There's nothing, of course, except some visits to a young American dangerously ill of pneumonia at his hotel.'

'Of which I knew and approved,' said Michael, without turning round.

'Could we call him?'

'I believe he's still at Bournemouth. But he was in love with Miss Ferrar.'

Sir James turned to Soames.

'If there's no question of a settlement, we'd better go for the gloves. Merely to cross-examine as to books and play and clubs is very inconclusive.'

'Have you read the dark scene in "The plain Dealer"?' Asked Soames; 'and that novel, *Canthar*?'

'All very well, Mr Forsyte, but impossible to say what a jury would make of impersonal evidence like that.'

Michael had come back to his seat.

'I've a horror,' he said, 'of dragging in Miss Ferrar's private life.'

'No doubt. But do you want me to win the case?'

'Not that way. Can't we go into Court, say nothing, and pay up?'

Sir James Foskisson smiled and looked at Soames. 'Really,' he seemed to say, 'why did you bring me this young man?'

Soames, however, had been pursuing his own thoughts.

'There's too much risk about that flat; if we failed there, it might be a matter of twenty thousand pounds. Besides, they would certainly call my daughter. I want to prevent that at all costs. I thought you could turn the whole thing into an indictment of modern morality.'

Sir James Foskisson moved in his chair, and the pupils of his light-blue eyes became as pin-points. He nodded almost imperceptibly three times, precisely as if he had seen the Holy Ghost.

'When shall we be reached?' he said to very young Nicholas.

'Probably next Thursday – Mr Justice Brane.'

'Very well. I'll see you again on Monday. Good evening.' And he sank back into an immobility, which neither Soames nor Michael felt equal to disturbing.

They went away silent – very young Nicholas tarrying in conversation with Sir James's devil.

Turning at the Temple station, Michael murmured:

'It was just as if he'd said: "Some stunt!" wasn't it? I'm looking in at *The Outpost*, sir. If you're going back to Fleur, will you tell her?'

Soames nodded. There it was! He had to do everything that was painful.

2

'NOT GOING TO HAVE IT'

In the office of *The Outpost* Mr Blythe had just been in conversation with one of those great business men who make such deep impression on all to whom they voice their views in strict confidence. If Sir Thomas Lockit did not precisely monopolise the control of manufacture in Great Britain, he, like others, caused almost anyone to think so – his knowledge was so positive and his emphasis so cold. In his view the country must resume the position held before the Great War. It all hinged on coal – a question of this seven hours a day; and they were "not going to have it". A shilling, perhaps two shillings, off the cost of coal. They were "not going to have" Europe doing without British produce. Very few people knew Sir Thomas Lockit's mind; but nearly all who did were extraordinarily gratified.

Mr Blythe, however, was biting his finger, and spitting out the result.

'Who was that fellow with the grey moustache?' asked Michael.

'Lockit. He's "not going to have it".'

'Oh!' said Michael, in some surprise.

'One sees more and more, Mont, that the really dangerous people are not the politicians, who want things with public passion – that is, mildly, slowly; but the big business men, who want things with private passion, strenuously, quickly. They know their own minds; and if we don't look out they'll wreck the country.'

'What are they up to now?' said Michael.

'Nothing for the moment; but it's brewing. One sees in Lockit the futility of will-power. He's not going to have what it's entirely out of his power to prevent. He'd like to break Labour and make it work like a nigger from sheer necessity. Before that we shall be having civil war. Some of the Labour people, of course, are just as bad–they want to break everybody. It's a bee nuisance. If we're all to be plunged into industrial struggles again, how are we to get on with Foggartism?'

'I've been thinking about the country,' said Michael, 'Aren't we beating the air, Blythe? Is it any good telling a man who's lost a lung that what he wants is a new one?'

Mr Blythe puffed out one cheek.

'Yes,' he said, 'the country had a hundred very settled years–Waterloo to the War–to get into its present state; it's got its line of life so fixed and its habits so settled that nobody–neither editors, politicians nor business men–can think except in terms of its bloated town industrialism. The country's got beyond the point of balance in that hundred settled years, and it'll want fifty settled years to get back to that point again. The real trouble is that we're not going to get fifty settled years. Some bee thing or other–war with Turkey or Russia, trouble in India, civil ructions, to say nothing of another general flare-up–may knock the bottom out of any settled plans at any time. We've struck a disturbed patch of history, and we know it in our bones, and live from hand to mouth, according.'

'Well, then!' said Michael glumly, thinking of what the Minister had said to him at Lippinghall.

Mr Blythe puffed out the other cheek.

'No backsliding, young man! In Foggartism we have the best goods we can see before us, and we must bee well deliver them, as best we can. We've outgrown all the old hats.'

'Have you seen Aubrey Greene's cartoon?'

'I have.'

'Good–isn't it? But what I really came in to tell you is that this beastly libel case of ours will be on next week.'

Mr Blythe's ears moved.

'I'm sorry for that. Win or lose–nothing's worse for public life than private ructions. You're not going to have it, are you?'

'We can't help it. But our defence is to be confined to an attack on the new morality.'

'One can't attack what isn't,' said Mr Blythe.

'D'you mean to say,' said Michael, grinning, 'that you haven't noticed the new morality?'

'Certainly not. Formulate it if you can.'

' "Don't be stupid, don't be dull." '

Mr Blythe grunted. 'The old morality used to be: "Behave like a gentleman." '

'Yes! But in modern thought there ain't no sich an animal.'

'There are fragments lying about; they reconstructed Neanderthal man from half a skull.'

'A word that's laughed at can't be used, Blythe.'

'Ah!' said Mr Blythe. 'The chief failings of your generation, young Mont, are sensitiveness to ridicule and terror of being behind the times. It's bee weak-minded.'

Michael grinned.

'I know it. Come down to the House. Parsham's Electrification Bill is due. We may get some lights on Unemployment.'

Having parted from Mr Blythe in the Lobby, Michael came on his father walking down a corridor with a short bright old man in a trim grey beard.

'Ah! Michael, we've been seeking you. Marquess, my hopeful son! The Marquess wants to interest you in electricity.'

Michael removed his hat.

'Will you come to the reading-room, my lord?'

This, as he knew, was Marjorie Ferrar's grandfather, and might be useful. In a remote corner of a room lighted so that nobody could see anyone else reading, they sat down in triangular formation.

'You know about electricity, Mr Mont?' said the Marquess.

'No, sir, except that more of it would be desirable in this room.'

'Everywhere, Mr Mont. I've read about your Foggartism; if you'll allow me to say so, it's quite possibly the policy of the future; but nothing will be done with it till you've electrified the country. I should like you to start by supporting this Bill of Parsham's.'

And, with an engaging distinction of syllable, the old peer proceeded to darken Michael's mind.

'I see, sir,' said Michael at last. 'This Bill ought to add considerably to Unemployment.'

'Temporarily.'

'I wonder if I ought to take on any more temporary trouble. I'm finding it difficult enough to interest people in the future as it is—they seem to think the present so important.'

Sir Lawrence whinnied.

'You must give him time and pamphlets, Marquess. But, my dear fellow, while your Foggartism is confined to the stable, you'll want a second horse.'

'I've been advised already to take up the state of the traffic or penny postage. And, by the way, sir, that case of ours *is* coming into Court next week.'

Sir Lawrence's loose eyebrow shot up:

'Oh!' he said. 'Do you remember, Marquess—your grand-daughter and my daughter-in-law? I came to you about it.'

'Something to do with lions? A libel, was it?' said the old peer. 'My aunt—'

While Michael was trying to decide whether this was an ejaculation or the beginning of a reminiscence, his father broke in:

'Ah! yes, an interesting case that, Marquess—it's all in Betty Montecourt's Memoirs.'

'Libels,' resumed the Marquess, 'had flavour in those days. The words complained of were: "Her crinoline covers her considerable obliquity." '

'If anything's to be done to save scandal,' muttered Michael, 'it must be done now. We're at a deadlock.'

'Could *you* put in a word, sir?' said Sir Lawrence.

The Marquess's beard quivered.

'I see from the papers that my granddaughter is marrying a man called MacGown, a Member of this House. Is he about?'

'Probably,' said Michael. 'But I had a row with him. I think, sir, there would be more chance with her.'

The Marquess rose. 'I'll ask her to breakfast. I dislike publicity. Well, I hope you'll vote for this Bill, Mr Mont, and think over the question of electrifying the country. We want young men interested. I'm going to the Peers' Gallery now. Good-bye!'

When briskly he had gone, Michael said to his father: 'If he's not going to have it, I wish he'd ask Fleur to breakfast, too. There are two parties to this quarrel.'

3

SOAMES DRIVES HOME

Soames in the meantime was seated with one of those parties in her 'parlour'. She had listened in silence, but with a stubborn and resentful face. What did he know of the loneliness and frustration she had been feeling? Could he tell that the thrown stone had starred her mirrored image of herself; that the words 'snob' and 'lion-huntress' had entered her very soul? He could not understand the spiritual injury she had received, the sudden deprivation of that self-importance, and hope of rising, necessary to all. Concerned by the expression on her face, preoccupied with the practical aspects of the 'circus' before them, and desperately involved in thoughts of how to keep her out of it as much as possible, Soames was reduced to the closeness of a fish.

'You'll be sitting in front, next to me,' he said. 'I shouldn't wear anything too bright. Would you like your mother there, too?'

Fleur shrugged her shoulders.

'Just so,' said Soames. 'But if she wants to come, she'd better, perhaps. Brane is not a joking judge, thank goodness. Have you ever been in a Court?'

'No.'

'The great thing is to keep still and pay no attention to anything. They'll all be behind you, except the jury—and there's nothing in them really. If you look at them, don't smile!'

'Why? Aren't they safe, Dad?'

Soames put the levity aside.

'I should wear a small hat. Michael must sit on your left. Have you got over that—er—not telling each other things?'

'Yes.'

'I shouldn't begin it again. He's very fond of you.'

Fleur nodded.

'Is there anything you want to tell *me*? You know I—I worry about you.'

Fleur got up and sat on the arm of his chair; he had at once a feeling of assuagement.

'I really don't care now. The harm's done. I only hope *she'll* have a bad time.'

Soames, who had the same hope, was somewhat shocked by its expression.

He took leave of her soon after and got into his car for the dark drive back to Mapledurham. The spring evening was cold and he had the window up. At first he thought of very little; and then of still less. He had passed a tiring afternoon, and was glad of the slight smell of stephanotis provided by Annette. The road was too familiar to rouse his thoughts, beyond wonder at the lot of people there always seemed to be in the world between six and seven. He dozed his way into the new cut, woke, and dozed again. What was this—Slough? Before going to

Marlborough he had been at school there with young Nicholas and St John Heyman, and after his time, some other young Forsytes. Nearly sixty years ago! He remembered his first day—a brand-new little boy in a brand-new little top-hat, with a playbox stored by his mother with things to eat, and blessed with the words: 'There, Summy dear, that'll make you popular.' He had reckoned on having command of that corruption for some weeks; but no sooner had he produced a bit of it than they had taken the box, and suggested to him that it would be a good thing to eat the lot. In twenty-two minutes twenty-two boys had materially increased their weight, and he himself, in handing out the contents, had been obliged to eat less than a twenty-third. They had left him one packet of biscuits, and those had caraway seeds, for which he had constitutionally no passion whatever. Afterwards, three other new boys had complained that he was a fool for having it all eaten up like that, instead of saving it for them, and he had been obliged to sit on their heads one by one. His popularity had lasted twenty-two minutes, and, so far as he knew, had never come back. He had been against Communism ever since.

Bounding a little on the cushioned seat, he remembered poignantly his own cousin St John Heyman pushing him into a gorse-bush and holding him there for an appreciable minute. Horrid little brutes, boys! For a moment he felt quite grateful to Michael for trying to get them out of England. And yet—! He had some pleasant memories even of boys. There was his collection of butterflies—he had sold two Red Admirals in poor condition to a boy for one-and-threepence. To be a boy again—h'm—and shoot peas at passengers in a train that couldn't stop, and drink cherry brandy going home, and win a prize by reciting two hundred lines of 'The Lady of the Lake' better than 'Cherry-Tart' Burroughes—Um? What had become of 'Cherry-Tart' Burroughes, who had so much money at school that his father went bankrupt! 'Cherry-Tart' Burroughes!

The loom of Slough faded. One was in rank country now, and he ground the handle of the window to get a little fresh air. A smell of trees and grass came in. Get boys out of England! They had funny accents in those great places overseas. Well, they had funny accents here, too. The accent had been all right at Slough—for if it wasn't a boy got lammed. He remembered the first time his father and mother—James and Emily—came down; very genteel (before the word was fly-blown), all whiskers and crinoline; the beastly boys had made personal remarks which had hurt him! Get 'em out of England! But in those days there had been nowhere for boys to go. He took a long breath of the wayside air. They said England was changed, spoiled, some even said 'done for'. Bosh! It still smelt the same! His great-uncle, one of 'Superior Dosset's' brothers, had gone as a boy to Bermuda at the beginning of the last century, and had he been heard of since? Not he. Young Jon Forsyte and his mother—his own first, unfaithful, still not quite forgotten wife—had gone to the States—would they be heard of again? He hoped not. England! Some day, when he had time and the car was free, he would go and poke round on the border of Dorset and Devon where the Forsytes came from. There was nothing there—he understood, and he wouldn't care to let anybody know of his going; but the earth must be some sort of colour, and there would be a graveyard, and—ah! Maidenhead! These sprawling villas and hotels and gramophones spoiled the river. Funny that Fleur had never been very fond of the river; too slow and wet, perhaps—everything was quick and dry now, like America. But had they such a river as the Thames anywhere out of England? Not they! Nothing that ran green and clear and weedy, where you could sit in a punt and watch the cows, and those big elms, and the poplars. Nothing that was safe and quiet, where you called your soul your own and thought of Constable and Mason and Walker.

His car bumped something slightly, and came to a stand. That fellow Riggs was always bumping something! He looked out. The chauffeur had got down and was examining his mudguard.

'What was that?' said Soames.

'I think it was a pig, sir.'

'Where?'

'Shall I drive on, or see?'

Soames looked round. There seemed no inhabitants in sight.

'Better see.'

The chauffeur disappeared behind the car. Soames remained seated. He had never had any pigs. They said the pig was a clean animal. People didn't treat pigs properly. It was very quiet! No cars on the road; in the silence the wind was talking a little in the hedgerow. He noticed some stars.

'It *is* a pig, sir; he's breathing.'

'Oh!' said Soames. If a cat had nine, how many lives had a pig? He remembered his father James's only riddle: 'If a herring and a half cost three-ha'pence, what's the price of a gridiron?' When still very small, he had perceived that it was unanswerable.

'Where is he?' he said.

'In the ditch, sir.'

A pig was property, but if in the ditch, nobody would notice it till after he was home. 'Drive on,' he said. 'No! Wait!' And, opening the near door, he got out. After all, the pig was in distress. 'Show me,' he said, and moved in the tail-light of his car to where the chauffeur stood pointing. There, in the shallow ditch, was a dark object emitting cavernous low sounds, as of a man asleep in a club chair.

'It must belong to one of them cottages we passed a bit back,' said the chauffeur.

Soames looked at the pig.

'Anything broken?'

'No, sir; the mudguard's all right. I fancy it copped him pretty fair.'

'In the pig, I meant.'

The chauffeur touched the pig with his foot. It squealed, and Soames quivered. Someone would hear! Just like that fellow, drawing attention to it—no gumption whatever! But how, without touching, did you find out whether anything was broken in a pig? He moved a step and saw the pig's eyes; and a sort of fellow-feeling stirred in him. What if it had a broken leg! Again the chauffeur touched it with his foot. The pig uttered a lamentable noise, and, upheaving its bulk, squealing and grunting, trotted off. Soames hastily resumed his seat. 'Drive on!' he said. Pigs! They never thought of anything but themselves; and cottagers were just as bad—very unpleasant about cars. And he wasn't sure they weren't right—tearing great things! The pig's eye seemed looking at him again from where his feet were resting. Should he keep some, now that he had those meadows on the other side of the river? Eat one's own bacon, cure one's own hams! After all, there was something in it—clean pigs, properly fed! That book of old Foggart said one must grow more food in England, and be independent if there were another war. He sniffed. Smell of baking—. Reading town already! They still grew biscuits in England! Foreign countries growing his food—something unpleasant about living on sufferance like that! After all, English meat and English wheat—as for a potato, you couldn't get one fit to eat in Italy, or France. And now they wanted to trade with Russia again! Those Bolshevists hated England. Eat their wheat and eggs, use their tallow and skins? *Infra dig*, he called it! The car swerved and he was jerked against the side cushions. The village church!—that fellow Riggs was always shying at something. Pretty little old affair, too, with its squat spire and its lichen—couldn't see that out of England—graves, old names, yew trees. And that reminded him: One would have to be buried, some day. Here, perhaps. Nothing flowery! Just his name, 'Soames Forsyte', standing out on rough stone, like that grave he had sat on at Highgate; no need to put 'Here lies'—of course he'd lie! As to a cross, he didn't know. Probably they'd put one, whatever he wished. He'd like to be in a corner, though, away from people—with an apple tree or something, over him. The less they remembered him, the better. Except Fleur—and she would have other things to think of!

The car turned down the last low hill to the level of the river. He caught a glimpse of it flowing dark between the poplars, like the soul of England, running hidden. The car rolled into the drive, and stopped before the door. He shouldn't tell Annette yet about this case coming into Court—she wouldn't feel as he did—she had no nerves!

4

CATECHISM

Marjorie Ferrar's marriage was fixed for the day of the Easter Recess; her honeymoon to Lugano; her trousseau with Clothilde; her residence in Eaton Square; her pin-money at two thousand a year; and her affections on nobody. When she received a telephone message: Would she come to breakfast at Shropshire House? she was surprised. What could be the matter with the old boy?

At five minutes past nine, however, on the following day she entered the ancestral precincts, having left almost all powder and pigment on her dressing-table. Was he going to disapprove of her marriage? Or to give her some of her grandmother's lace, which was only fit to be in a museum?

The marquess was reading the paper in front of an electric fire. He bent on her his bright, shrewd glance.

'Well, Marjorie? Shall we sit down, or do you like to breakfast standing? There's porridge, scrambled eggs, fish—ah! and grapefruit—very considerate of them! Pour out the coffee, will you?'

'What'll *you* have, Grandfather?'

'Thank you, I'll roam about and peck a bit. So you're going to be married. Is that fortunate?'

'People say so.'

'He's in Parliament, I see. Do you think you could interest him in this Electricity Bill of Parsham's?'

'Oh! yes. He's dead keen on electricity.'

'Sensible man. He's got Works, I suppose. Are they electrified?'

'I expect so.'

The marquess gave her another glance.

'You know nothing about it,' he said. 'But you're looking very charming. What's this I hear of a libel?'

She might have known! Grandfather was too frightfully spry! He missed nothing!

'It wouldn't interest you, dear.'

'I disagree. My father and *old* Lawrence Mont were great friends. Why do you want to wash linen in Court?'

'I don't.'

'Are you the plaintiff?'

'Yes.'

'What do you complain of?'

'They've said things about me.'

'Who?'

'Fleur Mont and her father.'

'Ah! the relation of the tea-man. What have they said?'

'That I haven't a moral about me.'

'Well, have you?'

'As much as most people.'

'Anything else?'

'That I'm a snake of the first water.'

'I don't like that. What made them say so?'

'Only that I was heard calling her a snob; and so she is.'

The marquess, who had resigned a finished grapefruit, placed his foot on a chair, his elbow on his knee, his chin on his hand, and said:

'No divinity hedges our Order in these days, Marjorie; but we still stand for something. It's a mistake to forget that.'

She sat very still. Everybody respected grandfather; even her father, to whom he did not speak. But to be told that she stood for something was really too dull for anything! All very well for grandfather at his age, and with his lack of temptations! Besides, *she* had no handle to her name, owing to the vaunted nature of British institutions. Even if she felt that–by Lord Charles out of Lady Ursula–she ought not to be dictated to, she had never put on frills–had always liked to be thought a mere Bohemian. And, after all, she did stand–for not being stuffy, and not being dull.

'Well, Grandfather, I tried to make it up, but she wouldn't. Coffee?'

'Yes, coffee. But tell me, are you happy about yourself?'

Marjorie Ferrar handed him the cup.

'No. Who is?'

'A hit,' said the marquess. 'You're going to be very well off, I hear. That means power. It's worth using well, Marjorie. He's a Scotsman, isn't he? Do you like him?' Again the shrewd bright glance.

'At times.'

'I see. With your hair, you must be careful. Red hair is extraordinarily valuable on occasion. In the Eton and Harrow Match, or for speaking after dinner; but don't let it run away with you after you're married. Where are you going to live?'

'In Eaton Square. There's a Scotch place, too.'

'Have your kitchens electrified. I've had it done here. It saves the cook's temper. I get very equable food. But about this libel. Can't you all say you're sorry–why put money into the lawyers' pockets?'

'She won't, unless I do, and I won't, unless she does.'

The marquess drank off his coffee.

'Then what is there in the way? I dislike publicity, Marjorie. Look at that suit the other day. Anything of this nature in Society, nowadays, is a nail in our coffins.'

'I'll speak to Alec, if you like.'

'Do! Has he red hair?'

'No; black.'

'Ah! What would you like for a wedding-present–lace?'

'Oh! no, please, dear. Nobody's wearing lace.'

With his head on one side, the marquess looked at her. 'I can't get that lace off,' he seemed to say.

'Perhaps you'd like a colliery. Electrified, it would pay in no time.'

Marjorie Ferrar laughed. 'I know you're hard up, Grandfather; but I'd rather not have a colliery, thanks. They're so expensive. Just give me your blessing.'

'I wonder,' said the marquess, 'if I could sell blessings? Your uncle Dangerfield has gone in for farming; he's ruining me. If only he'd grow wheat by electricity; it's the only way to make it pay at the present price. Well, if you've finished breakfast, good-bye. I must go to work.'

Marjorie Ferrar, who had indeed begun breakfast, stood up and pressed his hand. He was a dear old boy, if somewhat rapid! . . .

That same evening, in a box at the St Anthony, she had her opportunity, when MacGown was telling her of Soames's visit.

'Oh, dear! Why on earth didn't you settle it, Alec? The whole thing's a bore. I've had my grandfather at me about it.'

'If they'll apologise,' said MacGown, 'I'll settle it to-morrow. But an apology they must make.'

'And what about me? I don't want to stand up to be shot at.'

'There are some things one can't sit down under, Marjorie. Their whole conduct has been infamous.'

Visited by a reckless impulse, she said:

'What d'you suppose I'm really like, Alec?'

MacGown put his hand on her bare arm.

'I don't suppose I know.'

'Well?'

'Defiant.'

Curious summary! Strangely good in a way–only–!

'You mean that I like to irritate people till they think I'm–what I'm not. But suppose'–her eyes confronted his–'I really am.'

MacGown's grasp tightened.

'You're not; and I won't have it said.'

'You think this case will whitewash my–defiance?'

'I know what gossip is; and I know it buzzes about you. People who say things are going to be taught, once for all, that they can't.'

Marjorie Ferrar turned her gaze towards the still life on the dropped curtain, laughed and said:

'My dear man, you're dangerously provincial.'

'I know a straight line when I see one.'

'Yes; but there aren't any in London. You'd better hedge, Alec, or you'll be taking a toss over me.'

MacGown said, simply: 'I believe in you more than you believe in yourself.'

She was glad that the curtain rose just then, for she felt confused and rather touched.

Instead of confirming her desire to drop the case, that little talk gave her a feeling that by the case her marriage stood or fell. Alec would know where he was when it was over, and so would she! There would be precious little secret about her and she would either not be married to him, or at least not married under false pretences. Let it rip! It was, however, a terrible bore; especially the preparatory legal catechism she had now to undergo. What effect, for instance, had been produced among her friends and acquaintances by those letters? From the point of view of winning, the point was obviously not without importance. But how was she to tell? Two hostesses had cancelled week-end invitations: a rather prim countess, and a Canadian millionairess married to a decaying baronet. It had not occured to her before that this was the reason, but it might have been. Apart from them she would have to say she didn't know, people didn't tell you to your face what they heard or thought of you. They were going to try and make her out a piece of injured innocence! Good Lord! What if she declared her real faith in Court, and left them all in the soup! Her real faith—what was it? Not to let a friend down; not to give a man away; not to funk; to do things differently from other people; to be always on the go; not to be 'stuffy'; not to be dull! The whole thing was topsy-turvy! Well, she must keep her head!

5

THE DAY

On the day of the case Soames rose, in Green Street, with a sort of sick impatience. Why wasn't it the day after?

Renewed interviews with very young Nicholas and Sir James Foskisson had confirmed the idea of defence by attack on modern morality. Foskisson was evidently going to put his heart into attacking that from which he had perhaps suffered; and if he were at all like old Bobstay, who, aged eighty-two, had just published his reminiscences, that cat would lose her hair and give herself away. Yesterday afternoon Soames had taken an hour's look at Mr Justice Brane, and been very favourably impressed; the learned judge, though younger than himself—he had often briefed him in other times—looked old-fashioned enough now for anything.

Having cleaned his teeth, put in his plate, and brushed his hair, Soames went into the adjoining room and told Annette she would be late. She always looked terribly young and well in bed, and this, though a satisfaction to him, he could never quite forgive. When he was gone, fifteen years hence, perhaps, she would still be under sixty, and might live another twenty years.

Having roused her sufficiently to say: 'You will have plenty of time to be fussy in that Court, Soames,' he went back and looked out of his window. The air smelled of spring—aggravating! He bathed and shaved with care—didn't want to go into the Box with a cut on his chin!—then went back to see that Annette was not putting on anything bright. He found her in pink under-clothes.

'I should wear black,' he said.

Annette regarded him above her hand-mirror.

'Whom do you want me to fascinate, Soames?'

'These people will bring their friends, I shouldn't wonder; anything conspicuous—'

'Don't be afraid; I shall not try to be younger than my daughter.'

Soames went out again. The French! Well, she had good taste in dress.

After breakfast he went off to Fleur's. Winifred and Imogen would look after Annette—they too were going to the Court, as if there were anything to enjoy about this business!

Spruce in his silk hat, he walked across the Green Park, conning over his evidence. No buds on the trees—a late year; and the Royal Family out of town! Passing the Palace, he thought: 'They're very popular!' He supposed they liked this great Empire group in front of them, all muscle and flesh and large animals! The Albert Memorial, and this—everybody ran them down; but, after all, peace and plenty—nothing modern about them! Emerging into Westminster, he cut his way through a smell of fried fish into the Parliamentary backwater of North Street, and, between its pleasant little houses, gazed steadily at the Wren Church. Never going inside any church except St Paul's, he derived a sort of strength from their outsides—churches were solid and stood back, and didn't seem to care what people thought of them! He felt a little better, rounding into South Square. The Dandie met him in the hall. Though he was not over-fond of dogs, the breadth and solidity of this one always affected Soames pleasurably—better than that little Chinese abortion they used to have! This dog was a character—masterful and tenacious—you would get very little out of *him* in a witness-box! Looking up from the dog, he saw Michael and Fleur coming down the stairs. After hurriedly inspecting Michael's brown suit and speckled tie, his eyes came to anchor on his daughter's face. Pale but creamy, nothing modern—thank goodness! no rouge, salve, powder, or eye-blacking; perfectly made-up for her part! In a blue dress, too, very good taste, which must have taken some finding! The desire that she should not feel nervous stilled Soames's private qualms.

'Quite a smell of spring!' he said: 'Shall we start?'

While a cab was being summoned, he tried to put her at ease.

'I had a look at Brane yesterday; he's changed a good deal from when I used to know him. I was one of the first to give him briefs.'

'That's bad, isn't it, sir?' said Michael.

'How?'

'He'll be afraid of being thought grateful.'

Flippant, as usual!

'Our judges,' he said, 'are a good lot, take them all round.'

'I'm sure they are. Do you know if he ever reads, sir?'

'How d'you mean—reads?'

'Fiction. We don't, in Parliament.'

'Nobody reads novels, except women,' said Soames. And he felt Fleur's dress. 'You'll want a fur; that's flimsy.'

While she was getting the fur, he said to Michael: 'How did she sleep?'

'Better than I did, sir.'

'That's a comfort, anyway. Here's the cab. Keep away from that Scotchman.'

'I see him every day in the House, you know.'

'Ah!' said Soames; 'I forgot. You make nothing of that sort of thing there, I believe.' And taking his daughter's arm, he led her forth.

'I wonder if old Blythe will turn up,' he heard Michael say, when they passed the office of *The Outpost*. It was the first remark made in the cab, and, calling for no response, it was the last.

The Law Courts had their customary air, and people, in black and blue, were hurrying into them. 'Beetle-trap!' muttered Michael. Soames rejected the simile with his elbow—for him they were just familiar echoing space, concealed staircases, stuffy corridors, and the square enclosures of one voice at a time.

Too early, they went slowly up the stairs. Really, it was weak-minded! Here they had come—they and the other side—to get—what? He was amazed at himself for not having insisted on Fleur's apologising. Time and again in the case of others, all this had appeared quite natural—in the case of his own daughter, it now seemed almost incredibly idiotic. He hurried her on, however, past lingering lawyers' clerks, witnesses, what not. A few low words to an usher, and they were inside, and sitting down. Very young Nicholas was already in his place, and Soames so adjusted himself that there would only be the thickness of Sir James, when he materialised, between them. Turning to confer, he lived for a cosy moment in the past again, as might some retired old cricketer taking block once more. Beyond young Nicholas he quartered the assemblage with his glance. Yes, people had got wind of it! He knew they would—with that cat always in the public eye—quite a lot of furbelows up there at the back, and more coming. He reversed himself abruptly; the jury were filing in—special, but a common-looking lot! Why were juries always common-looking? He had never been on one himself. He glanced at Fleur. There she sat, and what she was feeling he couldn't tell. As for young Michael, his ears looked very pointed. And just then he caught sight of Annette. She'd better not come and sit down here, after all—the more there were of them in front, the more conspicuous it would be! So he shook his head at her, and waved towards the back. Ah! She was going! She and Winifred and Imogen would take up room—all rather broad in the beam; but there were still gaps up there. And suddenly he saw the plaintiff and her lawyer and MacGown; very spry they looked, and that insolent cat was smiling! Careful not to glance in their direction, Soames saw them sit down, some six feet off. Ah! and here came Counsel—Foskisson and Bullfry together, thick as thieves. They'd soon be calling each other 'my friend' now, and cutting each other's throats! He wondered if he wouldn't have done better after all to let the other side have Foskisson, and briefed Bullfry—an ugly-looking customer, broad, competent and leathery. He and Michael with Fleur between them, and behind—Foskisson and his junior; Settlewhite and the Scotchman with 'that cat' between them, and behind—Bullfry and his junior! Only the Judge wanted now to complete the pattern! And there he came! Soames gripped Fleur's arm and raised her with himself. Bob! Down again! One side of Brane's face seemed a little fuller than the other; Soames wondered if he had toothache, and how it would affect the proceedings.

And now came the usual 'shivaree' about such and such a case, and what would be taken next week, and so on. Well! that was over, and the Judge was turning his head this way and that, as if to see where the field was placed. Now Bullfry was up:

'If it please Your Lordship—'

He was making the usual opening, with the usual flowery description of the plaintiff—granddaughter of a marquess, engaged to a future Prime Minister . . .

or so you'd think! . . . prominent in the most brilliant circles, high-spirited, perhaps a thought too high-spirited. . . . Baggage! . . . the usual smooth and subacid description of the defendant! . . . Rich and ambitious young married lady. . . . Impudent beggar! . . . Jury would bear in mind that they were dealing in both cases with members of advanced Society, but they would bear in mind, too, that primary words had primary meanings and consequences, whatever the Society in which they were uttered. H'm! Very sketchy reference to the incident in Fleur's drawing-room—minimised, of course—ha! an allusion to himself—man of property and standing—thank you for nothing! Reading the libellous letter now! Effect of them . . . very made-up, all that! . . . Plaintiff obliged to take action. . . . Bunkum! 'I shall now call Mrs Ralph Ppynrryn.'

'How do you spell that name, Mr Bullfry?'

'With two p's two y's, two n's and two r's, my lord.'

'I see.'

Soames looked at the owner of the name. Good-looking woman of the flibberty-gibbet type! He listened to her evidence with close attention. Her account of the incident in Fleur's drawing-room seemed substantially correct. She had received the libellous letter two days later; had thought it her duty, as a friend, to inform Miss Ferrar. Should say, as a woman in Society, that this incident and these letters had done Miss Ferrar harm. Had talked it over with a good many people. A public incident. Much feeling excited. Had shown her letter to Mrs Maltese, and been shown one that she had received. Whole matter had become current gossip. H'm!

Bullfry down, and Foskisson up!

Soames adjusted himself. Now to see how the fellow shaped—the manner of a cross-examiner was so important! Well, he had seen worse—the eye, like frozen light, fixed on unoccupied space while the question was being asked, and coming round on to the witness for the answer; the mouth a little open, as if to swallow it; the tongue visible at times on the lower lip, the unoccupied hand clasping something under the gown behind.

'Now, Mrs—er—Ppynrryn. This incident, as my friend has called it, happened at the house of Mrs Mont, did it not? And how did you come there? As a friend. Quite so! And you have nothing against Mrs Mont? No. And you thought it advisable and kind, madam, to show this letter to the plaintiff and to other people—in fact, to foment this little incident to the best of your ability?' Eyes round!

'If a friend óf mine received such a letter about me, I should expect her to tell me that the writer was going about abusing me.'

'Even if your friend knew of the provocation and was also a friend of the letter-writer?'

'Yes.'

'Now, madam, wasn't it simply that the sensation of this little quarrel was too precious to be burked? It would have been so easy, wouldn't it, to have torn the letter up and said nothing about it? You don't mean to suggest that it made *you* think any the worse of Miss Ferrar—you knew her too well, didn't you?'

'Ye-es.'

'Exactly. As a friend of both parties you knew that the expressions were just spleen and not be taken seriously?'

'I can't say that.'

'Oh! You regard them as serious? Am I to take it that you thought they touched the hambone? In other words, that they were true?'

'Certainly not.'

'Could they do Miss Ferrar any harm if they were palpably untrue?'

'I think they could.'

'Not with you–you were a friend?'

'Not with me.'

'But with other people, who would never have heard of them but for you. In fact, madam, you enjoyed the whole thing. Did you?'

'Enjoyed? No.'

'You regarded it as your duty to spread this letter? Don't you enjoy doing your duty?'

The dry cackle within Soames stopped at his lips.

Foskisson down, and Bullfry up!

'It is, in fact, your experience, Mrs Ppynrryn, as well as that of most of us not so well constituted, perhaps, as my learned friend, that duty is sometimes painful.'

'Yes.'

'Thank you. Mrs Edward Maltese.'

During the examination of this other young woman, who seemed to be dark and solid, Soames tried to estimate the comparative effect produced by Fleur and 'that cat' on the four jurymen whose eyes seemed to stray towards beauty. He had come to no definite conclusion, when Sir James Foskisson rose to cross-examine.

'Tell me, Mrs Maltese, which do you consider the most serious allegation among those complained of?'

'The word "treacherous" in my letter, and the expression "a snake of the first water" in the letter to Mrs Ppynrryn.'

'More serious than the others?'

'Yes.'

'That is where you can help me, madam. The circle you move in is not exactly the plaintiff's, perhaps?'

'Not exactly.'

'Intersecting, um?'

'Yes.'

'Now, in which section, yours or the plaintiff's, would you say the expression "she hasn't a moral about her" would be the more, or shall we say the less, damning?'

'I can't say.'

'I only want your opinion. Do you think your section of Society as advanced as Miss Ferrar's?'

'Perhaps not.'

'It's well known, isn't it, that her circle is very free and easy?'

'I suppose so.'

'Still, *your* section is pretty advanced–I mean, you're not "stuffy"?'

'Not what, Sir James?'

'Stuffy, my lord; it's an expression a good deal used in modern Society.'

'What does it mean?'

'Strait-laced, my lord.'

'I see. Well, he's asking you if you're stuffy?'

'No, my lord. I hope not.'

'You hope not. Go on, Sir James.'

'Not being stuffy, you wouldn't be exactly worried if somebody said to you:

"My dear, you haven't a moral about you"?'

'Not if it was said as charmingly as that.'

'Now come, Mrs Maltese, does such an expression, said charmingly or the reverse, convey any blame to you or to your friends?'

'If the reverse, yes.'

'Am I to take it that the conception of morality in your circle is the same as in—my lord's?'

'How is the witness to answer that, Sir James?'

'Well, in your circle are you shocked when your friends are divorced, or when they go off together for a week in Paris, say, or wherever they find convenient?'

'Shocked? Well, I suppose one needn't be shocked by what one wouldn't do oneself.'

'In fact, you're not shocked?'

'I don't know that I'm shocked by anything.'

'That would be being stuffy, wouldn't it?'

'Perhaps.'

'Well, will you tell me then—if that's the state of mind in your circle; and you said, you know, that your circle is less free and easy than the plaintiff's—how it is possible that such words as "she hasn't a moral about her" can have done the plaintiff any harm?'

'The whole world isn't in our circles.'

'No. I suggest that only a very small portion of the world is in your circles. But do you tell me that you or the plaintiff pay any—?'

'How can she tell, Sir James, what the plaintiff pays?'

'That *you*, then, pay any attention to what people outside your circle think?'

Soames moved his head twice. The fellow was doing it well. And his eye caught Fleur's face turned towards the witness; a little smile was curling her lip.

'I don't personally pay much attention even to what anybody *in* my circle thinks.'

'Have you more independence of character than the plaintiff, should you say?'

'I dare say I've got as much.'

'Is she notoriously independent?'

'Yes.'

'Thank you, Mrs Maltese.'

Foskisson down, Bullfry up!

'I call the plaintiff, my lord.'

Soames uncrossed his legs.

6

IN THE BOX

Marjorie Ferrar stepped into the Box, not exactly nervous, and only just 'made-up'. The papers would record a black costume with chinchilla fur and a black hat. She kissed the air in front of the book, took a deep breath, and turned to Mr Bullfry.

For the last five days she had resented more and more the way this case had taken charge of her. She had initiated it, and it had completely deprived her of initiative. She had, in fact, made the old discovery, that when the machinery of quarrel is once put in motion, much more than pressure of the starting button is required to stop its revolutions. She was feeling that it would serve Alec and the lawyers right if all went wrong.

The voice of Mr Bullfry, carefully adjusted, soothed her. His questions were familiar, and with each answer her confidence increased, her voice sounded clear and pleasant in her ears. And she stood at ease, making her figure as boyish as she could. Her performance, she felt, was interesting to the Judge, the jury, and all those people up there, whom she could dimly see. If only 'that little snob' had not been seated, expressionless, between her and her Counsel! When at length Mr Bullfry sat down and Sir James Foskisson got up, she almost succumbed to the longing to powder her nose. Clasping the Box, she resisted it, and while he turned his papers, and hitched his gown, the first tremor of the morning passed down her spine. At least he might look at her when he spoke!

'Have you ever been party to an action before, Miss Ferrar?'

'No.'

'You quite understand, don't you, that you are on your oath?'

'Quite.'

'You have told my friend that you had no animus against Mrs Mont. Look at this marked paragraph in *The Evening Sun* of October 3rd. Did you write that?'

Marjorie Ferrar felt exactly as if she had stepped out of a conservatory into an east wind. Did they know everything, then?

'Yes; 1 wrote it.'

'It ends thus: "The enterprising little lady is losing no chance of building up her 'salon' on the curiosity which ever surrounds any buccaneering in politics.' Is the reference to Mrs Mont?'

'Yes.'

'Not very nice, is it–of a friend?'

'I don't see any harm in it.'

'The sort of thing, in fact, you'd like written about yourself?'

'The sort of thing I should expect if I were doing the same thing.'

'That's not quite an answer, but let me put it like this: The sort of thing your father would like to read about you, is it?'

'My father would never read that column.'

'Then it surprises you to hear that Mrs Mont's father did? Do you write many of these cheery little paragraphs about your friends?'

'Not many.'

'Every now and then, eh? And do they remain your friends?'

'It's not easy in Society to tell who's a friend and who isn't.'

'I quite agree, Miss Ferrar. You have admitted making one or two critical–that was your word, I think–remarks concerning Mrs Mont, in her own house. Do you go to many houses and talk disparagingly of your hostess?'

'No; and in any case I don't expect to be eavesdropped.'

'I see; so long as you're not found out, it's all right, eh? Now, on this first Wednesday in October last, at Mrs Mont's, in speaking to this gentleman, Mr Philip–er–Quinsey, did you use the word "snob" of your hostess?'

'I don't think so.'

'Be careful. You heard the evidence of Mrs Ppynrryn and Mrs Maltese. Mrs

Maltese said, you remember, that Mr Forsyte–that is Mrs Mont's father–said to you on that occasion: "You called my daughter a snob in her own house, madam–be so kind as to withdraw; you are a traitress." Is that a correct version?'

'Probably.'

'Do you suggest that he invented the word "snob"?'

'I suggest he was mistaken.'

'Not a nice word, is it–"snob"? Was there any other reason why he should call you a traitress?'

'My remarks weren't meant for his ears. I don't remember exactly what I said.'

'Well, we shall have Mr Forsyte in the Box to refresh your memory as to exactly what you said. But I put it to you that you called her a snob, not once but twice, during that little conversation?'

'I've told you I don't remember; he shouldn't have listened.'

'Very well! So you feel quite happy about having written that paragraph and said nasty things of Mrs Mont behind her back in her own drawing-room?'

Marjorie Ferrar grasped the Box till the blood tingled in her palms. His voice was maddening.

'Yet it seems, Miss Ferrar, that you object to others saying nasty things about you in return. Who advised you to bring this action?'

'My father first; and then my fiancé.'

'Sir Alexander MacGown. Does he move in the same circles as you?'

'No; he moves in Parliamentary circles.'

'Exactly; and he wouldn't know, would he, the canons of conduct that rule in your circle?'

'There are no circles so definite as that.'

'Always willing to learn, Miss Ferrar. But tell me, do you know what Sir Alexander's Parliamentary friends think about conduct and morality?'

'I can guess. I don't suppose there's much difference.'

'Are you suggesting, Miss Ferrar, that responsible public men take the same light-hearted view of conduct and morals as you?'

'Aren't you rather assuming, Sir James, that her view *is* light-hearted?'

'As to conduct, my lord, I submit that her answers have shown the very light-hearted view she takes of the obligations incurred by the acceptance of hospitality, for instance. I'm coming to morals now.'

'I think you'd better, before drawing your conclusions. What have public men to do with it?'

'I'm suggesting, my lord, that this lady is making a great to-do about words which a public man, or any ordinary citizen, would have a perfect right to resent, but which she, with her views, has no right whatever to resent.'

'You must prove her views then. Go on!'

Marjorie Ferrar, relaxed for a moment, gathered herself again. Her views!

'Tell me, Miss Ferrar–we all know now the meaning of the word "stuffy"–are public men "stuffier" than you?'

'They may say they are.'

'You think them hypocrites?'

'I don't think anything at all about them.'

'Though you're going to marry one? You are complaining of the words: "she hasn't a moral about her." Have you read this novel *Canthar*?' He was holding up a book.

'I think so.'

'Don't you know?'

'I've skimmed it.'

'Taken off the cream, eh? Read it sufficiently to form an opinion?'

'Yes.'

'Would you agree with the view of it expressed in this letter to a journal? "The book breaks through the British 'stuffiness', which condemns any frank work of art–and a good thing, too!" Is it a good thing?'

'Yes. I hate Grundyism.'

'"It is undoubtedly Literature." The word is written with a large L. Should you say it was?'

'Literature–yes. Not great literature, perhaps.'

'But it ought to be published?'

'I don't see why not.'

'You know that it is not published in England?'

'Yes.'

'But it ought to be?'

'It isn't everybody's sort of book, of course.'

'Don't evade the question, please. In your opinion ought this novel *Canthar* to be published in England? . . . Take your time, Miss Ferrar.'

The brute lost nothing! Just because she had hesitated a moment trying to see where he was leading her.

'Yes. I think literature should be free.'

'You wouldn't sympathise with its suppression if it were published?'

'No.'

'You wouldn't approve of the suppression of any book on the ground of mere morals?'

'I can't tell you unless I see the book. People aren't bound to read books, you know.'

'And you think your opinion generally on this subject is that of public men and ordinary citizens?'

'No; I suppose it isn't.'

'But your view would be shared by most of your own associates?'

'I should hope so.'

'A contrary opinion would be "stuffy", wouldn't it?'

'If you like to call it so. It's not my word.'

'What is your word, Miss Ferrar?'

'I think I generally say "ga-ga".'

'Do you know, I'm afraid the Court will require a little elaboration of that.'

'Not for me, Sir James; I'm perfectly familiar with the word; it means "in your dotage".'

'The Bench is omniscient, my lord. Then anyone, Miss Ferrar, who didn't share the opinion of yourself and your associates in the matter of this book would be "ga-ga", that is to say, in his or her dotage?'

'Æsthetically.'

'Ah! I thought we should arrive at that word. You, I suppose, don't connect art with life?'

'No.'

'Don't think it has any effect on life?'

'It oughtn't to.'

'When a man's theme in a book is extreme incontinence, depicted with all due emphasis, that wouldn't have any practical effect on his readers, however young?'

'I can't say about other people, it wouldn't have any effect on me.'

'You are emancipated, in fact.'

'I don't know what you mean by that.'

'Isn't what you are saying about the divorce of art from life the merest claptrap; and don't you know it.'

'I certainly don't.'

'Let me put it another way: Is it possible for those who believe in current morality to hold your view that art has no effect on life?'

'Quite possible; if they are cultured.'

'Cultured! Do you believe in current morality yourself?'

'I don't know what you call current morality.'

'I will tell you, Miss Ferrar. I should say, for instance, it was current morality that women should not have *liaisons* before they're married, and should not have them after.'

'What about men?'

'Thank you; I was coming to men. And that men should at least not have them after.'

'I shouldn't say that was *current* morality at all.'

In yielding to that satiric impulse she knew at once she had made a mistake–the judge had turned his face towards her. He was speaking.

'Do I understand you to imply that in your view it is moral for women to have *liaisons* before marriage, and for men and women to have them after?'

'I think it's current morality, my lord.'

'I'm not asking you about current morality; I'm asking whether in *your* view it is moral?'

'I think many people think it's all right who don't say it, yet.'

She was conscious of movement throughout the jury; and of a little flump in the well of the Court. Sir Alexander had dropped his hat. The sound of a nose being loudly blown broke the stillness, the face of Bullfry, K.C., was lost to her view. She felt the blood mounting in her cheeks.

'Answer my question, please. Do *you* say it's all right?'

'I–I think it depends.'

'On what?'

'On–on circumstances, environment, temperament; all sorts of things.'

'Would it be all right for *you*?'

Marjorie Ferrar became very still. 'I can't answer that question, my lord.'

'You mean–you don't want to!'

'I mean I don't know.'

And, with a feeling as if she had withdrawn her foot from a bit of breaking ice, she saw Bullfry's face re-emerge from his handkerchief.

'Very well. Go on, Sir James!'

'Anyway, we may take it, Miss Ferrar, that those of us who say we don't believe in these irregularities are hypocrites in your view?'

'Why can't you be fair?'

He was looking at her now; and she didn't like him any the better for it.

'I shall prove myself fair before I've done, Miss Ferrar.'

'You've got your work cut out, haven't you?'

'Believe me, madam, it will be better for you not to indulge in witticism. According to you, there is no harm in a book like *Canthar*?'

'There ought to be none.'

'You mean if we were all as æsthetically cultured—as you.'—Sneering beast!—'But are we?'

'No.'

'Then there is harm. But you wouldn't mind that harm being done. I don't propose, my lord, to read from this very unpleasant novel. Owing apparently to its unsavoury reputation, a copy of it now costs nearly seven pounds. And I venture to think that is in itself an answer to the plaintiff's contention that "art" so called has no effect on life. We have gone to the considerable expense of buying copies, and I shall ask that during the luncheon interval the jury may read some dozen marked passages.'

'Have you a copy for me, Sir James?'

'Yes, my lord.'

'And one for Mr Bullfry? . . . If there is any laughter, I shall have the Court cleared. Go on.'

'You know the "Ne Plus Ultra" Play-Producing Society, Miss Ferrar? It exists to produce advanced plays, I believe.'

'Plays—I don't know about "advanced".'

'Russian plays, and the Restoration dramatists?'

'Yes.'

'And you have played in them?'

'Sometimes.'

'Do you remember a play called "The Plain Dealer", by Wycherley, given at a matinée on January 7th last—did you play in that the part of Olivia?'

'Yes.'

'A nice part?'

'A very good part.'

'I said "nice".'

'I don't like the word.'

'Too suggestive of "prunes and prisms", Miss Ferrar? Is it the part of a modest woman?'

'No.'

'Is it, towards the end, extremely immodest? I allude to the dark scene.'

'I don't know about extremely.'

'Anyway, you felt no hesitation about undertaking and playing the part—a little thing like that doesn't worry you?'

'I don't know why it should. If it did, I shouldn't act.'

'You don't act for money?'

'No; for pleasure.'

'Then, of course, you can refuse any part you like?'

'If I did, I shouldn't have any offered me.'

'Don't quibble, please. You took the part of Olivia not for money but for pleasure. You enjoyed playing it?'

'Pretty well.'

'I'm afraid I shall have to ask the jury, my lord, to run their eyes over the dark scene in "The Plain Dealer".'

'Are you saying, Sir James, that a woman who plays an immoral part is not moral—that would asperse a great many excellent reputations.'

'No, my lord; I'm saying that here is a young lady so jealous of her good name in the eyes of the world, that she brings a libel action because someone has said in a private letter that she "hasn't a moral about her". And at the same time she

is reading and approving books like this *Canthar*, playing parts like that of
Olivia in "The Plain Dealer", and, as I submit, living in a section of Society
that really doesn't know the meaning of the word morals, that looks upon
morals, in fact, rather as we look upon measles. It's my contention, my lord,
that the saying in my client's letter: "She hasn't a moral about her", is rather a
compliment to the plaintiff than otherwise.'
  'Do you mean that it was intended as a compliment?'
  'No, no, my lord.'
  'Well, you want the jury to read that scene. You will have a busy luncheon
interval, gentlemen. Go on, Sir James.'
  'Now, Miss Ferrar—my friend made a point of the fact that you are engaged
to a wealthy and highly respected Member of Parliament. How long have you
been engaged to him?'
  'Six months.'
  'You have no secrets from him, I suppose?'
  'Why should I answer that?'
  'Why should she, Sir James?'
  'I am quite content to leave it at her reluctance, my lord.'
  Sneering brute! As if everybody hadn't secrets from everybody!
  'Your engagement was not made public till January, was it?'
  'No.'
  'May I take it that you were not sure of your own mind till then?'
  'If you like.'
  'Now, Miss Ferrar, did you bring this action because of your good name?
Wasn't it because you were hard up?'
  She was conscious again of blood in her cheeks.
  'No.'
  '*Were* you hard up when you brought it?'
  'Yes.'
  'Very?'
  'Not worse than I have been before.'
  'I put it to you that you owed a great deal of money, and were hard pressed.'
  'If you like.'
  'I'm glad you've admitted that, Miss Ferrar; otherwise I should have had to
prove it. And you didn't bring this action with a view to paying some of your
debts?'
  'No.'
  'Did you in early January become aware that you were not likely to get any
sum in settlement of this suit?'
  'I believe I was told that an offer was withdrawn.'
  'And do you know why?'
  'Yes, because Mrs Mont wouldn't give the apology I asked for.'
  'Exactly! And was it a coincidence that you thereupon made up your mind to
marry Sir Alexander MacGown?'
  'A coincidence?'
  'I mean the announcement of your engagement, you know?'
  Brute!
  'It had nothing to do with this case.'
  'Indeed! Now when you brought this action, did you really care one straw
whether people thought you moral or not?'
  'I brought it chiefly because I was called "a snake".'

'Please answer my question.'

'It isn't so much what *I* cared, as what my friends cared.'

'But their view of morality is much what yours is–thoroughly accommodating?'

'Not my *fiancé's*.'

'Ah! no. He doesn't move in your circle, you said. But the rest of your friends. You're not ashamed of your own accommodating philosophy, are you?'

'No.'

'Then why be ashamed of it for them?'

'How can I tell what *their* philosophy is?'

'How can she, Sir James?'

'As your lordship pleases. Now, Miss Ferrar! You like to stand up for your views, I hope. Let me put your philosophy to you in a nutshell: You believe, don't you, in the full expression of your personality; it would be your duty, wouldn't it, to break through any convention–I don't say law–but any so-called moral convention that cramped you?'

'I never said I had a philosophy.'

'Don't run away from it, please.'

'I'm not in the habit of running away.'

'I'm so glad of that. You believe in being the sole judge of your own conduct?'

'Yes.'

'You're not alone in that view, are you?'

'I shouldn't think so.'

'It's the view, in fact, of what may be called the forward wing of modern Society, isn't it–the wing you belong to, and are proud of belonging to? And in that section of Society–so long as you don't break the actual law–you think and do as you like, eh?'

'One doesn't always act up to one's principles.'

'Quite so. But among your associates, even if you and they don't always act up to it, it *is* a principle, isn't it, to judge for yourselves and go your own ways without regard to convention?'

'More or less.'

'And, living in that circle, with that belief, you have the effrontery to think the words: "She hasn't a moral about her", entitles you to damages?'

Her voice rang out angrily: 'I have morals. They may not be yours, but they may be just as good, perhaps better. I'm not a hypocrite, anyway.'

Again she saw him look at her, there was a gleam in his eyes; and she knew she had made another mistake.

'We'll leave my morals out of the question, Miss Ferrar. But we'll go a little farther into what you say are yours. In your own words, it should depend on temperament, circumstances, environment, whether you conform to morality or not?'

She stood silent, biting her lip.

'Answer, please.'

She inclined her head. 'Yes.'

'Very good!' He had paused, turning over his papers, and she drew back in the Box. She had lost her temper–had made him lose his; at all costs she must keep her head now! In this moment of search for her head she took in everything–expressions, gestures, even the atmosphere–the curious dramatic emanation from a hundred and more still faces; she noted the one lady juryman, the judge breaking the nib of a quill, with his eyes turned away from it as if looking at something that had run across the well of the Court. Yes, and down there, the lengthening lip of Mr Settlewhite, Michael's face turned up at her with a rueful frown, Fleur Mont's mask with red spots in the cheeks, Alec's clenched hands, and his eyes fixed on her. A sort of comic intensity about it all! If only she were the size of Alice in 'Wonderland', and could take them all in her hands and shake them like a pack of cards—so motionless, there, at her expense! That sarcastic brute had finished fiddling with his papers, and she moved forward again to attention in the box.

'Now, Miss Ferrar, his lordship put a general question to you which you did not feel able to answer. I am going to put it in a way that will be easier for you. Whether or no it was right for you to have one'—she saw Michael's hand go up to his face—'have you *in fact* had a—*liaison?*' And from some tone in his voice, from the look on his face, she could tell for certain that her persecutor knew she had.

With her back to the wall, she had not even a wall to her back. Ten, twenty, thirty seconds—judge, jury, that old fox with his hand under the tail of his gown, and his eyes averted! Why did she not spit out the indignant: No! which she had so often rehearsed? Suppose he proved it—as he had said he would prove her debts?

'Take your time, Miss Ferrar. You know what a *liaison* is, of course.'

Brute! On the verge of denial, she saw Michael lean across, and heard his whisper: 'Stop this!' And then 'that little snob' looked up at her—the scrutiny was knowing and contemptuous: 'Now hear her lie!' it seemed to say. And she answered quickly: 'I consider your question insulting.'

'Oh! come, Miss Ferrar, after your own words! After what—'

'Well! I shan't answer it.'

A rustle, a whispering in the Court.

'You won't answer it?'

'No.'

'Thank you, Miss Ferrar.' Could a voice be more sarcastic?

The brute was sitting down.

Marjorie Ferrar stood defiant, with no ground under her feet. What next? Her counsel was beckoning. She descended from the Box, and, passing her adversaries, resumed her seat next her betrothed. How red and still he was! She heard the judge say:

'I shall break for lunch now, Mr Bullfry,' saw him rise and go out, and the jury getting up. The whispering and rustling in the Court swelled to a buzz. She stood up. Mr Settlewhite was speaking to her.

7

'FED UP'

Guided by him into a room designed to shelter witnesses, Marjorie Ferrar looked at her lawyer.

'Well?'

'An unfortunate refusal, Miss Ferrar–very. I'm afraid the effect on the jury may be fatal. If we can settle it now, I should certainly say we'd better.'

'It's all the same to me.'

'In that case you may take it I shall settle. I'll go and see Sir Alexander and Mr Bullfry at once.'

'How do I get out quietly?'

'Down those stairs. You'll find cabs in Lincoln's Inn Fields. Excuse me.' He made her a grave little bow and stalked away.

Marjorie Ferrar did not take a cab; she walked. If her last answer had been fatal, on the whole she was content. She had told no lies to speak of, had stood up to 'that sarcastic beast', and given him sometimes as good as she had got. Alec! Well, she couldn't help it! He had insisted on her going into Court; she hoped he liked it now she'd been! Buying a newspaper, she went into a restaurant and read a description of herself, accompanied by a photograph. She ate a good lunch, and then continued her walk along Piccadilly. Passing into the Park, she sat down under a tree coming into bud, and drew the smoke of a cigarette quietly into her lungs. The Row was almost deserted. A few persons of little or no consequence occupied a few chairs. A riding mistress was teaching a small boy to trot. Some sparrows and a pigeon alone seemed to take a distant interest in her. The air smelled of spring. She sat some time with the pleasant feeling that nobody in the world knew where she was. Odd, when you thought of it–millions of people every day, leaving their houses, offices, shops, on their way to the next place, were as lost to the world as stones in a pond! Would it be nice to disappear permanently, and taste life incognita? Bertie Curfew was going to Moscow again. Would he take her as secretary, and *bonne amie*? Bertie Curfew–she had only pretended to be tired of him! The thought brought her face to face with the future. Alec! Explanations! It was hardly the word! He had a list of her debts, and had said he would pay them as a wedding-present. But–if there wasn't to be a wedding? Thank God, she had some ready money. The carefully 'laid-up' four-year-old in her father's stable had won yesterday. She had dribbled 'a pony' on at a nice price. She rose and sauntered along, distending her bust–in defiance of the boy-like fashion, which, after all, was on the wane–to take in the full of a sweet wind.

Leaving the Park, she came to South Kensington station and bought another paper. It had a full account under the headlines: 'Modern Morality Attacked.' 'Miss Marjorie Ferrar in the Box.' It seemed funny to stand there reading those words among people who were reading the same without knowing her from Eve, except, perhaps, by her clothes. Continuing her progress towards Wren

Street, she turned her latch-key in the door, and saw a hat. Waiting for her already! She took her time; and, pale from powder, as though she had gone through much, entered the studio.

MacGown was sitting with his head in his hands. She felt real pity for him–too strong, too square, too vital for that attitude! He raised his face.

'Well, Alec!'

'Tell me the truth, Marjorie. I'm in torment.'

She almost envied him the depth of his feeling, however unreasonable after her warnings. But she said ironically:

'Who was it knew me better than I knew myself?'

In the same dull voice he repeated:

'The truth, Marjorie, the truth!'

But why should she go into the confessional? Was he entitled to her past? His rights stopped at her future. It was the old business–men expecting more from women than they could give them. Inequality of the sexes. Something in that, perhaps, in the old days when women bore children, and men didn't; but now that women knew all about sex and only bore children when they wanted to, and not always even then, why should men be freer?

And she said slowly: 'In exchange for your adventures I'll tell you mine.'

'For God's sake don't mock me; I've had hell these last hours.'

His face showed it, and she said with feeling:

'I said you'd be taking a toss over me, Alec. Why on earth did you insist on my bringing this case? You've had your way, and now you don't like it.'

'It's true, then?'

'Yes. Why not?'

He uttered a groan, recoiling till his back was against the wall, as if afraid of being loose in the room.

'Who was he?'

'Oh! no! That I can't possibly tell you. And how many affairs have you had?'

He paid no attention. He wouldn't! He knew she didn't love him; and such things only mattered if you loved! Ah! well! His agony was a tribute to her, after all!'

'You're well out of me,' she said sullenly; and, sitting down, she lighted a cigarette. A scene! How hateful! Why didn't he go? She'd rather he'd be violent than deaf and dumb and blind like this.

'Not that American fellow?'

She could not help a laugh.

'Oh! no, poor boy!'

'How long did it last?'

'Nearly a year.'

'My God!'

He had rushed to the door. If only he would open it and go! That he could feel so violently! That figure by the door was just not mad! His stuffy passions! And then he did pull the door open and was gone.

She threw herself at full length on the divan; not from lassitude, exactly, nor despair–from a feeling rather as if nothing mattered. How stupid and pre-war! Why couldn't he, like her, be free, be supple, take life as it came? Passions, prejudices, principles, pity–old-fashioned as the stuffy clothes worn when she was a tot. Well! Good riddance! Fancy living in the same house, sharing the same bed, with a man so full of the primitive that he could 'go off his chump' with jealousy about her! Fancy living with a man who took life so seriously, that he couldn't even see himself doing it! Life was a cigarette to be inhaled and thrown away, a dance to be danced out. On with that dance! . . . Yes, but she couldn't let him pay her debts, now, even if he wanted to. Married, she would have repaid him with her body; as it was—no! Oh! why didn't someone die and leave her something? What a bore it all was! And she lay still, listening to the tea-time sounds of a quiet street—taxis rounding the corner from the river; the dog next door barking at the postman; that one-legged man—ex-Service—who came most afternoons and played on a poor fiddle. He expected her shilling—unhappy fellow! she'd have to get up and give it him. She went to the little side window that looked on to the street, and suddenly recoiled. Francis Wilmot in the doorway with his hand up to the bell! Another scene! No, really! This was too much! There went the bell! No time to say 'Not at home!' Well, let them all come—round her past, like bees round a honeypot!

'Mr Francis Wilmot.'

He stood there, large as the life he had nearly resigned—a little thinner, that was all.

'Well, Francis,' she said, 'I thought you were "through with that fool business"?'

Francis Wilmot came gravely up and took her hand. 'I sail to-morrow.'

Sail! Well, she could put up with that. He seemed to her just a thin, pale young man with dark hair and eyes and no juices in his system.

'I read the evening papers. I wondered if, perhaps, you'd wish to see me.'

Was he mocking her? But he wore no smile; there was no bitterness in his voice; and, though he was looking at her intently, she could not tell from his face whether he still had any feeling. She said:

'You think I owe you something? I know I treated you very badly.'

He looked rather as if she'd hit him.

'For heaven's sake, Francis, don't say you've come out of chivalry. That'd be too funny.'

'I don't follow you; I just thought, perhaps, you didn't like to answer that question about a love affair—because of me.'

Marjorie Ferrar broke into hysterical laughter.

'Senor Don Punctilio! Because of you! No, no, my dear!'

Francis Wilmot drew back, and made her a little bow.

'I shouldn't have come,' he said.

She had a sudden return of feeling for that slim unusual presence, with its grace and its dark eyes.

'I'm a free-lance again now, Francis, anyway.'

A long moment went by, and then he made her another little bow. It was a clear withdrawal.

'Then for God's sake,' she said, 'go away! I'm fed up!' And she turned her back on him.

When she looked round, he *had* gone, and that surprised her. He was a new variety, or a dead one, dug up! He didn't know the rudiments of life—old-fashioned, *à faire rire!* And, back at full length on the divan, she brooded. Well, her courage was 'not out'! To-morrow was Bella Magussie's 'At Home' to meet—some idiot. Everybody would be there, and so would she!

8

FANTOCHES

When Michael, screwed towards Sir James Foskisson's averted face, heard the
words: 'Well, I shan't answer', he spun round. It was just as if she had said:
'Yes, I have.' The judge was looking at her, everyone looking at her. Wasn't
Bullfry going to help her? No! He was beckoning her out of the Box. Michael
half rose, as she passed him. By George! He was sorry for MacGown! There he
sat, poor devil! with everyone getting up all round him, still, and red as a
turkey-cock.

Fleur! Michael looked at her face, slightly flushed, her gloved hands clasped
in her lap, her eyes fixed on the ground. Had his whisper: 'Stop this!' his little
abortive bow, offended her? How could one have helped sympathising with the
'Pet of the Panjoys' in so tight a place! Fleur must see that! The Court was
emptying—fine birds, many—he could see her mother and her aunt and cousin,
and Old Forsyte, talking with Foskisson. Ah! he had finished; was speaking:
'We can go now.'

They followed him along the corridor, down the stairs, into the air.

'We've time for a snack,' Soames was saying. 'Come in here!'

In one of several kennels without roofs in a celebrated room with a boarded
floor, they sat down.

'Three chump chops, sharp,' said Soames, and staring at the cruet-stand,
added: 'She's cooked her goose. They'll drop it like a hot potato. I've told
Foskisson he can settle, with both sides paying their own costs. It's more than
they deserve.'

'He ought never to have asked that question, sir.'

Fleur looked up sharply.

'Really, Michael!'

'Well, darling, we agreed he shouldn't. Why didn't Bullfry help her out, sir?'

'Only too glad to get her out of the Box; the judge would have asked her
himself in another minute. It's a complete fiasco, thank God!'

'Then we've won?' said Fleur.

'Unless I'm a Dutchman,' answered Soames.

'I'm not so sure,' muttered Michael.

'I tell you it's all over; Bullfry'll never go on with it.'

'I didn't mean that, sir.'

Fleur said acidly: 'Then what *do* you mean, Michael?'

'I don't think we shall be forgiven, that's all.'

'What for?'

'Well, I dare say I'm all wrong. Sauce, sir?'

'Worcester—yes. This is the only place in London where you can rely on a
floury potato. Waiter—three glasses of port, quick!'

After fifteen minutes of concentrated mastication, they returned to the
Court.

'Wait here,' said Soames, in the hall; 'I'll go and find out.'

In that echoing space, where a man's height was so inconsiderable, Fleur and Michael stood, not speaking, for some time.

'She couldn't know that Foskisson had been told not to follow it up, of course,' he said at last. 'Still, she must have expected the question. She should have told a good one and have done with it. I couldn't help feeling sorry for her.'

'You'd feel sorry for a flea that bit you, Michael. What do you mean by our not being forgiven?'

'Well! The drama was all on her side, and it's drama that counts. Besides, there's her engagement!'

'That'll be broken off.'

'Exactly! And if it is, she'll have sympathy; while if it isn't, he'll have it. Anyway, we shan't. Besides, you know, she stood up for what we all really believe nowadays.'

'Speak for yourself.'

'Well, don't we talk of everyone being free?'

'Yes, but is there any connection between what we say and what we do?'

'No,' said Michael.

And just then Soames returned.

'Well, sir?'

'As I told you, Bullfry caught at it. They've settled. It's a moral victory.'

'Oh! not moral, I hope, sir.'

'It's cost a pretty penny, anyway,' said Soames, looking at Fleur. 'Your mother's quite annoyed—she's no sense of proportion. Very clever the way Foskisson made that woman lose her temper.'

'He lost his, at the end. That's his excuse, I suppose.'

'Well,' said Soames, 'it's all over! Your mother's got the car; we'll take a taxi.'

On the drive back to South Square, taking precisely the same route, there was precisely the same silence.

When a little later Michael went over to the House, he was edified by posters. "Society Libel Action."

"Marquess's Granddaughter and K.C."

"Dramatic evidence."

"Modern Morality!"

All over—was it? With publicity—in Michael's opinion—it had but just begun! Morality! What was it—who had it, and what did they do with it? How would he have answered those questions himself? Who could answer them, nowadays, by rote or rule? Not he, nor Fleur! They had been identified with the Inquisition, and what was their position now? False, if not odious! He passed into the House. But, try as he would, he could not fix his attention on the Purity of Food, and passed out again. With a curious longing for his father, he walked rapidly down Whitehall. Drawing blank at 'Snooks'' and the 'Aeroplane', he tried the 'Parthenæum' as a last resort. Sir Lawrence was in a corner of a forbidden room, reading a life of Lord Palmerston. He looked up at his son.

'Ah! Michael! They don't do justice to old Pam. A man without frills, who worked like a nigger. But we mustn't talk here!' And he pointed to a member who seemed awake. 'Shall we take a turn before the old gentleman over there has a fit? The books here are camouflage; it's really a dormitory.'

He led the way, with Michael retailing the events of the morning.

'Foskisson?' said Sir Lawrence, entering the Green Park. 'He was a nice little chap when I left Winchester. To be professionally in the right is bad for a man's character–counsel, parsons, policemen, they all suffer from it. Judges, High Priests, Arch-Inspectors, aren't so bad–they've suffered from it so long that they've lost consciousness.'

'It was a full house,' said Michael glumly, 'and the papers have got hold of it.'

'They would.' And Sir Lawrence pointed to the ornamental water. 'These birds,' he said, 'remind me of China. By the way, I met your friend Desert yesterday at the "Aeroplane"–he's more interesting now that he's dropped Poetry for the East. Everybody ought to drop something. I'm too old now, but if I'd dropped baronetcy in time, I could have made quite a good contortionist.'

'What would you recommend for Members of Parliament?' asked Michael, with a grin.

'Postmanship, my dear–carrying on, you know; a certain importance, large bags, dogs to bark at you, no initiative, and conversation on every door-step. By the way, do you see Desert?'

'I have seen him.'

Sir Lawrence screwed up his eyes.

'The providential,' he said, 'doesn't happen twice.'

Michael coloured; he had not suspected his father of such shrewd observation. Sir Lawrence swung his cane.

'Your man Boddick,' he said, 'has persuaded some of his hens to lay; he's giving us quite good eggs.'

Michael admired his reticence. But somehow that unexpected slanting allusion to a past domestic crisis roused the feeling that for so long now had been curled like a sleepy snake in his chest, that another crisis was brewing and must soon be faced.

'Coming along for tea, sir? Kit had tummy-ache this morning. How's your last book doing? Does old Danby advertise it properly?'

'No,' said Sir Lawrence, 'no; he's keeping his head wonderfully; the book is almost dead.'

'I'm glad I dropped *him*, anyway,' said Michael, with emphasis. 'I suppose, sir, you haven't a tip to give us, now this case is over?'

Sir Lawrence gazed at a bird with a long red bill.

'When victorious,' he said at last, 'lie doggo. The triumphs of morality are apt to recoil on those who achieve them.'

'That's what I feel, sir. Heaven knows *I* didn't want to achieve one. My father-in-law says my hitting MacGown on the boko really brought it into Court.'

Sir Lawrence whinnied.

'The tax on luxuries. It gets you everywhere. I don't think I will come along, Michael–Old Forsyte's probably there. Your mother has an excellent recipe for child's tummy-ache; you almost lived on it at one time. I'll telephone it from Mount Street. Good-bye!'

Michael looked after that thin and sprightly figure moving North. Had he troubles of his own? If so, he disguised them wonderfully. Good old Bart! And he turned towards South Square.

Soames was just leaving.

'She's excited,' he said, on the door-step. 'It's the reaction. Give her a Seidlitz powder to-night. Be careful, too; I shouldn't talk about politics.'

Michael went in. Fleur was at the open window of the drawing-room.

'Oh! here you are!' she said. 'Kit's all right again. Take me to the Café Royal to-night, Michael, and if there's anything funny anywhere, for goodness' sake, let's see it. I'm sick of feeling solemn. Oh! And, by the way, Francis Wilmot's coming in to say good-bye. I've had a note. He says he's all right again.'

At the window by her side, Michael sniffed the unaccountable scent of grass. There was a south-west wind, and slanting from over the house-tops, sunlight was sprinkling the soil, the buds, the branches. A blackbird sang; a piano-organ round a corner was playing 'Rigoletto'. Against his own, her shoulder was soft, and to his lips her cheek was warm and creamy. . . .

When Francis Wilmot left them that evening after dinner at the Café Royal, Fleur said to Michael:

'Poor Francis! Did you ever see anyone so changed? He might be thirty. I'm glad he's going home to his river and his darkies. What are live oaks? Well! Are we going anywhere?'

Michael cloaked her shoulders.

' "Great Itch", I think; there's no other scream so certain.'

After their scream they came out into a mild night. High up in red and green the bright signs fled along the air: 'Tomber's Tires for Speed and Safety', 'Milkoh Makes Mothers Merry'. Through Trafalgar Square they went and down Whitehall, all moonlight and Portland stone.

'The night's unreal,' said Fleur. '"*Fantoches*"!'

Michael caught her waist.

'Don't! Suppose some Member saw you!'

'He'd only sympathise. How nice and solid you feel!'

'No. *Fantoches* have no substance.'

'Then give me shadow.'

'The substance is in Bethnal Green.'

Michael dropped his arm.

'That's a strange thought.'

'I have intuitions, Michael.'

'Because I can admire a good woman, can I not love you?'

'*I* shall never be "good"; it isn't in me.'

'Whatever you are's enough for me.'

'Prettily said. The Square looks jolly to-night! Open the doll's house.'

The hall was dark, with just a glimmer coming through the fanlight. Michael took off her cloak and knelt down. He felt her fingers stir his hair; real fingers, and real all this within his arms; only the soul elusive. Soul?

'*Fantoches!*' came her voice, soft and mocking. 'And so to bed!'

9

ROUT AT MRS MAGUSSIE'S

There are routs social, political, propagandic; and routs like Mrs Magussie's. In one of Anglo-American birth, inexhaustible wealth, unimpeachable widowhood, and catholic taste, the word hostess had found its highest expression. People might die, marry, and be born with impunity so long as they met, preferably in her house, one of the largest in Mayfair. If she called in a doctor, it was to meet another doctor; if she went to church, it was to get Canon

Forant to meet Dean Kimble at lunch afterwards. Her cards of invitation had the words: 'To meet' printed on them; and she never put 'me'. She was selfless. Once in a way she had a real rout, because once in a way a personality was available, whose name everybody, from poets to prelates, must know. In her intimate belief people loved to meet anybody sufficiently distinguished; and this was where she succeeded, because almost without exception they did. Her two husbands had 'passed on', having met in their time nearly everybody. They had both been distinguished, and had first met in her house; and she would never have a third for Society was losing its landmarks, and she was too occupied. People were inclined to smile at mention of Bella Magussie, and yet, how do without one who performed the function of cement? Without her, bishops could not place their cheeks by the jowls of ballet girls, or Home Secretaries be fertilised by disorderly dramatists. Except in her house, the diggers-up of old civilisation in Beluchistan never encountered the levellers of modern civilisation in London. Nor was there any chance for lights of the Palace to meet those lights of the Halls—Madame Nemesia and Top Nobby. Nowhere else could a Russian dancer go to supper with Sir Walter Peddel, M.D., F.R.S.T.R., P.M.V.S., 'R.I.P.' as Michael would add. Even a bowler with the finest collection of ducks' eggs in first-class cricket was not without a chance of wringing the hand of the great Indian economist Sir Banerjee Bath Babore. Mrs Magussie's, in fine, was a house of chief consequence; and her long face, as of the guardian of some first principle, moving about the waters of celebrity, was wrinkled in a great cause. To meet or not to meet? She had answered the question for good and all.

The 'met' or 'meetee' for her opening rout in 1925 was the great Italian violinist Luigi Sporza, who had just completed his remarkable tour of the world, having in half the time played more often than any two previous musicians. The prodigious feat had been noted in the press of all countries with every circumstance—the five violins he had tired out, the invitation he had received to preside over a South American Republic, the special steamer he had chartered to keep an engagement in North America, and his fainting fit in Moscow after the Beethoven and Brahms concertos, the Bach chaconne, and seventeen encores. During the lingering year of his great effort, his fame had been established. As an artist he had been known to a few, as an athlete he was now known to all.

Michael and Fleur, passing up the centre stairway, saw a man 'not 'arf like a bull'—Michael muttered—whose hand people were seizing, one after the other, to move away afterwards with a look of pain.

'Only Italy can produce men like that,' said Michael in Fleur's ear. 'Give him the go-by. He'll hurt you.'

But Fleur moved forward.

'Made of sterner stuff,' murmured Michael. It was not the part of his beloved to miss the hand of celebrity, however horny! No portion of her charming face quivered as the great athlete's grip closed on hers, and his eyes, like those of a tired minotaur, traversed her supple body with a gleam of interest.

'Hulking brute!' thought Michael, disentangling his own grasp, and drifting with her over shining space. Since yesterday's ordeal and its subsequent spring-running, he had kept his unacceptable misgivings to himself; he did not even know whether, at this rout, she was deliberately putting their position to the test, or merely, without forethought, indulging her liking to be in the swim. And what a swim! In that great pillared 'salon',

Members of Parliament, poets, musicians, very dry in the smile, as who should say: 'I could have done it better,' or 'Imagine doing that!' peers, physicians, dancers, painters, Labour Leaders, cricketers, lawyers, critics, ladies of fashion, and ladies who 'couldn't bear it'—every mortal person that Michael knew or didn't know seemed present. He watched Fleur's eyes quartering them, busy as bees beneath the white lids he had kissed last night. He envied her that social curiosity; to live in London without it was like being at the sea without bathing. She was quietly—he could tell—making up her mind whom she wanted to speak to among those she knew, and whom, among those she didn't yet know, she wanted to speak to her. 'I hope to God she's not in for a snubbing,' he thought, and when she was engaged in talk, he slipped towards a pillar. A small voice behind him said: 'Well, young Mont!' Mr Blythe, looking like a Dover sole above Kew Bridge, was squeezed against the same pillar, his eyes goggling timorously above his beard.

'Stick to me!' he said. 'These bees are too bee busy.'

'Were you in Court yesterday?' asked Michael.

'No; one read about it. You did well.'

'She did better.'

'H'm!' said Mr Blythe. 'By the way, *The Evening Sun* was at us again this afternoon. They compared us to kittens playing with their tails. It's time for your second barrel, Mont.'

'I thought—on the agricultural estimates.'

'Good! Governmental purchase and control of wheat. Stress use of the present machinery. No more officials than are absolutely necessary.'

'Blythe,' said Michael suddenly, 'where were you born?'

'Lincolnshire.'

'You're English, then?'

'Pure,' said Mr Blythe.

'So am I; so's old Foggart—I looked him up in the stud-book. It's lucky, because we shall certainly be assailed for lack of patriotism.'

'We *are*,' said Mr Blythe. '"People who can see no good in their own country. . . . Birds who foul their own nest. . . . Gentry never happy unless running England down in the eyes of the world. . . . Calamity-mongers. . . . Pessimists. . . ." You don't mind that sort of gup, I hope?'

'Unfortunately,' said Michael, 'I do; it hurts me inside. It's so damned unjust. I simply can't bear the idea of England being in a fix.'

Mr Blythe's eyes rolled.

'She's bee well not going to be, if we can help it.'

'If only I amounted to something,' murmured Michael; 'but I always feel as if I could creep into one of my back teeth.'

'Have it crowned. What you want is brass, Mont. And talking of brass: there's your late adversary! *She's* got it all right. Look at her!'

Michael saw Marjorie Ferrar moving away from the great Italian, in not too much of a sea-green gown, with her red-gold head held high. She came to a stand a small room's length from Fleur, and swept her eyes this way and that. Evidently she had taken up that position in deliberate challenge.

'I must go to Fleur.'

'So must I,' said Mr Blythe, and Michael gave him a grateful look.

And now it would have been so interesting to one less interested than Michael. The long, the tapering nose of Society could be seen to twitch, to move delicately upwards, and like the trunk of some wild elephant scenting man, writhe and snout this way and that, catching the whiff of sensation. Lips were smiling and moving closer to ears; eyes turning from that standing figure to the other; little reflective frowns appeared on foreheads, as if, beneath cropped and scented scalps, brains were trying to make choice. And Marjorie Ferrar stood smiling and composed; and Fleur talked and twisted the flower in her hand; and both went on looking their best. So began a battle without sign of war declared, without even seeming recognition of each other's presence. Mr Blythe, indeed, stood pat between the two of them. Bulky and tall, he was an effective screen. But Michael, on the other side of her, could see and grimly follow. The Nose was taking time to apprehend the full of the aroma; the Brain to make its choice. Tide seemed at balance, not moving in or out. And then, with the slow implacability of tides, the water moved away from Fleur and lapped round her rival. Michael chattered, Mr Blythe goggled, using the impersonal pronoun with a sort of passion; Fleur smiled, talked, twisted the flower. And, over there, Marjorie Ferrar seemed to hold a little court. Did people admire, commiserate, approve of, or sympathise with her? Or did they disapprove of himself and Fleur? Or was it just that the 'Pet of the Panjoys' was always the more sensational figure? Michael watched Fleur growing paler, her smile more nervous, the twitching of the flower spasmodic. And he dared not suggest going; for she would see in it an admission of defeat. But on the faces, turned their way, the expression became more and more informative. Sir James Foskisson had done his job too well; he had slavered his clients with his own self-righteousness. Better the confessed libertine than those who brought her to judgment! And Michael thought: 'Dashed natural, after all! Why didn't the fellow take my tip, and let us pay and look pleasant.'

And just then close to the great Italian he caught sight of a tall young man with his hair brushed back, who was looking at his fingers. By George! It was Bertie Curfew! And there behind him, waiting for his turn 'to meet', who but MacGown himself! The humour of the gods had run amok! Head in air, soothing his mangled fingers, Bertie Curfew passed them, and strayed into the group around his former flame. Her greeting of him was elaborately casual. But up went the tapering Nose, for here came MacGown! How the fellow had changed—grim, greyish, bitter! The great Italian had met his match for once. And he too, stepped into that throng.

A queer silence was followed by a burst of speech, and then by dissolution. In twos and threes they trickled off, and there were MacGown and his betrothed standing alone. Michael turned to Fleur.

'Let's go.'

Silence reigned in the homing cab. He had chattered himself out on the field of battle, and must wait for fresh supplies of camouflage. But he slipped his hand along till it found hers, which did not return his pressure. The card he used to play at times of stress—the eleventh baronet—had failed for the last three months; Fleur seemed of late to resent his introduction as a remedy. He followed her into the dining-room, sore at heart, bewildered in mind. He had never seen her look so pretty as in that oyster-coloured frock, very straight and simply made, with a swing out above the ankles. She sat down at the narrow dining-table, and he seated himself opposite, with the costive feeling of one who cannot find words that will ring true. For social discomfiture he himself didn't care a tinker's curse; but she—!

And, suddenly, she said:

'And you don't mind?'

'For myself—not a bit.'

'Yes, you've still got your Foggartism and your Bethnal Green.'

'If *you* care, Fleur, I care a lot.'

'*If* I care!'

'How—exactly?'

'I'd rather not increase your feeling that I'm a snob.'

'I never had any such feeling.'

'Michael!'

'Hadn't you better say what you mean by the word?'

'You know perfectly well.'

'I know that you appreciate having people about you, and like them to think well of you. That isn't being a snob.'

'Yes; you're very kind, but you don't admire it.'

'I admire *you*.'

'You mean, desire me. You admire Norah Curfew.'

'Norah Curfew! For all I care, she might snuff out to-morrow.'

And from her face he had the feeling that she believed him.

'If it isn't her, it's what she stands for—all that I'm not.'

'I admire a lot in you,' said Michael, fervently; 'your intelligence, your flair; I admire you with Kit and your father; your pluck; and the way you put up with me.'

'No, I admire you much more than you admire me. Only, you see, I'm not capable of devotion.'

'What about Kit?'

'I'm devoted to myself—that's all.'

He reached across the table and touched her hand.

'Morbid, darling.'

'No. I see too clearly to be morbid.'

She was leaning back, and her throat, very white and round, gleamed in the alabaster-shaded light; little choky movements were occuring there.

'Michael, I want you to take me round the world.'

'And leave Kit?'

'He's too young to mind. Besides, my mother would look after him.'

If she had got as far as that, this was a deliberate desire!

'But your father—'

'He's not really old yet, and he'd have Kit.'

'When we rise in August, perhaps—'

'No, now.'

'It's only five months to wait. We'd have time in the vacation to do a lot of travelling.'

Fleur looked straight at him.

'I knew you cared more for Foggartism now than for me.'

'Be reasonable, Fleur.'

'For five months—with the feeling I've got here!' she put her hand to her breast. 'I've had six months of it already. You don't realise, I suppose, that I'm down and out?'

'But, Fleur, it's all so—'

'Yes, it's always petty to mind being a dead failure, isn't it?'

'But, my child—'

'Oh! If you can't feel it—'

'I can—I felt wild this evening. But all you've got to do is to let them see that you don't care; and they'll come buzzing round again like flies. It would be running away, Fleur.'

'No,' said Fleur, coldly, 'it's not that—I don't try twice for the same prize. Very well, I'll stay and be laughed at.'

Michael got up.

'I know you don't think there's anything to my job. But there is, Fleur, and I've put my hand to it. Oh! don't look like that. Dash it! This is dreadful!'

'I suppose I could go by myself. That would be more thrilling.'

'Absurd! Of course you couldn't! You're seeing blue to-night, old thing. It'll all seem different to-morrow.'

'To-morrow and to-morrow! No, Michael, mortification has set in, my funeral can take place any day you like!'

Michael's hands went up. She meant what she was saying! To realise, he must remember how much store she had set on her powers as hostess; how she had worked for her collection and shone among it! Her house of cards all pulled about her ears! Cruel! But would going round the world help her? Yes! Her instinct was quite right. He had been round the world himself, nothing else would change her values in quite that way; nothing else would so guarantee oblivion in others and herself! Lippinghall, her father's, the sea for five months till vacation came—they wouldn't meet her case! She needed what would give her back her importance. And yet, how could he go until vacation? Foggartism—that lean and lonely plant—unwatered and without its only gardener, would wither to its roots, if, indeed, it had any. There was some movement in it now, interest here and there—this Member and that were pecking at it. Private efforts in the same direction were gathering way. And time was going on—Big Ben had called no truce; unemployment swelling, trade dawdling, industrial trouble brewing—brewing, hope losing patience! And what would old Blythe say to his desertion now?

'Give me a week,' he muttered. 'It's not easy. I must think it over.'

10

THE NEW LEAF

When MacGown came up to her, Marjorie Ferrar thought: 'Does he know about Bertie?' Fresh from her triumph over 'that little snob', fluttered by the sudden appearance of her past, and confronted with her present, she was not in complete possession of her head. When they had moved away into an empty side room, she faced him.

'Well, Alec, nothing's changed. I still have a past as lurid as yesterday. I'm extremely sorry I ever kept it from you. But I did practically tell you, several times; only you wouldn't take it.'

'Because it was hell to me. Tell me everything, Marjorie!'

'You want to revel in it?'

'Tell me everything, and I'll marry you still.'

She shook her head. 'Marry! Oh! no! I don't go out of my depth any more. It was absurd anyway. I never loved you, Alec.'

'Then you loved that—you still—'

'My dear Alec, enough!'

He put his hands to his head, and swayed. And she was touched by genuine compassion.

'I'm awfully sorry, I really am. You've got to cut me out; that's all.'

She had turned to leave him, but the misery in his face stopped her. She had not quite realised. He was burnt up! He was–! And she said quickly:

'Marry you I won't; but I'd like to pay up, if I could–'

He looked at her.

Quivering all over from that look, she shrugged her shoulders, and walked away. Men of an old fashion! Her own fault for stepping outside the charmed circle that took nothing too seriously. She walked over the shining floor, conscious of many eyes, slipped past her hostess, and soon was in a cab.

She lay awake, thinking. Even without announcement the return of presents would set London by the ears and bring on her again an avalanche of bills. Five thousand pounds! She got up and rummaged out the list, duplicate of that which Alec had. He might still want to pay them! After all, it was he who had spilled the ink by making her go into Court! But then his eyes came haunting her. Out of the question! And, shivering a little, she got back into bed. Perhaps she would have a brain-wave in the morning. She had so many in the night, that she could not sleep. Moscow with Bertie Curfew? The stage? America and the 'movies'? All three? She slept at last, and woke languid and pale. With her letters was one from Shropshire House.

DEAR MARJORIE,

If you've nothing better to do, I should like to see you this morning.

Affectionately,
SHROPSHIRE.

What now? She looked at herself in the glass, and decided that she *must* make-up a little. At eleven o'clock she was at Shropshire House. The marquess was in his work-room at the top, among a small forest of contraptions. With coat off, he was peering through a magnifying-glass at what looked like nothing.

'Sit down, Marjorie,' he said: 'I'll have done in a minute.'

Except the floor, there seemed nowhere to sit, so she remained standing.

'I thought so,' said the marquess; 'the Italians are wrong.'

He put the spy-glass down, ran his hand through his silvery hair, and drew his ruffled beard into a peak. Then, taking an eyebrow between finger and thumb, he gave it an upward twist, and scratched himself behind one ear.

'They're wrong; there's no reaction whatever.'

Turning towards his granddaughter, he screwed up his eyes till they were bright as pins. 'You've never been up here before. Sit in the window.'

She seated herself on a broad window-ledge covering some sort of battery, with her back to the light.

'So you brought that case, Marjorie?'

'I had to.'

'Now why?' He was standing with his head a little to one side, his cheeks very pink, and his eyes very shrewd. And she thought: 'After all, I'm his granddaughter. I'll plunge.'

'Common honesty, if you want to know.'

The marquess pouted, as if trying to understand the words.

'I read your evidence,' he said, 'if you mean that.'

'No. I meant that I wanted to find out where I stood.'

'And did you?'

'Very much so.'

'Are you still going to be married?'

Really, he was a spry old boy!

'No.'

'Whose doing? Yours or his?'

'He still says he'll marry me if I tell him everything. But I don't choose to.'

The marquess moved two steps, placed his foot on a box, and assumed his favourite attitude. He had a red silk tie this morning which floated loose; his tweed trousers were of a blue-green, his shirt of a green-blue. He looked wonderfully bright.

'Is there much to tell?'

'A good deal.'

'Well, Marjorie, you know what I said to you.'

'Yes, Grandfather, but I don't quite see it. *I* don't want to stand for anything.'

'Ah! you're an exception in our class—luckily! But it's the exceptions that do the harm.'

'If people took one as any better than themselves, perhaps. But they don't nowadays.'

'Not quite honest, that,' interrupted the marquess; 'what about the feeling in your bones?'

She smiled.

'It's good to mortify oneself, Grandfather.'

'By having a better time than you ought, um? So your marriage is off?'

'Very much so.'

'Are you in debt?'

'Yes.'

'How much do you owe?'

Marjorie Ferrar hesitated. Should she compromise, or blurt it out?

'No heel-taps, Marjorie.'

'Well, then, five thousand about.'

The old peer screwed up his lips, and a melancholy little whistle escaped.

'A good deal of it, of course, is due to my engagement.'

'Your father won a race the other day, I see.'

The old boy knew everything!

'Yes; but I believe it's all gone.'

'It would be,' said the marquess. 'What are you going to do now?'

She had a strong desire to answer: 'What are *you*?' but restrained it, and said: 'I thought of going on the stage.'

'Well, I suppose that might be suitable. Can you act?'

'I'm not a Duse.'

'Duse?' the marquess shook his head. 'One must go back to Ristori for really great acting. Duse! Very talented, of course, but always the same. So you don't choose to marry him now?' He looked at her intently. 'That, I think, is right. Have you a list of your debts?'

Majorie Ferrar rummaged in her vanity bag. 'Here it is.'

She could see his nose wrinkling above it, but whether at its scent, or its contents, she could not tell.

'Your grandmother,' he said, 'spent about a fifth of what you seem to on about five times the acreage of clothes. You wear nothing nowadays, and yet it costs all this.'

'The less there is, Grandfather, the better it has to be cut, you know.'

'Have you sent your presents back?'

'I've had them packed.'

'They must all go,' said the marquess. 'Keep nothing he or anyone else gave you.'

'Of course not.'

'To frank you,' he said, suddenly, 'I should have to sell the Gainsborough.'

'Oh, no!'

Gainsborough's picture of his own grandmother as a little girl—that beautiful thing! She stretched out her hand for the list. Still holding it, he put his foot to the ground, and stood peering at her with his bright, intent old eyes.

'The question is, Marjorie, how far it's possible to strike a bargain with you. Have you a "word" to keep?'

She felt the blood mounting in her cheeks.

'I think so. It depends on what I've got to promise. But Grandfather, I don't *want* you to sell the Gainsborough.'

'Unfortunately,' said the marquess, 'without doing your uncle Dangerfield in the eye, I've nothing else. It's been my fault, I suppose, for having had expensive children. Other people don't seem to have had them to the same degree.'

She stifled a smile.

'Times are hard,' went on the marquess. 'Land costs money, collieries cost money, Shropshire house costs money; and where's the money? I've got an invention here that ought to make my fortune, but nobody will look at it.'

The poor old boy—at his age! She said with a sigh:

'I really didn't mean to bother you with this, Grandfather. I'll manage somehow.'

The old peer took several somewhat hampered steps, and she noticed that his red slippers were heel-less. He halted, a wonderfully bright spot among the contraptions.

'To come back to what we were saying, Marjorie. If your idea of life is simply to have a good time, how can you promise anything?'

'What do you want me to promise?'

He came and stood before her again, short and a little bent.

'You look as if you had stuff in you, too, with your hair. Do you really think you could earn your living?'

'I believe I can; I know a lot of people.'

'If I clear you, will you give me your word to pay ready money in future? Now don't say "Yes", and go out and order yourself a lot of fallals. I want the word of a lady, if you understand what that implies.'

She stood up.

'I suppose you've every right to say that. But I don't want you to clear me if you have to sell the Gainsborough.'

'You must leave that to me. I might manage, perhaps, to scrape it up without. About that promise?'

'Yes; I promise that.'

'Meaning to keep it?'

'Meaning to keep it.'

'Well, that's something.'

'Anything else, Grandfather?'

'I should have liked to ask you not to cheapen our name any more, but I suppose that would be putting the clock back. The spirit of the age is against me.'

Turning from his face, she stood looking out of the window. The spirit of the age! It was all very well, but he didn't understand what it was. Cheapen? Why! she had *raised* the price of the family name; hoicked it out of a dusty cupboard, and made of it a current coin. People sat up when they read of her. Did they sit up when they read of grandfather? But he would never see that! And she murmured:

'All right, dear, I'll be careful. I think I shall go to America.'

His eyes twinkled.

'And start a fashion of marrying American husbands? It's not yet been done, I believe. Get one who's interested in electricity, and bring him over. There are great things for an American to do here. Well, I'll keep this list and work it off somehow. Just one thing, Marjorie: I'm eighty, and you're–what are you–twenty-five? Don't get through life so fast–you'll be dreadfully bored by the time you're fifty, and there's no greater bore than a bored person. Good-bye!' He held out his hand.

She took a long breath. Free!

And seizing his hand, she put it to her lips. Oh! He was gazing at it–oh! Had her lips come off? And she hurried out. The old boy! He was a darling to have kept that list! A new leaf! She would go at once to Bertie Curfew and get him to turn it over for her! The expression in his eye last night!

II

OVER THE WINDMILL

During his period of indecision Michael struck no attitudes, and used practically no words; the thing was too serious. Perhaps Kit would change Fleur's mood, or she would see other disadvantages, such as her father. The complete cessation, however, of any social behaviour on her part–no invitation issued, or received, no function attended, or even discussed, during that rather terrible week, proved that the iron had really seared her spirit. She was not sulky, but she was mum and listless. And she was always watching him, with a wistful expression on her face, and now and then a resentful look, as if she had made up her mind that he was going to refuse. He could consult no one, too, for to any who had not lived through this long episode, Fleur's attitude would seem incomprehensible, even ridiculous. He could not give her away; could not even go to old Blythe, until he had decided. Complicating his mental conflict was the habitual doubt whether he was really essential to Foggartism. If only his head would swell! He had not even the comfort of feeling that a sturdy negative would impress Fleur; she thought his job a stunt, useful to make him conspicuous, but of no real importance to the country. She had the political cynicism of the woman in the street; only that which threatened property or Kit would really ruffle her. He knew that his dilemma was comic. the future of England against the present of a young woman socially snubbed! But, after all, only Sir James Foggart and old Blythe so far seriously connected Foggartism with the future of England; and if, now, he went off round the world, even they would lose their faith.

On the last morning of that week, Michael, still in doubt, crossed Westminster Bridge and sought the heart of the Surrey side. It was unfamiliar, and he walked with interest. Here, he remembered, the Bickets had lived; the Bickets who had failed, and apparently were failing in Australia, too. Street after mean street! Breeding-ground of Bickets! Catch them early, catch them often, catch them before they were Bickets, spoiled for the land; make them men and women of property, give them air and give them sun–the most decent folk in the world, give them a chance! Ugly houses, ugly shops, ugly pubs! No, that wouldn't do! Keep Beauty out of it; Beauty never went down in 'the House'! No sentiment went down! At least, only such as was understood–'British stock', 'Patriotism', 'Empire', 'Moral Fibre'. Thews and productive power–stick to the clichés! He stood listening outside a school to the dull hum of education. The English breed with its pluck and its sense of humour and its patience, all mewed-up in mean streets!

He had a sudden longing for the country. His motor-cycle! Since taking his seat in Parliament he had not been on a machine so inclined to bump his dignity. But he would have it out now, and go for a run–it might shake him into a decision!

Fleur was not in, and no lunch ordered. So he ate some ham, and by two o'clock had started.

With spit and bluster he ran out along the road past Chiswick, Slough and Maidenhead; crossed the river and sputtered towards Reading. At Caversham he crossed again, and ran on to Pangbourne. By the towing path he tipped his machine into some bushes and sat down to smoke a pipe. Quite windless! The river between the bare poplars had a grey, untroubled look; the catkins were forming on the willows. He plucked a twig, and stirred it round the bowl of his pipe before pressing in tobacco. The shaking had done him good; his mind was working freely. The war! One had no hesitations then; but then–one had no Fleur. Besides, that was a clear, a simple issue. But now, beyond this 'to stay or not to stay', Michael seemed seeing the future of his married life. The decision that he made would affect what might last another fifty years. To put your hand to the plough, and at the first request to take it off again! You might be ploughing crooked, and by twilight; but better plough by dim light than no light; a crooked furrow than none at all! Foggartism was the best course he could see, and he must stick to it! The future of England! A blackbird, close by, chuckled. Quite so! But, as old Blythe said, one must stand up to laughter! Oh! Surely Fleur would see in the long run that he couldn't play fast and loose; see that if she wanted him to remain in Parliament–and she did–he must hang on to the line he had taken, however it amused the blackbirds. She wouldn't like him to sink to the nonentity of a turntail. For after all she was his wife, and with his self-respect her own was bound up.

He watched the smoke from his pipe, and the low grey clouds, the white-faced Herefords grazing beyond the river, and a man fishing with a worm. He took up the twig and twirled it, admiring the yellowish-grey velvet of its budding catkins. He felt quiet in the heart, at last, but very sorry. How make up to Fleur? Beside this river not two miles away, he had wooed–queer word–if not won her! And now they had come to this snag. Well, it was up to her now, whether or no they should come to grief on it. And it seemed to him, suddenly, that he would like to tell Old Forsyte. . . .

When he heard the splutter of Michael's motor-cycle, Soames was engaged in hanging the Fred Walker he had bought at the emporium next to Messrs. Settlewhite and Stark, memorialising his freedom from the worry of that case, and soothing his itch for the British School. Fred Walker! The fellow was old-fashioned; he and Mason had been succeeded by a dozen movements. But—like old fiddles, with the same agreeable glow—there they were, very good curiosities such as would always command a price.

Having detached a Courbet, early and about ripe, he was standing in his shirt-sleeves, with a coil of wire in his hand, when Michael entered.

'Where have you sprung from?' he said, surprised.

'I happened to be passing, sir, on my old bike. I see you've kept your word about the English School.'

Soames attached the wire.

'I shan't be happy,' he said, 'till I've got an old Crome—best of the English landscapists.'

'Awfully rare, isn't he, old Crome?'

'Yes, that's why I want him,'

The smile on Michael's face, as if he were thinking: 'You mean that's why you consider him the best,' was lost on Soames giving the wire a final twist.

'I haven't seen your pictures for a long time, sir. Can I look round?'

Observing him sidelong, Soames remembered his appearance there one summer Sunday, after he had first seen Fleur in that Gallery off Cork Street. Only four years? It seemed an age! The young fellow had worn better than one had hoped; looked a good deal older, too, less flighty; an amiable chap, considering his upbringing, and that war! And suddenly he perceived that Michael was engaged in observing him. Wanted something, no doubt—wouldn't have come down for nothing! He tried to remember when anybody had come to see him without wanting something; but could not. It was natural!

'Are you looking for a picture to go with that Fragonard?' he said. 'There's a Chardin in the corner.'

'No, no, sir; you've been much too generous to us already.'

Generous! How could one be generous to one's only daughter?

'How is Fleur?'

'I wanted to tell you about her. She's feeling awfully restless.'

Soames looked out of the window. The spring was late!

'She oughtn't to be, with that case out of the way.'

'That's just it, sir.'

Soames gimleted the young man's face. 'I don't follow you.'

'We're being cold-shouldered.'

'How? You won.'

'Yes, but you see, people resent moral superiority.'

'What's that? Who—?' Moral superiority—he resented it himself!

'Foskisson, you know; we're tarred with his brush. I told you I was afraid of it. It's the being laughed at Fleur feels so bitterly.'

'Laughed at? Who has the impudence—?'

'To attack modern morality was a good stunt, sir, with the judge and the jury, and anyone professionally pompous; but it makes one ridiculous nowadays in Society, you know, when everybody prides himself on lack of prejudice.'

'Society!'

'Yes, sir; but it's what we live in. *I* don't mind, got used to it over Foggartism;

but Fleur's miserable. It's natural, if you think of it–Society's her game.'

'She ought to have more strength of mind,' said Soames. But he was gravely perturbed. First she'd been looked on as a snob, and now there was this!

'What with that German actor hanging himself at Lippinghall,' Michael went on, 'and my Foggartism, and this Ferrar rumpus, our pitch is badly queered. We've had a wretched week of it since the case. Fleur feels so out of her plate, that she wants me to take her round the world.'

A bomb bursting on the dove-cote down there could not have been more startling. Round the world! He heard Michael murmuring on:

'She's quite right, too. It might be the very best thing for her; but I simply can't leave my job until the long vacation. I've taken up this thing, and I must stick to it while Parliament's sitting.'

Sitting! As if it were a hen, addling its precious eggs! Round the world!

But Michael ran on:

'It's only to-day I've quite decided. I should feel like a deserter, and that wouldn't be good for either of us in the long run. But she doesn't know yet.'

For Soames the dove-cote was solidifying again, now that he knew Michael was not going to take her away for goodness knew how long!

'Round the world!' he said. 'Why not–er–Pontresina?'

'I think,' answered Michael slowly, like a doctor diagnosing, 'that she wants something dramatic. Round the world at twenty-three! She feels somehow that she's lost caste.'

'How can she think of leaving that little chap?'

'Yes, that shows it's pretty desperate with her. I wish to goodness I *could* go.'

Soames stared. The young fellow wasn't expecting him to do anything about it, was he? Round the world? A crazy notion!

'I must see her,' he said. 'Can you leave that thing of yours in the garage and come up with me in the car? I'll be ready in twenty minutes. You'll find tea going downstairs.'

Left alone with the Fred Walker still unhung, Soames gazed at his pictures. He saw them with an added clarity, a more penetrating glance, a sort of ache in his heart, as if– Well! A good lot they were, better than he had thought, of late! *She* had gone in for collecting people! And now she'd lost her collection! Poor little thing! All nonsense, of course–as if there were any satisfaction in people! Suppose he took her up that Chardin? It was a good Chardin. Dumetrius had done him over the price, but not too much. And, before Chardin was finished with, he would do Dumetrius. Still–if it would give her any pleasure! He unhooked the picture and, carrying it under his arm, went downstairs.

Beyond certain allusions to the characteristics of the eleventh baronet, and the regrettable tendencies of the police to compel slow travelling over the new cut constructed to speed up traffic, little was said in the car. They arrived in South Square about six o'clock. Fleur had not been in since lunch; and they sat down uneasily to wait for her. The Dandie, having descended to look for strange legs, had almost immediately ascended again, and the house was very quiet. Michael was continually looking at his watch.

'Where do you think she's got to?' said Soames at last.

'Haven't an idea, sir; that's the worst of London, it swallows people up.'

He had begun to fidget; Soames, who also wanted to fidget, was thinking of saying 'Don't!' when from the window Michael cried:

'Here she is!' and went quickly to the door.

Soames sat on, with the Chardin resting against his chair.

They were a long time out there! Minute after minute passed, and still they did not come.

At last Michael reappeared. He looked exceedingly grave.

'She's in her little room upstairs, sir. I'm afraid it's upset her awfully. Perhaps you wouldn't mind going up.'

Soames grasped the Chardin.

'Let's see, that's the first door on the left, isn't it?' He mounted slowly, his mind blank, and without waiting for her to answer his mild knock, went in.

Fleur was sitting at the satinwood bureau, with her face buried on her arms. Her hair, again in its more natural 'bob', gleamed lustrously under the light. She seemed unconscious of his entry. This sight of private life affected Soames, unaccustomed to give or receive undefended glimpses of self, and he stood, uncertain. Had he the right to surprise her, with her ears muffled like that, and her feelings all upset? He would have gone out and come in again, but he was too concerned. And, moving to her side, he put his finger on her shoulder and said:

'Tired, my child?'

Her face came round – queer, creased, not like her face; and Soames spoke the phrase of her childhood:

'See what I've brought you!'

He raised the Chardin; she gave it just a glance and he felt hurt. After all, it was worth some hundreds of pounds! Very pale, she had crossed her arms on her chest as if shutting herself up. He recognised the symptom. A spiritual crisis! The sort of thing his whole life had been passed in regarding as extravagant; like a case of appendicitis that will not wait decently.

'Michael,' he said, 'tells me you want him to take you round the world.'

'Well, he can't; so that ends it.'

If she had said: 'Yes, and why can't he?' Soames would have joined the opposition automatically. But her words roused his natural perversity. Here she was, and here was her heart's desire – and she wasn't getting it! He put the Chardin down and took a walk over the soft carpet.

'Tell me,' he said, coming to a halt, 'where do you feel it exactly?'

Fleur laughed: 'In my head, and my eyes, and my ears, and my heart.'

'What business,' muttered Soames, 'have they to look down their confounded noses!' And he set off again across the room. All the modern jackanapes whom from time to time he had been unable to avoid in her house, seemed to have come sniggering round him with lifted eyebrows, like a set of ghosts. The longing to put them in their places – a shallow lot – possessed him at that moment to the exclusion of a greater sanity.

'I–I don't see how *I* can take you,' he said, and stopped short.

What was that he was saying? Who had asked him to take her? Her eyes, widely open, were fixed on him.

'But of course not, Dad!'

Of course not! He didn't know about that!

'I shall get used to being laughed at, in time.'

Soames growled.

'I don't see why you should,' he said. 'I suppose people do go round the world.'

Fleur's pallor had gone, now.

'But not you, dear; why, it would bore you stiff! It's very sweet of you, even to think of it; but of course I couldn't let you – at your age!'

'At my age?' said Soames. 'I'm not so very old.'

'No, no, Dad; I'll just dree my weird.'

Soames took another walk, without a sound. Dree her weird, indeed!

'I won't have it,' he ejaculated; 'if people can't behave to you, I–I'll show them!'

She had got up, and was breathing deeply, with her lips parted and her cheeks very flushed. So she had stood, before her first party, holding out her frock for him to see.

'We'll go,' he said gruffly. 'Don't make a fuss! That's settled.'

Her arms were round his neck; his nose felt wet. What nonsense! as if–! . . .

He stood unbuttoning his braces that night in the most peculiar state of mind. Going round the world–was he? Preposterous! It had knocked that young fellow over, anyway–he was to join them in August wherever they were by that time! Good Lord! It might be China! The thing was fantastic; and Fleur behaving like a kitten! The words of a comic ditty, sung by a clergyman, in his boyhood, kept up a tattoo within him:

> 'I see Jerusalem and Madagascar,
> And North and South Amerikee. . . .'

Yes! Indeed! His affairs were in apple-pie order, luckily! There was nothing to do, in Timothy's or Winifred's Trusts–the only two he had on his hands now; but how things would get on without him, he couldn't tell. As to Annette! She wouldn't be sorry, he supposed. There was no one else to care, except Winifred, a little. It was, rather, the intangible presence of England that troubled him, about to forsake her for months on end! Still, the cliffs of Dover would be standing, he supposed, and the river still running past his lawn, when he came back, if he ever came back! You picked up all sorts of things out there–microbes, insects, snakes–never knew what you'd run into! Pretty business, steering Fleur clear of all that. And the sightseeing he would have to do! For *she* wouldn't miss anything! Trust her! Going round among a lot of people with their mouths open–he couldn't stand that; but he would have to! H'm! A relief when that young fellow could join them. And yet–to have her to himself; he hadn't, for a long time now. But she would pick up with everybody, of course. He would have to make himself agreeable to Tom, Dick, and Harry. A look at Egypt, then to India, and across to China and Japan, and back through that great sprawling America–God's own country, didn't they call it! She had it all mapped out. Thank goodness, no question of Russia! She hadn't even proposed that–it was all to pieces now, they said! Communism! Who knew what would happen at home before they got back? It seemed to Soames as if England, too, must all go to pieces, if he left it. Well, he'd said he would take her! And she had cried over it. Phew! He threw the window up, and in the Jaeger dressing-gown, kept there for stray occasions, leaned into the mild air. No Westminster Square did he seem to see out there, but his own river and its poplars, with the full moon behind them, a bright witness–the quiet beauty he had never put into words, the green tranquillity he had felt for thirty years, and only permitted to seep into the back of his being. He would miss it–the scents, the sighs of the river under the wind, the chuckle down at the weir, the stars. They had stars out there, of course, but not English stars. And the grass–those great places had no grass, he believed! The blossom, too, was late this year–no blossom before they left! Well, the milk was spilled! And that reminded him: The dairyman would be certain to let the cows go out of milk—he was a 'natural', that chap! He would have to warn Annette. Women never seemed to understand that a cow didn't go on giving milk for ever, without being attended to. If he only had a man to rely on in the country, like old Gradman in Town! H'm! Old Gradman's eyes would drop out when he heard this news! Bit of old England there; and wouldn't be left long, now! It would be queer to come back and find old Gradman gone. One—Two—Three—Eleven! That clock! It had kept him awake before now; still—it was a fine old clock! That young fellow was to go on sitting under it. And was there anything in the notions that kept him sitting there, or were they just talk? Well, he was right to stick to his guns, anyway. But five months away from his young wife—great risk in that! 'Youth's a stuff'—Old Shakespeare knew the world. Well! Risk or no risk, there it was! After all, Fleur had a good head; and young Michael had a good heart. Fleur had a good heart, too; he wouldn't have it said that she hadn't! She would feel leaving the baby when it came to the point. She didn't realise, yet. And Soames felt within him the stir of a curious conflict, between hope that, after all, she might give it up, and apprehension lest she should. Funny—that! His habits, his comfort, his possessions . . . and here he was, flinging them all over the windmill! Absurd! And yet—!

12

ENVOI

Away from Fleur five months at least!

Soames's astounding conduct had indeed knocked Michael over. And yet, after all, they had come to a crisis in their life together, the more serious because concerned with workaday feelings. Perhaps out there she would become afflicted, like himself, with an enlarged prospect; lose her idea that the world consisted of some five thousand people of advanced tastes, of whom she knew at the outside five hundred. It was she who had pushed him into Parliament, and until he was hoofed therefrom as a failure, their path was surely conjoined along the crest of a large view. In the fortnight before her departure he suffered and kept smiling; wryly thankful that she was behaving 'like a kitten', as her father called it. Her nerves had been on edge ever since the autumn over that wretched case—what more natural than this reaction? At least she felt for him sufficiently to be prodigal of kisses—great consolation to Michael while it lasted. Once or twice he caught her hanging with wet eyes over the eleventh baronet; once found her with a wet face when he awoke in the morning. These indications were a priceless assurance to him that she meant to come back. For there were moments when possibilities balled into a nightmare. Absurd! She was going with her father, that embodiment of care and prudence! Who would have thought old Forsyte could uproot himself like this? He, too, was leaving a wife, though Michael saw no signs of it. One didn't know much about old Forsyte's feelings, except that they centred round his daughter, and that he was continually asking questions about labels and insects. He had bought himself, too, a life-saving waistcoat and one for Fleur. Michael held with him only one important conversation.

'I want you,' Soames said, 'to keep an eye on my wife, and see she doesn't go getting into a mess with the cows. She'll have her mother with her, but women are so funny. You'll find her first-rate with the baby. How will you be off for money?'

'Perfectly all right, sir.'

'Well, if you want some for any good purpose, go to old Gradman in the City; you remember him, perhaps?'

'Yes, and I'm afraid he'll remember me.'

'Never mind; he's a faithful old fellow.' And Michael heard him sigh. 'I'd like you to look in at Green Street, too, now and then. Your aunt-in-law may feel my being away a little. I'll let you have news of Fleur from time to time—now they've got this wireless she'll want to know about the baby. I'm taking plenty of quinine, Fleur says she's a good sailor. There's nothing like champagne for that, I'm told. And, by the way, you know best, but I shouldn't press your notions too far in Parliament; they're easily bored there, I believe. We'll meet you at Vancouver, at the end of August. She'll be tired of travelling by then. She's looking forward to Egypt and Japan, but I don't know. Seems to me it'll be all travelling.'

'Have you plenty of ducks, sir? You'll want them at this time of year in the Red Sea; and I should take a helmet.'

'I've got one,' said Soames; 'they're heavy great things,' and, looking suddenly at Michael, he added:

'I shall look after her, and you'll look after yourself, I hope.'

Michael understood him.

'Yes, sir. And thank you very much. I think it's most frightfully sporting of you.'

'It's to be hoped it'll do her good; and that the little chap won't miss her.'

'Not if I can help it.'

Soames, who was seated in front of 'The White Monkey', seemed to go into a trance. At last he stirred in his chair and said:

'The war's left everything very unsettled. I suppose people believe in something nowadays, but *I* don't know what it is.'

Michael felt a fearful interest.

'Do you mind telling me, sir, what you believe in yourself?'

'What was good enough for my fathers is good enough for me. They expect too much now; there's no interest taken in being alive.'

'Interest taken in being alive!' The words were singularly comprehensive. Were they the answer to all modern doubt?

The last night, the last kiss came; and the glum journey to the Docks in Soames's car. Michael alone went to see them off! The gloomy dockside, and the grey river; the bustle with baggage, and the crowded tender. An aching business! Even for her, he almost believed—an aching business. And the long desultory minutes on the ship; the initiation of Soames into its cramped, shining, strangely odoured mysteries. The ghastly smile one had to keep on the lips, the inane jokes one had to make. And then that moment, apart, when she pressed her breast to his and gave him a clinging kiss.

'Good-bye, Michael; it's not for very long.'

'Good-bye, darling! Take care of yourself. You shall have all the news I can send you, and don't worry about Kit.'

His teeth were clinched, and her eyes—he saw—were wet! And, then, once more:

'Good-bye!'

'Good-bye!'

Back on the tender, with the strip of grey water opening, spreading, between him and the ship's side, and that high line of faces above the bulwark–Fleur's face under the small fawn hat, her waving hand; and, away to the left, seen out of the tail of his eyes, old Forsyte's face alone–withdrawn so that they might have their parting to themselves–long, chinny, grey-moustached, very motionless; absorbed and lonely, as might be that of some long-distance bird arrived on an unknown shore, and looking back towards the land of its departure. Smaller and smaller they grew, merged in blur, vanished.

For the whole journey back to Westminster, Michael smoked cigarette on cigarette, and read the same sentence over and over in the same journal, and the sentence was:

'Robbery at Highgate, Cat Burglar gets clear away.'

He went straight into the House of Commons. And all the afternoon sat listening and taking in a few words now and then, of a debate on education. What chance–what earthly chance–had his skyscraping in this place, where they still talked with calm disagreement, as if England were the England of 1906, and the verdict on him was: 'Amiable but very foolish young man!' National unity–national movement! No jolly fear! The country wouldn't have it! One was battering at a door which everybody said must be opened, but through which nobody could pass. And a long strip of grey water kept spreading between him and the talkers; the face under the fawn hat confused itself with that of the Member for Wasbaston; the face of Old Forsyte above the bulwark rail appeared suddenly between two Labour Leaders; and the lines of faces faded to a blur on a grey river where gulls were flighting.

Going out, he passed a face that had more reality–MacGown's! Grim! It wasn't the word. No one had got any change out of that affair. *Multum ex parvo! Parvum ex multo!* That was the modern comedy!

Going home to have a look at Kit and send Fleur a wireless, he passed four musicians playing four instruments with a sort of fury. They had able bodies in shabby clothes. 'By Jove!' thought Michael, 'I know that chap's face!–surely he was in my company in France!' He watched till the cheeks collapsed. Yes! A good man, too! But they had all been good men. By George, they had been wonders! And here they were! And he within an ace of abandoning them! Though everybody had his nostrum, and one perhaps was as good as another, still one could only follow what light one had! And if the Future was unreadable, and Fate grinned, well–let it grin!

How empty the house felt! To-morrow Kit and the dog were to go down to 'The Shelter' in the car, and it would be still emptier. From room after room he tried to retrieve some sight or scent of Fleur. Too painful! His dressing-room, his study were the only places possible–in them he would abide.

He went to the nursery and opened the door softly. Whiteness and dimity; the dog on his fat silver side, the Magicoal fire burning; the prints on the white walls so carefully selected for the moment when the eleventh baronet should begin to take notice–prints slightly comic, to avoid a moral; the high and shining fender-guard that even Magicoal might not be taken too seriously; the light coming in between bright chintz. A charming room! The nurse, in blue, was standing with her back to the door, and did not see him. And, in his little high chair, the eleventh baronet was at table; on his face, beneath its dark chestnut curls, was a slight frown; and in his tiny hand he held a silver spoon, with which over the bowl before him he was making spasmodic passes.

Michael heard the nurse saying:

'Now that mother's gone, you must be a little man, Kit, and learn to use your spoon.'

Michael saw his offspring dip at the bowl and throw some of its contents into the air.

'That's not the way at all.'

The eleventh baronet repeated the performance, and looked for applause, with a determined smile.

'Naughty!'

'A–a!' said the eleventh baronet, plopping the spoon. The contents spurted wastefully.

'Oh! you spoiled boy!'

'"England, my England!"' thought Michael, 'as the poet said.'

BOOK III
Swan Song

SWAN SONG

'We are such stuff
As dreams are made on; and our little life
Is rounded with a sleep.'

The Tempest

TO F. N. DOUBLEDAY

PART I

I

INITIATION OF THE CANTEEN

In modern Society, one thing after another, this spice on that, ensures a kind of memoristic vacuum, and Fleur Mont's passage of arms with Marjorie Ferrar was, by the spring of 1926, well-nigh forgotten. Moreover, she gave Society's memory no encouragement, for after her tour round the world, she was interested in the Empire—a bent so out of fashion as to have all the flavour and excitement of novelty with a sort of impersonality guaranteed.

Colonials, Americans, and Indian students, people whom nobody could suspect of being lions, now encountered each other in the 'bi-metallic parlour', and were found by Fleur 'very interesting', especially the Indian students, so supple and enigmatic, that she could never tell whether she were 'using' them or they were 'using' her.

Perceiving the extraordinarily uphill nature of Foggartism, she had been looking for a second string to Michael's Parliamentary bow, and, with her knowledge of India, where she had spent six weeks of her tour, she believed that she had found it in the idea of free entrance for the Indians into Kenya. In her talks with these Indian students, she learned that it was impossible to walk in a direction unless you knew what it was. These young men might be complicated and unpractical, meditative and secret, but at least they appeared to be convinced that the molecules in an organism mattered less than the organism itself—that they, in fact, mattered less than India. Fleur, it seemed, had encountered faith—a new and 'intriguing' experience. She mentioned the fact to Michael.

'It's all very well,' he answered, 'but our Indian friends didn't live four years in the trenches, or the fear thereof, for the sake of their faith. If they had, they couldn't possibly have the feeling that it matters as much as they think it does. They might want to, but their feelers would be blunted. That's what the war really did to all of us in Europe who were in the war.'

'That doesn't make "faith" any less interesting,' said Fleur, dryly.

'Well, my dear, the prophets abuse us for being at loose ends, but can you have faith in a life force so darned extravagant that it makes mincemeat of you by the million? Take it from me, Victorian times fostered a lot of very cheap and easy faith, and our Indian friends are in the same case—their India has lain doggo since the Mutiny, and that was only a surface upheaval. So you needn't take 'em too seriously.'

'I don't; but I like the way they believe they're serving India.'

And at his smile she frowned, seeing that he thought she was only increasing her collection.

Her father-in-law, who had really made some study of Orientalism, lifted his eyebrow over these new acquaintances.

'My oldest friend,' he said, on the first of May, 'is a judge in India. He's been there forty years. When he'd been there two, he wrote to me that he was beginning to know something about the Indians. When he'd been there ten, he wrote that he knew all about them. I had a letter from him yesterday, and he says that after forty years he knows nothing about them. And they know as little about us. East and West—the circulation of the blood is different.'

'Hasn't forty years altered the circulation of your friend's blood?'

'Not a jot,' replied Sir Lawrence. 'It takes forty generations. Give me another cup of your nice Turkish coffee, my dear. What does Michael say about the general strike?'

'That the Government won't budge unless the T.U.C. withdraw the notice unreservedly.'

'Exactly! And but for the circulation of English blood there'd be "a pretty mess", as old Forsyte would say.'

'Michael's sympathies are with the miners.'

'So are mine, young lady. Excellent fellow, the miner—but unfortunately cursed with leaders. The mine-owners are in the same case. Those precious leaders are going to grind the country's nose before they've done. Inconvenient product—coal; it's blackened our faces, and now it's going to black our eyes. Not a merry old soul! Well, good-bye! My love to Kit, and tell Michael to keep his head.'

This was precisely what Michael was trying to do. When 'the Great War' broke out, though just old enough to fight, he had been too young to appreciate the fatalism which creeps over human nature with the approach of crisis. He was appreciating it now before 'the Great Strike', together with the peculiar value which the human being attaches to saving face. He noticed that both sides had expressed the intention of meeting the other side in every way, without, of course, making any concessions whatever; the slogans, 'Longer hours, less wages', 'Not a minute more, not a bob off', curtsied, and got more and more distant as they neared each other. And now, with the ill-disguised impatience of his somewhat mercurial nature, Michael was watching the sober and tentative approaches of the typical Britons in whose hands any chance of mediation lay. When, on that memorable Monday, not merely the faces of the gentlemen with slogans, but the very faces of the typical Britons, were suddenly confronted with the need for being saved, he knew that all was up; and returning from the House of Commons at midnight, he looked at his sleeping wife. Should he wake Fleur and tell her that the country was 'for it', or should he not? Why spoil her beauty sleep? She would know soon enough. Besides, she wouldn't take it seriously. Passing into his dressing-room, he stood looking out of the window at the dark Square below. A general strike at a few hours' notice! 'Some' test of the British character! The British character? Suspicion had been dawning on Michael for years that its appearances were deceptive; that Members of Parliament, theatre-goers, trotty little ladies with dresses tight blown about trotty little figures, plethoric generals in armchairs, pettish and petted poets, parsons in pulpits, posters in the street—above all, the Press, were not representative of the national disposition. If the papers were not to come out, one would at least get a chance of feeling and seeing British character; owing to the papers, one never had seen or felt it clearly during the war, at least not in

England. In the trenches, of course, one had–there, sentiment and hate, advertisement and moonshine, had been 'taboo', and with a grim humour the Briton had just 'carried on', unornamental and sublime, in the mud and the blood, the stink and the racket, and the endless nightmare of being pitchforked into fire without rhyme or reason! The Briton's defiant humour that grew better as things grew worse, would–he felt–gets its chance again now. And, turning from the window, he undressed and went back into the bedroom.

Fleur was awake.

'Well, Michael?'

'The strike's on.'

'What a bore!'

'Yes; we shall have to exert ourselves.'

'What did they appoint that Commission for, and pay all that subsidy, if not to avoid this?'

'My dear girl, that's mere common sense–no good at all.'

'Why can't they come to an agreement?'

'Because they've got to save face. Saving face is the strongest motive in the world.'

'How do you mean?'

'Well, it caused the war; it's causing the strike now; without "saving face" there'd probably be no life on the earth at all by this time.'

Michael kissed her.

'I suppose you'll have to do something,' she said, sleepily. 'There won't be much to talk about in the House while this is on.'

'No; we shall sit and glower at each other, and use the word "formula" at stated intervals.'

'I wish we had a Mussolini.'

'I don't. You pay for him in the long run. Look at Diaz and Mexico; or Lenin and Russia; or Napoleon and France; or Cromwell and England, for the matter of that.'

'Charles the Second,' murmured Fleur into her pillow 'was rather a dear.'

Michael stayed awake a little, disturbed by the kiss, slept a little, woke again. To save face! No one would make a move because of their faces. For nearly an hour he lay trying to think out a way of saving them all, then fell asleep. He woke at seven with the feeling that he had wasted his time. Under the appearance of concern for the country, and professions of anxiety to find a 'formula', too many personal feelings, motives, and prejudices were at work. As before the war, there was a profound longing for the humiliation and dejection of the adversary; each wished his face saved at the expense of the other fellow's!

He went out directly after breakfast.

People and cars were streaming in over Westminster Bridge, no buses ran, no trams; but motor-lorries, full or empty, rumbled past. Some 'specials' were out already, and everybody had a look as if they were going to a tea party, cloaked in a kind of defiant jollity. Michael moved on towards Hyde Park. Over night had sprung up this amazing mish-mash of lorries and cans and tents! In the midst of all the mental and imaginative lethargy which had produced this national crisis–what a wonderful display of practical and departmental energy! 'They say we can't organise!' thought Michael; 'can't we just–*after the event!*'

He went on to a big railway station. It was picketed, but they were running trains already, with volunteer labour. Poking round, he talked here and there among the volunteers. 'By George!' he thought, 'these fellows'll want feeding! What about a canteen!' And he returned post haste to South Square.

Fleur was in.

'Will you help me run a railway canteen for volunteers?' He saw the expression: 'Is that a good stunt?' rise on her face, and hurried on:

'It'll mean frightfully hard work; and getting anybody we can to help. I daresay I could rope in Norah Curfew and her gang from Bethnal Green for a start. But it's your quick head that's wanted and your way with men.'

Fleur smiled. 'All right,' she said.

They took the car—a present from Soames on their return from round the world—and went about, picking people up and dropping them again. They recruited Norah Curfew and 'her gang' in Bethnal Green; and during this first meeting of Fleur with one whom she had been inclined to suspect as something of a rival, Michael noted how, within five minutes, she had accepted Norah Curfew as too 'good' to be dangerous. He left them at South Square in conference over culinary details, and set forth to sap the natural oppositions of officialdom. It was like cutting barbed wire on a dark night before an 'operation'. He cut a good deal, and went down to the 'House'. Humming with unformulated 'formulas', it was, on the whole, the least cheerful place he had been in that day. Everyone was talking of the 'menace to the Constitution'. The Government's long face was longer than ever, and nothing—they said—could be done until it had been saved. The expressions 'Freedom of the Press' and 'At the pistol's mouth', were being used to the point of tautology! He ran across Mr Blythe brooding in the Lobby on the temporary decease of his beloved weekly, and took him over to South Square 'for a bite' at nine o'clock. Fleur had come in for the same purpose. According to Mr Blythe, the solution was to 'form a group' of right-thinking opinion.

'Exactly, Blythe! But what is right-thinking, at "the present time of speaking"?'

'It all comes back to Foggartism,' said Mr Blythe.

'Oh!' said Fleur, 'I do wish you'd drop that. Nobody will have anything to say to it. You might as well ask the people of to-day to live like St Francis d'Assisi.'

'My dear young lady, suppose St Francis d'Assisi had said that, we shouldn't be hearing to-day of St Francis.'

'Well, what real effect has he had? He's just a curiosity. All those great spiritual figures are curiosities. Look at Tolstoi now, or Christ, for that matter!'

'Fleur's rather right, Blythe.'

'Blasphemy!' said Mr Blythe.

'I don't know, Blythe; I've been looking at the gutters lately, and I've come to the conclusion that they put a stopper on Foggartism. Watch the children there, and you'll see how attractive gutters are! So long as a child can have a gutter, he'll never leave it. And, mind you, gutters are a great civilising influence. We have more gutters here than any other country and more children brought up in them; and we're the most civilised people in the world. This strike's going to prove that. There'll be less bloodshed and more good humour than there could be anywhere else; all due to the gutter.'

'Renegade!' said Mr Blythe.

'Well,' said Michael, 'Foggartism, like all religions, is the over-expression of a home truth. We've been too wholesale, Blythe. What converts have we made?'

'None,' said Mr Blythe. 'But if we can't take children from the gutter, Foggartism is no more.'

Michael wriggled; and Fleur said promptly: 'What never was can't be no more. Are you coming with me to see the kitchens, Michael – they've been left in a filthy state. How does one deal with black beetles on a large scale?'

'Get a beetle-man – sort of pied piper, who lures them to their fate.'

Arrived on the premises of the canteen-to-be, they were joined by Ruth La Fontaine, of Norah Curfew's 'gang', and descended to the dark and odorous kitchen. Michael struck a match, and found the switch. Gosh! In the light, surprised, a brown-black scuttling swarm covered the floor, the walls, the tables. Michael had just sufficient control of his nerves to take in the faces of those three – Fleur's shuddering frown, Mr Blythe's open mouth, the dark and pretty Ruth La Fontaine's nervous smile. He felt Fleur clutch his arm.

'How *disgusting*!'

The disturbed creatures were finding their holes or had ceased to scuttle; here and there, a large one, isolated, seemed to watch them.

'Imagine!' cried Fleur. 'And food's been cooked here all these years! Ugh!'

'After all,' said Ruth La Fontaine, with a shivery giggle, 'they're not so b-bad as b-bugs.'

Mr Blythe puffed hard at his cigar. Fleur muttered:

'What's to be done, Michael?'

Her face was pale; she was drawing little shuddering breaths; and Michael was thinking: 'It's too bad; I must get her out of this!' when suddenly she seized a broom and rushed at a large cockroach on the wall. In a minute they were all at it – swabbing and sweeping, and flinging open doors and windows.

2

ON THE 'PHONE

Winifred Dartie had not received her *Morning Post.* Now in her sixty-eighth year, she had not followed too closely the progress of events which led up to the general strike – they were always saying things in the papers, and you never knew what was true; those Trades Union people, too, were so interfering, that really one had no patience. Besides, the Government always did something in the end. Acting, however, on the advice of her brother Soames, she had filled her cellars with coal and her cupboards with groceries, and by ten o'clock on the second morning of the strike, was seated comfortably at the telephone.

'Is that you, Imogen? Are you and Jack coming for me this evening?'

'No, Mother. Jack's sworn in, of course. He has to be on duty at five. Besides, they say the theatres will close. We'll go later. "Dat Lubly Lady's" sure to run.'

'Very well, dear. But what a fuss it all is! How are the boys?'

'Awfully fit. They're both going to be little "specials". I've made them tiny badges. D'you think the child's department at Harridge's would have toy truncheons?'

'Sure too, if it goes on. I shall be there to-day; I'll suggest it. They'd look too sweet, wouldn't they? Are you all right for coal?'

'Oh, yes. Jack says we mustn't hoard. He's fearfully patriotic.'

'Well, good-bye, dear! My love to the boys!'

She had just begun to consider whom she should call up next when the telephone bell rang.

'Yes?'

'Mr Val Dartie living there?'

'No. Who is speaking?'

'My name is Stainford. I'm an old college friend of his. Could you give me his address, please?'

Stainford? It conveyed nothing.

'I'm his mother. My son is not in town; but I daresay he will be before long. Can I give him any message?'

'Well, thanks! I want to see him, I'll ring up again; or take my chance later. Thanks!'

Winifred replaced the receiver.

Stainford! The voice was distinguished. She hoped it had nothing to do with money. Odd, how often distinction was connected with money! Or, rather, with the lack of it. In the old Park Lane days they had known so many fashionables who had ended in the bankruptcy or divorce courts. Emily–her mother–had never been able to resist distinction. That had been the beginning of Monty–he had worn such perfect waistcoats and gardenias, and had known so much about all that was fast–impossible not to be impressed by him. Ah, well! She did not regret him now. Without him she would never have had Val, or Imogen's two boys, or Benedict (almost a colonel), though she never saw him now, living as he did, in Guernsey, to grow cucumbers, away from the income tax. They might say what they liked about the age, but could it really be more up-to-date than it was in the 'nineties and the early years of the century, when income tax was at a shilling, and that considered high! People now just ran about and talked, to disguise the fact that they were not so 'chic' and up-to-date as they used to be.

Again the telephone bell rang. 'Will you take a trunk call from Wansdon?' . . .

'Hallo! That you, Mother?'

'Oh, Val, how nice! Isn't this strike absurd?'

'Silly asses! I say: we're coming up.'

'Really, dear. But why? You'll be so much more comfortable in the country.'

'Holly says we've got to do things. Who d'you think turned up last night?–her brother–young Jon Forsyte. Left his wife and mother in Paris–said he'd missed the war and couldn't afford to miss this. Been travelling all the winter–Egypt, Italy, and that–chucked America, I gather. Says he wants to do something dirty–going to stoke an engine. We're driving up to the "Bristol" this afternoon.'

'Oh, but why not come to me, dear, I've got plenty of everything?'

'Well, there's young Jon–I don't think–'

'But he's a nice boy, isn't he?'

'Uncle Soames isn't with you, is he?'

'No, dear. He's at Mapledurham. Oh, and by the way, Val, someone has just rung up for you–a Mr Stainford.'

'Stainford? What! Aubrey Stainford–I haven't seen him since Oxford.'

'He said he would ring up again or take his chance of finding you here.'

'Oh, I'd love to see old Stainford again. Well, if you don't mind putting us up, Mother. Can't leave young Jon out, you know–he and Holly are very thick after six years; but I expect he'll be out all the time.'

'Oh, that'll be quite all right, dear; and how is Holly?'

'Topping.'

'And the horses?'

'All right. I've got a snorting two-year-old, rather backward. Shan't run him till Goodwood, but he ought to win then.'

'That'll be delightful. Well, dear boy, I'll expect you. But you won't be doing anything rash, with your leg?'

'No; just drive a bus, perhaps. Won't last, you know. The Government's all ready. Pretty hot stuff. We've *got* 'em this time.'

'I'm so glad. It'll be such a good thing to have it over; it's dreadfully bad for the season. Your uncle will be very upset.'

An indistinguishable sound; then Val's voice again:

'I say, Holly says *she'll* want a job—you might ask young Mont. He's in with people. See you soon, then—good-bye!'

Replacing the receiver, Winifred had scarcely risen from the satinwood chair on which she had been seated, when the bell rang again.

'Mrs Dartie? . . . That you, Winifred? Soames speaking. What did I tell you?'

'Yes; it's very annoying, dear. But Val says it'll soon be over.'

'What's he know about it?'

'He's very shrewd.'

'Shrewd? H'm! I'm coming up to Fleur's.'

'But why, Soames? I should have thought—'

'Must be on the spot, in case of—accidents. Besides, the car'll be eating its head off down here—may as well be useful. Do that fellow Riggs good to be sworn in. This thing may lead to anything.'

'Oh! Do you think—'

'Think? It's no joke. Comes of playing about with subsidies.'

'But you told me last summer—'

'They don't look ahead. They've got no more *nous* than a tom-cat. Annette wants to go to her mother's in France. I shan't stop her. She can't gad about while this is on. I shall take her to Dover with the car to-day, and come up to-morrow.'

'Ought one to sell anything, Soames?'

'Certainly not.'

'People seem dreadfully busy about it all. Val's going to drive a bus. Oh! and, Soames—that young Jon Forsyte is back. He's left his wife and mother in Paris, and come over to be a stoker.'

A deep sound, and then:

'What's he want to do that for? Much better keep out of England.'

'Ye-es. I suppose Fleur—'

'Don't you go putting things into *her* head!'

'Of course not, Soames. So I shall see you? Good-bye.'

Dear Soames was always so fussy about Fleur! Young Jon Forsyte and she—of course—but that was ages ago! Calf love! And Winifred smiled, sitting very still. This strike was really most 'intriguing'. So long as they didn't break any windows—because, of course, the milk supply would be all right, the Government always saw to that; and as to the newspapers—well, after all, they were a luxury! It would be very nice to have Val and Holly. The strike was really something to talk about; there had been nothing so exciting since the war. And, obeying an obscure instinct to do something about it, Winifred again took up the receiver. 'Give me Westminster oooo . . . Is that Mrs Michael Mont's?

Fleur? Aunt Winifred speaking. How are you, dear?'

The voice which answered had that quick little way of shaping words that was so amusing to Winifred, who in her youth had perfected a drawl, which effectually dominated both speed and emotion. All the young women in Society nowadays spoke like Fleur, as if they had found the old way of speaking English slow and flat, and were gingering it with little pinches.

'Perfectly all right, thanks. Anything I can do for you, Auntie?'

'Yes, my dear—your cousin Val and Holly are coming up to me about this strike. And Holly—I think it's very unnecessary, but she wants to *do* something. She thought perhaps Michael would know—'

'Oh, well, of course there are lots of things. We've started a canteen for railway workers; perhaps she'd like to help in that.'

'My dear, that would be awfully nice.'

'It won't, Aunt Winifred; it's pretty strenuous.'

'It can't last, dear, of course. Parliament are bound to do something about it. It must be a great comfort to you to have all the news at first hand. Then, may I send Holly to you?'

'But of course. She'll be very useful. At her age she'd better do supplies, I think, instead of standing about, serving. I get on with her all right. The great thing is to have people that get on together and don't fuss. Have you heard from Father?'

'Yes; he's coming up to you to-morrow.'

'Oh! But why?'

'He says he must be on the spot, in case of—'

'That's so silly. Never mind. It'll make two cars.'

'Holly will have hers, too. Val's going to drive a bus, he says—and—er—young—well, dear, that's all! My love to Kit. There are a tremendous lot of milk-cans in the Park already, Smither says. She went out this morning into Park Lane to have a look. It's all rather thrilling, don't you think?'

'At the House they say it'll mean another shilling on the income tax before it's over.'

'Oh, dear!'

At this moment a voice said: 'Have they answered?' And, replacing the receiver, Winifred again sat, placid. Park Lane! From the old house there—house of her youth—one would have had a splendid view of everything—quite the headquarters! But how dreadfully the poor old Pater would have felt it! James! She seemed to see him again with his plaid over his shoulders, and his nose glued to a window-pane, trying to cure with the evidence of his old grey eyes the fatal habit they all had of not telling him anything. She still had some of his wine. And Warmson, their old butler, still kept 'The Pouter Pigeon', on the river at Moulsbridge. He always sent her a Stilton cheese at Christmas, with a memorandum of the exact amount of the old Park Lane port she was to pour into it. His last letter had ended thus: 'I often think of the master, and how fond he was of going down the cellar right up to the end. As regards wine, ma'am, I'm afraid the days are not what they were. My duty to Mr Soames and all. Dear me, it seems a long time since I first came to Park Lane.

> 'Your obedient servant,
> 'George Warmson.

'P.S.—I had a pound or two on that colt Mr Val bred, please to tell him—and came in useful.'

The old sort of servant! And now she had Smither, from Timothy's, Cook having died—so mysteriously, or, as Smither put it: 'Of hornwee, ma'am, I verily believe, missing Mr Timothy as we did'—Smither as a sort of supercargo—didn't they call it, on ships? and really very capable, considering she was sixty, if a day, and the way her corsets creaked. After all, to be with the family again was a great comfort to the poor old soul—eight years younger than Winifred, who, like a true Forsyte, looked down on the age of others from the platform of perennial youth. And a comfort, too, to have about the house one who remembered Monty in his prime—Montague Dartie, so long dead now, that he had a halo as yellow as his gills had so often been. Poor, dear Monty! Was it really forty-seven years since she married him, and came to live in Green Street? How well those satinwood chairs with the floral green design on their top rails, had worn—furniture of times before this seven-hour day and all the rest of it! People thought about their work then, and not about the cinema! And Winifred, who had never had any work to think about, sighed. It had all been great fun—and, if they could only get this little fuss over, the coming season would be most enjoyable. She had seats already for almost everything. Her hand slipped down to what she was sitting on. Yes, she had only had those chairs re-covered twice in all her forty-seven years in Green Street, and, really, they were quite respectable still. True! no one ever sat on them now, because they were straight up without arms; and in these days, of course, everybody sprawled, so restless, too, that no chair could stand it. She rose to judge the degree of respectability beneath her, tilting the satinwood chair forward. The year Monty died they had been recovered last—1913, just before the war. Really that had been a marvellous piece of grey-green silk!

3

HOME-COMING

Jon Forsyte's sensations on landing at Newhaven, by the last possible boat, after five and a half years' absence, had been most peculiar. All the way by car to Wansdon under the Sussex Downs he was in a sort of excited dream. England! What wonderful chalk, what wonderful green! What an air of having been there for ever! The sudden dips into villages, the old bridges, the sheep, the beech clumps! And the cuckoo—not heard for six years! A poet, somewhat dormant of late, stirred within this young man. Delicious old country! Anne would be crazy about this countryside—it was so beautifully finished. When the general strike was over she could come along, and he would show her everything. In the meantime she would be all right with his mother in Paris, and he would be free for any job he could get. He remembered this bit, and Chanctonbury Ring up there, and his walk over from Worthing. He remembered very well. Fleur! His brother-in-law, Francis Wilmot, had come back from England with much to say about Fleur; she was very modern now, and attractive, and had a boy. How deeply one could be in love; and how completely get over it! Considering what his old feelings down here had been, it was strange but pleasant to be just simply eager to see Holly and 'old Val'.

Beyond a telegram from Dieppe, he had made no announcement of his

coming; but they would surely be here because of the horses. He would like to
have a look at Val's racing stable, and get a ride, perhaps, on the Downs before
taking on a strike job. If only Anne were with him, and they could have that ride
together! And Jon thought of his first ride with Anne in the South Carolinian
woods–that ride from which they had neither of them recovered. There it was!
The jolly old house! And here at the door–Holly herself! And at sight of his
half-sister, slim and dark-haired in a lilac dress, Jon was visited by a stabbing
memory of their father as he had looked that dreadful afternoon, lying dead in
the old arm-chair at Robin Hill. Dad–always lovable–and so good to him!

'Jon! How wonderful to see you!'

Her kiss, he remembered, had always lighted on his eyebrow–she hadn't
changed a bit. A half-sister was nicer than a full-sister, after all. With full sisters
you were almost bound to fight a little.

'What a pity you couldn't bring Anne and your mother! But perhaps it's just
as well, till this is over. You look quite English still, Jon; and your mouth's as
nice and wide as ever. Why do Americans and naval men have such small
mouths?'

'Sense of duty, I think. How's Val?'

'Oh, Val's all right. You haven't lost your smile. D'you remember your old
room?'

'Rather. And how are *you*, Holly?'

'So-so. I've become a writer, Jon.'

'Splendid!'

'Not at all. Hard labour and no reward.'

'Oh!'

'The first book was born to still for anything. A sort of "African Farm",
without the spiritual frills–if you remember it.'

'Rather! But I always left the frills out.'

'Yes, we get our objection to frills from Dad, Jon. He said to me once: "It'll
end in our calling all matter spirit or all spirit matter– I don't know which."'

'It won't,' said Jon; 'people love to divide things up. I say, I remember every
stick in this room. How are the horses? Can I have a look at them and a ride to-
morrow?'

'We'll go forth early and see them at exercise. We've only got three two-year-
olds, but one of them's most promising.'

'Fine! After that I must go up and get a good, dirty job. I should like to stoke
an engine. I've always wanted to know how stokers feel.'

'We'll all go. We can stay with Val's mother. It *is* so lovely to see you, Jon.
Dinner's in half an hour.'

Jon lingered five minutes at his window. That orchard in full bloom–not
mathematically planted, like his just-sold North Carolinian peach trees–was as
lovely as on that long-ago night when he chased Fleur therein. That was the
beauty of England–nothing was planned! How home-sick he had been over
there; yes, and his mother, too! He would never go back! How wonderful that
sea of apple blossom! Cuckoo again! That alone was worth coming home for.
He would find a place and grow fruit, down in the West, Worcestershire or
Somerset, or near here–they grew a lot of figs and things at Worthing, he
remembered. Turning out his suit-case, he began to dress. Just where he was
sitting now, pulling on his American socks, had he sat when Fleur was
showing him her Goya dress. Who would have believed then that, six years
later, he would want Anne, not Fleur, beside him on this bed! The gong!

Dabbing at his hair, bright and stivery, he straightened his tie and ran down.

Val's views on the strike, Val's views on everything, shrewd and narrow as his horseman's face! Those Labour johnnies were up against it this time with a vengeance; they'd have to heel up before it was over. How had Jon liked the Yanks? Had he seen 'Man of War'? No? Good Lord! The thing best worth seeing in America! Was the grass in Kentucky really blue? Only from the distance? Oh! What were they going to abolish over there next? Wasn't there a place down South where you were only allowed to cohabit under the eyes of the town watch? Parliament here were going to put a tax on betting; why not introduce the 'Tote' and have done with it? Personally he didn't care, he'd given up betting! And he glanced at Holly. Jon, too, glanced at her lifted brows and slightly parted lips–a charming face–ironical and tolerant! She drove Val with silken reins!

Val went on: Good job Jon had given up America; if he must farm out of England, why not South Africa, under the poor old British flag; though the Dutch weren't done with yet! A tough lot! They had gone out there, of course, so bright and early that they were real settlers–none of your adventurers, failures-at-home, remittance-men. He didn't like the beggars, but they were stout fellows, all the same. Going to stay in England? Good! What about coming in with them and breeding racing stock?

After an awkward little silence, Holly said slyly:

'Jon doesn't think that's quite a man's job, Val.'

'Why not?'

'Luxury trade.'

'Blood stock–where would horses be without it?'

'Very tempting,' said Jon. 'I'd like an interest in it. But I'd want to grow fruit and things for a main line.'

'All right, my son; you can grow the apples they eat on Sundays.'

'You see, Jon,' said Holly, 'nobody believes in growing anything in England. We talk about it more and more, and do it less and less. Do you see any change in Jon, Val?'

The cousins exchanged a stare.

'A bit more solid; nothing American, anyway.'

Holly murmured thoughtfully: 'Why can one always tell an American?'

'Why can one always tell an Englishman?' said Jon.

'Something guarded, my dear. But a national looks the most difficult thing in the world to define. Still, you can't mistake the American expression.'

'I don't believe you'll take Anne for one.'

'Describe her, Jon.'

'No. Wait till you see her.'

When, after dinner, Val was going his last round of the stables, Jon said:

'Do you ever see Fleur, Holly?'

'I haven't for eighteen months, I should think. I like her husband; he's an awfully good sort. You were well out of that, Jon. She isn't your kind–not that she isn't charming; but she has to be plumb centre of the stage. I suppose you knew that, really.'

Jon looked at her and did not answer.

'Of course,' murmured Holly, 'when one's in love, one doesn't know much.'

Up in his room again, the house began to be haunted. Into it seeemed to troop all his memories, of Fleur, of Robin Hill–old trees of his boyhood, his father's cigars, his mother's flowers and music; the nursery of his games,

Holly's nursery before him, with its window looking out over the clock tower above the stables, the room where latterly he had struggled with rhyme. In through his open bedroom window came the sweet-scented air—England's self—from the loom of the Downs in the moon-scattered dusk, this first night of home for more than two thousand nights. With Robin Hill sold, this was the nearest he had come to home in England now. But they must make one of their own—he and Anne. Home! On the English liner he had wanted to embrace the stewards and stewardesses just because they spoke with an English accent. It was, still, as music to his ears. Anne would pick it up faster now—she was very receptive! He had liked the Americans, but he was glad Val had said there was nothing American about him. An owl hooted. What a shadow that barn cast—how soft and old its angle! He got into bed. Sleep—if he wanted to be up to see the horses exercised! Once before, here, he had got up early—for another purpose! And soon he slept; and a form—was it Anne's, was it Fleur's—wandered in the corridors of his dreams.

4

SOAMES GOES UP TO TOWN

Having seen his wife off from Dover on the Wednesday, Soames Forsyte motored towards town. On the way he decided to make a considerable detour and enter London over Hammersmith, the farthest westerly bridge in reason. There was for him a fixed connection between unpleasantness and the East End, in times of industrial disturbance. And feeling that, if he encountered a threatening proletariat, he would insist on going through with it, he acted in accordance with the other side of a Forsyte's temperament, and looked ahead. Thus it was that he found his car held up in Hammersmith Broadway by the only threatening conduct of the afternoon. A number of persons had collected to interfere with a traffic of which they did not seem to approve. After sitting forward, to say to his chauffeur, 'You'd better go round, Riggs,' Soames did nothing but sit back. The afternoon was fine, and the car—a landaulette—open, so that he had a good view of the total impossibility of 'going round'. Just like that fellow Riggs to have run bang into this! A terrific pack of cars crammed with people trying to run out of town; a few cars like his own, half empty, trying to creep past them into town; a motor-omnibus, not overturned precisely, but with every window broken, standing half across the road; and a number of blank-looking people eddying and shifting before a handful of constables! Such were the phenomena which Soames felt the authorities ought to be handling better.

The words, 'Look at that blighted plutocrat!' assailed his ears; and in attempting to see the plutocrat in question, he became aware that it was himself. The epithets were unjust! He was modestly attired in a brown overcoat and soft felt hat; that fellow Riggs was plain enough in all conscience, and the car was an ordinary blue. True, he was alone in it, and all the other cars seemed full of people; but he did not see how he was to get over that, short of carrying into London persons desirous of going in the opposite direction. To shut the car, at all events, would look too pointed—so there was nothing for it but to sit still and take no notice! For this occupation no one could have been better framed by Nature than Soames, with his air of slightly despising creation. He sat, taking in little but his own nose, with the sun shining on his neck behind, and the crowd eddying round the police. Such violence as had been necessary to break the windows of the bus had ceased, and the block was rather what might have been caused by the Prince of Wales. With every appearance of not encouraging it by seeming to take notice, Soames was observing the crowd. And a vacant-looking lot they were, in his opinion; neither their eyes nor their hands had any of that close attention to business which alone made revolutionary conduct formidable. Youths, for the most part, with cigarettes drooping from their lips–they might have been looking at a fallen horse.

People were born gaping nowadays. And a good thing, too! Cinemas, fags, and football matches–there would be no real revolution while they were on hand; and as there seemed to be more and more on hand every year, he was just feeling that the prospect was not too bleak, when a young woman put her head over the window of his car.

'Could you take me into town?'

Soames automatically consulted his watch. The hands pointing to seven o'clock gave him extraordinarily little help. Rather a smartly-dressed young woman, with a slight cockney accent and powder on her nose! That fellow Riggs would never have done grinning. And yet he had read in the *British Gazette* that everybody was doing it. Rather gruffly he said:

'I suppose so. Where do you want to go?'

'Oh, Leicester Square would do me all right.'

Great Scott!

The young woman seemed to sense his emotion. 'You see,' she said, 'I got to get something to eat before my show.'

Moreover, she was getting in! Soames nearly got out. Restraining himself, he gave her a sidelong look; actress or something–young–round face, made up, naturally–nose a little snub–eyes grey, rather goggly–mouth–h'm, pretty mouth, slightly common! Shingled–of course.

'It's awf'ly kind of you!'

'Not at all!' said Soames; and the car moved.

'Think it's going to last, the strike?'

Soames leaned forward.

'Go on, Riggs,' he said; 'and put this young lady down in–er–Coventry Street.'

'It's frightf'ly awk for us, all this,' said the young lady. 'I should never've got there in time. You seen our show, "Dat Lubly Lady?"'

'No.'

'It's rather good.'

'Oh!'

'We shall have to close, though, if this lasts.'

'Ah!'

The young lady was silent, seeming to recognise that she was not in the presence of a conversationalist.

Soames re-crossed his legs. It was so long since he had spoken to a strange young woman, that he had almost forgotten how it was done. He did not want to encourage her, and yet was conscious that it was his car.

'Comfortable?' he said suddenly.

The young lady smiled.

'What d'you think?' she said. 'It's a lovely car.'

'I don't like it,' said Soames.

The young lady's mouth opened.

'Why?'

Soames shrugged his shoulders; he had only been keeping the conversation alive.

'I think it's rather fun, don't you?' said the young lady. 'Carrying on–you know, like we're all doing.'

The car was now going at speed, and Soames began to calculate the minutes necessary to put an end to this juxtaposition.

The Albert Memorial, already; he felt almost an affection for it–so guiltless of the times!

'You *must* come and see our show,' said the young lady.

Soames made an effort and looked into her face.

'What do you do in it?' he asked.

'Sing and dance.'

'I see.'

'I've rather a good bit in the third act, where we're all in our nighties.'

Soames smiled faintly.

'You've got no one like Kate Vaughan now,' he said.

'Kate Vaughan? Who was she?'

'Who was Kate Vaughan?' repeated Soames; 'greatest dancer that was ever in burlesque. Dancing was graceful in those days; now it's all throwing your legs about. The faster you can move your legs, the more you think you're dancing.' And, disconcerted by an outburst that was bound to lead to something, he averted his eyes.

'You don't like jazz?' queried the young lady.

'I do not,' said Soames.

'Well, I don't either–not reelly; it's getting old-fashioned, too.'

Hyde Park Corner already! And the car going a good twenty!

'My word! Look at the lorries; it's marvellous, isn't it?'

Soames emitted a confirmatory grunt. The young lady was powdering her nose now, and touching up her lips, with an almost staggering frankness. 'Suppose anyone sees me?' thought Soames. And he would never know whether anyone had or not. Turning up the high collar of his overcoat, he said:

'Draughty things, these cars! Shall I put you down at Scott's?'

'Oh no. Lyons, please; I've only time f'r a snack; got to be on the stage at eight. It's been awf'ly kind of you. I only hope somebody'll take me home!' Her eyes rolled suddenly, and she added: 'If you know what I mean.'

'Quite!' said Soames, with a certain delicacy of perception. 'Here you are. Stop–Riggs!'

The car stopped, and the young lady extended her hand to Soames.

'Good-bye, and thank you!'

'Good-bye!' said Soames. Nodding and smiling, she got out.

'Go on, Riggs, sharp! South Square.'

The car moved on. Soames did not look back; in his mind the thought formed like a bubble on the surface of water: 'In the old days anyone who looked and talked like that would have left me her address.' And she hadn't! He could not decide whether or no this marked an advance.

At South Square, on discovering that Michael and Fleur were out, he did not dress for dinner, but went to the nursery. His grandson, now nearly three years old, was still awake, and said: 'Hallo!'

'Hallo!' Soames produced a toy watchman's rattle. There followed five minutes of silent and complete absorption, broken fitfully by guttural sounds from the rattle. Then his grandson lay back in his cot, fixed his blue eyes on Soames and said: 'Hallo!'

'Hallo!' replied Soames.

'Ta, ta!' said his grandson.

'Ta, ta!' said Soames, backing to the door and nearly falling over the silver dog. The interview then terminated, and Soames went downstairs. Fleur had telephoned to say he was not to wait dinner.

Opposite the Goya he sat down. No good saying he remembered the Chartist riots of '48, because he had been born in '55; but he knew his Uncle Swithin had been a 'special' at the time. This general strike was probably the most serious internal disturbance that had happened since; and, sitting over his soup, he bored further and further into its possibilities. Bolshevism round the corner–that was the trouble! That and the fixed nature of ideas in England. Because a thing like coal had once been profitable, they thought it must always be profitable. Political leaders, Trades Unionists, newspaper chaps–they never looked an inch before their noses! They'd had since last August to do something about it, and what had they done? Drawn up a report that nobody would look at!

'White wine, sir, or claret?'

'Anything that's open.' To have said that in the 'eighties, or even the 'nineties, would have given his father a fit! The idea of drinking claret already opened was then almost equivalent to atheism. Another sign of the slump in ideals.

'What do *you* think about this strike, Coaker?'

The almost hairless man lowered the Sauterne.

'Got no body in it, sir, if you ask me.'

'What makes you say that?'

'If it had any body in it, sir, they'd have had the railings of Hyde Park up by now.'

Soames poised a bit of his sole. 'Shouldn't be surprised if you were right,' he said, with a certain approval.

'They make a lot of fuss, but no–there's nothing to it. The dole–that was a clever dodge, sir. *Pannus et circesses*, as Mr Mont says, sir.'

'Ha! Have you seen this canteen they're running?'

'No, sir; I believe they've got the beetle man in this evening. I'm told there's a proper lot of beetles.'

'Ugh!'

'Yes, sir; it's a nahsty insect.'

Having finished dinner, Soames lighted the second of his two daily cigars and took up the ear-pieces of the wireless. He had resisted this invention as long as he could–but in times like these! 'London calling!' Yes, and the British Isles listening! Trouble in Glasgow? There would be–lot of Irish there. More 'specials' wanted? There'd soon be plenty of those. He must tell that fellow Riggs to enlist. This butler chap, too, could well be spared. Trains! They seemed to be running a lot of trains already. After listening with some attention to the Home Secretary, Soames put the ear-pieces down and took up the *British Gazette*. It was his first sustained look at this tenuous production, and he hoped it would be his last. The paper and printing were deplorable. Still, he supposed it was something to have got it out at all. Tampering with the freedom of the Press! Those fellows were not finding it so easy as they thought. They had tampered, and the result was a Press much more definitely against them than the Press they had suppressed. Burned their fingers there! And quite unnecessary–old-fashioned notion now–influence of the Press. The war had killed it. Without confidence in truth there was no influence. Politicians or the Press–if you couldn't believe them, they didn't count! Perhaps they would re-discover that some day. In the meantime the papers were like cocktails–titivators mostly of the appetite and the nerves. How sleepy he was! He hoped Fleur wouldn't be very late coming in. Mad thing, this strike, making everybody do things they weren't accustomed to, just as Industry, too, was beginning–or at least pretending–to recover. But that was it! With every year, in these times, it was more difficult to do what you said you would. Always something or other turning up! The world seemed to live from hand to mouth, and at such a pace, too! Sitting back in the Spanish chair, Soames covered his eyes from the light, and the surge of sleep mounted to his brain; strike or no strike, the soft, inexorable tide washed over him.

A tickling, and over his hand, thin and rather brown, the fringe of a shawl came dangling. Why! With an effort he climbed out of an abyss of dreams. Fleur was standing beside him. Pretty, bright, her eyes shining, speaking quickly, excitedly, it seemed to him.

'Here you are, then, Dad!' Her lips felt hot and soft on his forehead, and her eyes– What was the matter with her? She looked so young–she looked so–how express it?

'So you're in!' he said. 'Kit's getting talkative. Had anything to eat?'

'Heaps!'

'This canteen–'

She flung off her shawl.

'I'm enjoying it frightfully.'

Soames noted with surprise the rise and fall of her breast, as if she had been running. Her cheeks, too, were very pink.

'You haven't caught anything, have you–in that place?'

Fleur laughed. A sound–delicious and unwarranted.

'How funny you are, Dad! I hope the strike lasts!'

'Don't be foolish!' said Soames. 'Where's Michael?'

'Gone up. He called for me, after the House. Nothing doing there, he says.'

'What's the time?'

'Past twelve, dear. You must have had a real good sleep.'

'Just nodding.'

'We saw a tank pass, on the Embankment–going east. It looked awfully queer. Didn't you hear it?'

'No,' said Soames.

'Well, don't be alarmed if you hear another. They're on their way to the docks, Michael says.'

'Glad to hear it–shows the Government means business. But you must go up. You're overtired.'

She gazed at him over the Spanish shawl on her arm–whistling some tune.

'Good-night!' he said. 'I shall be coming up in a minute.'

She blew him a kiss, twirled round, and went.

'I don't like it,' murmured Soames to himself; 'I don't know why, but I don't like it.'

She had looked so young. Had the strike gone to her head? He rose to squirt some soda-water into a glass–that nap had left a taste in his mouth.

Um–dum–bom–um–dum–bom–um–dum–bom! A grunching noise! Another of those tanks? He would like to see one of those great things! For the idea that they were going down to the docks gave him a feeling almost of exhilaration. With them on the spot the country was safe enough. Putting on his motoring coat and hat, he went out, crossed the empty Square, and stood in the street, whence he could see the Embankment. There it came! Like a great primeval monster in the lamplit darkness, growling and gruntling along, a huge, fantastic tortoise–like an embodiment of inexorable power. 'That'll astonish their weak nerves!' thought Soames, as the tank crawled, grunching, out of sight. He could hear another coming; but with a sudden feeling that it would be too much of a good thing, he turned on his heel. A sort of extravagance about them, when he remembered the blank-looking crowd around his car that afternoon, not a weapon among the lot, nor even a revolutionary look in their eyes!

'No *body* in the strike!' These great crawling monsters! Were the Government trying to pretend that there was? Playing the strong man! Something in Soames revolted slightly. Hang it! This was England, not Russia, or Italy! They might be right, but he didn't like it! Too–too military! He puts his latch-key into the key-hole. Um–dum–bom–um–dum–bom! Well, not many people would see or hear them–this time of night! He supposed they had got here from the country somewhere–he wouldn't care to meet them wandering about in the old lanes and places. Father and mother and baby tanks–like–like a family of mastodons, m–m? No sense of proportion in things like that! And no sense of humour! He stood on the stairs listening. It was to be hoped they wouldn't wake the baby!

5

JEOPARDY

When, looking down the row of faces at her canteen table, Fleur saw Jon Forsyte's, it was within her heart as if, in winter, she had met with honeysuckle. Recovering from that faint intoxication, she noted his appearance from farther off. He was sitting seemingly indifferent to food; and on his face, which was smudged with coal-dust and sweat, was such a smile as men wear after going up a mountain or at the end of a long run–tired, charming, and as if they have been through something worth while. His lashes–long and dark as in her memory–concealed his eyes, and quarrelled with his brighter hair, tousled to the limit of its shortness.

Continuing to issue her instructions to Ruth La Fontaine, Fleur thought rapidly. Jon! Dropped from the skies into her canteen, stronger-looking, better knit, with more jaw, and deeper eyes, but frightfully like Jon! What was to be done about it? If only she could turn out the lights, steal up behind, lean over and kiss him on that smudge above his left eye! Yes! And then–what? Silly! And now, suppose he came out of his far-away smile and saw her! As likely as not he would never come into her canteen again. She remembered his conscience! And she took a swift decision. Not to-night! Holly would know where he was staying. At her chosen time, on her chosen ground, if—on second thoughts, she wanted to play with fire. And, giving a mandate to Ruth La Fontaine concerning buns, she looked back over her shoulder at Jon's absorbed and smiling face, and passed out into her little office.

And second thoughts began. Michael, Kit, her father; the solid security of virtue and possessions; the peace of mind into which she had passed of late! All jeopardised for the sake of a smile, and a scent of honeysuckle! No! The account was closed. To reopen it was to tempt Providence. And if to tempt Providence was the practice of Modernity, she wasn't sure whether she was modern. Besides, who knew whether she *could* reopen that account? And she was seized by a gust of curiosity to see that wife of his—that substitute for herself. Was she in England? Was she dark, like her brother Francis? Fleur took up her list of purchases for the morrow. With so much to do, it was idiotic even to think about such things! The telephone! All day its bell had been ringing; since nine o'clock that morning she had been dancing to its pipe.

'Yes. . . ? Mrs Mont speaking. What? But I've ordered them. . . . Oh! But really I *must* give them bacon and eggs in the morning. They can't start on cocoa only. . . . How? The Company can't afford? . . . Well! Do you want an effective service or not? . . . Come round to see you about it? I really haven't time. . . . Yes, yes . . . now please do be nice to me and tell the manager that they simply must be properly fed. They look so tired. He'll understand . . . Yes. . . . Thank you ever so!' She hung up the receiver. 'Damn!'

Someone laughed. 'Oh! it's you, Holly! Cheeseparing and red tape as usual! This is the fourth time to-day. Well, I don't care—I'm going ahead. Look! Here's Harridge's list for to-morrow. It's terrific, but it's got to be. Buy it all; I'll take the risk, if I have to go round and slobber on him.' And beyond the ironic sympathy on Holly's face she seemed to see Jon's smile. He should be properly fed—all of them should! And, without looking at her cousin, she said:

'I saw Jon in there. Where has he dropped from?'

'Paris. He's putting up with us in Green Street.'

Fleur stuck her chin forward, and gave a little laugh.

'Quaint to see him again, all smudgy like that! His wife with him?'

'Not yet,' said Holly; 'she's in Paris still, with her mother.'

'Oh! It'd be fun to see him some time!'

'He's stoking an engine on the local service—goes out at six, and doesn't get in till about midnight.'

'Of course; I meant after, if the strike ever ends.'

Holly nodded. 'His wife wants to come over and help; would you like her in the canteen?'

'If she's the right sort.'

'Jon says: Very much so.'

'I don't see why an American should worry herself. Are they going to live in England?'

'Yes.'

'Oh! Well, we're both over the measles.'

'If you get them again grown-up, Fleur, they're pretty bad.'

Fleur laughed. 'No fear!' And her eyes, hazel, clear, glancing, met her cousin's eyes, deep, steady, grey.

'Michael's waiting for you with the car,' said Holly.

'All right! Can you carry on till they've finished? Norah Curfew's on duty at five to-morrow morning. I shall be round at nine, before you start for

Harridge's. If you think of anything else, stick it on the list–I'll make them stump up somehow. Good-night, Holly.'

'Good-night, my dear.'

Was there a gleam of pity in those grey eyes? Pity, indeed!

'Give Jon my love. I do wonder how he likes stoking! We must get some more wash-basins in.'

Sitting beside Michael, who was driving their car, she saw again, as it were, Jon's smile in the glass of the windscreen, and in the dark her lips pouted as if reaching it. Measles–they spotted you, and raised your temperature! How empty the streets were now that the taxis were on strike! Michael looked round at her.

'Well, how's it going?'

'The beetle-man was a caution, Michael. He had a face like a ravaged wedge, a wave of black hair, and the eyes of a lost soul; but he was frightfully efficient.'

'Look! There's a tank; I was told of them. They're going down to the docks. Rather provocative! Just as well there are no papers for them to get into.'

Fleur laughed.

'Father'll be at home. He's come up to protect me. If there really was shooting, I wonder what he'd do–take his umbrella?'

'Instinct. How about you and Kit? It's the same thing.'

Fleur did not answer. And when, after seeing her father, she went upstairs, she stood at the nursery door. The tune that had excited Soames's surprise made a whiffling sound in the empty passage. *'L'amour est enfant de Bohême; il n'a jamais jamais connu de loi; si tu ne m'aimes pas, je t'aime, et si je t'aime, prends garde à toi!'* Spain, and the heartache of her honeymoon! 'Voice in the night crying!' Close the shutters, muffle the ears–keep it out! She entered her bedroom and turned up the lights. It had never seemed to her so pretty, with its many mirrors, its lilac and green, its shining silver. She stood looking at her face, into which had come two patches of red, one in each cheek. Why wasn't she Norah Curfew–dutiful, uncomplicated, selfless, who would give Jon eggs and bacon at half-past five to-morrow morning–Jon with a clean face! Quickly she undressed. Was that wife of his her equal undressed? To which would he award the golden apple if she stood side by side with Anne? And the red spots deepened in her cheeks. Overtired–she knew that feeling! She would not sleep! But the sheets were cool. Yes, she preferred the old smooth Irish linen to that new rough French grass-bleached stuff. Ah! Here was Michael coming in, coming up to her! Well! No use to be unkind to him–poor old Michael! And in his arms, she saw–Jon's smile.

The first day spent stoking an engine had been enough to make anyone smile. An engine-driver almost as youthful, but in private life partner in his own engineering works, had put Jon 'wise' to the mystery of getting level combustion. 'A tricky job, and very tiring!' Their passengers had behaved well. One had even come up and thanked them. The engine-driver had winked at Jon. There had been some hectic moments. Supping pea soup, Jon thought of them with pleasure. It had been great sport, but his hands and arms felt wrenched. 'Oil them to-night,' the engine-driver had said.

A young woman was handing him 'jacket' potatoes. She had marvellously clear, brown eyes, something like Anne's–only Anne's were like a water nymph's. He took a potato, thanked her, and returned to a stoker's dreams. Extraordinary pleasure in being up against it–being in England again, doing something for England! One had to leave one's country to become conscious of it. Anne had telegraphed that she wanted to come over and join him. If he wired back 'No,' she would come all the same. He knew that much after nearly two years of marriage. Well, she would see England at its best. Americans didn't really know what England was. Her brother had seen nothing but London; he had spoken bitterly—a girl, Jon supposed, though nothing had been said of her. In Francis Wilmot's history of England the gap accounted for the rest. But everybody ran down England, because she didn't slop over, or blow her own trumpet.

'Butter?'

'Thanks, awfully. These potatoes are frightfully good.'

'So glad.'

'Who runs this canteen?'

'Mr and Mrs Michael Mont mostly; he's a Member of Parliament.'

Jon dropped his potato.

'Mrs Mont? Gracious! She's a cousin of mine. Is she here?'

'Was. Just gone, I think.'

Jon's far-sighted eyes travelled round the large and dingy room. Fleur! How amazing!

'Treacle pudding?'

'No, thanks. Nothing more.'

'There'll be coffee, tea, or cocoa, and eggs and bacon, to-morrow at 5.45.'

'Splendid! I think it's wonderful.'

'It is, rather, in the time.'

'Thank you awfully. Good-night!'

Jon sought his coat. Outside were Val and Holly in their car.

'Hallo, young Jon! You're a nice object.'

'What job have *you* caught, Val?'

'Motor-lorry—begin to-morrow.'

'Fine!'

'This'll knock out racing for a bit.'

'But not England.'

'England? Lord—no! What did you think?'

'Abroad they were saying so.'

'Abroad!' growled Val. 'They would!'

And there was silence at thirty miles an hour.

From his bedroom door Jon said to his sister:

'They say Fleur runs that canteen. Is she really so old now?'

'Fleur has a very clear head, my dear. She saw you there. No second go of measles, Jon.'

Jon laughed.

'Aunt Winifred,' said Holly, 'will be delighted to have Anne here on Friday, she told me to tell you.'

'Splendid! That's awfully good of her.'

'Well, good-night; bless you. There's still hot water in the bathroom.'

In his bath Jon lay luxuriously still. Sixty hours away from his young wife, he was already looking forward with impatience to her appearance on Friday. And so Fleur ran that canteen! A fashionable young woman with a clear and, no doubt, shingled head—he felt a great curiosity to see her again, but nothing more. Second go of measles! Not much! He had suffered too severely from the first. Besides, he was too glad to be back—result of long, half-acknowledged home-sickness. His mother had been home-sick for Europe; but *he* had felt no assuagement in Italy and France. It was England he had wanted. Something in the way people walked and talked; in the smell and the look of everything; some good-humoured, slow, ironic essence in the air, after the tension of America, the shrillness of Italy, the clarity of Paris. For the first time in five years his nerves felt coated. Even those features of his native land which offended the æsthetic soul, were comforting. The approaches to London, the countless awful little houses, of brick and slate which his own great-grandfather, 'Superior Dosset' Forsyte, had helped, so his father had once told him, to build; the many little new houses, rather better but still bent on compromise; the total absence of symmetry or plan; the ugly railway stations; the cockney voices, the lack of colour, taste, or pride in people's dress–all seemed comfortable, a guarantee that England would always be England.

And so Fleur was running that canteen! He would be seeing her! He would like to see her! Oh, yes!

6

SNUFF-BOX

In the next room Val was saying to Holly:

'Had a chap I knew at college to see me to-day. Wanted me to lend him money. I once did, when I was jolly hard up myself, and never got it back. He used to impress me frightfully–such an awfully good-looking, languid beggar. I thought him top notch as a "blood". You should see him now!'

'I did. I was coming in as he was going out; I wondered who he was. I never saw a more bitterly contemptuous expression on a face. Did you lend him money?'

'Only a fiver.'

'Well, don't lend him any more.'

'Hardly. D'you know what he's done? Gone off with that Louis Quinze snuff-box of mother's that's worth about two hundred. There's been nobody else in that room.'

'Good heavens!'

'Yes, it's pretty thick. He had the reputation of being the fastest man up at the 'Varsity in my time–in with the gambling set. Since I went out to the Boer war I've never heard of him.'

'Isn't your mother very annoyed, Val?'

'She wants to prosecute–it belonged to my grandad. But how can we–a college pal! Besides, we shouldn't get the box back.'

Holly ceased to brush her hair.

'It's rather a comfort to me–this,' she said.

'What is?'

'Why everybody says the standard of honesty's gone down. It's nice to find someone belonging to our generation that had it even less.'

'Rum comfort!'

'Human nature doesn't alter, Val. I believe in the young generation. We don't understand them–brought up in too settled times.'

'That may be. My own dad wasn't too particular. But what am I to do about this?'

'Do you know his address?'

'He said the Brummell Club would find him—pretty queer haunt, if I remember. To come to sneaking things like that! It's upset me frightfully.'

Holly looked at him lying on his back in bed. Catching her eyes on him, he said:

'But for you, old girl, I might have gone a holy mucker myself.'

'Oh, no, Val! You're too open-air. It's the indoor people who go really wrong.'

Val grinned.

'Something in that—the only exercise I ever saw that fellow take was in a punt. He used to bet like anything, but he didn't know a horse from a hedgehog. Well, Mother must put up with it, I can't do anything.'

Holly came up to his bed.

'Turn over, and I'll tuck you up.'

Getting into bed herself, she lay awake, thinking of the man who had gone a holy mucker, and the contempt on his face—lined, dark, well-featured, with prematurely greying hair, and prematurely faded rings round the irises of the eyes; of his clothes, too, so preternaturally preserved, and the worn, careful school tie. She felt she knew him. No moral sense, and ingrained contempt for those who had. Poor Val! He hadn't so much moral sense that he need be despised for it! And yet—! With a good many risky male instincts, Val had been a loyal comrade all these years. If in philosophic reach or æsthetic taste he was not advanced, if he knew more of horses than of poetry, was he any the worse? She sometimes thought he was the better. The horse didn't change shape or colour every five years and start reviling its predecessor. The horse was a constant, kept you from going too fast, and had a nose to stroke—more than you could say of a poet. They had, indeed, only one thing in common—a liking for sugar. Since the publication of her novel Holly had become member of the 1930 Club. Fleur had put her up, and whenever she came to town, she studied modernity there. Modernity was nothing but speed! People who blamed it might as well blame telephone, wireless, flying machine, and quick lunch counter. Beneath that top-dressing of speed, modernity was old. Women had worn fewer clothes when Jane Austen began to write. Drawers—the historians said—were only nineteenth-century productions. And take modern talk! After South Africa the speed of it certainly took one's wind away; but the thoughts expressed were much of her own thoughts as a girl, cut into breathless lengths, by car and telephone bell. Take modern courtships! They resulted in the same thing as under George the Second, but took longer to reach it, owing to the motor-cycle and the standing lunch. Take modern philosophy! People had no less real philosophy than Martin Tupper or Izaak Walton; only, unlike those celebrated ancients, they had no time to formulate it. As to a future life—modernity lived in hope, and not too much of that, as everyone had done, from immemorial time. In fact, as a novelist naturally would. Holly jumped to conslusions. Scratch—she thought—the best of modern youth, and you would find Charles James Fox and Perdita in golf sweaters! A steady sound retrieved her thoughts. Val was asleep. How long and dark his eyelashes still were, but his mouth was open!

'Val,' she said, very softly; 'Val! Don't snore, dear!' . . .

A snuff-box may be precious, not so much for its enamel, its period, and its little brilliants, as because it has belonged to one's father. Winifred, though her sense of property had been well proved by her retention of Montague Dartie 'for poorer', throughout so many years, did not possess her brother Soames's collecting instinct, nor, indeed, his taste in objects which George Forsyte had been the first to call of 'bigotry and virtue'. But the further Time removed her father James—a quarter of a century by now—the more she revered his memory. As some ancient general or philosopher, secured by age from competition, is acclaimed year by year a greater genius, so with James! His objection to change, his perfect domesticity, his power of saving money for his children, and his dread of not being told anything, were haloed for her more and more with every year that he spent underground. Her fashionable aspirations waning with the increase of adipose, the past waxed and became a very constellation of shining memories. The removal of this snuff-box—so tangible a reminder of James and Emily—tried her considerable equanimity more than anything that had happened to her for years. The thought that she had succumbed to the distinction of a voice on the telephone, caused her positive discomfort. With all her experience of distinction, she ought to have known better! She was, however, one of those women who, when a thing is done, admit the fact with a view to having it undone as soon as possible; and, having failed with Val, who merely said: 'Awfully sorry, Mother, but there it is—jolly bad luck!' she summoned her brother.

Soames was little less than appalled. He remembered seeing James buy the box at Jobson's for hardly more than one-tenth of what it would fetch now. Everything seemed futile if, in such a way, one could lose what had been nursed for forty years into so really magnificent a state of unearned increment. And the fellow who had taken it was of quite good family, or so his nephew said! Whether the honesty of the old Forsytes, in the atmosphere of which he had been brought up and turned out into the world, had been inherited or acquired—derived from their blood or their banks—he had never considered. It had been in their systems just as the proverb 'Honesty is the best policy' was in that of the private banking which then obtained. A slight reverie on banking was no uncommon affection of the mind in one who could recall the repercussion of 'Understart and Darnett's' failure, and the disappearance one by one of all the little, old banks with legendary names. These great modern affairs were good for credit and bad for novelists—run on a bank—there had been no better reading! Such monster concerns couldn't 'go broke', no matter what their clients did; but whether they made for honesty in the individual, Soames couldn't tell. The snuff-box was gone, however; and if Winifred didn't take care, she wouldn't get it back. How, precisely, she was to take care he could not at present see; but he should advise her to put it into the hands of somebody at once.

'But whose, Soames?'

'There's Scotland Yard,' answered Soames, gloomily. 'I believe they're very little good, except to make a fuss. There's that fellow I employed in the Ferrar case. He charges very high.'

'I shouldn't care so much,' said Winifred, 'if it hadn't belonged to the dear Dad.'

'Ruffians like that,' muttered Soames, 'oughtn't to be at large.'

'And to think,' said Winifred, 'that it was especially to see him that Val came to stay here.'

'Was it?' said Soames, gloomily. 'I suppose you're sure that fellow took it?'

'Quite. I'd had it out to polish only a quarter of an hour before. After he went, I came back into the room at once, to put it away, and it was gone. Val had been in the room the whole time.'

Soames dwelled for a moment, then rejected a doubt about his nephew, for, though connected by blood with that precious father of his, Montague Dartie, and a racing man to boot, he was half a Forsyte after all.'

'Well,' he said, 'shall I send you this man—his name's Becroft—always looks as if he'd over-shaved himself, but he's got a certain amount of *nous*. I should suggest his getting in touch with that fellow's club.'

'Suppose he's already sold the box?' said Winifred.

'Yesterday afternoon? Should doubt that; but it wants immediate handling. I'll see Becroft as I go away. Fleur's overdoing it, with this canteen of hers.'

'They say she's running it very well. I do think all these young women are so smart.'

'Quick enough,' grumbled Soames, 'but steady does it in the long run.'

At that phrase—a maxim never far away from the lips of the old Forsytes in her youthful days—Winifred blinked her rather too light eyelashes.

'That was always rather a bore, you know Soames. And in these days, if you're not quick, things move past you, so.'

Soames gathered his hat. 'That snuff-box will, if we don't look sharp.'

'Well, thank you, dear boy. I do hope we get it back. The dear Pater was so proud of it, and when he died it wasn't worth half what it is now.'

'Not a quarter,' said Soames, and the thought bored into him as he walked away. What was the use of having judgment, if anybody could come along and pocket the results! People sneered at property nowadays; but property was a proof of good judgment—it was one's *amour propre* half the time. And he thought of the *amour propre* Bosinney had stolen from him in those far-off days of trouble. Yes, even marriage—was an exercise of judgment—a pitting of yourself against other people. You 'spotted a winner', as they called it, or you didn't—Irene hadn't been 'a winner'—not exactly! Ah! And he had forgotten to ask Winifred about that young Jon Forsyte who had suddenly come back into the wind. But about this snuff-box! The Brummell Club was some sort of betting place, he had heard; full of gamblers, and people who did and sold things on commission, he shouldn't wonder. That was the vice of the day; that and the dole. Work? No! Sell things on commission—motor-cars, for choice. Brummell Club! Yes! This was the place! It had a window—he remembered. No harm, anyway, in asking if the fellow really belonged there! And entering, he enquired:

'Mr Stainford a member here?'

'Yes. Don't know if he's in. Mr Stainford been in, Bob?'

'Just come in.'

'Oh!' said Soames, rather taken aback.

'Gentleman to see him, Bob.'

A rather sinking sensation occurred within Soames.

'Come with me, sir.'

Soames took a deep breath, and his legs moved. In an alcove off the entrance—somewhat shabby and constricted—he could see a man lolling in an old armchair, smoking a cigarette through a holder. He had a little red book in one hand and a small pencil in the other, and held them as still as if he were about to jot down a conviction that he had not got. He wore a dark suit with little lines; his legs were crossed, and Soames noted that one foot in a worn brown shoe, treed and polished against age to the point of pathos, was slowly moving in a circle;

'Gemman to see you, sir.'

Soames now saw the face. Its eyebrows were lifted in a V reversed, its eyelids nearly covered its eyes. Together with the figure, it gave an impression of really remarkable languor. Thin to a degree, oval and pale, it seemed all shadow and slightly aquiline feature. The foot had become still, the whole affair still. Soames had the curious feeling of being in the presence of something arrogantly dead. Without time for thought, he began:

'Mr Stainford, I think? Don't disturb yourself. My name is Forsyte. You called at my sister's in Green Street yesterday afternoon.'

A slight contraction of the lines round that small mouth was followed by the words:

'Will you sit down?'

The eyes had opened now, and must once have been beautiful. They narrowed again, so that Soames could not help feeling that their owner had outlived everything except himself. He swallowed a qualm and resumed:

'I just wanted to ask you a question. During your call, did you by any chance happen to notice a Louis Quinze snuff-box on the table? It's–er–disappeared, and we want to fix the time of its loss.'

As a ghost might have smiled, so did the man in the chair; his eyes disappeared still further.

'Afraid not.'

With the thought: 'He's got it!' Soames went on:

'I'm sorry–the thing had virtue as an heirloom. It has obviously been stolen. I wanted to narrow down the issue. If you'd noticed it, we could have fixed the exact hour–on the little table just where you were sitting–blue enamel.'

The thin shoulders wriggled slightly, as though resenting this attempt to place responsibility on them.

'Sorry I can't help you; I noticed nothing but some rather good marqueterie.'

'Coolest card I ever saw,' thought Soames. 'Wonder if it's in his pocket.'

'The thing's unique,' he said slowly. 'The police won't have much difficulty. Well, thanks very much. I apologise for troubling you. You knew my nephew at college, I believe. Good-morning.'

'Good-morning.'

From the door Soames took a stealthy glance. The figure was perfectly motionless, the legs still crossed, and above the little red book the pale forehead was poised under the smooth grizzling hair. Nothing to be made of that! But the fellow had it, he was sure.

He went out and down to the Green Park with a most peculiar feeling. Sneak thief! A gentleman to come to that! The Elderson affair had been bad, but somehow not pitiful like this. The whitened seams of the excellent suit, the traversing creases in the once admirable shoes, the faded tie exactly tied, were evidences of form preserved, day by day, from hand to mouth. They afflicted Soames. That languid figure! What *did* a chap do when he had no money and couldn't exert himself to save his life? Incapable of shame–that was clear! He must talk to Winifred again. And, turning on his heel, Soames walked back towards Green Street. Debouching from the Park, he saw on the opposite side of Piccadilly the languid figure. It, too, was moving in the direction of Green

Street. Phew! He crossed over and followed. The chap had an air. He was
walking like someone who had come into the world from another age–an age
which set all its store on 'form'. He felt that 'this chap' would sooner part with
life itself than exhibit interest in anything. Form! Could you carry contempt for
emotion to such a pitch that you could no longer feel emotion? Could the lifted
eyebrow become more important to you than all the movements of the heart
and brain? Threadbare peacock's feathers walking, with no peacock inside! To
show feeling was perhaps the only thing of which that chap would be ashamed.
And, a little astonished at his own powers of diagnosis, Soames followed round
corner after corner, till he was actually in Green Street. By George! The chap
was going to Winifred's! 'I'll astonish his weak nerves!' thought Soames. And,
suddenly hastening, he said, rather breathlessly, on his sister's very doorstep:
    'Ah! Mr Stainford! Come to return the snuff-box?'
    With a sigh, and a slight stiffening of his cane on the pavement, the figure
turned. Soames felt a sudden compunction–as of one who has jumped out at a
child in the dark. The face, unmoved, with eyebrows still raised and lids still
lowered, was greenishly pale, like that of a man whose heart is affected; a faint
smile struggled on the lips. There was fully half a minute's silence, then the
pale lips spoke.
    'Depends. How much?'
    What little breath was in Soames's body left him. The impudence! And again
the lips moved.
    'You can have it for ten pounds.'
    'I can have it for nothing,' said Soames, 'by asking a policeman to step here.'
    The smile returned. 'You won't do that.'
    'Why not?'
    'Not done.'
    'Not done!' repeated Soames. 'Why on earth not? Most barefaced thing I
ever knew.'
    'Ten pounds,' said the lips. 'I want them badly.'
    Soames stood and stared. The thing was so sublime; the fellow as easy as if
asking for a match; not a flicker on a face which looked as if it might pass into
death at any moment. Great art! He perceived that it was not the slightest use to
indulge in moral utterance. The choice was between giving him the ten pounds
or calling a policeman. He looked up and down the street.
    'No–there isn't one in sight. I have the box here–ten pounds.'
    Soames began to stammer. The fellow was exercising on him a sort of
fascination. And suddenly the whole thing tickled him. It was rich!
    'Well!' he said, taking out two five-pound notes. 'For brass–!'
    A thin hand removed a slight protuberance from a side pocket.
    'Thanks very much. Here it is! Good-morning!'
    The fellow was moving away. He moved with the same incomparable
languor; he didn't look back. Soames stood with the snuff-box in his hand,
staring after him.
    'Well,' he said aloud, 'that's a specimen they can't produce now,' and he
rang Winifred's bell.

7

MICHAEL HAS QUALMS

During the eight days of the General Strike, Michael's somewhat hectic existence was relieved only by the hours spent in a House of Commons so occupied in meditating on what it could do, that it could do nothing. He had formed his own opinion of how to settle the matter, but as no one else had formed it, the result was inconspicuous. He watched, however, with a very deep satisfaction the stock of British character daily quoted higher at home and abroad; and with a certain uneasiness the stock of British intelligence becoming almost unsaleable. Mr Blythe's continual remark: 'What the bee aitch are they all about?' met with no small response in his soul. What *were* they about? He had one conversation with his father-in-law on the subject.

Over his egg Soames had said:

'Well, the Budget's dished.'

Over his marmalade Michael answered:

'Used you to have this sort of thing in your young days, sir?'

'No,' said Soames; 'no Trade Unionism then, to speak of.'

'People are saying this'll be the end of it. What's your opinion of the strike as a weapon, sir?'

'For the purposes of suicide, perfect. It's a wonder they haven't found that out long ago.'

'I rather agree, but what's the alternative?'

'Well,' said Soames, 'they've got the vote.'

'Yes, that's always said. But somehow Parliament seems to matter less and less; there's a directive sense in the country now, which really settles things before we get down to them in Parliament. Look at this strike, for instance; we can do nothing about it.'

'There must be government,' said Soames.

'Administration—of course. But all we seem able to do in Parliament is to discuss administration afterwards without much effect. The fact is, things swop around too quick for us nowadays.'

'Well,' said Soames, 'you know your own business best. Parliament always was a talking shop.' And with that unconscious quotation from Carlyle—an extravagant writer whom he curiously connected with revolution—he looked up at the Goya, and added: 'I shouldn't like to see Parliament done away with, though. Ever heard any more of that red-haired young woman?'

'Marjorie Ferrar? Oddly enough, I saw her yesterday in Whitehall. She told me she was driving for Downing Street.'

'She spoke to you?'

'Oh yes. No ill-feeling.'

'H'm!' said Soames. 'I don't understand this generation. Is she married?'

'No.'

'That chap MacGown had a lucky escape—not that he deserved it. Fleur doesn't miss her evenings?'

Michael did not answer. He did not know. Fleur and he were on such perfect terms that they had no real knowledge of each other's thoughts. Then, feeling his father-in-law's grey eye gimletting into him, he said hastily:

'Fleur's all right, sir.'

Soames nodded. 'Don't let her overdo this canteen.'

'She's thoroughly enjoying it–gives her head a chance.'

'Yes,' said Soames, 'she's got a good little head, when she doesn't lose it.' He seemed again to consult the Goya, and added:

'By the way, that young Jon Forsyte is over here–they tell me–staying at Green Street, and stoking an engine or something. A boy-and-girl affair; but I thought you ought to know.'

'Oh!' said Michael, 'thanks. I hadn't heard.'

'I don't suppose she's heard, either,' said Soames guardedly; 'I told them not to tell her. D'you remember, in America, up at Mount Vernon, when I was taken ill?'

'Yes, sir; very well.'

'Well, I wasn't. Fact is, I saw that young man and his wife talking to you on the stairs. Thought it better that Fleur shouldn't run up against them. These things are very silly, but you never can tell.'

'No,' said Michael dryly; 'you never can tell. I remember liking the look of him a good deal.'

'H'm!' muttered Soames. 'He's the son of his father, I expect.'

And, from the expression on his face, Michael formed the notion that this was a doubtful advantage.

No more was said, because of Soames's lifelong conviction that one did not say any more than one need say; and of Michael's prejudice against discussing Fleur seriously, even with her father. She had seemed to him quite happy lately. After five and a half years of marriage, he was sure that mentally Fleur liked him, that physically she had no objection to him, and that a man was not sensible if he expected much more. She consistently declined, of course, to duplicate Kit, but only because she did not want to be put out of action again for months at a time. The more active, the happier she was–over this canteen, for instance she was in her glory. If, indeed, he had realised that Jon Forsyte was being fed there, Michael would have been troubled; as it was, the news of the young man's reappearance in England made no great impression. The country held the field of one's attention those strenuous days. The multiple evidence of patriotism exhilarated him–undergraduates at the docks, young women driving cars, shopfolk walking cheerfully to their work, the swarm of 'specials', the general 'carrying-on'. Even the strikers were good-humoured. A secret conviction of his own concerning England was being reinforced day by day, in refutation of the pessimists. And there was no place so un-English at the moment, he felt, as the House of Commons, where people had nothing to do but pull long faces and talk over 'the situation'.

The news of the General Strike's collapse caught him as he was going home after driving Fleur to the canteen. A fizz and bustle in the streets, and the words: 'Strike Over' scrawled extempore at street corners, preceded the 'End of the Strike–Official' of the hurrying newsvendors. Michael stopped his car against the kerb and bought a news-sheet. There it was! For a minute he sat motionless with a choky feeling, such as he had felt when the news of the Armistice came through. A sword lifted from over the head of England! A source of pleasure to her enemies dried up! People passed and passed him, each with a news-sheet, or a look in the eye. They were taking it almost as soberly as they had taken the strike itself. 'Good old England! We're a great people when we're up against it!' he thought, driving his car slowly on into Trafalgar Square. A group of men, who had obviously been strikers, stood leaning against the parapet. He tried to read their faces. Glad, sorry, ashamed, resentful, relieved? For the life of him he could not tell. Some defensive joke seemed going the round of them.

'No wonder we're a puzzle to foreigners!' thought Michael. The least understood people in the world!'

He moved on slowly round the square, into Whitehall. Here were some slight evidences of feeling. The block was thick around the Cenotaph and the entrance to Downing Street; and little cheers kept breaking out. A 'special' was escorting a lame man across the street. As he came back, Michael saw his face. Why, it was Uncle Hilary! His mother's youngest brother, Hilary Charwell, Vicar of St Augustine's-in-the-Meads.

'Hallo, Michael!'

'You a "special", Uncle Hilary? Where's your cloth?'

'My dear! Are you one of those who think the Church debarred from mundane pleasure? You're not getting old-fashioned, Michael?'

Michael grinned. He had a real affection for Uncle Hilary, based on admiration for his thin, long face, so creased and humorous, on boyish recollection of a jolly uncle, on a suspicion that in Hilary Charwell had been lost a Polar explorer, or other sort of first-rate adventurer.

'That reminds me, Michael; when are you coming round to see us? I've got a topping scheme for airing "The Meads".'

'Ah!' said Michael; 'overcrowding's at the bottom of everything, even this strike.'

'Right you are, my son. Come along, then, as soon as you can. You fellows in Parliament ought always to see things at first hand. You suffer from auto-intoxication in that House. And now pass on, young man, you're impeding the traffic.'

Michael passed on, grinning. Good old Uncle Hilary! Humanising religion, and living dangerously—had climbed all the worst peaks in Europe; no sense of his own importance and a real sense of humour. Quite the best type of Englishman! They had tried to make him a dignitary, but he had jibbed at the gaiters and hat-ropes. He was what they called a 'live wire', and often committed the most dreadful indiscretions; but everybody liked him, even his own wife. Michael dwelt for a moment on his Aunt May. Forty—he supposed—with three children and fourteen hundred things to attend to every day; shingled, and cheerful as a sandboy. Nice-looking woman, Aunt May!

Having garaged his car, he remembered that he had not lunched. It was three o'clock. Munching a biscuit, he drank a glass of sherry, and walked over to the House of Commons. He found it humming in anticipation of a statement. Sitting back, with his legs stretched out, he had qualms. What things had been done in here! The abolitions of Slavery and of Child Labour, the Married Woman's Property Act, Repeal of the Corn Laws; but could they be done nowadays? And if not—was it a life? He had said to Fleur that you couldn't change your vocation twice and survive. But did he want to survive? Failing Foggartism—and Foggartism hadn't failed only because it hadn't started—what did he really care about?

Leaving the world better than he found it? Sitting there, he couldn't help perceiving a certain vagueness about such an aspiration, even when confined to England. It was the aspiration of the House of Commons; but in the ebb and flow of Party, it didn't seem to make much progress. Better to fix on some definite bit of administrative work, stick to it, and get something done. Fleur wanted him to concentrate on Kenya for the Indians. Again rather remote, and having little to do with England. What definite work was most needed in connection with England? Education? Bunkered again! How tell what was the best direction into which to turn education? When they brought in State Education, for instance, they had thought the question settled. Now people were saying that State education had ruined the State. Emigration? Attractive, but negative. Revival of agriculture? Well, the two combined were Foggartism, and he knew by now that nothing but bitter hardship would teach those lessons; you might talk till you were blue in the face without convincing anyone but yourself.

What then?

'I've got a topping scheme for airing "The Meads".' 'The Meads' was one of the worst slum parishes in London. 'Clear the slums!' thought Michael; 'that's practical, anyway!' You could smell the slums, and feel them. They stank and bit and bred corruption. And yet the dwellers therein loved them; or at least preferred them to slums they knew not of! And slum-dwellers were such good sorts! Too bad to play at shuttlecock with them! He must have a talk with Uncle Hilary. Lots of vitality in England still—numbers of red-haired children! But the vitality got sooted as it grew up—like plants in a back garden. Slum clearance, smoke abolition, industrial peace, emigration, agriculture, and safety in the air! 'Them's my sentiments!' thought Michael. 'And if that isn't a large enough policy for any man, I'm—!'

He turned his face towards the statement, and thought of his uncle's words about this 'House'. Were they all really in a state of auto-intoxication here—continual slow poisoning of the tissues? All these chaps around him thought they were doing things. And he looked at the chaps. He knew most of them, and had great respect for many, but collectively he could not deny that they looked a bit dazed. His neighbour to the right was showing his front teeth in an asphyxiated smile. 'Really,' he thought; 'it's heroic how we all keep awake day after day!'

8

SECRET

It would not have been natural that Fleur should rejoice in the collapse of the General Strike. A national outlook over such a matter was hardly in her character. Her canteen was completing the re-establishment in her of the social confidence which the Majorie Ferrar affair had so severely shaken; and to be thoroughly busy with practical matters suited her. Recruited by Norah Curfew, by herself, Michael, and his Aunt Lady Alison Charwell, she had a first-rate crew of helpers of all ages, most of them in Society. They worked in the manner popularly attributed to negroes; they craned at nothing—not even cockroaches. They got up at, or stayed up to, all hours. They were never cross and always cheery. In a word, they seemed inspired. The differences they had made in the appearance of the railway's culinary premises was startling to the Company. Fleur herself was 'on the bridge' all the time. On her devolved the greasing of the official wheels, the snipping off of red tape in numberless telephonic duels, and the bearding of the managerial face. She had even opened her father's pocket to supplement the shortcomings she encountered. The volunteers were fed to repletion, and–on Michael's inspiration–she had undermined the pickets with surreptitious coffee dashed with rum, at odd hours of their wearisome vigils. Her provisioning car, entrusted to Holly, ran the blockade, by leaving and arriving, as though Harridge's, whence she drew her supplies, were the last place in its thoughts.

'Let us give the strikers,' said Michael, 'every possible excuse to wink the other eye.'

The canteen, in fact, was an unqualified success. She had not seen Jon again, but she lived in that peculiar mixture of fear and hope which signifies a real interest in life. On the Friday Holly announced to her that Jon's wife had arrived–might she bring her down next morning?

'Oh! yes,' said Fleur. 'What is she like?'

'Attractive–with eyes like a water-nymph's, or so Jon thinks; but it's quite the best type of water-nymph.'

'M-m!' said Fleur.

She was checking a list on the telephone next day when Holly brought Anne. About Fleur's own height, straight and slim, darker in the hair, browner in complexion, browner in the eye (Fleur could see what Holly had meant by 'water-nymph'), her nose a little too sudden, her chin pointed and her teeth very white, her successor stood. Did she know that Jon and she–?

And stretching out her free hand, Fleur said:

'I think it's awfully sporting of you as an American. How's your brother Francis?'

The hand she squeezed was brown, dry, warm; the voice she heard only faintly American, as if Jon had been at it.

'You were just too good to Francis. He always talks of you. If it hadn't been for you–'

'That's nothing. Excuse me. . . . Ye-es? . . . No! If the Princess comes, ask her to be good enough to come when they're feeding. Yes–yes–thank you! To-morrow? Certainly. . . . Did you have a good crossing?'

'Frightful! I was glad Jon wasn't with me. I do so hate being green, don't you?'

'I never am,' said Fleur.

That girl had Jon to bend above her when she was green! Pretty? Yes. The browned face was very alive–rather like Francis Wilmot's, but with those enticing eyes, much more eager. What was it about those eyes that made them so unusual and attractive?–surely the suspicion of a squint! She had a way of standing, too–a trick of the neck, the head was beautifully poised. Lovely clothes, of course! Fleur's glance swept swiftly down to calves and ankles. Not thick, not crooked! No luck!

'I think it's just wonderful of you to let me come and help.'

'Not a bit. Holly will put you wise.'

'That sounds nice and homey.'

'Oh! We all use your expressions now. Will you take her provisioning, Holly?'

When the girl had gone, under Holly's wing, Fleur bit her lip. By the uncomplicated glance of Jon's wife she guessed that Jon had not told her. How awfully young! Fleur felt suddenly as if she herself had never had a youth. Ah! If Jon had not been caught away from her! Her bitten lip quivered, and she buried it in the mouthpiece of the telephone.

Whenever again – three or four times – before the canteen was closed, she saw the girl, she forced herself to be cordial. Instinctively she felt that she must shut no doors on life just now. What Jon's reappearance meant to her she could not yet tell; but no one should put a finger this time in whatever pie she chose to make. She was mistress of her face and movements now, as she had never been when she and Jon were babes in the wood. With a warped pleasure she heard Holly's: 'Anne thinks you wonderful, Fleur!' No! Jon had not told his wife about her. It was like him, for the secret had not been his alone! But how long would that girl be left in ignorance? On the day the canteen closed she said to Holly:

'No one has told Jon's wife that he and I were once in love, I suppose?'

Holly shook her head.

'I'd rather they didn't, then.'

'Of course not, my dear. I'll see to it. The child's nice, I think.'

'Nice,' said Fleur, 'but not important.'

'You've got to allow for the utter strangeness of everything. Americans are generally important, sooner or later.'

'To themselves,' said Fleur, and saw Holly smile. Feeling that she had revealed a corner of her feelings, she smiled too.

'Well, so long as they get on. They do, I suppose?'

'My dear, I've hardly seen Jon, but I should say it's perfectly successful. Now the strike's over they're coming down to us at Wansdon.'

'Good! Well, this is the end of the old canteen. Let's powder our noses and get out; Father's waiting for me with the car. Can we drop you?'

'No, thanks; I'll walk.'

'What? The old *gêne*? Funny how hard things die!'

'Yes; when you're a Forsyte,' murmured Holly. 'You see, we don't show our feelings. It's airing them that kills feelings.'

'Ah!' said Fleur. 'Well, God bless you, as they say, and give Jon my love. I'd ask them to lunch, but you're off to Wansdon?'

'The day after to-morrow.'

In the little round mirror Fleur saw her face mask itself more thoroughly, and turned to the door.

'I *may* look in at Aunt Winifred's, if I've time. So long!'

Going down the stairs she thought: 'So it's air that kills feelings!'

Soames, in the car, was gazing at Riggs's back. The fellow was as lean as a rail.

'Finished with that?' he said to her.

'Yes, dear.'

'Good job, too. Wearing yourself to a shadow.'

'Why? Do I look thin, Dad?'

'No,' said Soames, 'no. That's your mother. But you can't keep on at that rate. Would you like some air? Into the Park, Riggs.'

Passing into that haven, he murmured:

'I remember when your grandmother drove here every day, regular as clockwork. People had habits then. Shall we stop and have a look at that

Memorial affair they made such a fuss about?'

'I've seen it, Dad.'

'So have I,' said Soames. 'Stunt sculpture! Now, that St Gaudens statue at Washington *was* something.' And he looked at her sidelong. Thank goodness she didn't know of the way he had fended her off from young Jon Forsyte over there. She must have heard by now that the fellow was in London, and staying at her aunt's, too! And now the strike was off, and normal railway services beginning again, he would be at a loose end! But perhaps he would go back to Paris; his mother was there still, he understood. It was on the tip of his tongue to ask. Instinct, however, potent only in his dealings with Fleur, stopped him. If she had seen the young man, she wouldn't tell him of it. She was looking somehow secret—or was that just imagination?

No! He couldn't see her thoughts. Good thing, perhaps! Who could afford to have his thoughts seen? The recesses, ramifications, excesses of thought! Only when sieved and filtered was thought fit for exposure. And again Soames looked sidelong at his daughter.

She was thinking, indeed, to purposes that would have upset him. How was she going to see Jon alone before he left for Wansdon? She could call to-morrow, of course, openly at Green Street, and probably *not* see him. She could ask him to lunch in South Square, but hardly without his wife or her own husband. There was, in fact, no way of seeing him alone except by accident. And she began trying to plan one. On the point of perceiving that the essence of an accident was that it could not be planned, she planned it. She would go to Green Street at nine in the morning to consult Holly on the canteen accounts. After such strenuous days Holly and Anne might surely be breakfasting in bed. Val had gone back to Wansdon, Aunt Winifred never got up! Jon *might* be alone! And she turned to Soames:

'Awfully sweet of you, Dad, to be airing me; I *am* enjoying it.'

'Like to get out and have a look at the ducks? The swans have got a brood at Mapledurham again this year.'

The swans! How well she remembered the six little grey destroyers following the old swans over the green-tinged water, that six-year-gone summer of her love! Crossing the grass down to the Serpentine, she felt a sort of creeping sweetness. But nobody—nobody should know of what went on inside her. Whatever happened—and, after all, most likely nothing would happen—she would save face this time—strongest motive in the world, as Michael said.

'Your grandfather used to bring me here when I was a shaver,' said her father's voice beside her. It did not add: 'And I used to bring that wife of mine when we were first married.' Irene! She had liked water and trees. She had liked all beauty, and she hadn't liked him!

'Eton jackets. Sixty years ago and more. Who'd have thought it then?'

'Who'd have thought what, Dad? That Eton jackets would still be in?'

'That chap—Tennyson, wasn't it—"The old order changeth, giving place to new." I can't see *you* in high necks and skirts down to your feet, to say nothing of bustles. Women then were defended up to the nines, but you knew just as much about them as you do now—and that's precious little.'

'I wonder. Do you think people's passions are what they used to be, Dad?'

Soames brooded into his hand. Now, why had she said that? He had once told her that a grand passion was a thing of the past, and she had replied that she had one. And suddenly he was back in steamy heat, redolent of earth and potted pelargonium, kicking a hot water-pipe in a greenhouse at Mapledurham.

Perhaps she'd been right; there was always a lot of human nature about.

'Passions!' he said. 'Well, you still read of people putting their heads under the gas. In old days they used to drown themselves. Let's go and have tea at that kiosk place.'

When they were seated, and the pigeons were enjoying his cake, he took a long look at her. She had her legs crossed–and very nice they were!–and just that difference in her body from the waist up, from so many young women he saw about. She didn't sit in a curve, but with a slight hollow in her back, giving the impression of backbone and a poise to her head and neck. She was shingled again–the custom had unexpected life–but, after all, her neck was remarkably white and round. Her face–short, with its firm rounded chin, very little powder and no rouge, with its dark-lashed white lids, clear-glancing hazel eyes, short, straight nose and broad low brow, with the chestnut hair over its ears, and its sensibly kissable mouth–really it was a credit!

'I should think,' he said, 'you'd be glad to have more time for Kit again. He's a rascal. What d'you think he asked me for yesterday–a hammer!'

'Yes; he's always breaking things up. I smack him as little as possible, but it's unavoidable at times–nobody else is allowed to. Mother got him used to it while we were away, so he looks on it as all in the day's work.'

'Children,' said Soames, 'are funny things. We weren't made such a fuss of when I was young.'

'Forgive me, Dad, but I think *you* make more fuss of him than anybody.'

'What?' said Soames, 'I?'

'You do exactly as he tells you. Did you give him the hammer?'

'Hadn't one–what should I carry hammers about for?'

Fleur laughed. 'No; but you take him so seriously. Michael takes him ironically.'

'The little chap's got a twinkle,' said Soames.

'Mercifully. Didn't you spoil *me*, Dad?'

Soames gaped at a pigeon.

'Can't tell,' he said. 'Do you feel spoiled?'

'When I want things, I want things.'

He knew that; but so long as she wanted the right things!

'And when I don't get them, I'm not safe.'

'Who says that?'

'No one ever says it, but I know it.'

H'm! What was she wanting now? Should he ask? And, as if attending to the crumbs on his lapel, he took 'a lunar'. That face of hers, whose eyes for a moment were off guard, was dark with some deep–he couldn't tell! Secret! That's what it was!

9

With the canteen accounts in her hand, Fleur stepped out between her tubbed bay trees. A quarter to nine by Big Ben! Twenty odd minutes to walk across the Green Park! She had drunk her coffee in bed to elude questions–and there, of course, was Dad with his nose glued to the dining-room window. She waved the accounts, and he withdrew his face as if they had flicked him. He was ever so good, but he shouldn't always be dusting her–she wasn't a piece of china!

She walked briskly. She had no honeysuckle sensations this morning, but felt hard and bright. If Jon had come back to England to stay, she must get him over. The sooner the better, without fuss! Passing the geraniums in front of Buckingham Palace, just out and highly scarlet, she felt her blood heating. Not walk so fast or she would arrive damp! The trees were far advanced; the Green Park, under breeze and sun, smelled of grass and leaves. Spring had not smelled so good for years. A longing for the country seized on Fleur. Grass and trees and water–her hours with Jon had been passed among them–one hour in this very Park, before he took her down to Robin Hill! Robin Hill had been sold to some peer or other, and she wished him joy of it–she knew its history as of some unlucky ship! That house had 'done in' her father, and Jon's father, yes–and his grandfather, she believed, to say nothing of herself. One would not be 'done in' again so easily! And, passing into Piccadilly, Fleur smiled at her green youth. In the early windows of the club, nicknamed by George Forsyte the 'Iseeum', no one of his compeers sat as yet, above the moving humours of the street, sipping from glass or cup, and puffing his conclusions out in smoke. Fleur could just remember him, her old Cousin George Forsyte, who used to sit there, fleshy and sardonic behind the curving panes; Cousin George, who had owned the 'White Monkey' up in Michael's study. Uncle Montague Dartie, too, whom she remembered because the only time she had seen him he had pinched her in a curving place, saying: 'What are little girls made of?' so that she had clapped her hands when she heard that he had broken his neck, soon after; a horrid man, with fat cheeks and a dark moustache, smelling of scent and cigars. Rounding the last corner, she felt breathless. Geraniums were in her aunt's window-boxes–but not the fuchsias yet. Was *their* room the one she herself used to have? And, taking her hand from her heart, she rang the bell.

'Ah! Smither, anybody down?'

'Only Mr Jon's down yet, Miss Fleur.'

Why did hearts wobble? Sickening–when one was perfectly cool!

'He'll do for the moment, Smither. Where is he?'

'Having breakfast, Miss Fleur.'

'All right; show me in. I don't mind having another cup myself.'

Under her breath, she declined the creaking noun who was preceding her to the dining-room: 'Smither: O Smither: Of a Smither: To a Smither: A Smither.' Silly!

'Mrs Michael Mont, Mr Jon. Shall I get you some fresh coffee, Miss Fleur?'

'No, thank you, Smither.' Stays creaked, the door was shut. Jon was standing up.

'Fleur!'

'Well, Jon?'

She could hold his hand and keep her pallor, though the blood was in *his* cheeks, no longer smudged.

'Did I feed you nicely?'

'Splendidly. How are you, Fleur? Not tired after all that?'

'Not a bit. How did you like stoking?'

'Fine! My engine-driver was a real brick. Anne will be so disappointed: she's having a lie-off.'

'She was quite a help. Nearly six years, Jon; you haven't changed much.'

'Nor you.'

'Oh! *I* have. Out of knowledge.'

'Well, I don't see it. Have you had breakfast?'

'Yes. Sit down and go on with yours. I came round to see Holly about some accounts. Is she in bed, too?'

'I expect so.'

'Well, I'll go up directly. How does England feel, Jon?'

'Topping. Can't leave it again. Anne says she doesn't mind.'

'Where are you going to settle?'

'Somewhere near Val and Holly, if we can get a place to grow things.'

'Still keen on growing things?'

'More than ever.'

'How's the poetry?'

'Pretty dud.'

Fleur quoted:

'"Voice in the night crying, down in the old sleeping Spanish city darkened under her white stars."'

'Good Lord! Do you remember that?'

'Yes.'

His eyes were as straight, his lashes as dark as ever.

'Would you like to meet Michael, Jon, and see my infant?'

'Rather!'

'When do you go down to Wansdon?'

'To-morrow or the day after.'

'Then, won't you both come and lunch to-morrow?'

'We'd love to.'

'Half-past one. Holly and Aunt Winifred, too. Is your mother still in Paris?'

'Yes. She thinks of settling there.'

'Well, Jon—things fall on their feet, don't they?'

'They do.'

'Shall I give you some more coffee? Aunt Winifred prides herself on her coffee.'

'Fleur, you do look splendid.'

'Thank you! Have you been down to see Robin Hill?'

'Not yet. Some potentate's got it now.'

'Does your—does Anne find things amusing here?'

'She's terribly impressed—says we're a nation of gentlemen. Did you ever think that?'

'Positively–no; comparatively–perhaps.'

'It all smells so good here.'

'The poet's nose. D'you remember our walk at Wansdon?'

'I remember everything, Fleur.'

'That's honest. So do I. It took me some time to remember that I'd forgotten. How long did it take you?'

'Still longer, I expect.'

'Well, Michael's the best male I know.'

'Anne's the best female.'

'How fortunate–isn't it? How old is she?'

'Twenty-one.'

'Just right for you. Even if we hadn't been star-crossed, I was always too old for you. God! Weren't we young fools?'

'I don't see that. It was natural–it was beautiful.'

'Still got ideals? Marmalade? It's Oxford.'

'Yes. They can't make marmalade out of Oxford.'

'Jon, your hair grows exactly as it used to. Have you noticed mine?'

'I've been trying to.'

'Don't you like it?'

'Not so much, quite; and yet–'

'You mean I shouldn't look well out of fashion. Very acute! You don't mind *her* being shingled, apparently.'

'It suits Anne.'

'Did her brother tell you much about me?'

'He said you had a lovely house; and nursed him like an angel.'

'Not like an angel; like a young woman of fashion. There's still a difference.'

'Anne was awfully grateful for that. She's told you?'

'Yes. But I'm afraid, between us, we sent Francis home rather cynical. Cynicism grows here; d'you notice it in me?'

'I think you put it on.'

'My dear! I take it off when I talk to you. You were always an innocent. Don't smile–you were! That's why you were well rid of me. Well, I never thought I should see you again.'

'Nor I. I'm sorry Anne's not down.'

'You've never told her about me.'

'How did you know that?'

'By the way she looks at me.'

'Why should I tell her?'

'No reason in the world. Let the dead past–It's fun to see you again, though. Shake hands. I'm going up to Holly now.'

Their hands joined over the marmalade on his plate.

'We're not children now, Jon. Till to-morrow, then! You'll like my house. *A rivederci!*'

Going up the stairs she thought with resolution about nothing.

'Can I come in Holly?'

'Fleur! My dear!'

That thin, rather sallow face, so charmingly intelligent, was propped against a pillow. Fleur had the feeling that, of all people, it was most difficult to keep one's thoughts from Holly.

'These accounts,' she said. 'I'm to see that official ass at ten. Did you order all these sides of bacon?'

The thin sallow hand took the accounts, and between the large grey eyes came a furrow.

'Nine? No—yes; that's right. Have you seen Jon?'

'Yes; he's the only early bird. Will you all come to lunch with us to-morrow?'

'If you think it'll be wise, Fleur.'

'I think it'll be pleasant.'

She met the search of the grey eyes steadily, and with secret anger. No one should see into her—no one should interfere!

'All right then, we'll expect you all four at one-thirty. I must run now.'

She did run; but since she really had no appointment with any 'official ass,' she went back into the Green Park and sat down.

So that was Jon—now! Terribly like Jon—then! His eyes deeper, his chin more obstinate—that perhaps was all the difference. He still had his sunny look; he still believed in things. He still—admired her. Ye-es! A little wind talked above her in a tree. The day was surprisingly fine—the first really fine day since Easter! What should she give them for lunch? How should she deal with Dad? He must not be there! To have perfect command of oneself was all very well; to have perfect command of one's father was not so easy. A pattern of leaves covered her short skirt, the sun warmed her knees; she crossed them and leaned back. Eve's first costume—a pattern of leaves. . . . 'Wise?' Holly had said. Who knew? Shrimp cocktails? No! English food. Pancakes—certainly! . . . To get rid of Dad, she must propose herself with Kit at Mapledurham for the day after; then he would go, to prepare for them. Her mother was still in France. The others would be gone to Wansdon. Nothing to wait for in town. A nice warm sun on her neck. A scent of grass—of honeysuckle! Oh! dear!

10

AFTER LUNCH

That the most pregnant function of human life is the meal, will be admitted by all who take part in these recurrent crises. The impossibility of getting down from table renders it the most formidable of human activities among people civilised to the point of swallowing not only their food but their feelings.

Such a conclusion at least was present to Fleur during that lunch. That her room was Spanish, reminded her that it was not with Jon she had spent her honeymoon in Spain. There had been a curious moment, too, before lunch; for, the first words Jon had spoken on seeing Michael, had been:

'Hallo! This is queer! Was Fleur with you that day at Mount Vernon?'

What was this? Had she been kept in the dark?

Then Michael had said:

'You remember, Fleur? The young Englishman I met at Mount Vernon.'

'"Ships that pass in the night!"' said Fleur.

Mount Vernon! So *they* had met there! And she had not!

'Mount Vernon is lovely. But you ought to see Richmond, Anne. We could go after lunch. You haven't been to Richmond for ages, I expect, Aunt Winifred. We could take Robin Hill on the way home, Jon.'

'Your old home, Jon? Oh! Do let's!'

At that moment she hated the girl's eager face at which Jon was looking.

'There's the potentate,' he said.

'Oh!' said Fleur, quickly, 'he's at Monte Carlo. I read it yesterday. Could *you* come, Michael?'

'Afraid I've got a Committee. And the car can only manage five.'

'It would be just too lovely!'

Oh! that American enthusiasm! It was comforting to hear her aunt's flat voice opining that it would be a nice little run—the chestnuts would be out in the Park.

Had Michael really a Committee? She often knew what Michael really had, she generally knew more or less what he was thinking, but now she did not seem to know. In telling him last night of this invitation to lunch, she had carefully obliterated the impression by an embrace warmer than usual—he must not get any nonsense into his head about Jon! When, too, to her father she had said:

'Couldn't Kit and I come down to you the day after to-morrow; but you'll want a day there first, I'm afraid, if Mother's not there,' how carefully she had listened to the tone of his reply:

'H'm! Ye-es! I'll go down to-morrow morning.'

Had he scented anything; had Michael scented anything? She turned to Jon.

'Well, Jon, what d'you think of my house?'

'It's very like you.'

'Is that a compliment?'

'To the house? Of course.'

'Francis didn't exaggerate then?'

'Not a bit.'

'You haven't seen Kit yet. We'll have him down. Coaker, please ask Nurse to bring Kit down, unless he's asleep. . . . He'll be three in July; quite a good walker already. It makes one frightfully old!'

The entrance of Kit and his silver dog caused a sort of cooing sound, speedily checked, for three of the women were of Forsyte stock, and the Forsytes did not coo. He stood there, blue and rather Dutch, with a slight frown and his hair bright, staring at the company.

'Come here, my son. This is Jon—your second cousin once removed.'

Kit advanced.

'S'all I bwing my 'orse in?'

'Horse, Kit. No; shake hands.'

The small hand went up; Jon's hand came down.

'You got dirty nails.'

She saw Jon flush, heard Anne's: 'Isn't he just too cunning?' and said:

'Kit, you're very rude. So would you have, if you'd been stoking an engine.'

'Yes, old man, I've been washing them ever since, but I can't get them clean.'

'Why?'

'It's got into the skin.'

'Le' me see.'

'Go and shake hands with your great-aunt, Kit.'

'No.'

'Dear little chap,' said Winifred. 'Such a bore, isn't it, Kit?'

'Very well, then, go out again, and get your manners, and bring them in.'

'All wight.'

His exit, closed in by the silver dog, was followed by a general laugh; Fleur said, softly:

'Little wretch–poor Jon!' And through her lashes she saw Jon give her a grateful look.

In this mid-May fine weather the view from Richmond Hill had all the width and leafy charm which had drawn so many Forsytes in phaetons and barouches, in hansom cabs and motor-cars from immemorial time, or at least from the days of George the Fourth. The winding river shone discreetly, far down there; and the trees of the encompassing landscape, though the oaks were still goldened, had just begun to have a brooding look; in July they would be heavy and blueish. Curiously, few houses showed among the trees and fields; very scanty evidence of man, within twelve miles of London! The spirit of an older England seemed to have fended jerry-builders from a prospect sacred to the ejaculations of four generations.

Of those five on the terrace Winifred best expressed that guarding spirit, with her:

'Really, it's a very pretty view!'

A view–a view! And yet a view was not what it had been when old Jolyon travelled the Alps with that knapsack of brown leather and square shape, still in his grandson Jon's possession; or Swithin above his greys, rolling his neck with consequence towards the lady by his side, had pointed with his whip down at the river and pouted: 'A pooty little view!' Or James, crouched over his long knees in some gondola, had examined the Grand Canal at Venice with doubting eyes, and muttered: 'They never told me the water was this colour!' Or Nicholas, taking his constitutional at Matlock, had opined that the gorge was the finest in England. No, a view was not what it had been! George Forsyte and Montague Dartie, with their backs to it, quizzically contemplating the Liberty ladies brought down to be fed, had started that rot; and now the young folk didn't use the expression, but just ejaculated: 'Christ!' or words to that effect.

But there was Anne, of course, like an American, with clasped hands, and:

'Isn't it too lovely, Jon? It's sort of romantic!'

And so to the Park, where Winifred chanted automatically at sight of the chestnuts, and every path and patch of fern and fallen tree drew from Holly or Jon some riding recollection.

'Look, Anne, that's where I threw myself off my pony as a kid when I lost my stirrup and got so bored with being bumped.'

Or: 'Look, Jon! Val and I had a race down that avenue. Oh! and there's the log we used to jump. Still there!'

And Anne was in ecstasies over the deer and the grass, so different from the American varieties.

To Fleur the Park meant nothing.

'Jon,' she said, suddenly, 'what are you going to do to get in at Robin Hill?'

'Tell the butler that I want to show my wife where I lived as a boy; and give him a couple of good reasons. I don't want to see the house, all new furniture and that.'

'Couldn't we go in at the bottom, through the coppice?' and her eyes added: 'As we did that day.'

'We might come on someone, and get turned back.'

The couple of good reasons secured their top entrance to the grounds; the 'family' was not 'in residence'.

Bosinney's masterpiece wore its mellowest aspect. The sun-blinds were down, for the sun was streaming on its front, past the old oak tree, where was now no swing. In Irene's rose-garden, which had replaced old Jolyon's fernery, buds were forming, but only one rose was out.

'"Rose, you Spaniard!"' Something clutched Fleur's heart. What was Jon thinking–what remembering, with those words and that frown? Just here she had sat between his father and his mother, believing that she and Jon would live here some day; together watch the roses bloom, the old oak drop its leaves; together say to their guests: 'Look! There's the grandstand at Epsom–see? Just above those poplars!'

And now she could not even walk beside him, who was playing guide to that girl, his wife! Beside her aunt she walked instead. Winifred was extremely intrigued. She had never yet seen this house, which Soames had built with the brains of young Bosinney; which Irene, with 'that unfortunate little affair of hers' had wrecked; this house where Old Uncle Jolyon and Cousin Jolyon had died; and Irene, so ironically, had lived and had this boy Jon–a nice boy, too; this house of Forsyte song and story. It was very distinguished and belonged to a peer now, which, since it had gone out of the family, seemed suitable. In the walled fruit-garden, she said to Fleur:

'Your grandfather came down here once, to see how it was getting on. I remember his saying: "It'll cost a pretty penny to keep up." And I should think it does. But it was a pity to sell it. Irene's doing, of course! She never cared for the family. Now, if only–' But she stopped short of the words: 'you and Jon had made a match of it.'

'What on earth would Jon have done, Auntie, with a great place like this so near London? He's a poet.'

'Yes,' murmured Winifred–not very quick, because in her youth quickness had not been fashionable: 'There's too much glass, perhaps.' And they went down through the meadow.

The coppice! Still there at the bottom of the field! But Fleur lingered now, stood by the fallen log, waited till she could say:

'Listen! The cuckoo, Jon!'

The cuckoo's song, and the sight of bluebells under the larch trees! Beside her Jon stood still! Yes, and the spring stood still! There went the song–over and over!

'It was *here* we came on your mother, Jon, and our stars were crossed. Oh, Jon!'

Could so short a sound mean so much, say so much, be so startling? His face! She jumped on to the log at once.

'No ghosts, my dear!'

And, with a start, Jon looked up at her.

She put her hands on his shoulders and jumped down. And among the bluebells they went on. And the bird sang after them.

'That bird repeats himself,' said Fleur.

II

PERAMBULATION

The instinct in regard to his daughter, which by now formed part of his protective covering against the machinations of Fate, had warned Soames, the day before, that Fleur was up to something when she went out while he was having breakfast. Seen through the window waving papers at him, she had an air of unreality, or at least an appearance of not telling him anything. As something not quite genuine in the voice warns a dog that he is about to be left, so was Soames warned by the ostentation of those papers. He finished his breakfast, therefore, too abruptly for one constitutionally given to marmalade, and set forth to Green Street. Since that young fellow Jon was staying there, this fashionable locality was the seat of any reasonable uneasiness. If, moreover, there was a place in the world where Soames could still unbutton his soul, it was his sister Winifred's drawing-room, on which in 1879 he himself had impressed so deeply the personality of Louis Quinze that, in spite of jazz and Winifred's desire to be in the heavier modern fashion, that monarch's incurable levity was still to be observed.

Taking a somewhat circuitous course and looking in at the Connoisseurs' Club on the way, Soames did not arrive until after Fleur's departure. The first remark from Smither confirmed the uneasiness which had taken him forth.

'Mr Soames! Oh! What a pity – Miss Fleur's just gone! And nobody down yet but Mr Jon.'

'Oh!' said Soames. 'Did she see him?'

'Yes, sir. He's in the dining-room, if you'd like to go in.'

Soames shook his head.

'How long are they staying, Smither?'

'Well, I did hear Mrs Val say they were all going back to Wansdon the day after to-morrow. We shall be all alone again in case you were thinking of coming to us, Mr Soames.'

Again Soames shook his head. 'Too busy,' he said.

'What a beautiful young lady Miss Fleur 'as grown, to be sure; such a colour she 'ad this morning!'

Soames gave vent to an indeterminate sound. The news was not to his liking, but he could hardly say so in front of an institution. One could never tell how much Smither knew. She had creaked her way through pretty well every family secret in her time, from the days when his own matrimonial relations supplied Timothy's with more than all the gossip it required. Yes, and were not his own matrimonial relations, twice-laid, still supplying the raw material? Curiously sinister it seemed to him just then, that the son of his supplanter Jolyon should be here in this house, the nearest counterfeit of that old homing centre of the Forsytes, Timothy's in the Bayswater Road. What perversity there was in things! And, repeating the indeterminate sound, he said:

'By the way, I suppose that Mr Stainford never came here again?'

'Oh, yes, Mr Soames; he called yesterday to see Mr Val; but Mr Val was gone.'

'He did—did he?' said Soames, round-eyed. 'What did he take this time?'

'Oh! Of course I knew better than to let him in.'

'You didn't give him Mr Val's address in the country?'

'Oh, no, sir; he knew it.'

'Deuce he did!'

'Shall I tell the mistress you're here, Mr Soames? She must be nearly down by now.'

'No; don't disturb her.'

'I'm that sorry, sir; it's always such a pleasure to her to see you.'

Old Smither bridling! A good soul! No such domestics nowadays! And, putting on his hat, Soames touched its brim, murmuring:

'Well, good-bye, Smither. Give her my love!' and went out.

'So!' he thought, 'Fleur's seen that boy!' The whole thing would begin over again! He had known it! And, very slowly, with his hat rather over his eyes, he made for Hyde Park Corner. This was for him a moment in deep waters, when the heart must be hardened to this dangerous decision or to that. With the tendency for riding past the hounds inherited from his father James in all matters which threatened the main securities of life, Soames rushed on in thought to the ruin of his daughter's future, wherein so sacredly was embalmed his own.

'Such a colour she 'ad this morning!' When she waved those papers at him, she was pale enough—too pale! A confounded chance! Breakfast time, too—worst time in the day—most intimate! His naturally realistic nature apprehended all the suggestions that lay in breakfast. Those who breakfasted alone together slept together as often as not. Putting things into her head! Yes; and they were not boy and girl now! Well, it all depended on what their feelings were, if they still had any. And who was to know? Who, in heaven's name, was to know? Automatically he had begun to encompass the Artillery Memorial. A great white thing which he had never yet taken in properly, and didn't know that he wanted to. Yet somehow it was very real, and suited to his mood—faced things; nothing high-flown about that gun—short, barking brute of a thing; or those dark men—drawn and devoted under their steel hats! Nothing pretty-pretty about that memorial—no angels' wings there! No Georges and no dragons, nor horses on the prance; no panoply, and no *panache*! There it 'sot'—as they used to say—squatted like a great white toad on the nation's life. Concreted thunder. Not an illusion about it! Good thing to look at once a day, and see what you'd got to avoid. 'I'd like to rub the noses of those Crown Princes and military cocks-o'-the-walk on it,' thought Soames, 'with their—what was it?—"fresh and merry wars!"' And, crossing the road in the sunshine, he passed into the Park, moving towards Knightsbridge.

But about Fleur? Was he going to take the bull by the horns, or to lie low? Must be one thing or the other. He walked rapidly now, concentrated in face and movement, stalking as it were his own thoughts with a view to finality. He passed out at Knightsbridge, and after unseeing scrutiny of two or three small shops where in his time he had picked up many a bargain, for himself or shopman, he edged past Tattersall's. That hung on—they still sold horses there, he believed! Horses had never been in his line, but he had not lived in Montpelier Square without knowing the *habitués* of Tattersall's by sight. Like everything else that was crusted, they'd be pulling it down before long, he shouldn't wonder, and putting up some motor place or cinema!

Suppose he talked to Michael? No! Worse than useless. Besides, he couldn't talk about Fleur and that boy to anyone—thereby hung too long a tale; and the tale was his own. Montpelier Square! He had turned into the very place, whether by design he hardly knew. It hadn't changed—but was all slicked up since he was last there, soon after the war. Builders and decorators must have done well lately—about the only people who had. He walked along the right side of the narrow square, where he had known turbulence and tragedy. There the house was, looking much as it used to, not quite so neat, and a little more florid. Why had he ever married that woman? What had made him so set on it? Well! She had done her best to deter him. But—God!—how he had wanted her! To this day he could recognise that. And at first—at first, he had thought, and perhaps she had thought—but who could tell?—*he* never could! And then slowly—or was it quickly?—the end; a ghastly business! He stood still by the square railings, and stared at the doorway that had been his own, as if from its green paint and its brass number he might receive inspiration how to choke love in his own daughter for the son of his own wife—yes, how to choke it before it spread and choked her?

And as, on those days and nights of his first married life, returning home, he had sought in vain for inspiration how to awaken love, so now no inspiration came to tell him how to strangle love. And, doggedly, he turned out of the little square.

In a way it was ridiculous to be fussing about the matter; for, after all, Michael was a good young fellow, and her marriage far from unhappy, so far as he could see. As for young Jon, presumably he had married for love; there hadn't been anything else to marry for, he believed—unless he had been misinformed, the girl and her brother had been museum pieces, two Americans without money to speak of. And yet—there was the moon, and he could not forget how Fleur had always wanted it. A desire to have what she hadn't yet got was her leading characteristic. Impossible, too, to blink his memory of her, six years ago—to forget her body crumpled and crushed into the sofa in the dark that night when he came back from Robin Hill and broke the news to her. Perusing with his mind the record, since, Soames had an acute and comfortless feeling that she had, as it were, been marking time, that all her fluttering activities, even the production of Kit, had been in the nature of a makeshift. Like the age to which she belonged, she had been lifting her feet up and down without getting anywhere, because she didn't know where she wanted to get. And yet, of late, since she had been round the world, he had seemed to notice something quieter and more solid in her conduct, as if settled purposes were pushing up, and she were coming to terms at last with her daily life. Look, for instance, at the way she had tackled this canteen! And, turning his face homeward, Soames had a vision of a common not far from Mapledurham, where some fool had started a fire which had burned the gorse, and of the grass pushing up, almost impudently green and young, through the charred embers of that conflagration. Rather like things generally, when you thought of it! The war had burned them all out, but things, yes, and people, too—one noticed—were beginning to sprout a bit, as if they felt again it might be worth while. Why, even he himself had regained some of his old connoisseur's desire to have nice things! It all depended on what you saw ahead, on whether you could eat and drink because to-morrow you didn't die. With this Dawes Settlement and Locarno business and the General Strike broken, there might even be another long calm, like the Victorian, which would make things possible. He was seventy-one, but one could always dwell on Timothy, who had lived to be a hundred, fixed star in shifting skies. And Fleur–only twenty four–might almost out-live the century if she, or, rather the century, took care and bottled up its unruly passions, its disordered longings, and all that silly rushing along to nowhere in particular. If they steadied down, the age might yet become a golden, or a platinum, age at any rate. Even he might live to see the income tax at half a crown. 'No,' he thought, confused between his daughter and the age; 'she mustn't go throwing her cap over the windmill. It's short-sighted!' And, his blood warmed by perambulation, he became convinced that he would not speak to her, but lie low, and trust to that common sense, of which she surely had her share–oh, yes! 'Just keep my eyes open, and speak to no one,' he thought; 'least said, soonest mended.'

He had come again to the Artillery Memorial; and for the second time he moved around it. No! A bit of a blot–it seemed to him, now–so literal and heavy! Would that great white thing help Consols to rise? Some thing with wings might, after all, have been preferable. Some encouragement to people to take shares or go into domestic service; help, in fact, to make life liveable, instead of reminding them all the time that they had already once been blown to perdition and might again be. Those Artillery fellows–he had read somewhere–loved their guns, and wanted to be reminded of them. But did anybody else love their guns, or want reminder? Not those Artillery fellows would look at this every day outside St George's Hospital, but Tom, Dick, Harry, Peter, Gladys, Joan and Marjorie. 'Mistake!' thought Soames; 'and a pretty heavy one. Something sedative, statue of Vulcan, or somebody on a horse; that's what's wanted!' And remembering George III on a horse, he smiled grimly. Anyway, there the thing was, and would have to stay! But it was high time artists went back to nymphs and dolphins, and other evidences of a settled life.

When at lunch Fleur suggested that he would want a day's law at Mapledurham before she and Kit came down, he again felt there was something behind; but, relieved enough at getting her, he let 'the sleeping dog' lie; nor did he mention his visit to Green Street.

'The weather looks settled,' he said. 'You want some sun after that canteen. They talk about these ultra-violet rays. Plain sunshine used to be good enough. The doctors'll be finding something extra-pink before long. If they'd only let things alone!'

'Darling, it amuses them.'

'Re-discovering what our grandmothers knew so well that we've forgotten 'em, and calling 'em by fresh names! A thing isn't any more wholesome to eat for instance, because they've invented the word "vitamin". Why, your grandfather ate an orange every day of his life, because his old doctor told him to, at the beginning of the last century. Vitamins! Don't you let Kit get faddy about his food. It's a long time before he'll go to school–that's one comfort. School feeding!'

'Did they feed you so badly, Dad?'

'Badly! How we grew up, I don't know. We ate our principal meal in twenty minutes, and were playing football ten minutes after. But nobody thought about digestion, then.'

'Isn't that an argument for thinking of it now?'

'A good digestion,' said Soames, 'is the whole secret of life.' And he looked at his daughter. Thank God! *She* wasn't peaky. So far as he knew, her digestion was excellent. She might fancy herself in love, or out of it; but so long as she was unconscious of her digestion, she would come through. 'The thing is to walk as much as you can, in these days of cars,' he added.

'Yes,' said Fleur, 'I had a nice walk this morning.'

Was she challenging him over her apple charlotte? If so, he wasn't going to rise.

'So did I,' he said. 'I went all about. We'll have some golf down there.'

She looked at him for a second, then said a surprising thing:

'Yes, I believe I'm getting middle-aged enough for golf.'

Now what did she mean by that?

12

PRIVATE FEELINGS

On the day of the lunch party and the drive to Robin Hill, Michael really had a Committee, but he also had his private feelings and wanted to get on terms with them. There are natures in which discovery of what threatens happiness perverts to prejudice all judgment of the disturbing object. Michael's was not such. He had taken a fancy to the young Englishman met at the home of that old American George Washington, partly, indeed, because he *was* English; and, seeing him now seated next to Fleur, second cousin and first love–he was unable to revise the verdict. The boy had a nice face, and was better-looking than himself; he had attractive hair, a strong chin, straight eyes, and a modest bearing; there was no sense in blinking facts like those. The Free Trade in love, which obtained amongst pleasant people, forbade Michael to apply the cruder principles of Protection even in thoughts. Fortunately, the boy was married to this slim and attractive girl, who looked at one–as Mrs Val had put it to him–like a guaranteed-pure water-nymph! Michael's private feelings were therefore more concerned with Fleur than with the young man himself. But hers was a difficult face to read, a twisting brain to follow, a heart hard to get at; and–was Jon Forsyte the reason why? He remembered how in Cork Street this boy's elderly half-sister–that fly-away little lady, June Forsyte–had blurted out to him that Fleur ought to have married her young brother–first he had ever heard of it. How painfully it had affected him with its intimation that he played but second fiddle in the life of his beloved! He remembered, too, some cautious and cautionary allusions by 'old Forsyte'. Coming from that model of secrecy and suppressed feelings, they, too, had made on Michael a deep and lasting impression reinforced by his own failure to get at the bottom of Fleur's heart. He went to his Committee with but half his mind on public matters. What had nipped that early love affair in the bud and given him his chance? Not sudden dislike, lack of health, or lack of money–not relationship, for Mrs Val Dartie had married her second cousin apparently with everyone's consent. Michael, it will be seen, had remained quite ignorant of the skeleton in Soames's cupboard. Such Forsytes as he had met, reticent about family affairs, had never mentioned it; and Fleur had never spoken of her first love, much less of the reason why it had come to naught. Yet, there must have been some reason; and it was idle to try and understand her present feelings without knowing what it was!

His Committee was on birth control in connection with the Ministry of Health; and, while listening to arguments why he should not support for other people what he practised himself, he was visited by an idea. Why not go and ask June Forsyte? He could find her in the telephone book–there could be but one with such a name.

'What do *you* say, Mont?'

'Well, sir, if we won't export children to the Colonies or speed up emigration somehow, there's nothing for it but birth control. In the upper and middle classes we're doing it all the time, and blinking the moral side, if there is one; and I really don't see how we can insist on a moral side for those who haven't a quarter of our excuse for having lots of children.'

'My dear Mont,' said the chairman, with a grin, 'aren't you cutting there at the basis of all privilege?'

'Very probably,' said Michael, with an answering grin. 'I think, of course, that child emigration is much better, but nobody else does, apparently.'

Everybody knew that 'young Mont' had a 'bee in his bonnet' about child emigration, and there was little disposition to encourage it to buzz. And, since no one was more aware than Michael of being that crank in politics, one who thought you could not eat your cake and have it, he said no more. Presently, feeling that they would go round and round the mulberry bush for some time yet, and sit on the fence after, he excused himself and went away.

He found the address he wanted: 'Miss June Forsyte, Poplar House, Chiswick', and mounted a Hammersmith bus.

How fast things seemed coming back to the normal! Extraordinarily difficult to upset anything so vast, intricate, and elastic as a nation's life. The bus swung along among countless vehicles and pedestrian myriads, and Michael realised how firm were those two elements of stability in the modern state, the common need for eating, drinking, and getting about; and the fact that so many people could drive cars. 'Revolution?' he thought. 'There never was a time when it had less chance. Machinery's dead agin it.' Machinery belonged to the settled state of things, and every day saw its reinforcement. The unskilled multitude and the Communistic visionaries, their leaders, only had a chance now where machinery and means of communication were still undeveloped, as in Russia. Brains, ability and technical skill, were by nature on the side of capital and individual enterprise, and were gaining ever more power.

'Poplar House' took some finding, and, when found, was a little house supporting a large studio with a north light. It stood, behind two poplar trees, tall, white, like a ghost. A foreign woman opened to him. Yes. Miss Forsyte was in the studio with Mr Blade! Michael sent up his card, and waited in a draught, extremely ill at ease; for now that he was here he could not imagine why he had come. How to get the information he wanted without seeming to have come for it, passed his comprehension; for it was the sort of knowledge that could only be arrived at by crude questioning.

Finding that he was to go up, he went, perfecting his first lie. On entering the studio, a large room with green canvassed walls, pictures hung or stacked, the usual daïs, a top light half curtained, and some cats, he was conscious of a fluttering movement. A little light lady in flowing green, with short silver hair, had risen from a footstool, and was coming towards him.

'How do you do? You know Harold Blade, of course?'

The young man, at whose feet she had been sitting, rose and stood before Michael, square, somewhat lowering with a dun-coloured complexion and heavily charged eyes.

'You must know his wonderful Rafaelite work.'

'Oh yes!' said Michael, whose conscience was saying: 'Oh no!'

The young man said grimly: 'He doesn't know me from Adam.'

'No, really,' muttered Michael. 'But do tell me, why Rafaelite? I've always wanted to know.'

'Why?' exclaimed June. 'Because he's the only man who's giving us the old values; he's rediscovered them.'

'Forgive me, I'm such a dud in art matters – I thought the academicians were still in perspective!'

'*They!*' cried June, and Michael winced at the passion in the word. 'Oh, well – if you still believe in them –'

'But I don't,' said Michael.

'Harold is the only Rafaelite; people are grouping round him, of course, but he'll be the last, too. It's always like that. Great painters make a school, but the schools never amount to anything.'

Michael looked with added interest at the first and last Rafaelite. He did not like the face, but it had a certain epileptic quality.

'Might I look round? Does my father-in-law know your work, I wonder? He's a great collector, and always on the look-out.'

'Soames!' said June, and again Michael winced. 'He'll be collecting Harold when we're all dead. Look at that!'

Michael turned from the Rafaelite, who was shrugging his thick shoulders. He saw what was clearly a portrait of June. It was entirely recognisable, very smooth, all green and silver, with a suggestion of halo round the head.

'Pure primary line and colour – d'you think they'd hang *that* in the Academy?'

'Seems to me exactly what they would hang,' thought Michael, careful to keep the conclusion out of his face.

'I like the suggestion of a halo,' he murmured.

The Rafaelite uttered a short, sharp laugh.

'I'm going for a walk,' he said; 'I'll be in to supper. Good-bye!'

'Good-bye!' said Michael, with a certain relief.

'Of course,' said June when they were alone, 'he's the *only* person who could paint Fleur. He'd get her modern look so perfectly. Would she sit to him? With everybody against him, you know, he has *such* a struggle.'

'I'll ask her. But do tell me – why is everybody against him?'

'Because he's been through all these empty modern crazes, and come back to pure form and colour. They think he's a traitor, and call him academic. It's always the way when a man has the grit to fly against fashion and follow his own genius. I can see exactly what he'd do with Fleur. It would be a great chance for him, because he's very proud, and this would be a proper commission from Soames. Splendid for her, too, of course. She ought to jump at it – in ten years' time he'll be *the* man.'

Michael, who doubted if Fleur would 'jump at it', or Soames give the commission, replied cautiously: 'I'll sound her. . . . By the way, your sister Holly and your young brother and his wife were lunching with us to-day.'

'Oh!' said June, 'I haven't seen Jon yet.' And looking at Michael with her straight blue eyes, she added:

'Why did you come to see me?'

Under that challenging stare Michael's diplomacy wilted.

'Well,' he said, 'frankly, I want you to tell me why Fleur and your young brother came to an end with each other.'

'Sit down,' said June, and resting her pointed chin on her hand, she looked at him with eyes moving a little from side to side, as might a cat's.

'I'm glad you asked me straight out; I hate people who beat about the bush. Don't you know about his mother? She was Soames's first wife, of course.'

'Oh!' said Michael.

'Irene,' and, as she spoke the name, Michael was aware of something deep and primitive stirring in that little figure. 'Very beautiful–they didn't get on; she left him–and years later she married my father, and Soames divorced her. I mean Soames divorced her and she married my father. They had Jon. And then, when Jon and Fleur fell in love, Irene and my father were terribly upset, and so was Soames–at least, he ought to have been.'

'And then?' asked Michael, for she was silent.

'The children were told; and my father died in the middle of it all; and Jon sacrificed himself and took his mother away, and Fleur married you.'

So that was it! In spite of the short, sharp method of the telling, he could feel tragic human feeling heavy in the tale. Poor little devils!

'I always thought it was too bad,' said June suddenly. 'Irene ought to have put up with it. Only–only–' and she stared at Michael, 'they wouldn't have been happy. Fleur's too selfish. I expect she saw that.'

Michael raised an indignant voice.

'Yes,' said June; 'you're a good sort, I know–too good for her.'

'I'm not,' said Michael sharply.

'Oh yes, you are. She isn't bad, but she's a selfish little creature.'

'I wish you'd remember–'

'Sit down! Don't mind what I say. I only speak the truth, you know. Of course, it was all horrible; Soames and my father were first cousins. And those children were awfully in love.'

Again Michael was conscious of the deep and private feeling within the little figure; conscious, too, of something deep and private stirring within himself.

'Painful!' he said.

'I don't know,' June went on abruptly, 'I don't know; perhaps it was all for the best. You're happy, aren't you?'

With that pistol to his head, he stood and delivered.

'I am. But is she?'

The little green-and-silver figure straightened up. She caught his hand and gave it a squeeze. There was something almost terribly warm-hearted about the action, and Michael was touched. He had only seen her twice before!

'After all, Jon's married. What's his wife like?'

'Looks charming–nice, I think.'

'An American!' said June deeply. 'Well, Fleur's half French. I'm glad you've got a boy.'

Never had Michael known anyone whose words conveyed so much unintended potency of discomfort! Why was she glad he had a boy? Because it was an insurance–against what?

'Well,' he mumbled, 'I'm very glad to know at last what it was all about.'

'You ought to have been told before; but you don't know still. Nobody can know what family feuds and feelings are like, who hasn't had them. Though I was angry about those children, I admit that. You see, I was the first to back Irene against Soames in the old days. I wanted her to leave him at the beginning of everything. She had a beastly time; he was such a–such a slug about his precious rights, and no proper pride either. Fancy forcing yourself on a woman who didn't want you!'

'Ah!' Michael muttered. 'Fancy!'

'People in the 'eighties and 'nineties didn't understand how disgusting it was. Thank goodness, they do now!'

'Do they?' murmured Michael. 'I wonder!'

'Of course they do.'

Michael sat corrected.

'Things are much better in that way than they were–not nearly so stuffy and farmyardy. I wonder Fleur hasn't told you all about it.'

'She's never said a word.'

'Oh!'

That sound was as discomforting as any of her more elaborate remarks. Clearly she was thinking what he himself was thinking: that it had gone too deep with Fleur to be spoken of. He was not even sure that Fleur knew whether he had ever heard of her affair with Jon.

And, with a sudden shrinking from any more discomforting sounds, he rose. 'Thanks awfully for telling me. I must buzz off now, I'm afraid.'

'I shall come and see Fleur about sitting to Harold. It's too good a chance for him to miss. He simply must get commissions.'

'Of course!' said Michael; he could trust Fleur's powers of refusal better than his own.

'Good-bye, then!'

But when he got to the door and looked back at her standing alone in that large room, he felt a pang–she seemed so light, so small, so fly-away, with her silver hair and her little intent face–still young from misjudged enthusiasm. He had got something out of her, too, left nothing with her; and he had stirred up some private feeling of her past, some feeling as strong, perhaps stronger, than his own.

She looked dashed lonely! He waved his hand to her.

Fleur had returned when he got home, and Michael realised suddenly that in calling on June Forsyte he had done a thing inexplicable, save in relation to her and Jon!

'I must write and ask that little lady not to mention it,' he thought. To let Fleur know that he had been fussing about her past would never do.

'Had a good time?' he said.

'Very. Young Anne reminds me of Francis, except for her eyes.'

'Yes; I liked the looks of those two when I saw them at Mount Vernon. That was a queer meeting, wasn't it?'

'The day father was unwell?'

He felt that she knew the meeting had been kept from her. If only he could talk to her freely; if only she would blurt out everything!

But all she said was: 'I feel at a bad loose end, Michael, without the canteen.'

13

To say that Soames preferred his house by the river when his wife was not there, would be a crude way of expressing a far from simple equation. He was glad to be still married to a handsome woman and very good housekeeper, who really could not help being French and twenty-five years younger than himself. But the fact was, that when she was away from him, he could see her good points so much better than when she was not. Though fond of mocking him in her French way, she had, he knew, lived into a certain regard for his comfort, and her own position as his wife. Affection? No, he did not suppose she had affection for him, but she liked her home, her bridge, her importance in the neighbourhood, and doing things about the house and garden. She was like a cat. And with money she was admirable–making it go further and buy more than most people. She was getting older, too, all the time, so that he had lost serious fear that she would overdo some friendship or other, and let him know it. That Prosper Profond business of six years ago, which had been such a squeak, had taught her discretion.

It had been quite unnecessary really for him to go down a day before Fleur's arrival; his household ran on wheels too well geared and greased. On his fifteen acres, with the new dairy and cows across the river, he grew everything now except flour, fish and meat of which he was but a sparing eater. Fifteen acres, if hardly 'land', represented a deal of produce. The establishment was, in fact, typical of countless residences of the unlanded well-to-do.

Soames had taste, and Annette, if anything, had more, especially in food, so that a better fed household could scarcely have been found.

In this bright weather, the leaves just full, the mayflower in bloom, bulbs not yet quite over, and the river re-learning its summer smile, the beauty of the prospect was not to be sneezed at. And Soames on his green lawn walked a little and thought of why gardeners seemed always on the move from one place to another. He couldn't seem to remember ever having seen an English gardener otherwise than about to work. That was, he supposed, why people so often had Scotch gardeners. Fleur's dog came out and joined him. The fellow was getting old, and did little but attack imaginary fleas. Soames was very particular about real fleas, and the animal was washed so often that his skin had become very thin–a golden brown retriever, so rare that he was always taken for a mongrel. The head gardener came by with a spud in his hand.

'Good-afternoon, sir.'

'Good-afternoon,' replied Soames. 'So the strike's over!'

'Yes, sir. If they'd attend to their business, it'd be better.'

'It would. How's your asparagus?'

'Well, I'm trying to make a third bed, but I can't get the extra labour.'

Soames gazed at his gardener, who had a narrow face, rather on one side, owing to the growth of flowers. 'What?' he said. 'When there are about a million and a half people out of employment?'

'And where they get to, I can't think,' said the gardener.

'Most of them,' said Soames, 'are playing instruments in the streets.'

'That's right, sir—my sister lives in London. I could get a boy, but I can't trust him.'

'Why don't you do it yourself?'

'Well, sir, I expect it'll come to that; but I don't want to let the garden down, you know.' And he moved the spud uneasily.

'What have you got that thing for? There isn't a weed about the place.'

The gardener smiled. 'It's something cruel,' he said, 'the way they spring up when you're not about.'

'Mrs Mont will be down to-morrow,' muttered Soames. 'I shall want some good flowers in the house.'

'Very little at this time of year, sir.'

'I never knew a time of year when there was much. You must stir your stumps and find something.'

'Very good, sir,' said the gardener, and walked away.

'Where's he going now?' thought Soames. 'I never knew such a chap. But they're all the same.' He supposed they did work some time or other; in the small hours, perhaps—precious small hours! Anyway, he had to pay 'em a pretty penny for it! And, noticing the dog's head on one side, he said:

'Want a walk?'

They went out of the gate together, away from the river. The birds were in varied song, and the cuckoos obstreperous.

They walked up to the bit of common land where there had been a conflagration in the exceptionally fine Easter weather. From there one could look down at the river winding among poplars and willows. The prospect was something like that in a long river landscape by Daubigny which he had seen in an American's private collection—a very fine landscape, he never remembered seeing a finer. He could mark the smoke from his own kitchen chimney, and was more pleased than he would have been marking the smoke from any other. He had missed it a lot last year—all those months, mostly hot—touring the world with Fleur from one unhomelike place to another. Young Michael's craze for emigration! Soames was Imperialist enough to see the point of it in theory; but in practice every place out of England seemed to him so raw, or so extravagant. An Englishman was entitled to the smoke of his own kitchen chimney. Look at the Ganges—monstrous great thing, compared with that winding silvery thread down there! The St Lawrence, the Hudson, the Pótomac—as he still called it in thought—had all pleased him, but, comparatively, they were sprawling pieces of water. And the people out there were a sprawling lot. They had to be, in those big places. He moved down from the common through a narrow bit of wood where rooks were in a state of some excitement. He knew little about the habits of birds, not detached enough from self for the study of creatures quite unconnected with him; but he supposed they would be holding a palaver about food—worm-currency would be depressed, or there had been some inflation or other—fussy as the French over their wretched franc. Emerging, he came down opposite the lock-keeper's cottage. There, with the scent of the wood-smoke threading from its low and humble chimney, the weir murmuring, the blackbirds and the cuckoos calling, Soames experienced something like asphyxiation of the proprietary instincts. Opening the handle of his shooting-stick, he sat down on it, to contemplate the oozy green on the sides of the emptied lock and dabble one hand in the air. Ingenious things—locks! Why not locks in the insides of men and women, so that their passions could be dammed to the proper moment, then used, under control, for the main traffic of life, instead of pouring to waste over weirs and down rapids? The tongue of Fleur's dog licking his dabbled hand interrupted this somewhat philosophic reflection. Animals were too human nowadays, always wanting to have notice taken of them; only that afternoon he had seen Annette's black cat look up into the plaster face of his Naples Psyche, and mew faintly—wanting to be taken up into its lap, he supposed.

The lock-keeper's daughter came out to take some garments off a line. Women in the country seemed to do nothing but hang clothes on lines and take them off again! Soames watched her, neat-handed, neat-ankled, in neat light-blue print, with a face like a Botticelli—lots of faces like that in England! She would have a young man or perhaps two—and they would walk in that wood, and sit in damp places and all the rest of it, and imagine themselves happy, he shouldn't wonder; or she would get up behind him on one of those cycle things and go tearing about the country with her dress up to her knees. And her name would be Gladys or Doris, or what not! She saw him, and smiled. She had a full mouth that looked pretty when it smiled. Soames raised his hat slightly.

'Nice evening!' he said.

'Yes, sir.'

Very respectful.

'River's still high.'

'Yes, sir.'

Rather a pretty girl! Suppose he had been a lock-keeper, and Fleur had been a lock-keeper's daughter—hanging clothes on a line, and saying: 'Yes, sir!' Well, he would as soon be a lock-keeper as anything else in a humble walk of life—watching water go up and down, and living in that pretty cottage, with nothing to worry about, except—except his daughter! And he checked an impulse to say to the girl: 'Are you a good daughter?' Was there such a thing nowadays—a daughter that thought of you first, and herself after?

'These cuckoos!' he said, heavily.

'Yes, sir.'

She was taking a somewhat suggestive garment off the line now, and Soames lowered his eyes, he did not want to embarrass the girl—not that he saw any signs. Probably you couldn't embarrass a girl nowadays! And, rising, he closed the handle of his shooting-stick.

'Well, it'll keep fine, I shouldn't wonder.'

'Yes, sir.'

'Good-evening.'

'Good-evening, sir.'

Followed by the dog, he moved along towards home. Butter wouldn't melt in her mouth; but how would she talk to her young man? Humiliating to be old! On an evening like this, one should be young again, and walk in a wood with a girl like that; and all that had been faun-like in his nature pricked ears for a moment, licked lips, and with a shrug and a slight sense of shame, died down.

It had always been characteristic of Soames, who had his full share of the faun, to keep the fact carefully hidden. Like all his family, except, perhaps, his cousin George and his uncle Swithin, he was secretive in matters of sex; no Forsyte talked sex, or liked to hear others talk it; and when they felt its call, they gave no outward sign. Not the Puritan spirit, but a certain refinement in them forbade the subject, and where they got it from they did not know!

After his lonely dinner he lit his cigar and strolled out again. It was really warm for May, and still light enough for him to see his cows in the meadow beyond the river. They would soon be sheltering for the night, under that hawthorn hedge. And here came the swans, with their grey brood in tow; handsome birds, going to bed on the island!

The river was whitening; the dusk seemed held in the trees, waiting to spread and fly up into a sky just drained of sunset. Very peaceful, and a little eerie–the hour between! Those starlings made a racket–disagreeable beggars; there could be no real self-respect with such short tails! The swallows went by, taking 'night-caps' of gnats and early moths; and the poplars stood so still–just as if listening–that Soames put up his hand to feel for the breeze. Not a breath! And then, all at once–no swallows flying, no starlings; a chalky hue over river, over sky! The lights sprang up in the house. A night-flying beetle passed him, booming. The dew was falling–he felt it; must go in. And, as he turned, quickly, dusk softened the trees, the sky, the river. And Soames thought: 'Hope to goodness there'll be no mysteries when she comes down to-morrow. I don't want to be worried!' Just she and the little chap; it might be so pleasant, if that old love trouble with its gnarled roots in the past and its better fruits in the future were not present, to cast a gloom. . . .

He slept well, and next morning could settle to nothing but the arrangement of things already arranged. Several times he stopped dead in the middle of this task to listen for the car and remind himself that he must not fuss, or go asking things. No doubt she had seen young Jon again yesterday, but he must not ask.

He went up to his picture gallery and unhooked from the wall a little Watteau, which he had once heard her admire. He took it downstairs and stood it on an easel in her bedroom–a young man in full plum-coloured skirts and lace ruffles, playing a tambourine to a young lady in blue, with a bare bosom, behind a pet lamb. Charming thing! She could take it away when she went, and hang it with the Fragonards and Chardin in her drawing-room. Standing by the double-poster, he bent down and sniffed at the bed linen. Not quite as fragrant as it ought to be. That woman, Mrs Edger–his housekeeper–had forgotten the pot-pourri bags; he knew there would be something! And, going to a store closet, he took four little bags with tiny mauve ribbons from a shelf, and put them into the bed. He wandered thence into the bathroom. He didn't know whether she would like those salts–they were Annette's new speciality, and smelt too strong for *his* taste. Otherwise it seemed all right; the soap was 'Roger and Gallet', and the waste worked. All these new gadgets–half of them didn't; there was nothing like the old-fashioned thing that pulled up with a chain! Great change in washing during his lifetime. He couldn't quite remember pre-bathroom days; but he could well recall how his father used to say regularly: 'They never gave me a bath when I was a boy. First house of my own, I had one put in–people used to come and stare at it–in 1840. They tell me the doctors are against washing now; but I don't know.' James had been dead a quarter of a century, and the doctors had turned their coats several times since. Fact was, people enjoyed baths; so it didn't really matter what views the doctors took! Kit enjoyed them–some children didn't. And, leaving the bathroom, Soames stood in front of the flowers the gardener had brought in–among them, three special early roses. Roses were the fellow's forte, or rather his weak point–he cared for nothing else; that was the worst of people nowadays, they specialised so that there was no relativity between things, in spite of its being the fashionable philosophy, or so they told him. He took up a rose and sniffed at it deeply. So many different kinds now—he had lost track! In his young days one could tell them—La France, Maréchal Neil, and Gloire de Dijon—nothing else to speak of; you never heard of *them* now. And at this reminder of the mutability of flowers and the ingenuity of human beings, Soames felt slightly exhausted. There was no end to things!

She was late, too! That fellow Riggs—for he had left the car to bring her down, and had come by train himself—would have got punctured, of course; he was always getting punctured if there was any reason why he shouldn't. And for the next half-hour Soames fidgeted about so that he was deep in nothing in his picture gallery at the very top of the house and did not hear the car arrive. Fleur's voice roused him from thoughts of her.

'Hallo!' he said, peering down the stairs, 'where have *you* sprung from? I expected you an hour ago.'

'Yes, dear, we had to get some things on the way. How lovely it all looks! Kit's in the garden.'

'Ah!' said Soames, descending. 'Did you get a rest yester—' and he pulled up in front of her.

She bent her face forward for a kiss, and her eyes looked beyond him. Soames put his lips on the edge of her cheek-bone. She was away somewhere! And, as his lips mumbled her soft skin slightly, he thought: 'She's not thinking of me—why should she? She's young!'

PART II

I

SON OF SLEEPING DOVE

Whether or not the character of Englishmen in general is based on chalk, it is undeniably present in the systems of our jockeys and trainers. Living for the most part on downs, drinking a good deal of water, and concerned with the joints of horses, they are almost professionally calcareous, and at times distinguished by bony noses and chins.

The chin of Greenwater, the retired jockey in charge of Val Dartie's stable, projected, as if in years of race-riding it had been bent on prolonging the efforts of his mounts and catching the judge's eye. His thin, commanding nose dominated a mask of brown skin and bone, his narrow brown eyes glowed slightly, his dark hair was smooth and brushed back; he was five feet seven inches in height, and long seasons, during which he had been afraid to eat, had laid a look of austerity over such natural liveliness, as may be observed in—say—a water-wagtail. A married man with two children, he was endeared to his family by the taciturnity of one who had been intimate with horses for thirty-five years. In his leisure hours he played the piccolo. No one in England was more reliable.

Val, who had picked him up on his retirement from the pig-skin in 1921, thought him an even better judge of men than of horses, incapable of trusting them farther than he could see them, and that not very far. Just now it was particularly necessary to trust no one, for there was in the stable a two-year-old colt, Rondavel, by Kaffir out of Sleeping Dove, of whom so much was expected, that nothing whatever had been said about him. On the Monday of Ascot week Val was the more surprised, then, to hear his trainer remark:

'Mr Dartie, there was a son of a gun watching the gallop this morning.'

'The deuce there was!'

'Someone's been talking. When they come watching a little stable like this—something's up. If you take my advice, you'll send the colt to Ascot and let him run his chance on Thursday—won't do him any harm to smell a racecourse. We can ease him after, and bring him again for Goodwood.'

Aware of his trainer's conviction that the English race-horse, no less than the English man, liked a light preparation nowadays, Val answered:

'Afraid of overdoing him?'

'Well, he's fit now, and that's a fact. I had Sinnet shake him up this morning, and he just left 'em all standing. Fit to run for his life, he is; wish you'd been there.'

'Oho!' said Val, unlatching the door of the box. 'Well, my beauty?'

The Sleeping Dove colt turned his head, regarding his owner with a certain lustrous philosophy. A dark grey, with one white heel and a star, he stood glistening from his morning toilet. A good one! The straight hocks and ranginess of St Simon crosses in his background! Scope, and a rare shoulder for coming down a hill. Not exactly what you'd call a 'picture'–his lines didn't quite 'flow', but great character. Intelligent as a dog, and game as an otter! Val looked back at his trainer's intent face.

'All right, Greenwater. I'll tell the missus–we'll go in force. Who can you get to ride at such short notice?'

'Young Lamb.'

'Ah!' said Val, with a grin; 'you've got it all cut and dried, I see.'

Only on his way back to the house did he recollect a possible 'hole in the ballot' of secrecy. . . . Three days after the General Strike collapsed, before Holly and young Jon and his wife had returned, he had been smoking a second pipe over his accounts, when the maid had announced:

'A gentleman to see you, sir.'

'What name?'

'Stainford, sir.'

Checking the impulse to say: 'And you left him in the hall!' Val passed hurriedly into that part of the house.

His old college pal was contemplating a piece of plate over the stone hearth.

'Hallo!' said Val.

His unemotional visitor turned round.

Less threadbare than in Green Street, as if something had restored his credit, his face had the same crow's-footed, contemptuous calm.

'Ah, Dartie!' he said. 'Joe Lightson, the bookie, told me you had a stable down here. I thought I'd look you up on my way to Brighton. How has your Sleeping Dove yearling turned out?'

'So-so,' said Val.

'When are you going to run him? I thought, perhaps you'd like me to work your commission. I could do it much better than the professionals.'

Really, the fellow's impudence was sublime!

'Thanks very much; but I hardly bet at all.'

'Is that possible? I say, Dartie, I didn't mean to bother you again, but if you could let me have a "pony", it would be a great boon.'

'Sorry, but I don't keep "ponies" about me down here.'

'A cheque–'

Cheque–not if he knew it!

'No,' said Val firmly. 'Have a drink?'

'Thanks very much!'

Pouring out the drink at the sideboard in the dining-room, with one eye on the stilly figure of his guest, Val took a resolution.

'Look here, Stainford–' he began, then his heart failed him. 'How did you get here?'

'By car, from Horsham. And that reminds me. I haven't a sou with me to pay for it.'

Val winced. There was something ineffably wretched about the whole thing.

'Well,' he said, 'here's a fiver, if that's any use to you; but really I'm not game for any more.' And, with a sudden outburst, he added: 'I've never forgotten, you know, that I once lent you all I had at Oxford when I was deuced hard pressed myself, and you never paid it back, though you came into shekels that very term.'

The well-shaped hand closed on the fiver; a bitter smile opened the thin lips.

'Oxford! Another life! Well, good-bye, Dartie–I'll get on; and thanks! Hope you'll have a good season.'

He did not hold out his hand. Val watched his back, languid and slim, till it was out of sight. . . .

Yes! That memory explained it! Stainford must have picked up some gossip in the village–not likely that they would let a 'Sleeping Dove' lie! It didn't much matter; since Holly would hardly let him bet at all. But Greenwater must look sharp after the colt. Plenty of straight men racing; but a lot of blackguards hanging about the sport. Queer how horses collected blackguards–most beautiful creatures God ever made! But beauty was like that–look at the blackguards hanging round pretty women! Well, he must let Holly know. They could stay, as usual, at old Warmson's Inn, on the river; from there it was only a fifteen-mile drive to the course. . . .

The 'Pouter Pigeon' stood back a little from the river Thames, on the Berkshire side, above an old-fashioned garden of roses, stocks, gillyflowers, poppies, phlox drummondi, sweet-williams. In the warm June weather the scents from that garden and from sweetbriar round the windows drifted into an old brick house painted cream-colour. Late Victorian service in Park Lane under James Forsyte, confirmed by a later marriage with Emily's maid Fifine, had induced in Warmson, indeed, such complete knowledge of what was what, that no river inn had greater attractions for those whose taste had survived modernity. Spotless linen, double beds warmed with copper pans, even in summer; cider, home-made from a large orchard, and matured in rum casks–the inn was a veritable feather-bed to all the senses. Prints of 'Mariage à la Mode', 'Rake's Progress', 'The Nightshirt Steeplechase', 'Run with the Quorn', and large functional groupings of Victorian celebrities with their names attached to blank faces on a key chart, decorated the walls. Its sanitation and its port were excellent. Pot-pourri lay in every bedroom, old pewter round the coffee-room, clean napkins at every meal. And a poor welcome was assured to earwigs, spiders, and the wrong sort of guest. . . . Warmson, one of those self-contained men who spread when they take inns, pervaded the house, with a red face set in small, grey whiskers, like a sun of just sufficient warmth.

To young Anne Forsyte all was 'just too lovely.' Never in her short life, confined to a large country, had she come across such defiant cosiness–the lush peace of the river, the songs of birds, the scents of flowers, the rustic arbour, the drifting lazy sky, now blue, now white, the friendly fat spaniel, and the feeling that to-morrow and to-morrow and to-morrow would for ever be the same as yesterday.

'It's a poem, Jon.'

'Slightly comic. When everything's slightly comic, you don't tire.'

'I'd certainly never tire of this.'

'We don't grow tragedy in England, Anne.'

'Why?'

'Well, tragedy's extreme; and we don't like extremes. Tragedy's dry and England's damp.'

She was leaning her elbows on the wall at the bottom of the garden, and, turning her chin a little in her hand, she looked round and up at him.

'Fleur Mont's father lives on the river, doesn't he? Is that far from here?'

'Mapledurham? I should think about ten miles.'

'I wonder if we shall see her at Ascot. I think she's lovely.'

'Yes,' said Jon.

'I wonder you didn't fall in love with her, Jon.'

'We were kids when I knew her.'

'I think she fell in love with you.'

'Why?'

'By the way she looks at you. . . . She isn't in love with Mr Mont; she just likes him.'

'Oh!' said Jon.

Since in the coppice at Robin Hill Fleur had said 'Jon!' in so strange a voice, he had known queer moments. There was that in him which could have caught her, balanced there on the log with her hands on his shoulders, and gone straight back into the past with her. There was that in him which abhorred the notion. There was that in him which sat apart and made a song about them both, and that in him which said: 'Get to work and drop all these silly feelings!' He was, in fact, confused. The past, it seemed, did not die, as he had thought, but lived on beside the present, and sometimes, perhaps, became the future. Did one live for what one had not got? There was wrinkling in his soul, and feverish draughts crept about within him. The whole thing was on his conscience–for if Jon had anything, he had a conscience.

'When we get our place,' he said, 'we'll have all these old-fashioned flowers. They're much the sweetest!'

'Ah! Yes, do let's get a home, Jon. Only are you sure you want one? Wouldn't you like to travel and write poetry?'

'It's not a job. Besides, my verse isn't good enough. You want the mood of Hatteras J. Hopkins:

> '"Now, severed from my kind by my contempt,
> I live apart and beat my lonely drum."'

'I wish you weren't modest, Jon.'

'It's not modesty, Anne; it's a sense of the comic.'

'Couldn't we get a swim before dinner? It would be fine.'

'I don't know what the regulations are here.'

'Let's bathe first and find out afterwards.'

'All right. You go and change. I'll get this gate open.'

A fish splashed, a long white cloud brushed the poplar tops beyond the water. Just such an evening, six years ago, he had walked the towing-path with Fleur, had separated from her, waited to see her look back and wave her hand. He could see her still–that special grace, which gave her movements a lingering solidity within the memory. And now–it was Anne! And Anne in water was a dream! . . .

Above the 'Pouter Pigeon' the sky was darkening; cars in their garages were still; no boats passed, only the water moved, and the river wind talked vaguely in the rushes and among the leaves. All within was cosy. On their backs lay Warmson and his Fifine, singing a little through their noses. By a bedside light Holly read *The Worst Journey in the World*, and beside her Val dreamed that he was trying to stroke a horse's nose, shortening under his hand to the size of a leopard's. And Anne slept with her eyes hidden against Jon's shoulder, and Jon lay staring at the crannies through which the moonlight eddied.

And in his stable at Ascot the son of Sleeping Dove, from home for the first time, pondered on the mutability of equine affairs, closing and opening his eyes and breathing without sound in the strawy dark above the black cat he had brought to bear him company.

2

SOAMES GOES RACING

To Winifred Dartie the début of her son's Sleeping Dove colt on Ascot Cup Day seemed an occasion for the gathering of such members of her family as were permitted to go racing by the primary caution in their blood; but it was almost a shock to her when Fleur telephoned: 'Father's coming; he's never been to Ascot, and doesn't know that he wants to go.'

'Oh!' she said, 'it's too late to get any more Enclosure tickets. But Jack can see to him. What about Michael?'

'Michael can't come; he's deep in slums–got a new slogan: "Broader gutters!"'

'He's so good,' said Winifred. 'Let's go down early enough to lunch before racing, dear. I think we'd better drive.'

'Father's car is up–we'll call for you.'

'Delightful!' said Winifred. 'Has your father got a grey top hat? No? Oh! But he simply must wear one; they're all the go this year. Don't say anything, just get him one. He wears seven-and-a-quarter; and, dear, tell them to heat the hat and squash it in at the sides–otherwise they're always too round for him. And he needn't bring any money to speak of; Jack will do all our betting for us.'

Fleur thought that it was not likely father would have a bet; he had said he just wanted to see what the thing was like.

'He's so funny about betting,' said Winifred, 'like your grandfather.'

Not that it had been altogether funny in the case of James, who had been called on to pay the racing debts of Montague Dartie three times over.

With Soames and Winifred on the back seats, Fleur and Imogen on the front seats, and Jack Cardigan alongside Riggs, they took a circuitous road by way of Harrow to avoid the traffic, and emerged into it just at the point where for the first time it became thick. Soames, who had placed his grey top hat on his knee, put it on, and said:

'Just like Riggs!'

'Oh no, Uncle!' said Imogen. 'It's Jack's doing. When he's got to go through Eton, he always likes to go through Harrow first.'

'Oh! Ah!' said Soames. 'He was there. I should like Kit's name put down.'

'How nice!' said Imogen. 'Our boys will have left when he goes. You look so well in that hat, Uncle.'

Soames took it off again.

'White elephant,' he said. 'Can't think what made Fleur get me the thing!'

'My dear,' said Winifred, 'it'll last you for years. Jack's had his ever since the war. The great thing is to prevent the moth getting into it, between seasons. What a lot of cars! I do think it's wonderful that so many people should have the money in these days.'

The sight of so much money flowing down from town would have been more exhilarating to Soames if he had not been wondering where on earth they all got it. With the coal trade at a stand-still and factories closing down all over the place, this display of wealth and fashion, however reassuring, seemed to him almost indecent.

Jack Cardigan, from his front seat, had been explaining a thing he called the 'tote'. It seemed to be a machine that did your betting for you. Jack Cardigan was a funny fellow; he made a life's business of sport; there wasn't another country that could have produced him! And, leaning forward, Soames said to Fleur:

'You've not got a draught there?'

She had been very silent all the way, and he knew why. Ten to one if young Jon Forsyte wouldn't be at Ascot! Twice over at Mapledurham he had noticed letters addressed by her to:

> 'Mrs Val Dartie,
> Wansdon,
> Sussex.'

She had seemed to him very fidgety or very listless all that fortnight. Once, when he had been talking to her about Kit's future, she had said: 'I don't think it matters, Dad, whatever one proposes–he'll dispose; parents don't count now: look at me!'

And he had looked at her, and left it at that.

He was still contemplating the back of her head when they drew into an enclosure and he was forced to expose his hat to the public gaze. What a crowd! Here, on the far side of the course, were rows of people all jammed together, who, so far as he could tell, would see nothing, and be damp one way or another throughout the afternoon. If that was pleasure! He followed the others across the course, in front of the grandstand. So those were 'the bookies'! Funny lot, with their names 'painted clearly on each', so that people could tell them apart, just as well, for they all seemed to him the same, with large necks and red faces, or scraggy necks and lean faces, one of each kind in every firm, like a couple of music-hall comedians. And, every now and then, in the pre-racing hush, one of them gave a sort of circular howl and looked hungrily at space. Funny fellows! They passed alongside the Royal Enclosure where bookmakers did not seem to be admitted. Numbers of grey top hats there! This was the place–he had heard–to see pretty women. He was looking for them when Winifred pressed his arm.

'Look, Soames–the Royal Procession!'

Thus required to gape at those horse-drawn carriages at which everybody else would be gaping, Soames averted his eyes, and became conscious that Winifred and he were alone!

'What's become of the others?' he said.

'Gone to the paddock, I expect.'

'What for?'

'To look at the horses, dear.'

Soames had forgotten the horses.

'Fancy driving up like that, at this time of day!' he muttered.

'I think it's so amusing!' said Winifred. 'Shall we go to the paddock, too?'

Soames, who had not intended to lose sight of his daughter, followed her towards whatever the paddock might be.

It was one of those days when nobody could tell whether it was going to rain,

so that he was disappointed by the dresses and the women's looks. He saw
nothing to equal his daughter and was about to make a disparaging remark
when a voice behind him said:

'Look, Jon! There's Fleur Mont!'

Placing his foot on Winifred's, Soames stood still. There, and wearing a grey
top hat, too, was that young chap between his wife and his sister. A memory of
tea at Robin Hill with his cousin Jolyon, that boy's father, twenty-seven years
ago, assailed Soames–and of how Holly and Val had come in and sat looking at
him as if he were a new kind of bird. There they went, those three, into a ring of
people who were staring at nothing so far as he could see. And there, close to
them, were those other three, Jack Cardigan, Fleur and Imogen.

'My dear,' said Winifred, 'you *did* tread on my toe.'

'I didn't mean to,' muttered Soames. 'Come over to the other side–there's
more room.'

It seemed horses were being led around; but it was at his daughter that
Soames wanted to gaze from behind Winifred's shoulder. She had not yet seen
the young man, but was evidently looking for him–her eyes were hardly ever on
the horses–no great wonder in that, perhaps, for they all seemed alike to
Soames, shining and snakey, quiet as sheep, with boys holding on to their
heads. Ah! A stab went through his chest, for Fleur had suddenly come to life;
and, as suddenly, seemed to hide her resurrection even from herself! How still
she stood–ever so still gazing at that young fellow talking to his wife.

'That's the favourite, Soames. At least, Jack said he would be. What do you
think of him?'

'Much like the others–got four legs.'

Winifred laughed. Soames was so amusing!

'Jack's moving; if we're going to have a bet, I think we'd better go back, dear.
I know what I fancy.'

'I don't fancy anything,' said Soames. 'Weak-minded, I call it; as if they
could tell one horse from another!'

'Oh! but you'd be surprised,' said Winifred; 'you must get Jack to–'

'No, thank you.'

He had seen Fleur move and join those three. But faithful to his resolve to
show no sign, he walked glumly back to the grandstand. What a monstrous noise
they were making now in the ring down there! And what a pack of people in this
great stand! Up there, on the top of it, he could see what looked like half a dozen
lunatics frantically gesticulating–some kind of signalling, he supposed.
Suddenly, beyond the railings at the bottom of the lawn, a flash of colour
passed. Horses–one, two, three; a dozen or more–all labelled with numbers,
and with little bright men sitting on their necks like monkeys. Down they
went–and soon they'd come back, he supposed; and a lot of money would
change hands. And then they'd do it again, and the money would change back.
And what satisfaction they all got out of it, he didn't know! There were men who
went on like that all their lives, he believed–thousands of them: must be lots of
time and money to waste in the country! What was it Timothy had said:
'Consols are going up!' They hadn't; on the contrary, they were down a point, at
least, and would go lower before the Coal Strike was over. Jack Cardigan's
voice said in his ear:

'What are you going to back, Uncle Soames?'

'How should I know?'

'You must back something, to give you an interest.'

'Put something on for Fleur, and leave me alone,' said Soames; 'I'm too old to begin.'

And, opening the handle of his racing-stick, he sat down on it. 'Going to rain,' he added gloomily. He sat there alone; Winifred and Imogen had joined Fleur down by the rails with Holly and her party—Fleur and that young man side by side. And he remembered how, when Bosinney had been hanging around Irene, he, as now, had made no sign, hoping against hope that by ignoring the depths beneath him he could walk upon the waters. Treacherously they had given way then and engulfed him; would they again—would they again? His lip twitched; and he put out his hand. A little drizzle fell on the back of it.

'They're off!'

Thank goodness—the racket had ceased! Funny change from din to hush. The whole thing funny—a lot of grown-up children! Somebody called out shrilly at the top of his voice—there was a laugh—then noise began swelling from the stand; heads were craning round him. "The favourite wins!" 'Not he!' More noise; a thudding—a flashing past of colour! And Soames thought: 'Well, that's over!' Perhaps everything was like that really. A hush—a din—a flashing past—a hush! All life a race, a spectacle—only you couldn't see it! A venture and a paying-up! And beneath his new hat he passed his hand down over one flat cheek, and then the other. A paying-up! He didn't care who paid up, so long as it wasn't Fleur? But there it was—some debts could not be paid by proxy! What on earth was Nature about when she made the human heart!

The afternoon wore on, and he saw nothing of his daughter. It was as if she suspected his design of watching over her. There was the 'horse of the century' running in the Gold Cup, and he positively mustn't miss that—they said. So again Soames was led to the ring where the horses were moving round.

'That the animal?' he said, pointing to a tall mare, whom, by reason of two white ankles, he was able to distinguish from the others. Nobody answered him, and he perceived that he was separated from Winifred and the Cardigans by three persons, all looking at him with a certain curiosity.

'Here he comes!' said one of them. Soames turned his head. Oh! So *this* was the horse of the century, was it?—this bay fellow—same colour as the pair they used to drive in the Park Lane barouche. His father always had bays, because old Jolyon had browns, and Nicholas blacks, and Swithin greys, and Roger—he didn't remember what Roger used to have—something a bit eccentric—piebalds, he shouldn't wonder. Sometimes they would talk about horses, or, rather, about what they had given for them: Swithin had been a judge, or so he said—Soames had never believed it, he had never believed in Swithin at all. But he could perfectly well remember George being run away with by his pony in the Row, and pitched into a flower-bed—no one had ever been able to explain how; just like George, with his taste for the grotesque! He himself had never taken any interest in horses. Irene, of course, had loved riding—she would! She had never had any after she married him. . . . A voice said:

'Well, what do you think of him, Uncle Soames?'

Val, with his confounded grin; Jack Cardigan, too, and a thin, brown-faced man with a nose and chin. Soames said guardedly:

'Nice enough nag.'

If they thought they were going to get a rise out of him!

'Think he'll stay, Val? It's the deuce of a journey.'

'He'll stay all right.'

'Got nothing to beat,' said the thin brown man.

'The Frenchman, Greenwater.'

'No class, Captain Cardigan. He's not all the horse they think him, but he can't lose to-day.'

'Well, I hope to God he beats the Frenchman; we want a cup or two left in the country.'

Something responded within Soames's breast. If it was against a Frenchman, he would do his best to help.

'Put me five pounds on him,' he said suddenly to Jack Cardigan.

'Good for you, Uncle Soames. He'll start about evens. See his head and his forehand and the way he's let down–lots of heart room. Not quite so good behind the saddle, but a great horse, I think.'

'Which is the Frenchman?' asked Soames 'That! Oh! Ah! I don't like *him*. I want to see this race.'

Jack Cardigan gripped his arm–the fellow's fingers were like iron.

'You come along with me!' he said. Soames went, was put up higher than he had been yet, given Imogen's glasses–a present from himself–and left there. He was surprised to find how well and far he could see. What a lot of cars, and what a lot of people! 'The national pastime'–didn't they call it! Here came the horses walking past, each led by a man. Well! They were pretty creatures, no doubt! An English horse against a French horse–that gave the thing some meaning. He was glad Annette was still with her mother in France, otherwise she'd have been here with him. Now they were cantering past. Soames made a real effort to tell one from the other, but except for their numbers, they were so confoundedly alike. 'No,' he said to himself, 'I'll just watch those two, and that tall horse'–its name had appealed to him, Pons Asinorum. Rather painfully he got the colours of the three by heart and fixed his glasses on the wheeling group out there at the starting-point. As soon as they were off, however, all he could see was that one horse was in front of the others. Why had he gone to the trouble of learning the colours? On and on and on he watched them, worried because he could make nothing of it, and everybody else seemed making a good deal. Now they were round into the straight. 'The favourite's coming up!' 'Look at the Frenchman!' Soames could see the colours now. Those two! His hand shook a little and he dropped his glasses. Here they came–a regular ding-dong! Dash it–he wasn't–England wasn't! Yes, by George! No! Yes! Entirely without approval his heart was beating painfully. 'Absurd!' he thought. 'The Frenchman!' 'No! the favourite wins! He wins!' Almost opposite, the horse was shooting out. Good horse! Hooray! England for ever! Soames covered his mouth just in time to prevent the words escaping. Somebody said something to him. He paid no attention; and, carefully putting Imogen's glasses into their case, took off his grey hat and looked into it. There was nothing there except a faint discoloration of the buff leather where he had perspired.

3

THE TWO-YEAR-OLDS

The toilet of the two-year-olds was proceeding in the more unfrequented portions of the paddock.

'Come and see Rondavel saddled, Jon,' said Fleur.

And, when he looked back, she laughed.

'No, you've got Anne all day and all night. Come with me for a change.'

On the far side of the paddock the son of Sleeping Dove was holding high his intelligent head, and his bit was being gently jiggled, while Greenwater with his own hands adjusted the saddle.

'A race-horse has about the best time of anything on earth,' she heard Jon say. 'Look at his eye–wise, bright, not bored. Draft horses have a cynical, long-suffering look–race-horses never. He likes his job; that keeps him spirity.'

'Don't talk like a pamphlet, Jon. Did you expect to see me here?'

'Yes.'

'And it didn't keep you away? How brave!'

'Must you say that sort of thing?'

'What then? You notice, Jon, that a race-horse never stands over at the knee; the reason is, of course, that he isn't old enough. By the way, there's one thing that spoils your raptures about them. They're not free agents.'

'Is anyone?'

How set and obstinate his face!

They joined Val, who said gloomily:

'D'you want to have anything on?'

'Do *you*, Jon?' said Fleur.

'Yes; a tenner.'

'So will I then. Twenty pounds between us, Val.'

Val sighed.

'Look at him! Ever see a two-year-old more self-contained? I tell you that youngster's going far. And I'm confined to a miserable "pony"! Damn!'

He left them and spoke to Greenwater.

'More self-contained,' said Fleur. 'Not a modern quality, is it, Jon?'

'Perhaps, underneath.'

'Oh! You've been in the backwoods too long. Francis, too, was wonderfully primitive; so, I suppose, is Anne. You should have tried New York, judging by their literature.'

'I don't judge by literature; I don't believe there's any relation between it and life.'

'Let's hope not, anyway. Where shall we see the race from?'

'The rails over there. It's the finish I care about. I don't see Anne.'

Fleur closed her lips suddenly on the words: 'Damn Anne.'

'We can't wait for them,' she said. 'The rails soon fill up.'

On the rails they were almost opposite the winning-post, and they stood there silent, in a queer sort of enmity–it seemed to Fleur.

'Here they come!'

Too quickly and too close to be properly taken in, the two-year-olds come cantering past.

'Rondavel goes well', said Jon. 'And I like that brown.'

Fleur noted them languidly, too conscious of being alone with him–really alone, blocked off by strangers from any knowing eye. To savour that loneliness of so few minutes was tasking all her faculties. She slipped her hand through his arm, and forced her voice.

'I'm awfully worked up, Jon. He simply must win.'

Did he know that in focusing his glasses he left her hand uncaged?

'I can't make them out from here.' Then his arm recaged her hand against his side. Did he know? What did he know?

'They're off!'

Fleur pressed closer.

Silence–din–shouting of this name–that name! But pressure against him was all it meant to Fleur. Past they came, a flourishing flash of colour; but she saw nothing of it, for her eyes were closed.

'By Gosh!' she heard him say: 'He's won.'

'Oh, Jon!'

'I wonder what price we got?'

Fleur looked at him, a spot of red in each pale cheek, and her eyes very clear.

'Price? Did you really mean that, Jon?'

And, though he was behind her, following to the paddock she knew from the way his eyes were fixed on her, that he had not meant it.

They found their party reunited all but Soames. Jack Cardigan was explaining that the price obtained was unaccountably short, since there was no stable money on to speak of; somebody must have known something; he seemed to think that this was extremely reprehensible.

'I suppose Uncle Soames hasn't been going for the gloves,' he said. 'Nobody's seen him since the Gold Cup. Wouldn't it be ripping if we found he'd kicked over and had a "monkey" on?'

Fleur said uneasily:

'I expect Father got tired and went to the car. We'd better go too, Auntie, and get away before the crowd.'

She turned to Anne. 'When shall we see you again?' She saw the girl look at Jon, and heard him say glumly:

'Oh! sometime.'

'Yes, we'll fix something up. Good-bye, my dear! Good-bye, Jon! Tell Val I'm very glad.' And, with a farewell nod, she led the way. Of a sort of rage in her heart she gave no sign, preparing normality for her father's eyes.

Soames, indeed, was in the car. Excitement over the Gold Cup–so contrary to his principles–had caused him to sit down in the stand. And there he had remained during the next two races, idly watching the throng below, and the horses going down fast and coming back faster. There, quietly, in the isolation suited to his spirit, he could, if not enjoy, at least browse on a scene strikingly unfamiliar to him. The national pastime–he knew that everybody had "a bit on" something nowadays. For one person who ever went racing there were twenty–it seemed–who didn't, and yet knew at least enough to lose their money. You couldn't buy a paper, or have your hair cut, without being conscious of that. All over London, and the South, the Midlands and the

North, in all classes, they were at it, supporting horses with their bobs and dollars and sovereigns. Most of them–he believed–had never seen a race-horse in their lives–hardly a horse of any sort; racing was a sort of religion, he supposed, and now that they were going to tax it, an orthodox religion. Some primeval nonconformity in the blood of Soames shuddered a little. He had no sympathy, of course, with those leather-lunged chaps down there under their queer hats, and their umbrellas, but the feeling that they were now made free of heaven–or at least of that synonym of heaven the modern state–ruffled him. It was almost as if England were facing realities at last–Very dangerous! They would be licensing prostitution next! To tax what were called vices was to admit that they were part of human nature. And though, like a Forsyte, he had long known them to be so, to admit it was, he felt, too French. To acknowledge the limitations of human nature was a sort of defeatism; when you once began that, you didn't know where you'd stop. Still, from all he could see, the tax would bring in a pretty penny–and pennies were badly needed; so, he didn't know, he wasn't sure. He wouldn't have done it himself, but he wasn't prepared to turn out the Government for having done it. They had recognised, too, no doubt, as he did, that gambling was the greatest make-weight there was against revolution; so long as a man could bet he had always a chance of getting something for nothing, and that desire was the real driving force behind any attempt to turn things upside down. Besides you had to move with the times uphill or downhill, and it was difficult to tell one from the other. The great thing was to avoid extremes.

From this measured reflection he was abruptly transferred to feelings unmeasured. Fleur and that young fellow were walking across there down to the rails! From under the brim of his grey hat he watched them painfully, reluctantly admitting that they made as pretty a couple as any there. They came to a stand on the rails–not talking; and to Soames, who, when moved, was exceptionally taciturn, this seemed a bad sign. Were things really going wrong, then–was passion forming within its still cocoon to fly on butterfly wings for its brief hour? What was going on within the silence of those two? The horses were passing now; and the grey, they said, was his own nephew's? Why did the fellow have horses? He had known how it would be when Fleur said he was going to Ascot. He regretted now having come. No, he didn't! Better to know what there was to be known. In the press of people to the rails he could no longer see more than the young man's grey hat, and the black-and-white covering of his daughter's head. For a minute the race diverted him: might as well see Val's horse well beaten. They said he thought a lot of it; and Soames thought the less of its chance for that. Here they came, all in a bunch –thundering great troop, and that grey–a handy colour, you couldn't miss it. Why, he was winning! Hang it–he had won!

'H'm!' he said, aloud: 'that's my nephew's horse!'

Since nobody replied, he hoped they hadn't heard. And back went his eyes to those two on the rails. Yes, they were coming away silently–Fleur a little in front. Perhaps–perhaps, after all, they didn't get on, now! Must hope for the best. By George, but he felt tired! He would go to the car, and wait.

And there in the dusk of it he was sitting when they came, full of bubble and squeak–something very little-headed about people when they'd won money. For they had all won money, it seemed!

'And you didn't back him, Uncle Soames?'

'I was thinking of other things,' said Soames, gazing at his daughter.

'We thought you were responsible for the shockin' bad price.'

'Why!' said Soames, gloomily. 'Did you expect me to bet against him?'

Jack Cardigan threw back his head and laughed.

'I don't see anything funny,' muttered Soames.

'Nor do I, Jack,' said Fleur. 'Why should Father know anything about racing?'

'I beg your pardon, sir, I'll tell you all about it.'

'God forbid!' said Soames.

'No, but it's rather queer. D'you remember that chap Stainford, who sneaked the Mater's snuff-box?'

'I do.'

'Well, it seems he paid Val a visit at Wansdon, and Val thinks he picked up the idea that Rondavel was a real good one. There was a chap watching the gallop last Monday. That's what decided them to run the colt to-day. They were going to wait for Goodwood. Too late, though; somebody's made a pot over him. We only got fours.'

It was all Greek to Soames, except that the languid ruffian Stainford had somehow been responsible a *second* time for bringing about a meeting between Fleur and Jon; for he knew from Winifred that Val and his *ménage* had gone to stay at Green Street during the strike on purpose to see Stainford. He wished to goodness he had called a policeman that day, and had the fellow shut up.

They were a long time getting out of the traffic—owing to the perversity of 'that chap Riggs,' and did not reach South Square till seven o'clock. They were greeted by the news that Kit had a temperature. Mr Mont was with him. Fleur flew up. Having washed off his day, Soames settled himself in the 'parlour' to wait uneasily for their report. Fleur used to have temperatures, and not infrequently they led to something. If Kit's didn't lead to anything serious, it might be good for her—keeping her thoughts at home. He lay back in his chair opposite the Fragonard—a delicate thing, but with no soul in it, like all the works of that period—wondering why Fleur had changed the style of this room from Chinese to Louis Quinze. Just for the sake of change, he supposed. These young people had no continuity; some microbe in the blood—of the 'idle rich', and the 'idle poor', and everybody else, so far as he could see. Nobody could be got to stay anywhere—not even in their graves, judging by all those séances. If only people would attend quietly to their business, even to that of being dead! They had such an appetite for living, that they had no life. A beam of sunlight, smoky with dust-motes, came slanting in on to the wall before him—pretty thing, a beam of sunlight, but a terrible lot of dust, even in a room spick-and-spandy as this. And to think that a thing smaller than one of those dust-motes could give a child a temperature. He hoped to goodness Kit had nothing catching. And his mind went over the illnesses of childhood—mumps, measles, chicken-pox, whooping-cough. Fleur had caught them all, but never scarlet fever. And Soames began to fidget. Surely Kit was too young to have got scarlet fever. But nurses were so careless—you never knew! And suddenly he began to wish for Annette. What was she doing in France all this time? She was useful in illness; had some very good prescriptions. He *would* say that for the French—their doctors were clever when you could get them to take an interest. The stuff they had given him for his lumbago at Deauville had been first-rate. And after his visit the little doctor chap had said: 'I come for the money to-morrow!' or so it had sounded. It seemed he had meant: 'I come in the morning to-morrow.' They never could speak anything but their own confounded language, and looked aggrieved when you couldn't speak it yourself.

They had kept him a long time there without news before Michael came in. 'Well?'

'Well, sir, it looks uncommonly like measles.'

'H'm! Now, how on earth did he get that?'

'Nurse has no idea; but Kit's awfully sociable. If there's another child in sight, he goes for him.'

'That's bad,' said Soames. 'You've got slums at the back here.'

'Ah!' said Michael: 'Slums to the right of us, slums to the left of us, slums to the front of us–how can you wonder?'

Soames stared. 'They're not notifiable,' he said, 'thank goodness!'

'Slums?'

'No. Measles.'' If he had a dread, it was a notifiable disease, with the authorities poking their noses in, and having up the drains as likely as not. 'How's the little chap feeling?'

'Very sorry for himself.'

'In my opinion,' said Soames, 'there's a great deal more in fleas than they think. That dog of his may have picked up a measley flea. I wonder the doctors don't turn their attention to fleas.'

'I wonder they don't turn their attention to slums,' said Michael; 'that's where the fleas come from.'

Again Soames stared. Had his son-in-law got slums in his bonnet now? His manifestations of public spirit were very disturbing. Perhaps he'd been going round those places, and brought the flea in himself, or some infection or other.

'Have you sent for the doctor?'

'Yes; he'll be here any minute.'

'Is he any good, or just the ordinary cock-and-bull type?'

'The same man we had for Fleur.'

'Oh! Ah! I remember–too much manner, but shrewd. Doctors!'

There was silence in the polished room, while they waited for the bell to ring; and Soames brooded. Should he tell Michael about the afternoon? His mouth opened once, but nothing came out. Over and over again his son-in-law had surprised him by the view he took of things. And he only stared at Michael, who was gazing out of the window–queer face the young fellow had; plain, and yet attractive with those pointed ears and eyebrows running up on the outside–wasn't always thinking of himself like good-looking young men seemed to be. Good-looking men were always selfish; got spoiled, he supposed. He would give a penny for the young fellow's thoughts.

'Here he is!' said Michael, jumping up.

Soames was alone again. How long alone, he didn't know, for he was tired, and, in spite of his concern, he dozed. The opening of the door roused him in time to assume anxiety before Fleur spoke.

'It's almost certainly measles, Dad.'

'Oh!' said Soames, blankly. 'What about nursing?'

'Nurse and I, of course.'

'That'll mean you can't get about.'

'And aren't you glad?' her face seemed to say. How she read his thoughts! God knew he wasn't glad of anything that troubled her–and yet–!

'Poor little chap!' he said, evasively: 'Your mother must come back. I must try and find him something that'll take his attention off.'

'Don't trouble, Dad; he's too feverish, poor darling. Dinner's ready. I'm having mine upstairs.'

Soames rose and went up to her.

'Don't you be worrying,' he said. 'All children—'

Fleur put her arm out.

'Not too near, Dad. No. I won't worry.'

'Give him my love,' said Soames. 'He won't care for it.'

Fleur looked at him. Her lips smiled a very little. Her eyelids winked twice. Then she turned and went out, and Soames thought:

'She—poor little thing! I'm no use!' It was of her, not of his grandson, that he thought.

4

IN THE MEADS

The Meads of St Augustine had, no doubt, once on a time been flowery, and burgesses had walked there of a Sunday, plucking nosegays. If there were a flower now, it would be found on the altar of the Reverend Hilary's church, or on Mrs Hilary's dining-table. The rest of a numerous population had heard of these unnatural products, and, indeed, seeing them occasionally in baskets, would utter the words: 'Aoh! Look at the luv-ly flahers!'

When Michael visited his uncle, according to promise, on Ascot Cup Day, he was ushered hurriedly into the presence of twenty little Augustinians on the point of being taken in a covered motor-van for a fortnight among flowers in a state of nature. His Aunt May was standing among them. She was a tall woman with bright brown shingled hair going grey, and the slightly rapt expression of one listening to music. Her smile was very sweet, and this, with the puzzled twitch of her delicate eyebrows, as who should say placidly: 'What next, I wonder?' endeared her to everyone. She had emerged from a rectory in Huntingdonshire, in the early years of the century, and had married Hilary at the age of twenty. He had kept her busy ever since. Her boys and girl were all at school now, so that in term time she had merely some hundreds of Augustinians for a family. Hilary was wont to say: 'May's a wonder. Now that she's had her hair off, she's got so much time on her hands that we're thinking of keeping guinea-pigs. If she'd only let me grow a beard, we could really get a move on.'

She greeted Michael with a nod and a twitch.

'Young London, my dear,' she said, privately, 'just off to Leatherhead. Rather sweet, aren't they?'

Michael, indeed, was surprised by the solidity and neatness of the twenty young Augustinians. Judging by the streets from which they came and the mothers who were there to see them off, their families had evidently gone 'all out' to get them in condition for Leatherhead.

He stood grinning amiably, while they were ushered out on to the glowing pavement between the unrestrained appreciation of their mothers and sisters. Into the van, open only at the rear, they piled, with four young ladies to look after them.

'Four-and-twenty blackbirds baked in a pie,' murmured Michael.

His aunt laughed.

'Yes, poor little dears, won't they be hot! But aren't they good?' She lowered her voice. 'And d'you know what they'll say when they come back after their fortnight? "Oh! yes, we liked it all very much, thank you, but it was rather slow. We like the streets better." Every year it's the same.'

'Then, what's the use of sending them, Aunt May?'

'It does them good physically; they look sturdy enough, but they aren't really strong. Besides, it seems so dreadful they should never see the country. Of course we country-bred folk, Michael, never can realise what London streets are to children–very nearly heaven, you know.'

The motor-van moved to an accompaniment of fluttered handkerchiefs and shrill cheering.

'The mothers love them to go,' said his aunt; 'it's kind of distinguished. Well, that's that! What would you like to see next? The street we've just bought, to gut and re-gut? Hilary'll be there with the architect.'

'Who owned the street?' asked Michael.

'He lived in Capri. I don't suppose he ever saw it. He died the other day, and we got it rather reasonably, considering how central we are, here. Sites are valuable.'

'Have you paid for it?'

'Oh! no.' Her eyebrows twitched. 'Post-dated a cheque on Providence.'

'Good Lord!'

'We had to have the street. It was such a chance. We've paid the deposit, and we've got till September to get the rest.'

'How much?' said Michael.

'Thirty-two thousand.'

Michael gasped.

'Oh! We shall get it, dear, Hilary's wonderful in that way. Here's the street.'

It was a curving street of which, to Michael, slowly passing, each house seemed more dilapidated than the last. Grimey and defaced, with peeling plaster, broken rails and windows, and a look of having been abandoned to its fate–like some half-burnt-out ship–it hit the senses and the heart with its forlornness.

'What sort of people live here, Aunt May?'

'All sorts–three or four families to each house. Covent Garden workers, hawkers, girls in factories, out-of-works–every kind. The unmentionable insect abounds, Michael. The girls are wonderful–they keep their clothes in paper bags. Many of them turn out quite neat. If they didn't, of course, they'd get the sack, poor dears.'

'But is it possible,' said Michael, 'that people can *want* to go on living here?'

His aunt's brows became intricate.

'It isn't a question of want, my dear. It's a simple economic proposition. Where else *can* they live so cheaply? It's more than that, even; where else can they go at all, if they're turned out? The authorities demolished a street not long ago up there, and built that great block of workmen's flats; but the rents were prohibitive to the people who had been living in the street, and they simply melted away to other slums. Besides, you know, they don't like those barracky flats, and I don't wonder. They'd much rather have a little house, if they can; or the floor of a house if they can't. Or even a room. That's in the English nature, and it will be till they design workmen's dwellings better. The English like to live low down: I suppose because they always have. Oh! here's Hilary!'

Hilary Charwell, in a dark-grey Norfolk suit, a turn-down collar open at the neck, and no hat, was standing in the doorway of a house, talking to another spare man with a thin, and, to Michael, very pleasant face.

'Well, Michael, my boy, what think you of Slant Street? Each one of these houses is going to be gutted and made as bright as a new pin.'

'How long will they keep bright, Uncle Hilary?'

'Oh! That's all right,' said Hilary, 'judging by our experiments so far. Give 'em a chance, and the people are only too glad to keep their houses clean. It's wonderful what they do, as it is. Come in and see, but don't touch the walls. May, you stay and talk to James. An Irish lady in here; we haven't many. Can I come in, Mrs Corrigan?'

'Sure an' ye can. Plased to see your rivirence, though ut's not tidy I am this mornin'.'

A broad woman, with grizzled black hair and brawny arms, had paused in whatever she was doing to a room inconceivably crowded and encrusted. Three people evidently slept in the big bed, and one in a cot; cooking seemed to go on at the ordinary small black hearth, over which, on a mantel-board, were the social trophies of a lifetime. Some clothes were hung on a line. The patched and greasy walls had no pictures.

'My nephew, Mr Michael Mont, Mrs Corrigan; he's a Member of Parliament.'

The lady put her arms akimbo.

'Indeed, an' is he, then?'

It was said with an infinite indulgence that went to Michael's heart. 'An' is ut true your rivirence has bought the street? An' what would ye be doing with ut? Ye won't be afther turning us out, I'm thinking.'

'Not for the world, Mrs Corrigan.'

'Well, an' I knew that. I said to them: "It's cleaning our insides he'll maybe doing, but he'll never be afther putting us out." '

'When the turn of this house comes, Mrs Corrigan—I hope before very long—we'll find you good lodgings till you can come back here to new walls and floors and ceilings, a good range, no more bugs, and proper washing arrangements.'

'Well, an' wouldn't that be the day I'd like to see!'

'You'll see it fast enough. Look, Michael, if I put my finger through there, the genuine article will stalk forth! It's you that can't knock holes in your walls, Mrs Corrigan.'

'An' that's the truth o' God,' replied Mrs Corrigan. 'The last time Corrigan knocked a peg in, 'twas terrible—the life there was in there!'

'Well, Mrs Corrigan, I'm delighted to see you looking so well. Good-morning, and tell Corrigan if his donkey wants a rest any time, there'll be room in our paddock. Will you be going hopping this year?'

'We will that,' replied Mrs Corrigan. 'Good-day to your rivirence; good-day, sorr!'

On the bare, decrepit landing Hilary Charwell said: 'Salt of the earth, Michael. But imagine living in that atmosphere! Luckily they're all "snoof".'

'What?' said Michael, taking deep breaths of the somewhat less complicated air.

'It's a portmanteau syllable for "Got no sense of smell to speak of". And wanted too. One say "deaf", "blind", "dumb"—why not "snoof"?'

'Excellent! How long do you reckon it'll take you to convert this street, Uncle Hilary?'

'About three years.'

'And how are you going to get the money?'

'Win, wangle, and scrounge it. In here there are three girls who serve in "Petter and Poplins". They're all out, of course. Neat, isn't it? See their paper bags?'

'I say, uncle, would you blame a girl for doing anything to get out of a house like this?'

'No,' said the Reverend Hilary, 'I would not, and that's the truth o' God.'

'That's why I love you, Uncle Hilary. You restore my faith in the Church.'

'My dear boy,' said Hilary, 'the old Reformation was nothing to what's been going on in the Church lately. You wait and see! Though I confess a little wholesome Disestablishment would do us all no harm. Come and have lunch, and we'll talk about my slum conversion scheme. We'll bring James along.'

'You see,' he resumed, when they were seated in the Vicarage dining-room, 'there must be any amount of people who would be glad enough to lay out a small portion of their wealth at two-and-a-half per cent., with prospect of a rise to four as time went on, if they were certain that it meant the elimination of the slums. We've experimented and we find that we can put slum houses into proper living condition for their existing population at a mere fraction over the old rents, and pay two-and-a-half on our outlay. If we can do that here it can be done in all slum centres, by private Slum Conversion Societies such as ours, working on the principle of not displacing the existing slum population. But what's wanted, of course, is money—a General Slum Conversion fund—Bonds at two per cent., with bonuses, repayable in twenty years, from which the Societies could draw funds as they need them for buying and converting slum property.'

'How will you repay the Bonds in twenty years?'

'Oh! Like the Government—by issuing more.'

'But,' said Michael, 'the local authorities have very wide powers, and much more chance of getting the money.'

Hilary shook his head.

'Wide powers, yes; but they're slow, Michael—the snail is a fast animal compared with them; besides, they only displace, because the rents they charge are too high. Also it's not in the English character, my dear. Somehow we don't like being "done for" by officials, or being answerable to them. There's lots of room, of course, for slum area treatment by Borough Councils, and they do lots of good work, but by themselves, they'll never scotch the evil. You want the human touch; you want a sense of humour, and faith; and that's a matter for private effort in every town where there are slums.'

'And who's going to start this general fund?' asked Michael, gazing at his aunt's eyebrows, which had begun to twitch.

'Well,' said Hilary, twinkling, 'I thought that might be where you came in. That's why I asked you down to-day, in fact.'

'The deuce!' said Michael almost leaping above the Irish stew on his plate.

'Exactly!' said his uncle; 'but couldn't you get together a committee of both Houses to issue an appeal? From the work we've done James can give you exact figures. They could see for themselves what's happened here. Surely, Michael, there must be ten just men who could be got to move in a matter like this—'

' "Ten Apostles",' said Michael faintly.

'Well, but there's no real need to bring Christ in—nothing remote or sentimental; you could approach them from any angle. Old Sir Timothy Fanfield, for example, would love to have a "go" at slum landlordism. Then we've electrified all the kitchens so far, and mean to go on doing it—so you could get old Shropshire on that. Besides, there's no need to confine the committee to the two Houses—Sir Thomas Morsell, or, I should think, any of the big doctors, would come in; you could pinch a brace of bankers with Quaker blood in them; and there are always plenty of retired governor generals with their tongues out. Then if you could rope in a member of the Royal Family to head it—the trick would be done.'

'Poor Michael!' said his aunt's soft voice: 'Let him finish his stew, Hilary.'

But Michael had dropped his fork for good; he saw another kind of stew before him.

'The General Slum Conversion Fund,' went on Hilary, 'affiliating every Slum Conversion Society in being or to be, so long as it conforms to the principle of not displacing the present inhabitant. Don't you see what a pull that gives us over the inhabitants?—we start them straight, and we jolly well see that they don't let their houses down again.'

'But can you?' said Michael.

'Ah! you've heard stories of baths being used for coal and vegetables, and all that. Take it from me, they're exaggerated, Michael. Anyway, that's where we private workers come in with a big advantage over municipal authorities. They have to drive, we try to lead.'

'Let me hot up your stew, dear?' said his aunt.

Michael refused. He perceived that it would need no hotting up! Another crusade! His Uncle Hilary had always fascinated him with his crusading blood—at the time of the Crusades the name had been Kéroual, and now spelt Charwell, was pronounced Cherwell, in accordance with the sound English custom of worrying foreigners.

'I'm not approaching you, Michael, with the inducement that you should make your name at this, because, after all, you're a gent!'

'Thank you!' murmured Michael; 'always glad of a kind word.'

'No. I'm suggesting that you ought to do something, considering your luck in life.'

'I quite agree,' said Michael humbly. 'The question seems to be: Is this the something?'

'It is, undoubtedly,' said his uncle, waving a salt-spoon on which was engraved the Charwell crest. 'What else can it be?'

'Did you ever hear of Foggartism, Uncle Hilary?'

'No; what's that?'

'My aunt!' said Michael.

'Some blanc-mange, dear?'

'Not you, Aunt May! But did you really never hear of it, Uncle Hilary?'

'Foggartism? Is it that fog-abating scheme one reads about?'

'It is not,' said Michael. 'Of course, you're sunk in misery and sin here. Still, it's almost too thick. *You've* heard of it, Aunt May?'

His aunt's eyebrows became intricate again.

'I think,' she said, 'I do remember hearing someone say it was balderdash!'

Michael groaned: 'And you, Mr James?'

'It's to do with the currency, isn't it?'

'And here,' said Michael, 'we have three intelligent, public-spirited persons, who've never heard of Foggartism—and I've heard of nothing else for over a year.'

'Well,' said Hilary, 'had you heard of my slum-conversion scheme?'

'Certainly not.'

'I think,' said his aunt, 'it would be an excellent thing if you'd smoke while I make the coffee. Now I do remember, Michael: your mother did say to me that she wished you would get over it. I'd forgotten the name. It had to do with taking town children away from their parents.'

'Partly,' said Michael, with gloom.

'You have to remember, dear, that the poorer people are, the more they cling to their children.'

'Vicarious joy of life,' put in Hilary.

'And the poorer children are, the more they cling to their gutters, as I was telling you.'

Michael buried his hands in his pockets.

'There is no good in me,' he said stonily. 'You've pitched on a stumer, Uncle Hilary.'

Both Hilary and his wife got up very quickly, and each put a hand on his shoulder.

'My dear boy!' said his aunt.

'God bless you!' said Hilary. 'Have a "gasper".'

'All right,' said Michael, grinning, 'it's wholesome.'

Whether or not it was a "gasper" that was wholesome, he took and lighted it from his uncle's.

'What is the most pitiable sight in the world, Aunt May—I mean, next to seeing two people dance the Charleston?'

'The most pitiable sight?' said his aunt dreamily.

'Oh! I think—a rich man listening to a bad gramophone.'

'Wrong!' said Michael. 'The most pitiable sight in the world is a politician barking up the right tree. Behold him!'

'Look out, May! Your machine's boiling. She makes very good coffee, Michael—nothing like it for the grumps. Have some, and then James and I will show you the houses we've converted. James—come with me a moment.'

'Noted for his pertinacity,' muttered Michael, as they disappeared.

'Not only noted, Michael—dreaded.'

'Well, I would rather be Uncle Hilary than anybody I know.'

'He *is* rather a dear,' murmured his aunt, 'Coffee?'

'What does he really believe, Aunt May?'

'Well, he hardly has time for that.'

'Ah! that's the new hope of the Church. All the rest is just as much an attempt to improve on mathematics as Einstein's theory. Orthodox religion was devised for the cloister, Aunt May, and there aren't any cloisters left.'

'Religion,' said his aunt dreamily, 'used to burn a good many people, Michael, not in cloisters.'

'Quite so, when it emerged from cloisters, religion used to be red-hot politics, then it became caste feeling, and now it's a crossword puzzle—you don't solve *them* with your emotions.'

His aunt smiled.

'You have a dreadful way of putting things, my dear.'

'In our "suckles", Aunt May, we do nothing but put things—it destroys our motive power. But about this slum business: do you really advise me to have "a go"?'

'Not if you want a quiet life.'

'I don't know that I do. I did after the war; but not now. But, you see, I've tried Foggartism and everybody's too sane to look at it. I really can't afford to back another loser. Do you think there's a chance of getting a national move on?'

'Only a sporting chance, dear.'

'Would you take it up then, if you were me?'

'My dear, I'm prejudiced–Hilary's heart is so set on it; but it does seem to me that there's no other cause I'd so gladly fail in. Well, not that exactly; but there really is nothing so important as giving our town dwellers decent living conditions.'

'It's rather like going over to the enemy,' muttered Michael. 'Our future oughtn't to be so bound up in the towns.'

'It *will* be, whatever's done. "A bird in the hand," and such a big bird, Michael. Ah! Here's Hilary!'

Hilary and his architect took Michael forth again into 'The Meads'. The afternoon had turned drizzly, and the dismal character of that flowerless quarter was more than ever apparent. Up street, down street, Hilary extolled the virtues of his parishioners. They drank, but not nearly so much as was natural in the circumstances; they were dirty, but he would be dirtier under their conditions. They didn't come to church–who on earth would expect them to? They assaulted their wives to an almost negligible extent; were extraordinarily good, and extremely unwise, to their children. They had the most marvellous faculty for living on what was not a living wage. They helped each other far better than those who could afford to; never saved a bean, having no beans to save, and took no thought for a morrow which might be worse than to-day. Institutions they abominated. They were no more moral than was natural in their overcrowded state. Of philosophy they had plenty, of religion none that he could speak of. Their amusements were cinemas, streets, gaspers, public houses, and Sunday papers. They like a tune, and would dance if afforded a chance. They had their own brand of honesty, which required special study. Unhappy? Not precisely, having given up a future state in this life or in that–realist to their encrusted finger-nails. English? Well, nearly all, and mostly London-born. A few country folk had come in young, and would never go out old.

'You'd like them, Michael; nobody who really knows them can help liking them. And now, my dear fellow, good-bye, and think it over. The hope of England lies in you young men. God bless you!'

And with these words in his ears, Michael went home, to find his little son sickening for measles.

5

MEASLES

The diagnosis of Kit's malady was soon verified, and Fleur went into purdah.

Soames's efforts to distract his grandson arrived almost every day. One had the ears of a rabbit, with the expression of a dog, another the tail of a mule detachable from the body of a lion, the third made a noise like many bees; the fourth, though designed for a waistcoat, could be pulled out tall. The procuring of these rarities, together with the choicest mandarine oranges, muscatel grapes, and honey that was not merely 'warranted' pure, occupied his mornings in town. He was staying at Green Street, whereto the news, judiciously wired, had brought Annette. Soames, who was not yet entirely resigned to a spiritual life, was genuinely glad to see her. But after one night, he felt he could spare her to Fleur. It would be a relief to feel that she had her mother with her. Perhaps by the end of her seclusion that young fellow would be out of her reach again. A domestic crisis like this might even put him out of her head. Soames was not philosopher enough to gauge in-round the significance of his daughter's yearnings. To one born in 1855 love was a purely individual passion, or if it wasn't it ought to be. It did not occur to him that Fleur's longing for Jon might also symbolise the craving in her blood for life, the whole of life, and nothing but life; that Jon had represented her first serious defeat in the struggle for the fullness of perfection; a defeat that might yet be wiped out. The modern soul, in the intricate turmoil of its sophistication, was to Soames a book which, if not sealed, had its pages still uncut. 'Crying for the moon' had become a principle when he was already much too old for principles. Recognition of the limits of human life and happiness was in his blood, and had certainly been fostered by his experience. Without, exactly, defining existence as 'making the best of a bad job', he would have contended that though, when you had almost everything, you had better ask for more, you must not fash yourself if you did not get it. The virus of a time-worn religion which had made the really irreligious old Forsytes say their prayers to the death, in a muddled belief that they would get something for them after death, still worked inhibitively in the blood of their prayerless offspring, Soames, so that, although fairly certain that he would get nothing after death, he still believed that he would not get everything before death. He lagged, in fact, behind the beliefs of a new century in whose 'make-up' resignation played no part—a century which either believed, with spiritualism, that there were plenty of chances to get things after death, or that, since one died for good and all, one must see to it that one had everything before death. Resignation! Soames would have denied, of course, that he believed in any such thing; and certainly he thought nothing too good for his daughter! And yet, somehow, he felt in his bones that there *was* a limit, and Fleur did not—this little distinction, established by the difference in their epochs, accounted for his inability to follow so much of her restive search.

Even in the nursery, grieved and discomforted by the feverish miseries of her little son, Fleur continued that search. Sitting beside his cot, while he tossed and murmured and said he was 'so 'ot', her spirit tossed and murmured and said so, too. Except that, by the doctor's orders, bathed and in changed garments, she went for an hour's walk each day, keeping to herself, she was entirely out of the world, so that the heart from which she suffered had no anodyne but that of watching and ministering to Kit. Michael was 'ever so sweet' to her; and the fact that she wanted another in his place could never have been guessed from her manner. Her resolution to give nothing away was as firm as ever, but it was a real relief not to encounter the gimletting affection of her father's eye. She wrote to no one; but she received from Jon a little letter of condolence.

Wansdon.

June 22.

DEAR FLEUR,

We are so awfully sorry to hear of Kit's illness. It must be wretched for you. We do hope the poor little chap is over the painful part by now. I remember my measles as two beastly days, and then lots of things that felt nice and soothing all the way down. But I expect he's too young to be conscious of anything much except being thoroughly uncomfy.

Rondavel, they say, is all the better for his race. It was jolly seeing it together.

Good-bye, Fleur; with all sympathy,

Your affectionate friend,

JON

She kept it—as she had kept his old letters—but not like them, about her; there had come to be a dim, round mark on the 'affectionate friend' which looked as if it might have dropped from an eye; besides, Michael was liable to see her in any stage of costume. So she kept it in her jewel-box, whereof she alone had the key.

She read a good deal to Kit in those days, but still more to herself, conscious that of late she had fallen behind the forward march of literature, and seeking for distraction in an attempt to be up-to-date, rather than in the lives of characters too lively to be alive. They had so much soul, and that so contortionate that she could not even keep her attention on them long enough to discover why they were not alive. Michael brought her book after book, with the words: 'This is supposed to be clever,' or 'Here's the last Nazing.' or 'Our old friend Calvin again—not quite so near the ham-bone this time, but as near as makes no matter.' And she would sit with them on her lap and feel gradually that she knew enough to be able to say: 'Oh! yes, I've read *The Gorgons*—it's marvellously Proustian.' Or *'Love—the Chameleon?*—well, it's better than her *Green Cave*, but not up to *Souls in the Nude.'* Or, 'You *must* read *The Whirligig*, my dear—it gets quite marvellously nowhere.'

She held some converse with Annette, but of the guarded character, suitable between mothers and daughters after a certain age; directed, in fact, towards elucidating problems not unconnected with garb. The future—according to Annette—was dark. Were skirts to be longer or shorter by the autumn? If shorter, she herself would pay no attention; it might be all very well for Fleur, but she had reached the limit herself—at her age she would *not* go above the knee. As to the size of hats—again there was no definite indication. The most distinguished cocotte in Paris was said to be in favour of larger hats, but forces were working in the dark against her—motoring and Madame de Michel-Ange *'qui est toute pour la vieille cloche'*. Fleur wanted to know whether she had heard anything fresh about shingling. Annette, who was not yet shingled, but whose neck for a long time had trembled on the block, confessed herself '*désespérée*'. Everything now depended on the Basque cap. If women took to them, shingling would stay; if not, hair might come in again. In any case, the new tint would be pure gold; '*Et cela sera impossible. Ton père aurait une apoplexie.*' In any case, Annette feared that she was condemned to long hair till the day of judgment. Perhaps, the good God would give her a good mark for it.

'If you want to shingle, Mother, I should. It's just father's conservatism–he doesn't really know what he likes. It would be a new sensation for him.'

Annette grimaced. '*Ma chère; je n'en sais rien.* Your father is capable of anything.'

The man 'capable of anything' came every afternoon for half an hour, and would remain seated before the Fragonard, catechising Michael or Annette, and then say, rather suddenly:

'Well, give my love to Fleur; I'm glad the little chap's better!' Or: 'That pain he's got will be wind, I expect. But I should have what's-his-name see to it. Give my love to Fleur.' And in the hall he would stand a moment by the coat-sarcophagus, listening. Then, adjusting his hat, he would murmur what sounded like: 'Well, there it is!' or: 'She doesn't get enough air,' and go out.

And from the nursery window Fleur would see him, departing at his glum and measured gait, with a compunctious relief. Poor old Dad! Not his fault that he symbolised for her just now the glum and measured paces of domestic virtue. Soames's hope, indeed, that enforced domesticity might cure her, was not being borne out. After the first two or three anxious days, while Kit's temperature was still high, it worked to opposite ends. Her feeling for Jon, in which now was an element of sexual passion, lacking before her marriage, grew, as all such feelings grow, without air and exercise for the body and interest for the mind. It flourished like a plant transferred into a hot-house. The sense of having been defrauded fermented in her soul. Were they never to eat of the golden apple–she and Jon? Was it to hang there, always out of reach–amid dark, lustrous leaves, quite unlike an apple tree's? She took out her old water-colour box–long now since it had seen the light–and coloured a fantastic tree with large golden fruits.

Michael caught her at it.

'That's jolly good,' he said. 'You ought to keep up your water-colours, old thing.'

Rigid, as if listening for something behind the words, Fleur answered: 'Sheer idleness!'

'What's the fruit?'

Fleur laughed.

'Exactly! But this is the soul of a fruit tree, Michael–not its body!'

'I might have known,' said Michael ruefully. 'Anyway, may I have it for my study when it's done? It's got real feeling.'

Fleur felt a queer gratitude. 'Shall I label it "The Uneatable Fruit"?'

'Certainly not–it looks highly luscious; you'd have to eat it over a basin, though, like a mango.'

Fleur laughed again.

'Steward!' she said. And, to Michael bending down to kiss her, she inclined her cheek. At least he should guess nothing of her feelings. And indeed, the French blood in her never ran cold at one of whom she was fond but did not love; the bitter spice which tinctured the blood of most of the Forsytes preserved the jest of her position. She was still the not unhappy wife of a good comrade and best of fellows, who, whatever she did herself, would never do anything ungenerous or mean. Fastidious recoilings from unloved husbands of which she read in old-fashioned novels, and of which she knew her father's first wife had been so guilty, seemed to her rather ludicrous. Promiscuity was in the air; a fidelity of the spirit so logical that it extended to the motions of the body, was paleolithic, or at least Victorian and 'middle class'. Fullness of life could never be reached on those lines. And yet the frank paganism, advocated by certain masters of French and English literature, was also debarred from Fleur, by its austerely logical habit of going the whole hog. There wasn't enough necessary virus in her blood, no sex mania about Fleur; indeed, hereunto, that obsession had hardly come her way at all. But now—new was the feeling, as well as old, that she had for Jon; and the days went by in scheming how, when she was free again, she could see him and hear his voice and touch him as she had touched him by the enclosure rails while the horses went flashing by.

6

FORMING A COMMITTEE

In the meantime Michael was not so unconscious as she thought, for when two people live together, and one of them is still in love, he senses change as a springbok will sent drought. Memories of that lunch, and of his visit to June, were still unpleasantly green. In his public life—that excellent anodyne for its private counterpart—he sought distraction, and made up his mind to go 'all out' for his Uncle Hilary's slum-conversion scheme. Having amassed the needed literature, he began considering to whom he should go first, well aware that public bodies are centrifugal. Round what fine figure of a public man should he form his committee? Sir Timothy Fanfield and the Marquess of Shropshire would come in usefully enough later, but, though well known for their hobbies, they 'cut no ice' with the general public. A certain magnetism was needed. There was none in any banker he could think of, less in any lawyer or cleric, and no reforming soldier could be otherwise than discredited, until he had carried his reforms, by which time he would be dead. He would have liked an admiral, but they were all out of reach. Retired Prime Ministers were in too lively request, besides being tarred with the brush of Party; and literary idols would be too old, too busy with themselves, too lazy, or too erratic. There remained doctors, business men, governor-generals, dukes, and newspaper proprietors. It was at this point that he consulted his father.

Sir Lawrence, who had also been coming to South Square almost daily during Kit's illness, focused the problem with his eye-glass, and said nothing for quite two minutes.

'What do you mean by magnetism, Michael? The rays of a setting or of a rising sun?'

'Both, if possible, Dad.'

'Difficult,' said his progenitor, 'difficult. One thing's certain—you can't afford cleverness.'

'How?'

'The public have suffered from it too much. Besides, we don't really like it in this country, Michael. Character, my dear, character!'

Michael groaned.

'Yes, I know,' said Sir Lawrence, 'awfully out of date with you young folk.' Then, raising his loose eyebrow abruptly so that his eye-glass fell on to the problem, he added: 'Eureka! Wilfred Bentworth! The very man–last of the squires–reforming the slums. It's what you'd call a stunt.'

'Old Bentworth?' repeated Michael dubiously.

'He's only my age–sixty-eight, and got nothing to do with politics.'

'But isn't he stupid?'

'There speaks your modern! Rather broad in the beam, and looking a little like a butler with a moustache, but–stupid? No. Refused a peerage three times. Think of the effect of that on the public!'

'Wilfred Bentworth? I should never have thought of him–always looked on him as the professional honest man,' murmured Michael.

'But he *is* honest!'

'Yes, but when he speaks, he always alludes to it.'

'That's true,' said Sir Lawrence, 'but one must have a defect. He's got twenty thousand acres, and knows all about fatting stock. He's on a railway board; he's the figurehead of his county's cricket, and chairman of a big hospital. Everybody knows him. He has Royalty to shoot; goes back to Saxon times; and is the nearest thing to John Bull left. In any other country he'd frighten the life out of any scheme, but in England–well, if you can get him, Michael, your job's half done.'

Michael looked quizzically at his parent. Did Bart quite understand the England of to-day? His mind roved hurriedly over the fields of public life. By George! He did!

'How shall I approach him, Dad? Will you come on the committee yourself? You know him; and we could go together.'

'If you'd really like to have me,' said Sir Lawrence, almost wistfully, 'I will. It's time I did some work again.'

'Splendid! I think I see your point about Bentworth. Beyond suspicion–has too much already to have anything to gain, and isn't clever enough to take in anyone if he wanted to.'

Sir Lawrence nodded. 'Add his appearance; that counts tremendously in a people that have given up the land as a bad job. We still love to think of beef. It accounts for a good many of our modern leaderships. A people that's got away from its base, and is drifting after it knows not what, wants beam, beef, beer–or at least port–in its leaders. There's something pathetic about that, Michael. What's to-day–Thursday? This'll be Bentworth's board day. Shall we strike while the iron's hot? We'll very likely catch him at Burton's.'

'Good!' said Michael, and they set forth.

'This club,' murmured Sir Lawrence, as they were going up the steps of Burton's Club, 'is confined to travellers, and I don't suppose Bentworth's ever travelled a yard. That shows how respected he is. No, I'm wronging him. I remember he commanded his yeomanry in the Boer War. ''The Squire'' in the club, Smileman?'

'Yes, Sir Lawrence; just come in.'

The 'last of the squires' was, indeed, in front of the tape. His rosy face, with clipped white moustache, and hard, little, white whiskers, was held as if the news had come to him, not he to the news. Banks might inflate and Governments fall, wars break out and strikes collapse, but there would be no bending of that considerable waist, no flickering in the steady blue stare from under eyebrows a little raised at their outer ends. Rather bald, and clipped in what hair was left, never did man look more perfectly shaved; and the moustache ending exactly where the lips ended, gave an extreme firmness to the general good humour of an open-air face.

Looking from him to his own father–thin, quick, twisting, dark, as full of whims as a bog is of snipe–Michael was impressed. A whim, to Wilfred Bentworth, would be strange fowl indeed! 'However he's managed to keep out of politics,' thought Michael, 'I can't conceive.'

' "Squire"–my son–a sucking statesman. We've come to ask you to lead a forlorn hope. Don't smile! You're "for it", as they say in this Bonzoid age. We propose to shelter ourselves behind you in the breach.'

'Eh! What? Sit down! What's all this?'

'It's a matter of the slums, "if you know what I mean," as the lady said. But go ahead, Michael!'

Michael went ahead. Having developed his uncle's thesis and cited certain figures, he embroidered them with as much picturesque detail as he could remember, feeling rather like a fly attacking the flanks of an ox and watching his tail.

'When you drive a nail into the walls, sir,' he ended, 'things come out.'

'Good God!' said the squire suddenly. 'Good God!'

'One doubts the "good", there,' put in Sir Lawrence.

The squire stared.

'Irreverent beggar,' he said. 'I don't know Charwell, they say he's cracked.'

'Hardly that,' murmured Sir Lawrence; 'merely unusual, like most members of really old families.'

The early English specimen in the chair before him twinkled.

'The Charwells, you know,' went on Sir Lawrence, 'were hoary when that rascally lawyer, the first Mont, founded us under James the First.'

'Oh!' said the squire. 'Are you one of *his* precious creations? I didn't know.'

'You're not familiar with the slums, sir?' said Michael, feeling that they must not wander in the mazes of descent.

'What! No. Ought to be, I suppose. Poor devils!'

'It's not so much,' said Michael, cunningly, 'the humanitarian side, as the deterioration of stock, which is so serious.'

'M'm?' said the squire. 'Do you know anything about stock-breeding?'

Michael shook his head.

'Well, you can take it from me that it's nearly all heredity. You could fat a slum population, but you can't change their character!'

'I don't think there's anything very wrong with their character,' said Michael. 'The children are predominantly fair, which means, I suppose, that they've still got the Anglo-Saxon qualities.'

He saw his father cock an eye. 'Quite the diplomat!' he seemed saying.

'Whom have you got in mind for this committee?' asked the squire, abruptly.

'My father,' said Michael; 'and we'd thought of the Marquess of Shropshire–'

'Very long in the tooth.'

'But very spry,' said Sir Lawrence. 'Still game to electrify the world.'

'Who else?'

'Sir Timothy Fanfield–'

'That fire-eating old buffer! Yes?'

'Sir Thomas Morsell–'

'M'm!'

Michael hurried on: 'Or any other medical man you thought better of, sir.'

'There are none. Are you sure about the bugs?'

'Absolutely!'

'Well, I should have to see Charwell. I'm told he can gammon the hind-leg off a donkey.'

'Hilary's a good fellow,' put in Sir Lawrence; 'a really good fellow, "squire".'

'Well, Mont, if I take to him, I'll come in. I don't like vermin.'

'A great national movement, sir,' began Michael, 'and nobody–'

The squire shook his head.

'Don't make any mistake,' he said. 'May get a few pounds, perhaps – get rid of a few bugs; but national movements – no such things in this country.' . . .

'Stout fellow,' said Sir Lawrence when they were going down the steps again; 'never been enthusiastic in his life. He'll make a splendid chairman. I think we've got him, Michael. You played your bugs well. We'd better try the Marquess next. Even a duke will serve under Bentworth, they know he's of older family than themselves, and there's something about him.'

'Yes, what is it?'

'Well, he isn't thinking about himself; he never gets into the air; and he doesn't give a damn for anyone or anything.'

'There must be something more than that,' said Michael.

'Well, there is. The fact is, he thinks as England really thinks, and not as it thinks it thinks.'

'By Jove!' said Michael. '"Some" diagnosis! Shall we dine, sir?'

'Yes, let's go to the Parthenæum! When they made me a member there, I used to think I should never go in, but d'you know, I use it quite a lot. It's more like the East than anything else in London. A Yogi could ask for nothing better. I go in and I sit in a trance until it's time for me to come out again. There's no vulgar material comfort. The prevailing colour is that of the Ganges. And there's more inaccesible wisdom in that place than you could find anywhere else in the West. We'll have the club dinner. It's calculated to moderate all transports. Lunch, of course, you can't get if you've a friend with you. One must draw the line somewhere at hospitality.'

'Now,' he resumed, when they had finished moderating their transports, 'let's go and see the Marquess! I haven't set eyes on the old boy since that Marjorie Ferrar affair. We'll hope he hasn't got gout. . . .'

In Curzon Street, they found that the Marquess had finished dinner and gone back to his study.

'Don't wake him if he's asleep,' said Sir Lawrence.

'His lordship is never asleep, Sir Lawrence.'

He was writing when they were ushered in, and stopped to peer at them round the corner of his bureau.

'Ah, young Mont!' he said. 'How pleasant!' Then paused rather abruptly. 'Nothing to do with my granddaughter, I trust?'

'Far from it, Marquess. We just want your help in a public work on behalf of the humble. It's a slum proposition, as the Yanks say.'

The Marquess shook his head.

'I don't like interfering with the humble; the humbler people are, the more one ought to consider their feelings.'

'We're absolutely with you there, sir; but let my son explain.'

'Sit down, then.' And the Marquess rose, placed his foot on his chair, and leaning his elbow on his knee, inclined his head to one side. For the second time that evening Michael plunged into explanation.

'Bentworth?' said the Marquess. 'His shorthorns are good; a solid fellow, but behind the times.'

'That's why we want you, Marquess.'

'My dear young Mont, I'm too old.'

'It's precisely because you're so young that we came to you.'

'Frankly, sir,' said Michael, 'we thought you'd like to be on the committee of appeal, because in my uncle's policy there's electrification of the kitchens; we must have someone who's an authority on that and can keep it to the fore.'

'Ah!' said the Marquess. 'Hilary Charwell–I once heard him preach in St Paul's–most amusing! What do the slum-dwellers say to electrification?'

'Nothing till it's done, of course, but once it's done, it's everything to them.'

'H'm!' said the Marquess. 'H'm! It would appear that there are no flies on your uncle.'

'We hope,' pursued Michael, 'that with electrification, there will soon be no flies on anything else.'

The Marquess nodded. 'It's the right end of the stick. I'll think of it. My trouble is that I've no money; and I don't like appealing to others without putting down something substantial myself.'

The two Monts looked at each other; the excuse was patent, and they had not foreseen it.

'I suppose,' went on the Marquess 'you don't know anyone who would buy some lace–*point de Venise*, the real stuff? Or,' he added, 'I've a Morland–'

'Have you?' cried Michael. 'My father-in-law was saying only the other day that he wanted a Morland.'

'Has he a good home for it?' said the Marquess, rather wistfully. 'It's a white pony.'

'Oh, yes, sir; he's a real collector.'

'Any chance of its going to the nation, in time?'

'Quite a good chance, I think.'

'Well, perhaps he'd come and look at it. It's never changed hands so far. If he would give me the market price, whatever that may be, it might solve the problem.'

'That's frightfully good of you.'

'Not at all,' said the Marquess. 'I believe in electricity, and I detest smoke; this seems a movement in the right direction. It's a Mr Forsyte, I think. There was a case–my granddaughter; but that's a past matter. I trust you're friends again?'

'Yes, sir; I saw her about a fortnight ago, and it was quite O.K.'

'Nothing lasts with you modern young people,' said the Marquess; 'the younger generation seems to have forgotten the war already. Is that good, I wonder? What do *you* say, Mont?'

'"*Tout casse, tout passe*," Marquess.'

'Oh! I don't complain,' said the Marquess; 'rather the contrary. By the way–on this committee you'll want a new man with plenty of money.'

'Can you suggest one?'

'My next-door neighbour–a man called Montross–I think his real name is shorter–might possibly serve. He's made millions, I believe, out of the elastic band – has some patent for making them last only just long enough. I see him sometimes gazing longingly at me – I don't use them, you know. Perhaps if you mention my name. He has a wife, and no title at present. I should imagine he might be looking for a public work.'

'He sounds,' said Sir Lawrence, 'the very man. Do you think we might venture now?'

'Try!' said the Marquess, 'try. A domestic character I'm told. It's no use doing things by halves; an immense amount of money will be wanted if we are to electrify any considerable number of kitchens. A man who would help substantially towards that would earn his knighthood much better than most people.'

'I agree,' said Sir Lawrence; 'a real public service. I suppose we mustn't dangle the knighthood?'

The Marquess shook the head that was resting on his hand.

'In these days – no,' he said. 'Just the names of his colleagues. We can hardly hope that he'll take an interest in the thing for itself.'

'Well, thank you ever so much. We'll let you know whether Wilfred Bentworth will take the chair, and how we progress generally.'

The Marquess took his foot down and inclined his head at Michael.

'I like to see young politicians interesting themselves in the future of England, because, in fact, no amount of politics will prevent her having one. By the way, have you had your own kitchen electrified?'

'My wife and I are thinking of it, sir.'

'Don't think!' said the Marquess. 'Have it done!'

'We certainly shall, now.'

'We must strike while the strike is on,' said the Marquess. 'If there is anything shorter than the public's memory, I am not aware of it.'

'Phew!' said Sir Lawrence, on the next doorstep; 'the old boy's spryer than ever. I take it we may assume that the name here was originally Moss. If so, the question is: "Have we the wits for this job?"'

And, in some doubt, they scrutinised the mansion before them.

'We had better be perfectly straightforward,' said Michael. 'Dwell on the slums, mention the names we hope to get, and leave the rest to him.'

'I think,' said his father, 'we had better say "got", not "hope to get".'

'The moment we mention the names, Dad, he'll know we're after his dibs.'

'He'll know that in any case, my boy.'

'I suppose there's no doubt about the dibs?'

'"Montross, Ltd."! They're not confined to elastic bands.'

'I should like to make a perfectly plain appeal to his generosity, Dad. There's a lot of generosity in that blood, you know.'

'We can't stand just here, Michael, discussing the make-up of the chosen. Ring the bell!'

Michael rang.

'Mr Montross at home? Thank you. Will you give him these cards, and ask if we might see him for a moment?'

The room into which they were ushered was evidently accustomed to this sort of thing, for, while there was nothing that anyone could take away, there were chairs in which it was possible to be quite comfortable, and some valuable but large pictures and busts.

Sir Lawrence was examining a bust, and Michael a picture, when the door was opened, and a voice said: 'Yes, gentlemen?'

Mr Montross was of short statue, and somewhat like a thin walrus who had once been dark but had gone grey; his features were slightly aquiline, he had melancholy brown eyes, and big drooping grizzly moustaches and eyebrows.

'We were advised to come to you, sir,' began Michael at once, 'by your neighbour, the Marquess of Shropshire. We're trying to form a committee to issue an appeal for a national fund to convert the slums.' And for the third time he plunged into detail.

'And why do you come to *me*, gentlemen?' said Mr Montross, when he had finished.

Michael subdued a stammer.

'Because of your wealth, sir,' he said, simply.

'Good!' said Mr Montross. 'You see, I began in the slums, Mr Mont–is it?–yes, Mr Mont–I began there–I know a lot about those people, you know. I thought perhaps you came to me because of that.'

'Splendid, sir,' said Michael, 'but of course we hadn't an idea.'

'Well, those people are born without a future.'

'That's just what we're out to rectify, sir.'

'Take them away from their streets and put them in a new country, then–perhaps; but leave them in the streets–' Mr Montross shook his head. 'I know them, you see, Mr Mont; if these people thought about the future, they could not go on living. And if you do not think about the future, you cannot have one.'

'How about yourself?' said Sir Lawrence.

Mr Montross turned his gaze from Michael to the cards in his hand, then raised his melancholy eyes.

'Sir Lawrence Mont, isn't it? I am a Jew–that is different. A Jew will rise from any beginnings, if he is a real Jew. The reason the Polish and the Russian Jews do not rise so easily you can see from their faces–they have too much Slav or Mongol blood. The pure Jew like me rises.'

Sir Lawrence and Michael exchanged a glance. 'We like this fellow,' it seemed to say.

'I was a poor boy in a bad slum,' went on Mr Montross, intercepting the glance, 'and I am now–well, a millionaire; but I have not become that, you know, by throwing away my money. I like to help people that will help themselves.'

'Then,' said Michael, with a sigh, 'there's nothing in this scheme that appeals to you, sir?'

'I will ask my wife,' answered Mr Montross, also with a sigh. 'Good-night, gentlemen. Let me write to you.'

The two Monts moved slowly towards Mount Street in the last of the twilight.

'Well?' said Michael.

Sir Lawrence cocked his eyebrow.

'An honest man,' he said: 'it's fortunate for us he has a wife.'

'You mean–?'

'The potential Lady Montross will bring him in. There was no other reason why he should ask her. That makes four, and Sir Timothy's a "sitter"; slum landlords are his *bêtes noires*. We only want three more. A bishop one can always get, but I've forgotten which it is for the moment; we *must* have a big doctor, and we ought to have a banker, but perhaps your uncle, Lionel Charwell, will do; he knows all about the shady side of finance in the courts, and we could make Alison work for us. And now, my dear, goodnight! I don't know when I've felt more tired.'

They parted at the corner, and Michael walked towards Westminster. He passed under the spikes of Buckingham Palace Gardens, and along the stables leading to Victoria Street. All this part had some very nice slums, though of late he knew the authorities had been 'going for them'. He passed an area where they had 'gone' for them to the extent of pulling down a congery of old houses. Michael stared up at the remnants of walls mosaicked by the unstripped wallpapers. What had happened to the tribe out-driven from these ruins; whereto had they taken the tragic lives of which they made such cheerful comedy? He came to the broad river of Victoria Street and crossed it, and, taking a route that he knew was to be avoided, he was soon where women encrusted with age sat on doorsteps for a breath of air, and little alleys led off to unplumbed depths. Michael plumbed them in fancy, not in fact. He stood quite a while at the end of one, trying to imagine what it must be like to live there. Not succeeding, he walked briskly on, and turned into his own Square, and to his own habitat with its bay-treed tubs, its Danish roof, and almost hopeless cleanliness. And he suffered from the feeling which besets those who are sensitive about their luck.

'Fleur would say,' he thought, perching on the coat-sarcophagus, for he, too, was tired, 'that those people having no æsthetic sense and no tradition to wash up to, are at least happy as we are. She'd say that they get as much pleasure out of living from hand to mouth (and not too much mouth), as we do from baths, jazz, poetry and cocktails; and she's generally right.' Only, what a confession of defeat! If that were really so, to what end were they all dancing? If life with bugs and flies were as good as life without bugs and flies, why Keating's powder and all the other aspirations of the poets? Blake's New Jerusalem was, surely, based on Keating, and Keating was based on a sensitive skin. To say, then, that civilisation was skin-deep, wasn't cynical at all. People possibly had souls, but they certainly had skins, and progress was real only if thought of in terms of skin!

So ran the thoughts of Michael, perched on the coat-sarcophagus; and meditating on Fleur's skin, so clear and smooth, he went upstairs.

She had just had her final bath, and was standing at her bedroom window. Thinking of–what? The moon over the Square?

'Poor prisoner!' he said, and put his arm round her.

'What a queer sound the town makes at night, Michael. And, if you think, it's made up of the seven million separate sounds of people going their own ways.'

'And yet–the whole lot are going one way.'

'We're not going any way,' said Fleur, 'there's only pace.'

'There must be direction, my child, underneath.'

'Oh! Of course, change.'

'For better or worse; but that's direction in itself.'

'Perhaps only to the edge, and over we go.'

'Gadarene swine!'

'Well, why not?'

'I admit,' said Michael unhappily, 'it's all hair-triggerish; but there's always common sense.'

'Common sense–in face of passions!'

Michael slackened his embrace. 'I thought you were always on the side of common sense. Passion? The passion to have? Or the passion to know?'

'Both,' said Fleur. 'That's the present age, and I'm a child of it. You're not, you know, Michael.'

'Query!' said Michael, letting go her waist. 'But if you want to have or know anything particular, Fleur, I'd like to be told.'

There was a moment of stillness, before he felt her arm slipping through his, and her lips against his ear.

'Only the moon, my dear. Let's go to bed.'

7

TWO VISITS

On the very day that Fleur was freed from her nursing she received a visit from the last person in her thoughts. If she had not altogether forgotten the existence of one indelibly associated with her wedding day, she had never expected to see her again. To hear the words: 'Miss June Forsyte, ma'am,' and find her in front of the Fragonard, was like experiencing a very slight earthquake.

The silvery little figure had turned at her entrance, extending a hand clad in a fabric glove.

'It's a flimsy school, that,' she said, pointing her chin at the Fragonard; 'but I like your room. Harold Blade's pictures would look splendid here. Do you know his work?'

Fleur shook her head.

'Oh! I should have thought any—' The little lady stopped, as if she had seen a brink.

'Won't you sit down?' said Fleur. 'Have you still got your gallery off Cork Street?'

'That? Oh no! It was a hopeless place. I sold it for half what my father gave for it.'

'And what became of the Polo-American—Boris Strumo something—you were so interested in?'

'He! Oh! Gone to pieces utterly. Married, and does purely commercial work. He gets big prices for his things—no good at all. So Jon and his wife—' Again she stopped, and Fleur tried to see the edge from which she had saved her foot.

'Yes,' she said, looking steadily into June's eyes, which were moving from side to side, 'Jon seems to have abandoned America for good. I can't see his wife being happy over here.'

'Ah!' said June. 'Holly told me you went to America yourself. Did you see Jon over there?'

'Not quite.'

'Did you like America?'

'It's very stimulating.'

June sniffed.

'Do they buy pictures? I mean, do you think there'd be a chance for Harold Blade's work there?'

'Without knowing the work—'

'Of course, I forgot; it seems so impossible that you don't know it.'

She leaned towards Fleur and her eyes shone.

'I do so want you to sit to him, you know; he'd make such a wonderful picture of you. Your father simply must arrange that. With your position in Society, Fleur, especially after that case last year,' Fleur winced, if imperceptibly–'it would be the making of poor Harold. He's such a genius,' June added, frowing; 'you *must* come and see his work.'

'I should like to,' said Fleur. 'Have you seen Jon yet?'

'No. They're coming on Friday. I hope I shall like her. As a rule, I like all foreigners except the Americans and the French. I mean–with exceptions of course.'

'Naturally,' said Fleur. 'What time are you generally in?'

'Every afternoon between five and seven are Harold's hours for going out–he has my studio, you know. I can show you his work better without him; he's so touchy–all real geniuses are. I want him to paint Jon's wife, too. He's extraordinary with women.'

'In that case, I think you should let Jon see him and his work first.'

June's eyes stared up at her for a moment, and flew off to the Fragonard.

'When will your father come?' she asked.

'Perhaps it would be best for me to come first.'

'Soames naturally likes the wrong thing,' said June, thoughtfully; 'but if *you* tell him you want to be painted–he's sure to–he always spoils you–'

Fleur smiled.

'Well, I'll come. Perhaps not this week.' And, in thought, she added: 'And perhaps, yes–Friday.'

June rose. 'I like your house, and your husband. Where is he?'

'Michael? Slumming, probably; he's in the thick of a scheme for their conversion.'

'How splendid! Can I see your boy?'

'I'm afraid he's only just over measles.'

June sighed. 'It does seem long since I had measles. I remember Jon's measles so well; I got him his first adventure books.' Suddenly she looked up at Fleur: 'Do you like his wife? I think it's ridiculous his being married so young. I tell Harold he must never marry; it's the end of adventure.' Her eyes moved from side to side, as if she were adding: 'Or the beginning, and I've never had it.' And suddenly she held out both hands.

'I shall expect you. I don't know whether he'll like your hair!'

Fleur smiled.

'I'm afraid I can't grow it for him. Oh! Here's my father coming in!' She had seen Soames pass the window.

'I don't know that I want to see him unless it's necessary,' said June.

'I expect he'll feel exactly the same. If you just go out, he won't pay any attention.'

'Oh!' said June, and out she went.

Through the window Fleur watched her moving as if she had not time to touch the ground.

A moment later Soames came in.

'What's that woman want here?' he said. 'She's a stormy petrel.'

'Nothing much, dear; she has a new painter, whom she's trying to boost.'

'Another of her lame ducks! She's been famous for them all her life–ever since–' He stopped short of Bosinney's name. 'She'd never go anywhere without wanting something,' he added. 'Did she get it?'

'Not more than I did, dear!'

Soames was silent, feeling vaguely that he had been near the proverb, 'The kettle and the pot.' What was the use, indeed, of going anywhere unless you wanted something? It was one of the cardinal principles of life.

'I went to see that Morland,' he said; 'it's genuine enough. In fact, I bought it.' And he sank into a reverie. . . .

Acquainted by Michael with the fact that the Marquess of Shropshire had a Morland he wanted to sell, he had said at once: 'I don't know that I want to buy one.'

'I thought you did, sir, from what you were saying the other day. It's a white pony.'

'That, of course,' said Soames. 'What does he want for it?'

'The market price, I believe.'

'There isn't such a thing. Is it genuine?'

'It's never changed hands, he says.'

Soames brooded aloud. 'The Marquess of Shropshire – that's that red-haired baggage's grandfather, isn't it?'

'Yes, but perfectly docile. He'd like you to see it, he said.'

'I daresay,' said Soames, and no more at the moment. . . .

'Where's this Morland?' he asked a few days later.

'At Shropshire House – in Curzon Street, sir.'

'Oh! Ah! Well, I'll have a look at it.'

Having lunch at Green Street, where he was still staying, he walked round the necessary corners, and sent in his card, on which he had pencilled the words: 'My son-in-law, Michael Mont, says you would like me to see your Morland.'

The butler came back, and opening a door, said:

'In here, sir. The Morland is over the sideboard.'

In that big dining-room, where even large furniture looked small, the Morland looked smaller, between two still-lifes of a Dutch size and nature. It had a simple scheme – white pony in stable, pigeon picking up some grains, small boy on upturned basket eating apple. A glance told Soames that it was genuine, and had not even been restored – the chiaroscuro was considerable. He stood, back to the light, looking at it attentively. Morland was not so sought after as he used to be; on the other hand, his pictures were distinctive and of a handy size. If one had not much space left, and wanted that period represented, he was perhaps the most repaying after Constable – good Old Cromes being so infernally rare. A Morland was a Morland, as a Millet was a Millet; and would never be anything else. Like all collectors in an experimental epoch, Soames was continually being faced with the advisability of buying not only what was what, but what would remain what. Such modern painters as were painting modern stuff, would, in his opinion, be dead as door-nails before he himself was; besides, however much he tried, he did not like the stuff. Such modern painters like most of the academicians, as were painting ancient stuff, were careful fellows, no doubt, but who could say whether any of them would live? No! The only safe thing was to buy the dead, and only the dead who were going to live, at that. In this way – Soames was not alone in his conclusions – the early decease of most living painters was ensured. They were already, indeed, saying that hardly one of them could sell a picture for love or money.

He was looking at the pony through his curved thumb and forefinger when he heard a slight sound; and, turning, saw a short old man in a tweed suit, apparently looking at him in precisely the same way.

Dropping his hand, and deciding not to say 'Your Grace,' or whatever it ought to be, Soames muttered:

'I was looking at the tail–some good painting in that.'

The Marquess had also dropped his hand, and was consulting the card between his other thumb and forefinger.

'Mr Forsyte? Yes. My grandfather bought it from the painter. There's a note on the back. I don't want to part with it, but these are lean days. Would you like to see the back?'

'Yes,' said Soames; 'I always look at their backs.'

'Sometimes,' said the Marquess, detaching the Morland with difficulty, 'the best part of the picture.'

Soames smiled down the further side of his mouth; he did not wish the old fellow to receive a false impression that he was 'kow-towing', or anything of that sort.

'Something in the hereditary principle, Mr Forsyte,' the Marquess went on, with his head on one side, 'when it comes to the sale of heirlooms.'

'Oh! I can see it's genuine,' said Soames, 'without looking at the back.'

'Then, if you want to buy, we can have a simple transaction between gentlemen. You know all about values, I hear.'

Soames put his head to the other side, and looked at the back of the picture. The old fellow's words were so disarming, that for the life of him he could not tell whether or not to be disarmed.

'"George Morland to Lord George Ferrar,"' he heard, '"for value received–£80. 1797."'

'He came into the title later,' said Marquess. 'I'm glad Morland got his money–great rips, our grandfathers, Mr Forsyte; days of great rips, those.'

Subtly flattered by the thought that 'Superior Dosset' was a great rip, Soames expanded slightly.

'Great rip, Morland,' he said. 'But there were real painters then, people could buy with confidence–they can't now.'

'I'm not sure,' said the Marquess, 'I'm not sure. The electrification of art may be a necessary process. We're all in a movement, Mr Forsyte.'

'Yes,' said Soames, glumly; 'but we can't go on at this rate–it's not natural. We shall be standing-pat again before long.'

'I wonder. We must keep our minds open, mustn't we?'

'The pace doesn't matter so much,' said Soames, astonished at himself, 'so long as it leads somewhere.'

The Marquess resigned the picture to the sideboard, and putting his foot up on a chair, leaned his elbow on his knee.

'Did your son-in-law tell you for what I wanted the money? He has a scheme for electrifying slum kitchens. After all, we *are* cleaner and more humane than our grandfathers, Mr Forsyte. Now, what do you think would be a fair price?'

'Why not get Dumetrius's opinion?'

'The Haymarket man? Is his opinion better than yours?'

'That I can't say,' said Soames honestly. 'But if you mentioned my name, he'd value the picture for five guineas, and might make an offer himself.'

'I don't think I should care for it to be known that I was selling pictures.'

'Well,' said Soames, 'I don't want you to get less than perhaps you could. But if I told Dumetrius to buy me a Morland, five hundred would be my limit. Suppose I give you six.'

The Marquess tilted up his beard. 'That would be too generous, perhaps. Shall we say five-fifty?'

Soames shook his head.

'We won't haggle,' he said. 'Six. You can have the cheque now, and I'll take it away. It will hang in my gallery at Mapledurham.'

The Marquess took his foot down, and sighed.

'Really, I'm very much obliged to you. I'm delighted to think it will go to a good home.'

'If you care to come and see it at any time—' Soames checked himself. An old fellow with one foot in the House of Lords and one in the grave, and no difference between them, to speak of—as if he'd want to come!

'That would be delightful,' said the Marquess, with his eyes wandering, as Soames had suspected they would. 'Have you your own electric plant there?'

'Yes,' and Soames took out his cheque-book. 'May I have a taxi called? If you hang the still-lifes a little closer together, this won't be missed.'

With that doubtful phrase in their ears, they exchanged goods, and Soames, with the Morland, returned to Green Street in a cab. He wondered a little on the way whether or not the Marquess had done him, by talking about a transaction between gentlemen. Agreeable old chap in his way, but quick as a bird, looking through his thumb and finger like that! . . .

And now, in his daughter's 'parlour' he said:

'What's this about Michael electrifying slum kitchens?'

Fleur smiled, and Soames did not approve of its irony.

'Michael's over head and ears.'

'In debt?'

'Oh, no! Committed himself to a slum scheme, just as he did to Foggartism. I hardly see him.'

Soames made a sound within himself. Young Jon Forsyte lurked now behind all his thoughts of her. Did she really resent Michael's absorption in public life, or was it pretence—an excuse for having a private life of her own?

'The slums want attending to, no doubt,' he said. 'He must have something to do.'

Fleur shrugged.

'Michael's too good to live.'

'I don't know about that,' said Soames; 'but he's—er—rather trustful.'

'That's not your failing, is it, Dad? You don't trust *me* a bit.'

'Not exactly trust you!' floundered Soames. 'Why not?'

'Exactly!'

Soames sought refuge in the Fragonard. Sharp! She had seen into him!

'I suppose June wants me to buy a picture,' he said.

'She wants you to have me painted.'

'Does she? What's the name of her lame duck?'

'Blade, I think.'

'Never heard of him!'

'Well, I expect you will.'

'Yes' muttered Soames; 'she's like a limpet. It's in the blood.'

'The Forsyte blood? You and I, then, too, dear.'

Soames turned from the Fragonard and looked her straight in the eyes.

'Yes; you and I, too.'

'Isn't that nice?' said Fleur.

8

THE JOLLY ACCIDENT

In doubting Fleur's show of resentment at Michael's new 'stunt', Soames was near the mark. She did not resent it at all. It kept his attention off herself, it kept him from taking up birth control, for which she felt the country was not yet quite prepared, and it had a popular appeal denied to Foggartism. The slums were under one's nose, and what was under the nose could be brought to the attention even of party politics. Being a town proposition, slums would concern six-sevenths of the vote. Foggartism, based on the country life necessary to national stamina and the growth of food within and overseas, concerned the whole population, but only appealed to one-seventh of the vote. And Fleur, nothing if not a realist, had long grasped the fact that the main business of politicians was to be, and to remain, elected. The vote was a magnet of the first order, and unconsciously swayed every political judgment and aspiration; or, if not, it ought to, for was it not the touchstone of democracy? In the committee, too, which Michael was forming, she saw, incidentally, the best social step within her reach.

'If they want a meeting-place,' she had said, 'why not here?'

'Splendid!' answered Michael. 'Handy for the House and clubs. Thank you, old thing!'

Fleur had added honestly:

'Oh, I shall be quite glad. As soon as I take Kit to the sea, you can start. Norah Curfew's letting me her cottage at Loring for three weeks.' She did not add: 'And it's only five minutes from Wansdon.'

On the Friday, after lunch, she telephoned to June:

'I'm going to the sea on Monday–I *could* come this afternoon, but I think you said Jon was coming. Is he? Because if so–

'He's coming at four-thirty, but he's got to catch a train back at six-twenty.'

'His wife, too?'

'No. He's just coming to see Harold's work.'

'Oh!–well–I think I'd better come on Sunday, then.'

'Yes, Sunday will be all right; then Harold will see you. He never goes out on Sunday. He hates the look of it so.'

Putting down the receiver, Fleur took up the time-table. Yes, there was the train! What a coincidence if she happened to take it to make a preliminary inspection of Norah Curfew's cottage! Not even June, surely, would mention their talk on the phone.

At lunch she did not tell Michael she was going–he might want to come, too, or at least to see her off. She knew he would be at 'the House' in the afternoon, she would just leave a note to say that she had gone to make sure the cottage would be in order for Monday. And after lunch she bent over and kissed him between the eyes, without any sense of betrayal. A sight of Jon was due to her after these dreary weeks! Any sight of Jon was always due to her who had been defrauded of him. And, as the afternoon drew on, and she put her night things into her dressing-case, a red spot became fixed in each cheek, and she wandered swiftly, her hands restive, her spirit homeless. Having had tea, and left the note giving her address–an hotel at Nettlefold–she went early to Victoria Station. There, having tipped the guard to secure emptiness, she left her bag in a corner seat and took up her stand by the bookstall, where Jon must pass with his ticket. And, while she stood there, examining the fiction of the day, all her faculties were busy with reality. Among the shows and shadows of existence, an hour and a half of real life lay before her. Who could blame her for filching it back from a filching Providence? And if anybody could, she didn't care! The hands of the station clock moved on, and Fleur gazed at this novel after that, all of them full of young women in awkward situations, and vaguely wondered whether they were more awkward than her own. Three minutes to the time! Wasn't he coming after all? Had that wretched June kept him for the night? At last in despair she caught up a tome called *Violin Obbligato*, which at least would be modern, and paid for it. And then, as she was receiving her change, she saw him hastening. Turning, she passed through the wicket, walking quickly, knowing that he was walking more quickly. She let him see her first.

'Fleur!'

'Jon! Where are you going?'

'To Wansdon.'

'Oh! And I'm going to Nettlefold, to see a cottage at Loring for my baby. Here's my bag, in here–quick! We're off!'

The door was banged to, and she held out both her hands.

'Isn't this queer, and jolly?'

Jon held the hands, and dropped them rather suddenly.

'I've been to see June. She's just the same–bless her!'

'Yes, she came round to me the other day; wants me to be painted by her present pet.'

'You might do worse. I said he should paint Anne.'

'Really? Is he good enough for *her*?'

And she was sorry; she hadn't meant to begin like that! Still–must begin somehow–must employ lips which might otherwise go lighting on his eyes, his hair, *his* lips! And she rushed into words: Kit's measles, Michael's committee, *Violin Obbligato*, and the Proustian School; Val's horses, Jon's poetry, the smell of England–so important to a poet–anything, everything, in a sort of madcap medley.

'You see, Jon, I must talk; I've been in prison for a month.' And all the time she felt that she was wasting minutes that might have been spent with lips silent and heart against his, if the heart, as they said, really extended to the centre of the body. And for all the time, too, the proboscis of her spirit was scenting, searching for the honey and the saffron of his spirit. Was there any for her, or was it all kept for that wretched American girl he had left behind him, and to whom–alas!–he was returning? But Jon gave her no sign. Unlike the old impulsive Jon, he had learned secrecy. By a whim of memory, whose ways are so inscrutable, she remembered being taken, as a very little girl, to Timothy's in the Bayswater Road to her great-aunt Hester–an old still figure, in black Victorian lace and jet and a Victorian chair, saying in a stilly languid voice to her father: 'Oh, yes, my dear: your Uncle Jolyon, before he married, was very much in love with our great friend Alice Read; but she was consumptive, you know, and of course he felt he couldn't marry her–it wouldn't have been prudent, he felt, because of children. And then she died, and he married Edith Moor.' Funny how that had stuck in her ten-year-old mind! And she stared at Jon. Old Jolyon—as they called him in the family—had been his grandfather. She had seen his photograph in Holly's album—a domed head, a white moustache, eyes deep-set under the brows, like Jon's. 'It wouldn't have been prudent!' How Victorian! Was Jon, too, Victorian? She felt as if she would never know what Jon was. And she became suddenly cautious. A single step too far, or too soon, and he might be gone from her again for good! He was not—no, he was not modern! For all she knew, there might be something absolute, not relative, in his 'make-up', and to Fleur the absolute was strange, almost terrifying. But she had not spent six years in social servitude without learning to adjust herself swiftly to the playing of a new part. She spoke in a calmer tone, almost a drawl; her eyes became cool and quizzical. What did Jon think about the education of boys—before he knew where he was, of course, he would be having one himself? It hurt her to say that, and, while saying it, she searched his face; but it told her nothing.

'We've put Kit down for Winchester. Do you believe in the Public Schools, Jon? Or do you think they're out of date?'

'Yes; and a good thing, too.'

'How?'

'I mean I should send him there.'

'I see,' said Fleur. 'Do you know, Jon, you really have changed. You wouldn't have said that, I believe, six years ago.'

'Perhaps not. Being out of England makes you believe in dams. Ideas can't be left to swop around in the blue. In England they're not, and that's the beauty of it.'

'I don't care what happens to ideas,' said Fleur, 'but I don't like stupidity. The Public Schools—'

'Oh, no; not really. Certain things get cut and dried there, of course; but then, they ought to.'

Fleur leaned forward, and with faint malice said: 'Have you become a moralist, my dear?'

Jon answered glumly:

'Why, no—no more than reason!'

'Do you remember our walk by the river?'

'I told you before—I remember everything.'

Fleur restrained her hand from a heart which had given a jump.

'We nearly quarrelled because I said I hated people for their stupid cruelties, and wanted them to stew in their own juice.'

'Yes; and I said I pitied them. Well?'

'Repression is stupid, you know, Jon.' And, by instinct, added: 'That's why I doubt the Public Schools. They teach it.'

'They're useful socially, Fleur,' and his eyes twinkled.

Fleur pursed her lips. She did not mind. But she would make him sorry for that; because his compunction would be a trump card in her hand.

'I know perfectly well,' she said, 'that I'm a snob—I was called so publicly.'

'What!'

'Oh, yes; there was a case about it.'

'Who dared?'

'Oh! my dear, that's ancient history. But of course you knew—Francis Wilmot must have—'

Jon made a horrified gesture.

'Fleur, you never thought I–'

'Oh, but of course! Why not?' A trump, indeed! Jon seized her hand.

'Fleur, say you knew I didn't–'

Fleur shrugged her shoulders. 'My dear, you have lived too long among the primitives. Over here we stab each other daily, and no harm done.'

He dropped her hand, and she looked at him from beneath her lids.

'I was only teasing, Jon. It's good for primitives to have their legs pulled. *Parlons d'autre chose.* Have you found your place, to grow things, yet?'

'Practically.'

'Where?'

'About four miles from Wansdon, on the south side of the downs–Green Hill Farm. Fruit–a lot of glass; and some arable.'

'Why, it must be close to where I'm going with Kit. That's on the sea and only five miles from Wansdon. No, Jon; don't be alarmed. We shall only be there three weeks at most.'

'Alarmed! It's very jolly. We shall see you there. Perhaps we shall meet at Goodwood anyway.'

'I've been thinking–' Fleur paused, and again she stole a look. 'We *can* be steady friends, Jon, can't we?'

Jon answered, without looking up. 'I hope so.'

If his face had cleared, and his voice had been hearty, how different–how much slower–would have been the beating of her heart!

'Then that's all right,' she murmured. 'I've been wanting to say that to you ever since Ascot. Here we are, and here we shall be–and anything else would be silly, wouldn't it? This is not the romantic age.'

'H'm!'

'What do you mean by that unpleasant noise?'

'I always think it's rot to talk about ages being this or that. Human feelings remain the same.'

'Do you really think they do? The sort of life we live affects them. Nothing's worth more than a tear or two, Jon. I found that out. But I forgot–you hate cynicism. Tell me about Anne. Is she still liking England?'

'Loving it. You see, she's pure Southern, and the South's old still, too, in a way–or some of it is. What she likes here is the grass, the birds, and the villages. She doesn't feel homesick. And, of course, she loves the riding.'

'I suppose she's picking up English fast?'

And to his stare she made her face quite candid.

'I should like you to like her,' he said, wistfully.

'Oh! of course I shall, when I know her.'

But a fierce little wave of contempt passed up from her heart. What did he think she was made of? Like her! A girl who lay in his arms, who would be the mother of his children. Like her! And she began to talk about the preservation of Box Hill. And all the rest of the way till Jon got out at Pulborough, she was more wary than a cat–casual and friendly, with clear candid eyes, and a little tremble up at him when she said:

'*Au revoir*, then, at Goodwood, if not before! This *has* been a jolly accident!'

But on the way to her hotel, driving in a station fly through air that smelled of oysters, she folded her lips between her teeth, and her eyes were damp beneath her frowning brows.

9

BUT–JON!

But Jon, who had over five miles to walk, started with the words of the Old English song beating a silent tattoo within him:

> 'How happy could I be with either,
> Were t'other dear charmer away!

To such confusion had he come, contrary to intention, but in accordance with the impulses of a loyal disposition. Fleur had been his first love, Anne his second. But Anne was his wife, and Fleur the wife of another. A man could not be in love with two women at once, so he was tempted to conclude that he was not in love with either. Why, then, the queer sensations of his circulatory system? Was popular belief in error? A French, or Old-English way of looking at his situation, did not occur to him. He had married Anne, he loved Anne–she was a darling! There it ended! Why, then, walking along a grassy strip beside the road, did he think almost exclusively of Fleur? However cynical, or casual, or just friendly she might seem, she no more deceived him than she at heart wished to. He knew she had her old feeling for him, just as he knew he had it, or some of it, for her. But then he had feeling for another, too. Jon was not more of a fool than other men, nor was he more self-deceiving. Like other men before him, he intended to face what was, and to do what he believed to be right; or, rather, not to do what he believed to be wrong. Nor had he any doubt as to what was wrong. His trouble was more simple. It consisted in not having a control of his thoughts and feelings greater than that with which any man has hitherto been endowed. After all, it had not been his fault that he had once been wholly in love with Fleur, nor that she had been wholly in love with him; not his fault that he had met her again, nor that she was still in love with him. Nor again was it his fault that he was in love with his native land and tired of being out of it.

It was not his fault that he had fallen in love a second time or married the object of his affections. Nor, so far as he could see, was it his fault that the sight and the sound and the scent and the touch of Fleur had revived some of his former feelings. He was none the less disgusted at his double-heartedness; and he walked now fast, now slow, while the sun shifted over and struck on a neck always sensitive since his touch of the sun in Granada. Presently, he stopped and leaned over a gate. He had not been long enough back in England to have got over its beauty on a fine day. He was always stopping and leaning over gates, or in other ways, as Val called it, mooning!

Though it was already the first day of the Eton and Harrow Match, which his father had been wont to attend so religiously, hay harvest was barely over, and the scent of stacked hay still in the air. The downs lay before him to the south, lighted along their northern slopes. Red Sussex cattle were standing under some trees close to the gate, dribbling, and slowly swishing their tails. And away over there he could see others lingering along the hill-side. Peace lay thick on the land. The corn in that next field had an unearthly tinge, neither green nor gold, under the slanting sunlight. And in the restful beauty of the evening Jon could well perceive the destructiveness of love–an emotion so sweet, restless, and thrilling, that it drained Nature of its colour and peace, made those who suffered from it bores to their fellows and useless to the life of everyday. To work–and behold Nature in her moods! Why couldn't he get away to that, away from women? Why–like Holly's story of the holiday slum girl, whose family came to see her off by train–why couldn't he just get away and say: 'Thank Gawd! I'm shut o' that lot!'

The midges were biting, and he walked on. Should he tell Anne that he had come down with Fleur? Not to tell her was to stress the importance of the incident; but to tell her was somehow disagreeable to him. And then he came on Anne herself, without a hat, sitting on a gate, her hands in the pockets of her jumper. Very lissome and straight she looked.

'Lift me down, Jon!'

He lifted her down in a prolonged manner. And, almost instantly, said:

'Whom do you think I travelled with? Fleur Mont. We ran up against each other at Victoria. She's taking her boy to Loring next week, to convalesce him.'

'Oh! I'm sorry.'

'Why?'

'Because I'm in love with you, Jon.' She tilted her chin, so that her straight and shapely nose looked a little more sudden.

'I don't see–' began Jon.

'You see she's another. I saw that at Ascot. I reckon I'm old-fashioned, Jon.'

'That's all right, so am I.'

She turned her eyes on him, eyes not quite civilised, nor quite American, and put her arm round his waist.

'Rondavel's off his feed. Greenwater's very upset about it.'

' "Very", Anne.'

'Well, you can't pronounce "very" as I pronounce it, any more than I can as you do.'

'Sorry. But you told me to remind you. It's silly, though: why shouldn't you speak your own lingo?'

'Because I want to speak like you.'

'Want, then, not waunt.'

'Damn!'

'All right, darling. But isn't your lingo just as good?'

Anne disengaged her arm.

'No, you don't think that. You're awfully glad to be through with the American accent–you *are*, Jon.'

'It's natural to like one's own country's best.'

'Well, I do want–there!–to speak English. I'm English by law, now, and by descent, all but one French great-grandmother. If we have children, they'll be English, and we're going to live in England. Shall you take Green Hill Farm?'

'Yes. And I'm not going to play at things any more. I've played twice, and this time I'm going all out.'

'You weren't playing in North Carolina.'

'Not exactly. But this is different. It didn't matter there–What are peaches, anyway? It does here–it matters a lot. I mean to make it pay.'

'Bully!' said Anne: 'I mean–er–splendid. But I never believed you'd say that.'

'Paying's the only proof. I'm going in for tomatoes, onions, asparagus, and figs; and I mean to work the arable for all it's worth, and if I can get any more land, I will.'

'Jon! What energy!' And she caught hold of his chin.

'All right!' said Jon, grimly. 'You watch out, and see if I don't mean it.'

'And you'll leave the house to me? I'll make it just too lovely!'

'That's a bargain.'

'Kiss me, then.'

With her lips parted and her eyes looking into his, with just that suspicion of a squint which made them so enticing, Jon thought: 'It's quite simple. The other thing's absurd. Why, of course!' He kissed her forehead and lips, but, even while he did so, he seemed to see Fleur trembling up at him, and to hear her words: '*Au revoir!* It *was* a jolly accident!'

'Let's go and have a look at Rondavel,' he said.

In his box, when those two went in, the grey colt stood by the far wall, idly contemplating a carrot in the hand of Greenwater.

'Clean off!' said the latter over his shoulder: 'It's good-bye to Goodwood! The colt's sick.'

What had Fleur said: '*Au revoir* at Goodwood, if not before!'

'Perhaps it's just a megrim, Greenwater,' said Anne.

'No, ma'am; the horse has got a temperature. Well, we'll win the Middle Park Plate with him yet.'

Jon passed his hand over the colt's quarter: 'Poor old son! Funny! You can tell he's not fit by the feel of his coat!'

'You can that,' replied Greenwater: 'But where's he got it from? There isn't a sick horse that I know of anywhere about. If there's anything in the world more perverse than horses–! We didn't train him for Ascot, and he goes and wins. We meant him for Goodwood, and he's gone amiss. Mr Dartie wants me to give him some South African stuff I never heard of.'

'They have a lot of horse sickness out there,' said Jon. 'See,' said the trainer, stretching his hand up to the colt's ears; 'no kick in him at all! Looks like blackberry sickness out of season. I'd give a good deal to know how he picked it up.'

The two young people left him standing by the colt's dejected head, his dark, hawk-like face thrust forward, as if trying to read the sensations within his favourite.

That night, Jon went up, bemused by Val's opinions on Communism, the Labour Party, the qualities inherent in the offspring of 'Sleeping Dove', with a dissertation on horse-sickness in South Africa. He entered a dim bedroom. A white figure was standing at the window. It turned when he came near and flung its arms round him.

'Jon, you mustn't stop loving me.'

'Why should I?'

'Because men do. Besides, it's not the fashion to be faithful.'

'Bosh!' said Jon gently; 'it's just as much the fashion as it ever was.'

'I'm glad we shan't be going to Goodwood. I'm afraid of her. She's so clever.'

'Fleur?'

'You *were* in love with her, Jon; I feel it in my bones. I wish you'd told me.'

Jon leaned beside her in the window.

'Why?' he said dully.

She did not answer. They stood side by side in the breathless warmth, moths passed their faces, a night-jar churred in the silence, and now and then, from the stables, came the stamp of a sleepless horse. Suddenly Anne stretched out her hand.

'Over there–somewhere–she's awake, and wanting you. I'm not happy, Jon.'

'Don't be morbid, darling!'

'But I'm *not* happy, Jon.'

Like a great child–slim within his arm, her cheek pressed to his, her dark earlock tickling his neck! And suddenly her lips came round to his, vehement.

'Love me!'

But when she was asleep, Jon lay wakeful. Moonlight had crept in and there was a ghost in the room–a ghost in a Goya dress, twirling, holding out its skirts, beckoning with its eyes, and with its lips seeming to whisper: "Me, too! Me, too!"

And, raising himself on his elbow, he looked resolutely at the dark head beside him. No! There was–there should be nothing but that in the room! Reality–reality!

10

THAT THING AND THIS THING

On the following Monday at breakfast Val said to Holly:

'Listen to this!

DEAR DARTIE,–

I think I can do you a good turn. I have some information that concerns your 'Sleeping Dove' colt and your stable generally, worth a great deal more than the fifty pounds which I hope you may feel inclined to pay for it. Are you coming up to town this week-end? If so, can I see you at the Brummell? Or I could come to Green Street if you prefer it. It's really rather vital.

Sincerely yours,
AUBREY STAINFORD.

'That fellow again!'

'Pay no attention, Val.'

'I don't know,' said Val glumly. 'Some gang or other are taking altogether too much interest in the colt. Greenwater's very uneasy. I'd better get to the bottom of it, if I can.'

'Consult your uncle, then, first. He's still at your mother's.'

Val made a wry face.

'Yes,' said Holly; 'but he'll know what you can do and what you can't. You really mustn't deal single-handed with people like that.'

'All right, then. There's hanky-panky in the wind, I'm sure. Somebody knew all about the colt at Ascot.'

He took the morning train and arrived at his mother's at lunch-time. She and Annette were lunching-out, but Soames, who was lunching-in, crossed a cold hand with his nephew's.

'Have you still got that young man and his wife staying with you?'

'Yes,' said Val.

'Isn't he ever going to do anything?'

On being told that Jon was about to do something, Soames grunted.

'Farm—in England? What's he want to do that for? He'll only throw his money away. Much better go back to America, or some other new country. Why doesn't he try South Africa? His half-brother died out there.'

'He won't leave England again, Uncle Soames—seems to have developed quite a feeling for the old country.'

Soames masticated.

'Amateurs,' he said, 'all the young Forsytes. How much has he got a year?'

'The same as Holly and her half-sister—only about two thousand, so long as his mother's alive.'

Soames looked into his wineglass and took from it an infinitesimal piece of cork. His mother! She was in Paris again, he was told. *She* must have three thousand a year, now at least. He remembered when she had nothing but a beggarly fifty pounds a year, and that fifty pounds too much, putting the thought of independence into her head. In Paris again! The Bois de Boulogne, that Green Niobe—all drinking water, he remembered it still, and the scene between them there. . . .

'What have *you* come up for?' he said to Val.

'This, Uncle Soames.'

Soames fixed on his nose the glasses he had just begun to need for reading purposes, read the letter, and returned it to his nephew.

'I've known impudence in my time, but this chap—!'

'What do you recommend me to do?'

'Pitch it into the waste-paper basket?'

Val shook his head.

'Stainford dropped in on me one day at Wansdon. I told him nothing; but you remember we couldn't get more than fours at Ascot, and it was Rondavel's first outing. And now the colt's sick just before Goodwood; there's a screw loose somewhere.'

'What do you think of doing, then?'

'I thought I'd see him, and that perhaps you'd like to be present, to keep me from making a fool of myself.'

'There's something in that,' said Soames. 'This fellow's the coolest ruffian I ever came across.'

'He's pedigree stock, Uncle Soames. Blood will tell.'

'H'm!' muttered Soames. 'Well, have him here, if you must see him, but clear the room first and tell Smither to put away the umbrellas.'

Having seen Fleur and his grandson off to the sea that morning, he felt flat, especially as, since her departure, he had gathered from the map of Sussex that she would be quite near to Wansdon and the young man who was always now at the back of his thoughts. The notion of a return match with 'this ruffian' Stainford, was, therefore, in the nature of a distraction. And, as soon as the messenger was gone, he took a chair whence he could see the street. On second thoughts he had not spoken about the umbrellas—it was not quite dignified; but he had counted them. The day was warm and rainy, and, through the open window of that ground-floor dining-room, the air of Green Street came in, wetted and a little charged with the scent of servants' dinners.

'Here he is,' he said suddenly, 'languid beggar!'

Val crossed from the sideboard and stood behind his uncle's chair. Soames moved uneasily. This fellow and his nephew had been at college together, and had–goodness knew what other vices in common.

'By Jove!' he heard Val mutter. 'He does look ill.'

The 'languid beggar' wore the same dark suit and hat, and the same slow elegance that Soames had first noted on him; a raised eyebrow and the half-lidded eyes despised as ever the bitter crow's-footed exhaustion on his face. And that indefinable look of a damned soul, lost to all but its contempt for emotion, awakened within Soames, just as it had before, the queerest little quirk of sympathy.

'He'd better have a drink,' he said.

Val moved back to the sideboard.

They heard the bell, voices in the hall; then Smither appeared, red, breathless, deprecatory.

'Will you see that gentleman, sir, who took the you know what, sir?'

'Show him in, Smither.'

Val turned towards the door. Soames remained seated.

The 'languid beggar' entered, nodded to Val, and raised his eyebrows at Soames, who said:

'How d'you do, Mr Stainford?'

'Mr Forsyte, I think?'

'Whisky or brandy, Stainford?'

'Brandy, thanks.'

'Smoke, won't you? You wanted to see me. My uncle here is my solicitor.'

Soames saw Stainford smile. It was as if he had said: 'Really! How wonderful these people are!' He lighted the proffered cigar, and there was silence.

'Well?' said Val at last.

'I'm sorry your "Sleeping Dove" colt's gone amiss, Dartie.'

'How did you know that?'

'Exactly! But before I tell you, d'you mind giving me fifty pounds and your word that my name's not mentioned.'

Soames and his nephew stared in silence. At last Val said:

'What guarantee have I that your information's worth fifty pounds, or even five?'

'The fact that I knew your colt had gone amiss.'

However ignorant of the Turf, Soames could see that the fellow had scored.

'You mean you know where the leakage is?'

Stainford nodded.

'We were college pals,' said Val. 'What would you expect me to do if I knew that about a stable of yours?'

'My dear Dartie, there's no analogy. You're a man of means, I'm not.'

Trite expressions were knocking against Soames's plate. He swallowed them. What use in talking to a chap like this!

'Fifty pounds is a lot,' said Val. 'Is your information of real value?'

'Yes–on my word of honour.'

Soames sniffed audibly.

'If I buy this leakage from you,' said Val, 'can you guarantee that it won't break out in another direction?'

'Highly improbable that two pipes will leak in your stable.'

'I find it hard to believe there's one.'

'Well, there is.'

Soames saw his nephew move up to the table and begin counting over a roll of notes.

'Tell me what you know, first, and I'll give them to you if on the face of it your information's probable. I won't mention your name.'

Soames saw the languid eyebrows lift.

'I'm not so distrustful as you, Dartie. Get rid of a boy called Sinnet—that's where your stable leaks.'

'Sinnet?' said Val; 'my best boy? What proof have you?'

Stainford took out a dirty piece of writing-paper and held it up. Val read aloud:

'"The grey colt's amiss all right—he'll be no good for Goodwood." All right?' he repeated. 'Does that means he engineered it?'

Stainford shrugged his shoulders.

'Can I have this bit of paper?' said Val.

'If you'll promise not to show it to him.'

Val nodded, and took the paper.

'Do you know his writing?' asked Soames. 'All this is very fishy.'

'Not yet,' said Val, and to Soames's horror, put the notes into the outstretched hand. The little sigh the fellow gave was distinctly audible. Val said suddenly:

'Did you get at him the day you came down to see me?'

Stainford smiled faintly, shrugged his shoulders again and turned to the door. 'Good-bye, Dartie,' he said.

Soames's mouth fell open. The return match was over! The fellow had gone!

'Here!' he said. 'Don't let him go like that. It's monstrous.'

'Dam' funny!' said Val suddenly, and began to laugh. 'Oh! dam' funny!'

'Funny!' muttered Soames. 'I don't know what the world's coming to.'

'Never mind, Uncle Soames. He's taken fifty of the best off me, but it was worth it. Sinnet, my best boy!'

Soames continued to mutter:

'To corrupt one of your men, and get you to pay him for it. It's the limit.'

'That's what tickles me, Uncle Soames. Well, I'll go back to Wansdon now, and get rid of that young blackguard.'

'I shouldn't have any scruple, if I were you, in telling him exactly how you got the knowledge.'

'Well, I don't know. Stainford's on his beam ends. I'm not a moralist, but I think I'll keep my word to him.'

For a moment Soames said nothing; then, with a sidelong glance at his nephew:

'Well, perhaps. But he ought to be locked up.'

With those words he walked into the hall and counted the umbrellas. Their number was undiminished, and taking one of them, he went out. He felt in need of air. With the exception of that Elderson affair, he had encountered little flagrant dishonesty in his time, and that only in connection with the lower classes. One could forgive a poor devil of a tramp, or even a clerk or domestic servant. They had temptations, and no particular traditions to live up to. But what was coming to the world, if you couldn't rely on gentlemen in a simple matter like honesty! Every day one read cases, and for every one that came into Court one might be sure there were a dozen that didn't! And when you added all the hanky-panky in the City, all the dubious commissions, bribery of the police, sale of honours—though he believed that had been put a stop to—all the dicky-dealing over contracts; it was enough to make one's hair stand on end. They might sneer at the past, and no doubt there was more temptation in the present, but something simple and straightforward seemed to have perished out of life. By hook or by crook people had to get their ends, would no longer wait for their ends to come to them. Everybody was in such a hurry to make good, or rather bad! Get money at all costs—look at the quack remedies they sold and the books they published nowadays, without caring for truth or decency or anything. And the advertisements! Good Lord!

In the gloom of these reflections he had come to Westminster. He might as well call in at South Square and see if Fleur had telephoned her arrival at the sea! In the hall eight hats of differing shape and colour lay on the coat-sarcophagus. What the deuce was going on? A sound of voices came from the dining-room, then the peculiar drone of somebody making a speech. Some meeting or other of Michael's, and the measles only just out of the house!

'What's going on here?' he said to Coaker.

'Something to do with the slums, sir, I believe; they're converting them, I heard Mr Mont say.'

'Don't put my hat with those,' said Soames; 'have you had any message from your mistress?'

'Yes, sir. They had a good journey. The little dog was sick, I believe. He will have his own way.'

'Well,' said Soames, 'I'll go up and wait in the study.'

On getting there, he noticed a water-colour drawing on the bureau: a tree with large dark green leaves and globular golden fruit, against a silvery sort of background—peculiar thing, amateurish, but somehow arresting. Underneath, he recognised his daughter's handwriting:

'The Golden Apple. F.M. 1926.'

Really he had no idea that she could use water-colour as well as that! She was a clever little thing! And he put the drawing up on end where he could see it better! Apple? Passion-fruit, he would have said, of an exaggerated size. Thoroughly uneatable—they had a glow like lanterns. Forbidden fruit! Eve might have given them to Adam. Was this thing symbolic? Did it fancifully reveal her thoughts? And in front of it he fell into sombre mood, which was broken by the opening of the door. Michael had entered.

'Hallo, sir!'

'Hallo!' replied Soames. 'What's this thing?'

II

CONVERTING THE SLUMS

In an age governed almost exclusively by committees, Michael knew fairly well what committees were governed by. A committee must not meet too soon after food, for then the committee-men would sleep; nor too soon before food, because then the committee-men would be excitable. The committee-men should be allowed to say what they liked, without direction, until each was tired of hearing the others say it. But there must be someone present, preferably the chairman, who said little, thought more, and could be relied on to be awake when that moment was reached, whereupon a middle policy, voiced by him to exhausted receivers, would probably be adopted.

Having secured his bishop, and Sir Godfrey Bedwin, who specialised in chests, and failed with his Uncle Lionel Charwell, who had scented the work destined for Lady Alison his wife, Michael convened the first meeting for three o'clock in South Square on the day of Fleur's departure for the sea. Hilary was present, and a young woman, to take them down. Surprise came early. They all attended, and fell into conversation around the Spanish table. It was plain to Michael that the bishop and Sir Timothy Fanfield had expectations of the chair; and he kicked his father under the table, fearing that one of them might propose the other in the hope of the other proposing the one. Sir Lawrence then murmured:

'My dear, that's my shin.'

'I know,' muttered Michael; 'shall we get on with it?'

Dropping his eyeglass, Sir Lawrence said:

'Exactly! Gentlemen, I propose that the Squire takes the chair. Will you second that, Marquess?'

The Marquess nodded.

The blow was well received, and the Squire proceeded to the head of the table. He began as follows:–

'I won't beat about the bush. You all know as much about it as I do, which is precious little. The whole thing is the idea of Mr Hilary Charwell here, so I'll ask him to explain it to us. The slums are C 3 breeders, and verminous into the bargain, and anything we can do to abate this nuisance, I, for one, should be happy to do. Will you give tongue, Mr Charwell?'

Hilary dropped at once into a warm, witty and thorough exposition of his views, dwelling particularly on the human character of a problem 'hitherto,' he said, 'almost exclusively confined to Borough Councils, Bigotry and Blue Books.' That he had made an impression was instantly demonstrated by the buzz of voices. The Squire, who was sitting with his head up and his heels down his knees apart and his elbows close to his sides, muttered:

'Let it rip! Can we smoke, Mont!' And, refusing the cigars and cigarettes proffered by Michael, he filled a pipe, and smoked in silence for several minutes.

'Then we're all agreed,' he said, suddenly, 'that what we want to do is to form this Fund.'

No one having as yet expressed any such opinion, this was the more readily assented to.

'In that case, we'd better get down to it and draw up our appeal.' And, pointing his pipe at Sir Lawrence, he added:

'You've got the gift of the gab with a pen, Mont; suppose you and the bishop and Charwell here go into another room and knock us out a draft. Pitch it strong, but no waterworks.'

When the designated three had withdrawn, conversation broke out again. Michael could hear the Squire and Sir Godfrey Bedwin talking of distemper, and the Marquess discussing with Mr Montross the electrification of the latter's kitchen. Sir Timothy Fanfield was staring at the Goya. He was a tall, lean man of about seventy, with a thin, hooked nose, brown face, and large white moustaches, who had been in the Household Cavalry and come out of it.

A little afraid of his verdict on the Goya, Michael said hastily:

'Well, Sir Timothy, the coal strike doesn't end.'

'No; they ought to be shot. I'm all for the working man; but I'd shoot his leaders to-morrow.'

'What about the mine-owners?' queried Michael.

'I'd shoot their leaders, too. We shall never have industrial peace till we shoot somebody. Fact is, we didn't shoot half enough people during the war. Conshies and Communists and profiteers—I'd have had 'em all against a wall.'

'I'm very glad you came on our committee, sir,' Michael murmured; 'we want someone with strong views.'

'Ah!' said Sir Timothy, and pointing his chin towards the end of the table, he lowered his voice. 'Between ourselves–bit too moderate, the Squire. You want to take these scoundrels by the throat. I knew a chap that owned half a slum and had the face to ask me to subscribe to a Missionary Fund in China. I told the fellow he ought to be shot. Impudent beggar–he didn't like it.'

'No?' said Michael; and at this moment the young woman pulled his sleeve. Was she to take anything down?

Not at present–Michael thought.

Sir Timothy was again staring at the Goya.

'Family portrait?' he said.

'No,' said Michael; 'it's a Goya.'

'Deuce it is! Goy is Jewish for Christian. Female Christian–what?'

'No, sir. Name of the Spanish painter.'

'No idea there were any except Murillo and Velasquez–never see anything like *them* nowadays. These modern painters, you know, ought to be tortured. I say,' and again he lowered his voice, 'bishop!–what!–they're always running some hare of their own–anti-birth-control, or missions of sorts. We want to cut this C 3 population off at the root. Stop 'em having babies by hook or crook; and then shoot a slum landlord or two–deal with both ends. But they'll jib at it, you'll see. D'you know anything about ants?'

'Only that they're busy,' said Michael.

'I've made a study of 'em. Come down to my place in Hampshire, and I'll show you my slides–most interestin' insects in the world.' He lowered his voice again:

'Who's that talkin' to the old Marquess? What! The rubber man? Jew, isn't he? What axe is *he* grinding? The composition of this committee's wrong, Mr Mont. Old Shropshire's a charmin' old man, but–' Sir Timothy touched his forehead–'mad as a March hare about electricity. You've got a doctor, too. They're too mealy-mouthed. What you want is a committee that'll go for those scoundrels. Tea? Never drink it. Chap who invented tea ought to have been strung up.'

At this moment the sub-committee re-entering the room, Michael rose, not without relief.

'Hallo,' he heard the Squire say: 'you've been pretty slippy.'

The look of modest worth which passed over the faces of the sub-committee did not altogether deceive Michael, who knew that his Uncle had brought the draft appeal in his coat pocket. It was now handed up, and the Squire, putting on some horn-rimmed spectacles, began reading it aloud, as if it were an entry of hounds, or the rules of a race-meeting. Michael could not help feeling that what it lost it gained–the Squire and emphasis were somehow incompatible. When he had finished reading, the Squire said:

'We can discuss it now, clause by clause. But time's getting on, gentlemen. Personally, I think it about fills the bill. What do you say, Shropshire?'

The Marquess leaned forward and took his beard in his hand.

'An admirable draft, with one exception. Not sufficient stress is laid on electrification of the kitchens. Sir Godfrey will bear me out. You can't expect these poor people to keep their houses clean unless you can get rid of the smoke and the smells and the flies.'

'Well, we can put in something more about that, if you'll give us the wording, Shropshire.'

The Marquess began to write. Michael saw Sir Timothy twirl his moustaches.

'*I'm* not satisfied,' he began, abruptly. 'I want something that'll make slum landlords sit up. We're here to twist their tails. The appeal's too mild.'

'M'm!' said the Squire; 'What do you suggest, Fanfield?'

Sir Timothy read from his shirt-cuff.

' "We record our conviction that anyone who owns slum property ought to be shot," These gentlemen–'

'*That* won't do,' said the Squire.

'Why not?'

'All sorts of respectable people own slum property–widows, syndicates, dukes, goodness-knows-who! We can't go calling them gentlemen, and sayin' they ought to be shot. It won't *do*.'

The bishop leaned forward:

'Might we rather word it like this? "The signatories much regret that those persons who own slum property are not more alive to their responsibilities to the community at large." '

'Good Lord!' burst from Sir Timothy.

'I think we might pitch it stronger than that, Bishop,' said Sir Lawrence: 'But we ought to have a lawyer here, to tell us exactly how far we can go.'

Michael turned to the chairman:

'I've got one in the house, sir. My father-in-law–I saw him come in just now. I daresay he'd advise us.'

'Old Forsyte!' said Sir Lawrence. 'The very man. We ought to have him on the committee, Squire. He's well up in the law of libel.'

'Ah!' said the Marquess: 'Mr Forsyte! By all means–a steady head.'

'Let's co-opt him, then,' said the Squire; 'a lawyer's always useful.'

Michael went out.

Having drawn the Fragonard blank, he went up to his study, and was greeted by Soames's 'What's this?'

'Pretty good, sir, don't you think? It's Fleur's–got feeling.'

'Yes,' muttered Soames; 'too much, I shouldn't wonder.'

'You saw the hats in the hall, no doubt. My Slum Conversion Committee are just drafting their appeal, and they'd be most frightfully obliged to you, sir, as a lawyer, if you'd come down and cast your eye over one of two of the allusions to slum landlords. They want to go just far enough, you know. In fact, if it wouldn't bore you terribly, they'd like to co-opt you on the committee.'

'Would they?' said Soames: 'And who are *they*?'

Michael ran over the names.

Soames drew up a nostril. 'Lot of titles! Is this a wildcat thing?'

'Oh! no, sir. Our wish to have you on is a guarantee against that. Besides, our chairman, Wilfred Bentworth, has refused a title three times.'

'Well,' said Soames, 'I don't know. I'll come and have a look at them.'

'That's very good of you. I think you'll find them thoroughly respectable,' and he preceded Soames downstairs.

'This is quite out of my line,' said Soames on the threshold. He was greeted with a number of little silent bows and nods. It was his impression that they'd been having a scrap.

'Mr—Mr Forsyte,' said what he supposed was this Bentworth, 'we want you as a lawyer to come on this committee and keep us—er—straight—check our fire-eaters, like Fanfield there, if you know what I mean;' and he looked over his tortoiseshell spectacles at Sir Timothy. 'Just cast your eye over this, will you be so good?' He passed a sheet of paper to Soames, who had sat down on a chair slipped under him by the young woman. Soames began to read:

'"While we suppose that there may be circumstances which justify the possession of slum property, we nevertheless regret profoundly the apparent indifference of most slum owners to this great national evil. With the hearty co-operation of slum property owners, much might be done which at present cannot be done. We do not wish to hold them up to the execration of anyone, but we want them to realise that they must at least co-operate in getting rid of this blot on our civilisation."'

He read it twice, holding the end of his nose between his thumb and finger: then said: '"We don't wish to hold them up to the execration of anyone." If you don't you don't; then why say so? The word "execration"! H'm!'

'Exactly!' said the chairman: 'Most valuable to have you on the committee, Mr—Forsyte.'

'Not at all,' said Soames, staring round him: 'I don't know that I'm coming on.'

'Look here, sir!' And Soames saw a fellow who looked like a general in a story-book, leaning towards him: 'D'you mean to say we can't use a mild word like "execration", when we know they ought to be shot?'

Soames gave a pale smile: if there was a thing he couldn't stand, it was militarism.

'You can use it if you like,' he said, 'but not with me or any other man of judgment on the committee.'

At his words at least four members of the committee burst into speech. Had he said anything too strong?

'We'll pass that without those words, then,' said the chairman. 'Now for your clause about the kitchens, Shropshire. That's important.'

The Marquess began reading; Soames looked at him almost with benevolence. They had hit it off very well over the Morland. No one objected to the addition, and it was adopted.

'That's that, then. I don't think there's anything more. I want to get off.'

'A minute, Mr Chairman.' Soames saw that the words were issuing from behind a walrus-like moustache. 'I know more of these people than any of you here. I started life in the slums, and I want to tell you something. Suppose you get some money, suppose you convert some streets, will you convert those people? No, gentlemen; you won't.'

'Their children, Mr Montross, their children,' said a man whom Soames recognised as one of those who had married Michael to his daughter.

'I'm not against the appeal, Mr Charwell, but I'm a self-made man and a realist, and I know what we're up against. I'm going to put some money into this, gentlemen, but I want you to know that I do so with my eyes open.'

Soames saw the eyes, melancholy and brown, fixed on himself, and had a longing to say: 'You bet!' But, looking at Sir Lawrence, he saw that "Old Mont" had the longing too, and closed his lips firmly.

'Capital!' said the chairman. 'Well, Mr Forsyte, are you joining us?'

Soames looked round the table.

'I'll go into the matter,' he said, 'and let you know.'

Almost instantly the committee broke towards their hats, and he was left opposite the Goya with the Marquess.

'A Goya, Mr Forsyte, I think, and a good one. Am I mistaken, or didn't it once belong to Burlingford?'

'Yes,' said Soames, astonished. 'I bought it when Lord Burlingford sold his pictures in 1910.'

'I thought so. Poor Burlingford! He got very rattled, I remember, over the House of Lords. But, you see, they've done nothing since. How English it all was!'

'They're a dilatory lot,' murmured Soames, whose political recollections were of the vaguest.

'Fortunately, perhaps,' said the Marquess; 'there is so much leisure for repentance.'

'I can show you another picture or two, here, if you care for them,' said Soames.

'Do,' said the Marquess; and Soames led him across the hall, now evacuated by the hats.

'Watteau, Fragonard, Pater, Chardin,' said Soames.

The Marquess was gazing from picture to picture with his head a little on one side.

'Delightful!' he said. 'What a pleasant, and what a worthless age that was! After all, the French are the only people that can make vice attractive except perhaps the Japanese, before they were spoiled. Tell me, Mr Forsyte, do you know any Englishman who has done it?'

Soames, who had never studied the question and was hampered by not knowing whether he wanted an Englishman to do it, was hesitating when the Marquess added:

'And yet no such domestic people as the French.'

'My wife's French,' said Soames, looking round his nose.

'Indeed!' said the Marquess; 'How pleasant!'

Soames was again about to answer, when the Marquess continued:

'To see them go out on Sundays—the whole family, with their bread and cheese, their sausage and wine! A truly remarkable people!'

'I prefer ourselves,' said Soames, bluntly. 'Less ornamental, perhaps, but–' he stopped short of his country's virtues.

'The first of my family, Mr Forsyte, was undoubtedly a Frenchman–not even a Norman Frenchman. There's a tradition that he was engaged to keep William Rufus's hair red, when it was on the turn. They gave him lands, so he must have been successful. We've had a red streak in the family ever since. My granddaughter–' He regarded Soames with a bird-like eye–'But she and your daughter hardly got on, I remember.'

'No,' said Soames, grimly, 'they hardly got on.'

'I'm told they've made it up.'

'I don't think so,' said Soames; 'but that's ancient history.'

In the stress of the present uneasiness he could have wished it were modern.

'Well, Mr Forsyte, I'm delighted to have seen these pictures. Your son-in-law tells me he's going to electrify the kitchen here. Believe me, there's nothing more conducive to a quiet stomach than a cook who never gets heated. Do tell Mrs Forsyte that!'

'I will,' said Soames; 'but the French are conservative.'

'Lamentably so,' replied the Marquess, holding out his hand: 'Good-bye to you!'

'Good-bye!' said Soames, and remained at the window, gazing after the old man's short, quick figure in its grey-green tweeds, with a feeling of having been slightly electrified.

I2

DELICIOUS NIGHT

Fleur sat under a groyne at Loring. There were few things with which she had less patience than the sea. It was not in her blood. The sea, with its reputation for never being in the same mood, blue, wet, unceasing, had for her a distressing sameness. And, though she sat with her face to it, she turned to it the back of her mind. She had been there a week without seeing Jon again. They knew where she was, yet only Holly had been over; and her quick instinct apprehended the cause—Anne must have become aware of her. And now, as Holly had told her, there was no longer even Goodwood to look forward to. Everywhere she was baulked and with all her heart resented it! She was indeed in a wretched state of indecision. If she had known precisely the end she wished to attain, she could have possessed her soul; but she knew it not. Even the care of Kit was no longer important. He was robust again, and employed all day, with spade and bucket.

'I can't stand it,' she thought; 'I shall go up to town. Michael will be glad of me.'

She went up after an early lunch, reading in the train a book of reminiscences which took away the reputations of various dead persons. Quite in the mode, it distracted her thoughts more than she had hoped from its title: and her spirits rose as the scent of oysters died out of the air. She had letters from her father and Michael in her bag, and got them out to read again.

DEAR HEART (ran Michael's—yes, she supposed she *was* still his dear heart)—

I hope this finds you and Kit as it leaves me 'at the present time of speaking'. But I miss you horribly as usual, and intend to descend on you before long, unless you descend on me first. I don't know if you saw our appeal in the papers on Monday. People are already beginning to take bonds. The committee weighed in well for a send-off. The walrus put down five thousand of the best, the Marquess sent your father's Morland cheque for six hundred, and your Dad and Bart each gave two-fifty. The Squire gave five hundred; Bedwin and Sir Timothy a hundred apiece, and the bishop gave us twenty and his blessing. So we opened with six thousand eight hundred and twenty from the committee alone—none so dusty. I believe the thing will go. The appeal has been reprinted, and is going out to everybody who ever gives to anything; and amongst other propaganda, we've got the Polytheum to promise to show a slum film if we can get one made. My Uncle Hilary is very bucked. It was funny to see your Dad—he was a long time making up his mind, and he actually went down to look at the Meads. He came back saying—he didn't know, it was a tumble-down neighbourhood, he didn't think it could be done for five hundred a house. I had my uncle to him that evening, and he knocked under to Hilary's charm. But next morning he was very grumpy—said his name would be in the papers as signing the appeal, and seemed to think it would do him harm. 'They'll think I've taken leave of my senses,' was his way of putting it. However, there he is, on the committee, and he'll get used to it in time. They're a rum team, and but for the bugs I don't think they'd hold together. We had another meeting to-day. Old Blythe's nose is properly out of joint; he says I've gone back on him and Foggartism. I haven't, of course–but, dash it, one must have something real to do!

All my love to you and Kit.

MICHAEL.

I've got your drawing framed and hung above my bureau, and very jolly it looks. Your Dad was quite struck. M.

Above his bureau–'The golden apple!' How ironical! Poor Michael–if he knew–!

Her father's letter was short–she had never had a long one from him.

MY DEAR CHILD,

Your mother has gone back to 'The Shelter', but I am staying on at Green Street about this thing of Michael's. I don't know, I'm sure, whether there's anything in it; there's a lot of gammon talked about the slums; still, for a parson, I find his Uncle Hilary an amiable fellow, and there are some goodish names on the committee. We shall see.

I had no idea you had kept up your water-colours. The drawing has considerable merit, though the subject is not clear to me. The fruit looks too soft and rich for apples. Still, I suppose you know what you were driving at. I am glad the news of Kit is so good, and that you are feeling the better for the sea air.

Ever your affectionate father,
S.F.

Knew what she was driving at! If only she did! And if only her father didn't! That was the doubt in her mind when she tore up the letter and scattered it on Surrey through the window. He watched her like a lynx–like a lover; and she did not want to be watched just now.

She had no luggage, and at Victoria took a cab for Chiswick. June would at least know something about those two; whether they were still at Wansdon, or where they were.

How well she remembered the little house from the one visit she had paid to it–in the days when she and Jon–!

June was in the hall, on the point of going out.

'Oh! it's you!' she said. 'You didn't come that Sunday!'

'No, I had too much to do before I went away.'

'Jon and Anne are staying here now. Harold is painting a beautiful thing of her. It'll be quite unique. She's a nice little thing, I think,' (*she* was several inches taller than June, according to Fleur's recollection) 'and pretty. I'm just going out to get him something he specially wants, but I shan't be a quarter of an hour. If you'll wait in the meal-room till I come back, I'll take you up, and then he'll see you. He's the only man who's doing real work just now.'

'It's so nice that there's one,' said Fleur.

'Here's an album of reproductions of his pictures'–and June opened a large book on a small dining-table. 'Isn't that lovely? But all his work has such quality. You must look through it, and I'll come back.' And with a little squeeze of Fleur's shoulder, she fled.

Fleur did not look through the album, she looked through the window and round the room. How she remembered it, and that round, dim mirror of very old glass wherein she had seen herself while she waited for Jon. And the stormy little scene they had been through together in this room too small for storms, seven years ago! Jon staying here! Her heart beat, and she stared at herself again in that dim mirror. Surely she was no worse to look at than she had been then! Nay! She was better! Her face had a stamp on it now, line on the roundness of youth! Couldn't she let him know that she was here? Couldn't she see him somehow just for a minute alone! That little one-eyed fanatic–for so in her thoughts Fleur looked on June—would be back directly. And quick mind took quick decision. If Jon were in, she would find him! Touching her hair at the sides, the pearls round her neck, and flicking an almost powderless puff over her nose, she went out into the hall and listened. No sound! And slowly she began mounting the stairs. In his bedroom he would be, or in the studio—there was no other covert. On the first landing, bedroom to right of her, bedroom to left of her, bathroom in front of her, the doors open. Blank!—and blank in her heart! The studio was all there was above. And there—as well as Jon, would be the painter and that girl, his wife. Was it worth it? She took two steps down, and then retraced them. Yes! It was. Slowly, very silently, she went. The studio door was open, for she could hear the quick, familiar shuffle of a painter to his canvas and away again. She closed her eyes a moment, and then again went up. On the landing, close to the open door, she stood still. No need to go farther. For, in the room directly opposite to her, was a long, broad mirror, and in it—unseen herself—she could see. Jon was sitting on the end of a low divan with an unsmoked pipe in his hand, staring straight before him. On the dais that girl was standing, dressed in white; her hands held a long-stemmed lily whose flower reached to within an inch of her chin. Oh! she was pretty—pretty and brown, with those dark eyes and that dark hair framing her face. But Jon's expression—deepset on the mask of his visage as the eyes in his head! She had seen lion cubs look like that, seeing nothing close to them, seeing—what?—in the distance. That girl's eyes, 'what was it Holly had called them?—'best type of water-nymph's'—slid round and looked at him, and at once his eyes left the distance and smiled back. Fleur turned then, hurried down the stairs, and out of the house. Wait for June—hear her rhapsodise—be introduced to the painter—have to control her face in front of that girl? No! Mounting to the top of her bus, she saw June skimming round a corner, and thought with malicious pleasure of her disappointment—when one had been hurt, one wanted to hurt somebody. The bus carried her away down the King's Road, Hammersmith, sweating in the westering sunlight, away into the big town with its myriad lives and interests, untouchable, indifferent as Fate.

At Kensington Gardens she descended. If she could get her legs to ache, perhaps her heart would not. And she walked fast between the flowers and the nursemaids, the old ladies and the old gentlemen. But her legs were strong, and Hyde Park Corner came too soon for all but one old gentleman who had tried to keep pace with her because, at his age, it did him good to be attracted. She crossed to the Green park and held on. And she despised herself while she walked. She despised herself. She—to whom the heart was such *vieux jeu*; who had learned, as she thought, to control or outspeed emotions?

She reached home, and it was empty—Michael not in. She went upstairs, ordered herself some Turkish coffee, got into a hot bath, and lay there smoking cigarettes. She experienced some alleviation. Among her friends the recipe had long been recognised. When she could steep herself no more, she put on a wrapper and went to Michael's study. There was her 'Golden Apple'—very nicely framed. The fruit looked to her extraordinarily uneatable at that moment. The smile in Jon's eyes, answering that girl's smile! Another woman's leavings! The fruit was not worth eating. Sour apples—sour apples! Even the white monkey would refuse fruit like that. And for some minutes she stood staring instead at the eyes of the ape in that Chinese painting—those almost human eyes that yet were not human because their owner had no sense of continuity. A modern painter could not have painted eyes like that. The Chinese artist of all those centuries ago had continuity and tradition in his blood; he had seen the creature's restlessness at a sharper angle than people could see it now, and stamped it there for ever.

And Fleur–charming in her jade-green wrapper–tucked a corner of her lip behind a tooth, and went back to her room to finish dressing. She put on her prettiest frock. If she could not have the wish of her heart–the wish that she felt would give her calm and continuity–let her at least have pleasure, speed, distraction, grasp it with both hands, eat it with full lips. And she sat down before her glass to make herself as perfect as she could. She manicured her hands, titivated her hair, scented her eyebrows, smoothed her lips, put on rouge, and the merest dusting of powder, save where the seaside sun had stained her neck.

Michael found her still seated there–a modern masterpiece–almost too perfect to touch.

'Fleur!' he said, and nothing more; but any more would have spoiled it.

'I thought I deserved a night out. Dress quickly, Michael, and let's dine somewhere amusing, and do a theatre and a club afterwards. You needn't go to the House this evening, need you?'

He had meant to go but there was in her voice what would have stopped him from affairs even more serious.

Inhaling her, he said:

'Delicious! I've been in the slums. Shan't be a jiffy, darling!' and he fled.

During the jiffy she thought of him and how good he was; and while she thought, she saw the eyes and the hair and the smile of Jon.

The 'somewhere amusing' was a little restaurant full of theatrical folk. Fleur and Michael knew many of them, and they came up, as they passed out to their theatres, and said:

'How delightful to see you!' and looked as if they meant it–so strange! But then, theatre folk were like that! They looked things so easily. And they kept saying: 'Have you seen our show? Oh! You must. It's just too frightful!' or, 'It's a marvellous play!' And then, over the other shoulder they would see somebody else, and call out: 'Ha! How delightful to see you!' There was no boring continuity about them. Fleur drank a cocktail and two glasses of champagne. She went out with her cheeks slightly flushed. 'Dat Lubly Lady' had been in progress over half an hour before they reached her; but this did not seem to matter, for what they saw conveyed to them no more than what they had not seen. The house was very full, and people were saying that the thing would 'run for years.' It had a tune which had taken the town by storm, a male dancer whose legs could form the most acute angles, and no continuity whatever. Michael and Fleur went out humming the tune, and took a taxi to the dancing club to which they belonged because it was the thing, rather than because they ever went there. It was a select club, and contained among its members a Cabinet Minister who had considered it his duty. They found a Charleston in progress, seven couples wobbling weak knees at each other in various corners of the room.

'Gawd!' said Michael. 'I do think it's the limit of vacuity! What's its attraction?'

'Vacuity, my dear. This is a vacuous age–didn't you know?'

'Is there no limit?'

'A limit,' said Fleur, 'is what you can't go beyond; one can always become more vacuous.'

The words were nothing, for, after all, cynicism was in fashion, but the tone made Michael shiver; he felt in it a personal ring. Did she, then, feel her life so vacuous; and, if so, why?

'They say,' said Fleur, 'there's another American dance coming, called "The White Beam", that's got even less in it.'

'Not possible,' muttered Michael; 'for congenital idiocy this'll never be surpassed. Look at those two!'

The two in question were wobbling towards them with their knees flexed as if their souls had slipped down into them; their eyes regarded Fleur and Michael with no more expression than could have been found in four first-class marbles. A strange earnestness radiated from them below the waist, but above that line they seemed to have passed away. The music stopped, and each of the seven couples stopped also and began to clap their hands, holding them low, as though afraid of disturbing the vacuity attained above.

'I refuse to believe it,' said Michael, suddenly.

'What?'

'That this represents our age—no beauty, no joy, no skill, not even devil—just look a fool and wobble your knees.'

'You can't do it, you see.'

'D'you mean you can?'

'Of course,' said Fleur; 'one must keep up with things.'

'Well, for the land's sake, don't let me see you.'

At this moment the seven couples stopped clapping their hands—the band had broken into a tune to which the knee could not be flexed. Michael and Fleur began to dance. They danced together, two foxtrots and a waltz, then left.

'After all,' said Fleur, in the taxi, 'dancing makes you forget yourself. That was the beauty of the canteen. Find me another job, Michael; I can bring Kit back in about a week.'

'How about joint secretaryship with me of our Slum Conversion Fund? You'd be invaluable to get up balls, bazaars, and *matinées*.'

'I wouldn't mind. I suppose they're worth converting.'

'Well, *I* think so. You don't know Hilary; I must get him and Aunt May to lunch; after that you can judge for yourself.'

He slipped his hand under her bare arm, and added: 'Fleur, you're not quite tired of me, are you?'

The tone of his voice, humble and a little anxious, touched her, and she pressed his hand with her arm.

'I should never be tired of you, Michael.'

'You mean you'd never have a feeling so definite towards me.'

It was exactly what she had meant, and she hastened to deny it.

'No, dear boy; I mean I know a good thing, and even a good person, when I've got it.'

Michael sighed, and, taking up her hand, put it to his lips.

'I wish,' cried Fleur, 'one wasn't so complex. You're lucky to be so single-hearted. It's the greatest gift. Only, don't ever become serious, Michael. That'd be a misfortune.'

'No; after all, comedy's the real thing.'

'Let's hope so,' said Fleur, as the taxi stopped. 'Delicious night!'

And Michael, having paid the driver, looked at her lighted up in the open doorway. Delicious night! Yes—for him.

'ALWAYS!'

The announcement by Michael on the following Monday that Fleur would be bringing Kit home the next morning, caused Soames to say:

'I'd like to have a look at that part of the world. I'll take the car down this afternoon and drive them up to-morrow. Don't say anything to Fleur. I'll let her know when I get down to Nettlefold. There's an hotel there, I'm told.'

'Quite a good one,' said Michael. 'But it'll be full for Goodwood.'

'I'll telephone. They must find a room for me.'

He did, and they found for him a room which somebody else lost. He started about five–Riggs having informed him that it was a two-and-a-half hours' drive. The day had been somewhat English in character, but by the time he reached Dorking had become fine enough to enjoy. He had seen little of the England that lay beyond the straight line between his river home and Westminster for many years; and this late afternoon, less preoccupied than usual, he was able to give it a somewhat detached consideration. It was certainly a variegated and bumpy land, incorrigibly green and unlike India, Canada and Japan. They said it had been jungle, heath and marsh not fifteen hundred years ago. What would it be fifteen hundred years hence? Jungle, heath and marsh again, or one large suburb–who could say? He had read somewhere that people would live underground, and come up to take air in their flying machines on Sundays. He thought it was unlikely. The English would still want their windows down and a thorough draught, and so far as he could see, it would always be stuffy to play with a ball underground, and impossible to play with a ball up in the air. Those fellows who wrote prophetic articles and books were always forgetting that people had passions. He would make a bet that the passions of the English in 3400 A.D. would still be: playing golf, cursing the weather, sitting in draughts, and revising the Prayer Book.

And that reminded him that old Gradman was getting very old; he must look out for somebody who could take his place. There was nothing to do in the family trusts now–the only essential was perfect honesty. And where was he going to find it? Even if there was some about, it could only be tested by prolonged experiment. Must be a youngish man, too, because he himself couldn't last very much longer. And, moving at forty miles an hour along the road to Billingshurst, he recalled being fetched by old Gradman at six miles an hour from Paddington Station to Park Lane in a growler with wet straw on the floor–over sixty years ago–when old Gradman himself was only a boy of twenty, trying to grow sidewhiskers and writing round-hand all day. 'Five Oaks' on a signpost; he couldn't see the oaks! What a pace that chap Riggs was going! One of these days he would bring the whole thing to grief, and be sorry for it. But it was somehow *infra dig.* to pull him up for speed when there wasn't a woman in the car; and Soames sat the stiller, with a slightly contemptuous expression as a kind of insurance against his own sensations. Through

Pulborough, down a twisting hill, across a little bridge, a little river, into a different kind of country–something new to him–flat meadows all along, that would be marsh in the winter, he would wager, with large, dark red cattle, and black-and-white and strawberry roan cattle; and over away to the south, high rising downs of a singularly cool green, as if they were white inside. Chalk–outcropping here and there, and sheep up on those downs, no doubt–his father had always sworn by Southdown mutton. A very pretty light, a silvery look, a nice prospect altogether, that made you feel thinner at once and lighter in the head! So this was the sort of country his nephew had got hold of, and that young fellow Jon Forsyte. Well! It might have been worse–very individual; he didn't remember anything just like it. And a sort of grudging fairness, latent in Soames's nature, applauded slightly. How that chap Riggs was banging the car up this hill–the deuce of a hill, too, past chalk-pits and gravel-pits, and grassy down and dipping spurs of covert, past the lodge of a park, into a great beech-wood. Very pretty–very still–no life but trees, spreading trees, very cool, very green! Past a monstrous great church thing, now, and a lot of high walls and towers–Arundel Castle, he supposed; huge, great place; would look better, no doubt, the farther you got from it; then over another river and up another hill, banging along into this Nettlefold and the hotel, and the sea in front of you!

Soames got out.

'What time's dinner?'

'Dinner is on, sir.'

'Do they dress?'

'Yes, sir. There's a fancy dress, sir, this evening, before Goodwood.'

'What a thing to have! Get me a table; I'll be down directly.'

He had once read in a Victorian novel that the mark of a gentleman was being able to dress for dinner in ten minutes, tying his own tie. He had never forgotten it. He was down in twelve. Most people had nearly finished, but there was no one in fancy dress. Soames ate leisurely, contemplating a garden with the sea beyond. He had not, like Fleur, an objection to the sea–had he not once lived at Brighton for seven years, going up and down to his work in town? That was the epoch when he had been living down the disgrace of being deserted by his first wife. Curious how the injured party was always the one in disgrace! People admired immorality, however much they said they didn't. The deserted husband, the deserted wife, were looked on as poor things. Was it due to something still wild in human nature, or merely to reaction against the salaried morality of judges and parsons, and so forth? Morality you might respect, but salaried morality–no! He had seen it in people's eyes after his own trouble; he had seen it in the Marjorie Ferrar case. The fact was, people took the protection of the law and secretly disliked it because it was protective. The same thing with taxes–you couldn't do without them, but you avoided paying them when you could.

Having finished dinner, he sat with his cigar in a somewhat deserted lounge, turning over weekly papers full of ladies with children or dogs, ladies with clothes in striking attitudes, ladies with no clothes in still more striking attitudes; men with titles, men in aeroplanes, statesmen in trouble, race-horses; large houses prefaced with rows of people with the names printed clearly for each, and other evidences of the millennium. He supposed his fellow-guests were 'dolling up' (as young Michael would put it) for this ball–fancy dressing up at their age! But people *were* weak-minded–no question of that! Fleur would be surprised when he dropped in on her to-morrow early. Soon she would be coming down to him on the river—its best time of year—and perhaps he could take her for a motor trip into the west somewhere; it might divert her thoughts from this part of the country and that young man. He had often promised himself a visit to where the old Forsytes came from; only he didn't suppose she would care to look at anything so rustic as genuine farmland. The magazine dropped from his fingers, and he sat staring out of the large window at the flowers about to sleep. He hadn't so many more years before him now, he supposed. They said that people lived longer than they used to, but how he was going to outlive the old Forsytes, he didn't know—the ten of them had averaged eighty-seven years—a monstrous age! And yet he didn't feel it would be natural to die in another sixteen years, with the flowers growing like that out there, and his grandson coming along nicely. With age one suffered from the feeling that one might have enjoyed things more. Cows, for instance, and rooks, and good smells. Curious how the country grew on you as you got older! But he didn't know that it would ever grow on Fleur—she wanted people about her; still she might lose that when she found out once for all that there was so little in them. The light faded on the garden and his reverie. There were lots of people out on the sea front, and a band had begun to play. A band was playing behind him, too, in the hotel somewhere. They must be dancing! He might have a look at that before he went up. On his trip round the world with Fleur he had often put his nose out and watched the dancing on deck—funny business nowadays, shimmying, bunny-hugging, didn't they call it?—dreadful!—He remembered the academy of dancing where he had been instructed as a small boy in the polka, the mazurka, deportment and calisthenics. And a pale grin spread over his chaps—that little old Miss Shears, who had taught him and Winifred, what wouldn't she have died of if she had lived to see these modern dances! People despised the old dances, and when he came to think of it, he had despised them himself, but compared with this modern walking about and shaking at the knees, they had been dances, after all. Look at the Highland schottische, where you spun round and howled, and the old gallop to the tune 'D'ye ken John Peel'—some stingo in them; and you had to change your collar. No changing collars nowadays—they just dawdled. For an age that prided itself on enjoying life, they had a funny idea of it. He remembered once before his first marriage, going—by accident—to one of those old dancing clubs, the Athenians, and seeing George Forsyte and his cronies waltzing and swinging the girls round and round clean off their feet. The girls at those clubs, then, were all professional lights-o'-love. Very different now, he was told; but there it was—people posed nowadays, they posed as *viveurs*, and all the rest of it, but they didn't vive; they thought too much about how to.

The music—all jazz—died behind him and rose again, and he, too, rose. He would just have a squint and go to bed.

The ballroom was somewhat detached, and Soames went down a corridor. At its end he came on a twirl of sound and colour. They were hard at it, 'dolled up' to the nines—Mephistopheleses, ladies of Spain, Italian peasants, pierrots. His bewildered eyes with difficulty took in the strutting, wheeling mass; his bewildered ears decided that the tune was trying to be a waltz. He remembered that the waltz was in three-time, remembered the waltz of olden days—too well—that dance at Roger's, and Irene, his own wife, waltzing in the arms of young Bosinney; to this day remembered the look on her face, the rise and fall of her breast, the scent of the gardenias she was wearing, and that fellow's face when she raised to his her dark eyes–lost to all but themselves and their guilty enjoyment; remembered the balcony on which he had refuged from that sight, and the policeman down below him on the strip of red carpet from house to street.

'"Always!"–good tune!' said someone behind his ears.

Not bad, certainly–a sort of sweetness in it. His eyes, from behind the neck of a large lady who seemed trying to be a fairy, roved again among the dancers. What! Over there! Fleur! Fleur in her Goya dress, grape-coloured–'La Vendimia–the Vintage'–floating out from her knees, with her face close to the face of a sheik, and his face close to hers. Fleur! And that sheik, that Moor in a dress all white and flowing! In Soames a groan was converted to a cough. *Those two!* So close–so–so lost–it seemed to him! As Irene with Bosinney, so she with that young Jon! They passed, not seeing him behind the fairy's competent bulk. Soames's eyes tracked them through the shifting, yawing throng. Round again they came–her eyes so nearly closed that he hardly knew them; and young Jon's over her fichued shoulder, deep-set and staring. Where was the fellow's wife? And just then Soames caught sight of her, dancing, too, but looking back at them–a nymph all trailing green, the eyes surprised, and jealous. No wonder, since under her very gaze was Fleur's swinging skirt, the rise and falling of her breast, the languor in her eyes! 'Always!' Would they never stop that cursed tune, stop those two, who with every bar seemed to cling closer and closer! And, fearful lest he should be seen, Soames turned away and mounted slowly to his room. He had had his squint. It was enough!

The band had ceased to play on the sea front, people were deserting, lights going out; by the sound out there, the tide must be rising. Soames touched himself where he was sore, beneath his starched shirt, and stood still. 'Always!' Incalculable consequences welled in on his consciousness, like the murmuring tide of that sea. Daughter exiled, grandson lost to him; memories deflowered; hopes in the dust! 'Always!' Forsooth! Not if he knew it–not for Joe! And all that grim power of self-containment which but twice or three times in his life had failed him, and always with disastrous consequence, again for a moment failed him, so that to any living thing present in the dim and austere hotel bedroom, he would have seemed like one demented. The paroxysm passed. No use to rave! Worse than no use–far; would only make him ill, and he would want his strength. For what? For sitting still; for doing nothing; for waiting to see! Venus! Touch not the goddess–the hot, the jealous one with the lost dark eyes! He had touched her in the past, and she had answered with a blow. Touch her not! Possess his sore and anxious heart! Nothing to do but wait and see!

PART III

I

SOAMES GIVES ADVICE

On her return to Nettlefold from her night in town, Fleur had continued to 'eat her heart out' by 'the sad sea wave'. For still neither Jon nor his wife came to see her. Clearly she was labelled 'poison'. Twice she had walked over to Green Hill Farm hoping for another 'jolly accident'. She had seen there an attractive old house with aged farm buildings flanked by a hill and a wide prospect towards the sea. Calm, broad, and home-like, the place roused hostility in her. It could never be *her* home, and so was inimical, part of the forces working against her. Loose ends in Jon's life were all in her favour. In exploitation of those calm acres he would be secured to that girl his wife, out of her reach again, this time for good – the twice-burnt child! And yet, with all her heart-ache, she was still uncertain what, precisely, she wanted. Not having to grapple with actual decision, things seemed possible which, in her bones, she knew might not be possible. Even to fling her 'cap over the windmill' did not seem like rank and staring madness. To retrieve Spain with Jon! Her hands clenched and her lips loosened at the thought of it – an Odyssey together, till in the shifting, tolerant, modern world, all was forgotten, if not forgiven! Every form of companionship with him from decorous and platonic friendship to the world well lost; from guilty and secret liaison to orderly and above-board glimpses of him at not too long intervals. According to the tides in her blood, all seemed possible, if not exactly probable, so long as she did not lose him again altogether.

To these feverish veerings of her spirit, a letter from her Aunt Winifred supplied a point of anchorage:

'I hear from Val that they are not going to Goodwood after all – their nice two-year-old is not in form. Such a bore. It's the most comfortable meeting of the year. They seem to be very busy settling about the farm that Jon Forsyte is going to take. It will be pleasant for Val and Holly to have them so close, though I'm afraid that American child will find it dull. Holly writes that they are going to an amusing little fancy dress affair at the hotel in Nettlefold. Anne is to go as a water-nymph – she will make quite a good one with her nice straight legs. Holly is to be Madame Vigée le Brun; and Val says he'll go as a tipster or not at all. I do hope he won't redden his nose. Young Jon Forsyte has an Arab dress he brought from Egypt.'

'And I,' thought Fleur, 'have the dress I wore the night I went to his room at Wansdon.' How she wished now that she had come out of that room his wife; after that nothing could have divided them. But they had been such innocents then!

For at once she had made up her mind to go to that dance herself. She was there first, and with malicious pleasure watched the faces of those two when she met them at the entrance of the room. Her grape-dress. She could see that Jon remembered it, and quickly she began to praise Anne's. A water-nymph to the life! As for Jon—another wife or two was all he needed to be perfect! She was discretion itself until that waltz; and even then she had tried to be discreet to all but Jon. For him she kept (or so she hoped) the closeness, the clinging and the languor of her eyes; but in those few minutes she let him know quite surely that love ran in her veins.

'"Always!",' was all she said when at last they stopped.

And, after that dance, she stole away home; having no heart to see him dance with his water-nymph. She crept up to her small bedroom trembling, and on her bed fell into a passion of silent weeping. And the water-nymph's browned face and eyes and legs flitted torturingly in the tangled glades of her vision. She quieted down at last. At least, for a few minutes, she had had him to herself, heart against heart. That was something.

She rose late, pale and composed again. At ten o'clock the startling appearance of her father's car completed the masking of her face. She greeted him with an emphatic gratitude quite unfelt.

'Dad! How lovely! Where have you sprung from?'

'Nettlefold. I spent the night there.'

'At the hotel?'

'Yes.'

'Why! I was there myself last night at a dance!'

'Oh!' said Soames, 'that fancy dress affair—they told me of it. Pleasant?'

'Not very; I left early. If I'd known you were there! Why didn't you tell me you were coming down to fetch us home?'

'It just came into my mind that it was better for the boy than the train.'

And Fleur could not tell what he had seen, or if, indeed, he had seen anything.

Fortunately, during the journey up, Kit had much to say, and Soames dozed, very tired after a night of anxiety, indecision, and little sleep. The aspect of the South Square house, choice and sophisticated, and the warmth of Michael's greeting, quite beautifully returned by Fleur, restored to him at least a measure of equanimity. Here, at all events, was no unhappy home; that counted much in the equation of a future into which he could no longer see.

After lunch he went up to Michael's study to discuss slum conversion. Confronted, while they were talking, with Fleur's watercolour, Soames rediscovered the truth that individuals are more interesting than the collection of them called the State. Not national welfare, but the painter of those passion fruits, possessed his mind. How prevent her from eating them?

'Yes, sir. That's really quite good, isn't it? I wish Fleur would take seriously to water-colour work.'

Soames started.

'I wish she'd take seriously to anything, and keep her mind occupied.'

Michael looked at him. 'Rather like a dog,' Soames thought, 'trying to understand. Suddenly, he saw the young man wet his lips.

'You've got something to tell me, sir, I believe. I remember what you said to me some weeks ago. Is it anything to do with that?'

'Yes,' answered Soames, watching his eyes. 'Don't take it too much to heart, but I've reason to believe she's never properly got over the feeling she used to have. I don't know how much you've heard about that boy and girl affair.'

'Pretty well all, I think.' Again he saw Michael moisten his lips.

'Oh! From her?'

'No. Fleur's never said a word. From Miss June Forsyte.'

'That woman! *She's* sure to have plumped it all out. But Fleur's fond of you.'

'I belong.'

It seemed to Soames a queer way of putting it; pathetic somehow!

'Well,' he said, 'I've not made a sign. Perhaps you'd like to know how I formed my view.'

'No, sir.'

Soames glanced quickly at him and away again. This was a bitter moment, no doubt, for young Michael! Was one precipitating a crisis which one felt, deeply yet vaguely, had to be reached and passed? He himself knew how to wait, but did this modern young man, so feather-pated and scattery? Still, he was a gentleman. That at least had become a cardinal belief with Soames. And it was a comfort to him, looking at the 'White Monkey' on the wall, who had so slender a claim to such a title.

'The only thing,' he muttered, 'is to wait—'

'Not "and see", sir; anything but that. I can wait and not see, or I can have the whole thing out.'

'No,' said Soames, with emphasis, 'don't have it out! I may be mistaken. There's everything against it; she knows which side her bread is buttered.'

'Don't!' cried Michael, and got up.

'Now, now,' murmured Soames; 'I've upset you. Everything depends on keeping your head.'

Michael emitted an unhappy little laugh.

'*You* can't go round the world again, sir. Perhaps *I'd* better, this time, and alone.'

Soames looked at him. 'This won't do,' he said. 'She's got a strong affection for you; it's just feverishness, if it's anything. Take it like a man, and keep quiet.' He was talking to the young man's back now, and found it easier. 'She was always a spoiled child, you know; spoiled children get things into their heads, but it doesn't amount to anything. Can't you get her interested in these slums?'

Michael turned round.

'How far has it gone?'

'There you go!' said Soames. 'Not any way so far as I know. I only happened to see her dancing with him last night at that hotel, and noticed her—her expression.'

The word 'eyes' had seemed somehow too extravagant.

'There's always his wife,' he added quickly, 'she's an attractive little thing; and he's going to farm down there—they tell me. That'll take him all his time. How would it be if I took Fleur to Scotland for August and September? With this strike on there'll be some places in the market still.'

'No, sir. That's only putting off the evil day. It must go to a finish, one way or the other.'

Soames did not answer for some time.

'It's never any good to meet trouble half-way,' he said at last. 'You young people are always in a hurry. One can do things, but one can't undo them. It's not,' he went on shyly, 'as if this were anything new—an unfortunate old

business revived for the moment; it'll die away again as it did before, if it's
properly left alone. Plenty of exercise, and keep her mind well occupied.'

The young man's expression was peculiar. 'And have you found that
successful, sir, in your experience?' it seemed to say. That woman June had
been blurting out his past, he shouldn't wonder!

'Promise me, anyway, to keep what I've said to yourself, and do nothing
rash.'

Michael shook his head. 'I can't promise anything, it must depend; but I'll
remember your advice, sir.'

And with this Soames had to be content.

Acting on that instinct, born of love, which guided him in his dealings with
Fleur, he bade her an almost casual farewell, and next day returned to
Mapledurham. He detailed to Annette everything that was not of importance,
for to tell her what was would never do.

His home in these last days of July was pleasurable; and almost at once he
went out fishing in the punt. There, in contemplation of his line and the gliding
water, green with reflection, he felt rested. Bulrushes, water-lilies, dragonflies, and the cows in his own fields, the incessant cooing of the wood-
pigeons–with their precious 'Take *two* cows, David!'–the distant buzz of his
gardener's lawn-mower, the splash of a water-rat, shadows lengthening out
from the poplars and the willow trees, the scent of grass and of elder flowers
bright along the banks, and the slow drift of the white river clouds–
peaceful–very peaceful; and something of Nature's calm entered his
soul, so that the disappearance of his float recalled him to reality with a jerk.

'It'll be uneatable,' he thought, winding at his line.

2

OCCUPYING THE MIND

Comedy the real thing! Was it? Michael wondered. In saying to Soames that he
could not wait and see, he had expressed a very natural abhorrence. Watch, spy,
calculate–impossible! To go to Fleur and ask for a frank exposure of her
feelings was what he would have liked to do; but he could not help knowing the
depth of his father-in-law's affection and concern, and the length of his head;
and he had sufficient feeling to hesitate before imperilling what was as much
'Old Forsyte's' happiness as his own. The 'old boy' had behaved so decently in
pulling up his roots and going round the world with Fleur, that every
consideration was due to him. It remained, then, to wait without attempting to
see–hardest of all courses because least active. 'Keep her mind well occupied!'
So easy! Recollecting his own prenuptial feelings, he did not see how it was to
be done. And Fleur's was a particularly difficult mind to occupy with anything
except that on which she had set her heart. The slums? No! She possessed one
of those eminently sane natures which rejected social problems, as fruitless and
incalculable. An immediate job, like the canteen, in which she could shine a
little–she would perform beautifully; but she would never work for a remote
object, without shining! He could see her clear eyes looking at the slums
as they had looked at Foggartism, and his experiment with the out-of-works.

He might take her to see Hilary and Aunt May, but it would be futile in the end.

Night brought the first acute trouble. What were to be his relations with her, if her feelings were really engaged elsewhere? To wait and not see meant continuation of the married state. He suspected Soames of having wished to counsel that. Whipped by longing, stung and half numbed by a jealousy he must not show, and unwishful to wound her, he waited for a sign, feeling as if she must know why he was waiting. He received it, and was glad, but it did not convince him. Still!

He woke much lighter in spirit.

At breakfast he asked her what she would like to do, now that she was back and the season over. Did this slum scheme amuse her at all, because if so, there was a lot to do in it; she would find Hilary and May great sports.

'Rather! Anything really useful, Michael!'

He took her round to 'The Meads'. The result was better than he had hoped.

For his uncle and aunt were human buildings the like of which Fleur had not yet encountered–positively fashioned, concreted in tradition, but freely exposed to sun and air, tiled with taste, and windowed with humour. Michael, with something of their 'make-up', had neither their poise, nor active certainty. Fleur recognised at once that those two dwelt in unity unlike any that she knew, as if, in their twenty odd years together, they had welded a single instrument to carry out a new discovery–the unselfconscious day. They were not fools, yet cleverness in their presence seemed jejune, and as if unrelated to reality. They knew–especially Hilary–a vast deal about flowers, printing, architecture, mountains, drains, electricity, the price of living, Italian cities; they knew how to treat the ailments of dogs, play musical instruments, administer first and even second aid, amuse children, and cause the aged to laugh. They could discuss anything from religion to morality with fluency, and the tolerance that came from experience of the trials of others and forgetfulness of their own. With her natural intelligence Fleur admired them. They were good, but they were not dull–very odd! Admiring them, she could not help making up to them. Their attitude in life–she recognised–was superior to her own, and she was prepared to pay at least lip-service. But lip-service 'cut no ice' in 'The Meads'–Hand, foot, intellect and heart were the matter-of-course requirements. To occupy her mind, however, she took the jobs given her. Then trouble began. The jobs were not her own, and there was no career in them. Try as she would, she could not identify herself with Mrs Corrigan or the little Topmarshes. The girls, who served at Petter and Poplin's and kept their clothes in paper bags, bored her when they talked and when they didn't. Each new type amused her for a day, and then just seemed unlovely. She tried hard, however, for her own sake, and in order to deceive Michael. She had been at it more than a week before she had an idea.

'You know, Michael, I feel I should be ever so much more interested if I ran a place of my own in the country–a sort of rest-house that I could make attractive for girls who wanted air and that.'

To Michael, remembering the canteen, it seemed 'an idea' indeed. To Fleur it seemed more–a 'lease and release', as her father might have put it. Her scheming mind had seen the possibilities. She would be able to go there without let or cavil, and none would know what she did with her time. A base of operations with a fool-proof title was essential for a relationship, however innocent, with Jon. She began at once to learn to drive the car; for the 'rest-

house' must not be so near him as to excite suspicion. She approached her
father on the finance of the matter. At first doubtfully, and then almost
cordially, Soames approved. If he would pay the rent and rates of the house, she
would manage the rest out of her own pocket. She could not have bettered such
a policy by way of convincing him that her interest was genuine; for he
emphatically distrusted the interest of people in anything that did not cost
them money. A careful study of the map suggested to her the neighbourhood of
Dorking. Box Hill had a reputation for air and beauty, and was within an hour's
fast drive of Wansdon. In the next three weeks she found and furnished a
derelict house, rambling and cheap, close to the road on the London side of Box
Hill, with a good garden and stables that could be converted easily. She
completed her education with the car, and engaged a couple who could be left in
charge with impunity. She consulted Michael and the Hilarys freely. In fact,
like a mother cat, who carefully misleads the household as to where she is going
to 'lay' her kittens, so Fleur, by the nature of her preparations, disguised her
round-about design. 'The Meads Rest House', as it was called, was opened at
the end of August.

All this time she possessed her soul with only the scantiest news of Jon. A
letter from Holly told her that negotiations for Green Hill Farm were 'hanging
fire' over the price, though Jon was more and more taken with it; and Anne
daily becoming more rural and more English. Rondavel was in great form
again, and expected to win at Doncaster. Val had already taken a long shot
about him for the Derby next year.

Fleur replied in a letter so worded as to give the impression that she had no
other interest in the world just then but her new scheme. They must all drive
over and see whether her 'Rest House' didn't beat the canteen. The people
were 'such dears'–it was all 'terribly amusing'. She wished to convey the
feeling that she had no fears of herself, no alarm in the thought of Jon; and that
her work in life was serious. Michael, never wholly deserted by the naïveté of a
good disposition, was more and more deceived. To him her mind seemed really
occupied; and certainly her body, for she ran up from Dorking almost daily and
spent the week-ends with him either at 'The Shelter', where Kit was installed
with his grandparents, or at Lippinghall, where they always made a fuss of
Fleur. Rowing her on the river in bland weather, Michael recaptured a feeling
of security. 'Old Forsyte' must have let his imagination run away with him; the
old boy *was* rather like a hen where Fleur was concerned, clucking and turning
an inflamed eye on everything that came near!

Parliament had risen, and slum conversion work was now all that he was
doing. These days on that river, which he ever associated with his wooing, were
the happiest he had spent since the strike began–the strike that in narrowed
form dragged wearyingly on, so that people ceased to mention it, the weather
being warm.

And Soames? By his daughter's tranquil amiability, he, too, was
tranquilised. He would look at Michael and say nothing, in accordance with the
best English traditions, and his own dignity. It was he who revived the idea of
Fleur's being painted by June's 'lame duck'. He felt it would occupy her mind
still further. He would like, however, to see the fellow's work first, though he
supposed it would mean a visit to June's.

'If she were to be out,' he said to Fleur, 'I shouldn't mind having a look
round her studio.'

'Shall I arrange that, then, Dad?'

'Not too pointedly,' said Soames; 'or she'll get into a fantod.'

Accordingly at the following week-end Fleur said to him:

'If you'll come up with me on Monday, dear, we'll go round. The Rafaelite will be in, but June won't. She doesn't want to see you any more than you want to see her.'

'H'm!' said Soames. 'She always spoke her mind.'

They went up in his car. After forming his opinion Soames was to return, and Fleur to go on home. The Rafaelite met them at the head of the stairs. To Soames he suggested a bull-fighter (not that he had ever seen one in the flesh), with his short whiskers and his broad, pale face which wore the expression: 'If you suppose yourself capable of appreciating my work, you make a mistake.' Soames's face, on the other hand, wore the expression: 'If you suppose that I want to appreciate your work, you make a greater.' And, leaving him to Fleur, he began to look round. In truth he was not unfavourably impressed. The work had turned its back on modernity. The surfaces were smooth, the drawing in perspective, and the colouring full. He perceived a new note, or rather the definite revival of an old one. The chap had undoubted talent; whether it would go down in these days he did not know, but its texture was more agreeable to live with than any he had seen for some time. When he came to the portrait of June he stood for a minute, with his head on one side, and then said, with a pale smile:

'You've got her to the life.' It pleased him to think that June had evidently not seen in it what he saw. But when his eyes fell on the picture of Anne, his face fell, too, and he looked quickly at Fleur, who said:

'Yes, Dad? What do you think of that?'

The thought had flashed through Soames's mind: 'Is it to get in touch with *him* that she's ready to be painted?'

'Finished?' he asked.

The Rafaelite answered:

'Yes. Going down to them to-morrow.'

Soames's face rose again. That risk was over then!

'Quite clever!' he murmured. 'The lily's excellent.' And he passed on to a sketch of the woman who had opened the door to them.

'That's recognisable! Not at all bad.'

In these quiet ways he made it clear that, while he approved on the whole, he was not going to pay any extravagant price. He took an opportunity when Fleur was out of hearing, and said:

'So you want to paint my daughter. What's your figure?'

'A hundred and fifty.'

'Rather tall for these days—you're a young man. However—so long as you make a good thing of it!'

The Rafaelite bowed ironically.

'Yes,' said Soames, 'I dare say; you think all your geese are swans—never met a painter who didn't. You won't keep her sitting long, I suppose—she's busy. That's agreed, then. Good-bye! Don't come down!'

As they went out he said to Fleur:

'I've fixed that. You can begin sitting when you like. His work's better than you'd think from the look of him. Forbidding chap, I call him.'

'A painter has to be forbidding, Dad; otherwise people would think he was cadging.'

'Something in that,' said Soames. 'I'll get back now, as you won't let me take you home. Good-bye! Take care of yourself, and don't overdo it.' And, receiving her kiss, he got into the car.

Fleur began to walk towards her eastward-bound bus as his car moved west, nor did he see her stop, give him some law, then retrace her steps to June's.

3

POSSESSING THE SOUL

Just as in a very old world to find things or people of pure descent is impossible, so with actions; and the psychologist who traces them to single motives is like Soames, who believed that his daughter wanted to be painted in order that she might see herself hanging on a wall. Everybody, he knew, had themselves hung sooner or later, and generally sooner. Yet Fleur, though certainly not averse to being hung, had motives that were hardly so single as all that. In the service of this complexity, she went back to June's. That little lady, who had been lurking in her bedroom so as not to meet her kinsman, was in high feather.

'Of course the price is nominal,' she said. 'Harold ought really to be getting every bit as much for his portraits as Thom or Lippen. Still, it's so important for him to be making something while he's waiting to take his real place. What have you come back for?'

'Partly for the pleasure of seeing you,' said Fleur, 'and partly because we forgot to arrange for the first sitting. I think my best time would be three o'clock.'

'Yes,' murmured June doubtfully, not so much from doubt as from not having suggested it herself. 'I think Harold could manage that. Isn't his work exquisite?'

'I particularly like the thing he's done of Anne. It's going down to them to-morrow, I hear.'

'Yes; Jon's coming to fetch it.'

Fleur looked hastily into the little dim mirror to see that she was keeping expression off her face.

'What do you think I ought to wear?'

June's gaze swept her from side to side.

'Oh! I expect he'll want an artificial scheme with you.'

'Exactly! But what colour? One must come in something.'

'We'll go up and ask him.'

The Rafaelite was standing before his picture of Anne. He turned and looked at them, without precisely saying: 'Good Lord! These women!' and nodded, gloomily, at the suggestion of three o'clock.

'What do you want her in?' asked June.

The Rafaelite stared at Fleur as if determining where her ribs left off and her hip-bones began.

'Gold and silver,' he said at last.

June clasped her hands.

'Now isn't that extraordinary? He's seen through you at once. Your gold and silver room. Harold, how *did* you?'

'I happen to have an old "Folly" dress,' said Fleur, 'silver and gold, with bells, that I haven't worn since I was married.'

'A "Folly"!' cried June. 'The very thing. If it's pretty. Some are hideous, of course.'

'Oh! it's pretty, and makes a charming sound.'

'He can't paint that,' said June. Then added dreamily: 'But you could suggest it, Harold–like Leonardo.'

'Leonardo!'

'Oh! Of course! I know, he wasn't–'

The Rafaelite interrupted.

'Don't make your face up,' he said to Fleur.

'No,' murmured Fleur. 'June, I do so like that of Anne. Has it struck you that she's sure to want Jon painted now?'

'Of course. I'll make him promise when he comes to-morrow.'

'He's going to begin farming, you know; he'll make that an excuse. Men hate being painted.'

'Oh, that's all nonsense,' said June. 'In old days they loved it. Anyway, Jon must sit before he begins. They'll make a splendid pair.'

Behind the Rafaelite's back Fleur bit her lip.

'He must wear a turn-down shirt. Blue, don't you think, Harold–to go with his hair?'

'Pink, with green spots,' muttered the Rafaelite.

'Then three o'clock to-morrow?' said Fleur hastily.

June nodded. 'Jon's coming to lunch, so he'll be gone before you come.'

'All right, then. Au revoir!'

She held her hand out to the Rafaelite, who seemed surprised at the gesture.

'Good-bye, June!'

June came suddenly close and kissed her on the chin. At that moment the little lady's face looked soft and pink, and her eyes soft; her lips were warm, too, as if she were warm all through.

Fleur went away thinking: 'Ought I to have asked her not to tell Jon I was going to be painted?' But surely June, the warm, the single-eyed, would never tell Jon anything that might stop him being useful to her Rafaelite. She stood, noting the geography around 'The Poplars'. The only approach to this backwater was by a road that dipped into it and came out again. Just here, she would not be seen from the house, and could see Jon leaving after lunch whichever way he went. But then he would have to take a taxi, for the picture. It struck her bitterly that she, who had been his first-adored, should have to scheme to see him. But if she didn't, she would never see him! Ah! what a ninny she had been at Wansdon in those old days when her room was next to his. One little act, and nothing could have kept him from her for all time, not his mother nor the old feud; not her father; nothing; and then there had been no vows of hers or his, no Michael, no Kit, no nymph-eyed girl in barrier between them; nothing but youth and innocence. And it seemed to her that youth and innocence were over-rated.

She lit on no plan by which she could see him without giving away the fact that she had schemed. She would have to possess her soul a little longer. Let him once get his head into the painter's noose, and there would be not one but many chances.

She arrived at three o'clock with her Folly's dress, and was taken into June's bedroom to put it on.

'It's just right,' said June; 'delightfully artificial. Harold will love it.'

'I wonder,' said Fleur. The Rafaelite's temperament had not yet struck her as very loving. They went up to the studio without having mentioned Jon.

The portrait of Anne was gone. And when June went to fetch 'the exact thing' to cover a bit of background, Fleur said at once:

'Well? Are you going to paint my cousin Jon?'

The Rafaelite nodded.

'He didn't want to be, but *she* made him.'

'When do you begin?'

'To-morrow,' said the Rafaelite. 'He's coming every morning for a week. What's the good of a week?'

'If he's only got a week I should have thought he'd better stay here.'

'He won't without his wife, and his wife's got a cold.'

'Oh!' said Fleur, and she thought rapidly. 'Wouldn't it be more convenient, then, for him to sit early in the afternoons? I could come in the mornings; in fact, I'd rather—one feels fresher. June could give him a trunk call.'

The Rafaelite uttered what she judged to be an approving sound. When she left, she said to June: 'I want to come at ten every morning, then I get my afternoons free for my "Rest House" down at Dorking. Couldn't you get Jon to come in the afternoons instead? It would suit him better. Only don't let him know I'm being painted—my picture won't be recognisable for a week, anyway.'

'Oh!' said June, 'you're quite wrong there. Harold always gets an unmistakable likeness at once; but of course he'll put it face to the wall, he always does while he's at work on a picture.'

'Good! He's made quite a nice start. Then if you'll telephone to Jon, I'll come to-morrow at ten.' And for yet another day she possessed her soul. On the day after, she nodded at a canvas whose face was to the wall, and asked:

'Do you find my cousin a good sitter?'

'No,' said the Rafaelite; 'he takes no interest. Got something on his mind, I should think.'

'He's a poet, you know,' said Fleur.

The Rafaelite gave her an epileptic stare. 'Poet! His head's the wrong shape—too much jaw—and the eyes too deep in.'

'But his hair! Don't you find him an attractive subject?'

'Attractive!' replied the Rafaelite—'I paint anything, whether it's pretty or ugly as sin. Look at Rafael's Pope—did you ever see a better portrait, or an uglier man? Ugliness is not attractive, but it's there.'

'That's obvious,' said Fleur.

'I state the obvious. The only real novelties now are platitudes. That's why my work is important and seems new. People have got so far away from the obvious that the obvious startles them, and nothing else does. I advise you to think that over.'

'I'm sure there's a lot in it,' said Fleur.

'Of course,' said the Rafaelite, 'a platitude has to be stated with force and clarity. If you can't do that, you'd better go on slopping around and playing parlour tricks like the Ga-gaists. They're a bathetic lot, trying to prove that cocktails are a better drink than old brandy. I met a man last night who told me he'd spent four years writing twenty-two lines of poetry that nobody can understand. How's that for bathos? But it'll make him quite a reputation, till somebody writes twenty-three lines in five years still more unintelligible. Hold your head up. . . . Your cousin's a silent beggar.'

'Silence is quite a quality,' said Fleur.

The Rafaelite grinned. 'I suppose you think I haven't got it. But you're wrong, madam. Not long ago I went a fortnight without opening my lips except to eat and say yes or no. *She* got quite worried.'

'I don't think you're very nice to her,' said Fleur.

'No, I'm not. She's after my soul. That's the worst of women–saving your presence–they're not content with their own.'

'Perhaps they haven't any,' said Fleur.

'The Mohammedan view–well, there's certainly something in it. A woman's always after the soul of a man, a child, or a dog. Men are content with wanting bodies.'

'I'm more interested in your platitudinal theory, Mr Blade.'

'Can't afford to be interested in the other? Eh! Strikes home? Turn your shoulder a bit, will you? No, to the left. . . . Well, it's a platitude that a woman always wants some other soul–only people have forgotten it. Look at the Sistine Madonna! The baby has a soul of its own, and the Madonna's floating on the soul of the baby. That's what makes it a great picture, apart from the line and colour. It states a great platitude; but nobody sees it now. None of the cognoscenti, anyway–they're too far gone.'

'What platitude are you going to state in your picture of me?'

'Don't you worry,' said the Rafaelite. 'There'll be one all right when it's finished, though I shan't know what it is while I'm at it. Character will out, you know. Like a rest?'

'Enormously. What platitude did you express in the portrait of my cousin's wife?'

'Coo Lummy!' said the Rafaelite. 'Some catechism!'

'You surely didn't fail with that picture? Wasn't it platitudinous?'

'It got her all right. She's not a proper American.'

'How?'

'Throws back to something–Irish, perhaps, or Breton. There's nymph in her.'

'She was brought up in the backwoods, I believe,' said Fleur acidly.

The Rafaelite eyed her.

'You don't like the lady?'

'Certainly I do, but haven't you noticed that picturesque people are generally tame? And my cousin–what's his platitude to be?'

'Conscience,' said the Rafaelite; 'that young man will go far on the straight and narrow. He worries.'

A sharp movement shook all Fleur's silver bells.

'What a dreadful prophecy! Shall I stand again?'

4

TALK IN A CAR

For yet one more day Fleur possessed her soul; then, at the morning's sitting, accidentally left her vanity bag, behind her, in the studio. She called for it the same afternoon. Jon had not gone. Just out of the sitter's chair, he was stretching himself and yawning.

'Go on, Jon! Every morning I wish I had your mouth. Mr Blade, I left my bag; it's got my cheque-book in it, and I shall want it down at Dorking to-night. By the way, I shall be half an hour late for my sitting to-morrow, I'm afraid. Did you know I was your fellow victim, Jon? We've been playing "Box and Cox". How are you? I hear Anne's got a cold. Give her my sympathy. Is the picture going well? Might I have a peep, Mr Blade, and see how the platitude is coming out? Oh! It's going to be splendid! I can quite see the line.'

'Can you?' said the Rafaelite. 'I can't.'

'Here's my wretched bag! If you've finished, Jon, I could run you out as far as Dorking; you'd catch an earlier train. Do come and cheer me on my way. Haven't seen you for such ages!'

Threading over Hammersmith Bridge, Fleur regained the self-possession she had never seemed to lose. She spoke lightly of light matters, letting Jon grow accustomed to proximity.

'I go down every evening about this time, to see to my chores, and drive up in the morning early. So any afternoon you like I can take you as far as Dorking. Why shouldn't we see a little of each other in a friendly way, Jon?'

'When we do, it doesn't seem to make for happiness, Fleur.'

'My dear boy, what is happiness? Surely life should be as harmlessly full as it can be?'

'Harmlessly!'

'The Rafaelite says you have a terrible conscience, Jon.'

'The Rafaelite's a bounder.'

'Yes; but a clever one. You *have* changed, you usen't to have that line between your eyes, and your jaw's getting too strong. Look, Jon dear, be a friend to me—as they say, and we won't think of anything else. I always like Wimbledon Common—it hasn't been caught up yet. Have you bought that farm?'

'Not quite.'

'Let's go by way of Robin Hill, and look at it through the trees? It might inspire you to a poem.'

'I shall never write any more verse. It's quite gone.'

'Nonsense, Jon. You only want stirring up. Don't I drive well, considering I've only been at it five weeks?'

'You do everything well, Fleur.'

'You say that as if you disapproved. Do you know we'd never danced together before that night at Nettlefold? Shall we ever dance together again?'

'Probably not.'

'Optimistic Jon! That's right–smile! Look! Is that the church where you were baptized?'

'I wasn't.'

'Oh! No. That was the period, of course, when people were serious about those things. I believe I was done twice over–R.C. and Anglican. That's why I'm not so religious as you, Jon.'

'Religious? I'm not religious.'

'I fancy you *are*. You have moral backbone, anyway.'

'Really!'

'Jon, you remind me of American notices outside their properties– "Stop–look–take care–keep out!" I suppose you think me a frightful butterfly.'

'No, Fleur. Far from it. The butterfly has no knowledge of a straight line between two points.'

'Now what do you mean by that?'

'That you set your heart on things.'

'Did you get that from the Rafaelite?'

'No, but he confirmed it.'

'He did–did he? That young man talks too much. Has he expounded to you his theory that a woman must possess the soul of someone else, and that a man is content with bodies?'

'He has.'

'Is it true?'

'I hate to agree with him, but I think it is, in a way.'

'Well, I can tell you there are plenty of women about now who keep their own souls and are content with other people's bodies.'

'Are you one of them, Fleur?'

'Ask me another! There's Robin Hill!'

The fount of Forsyte song and story stood grey and imposing among its trees, with the sinking sun aslant on a front where green sun-blinds were still down.

Jon sighed. 'I had a lovely time there.'

'Till I came and spoiled it.'

'No; that's blasphemy.'

Fleur touched his arm.

'That's nice of you, dear Jon. You always were nice, and I shall always love you–in a harmless way. The coppice looks jolly. God had a brain-wave when He invented larches.'

'Yes, Holly says that the coppice was my grandfather's favourite spot.'

'Old Jolyon–who wouldn't marry his beloved, because she was consumptive?'

'I never heard that. But he was a great old fellow, my father and mother adored him.'

'I've seen his photographs–don't get a chin like his, Jon! The Forsytes all have such chins. June's frightens me.'

'June is one of the best people on earth.'

'Oh! Jon, you are horribly loyal.'

'Is that an offence?'

'It makes everything terribly earnest in a world that isn't worth it. No, don't quote Longfellow. When you get home, shall you tell Anne you've been driving with me?'

'Why not?'

'She's uneasy about me as it is, isn't she? You needn't answer, Jon. But I think it's unfair of her. I want so little, and you're so safe.'

'Safe?' It seemed to Fleur that he closed his teeth on the word, and for a moment she was happy.

'Now you've got your lion cub look. Do lion cubs have consciences? It's going to be rather interesting for the Rafaelite. I think your conscience might stop before telling Anne, though. It's a pity to worry her if she has a talent for uneasiness.' Then, by the silence at her side, she knew she had made a mistake.

'This is where I put in my clutch,' she said, 'as they say in the "bloods"!' And through Epsom and Leatherhead they travelled in silence.

'Do you love England as much as ever, Jon?'

'More.'

'It *is* a gorgeous country.'

'The last word I should have used—a great and lovely country.'

'Michael says its soul is grass.'

'Yes, and if I get my farm, I'll break some up, all right.'

'I can't see you as a real farmer.'

'You can't see me as a real anything—I suppose. Just an amateur.'

'Don't be horrid! I mean you're too sensitive to be a farmer.'

'No. I want to get down to the earth, and I will.'

'You must be a throw-back, Jon. The primeval Forsytes were farmers. My father wants to take me down and show me where they lived.'

'Have you jumped at it?'

'I'm not sentimental; haven't you realised that? I wonder if you've realised anything about me?' And drooping forward over her wheel, she murmured: 'Oh! It's a pity we have to talk like this!'

'I said it wouldn't work!'

'No, you've got to let me see you sometimes, Jon. This is harmless enough. I must and will see you now and then. It's owed to me!'

Tears stood in her eyes, and rolled slowly down. She felt Jon touch her arm. 'Oh! Fleur, don't!'

'I'll put you out at North Dorking now, you'll just catch the five-forty-six. That's my house. Next time I must show you over it. I'm trying to be good, Jon; and you must help me. . . . Well, here we are! Good-bye, dear Jon; and don't worry Anne about me, I beseech you!'

A hard hand-grip, and he was gone. Fleur turned from the station and drove slowly back along the road.

She put away the car, and entered her 'Rest House'. It was full, late holiday time still, and seven young women were resting limbs, tired out in the service of 'Petter, Poplin', and their like.

They were at supper, and a cheery buzz assailed Fleur's ears. These girls had nothing, and she had everything, except—the one thing that she chiefly wanted. For a moment she felt ashamed, listening to their talk and laughter. No! She would not change with them—and yet without that one thing she felt as if she could not live. And, while she went about the house, sifting the flowers, ordering for to-morrow, inspecting the bedrooms, laughter, cheery and uncontrolled, floated up and seemed to mock her.

5

Jon had too little sense of his own importance to be simultaneously loved with comfort to himself by two pretty and attractive young women. He drove home from Pulborough, where now daily he parked Val's car, with a sore heart and a mind distraught. He had seen Fleur six times since his return to England, in a sort of painful crescendo. That dance with her had disclosed to him her state of heart, but still he did not suspect her of consciously pursuing him; and no amount of heart-searching seemed to make his own feelings clearer. Ought he to tell Anne about to-day's meeting? In many small and silent ways she had shown that she was afraid of Fleur. Why add to her fears without real cause? The portrait was not his own doing, and only for the next few days was he likely to be seeing Fleur. After that they would meet, perhaps, two or three times a year. 'Don't tell Anne – I beseech you!' Could he tell her after that? Surely he owed Fleur that much consideration. She had never consented to give him up; she had not fallen in love with Michael, as he with Anne. Still undecided, he reached Wansdon. His mother had once said to him: 'You must never tell a lie, Jon, your face will always give you away.' And so, though he did not tell Anne, her eyes following him about noted that he was keeping something from her. Her cold was in the bronchial stage, so that she was still upstairs, and tense from lack of occupation. Jon came up early again after dinner, and began to read to her. He read from *The Worst Journey in the World*, and on her side she lay with her face pillowed on her arm and watched him over it. The smoke of a wood fire, the scent of balsamic remedies, the drone of his own voice, retailing that epic of a penguin's egg, drowsed him till the book dropped from his hand.

'Have a snooze, Jon, you're tired.' Jon lay back, but he did not snooze. He thought instead. In this girl, his wife, he knew well that there was what her brother, Francis Wilmot, called 'sand'. She knew how to be silent when shoes pinched. He had watched her making up her mind that she was in danger; and now it seemed to him that she was biding her time. Anne always knew what she wanted. She had a singleness of purpose not confused like Fleur's by the currents of modernity, and she was resolute. Youth in her South Carolinian home had been simple and self-reliant; and unlike most American girls, she had not had too good a time. It had been a shock to her, he knew, that he was not his first love and that his first love was still in love with him. She had shown her uneasiness at once, but now, he felt, she had closed her guard. And Jon could not help knowing, too, that she was still deeply in love with him for all that they had been married two years. He had often heard that American girls seldom really knew the men they married; but it seemed to him sometimes that Anne knew him better than he knew himself. If so, what did she know? What was he? He wanted to do something useful with his life; he wanted to be loyal and kind. But was it all just wanting? Was he a fraud? Not what she thought him? It was all confused and heavy in his mind, like the air in the room.

No use thinking! Better to snooze, as Anne said–better to snooze! He woke and said:

'Hallo! Was I snoring?'

'No. But you were twitching like a dog, Jon.'

Jon got up and went to the window.

'I was dreaming. It's a beautiful night. A fine September's the pick of the year.'

'Yes; I love the "fall". Is your mother coming over, soon?'

'Not until we're settled in. I believe she thinks we're better without her.'

'Your mother would always feel she was *de trop* before she was.'

'That's on the right side, anyway.'

'Yes, I wonder if I should.'

Jon turned. She was sitting up, staring in front of her, frowning. He went over and kissed her.

'Careful of your chest, darling!' and he pulled up the clothes.

She lay back, gazing up at him; and again he wondered what she saw. . . .

He was met next day by June's: 'So Fleur was here yesterday and gave you a lift! I told her what I thought this morning.'

'What *did* you think?' said Jon.

'That it mustn't begin again. She's a spoiled child not to be trusted.'

His eyes moved angrily.

'You'd better leave Fleur alone.'

'I always leave people alone,' said June; 'but this is my house, and I had to speak my mind.'

'I'd better stop sitting then.'

'Now, don't be silly, Jon. Of course you can't stop sitting–neither of you. Harold would be frightfully upset.'

'Damn Harold!'

June took hold of his lapel.

'That's not what I meant at all. The pictures are going to be splendid. I only meant that you mustn't meet here.'

'Did you tell Fleur that?'

'Yes.'

Jon laughed, and the sound of the laugh was hard.

'We're not children, June.'

'Have you told Anne?'

'No.'

'There, you see!'

'What?'

His face had become stubborn and angry.

'You're very like your father and grandfather, Jon–they couldn't bear to be told anything.'

'Can *you*?'

'Of course, when it's necessary.'

'Then please don't interfere.'

Pink rushed into June's cheeks, tears into her eyes; she winked them away, shook herself, and said coldly:

'I never interfere.'

'No?'

She went more pink, and suddenly stroked his sleeve. That touched Jon, and he smiled.

He 'sat' disturbed all that afternoon, while the Rafaelite painted, and June hovered, sometimes with a frown, and sometimes with yearning in her face. He wondered what he should do if Fleur called for him again. But Fleur did not call, and he went home alone. The next day was Sunday and he did not go up; but on Monday when he came out of 'The Poplars', after 'sitting' he saw Fleur's car standing by the kerb.

'I do want to show you my house to-day. I suppose June spoke to you, but I'm a reformed character, Jon. Get in!' And Jon got in.

The day was dull, neither lighted nor staged for emotion, and the 'reformed character' played her part to perfection. Not a word suggested that they were other than best friends. She talked of America, its language and books. Jon maintained that America was violent in its repressions and in its revolt against repressions.

'In a word,' said Fleur, 'young.'

'Yes; but so far as I can make out, it's getting younger every year.'

'I liked America.'

'Oh! I liked it all right. I made quite a profit, too, on my orchard when I sold.'

'I wonder you came back, Jon. The fact is—you're old-fashioned.'

'How?'

'Take sex—I couldn't discuss sex with you.'

'Can you with other people?'

'Oh! with nearly everyone. Don't frown like that! You'd be awfully out of it, my dear, in London, or New York, for that matter.'

'I hate fluffy talk about sex,' said Jon, gruffly. 'The French are the only people who understand sex. It isn't to be talked about as they do here and in America; it's much too real.'

Fleur stole another look.

'Then let us drop that hot potato. I'm not sure whether I could even discuss art with you.'

'Did you see that St Gaudens statue at Washington?'

'Yes; but that's *vieux jeu* nowadays.'

'Is it?' growled Jon. 'What do they want, then?'

'You know as well as I.'

'You mean it must be unintelligible?'

'Put it that way if you like. The point is that art now is just a subject for conversation; and anything that anybody can understand at first sight is not worth talking about and therefore not art.'

'I call that silly.'

'Perhaps. But more amusing.'

'If you see through it, how can you be amused?'

'Another hot potato. Let's try again! I bet you don't approve of women's dress, these days?'

'Why not? It's jolly sensible.'

'La, la! Are we coming together on that?'

'Naturally, you'd all look better without hats. You can wash your heads easily now, you know.'

'Oh! don't cut us off hats, Jon. All our stoicism would go. If we hadn't to find hats that suited us, life would be much too easy.'

'But they don't suit you.'

'I agree, my dear; but I know the feminine character better than you. One must always give babies something to cut their teeth on.'

'Fleur, you're too intelligent to live in London.'

My dear boy, the modern young woman doesn't live anywhere. She floats in an ether of her own.'

'She touches earth sometimes, I suppose.'

Fleur did not answer for a minute; then, looking at him:

'Yes; she touches earth sometimes, Jon.' And in that look she seemed to say again: 'Oh! what a pity we have to talk like this!'

She showed him the house in such a way that he might get the impression that she considered to some purpose the comfort of others. Even her momentary encounters with the denizens had that quality. Jon went away with a tingling in his palm, and the thought: 'She likes to make herself out a butterfly, but at heart–!' The memory of her clear eyes smiling at him, the half-comic quiver of her lips when she said: 'Good-bye, bless you!' blurred his vision of Sussex all the way home. And who shall say that she had not so intended?

Holly had come to meet him with a hired car.

'I'm sorry, Jon, Val's got the car. He won't be able to drive you up and down to-morrow as he said he would. He's had to go up to-day. And if he can get through his business in town, he'll go on to Newmarket on Wednesday. Something rather beastly's happened. His name's been forged on a cheque for a hundred pounds by an old college friend to whom he'd been particularly decent.'

'Very adequate reasons,' said Jon. 'What's Val going to do?'

'He doesn't know yet; but this is the third time he's played a dirty trick on Val.'

'Is it quite certain?'

'The bank described him unmistakably. He seems to think Val will stand anything; but it can't be allowed to go on.'

'I should say not.'

'Yes, dear boy; but what would you do? Prosecute an old college friend? Val has a queer feeling that it's only a sort of accident that he himself has kept straight.'

Jon stared. *Was* it an accident that one kept straight?

'Was this fellow in the war?' he asked.

'I doubt it. He seems to be an absolute rotter. I saw his face once–bone slack and bone selfish.'

'Beastly for Val!' said Jon.

'He's going to consult his uncle, Fleur's father. By the way, have you seen Fleur lately?'

'Yes. I saw her to-day. She brought me as far as Dorking, and showed me her house there.'

The look on Holly's face, the reflective shadow between her eyes, were not lost on him.

'Is there any objection to my seeing her?' he said, abruptly.

'Only you can know that, dear boy.'

Jon did not answer, but the moment he saw Anne he told her. She showed him nothing by face or voice, just asked how Fleur was and how he liked the house. That night, after she seemed asleep, he lay awake, gnawed by uncertainty. *Was* it an accident that one kept straight–was it?

6

SOAMES HAS BRAIN-WAVES

The first question Soames put to his nephew in Green Street, was: 'How did he get hold of the cheque form? Do you keep your cheque-books lying about?'

'I'm afraid I do, rather, in the country, Uncle Soames.'

'Um,' said Soames, 'then you deserve all you get. What about your signature?'

'He wrote from Brighton asking if he could see me.'

'You should have made your wife sign your answer.'

Val groaned. 'I didn't think he'd run to forgery.'

'They run to anything when they're as far gone as that. I suppose when you said "No", he came over from Brighton all the same?'

'Yes, he did; but I wasn't in.'

'Exactly; and he sneaked a form. Well, if you want to stop him, you'd better prosecute. He'll get three years.'

'That'd kill him,' said Val, 'to judge by his looks.'

Soames shook his head. 'Improve his health—very likely. Has he ever been in prison?'

'Not that I know of.'

'H'm!'

Silence followed this profound remark.

'I can't prosecute,' said Val, suddenly. 'College pal. There, but for the grace of God and all that, don't you know; one might have gone to the dogs oneself.'

Soames stared at him.

'Well,' he said, 'I suppose you might. Your father was always in some scrape or other.'

Val frowned. He had suddenly remembered an evening at the Pandemonium, when, in company with another college friend, he had seen his own father, drunk.

'But somehow,' he said, 'I've got to see that he doesn't do it again. If he didn't look such a "heart" subject, one could give him a hiding.'

Soames shook his head. 'Personal violence—besides, he's probably out of England by now.'

'No; I called at his club on the way here—he's in town all right.'

'You didn't see him?'

'No. I wanted to see you first.'

Flattered in spite of himself, Soames said sardonically:

'Perhaps he's got what they call a better nature?'

'By Jove, Uncle Soames, I believe that's a brain-wave!'

Soames shook his head. 'Not to judge by his face.'

'I don't know,' said Val. 'After all, he was born a gentleman.'

'That means nothing nowadays. And, apropos, before I forget it. Do you remember a young fellow called Butterfield, in the Elderson affair—no, you wouldn't. Well, I'm going to take him out of his publishing firm, and put him under old Gradman, to learn about your mother's and the other family Trusts. Old Gradman's on his last legs, and this young man can step into his shoes—it's a permanent job, and better pay than he's getting now. I can rely on him, and that's something in these days. I thought I'd tell you.'

'Another brain-wave, Uncle Soames. But about your first. Could you see Stainford, and follow that up?'

'Why should *I* see him?'

'You carry so much more weight than I do.'

'H'm! Seems to me I always have to do the unpleasant thing. However, I expect it's better than your seeing him.'

Val grinned. 'I shall feel much happier if you do it.'

'*I* shan't,' said Soames. 'That bank cashier hasn't made a mistake, I suppose?'

'Who could mistake Stainford?'

'Nobody,' said Soames. 'Well, if you won't prosecute, you'd better leave it to me.'

When Val was gone he remained in thought. Here he was, still keeping the family affairs straight; he wondered what they would do without him some day. That young Butterfield might be a brain-wave, but who could tell—the fellow was attached to him, though, in a curious sort of way, with his eyes of a dog! He should put that in hand at once, before old Gradman dropped off. Must give old Gradman a bit of plate, too, with his name engraved, while he could still appreciate it. Most people only got them when they were dead or dotty. Young Butterfield knew Michael, too, and that would make him interested in Fleur's affairs. But as to this infernal Stainford? How was he going to set about it? He had better get the fellow here if possible, rather than go to his club. If he'd had the brass to stay in England after committing such a bare-faced forgery, he would have the brass to come here again and see what more he could get. And, smiling sourly, Soames went to the telephone.

'Mr Stainford in the club? Ask him if he'd be good enough to step over and see Mr Forsyte at Green Street.'

After a look round to see that there were no ornaments within reach, he seated himself in the dining-room and had Smither in.

'I'm expecting that Mr Stainford, Smither. If I ring, while he's here, pop out and get a policeman.'

At the expression on Smither's face he added:

'I don't anticipate it, but one never knows.'

'There's no danger, I hope, Mr Soames?'

'Nothing of the sort, Smither; I may want him arrested—that's all.'

'Do you expect him to take something again, sir?'

Soames smiled, and waved his hand at the lack of ornaments. 'Very likely he won't come, but if he does, show him in here.'

When she had gone, he settled down with the clock—a Dutch piece too heavy to take away; it had been 'picked up' by James, chimed everything, and had a moon and a lot of stars on its face. He did not feel so 'bobbish' before this third encounter with that fellow; the chap had scored twice, and so far as he could see, owing to Val's reluctance to prosecute, was going to score a third time. And yet there was a sort of fascination in dealing with what they called 'the limit', and a certain quality about the fellow which raised him almost to the level of romance. It was as if the idolised maxim of his own youth 'Show no emotion', and all the fashionableness that, under the ægis of his mother Emily, had clung about Park Lane, were revisiting him in the shape of this languid beggar. And probably the chap would come!

'Mr Stainford, sir.'

When Smither—very red—had withdrawn, Soames did not know how to begin, the fellow's face, like old parchment, was as if it had come from some grave or other. At last he said:

'I wanted to see you about a cheque. My nephew's name's been forged.'

The eyebrows rose, the eyelids dropped still further.

'Yes. Dartie won't prosecute.'

Soames's gorge rose.

'You seem very cocksure,' he said; 'my nephew has by no means made up his mind.'

'We were at college together, Mr Forsyte.'

'You trade on that, do you? There's a limit, Mr Stainford. That was a very clever forgery, for a first.'

There was just a flicker of the face; and Soames drew the forged cheque from his pocket. Inadequately protected, of course, not even automatically crossed! Val's cheques would have to have the words 'Not negotiable; Credit payee' stamped on them in future. But how could he give this fellow a thorough scare?

'I have a detective at hand,' he said, 'only waiting for me to ring. This sort of thing must stop. As you don't seem to understand that—' and he took a step towards the bell.

A faint and bitter smile had come on those pale lips.

'You've never been down and out, I imagine, Mr Forsyte?'

'No,' answered Soames, with a certain disgust.

'I always am. It's very wearing.'

'In that case,' said Soames, 'you'll find prison a rest.' But even as he spoke them, the words seemed futile and a little brutal. The fellow wasn't a man at all—he was a shade, a languid bitter shade. It was as if one were bullying a ghost.

'Look here!' he said. 'As a gentleman by birth, give me your word not to try it on again with my nephew, or any of my family, and I won't ring.'

'Very well, you have my word—such as it is!'

'We'll leave it at that, then,' said Soames. 'But this is the last time. I shall keep the evidence of this.'

'One must live, Mr Forsyte.'

'I don't agree,' said Soames.

The 'shade' uttered a peculiar sound—presumably a laugh, and Soames was alone again. He went hastily to the door, and watched the fellow into the street. Live? Must one? Wouldn't a fellow like that be better dead? Wouldn't most people be better dead? And, astonished at so extravagant a thought, he went up to the drawing-room. Forty-five years since he had laid its foundations, and there it was, as full of marqueterie as ever. On the mantelpiece was a little old daguerreotype, slightly pinked in the cheeks, of his grandfather—'Superior Dosset' set in a deep, enamelled frame. Soames contemplated it. The chin of the founder of the Forsyte clan was settled comfortably between the widely separated points of an old-fashioned collar. The eyes—with thick under-lids, were light and shrewd and rather japing; the side-whiskers grey; the mouth looked as if it could swallow a lot; the old-time tail-coat was of broadcloth; the hands those of a man of affairs. A stocky old boy, with a certain force, and a deal of character! Well-nigh a hundred years since that was taken of him. Refreshing to look at character, after that languid seedy specimen! He would like to see where that old chap had been born and bred before he emerged at the end of the eighteenth century and built the house of Forsyte. He would take Riggs, and go down, and if Fleur wouldn't come–perhaps all the better! Be dull for her! Roots were nothing to young people. Yes, he would go and look at his roots while the weather was still fine. But first to put old Gradman in order. It would do him good to see the old fellow after this experience–he never left the office till half-past five. And, replacing the daguerreotype, Soames took a taxi to the Poultry, reflecting as he went. How difficult it was to keep things secure, with chaps like Elderson and this fellow Stainford always on the look-out. There was the country too, no sooner was it out of one than it was into another mess; the coal strike would end when people began to feel the winter pinch, but something else would crop up, some war or disturbance or other. And then there was Fleur–she had plenty of money of her own. Had he been wrong to make her so independent? And yet–the idea of controlling her through money had always been repulsive to him. Whatever she did–she was his only child, one might say his only love. If she couldn't keep straight for love of her infant and himself, to say nothing of her husband–he couldn't do it for her by threat of cutting her off or anything like that! Anyway, things were looking better with her, and perhaps he had been wrong.

The City had just begun to disgorge its daily life. Its denizens were scurrying out like rabbits; they didn't scurry in like that, he would bet–work-shy, nowadays! Ten where it used to be nine; five where it used to be six. Still, with the telephone and one thing and another, they got through as much perhaps; and didn't drink all the beer and sherry and eat all the chops they used to–a skimpier breed altogether, compared with that old boy whose effigy he had just been gazing at, a shadowy, narrow-headed lot, with a nervy, anxious look, as if they'd invested in life and found it a dropping stock. And not a tail-coat or a silk hat to be seen. Settling his own more firmly on his head, he got out at the familiar backwater off the Poultry, and entered the offices of Cuthcott, Kingson and Forsyte.

Old Gradman was still there, his broad, bent back just divested of its workaday coat.

'Ah! Mr Soames, I was just going. Excuse me while I put on my coat.'

A frock-coat made in the year one, to judge by the cut of it!

'I go at half-past five now. There isn't much to do as a rule. I like to get a nap before supper. It's a pleasure to see you; you're quite a stranger.'

'Yes,' said Soames. 'I don't come in much, but I've been thinking. If anything should happen to either or both of us, things would soon be in Queer Street, Gradman.'

'Aow! We won't think about th-at!'

'But we must; we're neither of us young men.'

'Well, I'm not a chicken, but you're *no* age, Mr Soames.'

'Seventy-one.'

'Dear, dear! It seems only the other day since I took you down to school at Slough. I remember what happened then better than I do what happened yesterday.'

'So do I, Gradman; and that's a sign of age. Do you recollect that young chap who came here and told he about Elderson?'

'Aow, yes! Nice young feller. Buttermilk or some such name.'

'Butterfield. Well, I'm going to put him under you here, and I want you to get him *au fait* with everything.'

The old fellow seemed standing very still; his face, in its surround of grey beard and hair, was quite expressionless. Soames hurried on:

'It's just precautionary. Some day you'll be wanting to retire.'

Gradman lifted his hand with a heavy gesture.

'I'll die in 'arness, I 'ope,' he said.

'That's as you like, Gradman. You'll remain as you always have been–in full charge; but you'll have someone to rely on if you don't feel well or want a holiday or what not.'

'I'd rather not, Mr Soames. To have a young man about the place–'

'A good young fellow, Gradman. And for some reason, grateful to me and to my son-in-law. He won't give you any trouble. We none of us live for ever, you know.'

The old chàp's face had puckered queerly, his voice grated more than usual.

'It seems going to meet trouble. I'm quite up to the work, Mr Soames.'

'Oh! I know how you feel,' said Soames. 'I feel much the same myself but Time stands still for no man, and we must look to the future.'

A sigh escaped from its grizzled prison.

'Well, Mr Soames, if you've made up your mind, we'll say no more; but I don't like it.'

'Let me give you a lift to your station.'

'I'd rather walk, thank you; I like the air. I'll just lock up.'

Soames perceived that not only drawers but feelings required locking up, and went out.

Faithful old chap! One might go round to Polkingford's and see if one could pick up that bit of plate.

In that emporium, so lined with silver and gold, that a man wondered whether anything had ever been sold there, Soames stood considering. Must be something that a man could swear by–nothing arty or elegant. He supposed the old chap didn't drink punch–a chapel-goer! How about those camels in silver-gilt with two humps each and candles coming out of them? 'Joseph Gradman, in gratitude from the Forsyte family' engraved between the humps? Gradman lived somewhere near the Zoo. M'm! Camels? No! a bowl was better. If he didn't drink punch he could put rose-leaves or flowers into it.

'I want a bowl,' he said, 'a really good one.'

'Yes, sir, I think we have the very article.'

They always had the very article!

'How about this, sir–massive silver–a very chaste design.'

'Chaste!' said Soames. 'I wouldn't have it as a gift.'

'No, sir; it isn't perhaps *exactly* what you require. Now, this is a nice little bowl.'

'No, no; something plain and solid that would hold about a gallon.'

'Mr Bankwait–come here a minute. This gentleman want an old-fashioned bowl.'

'Yes, sir; I think we have the very thing.'

Soames uttered an indistinguishable sound.

'There isn't much demand for the old-fashioned bowl; but we have a very fine second-hand, that used to be in the Rexborough family.'

'With arms on?' said Soames. 'That won't do. It must be new, or free from arms, anyway.'

'Ah! Then this will be what you want, sir.'

'My Lord!' said Soames; and raising his umbrella he pointed in the opposite direction. 'What's that thing?'

With a slightly chagrined air the shopman brought the article from its case.

Upon a swelling base, with a waist above, a silver bowl sprang generously forth. Soames flipped it with his finger.

'Pure silver, sir; and, as you see, very delicate edging; not too bacchanalian in design; the best gilt within. I should say the very thing you want.'

'It might do. What's the price?'

The shopman examined a cabalistic sign.

'Thirty-five pounds, sir.'

'Quite enough,' said Soames. Whether it would please old Gradman, he didn't know, but the thing was in good taste, and would not do the family discredit. 'I'll have that, then,' he said. 'Engrave these words on it,' and he wrôte them down. 'Send it to that address, and the account to me; and don't be long about it.'

'Very good sir. You wouldn't like those goblets?–They're perfect in their way.'

'Nothing more!' said Soames. 'Good-evening!' And, handing the shopman his card, with a cold circular glance, he went out. That was off his mind!

September sun sprinkled him, threading his way west along Piccadilly into the Green Park. These gentle autumn days were very pleasant. He didn't get hot, and he didn't feel cold. And the plane trees looked their best, just making up their minds to turn; nice trees, shapely. And, crossing the grassy spaces, Soames felt almost mellow. A rather more rapid step behind impinged on his consciousness. A voice said:

'Ah! Forsyte! Bound for the meeting at Michael's? Might we go along together?'

Old Mont, perky and talkative as ever! There he went–off at once!

'What's your view of all these London changes, Forsyte? You remember the peg-top trouser, and the crinoline–Leech in his prime–Old Pam on his horse–September makes one reminiscent.'

'It's all on the surface,' said Soames.

'On the surface? I sometimes have that feeling. But there is a real change. It's the difference between the Austen and Trollope novels and these modern fellows. There are no parishes left. Classes? Yes, but divided by man, not by God, as in Trollope's day.'

Soames sniffed. The chap was always putting things in that sort of way!

'At the rate we're going, they'll soon not be divided at all,' he said.

'I think you're wrong there, Forsyte. I should never be surprised to see the horse come back.'

'The horse,' muttered Soames; 'what's he got to do with it?'

'What we must look for,' said Sir Lawrence, swinging his cane, 'is the millennium. Then we shall soon be developing individuality again. And the millennium's nearly here.'

'I don't in the least follow you,' said Soames.

'Education's free; women have the vote; even the workman has or soon will have his car; the slums are doomed–thanks to you, Forsyte; amusement and news are in every home; the Liberal Party's up the spout; Free Trade's a moveable feast; sport's cheap and plentiful; dogma's got the knock; so has the General Strike; Boy Scouts are increasing rapidly; dress is comfortable; and hair is short—it's all millennial.'

'What's all that got to do with the horse?'

'A symbol, my dear Forsyte. It's impossible to standardise or socialise the horse. We're beginning to react against uniformity. A little more millennium and we shall soon be cultivating our souls and driving tandem again.'

'What's that noise?' said Soames. 'Sounds like a person in distress.'

Sir Lawrence cocked his eyebrow.

'It's a vacuum cleaner, in Buckingham Palace. Very human things those.'

Soames grunted—the fellow couldn't be serious! Well! He might *have* to be before long. If Fleur—! But he would not contemplate that 'if'.

'What I admire about the Englishman,' said Sir Lawrence suddenly, 'is his evolutionary character. He flows and ebbs, and flows again. Foreigners may think him a stick-in-the-mud, but he's got continuity—a great quality, Forsyte. What are you going to do with your pictures when you take the ferry? Leave them to the nation?'

'Depends on how they treat me. If they're going to clap on any more death duties, I shall revoke the bequest.'

'The principle of our ancestors, eh? Voluntary service, or none. Great fellows, our ancestors.'

'I don't know about yours,' said Soames; 'mine were just yeomen. I'm going down to have a look at them to-morrow,' he added defiantly.

'Splendid! I hope you'll find them at home.'

'We're late,' said Soames, glancing in at the dining-room window, where the committee were glancing out. 'Half-past six! What a funny lot they look!'

'We always look a funny lot,' said Sir Lawrence, following him into the house, 'except to ourselves. That's the first principle of existence, Forsyte.'

7

TO-MORROW

Fleur met them in the hall. After dropping Jon at Dorking she had exceeded the limit homewards, that she might appear to have nothing in her thoughts but the welfare of the slums. 'The Squire' being among his partridges, the bishop was in the Chair. Fleur went to the sideboard, and, while Michael was reading the minutes, began pouring out the tea. The bishop, Sir Godfrey Bedwin, Mr Montross, her father-in-law, and herself drank China tea; Sir Timothy—whisky and soda; Michael nothing; the Marquess, Hilary, and her father Indian tea; and each maintained that the others were destroying their digestions. Her father, indeed, was always telling her that she only drank China tea because it was the fashion—she couldn't possibly like it. While she apportioned their beverages she wondered what they would think if they knew what, besides tea, was going on within her. To-morrow was Jon's last sitting and she was going 'over the top'! All the careful possessing of her soul these two months since she had danced with him at Nettlefold would by this time to-morrow be ended. To-morrow at this hour she would claim her own. The knowledge that there must be two parties to any contract did not trouble her. She had the faith of a pretty woman in love. What she willed would be accomplished, but none should know it! And, handing her cups, she smiled, pitying the ignorance of these wise old men. They should not know, nor anyone else, least of all the young man who last night had held her in his arms. And, thinking of one not yet so holding her, she sat down by the hearth, with her tea and her tablets, while her pulses throbbed and her half-closed eyes saw Jon's face turned round to her from the station door. Fulfilment! She, like Jacob, had served seven years—for the fulfilment of her love—seven long, long years! And—while she sat there listening to the edgeless booming of the bishop and Sir Godfrey, to the random ejaculations of Sir Timothy, to her father's close and cautious comments—that something clear, precise, unflinching, woven into her nature with French blood, silently perfected the machinery of the stolen life, that should begin to-morrow after they had eaten of forbidden fruit. A stolen life was a safe life if there were no chicken-hearted hesitation, no squeamishness, and no remorse! She might have experienced a dozen stolen lives already, from the certainty she felt about that. She alone would arrange—Jon should be spared all. And no one should know!

'Fleur, would you take note of that?'

'Yes.'

And she wrote down on her tablets: 'Ask Michael what I was to take a note of.'

'Mrs Mont!'

'Yes, Sir Timothy?'

'Could you get up one of those what d'you call 'ems for us?'

'Matinées?'

'No, no—jumble sales, don't they call 'em.'

'Certainly.'

The more she got up for them the more impeccable her reputation, the greater her freedom, and the more she would deserve, and ironically enjoy, her stolen life.

Hilary speaking now. What would *he* think if he knew?

'But I think we *ought* to have a matinée, Fleur. The public are so good, they'll always pay a guinea to go to what most of them would give a guinea any day not to go to. What do you say, Bishop?'

'A matinée—by all means!'

'Matinées—dreadful things!'

'Not if we got a pleasant play, Mr Forsyte—something a little old-fashioned—one of L.S.D.'s. It would advertise us, you know. What do you think, Lord Shropshire?'

'My granddaughter Marjorie would get one up for you. It would do her good.'

'H'm. If *she* gets it up, it won't be old-fashioned.' And Fleur saw her father's face turning towards her as he spoke. If only he knew how utterly she was beyond all that; how trivial to her seemed that heart-burning of the past.

'Mr Montross, have you a theatre in your pocket?'

'I can get you one, Mr Charwell.'

'First rate! Then, will you and Lord Shropshire and my nephew here take that under your wings. Fleur, tell us how your "Rest House" is doing?'

'Perfectly, Uncle Hilary. It's quite full. The girls are delightful.'

'Wild lot, I should think—aren't they?'

'Oh! no, Sir Timothy; they're quite model.'·

If only the old gentleman could see over his moustache into the model lady who controlled them!

'Well then, that's that.'If there's nothing more, Mr Chairman, will you excuse me? I've got to meet an American about ants. We aren't properly shaking up these landlords, in my opinion. Good-night to you all!'

Motioning to Michael to stay behind, Fleur rose to see Sir Timothy out.

'Which umbrella is yours, Sir Timothy?'

'I don't know; that looks the best. If you get up a jumble sale, Mrs Mont, I wish you'd sell the bishop at it. I can't stand a fellow with a plum in his mouth, especially in the Chair.'

Fleur smiled, and the 'old boy' cocked his hat at her. They all cocked their hats at her, and that was pleasant! But would they if they knew! Dusk among the trees of the Square Garden, the lights just turned up–what luck to have such weather–dry and warm! She stood in the doorway, taking long breaths. By this time to-morrow she meant to be a dishonest wife! Well, not more than she had always been in secret aspiration.

'I'm glad Kit's down at "The Shelter",' she thought. *He* should never know, no one should! There would be no change–no change in anything except in her and Jon. The Life Force would break bounds in a little secret river, which would flow–ah, where? Who cared?

'My dear Mont, honesty was never the best policy from a material point of view. The sentiment is purely Victorian. The Victorians were wonderful fellows for squaring circles.'

'I agree, Marquess, I agree; they could think what they wanted better than anybody. When times are fat, you can.'

Those two in the hall behind her–dried up and withered! Fleur turned to them with her smile.

'My dear young lady–the evening air! You won't take cold?'

'No, thank you, sir; I'm warm all through.'

'How nice that is!'

'May I give you a lift, my lord?'

'Thank you, Mr Montross. Wish I could afford a car myself. Are you coming our way, Mont? Do you know that song, Mr Montross: "We'll all go round to Alice's house"? It seems to have a fascination for my milk-boy. I often wonder who Alice is? I have a suspicion she may not be altogether proper. Good-night to you, Mrs Mont. How charming your house is!'

'Good-night, sir!'

His hand; 'the walrus's'; her father-in-law's.

'Kit all right, Fleur?'

'First rate.'

'Good-night, my dear!'

His dear–the mother of his grandson! 'To-morrow and to-morrow and to-morrow!'

The rug wrapped round the cargo of age, the door shut–what a smooth and silent car! Voices again:

'Will you have a taxi, Uncle Hilary?'

'No, thank you, Michael, the bishop and I will walk.'

'Then I'll come with you as far as the corner. Coming, Sir Godfrey? Bye-bye, darling. Your Dad's staying to dinner. I'll be back from old Blythe's about ten.'

The animals went out four by four!

'Don't stand there; you'll get cold!' Her father's voice! The one person whose eyes she feared. She must keep her mask on now.

'Well, Dad, what have you been doing to-day? Come into the "parlour"—we'll have dinner quite soon.'

'How's your picture? Is this fellow taking care not to exaggerate? I think I'd better have a look at it.'

'Not just yet, dear. He's a very touchy gentleman.'

'They're all that. I thought of going down West to-morrow to see where the Forsytes sprang from. I suppose you couldn't take a rest and come?'

Fleur heard, without giving a sign of her relief.

'How long will you be away, Dad?'

'Back on the third day. 'Tisn't two hundred miles.'

'I'm afraid it would put the gentleman out.'

'Well, I didn't think you'd care to. There's no kudos there. But I've meant to for a long time; and the weather's fine.'

'I'm sure it will be frightfully interesting, dear; you must tell me all about it. But what with the portrait and my "Rest House", I'm very tied just now.'

'Well, then, I'll look for you at the week-end. Your mother's gone to some friends—they do nothing but play bridge; she'll be away till Monday. I always want you, you know,' he added simply. And to avoid his eyes she got up.

'I'll just run up now, Dad, and change. Those Slum Committee meetings always make me feel grubby. I don't know why.'

'They're a waste of time,' said Soames. 'There'll always be slums. Still, it's something for you both to do.'

'Yes, Michael's quite happy about it.'

'That old fool, Sir Timothy!' And Soames went up to the Fragonard. 'I've hung that Morland. The Marquess is an amiable old chap. I suppose you know I'm leaving my pictures to the nation? You've no use for them. You'll have to live at that place Lippinghall some day. Pictures'd be no good there. Ancestors and stags' horns and horses—that sort of thing. M'ff!'

A secret life and Lippinghall! Long, long might that conjunction be deferred!

'Oh, Bart will live for ever, Dad!'

'M'yes! He's spry enough. Well, you run up!'

While she washed off powder and put it on again Fleur thought: "Dear Dad! Thank God! He'll be far away!"

Now that her mind was thoroughly made up, it was comparatively easy to bluff, and keep her freshly-powdered face, smiling and serene, above the Chelsea dinner service.

'Where are you going to hang your portrait, when it's done?' resumed Soames.

'Why! It'll be yours, dear.'

'Mine? Well, of course; but you'll hang it here; Michael'll want it.'

Michael—unknowing! *That* gave her a twinge.

Well, she would be as good to him after, as ever. No old-fashioned squeamishness!

'Thank you, dear. I expect he'll like it in the "parlour". The scheme *is* silver and gold—my "Folly" dress.'

'I remember it,' said Soames; 'a thing with bells.'

'I think all that part of the picture's very good.'

'What? Hasn't he got your face?'

'Perhaps–but I don't know that I approve of it frightfully.' After this morning's sitting, indeed, she had wondered. Something avid had come into the face as if the Rafaelite had sensed the hardening of resolve within her.

'If he doesn't do you justice I shan't take it,' said Soames.

Fleur smiled. The Rafaelite would have something to say to that.

'Oh! I expect it'll be all right. One never thinks one's own effigies are marvellous, I suppose.'

'Don't know,' said Soames, 'never was painted.'

'You ought to be, dear.'

'Waste of time! Has he sent away the picture of that young woman?'

Fleur's eyes did not flinch.

'Jon Forsyte's wife? Oh! yes–long ago.'

She expected him to say: 'Seen anything of them?' But it did not come. And that disturbed her more than if it had come.

'I had your cousin Val to see me to-day.'

Fleur's heart stood still. Had they been talking?

'His name's been forged.'

Thank heaven!

'Some people have no moral sense at all,' continued Soames. Involuntarily her white shoulder rose; but he wasn't looking. 'Common honesty, I don't know where it is.'

'I heard Lord Shropshire say to-night that "Honesty's the best policy" was a mere Victorianism, Dad.'

'Well, he's ten years my senior, but I don't know where he got that from. Everything's twisted inside out, nowadays.'

'But if it's the best *policy*, there never was any particular virtue in it, was there?'

Soames took a sharp look at her smiling face.

'Why not?'

'Oh, I don't know. These are Lippinghall partridges, Dad.'

Soames sniffed. 'Not hung quite long enough. You ought to be able to swear by the leg of a partridge.'

'Yes, I've told cook, but she has her own views.'

'And the bread sauce should have a touch more onion in it. Victorianism, indeed! I suppose he'd call *me* a Victorian?'

'Well, aren't you, Dad? You had forty-six years of her.'

'I've had twenty-five without her, and hope to have a few more.'

'Many, many,' said Fleur softly.

'Can't expect that.'

'Oh yes! But I'm glad you don't consider yourself a Victorian; I don't like them. They wore too many clothes.'

'Don't you be too sure of that.'

'Well, to-morrow you'll be among Georgians, anyway.'

'Yes,' said Soames. 'There's a graveyard there, they say. And that reminds me–I've bought that corner bit in the churchyard down at home. It'll do for me as well as any other. Your mother will want to go to France to be buried, I expect.'

'Give Mr Forsyte some sherry, Coaker.'

Soames took a long sniff.

'This is some of your grandfather's. He lived to be ninety.'

If she and Jon lived to be ninety–would nobody still know? . . . She left him at ten o'clock, brushing his nose with her lips.

'I'm tired, Dad; and you'll have a long day to-morrow. Good-night, dear!'

Thank God he would be among the Georgians to-morrow!

8

FORBIDDEN FRUIT

Halting the car suddenly in the by-road between Gage's farm and the Robin Hill coppice, Fleur said: 'Jon, dear, I've got a whim. Let's get out and go in there. The potentate's in Scotland.' He did not move and she added: 'I shan't see you again for a long time, now your picture's finished.'

Jon got out, then, and she unlatched the footpath gate. They stood a minute within, listening for sounds of anyone to interrupt their trespass. The fine September afternoon was dying fast. The last 'sitting' had been long, and it was late; and in the coppice of larch and birch the dusk was deepening. Fleur slid her hand within his arm.

'Listen! Still, isn't it? I feel as if we were back seven years, Jon. Do you wish we were? Babes in the wood once more?'

Gruffly he answered:

'No good looking back–things happen as they must.'

'The birds are going to bed. Used there to be owls?'

'Yes; we shall hear one soon, I expect.'

'How good it smells!'

'Trees and the cow-houses!'

'Vanilla and hay, as the poets have it. Are they close?'

'Yes.'

'Don't let's go farther, then.'

'Here's the old log,' said Jon. 'We might sit down, and listen for an owl.'

On the old log seat they sat down, side by side.

'No dew,' said Fleur. 'The weather will break soon, I expect. I love the scent of drought.'

'I love the smell of rain.'

'You and I never love the same thing, Jon. And yet–we've loved each other.' Against her arm it was as if he shivered.

'There goes the old clock! It's awfully late, Fleur! Listen! The owl!'

Startlingly close through the thin-branched trees the call came. Fleur rose. 'Let's see if we can find him.'

She moved back from the old log.

'Aren't you coming? Just a little wander, Jon.'

Jon got up and went along at her side among the larches.

'Up this way–wasn't it? How quickly it's got dark. Look! The birches are still white. I love birch trees.' She put her hand on a pale stem. 'The smoothness, Jon. It's like skin.' And, leaning forward, she laid her cheek against the trunk. 'There! feel my cheek, and then the bark. Could you tell the difference, except for warmth?'

Jon reached his hand up. She turned her lips and touched it.

'Jon—kiss me just once.'

'You know I couldn't kiss you "just once", Fleur.'

'Then kiss me for ever, Jon.'

'No, no! No, no!'

'Things happen as they must—you said so.'

'Fleur—don't! I can't stand it.'

She laughed—very low, softly.

'I don't want you to. I've waited seven years for this. No! Don't cover your face! Look at me! I take it all on myself. The woman tempted you. But, Jon, you were always mine. There! That's better. I can see your eyes. Poor Jon! Now kiss me!' In that long kiss her very spirit seemed to leave her; she could not even see whether his eyes were open or, like hers, closed. And again the owl hooted.

Jon tore his lips away. He stood there in her arms, trembling like a startled horse.

With her lips against his ear, she whispered:

'There's nothing, Jon; there's nothing.' She could hear him holding-in his breath, and her warm lips whispered on: 'Take me in your arms, Jon; take me!' The light had failed completely now; stars were out between the dark feathering of the trees, and low down, from where the coppice sloped up towards the east, a creeping brightness seemed trembling towards them through the wood from the moon rising. A faint rustle broke the silence, ceased, broke it again. Closer, closer—Fleur pressed against him.

'Not here, Fleur; not here. I can't—I won't—'

'Yes, Jon; here—now! I claim you.'

The moon was shining through the tree stems when they sat again side by side on the log seat.

Jon's hands were pressed to his forehead, and she could not see his eyes.

'No one shall ever know, Jon.'

He dropped his hands and faced her.

'I must tell her.'

'Jon!'

'I must!'

'You can't unless I let you, and I don't let you.'

'What have we done? Oh, Fleur, what *have* we done?'

'It was written. When shall I see you again, Jon?'

He started up.

'Never, unless she knows. Never, Fleur—never! I can't go on in secret!'

As quickly, too, Fleur was on her feet. They stood with their hands on each other's arms, in a sort of struggle. Then Jon wrenched himself free, and, like one demented, rushed back into the coppice.

She stood trembling, not daring to call. Bewildered, she stood, waiting for him to come back to her, and he did not come.

Suddenly she moaned, and sank on her knees; and again she moaned. He must hear, and come back! He could not have left her at such a moment—he could not!

'Jon!' No sound. She rose from her knees and stood peering into the brightened dusk. The owl hooted; and, startled, she saw the moon caught among the tree-tops, like a presence watching her. A shivering sob choked in her throat, became a whimper, like a hurt child's. She stood, listening fearfully. No rustling; no footstep; no hoot of owl—not a sound, save a distant whir of traffic on the London road! Had he gone to the car, or was he hiding from her in that coppice, all creepy now with shadows?

'Jon! Jon!' No answer! She ran towards the gate. There was the car—empty! She got into it and sat leaning forward over the driving-wheel with a numb feeling in her limbs. What did it mean? Was she beaten in the very hour of victory? He could not—no, he could not mean to leave her thus? Mechanically she turned on the car's lights. A couple on foot, a man on a bicycle, passed. And still Fleur sat there, numbed. This—fulfilment! The fulfilment she had dreamed of? A few moments of hasty and delirious passion—and this! And, to her chagrin, her consternation, were added humiliation that, after such a moment, he could thus have fled from her; and the fear that in winning him she had lost him!

At last she started the engine, and drove miserably on, watching the road, hoping against hope to come on him. Very slowly she drove, and only when she reached the Dorking road did she quite abandon hope. How she guided the car for the rest of the drive, she hardly knew. Life seemed suddenly to have gone out.

9

AFTERMATH

Jon, when he rushed back into the coppice, turned to the left, and, emerging past the pond, ran up through the field, towards the house, as if it were still his own. It stood above its terrace and lawns unlighted, ghostly in the spreading moonlight. Behind a clump of rhododendrons, where as a little boy he had played hide-and-seek, or pursued the staghorn beetle with his bow and arrow, he sank down as if his legs had turned to water, pressing his fists against his cheeks, both burning hot. He had known and he had not known, had dreamed and never dreamed of this! Overwhelming, sudden, relentless! 'It was written!' she had said. For her, every excuse, perhaps; but what excuse for him? Among those moonlit rhododendrons he could not find it. Yet the deed was done! Whose was he now? He stood up and looked at the house where he had been born, grown up, and played, as if asking for an answer. Whitened and lightless, it looked the ghost of a house, keeping secrets. 'And I don't let you tell! . . . When shall I see you again?' That meant she claimed a secret lover. Impossible! The one thing utterly impossible. He would belong to one or to the other—not to both. Torn in every fibre of his being, he clung to the fixity of that. Behind the rhododendrons stretching along the far end of the lawn he walked, crouching, till he came to the wall of the grounds, the wall he had often scrambled over as a boy; and, pulling himself up, dropped into the top roadway. No one saw him, and he hurried on. He had a dumb and muddled craving to get back to Wansdon, though what he would do when he got there he could not tell. He turned towards Kingston.

All through that two hours' drive in a hired car Jon thought and thought. Whatever he did now, he must be disloyal to one or to the other. And with those passionate moments still rioting within him, he could get no grip on his position; and yet—he must!

He reached Wansdon at eleven, and, dismissing the car in the road, walked up to the house. Everyone had gone to bed, evidently assuming that he was staying the night at June's for a further sitting. There was a light in his and Anne's bedroom; and, at sight of it, the full shame of what he had done smote him. He could not bring himself to attract her attention, and he stole round the house, seeking for some way of breaking in. At last he spied a spare-room window open at the top, and fetching a garden ladder, climbed it and got in. The burglarious act restored some self-possession. He went down into the hall, and out of the house, replaced the ladder, came in again and stole upstairs. But outside their door he halted. No light, now, came from under. She must be in bed. And, suddenly, he could not face going in. He would feel like Judas, kissing her. Taking off his boots and carrying them, he stole downstairs again to the dining-room. Having had nothing but a cup of tea since lunch, he got himself some biscuits and a drink. They altered his mood—no man could have resisted Fleur's kisses in that moonlit coppice—no man! Must he, then, hurt one or the other so terribly? Why not follow Fleur's wish? Why not secrecy? By continuing her lover in secret, he would not hurt Fleur; by not telling Anne, he would not hurt Anne! Like a leopard in a cage, he paced the room. And all that was honest in him refused, and all that was sage. As if one could remain the husband of two women, when one of them knew! As if Fleur would stand that long! And lies, subterfuge! And—Michael Mont!—a decent chap! He had done him enough harm as it was! No! A clean cut one way or the other! He stopped by the hearth, and leaned his arms on the stone mantelpiece. How still! Only that old clock which had belonged to his grandfather, ticking away time—time that cured everything, that made so little of commotions, ticking men and things to their appointed ends. Just in front of him on the mantelpiece was a photograph of his grandfather, old Jolyon, taken in his 'eighties—the last record of that old face, its broad brow, and white moustache, its sunken cheeks, deep, steady eyes, and strong jaw. Jon looked at it long! 'Take a course and stick to it!' the face, gazing back at him so deeply, seemed to say. He went to the bureau and sat down to write.

I am sorry I rushed away to-night, but it was better, really. I had to think. I have thought. I'm only certain of one thing yet. To go on *in secret* is impossible. I shan't say a word about to-night, of course, until you let me. But, Fleur, unless I can tell everything, it must end. You wouldn't wish it otherwise, would you? Please answer to the Post Office, Nettlefold.

JON.

He sealed this up, addressed it to her at Dorking, and, pulling on his boots, again stole out and posted it. When he got back he felt so tired, that, wrapped in an old coat, he fell asleep in an arm-chair. The moonlight played tricks through the half-drawn curtains, the old clock ticked, but Jon slept, dreamless.

He woke at daybreak, stole up to the bathroom, bathed and shaved noiselessly, and went out through a window, so as not to leave the front door unfastened. He walked up through the gap past the old chalk-pit, on to the Downs, by the path he had taken with Fleur seven years ago. Till he had heard from her he did not know what to do; and he dreaded Anne's eyes, while his mind was still distraught. He went towards Chanctonbury Ring. There was a heavy dew, and the short turf was all spun over with it. All was infinitely beautiful, remote and stilly in the level sunlight. The beauty tore at his heart. He had come to love the Downs—they had a special loveliness, like no other part of the world that he had seen. Did this mean that he must now leave them, leave

England again—leave everything, and cleave to Fleur? If she claimed him, if she decided on declaring their act of union, he supposed it did. And Jon walked in confusion of heart, such as he had not thought possible to man. From the Ring he branched away, taking care to avoid the horses at their early exercise. And this first subterfuge brought him face to face with immediate decision. What should he do till he had heard from Fleur? Her answer could not reach Nettlefold till the evening or even next morning. He decided, painfully, to go back to breakfast, and tell them he had missed his train, and entered in the night burglariously so as not to disturb them.

That day, with its anxiety and its watchfulness of self, was one of the most wretched he had ever spent; and he could not free himself from the feeling that Anne was reading his thoughts. It was as if each passed the day looking at the other unobserved—almost unbearable! In the afternoon he asked for a horse to ride over to Green Hill Farm, and said he would be back late. He rode on into Nettlefold and went to the Post Office. There was a telegram: 'Must see you. Will be at Green Hill Farm to-morrow at noon. Don't fail me.—F.'

Jon destroyed it, and rode homewards. Wretchedness and strain for another eighteen hours! Was there anything in the world worse than indecision? He rode slowly so as to have the less time at home, dreading the night. He stopped at a wayside inn to eat, and again went by way of Green Hill Farm to save at least the letter of his tale. It was nearly ten and full moonlight before he got back.

'It's a wonderful night,' he said, when he came into the drawing-room. 'The moonlight's simply marvellous.' It was Holly who answered; Anne, sitting by the fire, did not even look up. 'She knows,' thought Jon, 'She knows something.' Very soon after, she said she was sleepy, and went up. Jon stayed, talking to Holly. Val had gone on from town to Newmarket, and would not be back till Friday. They sat one on each side of the wood fire. And, looking at his sister's face, charming and pensive, Jon was tempted. She was so wise and sympathetic. It would be a relief to tell her everything. But Fleur's command held him back—it was not his secret.

'Well, Jon, is it all right about the farm?'

'I've got some new figures; I'm going into them to-night.'

'I do wish it were settled, and we know you were going to be near for certain. I shall be awfully disappointed if you're not.'

'Yes; but I must make sure this time.'

'Anne's very set on it. She doesn't say much, but she really is. It's such a charming old place.'

'I don't want a better, but it must pay its way.'

'Is that your real reason, Jon?'

'Why not?'

'I thought perhaps you were secretly afraid of settling again. But you're the head of the family, Jon—you ought to settle.'

'Head of the family!'

'Yes, the only son of the only son of the eldest son right back to the primeval Jolyon.'

'Nice head!' said Jon bitterly.

'Yes—a nice head.' And, suddenly rising, Holly bent over and kissed the top of it.

'Bless you! Don't sit up too late. Anne's rather in the dumps.'

Jon turned out the lamp and stayed huddled in his chair before the fire. Head of the family! He had done them proud! And if—! Ha! That would, indeed, be illustrious! What would the old fellow whose photograph he had been looking at last night, think, if he knew? Ah, what a coil! For in his inmost heart he knew that Anne was more his mate, more her with whom he could live and work and have his being, than ever Fleur could be. Madness, momentary madness, coming on him from the past–the past, and the potency of her will to have and hold him! He got up, and drew aside the curtains. There, between two elm trees, the moon, mysterious and powerful, shone, and all was moving with its light up to the crest of the Downs. What beauty, what stillness! He threw the window up and stepped out; like some dark fluid spilled on the whitened grass, the ragged shadow of one elm tree reached almost to his feet. From their window above a light shone. He must go up and face it. He had not been alone with her since–! If only he knew for certain what he was going to do! And he realised now that in obeying that impulse to rush away from Fleur he had been wrong; he ought to have stayed and threshed it out there and then. And yet, who could have behaved reasonably, sanely, feeling as he had felt? He stepped back to the window, and stopped with his heart in his mouth. There between firelight and moonlight stood Anne! Slender, in a light wrapper drawn close, she was gazing towards him. Jon closed the window and drew the curtain.

'Sorry, darling, you'll catch cold–the moonlight got me.' She moved to the far side of the hearth, and stood looking at him.

'Jon, I'm going to have a child.'

'You–!'

'Yes. I didn't tell you last month because I wanted to be sure.'

'Anne!'

She was holding up her hand.

'Wait a minute!'

Jon gripped the back of a chair, he knew what was coming.

'Something's happened between you and Fleur.'

Jon held his breath, staring at her eyes; dark, unflinching, startled, they stared back at him.

'Everything's happened, hasn't it?'

Jon bent his head.

'Yesterday? Don't explain, don't excuse yourself or her. Only–what does it mean?'

Without raising his head, Jon answered:

'That depends on you.'

'On me?'

'After what you've just told me. Oh! Anne, why didn't you tell me sooner?'

'Yes; I kept it too long!'

He understood what she meant–she had kept it as a weapon of defence. And, seeming to himself unforgiveable, he said:

'Forgive me, Anne–forgive me!'

'Oh! Jon, I don't just know.'

'I swear that I will never see her again.'

He raised his eyes now, and saw that she had sunk on her knees by the fire, holding a hand out to it, as if cold. He dropped on his knees beside her.

'I think,' he said, 'love is the cruellest thing in the world.'

'Yes.'

She had covered her eyes with her hand; and it seemed hours that he knelt there, waiting for a movement, a sign, a word. At last she dropped her hand.

'All right. It's over. But don't kiss me–yet.'

10

BITTER APPLE

Life revived in Fleur while she went about her business in the morning. Standing in sunshine before the hollyhocks and sunflowers of the 'Rest House' garden, she reviewed past and future with feverish vigour. Of course Jon was upset! She had taken him by storm! He was old-fashioned, conscientious; he couldn't take things lightly. But since already he had betrayed his conscience, he would realise that what had happened outweighed what more could happen. It was the first step that counted! They had always belonged to each other. She felt no remorse; then why should he—when his confusion was over? It was for the best, perhaps, that he had run away from her till he could see the inexorability of his position. Her design was quite unshaken by the emotions she had been through. Jon was hers now, he could not betray their secret unless she gave him leave. He must and would conform to the one course possible—secrecy. Infidelity had been achieved—one act or many, what did it matter? Ah! But she would make up to him the loss of self-respect with her love, and with her wisdom. She would make him a success. In spite of that American chit, he should succeed with his farming, become important to his county, to his country, perhaps. She would be circumspection itself—for his sake, for her own, for Michael's, Kit's, her father's.

With a great bunch of autumn flowers to which was clinging one bee, she went back into the house to put them in water. On the table in the hall were a number of little bags of bitter-apple prepared by her caretaker's wife against the moth, which were all over a house that had been derelict for a year. She busied herself with stowing them in drawers. The second post brought her Jon's letter.

She read it, and spots of burning colour became fixed in her cheeks. He had written this before he slept—it was all part of his confusion! But she must see him at once—at once! She got out the car, and, driving to a village where she was not known, sent a telegram to the post office at Nettlefold. Dreadful to have to wait over the night! But she knew it might be evening or even next morning before he could call for it.

Never did time go so slowly. For now she was shaken again. Was she over-estimating her power, relying too much on her sudden victory in a moment of passion, under-estimating Jon's strength after resolve taken? She remembered how in those old days she had failed to move him from renunciation. And, unable to keep still, she went up lonely on to Box Hill, and wandered among its yew trees and spindleberry bushes, till she was tired out and the sun was nearly down. With the sinking light the loneliness up there repelled her, for she was not a real nature-lover, and for an anxious heart Nature has little comfort. She was glad to be back, listening to the chatter of the supper-eating girls. It had no interest for her, but at least it was not melancholy like the space and shadows of the open. She suddenly remembered that she had missed her 'sitting' and had sent no word. The Rafaelite would gnash his teeth; perhaps he had set her 'Folly' dress up on a dummy, to paint the sound from its silver bells. Bells! Michael! Poor Michael! But was he to be pitied, who had owned her for years while at heart she belonged to another? She went up to bed early. If only she could sleep till it was time to start! This force that played with hearts, tore them open, left them quivering—made them wait and ache, and ache and wait! Had the Victorian Miss, whom they had taken to praising again, ever to go through what she had gone through since first she saw her fate in front of that grotesque Juno—or was it Venus?—in the gallery off Cork Street? The disciplined Victorian Miss? Admit—oh! freely—that she, Fleur Mont, was undisciplined; still, she hadn't worn her heart upon her sleeve. She hadn't kicked and screamed. Surely she deserved a spell of happiness! Not more than a spell—she wouldn't ask for more than that! Things wore out, hearts wore out! But, to have the heart she wanted against her own, as last night, and then to lose it straightway? It could not be! And so at last she slept, and the moon that had watched over her victory came by, to look in through the curtain chinks, and make her dream.

She woke and lay thinking with the preternatural intensity of early morning thought. People would blame her if they knew; and was there any real possibility that they would not come to know? Suppose Jon remained immovably opposed to secrecy. What then? Was she prepared to give up all and follow him? It would mean more than in the ordinary case. It would mean isolation. For always, in the background, was the old barrier of the family feud; her father and his mother, and the abhorrence of union between her and Jon. And all the worldly sense in Fleur, brought to the edge of hard reality, shivered and recoiled. Money! It was not that they would lack money. But position, approval, appreciation, where in the world could they ever regain all that? And Kit? He would be lost to her. The Monts would claim him. She sat up in bed, seeing with utter clearness in the dark a truth she had never before seen naked—that the condition of conquest is sacrifice. Then she revolted. No! Jon would be reasonable, Jon would come round! In secret they would, they must, be happy, or if not happy, at least not starved. She would have to share him, he to share her; but they would each know that the other only pretended to belong elsewhere. But would it be pretence with him? Was he at heart all hers? Was he not, at least, as much his wife's? Horribly clear she could see that girl's face, its dark, eager eyes, with the something strange and so attractive in their setting. No! She would not think of her! It only weakened her power to win Jon over. Dawn opened a sleepy eye. A bird cheeped, and daylight crept in. She lay back, resigned again to the dull ache of waiting. She rose unrested. A fine morning, dry as ever—save for the dew on the grass! At ten she would start! It would be easier to wait in motion even if she had to drive dead slow. She gave her morning orders, got out the car, and left. She drove by the clock so as to arrive at noon. The leaves were turning already, it would be an early fall. Had she put on the right frock? Would he like this soft russet, the colour of gone-off apples? The red was prettier; but red caught the eye. And the eye must not be caught to-day. She drove the last mile at a foot's pace, and drew up in the wooded lane just where the garden of Green Hill Farm ended in orchard, and the fields began. Very earnestly she scrutinised her face in the small mirror of her vanity-bag. Where had she read that one always looked one's worst in a mirror? If so, it was a mercy. She remembered that Jon had once said he hated the look of lip salve; and, not touching her lips, she put away the mirror and got out. She walked slowly towards the entrance gate. From there a lane divided the house from the straw-yards and farm buildings sloping up behind it. In the fine autumn sunlight they ranged imposing, dry and deserted—no stock, not so much as a hen. Even Fleur's unlearned mind realised the stiff job before anyone who took this farm. Had she not often heard Michael say that farming was more of a man's job than any other in the England of to-day! She would let him take it, then that wretched conscience of his would be at rest on one score at least. She passed the gate and stood before the old house, gabled and red with Virginia creeper. Twelve had struck down in the village as she passed through. Surely he had not failed her! Five minutes she waited that seemed like five hours. Then, with her heart beating fast, she went up and rang the bell. It sounded far away in the empty house. Footsteps—a woman's!

'Yes, ma'am?'

'I was to meet Mr Forsyte here at noon about the farm.'

'Oh, yes, ma'am; Mr Forsyte came early. He was very sorry he had to go away. He left this note for you.'

'He's not coming back?'

'No, ma'am, he was very sorry, but he couldn't come back to-day.'

'Thank you.'

Fleur went back to the gate. She stood there, turning the note over and over. Suddenly she broke the seal and read:

Last night Anne told me of her own accord that she knew what had happened. She told me, too, that she is to have a child. I have promised her not to see you again. Forgive me and forget me, as I must forget you.

JON.

Slowly, as if not knowing, she tore the sheet of paper and the envelope into tiny fragments and buried them in the hedge. Then she walked slowly, as if not seeing, to her car, and got in. She sat there stonily, alongside the orchard with the sunlight on her neck and scent from wind-fallen rotting apples in her nostrils. For four months, since in the canteen she saw Jon's tired smile, he had been one long thought in her mind. And this was the end! Oh! Let her get away—away from here!

She started the car, and, once out of the lane, drove at a great pace. If she broke her neck, all the better! But Providence, which attends the drunk and desperate, was about her—spying out her ways; and she did not break her neck. For more than two hours she drove, hardly knowing where. At three in the afternoon she had her first sane impulse—a craving to smoke, a longing for tea. She got some at an inn, and turned her car towards Dorking. Driving more slowly now, she arrived between four and five. She had been at the wheel for nearly six hours. And the first thing she saw outside the 'Rest House' was her father's car. He! What had *he* come for? Why did people pester her? On the point of starting the engine again, she saw him come out of the front door, and stand looking up and down the road. Something groping in that look of his touched her, and, leaving the car, she walked towards him.

I I

'GREAT FORSYTE'

On the morning after the Slum Conversion Committee meeting Soames had started early. It was his intention to spend the night somewhere 'down there', look at his roots the following morning, and motor part of the way home. On the day after, he would return to town and see if he couldn't carry Fleur back with him to Mapledurham for a long week-end. He reached a seaside hostel ten miles from his origin about six o'clock, ate a damp dinner, smoked his own cigar, and went to a bed in which, for insurance sake, he placed a camel's hair shawl.

He had thought things out, and was provided with an ordinance map on an inordinate scale. He meant to begin his investigation by seeing the church. For he had little to go by except a memory that his father James had once been down, and had returned speaking of a church by the sea, and supposing that there might be 'parish entries and that, but it was a long time back and he didn't know.'

After an early breakfast he directed Riggs towards the church. As James had said, it was close to the sea, and it was open. Soames went in. A little old grey church with funny pews, and a damp smell. There wouldn't be any tablets to his name, he supposed. There were not, and he went out again, to wander among the gravestones, overcome by a sense of unreality – everything underground, and each gravestone, older than the last century, undecipherable. He was about to turn away when he stumbled. Looking down in disapproval at a flat stone, he saw on the worn and lichened surface a capital F. He stood for a minute, scrutinising, then went down on his knees with a sort of thrill. Two names – the first had an undoubted capital J, a y, and an n; the second name began with that capital F, and had what looked like an s in the middle, and the remains of a tall letter last but one! The date? By George – the date was legible! 1777. Scraping gingerly at the first name, he disinterred an o. Four letters out of the six in Jolyon; three letters out of Forsyte. There could hardly be a doubt that he had stumbled over his great-great-grandfather! Supposing the old chap had lived to the ordinary age of a Forsyte, his birth would be near the beginning of the eighteenth century! His eyes gimletted the stone with a hard grey glance as though to pierce to the bones beneath – clean as a whistle long since, no doubt! Then he rose from his knees and dusted them. He had a date now. And, singularly fortified, he emerged from the graveyard, and cast a suspicious look at Riggs. Had he been seen on his knees? But the fellow was seated, as usual, with his back to everything, smoking his eternal cigarette. Soames got into the car.

'I want the vicarage now, or whatever it is.'

'Yes, sir.'

He was always saying 'Yes, sir,' without having an idea of where places were.

'You'd better ask,' he said, as the car moved up the rutted lane. Sooner than ask, the fellow would go back to London! Not that there was anyone to ask. Soames was impressed, indeed, by the extreme emptiness of this parish where his roots lay. It seemed terribly hilly, and full of space, with large fields, some woods in the coombe to the left, and a soil that you couldn't swear by–not red and not white and not brown exactly; the sea was blue, however, and the cliffs, so far as he could judge, streaky. The lane bent to the right, past a black-smith's forge.

'Hi!' said Soames, 'pull up!' He himself got out to ask. That fellow never made head or tail of what he was told.

The blacksmith was hammering at a wheel, and Soames waited till his presence was observed.

'Where's the vicarage?'

'Up the lane, third 'ouse on the right.'

'Thank you,' said Soames, and, looking at the man suspiciously, added:

'Is the name Forsyte known hereabouts nowadays?'

'What's that?'

'Have you ever heard the name Forsyte?'

'Farsyt? Noa.'

Soames heard him with a disappointed relief, and resumed his seat. What if he'd said: 'Yes, it's mine!'

A blacksmith's was a respectable occupation, but he felt that he could do without it in the family. The car moved on.

The vicarage was smothered in creeper. Probably the vicar would be, too! He rang a rusty bell and waited. The door was opened by a red-cheeked girl. It was all very rustic.

'I want the vicar,' said Soames. 'Is he in?'

'Yes, sir. What name?'

But at this moment a thin man in a thin suit and a thin beard came out from a doorway, saying:

'Am I wanted, Mary?'

'Yes,' said Soames; 'here's my card.'

There ought–he felt–to be a way of enquiring about one's origin that would be distinguished; but, not finding it, he added simply:

'My family came from hereabouts some generations back; I just wanted to have a look at the place, and ask you a question or two.'

'Forsyte?' said the vicar, glancing at the card: 'I don't know the name, but I daresay we shall find something.'

His clothes were extremely well worn, and Soames had the impression that his eyes would have been glad if they could. 'Smells a fee,' he thought; 'poor devil!'

'Will you come in?' said the vicar. 'I've got some records and an old tithe map. We might have a look at them. The registers go back to 1580. I could make a search for you.'

'I don't know if that's worth while,' said Soames, following him into a room that impressed him as dismal beyond words.

'Do sit down,' said the vicar. 'I'll get that map. Forsyte? I seem to remember the name now.'

The fellow was agreeable, and looked as if he could do with an honest penny!

'I've been up to the church,' said Soames; 'it seems very close to the sea.'

'Yes; they used to use the pulpit, I'm afraid, to hide their smuggled brandy.'

'I got a date in the graveyard–1777; the stones are very much let down.'

'Yes,' said the vicar, who was groping in a cupboard: 'one's difficulty is the sea air. Here's the map I spoke of;' and, unrolling a large and dingy map, he laid it on the table, weighting down the corners with a tin of tobacco, an inkstand, a book of sermons, and a dog whip. The latter was not heavy enough, and the map curled slowly away from Soames.

'Sometimes,' said the vicar, restoring the corner, and looking round for something to secure it, 'we get very useful information from these old maps.'

'I'll keep it down,' said Soames, bending over the map. 'I suppose you get a lot of Americans, fishing for ancestors?'

'Not a lot,' said the vicar, with a sideway glance that Soames did not quite like. 'I can remember two. Ah! here,' and his finger came down on the map, 'I *thought* I remembered the name—it's unusual. Look! This field close to the sea is marked "Great Forsyte"!'

Again Soames felt a thrill.

'What size is that field?'

'Twenty-four acres. There was the ruin of an old house, I remember, just there; they took the stones away in the war to make our shooting range. "Great Forsyte"—isn't that interesting?'

'More interesting to me,' said Soames, 'if they'd left the stones.'

'The spot is still marked with an old cross—the cattle use it for a rubbing stone. It's close to the hedge on the right-hand side of the coombe.'

'Could I get to it with the car?'

'Oh, yes; by going round the head of the coombe. Would you like me to come?'

'No, thanks,' said Soames. The idea of being overlooked while inspecting his roots was unpleasant to him. 'But if you'd kindly make a search in the register while I'm gone, I could call back after lunch and see the result. My great-grandfather, Jolyon Forsyte, died at Studmouth. The stone I found was Jolyon Forsyte, buried in 1777—he'd be my great-great-grandfather, no doubt. I daresay you could pick up his birth, and perhaps *his* father's—I fancy they were a long-lived lot. The name Jolyon seems to have been a weakness with them.'

'I could make a search at once. It would take some hours. What would you think reasonable?'

'Five guineas?' hazarded Soames.

'Oh! That would be generous. I'll make a very thorough search. Now, let me come and tell you how to get to it.' With a slight pang Soames followed him—a gentleman in trousers shiny behind.

'You go up this road to the fork, take the left-hand branch past the Post Office, and right on round the head of the coombe, always bearing to the left, till you pass a farm called "Uphays". Then on till the lane begins to drop; there's a gate on the right, and if you go through it you'll find yourself at the top of that field with the sea before you. I'm so pleased to have found something. Won't you have a little lunch with us when you come back?'

'Thank you,' said Soames, 'very good of you, but I've got my lunch with me,' and was instantly ashamed of his thought. 'Does he think I'm going to make off without paying?' Raising his hat slightly, he got into the car, with his umbrella in his hand, so as to poke Riggs in the back when the fellow took his wrong turnings.

He sat, contented, using the umbrella gingerly now and then. So! To get baptised and buried, they used to cross the coombe. Twenty-four acres was quite a field. 'Great Forsyte'; there must have been 'Little Forsytes', too.

The farm the vicar had spoken of appeared to be a rambling place of old buildings, pigs and poultry.

'Keep on,' he said to Riggs, 'until the lane drops, and go slow, I want a gate on the right.'

The fellow was rushing along as usual, and the lane already dropping downhill.

'Hold hard! There it is!' The car came to a standstill at a rather awkward bend.

'You've overshot it!' said Soames, and got out. 'Wait here! I may be some time.'

Taking off his overcoat and carrying it on his arm, he went back to the gate, and passed through into a field of grass. He walked downwards to the hedge on the left, followed it round, and presently came in view of the sea, bright, peaceful, hazy, with a trail of smoke in the distance. The air beat in from the sea, fresh air, strong and salt. Ancestral! Soames took some deep breaths, savouring it, as one might an old wine. Its freshness went a little to his head, so impregnated with ozone or iodine, or whatever it was nowadays. And then, below him, perhaps a hundred yards away, above a hollow near the hedge he saw the stone, and again felt that thrill. He looked back. Yes! He was out of sight of the lane, and had his feelings to himself! And, going up to the stone, he gazed down at the hollow between him and the hedge. Below it the field sloped to the beach, and what looked like the ghost of a lane ran up towards the hollow from the coombe. In that hollow then, the house had been; and there they'd lived, the old Forsytes, for generations, pickled in this air, without another house in sight—nothing but this expanse of grass in view and the sea beyond, and the gulls on that rock, and the waves beating over it. There they'd lived, tilling the land, and growing rheumatic, and crossing the coombe to church, and getting their brandy free, perhaps. He went up and examined the stone—upright, with another bit across the top—lintel of a barn, perhaps—nothing on it. Descending into the hollow, he poked about with his umbrella. During the war—the parson had said—they had removed the ruins. Only twelve years ago, but not a sign! Grassed over utterly, not even the shape visible. He explored up to the hedge. They'd made a clean sweep all right—nothing but grass now and a scrubble of fern and young gorse, such as would seize on a hollow for their growing. And, sitting on his overcoat with his back against the stone, Soames pondered. Had his forbears themselves built the house there in this lonely place—been the first to seat themselves on this bit of wind-swept soil? And something moved in him, as if the salty independence of that lonely spot were still in his bones. Old Jolyon and his own father and the rest of his uncles—no wonder they'd been independent, with this air and loneliness in their blood; and crabbed with the pickling of it—unable to give up, to let go, to die. For a moment he seemed to understand even himself. Southern spot, south aspect, not any of your northern roughness, but free, and salt, and solitary from sunrise to sunset, year in, year out, like that lonely rock with the gulls on it, for ever and for ever. And drawing the air deep into his lungs, he thought: 'I'm not surprised old Timothy lived to be a hundred!' A long time he sat there, nostalgically bemused, strangely unwilling to move. Never had he breathed anything quite like that air; or so, at least, it seemed to him. It had been the old England, when they lived down here—the England of pack-horses and very little smoke, of peat and wood fires, and wives who never left you, because they couldn't, probably. A static England, that dug and wove, where your parish was your world, and you were a churchwarden if you didn't take care. His own grandfather–begotten and born one hundred and fifty-six years ago, in the best bed, not two dozen paces from where he was sitting. What a change since then! For the better? Who could say? But here was this grass, and rock and sea, and the air and the gulls, and the old church over there beyond the coombe, precisely as they had been, only more so. If this field were in the market, he wouldn't mind buying it as a curiosity. Only, if he did, nobody would come and sit here! They'd want to play golf over it or something. And, uneasy at having verged on the sentimental, Soames put his hand down and felt the grass. But it wasn't damp, and he couldn't conscientiously feel that he was catching rheumatism; and still he sat there, with the sunlight warming his cheeks, and his eyes fixed on the sea. The ships went up and down, far out–steamers; no smugglers nowadays, and you paid the deuce of a price for brandy! In the old time here, without newspapers, with nothing from the outer world, you'd grow up without any sense of the State or that sort of thing. There'd be the church and your Bible, he supposed, and the market some miles away, and you'd work and eat and sleep and breathe the air and drink your cider and embrace your wife and watch your children, from June to June; and a good thing, too! What more did you do now that brought you any satisfaction? 'Change, it's all on the surface,' thought Soames; 'the roots are the same. You can't get beyond them–try as you will!' Progress, civilisation, what were they for? Unless–unless, indeed, to foster hobbies–collecting pictures, or what not? He didn't see how the old chaps down here could have had hobbies–except for bees, perhaps. Hobbies? Just for that–just to give people a chance to have hobbies? He'd had a lot of amusement out of his own; and but for progress would never have had it. No! He'd have been down here still, perhaps, shearing his sheep or following a plough, and his daughter would be a girl with sturdy ankles and one new hat. Perhaps it was just as well that you couldn't stop the clock! Ah! and it was time he was getting back to the lane before that chap came to look for him. And, getting up, Soames descended once more into the hollow. This time, close to the hedge, an object caught his eye, a very old boot–a boot so old that you could hardly swear by it. His lips became contorted in a faint smile. He seemed to hear his dead cousin George with his wry Forsytean humour cackling: 'The ancestral boot! What ho, my wild ones! Let the portcullis fall!' Yes! They would laugh at him in the family if they knew he'd been looking at their roots. He shouldn't say anything about it. And suddenly he went up to the boot, and, hooking the point of his umbrella under what was left of the toe-cap, flung it pettishly over the hedge. It defiled the loneliness–the feeling he had known, drinking-in that air. And very slowly he went back to the lane, so as not to get hot, and have to sit all damp in the car. But at the gate he stood, transfixed. What was all this? Two large, hairy horses were attached tandem to the back of his car with ropes, and beside them were three men, one of whom was Riggs, and two dogs, one of whom was lame. Soames perceived at once that it was all 'that fellow'! In trying to back up the hill, which he ought never to have gone down, he had jammed the car so that it couldn't move. He was always doing something! At this moment, however, 'the fellow' mounted the car and moved the wheel; while one of the men cracked a whip. 'Haup!' The hairy horses moved. Something in that slow, strong movement affected Soames. Progress! They had been obliged to fetch horses to drag Progress up the hill!

'That's a good horse!' he said, pointing to the biggest.

'Ah! We call 'im Lion–'e can pull. Haup!'

The car passed on to the level ground, and the horses were detached. Soames went up to the man who had said 'Haup!'

'Are you from the farm back there?'

'Yes.'

'Do you own this field?'

'I farm it.'

'What do you call it?'

'Call it? The big field.'

'It's marked "Great Forsyte" on the tithe map. D'you know that name?'

'Farsyt? There's none of the name now. My grandmother was called Farsyt.'

'Was she?' said Soames, and again felt the thrill.

'Ah!' said the farmer.

Soames controlled himself.

'And what's *your* name, if I may ask?'

'Beer.'

Soames looked at him rather long, and took out his note-case.

'You must allow me,' he said, 'for your horses and your trouble.' And he offered a pound note. The farmer shook his head.

'That's naught,' he said; 'you're welcome. We're always haulin' cars off this 'ill.'

'I really can't take something for nothing,' said Soames. 'You'll oblige me!'

'Well,' said the farmer, 'I thank yeou,' and he took the note. 'Haup!'

The released horses moved forward and the men and dogs followed after them. Soames got into the car, and, opening his packet of sandwiches, began to eat.

'Drive back to the vicarage—slowly.' And, while he ate, he wondered why he had felt a thrill on discovering that some of his own blood ran in a hard-bitten looking chap called Beer—if, indeed, that *was* his name.

It was two o'clock when he reached the vicarage, and the vicar came to him with his mouth full.

'I find a great many entries, Mr Forsyte; the name goes back to the beginning of the register. I shall have to take my time to give you the complete list. That Jolyon seems to have been born in 1710, son of Jolyon and Mary; he didn't pay his tithes in 1757. There was another Jolyon born in 1680, evidently the father—he was churchwarden from 1715 on; described as "Yeoman of Hays"—he married a Bere.'

Soames gazed at him, and took out his note-case. 'How do you spell it?' he said.

'B-e-r-e.'

'Oh! The farmer up there said that was his name, too. I thought he was gammoning me. It seems his grandmother was called Forsyte, and she was the last of them here. Perhaps you could send me the Bere entries, too, for an inclusive seven guineas?'

'Oh! Six will be ample.'

'No. We'll make it seven. You've got my card. I saw the stone. A healthy spot, right away from everything.' He laid the seven guineas on the table, and again had an impression, as of glad eyes. 'I must be getting back to London now. Good-bye!'

'Good-bye, Mr Forsyte. Anything I can find out I shall make a point of sending you.'

Soames shook his hand and went out to the car with the feeling that his roots would be conscientiously pulled up. After all, it was something to be dealing with a parson.

'Go on,' he said to Riggs; 'we'll get the best part of the way home.'

And, lying back in the car, thoroughly tired, he mused. Great Forsyte! Well! He was glad he had come down.

12

DRIVING ON

Soames spent the night at Winchester, a place he had often heard of but never seen. The Monts had been at school there, and that was why he didn't want Kit to go. He himself would prefer his own Marlborough, or Harrow, perhaps—some school that played at Lords—but not Eton, where young Jolyon had been. But then one wouldn't be alive to see Kit play; so perhaps it didn't matter.

The town seemed an old place. There was something in a cathedral, too; and after breakfast he went to it. The chancel was in activity—some choir practice or other. He entered noiselessly, for his boots were rubbered against damp, and sat down at the point of balance. With chin uplifted, he contemplated the arches and the glass. The place was rather dark, but very rich—like a Christmas pudding! These old buildings certainly gave one a feeling. He had always had it in St Paul's. One must admit at least a continuity of purpose somewhere. Up to a point—after that he wasn't sure. You had a great thing, like this, almost perfect; and then an earthquake or an air-raid, and down it went! Nothing permanent about anything, so far as he could see, not even about the best examples of ingenuity and beauty. The same with landscape! You had a perfect garden of a country, and then an ice-age came along. There was continuity, but it was always changing. That was why it seemed to him extremely unlikely that he would live after he was dead. He had read somewhere—though not in *The Times*—that life was just animated shape, and that when shape was broken it was no longer animated. Death broke your shape and there you were, he supposed. The fact was, people couldn't bear their own ends; they tried to dodge them with soft sawder. They were weak-minded. And Soames lowered his chin. They had lighted some candles up there in the chancel, insignificant in the daylight. Presently they would blow them out. There you were again, everything was blown out sooner or later. And it was no good pretending it wasn't. He had read the other day, again not in *The Times*, that the world was coming to an end in 1928, when the earth got between the moon and the sun—it had been predicted in the Pyramids—some such scientific humbug! Well, if it did, he, for one, wouldn't much mind. The thing had never been a great success, and if it were wiped out at one stroke there would be nothing left behind anyway; what was objectionable about death was leaving things that you were fond of behind. The moment, too, that the world came to an end, it would begin again in some other shape, anyway—that, no doubt, was why they called it 'world without end, Amen.' Ah! They were singing now. Sometimes he wished he had an ear. In spite of the lack, he could tell that this was good singing. Boys' voices! Psalms, too, and he knew the words. Funny! Fifty years since his church-going days, yet he remembered them as if it were yesterday!

'He sendeth the springs into the rivers; which run among the hills.' 'All beasts of the fields drink thereof; and the wild asses quench their thirst.' 'Beside them shall the fowls of the air have their habitation; and sing among the branches.' They were flinging the verses at each other across the aisle, like a ball. It was lively, and good vigorous English, too. 'So is the great and wide sea also, wherein are things creeping innumerable, both small and great beasts.' 'There go the ships, and there is that Leviathan, whom Thou hast made to take his pastime therein.' Leviathan! That word used to please him. 'Man goeth forth to his work, and to his labour, until the evening.' He certainly went forth, but whether he did any work, any labour, was the question, nowadays. 'I will sing unto the Lord as long as I live; I will praise my God while I have my being.' Would he? He wondered. 'Praise thou the Lord, O my soul, praise the Lord.' The singing ceased, and Soames again lifted up his chin. He sat very still—not thinking now; lost, as it were, among the arches, and the twilight of the roof. He was experiencing a peculiar sensation, not unpleasant. To be in here was like being within a jewelled and somewhat scented box. The world might roar and stink and buzz outside, strident and vulgar, childish and sensational, cheap and nasty—all jazz and cockney accent, but here—not a trace of it heard or felt or seen. This great box—God-box the Americans would call it—had been made centuries before the world became industrialised; it didn't belong to the modern world at all. In here everyone spoke and sang the King's English; it smelt faintly of age and incense; and nothing was unbeautiful. He sat with a sense of escape.

A verger passed, glancing at him curiously, as if unaccustomed to a raised chin; halting just behind, he made a little noise with his keys. Soames sneezed; and, reaching for his hat, got up. He had no intention of being taken round by that chap, and shown everything he didn't want to see, for half-a-crown. And with a 'No, thank you; not to-day,' he passed the verger, and went out to the car.

'You ought to have gone in,' he said to Riggs; 'they used to crown the kings of England there. To London now.'

The opened car travelled fast under a bright sun, and not until he was in the new cut, leading to Chiswick, did Soames have the idea which caused him to say: 'Stop at that house, "The Poplars", where you took us the other day.'

It was not yet lunch time, and in all probability Fleur would still be 'sitting'; so why not pick her up and take her straight away with him for the week-end? She had clothes down at 'The Shelter'. It would save some hours of fresh air for her. The foreign woman, however, who opened the door, informed him that the lady had not been to 'sit' to-day or yesterday.

'Oh!' said Soames. 'How's that?'

'Nobody did know, sir. She 'ave not sent any message. Mr Blade is very decomposed.'

Soames chewed his thoughts a moment.

'Is your mistress in?'

'Yes, sir.'

'Then ask her if she'll see me, please. Mr Soames Forsyte.'

'Will you in the meal-room wait, sir.'

Soames waited uneasily in that very little room. Fleur had said she could not come with him because of her 'sittings'; and she had not 'sat'. Was she ill, then?

He was roused from disquiet contemplation of the poplar trees outside by the words:

'Oh! It's you. I'm not sorry you came.'

The cordiality of this greeting increased his uneasiness, and, stretching out his hand, he said:

'How are you, June? I called for Fleur. When did she come last?'

'Tuesday morning. I saw her late on Tuesday afternoon, too, in her car, outside–' Soames could see her eyes moving from side to side, and knew that she was about to say something unpleasant. It came. 'She picked up Jon.'

Feeling as if he had received a punch in his wind, Soames exclaimed:

'What! Your young brother? What was he doing here?'

'"Sitting"! of course.'

'"Sitting"! What business–!' and checking the words, 'had he to "sit",' he stared at his cousin, who, flushing a deep pink, said:

'I told her she was not to see him here. I told Jon the same.'

'Then she'd done it before?'

'Yes, twice. She's so spoiled, you see.'

'Ah!' The reality of the danger had disarmed him. Antagonism seemed to him, thus faced with a sort of ruin, too luxurious.

'Where is she?'

'On Tuesday morning she said she was going down to Dorking.'

'And she picked him up?' repeated Soames.

June nodded. 'Yes, after his "sitting". His picture's finished. If you think I want them to–any more than you–'

'No one in their sense could want them to–' said Soames, coldly. 'But why did you make him "sit", while she was coming here?'

June flushed a deeper pink.

'*You* don't know how hard it is for real artists. I *had* to think of Harold. If I hadn't got Jon before he began his farming–'

'Farming!' said Soames. 'For all we know they may–' but again he checked his words. 'I've been expecting something of this sort ever since I heard he was back. Well! I'd better get on to Dorking. D'you know where his mother is?'

'In Paris.'

Ah! But not this time would he have to beg that woman to let her son belong to his daughter! No! It would be to beg her to stop his belonging–if at all.

'Good-bye!' he said.

'Soames,' said June, suddenly, 'don't let Fleur–it's she who–'

'I'll hear nothing against her,' said Soames.

June pressed her clenched hands to her flat breast.

'I like you for that,' she said; 'and I'm sorry if–'

'That's all right,' muttered Soames.

'Good-bye!' said June. 'Shake hands!'

Soames put his hand in one which gave it a convulsive squeeze, then dropped it like a cold potato.

'Down to Dorking,' he said to Riggs, on regaining his car. The memory of Fleur's face that night at Nettlefold, so close to the young man's, so full of what he had never seen on her face before, haunted him the length of Hammersmith Bridge. Ah! what a wilful creature! Suppose–suppose she had flung her cap over the windmill! Suppose the worst? Good God! What should–what *could* he do, then? The calculating tenacity of her passion for this young man–the way she had kept it from him, from everyone, or tried to! Something deadly about it, and something that almost touched him, rousing the memory of his own pursuit of that boy's mother—memory of a passion that would not, could not let go; that had won its ends, and destroyed in winning. He had often thought she had no continuity, that, like all these 'fizz-gig' young moderns, she was just fluttering without basic purpose or direction. And it was the irony of this moment that he perceived how she—when she knew what she wanted—had as much tenacity of will as himself and his generation.

It didn't do, it seemed, to judge by appearances! Beneath the surface passions remained what they had been, and in the draughty corridors and spaces there was the old hot stillness when they woke and breathed. . . .

That fellow was taking the Kingston road! Soon they would be passing Robin Hill. How all this part had changed since the day he went down with Bosinney to choose the site. Forty years—not more—but what a change! '*Plus ça change.*' Annette would say—'*plus c'est la même chose!*' Love and hate—no end to that, anyway! The beat of life went on beneath the wheels and whirr of traffic and the jazzy music of the band. Fate on its drum, or just the human heart? God knew! God? Convenient word. What did one mean by it? He didn't know, and never would! In the cathedral that morning he had thought—and then—that verger! There were the poplars, and the stable clock-tower, just visible, of the house he had built and never inhabited. If he could have foreseen a stream of cars like this passing day after day, not a quarter of a mile off, he would not have built it, and all that tragedy might never—And yet—did it matter what you did?—some way, somehow life took you up and put you where it would. He leaned forward and touched his chauffeur's back.

'Which way are you going?'

'Through Esher, sir, and off to the left.'

'Well,' said Soames, 'it's all the same to me.'

It was past lunch-time, but he wasn't hungry. He wouldn't be hungry till he knew the worst. But that chap would be, he supposed.

'Better stop somewhere,' he said, 'and have a snack and a cigarette.'

'Yes, sir.'

He wasn't long in stopping. Soames sat on in the car, gazing idly at the sign—'Red Lion'. Red Lions, Angels and White Horses—nothing killed them off. One of these days they'd try and bring in Prohibition, he shouldn't wonder; but that cock wouldn't fight in England—too extravagant! Treating people like children wasn't the way to make them grow up; as if they weren't childish enough as it was. Look at this coal strike, that went on and on—perfectly childish, hurting everybody and doing good to none! Weak-minded! To reflect on the weak-mindedness of his fellow-citizens was restful to Soames, faced with a future that might prove disastrous. For, in view of her infatuation, what could taking that young man about in her car mean—except disaster? What a time Riggs was! He got out and walked up and down. Not that there was anything he could do—he supposed—when he did get there. No matter how much you loved a person, how anxious you were about her, you had no power—perhaps less power in proportion to your love. But he must speak his mind at last, if he had the chance. Couldn't let her go over the edge without putting out a hand! The sun struck on his face, and he lifted it a little blindly, as if grateful for the warmth. All humbug about the world coming to an end, of course, but he'd be glad enough for it to come before he was brought down in sorrow to the grave. He saw with hideous clearness how complete disaster must be. If Fleur ran off, there'd be nothing left to him that he really cared about, for the Monts would take Kit. He'd be stranded among his pictures and his cows, without heart for either, till he died. 'I won't have it,' he thought. 'If it hasn't happened, I won't have it.' Yes! But how prevent it? And with the futility of his own resolution staring him in the face, he went back to the car. There was the fellow, at last, smoking his cigarette.

'Let's start!' he said. 'Push along!'

He arrived at three o'clock to hear that Fleur had gone out with the car at ten. It was an immense relief to learn that at least she had been there overnight. And at once he began to make trunk calls. They renewed his anxiety. She was not at home; nor at June's. Where, then, if not with that young man? But at least she had taken no things with her—this he ascertained, and it gave him strength to drink some tea and wait. He had gone out into the road for the fourth time to peer up and down when at last he saw her coming towards him.

The expression on her face—hungry and hard and feverish—had the most peculiar effect on Soames; his heart ached, and leaped with relief at the same time. That was not the face of victorious passion! It was tragically unhappy, arid, wrenched. Every feature seemed to have sharpened since he saw her last. And, instinctively, he remained silent, poking his face forward for a kiss. She gave it—hard and parched.

'So you're back,' she said.

'Yes; and when you've had your tea, I want you to come straight on with me to "The Shelter"—Riggs'll put your car away.'

She shrugged her shoulders and passed him into the house. It seemed to him that she did not care what he saw in her, or what he thought of her. And this was so strange in Fleur that he was confounded. Had she tried and failed? Could it mean anything so good? He searched his memory to recall how she had looked when he brought her back the news of failure six years ago. Yes! Only then she was so young, her face so round—not like this hardened, sharpened, burnt-up face, that frightened him. Get her away to Kit! Get her away, and quickly! And with that saving instinct of his where Fleur only was concerned, he summoned Riggs, told him to close the car and bring it round.

She had gone up to her room. He sent up a message presently that the car was ready. Soon she came down. She had coated her face with powder and put salve on her lips; and again Soames was shocked by that white mask with compressed red line of mouth, and the live and tortured eyes. And again he said nothing, and got out a map.

'That fellow will go wrong unless I sit beside him. It's cross-country;' and he mounted the front of the car. He knew she couldn't talk, and that he couldn't bear to see her face. So they started. An immense time they travelled thus, it seemed to him. Once or twice only he looked round to see her sitting like something dead, so white and motionless. And, within him, the two feelings—relief and pity, continued to struggle. Surely it was the end—she had played her hand and lost! How, where, when—he felt would always be unknown to him; but she had lost! Poor little thing! Not her fault that she had loved this boy, that she couldn't get him out of her head—no more her fault that it had been his own for loving that boy's mother! Only everyone's misfortune! It was as if that passion, born of an ill-starred meeting in a Bournemouth drawing-room forty-six years before, and transmitted with his blood into her being, were singing its swan song of death, through the silent crimsoned lips of that white-faced girl behind him in the cushioned car. 'Praise thou the Lord, O my soul! Praise the Lord!' Um! How could one! They were crossing the river at Staines—from now on that fellow knew his road. When they got home, how should he bring some life into her face again? Thank goodness her mother was away! Surely Kit would be some use! And her old dog, perhaps. And yet, tired though he was after his three long days, Soames dreaded the moment when the car should stop. To drive on and on, perhaps, was the thing for her. Perhaps, for all the world, now. To get away from something that couldn't be got away from–ever since the war–driving on! When you couldn't have what you wanted, and yet couldn't let go; and drove, on and on, to dull the aching. Resignation–like painting–was a lost art; or so it seemed to Soames, as they passed the graveyard where he expected to be buried some day.

Close to home now, and what was he going to say to her when they got out? Words were so futile. He put his head out of the window and took some deep breaths. It smelled better down here by the river than elsewhere, he always thought–more sap in the trees, more savour in the grass. Not the equal of the air on 'Great Forsyte', but more of the earth, more cosy. The gables and the poplars, the scent of a wood fire, the last flight of the doves–here they were! And with a long sigh, he got out.

'You've been doing too much,' he said, opening the door. 'Would you like to go straight up to bed when you've seen Kit? I'll send up your dinner.'

'Thanks, Dad. Some soup is all I shall want. I've got a chill, I think.'

Soames looked at her deeply for a moment and shook his head; then, touching her whitened cheek with a finger, he turned away.

He went round to the stables and released her old dog. It might want a run before being let into the house; and he took it down towards the river. A thin daylight lingered, though the sun had set some time, and while the dog freshened himself among the bushes, Soames stood looking at the water. The swans passed over to their islet while he gazed. The young ones were growing up–were almost white. Rather ghostly in the dusk, the flotilla passed–graceful things and silent. He had often thought of going in for a peacock or two, they put a finish on a garden, but they were noisy; he had never forgotten an early morning in Montpelier Square, hearing their cry, as of lost passion, from Hyde Park. No! The swan was better; just as graceful, and didn't sing. That dog was ruining his dwarf arbutus.

'Come along to your mistress!' he said, and turned back towards the lighted house. He went up into the picture gallery. On the bureau were laid a number of letters and things to be attended to. For half an hour he laboured at them. He had never torn up things with greater satisfaction. Then the gong sounded, and he went down to be lonely, as he supposed.

I3

FIRES

But Fleur came down again. And there began for Soames the most confused evening he had ever spent. For in his heart were great gladness and great pity, and he must not show a sign of either. He wished now that he had stopped to look at Fleur's portrait; it would have given him something to talk of. He fell back feebly on her Dorking house.

'It seems a useful place,' he said; 'the girls–'

'I always feel they hate me. And why not? They have nothing, and I have everything.'

Her laugh cut Soames to the quick.

She was only pretending to eat, too. But he was afraid to ask if she had taken her temperature. She would only laugh again. He began, instead, an account of how he had found a field by the sea where the Forsytes came from, and how he had visited Winchester Cathedral; and, while he went on and on, he thought: 'She hasn't heard a word.'

The idea that she would go up to bed consumed by this smouldering fire at which he could not get, distressed and alarmed him greatly. She looked as if–as if she might do something to herself! She had no veronal, or anything of that sort, he hoped. And all the time he was wondering what had happened. If the issue were still doubtful–if she were still waiting, she might be restless, feverish, but surely she would not look like this! No! It was defeat. But how? And was it final, and he freed for ever from the carking anxiety of these last months? His eyes kept questioning her face, where her fevered mood had crept through the coating of powder, so that she looked theatrical and unlike herself. Its expression, hard and hopeless, went to his heart. If only she would cry, and blurt everything out! But he recognised that in coming down at all, and facing him, she was practically saying: '*Nothing* has happened!' And he compressed his lips. A dumb thing, affection–one couldn't put it into words! The more deeply he felt the more dumb he had always been. Those glib people who poured themselves out and got rid of the feelings they had in their chests, he didn't know how they could do it!

Dinner dragged to its end, with little bursts of talk from Fleur, and more of that laughter which hurt him, and afterwards they went to the drawing-room.

'It's hot to-night,' she said, and opened the french window. The moon was just rising, low and far behind the river bushes; and a waft of light was already floating down the water.

'Yes, it's warm,' said Soames, 'but you oughtn't to be in the air if you've got a chill.'

And, taking her arm, he led her within. He had a dread of her wandering outside to-night, so near the water.

She went over to the piano.

'Do you mind if I strum, Dad?'

'Not at all. Your mother's got some French songs there.' He didn't mind what she did, if only she could get that look off her face. But music was emotional stuff, and French songs always about love! It was to be hoped she wouldn't light on the one Annette was for ever singing:

> '*Auprès de ma blonde, il fait bon–fait bon–fait bon,*
> *Auprès de ma blonde, il fait bon dormir.*'

The young man's hair! In the old days, beside his mother! What hair *she'd* had! What bright hair and what dark eyes! And for a moment it was as if, not Fleur, but Irene, sat there at the piano. Music! Mysterious how it could mean to anyone what it had meant to her. Yes! More than men and more than money–music! A thing that had never moved him, that he didn't understand! What a mischance! There she was, above the piano, as he used to see her in the little drawing-room in Montpelier Square; there, as he had seen her last in that Washington hotel. There she would sit until she died, he supposed, beautiful, he shouldn't wonder, even then. Music!

He came to himself.

Fleur's thin, staccato voice tickled his ears, where he sat in the fume of his cigar. Painful! She was making a brave fight. He wanted her to break down, and he didn't want her to. For if she broke down he didn't know what he would do!

She stopped in the middle of a song and closed the piano. She looked almost old–so she would look, perhaps, when she was forty. Then she came and sat down on the other side of the hearth. She was in red, and he wished she wasn't–the colour increased his feeling that she was on fire beneath that mask of powder on her face and neck. She sat there very still, pretending to read. And he who had *The Times* in his hand, tried not to notice her. Was there nothing he could do to divert her attention? What about his pictures? Which–he asked–was her favourite? The Constable, the Stevens, the Corot, or the Daumier?

'I'm leaving the lot to the nation,' he said. 'But I shall want you to take your pick of four or so; and, of course, that copy of Goya's "Vendimia" belongs to you.' Then, remembering she had worn the "Vendimia" dress at the dance in the Nettlefold hotel, he hurried on:

'With all this modern taste the nation mayn't want them; in that case I don't know. Dumetrius might take them off your hands; he's had a good deal out of most of them already. If you chose the right moment, clear of strikes and things, they ought to fetch money in a good sale. They stand me in at well over seventy thousand pounds–they ought to make a hundred thousand at least.'

She seemed to be listening, but he couldn't tell.

'In my belief,' he went on desperately, 'there'll be none of this modern painting in ten years' time–they can't go on for ever juggling in the air. They'll be sick of experiments by then, unless we have another war.'

'It wasn't the war.'

'How d'you mean–not the war? The war brought in ugliness, and put everyone into a hurry. You don't remember before the war.'

She shrugged her shoulders.

'I won't say,' continued Soames, 'that it hadn't begun before. I remember the first shows in London of those post-impressionists and early Cubist chaps. But they ran riot with the war, catching at things they couldn't get.'

He stopped. It was exactly what she–!

'I think I'll go to bed, Dad.'

'Ah!' said Soames. 'And take some aspirin. Don't you play about with a chill.'

A chill! If only it were! He himself went again to the open window and stood watching the moonlight. From the staff's quarters came the strain of a gramophone. How they loved to turn on that caterwauling, or the loud-speaker! He didn't know which he disliked most.

Moving to the edge of the veranda, he held out his palm. No dew! Dry as ever–remarkable weather! A dog began howling from over the river. Some people would take that for a banshee, he shouldn't wonder! The more he saw of people the more weak-minded they seemed; for ever looking for the sensational, or covering up their eyes and ears. The garden was looking pretty in the moonlight–pretty and unreal. That border of sunflowers and Michaelmas daisies and the late roses in the little round beds, and the low wall of very old brick–he'd had a lot of trouble to get that brick!–even the grass–the moonlight gave them all a stage-like quality. Only the poplars queered the dream-like values, dark and sharply outlined by the moon behind them.

Soames moved out on to the lawn. The face of the house, white and creepered, with a light in her bedroom, looked unreal, too, and as if powdered. Thirty-two years he'd been here. One had got attached to the place, especially since he'd bought the land over the river, so that no one could ever build and overlook him. To be overlooked, body or soul—on the whole he'd avoided that in life—at least, he hoped so.

He finished his cigar out there and threw the butt away. He would have liked to see her light go out before he went to bed—to feel that she was sleeping as when, a little thing, she went to bed with tooth-ache. But he was very tired. Motoring was hard on the liver. Well! He'd go in and shut up. After all, he couldn't do any good by staying down, couldn't do any good in any way. The old couldn't help the young—nobody could help anyone, if it came to that, at least where the heart was concerned. Queer arrangement—the heart! And to think that everybody had one. There ought to be some comfort in that, and yet there wasn't. No comfort to him, when he'd suffered, night in, day out, over that boy's mother, that she had suffered, too! No satisfaction to Fleur now, that the young man and his wife, too, very likely, were suffering as well! And, closing the window, Soames went up. He listened at her door, but could hear nothing; and, having undressed, took up Vasari's *Lives of the Painters*, and, propped against his pillows, began to read. Two pages of that book always sent him to sleep, and generally the same two, for he knew them so well that he never remembered where he had left off.

He was awakened presently by he couldn't tell what, and lay listening. It seemed that there was movement in the house. But if he got up to see he would certainly begin to worry again, and he didn't want to. Besides, in seeing to whether Fleur was asleep he might wake her up. Turning over, he dozed off, but again he woke, and lay drowsily thinking: 'I'm not sleeping well—I want exercise.' Moonlight was coming through the curtains not quite drawn. And, suddenly, his nostrils twitched. Surely a smell of burning! He sat up, sniffing. It *was*! Had there been a short circuit, or was the thatch of the pigeon-house on fire? Getting out of bed, he put on his dressing-gown and slippers, and went to the window.

A reddish, fitful light was coming from a window above. Great God! His picture gallery! He ran to the foot of the stairs that led up to it. A stealthy sound, a scent of burning much more emphatic, staggered him. He hurried up the stairs and pulled open the door. Heavens! The far end of the gallery, at the extreme left corner of the house was on fire. Little red flames were licking round the woodwork; the curtains of the far window were already a blackened mass, and the waste-paper-basket, between them and his writing-bureau, was a charred wreck! On the parquet floor he saw some cigarette ash. Someone had been up here smoking! The flames crackled as he stood there aghast. He rushed downstairs and threw open the door of Fleur's room. She was lying on her bed asleep, but fully dressed! Fully dressed! Was it–? Had she–? She opened her eyes, staring up at him.

'Get up!' he said, 'there's a fire in the picture gallery. Get Kit and the servants out at once–at once! Send for Riggs! Telephone to Reading for the engines–quick! Get everyone out of the house!' Only waiting to see her on her feet, he ran back to the foot of the gallery stairs and seized a fire-extinguisher. He carried it up, a heavy, great thing. He knew vaguely that you dashed the knob on the floor and sprayed the flames. Through the open doorway he could see that they had spread considerably. Good God! They were licking at his Fred

Walker, and the two David Coxes. They had caught the beam, too, that ran round the gallery, dividing the upper from the lower tier of pictures; yes, and the upper beam was on fire also. The Constable! For a moment he hesitated. Should he rush at that and save it, anyway? The extinguisher mightn't work! He dropped it, and, running the length of the gallery, seized the Constable just as the flames reached the woodwork above it. The hot breath of them scorched his face as he wrenched the picture from the wall, and, running back, flung open the window opposite the door and placed it on the sill. Then, seizing the extinguisher again, he dashed it, violently, against the floor. A stream of stuff came out, and, picking the thing up, he directed that stream against the flames. The room was full of smoke now, and he felt rather giddy. The stuff was good, and he saw with relief that the flames didn't like it. He was making a distinct impression on them. But the Walker was ruined–ah! and the Coxes! He had beaten the fire back to the window-wall, when the stream ceased, and he saw that the beams had broken into flame beyond where he had started spraying. The writing-bureau, too, was on fire now–its papers had caught! Should he run down and get another of these things, all the way to the hall! Where was that fellow Riggs? The 'Alfred Stevens'! By heaven! He was not going to lose his 'Stevens' nor his 'Gauguins', nor his 'Corots'!

And a sort of demon entered into Soames. His taste, his trouble, his money, and his pride–all consumed? By the Lord, no! And through the smoke he dashed again up to the far wall. Flame licked at his sleeve as he tore away the 'Stevens'; he could smell the singed stuff when he propped the picture in the window beside the Constable.

A lick of flame crossed the Daubigny, and down came its glass with a clatter–there was the picture exposed and fire creeping and flaring over it! He rushed back and grasped at a 'Gauguin'–a South Sea girl with nothing on. She wouldn't come away from the wall; he caught hold of the wire, but dropped it–red hot; seizing the frame he gave a great wrench. Away it came, and over he went, backwards. But he'd got it, his favourite Gauguin! He stacked that against the others, and ran back to the Corot nearest the flames. The silvery, cool picture was hot to his touch, but he got that, too! Now for the Monet! The engines would be twenty minutes at least. If that fellow Riggs didn't come soon–! They must spread a blanket down there, and he would throw the pictures out. And then he uttered a groan. The flames had got the other Corot! The poor thing! Wrenching off the Monet, he ran to the head of the stairs. Two frightened maids in coats over their nightgowns, and their necks showing, were half-way up.

'Here!' he cried. 'Take this picture and keep your heads. Miss Fleur and the boy out?'

'Yes, sir.'

'Have you telephoned?'

'Yes, sir.'

'Get me an extinguisher; and all of you hold a blanket spread beneath the window down there to catch the pictures as I throw them out. Don't be foolish–there's no danger! Where's Riggs?'

He went back into the gallery. Oh–h! There went his precious little Degas! And with rage in his heart Soames ran again at the wall and snatched at his other Gauguin. If ever he had beaten Dumetrius, it was over that highly-coloured affair. As if grateful to him, the picture came away neatly in his scorched and trembling hands. He stacked it, and stood for a moment choked and breathless. So long as he could breathe up here in the draught between the opened door and window, he must go on getting them off the wall.

It wouldn't take long to throw them out. The Bonnington and the Turner–that fellow Turner wouldn't have been so fond of sunsets if he'd known what fire was like. Each time now that he went to the wall his lungs felt as if they couldn't stand another journey. But they must!

'Dad!'

Fleur with an extinguisher!

'Go down! Go out!' he cried. 'D'you hear! Go out of the house! Get that blanket spread, and make them hold it tight.'

'Dad! Let me! I must!'

'Go down!' cried Soames again, and pushed her to the stairs. He watched her to the bottom, then dashed the knob of the extinguisher on the floor and again sprayed the fire. He put out the bureau, and attacked the flames on the far wall. He could hardly hold the heavy thing, and when it dropped empty, he could barely see. But again he had gained on the fire. If only he could hold on!

And then he saw that his Harpignies was gone–such a beauty! That wanton loss gave him strength. And rushing up to the wall–the long wall now–he detached picture after picture. But the flames were creeping back again, persistent as hell itself. He couldn't reach the Sisley and the Picasso, high in the corner there, couldn't face the flames so close, for if he slipped against the wall he would be done. They must go! But he'd have the Daumier! His favourite–perhaps his very favourite. Safe! Gasping, and avidly drinking the fresher air, he could see from the window that they had the blanket down there now stretched between four maids, holding each a corner.

'Hold tight!' he cried; and tipped the Daumier out. He watched it falling. What a thing to do to a picture! The blanket dipped with the weight, but held.

'Hold it tighter!' he shouted. 'Look out!' And over went the Gauguin South Sea girl. Picture after picture he tipped from the sill; and picture after picture, they took them from the blanket, and laid them on the grass. When he had tipped them all, he turned to take the situation in. The flames had caught the floor now, in the corner, and were spreading fast along the beams.

The engines would be in time to save the right-hand wall. The left-hand wall was hopeless, but most of the pictures there he'd saved. It was the long wall where the flames were beginning to get hold; he must go for that now. He ran as near to the corner as he dared, and seized the Morland. It was hot to his touch, but he got it–six hundred pounds' worth of white pony. He had promised it a good home! He tipped it from the window and saw it pitch headlong into the blanket.

'My word!'

Behind him, in the doorway, that fellow Riggs at last, in shirt and trousers, with two extinguishers and an open mouth!

'Shut your mouth!' he gasped, 'and spray that wall!'

He watched the stream and the flames recoiling from it. How he hated those inexorable red tongues. Ah! That was giving them pause!

'Now the other! Save the Courbet! Sharp!'

Again the stream spurted and the flames recoiled. Soames dashed for the Courbet. The glass had gone, but the picture was not harmed yet; he wrenched it away.

'That's the last of the bloomin' extinguishers, sir,' he heard Riggs mutter.

'Here, then!' he called. 'Pull the pictures off that wall and tip them out of the window one by one. Mind you hit the blanket. Stir your stumps!'

He, too, stirred his stumps, watching the discouraged flames regaining their lost ground. The two of them ran breathless to the wall, wrenched, ran back to the window, and back again—and the flames gained all the time.

'That top one,' said Soames; 'I must have that! Get on that chair. Quick! No, I'll do it. Lift me!—I can't reach!'

Uplifted in the grip of that fellow, Soames detached his James Maris, bought the very day the whole world broke into flames. 'Murder of the Archduke!' he could hear them at it now. A fine day; the sunlight coming in at the window of his cab, and he light-hearted, with that bargain on his knee. And there it went, pitching down! Ah! What a way to treat pictures!

'Come on!' he gasped.

'Better go down, sir! It's gettin' too thick now.'

'No!' said Soames. 'Come on!'

Three more pictures salved.

'If you don't go down, sir, I'll 'ave to carry you—you been up 'ere too long.'

'Nonsense!' gasped Soames. 'Come on!'

''Ooray! The engines!'

Soames stood still; besides the pumping of his heart and lungs he could hear another sound. Riggs seized his arm.

'Come along, sir; when they begin to play there'll be a proper smother.'

Soames pointed through the smoke.

'I must have that one,' he gasped. 'Help me. It's heavy.'

The 'Vendimia' copy stood on an easel. Soames staggered up to it. Half carrying and half dragging, he bore that Spanish effigy of Fleur towards the window.

'Now lift!' They lifted till it balanced on the sill.

'Come away there!' called a voice from the doorway.

'Tip!' gasped Soames, but arms seized him, he was carried to the door, down the stairs, into the air half-conscious. He came to himself in a chair on the verandah. He could see the helmets of firemen and heard a hissing sound. His lungs hurt him, his eyes smarted terribly, and his hands were scorched, but he felt drugged and drowsy and triumphant in spite of his aches and smarting.

The grass, the trees, the cool river under the moon! What a nightmare it had been up there among his pictures—his poor pictures! But he had saved them! The cigarette ash! The waste-paper-basket! Fleur! No doubt about the cause! What on earth had induced him to put his pictures into her head that evening of all others, when she didn't know what she was doing? What awful luck! Musn't let her know—unless—unless she did know? The shock—however! The shock might do her good! His Degas! The Harpignies! He closed his eyes to listen to the hissing of the water. Good! A good noise! They'd save the rest! It might have been worse! Something cold was thrust against his drooped hand. A dog's nose. They shouldn't have let him out. And, suddenly, it seemed to Soames that he must see to things again. They'd go the wrong way to work with all that water! He staggered to his feet. He could see better now. Fleur? Ah! There she was, standing by herself—too near the house! And what a mess on the lawn—firemen—engines—maids, that fellow Riggs—the hose laid to the river—plenty of water, anyway! They mustn't hurt the pictures with that water! Fools! He knew it! Why! They were squirting the untouched wall. Squirting through both windows. There was no need of that! The right-hand window only—only! He stumbled up to the fireman.

'Not that wall! Not that! That wall's all right. You'll spoil my pictures! Shoot at the centre!' The fireman shifted the angle of his arm, and Soames saw the jet strike the right-hand corner of the sill. The Vendimia! There went its precious—! Dislodged by the stream of water, it was tilting forward! And Fleur! Good God! Standing right under, looking up. She must see it, and she wasn't moving! It flashed through Soames that she wanted to be killed.

'It's falling!' he cried. 'Look out! Look out!' And, just as if he had seen her about to throw herself under a car, he darted forward, pushed her with his outstretched arms, and fell.

The thing had struck him to the earth.

14

HUSH

Old Gradman, off the Poultry, eating his daily chop, took up the early edition of the evening paper, brought to him with that collation:

FIRE IN A PICTURE GALLERY.
WELL-KNOWN CONNOISSEUR SEVERELY INJURED.

A fire, the cause of which is unknown, broke out last night in the picture gallery of Mr Soames Forsyte's house at Mapledurham. It was extinguished by fire-engines from Reading, and most of the valuable pictures were saved. Mr Forsyte, who was in residence, fought the fire before the firemen were on the spot, and, single-handed, rescued many of the pictures, throwing them out of the window of the gallery into a blanket which was held stretched out on the lawn below. Unfortunately, after the engines had arrived, he was struck on the head by the frame of a picture falling from the window of the gallery, which is on the second floor, and rendered unconscious. In view of his age and his exertions during the fire, very little hope is entertained of his recovery. Nobody else was injured, and no other part of the mansion was reached by the flames.

Laying down his fork, old Gradman took his napkin, and passed it over a brow which had grown damp. Replacing it on the table, he pushed away his chop, and took up the paper again. You never knew what to believe, nowadays, but the paragraph was uncommonly sober; and he dropped it with a gesture singularly like the wringing of hands.

'Mr Soames,' he thought. 'Mr Soames!' His two wives, his daughter, his grandson, the Forsyte family, himself! He stood up, grasping the table. An accidental thing like that! Mr Soames! Why—he was a young man, comparatively! But perhaps they'd got hold of the wrong stick! Mechanically he went to the telephone. He found the number with difficulty, his eyes being misty.

'Is that Mrs Dartie's—Gradman speaking. Is it true, ma'am? ... Not 'opeless, I do trust? Aow! Saving Miss Fleur's life? You don't say! You're goin' down? I think I'd better, too. Everything's in order, but he might want something, if he comes to. ... Dear, dear! ... Ah! I'm sure. ... Dreadful shock—dreadful!' He hung up the receiver, and stood quite still. Who would look after things now? There wasn't one of the family with any sense of business, compared with Mr Soames, not one who remembered the old days, and could handle house property as they used to, then. No, he couldn't relish any more chop—that was flat! Miss Fleur! Saving her life? Well, what a thing.

She'd always been first with him. What must she be feelin'! He remembered her as a little girl; yes, and at her wedding. To think of it. She'd be a rich woman now. He took his hat. Must go home first and get some things—might have to wait there days! But for a full three minutes he still stood, as if stunned—a thick-set figure with a puggy face, in a round grey beard—confirming his uneasy grief. If the Bank of England had gone he couldn't have felt it more. That he couldn't.

When he reached 'The Shelter' in a station fly, with a bag full of night things and papers, it was getting on for six o'clock. He was met in the hall by that young man, Mr Michael Mont, whom he remembered as making jokes about serious things—it was to be hoped he wouldn't do it now!

'Ah! Mr Gradman; so good of you to come! No! They hardly expect him to recover consciousness; it was a terrible knock. But if he does, he's sure to want to see you, even if he can't speak. We've got your room ready. Will you have some tea?'

Yes, he could relish a cup of tea—he could indeed! 'Miss Fleur?'

The young man shook his head, his eyes looked distressed.

'He saved her life.'

Gradman nodded. 'So they say. Tt, tt! To think that he—! His father lived to be ninety, and Mr Soames was always careful. Dear, dear!'

He had drunk a nice hot cup of tea when he saw a figure in the doorway—Miss Fleur herself. Why! What a face! She came forward and took his hand. And, almost unconsciously, old Gradman lifted his other hand and imprisoned hers between his two.

'My dear,' he said, 'I feel for you. I remember you as a little girl.'

She only answered: 'Yes, Mr Gradman,' and it seemed to him funny. She took him to his room, and left him there. He had never been in such a pleasant bedroom, with flowers and a nice smell, and a bathroom all to himself—really quite unnecessary. And to think that two doors off, Mr Soames was lying as good as gone!

'Just breathing,' she had said, passing the door. 'They daren't operate. My mother's there.'

What a face she had on her—so white, so hurt-looking—poor young thing! He stood at the open window, gazing out. It was warm—very warm for the end of September. A pleasant air—a smell of grass. It must be the river down there! Peaceful—and to think—! Moisture blurred the river out; he winked it away. Only the other day they'd been talking about something happening, and now it hadn't happened to him, but to Mr Soames himself. The ways of Providence! For Jesus Christ's sake—Our Lord! Dear, dear! To think of it! He would cut up a very warm man. Richer than his father. There were some birds out there on the water—geese or swans or something—ye-es! Swans! What a lot! In a row, floating along. He hadn't seen a swan since he took Mrs G. to Golder's Hill Park the year after the war. And they said—hopeless! A dreadful thing—sudden like that, with no time to say your prayers. Lucky the will was quite straightforward. Annuity to Mrs F., and the rest to his daughter for life, the remainder to her children in equal shares. Only one child at present, but there'd be others, no doubt, with all that money. Dear! What a sight of money there was in the family altogether, and yet, of the present generation, Mr Soames was the only warm man. It was all divided up now, and none of the young ones seemed to make any. He would have to keep a tight hand on the estates, or they'd be wanting their capital out, and Mr Soames wouldn't approve of that! To think of outliving Mr Soames! And something incorruptibly faithful within that puggy face and thick figure, something that for two generations had served and never expected more than it had got, so moved old Gradman that he subsided on the window-seat with the words: 'I'm quite upset!'

He was still sitting there with his head on his hand, and darkness thickening outside, when, with a knock on the door, that young man said:

'Mr Gradman, will you come down for dinner, or would you like it up here?'

'Up here, if it's all the same to you. Cold beef and pickles or anything there is, and a glass of stout, if it's quite convenient.'

The young man drew nearer.

'You must feel it awfully, Mr Gradman, having known him so long. Not an easy man to know, but one felt—'

Something gave way in Gradman and he spoke:

'Ah! I knew him from a little boy—took him to his first school—taught him how to draw a lease—never knew him to do a shady thing; very reserved man, Mr Soames, but no better judge of an investment, except his uncle Nicholas. He had his troubles, but he never said anything of them; good son to his father—good brother to his sisters—good father to his child, as you know, young man.'

'Yes, indeed! And very good to me.'

'Not much of a church-goer, I'm afraid, but straight as a die. Never one to wear his 'eart on his sleeve; a little uncomfortable sometimes, maybe, but you could depend on him. I'm sorry for your young wife, young man—I am that! 'Ow did it 'appen?'

'She was standing below the window when the picture fell, and didn't seem to realise. He pushed her out of the way, and it hit him instead.'

'Why! What a thing!'

'Yes. She can't get over it.'

Gradman looked up at the young man's face in the twilight.

'You mustn't be down-'earted,' he said. 'She'll come round. Misfortunes will happen. The family's been told, I suppose. There's just one thing, Mr Michael—his first wife, Mrs Irene, that married Mr Jolyon after; she's still living, they say; she might like to send a message that byegones were byegones, in case he came round.'

'I don't know, Mr Gradman, I don't know.'

'Forgive us our trespasses, as we forgive them that trespass—'e was greatly attached to 'er at one time.'

'So I believe, but there are things that—Still, Mrs Dartie knows her address, if you like to ask her. She's here, you know.'

'I'll turn it over. I remember Mrs Irene's wedding—very pale she was; a beautiful young woman, too.'

'I believe so.'

'The present one—being French, I suppose, she shows her feelings. However—if he's unconscious—' It seemed to him that the young man's face looked funny, and he added, 'I've never heard much of her. Not very happy with his wives, I'm afraid, he hasn't been.'

'Some men aren't, you know, Mr Gradman. It's being too near, I suppose.'

'Ah!' said Gradman: 'It's one thing or the other, and that's a fact. Mrs G. and I have never had a difference—not to speak of, in fifty-two years, and that's going back, as the saying is. Well, I mustn't keep you from Miss Fleur. She'll need cossetting. Just cold beef and a pickle. You'll let me know if I'm wanted—any time, day or night. And if Mrs Dartie'd like to see me I'm at her service.'

The talk had done him good. That young man was a nicer young fellow than he'd thought. He felt he could almost relish a pickle. After he had done so a message came: Would he go to Mrs Dartie in the drawing-room?

'Wait for me, my dear,' he said to the maid: 'I'm strange here.'

Having washed his hands and passed a towel over his face, he followed her down the stairs of the hushed house. What a room to be sure! Rather empty, but in apple-pie order, with its cream-coloured panels, and its china, and its grand piano. Winifred Dartie was sitting on a sofa before a wood fire. She rose and took his hand.

'Such a comfort to see you, Gradman,' she said: 'You're the oldest friend we have.'

Her face looked strange, as if she wanted to cry and had forgotten how. He had known her as a child, as a fashionable young woman, had helped to draw her marriage settlement, and shaken his head over her husband many a time—the trouble he'd had in finding out exactly what that gentleman owed, after he fell down the staircase in Paris and broke his neck! And every year still he prepared her income tax return.

'A good cry,' he said, 'would do you good, and I shouldn't blame you. But we mustn't say "die"; Mr Soames has a good constitution, and it's not as if he drank; perhaps he'll pull round after all.'

She shook her head. Her face had a square grim look that reminded him of her old Aunt Ann. Underneath all her fashionableness she'd borne a lot—she had, when you came to think of it.

'It struck him here,' she said; 'a slanting blow on the right side of the head. I shall miss him terribly; he's the only—' Gradman patted her hand.

'Ye-es, ye-es! But we must look on the bright side. If he comes round, I shall be there.' What exact comfort he thought this was, he could not have made clear. 'I did wonder whether he would like Mrs Irene told. I don't like the idea of his going with a grudge on his mind. It's an old story, of course, but at the Judgment Day—'

A faint smile was lost in the square lines round Winifred's mouth.

'We needn't bother him with that, Gradman; it's out of fashion.'

Gradman emitted a sound, as though, within him, faith and respect for the family he had served for sixty years had bumped against each other.

'Well, you know best,' he said. 'I shouldn't like him to go with anything on his conscience.'

'On *her* conscience, Gradman.'

Gradman stared at a Dresden shepherdess.

'In a case of forgivin', you never know. I wanted to speak to him, too, about his steel shares; they're not all they might be. But we must just take our chance, I suppose. I'm glad you father was spared this, Mr James *would* have taken on. It won't be like the same world again, if Mr Soames—'

She had put her hand up to her mouth and turned away. Fashion had dropped from her thickened figure. Much affected, Gradman turned to the door.

'Shan't leave my clothes off, in case I'm wanted. I've got everything here. *Good*-night!'

He went upstairs again, tiptoeing past the door, and, entering his room, switched on the light. They had taken away the pickles; turned his bed down, laid his flannel nightgown out. They took a lot of trouble! And, sinking on his knees, he prayed in a muffled murmur, varying the usual words, and ending: 'And for Mr Soames, O Lord, I specially commend him body and soul. Forgive him his trespasses, and deliver him from all 'ardness of 'eart and impurities, before he goes 'ence, and make him as a little lamb again, that he may find favour in Thy sight. Thy faithful servant. Amen.' And, for some time after he had finished, he remained kneeling on the very soft carpet, breathing-in the familiar reek of flannel and old times. He rose easier in his mind. Removing his boots, laced and square-toed, and his old frock-coat, he put on his Jaeger gown, and shut the window, to keep out the night air. Then taking the eiderdown, he placed a large handkerchief over his bald head, and, switching off the light, sat down in the armchair, with the eiderdown over his knees.

What an 'ush after London, to be sure, so quiet you could hear yourself think! For some reason he thought of Queen Victoria's first Jubilee, when he was a youngster of forty, and Mr James had give him and Mrs G. two seats. They had seen the whole thing—first chop! the Guards and the procession, the carriages, the horses, the Queen and the Royal Family. A beautiful summer day—a real summer that; not like the summers lately. And everything going on, as if it'd go on for ever, with three per cents at nearly par if he remembered, and all going to church regular. And only that same year, a bit later, Mr Soames had had his first upset. And another memory came. Queer he should remember that to-night, with Mr Soames lying there—must have been quite soon after the Jubilee, too! Going with a lease that wouldn't bear to wait to Mr Soames's private house, Montpelier Square, and being shown into the dining-room, and hearing someone singing and playing on the 'pianner'. He had opened the door to listen. Why—he could remember the words now! About 'laying on the grass,' 'I die, I faint, I fail,' 'the champaign odours,' something 'on your cheek' and something 'pale.' Fancy that! And, suddenly, the door had opened and out she'd come—Mrs Irene—in a frock—ah!

'Are you waiting for Mr Forsyte? Won't you come in and have some tea?' And he'd gone in and had tea, sitting on the edge of a chair that didn't look too firm, all gilt and spindley. And she on the sofa in that frock, pouring it out, and saying:

'Are you fond of music, then, Mr Gradman?' Soft, a soft look, with her dark eyes and her hair—not red and not what you'd call gold—but like a turned leaf—um?—a beautiful young woman, sad and sort of sympathetic in the face. He'd often thought of her—he could see her now! And then Mr Soames coming in, and her face all closing up like—like a book. Queer to remember that to-night! . . . Dear me! . . . How dark and quiet it was! That poor young daughter, that it was all about! It was to be 'oped she'd sleep! Ye-es! And what would Mrs G. say if she could see *him* sitting in a chair like this, with his teeth in, too. Ah! Well—she'd never seen Mr Soames, never seen the family—Maria hadn't! But what an 'ush! And slowly but surely old Gradman's mouth fell open, and he broke the hush.

Beyond the closed window the moon rode up, a full and brilliant moon, so that the stilly darkened country dissolved into shape and shadow, and the owls hooted, and, far off, a dog bayed; and flowers in the garden became each a little presence in a night-time carnival graven into stillness; and on the gleaming river every fallen leaf that drifted down carried a moonbeam; while, above, the trees stayed, quiet, measured and illumined, quiet as the very sky, for the wind stirred not.

I5

SOAMES TAKES THE FERRY

There was only just life in Soames. Two nights and two days they had waited, watching the unmoving bandaged head. Specialists had come, given their verdict: 'Nothing to be done by way of operation;' and gone again. The doctor who had presided over Fleur's birth was in charge. Though never quite forgiven by Soames for the anxiety he had caused on that occasion, 'the fellow' had hung on, attending the family. By his instructions they watched the patient's eyes; at any sign, they were to send for him at once.

Michael, from whom Fleur seemed inconsolably caught away, gave himself up to Kit, walking and talking and trying to keep the child unaware. He did not visit the still figure, not from indifference, but because he felt an intruder there. He had removed all the pictures left in the gallery, and, storing them with those which Soames had thrown from the window, had listed them carefully. The fire had destroyed eleven out of eighty-four.

Annette had cried, and was feeling better. The thought of life without Soames was for her strange and–possible; precisely, in fact, like the thought of life with him. She wished him to recover, but if he didn't she would live in France.

Winifred, who shared the watches, lived much and sadly in the past. Soames had been her mainstay throughout thirty-four years chequered by Montague Dartie, had continued her mainstay in the thirteen unchequered years since. She did not see how things could ever be cosy again. She had a heart, and could not look at that still figure without trying to remember how to cry. Letters came to her from the family worded with a sort of anxious astonishment that Soames should have had such a thing happen to him.

Gradman, who had taken a bath, and changed his trousers to black, was deep in calculations and correspondence with the insurance firm. He walked too, in the kitchen garden, out of sight of the house; for he could not get over the fact that Mr James had lived to be ninety, and Mr Timothy a hundred, to say nothing of the others. And, stopping mournfully before the seakale or the Brussels sprouts he would shake his head.

Smither had come down to be with Winifred, but was of little use, except to say: 'Poor Mr Soames! Poor dear Mr Soames! To think of it! And he so careful of himself, and everybody!'

For that was it! Ignorant of the long and stealthy march of passion, and of the state to which it had reduced Fleur; ignorant of how Soames had watched her, seen that beloved young part of his very self fail, reach the edge of things and stand there balancing; ignorant of Fleur's reckless desperation beneath that falling picture, and her father's knowledge thereof–ignorant of all this everybody felt aggrieved. It seemed to them that a mere bolt from the blue, rather than the inexorable secret culmination of an old, old story, had stricken one who of all men seemed the least liable to accident. How should they tell that it was not so accidental as all that!

But Fleur knew well enough that her desperate mood had destroyed her father, just as surely as if she had flung herself into the river and he had been drowned in saving her. Only too well she knew that on that night she had been capable of slipping down into the river, of standing before a rushing car, of anything not too deliberate and active, that would have put her out of her aching misery. She knew well enough that by her conduct she had invited his rush to the rescue. And now, sobered to the very marrow by the shock, she could not forgive herself.

With her mother, her aunt and the two trained nurses she divided the watches, so that there were never less than two, of whom she was nearly always one, in Annette's bedroom where Soames lay. She would sit hour after hour, almost as still as her father, with her eyes wistful and dark-circled, fixed on his face. Passion and fever had quite died out of her. It was as if, with his infallible instinct where she was concerned, Soames had taken the one step that could rid her of the fire which had been consuming her. Jon was remote from her in that room darkened by sun-blinds and her remorse.

Yes! She had meant to be killed by that picture. She had stood there under the window in a moment of passionate recklessness, watching the picture topple, wanting it all over and done with. Distraught that desperate night, she did not even now realise that she had caused the fire, by a cigarette flung down still lighted, not even perhaps that she had smoked up there. But only too well she realised that because she had wanted to die, had stood welcoming sudden extinction, her father was now lying there so nearly dead. How good he had always been to her! Incredible that he should die and take that goodness away, that she should never hear his flat-toned voice again, or feel the touch of his moustache on her cheeks or forehead. Incredible that he should never give her a chance to show that she had really loved him—yes really, beneath all the fret and self-importance of her life. While watching him now, the little rather than the great things came back to her. How he would pitch a new doll down in the nursery and say: 'Well, I don't know if you'll care for this one; I just picked her up.' How once, after her mother had whipped her, he had come in, taken her hand and said: 'There, there. Let's go and see if there are some raspberries!' How he had stood on the stairs at Green Street after her wedding, watching, pale and unobtrusive, above the guests clustered in the hall, for a turn of her head and her last look back. Unobtrusive! That was the word—unobtrusive, always! Why, if he went, there would be no portrait—hardly even a photograph, to remember him by! Just one of him as a baby, in his mother's arms; one as a little boy, looking sceptically at his velvet knickers; one in '76 as a young man in a full-tailed coat and short whiskers; and a snapshot or two taken unawares. Had any man ever been less photographed? He had never seemed to wish to be appreciated, or even remembered, by anyone. To Fleur, so avid of appreciation, it seemed marvellously strange. What secret force within that spare form, lying there inert, had made him thus self-sufficing? He had been brought up as luxuriously as herself, had never known want or the real need for effort, but somehow had preserved a sort of stoic independence of others, and what they thought of him. And yet, as none knew better than herself, he had longed to be loved. This hurt her most, watching him. He had longed for her affection, and she had not shown him enough. But she had felt it—really felt it all the time. Something in him had repelled feeling, dried up its manifestation. There had been no magnet in his 'make-up'. And stealing to the bed—her mother's bed where she herself had been conceived and born—she would stand beside that almost deserted body and drawn dun face, feeling so hollow and miserable that she could hardly restrain herself.

So the days and nights passed. On the third day about three o'clock, while she stood there beside him, she saw the eyes open—a falling apart of the lids, indeed, rather than an opening, and no speculation in the gaps; but her heart beat fast. The nurse, summoned by her finger, came, looked, and went quickly to the telephone. And Fleur stood there with her soul in her eyes, trying to summon his. It did not come, the lids drooped again. She drew up a chair and sat down, not taking her eyes off his face. The nurse came back to say that the doctor was on his rounds; as soon as he came in he would be sent to them post-haste. As her father would have said: 'Of course, "that fellow" wasn't in when he was wanted!' But it would make no difference. They knew what to do. It was nearly four when again the lids were raised, and this time something looked forth. Fleur could not be sure that he saw anything particular, recognised her or any other object, but there was something there, some flickering light, trying for focus. Slowly it strengthened, then went out again between the lids. They gave him stimulant. And again she sat down to watch. In half an hour his eyes re-opened. This time he *saw*! And for torturing minutes Fleur watched a being trying to *be*, a mind striving to obey the mandate of instinctive will power. Bending so that those eyes, which she now knew recognised her, should have the least possible effort, she waited with her lips trembling, as if in a kiss. The extraordinary tenacity of that struggle to come back terrified her. He *meant* to be a mind, he *meant* to know and hear and speak. It was as if he must die from the sheer effort of it. She murmured to him. She put her hand under his cold hand, so that if he made the faintest pressure she would feel it. She watched his lips desperately. At last the struggle for coherence ceased, the half-blank, half-angry look yielded to something deeper, the lips moved. They said nothing, but they moved, and the faintest tremor passed from his fingers into hers.

'You know me, darling?'

His eyes said: 'Yes.'

'You remember?'

Again his eyes said: 'Yes.'

His lips were twitching all the time, as if rehearsing for speech, and the look in his eyes deepening. She saw his brows frown faintly, as if her face were too close; drew back a little and the frown relaxed.

'Darling, you are going to be all right.'

His eyes said: 'No'; and his lips moved, but she could not distinguish the sound. For a moment she lost control, and said with a sob:

'Dad, forgive me!'

His eyes softened; and this time she caught what sounded like:

'Forgive? Nonsense!'

'I love you so.'

He seemed to abandon the effort to speak then, and centred all the life of him in his eyes. Deeper and deeper grew the colour and the form and the meaning in them, as if to compel something from her. And suddenly, like a little girl, she said:

'Yes, Dad; I will be good!'

A tremor from his finger passed into her palm; his lips seemed trying to smile, his head moved as if he had meant to nod, and always that look deepened in his eyes.

'Gradman is here, darling, and Mother, and Aunt Winifred, and Kit and Michael. Is there anyone you would like to see?'

His lips shaped: 'No–you!'

'I am here all the time.' Again she felt the tremor from his fingers, saw his lips whispering:

'That's all.'

And suddenly, his eyes went out. There was nothing there! For some time longer he breathed, but before 'that fellow' came, he had lost hold–was gone.

16

FULL CLOSE

In accordance with all that was implicit in Soames there was no fuss over his funeral. For a long time now, indeed, he had been the only one of the family at all interested in obsequies.

It was then, a very quiet affair, only men attending.

Sir Lawrence had come down, graver than Michael had ever known him.

'I respected old Forsyte, he said to his son, while they returned on foot from the graveyard, where, in the corner selected by himself, Soames now lay, under a crab-apple tree. 'He dated, and he couldn't express himself; but there was no humbug about him–an honest man. How is Fleur bearing up?'

Michael shook his head. 'It's terrible for her to think that he–'

'My dear boy, there's no better death than dying to save the one you're fondest of. As soon as you can, let us have Fleur at Lippinghall–where her father and her family never were. I'll get Hilary and his wife down for a holiday–she likes *them*.'

'I'm very worried about her, Dad–something's broken.'

'That happens to most of us, before we're thirty. Some spring or other goes; but presently we get our second winds. It's what happened to the Age–something broke and it hasn't yet got its second wind. But it's getting it, and so will she. What sort of a stone are you going to put up?'

'A cross, I suppose.'

'I think he'd prefer a flat stone with that crab-apple at the head and yew trees around, so that he's not overlooked. No "Beloved" or "Regretted". Has he got the freehold of that corner? He'd like to belong to his descendants in perpetuity. We're all more Chinese than you'd think, only with them it's the ancestors who do the owning. Who was the old chap who cried into his hat?'

'Old Mr Gradman–sort of business nurse to his family.'

'Faithful old dog! Well! I certainly never thought Forsyte would take the ferry before me. He looked permanent, but it's an ironical world. Can I do anything for you and Fleur? Talk to the nation about the pictures? The Marquess and I could fix that for you. He had quite a weakness for old Forsyte, and his Morland's saved. By the way, that must have been a considerable contest between him and the fire up there all alone. It's the sort of thing one would never have suspected him of.'

'Yes,' said Michael: 'I've been talking to Riggs. He's full of it.'

'He saw it then?'

Michael nodded. 'Here he comes!'

They slackened their pace, and the chauffeur, touching his hat, came alongside.

'Ah! Riggs,' said Sir Lawrence, 'you were up there at the fire, I'm told.'

'Yes, Sir Lawrence. Mr Forsyte was a proper wonder—went at it like a two-year-old, we fair had to carry him away. So particular as a rule about not getting his coat wet or sitting in a draught, but the way he stuck it—at his age . . . "Come on!" he kept saying to me all through that smoke—a proper champion! Never so surprised in all my life, Sir Lawrence—nervous gentleman like him. And what a bit o' luck! If he hadn't insisted on saving that last picture, it'd never have fallen and got 'im.'

'How did the fire begin?'

'Nobody knows, Sir Lawrence, unless Mr Forsyte did, and he never said nothing. Wish I'd got there sooner, but I was puttin' the petrol out of action. What that old gentleman did by 'imself up there; and after the day we'd had! Why! We came from Winchester that morning to London, on to Dorking, picked up Mrs Mont, and on here. And now he'll never tell me I've gone wrong again.'

A grimace passed over his thin face, seamed and shadowed by traffic and the insides of his car; and, touching his hat, he left them at the gate.

'"A proper champion,"' Sir Lawrence repeated softly. 'You might almost put that on the stone. Yes, it's an ironical world!'

In the hall they parted, for Sir Lawrence was going back to Town by car. He took Gradman with him, the provisions of the will having been quietly disclosed. Michael found Smither crying and drawing up the blinds, and in the library Winifred and Val, who had come, with Holly, for the funeral, dealing with condolences, such as they were. Annette was with Kit in the nursery. Michael went up to Fleur in the room she used to have as a little girl—a single room, so that he had been sleeping elsewhere.

She was lying on her bed, graceful, and as if without life.

The eyes she turned on Michael seemed to make of him no less, but no more, than they were making of the ceiling. It was not so much that the spirit behind them was away somewhere, as that there was nowhere for it to go. He went up to the bed and put his hand on hers.

'Dear Heart!'

Fleur turned her eyes on him again, but of the look in them he could make nothing.

'The moment you wish, darling, we'll take Kit home.'

'Any time, Michael.'

'I know exactly how you feel,' said Michael, knowing well that he did not. 'Riggs has been telling us how splendid your father was, up there with the fire.'

'Don't!'

There was that in her face which baffled him completely—something not natural, however much she might be mourning for her father. Suddenly she said:

'Give me time, Michael. Nothing matters, I suppose, in the long run. And don't worry about me—I'm not worth it.'

More conscious than he had ever been in his life that words were of no use, Michael put his lips to her forehead and left her lying there.

He went out and down to the river and stood watching it flow, tranquil and bright in this golden autumn weather, which had lasted so long. Soames's cows were feeding opposite. They would come under the hammer, now; all this that had belonged to him would come under the hammer, he supposed. Annette was going to her mother in France, and Fleur did not wish to keep it on. He looked back at the house, still marked and dishevelled by fire and water. And melancholy brooded in his heart, as if the dry grey spirit of its late owner were standing beside him looking at the passing away of his possessions, of all that on which he had lavished so much time and trouble. 'Change,' thought Michael, 'there's nothing but change. It's the one constant. Well! Who wouldn't have a river rather than a pond!' He went towards the flower border under the kitchen garden wall. The hollyhocks and sunflowers were in bloom there, and he turned to them as if for warmth. In the little summer-house at the corner he saw someone sitting. Mrs Val Dartie! Holly—a nice woman! And, suddenly, in Michael, out of the bafflement he had felt in Fleur's presence, the need to ask a question shaped itself timidly, ashamedly at first, then boldly, insistently. He went up to her. She had a book, but was not reading.

'How is Fleur?' she said.

Michael shook his head and sat down.

'I want to ask you a question. Don't answer if you don't want; but I feel I've got to ask. Can you—will you tell me: How are things between your young brother and her? I know what there was in the past. Is there anything in the present? I'm asking for her sake—not my own. Whatever you say shan't hurt her.'

She looked straight at him, and Michael searched her face. There was that in it from which he knew that whatever she did say, if indeed she said anything, would be the truth.

'Whatever there has been between them,' she said at last, 'and there *has* been something since he came back, is over for good. I know that for certain. It ended the day before the fire.'

'I see,' said Michael, very still. 'Why do you say it is over *for good?*'

'Because I know my young brother. He has given his wife his word never to see Fleur again. He must have blundered into something, I know there has been a crisis; but once Jon gives his word—nothing—*nothing* will make him go back on it. Whatever it was is over for good, and Fleur knows it.'

And again Michael said: 'I see.' And then, as if to himself: 'Whatever it was.'

She put out her hand and laid it on his.

'All right,' he said. 'I shall get my second wind in a minute. You needn't be afraid that I shall go back on my word, either. I know I've always played second fiddle. It shan't hurt her.'

The pressure on his hand increased; and, looking up, he saw tears in her eyes.

'Thank you very much,' he said; 'I understand now. It's when you don't understand that you feel such a dud. Thank you very much.'

He withdrew his hand gently and got up. Looking down at her still sitting there with tears in her eyes, he smiled.

'It's pretty hard sometimes to remember that it's all comedy; but one gets there, you know.'

'Good luck!' said Holly. And Michael answered: 'Good luck to all of us!'

That evening when the house was shuttered, he lit his pipe and stole out again. He had got his second wind. Whether he would have, but for Soames's death, he did not know. It was as if, by lying in that shadowy corner under a crab-apple tree, 'Old Forsyte' were still protecting his beloved. For her, Michael felt nothing but compassion. The bird had been shot with both barrels, and still lived; no one with any sporting instinct could hurt it further. Nothing for it but to pick her up and mend the wings as best he could. Something strong in Michael, so strong that he hadn't known of its existence, had rallied to his aid. Sportsmanship–chivalry? No! It was nameless; it was an instinct, a feeling that there was something beyond self to be considered, even when self was bruised and cast down. All his life he had detested the ebullient egoism of the *crime passionnel*, the wronged spouse, honour, vengeance, 'all that tommy-rot and naked savagery'. To be excused from being a decent man! One was never excused from that. Otherwise life was just where it was in the reindeer age, the pure tragedy of the primeval hunters, before civilisation and comedy began.

Whatever had been between those two–and he felt it had been all–it was over, and she, 'down and out'. He must stand by her and keep his mouth shut. If he couldn't do that now, he ought never to have married her, lukewarm as he had known her to be. And, drawing deeply at his pipe, he went down the dark garden to the river.

The sky was starry, and with the first touch of cold a slight mist was rising, filming the black water so that it scarcely seemed to move. Now and then in the stillness he could hear the drone of a distant car, and somewhere a little beast squeaking. Starlight, and the odour of bushes and the earth, the hoot of an owl, bats flitting, and those tall poplar shapes, darker than the darkness–what better setting for his mood just then!

An ironical world, his father had said! Yes, queerly ironical, with shape melting into shape, mood into mood, sound into sound, and nothing fixed anywhere, unless it were that starlight, and the instinct within all living things which said: 'Go on!'

A drift of music came down the river. There would be a party at some house. They were dancing probably, as he had seen the gnats dancing that afternoon! And then something out of the night seemed to catch him by the throat. God! It was beautiful, amazing! Breathing, in this darkness, as many billion shapes as there were stars above, all living, and all different! What a world! The Eternal Mood at work! And if you died, like that old boy, and lay for ever beneath a crab-apple tree–well, it was the Mood resting a moment in your still shape–no! not even resting, moving on in the mysterious rhythm that one called Life. Who could arrest the moving Mood–who wanted to? And if some pale possessor like that poor old chap, tried and succeeded for a moment, the stars twinkled just a little more when he was gone. To have and to hold! As though you could!

And Michael drew in his breath. A sound of singing came down the water to him, trailing, distant, high and sweet. It was as if a swan had sung!